Titles by Marsha Ward

Fiction:

The Owen Family Saga
Gone for a Soldier
The Man from Shenandoah
Spinster's Folly
Ride to Raton
Trail of Storms

Promised Valley
The Zion Trail

Other Fiction
Blood at Haught Springs
Faith and the Foreman

Nonfiction:

Rapid Recipes for Writers . . . And Other Busy People
From Julia's Kitchen: Owen Family Cookery

Simple Book List and Purchase Links

marshaward.com/bookshelf/simple-list/

The Complete Owen Family Saga

Five Novels
In Chronological Order

Gone for a Soldier
The Man from Shenandoah
Spinster's Folly
Ride to Raton
Trail of Storms

Marsha Ward

WestWard Books
჻჻♦჻჻
Payson, Arizona

The Complete Owen Family Saga

ISBN: 9780996146340
Ebook ISBN: 9780996146319

WestWard Books
P O Box 53
Payson, Arizona

Table of Contents

Gone for a Soldier
Notes and Disclaimers

Since the Shenandoah River flows south to north to empty into the Potomac River, locals refer to points south on the river as *up*, and points north as *down*. Thus, one would go *up* to Harrisonburg from Mount Jackson, and *down* to Winchester. It's an elevation thing.

You will encounter words and phrases used differently here than in our century. *Dear* in one instance means costly. *Make love to* means *pay court to*, except where it doesn't. You will know the difference. I use the term *secesh* early on as an adjective. It was slang for *secessionist*. Waynesborough, Spottsylvania, and Harper's Ferry are spellings used in those times. Many people did not adhere to established spelling norms, although they considered themselves literate.

For purposes of story, the details of some military encounters may not align exactly with the historical record. I have, however, made such attempts as were possible after almost two years of intensive research, to use existing accounts with as much accuracy as possible in regards to troop movements, skirmishes, battles, and the like in this novel.

Where I have had characters enroll in military units, they are actual companies in actual regiments and brigades. Their commanders are genuine, in most cases.

The notable exception is the cavalry company raised by the character Roderick Owen. It is entirely fictitious, although I have inserted the "Owen Dragoons" into actual encounters with enemy forces.

Important Characters
Families

<u>The Owen Family of Shenandoah County, Virginia</u>
Roderick Owen, farmer, horse breeder
Julia Helm Owen, his wife, whom he calls Julie
Rulon – age 20, sometimes called Rule
Benjamin – age 19, also called Ben
Peter – age 17
Carl – age 16
James – age 14
Marie – age 13
Clayton – age 11, also called Clay
Albert – age 10, also called Bertie
Julianna – age 8, also called Jule or Anna

<u>The Hilbrands Family of Mount Jackson, Virginia</u>
Randolph Hilbrands, merchant
Amanda Hilbrands, his wife
Mary – age 14
Ida – age 13
Sylvia – age 11
India – age 7
Eliza – born late in 1861

<u>The Allen Family of Shenandoah County, Virginia</u>
Theodore Allen, wealthy businessman and landowner
Louisa Allen, his wife
Merlin, their son, who doesn't play much of a role
Ella Ruth, their daughter – age 16, who does

Other Characters of Importance

Ren Lovell, corporal in Rulon's company
Owen Leoyd, private soldier in Rulon's company
Garth Von, private soldier in Rulon's company
Vernon Earl, from whom Rulon learns a valuable skill

Chapter 1
Rulon — April 19, 1861

Rulon Owen hadn't intended that crisp Friday in April to be momentous.

In fact, when he'd saddled his horse in order to do an errand in Mount Jackson for his ma, he hadn't given much thought to anything but stealing a few moments to see Mary Hilbrands.

She was only a little bit of a thing, a girl with dark hair and eyes that shone like . . . well, they kind of smoldered nowadays whenever she looked his way. Those smoky dark eyes gave him a shaky feeling that spun his head in circles and tied his gut into knots that—

"Whew." Rulon realized he'd let the horse slow to a walk while he'd been off in a reverie, somewhere not in Shenandoah County, as far as he could tell. He got the horse loping again, and wished it was already a year from now. Mayhap folks wouldn't get their tails in a twist about them keeping company once Mary turned sixteen in May next year. He was almighty tired of Ben and Peter, and especially of Pa, accusing him of trying to rob the cradle because he'd taken such a shine to the girl. Yes. He'd concede that she was young, but when she spoke his name, his knees felt like they was composed of apple jelly.

Ma sides with me, he thought. *Pa was the true cradle-robber of the family when the two of them wed. Him twenty-four. Ma barely sixteen.*

He wasn't likely to throw his opinion on that subject in his father's face any day soon. Firm. Formidable. The entire county used those words to describe his father. Rulon shook his head. Receiving back-sass from his offspring did not sit well with Roderick Owen. But at age twenty, Rulon hadn't taken a licking for a long spell. *Maybe Pa's gone soft in his old age. That's likely, now that he has nigh onto forty-five years pressing him down.*

Rulon rode on, wondering what to do to get his father off his back on the subject of Mary Hilbrands. *It's time I ask Ma to say a word to Pa*, he determined at last. *She won't let him ride me once I begin to court Mary in earnest.*

He slowed the horse to a walk as he entered the town. Ahead, he spotted his brother Ben pulling sacks of grain out of a wagon parked in front of the mill where he'd taken employment over the winter. Glancing up, Ben saw Rulon, and stopped to raise his hand in greeting, a big grin splitting his face.

Rulon drew rein and halted. "Brother Ben." He clasped the outstretched hand. "What makes you so happy today?"

"I am put in a smiling mood from seein' you with that enraptured look on your face. Can't wait to thrust your hand into the cookie jar, huh?"

Rulon snorted at Ben's fancy.

Ben kept on talking his nonsense. "Oh yes, indeed. You're an enchanted man, spellbound and smitten, ready to do that girl's bidding."

"Speak for yourself, brother."

Ben laughed and said, "Give my best to Miss Mary," then smacked Rulon's horse on the rump, which caused it first to shy and then to run.

After a block atop the runaway, Rulon regained control of the animal.

"Heartless boy," he grumbled, his face hot with humiliation. He settled the horse down to a sedate walk once again as he proceeded on his errand.

As he came in view of Mr. Hilbrands' store, he saw a crowd of excited men, some coming, and some going. Some were running. *Running!* What was amiss?

He drew up and dismounted. As soon as he had his feet on the ground, a friend of Pa's shoved the newspaper from Harrisonburg into his hands and bid him take it home. Slapping him on the back, the man ran down the street.

Rulon watched the man's hasty departure, then looked at the immense black headlines of the special edition. **WAR**. He read the subtitles interspersed with the text on the front page. **Ft. Sumter surrenders. Lincoln calls for troops. Via. Conv. votes to secede. Ratification vote in May. Counties raising Companies. Defend the Homeland.** His heart went cold at the urgency of the words. It soon rebounded, and began to beat at a rate he'd not experienced many times in his life. He looked up from the paper, his breath as quick as his heart rate, and made a decision. Feeling the cogs of his life shuddering to a halt and then changing direction, he strode into the store to put his plan into action.

☙

Rulon hadn't stepped far into the store when he found himself surrounded by a torrent of men: men shouting at each other, men who flung their arms about with great abandon, men who thumped their fists into their hands. A woman whom he recognized as the baker's wife stood hunched in a corner, as though she were protecting herself from the volume of noise in the building. Two of her daughters hid behind her, clutching brown-paper-wrapped loaves of bread to their chests. The girls looked exactly alike, so they had to be her twins.

He spotted his Mary at the side counter, holding her hands to her ears. Excited at the prospect of getting her approval of his newly minted plan, he grinned at her and waved the newspaper, hoping she would look up and see him. She did so as he approached, and smiled at him, but kept her hands over her ears.

Pushing, shoving, elbowing his way, he got to the spot, leaned over the counter, and asked, "Will you have me if I speak to your Pa today?"

She shook her head. His heart constricted. He thought it had stopped. He drew back and searched her face.

Her countenance softened. She must have realized what she'd done, because she shouted, "I cannot hear you."

Rulon's heart began to work again. He held up a finger and went to the end of the counter. He moved behind it and pulled Mary toward the back room. When he figured she could hear him, he tried again. "Sugar, do you have any objection if I ask your Pa for your hand?" He couldn't resist planting a quick kiss on her earlobe. Then he stood back and awaited her reply.

Her eyes widened, and a small smile tugged one side of her mouth upward. The other resisted movement, and he wondered if fear had taken root in her heart.

"Please say you don't object, Mary. I'm fixin' to ask him, today. Right away."

"Why, Rulon? We pledged to wait for all that wedding talk until I'm sixteen. I'll only be fifteen the end of next month."

He showed her the newspaper, pointing to the headline. "We are in a precarious situation. It's to be war, Mary. Abe Lincoln is driving us to that, and I'm leavin' soon."

Mary read the banner and on down the page. Her half-smile fled. Her eyes grew even larger. She put out one hand as though she would grasp onto his shirt, then pulled it away and tucked her arm behind her back. "You're leaving?"

"It's my duty to defend my home, Mary. Give me a better reason. Give me the right to defend *you*."

He saw tears in her eyes, filming the gaze that was fixed on him as though she were already memorizing his features before he departed.

She breathed deeply. Once. Twice. Then she spoke. "You may ask Papa, Rulon."

At her answer, his heart began beating as rapidly as a tattoo rattling on a drumhead. He leaned in and brushed a kiss onto her cheek. "I'll go seek your pa's favor now."

He backed away and into the store, relief mixed with anxiety. What was Mary's father likely to think about marriage talk today? Was all this ruckus good for business?

As Rulon rounded the counter, Chester Bates, a friend of his father, clapped him on the shoulder and spun him around.

"I see you've heard the news. There will be a place for you in the Mount Jackson Rifles, I dare say."

"Hello, Mr. Bates." Rulon nodded a greeting to the man. "Isn't that an infantry outfit?"

"It is, and the finest company in the Valley."

"Thank you for thinking of me, sir, but I have my heart set on joining a horse troop."

Frank disappointment showed on the man's face. He tipped his hat. "Good luck. I haven't heard anyone speak to raise one here."

"I'm obliged for the good wish, Mr. Bates." He spotted Mr. Hilbrands coming in the front door with a broom. "Excuse me, sir. I'm on a quest."

Mr. Bates quirked his sandy eyebrow as he followed Rulon's gaze. A grin overtook his face. "Ah. Good luck on that adventure, young man. I reckon Randolph's not thinking about marrying off his daughter just now." He stuck out his hand.

Rulon shook it, and struggled to make his way across the room.

⁊

Mr. Hilbrands had such a dark look in his eye that Rulon thought he was about to twirl the broom above his head and bring it down on some miscreant's shoulder. However, the time was now, or it would never happen, so he pressed forward through the throng and got within speaking distance of the man.

Rulon tried to speak loudly enough for Mr. Hilbrands to hear him above the hubbub in the room. "Sir, may I have a word?"

"Not now," the man answered.

"I only need a moment," Rulon said, feeling his confidence ebbing away.

"I'll speak to you when I've dealt with this turmoil," the man said, his dark brows drawn together.

"That suits me, sir. Do you need assistance?"

"Not this minute." Mr. Hilbrands raised the broom above his head, in a startling imitation of Rulon's imaginings, and thundered at his neighbors, "This is a place of business. I have work to do, customers to tend to. If you can't moderate your voices, take your discussions to the street."

Rulon had never heard such a speech from his prospective father-in-law. He wondered about the timing of his petition. How would it be received when the man was so worked up by the interruption of his commercial enterprise?

However, when the subdued men about the room had lowered their conversations to a reasonable level, Mr. Hilbrands was evidently satisfied by his efforts, and turned to Rulon, bearing a smile on his face.

"What can I do for you, young man?"

Rulon gulped, trying to think what to say right off. Every thought, every carefully planned sentence had fled from his brain.

Mr. Hilbrands arched an eyebrow, and Rulon hastened to find words to start his own speech.

"Nice . . . nice day, sir."

The eyebrow inched higher.

"You must be aware that your daughter Mary and me have been keepin' company for some time," he began, feeling like a veritable dolt. Of course the man knew that. He'd sat in the parlor his fair share of time to accompany them.

Mr. Hilbrands nodded. "Yes, indeed. Go on."

Rulon swallowed. "Sir, Miss Mary has agreed that we should, um, wed before I go to serve my country in this coming squabble."

Both eyebrows rose toward the tin ceiling. The black, forbidding look had returned to Mr. Hilbrands' features.

"We had planned to wait another year to ask for your permission to marry, but sir, the state of affairs demands, um, requires a change in our circumstances." Rulon felt like his tongue was dragging through molasses with each word, forcing him to speak so slowly that he wasn't sure the man's patience would hold out much longer.

"You want to marry my daughter? Now? Before you traipse off to make war with the Yankees?"

Rulon squirmed. The man made his proposal sound somehow improper and self-serving.

"I reckon that's about the size of it, sir," he admitted, casting his gaze down to the tips of the man's shoes.

"This is a surprise, and not a welcome one, young man. My daughter is still of tender years. I think it a mite unseemly of you to talk marriage at this time. Hmm."

"Please consider my request, sir," Rulon said, feeling like a beggar. "Mary's wishes are in accord with mine."

Mr. Hilbrands eyed Rulon and stroked his thin moustache. "This will require discussion with my wife," he said, his voice also conveying that he did not favor such a turn of events. "She must have an opportunity to give her opinion on this matter."

Rulon felt his heart plummeting to the pit of his stomach. He gulped anew and screwed up his courage for a final feint. "When might you give me an answer, sir?" He had so little time before other Virginia patriots stole a march on him and whipped the enemy. He might lose out entirely.

Mr. Hilbrands looked even more startled, if possible. "I will speak to the missus today. I suppose you want a speedy reply?"

Rulon nodded.

Mr. Hilbrands raised his chin. "You may expect our answer on Sunday morning, then, before the Sabbath service."

"Yes, sir. Thank you, sir! I will see you then, sir." Rulon turned on his heel and marched out of the store. Only then did he recall the errand Ma had given him to purchase a pound of sugar. He squared his shoulders—feeling very foolish—turned around, and re-entered the mercantile.

80

Rulon arrived in the barnyard of the home place an hour later, and shouted "Pa!"

"I'm here," a voice called from inside the barn.

Rulon dismounted and shoved his hair out of his eyes. When had he lost his hat? He pulled the horse along, wondering how his announcement would be received.

"Pa," he repeated, almost breathless, as he halted beside a horse tied securely in a stall. Rulon paused to swallow in an attempt to ease his dry throat.

"Hmm?" Pa bent over an upraised hoof, his hammer held in midair as he evidently waited for Rulon to speak.

"Charleston's secesh boys fired on Fort Sumter last week. The Federals gave up the fort. Ol' Abe Lincoln called on Virginia for troops. What an insult he gives us!" He stopped to get a breath, then continued, his words tumbling over each other. "The Virginia Convention voted to secede, but there'll be a ratification vote in May. We're going to war, Pa. The counties are raising new companies in case we're called to fight. Of course we'll be called up."

"What?" His father spit a mouthful of nails into his hand. "Where'd you hear that secession news, boy?"

Rulon held out the newspaper, forgotten in his rush to impart what he had learned. "The Hilbrands' store. I was—"

"Hold on there." Pa let the horse's hoof down easy and straightened up. "You was making love to his daughter. She's too young for you." He took the paper Rulon still offered him and let it dangle at the side of his leg.

Rulon's belly tightened. "I was fetching the sugar Ma asked me to bring her," he replied. Knowing he was on the edge of anger over the subject of Mary's youth, he needed to move away and cool down.

He stepped back to his horse, wrapped his fingers around the side of the stirrup, and gripped it so hard his hand went white. When his breathing had slowed, he released the stirrup and dug the parcel out of the saddlebag. He held it up where Pa could see the proof. Trying not to bite off his words as he lowered the packet of sugar, he said, "Miss Mary an' me, we've had an understanding for quite a spell."

"She's barely out of the cradle. You leave her be."

Rulon took a deep breath and held it for a moment before he said, "That's up to Mary's pa. I've asked him for her hand."

"You've done that? Asked Rand?" Pa shoulders seemed to sag slightly. "Have you given this plenty of thought, son? Miss Mary is still a schoolgirl."

Rulon measured his words. "I can't help but think of her night and day. I know she's young, but she's coming up on fifteen. She wants to wed me, and she's got a right strong opinion on the matter."

"You can't wait till you whip the Yankees?"

"No, Pa. I reckon I'll take my chance for a bit of happiness before I leave."

His father shook his head in resignation. "I can't blame you for that wish, Rulon. I expect you considered that wartime is risky?"

"Yes, Pa. That figured into my decision."

Rod sighed. "If you're set on this course, bear in mind to give the girl her happiness, too. Treat her well, and with respect. You're committing for a lifetime, you understand?"

"I never thought otherwise."

"You keep them marriage vows in mind while you're away." He looked off into the distance, as though remembering another time. Then he slapped his leg with the newspaper and turned to Rulon again. "Temptations to break them will present themselves. They always do."

Rulon chewed the inside of his cheek.

"You won't get diseased if you avoid those temptations. That's not a thing you want to bring home to the wife."

Rulon shifted his weight from one leg to the other, then back again, wondering how they had gotten onto this subject. "I don't intend—" He stopped, his voice strangled in his tight throat.

"Then don't give in to mankind's carnal nature." Pa turned away and lifted the horse's hoof. "Don't do it."

&

When Rulon came in the house before supper, Pa sat near the fireplace, reading the newspaper brought from town.

Rulon took a seat on a stool, uneasy about striking up a conversation that could wander onto the previous topic. "Pa, are you about finished with the paper?" he asked, drumming his fingers on his knees.

Pa looked up. "Not quite. What has you all-fired curious to read the news?"

Rulon cleared his throat, not once, but twice. Pa continued looking at him. Rulon glanced at his father's face, then away, and cleared his throat a third time. When he could no longer fail to respond, he said, "I'm seeking a cavalry company to join." He swallowed, avoiding his father's eyes entirely now. "I figured the paper would have word about a company or two being formed."

"Cavalry, you say?"

"I been raised up with horses all my life long, Pa. I reckon it's natural I go to war riding one."

Pa nodded. "Good reasoning. Take a look, then." He held out the paper.

Rulon devoured the columns of print, moving his forefinger down each article. In a few moments, he flicked the paper with his nail in disgust. "There's nothing." He looked up to see his father watching him intently.

"Nothing in our county?"

"Yes. I cannot fathom it."

"There are several infantry companies forming up, one right over in Mount Jackson."

"I don't admire the thought of trudging along on the ground. I prefer to ride."

Pa shifted in his chair. "Did you take notice of the mention of the Harrisonburg Cavalry?"

"Yes, sir. It says they're called to muster on the twenty-second of next month. Weren't they formed a couple of years past?"

"That's right, after John Brown raised his ruckus. Valley folks feared his cock-eyed scheme to raise a rebellion among the Negroes would take root in the wrong minds." He put out his hand for the newspaper.

Rulon passed it over. "I recall the alarm that put into the ladies hereabouts. I'm glad Ma is made of sterner stuff than Mrs. Hilbrands. Her fit of the vapors is legendary."

"Would you consider enrolling with the Harrisonburg troop?"

Rulon ran his hand through his hair. "I doubt they'd let me enroll, Pa. I'm not from Rockingham County, and I sure haven't drilled with them none."

"Their captain is Tom Yancey."

Rulon stared at his father, not making a connection between his comments.

"The Yanceys are kin of ours. Not close kin, but cousins, none the less."

Rulon straightened. "I'd forgotten."

"Family ties should count for something. I'll write a letter, if you'd like."

"It might go down better if I do it."

Pa considered that, and finally nodded. "You have the right of it. Let me go over the family connection." He rose and got the family bible down, brought it back, and opened it to the center section.

As Pa and Rulon explored the kinship between the two families, Ben came in and sank heavily onto the hearth, mumbling under his breath. He rubbed his head hard with both hands. "When are you going to geld that colt, Pa?" he finally interrupted.

"Throwed you again?" Rulon asked, smirking.

"No, I flew off on my own," Ben said, looking askance at Rulon.

"You should leave the horse-breaking to James. He has the knack."

"He's a baby."

"He still has the knack and you don't."

"How's he do that?" Ben rubbed his head again.

"He was born to be a horseman," Rulon said, then went back to his talk with

Pa, who appeared amused at Ben's misadventure.

Before long, Rulon knew all about his relationship to Captain Yancey, and let Pa go back to reading his newspaper.

"Ben," Rulon said, standing up and putting a hand on his brother's shoulder. "Come set on the porch with me until supper's ready. It's too warm in here with the fire." He cast a glance at his father, but he had resumed reading. "*I* don't have old man's bones," he muttered in a soft voice.

Ben acquiesced, and followed Rulon outside. "You called Pa an old man? You're a brave soul, Rule. By the way, I found your hat fetched up against a blackberry thicket along the road as I came in from town. I left it hanging in the stable."

"That was kindly of you," Rulon said with a snort. "It wouldn't stay in your hand long enough to bring it to mine?"

"The colt needed working."

Rulon nudged a chair out from the wall with the toe of his boot. "I can't figure why there's no cavalry company forming up hereabouts," he mused as they settled into their seats.

"Cavalry? You won't see much action riding a horse around the country."

"I reckon I will. A horse will get a body to the heart of the action quicker than a footsore man can march there."

Ben cuffed Rulon on the arm. "A horse will get shot out from under you. Then where will you be? Afoot, brother. A mere camp dog."

"I'll take the risk. I like horseflesh between my legs."

Ben chortled. "You like—"

"Don't you dare say it." Rulon waggled his finger under Ben's nose. "The haughty Miss Allen can't be pleased that you prefer the mud-slogging infantry," he added, deftly turning the conversation in another direction. "You'd rather come home to her with brogans full of muck than clean boots?"

"It doesn't seem likely that I'll be comin' home to her at all, except in a brotherly fashion." Ben's face lost all humor. "Miss Allen's pa has forbidden her to consider a match with me."

Rulon raised an eyebrow. "An Owen boy ain't good enough for him?"

"This Owen boy don't have any property. That's all that matters to him. Property and possessions."

"That's hard luck, Ben. What does the lady have to say?"

Ben rubbed his nose with a knuckle. "I've a notion the lady is wavering a mite. I'm planning to see her tomorrow night. With a little luck, maybe I can talk her into eloping."

"You'd go that far?"

"I ain't content without her."

"I reckon I know that itch." Rulon tipped his chair back, balancing on the rear legs.

"Are you making any headway in scratching it?"

Rulon sat silent for a time. He pinched a crease in the leg of his trousers and adjusted the fabric. "A mite," he said finally.

"You randy dog," Ben said, and whistled.

Rulon smacked him on the side of the head, growling in his throat, "It's not what you think, brother."

"Ow! Spare the brainpan. It's had enough abuse today." Ben slapped away Rulon's hand. "You're always a-sniffing around the girl. What else can I think?"

"Good luck in your quest with Miss Allen, brother." Rulon leaned farther back in his chair. "We're heading for war. Soon enough we'll have other battles to win. Through the cavalry, of course."

Ben started to sweep his boot toward the legs of Rulon's up tilted chair, but Rulon forestalled him by settling it back to the floor, then grinned at his brother in triumph. "I'm fixing to write a letter to Captain Yancey to offer my sword to the Harrisonburg Cavalry."

Ben's guffaw exploded onto the soft evening air. "Your sword? Where do you reckon to get a sword to offer?"

"It's a metaphorical sword, you dolt. What will you offer? A bedroll?"

"I'm going to offer my own self, and see no impediment to being accepted. The Mount Jackson Rifles are taking enlistments soon."

"You'd best work fast on the girl's pa, then."

"Don't I know it!" Ben's voice took on a note of despair. He rubbed his hands up and down his thighs. "If she won't go away and marry me, you and me will have to beat back those Yanks quick so I can come home and change the man's mind."

හ

Rulon had just passed the fried potatoes down to Ben when he leaned back from the table, looked around at the family, straightened his shoulders, and cleared his throat with emphasis.

"Got something to say, brother?" Ben asked, his eyes twinkling in the lamplight.

"I do," Rulon declared. He fiddled with his fork, then laid it on the table and got to his feet. "I'm fixing to wed Miss Mary Hilbrands."

"Scratching your itch," Ben muttered.

Peter was next down the table from Ben. "Maybe in a year or two," he jeered.

Rulon sat down and picked up his fork. "No. We'll do it as soon as Mr. Hilbrands gives me his consent."

Pa spoke. "How long do you reckon before he has an answer for you?"

"He said he'll talk to Missus Hilbrands and let me know their decision before church on Sunday." Rulon wagged his head. "I hope Mary has occasion to converse with him and make her feelings known. He had a reluctant spirit about him."

Ben chuckled. "Miss Mary don't have enough age on her to have an opinion, brother. She ain't but a year older than James, and he's a veritable baby."

"Am not," James countered from across the table.

"Are too." Peter dived into the fray, grinning widely.

"Always stirrin' up trouble," Rulon said, glaring at Ben, who gave him a triumphant look.

"Quiet," Pa thundered, slapping the flat of his hand on the table top.

After a moment, once silence had been achieved, Ma spoke up. "Rulon, when did you ask Mr. Hilbrands?"

He looked down the table at his mother. "Today when I was in town. After I read the news, I figured I'd best not wait longer."

"What news?" demanded his sister, Marie.

"War news. Abe Lincoln asked for troops to put down the rebellion in the cotton states," he said. "I'm going to enlist in a troop of cavalry, if they'll have me." He picked up his fork, held it for a moment, then stabbed it into his potatoes. "I want Mary to wed me before I go."

"Oh Rulon," said Ma. "You're too young."

"Ma." The distress on her face disturbed him. "I aim to marry her in any case. Better now than later." *Or never*, he dared to think.

"To go for a soldier," she said, her voice low.

"I'm almost too old," he huffed.

"Can I go, Ma?" Albert was only ten.

"No!"

"They'll need drummer boys. Or fife players."

"You don't play drum or fife, either one." Carl reached out and attempted to deliver a blow to Albert's ear, but Albert ducked as Pa pounded the table again.

"Food's getting cold," Pa declared. "Discussion's over."

Rulon raised his fork and shoved a mouthful of potatoes past his lips, wishing he hadn't even begun to broach the subject. *What an unruly bunch!* The sooner he was off on his own, the better.

Chapter 2
Ben — April 20, 1861

Ben waited in the darkness of the lane that led up from the north fork of the river. Before him on a rise stood the grand house, the centerpiece of the prosperous farm owned by Miss Ella Ruth Allen's father. Behind him, tied to a low-hanging tree limb, his horse nickered softly and stamped a hoof.

Ella Ruth was late in arriving to their tryst, but that was to be expected. Ella Ruth was late for every occasion.

He smiled momentarily at her habitual tardiness, and then adjusted his leaning position against the smooth tree trunk. If he had his wish, he would scoop her up and run away to the nearest place he could marry her, but she hadn't yet agreed to elope with him. He hoped his powers of persuasion would be sufficient to the task tonight. If not, he only had a few more days to win her over to the idea.

Hearing footfalls on the lane, he pushed away from the tree and straightened.

"Ben?" Breathless. Timid. Hopeful.

"I'm here," he called, keeping his voice low.

The footsteps slowed. Hesitant. "Where? I cannot see you."

She was close, so close to him that he could smell the scent of the rose water she wore. He moved forward. "Here," he said, bringing the girl into his arms.

"Oh Ben," she sighed, snuggling against him, her head fitting into the hollow beneath his chin. "I worried you wouldn't come." Her anxiety showed itself in a constrained giggle.

"You can depend on me," he told her, repeating a phrase he'd said many times before in his attempts to woo and win her.

"You always say that," she said, a bright little chuckle in her voice.

"I want you to remember it. I want you to know I am true to you. There is no one in my heart but your dear person."

"Oh Ben," she repeated. "It's Poppa you need to convince, not me."

He sighed. "Don't I know it." He held her, rocking her slightly. "What's the secret? How do I make him see my worth?"

"I cannot advise you on that point."

He heard the despair in her voice. "Ella Ruth, what does your ma think? Does she influence him?"

"Oh no! Momma doesn't meddle in Poppa's affairs. She wouldn't dream of telling him to let you—" Her voice choked.

No help in that direction. Ben sighed again. "There has to be a remedy. Does your brother have influence?"

"Merlin keeps out of Poppa's business."

Gall rose in his throat, and he couldn't speak until he had cleared it away. "My pa always told me life wasn't fair, that I should buck up and realize it for truth. I reckon I didn't know what he meant until now."

"Don't you get disheartened, Ben. I adore you. Poppa will have to see, sooner or later, that you are not merely a farmer's son, but a person of real substance, real importance. Like I do." Her voice rose to a squeak.

Marveling at her remarkable speech, he patted her hair, then stroked her cheek. "I won't lose heart, but time is growing short. War is coming, the papers say. I expect I'll go fight for the Confederacy."

"Oh no. You can't. You would have to leave me." She snuggled tighter against him.

"That's the way it is with war. All the more reason to redouble my efforts. When can I talk to your pa again?"

"Not for days. He's on a trip for business."

"Humph." Ben pondered on the problem, still stroking Ella Ruth's cheek until she stayed his hand.

"Ben."

"Hmm?"

"How much do you care for me?"

He shook his head, drew all his focus together to answer the question. "There ain't a measure large enough, girl." Moonlight fell upon her brow. It gave him an idea. He took her chin between fingers and thumb and gently turned up her face so he could gaze directly into her eyes. "You are the sun, the moon, the stars to me. No man ever loved a woman more."

Ella Ruth giggled. "I wish Poppa had a romantic soul. He couldn't help being moved by such tender words." She shivered. "He's a businessman."

"A very wealthy businessman."

"Yes." She sighed. "Can't you make a pretty speech about business, Ben?"

His chuckle sounded rueful to his ears. "I could tell him about mill stones and sacking flour and the best method to repair a sluice. However, I don't own the mill."

"Tell him about all your pa's nice horses."

"They don't belong to me, neither."

"Don't you own anything, Ben?"

He drew her close. "I own the love I bear you."

"Oh Ben. Such a pretty speech. And all for naught." Ella Ruth turned her head and sighed against his chest.

Disappointment in himself and his prospects surged through his veins. He really didn't own anything of substance, anything that a wealthy businessman would count as property. Despite the momentary negative thrust of his thoughts, he knew he had to press on and gain the prize. "I will put my mind toward finding a solution, my darling," he murmured. "All is not lost."

"Yes, Ben."

He stood quietly for a long moment, rocking her again in his arms. He didn't dare kiss her and excite his yearning. Not right now. Instead, he rocked her.

She said nothing, evidently content to be enfolded in his arms.

When he could not bear the silence a moment more, he whispered, "We could go up to Staunton and find a judge to marry us."

Immediately she began to shake her head against his chest. "I couldn't. I just couldn't. That would be wanton."

He tightened his hold a fraction. "Oh girl, I am wantin' you to marry me. Don't you want to?"

She wiggled his embrace loose enough that she could look up at him. "Of course I do. I want a lovely wedding in the church, with six bridesmaids, and roses heaped alongside the pews and under the altar, and my poppa giving me over to your keeping, and my momma's special cake afterward. That's my dearest dream."

"Not me?"

She tilted her head to one side. "Not you what?"

"I'm not your dearest dream?"

She giggled and gave his chest a little shove. "That's my dearest dream of a wedding, silly boy. A girl must keep hold of her fond dreams."

And a boy has to damp down his passions, he thought, choking back his disappointment at her refusal to consider his suggestion. The company he intended to join, raised by her own cousin, was going to war soon. He didn't dare tell her that tonight and chance a quarrel.

"Once Poppa admits what a wonderful catch you are, we will have that lovely wedding, with all our friends and family to witness our happiness." Her eyes sparkled. She walked two fingers up his shirt. "Ben, you'll look so handsome in a frockcoat, with great long tails, just like in the novels."

"I've never seen such a coat," he said, dubious that a piece of raiment like that was to be had in the entire county.

"We can have it made to order in Boston, and shipped here by special coach."

Ben drew a breath and nearly choked at the thought of the expense. He turned aside and coughed. Ella Ruth took such wild fancies into her mind at times. "Girl, you do realize Boston is in another country now?"

"Oh, you men say that, but it's not important. Poppa can get anything."

Sometimes he simply wanted to shake sense into her, but knew it would do nothing to advance his cause. "Never mind," he crooned into her hair. "First things first. When will your poppa return from his trip?"

"I don't know. I'll have to ask Momma tomorrow." She stirred. "I can't chance being out too much longer, or she will suspect I'm meeting you." She raised her face and gazed into his eyes. "Kiss me, Ben, before I go back."

He knew it was folly to arouse the ache that kissing her would unleash, but such a frank appeal could not be denied. He bent to the task, trying for a brief encounter, but the soft curves pressed against him worked their charms, and he yielded to a second kiss. Fortunately for his resolve, Ella Ruth pulled out of his embrace and patted him on the cheek.

"Be good, Ben," she bid him. "Think of me, not of any other girls."

"I am not acquainted with any other girls," he murmured, half stupefied. "Only you. Only you."

She slipped away, turning briefly to blow him another kiss, then she was swallowed up amidst the trees surrounding the house.

Ben exhaled until he thought his lungs surely were as bereft as his arms, then slumped over to support himself with hands on shaky knees as he took in air once more. If a whirlwind had caught him and flung him against the side of a barn, he figured he could not have felt more battered than he did by his emotional and physical upheaval. How could one little girl do this to him?

He slowly straightened and went toward his horse, not sure if he even had the strength to haul himself into the saddle. "Brownie," he said, patting the animal's neck, "don't you let me drown crossing the river."

ℵ

Rulon — April 21, 1861

Rulon stood just below the bottom step of the stairway leading up to the door of the church, clasping his hands behind his back. He heard his shoe tapping rapidly against the brick. He simply could not control the foot as he waited.

"Young man!"

Rulon swung around at the sharp tone he heard in Randolph Hilbrands' voice. It sounded like the man intended to give him ill news. "Sir?" he said, hoping his face bore a conciliatory aspect.

The man descended the steps, a frown bending his thin moustache in a downward curve.

A chill raised the hairs on the back of Rulon's neck. Had he lost Mary? He couldn't feel his hands.

Mr. Hilbrands stopped on the step above where Rulon was standing, and stared down at him. He took a quick breath. "My daughter wants to be your bride," he said, a fierce look on his face. "She says it must be now, before you enlist. I told her that was a fanciful notion."

Rulon didn't dare say a word. He couldn't hear himself breathing.

"She is most persuasive in her reasoning. She is young, but she seems to have a firm grasp of what she is fixing to do. Given the circumstances, I am giving consent."

Rulon felt himself toppling, and slid his left foot back to maintain his balance. His ears rang with the man's words. *I am giving consent.*

"Tha-thank you, sir." He struggled to stand upright, instead of sagging as he felt inclined to do. In point of fact, his knees begged to kiss the steps, but he conquered the impulse after a long moment, and thrust out his hand to seal the bargain.

Mr. Hilbrands solemnly shook it, but added, "Her mother is not convinced as yet, but may come around in due course. You would do well to spend time in that effort."

"Yes, I will, sir. Thank you again." Rulon left off pumping the man's hand, expecting to take his leave and go to Mary's side to ask her to marry him.

Mr. Hilbrands forestalled him, saying, "Come to the house after the service to speak to my daughter. You will want to tell her that I spoke to the minister. It appears there are several weddings taking place due to this war fever. He does not have any open days until May 11th. Will that suit?"

Rulon hoped his mouth wasn't gaping as Mr. Hilbrands' words swirled in his brain. May 11th. That was an age away. He gulped. "Yes, sir. That suits just fine. Give Mr. Moore my thanks."

"He'll want your coin for the service. Two dollars."

Rulon gulped again. Two dollars. That was four days' wages hereabouts! He'd never thought of any cost involved in getting wed. Two dollars! What would Pa say?

ฆ

After he had spoken to Mr. Hilbrands, Rulon entered the church, found his place in the family pew, and craned his neck to look at his intended, but Ma's hand on his shoulder drew his attention to the proceedings at hand. The Sunday service had stretched to three hours, an interminable length, which gave him ample time to think on the moment of his encounter with Mary and its solemn significance.

Now he knelt before the girl in the gloomy parlor of the Hilbrands' home, his gut tied in knots.

"Mary?"

Dust motes danced in the sliver of light streaming between the drawn drapes. His throat felt dry as the dust lying underneath the table against the far wall. Which girl had stinted in her dusting duties the previous day? Perhaps his arrival had caught Mrs. Hilbrands so unaware that she had forgotten the sad state of her parlor.

Where *was* Mrs. Hilbrands? Should he and Mary be alone? They'd never kept company in this room without another person as chaperone.

Rulon fought his increasing panic, grateful that at least he was kneeling. The position gave his knees no chance to knock together. He knew he was squeezing

Mary's fingers too tightly, and willed his grip to loosen, his shoulders to lower from their hunched position near his ears.

What was he doing here? How had he come to be proposing marriage to this girl who he knew to be so pure and tender and full of hopes for the future? What was their future to be? Only days before, his thoughts had centered only in somehow quenching the fire that arose in him whenever he was in Mary's company . . . touched her hand . . . or merely thought about her. The swell of her bosom drove him insane with desire, and his constant thought up to now had been how he might coax her to be alone with him, to let him touch . . . her flesh.

He swallowed.

And now? Now war was upon then, hovering over their lives like an inky thundercloud. It changed everything: every path, every hope, every desire. His desire. *Oh God, help me to have solemn thoughts on this holy day, this portentous day, this . . . engagement day.*

He cleared his throat, glad Mrs. Hilbrands had *not* had the opportunity to throw open the drapes. If Mary saw his countenance, surely she would see the doubts that must be covering it as he rethought his rash decision. He must be mad.

"Mary," he tried again, his ears catching the tremor in his voice. What a shambles he was making of the affair! Hearing how his voice trembled, she might now tell him "no," guessing how much he doubted. Could she know that he was driven more by the burning in his loins than by a burning in his heart?

No, that wasn't right. Not right at all. *I love Mary more than life! I'm sure that's the truth of the matter.*

What would Ma think of him and his carnal desires? The truth was she'd never feared to lay down the law in their home, to broach a subject he'd quaked to speak about to his pa. She did not hesitate to tell her sons to keep their pants buttoned until they were duly wed.

Well, if I can carry off this speech properly, I'll soon be duly wed and she can set her mind at ease where I'm concerned.

"Mary," he said again, thinking, *I've been doing this all wrong. Think on how much you love the girl.* He pursed his lips and let out a long sigh. "I can scarcely bear the thought of going off to fight, of leaving you behind, without making you my wife."

Ah! This is fearsome work!

He bowed his head, closing his eyes to block out distractions while he tried to regain his courage. He breathed deeply, feeling a need for a larger volume of air in his lungs, then opened his eyes again, focusing on Mary's blue and gray striped skirt. The cloth shivered beneath his gaze. The realization that she was trembling as much as he, finally steadied him.

He looked up. Mary's face lay half in shadow, half in light as the sliver of sunlight illuminated one cheek, one side of her fair brow, one half of her raven-dark hair. She was biting her lip.

Rulon took another deep breath. "My tenderest feelings are toward you," he declared, voice steady at last. "My bosom swells with joy at the mere glimmer of hope that you bear me similar feelings." *Where was this flowery turn of phrase coming from?* He brushed away the errant thought. "Will you marry me, my sweet girl?"

"Yes."

Even though her answer was but a whisper, he heard it. Joy swelled his chest as he had just claimed it would, to such a degree that he felt he would suffocate. The next thing he knew, he was smothering both of Mary's hands with kisses, and oddly, her fingers were wet.

To his horror, he took note that the moisture came from his own streaming eyes. What shame! If his brothers ever heard of this—that he had cried like a mewling babe because a girl—

No. He would own up to his seemingly womanish response if he ever had the occasion to do so. Mary had given him her answer, and bolstered by thought of the consent he'd won this morning from her father—reluctant though it had seemed—he reckoned he was justified in shedding a few tears of elation and triumph.

"Rulon," she whispered, her voice quivering slightly, "my heart is yours, and ever has been." She inhaled quickly, twice, then said, "I saw you talking to Papa this morning. What did he say?"

"He gave consent," Rulon began.

Mary cut him off. "Thank the Good Lord!" She removed one of her hands from Rulon's grasp to dash the tears from her brimming eyes.

"He was somewhat reluctant, but did not seem inclined to demand a long courtship. He knows our time together is short with war coming upon us."

"Papa can be sensible when he puts his mind to it."

Rulon stroked the hand that Mary had allowed him to keep in his. "Your pa said he spoke to the minister about a ceremony."

She inhaled sharply. "He did?"

"Mr. Moore is available on May 11th. Three whole weeks away!"

"Only three weeks?" Mary shook her hand out of Rulon's and covered her face.

Rulon rocked backward at her strange reaction. "Sweet girl, three weeks is a lifetime to wait."

Mary peeked over her fingers. "Oh Rulon. I have only three weeks to get ready for my wedding day. I wonder what Mama will say?"

∞

Mary — April 21, 1861

Mama had plenty to say, Mary discovered soon after Rulon took his leave.

She had swept into the parlor almost before the front door had closed upon the man, dragging Mary with her by a tight grasp on her arm. She thrust her onto the same chair upon which she had sat when Rulon knelt before her, then dropped into the seat opposite.

"You are too young to be a wife," she said right off.

Mary attempted to turn away that argument, pointing out that her own grandmother had married at the tender age of thirteen.

Mama compressed her lips and wagged her head. "The society was much different in that era. I am raising you to be a lady, and ladies do not wed before a proper age."

"Mama, this is war time. Rulon is enlisting soon. If I let him go without, if I don't marry him now, perhaps I will miss my chance entirely." The idea that Rulon could die brought waves of sadness crashing upon her, almost knocking her against the back of the chair upon which she perched.

"I do not recall hearing any proclamation of war. Mr. Hilbrands has not imparted any such news to me. He would have done so, had there been a need."

"I read in Papa's newspaper that war with the North would commence soon." Mary offered up the news as further evidence of her need. "The headlines were the largest letters I've ever seen. The editor said Virginia will surely secede and join the other states in the Confederacy. Mayhap they won't even wait until the convention vote is ratified in May. Mama, I have to marry Rulon before he leaves the county."

"You do not have to do any such a thing," Mrs. Hilbrands stated, but her voice had dropped in volume and firmness. "I suppose—" She stood abruptly, and headed toward the door.

"Mama?" Mary got to her feet and called out her strongest argument. "We have an appointment to be wed. With the minister."

The door slammed.

Mary stood rooted in place for a few seconds, then began to pace the room.

Would Mama try to convince Papa that wedding Rulon was a bad notion? Did Mama have some unspoken objection to her marriage into his family? Her parents had known Rulon's folks for years. Her father and Mr. Owen were friends of long standing. The man had a fine reputation as a farmer and horse breeder. Mary stopped in mid-stride. Did Mama dislike Mrs. Owen?

No. That couldn't be true. When she came to town, Mrs. Owen often traded her eggs and cream for goods in her parents' mercantile establishment. Mary had never heard of any discord in their bartering of goods. Mama always conversed with her in a familiar manner.

Mary continued pacing. What could be causing her mother's opposition? Rulon and his family were upright people, God-fearing people. Perhaps a bit, oh, irregular in their thinking about slavery being unjust, but she knew a few other folks in the county had similar feelings. That was such a small thing. There could be no logical impediment to a match between their families.

Growing weary of her mindless tours about the room, Mary sat, hands in her lap, shoulders bowed. Impending war and Rulon's proposal had certainly turned her world on its ear. She had known for months that she wanted to marry this particular man, but had thought the event was a few years in her future. Now he was set on going to fight, and the time to wed was here and now. In three short weeks, in fact.

Joy flashed through her, causing her heart to beat at a furious pace. As quickly as it had come, the elation was replaced by anxiety brought on by the thought of her mother's unanticipated resistance. *How am I to prepare for my wedding alone?* She clasped her hands, twisting them against each other. *Mama, Mama. I need you.*

℀

Rulon — April 21, 1861

Ma met Rulon at the door of the kitchen. She didn't say anything, just waited for him to speak first, her face aglow, yet strangely reserved.

"I done it, Ma. Mary accepted my proposal to wed." Tiny moths skittered around inside his belly.

Ma beamed. "I knew she would, son. She bears you a great affection."

"Don't she, though. It half puts a man on his guard, thinking about the future."

Ma patted his arm. "You have a grand future, son. At least, we all have the hope of that." As she spoke the last few words, her voice dropped almost to a whisper, her fear plainly exposed.

"Ma, everything is going to be just fine. We'll whip those Yankees in a fortnight and be home before planting time is done." He jerked his chin for emphasis.

"That is my prayer, Rulon. Come. Sit. Tell me your plans. When will the happy day occur?"

Rulon took his accustomed place at the table, then picked up and fidgeted with the salt cellar. "Mr. Moore's first open date to hold a wedding service for us is May 11th." He looked up at his mother. "That's three weeks off."

"Only three weeks!"

"Mary said that too, 'only three weeks.' What does it mean?"

"There's so much work to do, son. Mary needs to come up with a pleasing and serviceable dress. Then she has to plan and do the decorating, make a party and write notes to invite folks. Bake a cake and whatever other refreshments she wants. Weddings don't come off without a passel of work."

Rulon took the salt spoon out of the cellar and examined it. He put it back into the salt. "That didn't enter my mind, I reckon. I only been worrying over two things. The first is earning the two dollars I need to pay Mr. Moore, and the second . . ." He paused and leaned his chair back on two legs. "I've been mulling over what to write in a letter to Captain Yancey up in Rockingham County. I figure I've got only one chance to convince him to take me into the Harrisonburg Troop before it leaves."

A deep furrow appeared between Ma's brows. "The fighting. Is that all you men think about?"

"No. No." Rulon let the chair return to the floor. "But Ma, I don't want this little squabble to be over before I can take part."

"I reckon there's time enough for you to join some other company, if it really is to be war. Armies don't form up overnight, son."

Rulon put the salt cellar back on the table and nudged it into place. "Didn't we beat the Mexicans in short order?"

"It took a while, a long while. Those were hard times."

He shrugged. "I own I don't recall a great lot."

"I don't wonder, you being nothing but a little sprout at the time."

"Pa don't talk about it much."

"No, he don't, and thankful I am of that." Ma wiped her hands on her apron. "What will we need to do for the pair of you and the celebration? Will the girl marry from her father's house or the church? Will there be a shiveree or a proper party? No question that I'll fix a place ready for her when you bring her home to us."

Rulon shifted in the chair, uneasy that he'd not thought of any such details, nor even where Mary would live when he left for war.

"Ah, we didn't get to that stage of talking, Ma. It's early times yet to worry on that."

"Humph. You want to wed in a hurry so you can go to war, but don't take the time to converse with your gal about your plans? Spoken like a man who don't have to do the work."

"Ma." He made more than one syllable of the word. "We was . . . we was busy."

"Less spooning and more talking would suit." She arose and squinted at him. "I reckon it never occurred to your mind to think beyond the needs of your body. A man needs to use his brain as well as his other parts when he's fixing to wed."

"Ma!" he said again, this time to her back as she turned it to leave the room. "You speak the most outrageous—We wasn't spooning." The rush of warmth to his face was echoed in his "other parts" as he thought of Mary. And spooning. And earning two dollars. His ardor deflated. This business of getting married had more complexity than he'd suspected.

Then there was that other business. He had to write that letter. Sighing, he got up and fetched the ink bottle, steel-nibbed pen, and a few sheets of paper. Then he set about the task, thinking about each word before he wrote it down, hoping his plea would convince the captain to accept him into the troop, worrying if his spelling was acceptable.

Chapter 3
Rulon — April 22, 1861

As soon as he awoke the next day, Rulon rushed to waylay Ben before he rode into town to his job.

"Have you heard of any work at the mill?" he asked as they washed.

Ben glanced up, startled. "You can't have my job."

"I don't want it. I need day work. I have to earn two dollars to pay the minister."

"That's the cost of taking a bride? I will keep that in mind." Ben ran a hand over the fine-haired stubble on his chin. "I don't believe I'll shave today." He looked at Rulon, who had already lathered his face. "How about down to the Columbia furnace?"

"I was hoping for work closer by."

"I know they was hiring Negroes for day labor from Mr. Allen. When

Virginia goes to war, that furnace will be hopping to get enough pig iron smelted for the Tredegar Works in Richmond." Ben wiped his face dry, then chuckled. "You didn't know I knew that. I keep my ears open at the mill."

"Good for you, brother," Rulon mumbled, paying close attention to shaving under his nose. "I reckon I will look into it."

"You'll have to stay at the iron plantation. It's too far away from the place to ride out there every day."

"I'll take a bedroll. Do we still have any of that jerked venison?"

"How am I supposed to know that? Ask Marie. She knows what's in the larder."

"I will do that." Rulon took a towel from around his neck and used it to wipe away the last bits of stray lather. "Thank you for the information." He grinned. "A few days of work, and I'll have the money to put into Mr. Moore's palm."

"Generosity becomes you, brother." Ben buttoned his shirt.

"Ha! Any amount will be worth having the girl as my wife."

"Ease up, Rule. Think on something else, for a change."

Rulon snorted. "Like breakfast? The smell of that bacon does make a man's mouth water."

Ben laughed as they finished up and followed their noses.

ℂ

"Marie, do we have any jerked venison?" Rulon asked his sister after breakfast.

"I do believe there is a bit down in the cellar," she answered. "Why do you need it?"

"I'm off to look for a job at the Columbia furnace. I reckon I'll stay over and work it, if I get on."

"That sounds reasonable, but don't Pa need you today?"

"The seed is all in the ground, and he's finished shoeing the horses, so I figure I'm free for a spell."

"You haven't asked him?" she asked as she opened the trapdoor to the cellar.

He fidgeted with his hat. "No. Do I have to account to him for all my comings and goings?"

"You do if you're fixing to go off that-a-way," she said, her voice getting muffled as she descended the ladder.

"Little sis, you're too nosy."

Marie's head reappeared after a moment. "Do you want this, or shall I feed it to the hogs?" She held up a tied bag, but out of his easy grasp.

"I want it."

"Then keep a civil tongue in your head. Apologize."

"I'm sorry. You're growing taller every day."

"Rulon! I mean say you're sorry for calling me nosy. That's Julianna's domain."

He laughed. "You have the right of that. I am sorry I called you nosy. I'll speak to Pa. Now, can I have the jerky?"

She grabbed the ladder with the hand holding the bag and held out her other hand for a boost up the last rungs. Rulon gave her the assist. She pushed the trapdoor into place and turned to face him. "Here it is. You'd best start minding your tongue real close if you think to take a wife. You can't call *her* names."

He raised his eyebrows. "I don't intend to, unless you mean 'Darling' and 'Dear' and 'Sugar' and the like. I plan to use them real often."

"You are incorrigible!"

"Am not. Where's the respect due me, sis?"

"For what?" she scoffed. "Being born first? That's purely happenstance. I've got more sense'n you. I most likely was busy tending to the Angel Gabriel's fire, or I would have come first of all."

"You don't say." Rulon shoved the bag into his pocket and grinned at his sister. "You've got a lively imagination, I'll give you that."

She stuck out her tongue. "Off with you. Talk to Pa. I don't want him stomping through the kitchen with muddy boots because he's cross with you."

He grinned again and took himself out of the house to speak with his father.

∞

Rulon topped the hill and pulled up his horse so they both could rest for a few minutes before making the descent. The trip up the hills from Edinburg had been grueling for the animal, and he dismounted and pulled a bottle of water from his saddlebag. He took a long drag, then used his hat to water the horse.

The village around the Columbia Furnace spread before him on the floor of the valley. Beside Stony Creek, the limestone and frame buildings lay, and back farther, against the hill, he saw the furnace itself. He wondered where he would locate the foreman, at the headquarters, or at the works.

He decided whoever did the hiring would more likely be in an office. He stowed his damp hat under a strap on his saddle to let it dry, climbed aboard the horse, and tongue-clicked it into movement.

At the office, he was directed to speak to a Mr. Harvey about employment.

"Yes, I reckon we'll be needing more workers with this war talk," the man said. "I can hire you today to fell trees for charcoal, or next week to drive a team to Edinburg. The teamster pay is higher, but you say you want day work?"

"Yes, sir. That suits my circumstances better."

The man looked Rulon over. "Well, it appears to me you have the shoulders and arms to handle the saw and ax work. The pay's fifty cents a day, and I'll put you on a gang tomorrow. Did you say you're from Mount Jackson?"

"Thereabouts, yes sir."

"I reckon that's too far to ride out every mornin'. If you brought a bedroll, I can let you make a camp over yonder." He gestured to a copse of trees.

"That will suit me fine, sir. I come prepared."

"Good, then. Take care of your animal, and I'll have a piece of paper for your X when you return."

"I can sign my name, sir."

"Interested in office work? No? All right. Come back around the front when you're ready and you can meet the gang boss."

"Thank you, sir. I'm obliged."

∞

Rulon — April 27, 1861

On Saturday, Rulon rode back home with two dollars in his pocket and sore arms, shoulders, and back. He could scarcely wait to see Mary and tell her about his week, but first, he needed to clean up to make himself decent for the visit.

When he'd washed up and put on clean clothing, he picked out another horse and saddled it.

Peter approached with a frown on his face. "Take me with you."

"What task would take you to town, boy? I already asked Ma if she had needs. She said 'no'."

Peter ducked his head and mumbled something so low Rulon couldn't make it out.

"Speak up, boy. I haven't got all day to set here waiting for you to talk at me."

"You know what I want," Peter replied, all but shouting.

"You reckon you're a man and should do the duty of a man to defend his home?" Rulon swung aboard his horse. "Nah. Ma won't have it."

"I am a man, Rule!" Peter swiped a hand across his dark-stubbled chin. "Anyone can see it."

Rulon's horse turned, and he brought it around before he spoke again. "Needing to strop a razor each day don't make you a man. You barely celebrated seventeen years."

"I reckon the ability to raise a beard will help when it comes time to sign the paper."

The horse started to rear, and Rulon got it under control, then dismounted to check the gear.

As he calmed the horse, he threw a comment over his shoulder. "The matter has been decided. Ma don't want you to go." He lifted the saddle and found he'd been careless with the blanket. A fold in the material had caused the animal discomfort. He smoothed it out, restored the saddle to its place, and turned to his brother. "Despite the whiskers, you can't pass muster with that baby face." He buckled the cinch.

"Can too."

"Can not." Rulon ruffled his brother's hair. "The company clerk will take one look at you and spy you out for a fraud."

Peter jerked his head away. "Rule, you surely take the joy out of a man's life."

"A man?" Rulon snickered. "Don't call yourself a man again in my hearing, baby boy."

Peter planted his fist next to Rulon's eye.

Rulon probed the spot as he held Peter off with his other hand. "That is going to raise color, boy."

"No more than you deserve," Peter blustered, trying to swing again. "Bear the mark as a sign of your unbridled tongue!"

"That I am obliged to do." Rulon gave the young man a healthy shove away from him. "You still ain't going to town with me. I got business where you ain't wanted." He mounted and trotted off before Peter could recover and answer back.

Rulon — April 27, 1861

Mary reacted predictably, Rulon thought, recoiling at his swollen eye, then bringing him a cold compress to apply to it.

"Who did this to you? Was it that bunch of rowdies who hang out at Fletcher's? You weren't drinking? Oh, Rulon, how could you?"

He took her hand, mostly to keep it from fluttering around his face. "No Mary. Peter did it. He socked me when we was fooling around."

"Why would he do that? Your brother is a beast."

"No he ain't. I called him a name, and he felt justified."

"Why were you quarreling?"

"Mary, Mary." She was becoming overwrought, and he sought to quiet her with a little kiss on her temple.

"Don't you kiss me. Answer my question."

"Humph. He wants to enlist. I said he would be caught out for lying about his age."

"You were doing a noble task, then, preventing him from—"

"He didn't think so. When I called him a baby, he hit me."

Mary sat back on the sofa. Her face became stone. "You were goading him?"

Rulon shrugged his shoulders. "That's the way it is with brothers, Sugar." Remembering she had none, he added, "Don't sisters tease and josh each other?"

"Not to the point of violence, we don't."

"You never hit Ida?"

She looked horrified.

"Pushed her? No. Pinched her, then?"

"Well, maybe I've pinched her a time or two, but only when she well deserved it!"

"Boys ain't so dainty. Our bodies are larger than girls' are, for the most part, and we flail our arms around some. From time to time, somebody's liable to get in the way of a knuckle."

"You won't be doing that with me?"

He drew her into an embrace. "No." He kissed her. "No. I'm no woman beater." Her lips tasted of honey.

Mary freed her lips long enough to ask, "You reckon I'm a woman?"

"No question," he muttered on an exhaled breathe. "No question at all."

"Um," she murmured, permitting him a second kiss before she pushed him away.

"We have plans to make, Rulon. There's so little time to get this wedding together. Papa gave me a bolt of fabric, and I had another piece that goes with it, so once I borrowed a pattern from Lucy Hayes I started cutting out my dress. It's going to be so lovely, Rulon. You will just adore it."

Rulon doubted he could 'adore' any dress, but kept his mouth shut on that head. He could certainly adore the figure within it.

Sister Ida says she'll help me bake the cakes." She took a deep breath. "Mama seems so listless. I cannot get her excited about helping with the preparations." She counted on her fingers. "Rulon, May 11th is just two weeks away," she said, a little wail in her voice.

He bent and kissed her cheek. "We'll get it done, Sugar."

She drew in a breath, then looked around. "Papa said we should have the ceremony right here in the parlor. It will take less time and effort to decorate it rather than the church, and besides, we won't have to pay a rental fee."

Rulon nodded at the sense of that. It was enough botheration that the minister was charging money to read the words over them. He remembered something and said, "Ma told me to ask if there is to be a party afterward. I reckon she wants to pitch in any way she can."

"That is so sweet of your mama. I will send her a message. We shall have a small celebration. Perhaps only our families and close friends. Sweet cake and punch will suit for the refreshments. I don't reckon we need to hire a band. What do you think, Rulon?"

"No," he said, fervently shaking his head at the thought of more expense. "I don't think that's needed."

She considered. "You are right. A band wouldn't fit in this room anyway."

"No band. No," he agreed. Right now he didn't care about music. He wanted to kiss her again. Taste that warm honey again.

Mary looked up at him, trouble drawing her brows into a frown. "You're determined to enlist on the 22nd next?" Her voice quivered.

"That's when the troop is mustering." He tapped her nose lightly with his forefinger. "It's only for one year."

She sighed. "One year. A very long year."

"I'll write you every day."

"You'll be riding around the countryside. Most likely you won't find a place to post a daily letter. Instead, promise to write me every week."

"Every week, I promise," he agreed, focusing on her trembling lips and wanting them pressed against his.

"Here is some good news. Mama has resigned herself to our wedding. Papa gave her to understand that it is right and proper that we marry now. When she finally agreed, she said she would have India's belongings moved into the nursery and Ida's things moved into Sylvia's room so we can have my bedroom to ourselves."

Rulon sat up straight. "No. We're going out to the farm. Ma has already fixed up a spot for your necessaries and clothes and such."

Mary looked at her hands, folded together in her lap. "Oh, I couldn't. Mama is so set on her plan." She looked up, appeal in her dark eyes. "We must allow her some small victory in exchange. After all, she did give in to Papa's reasoning."

"But you'll be my wife. You should live with my family while I'm—"

Mary's eyes filled with tears, and she took a shaky breath. "Rulon, don't say that. You're quarreling with me." She hid her face with both hands.

He ducked down, trying to move her hands aside. "No, sweet girl. I ain't. It's the normal way of things to go to your man's place." He shrugged one shoulder.

"Well, in usual circumstances, you'd have your own house, but—"

"But you're going away. We don't have time to set up housekeeping. Please, just stay here with me until you have to—" She began to sob on the word "go."

"With all your sisters?" he mumbled, suddenly alarmed at the notion of sharing a house with the girls.

Mary sniffed. "They won't be in the way. Our room is in the back of the house."

At her words, so innocently spoken, but so evocative of intimacy and a door closed against the world and prying eyes, Rulon felt his blood warm. He swallowed hard. *It's time to leave.*

Mary undid his resolve by leaning forward and kissing his cheek. "Then it's settled? You'll be with me here?"

He groaned, and moved her face so that her lips met his. "I'll be with you anywhere you wish," he whispered against them. "Ah, Mary." He shuddered, acknowledging to himself that he'd reached his limit of endurance. "I have to go now."

"What?"

He exhaled. "I can't stay here." He managed to get to his feet, and reached for his hat. "You rouse my senses, Mary," he explained in answer to her questioning look. "I can't bear to touch you without—" He gritted his teeth before he said more than he should to her. "I'm not in a proper state," he finished, knowing that his words hadn't reached her understanding. She had no knowledge of his condition. She was a babe, young and innocent of the ways of men, of married folk.

"You'll come again soon? We have more plans to make."

"When I'm able," he whispered. "When I can do so." He jammed his hat on his head, fled the parlor, and barged through the front door.

഻

Rod — April 27, 1861

Roderick Owen sat in his favorite chair, enjoying the peace of the evening now that the young ones had all gone upstairs. He stared into the fire, listening to the soothing crackle of the flames for a while before he bestirred himself to go to bed.

Julia came and stood behind Rod's chair, her hands resting on his shoulders. "The day is fast approaching," she murmured.

"The day?" Rod looked around, craning his neck in an attempt to see his wife.

"Rulon's wedding day. The ceremony will take place in two weeks. The eleventh of May. That is a Saturday." She straightened his head and her fingers began to knead his neck. "My baby boy is now a man." Her voice seemed sunken into her throat.

"He'd like to presume that of himself." He captured one of her hands underneath one of his. "There's a heap of impetuosity in his nature."

"Don't he come by that naturally!" Her free hand wandered up the back of his neck, spreading his hair between her fingers.

He shivered at the touch. "Woman, what do you mean by that?"

"Husband," she returned his bantering tone. "Who was bent on asking my uncle for my hand instead of traveling north to get my brother's permission?"

"It was a long trip—"

"And would have taken too long."

"Besides, Jonathan is formidable."

Julia laughed. "You didn't know that at the time. He's no more intimidating than you are."

"I have grown into my fearsome posture."

She chuckled. "How do you reckon Jonathan arrived there?"

He pulled her around the side of the chair and lifted her onto his lap. "You are my daily breath, Julie. I don't take a step without thinking on your beauty and grace."

"Changing the subject?" she whispered.

"'She walks in Beauty, like the night of cloudless climes and starry skies, and all that is best of dark and bright meet in her aspect and her eyes. Thus mellowed to that tender light which Heaven to gaudy day denies.'"

She stirred in his lap. "Your courting poem."

"Not mine. 'One shade the more, one ray the less, had half impaired the nameless grace—'"

She joined in. "' . . .which waves in every raven tress, or softly lightens o'er her face, where thoughts serenely sweet express how pure, how dear their dwelling-place.'"

"Lord Byron's," he whispered, and then recited the final stanza.

She took his earlobes between her fingers and stroked them. "Husband, what news are you trying to ease into breaking to me?"

He sighed, a long exhalation. "You know me too well, wife." He enfolded her in his arms and drew her close, nuzzling the top of her head. "I am fixing to raise a cavalry company."

She struggled against him, squirming until she was in a position to see his face. "You wouldn't! Can't you be satisfied that you went off when you were young and played at war in a foreign land?"

Her irritation pricked both his conscience and his pride, but he could choose to address only one or the other. He chose to be properly abashed, but to lay his actions to pressure.

"Chester Bates brought the idea to me. It seems sound."

"You'd blame your friend for the notion? Roderick Owen, you are a scoundrel."

"I . . . am a scoundrel," he agreed, tilting his head to the side. "But I'm your scoundrel, and my native land's scoundrel. I can't let the Yankees invade my home."

In a flash, she turned into a melting woman and sank heavily against his chest. "I had hoped to avoid losing you to this squabble," she murmured, her voice catching.

"Oh Julie, Julie." He felt the softening of his sinews that her distress brought upon him these days. Tenderness had not been native to his nature, but over many years, he had learned a hard-won lesson. Tenderness betwixt a man and his wife was well worth cultivating. "I cannot pretend to know what is in store for me. I cannot lie on that point to ease your feelings." He kissed her hair. "Know this, woman. I will love you beyond any power that death has to separate us."

She wept in his arms, soft sobs she surely was trying to keep within the bounds of their chair. He could only whisper endearments and hold her closer to his soul.

Chapter 4
Mary — May 1, 1861

Mary sat in a small room off the kitchen where light from the sun illuminated the purple fabric in her lap. The tip of her tongue peeked out from between her lips as she concentrated on taking small stitches to join two pieces of the material together. Her sister Ida sat across her, sewing a seam into another two pieces of fabric.

"This is such tedious work," Ida said with a sigh. "Why can't Papa buy us one of those sewing machines?" She batted at the golden curls against her neck. "It is so warm today."

"Those machines are too expensive, Ida. Papa cannot afford to buy us one." Mary bent over to bite off the end of a thread. "Besides, he cannot procure one soon enough. You know I have a limited amount of time to finish my dress. Keep stitching."

Ida took one stitch, then stopped to ask, "Why is Papa allowing you to marry? You're not even fifteen yet. Mama wants you to wait until this war is over."

"That is my affair. Mama already agreed that I can wed, and there isn't any time to spare. If you don't want to help me with this skirt, go see if India brought home the lard for my cakes, and send her in here. Her stitches may not be pretty, but they will serve."

Ida put her work in her lap. "I think your beau is selfish. He is going off to war, but first, he wants to get married and do those things to you, those things Papa does to Mama."

"Ida!" Mary felt a flush going up her neck.

"Disgusting!"

"What are you talking about?" The heat of the flush was spreading throughout her body, and Mary shifted her position on the hard chair.

"Lizzie Sue told me all about it. She said—"

"That meddling little gossip? You cannot pay any attention to what she says, Ida. She doesn't know anything." She herself didn't know anything, just that Rulon's kisses—when she allowed him to kiss her—drove her to distraction with feelings she had not experienced before he began coming around and they had come to an understanding.

"Yes she does. She's told me many things that are true."

Mary noticed her sister's idle hands, and waggled her finger at them, relieved to find something to divert her thoughts from Rulon. "You are talking about this so you don't have to help me."

Ida smirked. "You're going to do those disgusting things with Rulon."

Mary sniffed in pretended disdain. "I cannot imagine what you are talking about."

"You had better find out quick. Ask Mama."

"You know she won't discuss anything like that." Mary had tried to broach the subject.

"What won't I discuss?" asked Mrs. Hilbrands as she entered the room.

"Nothing, Mama," said Mary. "We were only talking nonsense."

"I can imagine." Mrs. Hilbrands turned to her younger daughter. "Ida, did you dust the parlor this morning? I swear there is dust laying on all the surfaces in the room."

"I'm sorry, Mama. Mary has been hounding me to help her finish sewing her skirt."

"You must not neglect your chores. Each one teaches you how to manage a household one day."

"Yes, Mama. Shall I go now and dust?"

"That is wise, daughter."

"Mama," Mary protested, but her mother cut her off.

"You must manage your dress by yourself, Mary. We cannot quit our tasks merely because you are going to be wed. Against my advice, I might add."

Ida arose and made a face at Mary behind their mama's back. Then she left the room with a flounce of her skirt.

"You could have chosen to wear your Sunday dress, after all, instead of making a new one."

"I deserve to have a new dress when I make such a large change in my life."

"I would rather you wait until you are sixteen."

"I cannot wait. We have discussed this time and again. I am determined to become Rulon's wife as soon as may be."

"That young devil will be the ruination of you. He is only thinking of his own interests."

Mary stood. "I will not listen to this talk against Rulon. I believe I will go sweep the porch now." She put down her unfinished skirt and left the room, feeling like crying, but holding her chin high. She *would* marry Rulon, and he would *not* be her ruination.

∞

Rulon — May 7, 1861

"You'll be needing a horse."

Rulon turned from scooping oats out of the grain bin to see his father leaning against the door frame. Since Pa almost never leaned against anything, Rulon wondered how long he'd been standing there surveying him.

"I reckon I will. What will you take in trade for the bay?"

"You've worked the farm since you were old enough to lift a shovel or hoe weeds in the field. I figure that labor is plenty in exchange for the bay and her tack."

Rulon felt his throat constrict with sudden emotion. "I'm obliged," he managed to get out in a husky voice.

"You sure it's the bay you want? The sorrel is well mannered."

"The bay has spirit and don't spook easily. I reckon she would make a good battle mount."

"That's canny thinking, son. I agree. She will be steady under fire."

Rulon nodded. In a matter of days, he would leave this farmstead to live in town with his bride. Soon after, he expected to be doing some kind of patrolling, or picket duty, or whatever it was a cavalryman did to defend his country. That is, if he ever got a reply to his letter. If he wasn't acceptable to Captain Yancey and the Harrisonburg Cavalry troop, he would have to start his search all over again. He found himself chewing on the inside of his cheek.

"What has you worried, boy?"

"I ain't heard from Harrisonburg yet."

"Give it time, give it time. Yancey's bound to be a busy man. A lawyer, I hear. It's likely he's wrapping up his business."

"You're right. But getting married also has me perplexed." He shook his head. "The tasks Mary has been doing make my head swim."

Pa chuckled. "The ladies like everything fancy, son. Take a deep breath. Enjoy your day. It will be here before you know it."

"I wish I could believe that. It seems a lifetime away."

Pa nodded his head in understanding. "The day will come. By the way, your ma says there is another item you'll be needing." He cleared his throat. "My ma passed down her wedding ring to me when she died. She intended that my wife wear it when I found one, but I had forgotten about it by the time I married, and gave your ma a new one. She said you should have your grandmother's ring to put on Miss Mary's finger. She'll give it to you when the day comes around." He raised his eyebrow. "Men don't think about such geegaws. I'm pleased she recalled that ring."

"Such a lot of to-do." Rulon whistled. At the same time, he thought Mary would be happy to have a family ring.

Pa came over and clapped his hand on Rulon's shoulder. "Silken entanglements, boy. All these arrangements for fancy ceremony and parties and such sometimes seem unnecessary, but they keep the ladies happy. That's what matters, after all. Keep the wife happy, and you'll have a happy life." He tightened his grip briefly, then removed his hand.

"That's the sum total of your fatherly advice?" Rulon grinned wryly. "No words of wisdom for, other matters?" His face felt hot as he said the words.

Pa stared at him for a long time, and Rulon noticed a pink tinge on his father's forehead.

"Words of wisdom?" Pa cleared his throat. "Be gentle." He paused for a long moment, then added, "Work out the rest yourself." He turned away, then looked back over his shoulder. "Treat the bay gentle. She's a lady, too."

He was gone in a moment, and Rulon was left alone to chew on both his cheek and the words that still seemed to hang in the air.

ം

Julia — May 8, 1861

When Rulon came into the house at noon for dinner, Julia had been so intent upon the project she was doing with the girls that she was caught at what had remained a secret for some days.

"Ma," he said, his rising voice reflecting his surprise.

She stood and tried to put the work in her lap off to the side where he could not view it, but knew he had seen what they were up to. Marie had similarly shoved worsted material down on the floor beside her, but Julianna wasn't so wise, and only froze with her needle caught in grey fabric.

"Is that a uniform? I haven't even heard back yet from Captain Yancey. Why would you—"

"The answer is 'yes,' and it doesn't matter if you go with the Harrisonburg Troop or some other company. I reckon you're a-goin', and we have to put the best shine on the matter." She knew she sounded a bit defensive, but couldn't help defending her action in preparing a proper send-off for her first born. "I know you are set on being a cavalryman in this tussle, so you'll go as the fine-looking son of Roderick Owen of Shenandoah County, with a grand new suit of clothes, even if it is a uniform." She stood as straight as she could, hoping she didn't dissolve into tears and shame herself.

"We're beholden to Miss Mary for keeping silent about the material your ma purchased," Rod said from behind Rulon. "It was difficult for Randolph Hilbrands to find the braid, but he persevered, and found it in a shop down to Richmond." He walked over and held up the decorative sleeve resting in Julianna's lap. "The outfit will serve you well, wherever you end up."

The other boys crowded into the room behind Rulon, who stood slack-jawed, half-blocking the doorway.

Ben crossed over behind Marie and picked up the pants she had been working on. "Ha! A gold stripe down the leg? This is too fine for you, Rule."

Rod swung around, saying, "That's enough, Benjamin."

Julia pursed her lips as she looked around. A swirl of male voices surrounded her. Did boys relish fighting all their lives? Her sons' excitement filled the space in the room, and she had to raise her voice to be heard over the hubbub. "Marie, is the table laid?"

"Yes, Ma," she answered. "Julianna, come help me serve."

Julia followed her daughters to the kitchen. How had her family become so firmly entangled in this war?

Mary — May 10, 1861

Mary stood in the garden, halting for a moment before she resumed her pacing beneath the bower made of lilac bushes. Was everything ready? She had gone over her lists time after time, but felt that she had neglected a detail, some tiny particular that would put a finishing touch on her preparations. She stepped out onto the path again.

Is Rulon this nervous tonight? He had come to see her, but she had refused to let him enter the house, too distraught to entertain him without knowing all was ready for the next day.

She was getting married tomorrow. No. She couldn't be ready for this huge step. Becoming a married lady. Bearing a ring on her finger. Hearing folks call her "missus" instead of "miss". This was momentous. She wasn't ready.

She wanted to flee. She could run away, down the Valley Pike to hide in a crag in the mountains. Somewhere that Rulon wouldn't find her.

Rulon. What was she thinking? Was Rulon the right man for her, the right husband, the right—she shuddered—lover?

I don't even know what that means. She made a turn before she got out of the shadow of the lilacs. *Ida's foolish prattle has unnerved me.* Her talk of "disgusting things" that went on between married folk was truly unsettling. *What does Rulon intend to do to me?*

She tried to calm herself, to curb her distraught state. *Rulon loves me. He would never give me injury. I'm sure he will want to kiss me, though.* But what would come after the kisses? What was she expected to do? It was far too late to attempt to coax her mother into giving her pertinent information. What had she committed herself to do?

She wrapped her arms around herself and began to cry. Stumbling to the bench, she sat and put her face into her hands and sobbed until she had exhausted her tears and herself. Then she dried her eyes and walked back to the house to try to get into bed without any foolishness from her sisters.

Rulon — May 11, 1861

Rulon swung down from the horse with great care, mindful of the clothing he'd borrowed from his father to wear on this much-anticipated day. Peter took charge of his horse, tethering it to the hitch rail in front of Randolph Hilbrands' home.

Ben pulled up beside Rulon, dismounted, and gave him a knock on the shoulder.

"What's that about?" Rulon said, brushing off any dust Ben may have left behind.

"Cranky, are you? I didn't expect crankiness on this fine wedding day." Ben looked him over and guffawed. "You did a fine job with those buttons. Lined 'em up right nice." He doubled over with laughter.

Rulon looked down. He'd mis-buttoned the suit coat. Alarmed that his nerves were so evident, he re-did the job and scowled at Ben. "Your day will come, little brother."

"He won't have to button his own coat. Massa Allen will give the job to a slave." Peter ducked as though he expected Rulon or Ben to throw a punch.

Rulon peered at his brothers. "Rowdy troublemakers," he pronounced them. "Try and keep at least one civil tongue between the two of you."

"Oh, we'll be good, big brother," said Ben.

"Yes indeed. Best behavior," Peter agreed, grinning.

Rulon groaned. "I am not convinced."

The two younger brothers turned to look at one another, their upturned mouths reflecting their merriment at Rulon's expense.

"I'll hammer you both into the ground if you disrupt my wedding," he warned them.

"I reckon you'll be too busy with other matters," Ben said, laughing out loud now.

"Not that you'd know anything about caring for a woman."

Ben cocked his head. "Maybe more than you."

Rulon drew back his fist, then caught himself and muttered a mild oath. He wouldn't spoil his own marriage day by tussling with his brothers. Instead, he turned and strode toward the door, hopeful that the first sight of Mary would change his unease to gladness.

Mrs. Hilbrands opened the door to Rulon's knock and bade him enter, a small unchanging smile pasted on her mouth. As he hung his hat on the hat rack, he wondered if he should try to charm her, call her "Mother Hilbrands," or perhaps kiss her on the cheek, but in the end, his terror left him meekly following in her wake without any attempts on his part to ease the tension. Perhaps the sight of the lingering yellow and black color around his eye had contributed to the lack of warmth in her welcome.

He heard Ben and Peter coming through the door behind him, laughing. They shut up as they closed the door. Were they being respectful or did the oppressive atmosphere affect them as much as it did him?

When he entered the parlor, the first thing he noticed was the drawn drapes, heavy barriers that forbade the sun to shine upon his marriage. He wondered if the darkness was a sign, an ill omen of some sort, and his anticipation deflated.

The furniture had been shoved up against the walls, making room for the families and their guests to stand to witness the proceedings. Candles in heavy pewter holders stood along the mantelpiece, ready to be lit.

"Wait here," Mrs. Hilbrands said, then left him in the dim room with only his brothers to attend him.

"It's a mite somber in here," Ben said, and going to the nearest window, he tied back the drapes. Peter joined in, as Rulon protested in vain.

"Don't make trouble for me," he implored his brothers, thinking he sounded like a feeble old woman as he untied a pair of sashes to let one of the windows fall prey to the darkness again.

"The missus don't like you?" Peter asked, cocking an eyebrow.

"Well enough, I reckon," he said. "It's the wedding she don't like."

"As long as the girl is satisfied she's getting the right Owen," Peter said, smoothing down his hair. "I'm closer to her in age. By rights, I should be standing up with her today."

With an effort of will, Rulon refused to rise to the bait. "How far behind us was Pa?"

"He climbed in the wagon and set out just after you rode off. He should be driving up the street any moment," Ben said, and craned his neck to peer out the window opening to the front of the house. "Yes, there they come. Don't Ma look fine in that getup?"

Rulon was too occupied with adjusting the tail of his coat to go over to the window to admire his mother's finery. Where was the minister? Had Mr. Hilbrands changed his mind? Where was Mary? He pulled at his binding collar.

The knocker fell on the front door with a boom, causing Rulon's heart to jump. From the sound of the greeting, one of the Hilbrands girls answered, and soon his parents and his siblings came into the parlor, trailed by the Bates family. To his relief, Mr. Hilbrands accompanied them, bringing the minister along at his side. However, Mrs. Hilbrands kept her whereabouts a secret, and Mary was nowhere in sight.

Mr. Hilbrands greeted his guests, planted the minister before the fireplace, and called out into the hallway for a lamp to light the candles.

Mary's younger sister, Ida, brought a light, and as she performed the task with the candles, Mr. Hilbrands left the room.

"Such comings and goings," Ben commented behind the mask of his hand.

"Hush," Rulon whispered, adjusting with a shrug or two the position of Pa's coat upon his shoulders.

Just then, Mrs. Hilbrands came back and stood in the doorway, looking somewhat pale as the light of the now brighter room fell upon her countenance. Ma went and greeted her, patting her cheeks with hands encased in lace mitts. *Where did Ma dig those up?*

Rulon counted his siblings. Carl, James, Marie, Clayton, Albert, Julianna. The entire Owen clan had come to either tease him unmercifully or make merry. *They had better behave*, he thought.

Mrs. Hilbrands looked toward Ida motioned with her head. The girl promptly left the room. Then the woman made gathering motions with her hands, and the guests pressed toward the door.

Rulon didn't know whether to remain where he was or go along with the crowd, but the minister nudged him, so he chose the latter.

People spilled out into the hall, and Rulon edged up to the parlor door. Youthful female voices began to sing a song about "this happy occasion," as Mary's three sisters descended the stairway, carrying more lighted candles. At the top of the stair, Mr. Hilbrands stood with Mary on his arm.

Rulon sucked in his breath.

His bride wore a right pretty dress, light colored with purple flowers on the top, and purple with white flowers on the bottom. The skirt was wide enough to fill the area between the bannister and the wall. On her head, a circlet of purple blossoms of some kind crowned her dark hair.

"Mary." His shallow breathing allowed only a whisper of her name before he choked with emotion.

Her gaze rested momentarily upon him as though she had heard him say her name. Her simmering look pierced his soul. Then she lowered her eyes, took on a shy aspect, and made her slow way down the treads, leaning on her father's arm.

He found himself being pulled backwards, stumbling, to his place alongside the minister. Ben pinched his arm, and he remembered to stand tall, but was scarcely able to draw breath.

His family formed an aisle. The girls came forward, still singing, until they stood at the front, at one side, lined up next to Mrs. Hilbrands. Mr. Hilbrands brought Mary toward him, stepping carefully, stopping before the minister with Mary on his far arm.

The girls stopped singing.

The minister opened a book and began intoning words that Rulon paid no mind to. Mary was half hidden beyond the bulk of her father's body. Why didn't the man step back? Then Mr. Hilbrands said "I bring her," and granted Rulon's wish that he leave Mary's side.

Rearranging the couple, the minister kept talking, but Rulon only heard sound. All he could absorb was the fact that Mary now stood beside him, hands clasped together, looking at the carpet, her elbow brushing the sleeve of his coat.

After an interminable time, the man before them said something incomprehensible, then smiled and nodded at Rulon.

Ben toed him in the ankle. "Your answer," he hissed.

Rulon woke from his stupor and said, "I do."

Mary echoed him in her turn.

Mr. Moore took hold of Mary's left hand and looked expectant. Rulon felt his grandmother's ring come sliding across his palm. Ben. Rulon got it between his fingers, turned and put it on Mary's finger.

The minister said something about "man and wife," and smiled again. Ma gasped in the background. Mary turned to him, eyes glowing.

Peter chuckled. "Kiss her, or I will."

Rulon inhaled. Was it over? He felt an elbow in his ribs, and decided it was. He turned to Mary, looked at her upturned face, then kissed her.

She smelled of soap, and the purple blossoms, and another scent he didn't try to identify. Instead, his brain asked the most vital question. When could he carry her up those stairs to seclusion and privacy?

ઠ

After a party that lasted far too long, Rulon accompanied Mary up the stairs. She led the way down the hall, holding his hand tightly. She opened the door to their sanctuary and entered. He closed the distance between them.

He took her in his arms, covering her face with kisses, moaning, "Mary, Mary." He felt the fabric of his father's best trousers pressing against the evidence of his lust. Yes, it was lust, he admitted with almost his last coherent thought; frighteningly powerful in its hold on him. He kicked the door shut, too far gone to bother to secure the latch.

Mary pulled away from his frantic kisses long enough to do the job, then he gathered her back, intent only upon fulfilling his need.

They bumped against the bed. He laid her upon it and shed the intolerable trousers with such abruptness that a few of the buttons flew from their moorings and scattered on the floor. He lifted her purple skirt and moved undergarments aside to the extent that was necessary for his purpose, all the while crooning her name, over and over, a paean to wedding and bedding the girl as so often he had craved to do. Daytime or night, his imagination had driven him toward this moment, and he reveled in the commencement and completion of the connubial act.

After, her clothing restored to its accustomed place, Mary lay in his arms, trembling and sniffling against his shirt.

A thread of guilt needled into his consciousness. Pa had advised him to be gentle. He had not been. What if he had injured Mary?

He looked down and asked, as tenderly as he could, considering he was still breathless, "Did I hurt you?"

"No," she whispered, her voice too shaky for him to believe her denial.

"Mary? The truth, girl."

"Yes. A little. I didn't expect . . . that."

He groaned, covering his eyes with his hand. At length, he mumbled contrite words. "I beg forgiveness for losing all control, for overtaking you with my lustful yearnings." He shook his head, abashed at his behavior. "I'm a cad."

He felt the negative movement of her head against his chest.

"I am. I was thoughtless."

Mary stirred again, then planted a hesitant kiss on the side of his chin.

"I wanted you," she said. "I didn't know all that meant."

He removed his hand from his eyes, turned and kissed her hair, then settled her head into the hollow of his neck.

She continued. "I didn't know what 'coming together' signified."

"Your ma never—"

She snorted. "Mama doesn't talk about, ah, carnal acts."

He barely heard the last two words, her voice was so low. He reckoned it had cost her considerable effort to speak them. "She didn't prepare you?"

"It gives her the vapors to mention the subject."

"Ah, Mary."

"It was your right, Rulon. I know that much."

He lifted her chin and kissed one eyelid, tasting the salt of her dried tears. "My right don't include being rough. I regret I caused you pain."

She seemed to think on that for a while. Then she spoke hesitantly, her voice very soft. "Pa looked at me peculiar one night when I was going on and on about being woman-wed soon. He said, 'Mind he don't injure you.' I laughed at him."

He rose up on an elbow and stared down at his wife. "I did."

"No!" Her eyes went dark, then narrowed. Her hand cupped his cheek. "I am your woman now." Her little finger moved across his mouth, light as a butterfly. "I have waited so long to say those words." She swallowed. "A slight pain now is nothing in comparison to the longing I have felt to be your wife."

Rulon watched the movement of her throat, wishing for nothing more than to kiss the skin above her pounding pulse. He bent his head and did so. Her hand crept around to the back of his neck.

"Do it again," she murmured.

He took note that her respirations had begun to flutter faster. Her pulse beat more strongly against his lips. "What?"

"Show me I am your woman," she managed to say.

Chapter 5
Ben — May 13, 1861

Ben was about to follow Pa from the supper table when Peter mentioned offhandedly that he had fetched the mail from town and Rulon had received a letter.

Ben let Marie take away his plate and utensils, then said, "That's probably from the Harrisonburg company captain." He took a toothpick from the supply at the center of the table. "Why didn't you leave it off for him at Hilbrands' store? Hand it over, boy. I'll see he gets it tomorrow."

Peter put on a truculent countenance. "Who says I have the letter in hand? Who says I didn't deliver it directly into his greedy palm?"

Ben eyed him as he worked the toothpick around his teeth. He stopped long enough to say, "I thought the lad was on his honeymoon."

Peter quirked an eyebrow. "I sent Ida to knock on the door with my message. It took him long enough to come downstairs." His smug grin disappeared when Ma bopped him on the head with a wooden spoon.

"Mind your thoughts, son," she said above his howl of pain. "Keep 'em out of married folks' business."

Ben chuckled, and she turned on him.

"The same goes for you, Benjamin. Have an ounce of respect. If not for Rulon, at least for that young wife."

"Don't you be a-chastening me with that thing," Ben protested, putting his arms up for protection. "I've taken a mite too many whacks from it." The fingers of one hand explored around his head. "Yup, I have lumps aplenty from that ol' spoon." He said as an afterthought, "I meant no harm to Mistress Mary."

Ma waggled the implement in his direction. "You're not too old to take another lick if you don't curb your tongue and shackle your unruly thoughts," she said.

"Rulon don't mind a bit of rough talk," Peter said, rubbing his head.

"I mind," Ma said, her voice firm as she gestured with the spoon. "I mind on my own account, and that of your sisters here, and because I don't want you growing up rough and godless. The Man Upstairs has put his bounds on loose talk, and I won't have it around my table, nor amongst my children."

"Yes, Ma," Ben said.

Peter muttered something, and Ben gave him a poke.

"Yes, Ma," Peter blurted out, then turned and cuffed Ben in the arm.

"No fighting at the table," Ma said. "If you want to wrassle, go out on the porch."

ഔ

Rulon — May 13, 1861

When Rulon surfaced from his indulgent weekend, he became aware that he and Mary were expected to eat meals with the Hilbrands family, particularly the evening meal. In addition, he was expected to wear his finest go-to-meeting clothing for the occasion. When he asked about the seriousness of the request, Mary's solemn face and raised eyebrows gave him his answer.

"But sweet Mary, I've outgrown my good trousers. That's why I borrowed Pa's for the wedding." He grinned in an abashed manner. "I have to get those buttons sewn back on so I can return them to him."

"I can do that before we dine," Mary said, picking up her sewing basket.

"Why is your ma so set on having grand suppers, anyway? I'll be wearing the same clothes I wore on Saturday, my best shirt and Pa's trousers. She wants the coat, too?" At his wife's nod, he made a face. "Your folks saw all that at the wedding. If they want something showy, I reckon I can't provide it, unless I'm to wear the uniform."

"I'd rather you didn't, but I don't expect this attitude to last for long," Mary said as she threaded a needle. "Ma will grow fatigued of putting on airs and washing the tablecloth and napkins every week. I don't rightly know why she thinks she has to make a great show for us, anyway. The truth is, we usually have an oilcloth on the table."

"Just like at home." He handed Mary the trousers and buttons.

Mary looked at him, a little smile playing around her mouth as she tilted her head.

He backed away. "I'd rather look at you in all your finery." As he dropped his hand, it slid across the edge of his belt buckle, and he let it linger there. "My wife." He watched the spread of happiness across Mary's face. "It gives me great satisfaction to say them words," he said, a little huskily.

Mary looked up with a full smile. "It gives me great satisfaction to hear you say them." She shook a finger in his direction. "Now don't you get any ideas, Mister Rulon Owen. I don't have time for sport if I'm to get the buttons back on these trousers and you dressed like a fat holiday turkey for my mother to admire."

Rulon hooted with laughter and went back to where she sat to give her a quick hug. She returned it with relish, gave him her cheek to kiss, and went back to work on the buttons.

Well into supper, Randolph Hilbrands cleared his throat. "Mr. Owen."

Rulon had taken notice that Mr. Hilbrands had begun to address him in that manner since the wedding. He looked up and gave the man his attention.

"I understand you received a letter today."

"I did, sir."

"Daughter Ida says it came from Rockingham County."

Nosy little chit. "Yes, sir, it did."

"Mr. Owen, may I know who sent you the letter?"

That's where Ida gets her nosiness. "Sir, it's from my cavalry troop's commander, Captain Yancey, who is kin to me."

"Ah, a military matter."

Although the man made a statement, a slight upturn to his voice made Rulon aware that it really was meant as a question.

"Sir, he welcomed me to the Harrisonburg Cavalry and gave me a date to report for duty." Rulon figured he may as well give the man what he wanted. He was, after all, paying for Rulon's and Mary's keep. "It's May 22nd, as I reckoned it would be. I will leave here on the 21st in order to arrive early on the appointed day." He glanced at Mary. Their discussion of the matter had been a mournful one.

"Ah," Mr. Hilbrands said again, evidently satisfied with the answer. "Have you a hat?"

"My everyday one is all, sir."

"That will not do." Mr. Hilbrands arose and went to the sideboard, where he opened a door and drew forth a round box. He brought it to the table and reseated himself. "Now this is an acceptable hat for a cavalryman," he said, lifting from the box a slouch hat decorated with a black plume and held up on one side with a pin. Holding the headgear in reverent hands, he murmured, "It is after the fashion of the one worn by Colonel J.E.B. Stuart himself. I imagine he will be your ultimate commander."

Rulon gulped. "I reckon that's a mighty fine hat, sir," he managed to say. "Much obliged."

"The best available." He put the hat to one side on the table and looked up. "You will require armaments?"

"Yes, sir. Whatever I can bring."

"I have a pistol I want you to carry." Mr. Hilbrands took one from the hat box and laid it on the table.

"Thank you, sir. I'm much obliged."

"I would extract your promise to bring it home, but I know I cannot."

Rulon looked at Mary. Her face had gone white. "Sir, if you don't mind, the ladies."

"I know of their tender sensibilities, man. I live with a passel of 'em, don't I?" Rand scowled and his face reddened.

"My wife—"

"My daughter knows she could lose you." Mr. Hilbrands's scowl deepened.

"I reckon that's why she was so insistent in the matter of your somewhat hasty marriage."

Mary made a little sound of distress, and Rulon reached for her hand under cover of the tablecloth. He bent his head close to her ear and asked in a low tone, "Have you had your fill?"

She nodded, and he stood up and looked at Mary's mother. "Excuse us, Mrs. Hilbrands. My wife and I are going to retire. With your permission, ma'am?" He glanced at Mr. Hilbrands' annoyed countenance. "I am very much obliged to you, sir, for the gifts of the splendid hat and the pistol. However, my wife is unwell. Goodnight, sir." He hoped that was sop enough to deflect Mr. Hilbrands' anger as he gave Mary his arm and beat a formal but hasty retreat.

ഇ

Rulon lay on his side, watching the rise and fall of Mary's bosom as she slept. His ardor spent for the time being, he only marveled at the mysteries kept hidden beneath the cloth of her nightdress. For a girl everyone told him was too young to be his wife, she was undoubtedly woman enough for him.

He regretted that he would have to leave her soon. The letter Peter had shoved at him earlier that day wiped out all his wonderings about their future. Captain Yancey had replied to his question and had agreed to take Rulon into the troop, but only on the strength of the family connection. The captain stated in no uncertain terms that he had to prove himself a worthy cavalier.

He could ride. That wasn't a problem. He could shoot a shotgun, rifle or pistol, as he had proven countless times. Since he had been old enough to hold a weapon, Pa had taken him along to hunt meat for the family. His ability to shoot with better-than-average accuracy wasn't a question in his mind. The question causing him disquiet was, could he kill a man?

He felt sweat break out along his upper lip, upon his limbs and his brow. Could he ride into battle, take aim at a human being, and squeeze the trigger? He ran a hand over his forehead and down his face.

Mary stirred and he froze. She mumbled something he couldn't catch and threw an arm over his body. Then she resumed her slow, regular breathing.

Rulon let out his breath and returned to his thoughts.

Could anyone who was already a member of the Harrisonburg Cavalry kill another man? As far as he knew, none of them had had occasion to meet an enemy on a battlefield. They likely had only drilled for the happenstance. Training. That was what he lacked. Training. How did one train to kill an enemy?

He swallowed. Captain Yancey's letter had given the date on which he was to appear at the Harrisonburg Cavalry's camp in that town. Next week. So soon. So soon.

He was to bring what arms he could gather, along with a good horse and tack, and whatever personal effects he would need to sustain his needs as a military man. He had the horse and tack as his father's gift, two changes of clothing, and the fine uniform his mother and sisters had sewn for him. Mr. Hilbrands' hat was a mite outlandish, but the pistol was a timely gift and would serve him in good stead. He supposed he would have to acquire powder and lead balls, but perhaps the company would provide that. He knew so little about the details of war.

He was to enlist for one year.

He gulped. A year! He would be gone from Mary for a year. Would she forget him during that length of time? Would his caresses be gone from her memory when he returned? Would time dim her recall of the fervor of their entanglements, flesh against flesh as he had convinced her was right and proper?

He carefully placed his hand over hers as desire returned. Dare he wake her? Dare he not? He brought her hand to his lips, and at his soft kiss, she awoke and turned to him, eyes hooded and dark.

"Rulon? I am glad you're here. I dreamed you had gone."

"No, it's not time to leave you. Not yet." His voice sounded a little uneven, perhaps hesitant, to his ears. "Not for several more days."

"You are troubled." She got her hand loose and touched his cheek.

How do women know these things? "A little. I'm worried that I'll show myself a coward in battle."

She made a small sound, a disbelieving sound. "Not you. You're strong, like your papa. Did he ever run from anything?"

She sounded sleepy, and Rulon regretted awakening her.

"No. Not to my knowledge."

"I like your papa." She closed her eyes and smiled a bit.

"I reckon he's a good man. Go to sleep, little wife. Morning will come early."

"It always does," she agreed, and turned her head away, sighing herself into sleep.

෨

Rulon — May 21, 1861

It's here at last, Rulon thought when he awoke on the day he was to leave for Harrisonburg. He looked at Mary's face in the dimness, lightly touching his arm, peaceful in sleep. *This ain't going to be easy.* Last night they had spent a considerable time finishing off their honeymoon before sleep overcame them. He had intended to leave this morning without further connubial contact, but the sight of Mary's slightly parted lips, and the curl of hair that lay across her throat aroused him.

He put out a finger to brush her cheek. She was awake in an instant, although her eyes opened only partway, like her lips. Her hand went around the back of his neck, and Rulon heard himself moan as his resolve slipped away.

Later, he thought, *It's still early. If I don't stop to eat, I can make camp tonight and arrive in good time tomorrow.*

Mary climbed out of bed as Rulon dressed. She had removed her nightgown, and held it so it covered her, but she dropped it, approached him, and put her arms around his neck.

"Woman, I can't take the time—"

"I know that. I'm searing myself upon your memory," she said, her voice a little flirty, and at the same time, a little desperate. "You go win this war and come back to me and . . ." She ducked her head.

"And what? There's no doubt what I'll do when I return." He hugged her fiercely. Excitement filled him, but it wasn't a renewal of lust. It was a prickling anxiety to begin the new adventure, to beat back any Yankee threat to his country.

"I don't mean 'and we'll have another go.' I reckon something is different about my body." Mary backed out of Rulon's embrace and touched her white belly. "I believe . . . it might be possible . . . that I'm increasing." She didn't give him a chance to draw her to him again, but bent out of his grasp, picked up her nightdress, and draped it over her arm as though it were a shield.

"Mary," he whispered, his hands dangling. He gulped. Was he a father already? "When will you know for certain?"

She shook her head, biting her lip. After a moment she could speak again. "I don't know. I don't know. Perhaps a month, two months? I don't know. You will be home soon, won't you?"

He had no idea how to answer her. The reckless youth in him yearned to answer yes, but the unknown stretched before him like a dense cloud he could not penetrate. He tried to nod, to agree, but could not. "I will try," was all he could force past his lips before he enfolded her in his arms for the last time today.

Today. The last time today. Not the last time forever. He shook off that spectral thought and turned away to finish dressing. He heard Mary's clothing rustling as she dressed in silence. *My wife. The mother of my child? God strengthen you, Mary.*

ॐ

Rulon cleared the outskirts of Mount Jackson and put the horse into a steady gait. Did he have time to bid his kinfolk farewell? His early morning dalliance with Mary had put him behind schedule, but he might have a moment to spare. Should he share Mary's incredible supposition with his ma? No. It was just that as yet, a supposing, a feeling not proven. Still, canny women had canny senses, and his Mary was . . . What *was* Mary?

A little bit of a thing. The young girl he'd yearned for, all right, lusted after, and won because the Yankees were raising an army. Had times been different, would he have been able to marry her so quickly? Would she have consented to become his wife, to bare her heart and soul, and so readily give him her body to satiate his needs?

Surprisingly, she had taken to the marriage bed with an avid desire he had not expected. Was that a woman's way in order to become with child? Was that what Mary had craved from him? A babe? Had his lovemaking pleased her, or was it a sham to collect his seed?

Rulon pulled up and dismounted, breathing heavily. Where had he picked up this doubt? He surely didn't need to be unmanned when he was on his way to who knows what encounters with men who would take away his rights as a Virginia citizen. He scrubbed his clean-shaven face in his hands. He removed a flask of water from his saddlebag and took a swig of the liquid. He swallowed, put the bottle away and straightened his shoulders. *Mary was pleased to become my woman. Those eyes did not lie. She rejoiced in being with me.*

Half afraid of the tug that drew him back to Mount Jackson, he mounted and gigged the horse forward, onward toward Harrisonburg.

A mile or two more and he saw the bend in the road ahead where lay the turnoff to a lane that he could find on the darkest of nights. At the end of the lane, his family would be going about their daily tasks, perhaps thinking about him, perhaps not. Rulon cleared the bend in the road and reined the horse into the wide path. He had to be quick. Harrisonburg wasn't far away, as the crow flies, but he would need most of the time left of the day to make the trip on horseback.

Julianna saw him first when she turned from feeding the hogs. "Rulon!" his younger sister shouted, then dropped her pails and ran toward him, braids flying, spindly legs showing beneath her swirling skirt, skinny arms outstretched to him.

He dismounted before she reached him and caught her in his arms, noting the tears streaking her face.

"Why are you going to fight?" The anxiety in her voice caused it to come out high and thin, and he hugged her tighter than before.

"Our country needs me," he answered, muffling his answer against her sunbonnet.

"What if you die?" she wailed.

He couldn't reply. When he raised his head to take a last look around the place, Ma was there with Marie beside her, their grave faces bringing a lump to his already tight throat.

Then Albert, the mischievous scamp, came running down the lane, with Pa and the rest of the boys walking behind him. Ben was the only one missing. They had made their farewells in town.

He had to hug them all, even Pa. Then Ma began a prayer, and they quit their hats, joined hands right there in the lane, and listened to her heartfelt plea for a short war and safety for the troops.

As Ma spoke the "amen" and the family joined in, Rulon was reminded that he hadn't left Mary with a prayer. Mayhap he should have, instead of bedding her one last time. Devotion to God should be in their marriage, as it was in his parents' union, he reminded himself. He climbed on the horse, pledging to be a better husband when he got the chance. *If I get the chance.*

ॐ

As Rulon approached Harrisonburg in late afternoon, he kept his eyes open for a place that would make a good camp. He would need water for the horse. The river lay nearby, rippling its way north to the Potomac.

The Potomac! He would be there in a few days. The federal armory stood on its bank at Harper's Ferry, and he'd heard a whisper that it was now in the hands of his countrymen.

A glow of anticipation began to grow in the pit of his stomach. Across that wide river, his enemies gathered. He imagined a city of tents occupied by rough men eager to put a musket ball into his forehead.

His fingers touched the supposed spot. With effort, he lowered his hand as he admonished himself to quiet his fear. *Don't go borrowing trouble, boy. You may soon have a baby to support, a child to raise up. Keep your thoughts on getting home to Mary, to Mary and your son.*

His son! But could the babe be a girl? No. He was sure that if his seed had taken root in Mary's body, he had made a son. There was no doubt in his mind. The elation rising in him, the warm conviction, assured him on that score.

His thoughts jumped to Mary, with her winsome smile and raven hair. How bold she had been this morning, tossing all convention aside with her nightdress to, what was it she had said? *To sear herself upon my memory*. He shivered. That moment was not to be forgotten. She had achieved her end.

Soon a fine meadow that stretched off the road a ways drew his attention. The lowering sun glinted on water beyond. Beside the meadow stood a barn and other outbuildings. Near to a chicken coop, a house—white paint gleaming on half the boards—occupied the space at the head of a lane.

He reined the horse off the road, followed the path, and halted in the dooryard.

"Hello," he called. "Is anybody home?"

A full-bearded man stepped out of the barn and approached. "Hallo," he said, his deep voice easily pushing through the mass of facial hair. "What might I do for you?"

Rulon doffed his hat. "I was seeking a camp spot for the night and noticed your fine pasture over yonder. Might I bed down alongside the river?"

"Going for a soldier, are you?"

Rulon nodded. "I am. Enlisting tomorrow."

"It will be my honor to have your company on the place. You are . . .?"

"Rulon Owen, Mount Jackson."

"Mr. Owen. I am Helmut Strauss. You will sup with us tonight, if you please."

The man offered his hand, and Rulon gave him his.

"Many thanks, Mr. Strauss." He looked around the farmstead. "Have any chores I can do?"

"I was milking cows, Mr. Owen. Come. Get off your horse and take him to the well. When you have seen to his needs, you may lend me a hand with the last few animals."

Rulon dismounted with a sigh. "You're mighty gracious, Mr. Strauss. I'm obliged for your kindness."

"We must do all in our power to repulse the threat to our lands, Mr. Owen. I am in your debt."

Chapter 6

Rulon — May 22, 1861

When he had spent an hour helping around the Strauss farm, Rulon enjoyed a hearty meal laid on the table by Mrs. Strauss, and after a bit of conversation with Mr. Strauss, he bedded down beside the murmuring Shenandoah.

He was up early so he could don his finery, but no earlier than Mrs. Strauss, who turned aside his protest that he could eat a johnnycake from his saddlebag for breakfast, and plied him with sausage, fried potatoes, and eggs, which he washed down with large amounts of creamy milk. He took his leave soon after, stuffed to the brim with good food, and with a parcel of sandwiches from the good woman, to boot.

A short ride brought Rulon into Harrisonburg. It was not difficult to locate the place he was to enlist, as a row of several tents stood in the town's courthouse square. He dismounted and asked a passing man where he should enlist, and was directed to one of the tents. He hitched his horse to a nearby post and ducked inside the flap.

"Mornin'," a cheerful voice welcomed him as he entered. "You the man from Shenandoah County?"

"That's me. Name is Owen, Rulon Owen. I live near Mount Jackson." He took off his hat, wondering if the plume was too ostentatious.

The other man got up from behind his camp desk, pulled down his jacket, and extended his hand. "Pleased to make your acquaintance, Owen. Ren Lovell. I'm from Hilton Crossing up the pike about two miles."

Rulon took the proffered hand and gave it a firm shake. "I'm glad to know you, Lovell. Mayhap I should clarify. I moved into town when I wed a little more than a week ago."

"Felicitations, I'm sure." The man was slightly taller than Rulon, and slender, with bright yellow hair and a full moustache. He wore a short jacket with golden bars slashing the front, brass buttons holding it closed, and pants not unlike his own. His unabashed smile showed off a crooked front tooth and two dimples just beyond the facial hair. "Must have been hard to leave the new missus."

Rulon grinned back. "You have the right of that. I don't want to miss the doings, though. I believe the wife understands."

"Don't you be certain of that. The ladies may nod and smile, but they don't comprehend the issues or our need to whup the enemy."

"They do pitch in, regardless. Mount Jackson is buzzing like a bee tree. The ladies have taken over the Union Church for sewing circles."

"They will do such. Are those ladies the ones who made your outfit?"

"No." Rulon felt as though the uniform marked him as an outsider. "My ma and sisters made it up for me. Wanted me to make a good showing for the family."

Lovell chuckled, said, "Nothing but the best for the honor of the family," as though he understood perfectly Rulon's discomfort, then reached back to his desk and snatched his cap, which he seated on his head. "I'm to take you to meet the captain. He'll want to size you up before we commence drilling today."

"Drilling? What do you do in the drills?"

"We run the horses around a bit, and get more familiar with Hardee's tactics." Lovell smiled again. "That's in a book the captain always totes around. I saw you tying up a horse. Yours? How are you armed?"

"The horse is mine. I brought a pistol I acquired not long ago. Gift of the wife's father."

"Uh huh. What is it?"

"A cap and ball five shot."

"That'll do to start," Lovell said. "Drop your gear in the corner and I'll make you known to Captain Yancey."

"It'll be fine to meet him at last. He and I are kin. Second cousins, my pa reckoned it." Rulon put down his saddlebags and followed Lovell out of the tent and down the row to a larger tent near the center. A guard stood beside the hanging flap, carbine on his shoulder.

"Captain in?"

The guard gave Lovell a smirk. "I'm a-standing here, ain't I?"

"Tell him the new man came up."

"Go ahead in and tell him yourself." He eyed Rulon from top to toe, then returned his gaze to the feather adorning the hat. "You the new boy from down in Shenandoah County?"

Rulon nodded slowly, then Lovell tapped him on the arm and held the tent flap open. "Let's go."

Unsure about what kind of welcome awaited him from his cousin, Rulon straightened immediately upon entering, side-stepped to let Lovell enter, and then stood stiffly to his estimation of attention.

ℰℛ

The man in front of Rulon looked up when he and Ren Lovell entered the tent. He was clothed in a military uniform with a dozen or more gold buttons up the front of the coat and copious amounts of braid adorning the sleeves. Even seated in his camp chair with one leg crossed over the other, he had an erect carriage. Several papers covered his lap, and others had spilled onto the floor around him.

"What do you want?" he barked.

"Captain Yancey, sir. Rulon Owen, come here from Shenandoah County, has reported to enlist, sir," Lovell said, snapping off a salute. "He is fixing to sign the paper, sir. I was told to bring him here when he arrived."

Rulon imitated Lovell's salute, but the captain gave him little notice after the first cursory inspection.

"Is he outfitted?"

"He has a pistol, sir."

"Humph. I expected more from Shenandoah County than a pistol, that, that uniform, and a fancy hat." He pointed his pencil disparagingly at Rulon.

Rulon shifted his weight forward and began, "Sir, I—"

"Shh," cautioned Lovell. He spoke to the captain again. "He reckons he's your cousin, sir."

"I allowed him to join the company on that foundation," Thomas Yancey said. "It won't buy him special favors."

"No sir," Lovell said.

"Dismissed."

Lovell threw Rulon a glance and motioned with his head toward the tent flap. Then he saluted, about faced, and dragged Rulon outside while he was trying to execute another salute.

Lovell maintained his hold on Rulon's jacket until they were clear of the tent and the guard. Then he let go and grinned. "You should see your face."

"Whew." Rulon let out a breath, not sure if this would be an everyday occurrence or not. He brushed his hands down his uniform. "I don't look as fine as he does."

"Not many of us do. When we get to Harper's Ferry, I reckon we'll get you outfitted with the uniform pieces you're missing and the gear you'll need, if you didn't bring anything more from home."

"Saddle and saddlebags with my personal necessaries is what I brought." Rulon felt his face go hot. Was the intense labor of his mother and sisters all for naught? He followed Lovell back to the tent where they had met.

"You'll bunk here with me'n Owen," Lovell said when they'd made it back.

"Owen? I'm Owen. Rulon Owen."

Lovell grinned, showing the ubiquitous dimples. "He's Owen Leoyd. What are the chances you two would end up in the same outfit, let alone be tent-mates?"

"What's he like?" Rulon asked, sitting on the blanket covering the one cot out of the four in the tent that gave the appearance of being unclaimed.

"You met him over yonder, guarding the captain from the Yankees."

"Hmm. I reckon we'll get along all right."

"He's not as easy-going as me, but there's no evil in him. I can't say the same about the other fellow sleeping here. He's over to the hospital, playing sick." Lovell aimed a kick at the leg of the nearest cot.

"He's not sick?"

"More like he's perverse," Lovell responded with some heat. "He'd as soon stick you with a knife as shake your hand."

Rulon arose with haste. "I'm not taking his cot, am I?"

"No. That's unused."

"What's he doing in the company?"

Lovell wore a sober face for the first time in their short acquaintance, and swore briefly. "He's the surgeon's pet, some kind of kin. The doc wouldn't leave home without the rooster fart, so he dumped him on us."

Rulon caught himself before he laughed at the man's epithet. After he could speak without chortling, he asked, "When do you reckon he'll show his face here again?"

"If I had my druthers, never." Lovell took a deep breath, apparently trying to return to happier thoughts. "Likely tomorrow before we leave. The other doctors won't keep him long before sending him on his way."

"I reckon I have to meet him one time or another."

"Too bad you can't add 'never' to that."

"What does the man look like? I don't want to come upon him unaware and get on his bad side."

"He don't have a good side, Owen. Stick close to me, and I'll endeavor to point him out before you're obliged to meet him here in the tent."

Rulon nodded slowly.

Lovell pulled a paper from a stack and put it on the table before Rulon, accompanied by a pen he had dipped into an inkwell. "Sign here, Owen. This says you're bound in service to Virginia for one year."

"I can read," Rulon muttered as he took the pen. He bent to the task, then straightened and handed back the pen. "The fight will be over long before a year comes around. What then?"

Lovell tilted his head to one side and scratched under his chin. "I reckon the boys in charge will let us off, unless we're needed to guard the border."

"Let's hope ol' Abe Lincoln sees the right of our argument before then."

Lovell sanded the paper, then stowed it under a paperweight. "Time for our final drill, Owen. Keep your eyes open. You have a lot to learn today, because we'll be on the road tomorrow."

ഇ

Rulon — May 23, 1861

The next morning, Rulon awoke to the touch of a pinching hand over his mouth and the prick of a knife to his throat under one ear.

"Get outta yore cot, sissy boy. We're packing up to move outta here."

Rulon scarcely breathed. The knife's tip moved fractionally. Then it lifted a bit, but still made contact with his skin as it traced a line across his neck toward his other ear. Lovell hadn't been joking about the danger of this man.

"Von! Leave the man be!" Lovell's voice barked. "Put that hog-sticker away and prepare to strike the tent."

The man named Von growled an obscenity and removed the knife. "He's not our kind. Look at that damn feather," he added, gesturing toward Rulon's fine hat. But he finally backed away, left the tent, and made his noises outside.

"Whew!" Lovell expelled a gusty sigh. "I couldn't be sure he would obey me," he said, approaching to eye Rulon's neck.

By this time, Rulon had arisen and was dressing in haste.

"He didn't leave you any permanent damage," his new friend observed. "The sooner we can put him on a patrol against the Yankees, the sooner he'll be able to do what he loves best."

"What's that?" asked Rulon, dreading the answer as he struggled to recover his dignity.

"Killing folks."

ഇ

As soon as the tents had been struck and stowed into a baggage wagon, the men of the Harrisonburg Cavalry were mounted and on their way to war. They made a steady progress down the Shenandoah Valley, passing through town after town where crowds gathered to cheer them on. Bands played rousing marches. Dogs nipped at the heels of the horses.

At last, Mount Jackson loomed before the troop. Rulon's stomach knotted with tension as he spied his father-in-law standing in the road before his store, hat uplifted. And there . . . there stood Mary—upright, graceful, her raven locks gleaming in the sun.

Her eyes swept the rows of horsemen, then found him. At last he was glad he was wearing the uniform and hat she could identify. She locked her gaze upon him as though to plumb the depths of his very being. She raised a white handkerchief aloft. It fluttered in the slight breeze before she brought it to her lips and bestowed a kiss upon it.

Rulon devoured the sight of her, the slender figure clothed in a summer dress of some purple stuff. She did so love the color. As he looked at her, she launched her body forward and, braving the mass of horseflesh, came to his side.

He feared for her safety, but she smiled up at him, reaching up as she kept pace with his horse, offering up the handkerchief into his hand. He took it, pressed it to his own lips, and tucked it into the front of his coat, right over his heart.

Her hand touched his lightly, and he moved to enfold it, but she pulled free of his grasp and threaded her way among the horses to the side of the road. She had not been quick enough to prevent him catching sight of the tears beginning to fill her dark eyes.

Oh Mary. Tears? Did she fear for him? For herself? Was she ill? Ah, how heavy a burden it was to leave her behind again and go off to face an uncertain future at the hands of an unknown, uncaring foe. Would a Yankee musket ball claim his life? Make Mary a widow? Make his child an orphan?

He turned in the saddle and searched through the people standing along the way, but Mary was gone from his sight. Perhaps she was shielded from his view by larger citizens. Mayhap she had fled into the store to hide her emotions.

His heart felt as though a hand were wrapped about it, squeezing it tightly and painfully, as he rode with the troop out of the town, onward toward Harper's Ferry.

∞

Rod — May 26, 1861

One evening, Rod kept his sons at the table after supper, and produced a sheaf of papers and a lead pencil.

"Boys," he said, "Rulon has gone into the fighting. Benjamin will leave soon, and so will I. I'm raising a company of cavalry."

"Pa, you didn't tell us," complained Peter, running his finger in a circle on the oilcloth covering the wood table.

"You didn't need to know," Rod answered. "But now things are moving along, and I reckon it's time to lay out the plan on what's what in running the farm for your ma."

Carl groaned and let his head fall forward. "Pa," he said as he raised it, "we know when to plant and how to milk the cows and butcher the hogs and break the horses, and—"

"I reckon you all think you do, but there's a good chance you could forget a thing or two of vital importance, like saving sufficient seed, and watching the mares for signs of their season so you get the best stud to cover her at the right time." He turned to his third-born. "Peter, I'm putting you in charge of the crops. See that you don't forget to harrow after you plow."

"Pa," Peter said with a snort. "I've done that plenty of times."

"See you don't forget. Carl, you're to manage the cattle herd and the hogs. Keep track of the weather when you go to butcher, and mind that Granny sow. She's vicious. If she weren't such a good breeder, I would have eaten her long ago. Clay is to help you." He looked at the younger son. "You're a good milker, so don't take any guff from Carl."

It was Carl's turn to whine "Pa," and he took full advantage, while Clay played with his folding knife and grinned.

"James," Rod said, pointing his pencil down the table. "You are to oversee the stable. I know you're young, but you have more horse-sense than many grown men of my acquaintance. I've written down instructions on breeding the dams. I want you to keep the lines as pure as you can, so watch that stud I bought from Kentucky. He'd have his way with every mare on the place, if you'd let him."

"Rod," Julia called from her chair.

"I'm not telling him anything he don't already know, Julie," he remonstrated. "Albert, you are to help Peter. Make sure the seed don't rot from planting at the wrong time. Help your ma with the pumpkins in the kitchen patch. She don't have to heft them when there's a strong boy on the place."

Albert grinned at the compliment. "Yes, Pa."

"I've made lists for the chores that need to be done at certain times, and in correct order. Mind that y'all study them out and help each other when you're not busy with your own tasks. Am I understood?"

"Yes Pa," came in a chorus from both sides of the table.

Rod nodded, and passed around the pieces of paper. "You may as well keep them all together in the farm journal, in case someone takes sick or has an injury and another one of you needs to fill in." He took a deep breath and looked at each boy in turn. "I'm putting my trust in all y'all to do your duty and support your mother."

"Jerusalem crickets! I feel left out," said Ben.

Rod narrowed his eyes at Ben while he considered if that was a profanity, or crude talk instead. Ben looked so innocent in his disappointment that he decided to let it go without any further notice. He looked down the table again. "You have your work cut out for you. Get a good night's sleep. I'll start easing you into your tasks tomorrow."

∾

Rulon — May 28, 1861

Garth Von brought out his knife a few days later as the tent mates cooked their rations for supper. He got Rulon's attention when he growled "Owen!" and began to stroke his bewhiskered neck from side to side with the thin blade.

Rulon tried—with little success—to suppress a shudder as he dropped a slab of pork into the kettle. What was wrong with the man? Why did he bear him a grudge? He'd not known of Von's existence a week ago. Surely he had done nothing inside of that interval to merit such menacing behavior.

Von continued to mimic slitting a throat for several minutes, eying Rulon all the while.

Rulon's stomach curdled with fear. He stepped back from the fire and fought the sensation, yet it sat heavily upon him. Was he a coward? He squirmed at the notion. He thought not, but he had never encountered such unwarranted ill will on the farm.

Sure, he had tussled with bullies, town boys with too much time on their hands. They were easily met, and usually beaten, at least after he began to get his growth and put weight on his spindly frame. This situation felt different, like pig iron cast from a defective mold. The man was certainly contrary, but there was something more, besides.

"He's mad, you know," Owen Leoyd muttered for Rulon's ear as he broke a loaf of hard bread over his knee and handed him a chunk.

Madness. Was that what glittered in the man's eyes, flitting away for a time, then returning, doubled in intensity?

Rulon felt the hairs on his neck raise, and knew it wasn't due to the night air.

Von lurched forward, and Rulon threw himself backward, smacking up against Ren Lovell, spilling his tin cup of coffee.

But even as Lovell cried out in protest, Rulon saw that Von's movement wasn't an attack. The man thrust his knife into the kettle and stabbed the pork several times.

He looked up and cackled at Rulon's discomfort. "That's what I do to sissies," he crowed, and stalked away.

Equal parts of shame and humiliation served to dampen Rulon's appetite as he apologized to Ren. *Hell's bells!* He was a coward for reacting to the man's erratic acts.

Chapter 7

Mary — May 30, 1861

Mary locked the door of her room before she undressed and changed into the shift she wore at night in the summer heat. She noticed that the touch of the fabric irritated the skin of her bosom that had been so tender of late.

Did I bump into something? she wondered. *I can't recall doing so.* She sat on the bed and began braiding her hair. Every time one arm or the other brushed against her breasts, she felt the annoyance of pain.

She must take a look, see if she had bruised herself.

She swallowed. A proper young lady did not look at her body. She kept it covered, always.

She swallowed again. *Except when Rulon asked me to disrobe so he could gaze upon me.*

The request had disturbed her, but she had finally come to terms with it and acquiesced. Several times. Over and over and over. She felt herself warm and swallowed again. She had done that to please her husband. That was permissible.

I have injured myself somehow, she temporized. *I must discover where.*

She took the lamp to the looking glass and set it down. She took a deep breath. Her mouth had gone dry and now she couldn't make saliva to swallow. Holding her breath, she took the shift from her body. She breathed out. She examined her form in the glass. She lifted the lamp aloft to cast a wider pool of light. She held her breath again and looked closely at her breasts, careful not to touch them. They looked larger than she had imagined they were, but they had no bruise upon them that she could see. It was evident that she had not run against anything that had injured her flesh.

She let out the held breath in a shaky sigh. Mortified that she had been gazing at her own body, Mary placed the lamp on a chest of drawers and blew out the light. She stumbled to the bed, frantically replacing the shift. Whispering a prayer for forgiveness, she got into bed and covered herself with the bedclothes, although the night continued warm.

She lay in the bed, clasping the quilt to her chin. Tears stung her eyes. Why had she done that? Why had she looked upon herself? A tear slid down her cheek. Would God punish her for that sin? She trembled. What if she was . . . what if Rulon had truly left a child in her belly? Would God strike out at that child? Cause it harm for her sinful glance? She sobbed, letting her tears soak the bedding. She couldn't believe in a vengeful god who would punish a baby that way.

Perhaps there was no god. No! No! That would mean there was no one to watch over Rulon, to keep him safe. She could not believe that, either.

Growing so hot that she began to perspire, Mary flung aside the bed covering, keeping only the sheet on her body. That was better. That was sensible.

The bed seemed so empty now that Rulon was not here to fill it with his vitality and strength. How she missed him! A scrap of contrariness arose in her and she ventured to touch one breast. It remained tender.

Something was happening to her body; that was sure. Was this a sign that she truly was increasing? Who could advise her?

She quickly ruled out speaking to her mother. Mama never talked about such matters.

She had no close friends who were married ladies.

In despair, she realized she had no one with whom she could counsel.

She lay quietly, thinking of Rulon's last embrace on the morning he had left. How she wished he were here to comfort her! Certainly her own mother had not been the most tender soul of late. But Rulon could be as tender as a mother when she needed that of him. Perhaps his mother had played a part in shaping a gentle part of his being.

His mother. Mother Owen. Mary inhaled deeply. *She can advise me.*

Mary covered her mouth with her hand, then thought how foolish that movement was. The audacious thought had come from her brain, not her mouth.

Mother Owen. She was a forthright, courageous lady if there ever was one. Did she shrink from discussing matters of . . . anatomy?

There was but one way to discover if she did or did not. Mary had to ask her.

&

Mary — May 31, 1861

The next day, Mary sat in the back room of the store, sorting skeins of embroidery thread by color, when her father entered and looked down at her. When she glanced up, her heart froze at the sight of his frown.

She had difficulty getting any words through her suddenly-dry throat. "Papa?" she finally forced out. *Has he some news of Rulon?*

He shook his head with an effort. "Rest easy, daughter. My mind was elsewhere."

"May I help, Papa?" What was causing him such a concerned look?

"You must not worry yourself, Mary." He forcibly thrust his hand through his dark hair. "Your mother is not as excited as I had hoped she would be about her condition."

"What do you mean, Papa?"

"Perhaps you shall have a brother by and by," he said. "That is my hope."

Mama is increasing? That certainly would account for her irritable attitude of late. "Felicitations, Papa," she said, a bit staggered to think that her parents partook of the same delights that Rulon and she had discovered together. She banished the thought, unable to lend it credence. Mama would not take delight in intimacies.

Papa extended his hand, in which he held a letter. "The missive is addressed to you. I'll leave you to read it in peace."

As her father left the room, Mary examined the folded paper, her hands shaking. Yes, it was from Rulon. She recognized his script from the notes he used to leave her in the fork of the elm in the backyard of her father's house. She got the letter open and smoothed it across her knees.

Berryville, Berkeley Co. Va.
Twenty-fourth May, 1861
My pretty wife,
We have arriv'd at camp. I only have a momunt to scribbl this note Thank you for the token which I will wear over my heart until I see you again.
The wether looks like rain. We hope it holds off until nite. The fellows in the company are mostly of the regular sort. I will get along with them.
A trumpet is soundin. Corp'rl Lovell tells me the call is ment to get us on the march. I must post this now. I will rite to you later. Tell the little one his papa lovs him. Mary, my sweet Sugar, I see yor face each nite in my dreems.
Yor husband
Rulon S Owen, Private
Co. I, 1st Reg't Va. Cav.

Mary sobbed as she clutched the note to her bosom. Rulon was well. He loved her. He hadn't written that, but she could feel the strength of his esteem from the words he used. She briefly touched her skirt where it covered her abdomen, hoping there was a "little one" there to whisper to, hoping it was the son Rulon seemed to expect.

After a while her tears dried, and she tucked the note into her bodice, listening—for the rest of the day—to the crackle of the paper every time she moved around, going about the tasks that earned her keep while her husband was at war.

Ben — June 5, 1861

Ben took his noon break alongside the creek behind the mill, eating the first of two sandwiches Ma had packed that morning. He had just begun to wash it down with a bottle of milk he'd retrieved from the creek when small hands crept across his face from behind him and covered his eyes.

"Guess who," demanded a voice he knew so well that he choked as desire rose in him.

Keeping himself very still, he said softly, "Marie? How'd you get here? Did Pa bring you into town?"

"No! Guess again."

"Julianna? You sound so grown up." He put as much incredulity into his voice as he knew how.

"No-uh," said the girl, exasperation making her draw out the word.

He put the bottle on the ground beside him and placed his hands over the top of the ones touching his face. "I do not know any other women but my ma and Ella Ruth Allen." He heard the huskiness of his voice. "Ma is busy weeding the truck garden today. I conclude that you are . . ." He brought the hands to his lips, kissing first one, then the other. "My love. My all. My Ella Ruth."

A long and satisfied sigh answered him. Then the hands were tugged free of his grasp and Ella Ruth dashed around, planted herself in his lap, and put her arms around his neck. "I'm not your Ella Ruth yet, Benjamin. You have to get Poppa to let us marry."

He groaned as he bent forward and found her mouth, muttering, "Lordy, lordy, don't tempt me so."

She let him kiss her for a while, then shoved him back.

"Ben, Poppa is home from his trip. Come to supper tonight and plead your case to him."

Ben felt his eyebrows rise. "He'll let me come to supper?"

"I haven't asked him, but I'm sure he won't mind. I told Momma I would invite you, and she shrugged her shoulders, so I do not feel she will object if you arrive about six o'clock."

"That's some progress, at least," Ben muttered. "I'm obliged that you've been working on your ma to change her opinion of me."

"Momma does not hate you, Ben. She quite likes you, in fact. She is concerned that you don't have property. You must be able to support a wife, after all."

"Sweet girl, you do remember I'm going off to fight the Yankee hoards?"

"Oh Ben, that is so tiresome. Don't talk about that anymore."

He took her face between his calloused fingers and held it still. He gazed into her eyes. "Ella Ruth. The Rifles are leaving this month. You know that, but you persist in disbelieving that I'm obliged to go. If I come to supper, it will be to ask for your hand on the spot, and to tell your pa that we're going to be married as soon as may be. There will be no fancy wedding. It'll be only you, me, and our folks." He swallowed. "Or it will be nothing at all."

Ella Ruth drew in a sharp breath. She let it out slowly, shakily. When at last she spoke, she said, "Benjamin, you do not mean that. You cannot rob a girl of her dreams."

"If you truly want me, girl, the time has come to act like it. Now . . . or never." His throat felt as though it burned as he uttered the ultimatum.

She stared at him, frowning slightly. "You are serious," she finally said.

"I never have been more."

She gave a little shake of her head. "This talk is so unlike a gentleman, Benjamin. You are mistreating me." She got off his lap.

"No. I am offering you my heart, my life." He felt himself quivering from the strain as he arose. "But you must take them now, or you must leave them alone."

She raised her chin. "I don't like this talk, Benjamin. When you can treat me nicely, you may see me again." She turned her back and picked her way across the yard toward the front of the mill.

Ben exhaled. The girl would not see reason, could not see that life was spiraling out of her grasp, that she must bend her will to the times or they would break her. He felt as though his heart were cracking into pieces as she slipped around the corner.

℥

Mary — June 7, 1861

Several days after Mary had determined to speak to her mother-in-law, Julia Owen came into the store with a basket of eggs. Mary headed off her father and beckoned her mother-in-law to the side counter.

"Mother Owen," she said, hoping her smile was bright and cheerful, and not the wan greeting she was afraid might be seen on her face. "This is a good lot of eggs. You must be delighted with your hens."

"Hello, Mistress Mary. They are laying well. I'm mighty pleased to see you. I received a letter from Rulon a few days ago. He is unhurt and busy. Have you heard from him?"

Mary dropped one hand behind the counter and started to touch her stomach, but thought better of it. She couldn't keep up that action every time Rulon's name was mentioned. What if she did it where others could see?

"Yes, ma'am, I mean Mother Owen. He wrote about the men in the company and the trumpets. He sounded very excited."

"Young men are excited by fighting, it seems. Are you well? You look a little green around the gills."

Oh, I'm feeling . . ." Mary hesitated, then lowered her voice to a whisper. "Ma'am, may I ask your advice about a delicate subject?"

Julia looked perplexed, but nodded.

"It is a somewhat personal question, a very personal, delicate question."

"Mary girl, you may ask me anything you have a mind to." She looked around the busy store. "Would you prefer that we speak in the back room, or the garden?"

"Thank you. The garden is a peaceful place." Mary removed her apron and came around the counter. "The eggs will be fine sitting there for a few moments.

I promise not to take much time. I—"

Julia took her arm. "Let's go to the garden, my dear."

Once they had settled themselves on a bench under the elm tree where Rulon used to leave notes for her, Mary began in a soft voice. "Mrs . . . Mother Owen. I cannot speak to my mama about this. You appear to be made of sterner stuff than she is. I must ask . . . please advise me . . . how am I to know—"

"If you are to have a babe?"

"Yes!" Mary's relief left her limp. Rulon's ma would not shy away from the difficult topic.

Julia smiled and took Mary's hand in her own. "You have a vital young husband. You are young and in good health. You undoubtedly have come together in the good Lord's way, if Rulon's dash up the stairs on your wedding day is any measure."

Mary felt herself blushing at the mention of her husband's haste. She nodded.

"It's not been a month since that time, but mayhap your visit did not come around?"

"My visit?"

"The monthly. The accursed nuisance of womankind."

"Oh. I understand. I did not think to notice."

"Pay heed if it don't appear." She looked Mary over, top to toe. "You may feel a strangeness, a difference in your being?"

Mary slowly nodded, feeling wonderment at her mother-in-law's knowledge.

"Are you overly fatigued?"

"Yes, ma'am."

Julia placed her arm across her own chest. "Do you have soreness in your bosom?"

"Yes. Certainly that."

"Do odors offend you?"

"Now that you mention it, ma'am, yes, there are particular odors I cannot bear to smell."

Julia smiled. "It is early to know for sure, but it appears I am to be a granny."

"Pardon me?"

"You are likely increasing, my dear girl. You will give me a grandchild."

Mary sighed at the woman's confirmation. She said in a shy tone, "Rulon hopes for a son."

"Of course he does," Julia said, then laughed. She added, "Every man upon this earth thinks only of sons." She sobered, her smile fading. "Daughters can come later, but sons are highly valued for the first of the offspring. For some reason, begetting a man child is a proof of manhood. I don't pretend to understand it. Men are strange creatures."

Mary stared at the woman. Unlike her own mother, Mrs. Owen wasn't afraid to speak about anything. She herself knew only a little about a man's pride, but did know it was a thing she dared not meddle with. Her own father had exhibited a longing for a son not many days ago.

Swallowing, Mary asked a final question. "Will there be other signs to mind?"

"There are many. You may have difficulty keeping food down. Experience aching in the back." Julia patted her chest. "These will swell, increase in size. You will need to alter your bodices. Then, of course, you will need to let out your waistbands, as your belly will gradually enlarge to accommodate the growing child. You must have seen that in your mother."

Mary lowered her head. "We were not encouraged to take notice, ma'am."

"Your ma is a mite squeamish on that head, but since she is with child, you might take heed, this go-around."

Mary gasped. Mother Owen knew everything. "I only learned that a little while ago. She has been so irritable, and treated Rulon in a miserable way."

"As long as you treated him well, I reckon he didn't even pay heed to that."

"Mother Owen, how you do talk!"

"No offense meant, my dear. I did mean treating with him in more ways than just the one. Always feed your man well. Tend whatever wounds he may carry, be they physical or to his spirit, with gentleness and a good try at understanding his pain. Listen to his complaints, and soothe his soul. Those are the secrets to happiness in a marriage."

"I will remember your words for when he comes home."

Julia nodded. "Store them up. This fight can't last many months. Mr. Lincoln must be given to understand he cannot invade our homeland. We will resist firmly."

Mary let go of Julia's hand and clasped her own hands together. Rulon would return soon. They would have a child to raise up together. She looked at her mother-in-law and remembered something.

"Mother Owen, this isn't your homeland. You weren't born in Virginia."

Julia Owen raised her chin. "This valley is my home, girl. I married my man here, and bore my children in the house he brought me to. This," she nodded, "this *is* my home."

Mary felt a slight rebuke in her words, but forgave her the bluntness of them, glad that Mother Julia Owen was like a rock, the firm foundation that had nurtured Rulon to manhood. Mother Owen would be a loving granny to her child. What kind of grandmother her own mama would be had yet to be determined.

∛

Mary — June 12, 1861

Upon arising one morning, Mary barely made it to the washbasin in time to empty bile and not much else into the ceramic vessel. Her stomach heaved past the point where there was anything left to expel, and when the cramping tightness in her abdomen had ceased, she sank back to the bed, shaking with weakness. Mother Owen had mentioned that one symptom she'd likely have was an inability to keep food on her stomach, but she had yet to eat anything today. Was this some other illness? She touched her face to check for fever, but there was none.

When she felt steady, she approached the basin for the purpose of emptying it into the slop bucket, but the smell made her gag. *Ohhh.* She retreated toward the bed. Who could she get to take this vile, odorous mess away? Ida wouldn't do it.

Of that she was sure. Perhaps she could bribe India with a sweet from the store? For now, she would have to leave it in place. The smell was insufferable. She could not bear to approach the basin to deal with it herself.

Brushing her hair away from her face, she made an attempt to make herself presentable for the day, but she hardly felt presentable. Instead, she felt queasy, and several times had to restrain herself from renewing the debacle at the basin.

She couldn't work at the store in this condition. What if she had an accident at the counter, or on the merchandise, or, worse yet, on a customer?

At last she gave up the attempt to dress, and crawled back into bed.

It must not have been much past eight o'clock when a quick rap on the door woke her up. Who was disturbing her hard-won sleep? She took a tentative breath and said "Come in," hoping the effort to use her voice wouldn't roil up her stomach.

Her mother entered, moving so rapidly that the scarf she wore in a vain attempt to cloak her condition fluttered aside, revealing a thickness in her waist and a roundness at the front of her skirt.

"What is this nonsense?" she asked. "Why were you not in the kitchen preparing breakfast? We had poor fare for your father's meal this morning. He works so very hard to meet our needs."

"Mama," Mary wailed. "I'm sick."

Mrs. Hilbrands laid the back of her hand on Mary's forehead. "There is no fever. What ails you?" She turned her head back and forth, sniffing. "What is that horrid stench?"

"I vomited," Mary confessed. "Please, get someone to take it away. I cannot bear the odor."

"You are—He—" Gasping, Mrs. Hilbrands put her hand to her mouth, then removed it so she could speak. "I told you not to marry. He has made you, gotten you, left you with child. How could you, daughter?"

"Beg pardon? How could I do what?" *Questions. Why is she asking so many questions when my stomach is reeling?*

"Engage in carnal intercourse with that boy." Mrs. Hilbrands looked as though she thought she herself had broken all the Ten Commandments by speaking of it.

"We are wed." Mary wanted to vomit again, and threw off the covers so she could swing her limbs out of the bed. "It's the way of married folk."

"And in this house!" She pointed at the bed, accusation written on her face.

"You wouldn't let me leave. Mother Owen had a place for me, but you—" Mary couldn't finish her thought, and she scurried to the basin to vomit again.

When she had finished, Mary begged, "Go away. Please, go away, and take this basin with you."

೩

Rulon — June 15, 1861

Rulon had spent the last three nights on picket near the Potomac River and had just come back to the camp. As he rubbed down his horse, thinking of nothing but getting into his blankets and catching a few hours of rest, Ren Lovell approached and gave him an envelope.

"I thought you might like to have this, Owen. It got here with a packet of dispatches after you left."

Rulon took the letter and stuffed it into his pocket. "I'm obliged, Lovell."

"Go get breakfast before you sleep. We might all be hauling our tails out of here later today."

"Where are we bound?"

"The general is moving his headquarters. I'm not certain if we're going along or staying put. The colonel likes being in the thick of the fray."

"I wish we were better armed."

"We're supposed to get sabres soon. Not that I'm convinced they're good for anything. Not when some Yank troop is shooting lead balls at us." Lovell grinned wryly.

"How soon can we expect carbines from Richmond?"

Lovell snorted. "Maybe in a month. Maybe longer. There is a good deal of confusion in the armaments department. I swear old Beauregard gets all the arms shipments before any thought is given to us here behind the Blue Ridge."

Rulon made polite conversation as long as he could stand to do so, itching to get away so he could pull out the paper burning a hole in his pocket. He was almost certain the letter was from Mary. He'd caught merely a glimpse of the script on the face of the envelope before he'd put it away, but those rounded letters could only have been written by a young female, and he doubted his sisters would think about writing to him.

When he finally found a moment to himself, he snatched the letter from its hiding place and tore it open. He forbade himself the assurance of looking at the signature, and instead started at the top.

Mount Jackson, Chenandoah County, Va.

Tenth of June, year of Our Lord one thousand Eight hundred sixty-One

Dear husband,

I cried from relief to receev your lettr Thank you for writin altho it must needs be in hast. All are well here.

I have discover'd the cause of my Mother's late ill humor toward you. She is ~~breeding~~ ~~with child~~ increasing. How much fun we shall have raising our children togethr.!! That is, if I am to have a child. I do not kno at this time if my suspicions are true. I only kno the joy that corses through my bosom when I think of the possibility. That thot warms my being.

Yor Mother was in the store three days back and sends you her greetings. I was able to converse with her for a few moments. She seems assured that the signs I told her that I have been having are good ones concurning carrying a child. She is hoping along with me that I will soon kno for certun ab't the matter.

I pray you will take caution in all your ~~manuvrs~~ ~~manoeavrs~~ whenever you move about in sight of the Yankees. Hold the memry I

left you close to your heart always.
The wife you love,
Mary Margaret Hilbrands Owen
*(That is the first time I have writ my name down to you in its
entirety)*

Rulon stood very still. Merely reading Mary's words about the memory she had branded upon his soul aroused him, and he fought to curb the need it brought before it engulfed his body. A handful of tents had been pitched behind the hill on the Winchester road. He knew who inhabited them, but with Mary dancing around the notion that they really would have a child, he felt a strong compulsion to renew the pledge he'd made to himself, and he supposed, to God, not to take himself off to seek relief there.

Von and a few others of his acquaintance in the company were not so circumspect. Their boastful talk would drive him mad today if they had been with the harlots last night.

Clamping his teeth on his lip to divert his pain elsewhere, Rulon put the letter away and went to eat whatever the cook had prepared.

Chapter 8

Ben — June 15, 1861

Ben signed his name, then took the uniform that had been made by the ladies of the town especially for the men of the Mount Jackson Rifles, which they also named "Allen's Infantry," in honor of he who was their captain. Ella Ruth's own cousin. He swallowed the bile that arose upon thinking of her name and their last encounter.

He went behind the church and found that he was not the only man in the company with the same idea for privacy. He chuckled wryly, then shucked his ordinary clothing and dressed himself in the finery befitting an infantryman. He stowed his regular clothes in a haversack that had been provided to him for the purpose of trucking some of his accoutrements about. After that, he went to find his mother.

"Don't worry for my sake," he told her, holding her hand and stroking it. "This won't last long. The shine won't be off our tent pegs before you'll see us come marching down that road and home."

Ma seemed a bit assured by his joke and made a little noise he took for a laugh, but the sound was very faint among all the conversations going on in the square. She looked around.

"Did your girl come?"

Ben scowled. Up to just a few minutes ago, he had attempted not to think about Ella Ruth's absence. Now Ma's innocent question brought a flood of pain. "She won't be comin'. She rejected my offer of marriage." The words cut deep.

Ma squeezed his hand and said in a low voice, "I'm sorry, son." Her face showed her deep concern as she tried to comfort him.

He tried to grin to reassure her that he didn't care anymore. The grimace he produced hurt his lips. "Never mind, Ma." He patted her hand. He'd tried so hard not to remember the gash in his soul as he had prepared for this day.

He inhaled and mentally shook himself. Never mind, indeed. He had much better things to occupy his thoughts from now on.

"You behave, now," Ma said. "Go to church services as often as you can. I hear Mr. Jackson is a godly man. You hold him for your example."

"Old Jack?" Ben saw the question on his mother's face. "I hear tell that's what the men call the general, Ma. 'Jack,' from his surname, Jackson."

"That's a mite disrespectful, don't you reckon?"

"If that's the worst he's called, he'll be mighty lucky, Ma." He turned as he heard a bugle call. "Hear that sound? I have to go now. Give my regards to Pa and the young'uns. Tell Peter his time will come, and not to hurry into anything." He let go of her hand, gave her shoulders a quick squeeze, and moved away, forming up with his squad in a line.

Then they marched away, followed by a baggage wagon full of tents and the accoutrements they could not carry on their persons.

ॐ

Julia — June 15, 1861

"Mama, where is Peter?"

Upon hearing Julianna's question, Julia looked down the table. She had only just become accustomed to seeing a gap where Rulon had sat for so many years. Now Ben's place beside it would also be empty, for only a short time, she hoped. But Peter? Where was he, indeed?

"Rod, did you send Peter on an errand?"

He looked up from his plate of stew, frowning. "I did not, Julie. I figured he went into town with you and Benjamin. He wasn't in the buggy with you?"

"No. It was only Ben and me. Belle is a well-mannered animal, so I figured I would have no difficulty driving her home myself." She took a moment to think when she had last seen the missing boy. Trepidation sent a chill racing along the nerves of her arms. This morning . . . this morning after breakfast Peter had given her a fierce hug before he returned to his chores. She had thought it had something to do with comforting her in the face of Ben's imminent departure.

Her nails dug into her apron as her hands formed claws around the fabric. "No," she said, deep in her throat. "No, he wouldn't." She felt the weakness brought on by blood leaving her head and raised her hands to support herself against the possibility of falling, bringing the apron clenched within them.

"Julie!"

She heard her husband rise, utensils clattering to the table, striking his plate, and the legs of his chair scraping the floor. Hurried footfalls. Then his hand was firm upon her shoulder.

"Julie." He breathed heavily. "One of the horses didn't come up to water this afternoon, the one we call Brownie. I thought perhaps it got loose from the pasture." He stood beside her, his breathing easing toward normal. "I was going to send one of the boys to look for it. No need for that now. He took the horse."

"Where would he go?" she asked, her voice muffled in the apron. She wanted to enfold her runaway son in her arms, redo the embrace she had shrugged off with such haste this morning.

"Ma." It was Carl. "Pete's been studying the newspapers. I reckon he—" His voice faltered and she heard him take several gulps of air before he continued his story. "I saw him cut something out, then tuck it in his shirt. I made him show it to me. It was a mention of the Shenandoah Rangers forming up. I thought he was going to pull a prank on somebody." He sniffed. "It's a cavalry company. That's why he needed a horse."

Her head drooped farther toward the table. The Shenandoah Rangers? She knew nothing about that outfit. Who would know? Who could she ask?

She got a hand loose from her apron, reached out, and clutched her husband's vest instead. "Rod," she whispered. "Will General Meem know anything?"

"I'll make inquiries, wife. There's aught we can do tonight. Eat. You'll want the strength." He patted her shoulder and shifted his weight. "Eat!" His command was directed to the children. Then he said in a weary voice, "I'll speak to you after supper, Carl."

ℬ

Rod — June 17, 1861

Rod cut short his day's work to ride into Mount Jackson to see what he could learn about his missing son. On the way, he encountered Chester Bates, who was headed into town on a different errand.

"Rod," said his neighbor. "Fine day. Have you given thought to my idea?"

"I have." Feeling grumpy, Rod didn't expand on his answer.

"It's been two months. Have you made any progress?"

Rod sighed. "I have. Several men have volunteered." He thumped his thigh. "I told Julie first thing."

"Well, at least you gave her warning. When does the company enlist?"

"Any day now. First I have to find my boy Peter."

"Find him? That sounds like he's run away."

"He has. We think he's joined up." Rod pursed his lips in anger. "Julie's fit to be tied."

"I can imagine. Do you have any notion where he's gone?"

"None, except that Carl thinks Peter may have taken a shine to joining the Shenandoah Rangers. Have you heard anything about them?"

"Shenandoah Rangers?" Chester scratched his head. "The name sounds familiar. I'll think on it."

"Let me know right quick if you remember," Rod said, his tone a bit brusque. "If Julie takes it into her mind to prevent me from going to the war over this affair, I'll be in the brine with the pickles."

After bidding Chester goodbye at the edge of the town, Rod made the rounds of places that would have information: the store, the drinking establishments, and the telegraph office. Monday was a work day, so there were few people hanging around, and none of them was interested in a military company formed anywhere else than in Mount Jackson. Rod decided that Monday probably wasn't the best time to expect a full crowd.

As he left the telegraph office, he spied Chester coming up the street toward him. He seemed anxious to waylay him, and spoke as soon as he arrived.

"Rod," he said, puffing from the exertion of his hurry, "I recalled where I heard the name of that company. Sam Myers, the man who used to run the Columbia Furnace. He raised the Shenandoah Rangers over to Edinburg. If they haven't rode away yet, Peter may be down there."

Rod felt his breath leaving his body in a sigh. Peter was as nearby as that? He looked at the sun. His search had eaten up the afternoon, but if he left now, he could get there by dark.

"Chester, can you get word to Julie that I've gone to Edinburg?"

"I'll tell her myself."

"Much obliged, friend." Rod clapped Chester on the arm in farewell. He made haste to where he had tied his horse, mounted, and rode off toward the north.

He arrived in Edinburg as night fell. Since it was too late in the day for him to go about searching for Peter, he was obliged instead to seek a meal and a place to sleep. He found a small tavern that served food, and dug into his pocket for the price of the victuals. The talk in the tavern of the brave Rangers having left the town disheartened him.

When he finished eating, he asked the proprietor about lodgings, and was directed to ask at the livery barn. He spent an uneasy night on a pile of hay, wondering what Julia would say about his failure to bring back their son.

The next day, his fears solidified into reality. The Company had indeed gone to war, and Peter with them.

SO

Rod — June 18, 1861

When Rod rode down the lane late that night, a lamp burned in the kitchen window, casting a checkerboard patch of light across the dooryard outside the house. Julia's disappointment lay ahead of him at the moment when he would give her the bad news. Wrapped in an unfamiliar sense of failure, he dismounted in front of the barn, struck a match and lit the lantern hanging inside the door, then cared for the horse.

He paused before he closed the barn door. The scores of feet between the barn and the house stretched through the darkness like a gulf of bitterness. Julie waited up for him in the house. He was sure of that. She wanted to know if he had brought back her boy. Surely she had looked out when she heard the approach of his horse. Surely she already knew that only one horse had come down the lane and passed through the stream of light. Surely she already knew he had failed her.

Rod's heart sank to his toes as he stepped away from the barn. It seemed that his boots tripped him time and again. Was he so old that he could no longer walk that distance without faltering? He stopped, struggling to purge feebleness and pain from his body, regret and despair from his soul by an act of will. Julie would need strength from him, comfort from him, solace and peace. He shook his head. He couldn't give her the latter two gifts. She would have to get them from God.

After a long time, he moved forward again. Julie waited. He couldn't put off speaking to her any longer.

Upon reaching the house, he opened the door, noticing a squeak in a hinge. He would have to oil that tomorrow.

Julia was not in the kitchen. Rod took the lamp from the window and carried it into the parlor. She sat in his chair in front of a fire that had sunk to embers. When he approached, he realized that her head lay against the wing of the chair. She had fallen asleep while she waited for him to come home.

His first reaction was relief that he wouldn't have to dash her hopes tonight. He set the lamp on the hearth and adjusted the guttering wick. Then he knelt before her, wondering if he should scoop her up and take her to bed or leave her in the chair for the night. She looked comfortable enough, but he needed her beside him to comfort his own soul.

He must have made a noise, perhaps cleared his throat unconsciously, because before he could rise and pick her up, she opened her eyes. Focus came slowly, but then her eyes sharpened with recognition.

"Rod?" She put out a hand and touched him lightly on the breast of his shirt. "Is Peter—"

Before she could ask, he shook his head and said, "No, I failed you, Julie. He'd already left before I got to Edinburg."

Her eyes softened, and he thought she would begin to weep, but she surprised him by saying quietly, "Such an impetuous boy. So like his pa."

He could only shake his head.

She continued. "You're wore out, husband. Did you eat? I saved you a plate of supper."

"I couldn't eat it this late, wife. I am bone-weary. Come. We need sleep."

Chapter 9
Rulon — June 27, 1861

Troopers from Company "I" had followed a Yankee patrol for an hour before they lost sight of the enemy and pulled up in a grassy meadow. An older member of the troop, Vernon Earl, was ordered to dismount and puzzle out the direction the patrol had taken. As Rulon awaited the command to move out, he dozed in the hot sun, gratified to catch a few moments of rest.

He started awake when someone slapped his leg and a gruff voice said, "Ho, Owen! You've slept long enough. Get down and lend the old man a fresh set of eyes."

His sergeant was the speaker, and Rulon hastened to swing off the horse, responding with a "Yes suh" that was half drawled and half garbled from drowsiness. He glanced around to find the man on whom they relied in such situations. Vernon Earl had learned his tracking skills over a lifetime of hunting game in the Blue Ridge Mountains. However, his sight had recently begun to give him trouble.

"Mind where you step!" the old man warned as Rulon approached. "Don't bend the grass."

Rulon stopped. What was he supposed to do for the man? He slapped at a whining mosquito, which put him in mind of an old bite now itchy. As he scratched it, Earl called to him.

"Tread there and there," he said, pointing with a grizzled forefinger. "Look down. Notice the hoof prints?"

Rulon took a step where the man had indicated, then glanced downward. He saw nothing resembling what Earl had mentioned. "No."

"Well, they ain't none. The horses didn't come this-a-way." He began to walk ahead at an angle, head down, and Rulon followed.

When he caught up, he asked, "What are you looking for?"

"Bent grass. Clumps of overturned sod. Horse apples." Earl chuckled. "If you ain't keerful, you'll find the horse apples first with your boots."

Rulon lifted a foot surreptitiously and peered at the bottom. It appeared damp from mashing down the grass where's he'd been stepping, but to his relief, it was not coated with horse dung. However, when he put his foot down again, he spotted a place where faint variations made him think perhaps the grass had been disturbed. When he took a step closer, he found sod scattered about in a regular pattern, on a line heading off towards a wooded area.

"Mr. Earl." Once he had the man's attention, Rulon pointed out the patch. "Is this what we seek?"

Earl knelt on one knee and examined the overturned sod. He stirred a clump with a finger to break it up, then bent over and smelled it. When he arose, he said, "That's it precisely, boy. You have a good eye."

Rulon felt a prickle of pride, but had no idea what the man had been about when he had worked with the clod of earth. He determined to discover the man's secrets by helping out at every opportunity and thereby learn the tracking skill.

∞

Julia — July 10, 1861

After spending a long day spinning yarn, Julia sat down to write a letter to her eldest.

July 10 1861
Owen Farm
Dear son Rulon,
We are well here on the farm. Yor father is raising a Cavalry company that will leave soon to Defend us. Ben marched off with Allen's Infantry. Peter ran away with the horse we called Brownie to join a cavalry company raised in Edinburg. Ben so cottoned to that horse. He will be mortified if any harm comes to it.

I am sorry to tell you that Peter left without our Blessing and a proper Send Off. He always had a streak of the willful, as you well know from Celebratin your nuptials with that Colorful eye. I will say no more of Peter's escapade. He will learn Discipline in the Army, no dout.

We had an excitement a few days ago when a large meteor, as the scientific men told us, came down from the sky and exploded with a great noise and shower of light. Not knowing the origin of the heavenly display at first, we imagined that we were under a surprise Yankee bombardment, and of corse went down to the Cellar for safety. After an hour's wait and no more Shells sent, as we supposed, we emerged to find that no Federal Army had come upon us. When we later learned the True Origin of the great sound, we felt chagrined and foolish at our actions and the time wasted. However, we safely escaped the supposed attack, and count our reaction as a fine drill for an actual event of that sort.

You may imagine how little Julianna carried on with a nervous fit for quite a time, but I hardly blamed her, as I was equally frightened by the great sound and show of light.

I must tell you that your dear wife has high hopes that she will have happy news to relate to you soon. I am overjoied at the prospect.

Be firm and stedfast at all hazards, dear son, and uphold the Good Owen Name. Your father and I bear you a great affection.

Your mother
Julia Helm Owen

When she had finished the task, she went to give the letter to Rod so he could post it on his next visit to town.

"Husband, it pains me that you are going off to fight a young man's war," she said, as she settled into her chair before the fireplace.

"Don't give in to your nerves, Julie," he said. "You know I can't keep away from this scrap."

She made a scoffing noise. "You don't have to relish it so."

"Am I relishing war? Not so. My intent is to keep you and my young'uns safe, to the best of my powers."

She wanted to go over to Rod's chair, curl up in his lap, gain comfort from his touch, but those young'uns were seated around the room, and she could not bear to display to them so much of her need. She must make a strong show before them.

"I've written to Rulon," she said instead. "I told him about the Great Noise." She dangled the envelope from her hand. "I wonder if cannon fire is louder than that meteor."

Her husband looked over at her.

She read concern for her in his eyes. It ever was there, his steadfast devotion to his duty toward her. At other times the look added affection, and at special moments, frank ardor heated the mixture to an explosive glance that quickened her vitals. But for tonight, the gaze contained concern and duty.

"It has been many years since I've had experience of cannon fire." He took the envelope from her, letting his index finger rest upon the back of her hand. "I'll take this to town on Friday."

She nodded, releasing the paper. So few folk understood her man as she did. He had just told her he cherished her. It was her turn to relish something in her life, and this bit of byplay between them would do nicely.

"Carl, bring the Bible," Rod said. "Time for devotions." He looked toward Julia.

She noted that his glance now contained more than merely the concern it had held. The crickets had barely begun to chirp. She laid her hand over her heart and felt the increase in its speed. A weeknight? She smiled to herself, trying to get her mind focused on godly pursuits to end the day.

∞

Mary — July 12, 1861

Two months had passed since her wedding day, and Mary was at last satisfied that she was with child. The totality of the evidence was overwhelming. She was quite queasy. She couldn't stand many smells about the house, especially the odor of her own vomit. Her breasts remained tender and felt huge. A part of them had changed color, and the whiter areas were laced with dark blue veins. Her body felt ungainly and somehow different. Most convincing of all, she had not been visited by the women's curse.

Once she had gained enough equilibrium to go to work and ensconce herself in the storeroom, she pulled a piece of paper from a sheaf and prepared to write to her husband.

She sat for a long time, pen un-dipped in the ink, trying to decide how to break the news. Did she dare to write in plain language all that was happening to her? What if the letter fell into enemy hands? This letter wasn't going to be a state secret, but it was private between herself and Rulon, and precious to her. What if one of the soldiers in his company got his hands on it and read out the words? Did men in such close quarters tease each other in such a way? She had to suppose they might, judging from the observations she had made of Rulon's brothers.

What a perplexity. She wanted to share with Rulon the wonderment of the changes in her body, the puzzling moods that sent her into a spiral of emotions, the yearnings to hold the babe she now sheltered inside her body.

What if he didn't care? What if his war work was too much of a burden upon his mind and he had no time for dithering about her?

In the end, she took the safe road, and wrote him a short note.

12 July, 1861
Mnt Jackson, Shen. Cty, Virg.
Dear Husband,
If you are able to come home this winter, you will notice changes in my person, as you will have a child after the turn of the year. I am as well as can be expected.
Mama is dificult. I reckon she gave no thot to being with child at her advanced age. She is past 30, after all. I hope she is breeding a boy, for it surely is her last chance.

I have no dout you left me a boy. Yor mama smiles and agrees.

Be safe, dear Rulon, I pray you. Hold this letter to yor heart and you will feel all the affection I put into it.

Yor own Mary

After she wrote and sealed it, she wished she had put in more of the feelings she was experiencing daily. Not the unhappy things like throwing up her food, but the more positive ones, like filling out her bodices more, and the euphoria of knowing she would bear him a child. No matter. It was a safe letter, and she hoped he would read between the lines to discover the full meaning of her words and sense her deep emotions.

ॐ

Rulon — July 16, 1861

One night after a very exciting day on patrol and in camp, Rulon wrote to Mary.

16 July, 1861
In Camp at Berkeley Co. Va.
My dear Mary,
Our troop has been much engaged in traveling about the county, traping the Federal boys when they venture out from Martinsburg to hunt, which causes them to Hate us. Today we got word that J.E.B. Sturt is now Colonel of our regiment in fact, having receeved that comission of rank. I may have told you Harrisonburg Cavalry is assigned as Company I in 1st Regt. Va. Cavalry. This is a Large regimnt, haveing twelve Companys in all on this Date.

Col. Sturt insists on drills every Morning and Parade in ev'n. He also takes the Companys out himself to Patrol, which can be exciting when we come up amongst the enemy. Have no fears, Mary, as He has always brung us Through without incident. He does not permit Us to retreet, if on Foot, with our backs to the foe, but must March backwards to where we left the horses. If mounted, we may only trot away, for he says we are to reserve a Gallop for the Charge. The Col stirs every mans blood with his bravery.

Dear wife, I hope You find yorself well. I delited to lern in your last lett'r that you hope for the best. I had a note from Ma in which she said you now have further news for me. which I am anxious to receev. I assure you that I carry each of yor letters against my heart until I am handed the next one.

With fondest remembrance of your kind soul,
Yor husband,
Rulon S. Owen, trooper
1st Regt. Va. Cav., Co. I

After he had signed his name, he re-read what he had told his wife. Perhaps he should not have mentioned about Colonel Stuart taking them into the enemy lines, but the deed was done, and he didn't have time to re-do the letter.

He sealed the envelope and gave the flap a quick kiss, feeling foolish as he did it, but it comforted him that Mary's fingers would touch the spot. Perhaps she would bring the paper to her own lips before she opened the flap. Thinking that was almost as good as feeling her lips under his.

He gave in the letter to be posted, and trudged back to his lonely cot.

႙

Ella Ruth — July 19, 1861

Ella Ruth breezed into her father's office one afternoon, glanced at the three other men whose buzzing conversation resembled a dispute, shrugged her shoulders, and approached her father anyway.

"Poppa, you really must send for this," she said, waving a sheet of paper under his nose. When his look held a stormy aspect, she seated herself on his lap and put her arms around his neck. "Please, Poppa? If you put in the order now, I will have it back from Paris before it goes out of style."

She watched as her father's neck and face went from the normal pink color to a glowing scarlet. Perhaps she should not have interrupted his little meeting, she mused. Business was, to him, important, but she was also important, was she not? Did not he enjoy pampering her as much as her heart desired? What a pity Ben would not do so.

"Daughter!"

To her surprise, the word exploded from her father's lips, and he put her off his lap with firm hands.

"I am engaged, as you can see," he added, his voice elevated and angry. "We are not to be disturbed!" He gave her a little shove back toward the doorway.

Under the impetus of his push, Ella Ruth stumbled out of the room, chagrined and confused. Poppa had never treated her in such a manner before. True, she had burst into his meeting, but he always had delighted in giving her whatever she had asked. Why was his behavior so odd today?

She decided to listen to the conversation spilling quite clearly through the still-open door. The loudest voice went on and on about "nothing ventured," while another voice agreed with every point. Her father and the third man countered with "risky" and "ships boarded," and "cotton prices."

After several minutes, her head began to hurt because the argumentative exchanges held no meaning for her. However, they seemed to hold significant meaning for Poppa, and they had turned his outlook sour. Perhaps it was in her best interest to pay better attention to his concerns. She must make a beginning another time, when her head had ceased pounding.

Was all of the nonsense because of this war Ben had insisted was going to change everything? Something had certainly changed Poppa.

She went up the stairs to her room to rest. That surely must cure her headache. She sighed as she opened the door. She missed Ben. Her plan had been to convince Poppa that her ultimate happiness depended upon becoming Ben's bride in a magnificent ceremony this September, which would have entertained her with a great many delightful activities this summer. Now she had nothing to do with her time.

She sat at her dressing table and stared at her reddened face in the mirror. She no longer envisioned a blissful summer of shopping and parties, a splendid wedding with many attendants, and a bright future as Ben's wife. Ben had left her flat, going off to take target practice against the Yankees. She sighed and tested her forehead with the back of her hand. Had she a fever? No. Evidently not, notwithstanding her flushed cheeks. She touched her lips. How she missed Ben's kisses. A chill raced down her spine. Why had he gone in such haste, without even coming around to say goodbye?

Upon several moments of reflection, she considered that in all fairness to Ben, she *had* treated him with a teensy bit of disdain at their final meeting behind the mill, when he had offered her his name, his hand, his heart. In that moment, those had not been enough. She had thought she needed the pomp, the dress, the flowers, the crowd of friends to admire her good fortune and her conquest. Her heart lurched, leaving a tightness in her chest.

She leaned her elbows on the table. What would Momma say about leaning on them? No matter. She didn't care if they became rough and red. She cupped her cheeks in her palms. The longer she stared at herself, the more desolate she felt as she realized she had been wrong. Of what worth to her was the lacy dress hanging in her armoire when she had lost the man she loved?

She thought back to how Poppa's recent rejection had made her feel: confused, chagrined, put out, unappreciated, even unloved. Her cheeks grew hot beneath her fingertips as shame overwhelmed her. She had rejected Ben's offer because it didn't come with the elaborate trappings she had always dreamed of. She had rejected *him*. How must he feel?

She knew now. Confused. Unappreciated. Unloved. She had wronged him. She had broken his heart.

Oh, Ben.

Ella Ruth put her head down on her crossed arms and sobbed.

Chapter 10
Rulon — July 21, 1861

Orders had come down from General Johnston's headquarters to keep eyes on the enemy army led by General Patterson that had invaded the Valley. For the last few days, Rulon's company had been engaged in riding in countermoves against the Federal troops.

Near Winchester, a patrol became a skirmish when four members of Company "I" encountered enemy soldiers willing to fight. After dashing at each other a few times with no significant injury on either side, the Federal patrol withdrew and must have come across an artillery battery as they retreated. Soon after, the foursome from the Harrisonburg Cavalry found themselves targets of a Yankee bombardment.

Rulon hunkered down in a ditch alongside Owen Leoyd while artillery shells explored the air above them.

Leoyd said, "Them shells always whistle that-a-way when they miss you. If you don't hear 'em, they're gonna get you, so bless the noise of 'em."

"Obliged for the advice," Rulon replied, covering his head at the sound of a particularly close whistle.

"We'd best leave here," Leoyd commented. "That was a mite too near for my taste. Can't you get rid of that feather?"

Rulon grunted. He'd grown fond of the embellishment on his hat, especially since their colonel sported one so like Rulon's on his own headgear. How long was his plume going to be a source of merriment and ridicule for the fellows in the company?

He didn't have time to dwell for long on the good-natured abuse he'd received. During a brief lull in the fire, he and Leoyd beat a retreat to their horses, and found the rest of their comrades to continue the patrol.

When they returned to their bivouac, Ren Lovell announced that the company was to make all haste to Manassas Gap to cross the Blue Ridge. "General Beauregard is in a bad way. McDowell is on the move, and he's got a right smart lot of soldiers with him. We're ordered to battle, boys."

After that, the company rode toward the fray through fields alongside the infantry-clogged road.

"Pull down that fence, Owen," Ren called out. Both Rulon and Owen Leoyd dismounted, cast a wry glance at one another, and took the rails down so the company could advance. Dodging sleeping infantrymen in the way, crossing ditches, and riding over uneven ground ate up the miles, but sapped their strength, as well. Rulon tried to keep behind Von, as the man's ugly temper had simmered over into vile curses at nightfall when he realized that the baggage train with rations had not kept pace with the cavalry.

Finally, after thirty-six brutal hours in the saddle, the men of the regiment dismounted alongside the Bull Run.

"Line up for rations," a fellow called out, and Rulon stumbled over to do so. Head pounding from the dust and confusion, he procured the raw makings of his meal and found a fire on which he hoped to make it palatable. After he ate, he found a spot of grass, lay upon it, touched the handkerchief Mary had given him to his lips, and fell immediately into stupor.

About daylight, he awoke to the sound of musketry and bugles, and rushed to follow the order to saddle his horse. Then he washed the sleep out of his eyes, watered and fed the horse, and ate a hasty breakfast.

Captain Yancey ordered the company into line alongside the others, and Rulon sat his horse as Col. Stuart and a small detachment crossed the Run on a scout. After a while, they returned, and Rulon watched a trooper ride toward General Johnston's headquarters. He figured the man would report the findings of the scouting party.

The day grew hot as the din of battle increased on their left. They had received no orders, so they sat on the earth in the sun beside their horses, listening to the wood-shrouded struggles around them, and dodging wayward artillery shells.

"Ah!" cried a man from the Howard County company, as a shell burst in their column. The horses scattered, riders futilely pulling on their reins and swearing profusely.

"Anyone hurt?" called their captain. By some lucky happenstance, neither men nor horses were injured.

One time, they were allowed to seek water for their horses. Soon, however, they formed back into company lines, but waited in vain for any action. He could see the restlessness of their colonel. After the noon, he began to send messengers off, and Rulon turned to Ren.

"Where are they going?"

"Humph. If it was me, I'd be sending word to the generals that we're a-sitting over here with our thumbs up our butts and nothing to do."

Rulon hadn't heard such coarse talk from Ren before, and figured he had as bad a case of nerves as any other man around.

"We have to wait, then?"

"I reckon so. We're the pawns in this chess game, Owen. We do what we're told."

Rulon eyed the man. "We're not the knights?"

"Mayhap we are. We still have to await the hand of the general to move."

Garth Von growled an excited curse, then added as he pointed a finger, "He's staff, ain't he?"

Rulon turned to see a mounted officer coming from the woods at the gallop. At the sight, he got to his feet and looked to his horse, hoping the officer brought orders.

Evidently he did, as he saluted Col. Stuart smartly and gave him a message.

"Boots and saddles," Ren said as the bugle sounded. "We're in action at last."

Rulon had never seen such chaos, nor before felt such a rush of energy as he experienced several times over the remainder of that day. Although worn out from the long ride out of the Valley through the pass, the cavalry companies nevertheless feinted and parried with Federal forces the rest of the day, capturing some here, some there, breaking away when necessary, but mostly pressing forward, as was Colonel Stuart's wont.

General Early's brigade came up and Stuart sent the general a message. Early's soldiers waded into the battle with courage and speed. Then Rulon's company dashed into another skirmish. Upon returning with prisoners, he noticed that a sixteen-gun artillery battery commanded by Lieutenant Beckham had become attached to their flank. After each cannonade from the guns he worried for his hearing, but the fire was most welcome, as the shelling drove the Federal troops into cover and prevented them turning the left flank.

They were on the move again once the company had secured the prisoners. As they rode around a house, Col. Stuart sent another messenger. Beckham's guns then opened fire upon a Federal regiment drawn up in front of a wood, and the enemy began to retreat. Troops from Early's brigade took over the chase while Beckham's guns continued the cannon fire, but when the enemy moved out of range, the battery fell silent. Rulon only had time to attempt to shake the ringing sound from his ears when his company moved on the chase once more, with Beckham's battery following.

Rulon and two others soon dropped out from following the Federal flight when they were detailed to the rear accompanying a squad of captives. He learned over the campfire that night that the very last of Stuart's chasers followed McDowell's army a full twelve miles.

He said to Ren Lovell, "The Colonel surely does cotton to the chase," to which Lovell replied with hoots of laughter.

"They name Jeb Stuart 'the dashing cavalier' in some parts," he said when he could talk. "He does love the chase, and all that it brings."

"Glory?"

"Yes."

"Honor?"

"Of course."

"The attention of the fairer sex?"

"Not as much as you'd think. To some degree, though."

"Is he a married man?"

"Yes, and reputed to be happy in his union."

"Good for him." Rulon thought of his little wife, of the privations of the day's campaign, and of the relief he now felt at being safely delivered from any harm he could have met on the field of battle. He needed to write to Mary again soon to let her know he was hale and hearty.

&

Rulon — July 22, 1861

Rulon's first opportunity to write home after the battle came the next day in camp, when he snatched a moment to pen a letter.

22 Jul 1861
Fairfax C-H, Va.
Dear Wife,
I rite in haste to inform you of my good health following the rout of the Federals at Manassas junction. We are all well in the Company except for one poor fellow who met His Maker upon the field of honor, and another who suffer'd two wounds. Now we have moved forward to picket posts at Fairfax court-house Upon our journey here we come upon much salvagable goods that will stand us in Good sted. We feast'd upon Yankee provisions, and I tell you, wife, it is good to have a full belly again.

I picked up a picnick-basket droped by some fair Yankee ladie come to watch us Confederates get our come-uppance. Instead, we sent the Federal boys flying back to Washington City, making as quick a retreat over the same ground as it took them two or three days to advance. Mr. Lovell and I enjoied the ham sandwiches therein, after which I gave the basket to a farmwife. She was happy to receive the striped tablecloth and napkins, along with silver tableware. We don't have a use for those fancies in the cavalry.

Our Colonel Sturt covered himself with glory in the late campaign. The men of a few companies feel he works them too hard, but I'm glad of his spirit and daring. I have lerned a good deal from his example.

Mr. Earl, the old tracker, tells me I have sum talent in the skill. I continu to lern what he teaches me. He says I may soon track for a patrol on my own. I reckon his prais gives me prideful feelins but I trust not to exces. I want yor pa's hat to fit my head when this war is won.

Mary, I look forward to coming home to you soon, sinse the Federal Yankees know we are fighting men and will keep our country.

Until that happy Day,
Yor husband, who holds you most dear,
Rulon S. Owen

When he had given in the envelope to be dispatched at the next opportunity, Rulon wondered when mail from home would catch up with them. Surely by this time, Mary had discovered if she was with child or not. He yearned to know if it were true. He hoped she was carrying his babe. If he should be taken by a shell or a musket ball, a child would be a comfort to Mary, and to Ma and Pa, as well. He whispered a silent prayer that he would not be taken from her, and went to curry his horse.

ಋ

Ella Ruth — July 22, 1861

Ella Ruth regretted her sporadic fits of crying over the last two days. All the thinking and the tears had given her a tremendous headache. Even so, excitement bubbled in her stomach. In an effort to cheer her up, Poppa was taking her with him to Harrisonburg. She planned to shop to her heart's content.

The day began too early for her taste, but Poppa insisted on an early start to avoid the likelihood of meeting with enemy troops on the move. The Yankees were said to be tucked in safely down the Valley in Martinsburg, unlikely to come up to battle against the steadfast Virginians holding the line, but Poppa seemed cautious lately.

She climbed into the buggy with his assistance. "It is mighty kind of you to include me in your trip, Poppa," she said with a smile as she settled into the seat and adjusted her hat and veil. She turned to look at the servant getting on a horse behind the buggy. "Will Thomas be able to keep up with your prize team?"

"He rides well enough." He lifted the lines and clicked his tongue at the horses. Once they were on their way, he said, "I will not be able to accompany you for shopping, but Thomas will be with you to carry all your baubles."

"Poppa! I will be just fine alone. I do not plan to buy more than five or six 'baubles,' as you put it. I must have a new hat, however. This old veil is too thin for the sun."

"You won't go unaccompanied, daughter. I cannot allow you that liberty."

"Pish and tush." She looked again at the old black-skinned man following them. "He does seem to know how to ride. If you insist on him coming along, I suppose I shall endure it."

"Thomas is reliable, Ella. You will treat him well."

"Of course I will, Poppa! To hear you speak, one would think I was heartless."

He glanced over at her, but said nothing.

"I'm not heartless. I treat everybody well."

"Then what of your tears the past days?"

Ella Ruth sniffed. He knew she had been crying over her lost love affair. "You should have permitted me to marry Benjamin. If you had been agreeable, I would not have rejected him when he surprised me, when he told me out of the blue that we had to marry right away, without any friends around us. I was caught off guard, and yes, I did treat him badly. I'm sorry I did."

"You've had the household in quite an uproar, daughter."

"I miss Ben. I was wrong to turn him down so precipitously." She turned away. "Don't make me think about it now. I am on the point of crying again."

After the day-long drive, Poppa got them situated at the finest hotel the city offered, although it seemed to be teeming with people. As a result, she was obliged to sleep on a cot in the same room with Poppa, and Thomas was sent off to take a spot in the stable. How scandalous to share quarters with her father at her age!

During the evening she kept to the room reading a lady's fashion magazine while Poppa met with a business partner. Growing restless, she went to the window, lifted aside the drapes, and peered out. A group of men carrying torches had gathered opposite the hotel, and she shivered at the ominous looks on their faces. What had occurred to give them such long jaws?

After a while spent gazing at the men, she was no more enlightened on the matter, and let the drapery fall closed. She picked up her magazine once again and tried to find the most delightful items with which to make a shopping list.

However, she could not concentrate on that simple task. She had been so thrilled to accompany Poppa on this excursion to town, but now disturbing thoughts of Ben intruded. Where was he these days? Was he well? She supposed he was somewhere down the Valley, guarding the river against a Yankee invasion. She hoped he was getting enough to eat. How the man liked to eat!

She put down the magazine, unable to keep to her task. Poppa seemed to be worried these days. Did he entertain thoughts that Mr. Lincoln's army would come up the Valley and wreak havoc upon his business? Everyone prattled on about how the Yankees would try to overrun Virginia, but with men the likes of Ben on duty, she was sure that could never happen.

He always talked about how much he loved his native land, Virginia. Surely no one would stand stronger against the enemy threat. Her stalwart Ben! How hard he had worked at the mill, throwing about those bags of grain like a common laborer. She adored how his muscled arms were built like iron. How could a girl have any fears when Ben guarded the border, protecting her?

A chill disturbed her reverie and she wrapped her arms around herself. She could not help remembering the look on his face before she had whirled in anger and left the yard behind the mill on that horrible day. She felt as though a leaden casing wrapped around her heart. Ben wasn't standing guard for her. She had ruined their bond with her foolish pride and fancy dreams.

Perhaps it was just as well when Poppa came into the room, his face a thundercloud.

He said right away, "I'm sorry to spoil your outing. We leave before the crack of dawn to return home."

"But Poppa—"

"Not a word, Ella Ruth. There's been a battle. The war has come into Virginia."

She inhaled sharply. Ben!

"There, there," he said, softening his countenance as he approached. "We're not in immediate danger. We'll arrive home in time if we leave early enough."

"Poppa, I'm afraid." She heard how thin her voice sounded, and it frightened her still more.

He put his arms around her and she nestled into them. Poppa wasn't as strong as Ben, but he would do, for now.

℘

Ella Ruth — July 23, 1861

The journey home began even earlier in the day than had the one to Harrisonburg. The buggy moved through a ghostly mist that swirled as high as the tops of the wheels and obscured Ella Ruth's sight of the hills and gaps that she knew lay out there in the semi-darkness.

She sighed. Mist nearly always made her feel giddy, a bit excited, especially if she were on her way to meet Benjamin. But such was not the case today. *Today*, she thought, *today is not the same*. Today the mist caused her an unfamiliar sense of unease, a chilling sensation that all was not well, that the mist was not friendly, would not hide her escape from the house to meet Ben.

Ben. Perhaps she would never, ever see him again. That was entirely her own fault. She might never see Ben because— She drew a quick breath.

Please don't let Poppa hear me if I cry, she thought, struggling against the emotion sweeping through her body. Grief, hard as granite and bitter as quinine, ripped at her insides, tearing open a hole in her heart that only Ben could fill. She had nothing upon which to lay the blame but her own stiff pride.

Only that stubborn pride would get her through this moment, mask the trouble in her soul from Poppa, keep her alive in the unfulfilling future she saw stretching before her, endless and sterile. A future without Ben.

"You're quiet this morning." Poppa's voice broke into her solitary thoughts. "Disappointed not to spend my money on a new bonnet?"

She shook her head. "I suppose I'm tired," she answered, knowing it to be partly true. Her brain and bones and sinews reeked of tiredness. Was she disappointed that her shopping party had been terminated so abruptly? No. Not really. Her overwhelming pain stemmed from the grief, and yes, anxiety, on top of it all.

Poppa had mentioned a battle. Ben had gone for a soldier. Had he been involved? Was he wounded? Had he been. . . . She couldn't even bear to think of the word. Ben, so alive, so vital.

She shifted on the seat cushion. He would not be dead. She would not entertain the notion. She glanced sideways at her father. Perhaps engaging in conversation would rid her of this pall.

"You're a mite quiet yourself," she said, struggling to put a tease into the words.

Poppa looked over at her. "I have a few things on my mind," he said. "I don't fancy ruination, daughter."

Ella Ruth did not answer. Poppa seemed too preoccupied to pay mind to her. So be it. She would be silent and endure the ride home as best she could.

When the sun finally lifted above Massanutten Mountain, the mist began to burn away, revealing first the treetops, then more foliage, then entire trees, glistening with dew, green and tall and comforting, and at last, the pike.

They were alone on the Valley Pike, she and Poppa. The wheels chattered slightly on the rock surface. The clip-clop of hooves behind them reminded her that one other person accompanied them. Thomas. She wondered if he was annoyed at Poppa's early start for a second day in a row. He was growing older, with grizzled white patches on his head where there had always been black kinks before. Older folks sometimes complained of rheumatism and such. No matter. It was his duty to obey Poppa's directions, even if they were tiresome at times. Like this morning.

Presently, another vehicle approached, coming toward them in some haste. Poppa moved the horse from the center of the road to allow the wagon van to pass their buggy. The wagon had canvas sides, rolled down and tied, and several dark, blotchy stains on the material caught her eyes, but not before the appalling sounds of moans came to her ears. Hideous, terrible moans.

"Poppa, what is th—"

"Cover your ears!"

Her hands flew up to do so. What was causing that noise?

"Ambulance wagon," he muttered as the din faded in the distance. "Do not look next time," he added.

Those blotches on the sidewalls. Her heart shrank. Blood. Of course they were blood. An ambulance carried wounded men to the hospital. Were they going all the way to Staunton? She looked back, unable to restrain herself. How many of the wounded would be alive when they arrived?

Was Ben among those poor boys in the wagon?

She asked herself the same question each time they passed another ambulance, until the flood of them moving south up the pike had her sobbing, biting her veil to bits with the anxiety of not knowing the answer.

Chapter 11
Rod — July 31, 1861

Captain Roderick Owen of the Owen Dragoons mounted his mare, spur jingling as he swung his leg over and found the stirrup, feeling slightly chagrined that he was getting into the action so late. He figured all that was left was a clean-up, or some kind of defensive movement to enforce upon the Yankees the notion that everything was over but the shouting.

Julia came over and leaned against Rod's leg. "You come back safe, husband," she murmured in a voice stripped of emotion, as though she had spent it all. "We have that grandchild a-coming."

"That will be a joyous day." He rubbed the thigh of his other leg.

"Peter?"

He barely heard her thin voice above the pounding in his chest.

"I'll see about finding the boy after I join the regiment," he said, putting his hand on the side of her head, lightly, briefly. "If I can locate him, I'll send him home."

"They won't shoot him for desertion?"

"Nah, not that. I'll do it proper, get him discharged for being underage."

"Will they do that? Send him home?"

"I reckon. The government didn't make a call for young'uns." He cleared his throat. "I don't see this to-do extending for much longer, but he may yet have a chance to join in."

"No." Julia's voice found an emotion at last as she wailed the word. "Rulon and Ben are enough to send," she finished, head down, pressed tight against Rod's trouser leg. "And now, you."

"Julie," he began, but couldn't find any words to comfort her. Finally, he drew on the ancient faith. "Put the future in the Good Lord's hands, woman. He will see us through."

She let him loose and backed up, firming her shoulders. "Indeed," she said, with one last sniff, and made a "get along with you" gesture.

Rod rode down the lane without looking back, knowing if he did, he likely wouldn't leave his wife and home. But the pull of war was strong, and he gave in to it, even knowing what he knew of conflict, and blood, and the rancid taste of conquest.

&

Rulon — July 31, 1861

Rulon sat his horse in a driving rainstorm, grateful for the Federal overcoat he had acquired after the late battle. A biting wind added misery to the wet weather. Staring across the Potomac River, he could see the fortifications of the enemy capital. Soldiers drilled in the rain on a parade ground off to the left. Around the city, flag snapped so smartly on their poles he imagined he could hear them. Vidette duty often sent him within close proximity to the Yankees. In fair weather, he enjoyed acting as a sentinel for his country. This foul weather made the long hours of observation more challenging.

The wind shifted, and he adjusted his hat and collar to deflect the water attacking from a different angle. The skin of his neck seemed warm to the touch, even with the rain cooling the air. He shrugged off the notion that he might be taking sick. He didn't have time for that nonsense.

"Owen, we're moving back," said Owen Leoyd.

Rulon reined the horse around to follow the other man, and experienced a momentary dizziness. It wasn't enough to unseat him, but did give him another fleeting thought about taking ill. He shook it off as before. Too many of his comrades were sick. He couldn't let down the company and the regiment by joining them.

Leoyd led the way to a thicket about a mile away. There the two men dismounted and sheltered as best they could as the storm beat its fury upon them.

After a while, Rulon noticed himself shaking. He hunched into the greatcoat, putting his hands up the opposing sleeves so he could rub his arms inside the wool, and then chafed his hands together. When his teeth began to chatter, he began to feel concern.

"You ailing, Owen? Don't you make me sick or nothing," Leoyd said. He had mentioned repeatedly how much he enjoyed using Rulon's last name as much as possible as sort of a joke, seeing as how it was his own first name. He didn't seem like he was joking now, though, as he added, "I don't cotton to taking a fever from you."

"It's the cold wind," Rulon replied. Several of the men in the regiment had been so sick they'd been discharged and sent home, and a few had even died. Rulon did not intend to be among either group.

At last the wind died down.

"We should keep our eyes peeled for the relief vidette," Leoyd said. He squinted into the rain. "They should be along before sundown." He chuckled wryly. "It's not dark yet, is it? Hard to tell with all this bad weather."

Rulon shook his head. "I reckon it's early yet. Shouldn't we take another look across the river?" He could barely get the words out for the tremor in his jaw that made his teeth click together.

"Nope. The Yankees are still over there, all right. I don't figure they're going to be doing any marching in this rain."

"I s-suppose you're r-r-r-right," Rulon stammered.

Leoyd squinted in his direction. "You better git seen by the doc when we git to camp. I don't like the look of you."

"You n-n-never did."

"Well, yeah, but you look kinda mealy-mouth an' green just now."

"I'm fine. N-n-never b-b-better."

"Don't lie to me, Owen."

"Leoyd?" A low voice called from behind them.

"Over here," he answered. "'Bout time you boys showed up."

After a few verbal jabs back and forth, the new vidette took over the watch, and Rulon and Owen Leoyd made their way to their mounts and started back to camp.

"Doctor," Leoyd muttered after a few miles.

"If I don't f-feel better t-t-tomorrow, I'll c-c-consider your adv-v-vice."

≈

Rulon — August 1, 1861

Even with his heavy wool coat pulled up over his blanket, Rulon shivered all night and awoke feeling like he'd been stomped underneath a herd of stampeding mules. His face ached, his shoulders ached, and he knew the signs of a galloping fever when he felt them.

Someone in the tent was tending the stove, from the sounds of a chunk of wood settling into the ashes, but the heat might as well be going up the chimney, for all he felt of it.

"You've had a chill all night," Ren said quietly. "I recommend you get over to the hospital. I'll cover for you at roll call."

"I'm f-f-fine," Rulon protested, opening his eyes to find Ren staring down at him.

"I can't make you go," Ren replied, "but we're better off if you go be sick with the other fellows instead of staying here with us." He rubbed lather onto his face. "No offense meant."

"None t-t-taken. Do I appear to be sick?"

Ren quirked an eyebrow. "I'd say yes. No spots on you, but I'm not a medical man. Let the doc look at you."

Rulon got up and dressed as quickly as he could. "Still raining?" he asked, looking at his still-soggy hat.

"Not so much as yesterday. If you need help, I'm almost finished shaving."

"I'll make it, thank you kindly."

When he arrived at the hospital tent, an orderly had him wait for almost an hour before the doctor appeared to ask, "Symptoms?"

"Ch-ch-chills, f-fever, aches. P-pain in my j-jaw now."

"You had that stammer all your life?"

"Sh-showed up yesterday with the ch-chills."

"Hmm. Any spots?"

"Haven't looked."

"You a drinking man?"

"On s-special occasions, yes."

The doctor got a bottle and tumbler, filled the glass half full of amber liquid, and thrust it into Rulon's hand. "This is a special occasion. Drink it down. If it doesn't help or you get further symptoms, come back tomorrow or the next day."

Rulon looked at the doctor, then at the tumbler, then did as directed, got up, and went back toward his tent, his gullet burning, but his body warmer.

෴

Ben — August 2, 1861

When Ben's company had gone into camp following the battle of Manassas, he was persuaded that he ought to write home, and hunted up a pencil and paper to accomplish the task.

Dear Ma,
I reckon you will be pleased to heer that Me and the other fellows

---

in the Company hav been fending off the foe as admirably as we can. Our Company is called "G" in the 33rd Regiment of Virginia Volunteers of Infantry. We are, as I had supposed, fightin in the Brigade of "Old Jack". We Took part in the big Battle at Manassas junction after we rode the rail cars over hill and thru vale. I tell you, it was mighty fierce sittin atop them cars and feelin the wind pushin aganst us so hard it like to blow us away before we got to the station at M. We lost a few boys in the fight. I will mention, not to worry you, but to inform, as there is naught to worry you in the tale, that I receev'd a slight injury to my limb from a ball hitting upon a drummer boy and coming through him to smite me. I'm O.K. The Surgeon took out the ball and gave me a piece of cotton Lint to press on the scrape, and I'm right as rain now. I can't say the same for the unfortunate drummer boy.

The sting of the gunpowder smoke gettin in our eyes and up into our noses and choking our breth was the worst part of the battle. That, and the bellowing of the Yankees long guns as they spoke out real sharp and threw their shells acrost the fields and into our lines. When we could no longer bear to receev the shells in our ranks, we broke over the crest of the rise called the Henry House Hill and battled our weigh to the long guns to silents them. When the task was done and the shelling ceased, I wondered woud I ever hear right again.

"Old Jack" has a new name, giv'n him by a General what was shot dead soon after he spoke it out. The story goes this general Bee saw our troops drawn up Firm upon the ridgeline and said somethin like "There stands Jackson like A stone Wall," and he's been called Stone Wall Jackson ever since. He don't much like it, as I hear.

Give my affection to Pa and the young'uns, and accept my kiss upon your brow in grateful thanks for all you done for me thruout my years. I hope you have good news from Rulon and that he is well. Tell the rascal Peter to stop hounding you to go to war. There's plenty of fightin to go around, but I hope his time don't come soon to protect his native country. We bigger boys are risin to the task.

Your faithful son Benj'n

Chapter 12
Rulon — August 4, 1861

By Sunday, Rulon knew he was in trouble. With no appetite, he had grown weak over the last few days, and yesterday he had fallen from his horse. This morning he awoke with a swollen jaw and a tingling near his ear. Although he ached from the fall, he hadn't landed on his head, so the swelling puzzled him.

He sat on the edge of his cot, hand to his ear, dizzy and faint.

"Owen, what's wrong with your face?" Ren squatted down to get a better view.

"Swollen jaw."

"Hmm." Ren got up and backed away. "Mumps! You've got mumps."

"No."

"Yes. Get out of here."

"I reckon you're right," Rulon admitted. He pushed himself off the cot, caught his balance, and pulled on his trousers. Ren threw him his overcoat, and Rulon picked up his hat. As he shuffled toward the flap of the tent, Ren called to him.

"Wait. This came yesterday." He picked up an envelope from his camp desk and held it out. "From your wife, I imagine."

Rulon reached over to get the letter, and thrust it into his pocket. All the movement made his head swim, and he stopped for a moment to get over the feeling.

"Need help getting to the hospital?"

"I'm fine," Rulon said, his voice so weak he barely recognized it. He turned cautiously, lifted the flap, and stepped into a chilly wind.

ลง

Mary — August 5, 1861

Mary looked up from the list she was filling for Mrs. Bingham to see Miss Ella Ruth Allen hovering around the dry goods. She cast a furtive glance toward Mary.

When Mary had finished with the baker's wife, she noticed that the girl was looking her way again, but another customer claimed her attention, and she forgot about her for a time.

Sighing when she had finished filling the order, Mary straightened her shoulders and looked around the store. Ella Ruth was still in the same spot, fingering cloth and glancing her way every three seconds.

"May I assist you?" Mary called.

Ella Ruth took a tentative step in Mary's direction. She picked up speed, and was practically running when she reached the counter. She inclined her head as though the motion accompanied a curtsy, and said, "I am Ella Ruth Allen. Perhaps Benjamin has spoken of me?"

"Mary Owen, at your service. What may I get for you, Miss Allen?"

"Oh, you do not understand. I am not here to purchase anything. I only want—" She turned her head away sharply, sniffed, then collected herself. "I wish to know if you have heard from Benjamin."

"Benjamin?"

"Benjamin Owen. You know who he is. Your husband's brother?"

Now the situation came clear. This was the girl whom Brother Ben loved. Rulon had spoken of his sibling's difficulties with obtaining permission to marry the girl. Mostly as a contrast to his own happiness. Mostly between their bouts of intimacy. Mary felt herself grow warm. She wondered if her face was glowing.

"I cannot think why Brother Ben would communicate with me," she said, dodging the girl's searching gaze. "Have you not heard from him?" She knew her words would sound cruel, so she had softened her tone as much as she could to deflect any implied criticism. "Perhaps he is not in a place where he can write."

Mary watched in fascination as the girl's face seemed to crumple into what looked like a dried-apple doll's face.

"I, I, I would not marry him," she said, her voice breaking. "I was too full of pride. Now he is gone, and it is too late. I am so sorry. Tell him I am sorry."

"Brother Ben will not write to me," Mary repeated. "There is no cause for him to do so. If he has been able to write home, Mother Owen will have his address. You must petition her for that." Mary reached across the counter and patted Ella Ruth's hand where it gripped the edge of the counter. "I cannot help you, although I wish I could."

Her own happiness felt like a betrayal of this grieving girl, but that was nonsense. She barely knew her, and what she did knew of her selfish nature boded ill for any future with Ben. He had taken the rejection of his offer of marriage very hard, and had gone away with the taste of bitter ashes in his mouth.

Ella Ruth grabbed Mary by the wrist. "I cannot approach the woman. You must ask her for me. Please." She finally seemed to notice that she was detaining Mary, and released her arm.

The gasping way in which the Allen girl said the word "please" told Mary what a price she was paying in asking the favor. She was used to getting everything her own way in life. She had spurned Brother Ben. Perhaps she should pay for her foolishness a while longer.

But Mary knew she couldn't poison her babe by harboring rancor. She cupped her swelling stomach behind the cover of the counter, and nodded her assent. "I will ask Mother Owen for news the next time I see her. If she has any, I will pass it along to you."

How desperate was the countenance of the contrite girl! Mary almost felt sympathy for her plight, but not quite yet. Ella Ruth must prove her worth by coming to fetch any tidbit of information Mary might glean.

"Be here in a fortnight. I will give you any information I possess," she said, and tried softening her demand with a smile.

"Thank you." The girl pressed Mary's hand between hers. "Thank you," she said again, this time in a whisper.

As the girl left the store, Mary wondered if she would actually come through the door again.

෨

Rulon — August 6, 1861

After two days in the hospital tent, and several draughts a day of quinine mixed in water, Rulon still hadn't shaken off the chills and fever. His jaw ached, and now his ear was beginning to ring as though a troop of spur-jingling cavalry kept passing through his head. Worse still, he hadn't mustered the strength to read Mary's letter.

Feeling like a mewling new-born calf, Rulon struggled to sit up, determined that he would open the envelope at the very least. Once that was accomplished, perhaps it would be easier to read out the words she'd sent him.

When he had worked the flap loose, he saw that the letter was three weeks old, dated on the 12th of July. The first line told him Mary had confirmed her hopes that she was carrying his child. Joy surged through him, momentarily giving him the strength to sit longer and finish the letter. Further down the page, his heart lurched with additional gladness as he read that she was sure the child would be a boy. How could she know that, he wondered? He supposed her assurance came because he had so strongly and repeatedly expressed his wish for a son. She believed it because he wanted it. Dear sweet Mary.

Exhausted from the effort of reading the letter, Rulon lay back on his cot, his eyes wet from emotion. Yes, he had said he wanted a son. He didn't know much about young'uns and how they formed in the mother's womb, but he imagined the outcome was fixed by now.

A young'un. A child. He was going to be a father. He sucked in a long breath. He hadn't been much interested, as his brothers and sisters came along, in the months of progress toward what women called "the happy event." His happy event. Would this fussing and fighting be over in time for him to be there when Mary brought forth his son?

He thought about Mary. What was she going through? What would she endure when the time came to birth his child? He'd never wanted to know about the birthing part of the child-bearing process.

Would she suffer during her travail? The word itself brought to mind adversity. Burdensome toil. Pain. He shuddered to think about what women must suffer in delivering the young of mankind. Ah, Mary. She was such a little thing. She surely would be inconvenienced by giving birth. Might she die?

But Ma hadn't— He cringed. His mind would not even go toward relating the totality of such events with his mother. She was Ma! She never even—

After a long moment of the blankness of avoidance, he had to admit that she and Pa must have done some measure of . . . getting together, else they would not now have their sons and daughters.

He wiped his feverish face. He must be hallucinating to be thinking of carnal knowledge in the same context as his parents. But no. He was lucid. This was real. He held Mary's letter here in his hand, and he returned to worrying about her in the coming travail. It was true Ma had not died in birthing ten children, but he had heard her mutter something daunting about "the valley of the shadow of death" before Julianna put in her appearance.

He would have to redouble his prayers, make a greater effort to live a stalwart life in order that God would bless Mary in her hours of pain and labor and giving birth.

When she had successfully come through that time, he was going to be a father.

What kind of father would he be? Strong and autocratic, like his own? Of a willy-nilly persuasion who sought the fashion of the moment, like a man he knew in New Market? Stern, but fair to his children? What if this young'un was a daughter, instead of a son? Could he be kind, but firm, to keep her safe from predators? Predatory males, like, like, himself?

He thought long and hard about the concept that the coming child could be a tender daughter who needed a father on hand to protect and cherish her. He had to make it through this illness, this war against the Yankees. Son or daughter, it really didn't matter now. Sometime early next year, he needed to be home to welcome the new little one into his heart and home.

"God, let me live to see my child," he whispered. "Don't let me die in camp because of the mumps." Annoyingly, his eyes leaked as he said the words, and he had to wipe them furtively.

He didn't know if mumps was a fatal disease. The doctor had said it was usually one of the ailments a child went through, but hadn't added whether or not children died from it, like they often did with the measles, which thankfully, he'd survived. How he'd avoided contracting this mumps illness up to now was a mystery to him.

The doctor had mentioned one other thing, and Rulon thought on it now, wondering if he should include a special appeal to God about it in his improvised prayer. He finally decided that given the risk, he would take a chance on annoying God with the plea.

"Dear God," he started again, whispering as before. "Don't let my parts swell up."

The doctor had told him to take notice if his "testicles" became swollen, and to let him know if they did. Rulon had asked for a translation of the unknown word, and was horrified to be told what it meant, and that he might lose the power to engender children should the ailment spread to that site.

"Please," he added, knowing his vanity had partially prompted him to ask this boon, but hoping such a thing was important to a God he had been taught was the Father of All. Mary wanted several children, and the thought that a misplaced childhood disease could rob her of that fulfillment had been causing him a good deal of anguish. "Thank you for any mercy you can spare to Mary an' me," he concluded his appeal, and turned his head so his tears would be less apparent to the other patients in the tent.

ɞ

Mary — August 9, 1861

"Mother Owen," Mary greeted her mother-in-law later that week. "Welcome. That is a fine basket of eggs."

"And here is a can of cream," Julia said, indicating the metal armful Albert bore into the store.

"Cream! That is priceless these days," Mary said. She patted the counter, and Albert hoisted his burden onto it, then moved off to explore the inventory.

"How are you, my dear?"

"I feel better on some days than others. Today has been a good day. Do you suppose the sickness will lessen in time?"

"Most times it does, Mistress Mary. How long has it been, now?" She ticked months off on her fingers. "Almost three months gone. I predict a spate of better times a-coming."

"That will be most gladsome." Mary gave in to the desire to covertly pat the place on her abdomen that would be expanding more each future day. "Are all well in the family?" she asked in order not to neglect the social niceties.

"As well as can be expected, I reckon. We miss those not present, but are doing our best to carry on with the chores." Julia lifted her hands in resignation. "Mr. Owen apportioned the tasks to the boys, but we miss Peter's help. The scamp!"

"Have you had news from your sons?"

"Rulon has had the most time to send a letter, and I have received his. I have not heard from Ben or Peter. Or Mr. Owen," she added.

"I am sure you will hear from all of them, given time," Mary said, hoping her words would comfort her mother-in-law. "You might be surprised to learn that I had a visitor on Monday."

"Not the monthly?" Julia's face grew grave.

"Oh, no. No. I mean Miss Ella Ruth Allen came into the store to speak to me."

"That girl?"

"I know she rejected Brother Ben's offer of marriage. It appears she has repented of her pride. She seemed very contrite for her actions."

"What did she want with you?"

"She asked for news from Brother Ben. I reckon she also wants to obtain his address for correspondence."

"Hm. I wonder if he will welcome that from her."

Mary shrugged her shoulders. "I agreed to ask you for an address, once you have one to share, of course. If she has the gumption to attempt to correspond after turning him off, I figure she deserves the chance to ask for forgiveness, at the least."

Julia sighed. "Mary, you have the right of it. When Ben deigns to write, I will bring you the particulars."

"Thank you, Mother Owen. I knew you would rise to your good reputation."

"My good reputation?"

"Miss Allen was afraid to approach you. I told her how good you are. Perhaps one day she will have the courage to speak to you yourself."

"You're a caution, daughter Mary. Talking me up that-a-way. I'm plain Julia Owen. She has no reason to fear me."

"I'm hoping she will come to know that, ma'am."

Chapter 13
Rulon — August 10, 1861

Throughout the week, Rulon suffered a great deal of pain from his ailment. He began to write a rough journal of what was happening to him in case he didn't survive the disease, and got Ren to promise he would send the account of his illness to Mary in that event.

He wrote of fever coming and going, of nights of torment spent pacing beneath a tent upon which drummed incessant rain, of keen pains darting through his jaw and each tooth, of muscles and nerves jerking and quailing at the pain, of tremors, then more pain that the doctor could not ease.

One night he found that sitting alongside the stove with his mouth full of cold water brought a small amount of relief. Finally, the pain, fever and swelling abated, and he looked forward to being discharged the next morning.

He awoke while it was yet dark and screamed in agony. The other side of his jaw had risen in the night, and all the pain, fever, and throbbing were back. One of the men assigned to nurse the patients came running with a light, and tried to shush him.

"Quiet, man. What ails you?" He held up the light, then swore when he saw Rulon's cheek. "That must pain you a mite."

Rulon tried to tear his jaw off to relieve his distress, but the nurse tied his hands down and summoned the physician.

The doctor swore in his turn. "It's four o'clock in the morning. Keep silent!"

Rulon clamped his teeth shut, shame crowding him into desperation. He thrashed on the cot. He could not endure this torture further. He wanted to die.

"Oswald, bring me the laudanum."

"Should you waste it on him?"

"Do as I say." The doctor flung out his arm, indicating his disgust. "Dying men shouldn't deal with all this noise."

Sometime after the doctor administered part of a tumbler of bitter liquid to him, Rulon began to drift in a half-lit world of haze and buzzing. Then he went into a dark place and knew no more.

When he awoke to full sunlight, he vowed to comport himself with more order despite the pain, and apologized to his fellow patients. When he was allowed to go relieve himself, he discovered that his worst nightmare had become reality. Harboring icy despair at his predicament, he asked to speak to the doctor.

After an examination, the man said, "The swelling is not severe. Time will tell if there is a diminishment in your vigor. You have a wife?"

Rulon could hardly bear to speak. "Yes," he finally said through gritted teeth. "Children?"

"One coming soon," he managed.

"That's good. You'll have one child, at least. Bear up, man. Another two weeks and you'll be in the field again." The doctor gave Rulon a pat on the shoulder, a curt nod, and then hurried off.

Rulon lay down, the pain in his soul vying with the pain in his jaw for supremacy.

∞

Rod — August 11, 1861

Having arrived at his duty post, Rod wrote home to Julia.

11th Aug'st 1861
Outside Charles Town, Via.
My dear Wife,
I take pencil in hand to inform you of my safe arrival to the place
of our posting. The Men of the Owen Dragoons have covered
themselves with glory in the past week, firstly, in arriving without

incident, and secondly, in defending the Bord'r with dispach and zeel.

We have been assigned to tear up rails and Ties from the Baltimore & Ohio Rail Raod so that the Enemy does not have Use of it to invade our Land. Deer Wife, yu shoud see the hearty manner in wich my boys attack there task. Altho we do not ride as much as sum woud like, whatever we are commanded to do is honorabl, as I tell the boys.

Do you heer from our Sons who are servin the Comnwelth of Virginia? My hope is that they will bear themselves well and bring honor to the Owen Name.

My devoshun to you is without ceasin. Embrace the young'uns for me, and acept a kiss upon yor brow from

Yor husband,
Capt'n Roderick Owen
Commanding, Owen Dragoons
7th Reg'ment Via. Cav.

৪১

Mary — August 14, 1861

Mary sat at the table one evening, picking at her food. Nothing appealed to her. Some of the odors made her gag. The stink of the cabbage was insufferable. She passed the dish to Ida as quickly as she could.

Ida thrust an elbow into her side. "Don't throw up on me," she warned in a hiss.

"I'm not sick," Mary hissed back.

"You look green. Excuse yourself."

"I'm not ill," Mary repeated, a little louder.

"Mary," her mother's voice broke in. "Are you ailing? If that is the case, it would be best if you left the table."

"I am not ailing," Mary reiterated. "I merely do not have a strong appetite this evening." She laid her fork on the oilcloth. "Was there a post today?"

"No letters," Mr. Hilbrands announced.

Mary felt her blood congeal in her veins. No letters. No word from Rulon again today. Weeks had passed since she had received a message from him. She hadn't read of any battles since the big one at Manassas. What was going on? Was he ill, injured, dead?

"Did the Rockingham paper arrive?" Perhaps that weekly newspaper carried additional information about Rulon's company that the papers from New Market and Woodstock did not.

"I expect it tomorrow, daughter."

She felt like screaming, pulling on her hair, falling to the floor and drumming her heels on the carpet. That would get her nothing but a reprimand from her mother. Every day Mama found a new fault to point out, a new action that didn't suit her fancy, for which she spoke to Mary as though she were a naughty child.

I wish I had never pressed Rulon to let me live with my parents, she thought.

How much better it would be to live at the Owen farm. But the die had been cast, and she knew her mother would not let her move from the house now.

She held her breath for a moment, then let out a sigh. "I believe I am ailing after all," she said. "With your permission, I'll retire."

She scooted back her chair and escaped the room as quickly as she could. *Oh Rulon. Please be in good health. Please come home soon.*

℘

Peter — August 18, 1861

After thinking for a long time about how to couch his first letter home, on a bleak Sunday Peter finally decided he knew what to write.

18 August 1861
Der Pa and Ma,
I greet you with tha hope that yu are all well at home. I regret that I took off in such a great hurry and was neglectful about sayin my goodbyes. My intent never was to hurt you. and I hope you will be forgivin of my tresspass. I reckon a man is obliged to be about the busines of defending his country from the invader.

The Rangers have been put into the 7th Virginia Cavalry Regim't commanded by Colonel Angus Wm McDonald. He is an older man, but spry enuf despite a bad case of rumitizm. I hav been took into several brawls with the Yankees from which I emerged unskathed except for a paltry sabr cut upon my side wich is healin nicely. I wil bear a pretty scar to show my future wife as proof of my valor in battel.

Not havin much else to report, I will end. again beggin your forgiveness for the manner in which I took myself and the horse Brownie off from the place. Give my affection to my brothers and sisters. Tell Marie I miss her shortbread. We count ourselves lucky if we eat twice a day, and then our meals are beans and hardtack biskets.

I send you my deepest regards and love,
Yor son Peter

℘

Mary — August 19, 1861

On the 19th of August, Mary had conquered her stomach enough to show up for work in good time, and was removing the dust cloths covering the goods set up in the windows when she heard a tap on the front door. She looked out the glass pane to discover Ella Ruth Allen outside, an anxious expression on her face.

Mary unlocked the door and opened it a crack.

"We have not yet begun the day," she said after giving her a brief greeting.

"Please, won't you admit me? Father is on his way to the courthouse and agreed to let me come to buy a trifle if I didn't delay him but five minutes. I haven't a moment to spare. Please?"

The young woman's use of the word 'please' twice impressed Mary as to the urgency of her errand, and she bade her enter. "What trifle did you have in mind to buy?" she asked, turning to the wares.

Ella Ruth raised her shoulders, evidently in a protective motion, as she wrung her hands. "That was a subterfuge," she finally said. "I came for news of Benjamin. Do you have any word? An address where I might write him?"

Mary studied the pinched face, and put out her hand to lay it on Ella Ruth's. "You must compose yourself," she said.

Ella Ruth's face blanched. "Ah!" she wailed. "He is gone?"

"No. No, no. I merely mean that Mother Owen has not heard from him as yet. However, you may take comfort that his name has not been published on a list. Come back on Monday next. Perhaps there will be word this week."

Ella Ruth sighed raggedly. "Thank you for your kindness. You are a dear girl. I am sure your husband is happy in his choice of a bride." She cast her eyes down, then up again. "Are you well? You seem a trifle pale."

"I am as well as may be," Mary replied, with a small, secretive smile she kept from blossoming further with strong effort.

"What do you mean?"

"I am to have a child," she answered, and could not restrain her lips from their upward course.

Ella Ruth looked stricken. "If only, ah, if only I had not been prideful, I might have been even now carrying a child of my own. Benjamin's child."

Mary wondered if Ella Ruth realized how unseemly her thought was. She and Brother Ben were not married, and she should not talk of such things.

Ella Ruth spoke again. "I wish you every happiness, Missus Owen." She clasped her entwined fingers in front of her face, and seemed about to burst into tears.

Mary said nothing for a moment, then decided she must be gracious. "You're very kind in giving me that sentiment, Miss Allen. You may yet rejoice in a happy interval of your own. Rulon tells me this conflict cannot last for long. He and Brother Ben and the rest of the family will surely return soon."

"I can only pray for that glorious day," Ella Ruth squeezed out in a choked voice. "Thank you once more for being my intermediary. My go-between," she hastened to explain. She looked out the window. "I must go now. Poppa will be waiting."

"Do not forget your trifle, Miss Allen," Mary said, fishing out a stick of peppermint candy from a jar and wrapping it quickly in brown paper. "Here now. Take it. You have need of a smile."

Ella Ruth nodded as she accepted the parcel, then slipped away and closed the door quietly behind her.

Chapter 14
Julia — August 21, 1861

Clay brought mail from town, and in it was a letter addressed to Julia. She took it, looked at the inscription, and hugged it to her heart. "Your brother Ben always makes his letters with fancy doodiddles," she said to the girls, and sat down at the kitchen table in the middle of her work day to read the letter from her boy.

Marie and Julianna crowded around, and Clay hovered in the background as she read it aloud.

Julia smiled at Ben's description of riding atop a railroad car, frowned at the mention of a slight wound, wondering if he was making light of a more serious injury, and wept a bit for the mother of the unfortunate drummer boy. Beside her, the girls sniffed in sympathy.

"Stonewall Jackson," she murmured, thinking it a fitting name for the dour professor from the Virginia Military Institute. She had heard of his fondness for lemonade, and wondered if she ever would have occasion to serve it to the man. However, he would surely not be in the Valley for any cause except to do battle, so cast aside her notion as a flight of fancy.

As she folded up the letter to put it away, she recalled Mary's visitor, and the request for Ben's mailing address. She hesitated. The girls did not need to know of the foibles of romance at their young ages, so she arose and said, "Back to your chores, daughters. We have had a pleasant interval, but there remains work undone." She also shooed Clay out of the kitchen so she could be alone.

When her children were out of the way, she wrote out the directions on a scrap of paper, and tucked it behind a wooden box sitting on the mantelpiece. When she went into town later in the week, she would give Mary the paper.

෨

Mary — August 26, 1861

The next Monday, Miss Ella Ruth Allen showed up bright and early at the Hilbrands' store.

Glimpsing the wan, earnest face as Ella Ruth came through the door, Mary smiled to herself. This time, she had good news to impart. Not only had Mother Owen given her a slip of paper with the particulars of where it was that Brother Ben could receive mail, she had also allowed her to read the letter he had sent to his mother.

Although he mentioned that he had received an injury, he had made light of it. She wasn't about to mention it to Ella Ruth and get her all a-flutter with worry. If Brother Ben was willing to enter into correspondence with the girl, he could apprise her of the facts himself. Mary put on a bright smile to greet her visitor.

"You must have good news for me," Ella Ruth said as she approached, her anxiety showing in a pinched look of anticipation.

"I do indeed," Mary replied.

"Missus Owen has received word?"

"Yes. A letter came to her." She placed the scrap of paper on the counter. "She wrote out this address for you, and wishes you all success in the delivery of your correspondence."

"You were right," Ella Ruth breathed as she picked up the paper. "Missus Owen is a good woman."

Mary moved her head slightly, as though to say, "I told you she was," but she had no intention of speaking the rebuke out loud.

Ella Ruth smiled at last and Mary saw the comely face that had attracted the notice of Brother Ben.

"Have you any leather pocket books, the kind with writing paper inside, and perhaps a leaden pencil attached? I would like to purchase such an item."

Mary raised her eyebrows at the request. Surely she didn't intend to send a gift like that upon her first contact with Brother Ben.

Ella Ruth must have guessed her concern, for she said quickly, "I wish to write a note as soon as possible. If Benjamin is disposed to renew our . . . friendship, I shall dispatch the wallet to him on a later occasion." She ducked her head. "If he is not, I shall use the paper for other letters."

"I will ask my father," Mary said, and went in search of Papa. He found a pocket book which, when Ella Ruth saw it, placed a smile of satisfaction upon her lips.

"That will do splendidly," she said, somewhat more shyly than Mary had supposed her response would be. Mr. Hilbrands supplied the price, which Ella Ruth paid immediately.

When her father had gone about other business, Mary asked if her customer had other wishes, since she had not left once the money had changed hands.

Ella Ruth asked, her voice low, "Might there be a private place where I can write a letter? I do not dare write it at home and post it through my father."

"Certainly. You may use the desk in the back room. Just pass through here and follow me."

Mary showed the way, and was about to turn to leave the room when Ella Ruth put out her hand and touched her belly. Shocked, Mary said, "Ah!" and stepped backward. Ella Ruth pulled away her errant hand.

"I do beg your pardon," said the girl, speaking rapidly. "I have not had any experience of children, or ever been near a woman who is increasing. I so want to bear Benjamin's child."

Mary looked at her, stunned. She finally said, "But you hurt him sorely. He may not even—"

"I know my folly," Ella Ruth cried out. "My pride may have prevented any happiness I could have in this life. I may never have the chance to marry him." She put forward her hands in a supplicating gesture. "Do forgive me the indelicacy, Mistress Owen. Ah! How I wish to bear that name. You are fortunate."

"Yes," Mary agreed, still shaken by the intimacy of the cupping hand upon her skirt. "I married a good man, and I am bearing his child. I wish you every fortune, Miss Allen. Now I must return to my duties."

"Thank you." The girl inhaled sharply. "I hope that you and I may become friends. I hope we may share a name someday."

"Perhaps," Mary said, and turned away before the prospect that the tears stinging behind her eyelids could slide down her cheeks to reveal the reality of her loneliness. Rulon had not yet had the opportunity to touch her as Ella Ruth had. How long would it be before he could return from war and do so?

ဆ

Ella Ruth — August 26, 1861

Once Mary left her to herself in the back room, Ella Ruth crossed her arms on the desk and rested her forehead upon them. At last, after all the waiting, she had received the directions to which she could write to him, and she had no idea what words to put on the paper.

Whatever she wrote, it must appeal to his sense of fairness, and must convince him that she had undergone a true change of heart. She knew she had done wrong by him, but it wasn't enough to convey only that important message. She had to somehow soften Ben's heart toward her, for she knew she had caused it such pain that he would guard it most carefully against further hurt from her.

"I was so unbelievably heartless to you, my love," she whispered. "I refused to acknowledge how the world would change."

She raised her head and took up the pencil. There was plenty of paper in the pocket folio. She would simply have to try setting down what was in her heart, and if the first try did not suit, she would make another attempt . . . and another, and another, until she had it right.

She took several deeps breaths, licked the tip of the pencil, and poised it above the top of the sheet of paper.

Her fingers seemed to have no bones, and she dropped the implement. It rested where it had fallen, rebuking her for such absurd folly.

She hung her head. This was a senseless endeavor, foolish and vain. He would never forgive her.

Before despair could overcome her, however, a stubborn voice arose in her head. "You must try," it said. "You cannot give up before you make an attempt."

She recognized the inner voice. It was an echo of what she had heard throughout her life: her father's voice, encouraging her and her brother to take hold of every advantage in life.

The lesson had been taught. It had been received. It had become ingrained. Now it was time to execute the plan she had formulated. The tenacious Miss Ella Ruth Allen, daughter of a bull-headed and very successful businessman, straightened her shoulders, picked up the pencil, and went to work.

It took her three tries before she was satisfied with her labors. She had either written a letter that would cause Ben's heart to melt with compassion, or it was the wrong approach entirely, and he would reject her overture and cast her aside as she had done with him. However, she had made the attempt. Now she would have to allow time to show her the results.

ဆ

Rulon — August 31, 1861

At long last, Rulon found himself discharged from the physician's care, and not a moment too soon, as Garth Von strode up to the hospital, evidently bent on taking a rest from picket duty.

"Outta my path, Shenandoah sissy," growled the man, shoving Rulon as they both tried to use the door.

Rulon backed out of the way, assessing the threat. The man clearly was unhappy, but was he dangerous? Figuring caution was the better part of valor on this occasion, he took his departure and discovered that his company had moved away from the headquarters. Ren Lovell had left word that he had custody of Rulon's belongings, including his horse, so he was obliged to trudge on foot over a considerable part of the muddy countryside to rejoin his outfit.

When Ren Lovell saw him at evening, he greeted Rulon with a touch of deliberation. "Got rid of your contagion, have you? You still look a little swollen up."

Rulon shook his head. "That's your imaginings, Lovell. Mayhap I've grown plump on hospital gruel."

"Did it spread any?" He pointed downward. "A couple of the men made bets on it."

Rulon was unwilling to discuss his fears or be the butt of jokes, and put Lovell off with a few curt words. "That's none of your business. I'm sound now."

"You seem a tad bitter, Owen." Lovell laughed, showing his dimples. "I didn't bet on your misfortunate contagion, by the way, and you haven't missed any fighting, if that's what worries you. Not so you'd notice, anyway. We've had a minor fracas here or there, but this rain has kept us from doing more than simply keeping the Federals out of our land."

Rulon relaxed his guard and dropped his prickly attitude. He said, "I come across Von down to the hospital. "What's his story?"

Lovell made a face. "He says he has boils. He won't ride. I reckon we weren't getting enough killing action for him."

"Boils? On his butt?"

"That's what he says. I'm not surprised a bit. You know the man doesn't keep himself clean." Lovell rearranged a few papers on his desk. "Captain Yancey was happy to let him go for a while. Von's an unpleasant man when he's not busy."

"He's unpleasant most any day."

Rulon took advantage of the evening to borrow pen, ink, and paper to write to Mary. It had been a very long time since he had sent her a letter. She must be frantic with worry.

Septemb'r 2, 1861

He paused to reflect. Did he have the date correct? It didn't matter, he supposed. He bent over the paper again.

Near Fairfax C-H
My dearest love Mary,
*   You have been in my thoughts constantly during the Past month*
as I lay sick in the Hospital. I am recover'd now, and enjoying Good
helth, but I fared very poorly for a long while with the Mumps

swelling sickness. first in one side of my Jaw and then the other. I will not harow your thots. with a descripshun of my pains. Suffice it to say I had many agonies to get thru before the physician would Release me.

Such a lot of dying, Mary. The Hospital was not only for the Ill but the Wounded and Dyeing from the big Battle. I shudder now to think of it.

I will leave off talking of unpleasantries. Insted I will tell you that My heart was full to Bursting when I read of your good news. Are you well? Do you lack for anything? You must ask my Ma to bring you fresh eggs to eat. She will do that if you Say I asked.

Did Ben marry the Allen girl? He was very set on running away with her to Staunton to elope. Did he get his wish?

Is Peter behaving himself? He gave Ma the flutters with his talk of Enlisting. I hope he waits a while. I think this war will be longer than we at first thot. The Yankess do push back, although I reckon we will win out.

That is enouf news and questions for now. I miss your dear person and think of you every day.

Receiv a kiss from yor husband who adores you and wishes to see you soon

Rulon

Chapter 15
Mary — September 1, 1861

One Sunday after church services, the Hilbrands family was surprised by an afternoon visit from Dr. Meem, a prominent physician in the area. He asked to speak with Mrs. Owen, and Mary agreed to entertain him in the parlor.

"We are most honored by your visit," Mrs. Hilbrands said, and turned to lead the way into the room.

"Mama," Mary said so low that the visitor could not hear. "He wishes to speak to me."

"Nonsense," retorted her mother in the same fashion. "You cannot be alone with the man."

And so, Dr. Meem sat down to converse with the two ladies of the house, senior and junior.

As soon as he had taken a bit of refreshment, the doctor put down his cup and cleared his throat. "Mrs. Owen, I have been appointed as director of a new soldier's hospital that is to be built upon land donated by Colonel Rinker. We will have a need for ladies from Mount Jackson to lend a hand with some of the tasks suited to their station and nature. Your name has been presented as one who might wish to give such service, since you have a husband, I believe, at the front, serving his country?"

Mary bent her head, basking for a moment in the recognition of her married state and of Rulon's sacrifice. At last she smiled and lifted her eyes to give the doctor her assent, but her mother's voice cut across her train of thought.

"Certainly not. My daughter is in a delicate condition. It is not fitting for her to be among those of the opposite gender while she is, um, that is, while she remains, um, so indisposed."

"Mama! I am perfectly able to nurse the poor men who have given so much to our country. When will the building of the hospital be finished, Doctor?"

"Next spring, madam. It will—"

"I forbid it, daughter. Think of the odors, the contagion. You can scarcely hold food upon your stomach as it is."

"I am told that the sickness will go away soon, Mama. I will manage."

"No." She gave Mary a stern look, then turned to the doctor and said, "My daughter is unwell on many days. I am sure you will understand, Dr. Meem. She cannot help you." She arose. "Good day to you, sir."

While Mrs. Hilbrands showed the unhappy doctor to the door, Mary could hardly hold her temper in check. She stood beside her chair in the parlor, quivering with indignation that the decision had been so rudely taken from her power. When it was clear that her mother would not be returning, Mary went after her.

"How dare you speak for me?" she said, almost overcome with rage. "That was unconscionable. Mr. Owen would want me to help in any way possible."

"You forget yourself, Mary. You live in my house, under my roof and your father's protection. That husband of yours has no concern in the matters of my household. He was happy enough to leave you in my care, and I shall do as I see fit to keep you safe." She took a step away, then half turned and threw a cruel thought over her shoulder. "He is young and reckless. You cannot trust him. He is likely going to take up with the sort of women who follow the soldier camps."

Mary dug her fingernails into her hands and bit the inside of her cheek until it bled. She would not faint or carry on for her mother's benefit. She watched her go, with a bleak question sitting in the pit of her stomach. *What if Mama is right?*

છ

Ben — September 18, 1861

When Ben received more than one letter one drizzly afternoon in camp, he took the mail into the tent and sat on his cot. He looked at the first envelope, addressed to him in his mother's familiar hand, then shuffled the paper to inspect the second. The handwriting looped and dipped in a grand fashion, clearly a feminine characteristic, but was unknown to him. Perhaps the ladies of Mount Jackson had got up a campaign to write to lonely soldiers? If that were so, would this missive be from some lonely maiden lady, hoping to receive a note of gratitude from a male person?

As he examined the writing on the sturdy envelope, he spotted a miniscule set of initials in an upper corner, the sight of which sent a jolt of surprise through his soul.

E. R. A.

His head buzzed in shock. E. R. A. He knew a person with those initials. Ella Ruth Allen.

Miss Ella Ruth Allen had cruelly cast him aside like a dried corn husk. She had not wanted him. She had soundly rejected him. Had she now drawn the short straw in the bolster-the-spirits-of-the-lonely-soldier letter-writing assignment? Well, she could go whistle for any reply from him!

He turned the envelope over and over in his hands, thinking of going outside the tent and throwing it—unopened—into the cooking fire, but as he handled it, curiosity grew to overcome his ire. Had she written under the pressure of civic duty? Had she come to miss having him around to abuse? Or might she possibly have had a change of heart?

A seed of hope began to grow in his chest. He told himself not to build happy expectations on an unopened envelope, but his fingers refused to break the seal. He stared at the letter. Perhaps he should save it until he had read the news from home. Yes, he told himself. That was the best course to take. Let his mother's loving words buffer him from whatever unpleasant surprise Ella Ruth's note had in store. He put the letter beside him on the cot and opened the one from home.

Ma wrote that all at home were well except Julianna, who had a touch of grippe. She was glad he had found the time to correspond at last, and that he must take all good care with his wound. Then she recounted the outstanding events in the county since he had left home, including a tidbit about Peter stealing his horse—*his horse*—and enlisting from Edinburg.

"The scoundrel," he muttered. *Brownie, a war horse?*

She wrote that both Mistress Mary and her mother, Mrs. Hilbrands, were awaiting a happy event, and that James was overseeing the crops as well as the horses, due to Peter's hasty departure. She mentioned that his father had chafed sorely at delays in raising his cavalry company that caused him to miss the action at Manassas Junction, but that he and his troopers finally rode off, much to his satisfaction.

Ben imagined how sad that parting must have made Ma feel, even though there was not a hint of reproach against his father in her words. He knew she was strong, but she surely drew part of that strength from Pa. They had always been so close-knit, not like squabbling couples he'd seen in Mount Jackson.

Finally, Ma urged him to remember his prayers and to seek out church services as often as he could, and said that she bore him great affection. She signed it "your mother, Julia Helm Owen." A line from Marie had been added at the bottom of the paper, then the letter was finished.

Ben tucked the sheet back into the envelope, rose to put it into his knapsack, then glanced at the other letter lying on the cot.

The letter marked with E.R.A.

The letter he was sure had come from Ella Ruth.

The letter he should chuck into the cook fire.

He picked it up, and almost turned toward the tent flap to follow thought with deed, but knew it would be cruel of him to fail to acknowledge her efforts, whatever they might have produced in the way of words.

Sighing and steeling himself against further heart-break by way of Miss Ella Ruth Allen, he sat and opened the envelope.

Glancing down the page, he spotted imperfections, smudges in the pencil lead. He brought the paper close to his face to puzzle out the cause. Oh lordy, those were tear splotches.

He dropped his hands to his lap. Ella Ruth crying? Pouting, giggling, feigning anger, arching her eyebrows. He was familiar with all those wiles. He had never seen her in tears.

After a moment spent in reflecting on their last harsh encounter, Ben lifted the letter and began to read.

Benjamin,

Many a time you have chided me for coming late to an appointment. It is true. I have an intolerable habit of running behind times in all my endeavors in life.

So too, am I late in realizing the truth of what you tried so expressively to tell me. We are at war. Men must fight for their country else their liberty be taken from them. You have gone upon that endeavor.

Oh Ben. I have done wrong. I have taken your trust and love and ground them to pieces beneath my foolish heel. I know this now, and I have come to acknowledge this at a later date than gentility demands.

My heart is broken at the grievous hurt I caused you. I am contrite. I scourge my spirit daily at remembering my unwise action and unreasonable pride. I was lost in impossible dreams that cannot, and should not, be included in my daily walk.

Can you find it in your generous soul to forgive me? I cannot expect that you will do so, but I am compelled to ask this boon of you. I hope that I may ever call myself your friend, however imprudent I have been.

Ella Ruth /

From a partial stroke of her pen at the conclusion of her signature, Ben surmised that she had nearly added her surname, then decided against it. This was an intimate apology, not a formal one. He held his breath, assessing what that could mean.

Was she begging to resume their friendship at the point to which it had arrived? That was unclear. Perhaps she only felt a good dollop of remorse and wished to be Christian friends. She seemed to be suffering under a great weight, at the very least, and wished his forgiveness to get out from under it.

He expelled the breath. Her petition required an answer. He was too wrung out at the moment to reply. It would have to wait for another day, and for a much clearer head than the one he possessed at this time.

Ella Ruth. The golden girl he had hoped to woo and win. He recalled his ultimatum. He had offered her his heart and his life, then said, "But you must take them now, or you must leave them alone."

She had chosen in haste, and now she wanted to repent of throwing him over. His brain refused to hand him a fitting response. Did he want the girl back, or was he done with her?

A few moments spent in a muddle did him no good, but the call of the bugle broke him free of the need to make an instant decision. He put the letter away and sprinted to do his duty.

∞

Rulon — September 24, 1861

Rulon continued to write in his mumps journal, but now he made notes about things he experienced, some of which he would share with Mary in his letters.

On September 12, he noted that the regiment had been reorganized that day. The extra companies that had been added over time were transferred to other regiments and ten companies remained. The Harrisonburg Cavalry troop was kept, and continued with the designation of Company "I".

Later that month, a greater change came about when the regimental commander, Colonel J. E. B. Stuart, ascended to the rank of brigadier general and rose to command of the brigade.

He discussed the changes with Ren and Owen later that day over supper.

"Where is Colonel Jones from?" he asked about their new commander.

Owen answered. "He brought in the Mounted Rifles, Company 'L,' from Washington County. My sister married a fellow from Abington, where they raised the company. He has a crooked leg."

"The colonel?"

"No. My sister's husband. He couldn't get into the fight on account of the leg."

"Ah."

Ren spoke up. "I'm going to miss those Company 'K' fellows from Rockingham County. It was comforting to fight alongside folks we knew."

"They have spunk, I will say," Rulon said, nodding. "Any kin of yours in that group?"

"No, but their captain is brother to ours. I reckon it will be hard on them to be separated."

"Why do they call the colonel 'Grumble' Jones?" Rulon asked.

"I hear tell it is because of his irritable nature," Ren replied, and got to his feet. "We'd best keep our behavior on the impeccable side. Who is on guard duty tonight?"

Owen answered. "I'm your boy."

"Finish up and see to it," Ren said, and strode away.

∞

Rod — September 27, 1861

The stars must finally have aligned for Rod Owen, for in late September, when the breezes blew chill and the sun shone less each day, he came upon a young cavalryman with his back turned to him who was grooming the stolen horse Brownie.

"Son?" Rod queried, not sure this strapping lad was his offspring, but certain that the horse was his.

The boy pivoted and faced him. "Pa?" he said, his voice a bit defensive.

"My boy." A wash of relief caused Rod to abandon any pre-conceived plan to harangue Peter for his misdeeds. He opened his arms to embrace him, and Peter met him in like fashion.

"Pa," Peter said when they had broken the embrace. "I reckon it was wrong of me to take Ben's horse, although he wasn't going to use it for a while. I had the need. I figured you would come to know that, in time."

"You should have waited for your birthday before you enlisted, son. Surely there is war enough that it would have lasted until then."

"I didn't want to lose my chance."

"You grieved your ma."

Peter hung his head for a moment. When he raised it, he said, "I reckon that's true. I did write an apology to her. Your name was on the letter, as well. I had half a notion you would linger a mite longer at home, instead of leaving Ma to her own devices."

Rod felt a moment of ire at the hint of reproach his son had cast upon him at leaving his wife. It was true. He had left Julia to carry on, but was it not expected of an honorable man that he would defend his family and his country? There were capable boys at home to give her every aid. Instead of answering the charge, he turned the topic. "I told your ma I would get you sent home for being underage."

"No. Don't do that." Peter yanked up his shirt, unbuttoned his undershirt, pulled it aside, and revealed a lengthy red scar from which the scab had already fallen. "I've been bloodied in battle. I won't leave the defense of my land to lesser men."

"I'm sure a word to your captain—"

"He knows my age, Pa. He don't care. He said I was a valiant fighter and he wished he had a dozen men like me under his command." Under the truculent manner, Peter's face shone with an expression of satisfaction.

"Hmm," Rod said. "I didn't know about your injury."

"Ma knows of it. I wrote in the letter that it was a trifle."

"I'm sure you did." He wondered what argument was left to him with the boy. Clearly he had won the good opinion of his company commander. Peter's reasons for coming into the cavalry were much the same as his own—the defense of family and country, mixed with a youthful exuberance he himself now lacked.

"I ain't going home until the fight is won," Peter said, setting his jaw.

"You always were a stubborn lad," Rod said. "Much like me, unfortunately. If you give me your word to be cautious in the face of the enemy, I won't press the matter."

"Cautious? I can't promise that, Pa. I can promise to remember my mother and sisters, and to defend their honor with all my body and soul. That's all I can promise."

Rod's sigh lasted for several seconds, it seemed, all the breath leaving his body as though in terrible resignation. The boy would not be moved. As his father, his emotions warred in his breast. Love. Concern. Pride for the man his son had become in a few short weeks.

Life was a muddle of a knot, and he couldn't always make out the right way to cut through it. Should he leave the boy alone? If he let the issue die of natural causes, what was he to tell Julia?

He could only say he had found the boy, and determined that the war situation was desperate enough that the army needed Peter more than the farm and his kin did. He knew that was the truth of the matter, even as his heart urged him to carry the boy home to his mama, where he would be safe from harm.

At length, Rod said, "I reckon that's all I can ask."

଺ଠ

Mary — October 31, 1861

Mary held her belly and bent double, gasping at the force of the kick the creature inside her had dealt. Surely this child was a boy. No female could be so unruly.

She straightened with care, then grasped the supportive back of the chair beside her. Two weeks gone since she had last written to Rulon, and no letter had come back in that time. Was he even alive? Perhaps he was too busy to think of her. Or . . . perhaps those cruel words Mama had flung at her were true, especially with the seemingly confirming whispers she had heard of "camp followers" setting up tents— No! Those boys joking and laughing outside the store, what did they know? She wouldn't pay heed to them. She couldn't.

But the black thoughts continued. Rulon had needs. What had he called them? She searched through her swirling mind to remember their wedding day. *Lustful yearnings*. Yes. Very powerful yearnings. The two of them had spent a good deal of time assuaging his yearnings before their honeymoon days were spent. How could he set those urges aside now?

Another strong message from her babe demanded her attention, and for the moment, her body's needs prevailed over thoughts about Rulon's.

When the child had calmed himself, Mary thought about Rulon again. How could she turn *his* thoughts to *her*? How could she make him recall her attempt to brand him with the remembrance of her bared body pressed against him in the light of day? *What a foolish gesture*, she thought. A vain and feeble bid to claim his affection forever. Men's thoughts wandered. She had heard of a woman whose husband had strayed quite publicly, shaming the woman to such an extent that she had taken sufficient poison to end her pain. That had caused a terrible scandal. The man had buried his wife and fled north, taking his paramour with him, but leaving three poor children orphaned and at the mercy of relations.

Lust is a vicious drive, she tortured herself. She envisioned Rulon in the arms of a painted harlot, and cried out in despair. How could she return his thoughts, his allegiance to her? Had he not taken vows? Did he not give them uppermost value in his life?

She paced the room, their room, where he had whispered words of affection as he took her body beneath his own, entangling her in his needs, opening her to lustful emotions of her own as he spilled his seed within her. She paused to endure another attack from the babe. Rulon had planted this child that hurt her so sorely. When the kicking had passed, she thought, *I have given you body and soul, husband. What more must I do to ensure your fidelity?*

She spied a likeness of her parents that hung against the wall. Should she have a likeness made, wear a low-cut dress to entice him into remembering their nights of passion together? She had nothing of the sort in her wardrobe. Perhaps that would have an opposite effect, and drive him to seek relief. Should she turn in profile, to show him an outline of what he had left behind? She bowed in shame at the thought of revealing her condition so blatantly to a photograph maker. She sighed, then straightened and made a decision. She would have a likeness made of her face and hope it would be sweet and enchanting enough to give him thoughts of home and respite from battle.

The child brushed gently against her insides, giving her what she took as approval. Yes. She must be the sweet wife Rulon claimed to love, and show him that side of her in the likeness she would send. Having settled her mind on a course of action gave her the first peace she had felt for some time, and she went to the door with a new sense of resolve.

Chapter 16

Ben — November 4, 1861

On November 4th, General Jackson addressed his brigade. Ben stood on a hill with the rest of the troops, trying to keep his emotions in check. Old Jack, who now held the name Stonewall Jackson, was headed for the Shenandoah Valley to take commend there, but the brigade that also bore the nickname would hold the hard-won line before Washington.

The General said he was not making a speech, but was there to bid them farewell. After making more speech than Ben had ever heard from him, he stood in his stirrups and exclaimed, "In the Army of the Shenandoah you were the *First* Brigade, in the Army of the Potomac you were the *First* Brigade, in the 2d Corps of this army you are the *First* Brigade . . .."

Ben swallowed down the lump in his throat as the General went on.

"You are the *First* Brigade in the affections of your general, and I hope by your future deeds and bearing you will be handed down to posterity as the *First* Brigade in this, our second war of independence. Farewell!"

The hush extended for a moment only, then the men around him raised cheer after cheer. Ben joined in until his throat felt raw. General Jackson briefly waved farewell and rode away at a gallop.

The man next to Ben groaned. "I wish I was a-going with him," he said. "I'd cotton to seeing my Sara right about now."

Ben turned to him and nodded, remembering the strange letter he had received a few weeks ago from Miss Ella Ruth Allen. He'd done nothing about it. What was there to do? Not knowing what the girl expected of him, he'd put it away and forgotten it.

Now the pangs of homesickness hit him like the concussion from a cannon. He'd wanted a future with Ella Ruth, but now his future lay with fellows like the man beside him, Tom something. He searched his memory. Tom Grace. He was in the company from Hardy County.

He went back to camp, disheartened by the departure of the general he had come to respect. The rest of his company appeared to be out of humor, as well, so he decided to stay out of the way and write a letter home.

Instead of "Dear Ma," he stared at the words "Dear Miss Allen." No. He had no idea what to say to Ella Ruth. He thought about crumpling the sheet, but paper was in short supply in camp. Perhaps he would figure out what to say to the girl at some future day, so he put the paper back in his rucksack and pulled out another piece to write to Ma.

⅋

Mary — November 5, 1861

Mary entered the front door of the house, having taken the morning to go to the photographer's studio to have her likeness made to send to Rulon. She had not even had time to close the door when Ida's voice came down the stairs in a screech.

"Mama needs you. Come here at once!"

Mary's warm sense of worth and contentment vanished in the instant. What could be wrong with Mama? She hastily shed and hung her wrap, and trudged up the steps.

The second floor was a complete hub-bub. Her sisters yelled or wrung their hands, according to their nature. Mary followed the loudest noise, which came from her parents' room. Ida flapped about, urging their mother not to worry, that Mary would arrive soon. Mama lay on the bedspread, fully clothed, gritting her teeth through some paroxysm of pain, her eyes tightly closed and her face set.

Well, she was here now, and what was she supposed to do about this unusual situation? Had Mama fallen? Broken a limb?

Mama's fingers gripped the chenille bed covering. Her head quivered.

Mary gazed at the mounded fabric covering her mother's abdomen, and was astounded to see it move of its own accord; a sort of cramping or squeezing seemed to be taking place.

Then the idea of what was occurring hit Mary like a slap upon the side of her head. Mama was in the throes of giving birth to her baby. What was she to do about it? She had not had the same experience yet, and could not imagine herself dealing with the event.

She went to the side of the bed, stooped and took Mama's hand, then asked, "What arrangements have you made? Who is to attend you?"

"Char—Mrs. Bingham," Mama gasped. "Send Ida." She panted, worn out from such a small bit of talk. "Hurry!" Her voice came out low and strained, a harsh gargle.

Mary almost drew back at the venom in the command. Instead, she swallowed and looked at Ida. "You heard her. Make haste."

Ida left the room, looking back over her shoulder, and Mary saw tears brimming in widened eyes, a demonstration of emotion so unlike the saucy girl. How long had Mama been lying here in pain? Guilt at being absent swept through her. How was she to know this day had been set aside for a birth?

"Mama, is there anything I can do to relieve your pain?"

"No," her mother answered in the same harsh voice. "Bring my clean nightgown." Her hand flew up, indicating the wardrobe on the other side of the room.

Mary pushed herself around the bed and found the required article, which lay apart from the other clothing on top of a stack of clean sheets and towels. Was this all designated for the birthing? She picked up the stack and went back to Mama's side, laying the pile upon a nearby chair.

"Am I to help you change?" Mary's voice shook. Such an intimate act was beyond the limits of her sense of modesty. Mama could not wish it of her, for her thoughts on the subject were even more extreme.

"No!" she barked. "Unless." She waited for some reason, and Mary saw that the belly was in the grip of another contracting squeeze. "Unless she doesn't come in time," Mama finished her thought in a rush.

Mary fervently hoped Mrs. Bingham would do so. She had no idea of the stage of Mama's laborings. Was she to the point of expelling the infant? How was that done? Momentary panic froze her mind. How did babies arrive? Up to this time, she'd only known that a midwife came, assisted Mama in whatever the process had been, and left, after many hours behind a shut door.

She quailed to think of the only path she knew about by which a man delivered the seed of his loins to his woman. A baby didn't— It was impossible. The inlet was too small, too delicate, too sensitive. Her mouth dried. A baby would not fit. She squeezed her limbs together.

Her babe gave a kick as if to refute the silly notion. The purveyor of the activity would never deign to quiet himself enough to tunnel through—

"Mary," her mother grunted. "Is Charity here?"

"No, Mama. You must hold on."

Mama responded by gripping Mary's hand as though it were caught in a loop of rope drawn tight by a runaway horse. She made no other sound but a low moaning from time to time that rasped against Mary's heart, laying it open to pain and humility.

In ten more minutes, Mrs. Bingham arrived, bustling in and taking charge.

Mary sighed in relief to see the woman, and was on the verge of removing herself from the scene when Mrs. Bingham said, "Mary, help me with your mother."

She turned, cringing. Mama would not welcome her assistance.

"Hand me the nightgown," the woman said.

Mary went right to the pile on the chair, eyes half-closed in an effort to maintain her mother's dignity. She heard the rustle of clothing, a sharp gasp from Mama, a word of comfort from Mrs. Bingham. When would this be finished?

A hand brushed her sleeve. The nightgown was wanted. Mary handed it over, eyes averted. Mama groaned, muffled it, tried to keep another outburst contained.

I would not keep the pain to myself, Mary thought. *I believe I will scream when my time comes, if I need to do so.*

She berated herself. How did she know what her reaction would be to childbearing? She might be a perfect ninny. On the other hand, it was possible she could follow her mother's example of stoicism under travail.

The baby kicked, and she muffled her own outcry. There now. She would be silent. Strong. Brave.

Brave? What was there of bravery to stifling a great ordeal?

She ventured a glance over her shoulder. Mrs. Bingham had peeled the bed clothes back and spread a new sheet on top of the old. Mama lay upon it, clad in the nightgown, in a curled position. Her shoulders heaved as she panted.

"How bad is it?" Mary asked.

"Bad?" Mrs. Bingham gave Mary a quick glance. "It's good, girl. She's nearly ready." She looked at Mary again. "You'll be doing the same in a few months." She raised an eyebrow. "I can't believe how fast little Rulon Owen grew up."

Mary's face went hot in reaction to the comment. Mrs. Bingham knew what Rulon had done with her. Her fingers twitched. She had to get out of this room!

Mrs. Bingham chuckled. "There, there. No sense getting hot and bothered. Your ma needs you close by."

Did the woman know her every thought?

"Hand me a towel."

She did so, catching a glimpse of white limbs as Mrs. Bingham raised the hem of her mother's gown and tugged it obscenely high. She turned away. What was the woman doing?

"Mary. Another towel." A brief moment later, "Come over here."

Mrs. Bingham's sharp command brought her up short. She shuddered, and went to the woman's side with the towel.

She caught herself before she said more than "Ah!" at the sight of her mother's knees apart, white flesh spotted with blood, and the junction of her limbs bulging with a strange distortion that seemed bent upon emerging. The child!

Mary shut her eyes, trying not to faint. She felt her body quivering as Mrs. Bingham put herself in the middle of the action, holding the infant's head and crooning words of encouragement. In making their appearance, babies did violate that sacred area. She wondered how it could survive the onslaught to be of use again.

But this was Mama's fifth child. Five times Papa had put—

She wrapped her arms tightly around herself and squeezed the fruit of her own actions. She would not think of Papa. Parents did not— Surely not so late in life.

But the evidence lay between Mrs. Bingham's hands, coming forth from Mama's body. Her parents *had* done that.

Enwrapped in Rulon's arms, she had thought of what they did as a special act reserved for young people. Mama could not possibly take pleasure in it. She deemed it shameful. No wonder she hated Rulon so. She had no notion that such an act could be glorious and pleasurable. Poor Mama.

Mama screamed, and Mary jumped. With a squishy sound, the child popped onto the towel on Mrs. Bingham's hands. She swiveled and gave the baby to Mary, who almost dropped the burden.

"What am I to do?" she squealed.

"Wipe the face," the woman replied, busying herself with other matters. "Clear the mouth. Make sure it's breathing."

Mary stood still for a moment, overcome with the responsibility of making sure life began.

"Now, girl."

She looked to the task, noticing that she had a new sister, and gave a moment of thought to her father's wish for a son. Not this time. Would there be another? She doubted it as the baby took breath and wailed.

ℰ

Rulon — November 28, 1861

28th Nov'br, 1861
Near Fairfax C-H
My belov'd wife,
The days grow shorter. The army is quiet, and long evenings of Idleness beside the fire strech before me. I think of you and the preshus burden you carry under yor heart. Several other fellows in The Troop have left their wives in a Delicate condition. Not long ago we discussed what Names our young'uns should carry. If it be in accordince with your Favor, I should Like for ~~my~~ Our Son to bear the name of my Father, Roderick Owen. He is a stalwart man, and worthy of such Respect and Honor. If it should be within my Pow'r, I will be there for our Child's birth, but I do not kno what God or the Fates has in store for my appointments at that time.

I can only think of You, dear heart. My arms ache to hold you again, even more so since you had the Likeness made and sint to me and I can gaze upon your sweet Face once more. I kiss the Likeness a dozen times a day, pretendin it is you, my Darling. Alas it is not. There is no warmth of flesh Beneath my fing'rtips, no sweet breath coming from between The lips portraied with such realism. I yearn for the day when I can gaze upon the true Face and not the likeness, kiss the dear lips of flesh and Blood, and explore the delights that entranced Us in days of yore.

Receev a kiss from me upon your brow and upon your lips. Extend it to our Son, residing in warmth and comfort within his mother's woom. How I wish I could be by yor side, to hold you close and sooth your burdens and wipe away yor despair. I am yor true love, and my body and vig'r are yors alone.

Ever, yor Rulon

ℰ

Mary — December 14, 1861

Wondering what Christmas would be like during a war, Mary tried to be cheerful for the sake of her younger sisters, but the absence of her husband and the unsteady gait caused by her increased weight pulled her spirits downward. Although no word had been published of conflicts with the Federal army, the men defending Virginia and the Confederacy had not come home during the cold weather, as her father had said they would. This was a grave disappointment, but with the excitement of a new baby in the house, Mary was putting the best face possible on her outlook for the holidays.

Papa brought the mail home at noontime, and there was a letter for her! She snatched it away from his hand, and opened it in the kitchen with the aid of a sharp knife.

"My belov'd wife," Rulon had written. Mary could have burst into tears at the swell of emotion this brought forth, but if she did, she would wash out the ink, so she restrained herself and commenced to read of her husband's desire that she name the child for his father.

"Mama wants her dinner right away," Ida said as she entered the kitchen. She paused to look at Mary's rapt attention to her mail, and said in a nasty tone, "Stop lally-gagging around with that moon face and dish it up. I'm giving you fair warning. Don't you dare be as demanding as Mama when you drop that brat."

It was all Mary could do to keep from slapping Ida's insolent face, but she gathered her wits without a retort and folded the letter to tuck it into her apron pocket, out of sight. When would this war be over so she and Rulon could get their own place?

When dinner was finished, Papa had returned to the store, Mama was placated, and the dishes were washed and put away, Mary retired to her room to read the rest of Rulon's letter. She put her hand into her pocket as she sat, but her fingers did not find the precious envelope. She stood, digging deeper into the material, but her letter was not in evidence.

Horror rising in her throat, Mary clung to the bannister as she made her way as quickly as she could back down the stairs and into the kitchen. Where had she been standing? There, beside the food safe. But she could see nothing on the floor. Of course. Sylvia had swept. She went to the dust bin. Nothing. Had the letter been kicked underneath the food safe or a cabinet? How was she to find it if it had? As big and ungainly as she was now with her belly full of child, she would never be able to get down on her hands and knees to look. Even if she did get down on the floor, she would never be able to get up again.

Sobbing now, Mary tried to get the broom underneath the most likely hiding spots, but she could coax nothing from beneath them. Again and again she tried to maneuver the broom straws to her advantage, but it was not to be. Wherever the letter had gotten to, it was as good as lost.

Rulon — December 31, 1861

Dec 31, 1861
Below Fairfax CH
Dearest Mary,

It is the last day of the year as I rite to you. We have past a joyful Christmas in our tents on the Cemetery road. One fellow got his father to send him a cask of brandy to celebrate the Holiday, which he shared out to the company. I admit I took a sip of the stuff, but being only lately recovered of my good health, I felt it the better part of good sense to forbear imbibing a greater amount.

We received presents gathered by ladies of the Lutheran church in Richmond. shirts, blankets and shoes were much appreciated by the boys and me. A blanket made of wool was my portion, which I gratefully accepted. The minister brought us the gifts, adding small Testaments for each man. For myself, I am happy to have The Word about my person.

Our corporal, Ren Lovell, says this place is unhealthy, and I believe that to be true, as there has been much sickness in the regiment. We have even suffered a number of deaths unrelated to wounds received on the field of battle.

Our Captan is one whose health has not been good. He was away from the company for ten days earlier this month, and has just returned yesterday. Ren says the rumor is he has been taken with a typhoid fever. You must join your prayers with mine for his rapid recovery.

Sweet Mary, we did not speak much of our Christian Faith before we joined together in wedded bliss. This was a sore neglect on my part, as I was to be the head of our union and your guide in spiritual matters. I regret not discussing this with you. I will state that I have an abiding Faith in the goodness of God and His Holy Son, Christ Jesus. It is my hope that yor faith is in Him, as it is good to be equally yoked in Christ. I count my parents as a good example of being equally yoked. Pa has led the family in nightly devotions as long as I can remember, with Ma at his side. If it is agreeable to your dear self, I wish to do the same when we are once more united. How I long for that day of reunion. May the new Year bring it about.

Yor own Rulon

After he had taken his letter to be posted to Mary, Rulon kissed his wife's likeness, wrapped up in his Christmas blanket, and lay staring into the embers flickering in the fireplace they had built for the tent. When sleep did not close his eyes, he wondered what he had forgotten to do. He grunted softly as he remembered professing his beliefs to his wife; perhaps he should end the day with prayer.

He hoped Garth Von was asleep as he hoisted his legs over the edge of the cot and knelt beside it. For once, he was unmolested as he asked for safety for his wife, the coming child, his captain and the cause of the Confederacy, then tacked on a postscript concerning himself.

By the time he got back onto his cot, the cold of night had deepened, and he shivered until his body warmth filled the blanket cocoon and he relaxed into sleep.

ℰℴ

The prick of a well-honed knife point just below his chin brought Rulon awake. He held himself rigid as Von's low chuckle reached him.

"Thought I didn't see, did you?" He swore, then spit out, "Think you're better 'n me, with your Shenandoah pathway to heaven? Want to be a martyr, boy?"

Then he was gone as though he had not been poised to slit Rulon's throat. The tent flap rustled and cold air entered, but it could not chill Rulon's blood more than it already was. He got up and went through his pack until he had his pistol in hand, loaded and primed.

Owen Leoyd mumbled, "What's the matter, Owen?"

Rulon licked his lips and cleared his throat before he got out an answer. "Von." He took two quick breaths before adding, "I'd like to relieve him of that hog-sticker someday, and cut a boil or two off his butt."

Owen chuckled. "Good luck to you. He sleeps light."

"Mayhap I should learn the trick," Rulon muttered as he lay down with the pistol at his side.

In a few moments, the flap twisted once more, and Von came in, cursing the cold, the lack of a wind-proof privy, and Rulon. The man made no further attempt toward violence, however, and when he began to snore, Rulon let his grip on the pistol relax.

Chapter 17

Ben — January 26, 1862

As soon as his sodden company entered the camp near Winchester and erected a tent, Ben found his pent-up emotions over being half dead from exposure to the cold needed an outlet.

Ma would frown on any communication that had the least bit of complaint. He was sure of that, so writing a letter home was out of the question. He pulled out a sheaf of letters he had received from Miss Allen, all unanswered. Perhaps it was not too late for him to write to her. Would she censure him on account of his lack of civility in replying?

He wasn't sure. All he knew was that he had to write to someone who cared for his welfare. Perhaps Miss Ella Ruth would welcome some kind of word from him, even though it be full of an excess of frustration.

He began reading again the letters she had sent to him. The first, which he had wondered if she wrote as a civic exercise, was quite intimate for a first communication. It was the one in which she had begged his forgiveness for her rejection of his love.

A second letter had followed, and she had not again petitioned for a restoration of their friendship. Indeed, she had been bold enough to write as though he had agreed. He had wondered at the time he received the note why she had been so sure he would accept a renewed friendship with her, and had put off replying, just as he had put off answering the first letter.

By the time the third missive had appeared, Ben's feelings in the matter had become quite soothed, but still, he did not find the time to answer her almost brazen remembrance of a certain tryst within a potting shed where he had tried mightily to seduce her, and she had withstood his advances. He read again her mention of how close she had come to giving in to his caresses.

He hesitated before he reread the fourth letter. He had received it just before the regiment's trek to Romney, and he had not had time to formulate a reply, although he knew at the time that he would have to do so soon. Almost a month had passed since then. He could not forget the words she had written professing to love him, and telling him how she had pressed each and every letter she had written to him to her lips in multiple places so that he might feel the warmth of her affection. Even now, he could almost feel his fingertips burning as he held the sheet of paper. He wondered if the married fellows in the company received such astounding letters from their wives. He had not dared to bring up the subject to the men, and then all desires had been squelched in the snow and sleet of their expedition.

He thought very carefully for five minutes on how he should begin his side of the correspondence, then threw all caution to the wind and began as he felt, calling her his darling Ella Ruth.

He filled two sheets of paper, put down his pencil, and began to re-read the letter before he sealed it. He almost blushed to see his words of yearning instead of complaint. Let the snow fall. Let the wind howl. He had warmed to his subject, and did not regret a single word of affection. Although his pride had taken a severe blow when she had refused to marry him, he knew now he had never ceased to love Ella Ruth. For all her follies and foibles, he wanted her more now than ever, and looked to a day when he could flee warfare and begin a new life as her protector and husband.

§Ი

Rulon — February 13, 1862

Rulon found the inclement winter weather almost intolerable. Coming off a three-day picket assignment, he wiped down the bay horse as best he could under a makeshift shelter. After feeding his mount, he ran to his own shelter.

Ren was in the tent. Rulon entered to find him moving a chamber pot to catch a drip coming from the ridge.

"If we had tar, we could stop that leak," Rulon said.

"If we had tar, it would still be raining and the stuff wouldn't stick," Ren answered.

Rulon had no response. He felt the shirt that three days ago he had laid out on his cot to dry. It remained damp along every seam. He wiped his nose and made a derisive sound. What did he expect? With the air so saturated, the moisture in the material had little chance to evaporate.

"Any word on Leoyd?" he asked Ren, who had sat down to shuffle through paperwork.

"He's fortunate. The doc pulled him through the worst of the fever. That typhoid is nasty stuff. Doc is sending the captain home."

Rulon stood up straight, shocked. "You don't mean it."

"I'm afraid so. Herring is in charge until he returns." He shook his head, and added in a softer voice, "If he does."

Rulon absorbed the somber news. He felt bad asking, but with the change of leadership, he felt he had to broach the subject uppermost in his mind. "Do you reckon I can get a furlough?"

Ren shook his head. "Herring won't let you go with so many men laid up."

"Mary is nearing her time. I've got to go home and be with her."

"I'm sorry, Owen. We need every able-bodied man out there with their eyes open."

"And rain running down their collars. It's brutal detail. The Yankees aren't leaving their cozy tents."

"Spring will draw them out."

"Spring," Rulon said, and snorted. "I'm not sure I believe in it anymore."

A few days later, Rulon slogged through eighteen-inch deep mud to saddle his horse for another three days on duty away from camp. He spent twenty-four hours as a vidette, mounted almost all that time and hidden in a copse of trees keeping watch on a Yankee camp. For hours he shivered and wished for the fire he knew General Stuart had forbidden. Of course he knew a fire was impossible so close to the enemy, but the cold did suck the soul out of a man.

He worried about Mary. Centreville seemed so far away from Mount Jackson. He worried about catching cold and dying before he could see her again. He worried that the mumps would return.

After he returned from the patrol, he worried over how to impart to his wife the devastating news that greeted him. Captain Yancey had succumbed to the typhoid fever. He shouldn't tell her. She would be concerned about him catching the fever. At long last, he kept his explanation of the situation brief, and sent Mary his wishes for every good prospect in her coming ordeal.

After he sealed and posted the letter, he worried that he couldn't recall if he had used the word "ordeal." He should have been more positive, giving her his assurances that she had nothing to fear. After all, his mother had birthed ten children without dying. No, it was better that he hadn't talked any more on that subject. His mention of the captain's death was enough for her to deal with.

∽

Mary — February 19, 1862

On a chilly day in February, Mary sat at the dinner table at noon, more for appearances than to actually take nourishment. She was so large in the belly that the mere thought of trying to fit food in with the child gave her qualms of anxiety. When would this torture be over? She waddled when she walked. Her arched back ached. Every little occurrence irritated her. A great sense of heaviness lay upon her soul, and she had not heard from Rulon for longer than she cared to think about.

Since entering what Mama had called "confinement" a few weeks ago, she had naturally not been to church services. Mama had tried to bring Mr. Moore around. Mary refused to see him, begging off with so much force that her mother had given up trying to persuade her that she must needs prepare her immortal soul for her coming journey through the Valley of the Shadow of Death. She could scarcely stand to be in the company of family members. Entertaining a visitor, even the minister, was more than she could support. Her only desire was to build a cozy nest in her bedroom and retreat into it.

"Mama, Mary won't eat," Ida complained.

Her mother turned to Mary and gave her the eye. "Mistress Mary, your babe will not be strong if you neglect your duty. Eat the pumpkin, at least. Your sister is quite proud of her dish."

Mary sighed. Ida had a tiresome streak that strained her forbearance. "I will make an attempt," she said, and took one bite of the mushy vegetable. Then she felt a heavy flow of liquid pass from between the juncture of her lower limbs. Alarmed, she choked, sputtered until the pumpkin lay upon and beside her plate, and cried out, "Fetch the doctor. Something has gone wrong."

A spasm crushed her stomach, and she bent as far forward as she could to contain it. "Oh Lordy, I'm dying," she gasped when she could breathe.

"Good heavens, daughter, what is amiss?" asked her father.

By this time, Mary was in the throes of another cramp, and could only shake her head. She had somehow pushed back from the table, but without arising. Looking down, she spied a stain on the carpet that looked vaguely pink. Could she have commenced to bleed? Blood had more of a crimson hue. What had rushed out of her body?

She felt herself swaying, and her father was there, stopping her from falling.

"Ida, go bring the doctor," he commanded.

The next thing Mary knew, she was ensconced on her bed, and Sylvia was bathing her face with a cold cloth. Her dress felt odd, and she glanced at the skirt to discover that it clung damply to her limbs. Perhaps she had lost control of her bodily process. No, there was none of the stink of that fluid in the room. Her instinct told her it was appropriate to be lying upon her bed, but she didn't want the dress to soak the bedclothes, and she begged Sylvia to help her remove it.

After that task had been accomplished, her focus narrowed to one thing, the cramping in her belly that caused her such pain and forced her to groan and shriek in terror. The loss of self-control frightened her. She had never been given to vapors and screaming fits. Why was her throat giving voice to all manner of sounds? Her belly again contracted in a mighty spasm and she let loose a horrid moan. Bending forward, she cradled the offending portion of her body with hands and arms that were powerless to rip the agony away. Was this the dreaded childbirth?

"Yes," said the doctor when he arrived an hour later and had persuaded her that he must give her an examination or he might pronounce an incorrect diagnosis. When he had finished, his conclusion was that she was indeed laboring to bring forth her child. He would send for Granny Pankwurst, the midwife, to attend her. Did she want him to notify Mrs. Julia Owen to be present?

Mrs. Owen? Rulon's mother? Yes, yes, she nodded, over and over, until the doctor left the room. Another agonizing moment gripped her. She screamed. She seemed to make an outcry each time a spasm came. Where was her mother's stoicism, the tightly gritted teeth that permitted no utterance? She knew herself to be a failure, an unworthy daughter who had no self-dignity or control.

"Mama, Mama," Mary keened when her mother came in and sat beside the bed, tight-lipped and unsmiling. "Mama," she sobbed when she went away to suckle her new child.

She craved a tender touch, a soothing hand upon her sweat-beaded brow, but she knew there would be no such approving gestures from her mother. She had done the unthinkable deed in this very room, and was thus to be punished for marrying, for breeding, for having an absent husband.

Ida came into the room what must have been hours later, bringing Granny Pankwurst. Just then Mary let loose an ear-piercing wail, and the girl covered her ears and hid in the corner by the door.

"Here now," said the midwife. "None of that caterwauling noise around when I deliver *my* babies."

Her babies? Mary didn't understand. This was Rulon's baby, *her* baby. She was the one undergoing this terrible pain to give birth. She wanted to protest, but she had no energy.

Then the woman demanded that she stand and stride about the room. What did she mean? As it was, Mary could scarcely bear to lie here now. How could she be expected to walk? But walk she did, half carried between the wizened old woman and a protesting Ida: shuffling, doubling over, clutching herself when the pains returned and she sank to her knees in agony.

When she wanted to sit, the midwife forbade it. When she panted, the midwife told her to stop, to breathe naturally. She wanted to shout at her, to send her from the room, but she had no energy.

Then the woman told her to get onto the bed, which was what she had wanted to do all the while she had been forced to ambulate. But once she had crawled upon it, belly pressing deep into the mattress, the woman pushed her over onto her back. She then sent Ida from the room, which surely pleased her craven sister. Oh horror! The midwife wanted to inspect the place only Rulon and the doctor had ever viewed.

The midwife pawed at her knees. Mary resisted. The woman slapped her upon one lower limb. Mary cried out at the ignominy. She tried to hold her limbs together, but she had no energy, and the woman succeeded in violating the privacy of her sanctuary.

"Rulon!" she wailed, guilt flooding her senses. She had allowed an invasion into the intimate place they had shared. The doctor had been persuasive of the need; this detestable woman had forced her to give way to her will. But where was Rulon? Her mind ceased to give her answers for a time, then she remembered that he was at war, off where lewd women followed the soldier camps to ply a trade both ancient and sordid. Was Rulon partaking of their filthiness? He should be here, beside her as she offered up the gift of a child to him from her very loins.

As the woman probed between her limbs, Mary sobbed at the robbery of both her dignity and her guardianship. Had Rulon matched her betrayal with one of his own? How could she know? He surely would not tell her if he had broken his vows. She whimpered his name in despair.

The midwife mocked her. "Leave off hollering for your man. He ain't nowhere around."

Yes, the fact was that he was nowhere around. Rulon could be dead and buried, for all she knew. Was this child to have no father? Would she die from shame if this perverse woman kept peering between her limbs? If she did, the child would die within her, having no chance to come forth into the world.

The interminable pain came again, wearing her out, scouring her body until she had no bones to bear her up.

The midwife finished her probing and left the room, carrying away the only light. Mary sensed that she was alone. Was she dying, then? Had the woman abandoned her? Another spasm beset her. *Rulon, can having a child be worth this pain?*

A cool hand touched her brow. She started, unaware that anyone had entered the room. A soft voice assured her, "Mary. You're doing fine, girl. The babe will arrive soon."

Mother Owen. She had come. Would she be able to remove this awful burden of pain?

But no. A soothing voice and a cooling hand were all she could offer, and Mary's disappointment ran bone deep.

No one could save her. She must go through this all alone. She alone could enter the Valley of the Shadow of Death. What outcome would she find in that dismal place? Would she cheat Death, or would it cheat her? Her and Rulon? Her and Rulon and the babe?

Finally, the wicked old woman returned, elbowing Julia Owen quite cruelly, Mary thought, but her mother-in-law gave no protest. She simply sat at Mary's head and spoke comforting words.

"Hold on to my hand, Mary. Listen careful and do as the midwife tells you."

Mary could do no more than nod as the sweeping, all-encompassing torment came again.

Later, Mother Owen said, "Allow me to rub your neck, girl. Your shoulders have had quite a workout, bending and stretching so."

The tender fingers brought momentary relief before the onslaught of the next wave of affliction.

Then, when Mary was grunting and panting and holding apart her own limbs, a great despair upon her, Mother Owen whispered urgently, "It will soon be finished. Push on that babe. Push for your life, girl."

Some other creature cried out, high-pitched and protesting, wailing more robustly than she could find energy to do.

"A boy child," stated a self-satisfied voice.

Mary wanted only to sink into a mass of jelly and limp skin and cease to labor. She had worked so hard, harder than she ever had in her life up to this time. Her belly hurt from straining. Her back bore unremitting pain. Her special part burned as though torn. Her breasts ached from tension. Her arms yearned to hold the caterwauling creature she knew was Rulon's son. Her son. Their son.

ဢ

Mary watched the midwife pack up her belongings and leave the room. Sweet relief enveloped her. She would never see that woman again, if she could possibly help it.

"Here is your babe," Mother Owen said, and lay the sleeping infant, who she had wrapped in a soft blanket, in Mary's arms. "What name will you put on him?"

Cradling her son, Mary crooned to him, "Roddy, sweet little Roddy, my precious boy." She undid the covers enough to check something and sighed with satisfaction. "Ten wee fingers. Ten wee toes. A miniature likeness of your papa."

"Roddy, then?"

"Roderick Rulon Owen, but he is so tiny. Roddy will do for now."

Mother Owen smiled and resumed her seat in the shadow beside the bed.

Mama bustled into the room, carrying the baby Eliza. "Now that the excitement has ceased, let me look at little Randolph. I suppose you will do him the indignity of shortening his name to Randy?"

"No, Mama. His short name will be Roddy. His long name is Roderick."

"Roderick! You want to name him after that strutting rooster of a man?"

"Good morning, Amanda."

"Julia!"

Mary looked at Mother Owen, expecting some sort of outburst in defense of her husband. She herself certainly felt offense at her mother's characterization of the man. She liked Father Owen.

"He's not such a bad sort," Mother Owen said, a little smile quivering at the corner of her mouth.

"I beg your pardon. I did not see you there, and meant no offense to you."

"You meant every offense to Mr. Owen," she rejoined, but in a mild tone.

Mama turned back to stare at Mary. "I prefer the name Randolph, in honor of your father."

Mary took a deep breath and steeled her spine for the encounter. "He is named Roderick, to give honor to my husband's father. The next boy can bear Papa's name."

"I must protest. You live in your father's house."

"Mama, I will not be dissuaded. Mother Owen, please go to the minister to record the name as I have said it to you."

"You cannot dishonor your father."

"Amanda," Mother Owen said, her voice indicating rising ire. "Leave the girl be. You did not bring the child into the light. She did the job, and a fine job it was."

Mama rounded upon Mother Owen. "She herself is a child, play-acting at being a wife. Now she pretends to be a mother, as well? I won't have it."

Mother Owen's eyebrows went up. She patted Mary's shoulder. "Amanda, we've been friends for many a year. I cannot speak any plainer than this. Mary is a wife, woman, and mother. She ain't acting at it. She earned the right to name her own babe with her labor and blood. If you can't reckon with the broad fact of it, I'll move her and the boy out to the place."

"You would not."

"She bears the Owen name. By rights, she should be with us. Mary stayed here because she wanted to sooth your feelings, so Rulon told me. She's welcome on the Owen farm."

Mary watched as the starch went out of her mother's spine. She sagged against the chest of drawers, her face going pale. At length, she said in a strained voice. "I may have spoke out without thinking. Mary, I bear you no ill will. Name the boy as you please. Don't leave us."

"Mama." Mary couldn't say more for the lump in her throat. She had never seen such a transformation.

"That's sensible, Amanda. It's high time you give the girl the affection you've been withholding these long months, heaping on her head your disapproval of my son."

"It's not himself—"

"I reckon. You didn't cotton to his haste. It was better that they married than take other paths." Her eyes softened. "They had so little time together, Amanda. Mayhap it's all they get."

"No!" Mary felt her throat go raw. The two women turned to her, distress written across their countenances. Realizing they thought she had not faced reality, she added, "Don't speak of it now. Don't haunt my wee boy's dreams with that sad vision."

They looked at each other, her mother, Rulon's mother. Eliza began to wail. Roddy woke up and whimpered. "Let us be reconciled," Mary begged, bouncing the boy gently.

Mama extended her hand toward Mother Owen, who took it and gave it a squeeze.

"We will say no more of this," said Mother Owen. "We will be good Christian neighbors. This upset in our country can't last forever. Rulon will come home and make his family complete. At that time, we all must leave the young'uns be."

"I will say no more, "Mama said.

Mother Owen gave a slight nod. "See that you keep your resolve."

Mary sensed the balance shifting in the room. What had she just experienced? Mother Owen had gained the upper hand, and Mama had willingly allowed it.

"Mary," Mother Owen said softly, turning toward her, "I'll go see Mr. Moore now. It will be as you wish."

༄

Not much time had elapsed after Mother Owen left that the wee babe awoke and began to sniffle. Then he started to cry, a long wail at first, then robust and alarming demands for attention.

"What does he want?" Mary asked her mother.

"He is most likely hungry, if he has not wet himself" she said, and approached the bed. "You must give him suck."

Mary touched her bodice above her swollen breast, self-conscious in the presence of her mother. "Will it hurt?" she whispered.

"I do not recall any pain," Amanda said, her words clipped. "Merely put him to the teat. He will know what to do." She hoisted Eliza into a more comfortable position, nodded once, and left the room.

Mary slowly unbuttoned her bodice, making shushing sounds all the while to try to appease her squalling infant. She wanted to join him in his howls, but that would never do. She must now be the adult lady she professed to be, and give her child sustenance.

Roddy did not know what to do when Mary brought him to her breast. He rooted around, whimpering, but did not seem to know what to do with his mouth, which Mary imagined was supposed to clamp around her tender nipple, or something of the sort. She tried guiding his efforts, but he would not take it into his mouth, preferring to cry instead.

After a while, she had joined him, weeping in frustration and pain. Even when she tried to squeeze out liquid, none appeared, and she only succeeded in making herself sore.

Was he only wet? She discovered that he was not, but could not ease his distress.

After at least an hour of the most humiliating effort that Mary had ever experienced, the baby had exhausted himself with crying, and fell into a fitful sleep. She sat with him resting on her lap, weeping silent tears, her shoulders shaking convulsively.

A rap sounded on the door, and immediately thereafter, it opened. A dark woman not much older than herself appeared in the doorway. "Pardon, ma'am," she said. "The lady says I am to nurse the boy baby for you."

Mary endeavored to compose herself in the face of this stranger. "My mother brought you here?"

"I comes from Mount Airy," the girl explained. "Your mama have rented me."

"Rented you? To feed my child? I don't even know who you are."

"Marse Meem call me Pansy, ma'am. I's a wet nurse." She gestured to her bosom. "I has milk, ma'am, for the young'un."

Mama's repentant spirit has not lasted for long, Mary thought as she felt Roddy stir against her limbs. Their voices must have disturbed him, and he worked himself awake and resumed his wails.

Embarrassed, Mary held him out to the Negro girl. "Feed him," she said, barely able to restrain her own wails as the girl took him and went to the chair beside the bed.

As her baby began to suck greedily at the dark breast, Mary sank into her pillow and turned away, trembling with shame that she could not fulfill her most basic role as a mother, that of suckling her own child.

Chapter 18

Mary — February 26, 1862

A week later, Mary got herself out of bed, lit a candle, pulled on a dressing gown, and took on the task of writing a letter. She had neglected her correspondence with Rulon for some time, and it pained her to admit her sloth. But if truth be told, she had been under a great strain of late, what with her baby's birth last week and all the turmoil afterward. Now it was past time for her to catch her husband up on those matters.

Biting her lip, she began:

26 February, 1862

My darling Rulon,

I send news which I hope is agreable to you. On Wednesday last I was delivr'd of a helthie baby boy. Yor wishes prevailed over those of my mother, and I have named the child Roderick Rulon Owen. Yor ma recorded the name for me so my moth'r could not have her way.

I hope you do not mind that I put your name to the boy along side that of yor father, as you had asked for. I call the baby Roddy, as he is much too tiney to bear yor papa's long name at present.

Sister Marie brought baby Roddy the most cunning rattle, whittled out by Carl, I believe, or perhaps James. I fear I am distracted by dificulties I have experinced folowing the birth.

I hope to use the rattle to appease Baby when he cries from hunger. I continue trubled with ~~diffacultyies~~ failing in ~~giving him su~~ feeding him properly. He is not patient with me. Mama brings in a wet nurse to feed the boy, but it distreses me sorely to see Baby fed by a slave girl rented from Mount Airy. Such a scene harows me with guilt that I cannot do my duty as well as he demands. He is a very robust child. I promise I will continue my efforts to feed him.

Dearest husband, please take all mesures to avoid harm's way. Altho we do not hear of battels with the foe as yet, I pray The Telegraf does not return to bringin in horible casualty lists like we read last summ'r. They were most distresing. I prey for you nite and morning, for my bosom aches with fear over yor well-being as the seas'n for war approches.

Plese excuze my poor spelling. I cannot seem to make my brain fathum the proper letters I need to express myself to you.

Accept the kiss I place upon this X as tho it was put upon yor brow by my own lips. It is ment to convey all the love of my heart to you.

Yor wife,

Mary

She finished, tongue sticking out from between her bitten lips, and paused to place a kiss upon the mark. Then she shook sand over the ink. She carefully poured it back into the shaker, folded the paper as though it were an envelope, turned it over, and affixed Rulon's last known address.

She heard Roddy stirring in his cradle at the foot of her bed, and hurried her task as he began to cry.

Mary sealed the improvised flap shut with a few drippings from her melting candle, wishing she had a grand signet ring to press into the wax seal. She shrugged, used her thumb to smash it flat instead, then winced at the momentary burn.

"There," she said, satisfied that she had finished the long-pending task. "I have suffered long, husband," she said to the letter as she quickly moved it through the air in order to cool the seal. "The baby is crying. I had better go try to feed him with these poor, chapped breasts, or Mama will interfere again." She stuck her burned thumb in her mouth to alleviate the pain, and leaving the letter on the table, prepared to attempt to nurse her son.

෨

Julia — February 28, 1862

When Julia had finished her town business at the Hilbrands store on Friday, she began to pull herself up into the buggy for the return trip home, but something stopped her, and she put her foot back on the ground.

She looked in the buggy. Her egg basket, now heaped with parcels, lay on the floor of the vehicle. Had she forgotten some task, an item she was to buy or sell? No. Had she neglected to ask for the mail? The envelope addressed to her in Rod's firm hand that seemed to burn a hole in her pocket belied that notion.

Her grandchild. Oh lordy, she had forgotten to pay a visit to Mary and the baby!

Taking herself in hand, she walked around the block to the Hilbrands' home and let the knocker fall on the brass plate. Ida bade her enter, and she soon knocked on Mary's door.

She found the girl in her bed, in tears, her bodice open, and the baby lying across her limbs squalling in counterpoint to his mother.

"Ah, Mary girl! What's this?" She picked up Roddy and put a finger into his mouth. "Shush, sweet boy. Shush," she crooned.

"I am a failure," Mary wailed. "I cannot feed him." She covered her face. "Mama rents a wet nurse."

"There, there." Julia tried to sooth both mother and son.

Mary put her hands across her bosom and gasped out, "I've tried so hard. Mama says they are too small, which prevents the milk from coming."

"Nonsense," Julia said. "I am small, and have not lacked milk for my young'uns." She bounced Roddy as she commenced walking about the room. "You are anxious. That is causing the stoppage." She returned to the side of the bed. "Have you been up? Hasn't it been two weeks now since he came along?"

Mary shook her head. "I am to stay quiet until I cease passing blood."

Julia raised her eyebrows. "That will take a time. You must arise and go on living. Activity will stimulate the milk. The baby's cries should also help."

"They swell," Mary said, sniffing. "Nothing lets loose."

"May I see them?"

Mary allowed her to view one breast, then the other.

"There is chapping, but perhaps no fever. May I touch?"

Mary drew a sharp breath. She let it out slowly. "Must you?"

"I think it's needful," Julia replied, and put out her hand to check for a raised temperature in the skin. "Ah, yes. This one requires a warm, wet cloth applied here for fifteen minutes at a time, once an hour, until you feel relief. Do not nurse from it until the redness goes out of it. I would not recommend a mustard plaster, but perhaps a warm poultice once a day." She explained which herbs should be mixed for the application. "And you must get out of bed. You will only wither, lying in bed all the day. That is not healthy."

Mary began to cry. "Why doesn't Mama tell me these things?"

"She is not forthcoming in such matters," Julia explained. "You know her reticence about physicality. You must bear affection for her in spite of her foibles."

"I do love my mother. Whether she returns the feeling is in question."

"Then now, girl. You know she loves you. She is going through her own child-bearing cycle, and a surprise it was, too. Give her time to return to normal."

"She is usually affectionate and kind. I have missed that in her."

"We have all, none more so than your pa." Julia smiled. "You may have noticed that menfolk need affection more than women."

"Papa? He's busy with his work."

"Don't you go to thinking that he has no need of your mother's time and care."

Mary shuddered. "He's my papa."

"He's a man. Like your own."

"Please, Mother Owen."

Julia laughed. "I have embarrassed you. I beg your pardon. At times I speak too plainly for my own good." She stooped and helped Mary out of the bed and into the chair alongside it. Then she gave Roddy to her. "Put him to the breast and think of a pleasant scene." She continued with advice in a soothing voice. "Lean back against the cushion. Feel its softness enveloping you. Here. Try this with your fingers." She showed Mary how to guide her nipple into Roddy's mouth. "It will soon be second nature to you, if you will heed my words. Remember to be calm. Don't think about difficulty. Think of pleasant views."

"He is sucking," Mary said. "He has not done that before."

"Relax," Julia advised in a low tone. "Rain coursing down a window pane. Water squeezed from a sponge. Sipping warm milk from a cup." She could see Mary lowering her hunched shoulders. "That's the way, girl. Give the babe of your strength."

"I am not strong," Mary murmured.

"More than you suspect," Julia answered. "More each passing day."

Mary — March 4, 1862

Mary cowered in the cellar of the house, arms wrapped around her baby. Another shell whistled overhead and exploded in the distance. Ida shrieked in her ear, and Mary elbowed her sister in an attempt to quiet her. Sylvia and India huddled together. Mama sat in the corner, covering Baby Eliza with her shawl.

Poor Papa. He must be taking cover in the storeroom, Mary thought. She was glad the little girls had come home for dinner. She wondered how long the school would remain open. She shuddered at a boom that was too close at hand. *God, help us*, she begged. *Help Rulon*. She wasn't sure where he was now. She had lost track of all the different armies while these invaders were threatening her baby's life. *God, please don't let them kill my baby.*

Dust drifted down from the ceiling as a shell thudded into the ground nearby. Sylvia and India joined Ida's outcry, and now Roddy also raised his voice.

"Hush, hush," she said, trying to sooth him.

Mary could hear little Eliza greedily sucking from her mother's breast, unheeding of the bombardment. *Why is it so easy for Mama to give nourishment and at the same time, she prohibits me from doing so?* she wondered. *I will not let her rent the wet nurse again.*

She had been putting the warm herbal compresses upon her sore breast, as Mother Owen had advised, and the infection had now gone. It was time to be the strong mother Rulon's mama thought her to be.

Defiantly, Mary opened her bodice, brought Roddy to her breast, and concentrated on remembering what Mother Owen had told her.

"You must relax," she had said. "Do not pay heed to your bosom or to pain. Think of a pleasant scene, a meadow with sheep grazing, or the mountains beyond the river. Think on the flow of water. Be peaceful in your soul, and milk will come through to the boy."

Roddy opened his mouth, latched onto her nipple and began to suck. She thought of the flowing river, nurturing the land with needed moisture. She thought of rain gently falling on the bean crop in the garden. She thought of Sylvia pouring a can of water onto the base of the azaleas. She felt an unfamiliar sensation, and looked down to discover that her son was gustily drawing liquid into his mouth, a drop dribbling from the side of his lips. A patch of darkness marked her bodice above the unused breast. Her milk had let down, and she was nursing her child as easily as ever her mother had.

Almost sobbing with relief, she took a moment to say a grateful prayer, and to bless her mother-in-law for her kindness and wisdom. When another bomb burst overhead, she scarcely noticed.

Rulon — March 6, 1862

The Yankee cavalrymen came out of their winter camps.

Nearly every day they accosted the Confederate pickets in fierce skirmishes. One evening, Rulon limped into the tent, dropped his saddlebags and weapons on his bed, and spread his hands before the warmth of the stove.

Owen Leoyd came in behind him and said, "Holy Hepzibah! You're dripping blood all over the floor."

Rulon examined his arms and didn't see any wounds. "Where, man?"

"The back of your right leg. You don't feel it?"

Rulon snorted. "I'm so cold I can't feel my own nose." He looked over his shoulder and winced at the sight of the blood on the limb Leoyd had indicated.

"That needs to be tended. Do you want to see the doc?"

"I'd rather not. He'll likely take the leg off." Rulon unfastened his uniform trousers and kicked them off, then rummaged in his saddlebag. "My Ma sent me a bandage for Christmas. I hoped I wouldn't need it anytime soon." He held out a knitted roll to Leoyd. "I'd be obliged if you'd do the honors."

Leoyd acquiesced and splashed a small amount of spirits on the wound, at which Rulon gritted his teeth to avoid crying out. Leoyd held the edges of the gash together until he'd wrapped the knitted bandage around Rulon's calf.

"The cut's not deep, but it surely dripped a fair amount. Too bad it spoiled your fancy trousers."

"Don't you speak ill of my mother's fancy work," Rulon said, grinning to defuse his words. "She cared enough to make it pretty for me. I count her a true Virginia patriot, even if she did come from up North."

"Your ma's a Yankee?"

"No, no. She hasn't been that for a long spell. One summer when she was a slip of a girl, she went down to Shenandoah County to visit a cousin, and never returned home."

"Uh huh. What kept her in the county?"

"Her stay was prolonged on account of my Pa's persuasive words on behalf of his bright future and overwhelming manliness. When he asked if she would be his bride, she told him 'yes' and never looked back."

"A Yankee, huh?"

"Not anymore." He looked ruefully at his trousers, then donned them again. "I'll ask that you don't share the facts of my heritage with Von. He already thinks I'm not worthy of fighting for Virginia."

"He's mighty peculiar, for sure" Leoyd said. "I don't think he's right in the head."

"I will give him credit that he fights the Yankees like a devil from hell," Rulon said. "However, I never want to be in front of that blade of his when he's not set on toying with me."

Leoyd raised his eyebrows. "You think he's playing with you? He's got some kind of grudge against you, Owen. I don't know what caused it."

Rulon shook his head. "He took a dislike to me from the moment he first saw me. I reckon it's mighty awkward to have to sleep with one eye open and not even know why."

"Huh," said Leoyd. "Let's go grab whatever's left of supper."

On the way to eat, someone thrust a couple of letters into Rulon's hands. While he ate, he opened Mary's to read.

In only seconds, he was on his feet, whooping and hollering, his wound forgotten and the contents of his plate scattered on the ground.

One of the men looked up and asked, "What ails you, Owen?"

Rulon tried to calm himself enough to answer, but the powerful emotion Mary's words had evoked prevented him from giving a coherent reply for some minutes.

"I'm a papa," he finally gasped. "I have a son." The strength left his legs as the enormity of that responsibility swept through him. He sat with a whoosh as the air left his lungs.

The troopers of Company "I" gathered around, pounding him on the back and offering congratulations. All except for one, who eyed him with a resentful air.

∞

Ella Ruth — March 11, 1862

Poppa stormed into the parlor, bearing aloft an envelope.

"What is the meaning of this?" he said, his voice raised and angry.

Ella Ruth patted a wrinkle out of her skirt before she replied, striving to put on a coquettish smile. "Why, Poppa. I have no idea. Pray tell, what do you have there?"

He approached on stiff legs, his face crimson, and waved the paper in the air. "This, young lady, is a letter. It is addressed to you. It comes from that young man you professed to love, then cast aside. Why does he presume to write?"

Ben wrote to me? She felt her legs begin to tremble, then stilled them with an effort. *He finally wrote?* It had been several months since she first assayed to forge a tie with him, but when he hadn't responded to any of her missives, her hopes of hearing from him had diminished almost to despair.

"Poppa, I cannot say," she replied, trying to be arch, and finding herself failing miserably. Her stomach clenched.

"I fail to see why he would think you desired a correspondence with him." He stared back at Ella Ruth, pursing his lips and gripping the letter in two hands at the level of his watch chain.

After a long moment, she put out her hand and said in a meek voice, "May I have it?"

Poppa seemed startled by her request. "What? You may not." He held it out of her reach.

Ella Ruth raised her chin. "Perhaps he has sent me news of the progress of the war. Or a warning about the advance of the enemy. I must have it."

He considered. "I hardly dare think a lowly private soldier would be in possession of such information." He narrowed his eyes. "Did you write to him?"

She raised her chin even higher. "What if I did? It cannot matter to you. We are at war, and it behooves the women of this county to support our brave soldiers."

"Ella Ruth, you are not to encourage this young scoundrel. I forbid further contact with him."

She rose and attempted to snatch the letter from his hands, but he held it above her head. She cried out, "Poppa, you cannot deter me from having affection for Benjamin. If you had only bent your will the tiniest little bit, I would have been a bride and out of your hair long ago."

He snorted. "You were ill suited to be the bride of a farmer. You still are, even in these hard times."

She smiled, feeling her lips quivering the slightest amount. *I will not cry*, she decided. "You think poorly of me, Poppa, but you shall not forbid me to love this man."

"Love. What do you know of love, daughter? You imagine the emotion makes the world revolve. I know it helps, but does not do the job alone."

"Such a cynical Poppa."

He looked down at her, his heightened color fading. "I'm a realist. Our world is undergoing a tumult that may crush us, and you only think of that Owen boy."

"Man, Poppa. He's a soldier."

"Not even of the age of majority." He turned and strode around the room.

"I don't care. He's done the work of a man for years."

He stopped before Ella Ruth, waved the envelope in her face and said, "And he's tried to seduce my daughter into dalliance on more than one occasion."

"Poppa!" She felt her face grow warm. "What a thing to say to me." Her stomach twisted in dismay at the insult.

"Don't deny it. I have eyes." His voice began an upward march into renewed anger. "I've seen you come back from meeting him, your face flushed and your eyes filled with stars. He's not the right sort of man for my daughter."

"Oh Poppa. If you only knew him as I do." More than her lips trembled now. Her entire body vibrated with emotion. "He wanted only to marry me." She inhaled.

"I won't have it," he said, his voice hard and brittle. He tore the letter to bits, dropped them into a tin wastebasket beside a table, and left the room.

Ella Ruth let her breath go in a rush as she dropped to her knees beside the basket, feeling a sob clog her throat. *Poppa, what have you done?*

හ

Julia — March 11, 1862

Julia waited on the porch of the Hilbrands' home while James knocked on the door a second time. He stepped back, frowning. She placed a hand on his arm to forestall any complaint. She had no idea why it was taking so long for the family to respond, but surely someone would answer sooner or later.

At last, Julia heard footfalls approaching, and the door opened as though it were jerked backward. Ida stood in the opening, hair disheveled and apron rumpled. She held a squalling child on her shoulder.

"Go away," Ida said. "I'm too busy to entertain." She patted the baby and moved side to side in a futile attempt to sooth the child.

Julia couldn't determine if the babe was Amanda's girl or her grandchild, Roddy. She put out her hands to give aid, but Ida wasn't ready to accept help, for she turned away, kicking the door shut behind her.

Feeling anger rising up in her, Julia was on the point of snatching the door latch and pushing the door open again, but James grabbed her by the upper arms.

"Whoa, Ma. Ida is a mite overwrought. She won't welcome your help." He cocked his head. "She's ornery enough to see it as interfering."

Julia sighed. He was correct. Even so, she took the slight to heart, feeling as though she had been stung by a passel of wasps.

She looked up. James gazed at her, his dark eyes reflecting his concern. She patted his arms as the anger drained away. "You're so right, son. She's prickly as a bundle of nettles. We'll go."

She wanted to see Mary. She wanted to hold Roddy. Now was not the right moment. "We'll go," she repeated, and stepped off the stoop.

Chapter 19
Rulon — March 13, 1862

March 13, 1862
In Camp, Warrenton Junc. Via.
My Dearest Wife,
My joy upon hearing our blessed news new no bounds when I recved your letter the past week. I wood have ritten you at the time to thank you for producing a fine heir, but events with the Enemy prevented me taking pen in hand.

The Yankees have come up in such numbers that our general Johnston decided to remove the army from the thret. As a consequence, many suplys had to be destroyed, along with a mountain of private soldiers baggage. Oh Sugar, the smell of bacon burning about drove us mad. Also grain was set afire to keep it from the Yankees hands. Flour broken from barr'ls and heeped on the ground resembl'd a strange snowfall. I warrant we will rue the day we had to waste these provisions, but we had no way to carry them off from Manassas Junc.

My little Wife, I miss you with all my heart. Conserve your health in all ways. Kiss my Dear Son upon his brow and tell him of my boundless affection for him.
I remain, yor husband,
Rulon Owen

∞

Ella Ruth — March 15, 1862

For several days, Ella Ruth barely left her room, trying to find a way to read Ben's destroyed letter. Putting the pieces together was like trying to assemble a picture puzzle. At first, she thought she would make up a paste of flour and water and affix the mangled bits onto another piece of paper. After only a moment, she knew that wouldn't work. Ben had written on both sides of the paper. She wanted to read all that he had written, especially when it became evident from the first few words that he had forgiven her, and wanted her friendship.

She tried laying the pieces out and simply turning them over, but they were so small and lightweight that the slightest breath sent them fluttering to the floor, and all her labor was for naught.

Despairing, she stared out the window, seeking solace in the sunlight bathing the tops of the trees. She stared so long that her eyes became dry, and she blinked to moisten them.

Dear Ben. His letter deserved to be read so that she might answer.

She sniffed. She reached around to pick up her handkerchief to wipe her nose, and her elbow bumped the window pane.

The window pane. Glass. If I place the pieces on a sheet of glass, I can cover them— She stopped. How was she to get two sheets of glass? Poppa would scarcely buy them for her, if indeed, any were to be had. Where was she going to obtain glass?

It was not long before Ella Ruth decided that she would remove two of her window panes and use them to encase the pieces of paper. No matter if a little cold seeped into the room. She could sacrifice a bit of comfort for a desirable outcome to her letter dilemma.

After the midday meal, she hid a table knife in the folds of her skirt, told her mother she was going to take a nap, and mounted the stairs as quickly as she dared. She locked her bedroom door and surveyed the windows of the chamber. It wouldn't do for her maid to discover that she had cannibalized her window panes, so she chose the casement that had the least use, and regularly remained covered by the thick draperies that had hung in place for ages.

She laid an old pillowcase on the floor beneath the window, and began to attack the putty that held one pane of glass in the frame with her purloined knife. Was Mama likely to discover a knife was missing? She decided not to let that fret her. *Who counts silver anymore? There are larger issues at hand.*

Soon she had chiseled a quantity of putty from the bottom of the frame. Her hands quivered from the effects of the unaccustomed labor, and one was red and abraded. She determined to find another solution than hitting the base of the knife with the heel of her hand to dig out the stubborn putty.

After looking around in her room, she found a wooden figurine that would serve to hammer on the knife handle, and then the work went more rapidly and with far less pain.

At last the moment came when one window pane was free, and she carefully pried it loose from the last remnants of the putty keeping it in the frame. *Ha!* she thought. *I will not be defeated, Poppa.*

She took the glass to her dressing table and wrapped it in a towel, then went back to work on a second panel.

The putty in this frame had hardened unevenly, and at one point, she held her breath as the knife blade skittered across the glass, fearing that the pane would shatter. It chipped a bit on the edge, but that probably was acceptable, as long as she watched where she held the glass later.

At last she had two sheets of glass free and out of the window frame. Now, what was she to do with the putty? If she put it in the wastebasket, Lula would find it as she cleaned the room. No, Ella Ruth must dispose of it herself.

She gathered up the pillowcase and hid it in the back of her armoire, behind a pair of shoes. Lula would not be cleaning in there. Later, she would think about how to get the putty safely out of the house.

But first, she must clean the glass.

She poured a small amount of water into her wash basin and wet a face scrubbing rag. Then she rubbed the surface of the glass with it. *My goodness, how dirty the glass is!* Lula must not have washed the lesser-used windows much. She would speak to her about—

No, I won't. I can't let her know I've taken the glass.

When the panes were clean and she was at the point of laying the paper puzzle of Ben's letter down on the first sheet of glass, someone knocked on the door.

She squeaked involuntarily and almost dropped the glass.

Remembering that she was supposed to be napping, Ella Ruth let the knocking continue for a moment while she hid the glass, then answered in what she hoped was a sleepy voice.

"What is it?"

Lula said, "Miss Ella Ruth, you have a caller."

"Who is it?"

"It's the preacher man, Mr. Moore."

Ella Ruth groaned. The man probably wanted her to sing in the choir. "Send him away. I'm tired."

"No, miss. I ain't gonna send away no preacher man. That'd be scandalous."

This time, Ella Ruth sighed. "He won't bite you."

"He's the preacher!"

She supposed she would have to appease the man, and her maid, for sure. "All right. Let him know I will be down shortly."

"Yes, Miss Ella Ruth. I surely will."

Mr. Moore did not want her to join the choir. He wanted to counsel her about her soul.

After the formalities had been seen to, he said, "Your father is concerned for your welfare. He says you have fallen under the influence of a, ah, I believe he said 'a reprobate,' Miss Allen."

Ella Ruth felt her eyes widen. *Poppa can only mean Ben, but surely he isn't a reprobate.* "I'm sure I don't know what you mean, Mr. Moore." She refused to call him *sir* after such a beginning.

The minister tugged on his coat by the lapels, clearly nervous. "He, ah, claims you received a letter from an undesirable person."

Ella Ruth fixed her gaze upon him. "Do any of your parishioners fall into those categories? Reprobate? Undesirable?"

"I don't believe so, Miss Allen."

"This person my father brands with those pejoratives comes from one of our oldest county families. My father is mistaken." She got to her feet. "There you have it, Mr. Moore. You cannot think the son of Roderick Owen is some wanton beast."

He hastily rose. "No, Miss. A fine family, indeed."

She wanted to know if Poppa had mentioned that he had destroyed the letter before she had a chance to be "influenced" by it, but decided not to prolong the interview.

"Good day, sir. I'm sure you have other calls more pressing than this little misunderstanding." She hurried the minister to the door, shut it almost before he was clear, and hurried up the stairs. A puzzle awaited her.

℘

Determining which of the pieces of paper constituted the first page of the letter was more difficult than Ella Ruth supposed it would be. After an hour's work, however, she finally had assembled the page on one sheet of glass, placed the second sheet atop the first, and was ready to begin reading.

She had scarcely begun when the supper bell rang.

She made an unladylike sound, and then got to her feet and looked around for a place to hide the letter in its glass encasement. She finally decided it could be hidden under the bed if she arranged a few carelessly-dropped items of clothing in front of it. She added one slipper behind the clothing, just in case, and firmly shut the door behind her as she left the room.

Supper went on forever. She sustained herself through the hour by repeating to herself time and again the salutation with which Ben had begun: *My darling Ella Ruth.*

That was not the greeting of a polite correspondent replying to an acquaintance. It most certainly was the heartfelt greeting of a friend. She remembered the tingle of pleasure that swept through her upon setting her eyes on the words. She was understating the case. Ben wrote not as a friend, but as a lover.

Momma asked her something. Ella Ruth had to beg her pardon and ask her to repeat the question. It was a matter of passing around the biscuits, and Ella Ruth felt her face warm. Poppa was looking her way with a wary expression. She would have to lend more attention to the business of supper if she were to get through it with good grace and no suspicion.

Afterward, Momma wanted a family hour of music, and Ella Ruth had to endure hearing Merlin sing "Lorena" as though he were on the battlefront, pining after a girl. She wondered if he were going to join the army, or if Poppa had pressured him to complete his university education first. What a shame it must be to her brother to remain home when all his friends had enlisted straight away. Ben had been eager to serve.

Ben. Ella Ruth repeated to herself his greeting. *My darling Ella Ruth.* She was his darling. No matter what he thought, Poppa could never take that from her.

Suddenly the music ended, and Momma went about kissing everyone goodnight. At last! Ella Ruth fled to her room, shut the door, and leaned against it. Had Lula turned down her bed and removed her discarded clothing from the floor?

Yes. She had. However, the slipper still masked the letter sufficiently that she thought it safe to assume that her secret had not been discovered. She would have to find a better hiding place tonight. That could come after she read Ben's words.

Setting the glass sheets on her dressing table, she remembered to return to the door and lock it, slipping the key into the pocket of her dressing gown. She placed the lamp where it would shine upon the paper puzzle, and bent to her task.

Ben most certainly had feelings for her. His words warmed her, body and spirit, and when she had perused the first side of the first sheet, Ella Ruth very carefully rotated the sheets of glass to read the back side.

Although he told her a great deal about the grueling campaign he had survived in western Virginia, he spent time reminiscing about moments he and she had spent together.

He had not yet written a word of love for her, but the undercurrent ran deep, and she pressed forward, reading Ben's account of one time when he took her inside the mill after everyone had left. She recalled the air being hazy with dust from the day's wheat grinding. She had sneezed again and again, and he lent her his handkerchief, tying it around her head to filter what she breathed.

Was that the action of a reprobate? No. He cared for her then, and she imagined he cared for her now.

She sat back with a sigh when she came to the end of the first sheet of the letter. She wondered how long it would take to piece together the second half.

Before she disassembled the puzzle, a thought came to her. She might wish to read Ben's words again. Perhaps she should take the time to write out a copy of his missive.

This prompting sent her on a mental search for suitable paper on which to transcribe the precious words. *I can't use writing paper. I dare not use up what I have on hand.* Would parcel paper serve? The kitchen storeroom had a supply. Though it was coarse paper, it surely would take the impression of a lead pencil.

By now, the house had fallen into rest. She rose from the dressing table and carefully opened her door. She would have to be quiet as she descended the stair and went into the kitchen.

Careful! That is the squeaky tread. To bypass it, she supported her weight on the railing with one hand so she could take a large step while holding her candle with the other hand.

What was that moaning noise? She froze, listening. It could only be the wind. Funny, she had never noticed wind howling around the eaves before. But then, she was accustomed to being asleep at this hour.

Ella Ruth finally got safely to the bottom of the stair and listened before she ventured toward the back of the house. No sounds. Lula slept in an upper room, and the other house workers did, as well, so she needn't worry about disturbing anyone on the ground floor.

Unless Poppa was up doing some kind of business accounts.

She looked toward his study. *Good. There's no light showing.* She took a great breath and stepped around the newel post. Something ran over her foot, and she scarcely kept from screaming.

Shivering, she stood on tiptoe, trying to regularize her breathing. Had it been a rat? Lula had complained of vermin in the storeroom, and now she was headed right there.

It's only a small creature, she told herself. *One of God's creatures, so it must have a purpose.* Still, she shivered almost uncontrollably. She dearly wanted to fly up the stairs and retreat to her bed, but that would not do. She had to get paper if she were to preserve Ben's precious words.

Coaxing herself forward, step by step, she made it into the kitchen proper and held her light aloft to make sure she found her way to the storeroom without mishap.

Then, as quickly as she could, she pulled open the door, searched for the parcel paper, found it, ripped off a lengthy piece, and hurried back up to her room in such a rush that she didn't even care if the stair tread made a noise.

She stood with her back against the closed and locked door, breathing, breathing, breathing, until her heart and respirations returned to normal. Then she sat and carefully began the task of transcribing Ben's words.

She had no idea of the time when she finished the task with the first page, but it was far too late to begin her puzzle work for the second sheet of the letter. Reluctantly, she hid all her tools and the paper away underneath her shoes in the back corner of her wardrobe, changed into her nightdress, blew out the candle, and slipped into bed.

℘

Ella Ruth — March 17, 1862

The next night, after meticulous labor had resulted in Ella Ruth reading and preserving the sweet words found on the second sheet of Ben's letter, she sat up from a dead sleep. *Ben mustn't send letters here*, she thought. *Poppa will only destroy them.*

She lay back down on her pillow, worry creasing her forehead as her eyebrows pinched together. She hadn't ever received a letter before, and didn't know how delivery was accomplished. Poppa knew, but she could hardly ask him about the subject. Momma would suspect something strange was in the air if Ella Ruth were to approach her. Who could she ask about letters?

Mrs. Julia Owen would know, but Ella Ruth still had a nervous fascination with the mother of her Ben. She imagined that such an accomplished woman would take no notice of her problem. But perhaps the *other* Mrs. Owen would.

She thought about that for a while. She hadn't seen Mistress Mary in the store for ever so long, but then, perhaps it was time for her confinement. She was having a child. Rulon Owen's child.

Ella Ruth thought about how it would be if she were carrying Ben's child, and felt an odd tingle in the pit of her stomach. Would she ever get the opportunity? This horrible war threw such complications into her life. Would she never be able to marry Ben, join with him in conjugal bliss, bear him a child?

She wanted to weep at the thought of never. That was not acceptable to her. She would begin prayers every night and every morning to ensure that Ben returned to her. *Fervent prayers.* God would surely heed prayers offered with all the fervor of which she was capable.

But first, she must think of a way to ensure that their courtship by correspondence, if such it had to be, was not interrupted by her father's heavy hand.

She went to sleep with that problem foremost in her thoughts, trusting that her brain would arrive at a solution by morning.

When Ella Ruth awoke at daybreak, she determined to go to the store and see about Mistress Mary's situation. Perhaps she had given birth by now and would return soon. If not, perhaps one of her sisters would be amenable to the idea of keeping letters aside for her. Mrs. Hilbrands occasionally took a turn behind the counter, but Ella Ruth discarded the notion of approaching her. She seemed . . . prickly. Certainly not welcoming of unorthodox ideas.

After breakfast, Ella Ruth had another problem. How was she to get to the store? Poppa had not announced plans to go anywhere today, so she couldn't conjure an excuse to accompany him to town. Momma wasn't thinking of going out. Merlin never took the buggy if he was off to see a friend.

She wandered into the kitchen to see if the cook Sadie needed supplies, but found no answers from that quarter. Sadie was occupied with making the noon meal. As she took a jar of applesauce from the storeroom shelf, she shrugged off Ella Ruth's suggestion that she might need to go shopping. She opened the jar with a flourish as Ella Ruth's mouth began to water at the smell of the ham in the oven. With no options left, she removed herself from the kitchen.

Fuss and feathers! How am I to get to Mount Jackson?

As she sat in the parlor, idly flipping through a year-old copy of a magazine of ladies' fashions from New York, an idea came into her head. It was a rather unheard-of concept, but it would not leave her, so she let it free and examined it.

She could walk.

She swallowed.

Walk?

She had never walked the distance from her home to Mount Jackson, but surely it could be done. She had seen darkies and farm lads trudging along the road when she had passed by in the buggy, thinking nothing of their feat. Surely it wasn't difficult to put one foot in front of another and traverse a mile or two, even three. She enjoyed robust health, and had no impairment to her limbs. So what if the way was dusty? She could accomplish her objective with a little persistence. Indeed, she must.

Another thought came to her. What if Mary, or her sister, if it came to that, required coaxing to come to an agreement? She only had enough coins to post a note to Ben if she could make arrangements. What else did she have that she could use to sweeten her request?

A jar of applesauce.

Ella Ruth threw down the magazine and rose, excited that her problem was melting away after she had put so much mental energy into solving it. She would not let Poppa's attitude defeat her, now that Ben had come around to the point to responding to her letters. Ben loved her. She knew it. Nothing must become an obstacle to seeing their tenuously renewed friendship blossom into the full flower of courtship.

She hurried toward the kitchen, then slowed her pace so the cook would not become suspicious of her motives. She would say she had come for a tumbler of water. Yes, that was reasonable.

She entered the warm room and surveyed it.

Sadie had her head and arms extended toward the oven, preparing to remove the ham. She saw Ella Ruth and frowned. "What you doing back in my kitchen, child? I won't feed you nothing this close to dinner."

"Pay me no mind. Sadie. I'm parched, so I've come for a drink of water."

The cook cast a skeptical eye at Ella Ruth, then said, "Humph," and turned her back to complete her task.

Ella Ruth walked to the storeroom for a tumbler and removed a jar of applesauce from the shelf as well. She concealed the jar in the folds of her skirt, quickly filled the glass with water and drank it, then hurried out of the room.

She hid the applesauce in her room, knowing it was too close to the noon meal to leave. It would be counted odd if she did not show up.

When the bell sounded, she went downstairs and ate as fast as she could without drawing undue attention to herself. Unfortunately, she could not think of an excuse for leaving the table early, and had to sit, enduring the family small talk until her mother rose, the signal that everyone was dismissed to go about their activities.

Ella Ruth retrieved the applesauce, professed the desire to take a turn around the garden to see if anything had sprouted yet, and fled.

She crossed the river on a footbridge her brother had built last summer, climbed out of the bottom to the Valley Pike, and began her journey. After walking down the side of the pike for what seemed like forever, Ella Ruth looked behind her and realized that she wasn't all that far from home. The road stretched endlessly before her, white in the sunlight. The jar of applesauce she clutched felt like an andiron at the end of her arm. Why hadn't she thought to bring a basket?

She paused to catch her breath opposite the lane that led to the Owen farm, and ease her toes within her shoes. Was that dull pain from a blister rising?

She began to wonder if her plan had merit. What if she couldn't arrive in town before the store closed? She inhaled resolutely and set off once more, ignoring the pinching of her shoes. She had to achieve her goal.

Resting again sometime later, Ella Ruth wished she had thought to bring a basket and a container of water. Her mouth felt dry as the dust that covered her skirt and bodice. She was sure now that she had not one, but several blisters on her feet. She might make it to town and interview Mary or one of her sisters, but *how* was she to make it home again?

What would Ben do? *Silly girl, Ben would have a horse or a wagon to travel this great distance.*

She set her mouth in a grim line. She would walk until she reached the next fence post, and then go on to the next one. Accordingly, she began to walk, limping, but making progress along the pasture fence bordering the road.

After an interval of halting advancement that sapped her strength to the very limits of her constitution, Ella Ruth arrived in Mount Jackson. She dusted her dress, straightened her aching back, and walked with as much dignity as she could muster on blister-ravaged feet down the street toward the store.

She entered, then felt like crying when she espied Mrs. Hilbrands at the counter. Was all her labor for naught? She lingered beside the door, mastering her emotion before she decided what to do. A baby wailed from a back room. Was Mistress Mary here after all?

Mrs. Hilbrands made a resigned face and left the counter. She encountered one of her daughters coming out of the room, but it wasn't Mary. It was the next one, a selfish twit named Ida.

Ella Ruth caught a fragment of the girl's side of the conversation, something expressing dissatisfaction with tending the child and a question of when Mary was going to return to help with the work.

"Perhaps next week," the mother said curtly, and hurried to take care of the youngest offspring.

Ella Ruth turned and left the store. Mary lived at the Hilbrands' home, and must be there now. That was just around the block, and she hurried as fast as she could to get there, glad of the turn of events. Mary was much easier to talk to than the other ladies of the family. She could make a social visit of the occasion and still achieve her end.

One of Mary's younger sisters conducted her upstairs into Mary's room, where Ella Ruth cooed at the baby, and presented the jar of sauce. After what she adjudged was a decent period, she asked Mary if she would accommodate her desire to receive mail at the store.

"Brother Ben has replied to you, then?" Mary asked, a conspiratorial smile creeping onto her face.

"He has. But Poppa— My father is still opposed to our friendship." She hung her head. "I've been put to a great deal of trouble to rescue his letter from the trash."

"Oh my. Were you obliged to iron out the creases?"

"Oh Mary, if it were only so easy as that! I had to piece together the fragments after Poppa tore it to bits."

Mary frowned. "Do you truly love Brother Ben?"

Ella Ruth slapped her hands to her mouth to keep from crying out.

Mary must have seen that her question had caused Ella Ruth anguish. She nodded once, then said, "I will assist you. Now you must write to him that he is to direct your mail to Papa's store." She paused and patted Ella Ruth on the arm. "I wish you happiness, friend. I may call you *friend*?"

Ella Ruth nodded, not yet able to speak.

Mary gestured to a writing desk. "You may use that paper, but I have no stamps."

"I have enough coins to post the letter."

"Then you must get to the task." Mary put down her babe and went to the window to shut off a rising breeze. She turned away before she did so and asked, "You are footsore. How are you to return home?"

Seeing that Mary understood how she had arrived, Ella Ruth shook her head. "I haven't a plan."

Mary turned back, called out the window, "James! Hold, please. Wait there," and dashed out of the room.

Ella Ruth's heart throbbed with relief when Mary returned and told her James Owen would convey her home on the back of his horse. "You are a dear," she whispered as she finished sealing the note and handing it over.

"I said it before, friend Ella Ruth. I wish you happiness."

Ella Ruth hugged Mary, took her leave, and made her way carefully down the stairs to thank another kind soul for helping her in this time of dire need.

Chapter 20
Ben — March 20, 1862

When Ben first read his mother's letter exhorting him to attend church every time he had a chance, and to curb in himself the carnal nature of mankind, he felt his ears burn. Anger rose in his chest. Ma had no call to give him such advice. He wasn't a little child sitting at her skirts, owing her his attention and paying heed to her words. He was a man now, a soldier with a man's responsibilities for killing or being killed. He had precious little opportunity to attend prayer services when his time was spent on the battlefield or building roads over the muck and mud so wagons could bring provisions to the brigade. He was a man. With time on his hands this evening. With temptation in the form of perfumed and painted women calling to him from just beyond the camp.

He was on the point of casting Ma's letter into the fire and joining the fellows who were brushing the mud off their coats with the prospect of an evening's pleasure when his eye fell upon a word in Ma's fine handwriting. Disease.

He scoffed, but with a sense of unease as he recalled her words. Ma was a forthright woman, but she did have a sense of delicacy and had never come right out before and mentioned in such searing detail the dangers of partaking of forbidden fruits.

He reread the portion where her warnings had become particularly pointed. " . . .many cases of syphilis in the Soldier's Hospital . . . suffering . . . go mad . . . treatment almost worse than the disease."

Was Ma helping in the hospital, exposed to the results of man's corruptible nature?

He'd never heard the proper name for French sickness before, but Ma knew it, and had warned him against venturing into a path that might bring such a vile retribution upon him. A thought chased through his mind that curdled the contents of his stomach. Pa had gone to war. Had he—?

"Impossible," he muttered. Pa would never sin against his wife. He was a man of honor.

Where did that leave him, Ben? Where was his honor if he was contemplating lifting the skirt of a camp follower for a moment of relief?

The feeling of sickness caught him so quickly that he almost lost his supper. He fought the nausea, swallowing over and over. His thoughts swirled in a dizzy array, but one swam to the top of the whirlwind. He'd made up his mind that when he got a chance, he would ask Ella Ruth to be his bride. Did he want to take home an evil sickness to pass to her?

Sweat drenched his brow and ran in rivulets down his cheeks. He took out his handkerchief and mopped at his face. What would Ella Ruth think if he came home to her bearing the burden of worldliness? He could not stomach the thought of tainting her in such a manner. If he sinned in this fashion, he would lose her forever.

The dampness of the handkerchief seemed to freeze his hand. Ma was right. He needed to get his appetites under control. He needed to go to church. He needed to get right with God. Above all, he needed to forestall any barrier between himself and Ella Ruth.

∞

Peter — June 10, 1862

The fight had moved into the Shenandoah Valley, and Peter's cavalry regiment fought up and down the road that summer, as General Jackson's army chased Yankees. The enemy chased back, and the competing forces alternated driving and being driven.

On a retreat through Mount Jackson, skirmishing with Frémont's cavalry, Peter wished times were different and he could stop off at the farm for a visit. That would have to wait, as they were hard-pressed by vengeful Federals eager to take action against the Confederates for a defeat in the last battle.

A few days later, close by Harrisonburg, the Yankees got an unexpected benefit from a relatively minor engagement. A regiment of New Jersey cavalry led by an English adventurer attacked the Confederate cavalry, and in the fight, Colonel Turner Ashby's horse was shot from under him. He rose to lead his men on foot, and fell almost immediately, pierced by a Yankee bullet. He died almost instantly.

Jun 10, 1862
In camp at Brown's Gap, Vir.
Der Ma,
I wish I cood have pressed my lips to your browe when last I past the Farm, but Alas! the yankees drove us throu and we went up the Valy to a acursed place. You no dobt herd of our misfortunate encounter near Harisonburg. We are distrawt at the loss of Col. Ashby. Where will we find another leder of his dash and skill?
The boys are very loe of mind at his passing, as am I. We do not know who will become our comander. Pray for us to get a good'un.
I will leave off whinin, altho I coud speak my grief all the day.
I hope to be able to see you next time we pass nearby. If not, I will wave my hand in fond greetin. Does Pa ever stop by? I see him from time to time, but not often.
How big is Rulon's little Baby now? Do you see him or does the Hilbrands family keep you away from him? I recall Rulon wanted Mistress Mary to live with you at the farm. Will she be moving there, now that she has presented an eir?
I must close now. I am told we will be on picket duty tonight.
With a heavy heart but most Affectionately,
Your son, Peter

∞

Rulon — June 17, 1862

June 17, 1862 in Camp near Charles City C-H, Va.

Mary love,

Our company has returned from a great Adventure, riding clear around the entire Army of the Federals. This is McClellan's bunch of invaders. The boys were ready for patrol duty, as we did not engage in the late affair at Seven Pines, although we stood in readiness to support the infantry.

What a time we had! It began when about a thousand of us were ordered to move to Kilby's Station, where we were bid to cook three days' rations, but given no further orders. You may imagine our surprise to be woke up in the middle of the night and told to be mounted in ten minutes! Oh Mary, what juices flowed in our veins at the prospect of a fight! I swear to you the very horses felt their oats that night.

When we started off, from the direction we took, we thought we were marching to the Valley, and I had hopes of catching a glimpse of yor sweet face, but soon it became apparent we were going to observe the enemy close to hand, and do our utmost to gain intelligence and cause what trouble we could behind their lines.

Our spirits were high, despite the grave danger of our situation at times. Col. Fitz Lee took us on a little jaunt down a side road in hopes of cutting off a squad of Yankees, which exployt ended up with us crossing a swamp with some difficulty. Most of the enemy fled, and we took only one prisoner.

Another day, Col. Rooney Lee's 9th Reg't got into a close fight with sabrs and pistols, but prevailed. The Yankees took off and our colonel begged to be permitted to make a pursuit, and gaining consent, we were off on the road to Old Church.

I have been doing a bit of tracking under the instruction of old Mister Vernon Earl. I do not recall if I told you of him before. He is a hunter from the Blue Ridge who has good skills that he is imparting to me. He has taut me how to find the spots where animals go besides where the human animals pass. We've been looking for the latter, of course. Mayhap I will have a use for the animal tracking after this war is done.

On one occasion, our Col. put me to work practicing the knowledge I have gained from Mr. Earl. I am happy to report that I did not lead us into a swamp, but with only one mistake on my part, we ended up on the trail of a patrol of Yankees, of which we captured a great lot.

There is so much more to recount, but my paper is almost used up, and I have other words to say to you. Mary, how I miss you. How I miss the little son you have borne me, even though I have not seen him with my own eyes. I wish you could get a likeness made of the boy to send to me. I would keep it upon my heart at all times. I treasure the one you sent to me of yor dear person. I kiss it every night. Oh my love. I dream of the sweet day when I can return home to you, greet you with an embrace, and lay with you once again cradled in my arms. Do you not dream of the same? Do not be shy in riting affectionate words to me, my darling. I hold sacred yor trust. Feer not. My body and soul are yors alone.

I figure we are going into battle again within a short time. I am informed that when the spring and summer come, with them arrives a new season of battles. General Lee will not hesitate to move on the enemy. I will do everything in my power to remain whole and safe.

With all the tender feelings of my soul,
Yor husband, Rulon

ೞ

Mary — June 24, 1862

One morning, Rand Hilbrands came into the store with his arms full of letters and packages. "Ida, come take this parcel," he said, glancing in her direction.

Mary, who was closer to him, put out her arms to receive it, but he gave it into Ida's charge instead.

"Here is a letter for you, Mistress Mary. From your husband, I suspect."

Mary took it, relief sweeping through her breast at having evidence of his good health in her hand. "Thank you, Papa. We have no customers in the store. May I go to read it?"

"Can I prevent you from doing so?" he replied in a jovial manner. "I hope it is good tidings."

"Thank you, Papa," she said, and hurried into the back room where Roddy slept in his cradle, his breathing even, except when he made an occasional little snuffling sound.

Mary sat, unsealed the envelope flap, and took out one sheet of paper, written on both sides to the very margins. Rulon had been on a grand adventure, he said, and recounted some of the events. He seemed to have a liking for the art of tracking. Mary shrugged. That was a man's concern.

She caught her breath. He missed her. He spoke longingly of Roddy. She had not thought of sending a likeness of the boy, but must now certainly see about having one made of him, because Rulon wanted to have it.

Oh my, she thought, her heart leaping. She had just read his words of how he treated her likeness, and what effect it had upon him. Hungrily, she scanned the next sentence. "Oh my love," it read. She scarce could breathe for the tightness in her chest. How long had it been since she had heard his voice whisper those words to her? The next bit caught her by surprise, and she froze.

Rulon longed for her to be in his embrace, to lie beside him, in his arms. And then she read, "Feer not. My body and soul are yors alone."

She began to weep. Rulon had remained true to her. His letter clearly expressed his devotion. She had fretted and worried herself sick of mind for no reason. Her self-afflicted pain had been a misuse of her energies, and she regretted the waste of contentment while she had been engaged in doubting her husband's fidelity.

Conscious of her precarious location, and fearing to awaken her babe, she wiped her eyes and breathed slowly until her tears were under control. She reckoned she must make every effort to put doubt out of her mind. She must aid Rulon in being true. He desired her to use words of affection in her letters. Her mind shrank at the idea of putting her private thoughts on paper. She hadn't been a wife long enough to be comfortable in saying such things as he had included in this letter. He was a bolder creature than she. Even though he had taught her to relish certain intimacies, she certainly would not speak of them. Must she devise a code? Perhaps she would give thought to that notion. For now, it sufficed that Rulon bore bountiful affection for her and honored his vows.

Chapter 21
Rulon — August 30, 1862

Rulon had a great surprise upon the field of battle at Manassas late on the third day. He had been detailed as a courier for General Stuart and was carrying orders to General Robertson when he encountered his father.

"Pa!" he shouted, reining up. "Pa!" he tried again to get his attention.

His father turned his head, and seeing Rulon, spurred his horse in his direction.

"Son. Be safe. This fight is vicious."

"I will. Have you seen Ben or Peter?"

"Peter is in the thick fighting near the plantation house. I haven't caught sight of Ben. God speed, son," he said, and was off, leading his company in a different direction.

"Lordy, lordy," Rulon whispered in a demi prayer, relieved to see Pa was whole, but now concerned about Peter. The rascal would manage to go into the hottest part of the fray. Nothing would prevent him seeking glory.

Then Rulon could put no thought to his brother's pride, as he was on the move again, looking for the brigade colors that marked the spot from which the General directed his regiments. He had orders to deliver.

ଙ

Julia — September 2, 1862

After a year of war, Julia had grown used to the exercise of scanning the casualty lists published by the newspaper after the big battles. She would never become accustomed to the clutching sense of dread that accompanied the perusal.

Carl came home from town in late afternoon and handed the list to her, folded with such sharp edges that he must have run pinching fingers over the fold several times to leave a tight crease.

"Did you read it yet?" she asked.

He shook his head, eyes cautious. Albert stood half behind him, clutching white-knuckled hands together.

She held the sheet for a moment, then turned away from her sons, the dread closing her throat already.

She took a seat at the table. Marie came into the room, followed by Julianna. Julia said, "Sit down, daughters." Her quavering voice startled her.

Marie sat on one side and Julianna on the other. Julia heard Carl and Albert go outside, but they hadn't closed the door, and she could feel their eyes boring into her shoulder blades. She didn't know where James and Clayton were.

Marie twisted a handkerchief. Julianna folded her arms on the table top and put her head down on them. She squeezed her eyes shut.

Julia unfolded the paper and looked at it. The list was neither alphabetized nor ordered by unit, which meant she had to read each name. She did not want to see any name ending in Owen. She ran her tongue across her bottom lip. She struggled to take a breath.

She exhaled and began, drawing her forefinger slowly down the first column as she read the names. She noticed that her finger trembled, and she paused to get herself in hand.

Marie made a small sound.

Julia looked at her, then back to the paper. Her heart pounded in her ears. She slowly began to read again, her lips forming each name.

Near the bottom of the third column, her finger stopped. She shrank back, a cry arising from the depths of her soul.

"Mama?" moaned Julianna.

Peter. The entry said Peter Owen. It gave his regiment and company.

Julia whispered his name once, disbelieving the printer's ink under her finger. Her hands convulsed, opening and closing above the sheet before her. Her ears buzzed. *I dasn't faint. I dasn't!*

Shadows moved in front of her as the girls peered at the spot her finger had marked. Julianna whimpered and sat back. Julia forced herself to focus her eyes on her daughter. The girl's face had gone white as alabaster. She appeared about to topple to one side.

Julia found the strength to thrust out her arm and grasp her daughter's wrist. She heard a chair's legs scrape against the floor. Marie was on her feet, pacing, tears streaming down her cheeks as she sobbed.

"Ma?" Carl put his hands on her shoulders.

All she could do was point. She had no voice to speak his name again. Gone. The boy was gone.

Carl must have located the awful bit of news. She heard his sharp inhalation, and Albert's "Who is it, Carl?" as he came around her side. Carl's hands had slipped off her shoulders. The boys whispered to each other, then Albert choked off a sob.

Julianna had gone limp, leaning backwards, almost off the bench. Julia knew she couldn't hold her upright from her chair. She somehow got her feet underneath her, levered herself upright, and pulled the girl back to lean on the table, all the while chills ran races along her spine. Peter was dead. She had no time to mourn while her other children were in such sore straits.

༄

Julia — September 12, 1862

For days, Julia navigated the paths of her everyday life with her heart torn to shreds. Peter was gone. Peter, whose reckless spirit had led him to seek the adventures of war, was no more. She couldn't fathom it. Yes, she had been forced to lay a babe in a grave before this, but to have a half-grown child wrested from her? It was unthinkable.

She wondered if Rod knew of the loss. The two of them had been in the same regiment, so it was possible that he had found out. She longed to have his arm around her shoulders, to gain solace from his sturdy body held next to hers, but that was impossible just now. She would have to travel this path of sorrow alone.

No. She wasn't alone. She had children beside her, children who were grieving the taking of their playmate, older brother, and friend. Tease. Rapscallion. Jokester. He was all of those. But he was also a hard worker.

Had been. Not now. Julia felt her soul was stripped to pieces.

Peter would never again come up behind her and tie the tails of her apron strings where she couldn't reach them. He would never again curry the buggy horse and put it into harness for her. He would never again object to her swift kiss on his cheek at night.

Peter was gone, dumped into a hole on a battlefield and covered over with a few spades of Virginia earth.

She sank into a chair, ready to weep, knowing she should comfort Julianna, who went about the house like a ghost. Marie sobbed in her room at night. Carl wore the face of a martyr, white as alabaster. James kept himself occupied in the fields until after dark. Clay and Albert huddled on the fireplace hearth in the evenings, shoulders drooping, each one looking at the other then away, too proud to cry.

She had no strength. Peter. The dark-haired child who'd come along after two little tow-headed boys. How was she to do without him?

She rested for a few moments, imagining him dashing into the thick of the battle, then shied away from following that thought. She must not mope here. It would lead her into dark avenues. She gathered her resources into a tiny ball of resolve, and rose to get a basket and go outdoors to take the clothes off the lines. She hoped the open air would sooth her battered soul.

৵

Rulon — September 20, 1862

Rulon's regiment had pressed forward into Maryland as General Lee sought to gain an advantage by invading the North. One evening, shortly after the bloody days at Sharpsburg, he got a letter. He leaned on his horse to rip it open, having recognized Mary's hand.

September 4, 1862
Dear Husband,
I scarce can hold a pen to write these words for the great sorrow enwrapping my soul. Your sister Marie came to see our dear child

*and me. Soon after coming through the door, she commenced to
weep as though she would perish from grief, bringing the most
fearful news. Your brother Peter is no more. His name was writ on
the casualty list from the second fight about Manassas railway
junction. No one knows where his erthly remains are laid to rest. I
am terriby distracted by the evil news of your brother's demise.*

*Your mama is beside herself with mourning, Marie tells me. She
herself is almost in the same state. I endeavered to tell her to be
brave so she wood be fit to help your mama bear her burden. After
a time, she cried her final tears and agreed to do what she could.
We must now find or make black material for mourning clothes.
However, I do not kno of a weaver left in the county.*

*Dear husband, I pray you are well and can take the terribl loss
of your broth'r in stride. We hear many reports of your bravery and
skill in fighting the dred foe in Maryland. I tell Baby Roddy about
his Papa every night before I lay him in bed. Do not put yourself in
Harm's Way. My love for you is unending.*

Yor faithful wife,
Mary Hilbrands Owen

Halfway through his reading of the letter, he felt himself sliding down the
withers of the horse, and then he was sitting on the ground, distraught and trying
to hold himself together. Peter dead? It did not seem possible.

"No," he groaned. "No, not my brother. Dear God, why Peter? Why not me
instead?"

Ren found him there, and led the horse away so it wouldn't do him damage.
He returned and squatted beside Rulon.

"Ill news?"

"Oh God in heaven," Rulon cried out as though he petitioned the Lord for a
different outcome. "It's my brother. Gone. Dead."

He felt Ren's hand touching him lightly on the shoulder. "I'm sorry, Rule.
That's a terrible loss." The voice was so quiet Rulon could barely hear it.

He crumpled Mary's letter in his two fists, crying unashamed tears.

Ren stayed still and silent for a time, then arose. "You'd best take a mouthful
or two of rations, man. You may not think it will help, but it will keep you from
wasting in this hard time."

Rulon shook his head. How could he think of eating when his rascally brother
would never take sustenance again? "My poor ma. She don't deserve this."

Ren gave a little snort. "No mother does, but you know the truth. Our men are
dying most every day. Some poor mothers who don't get any notice are left to
wonder why their dear boy don't write home anymore."

"That don't help the pain, Ren."

"It's fresh, man. Don't dwell on it for more than a little space. You've got
your duty."

Rulon remembered the picket he was supposed to relieve. "Give me a minute.
I'll pull myself together."

"You will do. Riding by your side these months past, I've learned you've got the mettle."

"I—" Rulon scrubbed his eyes with the backs of his hands, almost tearing the letter in the process. "God have mercy on his soul," he muttered, then got to his feet. He carefully folded the letter to finish later, and tucked it into his jacket. "Oh Mary," he groaned. "Don't let the boy come to any harm."

₯

Ella Ruth — September 21, 1862

Weeks after Ella Ruth heard of Mrs. Owen's loss of her son, her parents invited Doctor Allen and his wife to Sunday dinner. The dinner conversation between the two brothers centered on the conflict just past at Sharpsburg, and the influx of wounded men into the new soldier's hospital just outside Mount Jackson. While the ham was served, Dr. Allen mentioned that he was looking for ladies from the town to volunteer several hours a week to come nurse the new patients. "My own dear wife helps as she has time, but the children do need her at home."

Mrs. Doctor Allen nodded and murmured a bit about how the little ones kept her quite occupied.

"Brother Joseph," Ella Ruth's mother said in a tone firm enough to catch the doctor's attention. "What kind of topic is this for the dinner table?"

"A war time topic, my dear," the doctor said. "These soldiers need care. Our country owes great thanks to these young men. What better way than to tend to their needs?"

Did Peter Owen die because no one was there to tend to his needs? Ella Ruth gave a little shudder, imagining Ben lying on a field strewn with the injured and dying. *Mama should let Uncle have his say.*

"Perhaps you should speak to Theodore on the topic after we dine. He can offer you several helpful ideas, I am quite sure. That would be more proper, don't you agree?" Mrs. Allen turned to her husband for support.

"Uncle," Ella Ruth surprised herself by speaking up. "What are your requirements for nurses?"

"Miss Ella Ruth, they need only have a pair of willing and able hands, a compassionate heart, and spare time." He wiped a dripping of sauce off his chin with his napkin. "We will give any needed training to the nurses as they work."

Ella Ruth let the conversation go on as she thought about his answer. She certainly had spare time, and her hands were capable, if not willing. Did she have a compassionate heart? Perhaps not. She wanted to be compassionate, but either it was a trait she lacked, or she had not been taught about compassion.

Was that the same thing as kindness? She thought of herself as kind. She always treated her maid Lula kindly. She never struck her, or spoke harshly to her. Was not that being kind? Was it compassionate? Perhaps so.

Or was compassion sympathy? She inhaled, contemplating the muddle in her brain. She was only confusing herself, putting too much thought into the affair. Why did it matter in the end? The doctor needed more hands to aid the soldiers in the hospital. She felt a chill run up her spine. Should Ben be wounded during his next encounter with the enemy and enter a hospital, would it not be her fondest desire that he have competent nursing care from some kindly woman? Yes, indeed it would.

"Dr. Allen," she blurted out, interrupting her father in mid-sentence. "I should like to serve in the hospital."

"Daughter, that is impossible," her mother said, drawing herself into a stiff posture.

"No, it is not. I have very little work to do here at home, no purpose in my life. This is what I will do as my thanks to our fine soldiers."

Her mother made a sound of protest, but her father jumped into the conversation with, "You see how it is, Louisa. She has set her mind to do this thing, and she will not be dissuaded." He turned to his brother. "It seems you have a volunteer, Joseph. Be sure she is treated well."

And that, Ella Ruth thought, *is that. I shall be an excellent nurse.*

ɛ৯

Julia — October 4, 1862

On a Saturday morning, Julia entered the kitchen to begin breakfast, and found a folded sheet of paper propped against her large mixing bowl. Immediate dread flowed down her spine as though an icy finger had stroked her bare skin. She sank into her chair, holding the paper where her blurred eyes could see the words on the outside.

To Ma

"No," she moaned, knowing what must be inside. "No." This time, the word escaped her throat as a sob.

Almost as though her hands were controlled by another person, they unfolded the paper.

Ma,

I kno you will take this hard, but I am hon'r-bound to take Peter's place. We lost so many good men at Manassas, and now that the Yankeys have been fot at great cost at Sharpsburg, Gen'l Bobby Lee needs me.

Do not dispare. I will be as a ghost in the mist attacking the foe. I sware to you I will return.

Your son, Carl

ɛ৯

Rulon — December 31, 1862

31st day of Decemb'r 1862
Culpepper C.H.
Dear Wife,
You will have heard about the Yankees bringing war to us in Fredricsburg. They did not prevale, due to much delay in bringing

the fight across the river. Our regimn't was not much employed in the battle at Fredricsburg but We afterward embarked upon a bold raid across the Rappahannoc and into the realm of the foe. Nearly two Thousand of troops in three Brigades under Gen'l Stuart's own leadership made the raiding party. We rode as far north as Dumfries before we went in other directions to impede the enemy's designs and give him pause. Near a place called Greenwood Church, our Regmt had a encounter with some boys from Penn, who turned tail and ran when we charged into them. The command routed, at which we pursewed them for about two miles, taking many prisoners.

Gen'r Stuart captured a telegraph house and made fools of the Yankees in Washington, getting information that helped him decide where to attac next. Our Brigadeer Gen'l, Fitz Lee, took a party and pulled down the rail road brige over a creek.

We coold not attac Fairfax C.H., as the enemy seemed to know of our activities, but we have returned to safety in this place.

I hope our little son and yor dear person had a plesent Christmas celebration. I wish I coold be there to hold you in my arms and see the New Year come in. This war must end soon. The Yankees surely by now see our determination to be a country separate from them. They cannot carry on this conflict much longer.

If you see my mother soon, give her a kiss for me. Receev a special kiss from my lips as if it were placed upon your brow and all other places. I miss my sweet Sugar.

Yor Husband,
Rulon Owen
1st Virginia Regiment, Cavalry

Chapter 22
Rulon — February through May 10, 1863

Despite sorry weather, in February General Fitz Lee's Brigade moved from their winter foraging in King William and Caroline counties back to Culpeper Court House to relieve Wade Hampton's Brigade on picket duty. Across the upper Rappahannock, the Federal troops sheltered for the winter, but Rulon's regiment picked away at the Federal videttes and lines of communication, in company with the other three regiments of the command.

The successful cavalry raids brought a response once the weather warmed a trifle. Rulon found himself tagged for courier duty during one of the encounters, and wrote to Mary of the recklessness of the task, dashing about the battleground taking messages from one commander to another. He embellished the patriotic elements of the duty while toning down the danger.

For the rest of the month of April, Rulon was occupied with picket duty and riding in support when a picket post at Rixeyville was reported under attack.

On the way back the next day, Ren said, "I reckon false reports will wear a body out quicker than a nice fight."

"It surely gets the blood up to no good purpose," Rulon replied. "My horse is about beat to death."

At the end of the month, though, Hooker's army crossed the Rappahannock. The 1st Virginia Cavalry struck the Federal advance on the Germanna Ford road, but Rulon's company was ordered to guard another road, and while there, captured enough prisoners to send good information to General Robert Lee about the Federal commands opposing them. The regiment rode all night through the Wilderness on winding roads, then was put into a fight the next day, without rest.

Moving through the woods, the column came to a standstill when they came in contact with the enemy. After a courier had come from General Stuart several times, bidding Colonel Drake to hurry on to Chancellorsville, and the colonel had sent him back with the ill tidings that they could not fulfill the order, Colonel Drake sent Rulon with the courier to emphasize the futility of the dispatch.

Soon General Stuart came up with a brigade of infantry, and although the soldiers were deployed in front of the regiment, the enemy was firmly entrenched in an old railroad cut and could not be dislodged.

General Jackson's corps later rolled up the Federal flank, and the Yankees retreated toward Chancellorsville.

Although the enemy was on the run, matters turned deadly serious when General Jackson rode out in front of his lines on a reconnaissance and was mortally wounded by his own men on his return.

Caught out of position during the battle, Rulon's company joined General Rooney Lee's Brigade in chasing the Federal cavalry south led by General Stoneman toward the James River. The pursuit lasted over eight days and nights, and although no major battles ensued, they skirmished with the Yankees nearly every day.

When General Stoneman's cavalry eluded capture, the 1st Regiment camped at Orange Court House.

Rulon threw himself onto the ground after he saw to his horse. "I declare I am dead of hunger," he said to Ren.

"Did you find any more crackers in your saddlebags?"

Rulon snorted. "I'm not a magician. I ate the last one two days ago."

Ren expressed his disappointment in sharp words.

"I can hear your stomach growl from over here," Rulon retorted, and tore up a handful of grass. He looked at the bright blades. "Do you reckon it's edible for humans?"

"Cats eat it. And goats. Horses graze on it." He sat beside Rulon and picked a blade of grass. "Why not us?" he said, and stuck the grass into his mouth.

જી

Ben — May 13, 1863

Word spread through the Confederate Army like wildfire that General Jackson had died. Some said losing his arm had disheartened him. Some said being shot by his own troops had put him in a mortal state of grief. After a time it was understood that the great general had died from pneumonia. That did not erase the sense of gloom that overshadowed his command.

My darling Ella Ruth,

I hope this finds you well and happy as can be expected, given the circumstances.

You cannot imagine the pain we endure in the Brigade. I do not know your feelins toward the General, but his death has thrown us into despair.

The heart within me seemed to break when the news came that the dread day had arriv'd. We hoped and prayed that God would spare Gen'l Jackson to lead us agin. I suppose God wanted him more than we did, but oh! The grief cuts us sore and deep.

The Yankees have so many men they seem to come from a deep well. We are drafting schoolboys and greybeards. Some come with no weapons, no shoes. I suppose they dragged them off a hill hideout in Tennessee. North Carolina sent good fighters early on, but the recroots now are reluctant to stand. Pray for the Cause, sweet girl. Pray with fervent heart that we will overcome the foe, and soon. We cannot go on like this forever.

Ben added a few lines about his plans for expanding crop production on the farm after the war, then continued.

I reckon you have had every good thing in your life. My hope is that as you consider becoming my little farm wife you will hav no regrets. Be assured that I adore you, but you will need to learn many tasks that will dirty your hands. My ma has felt great satisfaction in doing hard work for her family. You will feel the same joy as you learn the work.

He ended the letter expressing his fervent love, and then, signed it simply,

Ben

℘

Mary — May 15, 1863

Dear Husband,

My, how my arms do ache! We made soft soap today from the winter's ashs. Mama sent India to the store in my place so I could pitch into the labor. I hope Papa did not take offence at having a jun'r worker instead of his right-hand Mary.

The fire roared, the kett'l bubbled and splash'd, and Roddy lern'd how to hold up his dress to toddle toward the center of the excitment. I could not let harm come to yor son, so I fashn'd a pen of

chairs and blankets in the hedge of the garden. He is a smart creature for merely 15-months-old, and found a way to dig out between the bushes. I was forev'r putting him back in place and piling dirt up to keep him contain'd. Mama became so alarmed that she sent Ida to the store and India returned to tend the boy.

This made more work for Sylvia and me, but at the end of the day, we had poured out a quantity of soap for bars. I enclose one, wich I hope did not leek on the paper, as I wrapped it in the last oilcloth I could find.

I must hide my pleasure to see Papa treating with his grandson. With only girls in his projeny, havin a boy about the place is a novelty. I hast'n to add it is a joy to him. He looks for trinkets in the store to bring home to Roddy. I am ever cautining Papa about small items, for the boy still puts everything to a taste-test before he plays with it. I do not want him to choke, as a child did in New Market the past week. The moth'r is inconsoalable. She blames the Yankees, passin down the Valley again, for scaring the baby into swallowing his sugartit. I keep Roddy out of their way when they come thru town.

Yor Mother had a siege of sickness amongst your kin during the winter. All have recover'd and pray for an end to this conflict. Rulon, my prayers are constant on yor behalf. Keep safe, dear Life, and return to me whole and strong.

I take Roddy's hand in my own to make his mark
X
All our love,
Mary

∽

Rod — May 17, 1863

My dear Julie,

I am well. The cough that playged me during the cold spell has gone away. When I lost my good horse I had a rough time finding a remount, but finally acquired a sturdy bay mare that is coming along well.

When you rote me Carl had gone into the army I was not much surprised. I have kept my eyes open for him. He was in a regular horse company, but Jeb Stuart gave John Mosby permission to form up a company of partisans under the Act thet Congress passed. As soon as he could, Carl joined Mosby's Men.

How I wish I could see you and comfort you as you continue this year of mourning. If it will give you peace, Peter's captain told me of his valor upon the field of combat. He fought with bravery and honor. Cap'n Thomas said our boy passed quickly and painlessly in a charge against the foe at Portici Plantation. I hope that knowledge will suffice to give you pride in our son and comfort at his loss.

We have been much exercised in determining the position of the enemy as their army moves. It is fortunate that we have good forage for the horses now. I'm sure yor prayers have been effective, little Wife. Thank you for keeping our sons and me and my men in them.

Give the girls a kiss for me and embrace my sons at home.
Receive a kiss upon yor brow and an especial sincere hug from yor husband,

> Roderick Owen
> Cap'n, Owen Dragoons

℘

Rulon — June 5 through 9, 1863

The ranks of the cavalry had swelled considerably with new recruits and the return of a couple of brigades, and Jeb Stuart called for a general review of the entire command for June 5.

Such a hullabaloo, Rulon thought as the 1st Virginia Cavalry Regiment passed in rigid order before a group of ladies and invited guests. The invitees included 10,000 Texans of Hood's Division, who were neither quiet nor politic in their assessments of the Virginians. *Things might get rowdy tonight.*

The regiment avoided much of the shenanigans planned for them by Hood's veteran scrappers by marching across the ford on Hazel River and riding until two the next morning to Jeffersonton. Rulon dismounted as though his legs were made of apple jelly after the extended ride. He planted the side of his head against the saddle blanket and breathed deeply, trying to get enough air flowing to clear the dust from his lungs.

"Imagine walking that far," Ren Lovell said, his crooked smile a pale imitation of the one he used to turn on Rulon. "I'll go see if the Captain has orders."

Rulon hadn't shifted from leaning against his horse when Ren returned.

"Don't unsaddle. We're going on picket as soon as we get some grub into our bellies."

"I'd rather sleep," Rulon muttered.

"Do it quick, then. We're riding at sunrise over to Waterloo Bridge."

Rulon fished a portion of a hard tack cracker out of his saddlebag, just in case he had a yen to put something the army called food into his mouth, and led the horse to a lane. He tethered it to a tree and lay down nearby.

Owen Leoyd shook him awake before the sky had lightened. "Time to go, Owen," he said, the old joke worn thin by now.

Rulon stirred, opened his eyes, and got to his feet. The inside of his mouth made him think he'd ingested sand during the night. He took a swig of water from his canteen, swished it around, and spit. He found the cracker and put it into his cheek to soften until he could chew it. A roast chicken would taste better about now. He wondered if there were any chickens in the county. He shrugged off the thought. He didn't have any money to buy one if they were to be had.

When he was ready to mount up, Ren came by and said, "General Lee's stove up with rheumatism. Colonel Munford is taking the brigade until he comes back."

Rulon groaned. Every commander had a distinct leadership style. He was too tired to deal with Munford, so he hoped Old Fitz got well in a hurry.

Rulon drew a short straw and paired with Garth Von at a picket post. The surly fellow proceeded to pare his fingernails with his knife, and Rulon determined not to blink while he was in the company of Von.

Shortly after noon, Rulon's eyes sprang open when he heard carbine fire from a position closer to the bridge. Surprised he was still alive, he drew his weapon and looked around. Von had gigged his horse out of the trees toward the fight, and Rulon followed, gnashing his teeth at the thought that he had slumbered.

The other men from "I" Company joined the skirmish with a small detachment of Yankee cavalrymen. When the enemy had been driven off, Ren assessed the squadron and discovered that Private Whitmore had been injured.

Rulon promptly volunteered to take the man back to the surgeon at Rixeyville, and Ren let him go.

"Coward," Ren whispered as he bent near.

Rulon shook his head and mouthed, "Von."

Ren raised an eyebrow, but nodded and waved Rulon and Whitmore off in the direction of the regiment's headquarters.

A few days later, a buzz went around the brigade. The Yankee cavalry had crossed the Rappahannock and attacked Stuart's main encampment near Brandy Station. "Boots and Saddles" blared from multiple bugles, and men ran around the camp as though demons chased them. Although the distance to the battle wasn't that far, moving the men and horses of the Brigade effectively was a daunting task for a newly designated commander.

Colonel Drake wanted the 1st to leave first, but Munford had other ideas, and with all the hubbub, the brigade didn't arrive on the field until about four o'clock.

The 1st was ordered forward, and Rulon drew his sabre and galloped forward at the charge, yelling at the top of his voice. He heard Ren scream, "Give 'em the sabre, boys!" Desperate to drive back the Yankees, the men of the 1st Virginia called on all the boldness and dash they possessed.

A melee of men swirled around Rulon as the charge disintegrated into small fights in isolated pockets. He found himself in the midst of fierce action with his weapon, clashing in individual contest with one Yankee after another. One almost slashed his arm with a thrust but he parried at the last moment and the man went off his horse instead. Rulon incapacitated the man with a quick thrust of his own, not pausing to wonder how he did this so callously, as he had done at the beginning of the war. It was wound, or be wounded, kill or be killed, and the clash of sabres around him, the smoke and dust clogging the air, the screams of downed horses, the rattle of balls, and the roar of artillery reminded him that combat of this sort was intensely personal.

When he had a second to catch his breath, Rulon wondered how the brigades encamped around Stuart's headquarters had been caught with their pants down. Then he had no more time for thought, as another foeman rode toward him.

Then the Yankees began to retreat, their bugles calling them back from the field. Rulon engaged one last holdout, then the man turned and galloped off.

Rulon pulled his horse around in response to his own regiment's bugles, his heart still racing with the effects of the chaos and excitement, and saw Garth Von dismount and slit the throat of a downed Yankee officer. Von looked about, lifted the man's head by his hair, and with his bloody blade, carved a circle around the top of the Yankee's head, then sliced the scalp from the man's cranium.

Rulon fought back the urge to vomit, but Von wasn't finished.

He stuffed the ghastly prize into his saddlebag, then slit the officer's trousers up the front. He let out a keening yell of triumph, then mutilated the man's crotch. Lifting the remains, he ran to his horse and mounted.

Rulon lost his battle against nausea. Retching, he kicked his horse away from the scene, back toward the regiment, putting a fair amount of distance between himself and the man he had thought of as merely crazy. Ren's assessment had been correct. Von was evil.

⃞

Rulon — late June through early July, 1863

After the sickening events at Brandy Station, Rulon kept as far as he could from Garth Von as the regiment rested in camp at Rixeyville. He invited Owen Leoyd to join him for an entertainment.

"Come on, Leoyd. Company 'B' is putting on a race."

"They ought not to wear out the horses," Leoyd said, his face set in solemn lines.

"Oh, these critters have plenty of go in them."

"Critters? Where did they get racing hounds?"

"Not hounds. Come on. You'll see."

Rulon led the way to where the men of Company "B" had gathered in a flat area. A small patch of tent canvas lay on the ground, with the men shouting encouragement.

"What are they yelling about?" Leoyd asked.

Rulon dragged him into the circle. Several tiny dark objects scurried across the canvas, guided by splinters of wood held by the men closest to the fray.

"Fleas? They're racing fleas?" Leoyd scoffed at the sight, and would have turned away but for Rulon's hand on his sleeve.

"Don't matter what they're doin'. At least we're away from Von."

At that, Leoyd sat right down on the ground and observed.

Within days, the army was on the move, sending out pickets to warn of the approach of the enemy. They found them near Aldie, and the 1st held the road, fighting dismounted from behind stone walls.

After the skirmish, the 1st was on picket at Mountsville, but had to battle to keep the position. This continued until General Fitz Lee took command of his brigade again.

"We're heading east," Ren told the squadron. "General Bobbie Lee took the infantry boys over the river into Maryland. We're to do damage behind the lines."

The cavalry brigades destroyed canal boats, captured wagons and supplies, burned bridges and tore up railroad tracks as they advanced into Maryland and Pennsylvania. They skirmished in Westminster, and fought their way out of an encounter with overpowering numbers at Hanover.

"Stuart's lost, ain't he." Rulon observed to Ren when they reached Dover, Pennsylvania at daylight after riding through the night. "I don't see any sign of Early's army."

"Maybe so, but I see plentiful forage hereabouts."

"I hope Stuart lets us find provisions," Rulon said. "My stomach thinks my throat's been cut."

"They don't like us here."

"We don't like them in Virginia, either. It's time the Yankees learned that turn-about is fair."

After filling their bellies, they were on the march again by night.

"Jeb heard that Dick Ewell's in Carlisle," Ren said.

Rulon only groaned in reply. He'd managed to keep himself on his horse, but several men had gone to sleep and fallen from theirs.

Stuart sent Fitz Lee's brigade to lead the advance on the town, but it was full of Pennsylvania militiamen who refused to surrender.

Garth Von muttered, "Burn the Yankees out," and after a second attempt to convince the militia to surrender, Lee proceeded to bombard the town with shells from the guns of his horse artillery.

A courier came with orders for the 1st to burn the Carlisle Barracks, then join the rest of the cavalry on the way to Gettysburg.

"Gettysburg?" Owen Leoyd asked. "What's going on there?"

"Jeb found Bobbie Lee," Ren replied. "Bobbie Lee found Meade. I reckon it's going to be a big fight."

ഇ

Rulon — July 3, 1863

Rulon crouched in a farmer's field behind a fence, trying not to yawn. It was a good thing General Stuart had ordered the 1st Virginia to get into this fight dismounted. He didn't think his horse could take another step, much less gallop into a fray. He squelched another yawn behind his hand. His brigade hadn't arrived until the wee hours this morning after riding long miles from Carlisle, and here it was after noon. He'd not slept since arriving. Who could, with the Yankees flinging shell and shot at the Confederate cavalry for the last hour? They had stopped the ruckus only a few minutes ago. The air lay flat and calm around him, without a human sound to interrupt the flow of nature.

Ren coughed at his side. "Get ready," he said.

"I am ready," Rulon replied, a bit irritated by the wait. "Were those boys using Spencer rifles?"

"Yes, and the next brigade probably has them, too." Ren dug in his cartridge box. "Damn Yankee repeaters."

Then the bugle sounded, and Rulon was up and over the fence, yelling as he fired, reloading on the run, trying to beat back the Federal skirmishers in his path so the cavalry could take yonder intersection and sweep around the Yankee flank to their rear.

A barrage of cannon fire began and Rulon tripped and fell flat. The sound was wrong. It came from behind and to the left, and it was distant. It shook the earth beneath his belly, however, rolling thunder replacing the calm of moments before.

Rulon got to his feet and continued across the field, the 1st driving the Yankees down and across another fence line. But now, he heard screams of "Come on, you Wolverines!" The Yankees pushed back. Hampton's brigade came up from behind on horseback, and the 1st was signaled to withdraw and let the mounted troops take over the fight.

What a furious affair! Men fought with carbines, pistols, sabres, all the while screaming invective at each other. As he backed out of the battle, Rulon saw horses collide along the fence with a crash so hurtful that he imagined bones snapped. One horse went end over end and the rider screamed in agony as he was pinned by half a ton of horseflesh.

Now the Yankees were on three sides of them, and Hampton bled from a sabre cut. Frantic bugle calls summoned the men to withdraw, and so they did. No one came after them. The Yankees must have had enough, too.

છ

Ella Ruth — November 16, 1863

Christmas was coming in about a month, despite the war dragging on and on. Ella Ruth sat down after a long stint helping her Uncle Joseph with a wounded soldier, arching her aching back in an attempt to work the kinks out. If she was going to send a gift to Ben, it would have to be done soon or he would never receive it in time.

She knew he had survived that awful fight in Pennsylvania last summer. Thank the Good Lord he wasn't in General Pickett's division. Since July she had received a few letters from Ben, and the last note said he was somewhere in Orange County, below the Rapidan.

"Miss Allen," Uncle Joseph called to her. "I need your assistance."

With a sigh, Ella Ruth went back to work in the surgery room. What could she send to Ben?

Her answer came several days later as she read a letter to a young man whose bandages on a head wound made it impossible for him to see. His wife talked about a likeness she had sent to the soldier, and after she read that part, she glanced up to see him fumbling in his pocket to be sure he had the cherished item.

"Ain't she the most comely woman you ever saw?" he asked, moving the likeness where Ella Ruth could view it. She hoped he could not see her widened eyes at the sight of a very homely creature, but she made polite sounds and went back to reading.

Something about the man's devotion to his wife stirred Ella Ruth's heart. No matter what the girl's appearance, the remembrance she had sent was important to him.

Would Ben take such pride in my portrait? she wondered. A soft emotion swelling in her breast told her that he would. That was settled, then. She would take her pearl earrings to the photographer's studio to barter for a likeness of herself for Ben's Christmas gift.

Chapter 23
Rulon — May 13, 1864

Dear Wife of my very soul

We had a skirmish two days ago that causes my heart to quail within me as I think on it. Our Cause has lost its noble Cavalier to mortal wounds. Oh my love, JEB Stuart is gone. I am as desolate as tho another of my brothers has died. We all feel as low as can be. There is no one to take his Place. The spirit of every man in the Cavalry is broken to peaces.

My heart hangs heavy in my bosom today. We are in camp. It has been silent as a toomb. A short while ago, I listened as a comrade began playin' the tune "Lorena" on his banjo, and another fellow started in singing the words. My dear Mary, I about fell to weeping for the melancholy of the sound.

My sweet Sugar, I am so lonely for you and the brillunce of yor smile. I yearn to feel yor dear love encircling me to comfort my body and soul.

These days have been long and burdensome. Besides our Great Cavalier, many of our comrades have fallen. Mary, my love, I long for the day when this war will end and I can return to yor sweet embrace.

Rulon

ಬ

Julia — May 16, 1864

Julia heard an insistent thumping on the front door, and ran to answer it, her heart in her throat. *Are the Yankees back?* To her immense relief, a Confederate officer and several infantrymen stood outside.

"Yes?" She looked at the man's uniform. He appeared to be a lieutenant.

"Am I addressing Mrs. Owen?" he asked.

Julia raised her chin a fraction. His manner was too brusque for her taste. "You are. What is wanted?"

The lieutenant consulted a paper in his hand, then looked up. "Do you have a son, James Owen, living here?"

Julia nodded, very slowly, her throat so constricted that she had no voice.

"I have papers for his conscription."

She cleared her throat and inhaled. "He's the man of the house now."

He glanced at the paper, then back at her. "That may be, ma'am, but his country needs him in the army."

"I've sent four sons and a husband, and one gave his life defending his country. Isn't that enough?"

The man's eyes softened, but he straightened his shoulders. "No, ma'am. The Yankees are in the Valley again. We need your son."

A chill swept through her. "How long does he have before you collect him?"

"No time, ma'am. I'm to bring him with me."

She sucked in her breath. "Y'all can wait here. I'll gather his necessaries." She half turned away, then stopped. "You won't be needing my twelve-year-old, will you?" She turned back to hear the man's answer.

"No ma'am. Not today." His gaze fixed on hers, and a bit of dizziness swept through her.

How long will this warring last? Will it come down to sending Clay and Albert to the front?

She closed the door, ran through the parlor into the kitchen and opened the back door. She saw Albert hoeing weeds in the kitchen garden.

"Albert!" she called, her voice sounding as rough as though she gargled vinegar.

The boy paused at his work and looked up.

"Go fetch James. Give him a tight hug, while you're at it."

"Ma?"

"He's been drafted." Her voice broke.

Albert gave her a horrified look, dropped his hoe, and sprinted off into the fields.

Julia held back her tears and went up the stairs to put together a bundle for James.

℘

Ben — May 19, 1864

May 19 or 20 1864

My beautiful Friend,

I know not what the day is. We have come through such a terrible fight. If you have heard reports of "The Bloody Angle" in the newspaper, I was there. I saw many of my comrades reduced to lifeless corpses by forces that overcame our best made brestwerks. I must tell the truth that I was scared more than at any other time of my life. In the rain our weapons would not fire. Only by the grace of the Great God am I alive to rite to you. The fact is, the Stonewall Brigade is no more. we are so reduced in numbers that a small Brigade has been patched together from the leavings of the 33d and two or three others, Colonel Terry of the 4th Va, commanding.

My sweet heart, we are somewhere near what I think is the North Anna river. Mercifully, Grant's forces withdrew so that we could quit the vicinity of Spottsylvania, and before that, the wilderness.

I suffered a wound of no consicuence, which I will beg of you to kiss into wholeness when I return to the Valley. Before that may occur, you must agree to marry me. I beg this boon of you, sweet Ella Ruth. I can no longer go without a promise from you that you will be my own bride. I look at yor likeness ten times a day unless we are marching or fighting. It has a place of honor in my pock't over my heart. Each night I kiss the representation of yor lips in hopes that you will feel a ghost of mine upon yors. I beg again that you will give me yor heart and hand.

I close with a prayr that you are well and have enouf to eat and cloths to warm you. I kno what privation is. My heart fails me to think you may as well.

Accept a kiss and my everlasting love.

Yor Benj'n

ჽ

Mary — May 30, 1864

Mary read Rulon's brief letter again. *I wish I could be there to comfort him,* she thought. *He does sound very low. What can I do to brighten his spirits?*

A customer came into the store, sniffed at the scarcity of goods on the shelves, asked for eggs—of which Mary had none at that moment—and settled upon purchasing a jar of pickles that Mrs. Moore, the minister's wife, had exchanged for goods the previous week.

Mrs. Bingham and her three daughters brought in several loaves of fresh bread. The baker's wife traded for groceries, such as there were, and left with two of her daughters in tow, each carrying parcels. The youngest, Jessie, lingered behind, cradling her two parcels in one arm.

Mary smiled at her, and spoke. "Did you forget something, Miss Jessie?"

The girl ran the fingers of her free hand along the edge of the counter. "I wondered . . . I was wondering if y'all had heard anything of James."

"James Owen?"

"Yes, ma'am."

Mary almost giggled at being called *ma'am*. Most of the older matrons of Mount Jackson still called her *Miss Mary*, even after she'd been wed for three years with a little boy hugging her skirts. Instead, she put on a sober—but she hoped comforting—face and said, "We haven't yet. He's not been gone so long. I'm sure Mother Owen will bring word as soon as she receives a letter." Mary now smiled at the girl, recognizing the faraway look in her eyes. *I didn't know she was interested in young James.*

Jessie bent her head as though she made a curtsy, said, "Thank you, ma'am. You're most kind," and hurried out of the store.

Well, well. I hope the lad comes back, for Jessie's sake.

Mary arranged the vegetable display so that it seemed to hold more items, then cleaned a dusting of flour from the counter. Foodstuffs were so dear nowadays. She couldn't believe the cost of the peck of flour she had sold today. Of course the value of Confederate bills was inflated, but the war's cost wasn't only in lives lost.

As she sorted potatoes, she wondered how the Owen brothers were faring. She could only judge Ben's welfare from the aspect of Miss Allen's face whenever she dropped by the store, which wasn't often. He never had cause to write to Mary, and Mother Owen didn't impart news about him. She felt a twinge of sadness when she ran Peter's name through her mental countdown. His loss was still sorely felt on the farm. Carl? Carl was with Mosby, whose men seemed to lead a charmed existence. She actually had no idea where James had gone. She supposed he was with the infantry somewhere in eastern Virginia.

Father Owen had come into the store once when his company moved down the valley. He'd latched onto Roddy right away, and left with great reluctance, she'd judged.

She knew about Rulon's movements from his letters, and from the last one, he was well in body, but not doing well in his soul. She couldn't help sighing. *I must write something that will give him cheer*, she thought. Perhaps it was time to quit being a shy sister and let him know exactly what she planned for their reunion—behind closed doors—when this war had been won. An unfamiliar yearning filled her, a stirring that had long been dormant.

Mary closed her eyes. Yes. The time had come. She breathed deeply. Then she opened her eyes, went into the back room, and sat at the table. Writing paper was precious, but she determined to use as much as the task required to take Rulon's mind off his present sorrows.

ഇ

Ella Ruth — June 17, 1864

Ella Ruth stood on the edge of the road and eagerly attacked the letter she had only just picked up from the Hilbrands' store. Ben had written at last.

It began "My beautiful Friend." She smiled. Ben had so many ways of telling her how closely connected he felt to her. Her skin tingled to know that he counted her as his friend.

From there on to the end of the paragraph, his tone became so somber she wanted to weep. She had devoured news from the battle front, and had indeed heard of the Bloody Angle, where so many valiant Southern men had lost their lives. She had not found his name on the casualty lists, thank the good God, but from his words, he suffered nevertheless from the indignities and slaughter the Yankees had heaped upon the men of Virginia on home soil.

Sweet Ben, you are well away from the fray, she thought. Then she gasped to read he had been wounded, and clutched the letter to her bosom. How like him to discount the severity of his injury. He might have his heart half torn from his body and he would say, *it's of little consequence*. She shuddered, and resumed reading where he begged her to restore him to wholeness, upon condition of marrying him.

Her heart bounded with joy. She and Ben had skirted around the topic of a marriage ever since she had regained his trust. She knew from the top of her head to the tips of her toes that they were destined to marry one day, but he had not come right out and asked her until now. This very day. Actually, several weeks ago, but what did that matter? He was asking her to be his bride. No. He was *begging* her. She wanted to skip down the street, yell her news at the top of her lungs, and scandalize the entire neighborhood. Ben wanted to marry her!

She rejoiced that the sacrifice of her earrings had been for such an excellent reward, as he treasured her likeness as much as the wounded soldier in the hospital had done with that of his wife.

I will be Ben's wife! The very idea made her want to sing.

She read the final words with a bit less joy. *Privation.* Such a nasty word. She would not venture to recount to Ben the hardships on the home front. They would dishearten him at a time when she must instill joy into his heart as his letter had, overall, done in hers.

I will be Ben's wife, she repeated to herself. Nothing could take away the glory of that bright future promise. She took a step that, oddly enough, resembled a skip. How she wished the day were here when they would wed. She desired no friends or strangers to gawk at them, only their parents and families surrounding them with love and gladness to wish them well on their most happy day.

"Accept a kiss and my Everlasting love. Your Benj'n." She sighed and put the letter to her cheek to receive the kiss she imagined Ben had bestowed upon it. Maybe he hadn't actually done that. For all his sentimental talk, Ben was, after all, a man. In her experience of soldiers in the hospital, she had observed that men didn't always follow through with certain actions, especially if other men were close by. She had no idea how much privacy a soldier in camp could command. Perhaps they were crammed together like peas in a pod, arms constrained by the shoulders of comrades in arms.

"Even if you didn't kiss the letter, I will pretend that you did," she murmured to a far-off Ben, and hurried down the street, planning what she would write to tell him she would, indeed, marry him.

හ

Rulon — September 19, 1864

The battle had scarcely begun when Rulon heard bullets whizzing past his ears. Garth Von, riding on his left, rolled out a string of swear words. Most of the invective was directed at him, Rulon.

What did I do? he wondered, parrying a Yankee trooper's sabre blow with his own blade. He slashed at the next trooper to approach, Von's curses ringing in his ears.

" . . .your foppish feather!" Von screamed.

Feather? This animosity is about my plume? Rulon swept a different Federal cavalryman off his horse.

" . . .think you're a stinking officer!" Von added.

Dumbfounded, Rulon froze, but his horse shied, taking him just beyond the reach of the blue-coated Yankee whose sabre swished past his ear.

When he finally got his horse under control, Rulon found himself staring at the distant hills full of troopers and infantrymen as the heat of the battle moved elsewhere.

An artillery shell screamed overhead, and Rulon ducked reflexively. Wheeling around, he looked for Garth Von, but the man was not in sight. He rode toward his comrades gathered around the company's ragged guidon.

My feather. He envies me for that? It didn't make any sense that the man hated him so for want of a feather of his own.

He thought of Mary's father, presenting the stylish hat with such pride and pompous words. By now the hat was so bedraggled that he only wore the thing to keep the sun off his head. There was no fashion to it now. And the feather. *Great lands! That feather would make the ostrich weep.*

The company had been ordered into reserve. Rulon spotted Von in the midst of the pack, but rode silently back into position, keeping distance between himself and the man.

After an hour of waiting, Company "I" was put back into the battle. The squadron rode together, Garth Von among the men strung out in the line. Von hung back a slight bit, and Rulon, sensing danger from the scowling man, did so as well so he could keep the man in view.

A bugle blew for the charge, and Rulon put spurs to his mount. Again, bullets pinged around him. He felt a tug on his sleeve, but no pain. The ball had passed through the fabric. Then a horse shrieked and a man yelled obscenities as he fell. Rulon didn't dare turn to check who had lost his horse, for they were among the Yankee cavalry, slashing and parrying and being driven back. Soon they were retreating over ground they had held previously.

When they bivouacked that night up the valley at Fisher's Hill, Rulon looked around at the diminished company. Owen Leoyd was among the missing.

Overwhelming sadness tore at him. He'd fought beside Leoyd, rode around McClellan at his side, endured three-day vidette duties with him, and learned tricks from him that kept him alive.

It wasn't long before Rulon learned that Garth Von had survived the battle.

Von flew at him, a fist cocked. "It's your damn fault my horse is kilt, Owen," he raged. "Your damn swooping feather makes the Yankees think you're an officer."

Rulon fended him off, dancing backwards. "Hold on. The captains never said I was doing wrong to look like a cavalier. Why do you object?"

"The damn Yankees shoot at officers," Von answered, adding extra invective. "Anyone riding near you could be kilt."

Rulon snatched the now-bedraggled plume off his hat and stomped on it, but he knew the damage had been done long ago.

Von took a swing and missed as Rulon retreated. "You made me a camp dog," Von said. "I should have shot you dead the day you rode in wearing that ridiculous getup, thinking you was the King of Prussia."

"That's enough," Ren roared, coming up to the argument with a bandage around his sleeve. He pushed his way between Rulon and Von, and turning to Von, said, "Save that ire for the Federals. You'll need it. We've lost a fair amount of men, so go catch yourself a loose horse." He turned to Rulon. "Stay out of his way. They're coming for us tomorrow, I'll warrant."

$\wp$

Julia — October 7, 1864

When Clay burst into the front room, screeching like he'd been attacked by a lion, Julia dropped the shirt she was patching.

"Ma! Mr. Bates rode through. The Yankees are coming down the pike." He rubbed his neck. "They're taking the stock and burning the crops and harvests. Ma, they will surely burn the barn."

Julia stood. "Son. Quiet down. Let me think." She walked to the fireplace and put three fingers to her forehead. She tapped them, one at a time against skin and bone, thumping multiple times, the sound echoing like a horse crossing a bridge until her brain engaged and an idea came to her.

She took a breath and looked up. "Here's what to do. Get Albert and Marie." She looked at her youngest child, who had followed Clay into the room. "Anna, you go with them. Clay, all y'all drag out the corn sacks. Tie them closed. Put as many sacks on the backs of the cattle as they will tolerate. Tie them on secure. You don't want to spook them with shifting loads or they'll run off from you."

She laid a hand on his shoulder to steady his quaking frame. "When you finish up, take your brother and drive the cows up the mountain. Stay till the Yankees pass. I reckon you'll be there a few days, so I'll rustle up provisions for your stay." She squeezed his shoulder. "Go, you two. Get a wiggle on!"

Clay hesitated. "Mr. Bates said they're a mean bunch. They burned his house."

Julia set her jaw. That would not happen here. She shooed her son away and went to the kitchen. She fried the last of the pork skin to make cracklings, boiled eggs she'd been collecting from the last laying hen about the place, and wrapped corn pone in brown paper she had saved for stationery. No matter. Rod hadn't received but half of her letters. She would be spared the trouble of making ink from ground walnut hulls and stove soot. She never could achieve the proper fluid mixture to get it to flow smoothly from her nib anyhow.

She gathered the food and stuffed it into a carpetbag that would have to serve. She ran with it to the barn. Far to the south, smoke wreathed above the windbreak trees marking the lanes of their neighbors. The Yankees were coming.

The boys drove the dairy herd across the road and into the fields, riding after them on nearly the only horses left. Julia called after them, "Muffle that clattering bell or take it off." She and her daughters watched them go into the trees and down the creek bed, heading toward the Massanutten. She hoped her sons remembered the way to the hidden spot Rod used to take them to when hunting. It was their only hope for saving the herd and the corn.

She turned and stared down the pike. The smoke now billowed in black shafts in the distance. The Yankees were coming.

Julianna began to sob, tears coursing down cheeks smeared with corn silk and pollen from her labors.

"Stop that, child," Julia scolded, wiping the girl's face with her apron. "Show them your spirit, not your fear."

The three of them stood in the lane, waiting, watching as the Union soldiers advanced down the pike, marching unevenly as they came. Men broke out of the main body to torch the fields on each side. On they came. The Yankees were here.

❧

As the Union troops drew near enough that the soldiers started looking their way, Julia spoke in a low voice. "Girls, get to the house. I'm going to put a chair in the doorway and set down in it. Marie, bring me that Sharps rifle your pa left behind. Then you two stay upstairs unless I call you."

"Yes, Ma." Marie's voice quivered, but she turned her back and walked away to fetch the weapon.

"Mama, I'm scared." Julianna appeared to be keeping her tears in check, but her voice shook worse than Marie's had done.

"You will both be fine, Anna-girl. Just do as I tell you, mind?"

"Yes, Mama." She walked backward down the lane for a few paces, then turned and ran toward the house.

Julia walked backward herself for a few steps, then turned her back on the oncoming Union soldiers and strode toward her home, trying to give her daughters confidence in her, even if she barely felt any herself. The girls must not see her knees or her hands shake. Mothers must be brave in the face of danger.

She let the sight of the burning fields and the knowledge that her barn would likely be destroyed build indignation, then irritation, and finally anger in her. By the time she saw the Yankees coming toward her home, she sat in her rocker, holding the rifle down at her side, hidden by her skirt and apron, and she was in a righteous rage. Let a Yankee try to disturb her home. He would think twice before he attacked a southern woman's abode again.

"Mama!"

Marie hardly ever called her "Mama" these days. Something must be wrong to bring her down the stair in disobedience to instructions.

"Marie?"

"I tied Sheba in the barn. She'll burn up, Mama."

"Stay here."

"I can't leave her to die!" Marie slipped through the small space between Julia and the door jamb and set off toward the barn.

"No! Come back, daughter."

Marie glanced over her shoulder, but kept going.

Julia, faced with approaching soldiers bearing torches, didn't know which she should do first, drive the Yankees away from the house and her daughter upstairs, or get Marie and the dog out of the barn. She turned to gauge how close the soldiers had come. One man was intent upon torching the trees along the lane. She ground her teeth. Those trees broke the wind. They didn't bear any fruit. This was an unruly bunch. Three more soldiers brought their firebrands straight toward her. Her indecision past, she arose, kicked the rocker backward into the room, raised the rifle, and pointed it at the nearest man.

"Drop your torch. My home won't burn."

"Now ma'am," the soldier under her eye said, "we've got orders to take your crop."

"There's no crop here. Move yourself back."

"Ma'am. You do yourself no good turn holding a weapon on us," he said, his voice a little shaky as he looked down her barrel.

She raised her voice a mite. "Git off my property. Turn around and go!"

"We can't do that, little lady," another man said, approaching the first. He edged out of her vision, then broke into a run toward the barn. The third soldier joined him, and the tree-burner came closer by the second.

Julia could feel the heat coming from the trees. The snapping of the fire reminded her of pistols cracking in the distance. She couldn't contain all the men, couldn't leave the first man unguarded to deter the others.

"Marie!" she screamed, knowing she dared not turn her head. "My girl's in that barn," she told the man under her gun, knowing she was pleading, hating herself for doing so.

"Sam!" he barked. "Let the girl clear out."

As the man spoke, she noticed several stripes on his uniform sleeve. She had picked a sergeant to threaten. Was that good, bad? He had some part of decency in him, judging from his last words.

"You can destroy the barn." Her voice sounded strident, but she couldn't do anything about that. "Leave me my home and my girl."

She heard the report of a rifle and Marie's shriek, then a wail. She almost looked in her daughter's direction, but kept her eyes on the sergeant. If Marie had voice, she was alive.

"Your men will shoot a defenseless girl?"

The sergeant flicked a glance in the direction of the barn. "She's whole, ma'am," he reported, looking relieved, but at the same time, disgusted.

"Just tormenting her, then?"

"No ma'am," he said in a low voice. "He shot the dog."

Julia heard herself crying, out of control, losing herself in pain.

"Ma'am, you need to lower that rifle and go inside," the sergeant pleaded. "We have to be about our business."

Marie was thrust against her then, momentarily throwing off her aim. The barrel of her rifle dipped, and the sergeant took the opportunity to escape toward the barn.

"Mama. Sheba." Marie sobbed, then leaned against her, gasping and scrubbing the tears from her eyes with balled fists.

"Inside," Julia managed to say, and shoved the girl behind her. She backed through the doorway, waving the barrel of the rifle from side to side. Once clear of the doorway, she slammed and bolted the door.

"Mama. Why didn't you shoot them?" Marie asked in a broken voice.

Julia took several breaths, fighting the weakness of her knees until she got the rocker upright and sank into it, laying the weapon across her lap.

"It's not loaded," she said, her voice sounding like a raven's caw.

Chapter 24
Rulon — October 9, 1864

The base of the hill bristled with dismounted men waiting for action behind stone fences. Under a sky lightened by dawn, Rulon watched the skirmishers from the brigade move forward across the meadow toward Tom's brook. Behind him on the hill, wheels squeaked as artillerymen dragged the guns of the battery around, bringing them to bear on General Custer's cavalry. Rumor said the Yankees were finally going to fight back.

The 1st Virginia and other regiments in the brigades had harried Custer's retreating troopers for the last few days. The Union general had not turned his men and given them tit for tat, but had continued down the Valley, relying on his rearguard to keep General Rosser at bay. Yesterday, it seemed that Custer's patience had finally grown thin enough to let his boys give them a fight, but they had only engaged in a brief skirmish along the Back Road.

A shell whistled overhead from the rear. The battery had sent a message amongst the horses lined up in the distance, hazy through smoke. On a hill to the north, an echoing gun boomed to hurl disdain their way.

Damn the Yankees! It wasn't enough they had put in the ground all the decent men he'd served with the past years? Now they had busied themselves burning barns, mills, crops, and even the occasional abode, making his country a barren wasteland under a pall of smoke. How could God allow it?

He heard a groan, glanced at the fellow crouching beside him, then discovered he had made the sound himself. *Rulon, find your mettle,* he chided himself, but still groaned again. He knew he'd lost a great deal of courage the day General Stuart had been mortally wounded at Yellow Tavern. He ground his teeth to keep from crying out again at the waste. The glorious General gone. He bowed his neck under the pain.

That same day, he had lost his well-trained bay horse, shot from under him as he parried a sabre thrust with the stock of his rifle. Although toppling with the dying horse had saved his life, the loss was much to bear. He'd kept the horse healthy longer than he would have thought possible. Now his mount was a plow horse, ill-fitted for battle.

He took a deep breath to settle himself, then regretted it as he went into a spell of coughing to clear smoke from his lungs. When he had finished, he shivered as though a ghost had stepped on his grave. *Has God turned His face away from my country?*

Gone were the men who had ridden alongside him, fought beside him, shared a tent, tended fire, cooked rations. First Owen Leoyd had fallen, then Ren Lovell. *Good old Ren.* He shook his head. He doubted he would have survived his first days in the Troop without him. All were gone save one. Garth Von.

He almost let loose with a mighty curse, but managed to restrain himself at the last moment. He hated the loathsome, evil man.

Thinking about Von, one hand went to his head, to the once-fine hat Mary's father had presented to him with great ceremony. He jammed the filthy head-gear tighter onto his head, glad that he'd stomped the plume into the dust. If he had known the trouble it would bring him, he would have torn off the feather the second he left Mary behind. He remembered the strong emotion on her face as he and the company paraded through Mount Jackson in their splendid array, horses lined up just so, backs straight, heads up, off to beat the Yankee foe.

Oh Mary. He bent his head to mask his face. He missed her above all else. Even though they'd been here in the Valley since—when had it been? August? It was so hard to account for the days, let alone the months anymore. Even though the cavalry had passed through Mount Jackson what seemed like countless times, going up, going down, chasing or being chased, he had not been able to so much as rein in his horse and throw a kiss to his wife. War had robbed him of that simple pleasure. War occupied his every waking moment. Only at night could he spare Mary a thought, touch her likeness, and dream of the future. Would there be a future?

A great weariness swept him. How long had it been since he had eaten a home-cooked meal? Slept on a mattress tick filled with soft goose feathers and down? Held Mary in his arms?

He took a shallow breath, wary now of the smoke filling the countryside. He despised the mindless carnage, the cold and the heat and the dying, and being apart from his wife. He hated the war.

But much as he hated Garth Von and the war, he hated the Yankees more. They had given provocation from the first, invading his native land with their immense armies, but now their actions went beyond the pale as they proved themselves to be ravishers of the land.

As the sky brightened more, Rulon could see in the countryside below where smoke hung low over still-flickering flames. Damn Phil Sheridan! For the last three days, the Yankees had carried out their general's orders to burn, to ruin, to destroy.

How many houses had gone up in smoke and flames? Did Mary have a place to lay her head? Anger curled up from his toes, much as the smoke curled upward from the hay stacks off to the right. Pillagers! Vandals! Whatever provisions they could not use for themselves, they were leaving in ashes so Early's men and the Valley's inhabitants would starve.

Rulon thought of his little boy, the son he had never met. As though it rose upward, caused by friction through resistance from his clenched muscles, white heat seared his belly. The Yankees were starving his son! Surely God did not intend for this to happen? Sheridan and his minions could only be fiends from the deepest hell.

Smoke danced before his eyes, burning them. His stomach churned with fury as he waited for Yankees to come so he could kill them. The hardship to his baby would be avenged.

಄

The charge came suddenly, as Custer's men, their throats raising a cry of challenge, came out of the smoke at a gallop, sabres aloft. Rulon expected the men around him to mount at any moment to counter the Yankee charge, but instead, they remained dismounted, ordered to make a stand behind this stone wall to defend the line.

Is Rosser mad to keep us dismounted? The company, indeed, the whole brigade, would be swept before the fury of Custer's cavalry.

But the command had come down the line, and Rulon obediently shouldered his weapon. The 1st Virginia held the left flank, and if they were turned . . . He didn't want to think about the consequences.

Somewhere to the front, cannon boomed. Where were their answering guns? He looked over his shoulder. The battery stood silent, men lying broken around the guns. As he turned back to the front, a cry went up at the end of the line. Custer's troopers came on at their front, approaching with blood in their eyes, but the canny cavalier also had sent another unit to flank them. It was breaking through. It threatened what remained of the battery. It threatened them.

Rulon shivered. Fear flooded into his throat. The Yankees were in front and behind him.

A man or two threw themselves onto their mounts and rode off to the right. The bugler sounded retreat, and they kept on going. Soon, the trickle became a torrent, as the Yankees beat them back from their position.

He fought to find his horse, the nag he'd liberated after he found it chomping grass in a meadow. He reached it at last, threw himself into the saddle, and followed the others. Cannon boomed behind him and he pulled the fleeing horse to the left to avoid a shower of canister. He wondered if he would ever see Mary's face in this life again.

"Owen! Mind your back!"

Rulon did not know who screamed the warning. Mr. Earl? He pivoted in his saddle in time to grab hold of Garth Von's arm above the wrist with both hands before the man could stab him in the kidney.

The knife now veered toward his ribs, but Rulon jerked the arm sideways. In doing so, he unseated Von, but the man's falling weight served to drag him off his own mount. He fell heavily onto his side, still gripping Von's forearm. A shell ripped the air above them.

It had come to this: close combat with a supposed comrade under fire of the enemy.

He held on, struggling to best the man, sensing that if he did not come off victorious, it would mean the death of him.

Von got a foot up and kicked, aiming his holey boot at Rulon's jaw.

He twisted away, and they rolled, fury driving both of them, fueling a desperate engagement that never should have come about. All because of a feather.

Von clawed at Rulon's eyes with his free hand. Rulon evaded the gouging fingers and butted his forehead into the man's breastbone, felt it give. Von howled, cursing and exerting himself to rise, hauling Rulon to his feet as well.

Hampered by the need to keep the knife away from his gizzard, Rulon attempted to swing the man, to shake him until he dropped the wicked blade. He thought he was succeeding when the world exploded into scarlet and black, reducing Von to bits while shards of metal pierced his own chest and belly in multiple places.

A massive force threw him onto his back against the unforgiving surface of the road as shattered bone splinters and gouts of blood spattered him. He thought that he clutched the man's arm still, but its lightness refuted the notion as implausible. The knife dropped from the hand at last, and he heaved a sigh of relief, even as he slipped into the timeless world beneath the blare of battle.

&

Rulon — October 12, 1864

Rulon awoke with nightmares haunting his memory. Drenched in sweat, he endeavored to put the cursed visions into a deep pocket of his brain, but they escaped to torment his wakeful moments. It seemed he had been traveling in a wagon, but he wasn't the driver. He was inside, lying down on a rough pallet of burlap, trapped within canvas sidewalls that blocked the light of the sun but encased him in heat and misery.

Other unfortunate souls lay next to him, moaning each time the wagon took a bump on what must have been a very primitive path. He was horrified to discover that the loudest voice crying out was his own as pain, no, agony thrust a thousand spears into his chest and belly with each jolt. Finally, darkness came upon him.

Later, he battled the sensation that someone took him by the feet and pulled him toward the rear of the rickety vehicle. Another person lifted his shoulders seconds before he would have fallen headfirst to the ground. The two carried him a distance while he writhed in distress.

Rulon fought to subdue remembrance of the nightmare, but it only skipped forward. He found himself half-lying in a muddy ditch. Was he dead? No. Pain refuted that notion. He moved slightly and his head slipped downward on the muck and splashed into water, which immediately entered his nose. He sputtered frantically, trying to raise his head out of the murky liquid, but seemed to have no ready muscles in his torso. That part of his body cried out to die to escape the constant attacks from sharp instruments. In a moment, he discovered that his arms were whole, and succeeded in using them to raise his face above the surface of the water.

He opened his mouth and sucked air into his lungs, greedy to prolong his life. Yes, that was it. He wanted to live. Despite the immense pain inhabiting his body, he was not ready to die.

"Mary," he whispered. "I want to live."

"Shush, shush," she replied.

Stillness enveloped him at the sound of her voice. He opened his eyes to a dim space lit by one candle. Alas! He was dead after all. Mary's shimmering face hovered over him. She must have called him to join her in death.

He struggled against the thought, the despair that encompassed him at the notion. No. That wasn't right. He'd received no word that Mary had passed to Eternity. As far as he knew, she was alive. Did that mean—?

He tried to sit, found it impossible, struggled to focus and hold on to the spot of candlelight through the great wash of pain.

A glass pressed against his lips, forcing them open. A bitter liquid assailed his tongue. He struggled against swallowing, but a soft voice whispered, "Take the laudanum, dear husband," and a soft hand stroked his throat until he did so.

Could it be true that Mary had come here to nurse him? Where was *here*? How had he escaped the watery grave? Soon he felt himself slip into darkness, soothed by soft whispers of "There, there. I'll be here when you wake."

৪০

Mary — October 12, 1864

"Papa. We must have the small house. Rulon cannot abide all the noise here."

"What would you have me do?" her father asked. "Boot the Yankee company out on their ears?"

"They will go soon. Everyone says they are pushing up the Valley."

Mr. Hilbrands stroked his chin. He patted his stomach beneath his store apron. "It will be filthy."

"I will clean it somehow. He must have quiet. Have you seen the—" She broke off, afraid she would lose her supper if she thought long upon the horrible wounds in Rulon's body.

He patted her shoulder, nodding. "I marvel that he yet lives."

"He came home to me." She looked at her father, and began to shake. "I owe him a pleasant place to die." Her voice broke. "Roddy will be fatherless! Oh Papa!"

He wrapped his arms around her, holding her tight. "There now. I'm sure we can find someone to clean up the mess." He smoothed her hair. After a while, he held her at arm's length and peered down at her. "You go see to your husband now. He is still strong at the core. He's Rod Owen's son, after all."

Mary sniffled and wiped her eyes with a soft bit of worn fabric. Yes, and Mother Owen's as well. Perhaps she would not need to find walnut husks to dye her dress black. Perhaps she could bring him through this nightmare.

∞

Rulon — October 15, 1864

Rulon came out of blackness and into pain. Thrashing against whatever held his wrists immobile, he opened his eyes to slits, looking about for relief.

He spied purple fabric. Maybe it was a skirt. Where had he seen it before? He thought perhaps it had something to do with his wife, but couldn't look up far enough to see if she was encased within it.

"Rulon, husband," he heard. "Calm yourself. Are you in pain?"

He made a noise. Was he whimpering? He closed his eyes. *Dear God*, he begged, *don't let me cry*.

He felt a light touch on his shoulder. "I will return shortly, dear husband," came Mary's voice. He knew it now. How long had it been since he had heard her speak his name? Was there a burr of tears overlaying the sound?

Soon he heard a rustle of cloth. Mary must have sat beside him. She put a spoon between his lips and tilted rancid liquid into his mouth. She did it several times, and he swallowed, under the power of her urgings.

It was laudanum again. He hated the taste. At the same time, he yearned for the stupor and surcease from pain he knew would come soon. Mary took his hand, and he clung to it before the drug began its work, beset all the while by the stabbing knives of the injuries, feeling every chunk of the foreign objects lodged in his body. He recalled a moment of twilight when a surgeon had reckoned him to be a dead man and had barely closed the wounds with a score of stitches. He had not wasted a pain-killer or a slug of liquor on the patient.

Rulon remembered receiving the stitches. No man should have such a memory.

He waited to sink into the numbness of the narcotic slumber, anxious for the agony to be gone.

"Papa?"

Whose was that tiny, piping voice? It called him "Papa." Who could it be?

"This is your son, my husband," Mary whispered, as though she guessed his perplexity. "We call him Roddy."

Tiny fingers touched the back of his other hand, no more than a feather's stroke.

His boy. His son!

Rulon struggled to open his eyes. Through slits he saw him, dark curls framing his cherubic face. The wonder of creation that began so long ago. His son.

"Roddy?" he whispered, aware that moisture seeped down his cheek.

"Please Papa. You must get well," the small voice quavered, then the boy reached up and kissed Rulon's cheek.

"Come, child. Leave your papa to rest," another woman's voice said.

Someone in a brown dress took the lad by the hand and led him from the room.

Rulon closed his eyes. He had made that wondrous creature, he and Mary. Out of their union had come the miracle that was their son.

Would he live to take Mary into his arms again? He tried to squeeze her hand, but felt the effects of the laudanum overcoming him at last. Even as the pain faded, he felt robbed of that expression of affection between them.

Chapter 25

Ben — October 19 through 20, 1864

Why is it always my leg? Ben wondered, fighting to reach something to tie around the wound. This wasn't like the inconsequential leg injury he had suffered before. This one was bleeding to beat the band, and he had to stop it.

He discovered his belt would do to wrap around the leg above the flow. Now he had to get out of the field before the Yankees renewed their attack, pressed forward, and captured him.

He struggled to his feet, bearing his weight upon his rifle. The leg was not broken, he was relieved to discover. He looked around him. A body or two lay in the field below, but the losses weren't great this time. His company had left him, it appeared, as he was the only one of his fellows still here. Perhaps the shot had come from one of his own comrades?

Hunched over, he dragged his unresponsive leg and the rest of himself toward a hill covered with broken apple trees. Not the best cover, but perhaps it would serve until he located his company or someone who could take him to a surgeon to stitch him up. Once he achieved the shelter of the trees, he would allow himself to rest and survey the ground.

Fortunately, the rails of the fence surrounding the orchard were missing, so he didn't have to make a struggle to climb over. He found a spot high on the side of the hill where he could keep watch for anyone passing, and sat down with his back against a trunk. He promptly fell asleep.

Night came before he awoke. He could see campfires of the Federal troops off to the north, but the hill impeded his sight to the south. How far could the company have retreated before it stopped to regroup?

He checked his leg by moonlight. The bleeding seemed to have ceased, and he loosened the belt so the flesh would not die. Good. The wound was crusted over, and the flow of blood did not begin anew.

Where was he? He couldn't be far from Mount Jackson, or maybe his own home, but he had lost track of his precise location. Who still had an apple orchard that hadn't been entirely cut down for fuel? A rich man, he presumed, with enough slave hands to keep shivering soldiers at bay.

It wasn't possible that he was on the Allen farm, was it? What a comedown if he were to be lying in an orchard owned by his girl's father. He sighed, turned to get a better position, and went back to sleep.

He awoke at dawn, ravenous and in pain. He wondered if he had been moaning. He hoped not. He didn't want some darkie to come upon him and drag him to the Massa for trespassing.

He attempted to rise so he could move on south, and almost made it, but weakness and pain prevailed and he had to sit in a heap and husband his forces for another try.

Before he could do it, he heard a pistol clicking to full cock behind him.

"Do not move," came a voice. Feminine. "I will shoot you if you do not raise your hands."

He did so. "I'm wounded," he ventured. "You a Yankee?"

"Damn the Yankees to hell!" the voice replied, breaking a bit on the expletive. "Who are you?"

"Benjamin Owen, Company, Company. . . . I don't rightly know what company I'm in anymore. Was in the 33rd Virginia Infantry Regiment, but I've been sent hither and yon until I give up knowin'."

"Wait. Wait! Did you say 'Benjamin Owen'?"

"I did."

"From Allen's Infantry?"

"Yes, in the beginning."

"Ben?" Skirts rustled as the woman came into view. She laid the pistol down and dropped to her knees. "Ben?" she shrieked. "Oh, my Benjamin."

She was crying now, but underneath the mob cap, Ben recognized the gaunt features of Miss Ella Ruth Allen.

ℐ

Ben — October 20, 1864

"Jerusalem crickets!" he said as she fell upon him. "I scarce can believe it."

She held him tightly, rocking him back and forth, crooning his name.

"Mind the leg," he petitioned as her knee slid across his thigh. He gritted his teeth to avoid crying out.

She pulled back. "You are hurt? My poor Benjamin. Let me look."

"I'd druther you didn't," he said. "I told you I was wounded at the outset. Get me to a surgeon."

"I do not know where one is to be found who is not engaged in treating others," she said. "However, I have worked at the hospital under my uncle's eye. I can help you."

He wilted under the force of her assurances, and the pain, besides. "Go ahead. I can't bear the pain much longer."

Ella Ruth began by trying to open the hole in his trousers that had been cut by the Yankee ball sufficiently wide enough to assess the wound, but could not get a good look.

"Ben," she said, a bit timidly. "You will have to shuck your britches."

"The devil you say!"

"I cannot see the wound. I am sorry, but if I cannot see it, I cannot find the ball to remove it."

Ben shook his head. "No. Get me under a roof and bring me something to wrap about myself, and I'll decide then what course to take."

"You are so stubborn," she declared, sighing.

"I've quit bleeding. Help me rise, and shelter me in the shed or the stable." He held up his arm to be steadied by her. "Besides, you have no instruments here."

"All right. The old nursery shed is closest." She picked up the pistol, uncocked it, then helped him rise. "Lean on me, Ben. I can bear your weight."

"I doubt it."

"Yes I can. I have had lots of practice walking men about in the hospital."

She grunted a bit when he slung his arm around her shoulder and leaned on her. Despite his sleep, he was exhausted, and panted with the exertion of forward movement.

"Are you still in pain?" she asked a bit later as she bore him slowly along.

"A mite," he lied through gritted teeth, trying to use the rifle as a crutch. "Some little bit," he amended after a few more steps. As they neared the goal, he finally admitted, "More than I'd like to say."

"Oh Ben," she wailed, then tsked several times with her tongue. "Do not tell me lies. I must know your state before I endeavor to fish out the ball."

"You're not a surgeon, Ella Ruth."

"No, but I have seen many balls removed from wounds by my uncle and other surgeons. I believe I can do the task." She propped him against a work bench used in former times to prepare apple grafts. "Hold onto that rail," she commanded. "I shall return in no time at all with assistance."

"Leave me the pistol," he said. "It looks heavy."

"It is heavy, and I can shoot it," she said, and kept it with her as she hurried off.

Ben sank into a semi-dazed state while he waited for her to return. Perhaps she would think better of her plan and bring someone else to perform a surgery on him. Or mayhap she would find a vehicle to cart him to the hospital, if it wasn't within Yankee lines now.

After a time that seemed interminable, Ella Ruth came back with her arms full, but no one else accompanying her. Hadn't she mentioned seeking someone's assistance? Instead, she carried two tattered but clean-looking blankets, a handful of kitchen utensils, a roll of bandage, and most of a bottle of whiskey. She had donned an apron to cover her skirt and bodice, and the handle of the pistol poked out of a pocket.

"Where are your pa and ma? Did you tell them I'm here?" he asked, concerned that she had not brought anyone back with her to help attend to his wound.

Ella Ruth made a face. "They removed themselves to Charlottesville, but I refused to accompany them."

"You did what?" He felt a fever rising as he spoke sharply to her.

"You must be quiet, Ben. Your face is looking very pale. I fear you have lost a great deal of blood." She placed the items in her arms on the bench, then spread one blanket on the floor of the shed. She cocked her head to one side, then said, "No, I believe it is better if you lie on the work bench so you are high enough to tend to." Moving the items to the floor, she retrieved the first blanket, shook it with a snap to free it of dirt and straw, and spread it upon the bench as best she could with him leaning over it. Breathing rapidly, she surveyed her work. "Ben, you must get atop the bench with my help alone. We do not have any male darkies about. The ungrateful wretches all ran off to the enemy when the Yankees started up the Valley this year."

He groaned, half from disbelief that she persisted in her notion that she could tend him, and half from pain.

She glanced around the shed. "Oh, that stool will help," she said, going to a corner of the building and bringing it back. "Darling Ben, I knew I must be here if you came through. How else could we marry? Besides, Uncle Joseph had need of me at the soldier's hospital." She put her arms around Ben's chest and assisted him in mounting the stool and climbing onto the bench.

Ben's head felt as though he had already drunk the whiskey, as a profound lightness was affecting his reasoning. He must be crazed to think about letting this girl do an operation on him. But what recourse did he have? She seemed to be the only person about the place, and mayhap her uncle's skill ran in the family.

"Are you here alone, then?" he managed to ask. That would account for her fondness for keeping the pistol with her.

"No. One of the darkies, my maid Lula, stayed to care for me. She was rather mortified that I refused to go as a refugee with my parents, but I'm very glad she decided to stay with me. She is making you a bit of gruel."

"You are a caution, girl," he said, and that was all he could whisper as he lapsed into blackness.

๕

When Ben awoke, his leg throbbed abominably, but he seemed not to have any fever. His stomach grated against his backbone, he was so hungry. Lying on the bench, covered by the second blanket, he felt vulnerable, and struggled to rise, but gave up the attempt because of the pain it caused.

He looked around. He was alone. His rifle and accoutrements lay heaped in a jumble by the wall. What was that cloth? As he was puzzling out the question, he recognized the patchwork handiwork on the fabric. Jerusalem crickets! His trousers!

He groaned. He did not recall having removed them. That could only mean Ella Ruth had done so. Embarrassment flooded his thoughts and his hands clutched at the blanket. He had quit wearing underclothes when the last pair to his name became holey enough to let the breezes through. Had Ella Ruth been so fully caught up in her self-appointed task that she had accidentally or willfully gazed upon his parts?

Her bold actions in the last few hours confirmed to him that her streak of doggedness, her obdurate, unyielding nature had not changed. Gaining her way was of great importance to her. Whatever he wanted could go hang.

But yet, she may have saved his life by her persistence. Removing a poisonous lead ball from a wound was of equal importance to modesty, wasn't it? He chewed on that notion for a few moments. Would Ma be scandalized or practical about the matter? She had always appeared to have a direct conduit to God and His ideas of proper conduct. What advice would Ma give him, if he were to have the courage to ask for it?

The unseemly viewing had most likely taken place. He had an uncomfortable sense that this fell into the "offense to God" department. As soon as he could get around, even before he sought to rejoin his company, he would have to seek out a minister.

These circumstances accelerated the need for their wedding to take place as soon as may be. Otherwise, he could not make the matter right and assuage these overwhelmingly guilty feelings.

As he was musing on where he would get money to pay for a ceremony—which most likely cost more nowadays than the two dollars Rulon had paid over—Ella Ruth came through the shed door, bearing a bowl covered with a cloth.

"I'm sorry I don't have a tray for your food," she apologized. "The pewter was melted down ages ago for munitions, and Momma took the silver with her."

Ben eyed the bowl. "No matter. I'm starving, girl."

She came to the bench, propped him up, and handed him the food. "It is only corn gruel, but we do not have much in the way of provisions. Does your wound pain you?"

He paused between shoveled spoonsful. "Yes, a mite."

"I have whiskey left over from cleaning out the injury. When you have finished eating, I will give you a portion to dull the pain."

Ben wanted to finish eating before he got onto the tricky subject of clothing removal and its consequences. When he had scraped the dish clean, he handed it back to her. At least his stomach felt better for the food, if not for the nerves.

As she helped him lie back on the bench, he racked his brain for a suitable opening to the topic. He couldn't merely blurt out a question about how much of him she had seen. Perhaps he could approach in a sideways fashion.

"I'm obliged to you for tending my wound," he began. "I reckon I need the limb for later."

"Indeed," she said, giving him a smile.

"As soon as it can bear weight, I must take myself back to the army." No, that wasn't right. The pain must have muddled his brain, and he'd completely gone astray from speaking of the obligation they had to marry.

He noticed that Ella Ruth had stopped smiling.

"Remember what I promised you? You were quite insistent about the matter."

"Of course." What, exactly, was she thinking about amongst all the things they had written about?

"You are here now. You are injured, which is unfortunate, but my hope is that you will recover, given time and rest."

"I am agreed with that notion. I don't want to be reported absent without leave, though. I'm not a deserter."

"Then do not desert me."

He thought about her words for a long time. How had this conversation gone off from his planned topic of discussion? The silence stretched on. It was his turn to speak, and Ella Ruth was clearly waiting for him to do so.

"I don't intend to desert you." He had to get back on track. He swallowed. "I do have a question."

"Ask it, Ben."

He cleared his throat. What a fix he was in. The words he needed didn't appear as he had hoped. Where had his gift for fine words gone? All his charms had gone missing. Finally, he blurted out, "How much of me was uncovered and in your sight during the wound-tending?"

Oh, shame! He'd gone and done what he had determined not to do. He covered his eyes with his wrist, then let the arm fall to his side.

"Darling Ben," Ella Ruth said, after a very long time. "I caught sight of all of you." She stopped, and he could see her throat moving in a swallow of her own. When she continued, her voice had acquired a huskiness that he found no less disturbing than her words. "My work with Uncle Joseph obliged me to nurse men with injuries in every possible place. I suppose I have no reputation at all, anymore." She inhaled deeply before she went on. "You may find me unattractive, now that you know I have seen other men's most intimate parts."

Certainly not. Even in her gaunt, war-worn state and well-laundered attire, she was lovely as could be. A yearning for her began to grow, but he squashed it in order to set matters back on an orderly course.

"I've compromised you, girl."

"I just told you—"

"We must be wed, and soon."

"I have washed those men."

He shuddered. "For the honor of Virginia."

"As I have you," she said in a halting voice.

"No," he moaned.

"Yes. There was blood everywhere."

"We have to marry now. Today. Is Mr. Moore in the town?" He struggled to sit up, and his agitation gave him the strength to achieve that end.

"Ben, lie quiet."

"You must send the woman for the minister."

"He is gone, Ben. He was arrested by the Yankees for preaching against them."

"The Dunker preacher?"

"Dead."

"The German—"

"There is no one, Ben. We cannot have a church ceremony."

"But you saw—"

"I do not care." She lifted her chin a slight bit. "I have pledged myself to you, as you have to me. I promised to marry you, but we cannot have a regular ceremony. Let us make marriage vows to each other, Ben. That will put things right."

"Ella." He could hardly speak for the pain in his soul. "We must marry. Bring the judge."

"He went for a soldier."

"The mayor."

"He is gone."

"There is truly no one around?"

"Only the armies."

He clutched at a straw. "Can an officer—"

"I do not know, Ben." She shook her head. "General Early has gone south, and I will not be married by a Yankee."

That prospect alarmed him. He could be captured and sent off to a prison. Exhausted, he let himself sink back onto the blanket. He had to make Ella Ruth his wife, but his options seemed to have run out.

Chapter 26
Ella Ruth — October 20, 1864

Ella Ruth leaned forward and laid her forehead on Ben's chest. He put an arm over her shoulders. *He is in such a weakened state. Does he know how much blood he lost?* She thought not.

She turned her head slightly until she could see a part of his face. He was not looking at her, but at the roof above them. Such a puny roof. It leaked abominably, and she feared for his health if she kept him hidden here in the shed.

I need to move him to the house. He won't last in this rain and cold.

How was she to manage that? Would Lula help her? Could she count on the woman's loyalty if the Yankees came up the Valley again, or would the servant reveal Ben's presence? Lula had been a trifle uppity the last time Ella Ruth spoke with her. *Best not to take the chance.*

She took a deep breath and expelled it slowly. How many more obstacles to keeping Ben safe did she have to overcome?

Her mind skipped to her main concern. How were they to marry?

All the answers she had given to Ben's half-frantic questions were true. There was no religious or civil authority left to say any words over them, to sanction the union they had promised to make.

She felt a welling sadness rise from her middle. She wanted what Mary Owen had. The husband, even though he be horribly wounded. The child. The name. She no longer cared about the external appearances, the magnificent clothing and pomp of a church ceremony. She only wanted this man, her Ben, to hold her close, to caress her, to make her his woman.

What did words matter? They could say words, whisper to each other vows of fealty and devotion. She would promise whatever he wanted, if he would give her his name and his child.

A thought came to her mind, an image from her early childhood. The darkies had held a celebration she did not understood at the time. Now the meaning came clear to her, vivid in its import. Denied a Christian marriage ceremony, the slaves had devised their own.

"We will jump the broomstick," she murmured against Ben's shirt.

He lifted his head. "That's the Negro way."

"It's the only way," she whispered. "The only way left to us."

She saw that he would shake his head, and stopped him with a brief kiss on his cheek. "We can have a minister when this awful war ends," she whispered. "In the meantime, I will become your wife in the same way our servants have done."

"Ella—"

She cut him off. "Poppa always looked on such unions as legal. He considered the couple married. He wouldn't sell off one or the other and put them apart."

Ben rested his head on the bench, stared at the roof again. "We must do right."

"This will be right for us," she answered. "You want to marry me. I want you . . . to marry me," she added in a husky voice. "This is our solution."

"The minute Mr. Moore comes back—"

"We will have words said in the regular way," she promised, kissing his cheek again to seal the bargain.

℘

Ben — October 21, 1864

The next day at noon, Ella Ruth brought Ben a plate heaped with applesauce, what could be mashed potatoes or maybe turnips, and one little piece of meat of an indeterminate origin.

"Did you eat today?" he asked her.

She tilted her head and smiled, shrugging one shoulder in a coquettish manner.

"Well then, we will share," he said, and cut into the meat substance to divide it.

She tried to refuse, but he stared her down until she opened her mouth and accepted a bite from his fork.

"You really are a caution, Benjamin," she said in the old voice full of lightness and charm. "You need the nourishment to overcome that terrible injury."

He knew what she said was true, but seeing her face, so thin and drawn, tore at his sense of the right way to treat a lady, and his notion of who should go first in matters of polite society.

When he had consumed what he deemed was his fair share of the meal, he gave the leavings to Ella Ruth, and insisted that she finish the food.

She did so under protest, and then set the plate aside.

"I must change the dressing on your wound," she said.

His heart pounded with anxiety. "I don't reckon it's been bleeding or nothing of the sort," he said. "You don't need to bother."

"I know more than you about treating a variety of wounds, Ben." It was her turn to stare him down, and she did it with relish. "I will mind your sensibilities, but the flesh must be inspected for infection." She began to lift his blanket.

He cringed.

Noticing it, she said, "Benjamin! Your brother Rulon recently took a number of wounds from an exploding shell. He's struggling to survive from the effects of putrefying flesh. You don't want that sort of problem, do you?"

"Rulon's hurt? Lordy, I must go to him!"

"You are much too weak for that. Besides, the Yankees are still in the area. I cannot get you to Mount Jackson."

"Cannot, or will not?"

"I cannot. Truly. Please trust me, Ben. Have I not proven myself to you by now?" Tears started into her eyes, and she appeared to be on the verge of weeping.

"There now, don't you go to crying, sweet girl. He made a hand sign of resignation. "Look at the wound all you want, but don't take any notions of, of—" He stopped, unable to speak further.

Ella Ruth took a shuddering breath. "I will be circumspect, my love."

She raised the blanket enough to get a good field of vision of the wound site, and proceeded to take off the bandage she had applied previously.

Ben looked down his body at her busy hands, noting that they did not stray into forbidden areas. Since that issue was settled, he thought about the news Ella Ruth had sprung on him. Rulon was fighting for his life. The notion brought a sweep of nausea upon him. His next younger brother was gone. He couldn't bear to lose his big brother, too.

A sharp pain interrupted his worries about Rulon. "Ow!" He should have kept an eye on Ella Ruth's ministrations. She seemed to be probing his flesh with some cold metal implement. No, she was *cutting* his flesh! "Ella! For the love of—"

"Shush, Ben. Act the part of a man. I must remove this infection or you could lose the leg." Her look was stern, but quite concerned, and he gritted his teeth so hard he was afraid he would break them.

"Go ahead," he muttered. "Give me warning when you're fixing to cut me again."

"I'm sorry. It must be done. I wish I could give you a tumbler of liquor to dull your senses, but I cannot spare it. It is all I have to wash your wound afterward." She held up a bottle of amber liquid.

He nodded his understanding.

She returned to her work, and after a bit said, "Prepare yourself. I have one more cut to make."

He thought perhaps he blacked out for a while, because when he opened his eyes again, the blanket covered him. Ella Ruth wadded up the waste and put it into a basket. Then she turned to him and placed her hand on the blanket, uncomfortably close to his parts.

"Now you must rest. Tonight I will take you into the house. It's too dangerous to leave you here. You could be discovered."

"Ella?"

"Yes?"

"I owe you a debt of gratitude for taking me in and using your healing arts on me."

She stared at the ground, nervously working the fingers of the hand on the blanket against her thumb.

"Your devotion to me is clear. Will you forgive me for my doubts?"

She nodded. "With all my heart."

"I reckon you gave me that already."

"Yes." She joined her hands together before her mouth, and oh horror, a tear slid down her cheek.

"Don't weep, girl. We'll find a minister."

She sniffed and bowed her head, not saying anything further before she turned and left with her basket and his dinner plate.

⁊

Ben — October 21, 1864

After nightfall, Ella came back to the shed and whispered, "Ben. Are you awake?"

He was nearly asleep, truth be told, but got himself in hand enough to answer, "Yes, mostly."

"Good," she said. "Swing your limbs over the side of the table. I will assist you."

"Why?"

"I'm taking you to the house. The Yankees are about, and I don't want them to discover you."

Alert, now that she had reminded him of his dangerous circumstance, Ben struggled upright and did as Ella Ruth had bid him.

She took his arm and guided him onto the stool, then down to the ground. "Mind your wound," she murmured. "Let me bear your weight."

He looked around for his gear, but could see nothing in the dimness.

"Have no fear," she said. "Your rifle is safe in the house."

"I thank you," he whispered, wrapping his arm around her shoulder and venturing a step. Pain shivered up his leg, but he could hardly cry out and bring the enemy down upon them, so he bit his lip and bore the pain as well as he could while Ella Ruth tugged him toward the house.

He stumbled a time or two, both from weakness and from encountering unknown obstacles in the path, but they made good progress, and soon approached the house.

"Shh!" Ella Ruth cautioned, standing still.

Ben stopped, now clutching the girl for all he was worth in an attempt to keep his balance.

"Now go," she muttered, and tugged him forward.

Ben stumbled again, stepping on a rounded object that must have some length to it, as both feet found it.

"Careful. It's only a stick," she said, a little catch in her voice.

"I will make it, if we haven't far to go," he replied.

"Just a bit more," she promised, and soon they did arrive at the back of the house.

Ella Ruth pulled on the latch and opened the door to the darkened wash room. The kitchen showed no light either. They paused so she could close and bolt the door. Then they passed through the wash room and into the kitchen.

"Here," Ella Ruth said, pulling back a chair and easing Ben into it. "You must rest, dear husband."

Husband? Figuring his ears had stopped up to the extent that he had misheard her, he put a finger into one and wiggled it around.

Ella Ruth lit a candle, placed it on the table, took his hand from his ear, and said, "Ben, we've stepped over the broomstick. We're now husband and wife."

Even as he groaned in disbelief, he recalled the rounded stick near the back of the house. "I stepped *on* it," he whispered. "That's not the same as jumping over it."

She held herself rigidly erect, grasping his hand with hers. "No matter. You crossed over the broomstick. You are my husband, according to the rites of the servants." She paused, then took a breath and continued in a softer tone. "If you need words, I will say words to you, words of fealty and devotion, words of love and adoration."

"You can speak them later, once I've rested," he said, his mind reeling with the notion that they were married. Pain dulled his senses. He longed for sleep, could barely keep himself awake, but he would have to deal with Ella Ruth's conviction sooner or later. "If you're set on this rite, I'll come up with words to speak. Right now, I have to sleep."

ഌ

Ben — October 22 through November 6, 1864

Ben awoke the following morning with words in his brain that led him to believe that he had been mulling over the state of affairs during the night.

Ella Ruth had ensconced him in her parent's bed despite his strenuous objections. The girl would not be denied, which he already knew from sad experience, but at least he had put his mind to ease once he had spoken his doubts.

Now he felt a mite off. When he took stock of himself, he discovered that his leg had swollen up to a tremendous extent, and he feared infection and fever had set in.

Jerusalem crickets! He didn't have time or inclination to be laid up in bed for an extended period. He had to get back to his company.

He tried calling out for Ella Ruth. The weakness of his voice frightened him. He tried again, and this time he achieved some volume. She came quickly, worry written upon her face as she examined his leg.

"Ben, you must lie still. I'll bring an herbal powder for the wound. We must bring down that swelling and the fever. Bear with me, and I'll pull you through this rough spot."

At times in the days that followed, Ben doubted he would survive. At others, he wished for a surgeon to cut off the limb. But at the end of a fortnight, Ella Ruth's faith and labors were rewarded. Ben had come through the daunting hours of intense pain and weakness and finally felt he had regained his strength.

"Darling Ben," his miracle worker said as she spooned a thick soup into his mouth.

"Yes?" he asked between swallows. He could pull off the task of feeding himself, but at the moment, he enjoyed the luxury of lying in bed without pain at last.

"You must begin to walk around more."

"In due time," he said, not wanting to exercise at the moment.

"I will assist you."

"As ever." He noticed the brightness of her blue eyes against the dark hollows around them. Could she be starving? She should be eating this soup. Heaven only knew where she had acquired the ingredients. "Ain't you tired? Hungry?"

She gave a small shrug with one shoulder. "A little."

"You've gone without food and sleep to serve me."

She made a face of denial.

"Come rest beside me. I'll feed you what remains of the soup." He moved over to make room for her and took the bowl from her hand.

She raised an eyebrow. "Do you have any fever?"

"No. You have cured me of the infection."

She sat on the bed. A bird cawed outside the window. "I own I am a mite tired."

"Lie back. Eat."

He fed her the soup remaining in the bowl until she had taken it all and ran her tongue across her bottom lip in search of any lingering sustenance. The sight sent a stirring through his nether regions. He reached across her to put the bowl on the small table beside the bed and sensed the warmth of her breast beneath his arm.

His body responded with a yearning so sharp he barely could contain it. He sucked in a breath and held it. Had she spoke the truth when she had insisted he was indeed her husband? Could a step over a stick make it so?

He used the breath to ask, "Ella? You are truly my wife?"

She nodded, and he read conviction in her eyes, and yes, a spark of hunger. "And I am your husband?"

"Please," she said.

Chapter 27

Ben — November 7, 1864

Ben awoke at daybreak, his heart hammering, and his breathing—ragged, labored—took a long time to regularize.

What have I done?

He looked at the girl in his arms. She had murmured words to him, binding words of love and devotion and marriage. He dimly recalled some such pledge had come from his mouth in response. The details were hazy, but he had spoken of his undying adoration and claimed her as his wife.

Then he had done so in a carnal manner.

What have I done? his mind screamed. His heart replied that she was his own bride, but his innermost being cried out that he had sinned against Heaven and against Ella Ruth.

"No," he moaned, and felt her stir.

"Ben?"

He stiffened, felt his arms tighten around her. "I'm here," he muttered.

"Husband," she sighed.

He dared not speak. The idea that stepping over the broomstick was a legal and lawful marriage ceremony had lodged deep in her brain, convincing her that they were man and wife. He knew they were not. How could they be? They were not slaves.

He breathed slowly, deeply, trying to loosen his grip on the woman whose favors he had taken with such relish.

He shuddered. Slaves. Perhaps they were. Slaves to passion. Slaves to carnal actions. Slaves to the Eternal Pit. He had dragged her down to damnation.

He groaned, and she was instantly awake and aware.

"Are you ill?" Her voice was sharp.

"God forgive me. I have sinned."

"No." She sat up. "Look at me, Ben." She took his face between her palms to make sure he did. "Do I have the aspect of a sinner?"

She did not. Her countenance was radiant, peaceful. Could she be right in her conviction?

"We crossed over the broomstick. We spoke the words. We are wed, as perfectly wed as Mistress Mary and brother Rulon. Is that not so?" Her eyes bore into his.

He had to nod. He must not let her doubt her status. He knew the truth. He had violated her trust as much as her body, and he was damned to enter Hell for his sin.

∞

Julia — November 20, 1864

Owen Farm

Mt. Jackson, Via.

My dear husband,

How I long for your company. Instead, I am putting up three left-behind fellows who need nursing before they can go back to their companies. Yes, they should be in the soldier's hospital or in Staunton, but capacity having been reached, we are obliged to provide room, board, and bandages.

I do not let Marie or Jule anywhere near these young men, for they are a low sort of person from another state not known for gentility. I hope to see the last of them off in the next week, food being in short supply from the time of Sheridan's burning.

I fear it will be necessary to send the girls into town, perhaps to stay with Rulon and Mary. I hesitate to do so, as Mary has her hands full nursing Rulon. Husband, his wounds are grievous. At first, I despaired for his life, but Mary would not let him die. If I had the surgeon who ill-treated him in my rifle sights, I cannot say what I would do.

Surely you do not wish to hear blood-thirsty threats from your wife, so I will cease such talk, but my anger does not abate when I remember how my son was dumped in a ditch to die! I am weary of war and of trying to cope with a dire new situation nearly every day. When will it end, dear husband?

Ben is with Gen'l Early's army here in the Valley. Carl still rides with Mosby. James is besieged at Petersburg. He is certain Gen'l Lee will bust them out this coming Spring.

I pray for you and our sons every morning and every night. If Heaven has ears, surely the Father will give heed to our noble cause and bring this conflict to a close.

Craving to feel your arms about me, I remain,

Your loving wife, Julia

❧

Ben — November 24, 1864

Ben stood in the entryway, holding Ella Ruth tightly against his chest. She had been trying to put on a brave face, but he could tell from the riotous rhythm of her heart that she was profoundly affected.

"It won't be long before I'm back," he swore. "We'll find a true minister to unite us when warring is done."

"Ben," she sighed into his shirt. "There is no need. We are wedded as firmly as though we had said words in the church." She tilted up her face and planted a kiss on his lips. "I wish you would believe me."

He wished he could. He cupped her cheek in his hand. How she had changed since that fatal day. Her face radiated joy. She took pleasure in fetching and carrying for him, even though he knew his health had been restored, except for a slight limp. No more the heedless coquette, she had become the little wife she believed herself to be. His little wife.

Hating to erase the happiness from her brow, he had prolonged his stay as long as he could and still feel his absence was honorable. However, yesterday he had stated his intention to rejoin his company, which he figured to be wintering in a gap in the Blue Ridge.

Now the moment of parting had come and his heart ached, even as it beat wildly in anticipation of traveling back to the regiment.

"You will write?"

"Must I send letters to the store?"

"No. While Poppa is gone I shall take delivery here. Don't forget to begin with 'Missus,' or I won't know to whom you've addressed your note."

He smiled at the bantering tone in her voice. "You are a little scamp." Becoming serious, he tapped her on the nose. "That could be dangerous for you. Don't be surprised if I use the Allen surname." He saw the beginning of a frown on her lips, and hastened to add, "Just until the war is over."

"Then I may claim your name?"

"I promise." He felt a bit of unease at giving the vow, but shook off the doubt. They would be wed by proper authority as soon as he returned, and then she could call herself "Mrs. Benjamin Owen" to her heart's content. He sealed the promise with a long, yearning kiss.

"I must go, my love," he said at last, squeezed her gently, and turned on his heel.

&

Ella Ruth — December 3, 1864

Ella Ruth woke and faced the day ahead with a sigh. Ben had scarcely been gone a week, but she missed his grin, his warm presence beside her in her parents' bed, his tantalizing scent of manhood. She had waited such a long time for the caresses that had carried her away to the realm of womanly fulfillment.

She could hardly believe her good fortune when she had come upon him so unexpectedly in the battered orchard. She had gladly nursed him back to health, clinging to the promises they had made to marry when next they met. But she had not foreseen the impediment to their plans of a lack of ministers of the gospel.

The old Ben would not have cared. How many times had he urged her to give him her favors just one time? As many times as she had refused him. However, the Ben she had kissed last week and sent back to Jubal Early's army cared very deeply about the risk of carnal temptations.

She sat up. That didn't matter now. Poppa would acknowledge her marriage, wouldn't he? He had never denied the Negro servants their ceremonies. Ben's reservations would be overcome when he returned and they would be united in connubial bliss once more.

As she dressed, she considered if there were any changes in her body that would indicate coming motherhood. She knew the signs to watch for, but so far, there were none. Perhaps the handful of encounters she had teased out of Ben after that first night was not sufficient. When he returned, she intended to keep him to herself for a very long honeymoon. She had no desire now for a trip to Europe. Anywhere private would suit her, even a barn or a ferny dell. All she wanted was Ben's arms around her and the delightful exertions of marriage. She smiled to herself. Sooner or later, a child would come.

ຂາ

Rulon — December 31, 1864

Rulon looked down at the puckered scars on his stomach and chest and grimaced. How would Mary react to his unsightly body when time came for them to change their relationship from casualty and nurse to man and wife?

They lived in their own house. No one but the little son was around to impede them. The boy went to bed early, but would the awful mess of wounds cause his Mary's heart to shrink?

She had seen the wounds, true, but as his nurse, not as his lover.

He had fought back from the brink of extinction, holding fast to the longed-for reward of Mary's arms about his neck and her ready response to his embrace. Ever since he had returned home, his enemy had been the exhaustion that came hurtling out of the corner of the room to ensnare him after each attempt to begin an everyday activity. He had husbanded each gain in strength as a victory over the specter of death and defeat.

He had won the ability to feed himself. How sweet that was! He could draw himself to a sitting position, even swing his limbs over the side of the bed without pain lancing through his vital organs. He had advanced to being able to take short steps to sit in the armed chair Mary had dragged up the stairs from the kitchen. His greatest victory thus far was the ability to use the chamber pot by himself.

Be that as it may, he still was a prisoner of the second floor of the house. Two days ago, he had ventured as far as the stairs, but fell and tumbled down the steps to the landing. Mary would not permit a second try at escape now. He gingerly twisted his torso. The ache was still in his ribs. Descending the stairs was a victory yet to be gained.

Christmas had come and gone, celebrated here in this cell. He had not had anything to give to his son. Mary had produced a tin whistle and told the boy it was from Papa and herself, but Rulon felt the sting of uselessness.

He suppressed a groan as he lay back and drew up the sheet. He had never thought about how well his body had worked until his vitality had been stripped away in that horrible moment on the battlefield at Tom's Brook. Now he struggled to make it perform simple tasks.

All he wanted on this New Year's Eve was enough strength to hold Mary and make love to her. He'd been resting all day and thought he was ready, but how would she receive his advances? Would she reject any attempt to begin a connubial interlude because of concern, or would she be repulsed by his scars?

An hour ago, Mary brought the boy in for nightly devotions, then tucked him into bed in the next room. He'd listened to the murmur of their voices as she told him a Bible story. It had sounded like Abraham and Isaac, because Roddy asked about the ram in the thicket. Mary told him about miracles. Rulon wondered when his own miracle would come and *he* could tell his boy the stories. Ma had been their family's storyteller. Maybe that was Mary's role.

He sighed. After the boy had quieted, Mary returned to the kitchen downstairs. Had she turned left or right at the foot of the stairs? He didn't even know the rooms of his dwelling place.

The light behind the curtained window faded. Sundown. How long would Mary remain below, tidying up her house? Was she putting away Roddy's toys? Papa Hilbrands had found a toy bugle for the boy, which he tooted endlessly, except when he used the tin whistle. From the sounds during the day, he also galloped around the parlor on some sort of horse.

Rulon smiled. A horseman like his papa.

Was that Mary's tread on the stairs? He held his breath, listening to be sure. Yes. She paused on the landing. Gave a little cough. She wasn't coming down sick, was she? He'd have to— Have to do what? She was the nurse and he, the patient.

No. Not tonight. Tonight he would become a husband again.

Excitement thrummed through his veins. Mary came through the door, carrying a lamp. She set it on the washstand, then left the room again.

"Mary?"

She was back almost before the words died, carrying two mugs. She smiled. "These aren't Mama's fancy glassware, but they'll do for raspberry wine."

Raspberry wine? Strength flowed to where he'd hoped it would.

"It's New Year's. I thought a little celebration was in order."

Indeed. He felt a grin rise.

She handed him one of the mugs. "Roddy wanted a taste when I brought out the bottle, but I told him Papa would have to approve. He seemed satisfied to wait until you speak to him."

She drew the chair forward and sat at the bedside, her knees pressing against the mattress tick. He heard the rustle of the corn husks as she adjusted her position.

"I don't mean to keep you up until midnight," she said, smiling with a hint of mystery. "A toast and a wish will have to do to ring in the New Year together."

"Together," he muttered, feeling the burn of desire.

"Our first New Year's." Mary's smile quivered. Perhaps it was a trick of the light. Perhaps she bore a strong emotion. "Shall you make the toast?" she asked.

Rulon cleared his throat and extended his mug toward Mary's. "To our family," he said. "To being together again."

"To our family," she repeated. "Together," and tapped her mug against his.

Rulon lifted the mug and took a swallow. The wine was sweet, as he'd expected. *No sweeter than Mary's lips,* he imagined. He looked over the rim at her.

She sipped the wine sedately.

"A kiss?" he proposed.

"Of course." She leaned close and pecked his lips. Before he could put his hand behind her head, she withdrew.

"Mary." The word came out sounding rougher than he had intended. She didn't seem alarmed, and he went on. "I want a true celebration."

"Of course." The huskiness in her voice told him all he needed to know.

She stood and took his mug and set it, with her own, on the washstand. She didn't come back right away, but stood blocking the light of the lamp, wisps of her hair creating a halo around her head. Something occupied her attention for some while.

He finally decided she was undoing the buttons of her bodice. That would take time. Women used too many fastenings.

She turned at last, doffing pieces of attire. When she approached the bedside, he caught his breath. She was clothed in naught but lamplight.

"Husband," she said as she slipped under the bedding.

He kissed her as he had dreamed for so long of doing. She responded with verve. But before he could accomplish his goal, the daunting enemy, exhaustion, overtook him. His disappointment was mirrored on Mary's face.

"Are you unwell?" she whispered as he groaned and turned onto his side.

He trembled from the weakness that encompassed him, could not give her an answer.

"Rulon!" The sharpness in her voice pricked him.

"I'm well enough," he muttered, "but I have no strength." He watched fear and concern battle on her face until she cradled him in her arms and rocked him as she would a babe.

"There now," she crooned. "You must rest."

Rulon could only cling to her, disheartened by his body's betrayal.

Chapter 28
Rod — March 1, 1865

Rod held the torch to the flooring timber at the end of the bridge, grumbling to himself, because the air was so damp due to the continuous rain that nothing was catching fire. General Rosser wanted this bridge down. Sheridan was on the march again, and even if the cavalrymen's actions only slowed him down a bit, it was something.

He looked up when Wylie called him.

"Captain, it's slow to burn," Wylie said.

Rod thought a moment. "Hmm. Take your knife and pare down the wood, but leave it hanging," he said. "Make it like kindling."

Wylie did as he suggested, and Rod took out his knife to follow his own suggestion. The wood finally blazed up, and Rod and his men retreated down the covered bridge, leaving dancing fire in their wake.

He heard a shot, and dashed toward the south end of the bridge, heart pounding. *They're here!* He and Wylie made it to the road leading out from the bridge as a volley of firing sounded to the west.

Evans rode up with Rod's horse in tow and said, "They're swimming the river, captain. It's Custer."

Rod flung his torch onto the bridge and mounted. His horse reared from the excitement, and he brought it under control with difficulty. While he worked to settled it down, he shouted, "Cut them off when they come up the bank."

He and his men rallied to the other horsemen, and fired a second volley at the Yankees emerging from the river. The Yankees kept coming across the river through the water. Now they were also on the bridge, fighting the blaze.

An eerie, high sound from many voices echoed in the void under the bridge's cover. The Union horsemen charged across the burning timbers and into the open, still yelling.

"Back, back," Rosser yelled, gesturing to the woods, and Rod rode in that direction, urging his men to follow.

They'd done all they could here, but the numbers were on the enemy's side. It was time to retreat.

⁊ひ

Ben — March 1 through 2, 1865

Even though several months had gone by since Ben had left Ella Ruth, he continued to sleep badly, haunted by guilt. He'd been attempting to pray every night since he had been caught in the trap of lust. It wasn't any good. God already knew of his great transgression. He felt the disapproval and sorrow from the heavens every minute of the day, and all night long.

As he lay one evening staring into the stars, he finally came to the conclusion that he must confess his sin to someone who could guide him through the process of making amends for his act of ultimate robbery. Who could help him? Mr. Moore? He and the minister had never hit it off well, so he didn't really want to approach him. Besides that, he didn't know if the Yankees had let the man loose yet.

Perhaps he could speak to the Catholic priest who came around whenever they camped near Harrisonburg. Ben wondered if the man would refuse his assistance unless he converted to the faith. Who else might be suitable to help him cleanse his soul? He could think of no one. Would he have to venture toward repentance all on his own?

He supposed a first step would be to write to Ella Ruth and beg her forgiveness. He wondered what her response would be. She had been the one who had planted the seed of the idea, who had insisted they were married by virtue of them stepping on and over a broomstick in the dark. She sincerely believed they were wed. He knew they were not. Did that leave Ella Ruth blameless? His mind quivered to think that perhaps not. Perhaps her soul was in as much everlasting peril as his own.

He bore the ultimate blame for giving in to his passion. Under her coaxing, he had done so more than one time. Now he had to own up to the fact that they had sinned against each other, and against God.

He groaned, thinking about how far he had wandered from grace. Ma would be devastated. What a blow it would be upon her God-fearing heart to know that her son had distanced himself from his Creator in such a tawdry fashion. Could he bring himself to write to Ma, to beg her forgiveness, as well? Would that give him any relief from the chains of sin he felt tightening around his soul?

He felt the Testament digging into the small of his back. He needed to move it into a pocket, he thought, then refrained from doing so. Perhaps he needed a goad, a reminder of his fault, until he took steps toward making his soul clean.

After a long period of thinking, he arose and went to the campfire that had burned down to embers. Ella Ruth had given him a pocketbook with a sheaf of writing paper within. In addition, a lead pencil was affixed under the flap. He drew the object out of his pocket, and by the puny light of what remained of the fire he wrote,

My darling Ella Ruth,

I hope you are well, as I am not. Great sorrow weighs me down every day since we erred against our Maker in committing the sin of lust and acting upon our passion. We should not have done so, my dear girl. I forever regret that I was driven by unseemly appetites to rob you of virtue, and I cannot forget my wrong.

I cannot return to you that wich I stole. I can merely ask your forgivness for what I did to you. I pray you to grant me that favor, at leest - To forgive me as I forgive you.

I am weary of battle. The yankees have more men than we. They have provisions were we have none. We run short on munitions. They have all they need. Even so, I fight on for my dear Country until the end, whether it be the end of the fightin or the end of me.

I love you as man has never loved a woman before. I despise the thot that I have become a low sort of man, unable to keep myself strait with God. I beg your forgivness. Set my mind at ease so I mite petition God for His Grace and Forgivness.

Keep this note from the sight of strangers.

Your unworthy suitor, Ben

A bit of an old hymn ran through his mind as he signed and folded the letter. "Prone to wander, Lord, I feel it, prone to leave the God I love." Yes. He had left God, had run away to an enticing episode of carnal satisfaction, blinded by thoughts and acts of fleshly desire. How had he sunk into such depravity? How could he rise from it again?

He started writing a letter to Ma.

Julia Owen
Owen Farm outside Mount Jackson, Via.
Dear Ma,

I hope all is well with you. We are retreating before an overwhelming host, but my dread is that I won't be able to send this note before we come into another battle.

It pains me to tell you that I have done wrong. I sinned in givin in to lust. I let my pashun carry me into the forbiden gardin with a girl

I know. She is also known to you, but I will not divulge her name unless forced by circumstances. How I regret my sinful acts!

Unable to formulate more words at the moment, he tucked away the pocketbook and, having made a start to his atonement, slept soundly for the first time in months.

The next morning, he gave the letter meant for Ella Ruth into the hands of the adjutant, hoping he could find a way to post it, but because he had not finished the one to Ma, Ben kept it in his pocket book.

Later that day, he found himself trudging south up the Valley, falling sleet threatening to freeze upon his face. Ole Jube Early had sent his larger force of infantry toward Lynchburg, but Ben was marching with his company to Waynesborough, a bit east. Sheridan would chase after one of the ragtag armies. Ben hoped he would go to Lynchburg.

He stole a glance over his shoulder, wishing for a sight of a long-gone comrade's countenance. So many had been cut down in the months behind them. Now Sheridan was chasing the Confederates with a vengeance. All the armies could do was march to a place of resistance, somewhere they could stand their ground against Federals who wanted them dead.

"Company, halt," came to his ears. They had approached the outskirts of the town. Here on the west side, a little ridge rose before them. Would that do for a defensive ground? He didn't pretend to know strategies or tactics. Those were up to the colonels and captains to figure out. He was merely cannon fodder, a foot soldier doing his best to keep a hold on a little piece of the Southern dream. What was that dream? He could scarcely remember the long discussions at the home table about freedom of conscience and state's rights, and fighting for home and country.

Virginia was his country, and when it had joined the great secession, the Confederacy had become his country. But how much longer could he arm his weapon, raise it to his shoulder, and fire upon other men?

Now the order came to dig rifle pits. Weariness overtook him, but he dropped his gun and haversack, received a pick that was passed to him, and advanced to the appointed line. Heave. Swing. Heave. Swing. Heave. Swing. The rhythm caught him, and he continued blindly to heave and swing until told to stop.

How long could this defense last? Rain sluiced down his face. He could hear the roaring waters of the South Fork of the Shenandoah behind him. If the Yankees overran them, they were stuck between the enemy and the river without a place of refuge. What was Jubal Early thinking?

He hadn't been thinking well for a while, Ben mused. Even General Lee thought so. The General had been stripping away bits and pieces of Early's command, until now their strength was about 1500 or so, he'd been told. How could they stand off Sheridan? The Yankee general had more than ten thousand troops with him. Ten thousand!

He was told to pack the dirt beneath his feet and prepare to defend his pit. Yes, they said "dirt." It wasn't dirt, as any fool could see. Tromping the mud with his almost bare feet, Ben felt it squishing between his toes, clammy clay. He wondered if it held good fishing worms.

Fishing? Well, the river wasn't so far off. If he weren't a soldier priming to fight off a hoard of enemy invaders, he would go fishing. Or swimming. No, the river was too high for either leisurely pursuit.

Jerusalem crickets! When had he last had leisure? Time to himself for reflection? He had spent the last such moments sinning as though there was no tomorrow! Maybe there was no tomorrow for him. Maybe his sin had doomed him to Hell forever. He had to finish the letter to Ma, to confess his sin and express his regret, to seek forgiveness.

Someone, possibly Ma, had told him in the dim past that Jesus had died for his sins. Why then did he feel so forsaken for having been with Ella Ruth? The moments should have been sweet. Instead, the Jaws of Hell yawned open beneath him, and he couldn't shake a sense that his time was running out.

He knew the Federals had caught up to them when a shell screamed overhead, followed by a bee's swarm of balls. He ducked into the rifle pit and steeled himself for the fight to come.

"Oh dear God, forgive me," he whispered, popping up from the hole to fire his rifle at the attackers. "Lord Jesus, forgive my trespasses. Come and save me from my sins!"

The battle soon became a thunder of artillery pieces interspersed with the rattle of rifles in a frontal assault. Then a bugle sounded to the left of the line of breastworks.

That's not our bugle.

Shortly afterward, a hoard of yelling men broke from the trees on the left flank, firing rifles they didn't have to pause to load. *Spencers. Repeaters. Seven-shots.* At the same time, artillery shells pinned Ben's company in place. Surely Hell could be no worse than this.

A man next to him shrieked briefly and lay still. Another lifted his rifle and shot toward the Yankees approaching on the left. A ball caught him in the face, and he fell into the pit at Ben's feet.

"I'm not staying here to die," said another soldier, and slithered out of the pit on his belly toward the river. He crab-walked a few feet, stopped, then began again to move toward the rear. After he was out of rifle range, he stood and ran. Other men copied his thinking, and soon, the field was full of men running to the rear.

Emboldened by mass escape, Ben tried the same moves. He knew he had miscalculated the distance the Spencer rifle could shoot accurately when he felt himself being lifted off his feet by a round striking his body.

When he hit the ground, Ben lay unmoving on his side in a crumpled position, wondering why he didn't feel any pain in his leg, as he could see it had suffered a wound. He tried to dig his other heel into the ground to get himself onto his back, but it would not obey his thought.

A man from the regiment knelt beside him for a moment, grabbed him under the arms and dragged him toward the line of trees bordering the river. He gave him a drink from his canteen, and said, "Lie still, Owen."

"Help me up," Ben begged. "Take me with you."

The man tried to lift Ben, then swore softly. "Here's another hole." He lowered Ben to the ground.

"Where? I don't feel it."

"Here on your side." He checked Ben's opposite side. "Didn't go through. Is your spine broke, Owen?"

"I can't tell."

The man gave him another drink, then picked up his rifle, said "Lie still" again, and ran into the trees.

Ben craned his neck to where he could see his side and noticed his blood spilled steadily from the hole. Not much blood, it appeared, but he had nothing with which to staunch the flow. No part of his body below the hole in his side made response to his mental commands to move. Melancholy gripped his spirit as he felt a subtle weakness overcoming him, rising from his waist upward.

So I am to die, he thought. *Have I any valor left?*

He took Ella Ruth's likeness from his pocket, kissed it tenderly, struggling against tears, and laid it on his breast above his heart. He dug out his pencil and pocket book and added to his letter to Ma.

Waynesborough battle
Ma,
This note is short. My life is forfeit, as I am sorly wounded and bleedin my strength away. I am griev'd to leave without seeing you again. God has struck me down for my sin. Treat Miss Ella Ruth All'n with kindness as she was to be my wife.

If my seed took root, guard her as you woud your own child. I do not know how her pa will treat her if she is increasin with a poor man's bastard. It is to late for me to make it right.

I feel life ebbing. My last hope is this note will be found and sent to you.

With tender affect'n
Your dying son, Benj'n Owen

Knowing he was spending his last bit of strength, Ben folded the letter with clumsy fingers, put it into the pocket book, and placed the leather case on his chest beside Ella Ruth's likeness. His hands dropped to his sides. He whispered, "Jesus God, forgive my sins," and said no more.

&

Rod — March 3, 1865

When Rod Owen was rousted out of his blankets with orders to report to General Rosser, he wondered what news had come. Once the regimental commanders and several other company captains had been gathered, he found out. A scout had come early in the morning with word that General Early's command at Waynesborough had been almost entirely captured. The general and some of his staff had escaped across the Blue Ridge, but about 1,100 men under guard of the Yankee cavalry would soon be passing through Staunton toward Winchester.

Rod wondered what Rosser was going to do about the situation.

The cavalry general sheltered underneath a spread canvas, on his knees, drawing a map in the mud. "We won't leave those boys in Yankee hands," he said. "With so many prisoners, they'll likely take this road. We'll hound them on the flanks, and attack here, near Harrisonburg, tomorrow night." He shook his finger at his commanders. "They'll be on the alert. They know I won't rest while my countrymen are held captive." He pointed to a pair of company commanders. "You will hold the fords here and here." He drew the fords across the line designated as the Shenandoah River. "Keep them bottled up until we get those boys free." He looked up. "Owen, you're my spy. Take a squad to mingle with the prisoners. Incite them to revolt and escape when we attack. If you find your boy, get his cooperation to help you. Be cautious. I don't want you to join the prisoners permanently."

"Yes sir," Rod said, feeling the tingle of anticipation that danger always raised in his belly.

Rosser got to his feet. "The Yankees need to think we have a larger force, so we'll ride past them, double back, and pass 'em again." He pointed to three other captains. "That's your duty," he said, and took a lungful of air. "Boots and saddles, gentlemen."

Rod went back to his company, sorting out in his mind who best could join him in the delicate business. How he wished Rulon were in his company. He would keep a cool head.

No matter. He would take Evans, Wylie, and Court. He could risk no more than the four of them.

By now, the company was awake and the men were cooking rations over small fires. He snorted. What passed for rations. The days of full rations had ended long ago, when Sheridan burned the Valley.

Rod pulled his chosen few aside, gave them instructions, and left the lieutenant in command of the company. Then he pulled a worn coat over a linsey-woolsey shirt and wool pants, and they set off on the mission.

Once they found the army and their prisoners, it wasn't difficult to slip in among the dispirited captives and spread out. What was difficult was reanimating the men, trying to give them heart enough to agree to revolt when the attack from Rosser began. More times than not, he and his men encountered negative shakes of the head and little support for Rosser's plan. These men had lost all nerve and only wanted to get to a Federal camp where food was available.

Worse still, Rod couldn't find Ben. Few of the men knew him. Those who did know him had no news. The prisoners were too tired, too disheartened to care. Feeling sick to the depths of his soul, Rod stuck to his task, but when night came and Rosser with it, the captives made no attempt to break free. Rod and his men got away only because they carried pistols and made judicious use of them to extract themselves from the tender guardianship of the Union soldiers.

80

Rod — March 4, 1865

Chafing that the mission had not succeeded, but even more because he hadn't found Ben among the captives, Rod and his three spies rejoined Rosser's command. The general decided to give up the rescue effort and turned to follow Sheridan, who had continued toward Petersburg.

"He's joining Grant, blast him," Court said.

"We'll slow him down some," Rod answered, swinging up into his saddle for another day's hard ride.

When the Owen Dragoons entered Waynesborough, Rod found that a complement of citizens had buried the dead in the rifle pits behind the fortifications they'd defended. His belly crawling with dread, he went to the town hall and asked for information about the casualties.

"We kept the effects from the lads," the clerk said. "Some had very little, but one boy had time to write a letter. What's your name again?"

"Owen. Roderick Owen. I'm looking for my son, Benjamin."

"Owen. Where do you hale from, captain?" The man rubbed his ear.

"My farm's outside Mount Jackson, Shenandoah County."

The clerk's face went solemn, and he shook his head as though to clear a bad memory. "I'm sorry, captain. We kept a few things from a boy—"

"What do you have?" Rod kept himself from grabbing the man's lapels by a strong effort.

"There's a pocketbook with a few notes addressed to Ben or Benjamin Owen, and a likeness of a young lady."

Rod's legs quivered. He felt a peculiar weakness sapping his vitality, as though he were gushing blood from his heart.

"What is your wife's name, sir?"

"Julia." Was that faint voice his own?

"I'm so sorry, sir." He retrieved a parcel wrapped in a cloth from a cubbyhole and handed it to Rod. "We took these from your son's body. There's a letter for your missus."

Rod cleared his throat several times before he could manage a "thank you." He took the parcel, left the hall, and struggled to his horse on legs so weak he barely made the short distance before clutching the saddle to keep himself from falling.

"Sir?" It was Evans, his corporal.

"Ben," Rod whispered in a hoarse voice. "He's gone." He heard the man swear, but had no strength to reprimand him for his language. He was sucked dry. His voice had crackled like an old corn husk left on the ear too long. He thought of Julia. This news would kill her. He must not send her word until he could be with her.

He unbuttoned his shirt and tucked the parcel inside. It was too soon to look at the last remaining vestiges of Benjamin's life. He had spent too much time in this town, and Rosser needed him to harass Sheridan. Duty called.

He swallowed with great effort. Honor. Duty. At least he still had those. He clucked to his horse. He was still at war. With Sheridan. With Grant. With the Federals.

Chapter 29
Julia — April 7, 1865

Julia heard a noise outside and looked through her kitchen window. Someone trudged down her lane from the Pike. The man didn't wear a blue uniform. She could be thankful for that. However, he could be a straggling soldier come to ask for food. She grabbed her rifle and moved toward the back door.

Should she wait until the man knocked, or stand where he could see her? Show that she was armed?

She called to the girls to go into hiding, opened the door, and took a step out onto the stoop.

The man hesitated when he saw her, then set down his gear and began to run toward her.

Julia felt a shiver of fear. What compelled the man to do that? She lifted the rifle into view.

The man stopped, raised one hand in surrender and called, "Ma?"

That was confusing. Who would call her that? She saw the man bore a bandage about his left shoulder. Perhaps he was playing on her sympathies.

"Who are you?" she asked, leveling the weapon.

"Six little beans!" he spat out in disgust.

Julia dropped the rifle, running, running, running down the lane to her son, her James, her boy who wore Peter's hair but had come home. His arms were out, ready to embrace her, and she gladly flew into them, bumping against him with a thud that drew a groan from his body.

She cried out in wordless wonder, kissing his neck, his scruffy chin, his lips, his eyes, her arms about him, enfolding him against her breast.

"Ma," he protested. "Mind the shoulder."

She stood back then, holding his forearms and taking in the sight of him.

"How bad?" she murmured.

"Not so bad if you don't bump it," he replied in a strangled voice.

"Oh my dear son," she said, sniffling. "I beg pardon. Come. Let's get you under a roof."

ഌ

Rod — April 13, 1865

Rod led his horse up the lane, his heart thumping from equal parts relief, joy, and dread. The war was over. He'd never leave Julie again. He had a burdensome task ahead of him.

He figured if the telegraph wires were up, news had spread of the surrender, and she must be aware he would be on the homeward road.

The kitchen door opened. Mayhap she had been watching, or heard his step crunching on the gravel of the lane.

She stepped through the door, halted, put the rifle in the corner and ran toward him.

He dropped the reins and strode toward her, then quit all pretense of age and dignity and broke into a run.

His heart stopped when he saw her smile. He would wipe it from her face with his tidings. But for a moment, he could savor the sweetness of her welcome and hold her close before he broke the news.

She came into his embrace smelling of soap and wind, nuzzling into the space below his jaw that fit her like a glove. He knew his beard scratched, but she made no protest as she laid her lips on his cheek, then settled into his arms for a long, hungry kiss.

He gave what was due and more. Sorrow drove him as much as longing. His heart shrank that he had to break hers.

"Rod," she murmured when he let her breathe. "Is it truly over?"

"The fightin' is done," he answered, and she looked up at him. Did she sense that he had more to impart? Was this the best time and place to tell her Benjamin wasn't coming home?

He felt naked out in the air. Better to tell her indoors, where she could weep unashamed and away from prying eyes.

He should put up the horse. He looked toward the barn. No barn. No wellhead. No stock pens. No stock.

He set his jaw. This is what it meant to be the loser in the conflict.

"Albert," she called, startling him.

He looked down at his wife. She had already adjusted to losses around the farm. He would have to make an effort. He retraced his steps, brought the horse to where his Julie stood.

The boy came. He gave him an embrace, then handed him the reins.

"What more?" she asked.

He nodded to the house. "Indoors." The huskiness in his voice disturbed him. He had to be strong.

"Rod?" Julia asked once they were inside the main room.

"Julie." He swallowed the lump tightening his throat. "Sit."

She eyed him, then did as he bid her, but sitting upright, not relaxed.

God help him. He did not want to say the words. He looked into her eyes and dug in his shirt for the parcel he'd kept close to his heart for the last few weeks. He had not looked at it. They would have to do that together. He steeled himself and unwrapped the cloth.

The bundle contained three items, a leather pocket notebook, a folded frame that probably contained a photographic likeness, and a letter folded over and addressed to Julia.

He looked over at her and caught deep fear that shadowed her eyes. She already knew the items meant something very bad.

He cleared his throat. His voice came out more ragged than he would have liked when he said, "We chased Sheridan through Waynesborough after the fight there." He paused to clear his throat again. "Julie, Ben wasn't among the prisoners Sheridan sent north. A fellow at the town hall gave me these." He held out the letter to her, and she took it, her face set and as white as he had ever seen it.

She read the note, her breathing irregular, her hands shaking. She stopped once and laid the paper in her lap. She bowed her head and pinched the bridge of her nose, then took the paper up again.

He watched her read it, his soul shivering. Ben. What had he written that harrowed her up so badly? Unable to watch her pain, he looked at the other items he still held. He opened the picture frame and drew in a sharp breath.

Theodore Allen's daughter. Miss Ella Ruth. He hadn't known they had reconciled after their quarrel, but it had been a long war. If he had carried her portrait . . . the situation between them must have been serious.

He opened the pocketbook. It contained writing paper, and several letters, all from Miss Allen. He flipped the latest one open, ashamed to read a private message, but astonished to see her greeting.

"Dearest husband," she had begun. He closed the paper.

Julia sat with her head bowed again, the letter resting in her lap. From what he could see, she wasn't crying. How could she not cry? His own grief had gnawed at him, causing tears to fall in the dark when he could mourn privately.

She looked up. Her eyes had dark hollows around them, as though the news she read had caused them to sink into the sockets.

He held out the likeness and she took it. "Miss Allen," he said. "Somehow, they married. I'll pay a visit and inform her." He huddled against his crossed arms.

She whispered something so low he bent toward her and asked, "What's that?"

"Ben thinks they did not wed." She traced the curve of the girl's cheek.

He straightened up, rubbing the back of his neck. Then he held out Ella Ruth's letter. "She calls him 'husband.' That's as far as I read."

She shook her head, refusing to take the letter.

He watched her swallow, breathe deeply, and shut her eyes against the pain.

"Julie?" He wanted to offer comfort, and didn't know how.

"You must be tired," she said, her voice quivering just slightly. She rose and stepped into his arms.

He held her gently. "Bone deep," he answered, his shoulders sloping downward as renewed grief dropped its load onto them.

ℬↃ

Ella Ruth — April 14, 1865

Ella Ruth went to answer the knock on the front door, since Lula was busy in the kitchen. She didn't expect anyone in particular, but when she opened the door, she put her hand to her mouth. The formidable Mrs. Owen and her husband stood on her porch and stared at her with grave eyes.

A moment later, she remembered her manners and stepped back, uttering polite words bidding them to enter.

Mr. and Mrs. Owen had never been to her home. She watched to see if Mrs. Owen would look around in admiration of—of what, exactly? The furniture had grown almost shabby over the duration of the conflict.

But no, Mrs. Owen never turned her head. She gazed straight at Ella Ruth, which was a bit disconcerting. Mr. Owen's head was more bowed, like he had the weight of the fall of Petersburg on his shoulders. How did a man bear surrendering to a victorious foe? Not well, she supposed, as she ushered them in silence toward the parlor.

Something must be wrong with Ben, she thought. Why else would his parents visit her?

She felt her limbs go numb as she tried to gesture toward the sofa. *Something is very wrong with Ben.* She sank into a chair as they took places on the sofa opposite her. Her heart became a block of ice.

"May I get you a refreshment?" she asked, her voice shaking. Shaking terribly. Shaking as though she spoke into a windstorm.

Mr. Owen moved his hand to dismiss the thought of food or drink.

"Miss Allen," he began. He bowed his head. It seemed like hours passed before he raised it again. "Miss," he began again and stopped. "Daughter Ella Ruth," he managed to say at last.

She knew for certain then, and her heart cracked as she lurched upright, a moan starting in the pit of her stomach and rising through her chest and up into her throat to emerge as a cry of grief so terrible she could not stand the sound of it. She collapsed back into the chair, limp as the babe she would never carry. The sounds coming from her body hurt her ears, yet she could not stop them. They came in waves of agony more desolate than could be borne.

Mr. Owen was on his feet, coming over, then stopping as his wife rose unsteadily and dropped to her knees beside Ella Ruth.

"Go ahead," she whispered. "Let it out." Mrs. Owen's voice also shook, but she remained dry-eyed.

Doesn't she care?

Ella Ruth's keening continued, the sound hollow as a wolf's at a distance. Surely her heart must burst due to the bubble of anguish that rose in her midsection, pressing against her lungs, shredding her dignity, killing her soul.

Her mind managed a few thoughts. *Ben. Gone. I won't see him again. Ever.* "Nooo," her wail began again, rising to the rafters, a howl so primal she drew up her knees and curled into a ball.

She would have fallen to the floor and remained there for the rest of her existence, screaming in an overabundance of woe if not for Ben's father, who gathered her up in his arms and muttered to someone, who stuttered a reply. *Lula.*

He carried her, lightly as she imagined Ben would have done had he been here to do the task, out into the vestibule and down the long hall to her parent's room, where Mrs. Owen stripped back the bed covers so Mr. Owen could lay her tenderly upon the sheet. Lula sobbed in the background, rooted to the floorboards, immovable.

"Water," Mrs. Owen said to Lula, a bit sharply, as though to get her attention. "Bring her a glassful."

By now Ella Ruth's cries had subsided to moans, but still came, unrestricted, from her lips. I must die, she thought. I must join Ben. Her eyes streamed now.

"No," said Mrs. Owen.

You're reading my mind.

"No. You're speaking aloud, child."

She had no sense of having spoken. *I am losing my mind.*

"It will return," Mrs. Owen said, her voice soft, but the sound grating as though her throat were raw. "The first shock will pass. You will be clear in your mind . . . someday." Mrs. Owen's voice broke, but she still did not shed a tear.

Ella Ruth stopped moaning, but the flood of tears continued. She tried to put up her fist to dash them away, but her arm would not move, and they slid down her cheeks and onto the pillow. She looked from Mrs. Owen to Ben's father. He held his hand over his eyes, and she knew he was hiding his own emotion. Mrs. Owen's eyes were filled with affliction, but not tears.

"Mama." Pain washed over her again. Mama wasn't here to blunt her sorrow. Mama was in Charlottesville. She didn't know about Ben.

Mrs. Owen patted her hand. "There, there."

Ella Ruth's muscles finally moved, and she gripped the woman's hand. *She's kin, my mother-in-law.*

"Mama," she cried again, and Mrs. Owen enfolded her in her arms. Ella Ruth sobbed and wailed and cried anew. Hours must have gone by while she grieved, but Mrs. Owen never left her alone. She pressed a drink of water upon her, whispering soft words of comfort that seemed to come from a deep inner well. And yet, she did not join Ella Ruth in crying.

At last, exhaustion came, and the tears dried to crusts on Ella Ruth's cheeks. Mrs. Owen called for a cloth and warm water, and bathed Ella Ruth's face.

Relief touched Ella Ruth when she felt the cloth on her skin. *Mary was right. Mama Owen is not hard to know. Mary loves her. I will too.*

℘

Mary — April 14, 1865

Father Owen left. Mary closed the door, went back into the parlor, and stared toward Rulon. He sat on the sofa, stunned, shriveled beyond anything she had yet seen. She wondered how she would get him back upstairs. He had come down on his own power when she told him his father had called in, but this news, this brutal news obviously had chopped him down to mincemeat.

He looked up. There was no light in his eyes. They appeared sunken, anguished beyond her understanding. His gaze quickly dropped to his lap where his fisted hands pounded upon his thighs.

His sense of loss was too great for her to comprehend. She had no brothers. She had come to know that Rulon had fought, teased, joked, wrestled, and loved Ben from the time of his birth. They'd worked and played side by side on the farm, teaming up against their younger brothers to teach them the lessons of life and the ways of boys. Now that bond with his next younger brother had been severed. He had every appearance of a devastated soul.

Since she had become involved in Rulon's life, she had learned that sisters were different. She supposed she loved them, but Ida was a handful, and prickly as a pincushion. Mary's relationship with her next younger sister was not the same as Rulon's had been with Ben.

She sat gingerly beside him. He still thumped his legs, as though beating some understanding into a willfully heedless body.

"Rule?"

He turned to her, his eyes deep pits of despair. Still he kept up the thumping, looking away again, shaking his head now from side to side. Then he opened his mouth and cried out, "Bennnnnn," so dolefully that Mary thought her heart would break at the pain he expressed. She thought of Roddy, perhaps awakening from his nap to the eerie sound, but Rulon's need superseded that of her child, and she leaned in to put an arm around him.

He shook her off, his face set in a grimace of stone.

Her arm fell away, unwanted, unneeded. Her heart shrank at the rejection, but she struggled to bring reason to bear on the situation. *He is hurt. Perhaps he wants to be alone just now*. She didn't want to leave him, but she rose and went away, trying to understand his need for isolation. *I'll check on Roddy*, she decided. *It won't do for him to become frightened.*

Chapter 30
Mary — April 22, 1865

A week later, in an attempt to ease Rulon's grief, Mary decided to wear a dress that had sweet memories for them, the dress with the lavender skirt that she wore the day she married him. The dark shade would keep their mourning, although the light bodice would not. She hoped he would forgive her the lapse when he saw her in it, if it brought to mind happier days.

A happy surprise will do him good, she thought, searching through the wardrobe when he was asleep. She did not find the outfit there.

Hoping it was in the attic, she got up into the small space, but did not find it. However, Roddy took delight in holding up his toy sword and prancing around the attic as though he rode a horse.

Curbing her smile at the antics of her son, she wondered if she had left the dress behind at Papa's house. Mary sighed, remembering the fuzzy state of her mind when Rulon had returned in such dire straits. Yes, it probably still occupied a place in Ida's wardrobe.

"Come down now, Roddy. We must go wake Papa." She brushed dust off the boy. "He will have charge of you while I run an errand."

"Papa will play with me? Yippee!" he crowed, and dashed down the stair ahead of her.

"Quiet, dear son. We must wake Papa slowly, lest he become startled."

"Papa, Papa, Papa," Roddy whispered with enthusiasm.

Mary shushed the boy and took him into the larger bedroom of the two in the house.

"Rulon," she said softly as she passed through the doorway. She put a finger to her lips for Roddy's benefit, and approached the bed. "Husband? Will you wake?" When Rulon opened his eyes she continued. "Could you tend to Roddy for an hour? I must go do an errand."

Rulon raised himself on an elbow. He smiled at the child. "He gives me joy, Mary. I don't mind playing nursemaid for a spell."

She smiled, grateful that in the last two days Rulon had found his strength returning. A week ago, what a horror to learn of another great loss! It had laid Rulon low again, a setback to all the progress he had made in healing from his injuries. But yesterday he was much improved, and she took heart that his grief had taken on a yearning, almost accepting aspect, which helped soothe her own pain. Brother Ben had treated her kindly. She would miss him terribly. How Miss Allen must feel!

Once Roddy was safely in Rulon's charge, Mary hurried to the home of her childhood, watching out for Yankee soldiers, and went straight into her old room to search the wardrobe.

She found Ida in the room, sitting before the mirror, hunched over something she held close. She appeared to be in an unusual state, moaning softly to herself.

"Ida! What are you up to?"

Ida shrieked, jumped up, and backed away, trying to hide the object in her hand behind her back, but Mary was too quick for her, and snatched away a piece of paper.

Ida's red face turned petulant. "I'm only exploring the delights that entranced you," she blustered. "I deserve a few delights."

Mary looked at the paper and froze. A letter. Her letter. The lost letter from Rulon. Horrors! Ida had stolen it.

"'My body and vigor are yours alone'," Ida sneered. "They can't be anything special, now that he's all full of holes."

"You read my letter." Mary's ears rang, and she grabbed the back of Ida's chair to support herself.

"Perhaps he is missing his Things," Ida taunted, pointing downward. "Is that why he's so cross?"

"You read my letter and kept it from me." Mary's toes gripped the insides of her shoes.

"You don't know, do you? Six months, and you haven't even bothered to lay with him." Ida's mouth twisted in a smirk.

"What sort of tramp are you?" Mary asked in a low voice.

"I am not a tramp."

Mary spoke the worst insult she could think of. "Are you servicing Yankees?"

Ida cried out at the accusation and came at Mary with her nails bared.

Mary socked her in the eye. "You shame yourself," she hissed as Ida fell backward on her hind end. She turned and left the room.

She ran down the stairs, amazed at the rage that would not abate. Shaking out the pain in her violent hand, she hustled down the blocks, heedless of any Yankees standing about. Just let them try to molest her!

What Ida had said was true. She had not lain with Rulon. They had tried, but bitter circumstances prevented their union.

She stormed into her own house, shaking, wishing she had torn out Ida's hair, but knowing it was better to get away from the wayward minx. Shivering, she escaped toward her room, found Rulon alone, and stood in the doorway holding the letter she had never finished reading.

"I wore him out," Rulon said in a sleepy voice. "He's taking a nap."

She began to cry, almost certain he had all his manly parts, but ashamed that she had not been more attentive, more loving. Perhaps he now had no interest in her. After all, it had been months since that distressing attempt on New Year's Eve. In truth, his distressing weakness had frightened her. She had not wanted to press him with her needs, but perhaps he no longer wanted her. She gulped, hiccoughing now, then sobbing again as Rulon rose and came toward her.

"Mary?"

"Do you want me?"

"Mary, Sugar," he sighed, wrapping his arms around her. "Hush, now. Hush."

She leaned into his chest, wetting his shirt. She thumped his shoulder, away from his wounds. "Do you want me?"

"I do," he whispered into her hair. His arms tightened.

"She stole my letter." She shook it until the paper rattled. "I had not read it through." She listened to the horrible breaking of her voice. *How can he care for such a ninny?*

He didn't ask who she meant. "My precious Mary. Come. Sit. I will read it to you." He sat in the rocking chair, holding her on his lap, and took the paper from her hand. "My beloved wife," he began, and read it to the end, his voice trembling with emotion. He ended with, "Ever, your Rulon," and held her closer than before.

Mary turned her head and stretched up to kiss him on the mouth. "Show me," she whispered against his lips.

No dunce, he did.

೩

Rod — April 28, 1865

Rod stalked around the room, slapping one fist into the other. "Carl should be home by now."

Julia glanced up from her ever-present mending. "Husband, he may have gone south. You told me about the army in the Carolinas." She paused, then said quietly. "He's stubborn enough to not give up."

He turned on her, scowling. "He may be rotting in a grave and us without a whit of knowing."

"Could he be a prisoner?"

Rod looked at his wife. She had sounded hopeful, as though being in prison was better than being dead. He immediately repented of his scornful thought. Even if his son was in prison, he was still breathing. Not like Peter. Not like Ben. Alive.

He stood still and let his ire drain away. It wouldn't help his thinking. He had to admit to himself that anger never did. At last he was ready to consider the possibilities with rational purpose. "His name hasn't shown up on a casualty list." He said it almost like a sigh.

"No," Julia agreed.

"If he went south, there's no way to know until he comes home."

"Yes."

He wished Julia would cry, mourn Ben's death as the Allen girl had done. It worried him that she hadn't shed a tear yet. It couldn't be doing her any good.

The Allen girl. He had to stop thinking of her by that name. She counted herself an Owen now. He shook himself. His mind seemed to wander off too much lately. He wondered if grief did that to a body.

Carl. "If he's a prisoner, we won't get word."

"They wouldn't keep him now that the war's done, would they?"

He didn't know. He shook his head.

"Then we wait." She looked down and took a stitch.

She seemed so calm.

"One thing I learned about the Yankees," he said, "is they keep records. Good records. If he's a prisoner, there will be a record of him in Washington City." He rubbed his thumb across his forefinger. "I should leave this week."

"No!"

He jumped at the harshness in Julia's voice.

"I can't wait around forever."

"We wait and give the boy time to get home. If he doesn't come in a month's time, you can go."

Simple. Direct. His Julie's mind was working clear and true, even in the midst of this trouble. He moved behind her, put his hand on her shoulder. He gave it one pat. She placed her hand over his. The warmth eased his anxiety. For Carl. For her. If her mind was working, her tears would come loose sometime.

೫

Mary — May 10, 1865

Mary stood on the corner, watching the Federal cavalrymen parading themselves down the street like they owned Mount Jackson outright. She shivered. Men ought not to take upon themselves such self-righteous airs.

When they had passed, she stepped into the street to cross, but hesitated as one horseman wheeled and gave her the eye, then smirking, joined his fellows in their haughty procession.

"Yankees!" she said, spitting into the dust. The action made her half ashamed of herself, but she had been through just about enough turmoil for a lifetime. She didn't need to feel insulted every time she put a foot outside her door.

She finished crossing the street, slowing her pace so as not to show a shred of fear. *I won't give them the satisfaction.*

She walked a block, then turned a corner to a blast of laughter coming from Fletcher's Tavern. She stopped. Did she dare to walk past the door where a bunch of soldiers had congregated in plain daylight to drink spirits and behave in outrageous ways? She crossed her arms against her bosom, shivering again. She'd heard whispers of women being assaulted when they ventured into the streets of Mount Jackson at night. Did the same danger present itself here? She decided to be on her guard and take another route to her destination.

Another peal of laughter unnerved her, and she backed around the corner, chest heaving as she took in great gulps of air. *Oh Rulon. I wish you were strong and whole again.*

೫

Julia — May 16, 1865

The rap on the front door startled Julia. Strangers used that entrance. Someone at the front door almost always meant bad news or unwelcome company.

She got slowly to her feet, abandoning her mending. Everyone in the family but Carl was accounted for. Was someone here to tell her that he, like Peter and Ben, would never come home?

She moved toward the door on limbs that felt as heavy as pig iron bars. She opened the door. Ella Ruth Allen stood on the porch, dressed from bonnet to hem in black. Only her white face broke the somber color of the trappings of grief.

"Oh!" Julia said, and swung the door wide.

The girl stepped inside and put out her black-mitted hand, seemingly unsure what manner of greeting to offer.

Julia took it, pressed it between her two hands, then led her deeper into the room.

"I don't know how to call you," Ella Ruth said in a whispery voice. "Your comfort when you came— You are Ben's— I am Ben's—" She sank into the chair Julia offered.

"I reckon we're beyond the stage of formality," Julia replied as she sat.

Ella Ruth nodded. "We cannot be formal. He was . . ." She faltered, looked at her hands, clenched them until they went white, pulled her back straight and erect, and looked at Julia again. "You are my mother-in-law."

"Ben thought not."

"He is . . . was mistaken." Ella Ruth stopped speaking for a moment, and Julia allowed her time to compose herself and gather her thoughts.

"There was no one to marry us. Mr. Moore, the mayor, even the Dunker preacher, they were all gone." Ella Ruth's voice had a tinge of desperation. "We even considered a military officer, except I would not be married by a Yankee." She paused again. "Ben agreed. He was in danger of capture every moment he was away from the army."

Julia asked a question that had been burning a hole in her soul. "Why was he with you? Did he desert?"

"Never! He was shot in battle. I kept him safe while he healed."

Julia let the anxiety leave and replaced it with unease of another sort. "You could not marry, yet you claim kinship to me."

The statement hung between them for a moment. Ella Ruth broke the silence with a sigh, then said, "Poppa's slaves. They used a wedding ceremony that he recognized as binding. Ben and I jumped the broomstick."

"Jumped the what?" Julia entwined her fingers and rubbed her thumbs together.

"Broomstick. It's an old custom among the servants," Ella Ruth said. She looked thoughtful, narrowing her brows briefly. "Actually, Ben stepped on the broomstick. He was not sound enough to hop."

Julia nodded. "I see. That made a marriage?"

"We also said words. Vows. He loved me."

"And you loved him?"

"I love him still," she said.

Julia sensed the girl's deep conviction in the matter of her marriage being as real as though they had been church-wed. She let the conviction come across the space between them and into her own soul, felt the comfort it brought. The girl had married Ben. She basked in that surety. Then she remembered a phrase from his letter. She unclasped her hands and placed them in her lap.

"Will there be a child?"

Ella Ruth's face crumpled and she made a sound of woe. Then she said, "No," in an agony-wracked voice. She choked back a further sob.

Another silence wrapped around them, and they sat in its embrace.

At length, Julia spoke. "I will call you 'Daughter'. What will you call me?"

Ella Ruth came off her chair and to her knees before Julia. She grasped her hands. "Will you be 'Mama Owen'?"

"With all my heart," she answered.

Ella Ruth buried her face in Julia's lap and began to cry. When she raised her tear-streaked face, she said, "Poppa and Momma are taking me away to Charlottesville. I may never see you again."

"You cannot know that," Julia said. "Charlottesville is not so far from here."

"Perhaps not." She sniffed and delicately touched the tip of her nose with her knuckle. "I will not remarry," she stated flatly. "I will always be Ella Ruth Owen."

"You will always be my daughter," Julia replied. "Daughter Ella Ruth."

છ

Julia — May 21, 1865

Julia heard the sound of running footsteps coming from the direction of the lane. She stopped grinding corn and looked up as Albert ran in, yelling like the Yankees were still warring with the neighborhood.

"Ma!" The boy stopped, panted, went on. "Somebody's riding in, mighty confident like."

She pushed back a loose lock of hair. "Confident, you say? Does he look like a Yankee?"

Albert hung his head. "I mostly just saw him a-coming before I ran in, Ma. But he's riding real straight and sure of himself."

"Get your pa," she said, walking to the corner and grabbing the Sharps rifle. "No Yankees will set foot in this house."

Julia walked through the doorway with the Sharps in firing position and watched as a horseman in a mud-covered gray coat came down the lane from the pike. *That man rides bold*, she thought. *Bertie spoke the truth.*

"Hold up right there," she called out. "Put your hands where I can see 'em, and get down off that horse." She could see now that he was a young man. Maybe a Confederate cavalier on his way home? Best she found out before she lowered the weapon.

He halted the horse and raised his hands but made no other move than to laugh. "You always did look fine with fire in your eye, Ma."

She sucked in her breath, almost disbelieving the sight of her son's familiar grin. "Carl?" She took a step, lowering the rifle barrel toward the ground. "Carl! Is it really you? Lawsy, boy, we almost gave up on ever seeing you again."

Her eyes started to tear up, and she swiped at them with one hand. "Get off that horse and hug your ma."

He dropped gingerly to the muddy ground and approached with long strides. "Ma, I'm home." He grabbed her—rifle and all—and swung her into the air.

As he lifted her, she caught sight of a wince that he tried to cover. That, coupled with the dried blood on his face, sent her into a tizzy of worry over his health.

Carl set her on her feet at last, and brushed at the mud he had transferred to her dress. "I'm sorry about the mud, Ma. I had a little trouble with some fellers down the road a piece, and we wrasseled around a bit. Here, let me put that rifle aside. I reckon you don't want to put a ball into me."

He took the rifle from her nerveless hands and began to walk toward the front of the house.

She followed him, trying to stop him so she could get a clear view of his face, but he kept walking. "You're not hurt? What's the meaning of that blood on your chin, then?" She watched him lean the rifle against the stone wall and took the opportunity, when he straightened up, to get close.

"Here, let me look at you." She grabbed his arm, and turned him so she could inspect the source of the dried blood. As he squirmed in her grasp, she noted that he appeared to be not much damaged, beyond a split in his lip and several bruises. She moistened the corner of her apron with her tongue and dabbed at his face.

"Ma!" he protested. "It's just a little cut."

"And it needs tending to," she insisted, then hugged him again.

"Look here!" Rod's voice. Threatening. He could be so formidable.

Julie looked at him, feeling her smile spreading wide as a rainbow. Before she could speak, Carl turned to him.

"Have I changed so much, Pa?" He grinned under his camouflage of smeared mud.

"Rod, it's Carl. He's home at last." Julia swiped at the mud on her face with the apron.

Without a word, Rod wrapped his arms around Carl. After a long embrace, he held him off to look at him, and shook his head. "By gum, you sure got your growth dashing around with Mosby. We thought you were dead, boy, not hearing from you, nor seeing you home yet."

"Your pa was set on going to Washington City to ask after you." Julia could not stop smiling.

"I took the long road home. The Colonel disbanded the Rangers about three weeks into April, but me and some thirty others wouldn't leave him, so he took us south to join up with General Johnston in the Carolinas. Before we got there, we learned the General had surrendered, so Colonel Mosby cut us loose and made us go in to get paroled." He paused a moment, rubbing at a patch of mud on his nose. "They won't give him a parole, Pa. There's a price on his head!"

"I reckon there's mighty little justice around now, son. Your colonel won't get fair treatment since Booth shot the President. There's rumors Mosby had a hand in it."

"Somebody shot Jeff Davis?"

"The other president, Abe Lincoln."

"Is he dead?"

Rod set his jaw and turned his back on Carl. Julia reached out for him, but he walked off toward Carl's horse.

He picked up the trailing reins and came back. "Yes, and it brings hard times upon us. There's no mercy in the boys running the country now."

"Mosby had no part in it, Pa." He turned toward Julia. "Ma. I rode with him day and night for over two years." He pivoted back toward Rod. "He done no such a thing."

"I reckon," Rod said.

"He didn't. That's all." Carl's stomach growled. He looked at Julia. "Sorry my gut's so ill-mannered." He glanced around the ruined dooryard. "It sure don't look like Phil Sheridan left much hereabouts. We heard about his orders to burn the Valley, but we laughed. Not one of us believed he could do it as long as Jeb Early's troops were on home ground. How did he do it, Pa?"

"They sent in two and three times our number, son. All we could do was pester them around the edges some."

"Well, here I am now. I'll help rebuild the place. This ground will still grow food—if we can get seed."

Julia watched Albert come out of the shadow of the corner of the house. "Here's your brother, Bertie. Home safe."

Carl said, "You can't be Bertie. He were a little bitty sprout when I left."

"I ain't a sprout now. I been growing." His face bore a frown. "I go by Albert," he added, his voice a touch heated. "I'll be fourteen nigh on to Christmas time."

"You aged a right smart bit, Albert. Been doing most all the chores, I reckon."

"You left 'em to do."

Carl nodded. "I figured you three boys could handle the farm. When Peter died, I was obliged to take his place in the fight."

"I reckon." Albert looked at the ground and kicked the mud.

"I didn't know James would go, too."

Julia said, "They drafted him." She moved forward and pulled on Carl's arm. "Come in and set, boy. Doubtless you're weary, riding all day. I'll finish the pone we're having for supper while you tell your pa what shape the Valley's in south of here. He's been seeking news of the state of the Valley ever since he got home."

"Now Julie, the boy's just got here. I can quiz him later while he eats." Rod turned to Albert. "Take your brother's horse out back and put him in the pen behind the barn. See if you can find some grain. That animal's come far."

"Yes, Pa." Albert took the reins and led the horse around the corner of the house.

Julia got her rifle and went inside. She restored the weapon to its place behind the door, then went back to grinding corn. Carl and Rod came into the house and began to converse before the fire, something about buttons and uniforms and Yankees who had knocked him around.

She asked him, "That's where you got the cuts and bruises and the mud?"

"I reckon, but they didn't hurt me none."

He eased his body to a new position, and she figured he would be plenty sore tomorrow. She'd best give him the bottle of liniment before bed.

Rod's reaction was typical of his attitude nowadays. He slapped his thigh and spat out, "Yankees!"

Julia dumped the batch of cornmeal into a bowl with the rest she had ground. Pone was getting old, but at least they had corn to make it. Carl and Rod kept up the buzz of their talk as she mixed the meal with a bit of leavening and poured water over it.

As she mixed the bowl's contents with her large wooden spoon, Carl turned toward her.

"Ma, where's Marie and the little girl? Ain't they supposed to help you?"

Julia shook her head at his characterization. "Your little sister is nigh on to twelve years old, boy. We kept having birthdays while you were away." She looked over at him. "You've had a couple yourself. Ain't you about nineteen now?"

"Closer to twenty, Ma. I ain't a young'un no more."

Julia looked at the week-old stubble on Carl's face. He had grown into a man. "I see you been over the mountain, son." She laid down the spoon and began the task of forming corn cakes between her hands. "To answer your question, I sent the girls to Mount Jackson to Rulon's place. Mary's not feeling well. She's got Rulon to tend to, so they're helping out with young Roddy. I wrote you Rulon got hurt bad. Did you get my letter?"

Carl nodded.

"There's a mite more food in town," Rod said. "Your ma has her wits scraped down to a nubbin to find us enough to eat since Sheridan paid his call."

"I sent Clay in with the girls," Julia added. "He got himself a job at the livery. I only have to find victuals for your pa, James and Albert."

"And Benjamin," Carl reminded her.

Julia stiffened. The boy didn't know. She didn't fault him for bringing up her deepest sorrow, but his words caused pain to well up out of the place where she'd hidden it away. It swept over her with such force that she thought she would fall to the floor. She saw Rod take a step toward her. Silence hung in the room like a curtain made of combed cotton fibers, thick and heavy and oppressive. Then Rod spoke, his words muffled and measured.

"Benjamin fell at Waynesborough. I had no way to get word home. Your ma only found out when I got here."

Carl sagged on his stool and dropped his head against his hands. Julia felt her ears ringing hollow, filling her skull with a soft buzzing. She thought she should sit before she fell, but Carl was getting to his feet, turning to face Rod and her.

"I'm powerful sorry," he said standing stock still. "Benjamin was always such a lucky cuss, full of life, and all. It don't seem right he's gone." Carl bowed his head, took a deep breath, and began again. "Ma, I know he was your favorite son, and I don't hold it against him. He was the favorite of everybody."

She felt herself toppling, her face going slack like she was blacking out. Carl took two steps and had her in his arms, holding her up, patting her on the head and shoulders. She clung to him, struggling against the dammed emotions she needed so badly to unleash. She felt as though a serpent wrapped around her ribs so tightly she could scarcely breathe.

"There now, Ma, you cry. It'll do you good."

She wanted to cry. She hadn't been able to do it since Rod had brought her word.

Rod's arms came around the two of them. "The boy talks sense, Julia. You ain't cried since you got the news. Let tears come and wash out the grief you been carrying around." His voice became gruff as he said, "I reckon I already done my sorrowing."

The remembrance of her husband sobbing over the loss of his sons cut through the snake binding her heart. The tears came in a great torrent that let her heart expand. She wailed. She cried out. She drummed her fists against Carl's chest.

Her men waited, suspended, as her sobs tore the air. After a long, long time, she quieted, wiped the tears from her cheeks with her apron, and stepped out of the men's arms.

Exhausted, yet strangely renewed, she said, "I reckon that'll have to do for Benjamin. The living need their daily bread." She went back to the table, wiped her hands, and went to work again on her supper preparations. Carl was home. Rulon was on the mend. The family was now as whole as it could get after the terrible conflict. Somehow, they would survive.

ॐ

Mary — May 24, 1865

Mary sat on the edge of the bed, facing away from her husband. She found her voice and asked, "Rule?"

After a moment, he answered in a voice burred with sleep, "Love?"

In truth, she'd been sitting there for some time, endeavoring to find more courage than she thought she possessed. Butterflies flitted through her stomach. *Will he be pleased?*

Exhausted with the emotion she'd been wrestling all afternoon, she felt the need to rest her dithering head, to lie close to him. She rose, pulled the sheet free, and slipped beneath the covers. Rulon turned on his side and laid his arm across her body, just under her bosom. The warmth from his skin heartened her, and she asked again, "Rule?"

A sigh escaped her lips before she could tumble any more words out, and she sensed him coming awake.

"I'm here."

Let him be pleased. She turned toward him, lightly touching his cheek.

"Husband." She paused, choking back her joy until she knew his mind. "Rulon. I am . . . increasing."

His arm tightened, drawing her closer, pulling her against him. "Sugar," he murmured against her lips. "My sweet Sugar."

:::::

The Man from Shenandoah
Introduction

Parole signed by Robert E. Lee on April 9, 1865:

"We, the undersigned prisoners of war belonging to the Army of Northern Virginia, having been this day surrendered by General Robert E. Lee, C.S. Army, commanding said army, to Lieutenant General U. S. Grant, commanding Armies of the Unites States, do hereby give our solemn parole of honor that we will not hereafter serve in the armies of the Confederate States, or in any military capacity whatever, against the United States of America, or render aid to the enemies of the latter, until properly exchanged, in such manner as shall be mutually approved by the respective authorities. . . . The within named officers will not be disturbed by the United States authorities so long as they observe their parole and the laws in force where they may reside."

This was the Beginning of the End of the American Civil War

After General Lee surrendered to General Grant, a few outfits, not hearing of the end to hostilities, fought on past April 9. Other units, hoping against reality that the Cause was not lost, turned further south in join with forces in the Carolinas. One such group was the irregular cavalry outfit, Mosby's Rangers.

When the shabby boys of the unit finally disbanded and received their individual "paroles" as prisoners of war, they ceased to be soldiers, and were admonished not to wear uniforms of the Confederate States of America. An official determination was reached that when the embossed buttons were removed, the clothes they wore were no longer considered to be uniforms.

This is the story of one young veteran's introduction to that rule, and his life after the end of formal hostilities.

Chapter 1

The gaunt-featured young man with the lanky build choked down the last of his moldy bread, then got to his feet and climbed atop the stone wall against which he'd been sitting. Carl Owen looked as far as he could see down the Valley Pike, about two hundred yards, but no one was in sight. Turning to look at the burned-out field the wall enclosed, he surveyed the gray-toned devastation made muddy by today's intermittent rain.

Rage rising in him, thundering in his ears as his heartbeat quickened in frustration and hate, he shook his fist at the sky.

"Phil Sheridan, may God spit in your eye for the ruin you brought to this valley. Rot in hell, Sheridan!"

"Get him!" he heard, just before he was tackled from behind, tumbling him off the wall and into the mud. Carl came up sputtering muck. As he wiped gluey sludge from his eyes, someone kicked him. He was hauled to his feet—arms brutally twisted behind his back—and dragged over the wall to where a huge, red-faced sergeant in a faded blue uniform stood waiting for him.

"Yankees," Carl groaned, berating himself for letting his guard down enough to miss their approach. Panic coursed through his belly. He tried to tear free, but two soldiers gripped his arms, and he finally quit struggling.

The sergeant stood with his legs spread apart, looking Carl up and down. "Johnny Reb, you're on the loose. We have a stout prisoner of war camp for you up in Washington City." He bent forward, laughing in Carl's face, who involuntarily wrinkled his nose and squinted shut his eyes at the overpowering odor of liquor fumes. The man frowned, drew a knife from a sheath on his belt, and tested it on his thumb.

"You look at me, Johnny Reb," he snarled. "Look at me when I speak to you!"

Carl opened his eyes and stared into the Yankee's mean eyes. "I have parole papers," he said, raising his muddy, stubbled chin in defiance.

"You're violating your parole, wearing the uniform of the Confederate Army," the Yankee said. He put his blade against Carl's throat, who sucked in a breath, then held it, careful not to move.

Just then, a burly soldier came up behind the sergeant. "Sarge, you told us we were going to find some Southern belles to entertain us," he complained. "Let's dump him in the woods."

"Keep your nose out of official business. I'll open him up a bit and teach him how to act around his betters."

From the north, a rider came pounding up the road, spurring his horse, then sawing on the reins to bring it to a halt. He alighted and ran to the sergeant.

"The major's coming down the road. You'd better not let him catch you cutting another Reb."

The sergeant cursed and turned back to Carl, grabbing the front of his coat.

"You got no right to wear a uniform, you dirty Rebel pup." He took a fresh grip on his knife and addressed the soldiers restraining Carl. "Hold him tight while I teach him a lesson."

Carl felt the tight prickle of fear racing up his spine as the soldiers freshened their hold on his arms. The sergeant looked around at the road, cursed again, turned to Carl, and cut the embossed buttons from his coat. He jerked the coat open, grinning evilly, and cut the buttons from his shirt, as well.

"Now you're not a soldier." The man cackled as he pocketed the buttons and sheathed his knife. "Let him loose," he ordered, motioning to the soldiers. As they dropped his arms, he looked Carl up and down once more, his expression changing to hatred. The sergeant half turned away, then spun back, and with a massive fist knocked Carl flat. "Mount up," the sergeant barked, and strode toward his horse, weaving a bit.

Lying in the mud, propped on one elbow, Carl wiped blood from his jaw, tasting salt as he tongued his molars to see if they were still tight. He watched the patrol leave, hate burning his belly. He turned over onto his knees and got to his feet, wincing at the pain, then whistled for his horse. Looking around for his hat, he found it on the wall where it had landed when he was attacked. He brushed at the soft, shapeless felt, removing a splash of mud, then he jammed it onto his head.

Sherando came trotting out of the trees, gray coat glistening in the misty rain that had once again begun to fall. The horse jumped the fence to reach Carl and nickered softly. Carl checked to see that the Yankee rifle was secure in the scabbard. "Sure glad them Billy Blues was so drunk they didn't find you, boy," he whispered through raw lips.

He swung into the saddle and straightened his back, swiped at his face with both hands to remove as much mud as he could, then ran his fingers through the blond hair at the nape of his neck, tugging loose both tangles and mud. He hoped someone at home had a comb, for he had lost his personal gear in a wild, last-ditch ride for freedom with Colonel John Mosby. Carl's patrol had ridden into a Yankee camp to surrender after the war's end. Union officers gave the Confederate cavalrymen parole papers and turned them free instead of holding them as prisoners of war. Carl had stolen the rifle as he left camp, but hadn't had a chance to replace other gear.

Carl turned his horse onto the Valley Pike, laughing as joy surged through him. "Benjamin will have a comb. It'll be fine to see him again." Carl kneed Sherando to a trot, and launched into a tune he'd heard somewhere. "Oh Shenandoah, I'm coming to ya. I'm here, you rolling river."

Carl looked toward the shallow river flowing beside the road and grinned at the cleverness of his new words to an old song. "Hold up that head, horse. We'll show the folks that a passel of Yankees can't lick a Virginia boy. We're goin' home!"

∽

"Ma!" Albert ran in yelling from the trees at the corner of the yard. "Somebody's riding in, mighty confident like," he panted.

Julia Owen looked up from the corn she was grinding and pushed back a loose lock of dark hair.

"Confident, you say? Does he look like a Yankee?"

Albert hung his head. "I mostly just saw him a-coming before I ran in, Ma. But he's riding real straight and sure of himself."

"Get your pa," she said, grabbing the Sharps rifle from the corner. "There won't be no Yankees set foot in this house."

Julia walked through the doorway with the Sharps in firing position and watched as a horseman neared the end of the lane from the pike. *Albert spoke the truth*, she thought. *That man rides bold.*

"Hold up right there," her voice rang out. "Put them hands where I can see 'em, and get down off that horse."

The mud-covered young man in the gray coat laughed. "You always did look fine with fire in your eye, Ma."

"Carl?" She took a step, lowering the rifle barrel toward the ground. "Carl! Is it really you? Lawsy, boy, we almost gave up on ever seeing you again." She swiped at her eyes with one hand. "Get off that horse and hug your ma." Her son dropped gingerly to the muddy ground and approached with long strides.

"Ma, I'm home." He grabbed her—rifle and all—and swung her into the air.

She caught sight of the wince that he tried to cover and the dried blood on his face, and immediately began to worry over his health.

Setting her on her feet, Carl brushed at the mud he had transferred to her dress. "I'm sorry about the mud, Ma. I had a little trouble with some fellers down the road a piece, and we wrasseled around a bit. Here, let me put that rifle aside. I reckon you don't want to put a ball into me."

"You ain't been hurt? What's that blood?" She followed him to the front of the house, where he leaned the rifle against the stone wall. "Here, let me look at you." Julia grabbed his arm, moistened the corner of her apron with her tongue, and dabbed at his face.

"Ma!" he protested. "It's just a little cut."

"And it needs tending to," she insisted, then hugged him again.

∽

Roderick Owen came around the corner of the house, puzzled by the sounds in the front yard, but ready for Albert's Yankee invasion. He stopped short at the sight of a tall, very grubby man embracing his wife, and Albert bumped into his father from behind.

"Look here," Rod threatened, stepping forward.

Carl turned to meet him. "Have I changed so much, Pa?" He grinned under his smeared camouflage.

"Rod, it's Carl. He's home at last." Julia wiped the mud from her face with the apron.

Without a word, Rod enveloped his son in his arms. After a long embrace, he held him off to look at him, and shook his head. "By gum, you sure get your growth dashing around with Mosby. We thought you were dead, boy, not hearing from you, nor seeing you home yet."

"I took the long road home, Pa. The Colonel disbanded the Rangers about three weeks into April, but me and some thirty others wouldn't leave him, so he took us south to join up with General Johnston in the Carolinas. The General gave up before we got there, so Mosby cut us loose and made us go in to get paroled." He paused a moment, scratching his nose. "They won't give him a parole, Pa. There's a price on his head!"

"I reckon there's mighty little justice around now, son. Your colonel won't get fair treatment since Booth shot the President. There's rumors Mosby had a hand in it."

"Somebody shot Jeff Davis?"

"The other president, Abe Lincoln."

"Is he dead?"

Rod set his jaw, turned his back on his son, and walked toward Carl's horse, his hand worrying the mud at the front of his shirt and pants. He picked up the horse's trailing reins and approached his son. "Yes, and it brings hard times upon us. There's no mercy in the boys running the country now."

"Mosby had no part in it. I rode with him day and night for over two years. He done no such a thing."

"I reckon."

"He didn't. That's all." Carl's stomach growled aloud, and he looked at his mother. "Is there anything to eat? It sure don't look like Phil Sheridan left much. We heard about his orders to burn out the Valley, Pa, but we laughed. Not one of us believed he could do it with you and Jeb Early's troops on home ground."

"They sent in two and three times our number, son. All we could do was pester them around the edges some."

"Well, I'm home now, and this ground will grow food—if we can get seed." Carl looked about the yard. Albert stood in the shadow at the corner of the house.

"Who's that young'un? I don't recollect leaving anybody that big at home when I left."

"It's me, Albert. I growed a mite."

"Can't be. You were just a little bitty sprout."

Albert came out of the shadow and stood where Carl could see him. "I ain't a sprout now." His voice was a touch heated. "I'll be fourteen nigh on to Christmas time."

"You aged a right smart bit, Albert. Been doing most all the chores, I reckon."

"You left 'em to do."

Carl nodded. "I figured you three boys could handle the farm. When Peter died, I felt obliged to take his place in the fight."

"I reckon." Albert looked at the ground and kicked the mud.

"I didn't know James would go, too."

"They drafted him."

Julia moved forward and pulled on Carl's arm. "Come in and set, boy. Doubtless you're weary, riding all day. I'll finish the pone we're having for supper while you tell your pa what shape the Valley's in down south of here. He's been asking after news of the state of things since he got home."

"Now Julie, the boy's just got here. I can quiz him later while he eats." Rod turned to his youngest son. "Albert, take your brother's horse out back and put him in the pen behind the barn. See if you can find some grain. That animal's come far with your brother."

"Yes, Pa." Albert took the reins and led Sherando around the corner of the house.

℘

After knocking the mud from his boots, Carl entered the house, shrugged out of his wet coat, and hung it on a peg inside the door. He pulled his shirt together the best he could and glanced around the room, savoring its warmth and cheerfulness. Then he took the stool his father indicated and moved it close to the fire before sitting.

"What happened to your buttons, boy?" Rod asked. "Were you obliged to sell them for food?" He also sat, and crossed one leg over the other.

"Naw. Some fat Yankee sergeant down the road a ways cut them off me. Said I was in uniform and didn't have the right."

"That's where you got the cuts and bruises and the mud, Carl?" his mother asked.

"I reckon, but they didn't hurt me none." He eased his rib cage from side to side to be sure.

Rod slapped his thigh in anger. "Yankees," he spit out.

Carl looked up, feeling a similar heat. "They ain't mannerly, that's for sure, but I came out lucky anyhow. Didn't lose nothing but my buttons. I hid my horse back in the willows along the creek, and they were too drunk to spot him, so they missed the rifle I snuck off the Yankee weapon pile after I got my parole."

"Drunk, you say? That sounds like the same Yankee bunch that's been back and forth through this part of the Valley, teasing and tormenting the folks."

"Could be them." Carl shrugged, then looked around the room once more. "Ma, where's Marie and the little girl? Ain't they supposed to help you?"

Julia smiled. "Your little sister is nigh on to twelve years old, boy. We kept having birthdays while you were away. You've had a couple yourself. Ain't you about nineteen now?"

"Closer to twenty, Ma. I ain't a young'un no more."

Julia looked at Carl's bearded face. "I see you been over the mountain, son." She paused to form a corn cake. "I sent the girls in to Mount Jackson to Rulon's place. Mary's not feeling well, and she's got Rulon to tend to, so they're helping out with young Roddy. You heard Rulon got hurt bad?"

Carl nodded.

"There's also more food in town," Rod explained. "Your ma has her wits scraped down to a nubbin to find us enough to eat since Sheridan paid his call."

"Clay went in with the girls," Julia added. "He's got a job at the livery, so there's just Pa and James and Albert to fix for."

"And Benjamin," Carl reminded her.

He watched his mother's body stiffen, and saw his father take a protecting step toward her. Silence hung in the room like a curtain made of combed cotton fibers, thick and heavy and oppressive. Then Rod spoke, his words muffled and measured.

"Benjamin fell at Waynesboro. I had no way to get word home. Your ma only found out when I got here."

The words bucked into Carl with the kick of a mule. He sagged on the stool and his head dropped against his hands. First, Peter had fallen at the Second Battle of Manassas, or Bull Run, as the Yankees called it. Then Rulon, the eldest, was sorely wounded in the battle of Tom's Brook last October. Now Benjamin was gone. Carl felt his ears ringing hollow, filling his skull with a soft buzzing.

He rose to his feet and faced his parents. "I'm powerful sorry," he said, holding himself still. "Benjamin was always such a lucky cuss, full of life, and all. It don't seem right he'd be gone."

Carl bowed his head, took a deep breath, and began again. "Ma, I know he was your favorite son, and I don't hold it against him. He was the favorite of everybody."

He took a step toward his mother, watching her white, crumpling face. With another step he had her in his arms, patting her head and shoulders. "There, Ma, you cry. It'll do you good."

Rod's arms went around the pair. "The boy talks sense, Julia. You ain't cried since you got the news. Let the tears wash out the grief you been carrying around." He continued gruffly, "I reckon I already done my sorrowing."

The men waited, suspended, as Julia's sobs tore the air. After a long time, she quieted, wiped the tears from her cheeks with her apron, and stepped out of the men's arms. Her face was changed, resigned. "I reckon that'll have to do for Benjamin, 'cause the living need their daily bread." She went back to the table, wiped her hands, and continued to fix supper.

Rod approached his chair and sagged into it, while Carl returned to his stool. Both men sat slumped for a time, saying nothing as the pain sat upon their shoulders. After a time, Rod threw back his head.

"Your ma's kept the family going whilst we were gone, son, and she's the one saw to it that we didn't starve when we returned. I got a leave to come home in December, on account of our mounts were starving for lack of forage, and I'll be switched if she hadn't outsmarted that cocky Phil Sheridan. She saved most of the corn by tying the sacks on the backs of the stock, and sending Clay and Albert to the hills with the animals. She saved the crop and the herd, both. I'm mighty proud of her."

"Ma, that was right canny thinking. I'd like to see Sheridan's face should he find out you outfoxed him."

Julia shook her head and continued with the meal.

"We ain't tooting our horn about the food we got, Carl," Rod said. "It's mighty little for our needs, and even so, we had to send the girls into town."

"How serious was Rulon hurt, Pa?"

"Well, he had a right smart mess of holes in him. The surgeon sent him home to die, but there ain't no quit in Rulon. That little wife of his nursed him along real well, too. He's mostly out of bed now, finally on the mend." Rod rose to his feet. "Say, come out and help me milk, son. That brindle cow the Yankees stole last fall wandered up to the fence today, bawling and kicking and carrying on to be let in the gate, but she's still half wild. There's a calf trailing her, so she must have milk."

Carl nodded. "Sure, Pa. I reckon a body don't forget how to do the chores."

As the men stepped out the back door, Carl glanced around at what was left of the yard behind the house, and took in a rasping breath. The vegetable garden was a sea of mud, while out yonder, wreckage marked where the barn had been. All that remained were the burned beams and blackened supports that had fallen onto the floor. Two mounds of gray ashes, scattered by wind and rain, showed where the hay had been stacked. The animal pens were in ruins, poles broken and strewn about. Someone had piled brush in the gaps until new poles were cut.

Carl waved an arm at the view. "Was it like this when you got home, Pa?"

"Pretty near. The boys and I ain't had a lot of time to clean up much."

The brindle cow tied in the pen rolled her eyes and lowed in fright at the men's approach. Rod expelled his breath. "She always was skittish, Carl. I reckon she got away from Sheridan's soldiers and wintered back in the oak groves. She had her calf, then got lonely for home."

Carl stepped around behind the cow. "Mind that hoof." Rod spoke sharply as the brindle kicked out.

Carl dodged away and snorted. "She must be a Yankee lover. Welcome home to you too, cow." He patted her flank.

"Grab the pail and set to work, son. She wants milking."

Just then the hungry calf tied behind the remains of the barn began to bawl. Brindle pulled her head backward, and Rod reached for the rope to snub her on a shorter line. Lacking a stool, Carl squatted on his heels and began to milk.

The cow sidestepped, nearly catching Carl's foot. He avoided her hoof, and then she whipped her tail against his face. He turned away, saving his eyes from the coarse hair. Then she lifted her hoof and banged it hard against the pail, but Carl snatched it away in time to save the contents from spilling.

"Whoa, cow!" he yelled, as she swung her hindquarters against him. "You're right, Pa. She's gone wild." He scrambled out of the way, bringing the pail with him. "I call the job done. Let that calf come over here."

Rod grinned, went for the bawling creature, and untied the tether rope. "We're all out of practice of milking, son," he called. "I reckon I'd druther fight Yankees than get stepped on by a wild cow. I know James feels the same, after milking the white-face cow."

"Is he in one piece?" Carl asked, looking sidelong at his pa.

Rod turned the calf loose, and it ran to its mother. He grinned again as it began to suckle. Then his face went somber. "He got a flesh wound at Five Forks, outside Richmond, but it's healing clean. He can swing an ax, so I sent him up by the mountain to cut wood. Likely he'll be home tomorrow night with a load of fence poles."

"It'll be good to see him." Relief softened Carl's voice.

The two men headed for the house as the sun dropped toward the horizon. The rain earlier in the day had left the air cool and sweet, and a light breeze was blowing the final clouds away. Carl handed the milk pail to his father at the door.

"I'm all covered with mud, Pa. Best I wash up before I eat."

"You'll have to use the crick, son. The Yankees knocked the top of the well apart and dumped it into the shaft. I ain't got it cleaned out yet."

"Then I'll bring back some water."

Carl took two pails from the back stoop and slogged his way through the muck of the yard to the creek path. He felt like a small boy again, recalling the times he'd walked this path before the well was dug.

Carl came up to the creek, knelt, and dipped the pails into the deepest part of the water. After he set them high on the bank, he removed his shirt, tossed it aside, and plunged his arms into the water. Gasping with the impact of the cold, he splashed it onto his head and chest.

Once his face was clean, he wiped off his boots and rubbed most of the mud from his pants, then rinsed his shirt in the stream and wrung it out several times. He shook out the shirt and put it on, shivering when the cold, wet cloth made contact with his flesh.

Twilight took away most of the daylight as Carl paused to look into the water of the creek where it pooled below him. He saw a distorted reflection of the outline of his form in the dim light. Nineteen years had built his body well and tall, but the last four, with the privations of war, had hardened the muscles of his frame and made his features gaunt. His hair was too long, and the week's growth of sandy red beard itched. He'd have to hunt up scissors and a razor as well as a comb.

As night fell, Carl shrugged his shoulders to rearrange the damp shirt, picked up the pails, and headed back to the house, guided by the lamplight from the kitchen window. Breeze on the shirt chilled him, and he walked a little faster. At the steps he re-scraped his boots, then opened the door and went inside.

"We're just fixing to eat," Julia called. She turned and saw the water buckets. "Thank you, son. You saved me a trip."

Carl pulled up a chair to the table and joined Rod and Albert.

"It ain't much, Carl, but it'll keep you from blowing away." Julia waved her hand toward the food. "We're lucky to have greens. They popped up down by the crick, and I picked them late this afternoon. 'Course, there's corn pone, and we have milk, but there ain't no real coffee, just roasted chicory." She sighed as she sat at her place. "We'll have real food again once we get a crop up."

"That's something we need to do some talking about," Rod declared. "First, let's give thanks for Carl's safe return, and for this food we got."

At the end of the grace, Carl glanced across the table at his father. There'd been something in his voice that foretold serious business. Rod must have felt his stare, for he looked up, his beard wrinkling as he chewed.

Rod swallowed. "Tell me how it looks south of here, son. What did Sheridan leave for the folks in the south end of the Valley? You came from Staunton, I reckon?" Rod took a bite of greens.

"He burnt or pulled down homes, barns, crops, orchards, 'most everything, all the way to Staunton and beyond. It's a famine time. A crow flying by would have to bring his own rations." He paused to chew a piece of pone. "Ma, it's a wonder to me the Yankees left our house alone when they came back through."

"I had my good Sharps rifle, and I set right there in the doorway and wouldn't budge none. After a while they left me be and went out back to burn the barn."

"Marie could-a been killed," Albert said, frowning. "Them dirty Yankees didn't wait 'til she was out of the barn to set it afire." Albert's eyes looked dark and fierce. "I wish I'd a been down here shooting me some Yankees instead of up in the hills with Clay and all them cows!"

"Likely they'd have shot you, Albert," Carl said. "Praise God you was up there!"

Rod's mouth tightened. "What about livestock, son? What did you see?"

"I reckon we've got more cattle than any five stock men down the Valley, Pa. Maybe five pigs, thin stuff; not more'n ten hens anywhere. I reckon Grant didn't want no more supplies coming out of the Shenandoah. He meant for little Phil Sheridan to clean us out, and he did the job."

"Lucky I was warned some," Julia said, "or I wouldn't have had time to send the boys off up the hill."

Rod chewed his food slowly, his face looking thoughtful. "I reckon we're eating about as well as Rand Hilbrands. The Yankees missed burning the store in Mount Jackson, so he still has food to put on his table."

"What happened over to Chester Bates' place, Pa?"

"He lost his barn, and the house is gutted out. They burned his fields bare. The Bates family is about wiped off the face of the earth, I'd say."

"Are they all dead?"

"They've got their lives and little else."

"That's sure a pity." Carl wiped his mouth with his hand. "They had the prettiest stone house I believe I've ever seen. Where are they living now?"

"Right on the place, in the old tool shed."

"Hush, that's a shame. There's no finer man than Chester Bates, 'cept for you and John Mosby, Pa."

"Andy Campbell says his pa's so mad about his place being wrecked, he wants to clear out and go someplace else," Albert reported.

Rod Owen cleared his throat. "That's just what I aim to do."

Chapter 2

Rod's words seemed to echo in the room, fading into silence. Stunned, no one moved or spoke for several seconds, then the air was split with the clamor of the family reacting to his declaration.

Julia raised her chin a bit as she stared down the length of the table. "This has been my home since we wed."

"Pa, I took an oath I'd come home and wait to be exchanged proper. I don't reckon the Yankees will let me leave." Carl shifted in his chair, sitting up straight.

Albert jumped to his feet. "But Pa, I was born right here in this house."

Rod waved away the arguments and held up his hand for silence. "I've decided to sell the farm and go to the Colorado Territory. You ma's brother Jonathan is out there somewhere, and we'll find him. There's gold and silver to be mined, but I been contemplating." Rod paused to lift his cup and try the chicory. He made a face, then drank some more before setting down the cup.

"There's no future for us here in the Valley. Since we're going to cross the country to make a new start, why not start a cattle ranch?" Rod looked around at his family. "We have good cattle here that we can sell as beef to the miners," he said. "There's a sight of folks out there that like to eat. I reckon raising cattle is as good a way to earn a living as digging in the ground for metal."

"I took an oath, Pa." Carl leaned forward. "I'm bound to stay here until my papers come."

"Carl, an Owen's oath is sacred word, but you saw the way of things out there. Since the Yankees paid their call, if we stay here our only choice is to starve. I reckon your oath is null and void."

Carl slouched against the back of his chair. "Who'll buy a burned-out farm? Nobody around here has any federal cash to give you."

"There was a feller here last week from New York State, looking for farmland. His brother was one of Sheridan's torch men, and told him all about the fine crops he set fire to. Well, the man offered a good price, and I took it."

"But Pa," Albert burst out, "he's a damned Yankee!"

"Watch your tongue, young'un. Yes, he's a Yankee, but he has good Yankee currency and coin to give me. Now that you're home, Carl, I aim to leave in two weeks."

"Two weeks!" Julia echoed. "We can't be ready by then."

"How long did it take you to send the boys off up the mountain with the corn?"

Julia stared at her plate.

"We'll be ready in two weeks, because Mr. Avery will take possession then. He'll be back from Washington next week with the money, then he's off to get his family to move them here." Rod slapped the table and stood up.

"You really sold the place?" Julia got to her feet. "You never thought to ask me?"

"We're bound for Colorado. That's all." His words were sharp, final.

Julia reached down for her plate and turned her back in silence.

∞

Rod climbed into bed. Julia turned away from him.

"Still mad at me?" Disappointed, he reached out to touch her shoulder. She shrugged off his hand.

"I got a right."

"I figured you'd want to leave this place."

"I defended the house. I saved it, and I aimed to live in it." She turned over to glare at him.

"You need a change. This war has took your spirit, along with your boys, Julie. I figured you'd want to go."

"There ain't nothing wrong with my spirit, Rod Owen. I've plenty left to tell you what I think. It's a low-down, slimy, snake trick to take a gal's home away from her, without even a by-your-leave."

Rod pushed himself up with his elbows and stared at Julia. "You've changed a right smart whilst I was gone."

"I've had to fend for myself and the young'uns, Rod. I got so I was the boss around the place. I did my chores and yours, too. Now you come home and sell my place without considering my side of the matter. Yes, I've changed a right smart, and I'm mad at you." Julia turned away and hit the wall with her small, work-worn fist.

Rod sank back into the featherbed and let the air leave his lungs in one fast exhalation. When he spoke again, his voice was contemplative.

"I reckon we've both changed. Me, I got used to having my orders obeyed without a word of question coming back at me. It was do it right now or die. My guess is we've lost the habit of working together like we used to." He screwed up his face and rubbed his beard with both hands. "I just hope we ain't lost the habit of loving together," he added, barely audible.

"Um," she sighed, almost a sob, and after a long silence, she turned to look at Rod.

He put out his hand, touched her cheek, and said, "My Julie."

"I never got free of needing you to love me," she whispered. "We need to learn again how to get on with one another, is all."

"I give you my word I'll work hard to look after you like I used to."

"I don't need looking after like I did before the war took you away. I need you to work with me and think about my feelings and thoughts before you jump into something like this."

"I can't change what I did. The paper's signed."

"Oh, Rod, that means we have to leave Baby John lying over yonder in the burying ground." She clutched his forearm, then relaxed her grip to smooth the grizzled hair. "It about breaks my heart."

"Julie, I ain't an unfeeling man. I know it pains you to leave him, and Peter and Benjamin, too, but this is our chance to make a new start." Rod sat up, and the covers fell forward from his torso, exposing his long underwear. "We'll have the cash to buy an outfit to get to Colorado Territory. I'll try to shed my bossy ways, if you'll forgive me, and go with a willing heart."

Julia looked at Rod's back, gauging his excitement by the rapidity of his breathing. It finally returned to normal, and he sank back into the tick.

"Twenty-five years ago I made my vow to love you and to live with you wherever you went," she whispered. "Since you're bound to go, I'd best keep my promise."

Rod turned and looked at Julia. "I love you, woman," he sighed, gathering her into his arms.

൭

Carl woke up in his bed. *I'm home*, he marveled, rolling over in the quilt. He was warm under the covers, barricaded against air chilly from the night's rain.

Looking over at Albert, he saw the regular rise and fall of his brother's chest. *He's such a young'un,* Carl mused. *He's been doing all my chores for three years. It's time I took some of 'em back and let him sleep.*

He sat up and flicked the covers back from his bare legs. It had been a long time since he'd had a chance to get out of his pants at night. On the run with the Rangers, he had practically slept in his saddle. Carl got up and dressed quickly, yearning for a change of clothes.

He left Albert still asleep and went downstairs to stir up the fire. As he made it blaze to life, the chill around the fireplace faded, and he put a boiler of water on the hearth to heat for washing up later.

Carl crossed the room and got his coat before he went outdoors. From the doorway he looked at the morning sky. The clouds were thinning out, waiting for the sun to rise, and the rain had quit falling. Toward the east, the bulk of Massanutten Mountain rose up to prevent Carl from seeing the Blue Ridge Mountains, but he knew they were there, and he knew they were hazy and covered with fog on such a morning as this. He'd spent enough time dodging the Yankees, riding up into the sanctuary of the isolated gaps and hollows, that he knew the moods of the mountains.

The yard was under water from the night's rain, and Carl wondered how the animals would fare in the open in this weather. Then he recalled with a jolt that soon they would be used to it. There were no barns on the way to Colorado Territory.

Carl set about feeding the animals, and with courage born of morning freshness, he decided to tackle milking Brindle by himself.

"Cow, I been over the hill and down the river in the last few years. I ain't going to be licked by the likes of you."

Brindle promptly knocked him over, sprawling him into the mud and water. He scrambled up, soaked and sputtering, and went back to work, wiping his hands on his pants.

"I reckon I'll milk you, so you'd just as well surrender, you crazy cow." Carl set his jaw and grabbed a handful of teat. Brindle turned her head and rolled her eyes, unconvinced of Carl's prowess. He went on the attack, and the cow mooed with fright.

When he had a half-pail of milk, Carl figured he'd won the battle, and let the calf have its breakfast. He straightened his back, then probed the sore spot on his side where the cow had kicked him, but decided it was nothing to worry about.

Carl took the milk to the house and washed up with the water he'd left heating. Checking the wood box, he found it half empty and returned to the yard for an armful. From the looks of the stack of firewood on the left edge of the clearing, James had made more than one trip to the mountain for wood. Carl pulled some logs from the center of the pile where the wood was dry, and took them into the house.

Julia was up, tending the fire and baking bread for the day. She looked up at Carl, then down at his feet.

"Hush, Ma, I'm sorry. I forgot to wipe 'em. I ain't used to living in a house, but I'll try to keep the mud in the yard where it belongs."

Albert came into the room, yawning and stretching, and looked accusingly at Carl. "You left me a-sleeping. I got critters looking to be fed."

"You was up late, and looked like you were relishing your sleep. I took the liberty of doing your chores this morning. Set and eat."

"Thanks, Carl. Don't mind if I do." Albert sat and attacked his breakfast.

Rod came into the room, looking pleased with himself. He carried a list of purchases to make as soon as the Yankee money passed into his hands. He sat and greeted his family.

"Morning, Julia, boys. Fine day. Carl, you make ready to ride into town with me after breakfast. We'll fetch back your sisters to help your ma get the foodstuffs together." Rod paused to chew a mouthful of cornbread, then turned to his youngest son. "Albert, who did you say was willing to leave the Valley on account of his place was wrecked?"

"That would be Andy's pa, Angus Campbell."

"Pa," Carl broke in ahead of Rod's next speech. "How are we going to get out to Colorado? Me and my outfit blew up so much track hereabouts, I reckon the railroad's useless."

"I been studying on that, son. We'll take wagons, like those who went to Oregon in the early days, and the Mormon folk in the forties. I reckon we'll keep off the northern trails. I can just see a Yankee farmer taking pot shots at us, calling us wild Rebs. Likely we can get through Kentucky and Missouri on the back roads and hit the Santa Fe Trail at the city of Kansas. We'll follow it along the Arkansas River into Colorado, then turn north and strike out for Denver City to find your uncle."

"We're getting a mighty late start."

"I know, and wagons are slow, but I figure we can haul more goods for less cost that way. I reckon we'll need four, five months on the trail, but the weather should hold pretty fair until then." Rod turned his head to his wife. "We'll take that old box of Jonathan's to him."

Carl's gaze shifted from his father's face to the leather-covered strongbox on the mantel. Uncle Jonathan brought it with him when he returned from his trip to the Territory in 'Fifty-nine. He told his sister it was hers if they ever got word of his death. Then he went back west to his gold fields. The box had never been opened, and sat, padlocked and dusty, where he'd placed it.

"How long since you heard from Uncle Jonathan, Ma?" asked Carl.

"It's been a couple of years, but mail has been real chancy with the war on."

"It'll be good to see him again." Carl rose from the table. "I'll saddle the horses, Pa."

"I'm nearly through here." Rod paused to wipe his mouth. "Albert, you'd best get to shelling the corn. Your ma will need to make it all up into cornmeal before we leave."

"Yes, Pa."

Chapter 3

Carl rode with his father down the Valley toward Mount Jackson, feeling a wrenching in his gut at the desolation and ruin in the homesteads they passed. These folks had worked for years, generations even, and now everything was gone, wiped out by the advance of Sheridan's army. Some of these farmers might listen to Pa's plan to go west.

As they rode through the gray mist and green trees, they approached Mount Jackson, which sat near the Shenandoah River. The damage here was not so heavy. Old stone houses still lined the streets of the residential section, where the town folks were scratching out a post-war living. An occasional empty lot in the business district gave testimony of a wooden building gone up in smoke.

Rod pulled up his horse at an intersection and turned to Carl. "We'll go to Rulon's house first, let the girls know to pack up their bundles. Then I'll go talk to Randolph Hilbrands. He could make a pile of money with a store in Colorado, and he's always been partial to money." Rod chuckled. "Let's see how long it takes me to convince him."

Rulon lived on a quiet back street in a brick house owned by his father-in-law, that same Randolph Hilbrands. Rulon and Mary had lived there since he was sent home to die.

As Rod and Carl rode up to the door of the house, someone pulled aside the curtains of a window on the ground floor and peeked out. The men dismounted and tied their horses to the fence, then the door of the house was flung open, and out boiled two young females.

"Papa!" Julianna, fair colored and exuberant, with the energy of eleven years, threw herself into Rod's arms.

"It's Pa," squealed Marie. "And Carl's here, too!" Despite the decorum she had gained in sixteen years, she wrapped her arms around Carl, nearly knocking him off balance.

"Whoa, hold up there, Sis." He put out his hand to steady the two of them against the fence. "You've growed up," he said, astonished.

"Sure have." Marie giggled, tossing her dark head. "And you're a man, looks like." She backed away for a long appraisal.

Carl went hot with embarrassment. His sister was looking at him with woman's eyes.

"I'm just real skinny," he protested. "It makes me look taller."

"Wait 'til the girls get a look at you," laughed Marie. "You'll have to drive 'em off with a hay fork. It's been a long time since we've had any suitors around."

"Suitors! You and your friends ain't never had no suitors. You was just babies when us men went off to fight." Carl took a deep breath, on home ground now that he was bantering with Marie.

"That's all you know," she replied.

Julianna dragged Pa toward the house, so Carl grabbed Marie's hand and followed.

Mary Owen stood in the doorway, offering a hand to her father-in-law, who gave her a bear hug instead. She looked pale, and a crease appeared on her forehead as she endured the hug.

"Roddy," she called to a small, dark-haired child playing by the hearth. "You come over here. Your granddaddy just came. Give him a welcome."

The boy looked up, then jumped to his feet.

"Poppy!" he cried, and ran over to grasp Rod by the knees. Rod bent down and boosted him up onto his shoulders. The boy whooped, and held on to Rod's ears.

Julianna plumped a pillow in the best chair in the house, saying, "Papa, come an' set down."

Rod put the youngster on the floor, and Roddy scampered off to play with his blocks.

"Pa, it's right nice to see you again," Marie said, hugging her father. "Carl, come over here and set a while," she urged her brother, placing a chair for him.

The men sat, and Julianna tiptoed behind Carl, then ambushed him with a big hug, startling him into standing again.

"Jule! You'd best not surprise a man thataway. I might've hurt you."

"Carl's home, Carl's home," she sang, dancing her way around the room, heedless of his discomfort.

Rulon, hearing all the uproar, came down the stairs, leaning against the wall for support. Upon seeing his father and brother, he lowered the pistol he carried and entered the room. Mary glanced up and gave a little cry of alarm, but he waved aside her concern.

"I'm fine, Mary," Rulon grinned, sweeping his hair out of his eyes. He tucked the pistol into the waistband of his trousers and held out his hand to his father. "Just the sight of my kin makes me feel strong."

Rod arose and took Rulon's outstretched hand, then passed him on to Carl, who carefully embraced him.

"You look a mite thin, Rule, but likely you'll never get as skinny as me." The younger brother measured himself against the older, found himself to be taller, and grinned with delight. "Seems you've shrunk a mite, too."

"Taller don't make better, Carl. I still outweigh you in a wrestling match. Wait 'til I get my strength, and we'll have a go at it." Rulon stepped back to look at Carl's spare frame. "'Pears to me you're healthy. Did you catch any Yankee lead?"

Carl grinned. "Colonel Mosby kept us riding fast enough to beat the bullets. That's not saying we didn't lose a few men here and there." His expression changed. "We lost more than a few. I reckon we paid a powerful price."

"Amen, brother."

"Leastwise, you made it home, Rule. Pa just told me about Ben yesterday. That's a mighty blow, I tell you."

Rulon nodded, clapped Carl on the shoulder, and took a chair. "Pa, what brings you into town in the middle of the morning?"

"I've come to fetch your sisters home to help your ma. We've got a right smart job of work to do in the next fortnight. Well, so do you, come to think of it."

"What's that you mean, Pa?"

"I've sold the farm, and we're going to the Colorado Territory to hunt up Uncle Jonathan. I aim to thumb my nose at these Yankees, light a shuck out of here, and make a new life growing cows for all them miners to buy."

"Do miners need lots of milk and butter, Papa?" asked Julianna. She looked around, confused by the hoots of laughter that greeted her question. "Well, do they?"

"I don't mean milk cows, daughter. We're going to raise beef critters."

"Are you asking us to go with you, Pa?" Rulon asked.

"I'd like it, Rulon. It'd be best to keep the family together. You need good clean air to help you mend proper, and Mary here could use a change, her feeling so poorly just now."

Mary sank to her knees beside Rulon's chair, looking anxiously up at him. "I don't feel like I can leave Pa and Ma and go traipsing over the countryside dodging Yankees, Rulon. Please say 'no'," she implored him.

"Don't you go to fretting, Mistress Mary," Rod chuckled. "I aim to fix things with your pa right now. Marie, you girls gather up your things into a bundle and get ready to leave with us."

Rod turned to Rulon. "I'll leave Clay to help you get things together. He's a handy young'un, for his age."

Marie wagged her finger at her father. "Pa, don't let Clay hear you talking like that. He's done more than his share of the work since Carl took off to ride with Mosby. Then when James got drafted, well, he was the man on the place, and he's mighty proud of the job he done."

Rod laughed and tipped his hat onto his head. "Coming, Carl?"

"Ready, Pa." Carl rose to his feet and accompanied his father through the door.

"We'll go over and catch Rand in his store. He won't know what hit him." Rod laughed as he mounted his horse.

⁊つ

When he entered the Hilbrands Mercantile a few minutes later, Carl sniffed the spicy odors of the candy counter, just as he had in years past. This was a friendly place, as well known to him as his home or his saddle.

Pa walked in as though he owned the mortgage, moving with an easy, strolling gait. "Rand," he greeted Mr. Hilbrands, hand outstretched.

"Well, Rod Owen, you old nag-rider, you found you another son." Randolph Hilbrands took Pa's hand and shook it. "Seems like a new one comes home every day."

"Just got in yesterday. Colonel Mosby kept his boys in after school let out."

"You, with five sons left to you, you can joke. Me, with five daughters, and only one married, well, I'm past laughing." Mr. Hilbrands stroked his thin black moustache.

"Now Rand, it hardly seems likely that your girls are all of a marrying age.

Why, wasn't Amanda just having a child about the time I left for the fighting?"

"That would be Eliza. But Ida, now. She fancies herself quite a lady, and her not yet seventeen. Always going around worrying about when she will marry. I'm afraid Mandy's filled that girl's head with a mess of nonsense." Mr. Hilbrands shook his head and eased his tall, fleshy frame back onto his stool.

"She's just the age of my Marie. I reckon she's the same way."

"Not like my girl Ida. You never heard the like of the plans she makes to catch her a beau. It'd curl your hair, Rod."

Carl felt the heat of embarrassment creeping into his face, and turned away from Mr. Hilbrands' somber description of his daughter's antics. Looking around at the displays to find one out of earshot, he bumped into the saucy Miss Hilbrands herself, who had just entered from the street.

"I declare, you are the clumsiest—" As Ida got a good look at the object of her verbal attack, she backed up a step and started over. "I *am* so sorry," she drawled. "Silly me, can't help but trip on this old floor. Now let me think. You must be Carl Owen, Rulon's brother. I declare, you *have* grown up so nicely."

Carl stared at her, hoping his mouth wasn't open. Ida Hilbrands had grown up very nicely herself. Above a pair of merry blue eyes was the blondest, silkiest mop of curls he had ever seen. Her nose was tiny, with a hint of mischief to its tilt. Her mouth looked as though it laughed a great deal of the time, and was just now curled upward as she smiled gaily at her prize.

Ida threw back her head and gave a little sigh, and Carl became aware of other curved portions of her body.

"Carl Owen, I declare, has the cat got your tongue? You haven't said one little word since you bumped into me!" Ida smiled encouragingly, tapping her foot.

"I— I'm truly sorry, Miss Ida. I'm not used to being home yet, and in the company of such a pretty little thing as yourself. You have surely changed since last I saw you." Carl vaguely recalled a female child with long braids and knee-length skirts.

"Have you been home long?" Ida inquired sweetly.

"I arrived last evening. Got my parole last week near Charlottesville."

"All this talk of paroles! Makes our men folks out to be a passel of criminals."

"We was prisoners of war. The paroles mean we're on our honor to come home and wait for an exchange. I got my parole, like I said, then snuck me a Yankee rifle. Almost got caught, but I slipped away."

"Well, I never heard of such a thing," Ida exclaimed. "Why on earth would you want a dirty Yankee rifle?"

"Because it's an almighty good one, a repeater. I needed me a good firearm."

"I don't know anything about rifles and such," Ida murmured, looking at Carl with dreamy eyes.

"I have to see if Pa needs any help," Carl gulped, anxious to be away from the gaze of those eyes. "It was wondrous fine to see you again, Miss Ida."

"You'll have to come around and see us from time to time, now that this nasty war is over," she countered.

"I'd be pleased to," Carl nodded. He looked down and stared at his boots.

Ida tossed her head, greeted her father, and went into the back room of the store, sending one last smoldering look towards Carl.

He dropped a sigh of relief, then walked over to where his father and Ida's were deep in discussion.

"I've got my store," Mr. Hilbrands said. "I can make a living. You go ahead on. I'll not set the Yankees to your trail."

"I hope you'll give it a bit more thought, Rand. You've got goods here for a store in the Territory. Look around you and see the conditions hereabouts. Folks are starving, and all you can do is hand out credit and pray they'll get a good crop to repay you." Pa paused to scratch his nose. "Those miners in Colorado Territory have good hard money, gold dust and nuggets, mostly, and dug fresh out of the ground by their own hand. The things they lack are the goods you have right here. It don't seem right when you could make a bunch of money, were you in Colorado. It's not fair, somehow."

Carl wondered how long the silence would last. He glanced at Mr. Hilbrands, and nearly laughed out loud at the hungry look that came across the older man's face.

"Gold dust and nuggets, you say?" Mr. Hilbrands passed his hand over his face. "I'll go with you Rod, but with all this inventory and my house goods, too, I'll be needing an extra driver, and I'm willing to pay a good wage. Will you give me Carl, here?"

Pa turned and looked at Carl, his eyes twinkling. "Will you drive Mr. Hilbrands' wagon, son?"

"I reckon. You've got help a-plenty with the other boys."

"It's done then, Rand." Pa shook hands with his friend. "Have your wagons ready to go in a fortnight. We'll meet at my farm, and get an early start."

"Good. I want to get out there before some other merchant garners all the business." Mr. Hilbrands chuckled, and rubbed his hands along his apron front.

Pa waved good-bye and left the store, followed by Carl, who waited until they were outside, then said, "It didn't take so long to change his mind."

"I reckon I saved the best for last, son. I knew Rand Hilbrands could never stand the thought of good hard gold a-slipping through his fingers." Pa mounted his horse.

"It surely was comical to watch his face change." Carl swung into his saddle. "Who else do you aim to see here in town, Pa?"

"I'm going over to speak with the blacksmith. I hear he's been itching to go west since his wife died last winter. If he goes with us, Tom can take his little ones along, not leave them with the Campbells."

"Isn't Tom O'Connor some kind of kin to the Campbells?"

"Closer than most. Mistress Molly is Tom's sister. Now if Angus will agree to go with us, the whole passel of them can stick together and make a new start in the Territory."

"Why don't I go give the girls a hand, Pa? You don't need me to talk to Mr. O'Connor."

"Have them ready to go when I get back. Look, there's Angus Campbell himself, crossing the street up yonder. I may be gone for a while, son. I'll see you back at the house." Pa nudged his horse into a trot, and little puffs of dust arose as he went up the street.

Carl turned off toward Rulon's house. The sun had come out bright and strong, and it felt good and warm on his back. He grinned. "Hush, we're going west."

As he reached the corner, Carl saw a group of mounted men dashing up the cross street in front of him. Panic rose in his throat as he recognized the Yankee patrol that had jumped him, and he wheeled his horse to find a place of concealment. Then he realized where he was, turned Sherando again, and tried to calm his pounding heart. The soldiers were probably racing through the streets of Mount Jackson to make a ruckus, and he felt foolish to be caught in their trap.

"Easy, boy," he told his horse. "It ain't likely they'll take after me in town."

The Yankees drew up at the far end of the street, then turned and started back to town. As they thundered toward him, Carl noticed a young girl opposite him, evidently trying to decide whether to cross. She hesitated a moment, then bolted out into the street. In the middle, she looked around at the approaching soldiers, tripped, and fell into the road.

Without thinking, Carl spurred his horse into the street, leaned out from his saddle, and plucked the arising girl from the muck. Sherando carried them across the road while the Yankees whooped and whistled as their horses rushed by, venting their disappointment. Carl got down the street, turned a corner, then pulled up and set the girl on her feet and slid off his horse.

"Hush my mouth! That was the foolest thing I ever seen a body do!" Carl made no attempt to stop the hot words from tumbling out of his mouth. He glared at the girl, standing in the street with her chin up and her eyes flashing, auburn hair disheveled, the front of her clothes mud-caked and dripping. "You surely could have been killed, and that's a fact! You keep clear away from that gang of Yankees, you hear? Darn fool girl, anyhow." He got on his horse and left her standing there, pridefully biting back tears of relief. Then he rode away, shaking mud and slime off his arm, and muttering to himself.

∞

Carl dismounted at Rulon's fence and tied his horse, then rapped on the door. Marie answered and looked him over a moment before letting him enter.

"Did you fall off your horse, brother?" she asked, arching an eyebrow.

Carl glared at her. "Don't start in a-teasing me, Marie," he warned, stalking into the room. "Where can I clean up?"

"The well is in the back. I'll bring you soap and a towel if you'll tell me how you got so dirty."

"Keep them. I ain't going to give you the satisfaction." Carl left through the kitchen.

Marie heard the squeak of the windlass as she headed toward the stairs. "Stubborn," she proclaimed. Before she had gone up two steps, someone rapped in the front door again. Marie sighed, came back down, and opened the door.

"Ellen Bates! Whatever happened to you?"

"Please let me come in. I'm afraid those nasty Yankees will bother me again." Ellen's voice quivered dangerously, and Marie stepped back to admit her. Then she closed and bolted the door.

Ellen Bates was covered in the front with a slimy layer of mud. She stood by the door, shaking and dripping on the floor. Marie grabbed her arm and led her to the fire.

"Set here by the hearth while I get some water to clean you up." Marie went toward the kitchen, then halted. "Ellen, my brother Carl just went into the back yard with his arm all covered with mud, and in such a rage. Does he have anything to do with the state you're in?"

Ellen moaned and covered her face with her hands. "Is that who he was? I'll never be able to face him." She got up and moved toward the door. "I have to leave."

"Oh now, you ain't going anywhere." Marie barred her way. "I won't let you go out there looking like you fell down in the road. Oh lawsy! That's what happened, ain't it."

"I was crossing the street in front of those stupid Yankee soldiers running their horses down the way, and I tripped and fell. Your brother kicked that big horse of his and fetched me out of there. Then he set me on my feet and cussed me up and down. He really flapped his tongue some at me," she mumbled. "You've got to hide me before he comes in."

"You're not afraid of Carl, are you?"

"Not afraid. Just shamed. It was highly foolish of me to try to beat those Yankees across the street, and to get plucked out of the mud like a rag doll." She shuddered. "I'll never be able to hold up my head around him my whole life long."

"That's likely, but you can't keep from seeing him. He's here to take me on home. Ma needs me right now. We're going . . ." Marie looked sideways at Ellen. "I mean, we're going to be busy with . . . the planting."

"Marie, you're telling a fib. What's happening?"

"I'm sorry, Ellen. I can't say." She sighed. "But I will tell you, real soon, I promise. We'll clean you up, and I'll find some clothes so you can go home."

Marie left Ellen by the fire and went into the yard. She found Carl washing his shirt in a bucket of water. As she approached the well, Carl flicked drops of water at her and grinned.

"I'm sorry I was so fierce with you," he said. "Seems like ever since I got home, I've been muddy more than clean, and it's wearing on my nerves. Once, a cow knocked me into the mud, and now I'm filthy on account of a dumb girl."

"Well, that 'dumb girl' was coming to visit me, and she's out in the parlor dying of fright that you'll cuss at her again. Carl, how could you?"

"What? She's here?"

"She's my best friend."

"You surely do pick dumb friends."

"I ain't looking to fight with you, Carl. You had no business yelling at her, though."

"She nearly got us killed by a bunch of Yankees I had trouble with once before." He held up his dripping shirt. "Look at that. I was on my way home and they cut off all my buttons. Claimed I was violating my parole. I do not favor them casting their eyes on me again, seeing as how they're running the show hereabouts."

"Ellen knows she done a fool thing, but she's sorry. You'd best come in and make amends for yelling at her."

"Not me, Sis. Let her die of fright. I ain't apologizing for giving her something she earned." Carl put on his wet shirt and tied it closed with some bits of string.

"I see. Well, she needs to clean up, so if you don't aim to meet her, you'd best remain out here."

Carl mumbled something.

"What did you say?"

"You don't want to hear it."

Chapter 4

Two hours later, Rod Owen whistled as he tossed little Roddy into the air.

"Please, Mr. Owen," Mary cried out. "The baby is so delicate."

"Mistress Mary, you worry too much. This young'un is strong as an ox. And he'll need strength where we're going."

"You're still trying to get us to go with you? Rulon, tell him we can't go," she pleaded.

Rod continued. "Would you druther stay here and bid good-bye to your folks? Your pa agreed to go with me. Not only him, but Tom O'Connor, Angus Campbell, and Ed Morgan are going. I figure we need only one other family, and I'll talk to them on the way home."

Mary found a chair and sank down into it. Rulon crossed the room to squat by her side, and lifted her chin with his blunt fingers. "It won't be as bad as you figure, Sugar. I'm getting stronger every day, and you'll have your ma and sisters along. Look here, it'll mean a good start for us, and we've never had one, with this war. Mary, we're four years wed, and all we have to show for it is Roddy and some pots and pans." He got up and turned to his father. "Pa, we're going with you."

"Rulon, I'm pleased. You won't regret it none. Well now, are those girls ready to go home? I expect I'll need a wagon to haul their things."

Mary got up, sighing heavily, and went to get the girls, and as she passed her husband she gave him a long, despairing look.

"Afternoon, Mary," a young male voice called from the kitchen.

"That's Clay home for lunch," Rulon said. "He likely don't know you're in town, Pa. Clay," he called. "Come here a minute. Someone's here to see you."

A slim youth entered the room with his hat still on his head, brushing specks of straw off his colorless homespun shirt and faded brown trousers. "Pa!" he exclaimed, hastily taking the hat off his blond head. "When did you get into town?"

"I been here all morning, son. I bring happy news. We're pulling up stakes and heading for Colorado Territory."

"We're what? Where Uncle Jonathan lives? What do you want to do that for, Pa?"

"I've sold the farm, Clayton. We need a fresh start, and I'm sick of the sight of Yankee soldiers."

"You sold the farm? Our home, Pa?"

"I've decided, son."

Clay stood silent for a while, then said, "All right, Pa."

"By the way, your sisters are going home with me, but you stay here and help Rulon get ready to travel."

"What about my job, Pa?"

"Give in your notice this afternoon. Your brother needs you full-time, him not being so spry yet."

"Oh lawsy," Marie interrupted, coming down the stairs. "This house has been full of people all day." She came into the room with her bundle, trailed by Julianna, Mary, and Ellen, whose dignity had been restored by a wash-up and a change of clothes.

"How're you going to get us home, Papa?" Julianna did not like to walk if she could ride.

"I'll hire a team and buggy with Clay to drive us," Rod teased.

"Papa," Julianna wailed. "That takes money, and the Yankees have all of it."

"You'll ride behind me, and your sister will double with Carl." Rod looked around the room. "Where is Carl?"

"He's in the yard being a blue-nosed, stubborn fool," Marie told him.

"He's angry on account of me, Mr. Owen," said Ellen.

Rod finally noticed the extra face. "You're Chester's girl. Is your pa home?"

"Yes, sir, he was when I left this morning."

"Well, we're heading out to your place, so you can come along with us. You can ride with Marie, and Carl can walk."

"Oh, please, Mr. Owen. I'll be happy to walk. You don't need to bother Carl none."

"He's already almighty bothered." Marie giggled into Ellen's ear.

"We'll work something out," Rod declared.

∾

As Ellen walked down the pike with Marie, she daydreamed herself onto the back of Carl's horse. She imagined she felt the hard muscles of his torso under her encircling arms, bit her lip, and gave a shudder of delight. Then she realized her arms were wrapped around her own front. "Pleased, God," she prayed under her breath, "let him forgive me for being a fool." She squeezed her eyes shut in her fervor.

"Miss Ellen, are you ailing?"

Ellen jumped, and opened her eyes as Rod Owen came alongside her, leading his horse with Julianna aboard.

"You were making such a face, I wondered if you was feeling poorly."

"Oh, no," she hastened to assure him. "I was doing a mite of thinking."

"Would you favor riding for a spell? You can hop up there with Julianna and the baggage."

"I'm fine, Mr. Owen. I like to walk."

"You don't always do it so good," a scoffing voice broke into the conversation.

Ellen whirled around, her face flushing with anger. "That's not fair, Carl Owen. Tripping was an accident. You wasn't invited to busybody your way into my bad luck. Better for me had the Yankees run me over." She turned and ran off a ways before walking once more.

"You do have spunk, I'll say that," Carl called after her.

Rod scowled at his son. "That's no way to treat the little lady. You apologize to her."

"Pa!" Carl protested. "It's a misunderstanding betwixt her and me. Them Yankees were hoorayng her in town, and I got some riled at her for getting in their way."

"No son of mine ever spoke to a girl in like manner, Carl, and you ain't going to behave in a new fashion because your temper's short. You get along and make sure she's smiling when she gets home."

Carl shrugged his shoulders and set out after Ellen, frowning as he trotted his horse up the road. Ellen had gotten about ten yards ahead of his sister even though Marie called for her to wait and ran after her.

Carl slowed his horse to a walk alongside Marie, who was breathing hard and holding her side. "Save your breath, Sis. Go back and walk with Pa."

Marie looked up and giggled. "You're going to apologize, ain't you. Afraid I'll listen?"

"You'll try. Go along back to Pa. This is all his idea."

"I told you to say you was sorry, but you wouldn't listen to me."

"Go along, or I'll help you," he threatened.

"I'll go. I obey Pa better than you." Marie wrinkled her nose and stuck out her tongue, then stopped walking to wait for her father and sister.

Carl heeled Sherando into a faster gait to catch Ellen. As he came up beside her, he slowed the horse again and looked down at her angry, set face. "Say, you ain't still sore at me, are you?"

Ellen kept walking.

"I was mean as a mad dog to you back there in town. I'm sorry."

Still she walked, facing front, giving no notice to his words.

"I was worried about you. Looked like you were going to get yourself killed."

She stopped, hesitated, then looked up at him, shading her eyes. "You were worried? Why?"

Carl reined in the horse. "That was no way to treat any girl, especially a Southern girl. Them Yanks figured to hurt you. That scared me."

"You were scared?" She began to walk again, and Carl followed, walking his horse.

"Yes. You was, too."

"I saw them horses coming faster than I had figured, and that's what made me trip. I about died of fright."

"You about died of trampling!"

"I'm sorry you got so muddy, and worried, but I'm most sorry I didn't get a chance to thank you. You saved my life, I reckon."

Carl was silent for a moment, wondering why the conversation was so easy. *One thing*, he told himself, *this girl don't talk funny like that Hilbrands gal, playing a man like a fish on a hook.* After a while he asked, "Is your pa planning to rebuild the farm?"

"What choice does he have? We got to put the crops in, and I guess the barn goes up after that. But I reckon we don't need much of a barn, since the Yankees came through and took almost all the stock!"

"You've got you a temper, girl. Almost as bad as mine." He laughed.

"That's what my ma keeps telling me. She says, 'Girl, you're never going to catch—'" Ellen's face turned red again.

"What's that she says?"

"Never mind. Not important." Ellen began to walk faster again.

Carl nudged Sherando to a faster gait and caught up to her.

"If you're in such a hurry, you can ride behind me for a ways. Likely Marie's bag is soft enough to sit on." He put down his hand to help her up.

Ellen stood still in the road for a moment, then she accepted Carl's offer, took his hand, and he boosted her up on the baggage behind him. "Hang on tight," he advised. She slowly put her arms around his waist, and he felt the warmth of her body against his back. Then she rested her cheek against him, and he noticed that the thud of her heart matched the beat of his.

෨

"Chester, you been wiped out. Come with me to Colorado. You can grow acre after acre of wheat there." Rod Owen sat in the Bates' front yard on a tree stump, looking from Chester to his wife, Muriel.

Chester Bates was a mild, weather-beaten man, thick of chest and shoulder, but with no spare fat on his bones. His reddish hair was thinning a little on top, and his square jaw made a proper floor for his square face. Rod had seen the light fade from his dark blue eyes when he returned from the war to find his wife and daughter living in the former tool shed, compliments of the Yankees who burned his home. Now the light was back.

Chester glanced from his dark, matronly wife to his friend. "You're a God-send, Roderick Owen. I'll go with you," he replied. "I'll leave this place and go with you, and the Yankees be damned!"

"Chester, the young ladies," Muriel scolded, smiling.

Ellen pounced on Marie. "This is your secret," she burst out. "And now we're going with you. Lawsy me, if we didn't go, I'd just die!"

෨

"James is back," Julia greeted Rod. "He brought in all that wood. What are we going to do with it? It's no use to us on the road."

"We'll sell it. Likely there's some lazy man around who'll take it off our hands. Did Albert get the corn shelled for you?"

"That boy's been working his fingers to the bone—not to mention his tongue—with all his questions. I reckon he's anxious to go west." Julia hugged the girls. "How's Mary? Were you a help to her? Is Rulon on the mend?"

"He's up and about, Ma," said Marie. "Soon he won't even limp no more."

"Mama, Clay's going to quit his job. Papa told him to," Julianna reported. "Mary always looks sick, and she didn't want to go when Papa told her about his plan."

"I wonder what's making that girl feel so poorly?" Julia glanced over at his husband, catching his eye. "Just how well is Rulon?"

"Well enough, and surely home enough, I reckon," he replied, winking over Julianna's head. "And high time, too."

"Hush now, Rod," Julia cautioned.

മ

Carl took the horses to the pen and stripped off the saddles. Hearing a faint scraping sound behind him, he crouched in the brush. A short ways off he saw a young man seated on the bank of the creek, stropping a razor. At his side he had a basin of water and a pistol. After a while he laid the strop down and began to remove the curly black beard from his lanky face.

"James!" Carl called out. He rushed from the bushes and ran to the creek. The younger man threw down the razor and grabbed the pistol, then dropped it and gave a rebel yell.

Meeting on the bank like two young bulls, the brothers crashed together in a welter of arms and heads, wrestling each other to the ground.

Laughing, Carl declared, "You're just the feller I want to see. And you got you a razor, besides." He rubbed his red stubble while James punched him fondly in the side. "You be through shaving when I'm finished with the horses, you hear?"

"Carl, you coon-faced old lard bucket, we thought you got took prisoner or something. Pa was ready to go to Washington City to see what become of you."

"You're joshing me!"

"No sir, not me. He and Ma were sure worried some. I never seen them so worked up about a body. I reckon Ben going and getting himself killed there at the end of the fighting took some of the sand out of both of them."

"You old liar, you. Pa never had more sand than now. He's ripping us out of this valley, lock, stock, and barrel, and taking us to Colorado. Says we're going to raise beef cattle for the miners."

"He's what?"

"We're going to find Uncle Jonathan and set up a cow ranch, or something like that. Pa's spoken to a bunch of men, and they're going with us."

"You mean we're leaving Ma and the young'uns here?"

"No!" Carl tapped James on the head. "You got mush for brains? We're all going west. Ma and the girls, and everyone. Rulon, too."

"Which men did he talk to?"

"Rand Hilbrands, Ed Morgan, um, Angus Campbell, and Chester Bates."

"Not Joseph Bingham?"

Carl frowned at his brother. "Mr. Bingham lost his legs at Petersburg, James."

"I know that."

"Even though he's Pa's good friend, he's not fit for a trek over the countryside. I'm sure that's why Pa didn't ask him."

"Then I'll speak to Pa. I can tend to a wagon and chores for the Binghams. I have to change Pa's mind."

"You're fussing about something, James. What's nettling you?"

"Miss Jessica. I can't leave here without her."

Carl nodded. "You've been sparking her, I take it?"

"She's let me walk out with her. I think she'll marry me if I ask her."

"You've got yourself a lot of talking to do, brother. Good luck on changing Pa's mind."

"I'll take the offer of luck. Hey, you better finish with them horses, or you'll need the luck back with Pa after you. You know he sets great store by dumb animals."

"That must be why he was so worried about me," Carl quipped, rising to his feet. "Mind, as soon as you're done shaving, it's my turn."

Carl returned to the horses, fed and watered them, and brushed their coats down with an old rag. Then he went back to the creek bank and picked up the basin and razor.

"James, what I need is a bath and a change of clothes."

"Can't wait for Saturday, huh?"

"That foolish brindle cow keeps pushing me in the mud."

"Brindle always was a mite spooked. Well, I got a spare pair of trousers that might do. We're near the same length, looks like. Maybe Ma has an old shirt tucked away that Ben or Peter left behind."

"It's going to be hard to ask that of her."

"Yeah. But you need the clothes."

"Well, I'm bound for that old swimming hole downstream. Thanks for the loan of the razor."

As Carl turned away, James stopped him, holding something out. "Brother, don't forget the soap."

∾

James had to wait two days before both courage and opportunity to speak to his father coincided. As they worked together reinforcing a wagon, James said, "Pa, did you forget to ask Mr. Bingham to bring his family with us?"

"You mean Joseph Bingham, son?"

"Yes. He's your friend."

"He is my friend. He's a kind and gentle man."

"Then he and his family should come with us."

Rod put down his hammer and looked across the wagon bed at James. "He's a cripple. He can't go."

"He's getting better all the time, Pa. I can drive his wagon, do his chores."

"What would he do in Colorado, son? He has a home and a business here, and his wife can manage the bakery. He's not up to building again in a different place." Rod picked up his tool and began to pound a nail into a sideboard.

"Then give me your leave to ask Miss Jessica to go with us."

"What? Leave her family? Why?"

"I'll be her family. I want to ask her to marry me."

"That wouldn't be fair to her, asking her to go across the country where she'd never see her kin again. No."

"She'd do it, Pa. I've been sparking her on Sunday nights."

"I won't break up a family. Since Joe can't go, no one else of his kin goes."

"Pa—"

"No, James. They don't have time to get ready."

℘

Rod turned over in bed in the middle of the night and whispered in his wife's ear. "Julie."

She sat up with a rustle of the tick beneath her, eyes blank and staring in the moonlight that poured into the room from the un-curtained window. Rod pulled her down beside him.

She released a rush of air. "You startled me, Rod. What do you need, this time of night?"

"Julia, I've been thinking."

"In the night? Thinking?" She squirmed into the hollow of his elbow. "You're almost too old for anything else, I reckon." She chuckled, then yawned largely.

Rod squeezed her, then released her shoulders, slipped his arm free, and sat up. "We got to have a wedding before we leave."

"What?" Julia sat up again, wide awake.

"Yes. I've been thinking on the matter of our journey. For one thing, it'll take several months, and for another, it'll take us into land that isn't settled."

"What does that have to do with a wedding, Rod?"

"We've got us a couple of young men who need good wives. We're also taking several young ladies along with us, and they need men to take care of them."

"Roderick Owen! You're not thinking—"

"When Carl met young Ida Hilbrands, I reckon some sparks flew around her pa's store. He's going to drive a wagon for Randolph, and he might as well marry into the family, same as Rulon did. Since James has a hankering to marry, Chester's girl strikes me as a strong, likely match."

Julia sat mute.

"It's a good plan, Julie. You know it is. We won't have a lot of carrying on if the boys are safely wed, and it'll make tight bonds between our families."

"You're meddling where it isn't wanted, Rod," Julia finally managed to say. "You know James is heart-broke that the Binghams aren't coming with us."

"Nonsense, Julie. I'm sorry I can't accommodate his yearning. He'll get over the Bingham girl."

"I fear you're going to live to regret such thoughts. This will stir up more trouble than a bear putting its paw into a bee tree."

Rod laughed softly. "I'm not wrong, dear wife. The more I think on it, the better it sounds. I know Rand is anxious to marry Ida off, and I'll give Chester that wagon I picked up the other day in exchange for his word on his daughter's hand."

"Oh, I never heard the like. That's just—I don't know what to say about such conniving, Roderick Owen."

"Come on, Julie. You want them boys settled into their lives now that the war's over, and those are good girls. Well, that Ida is a mite flighty, but Carl can handle her fine. James is a tad distracted right now, but he and Ellen will get on very well, I wager. I'll talk to their fathers later this week." He idly rubbed the sunburned flesh below his Adam's apple.

Julia sucked in her breath. She held it a long time, then let it go in a rush of sound, bowing her head. "I'm near speechless at your meddling, Rod, but I know you're bound to try to work your will. I hope it don't return to bite you like a water moccasin."

Chapter 5

The next days sped by. Rod was here and there, at one farm or another, directing the preparations for departure. At last night fell, with only one day left to complete the work before they left the Shenandoah Valley forever.

Rod sighed deeply and settled into the tick that lay on the floor of the bedroom. "It's all set, Julie. Tomorrow, late in the afternoon, we will gather at Hilbrands' store to check the final details and see that everyone has their instructions. I've arranged for Reverend Halsey to come and speak the marriage words for Carl and James. I can trust Halsey not to say anything. The young people will have their wedding nights together before we all leave the next morning."

Julia slowly brushed the surface of the quilt with her hand three times, then said softly, "Wouldn't it be a good idea to tell the boys?"

"I don't want to spook them, especially James. You know he is still half ready to stay here."

"Rod, you're going to have to pay the piper someday."

He laughed and nuzzled her neck. "A man needs a wife, Julie. With good luck, they'll have love, too. No, I'm sure of it. Love will come along for both those boys."

Julia sighed. "I pray that will happen. I can hardly stand to look at James's long face. I hope he don't end up hating you, Rod."

He chuckled. "I'm right in this. He'll come to see it."

&

Rod paced the floor of the Hilbrands' store, then turned to glare toward the two couples standing uneasily at the counter in the back of the room. All the members of the company were present except for Clay, who Rod had dispatched to find out what had happened to the Reverend Halsey. They stood around in family groupings, talking quietly.

"Damnation! Where is the man?" Rod fumed, ignoring the furrowed brow that Julia turned toward him. "He's late. I paid him good money, and he's not here."

"What time did you say—?"

"He's two hours late, Julie. If he doesn't come soon, the whole plan will be ruined."

Chester Bates approached Rod. "Not ruined, surely. Just put off for a while. We can find someone farther down the road to marry the young people."

Rod pressed his lips together, his beard bristling. He grunted.

Chester went on, his voice pitched lower. "Mayhap it's a good thing they don't wed yet. We'll need to build houses and get crops in the ground. If those boys are working hard to build homes for their brides, they may not take it into their heads to go somewhere else to settle."

Rod growled a surly reply, then looked up as Clay came through the door. "Speak up, boy. Where's the minister?"

"He went off into the hills to give comfort to Mother Whitwell. She's dying."

"Humph!" Rod snorted. "When will he be back?"

"Mrs. Halsey didn't know for sure, but thought he wouldn't be back until after the burying."

Rod groaned, then gathered his wits and addressed the gathered company. "We'll put the weddings off until later." He shrugged his shoulders. "I suppose it's best that the young ladies don't have to travel with buns in the oven."

Several shocked faces turned his way.

"Well, git on home." He made a shooing motion with his hands. "We meet mighty early tomorrow."

&

After he set fires in the house and walked to the waiting wagons, Rod did not look back. He mounted to his place on the seat, turned to look at his wife, and gathered the lines into his hands.

"Avery can't live in your home now, Julie."

"Oh, Rod! Did you have to burn it?"

He let out his breath. "Hard work is what's needed, Julie. We can't undo the war, nor bring back our dead sons, and the land belongs to Avery now, but we can begin a new life where we won't have cruel memories."

He started the team, and the wagons of his neighbors turned into a line behind him. Albert and Andy Campbell, driving the livestock, took up the rear, and the animals provided the only island of noise amid the silent pioneer party.

They were anxious to get on the road, and to avoid the pursuit that might come when Malcolm Avery discovered that all he had bought with his Yankee money was land.

Julia sat on the seat of the wagon, hearing the stern command of her husband not to look back, but her body turned with a will of its own, to look at her home for one last time. She watched in fascination as the flames caught on the roof of the house. The fire rose in fingers of red and orange, falsifying the dawn and lighting up the bulk of Massanutten Mountain. Then her trance was broken by Rod's hand on her arm.

"Julie, don't!" he pleaded, and she turned around on the seat.

"Rod, it's my home," she said, feeling tears run down her cheeks. She drew herself up, setting her back rigidly against the glow of the fire.

Rod pulled on the lines, bringing the team to a halt. He set his jaw and put his arm around his wife. "It'll be ashes and rubble soon, just like the rest of the buildings, and we must be on our way." He looked down at her head, made his voice rough, and continued. "Let's go on, Julie. We'll get through this pain."

"I know," she whispered.

℘

Julianna huddled with her sister in the back of the wagon, numb from the long journey down the Valley Pike. She could not recall a more dismal experience than sitting in the wagon hour upon hour, cramped and jostled by the churn and the provision box. Their father had cautioned them to stay in the wagon, for he wanted to travel as fast as possible this first day.

She eased her muscles the best she could, and wondered how soon they would stop for the night. Passing scenery no longer amused her, and she wanted to stretch her legs.

"Jule, do you remember Uncle Jonathan?" Marie asked.

Julianna turned to look at her older sister. "I remember his beard. It always scratched me when he picked me up." She yawned. "But that was such a long time ago."

"I remember when he put his box on the mantel. I didn't want him to go back to Colorado." Marie sighed. "It's been so long since his last letter came. I reckon that's because of the difficulty lately."

"Marie, do you reckon he could be—dead?"

"No. Not Uncle Jonathan. Ma says the mail's been cut off with all the fighting. She says we'll catch up with him sooner or later."

Julianna yawned again, and wished Pa would make a rest stop.

℘

The light of the afternoon sun slanted sideways through the trees when Rod sighted the meadow. A small stream ran through it, and oak limbs were blown down in the surrounding woods. They didn't need anything else for a campground.

The wagon came even with the edge of the forest and Rod pulled his team off the road. He drove on a ways, back into the meadow where the forest put out a feeler into the grassland. Hauling on the lines, Rod stopped the wagon close to the stream. The others followed, stopping their wagons alongside his. Rod jumped down from the seat and helped Julia climb down from the seat as the men from the other wagons gathered.

"We'll make our first camp here, with two small fires, and two guards out toward the road."

"You're not still in the Army, Rod," interrupted Rand Hilbrands.

"Caution pays, Rand. We don't know who might follow us, or when they'd come."

"Not for a couple of days. You must be joking," Rand scoffed.

"I burned my house," Rod reminded him. "Most of us are paroled soldiers. There may be someone who'll object to our leaving."

"There's still soldiers going north," Chester said. "Some I've seen are hungry and mean. You can't trust them not to take what little we've salvaged. I'll take the first watch, Rod."

Rod laid his hand on Chester's shoulder and gripped it. "Thank you. Rulon will join you. Somebody will bring your supper, so don't get spooky and shoot them."

Carl got down from the last wagon and helped Ida Hilbrands to the ground. "Now you, Missy," he said, and swung down Eliza, her youngest sister. The girls gave their thanks, and walked off in the direction of their family wagon.

Even though their wedding had been postponed, Ida had insisted that she should ride on the seat of the freight wagon with Carl so they could "get to know each other better." Her mother agreed, as long as she took small Eliza along for "company."

Carl stretched, then shook out his tired arms. He hadn't driven a team in nearly three years, and today's trip had been extra long. He took his Spencer rifle from under the wagon seat, sought out his father, and volunteered to get firewood. Being still unused to the company of women since his war service, he was a little shy of Ida, with her head tossing and giggles, and was anxious to be off by himself in the woods for a while.

He jumped across the creek and strode into the trees. Carefully, he circled back toward the road and scouted the area, checking for signs of other travelers or pursuit. When he was satisfied that the group was alone, he returned to the vicinity of the camp and began to gather deadfalls and dried limbs for fuel. He arranged his load to leave his right hand free to carry the Spencer, and turned back to the camp. As he came out of the woods, he noticed Ida standing on the bank of the stream, waiting for him.

"Yoo-hoo," she called. "I've come to help you gather wood."

Carl approached the bank and grinned. "Seems you're on the wrong bank. I've got plenty, thanks."

"Oh-h-h," Ida pouted. "I couldn't get across this river."

Carl laughed. "Well, I can't let you go back empty-handed." He shifted his load to get a chunk of wood into his other hand, then awkwardly tossed the piece across the creek. It hit the bank and bounced into the water, and Ida scrambled after it, lost her footing on the slick bank, and landed in the water with a little cry.

Carl dropped his load and waded into the creek to retrieve her, struggling to stifle his laughter. Gathering her up in his arms, he became conscious of how the wet bodice of her dress accented her shapely form. His body reacted, and uncomfortable, he looked away from Ida and hurried to get her out of the stream.

"Are you hurt?" he asked, placing her on the bank. He stepped back and linked his hands together in front of his body.

She sighed. "Only my pride."

"You'd best get back to camp and dry off. You could take the ague, wet like that." Carl turned and splashed back through the creek for the wood, grateful the water was cold.

ঙ

After supper, Rod approached Carl and squatted on the ground beside him.

"You and James take the second watch. Get some sleep, and Rulon will wake you. I gave him first watch so he could sleep the rest of the night through."

"He seems much improved, Pa."

"There's no quit in Rulon, not even for a Yankee mortar shell. I can't figure why his wife's feeling so poorly, though."

"Woman's complaint?"

"Woman's ways, likely. Changeable creatures, they are. Take your ma. She was colder than wet socks when I told her I sold the farm, but she calmed down, and took right to the victual making and all. Except this morning, she was broke up some about leaving. She didn't like to see the house burning."

"You told her not to look, Pa."

"Well, she did."

"There ain't no accounting for women, Pa. I can't figure out Ida Hilbrands."

Rod chuckled. "I've seen the way she acts. She ain't had a man to work her womanly wiles on since she grew up and learned them, son." He placed his hand on Carl's shoulder. "You be cautious. Don't let her work you into a dither. If you fool with her before you have the marrying words said, Rand will take a shotgun to you. Mind my words."

"I will remember. Goodnight, Pa."

Carl crossed over to the Owen wagon and got his bedroll out of the back. He picked his way through the sleeping camp to the spot where James was already stretched out in his bedding. Carl unrolled his own blankets on the ground. He sat and pulled off his boots, then lay back and drew the covers around him.

"Night, James."

"Wake me when Rulon comes," James mumbled.

As he drifted off to sleep, Carl recalled the feel of Ida in his arms, the sight of her clinging dress. He groaned as his body betrayed his good sense, and half-woke James, who stirred in his sleep.

Carl sat up and shook his head to clear out the thought of Ida.

"Remember what your daddy said," he told himself, turned over, and eventually went to sleep.

Chapter 6

The city of Kansas lay ahead, hot in the sun, as Carl drove the freight wagon through the ford at Blue River. Three months of exposure to wind, dust, and sun had weathered his face and forearms to a dark brown. Three months of driving the mule team made it a matter of routine to urge the animals up the riverbank and into the meadow.

Those same three months of Ida Hilbrands' company had broken through some of Carl's reserve, and when he had pulled the team to a halt and applied the brake, he stood up, threw off his hat, bent over, and grabbed Ida off the seat. She squealed and grabbed for the wagon, but Carl held her fast and squeezed her.

"Look at that, girl. We made it all the way to the beginning of the Santa Fe

Trail, this here town. Purty soon we'll be on the last leg of the trip."

"Well, I declare, Carl Owen," she protested. "You put me down! I don't hanker to fall off this big old wagon."

"Hush, I ain't going to drop you." Carl let go of Ida's waist with his right arm to prove his strength, holding her with his left.

"Put me down! I'll have Papa speak to you." Ida struggled and kicked against Carl. "You ain't to be trusted!"

"Ida, you make me laugh. Your pa has trusted me for three months now with no complaints, and you been left in my entire care and keeping the whole time."

"You put me down, or I'll go ride with my mama and the other girls. I would be hurt real bad was you to drop me."

Carl frowned and eased her down to the seat. "Go along if you care to. I'll not stop you." He hoped she would ignore his retort and say something bright and witty, but she flounced down on the seat beside her little sister and folded her arms across her chest.

He swung down from the tall wagon, then put up his arms to help Ida get down. She was gone, climbing down the other side, taking Eliza with her. He fisted his hand and punched the wagon rim, then shook his hand and sucked his sore knuckles.

"This is a fine mess," he muttered, scuffing his boot through the dust. He sighed, and wondered what he'd done wrong.

Ida was fun to be with, most of the time. She excited his imagination, calling his attention to fantasy details in passing clouds, and had been an amusing and entertaining companion through the long, wet days of flight through Kentucky. Ida had kept him awake while he drowsed his way up the old King's Trace in eastern Missouri, feverish and weak. She had made him feel like a man, and many times he had had to dig his heels in and think "whoa" before he grabbed her and stole a kiss. But times like these confused him, with Ida willful and quarrelsome. He wondered what kind of a trick she was playing on his this time. Finally, he shrugged his shoulders and turned away from the wagon to find his pa.

As he walked along, a female voice called his name, and he stopped to find the speaker. Glancing around, he saw Ellen Bates peering from the back of her father's wagon. She was on her knees, searching for something, and her sunbonnet hung down her back, letting her auburn hair spill over her shoulders. Carl thought how pretty and peaceful she looked, and wished that Ida were as gentle.

Grinning, Carl approached the wagon. "Hello, Miss Ellen. Seems like forever since we last spoke."

"There ain't been much need." She looked down at her hands. Then she raised her head, looking him straight in the eye. "You been busy, driving that big wagon, and looking after the Hilbrands girls."

"It's been a lot of work, getting the knack of it, but I manage pretty well with the mules now. The girls ain't been too much trouble."

"Do we make camp here?"

"I was on my way to find out." Carl noticed for the first time the little flecks of brown in Ellen's green eyes. "I'll come back and tell you, if you like."

"Oh, don't go to any bother. Likely Pa will come back and tell us."

"You sure now?" There were also little flecks of brown across the bridge of Ellen's nose. *Sun freckles, like as not*, he thought, liking them.

Ellen nodded and disappeared into the wagon.

Hush, she's a fetching looking girl, he mused, never suspecting the hot tears that she wept onto her blanket at night, raging against Ida's good fortune.

Carl found his father and asked, "Is this our campground?"

"Howdy, son. No, I want to get closer to town before we settle in, but you can unhitch your mules and water them. By the way, I'm riding in to town later on to get some supplies. I'd be pleased if you boys would ride along with me."

"Sure, Pa. How much longer you figure before we hit Colorado?"

"If we don't have no major breakdowns, I reckon we got a month or forty-five days' travel ahead of us. Git going, son, and tend to your animals."

"Yes, Pa." Carl returned to the wagon and unhitched the mules, then drove them down to the river. Albert was there with the loose livestock, and Clay came down the bank with the spare horses.

Carl's horse, Sherando, caught his master's scent and tossed his head, whinnying in greeting. Carl waded over to his horse and patted the big gray gelding on the neck.

"Sherando, have you been keeping out of trouble? Hush, I miss riding you, you old war horse!"

Sherando nickered softly, pushing his muzzle into Carl's chest. Carl took a step backward and kept his balance.

"Oh no you don't, boy. I'll take a bath when I've got the time."

Albert came and patted the gray's flank. "He's a mighty fine horse, Carl. Why'd you name him 'Sherando?' It ain't a name I ever heard."

"It's the name of an old Indian chief, Albert. There's a legend that the Shenandoah Valley was named after him."

"An Indian, huh? In the Shenandoah?"

Carl ruffled the boy's hair. "It's so, Albert. There used to be Indians all over the woods and valleys, about a hundred years ago."

Bidding his brother and his horse good-bye, Carl returned to the mules and drove them out of the water. He took them to the wagon and re-hitched them. Somewhere from his belly came the pinching cramps of hunger, and he climbed up to the wagon seat to retrieve a packet of cornbread from underneath.

By gum, I never figured to eat cornbread again once I left the army, he thought, then shame swept over him as he remembered that he would be starving now if it hadn't been for his mother's quick thinking and courage. He finished the bread in silence.

"Tarl, lift me up," a small person with a lisp demanded.

Shoot, she sounds just like Ida, he thought, helping Eliza into the wagon.

"Where's your sister?"

"She's helping Mama. I'm 'posed to tell you that India is coming with us now."

Carl groaned. Ida was making good her threat. "Girls!" he exclaimed, and dropped to the ground, leaving the child on the seat.

He found Ida next to her father's wagon, doing nothing more needful than rearranging her hair. Silently, he caught her by the wrist and pulled her along with him, out into the meadow, away from the wagons. She didn't resist him physically, but protested a little with squeaks and squeals as they went along.

Carl stopped suddenly and spun around to face her, gripping her by the shoulders. "It's time we stopped the game-playing, Ida. You started it, but I'm ending it my way." He bent down and kissed her full on the lips. "That's how I feel about you. My pa arranged our betrothal to suit himself, but I like you a lot, and I reckon I want you for a wife. We can wed once we're settled in Colorado, but I'm telling you now, you stop picking fights with me!"

Ida stood rooted to the ground, looking up into Carl's eyes, and he watched the changing expressions on her face. He waited as she thought over what he had said, still holding her shoulders.

"I'm sorry I riled you," she blurted out. "I'll be a good wife to you." Ida gave a little gasp and clapped her hand over her mouth. "Carl, why don't we get married in the town? I know Papa will be much happier, and Mama will be glad to see me married safe."

"My pa wants me to ride with him into town in a little while. I'll see what I can arrange."

"Oh, Carl. It'll be so much fun!" She turned and ran back towards the wagon, and Carl slowly followed, his head reeling and his heart thumping in his chest.

૭

"It surely does feels fine to ride this horse again," Carl said to James as they followed their father and younger brothers into town. "I don't know as I would favor becoming a freighter for good. I would miss riding."

On his other side, Rulon rolled his shoulders, stretching them in a circle. "I'm surely glad I've got well enough to ride. Mary gets a bee in her bonnet from time to time, and it's a relief to get out of the wagon for a while."

"The old married man," James laughed. "Tell me, what makes her so touchy?"

"Why, she's making us up another young'un." Rulon's grin almost split his face in two.

"You don't say! Rulon, who would've figured you mended so quick?" James rode his horse up by Rulon and punched him lightly on the shoulder.

Rulon slugged him back. "Keep your nose wiped, little brother. Your time will come soon enough."

James made a growling sound deep in his throat. "I'm none too happy with Pa's meddling. If it weren't for Ma, I would have stayed behind. I'll never see Miss Jessica again."

Rulon reached out and patted James' shoulder. "I'm sorry your plans got thrown away, brother. It's hard to take leave of such good friends. Our family has to stay together to survive, though. Pa's right about that."

James only grunted and made a dour face.

Rod Owen pulled his horse to a halt by the tie rail in front of A. G. Boone's store. He dismounted and waited for his sons to join him before he spoke.

"Rulon, you take James and Albert and hunt up the law in town. We missed the trading caravans to Santa Fe by a long time, so find out what measures we need to take for safety. Carl and Clay, you come with me. I'll hunt up Mr. Boone. Your Uncle Jonathan told me to trade with him if ever I got this far west."

Rod wrapped his reins around the rail and swung under it, stepping onto the board sidewalk. Carl and Clay followed him, while the other three went off down the street.

Before entering the store, Carl turned and surveyed the bustling street. Even though the traders were gone, the traffic seemed constant. He glimpsed some soldiers up the street, loading a wagon with supplies, and recalled that his father had mentioned Fort Leavenworth up north a ways.

Wagons passed the store, narrowly missing each other in the intersection, their drivers yelling obscenities at one another, filling the air with strident shouts. Then the street was empty for a moment, and Carl's attention was drawn across the street by a group of three men lounging outside a saloon.

From the loudness of their talk, Carl guessed they had already visited the bar at some length. Two of the men were of average height and weight, wore nondescript trousers and shirt, and had full beards and shaggy hair. The third man was swarthy, tall, and of a powerful build. He wore tight black pants of a cut Carl had never seen before. His shirt was white, topped by a black vest that was embroidered with a light-catching thread. On his head he wore a hat with a wide brim and flat crown. The hat, too, was embroidered—with colored threads in fancy designs. The man's face was clean-shaven, except for a full-flowing moustache.

Carl gazed at the man for several seconds, until the dark, fancily dressed man removed the thin black cigar from his mouth, chuckled, and said something amusing to his companions. They laughed, and looked over at Carl, who noticed the whiteness of the big man's teeth beneath his moustache. *I reckon he's a Mexican*, he thought, and turned and entered the store.

He glanced around the crowded establishment. Three areas of commerce— dry goods, hardware, and groceries—shared the room, crowding the shelves and aisles. Pa was headed for the hardware counter, where a solidly built redhead in his fifties minded the store. Clay looked like he was enjoying himself browsing through the dry goods section, and Carl joined him.

Rod stopped at the counter. "I'm looking for A. G. Boone. You be him?"

"I am not. Mr. Boone is out to lunch. I am his clerk, Samuel P. Flaherty, at your service."

"Well, it ain't anything you can't handle, I reckon." Rod looked around the empty store. "You don't have much business today."

"It's the lunch hour. If you want to see business, sir, stick around until the end of the month when the traders return. Then you'll see business!" Mr. Flaherty bobbed his head in anticipation.

"I don't plan to stay that long. I'm here for provisions. That's my list. Can you fill it?" Rod put a bit of paper on the counter.

The man took up the list and peered at it. "Surely. If we don't have it, you don't need it." He looked up at Rod. "You going far?"

"We have kin west of here," Rod answered warily.

"Well, I wouldn't presume to ask, except if you're going to the Colorado Territory, you'd better check your supply of guns, powder, and lead."

"Is that a fact?"

"Yes, sir. The Indians are on the warpath out there. Seems some militia colonel named Chivington wiped out a bunch of Cheyenne and Arapahoe at Sand Creek last winter, and three or four tribes took exception to the action. They're raiding all the way from the Platte to the Arkansas, and on east into Kansas." Mr. Flaherty stopped to pull some cans from the shelf. "Indians favor sneaking up on a body when they attack. It's almost like they're invisible until they're on top of you." The clerk scratched his chin.

"Dangerous fellows," said Rod.

"Yes sir. I see you're not wearing handguns. Handguns are right handy to have when an Indian is five feet away and swinging a hatchet at your head. I expect you're a rifle man, yourself. Well, a rifle'd just get in the way with an enemy so close and set on revenge. Some of them don't care if they lives or dies, just so their kinfolks is avenged."

"You don't say."

"But I do say. If I was you, I would outfit my entire party with handguns, belts, and holsters. That's if I was you and going out to the Colorado Territory." Mr. Flaherty folded his arms and leaned forward on the counter.

Rod looked at the clerk, waiting there for a sale. He said nothing, but tucked his chin into his chest for a moment, then moved over to the dry goods section of the store.

Carl had spent his time admiring the clothes on display on the counter. There was a pair of blue jean trousers, waist overalls, that would suit him fine. He wished he had a couple of coins to rub together, or better yet, to spend on new trousers.

His father looked around for Clay, who had moved over to examine the candy counter. He saw Carl looking at the trousers, and approached him.

"They would look mighty nice, son, and you surely do need them, but I can't spare the cash right now. If what the clerk says is right, looks like we'll be needing handguns worse than a change of clothes." Rod looked chagrined. "I was hoping to get a little keepsake for your ma, but I reckon our safety comes before trinkets."

"Trouble on the trail, Pa? Outlaw?"

"Indians. Somebody broke a treaty, and the whole east part of Colorado Territory is running with blood. We might have to fight our way in." Rod grinned and winked. "Don't mention it to Rand Hilbrands. He's not much for fighting."

"Now, Pa," Carl responded. "Mr. Hilbrands ain't so bad. I don't reckon he's a cowardly sort. He just spent the whole war behind a store counter, and didn't get the chance to harden up like we did."

"That's so. And he saw a right smart lot of Yankees going up and down the Valley, but he sometimes wears my patience mighty thin."

"Pa, speaking of the Hilbrands, don't you think we could rustle up a preacher in this town so Ida 'n me can get married?"

Rod looked sharply at Carl. "Are you sparking on that wagon seat, boy?"

"I'm driving. Ida does the sparking." Carl grinned. "It's time I got wed, Pa."

"I'll see what I can do. It's surely a shame that preacher never came around back home. He put a bad crimp in my plan." Rod gripped Carl's shoulder and turned away toward the counter where Flaherty was loading his order into a couple of emptied grain sacks. "What are you asking for a handgun set?" he asked the clerk. "I might be persuaded that I'm interested if the price is right."

"Well now, we've got a mighty nice piece of goods for twenty-five dollars, complete with belt and holster. It's an Army model 1860 by Colt, .44 caliber with six shots. It's your standard percussion cap revolver, ain't been used much. Twenty-five dollars, ammunition extra." He brought out a big revolver for Rod to examine.

"If it saw action in the war, it's been used more than a mite." Rod looked it over, checking the cylinder and the heft of the nearly three pound gun in his hand. "You got any more like this?"

"Some. The Army dumped them on the market a while back, and they've been selling good."

"Let me have my pick of six pistols, you throw in the belts, holsters, and a thousand rounds of shot, with caps and powder enough to shoot them, and I'll give you a hundred dollars, Federal cash."

"Done!" said Mr. Flaherty.

𝕤𝕠

"Hallelujah, Pa! You got me a gun!" Albert's voice cracked in his excitement. "You really got me a gun, a humdinger. Thanks, Pa." The boy lifted the pistol in two hands, sighted down the barrel, then put it back into his holster.

"Albert, we're likely to run into some trouble up the road. I expect you to learn to use that pistol, but it's for protection. I won't stand for gun play. Don't forget that!"

"No, Pa, I surely won't. Boy, wait until I show this to Andy. His eyes will pop out of his head."

Rulon hitched his gun belt to a more comfortable position. "It feels strange, Pa. I'm more at home with a rifle."

"Rulon, it's mighty handy to have a weapon strapped on with enemies coming right at you. Mr. Flaherty spoke of Indian raids in the Territory. If we aim to find your Uncle Jonathan, we'll need guns at hand, I reckon." Rod hitched up his own belt.

James swung into his saddle, and retrieved his pistol as it slipped loose. "Pa, how do I keep the revolver from falling out of the holster when I'm mounting, or jogging loose as I ride?"

"Look at this thong, here. Loop it over the hammer, and the gun will stay in there real snug. If you expect trouble, just slip off the loop, and you're ready."

James fixed the rawhide thong as Rod had directed, then kneed his horse into the street. He cantered down a block, dodging wagons, then waited for a clear moment and returned at a gallop.

He pulled up before his father and brother, checked his pistol, and declared, "That works right fine."

Rod caught Carl's arm and spoke confidentially. "I found a preacher, son. He's willing to speak your wedding words this evening."

"That's good, Pa."

"See if you can talk James into marrying Miss Ellen, too."

Carl nodded and got on his horse. "Pa, I reckon I'll ride ahead and give Ida the news. She'll be happy to hear it."

"I'll go with you," Rulon volunteered. Rod and the others mounted their horses, and rode out of Kansas town in a cloud of dust.

As they completed the first mile of their ride back to camp, they heard gunfire and rode forward cautiously. Before them in the road, the big Mexican with the fine clothes trotted his horse in a circle, shooting his gun and laughing, while his two cronies followed him, enclosing three young women, who huddled together in fright.

Carl and Rulon, ahead of the other men, looked at each other, anger darkening their features.

"That's Marie, and Ellen Bates," Rulon shouted.

"And Ida Hilbrands," finished Carl.

Chapter 7

Carl spurred his horse into the midst of the rowdies, knocking the guns from the hands of two of them before Rulon arrived. As he whirled Sherando to face the man in the black vest, Carl saw the gun pointed at his chest.

"Do not be foolish, *señor*," Black-Vest warned him. "I shoot very fast, and I do not miss." He drew back his lips in what passed for a smile, and his teeth, white beneath his moustache, seemed large as headstones.

The other Owen men arrived, and noting the gun covering Carl, sat their horses in stolid silence, hands held carefully in sight. The two bearded men dismounted and retrieved their pistols, laughing as they brought them to bear on the Owen party. One man stepped backward and tried to caress Marie's cheek with his free hand. Marie shrank back and cried out.

Ellen's eyes went dark and glittering, and she snapped at the big Mexican, "What kind of cowards are you, picking on girls and honest men?"

Black-Vest's smile vanished. "Coward! You will see that Berto Acosta is not a coward. I withdraw my gun." He holstered the weapon and lifted his hands. "Now you see I am no coward. *Joven!* You with the quick temper. Let us see if your hand is as quick as your anger." He motioned to Carl to try to outdraw him.

Carl shrugged his shoulders. "I can't beat you. I just got the gun today."

"Ah," said Acosta. "But when a man puts on a gun he must be prepared to use it. What do we do now?" His hand dropped toward his gun.

"You're still a coward, or you'd let us go," Ellen hissed.

"That little one has fire," Acosta said, then leaned over to stroke Ida's blonde curls, "but I choose this white little goddess."

"No you don't!" shouted Carl, looking at Ida's chalky face. "I can't meet you with guns, but I sure can beat you with my bare hands!"

"A champion," laughed Acosta, baring his teeth. "*Mis amigos*," he addressed his friends, "we will have here a fine contest, and all will know I am no coward. If he wins, they will all go free." He threw back his head and laughed a long time. "But I will win, and then we shall enjoy the spoils!"

Carl flung himself off Sherando and stripped away his gun belt and shirt. Acosta seemed confident, dismounting with a lazy grace that spoke of long, hard muscle and great control. The big man gave his holster and belt to one of his companions, but he made no move to take off his vest or shirt.

As he looked at the Mexican, Carl imagined him holding Ida in his arms, and a cold rage welled up into his throat, nearly choking him. He stepped up to the older man and threw the first punch with his right fist. Acosta ducked and laughed, and hit Carl a short, sharp jab to the stomach. Carl backed up, sick from the powerful blow.

Acosta followed and slugged him again. When Carl doubled over, Acosta chopped down from above, aiming for the back of Carl's neck. The youth twisted out of the way, and Acosta's joined fists glanced off his shoulder. Carl stumbled sideways, knowing his opponent was following him, then he thudded up against Sherando. He gasped for breath, then moved out to meet Acosta's attack.

This time the blows caught him on the face, and he tried to escape by ducking as Acosta had done. The Mexican swung into air, and Carl, surprised by the success of his maneuver, followed up by butting Acosta with his head. Caught off guard, the rowdy went down, Carl on top of him.

They rolled together, dust filling their lungs and coating their bodies and clothes. Carl broke away first and got to his feet, coughing and shaking his head.

His rage was now a steady, burning drive to defeat the older man. He tasted blood as he licked his upper lip and realized that the Mexican was still unbloodied. "I'll change that now," he muttered, setting himself for the next attack.

Acosta got to his feet, threw back his head in anger, and cried out, "You have soiled my clothing, señor. This I do not forgive."

He's prideful, Carl thought. *It makes him angry to be mussed.* Carl raised his arms to turn aside Acosta's renewed attack, then hit his foe in the face as hard as his work-toughened muscles would allow. He heard the crunch of the nose breaking, felt the moistness of blood on his knuckles, but he hit again, with his left, opening a gash over Acosta's right cheekbone.

Stunned with the blow, unused to having his own blood flow, Acosta panicked, jabbing ineffectually at Carl's body. He paused once to wipe the blood from his ruined nose, and the sight of it on his hand seemed to cause him more alarm.

He swore at Carl, words that lost no venom for being in a foreign tongue. "You have ruined my face," he finished.

Carl gathered his strength and punched Acosta on the side of the head. The Mexican went down and stayed down, and Rod and young Albert pulled their pistols, covering the three rowdies, while Carl climbed on Sherando and his brothers boosted the girls up behind them on their horses. They all left at once, as the two men tried to revive their unconscious amigo.

When the Owens arrived in camp, Carl slid off Sherando and ran to gather Ida into his arms as Rulon lowered her to the ground from his saddle. Carl held her close to his dusty chest and stroked her hair, feeling the shivers that seized her body.

"There now, Ida," he soothed, calming her with little pats and strokes. "I took care of him. He won't never bother you again."

"Oh Carl, I thought he was killing you." She sneezed from the dust, then peered at his bruised and bloody face, and patted the puffiness under his left eye. "Oh, Carl!" Ida covered her mouth with her hand. "He spoiled your handsome face."

"I left him more a mess than he left me," he said, flexing his swelling hands.

∞

Marie and Ellen slipped to the ground and tried to get to their wagons, but Rod Owen barred the way, and he was soon joined by Chester Bates. Then Julia and Muriel ran up, with the rest of the party close behind.

"Marie," demanded Rod. "Why were you on the road back there?"

The girl took one look at her father's contorted face and began to blubber hysterically. Ellen put an arm around her and tried to smile.

"Ida said she needed to get some things from the store, and we agreed to go with her. We was almost there when those men rode up and began to torment us, shooting off their guns and making rude comments." Ellen looked up and saw Ida in Carl's arms. "If Carl and the rest of you hadn't come just then—" She turned her face and broke into sobs.

"Ellen," Marie cried out, and wrapped her arms around her friend. "You been so brave, and you talked back to that awful man. Don't cry."

Ellen shook her head and wept on, throwing her arms around Marie's neck.

"There, now," Muriel soothed her daughter. "We'll take you over to the wagon, you can lie down a spell, and you'll feel better tomorrow."

"No," she sobbed. "Leave me be." Then she whispered through her tears into Marie's ear, "Take care of your brother's face. It wants cold cloths, and Ida sure ain't going to think of that."

Marie drew back and gave her a sharp glance, then looked over at Carl and Ida. "I'll take her, Mrs. Bates," she volunteered. "We'll both be fine with a little rest." Marie took Ellen's hand and led her away from the buzzing group.

When the girls arrived at the Bates' wagon, Marie turned to Ellen. "You're not crying because you're scared. You're crying over my brother!" She scrutinized Ellen's face, not allowing her to cover her eyes with her hand. "You like my brother. I do declare!"

Ellen wiped her tears. "He saved my life. Twice, now. And I can't go over there and fix him up. You'll have to tend to that."

"You're right. Ida won't think of it, and Carl sure won't bother. Why, he ain't even got the sense to put his shirt back on. And I reckon his hands could use some tending, too. Ellen, you bathe your face, and I'll tend to Carl's."

∞

Rod spoke to the men gathered around the blowing horses. "We'll likely need extra guards tonight. I don't know if them rowdies have other friends, nor if they'd be foolish enough to attack an armed camp, but we'd best be prepared for them. Clay, Albert!"

"Yes, Pa," responded the two boys.

"You bunch the stock and put them on pickets, those you can. We'll give you more guards. Folks, let's form a square with the wagons. Angus, you and Ed put yours on the east side, Tom and Chester, take the south. Rand, you pull into the west, and Rulon and me'll make the north side."

"Rod, I reckon I need some supplies," Tom O'Connor said.

"This is a good time for everyone to take stock. Look over your goods, and if you need victuals, or extra shot, go into town together to buy." The men dispersed, except for Rand Hilbrands, who approached Rod.

"Where's Carl? My driver?"

Rod gestured toward the family wagon. "Getting his wounds tended. Say, Rand, the young ones wanted to get wed today, but I don't think it's a good idea now. Will you let Carl know?"

Rand grimaced. "I will." He walked up to Carl, who was seated on a barrel of cornmeal undergoing Marie's ministrations. "Carl, my boy, you done a fine, brave thing. I'm mighty grateful to you for rescuing my girl Ida from those thugs." Rand reached into his trousers pocket. "Here, take this coin with my thanks." He pressed it into Carl's puffy hand and continued. "Your pa said to say today's not a good time to wed."

"No, I—" Carl began, but Marie muffled her brother's voice with the cold cloth she held tightly to his mouth as Rand walked toward his wagon.

Marie removed the cloth when Rand was safely out of hearing range. "You were going to get married today?"

"Yep. That Acosta fellow surely messed up my plans."

Marie bit her lip, and ached for Ellen. When she had finished with Carl's face, she said, "Your hands are a mess, your lip is split, and you'll likely have a black eye for a spell, but you'll soon make Ida's heart go 'pitty-pat' again."

Carl squinted at his sister and gave a quick shrug of his shoulders, then got up from the barrel. "Thank you for tending my face. You didn't have to do that."

"I know it. Put your shirt on. You surely look foolish parading around half-naked." She put her fist on a hip. "Then go thank Ellen Bates. She's the only one of us who thought of caring for your ugly mug."

Carl felt his swollen lip with bruised fingers. "That was right sisterly of her."

Marie stared at her brother, unable to think of a proper response.

"What do I do with all this money, Sis? I've got my eye on a change of clothes, and I want to get something pretty for Ma, but I expect I'll have a bit left over."

"It's your money, and I reckon you took a beating to earn it, but I wouldn't fuss if you was to bring me a bite of something sweet."

"The store has a candy counter. I'll do it. I reckon that'll pay you back for washing up my face."

"Mind you, it was Ellen's idea. If you bring me some candy, you have to bring her some likewise."

"I wonder why she didn't fix me up herself?" he asked, putting on his shirt.

ഇ

Six cautious men went back into town to buy provisions, and Carl was among them. He picked out his clothes quickly, and then lingered over a selection of gifts for his ma, finally choosing a bright yellow Spanish shawl with colored embroidery and fringes around the edge. He spent a whole quarter dollar at the candy counter, and came away with plenty of sweets for the young people at the camp.

On the return trip, Chester Bates matched the gait of his horse to Carl's. The furrows between the older man's nose and mouth deepened and widened as he smiled at Carl and motioned for him to slow his mount.

When they had their horses walking, Chester put his hand out and gripped Carl's shoulder. "I'm beholden to you for defending the girls today. My Ellen has a strong mind and will, but she's no match for a bully of that kind. I thank you."

"Your daughter spoke out well for the girls. She is a brave one, Mr. Bates. If she had been armed, likely there'd have been no need for my help."

"You're a modest lad, and well-spoken yourself. Your pa can be proud of such a son."

Carl squirmed under this praise, knowing he had not earned it for defending Ellen or his sister. He said nothing, and Chester nodded to him and rode off up the trail.

When he reached camp, Carl went directly to his family's wagon and changed into his new clothes. As he dropped from the wagon box, his mother straightened up from the fire and looked him over.

"Don't you look fine! I count myself lucky that my sons are as fair of deed as they are of figure."

"Oh, Ma!" he protested, then advanced to the fire and placed a bundle into her busy hands.

"What's this, Carl?"

"Something I thought you'd like, Ma."

"For me?"

"You're the only ma I got."

She moved to the barrel beside the wagon and sat, smoothing the paper wrapping. "For me?" she asked again.

"Go ahead, open it, Ma."

She worried over the knots, until Carl stepped forward with his knife and cut the string. Then she wrapped it into a ball over her fingers and tucked it into a pocket of her apron.

"Come on, Ma," Carl urged.

She spread apart the paper, and the yellow silk burst into the light. Julia caught her breath. "Oh, Carl, it's lovely!" She laughed and held the shawl to her face, pressing the softness of the fabric against her cheek. "Where'd you get the coin for this, boy?"

"Mr. Hilbrands gave me a little 'thank you' present. He was grateful Ida wasn't harmed."

"And well she might have been." Julia sighed. "I don't know what got into those girls, even to think of going into a strange town without a man to escort them. I'm glad you boys happened along in time."

Basking in his mother's grateful reception of his present, Carl went in search of the girls.

"Here you go, Sis," he said, and gave Marie a twist of paper. "Thank you." He turned to Ellen and presented her with a similar paper twist. "I reckon thanks goes to you, too. Marie says so."

Ellen looked at Marie. "What's this for?"

"Tell her, Carl."

"Marie says you sent her over to fix up my wounds. I'm obliged."

Ellen turned to her friend. "Marie!" she protested, fidgeting with the paper in her hands. Then she held the candy out to Carl. "I didn't do nothing. I can't take it."

"Nonsense. It's for keeping your head, like."

She looked down. "Thank you."

"Enjoy your sweets."

Carl turned away, and Marie whispered to Ellen, "Look there, he's bringing you presents. And Ida ain't married him yet. He's still fair game."

"Marie, he treats me like he treats you. I'm an extra sister, to his mind."

Marie took hold of Ellen's upper arm and gave it a shake. "Don't give up, Ellen. Sometimes he's a bother, but my brother Carl's worth having. You keep in his sight. Don't let him forget you're around." She let go of her friend's arm. "Mind you, Ida's fun, and I reckon Carl thinks so, too, but I don't think she'll make him a good wife out in the Colorado Territory. She ain't the pioneering kind."

Ellen held the twist of candy over her heart. "But there's James to consider."

Marie sighed. "There's nothing wrong with James," she said. "He's nice enough: he's kind, and he's brave—he's got a bayonet wound to prove that."

"I don't want James," Ellen said, shaking her head, her face gone somber. "He's got that grin, and a quick wit, and I feel so ashamed that I can't find a morsel of affection for him." She hid her eyes behind her hands for a moment, then added, "I was so glad when Reverend Halsey didn't come. I know James was, too. But now he comes to our fire and sits with me, and tries to pretend he's happy a-courting me. He'll even kiss my hand from time to time before he goes back to your fire, but there's no . . . no loss in my bosom when he leaves."

Marie's eyes were wet with tears. "Oh, Ellen," she sniffed. "Why is life so hard?"

જી

"They will regret they ever came to *Ciudad* Kansas," the Mexican swore, breathing with difficulty through his smashed nose. "The young one, he will watch Berto Acosta have his way with the girl." He drained the beer from the mug he held in his fist, then turned and shouted, "I will follow them, and the *muchacha* will be mine!"

"You need rest, Berto," Willy murmured, taking hold of his arm.

"Shore, that nose won't heal proper if you sit here drinking all night," Rankin agreed, grabbing the second arm. "Let's get some sleep. We'll pick up their trail easy in a couple of days. Them tenderfeet are always easy to track."

Chapter 8

For several days after leaving the city of Kansas, the travelers had the road to themselves. Although stage stops and farms stretched all along their path, the other men agreed with Rod that camping and cooking their own food was both cheaper and safer than stopping to eat ready-made meals. However, Rod did inquire for news of Indian movements along the trail ahead.

A week later, the party came upon a fork in the trail, and Rod pointed out to Julia the branch angling off toward the northeast.

"That there's the road to Oregon. There used to be a sign here, telling folks which way was what. It was mostly a joke."

"But we don't go that way?"

"Nah. We take the left fork, keep going west until we hit the Arkansas River."

"Looks easy to follow, Rod."

"Should be. This trail is over forty years old. I reckon we could hold to the road in a snowstorm. The tracks are worn deep and wide."

"How come there is more than one trail going to the same place, like over there?" Julia gestured toward another track fifty yards away.

"I've been told folks would strike off on a path to one side, or where the grass was thicker for the stock. All the trails go to the same place—Santa Fe."

"I like the trees along here. They remind me of home." She pointed to a stand of oaks interrupting the waves of blue-stemmed grass.

"Enjoy them now, woman. There's a long stretch ahead of us without trees at all, and it goes for hundreds of miles. Jonathan said folks call it the 'Great American Desert'. That's where all them buffalo are supposed to cover the land from one horizon to the other."

"Rod, ain't there no trees in the Colorado Territory?"

"We'll have trees, Julie. I promise you we'll have trees if I have to plant 'em myself."

"That'll take years, Rod. I'd hanker for shade."

"You'll have it. I didn't bring you out here to pioneer forever. We'll have all we had back in the Shenandoah, and more. I figure to make a heap of money. I aim to have my share of this country, especially since the Yankees took as much of mine as they did. If I've got to start over, I mean to end big."

"Rod." Julia changed the subject. "I've been watching that dust cloud out there on the horizon, and it's growing mighty fast. Somebody's in a powerful hurry."

Rod studied the dust for a moment, noting how it boiled up out of the distant roadway. "No telling what trouble that could be. We'd best get off the road and circle the wagons."

Rod directed his team off the road, and the others followed him, wondering what was causing the delay. At Rod's explanation, they drew the eight wagons into a tight circle, unhitched the teams, and led them into the center along with the extra livestock. Then they found their rifles and waited as the dust cloud drifted nearer.

A few minutes later, a loud thundering sound accompanied the dust. Soon, the nervous watchers made out a dark, bulky shape, like a covered freight wagon, bearing down on them at high speed.

As it drew closer, Rulon called out to his father. "Pa. I reckon that's the mail stage." He walked nearer, and continued in a lower voice. "I reckon I forgot to tell you it was expected about now."

Rod expelled a lungful of air, and looked at his eldest son. "No harm done, I guess. Next time I send you to a stage stop for information, it would pleasure me if you would tell me all you dig up, boy."

"I'm sorry I forgot to give you that word, Pa. I reckon I ain't a boy no longer, though. Not with a wife and young'uns."

"You'll always be my boy, Rule. That's the way of fathers." Rod suddenly focused on his son's face. "Wait a minute. You said 'young'uns'?"

"You been preoccupied, Pa. Mary and me, well, Mary, anyway, is a-brooding chick number two. We reckon it'll hatch just before spring."

"That's why she didn't want to come west. A gal gets mighty particular about her nest during these times. Is she taking this traveling well, son?"

"Well enough. Look at that stage, Pa."

Six horses pulled the coach abreast of the wagons. The stage, blue- and red-painted sides gleaming through the dirt, sped by with only a wave of the hand from the guard, and then the stage, passengers, guard, and driver all blended into the dirty ball of dust following them.

Edward Morgan laughed. "That's a good joke on us, Rod. We're sitting here all ready for Indians."

"Practice makes perfect, they say," Rod said, his mouth set in wry lines. "Let's hitch up and get on the road again."

∞

Several hours later, Ida turned to Carl on the wagon seat. "What if that had been Indians?" she asked.

"What?"

"Back there. The stage. What would we do if they did come down on us?"

"Ida, a lot of us came through the war because we were pretty good with our rifles. That, and lucky. We've been practicing with our new revolvers, too. I reckon we'll fight them off, girl. A bunch of Indians can't be much different than a bunch of blue-belly Yankees."

Ida sighed. "I expect I'd die of fright. I still shudder when I think what might have happened to little ol' me." She gave an illustration of her best shudder.

Carl clamped his mouth shut against angry words. Her games grated on his nerves, what with the edgy feeling he'd had as soon as he woke that morning.

Ida continued to prattle on about her fright, and when he could bear no more, Carl turned his head to stare at her, trying to get his anger under control before he spoke.

Ida arched her eyebrows and remarked, "You're a cranky ol' fuss-budget today, Carl Owen. What ails you?"

Carl turned back to the lines, thinking, *I got a bad feeling*, and when James rode up alongside the wagon, Carl hailed him.

"Hey, James. Come take the mules for a spell."

James looked surprised, but traded places with Carl and greeted Ida, who sat frowning next to Eliza. "Hello, Miss Ida. Bet you could use the sight of a handsome face for once."

"Hello, James," she said in a monotone.

"Well, you'll get over that snit," he replied. "You always do."

"Humph," she replied, and bounced nearer her sister.

Carl rode off on James's horse, breathing deeply, feeling his anger drop away as he put distance between himself and the wagons. He headed east, checking the back trail, easing off toward the north. Searching the prairie, not knowing what he expected to find, he gained composure in the act of working.

After a few miles of riding through tall grass, Carl turned south again, and stopped to let his horse breathe. A rider approached from the direction of the wagon train, and he sat the horse and waited. Once he made out Rulon's blunt face, he walked the animal forward to meet his older brother.

"Find anything, Carl?" Rulon drawled.

"Nothing. And what's more, I don't know what I expect to find, but I been nervy as a bird waiting for the cat to pounce. I sure would admire to know why."

"I felt the same. Say, did you ride all the way back to that knoll over yonder?"

"Not yet."

"Let's go check it."

After riding for a time in silence, they reached the hill and cautiously circled wide behind it, approaching from the rear side. Rulon pulled up his horse, and pointed toward the east.

"See where that grass has been pushed aside? Somebody rode through that blue stem, probably early today."

The brothers dismounted and let the reins drag, ground-tying their horses. Rulon took the east approach, and Carl the west, and they advanced slowly, eyes sweeping the earth at the foot of the knoll.

"Look here," Rulon sang out, excitement registering in his voice.

Carl arrived to see Rulon down on his knees, picking up the stub of a thin black cigar. The grass was trampled in a large area, and included sign that several men and horses had met. Deep heel tracks marked where someone had squatted down. He had drawn in the dirt, then smoothed away the drawing.

"Did they watch the trail?" Carl asked, looking up at the knoll for signs of ascent.

"I reckon. I'll go up and see what's to be found there."

As Rulon climbed the hill, Carl walked over the area again, searching for more sign of what had taken place. He found a spot where a man had stretched out on his back, and the grass was still bent over, showing the outline of his body.

Rulon gave a shout as he skidded down the last few feet of the hill. "Somebody bellied-down there for quite a spell," he puffed, then caught his breath and went on. "Watching for us, maybe. The way I read it, they came before daylight and waited until we passed by, then up and returned the way they came." He gestured around. "How many do you figure in the party, Carl?"

"I count two over here, then two more came up. How many climbed up yonder?"

"Just the one, and he smokes these thin cigars. I found three more stubs up there. Something puzzles me, though. I thought maybe these folks might be those toughs from back yonder in Kansas town, but the feller up the hill didn't mind getting a little dirt on his britches. Your Mexican friend was powerful upset when you dusted up his clothes, so was it really him and his cronies?"

"I mussed up his fancy duds, but he's not likely to wear them on the trail. I got a crawling up my back tells me we got Berto Acosta and his pals tracking us."

Rulon took one last look around the base of the knoll. "Well, we'd best get back. I'll report to Pa. I've a feeling he won't like what I have to tell him." He laughed and shook his head.

"There ain't nothing funny about this, Rule."

"Only funny thing is that you have to sit up there day after day alongside the girl who brought this whole mess upon us."

"What're you saying?" Carl demanded.

"Mary's fool sister couldn't wait for an escort to get into town, so she drug the other two girls along with her, and almost got the three of them despoiled. I'd say that makes her to blame for this mess."

"I'd just as soon take a poke at you here and now, Rulon. Ida didn't mean anything, heading into town. If anybody's to blame, it's them three rowdies, especially Berto Acosta. Ida's blameless, and I won't allow you nor anybody else to pin the fault on her."

"You got yourself a case of hot blood there, little brother. Mind it don't get you into trouble."

"Don't push me, Rule." Carl climbed on his horse and started back toward the wagons, biting his tongue in regret at his hard words. He didn't know why he felt compelled to defend Ida, because he knew she was partly to blame for the trouble.

∽

Carl relieved James at the lines of the freight wagon, and spent the rest of the morning in grim silence. When the wagons stopped for the nooning, Carl helped Ida down from the wagon seat and looked at her gravely. "I ain't been good company this morning, and I'm sorry for it."

Ida smiled. "I'll pay it no mind, Carl."

"I've got to go talk with my brother. You stay put. No wandering away from the wagons, you hear? It's important, girl." He looked sternly into her blue eyes, and wagged his finger under her nose for emphasis.

"You're mighty serious, Carl," she giggled.

"I'm mighty serious," he agreed, nodding as he escorted her and her sister to the Hilbrands' family wagon.

"Sorry I left you out there, Rulon," Carl apologized stiffly once he located his brother. "I reckon my fool temper is stronger than my sense. Did you talk to Pa?"

"Yep."

"Well, what did he say about our watchers?"

"He thinks we're most likely right about who they are and who they're laying for."

"Well? What's he going to do?"

"He didn't say, Carl. You know Pa. He'll contemplate on the situation for a spell before deciding what action to take. We'll have to wait."

"That's so."

✫

Before the travelers hitched up for the afternoon march, Rod sent word around that he wanted to talk to the men. When they had gathered, he told them what Carl and Rulon had discovered behind the hill. Rod rubbed his beard and squinted around the horizon.

"There's no need to alarm the women folks. I reckon if we keep a sharp watch behind us, we can go along about like we have."

"Are you crazy, man?" Rand Hilbrands sputtered, his face red and mottled. "I say we should stay here and circle the wagons, wait for them ruffians to appear, and meet them from a position of strength."

"We could sit here for a week, waiting for trouble to find us, our food and water running out, when we should be miles down the road toward the Territory. That's not good tactics, Rand."

"You think because you were an officer and I stayed home, I don't know anything. Well, this I know: I'll not run from a fight. You go along with your two wagons, if you're too scared to stick and defend yourself and your women folks."

"Don't be a fool, Randolph. If they want to make trouble, together we have twice their number. You'll sit here and divide us up with your fool talk, and make it easy for them to wipe you out."

"I ain't going, Rod Owen. I aim to stay right here and fight it out, and yes, with your boy at my side. I paid for his work, and I'll keep his rifle here." He turned to the other men. "Tom O'Connor, you never ran from a fight, either. Stay with me."

The brawny blacksmith nodded. "I never ran, for a fact. I'm bound to back a man who'll stand and fight."

"Will the lot of you sit around and burrow into the trail then, waiting for those men to spook you like a bunch of rabbits?" Scorn thickened Rod's voice. "Devil take the ruffians. Who'll go on with me to Colorado?"

"I'll go, Rod," answered Chester Bates. "I see no sense in waiting for trouble to find me."

"The farther we go, the nearer we are to home," observed Ed Morgan. "I'm with you, Rod. You have my son Tom's rifle, too."

Angus Campbell glanced around at the angry faces. "I'd favor going on, Rod, but I can't leave Tom and his little ones. I reckon I have to stay with my kinfolks."

"You're a good man, Angus. I'm sorry to lose you. Godspeed to you, then. We'll go on." Rod turned his back on those who elected to stay, and took Carl by the shoulder.

"You ma will take this parting hard, Carl, but you've a duty to stay and see that fool and his freight wagon get on the way again. He's putting us in double danger, splitting our firepower, but I won't sit and wait. The season is late enough now."

Carl nodded dumbly, his throat choked tight with shock. He shook hands with his father, then, as Rod walked away, Carl called out.

"Pa! How'll I find you in Colorado?"

"Follow the trail, son. Once you catch sight of the mountains, you look sharp for my sign."

Carl got his gear and his saddle out of the family wagon, dumped it in a pile, and tied Sherando to the back of the freight vehicle. The day burned hot, with no beauty to temper his misery, and Carl felt dull-witted while the Owen group got under way. He stood gazing at his family as the four wagons turned miniature in the distance, finally being swallowed up in a cloud of dust. Then he turned and sat down against a wagon wheel, his rifle across his knees.

Rand Hilbrands swaggered a little with his new position of command. The other men hitched up their teams and drove them into a square. He walked around and around the puny shelter of the four wagons, assigning men to stand watch.

"You there, Carl. Get some rest. You'll have the first watch after nightfall."

Carl got his bedroll from the pile where he'd dumped his gear. He unrolled it and lay down beneath the wagon, but sleep would not come in the afternoon heat. Turning over on the blanket, he opened his eyes to see the hem of Ida's skirt.

The girl bent over to look at him. "I'll rub your shoulders, Carl, help you relax a bit," she offered.

"It wouldn't be seemly," Carl said, "you scooting under here with me."

"Fiddlesticks!" she declared, and crawled under the wagon beside him. "You're my man, and you need to get your mind and body laid to rest before you can sleep. I reckon it's my duty to help us all, you going on watch later, and all."

Carl looked up at her, keeping silent.

"I'm sorry your pa took off in such a hurry, Carl. If that nasty brute is following us, we could use a few more guns to chase him away. I think my pa is so brave to set here ready to stand him off. I am so thrilled."

Carl sighed wearily and declined to answer.

Ida leaned over him and began to rub his shoulders. He sensed the nearness of her body to his, smelled a faint odor of lilacs, then willed his muscles to go slack under her hands. Soon, her kneading manipulations eased the pain of tension. "That feels mighty good," he grunted, not caring any longer about the possessive way she was touching him. If Ida didn't care that her pa saw what she was doing, he wouldn't care either. Then, he succumbed to the heat and his fatigue and shock, and slept.

When he awoke, the sun was gone and supper was ready, cooked over a large campfire. Uneasy at the amount of light cast upon the prairie, Carl looked around for his father to protest. Then, remembering the split that the group had undergone, he shrugged his shoulders and yawned.

Ida smiled at him across the camp as he crawled from under the wagon, and a shiver of warning went up Carl's spine. *By gum, that girl has something on her mind, and I ain't got no taste to find out what it is just now*, he thought. He arranged his blankets into a neat bed, then stood, got his plate, and approached the fire.

Amanda Hilbrands served him a scoop of beans, some biscuits, and a mug of chicory coffee, eyeing him from under her pale brows. "You slept well enough after Ida tended to you, I see," she said. "My daughter has healing hands. Her daddy sent her to rub those tired muscles of yours. He says she's got a real talent."

Carl stared woodenly at Mrs. Hilbrands, thinking he had not heard right, then walked over to a barrel and sat. He ate silently, gulping down the hot brew in his cup. When his food was gone, Carl drained his mug and threw the grounds into the fire. He dropped his plate and mug into the washtub, wiped his knife on his trousers, and got his rifle from the wagon wheel. Then he walked out a ways from the hubbub of the camp and took his turn on watch.

Gradually, the noises of the camp subsided as the women washed and put away the dishes and the travelers retired to their beds. Glad when the fire died, Carl walked around the outside of the wagons, listening to the night sounds, alert for any unfamiliar noise. He took up a position for a time, then circled the wagons again, never keeping to a set pattern that a watcher could count on.

He listened as the night insects chirped early in the evening, then they, too, went to sleep and he was left in the solitude.

Dwarfed by the immensity of the night sky, Carl wondered where his family was that night. He drove his fist into his hand in frustration at the lowly rank he held in this company that kept him from talking sense into Rand Hilbrands. In Rand's eyes, he was barely more than a kid, a hired driver, not yet a son-in-law, and not worth listening to. Besides, he was Rod's son, and right now, that was a count against him. How long would they be here, perched on the side of the road, waiting, and sitting, and eating up the food and drinking the water barrels dry?

When his hours of watch were up, he awakened Tom O'Connor, then prevented him from throwing an armful of fuel onto the fire.

"Let's don't show them where we are, Mr. O'Connor."

"Right, lad. I guess I'm still used to a roaring fire in the hearth of the smithy. It comforts a man, somehow." Tom went off to take up his position, while Carl returned to the freight wagon to crawl into his blankets.

The next day, Carl spent several hours in Sherando's saddle, scouting the back trail. He wished Rulon was with him, with his tracking experience, but even without him, he was sure he had not missed anything when he returned and reported to Rand.

"There's nobody out there, Mr. Hilbrands. Not a sign of folks watching us, not a cigar stub, not a blade of grass bent down for miles around."

"You're sure you missed nothing, boy?" asked Angus Campbell. "If they're not out there, we might as well go on, don't you think, Rand?"

"No! We'll wait and fight them from a position of strength!" he trumpeted. "They're out there, all right. They're just waiting for a weak moment, a wavering on our part, to close in and destroy us. We'll wait, I say, and outwit them."

Carl turned away and went to rub down Sherando. *The man is hell-bent on staying until we all take root*, he thought. *There's no turning his mind to the righteous path.* Grumbling to himself, Carl worked with his horse, cooling it down from the exercise of the morning. Tom O'Connor walked over, and rubbed the horse's nose.

"Nothing to be seen, lad?"

"Maybe they went back to the last stage stop to drink some courage," Carl mumbled. "Acosta saw we were well armed when he spied on us, Mr. O'Connor. He'll have to make a plan other than 'catch up and shoot'."

Tom clapped Carl on the shoulder with his massive hand. "That's thinking, boy. We're ready for anything, here. But things have changed. There's less of us now."

"And he doesn't know it yet. I don't reckon there's any chance of fooling him when he shows up. Eight wagons, take-away four leaves us with the odds about even, and he'll know it sure as daylight spills over the edge of that prairie when the sun rises."

Tom's black brows drew together. "I'm beginning to think twice about this plan of Rand's. We should have stuck together."

Carl spun around to face the blacksmith. "It's too late to change your mind now," he said, gritting his teeth against striking out at the man. "You should've said that when Pa gave you the chance. We're double-dyed fools to sit here and waste time."

"Wait a minute, boy. Are you calling me a fool? Better think twice, yourself."

Carl stood himself up straight. "We're all fools, one day or another. And I ain't a boy, *Mr.* O'Connor. I ain't been a boy since I joined Mosby." He jabbed his finger into Tom's chest.

Tom grabbed Carl's fist, sucked in a breath, held it, and let it out slowly. "I reckon you're riled some, Carl. I can't see as I blame you, getting cut off from your kin." He loosened his grip on Carl's fist and dropped it. "If my babies was split up from me, why, I'd—"

"I'm sorry I let go of my manners, sir," Carl interrupted. "I guess one day or another I'm still a boy."

"Well, it takes a man to own it, I reckon," the blacksmith drawled. "Here, let me take that saddle."

Carl staked Sherando on a fresh patch of grass, then, with his arms full of tack, followed Tom back to the wagons. He dumped the headpiece, bit, and other gear in a heap beside the freight wagon, and accepted the saddle from Tom, who took his hat off, put it back on, then left.

Douglas Campbell wandered up as Carl inspected a loose cinch buckle on his saddle. "Ma says you're invited to eat dinner with us, come noon."

"Thanks, Doug. I don't mind if I do," Carl replied, recalling that Molly Campbell made the best biscuits he'd ever eaten. "Does your ma have any flour?"

"Sorry, no. But she's going to open a tin of peaches, I believe. She got it out of the supply bin."

Carl grinned. "I'll be there."

જી

The day was long in passing, and the enforced idleness weighed heavily on the members of Rand Hilbrands' rear guard. A quarrel developed between the most tolerant of men, Angus Campbell, and his brother-in-law, Tom O'Connor, over where their stock should be picketed. Rand tried to smooth over their feelings, but he lacked Rod Owen's mediating skills, and bad feelings persisted into the next day.

Again Carl scouted the surrounding area as soon as light broke over the eastern grasslands. He found nothing, even though he went farther afield. When he returned, he gave his report to each of the three men at the camp, for they were not willing to endure each other's company in order to hear his news at one time. Disgusted, Carl sought his bedroll before noon, and tried to sleep amid the noise of fighting children and quick-tongued wives.

He woke when someone called his name in an urgent whisper, and he sat up hurriedly, bumping his head on the bottom of the wagon box. He swore, wincing at the pain, and rubbed his head.

"Carl Owen, I declare," exclaimed Ida. "You oughtn't to say such words in the presence of a lady."

Carl groaned and shook his head. "Beggin' your pardon, Miss Ida. Somebody woke me up real sudden like, and now I've got a headache would make a lap dog turn vicious. Whew!" he shook his head again. "What do you want?"

She slid under the wagon and sat beside him. "Only some company. It's so boring sitting out here, getting hot and sunburned, and swatting flies and 'skeeters and other horrid little bugs." She grimaced. "Mama made me scrape some meat this morning. It had maggots on it, and she made me touch it." She shuddered. "I don't think she will find me under here with you."

Carl moved around in his bedroll until the sitting was comfortable and he could face Ida. "Seems like not long ago this setup pleased you mighty fine, your daddy being in charge, and all."

"Well, it's dreadful boring now, just like I told you. I'm sorry I ever let him talk us into staying."

"I didn't think we had much choice."

"Fiddle-dee-dee! I could have talked Papa into going on, if I'd have wanted to. I just didn't want to, at the time."

"Know your own mind, is it?" Carl's voice grated in his own ears as he looked Ida up and down.

She flushed. "You're making fun of me, Carl Owen. It's not fair for you to tease me."

But a woman can tease a man all she wants, and nobody says a word, Carl thought. "I was trying to get some sleep, girl," he said, hunching his shoulders and preparing to lie down again.

"Let me stay here beside you so Mama won't make me help her again. I fair liked to faint, working this morning." At Carl's scowl, Ida put on a smile and put a pleading note into her voice. "Please, Carl. I won't say another word, just sit real quiet and watch you sleep."

"Ida, you got the dangedest notions. It ain't fitting for a girl to stay around when a man sleeps, not unless the two of them is wed."

"I don't care. We were supposed to be wed by now. Twice, even. Let's pretend we are. Then I can cuddle up beside you and get some—"

"Ida Hilbrands! You get along with you. Scoot outta here! I won't play them kinds of games with you, not here, and not likely anywhere else on this trip. You git!"

Ida went, reluctantly, but finally. Carl let out a shuddering breath, wiping his sopping forehead on his sleeve, and ran his moist hands down the front of his shirt.

He swore mildly, and thought, *I'm set to marry one forward gal. We're sitting here under God's great sky, not getting one foot nearer to Colorado Territory. I'll never get that cabin raised before winter sets in*. He shook his head and sighed. *And I won't take her to wife, or anything like unto it, until I have a place for us to call our own.*

Chapter 9

The next day dragged on like the three before it: hot, humid, and full of quarrels. Carl again went out to scout, but this time, Angus insisted on going along with him.

They didn't say anything much to each other; there wasn't a lot to say about riding large circles through the dusty grass, squinting into the sun looking for trampled grass or hoof prints, and feeling the sweat dripping down their chests, backs, and arms. They stopped from time to time to share a gourd of water or to rest their animals, but they still didn't talk.

Carl and Angus rode all the way back to the knoll where the brothers had discovered the signs of pursuit several days before. The younger man got down from his horse and walked around, looking at the bare patch of ground where men had met and plotted.

He squatted on his heels for a time, backtracking his and Rulon's movements to determine if there was something here that they had missed. He climbed the hill, stood on the top of the rise, took off his hat and wiped the sweatband, replaced it on his head, and looked out toward the north. A half-mile away, a band of chewed-up earth stood out from the blue stem, catching his eye. *Rulon and I came up from behind the hill*, he thought, *but we didn't make them tracks out yonder*. He stared toward the track in the grass, then turned and ran down the knoll to where Angus waited with the horses.

"We've got trouble." He bowed his head, his chest heaving, then looked up. "No, Pa's got trouble. Those fellows didn't go back to town."

"What?"

He gestured to the north, then around the area. "There's a big track out there Rulon and I didn't see before the grass died. They stopped here and had a discussion, and if I'm reading sign rightly, left toward the east, then circled around out that-a-way, rode hard, and set up an ambush for us along the road a piece." He swore and scrambled into his saddle. "My family and a lot of other good folks moved right into it, and I don't think they're going to come out alive, because we're sitting here on our thumbs waiting for the moon to rise blue!" He clucked to Sherando, and started for the wagons.

"Now, calm down, son. Maybe they did go back after they saw how strong we was," Angus called.

"No chance," Carl threw back over his shoulder. "I saw the hate in that man's eyes when he flung them strange words at me, and he ain't one to quit on us."

Angus got his horse started as well, and caught up to Carl. "Maybe he thought better of it after a time," he shouted.

"You weren't there, Angus. He's after my blood, and the blood of my kin, and the girls, too. He won't give up on the girls," Carl yelled, his words bouncing out of his mouth.

When Carl and Angus rode into the camp, Tom and Rand were standing nose to nose, shaking fingers in each other's faces. Carl slid off his horse and ran up to the overheated men.

"Stop it! Stop it right now," he commanded. "Rand, if you want to prove how much courage you've got, then you'll have to go down the road a piece."

Randolph turned on Carl. "You're crazy, boy. We'll fight off them ruffians right here."

"Well, they ain't coming here. They holed up ahead, laying for my ma and pa, and my brothers and sister, and your daughter and little grandchild, and all them good people."

Tom turned to him. "Speak plain, boy."

Carl threw out his hands. "Berto Acosta and his bunch circled around and got ahead. My folks could be dead right now."

"Well, what're we sitting here for?" Rand sputtered. "We'd better get on the road." He turned on his heel and strode toward his wagon, then wheeled and returned. "How do you know, boy?"

"The sign all adds up now. Besides," he continued in a low voice, "I got a feeling in my bones."

Rand shuddered and moved away, bawling out orders for breaking camp.

They got underway, pushing the animals hard to eke out extra miles of travel. Carl looked around at the waving grass, and wished the wind would push them along with as much speed. He glanced at Ida. She sat scowling, holding on to the seat of the jolting wagon as he coaxed the mules to pull a little harder, move a little faster. Eliza played with her doll, looking like she was content to be moving again.

When the road made a curve around a stand of trees, he looked back the way they had come and caught sight of a mass of dark clouds on the horizon. *Rain,* he thought. *Good and bad, both. Cool us off, but it'll muddy up the road.*

Later, Carl saw the clouds again, but instead of growing upward to pile high into the heavens, these clouds grew sideways, spreading out to cover a good part of the eastern skyline.

Carl stared a moment longer at the cloud, then a mounting dread filled the pit of his stomach as he realized the blackness bearing down on them was not cloud, but smoke. He stopped the mules, threw himself off the wagon to the sounds of Ida's protests, and ran up the line to Rand's wagon.

"Rand, hold up a minute. Look at that," he shouted, pointing to the smoke enveloping the east. "That's a prairie fire, or I'm not my father's son."

"Prairie fire!" Rand exploded, then went white in the face. "What'll we do, boy?"

"We've got to make for the next stream and drive the wagons down into the water. Hurry, man, we ain't got much time to outrun it." He left Rand's wagon and ran back down the line, shouting, "Angus, Tom!" The men started to halt their teams and climb down from their wagons.

"No, keep moving," Carl yelled, waving his arm. "Fire! Get down to the next creek. Move on."

He ran back toward the freight wagon, calling out to Andy Campbell. "Throw them stock animals ahead of us. If they stampede, maybe the teams will follow."

Carl climbed to the seat and cracked his whip. The mules were reluctant to start pulling, and Carl assaulted the air again with the whip until he had provoked the animals into a shambling sort of hurry. He wished the girls weren't on the seat with him. Maybe then he'd feel like telling the team what he thought of their efforts.

Looking back at the smoke, Carl gauged the fire's advance. He could see flame now, growing dark orange as the fire paused to engulf a grove of trees. The smoke became black, towering upward into the blue heaven.

Hush, he thought, *we ain't going to outrun this fire.*

He turned to urge the beasts onward at a faster pace and caught sight of Ida's white, set face. She stared straight ahead, fingers tightly gripping the edges of the seat.

"We'll make it," he grunted, forcing himself to sound confident. "I ain't come this far west to burn up in no fire!"

Ida gave no sign of having heard him, but continued to stare ahead. Carl took his gaze from her face and whipped the mules a little faster. The trotting animals smelled the smoke on the wind from the east and lurched into the hames, frightened by the volume of the odor.

He turned to check the fire's progress again, and a groan escaped his tightly compressed lips, startling Ida out of her trance. She turned and hurled herself against Carl, grabbing him around the neck and cutting off his control of the team.

"Carl, Carl!" she screamed. "Don't let me get burned. I don't want no scars!"

He struggled with the panicked girl, trying to loosen her hold on his neck, trying to catch his breath. His right arm came free of her grasp and brushed against his holstered gun. Slipping off the rawhide loop, he drew the Colt and held it overhead, then fired one shot.

Ida jumped at the report of the gun, shrank back from Carl, and huddled on the lurching wagon seat.

At the sound of the gun, the mules took on a new spirit of cooperation and stretched out in a lope, faster than before. Carl replaced his pistol, and seeing that Ida was safe, tried to sooth her with quiet talk.

"Ida, settle down. You're going to be just fine," he said softly, his words jolted and cut up from the movement of the wagon. Smoke billowed on all sides of them now as the wind blew fiercely from the rear. Carl's belly twisted as he realized that time was short, too short, before the fire overtook them.

Like a sentinel of salvation, a lone oak tree stood out against the western sky just ahead. Carl's heart swelled with hope, and he stood up and popped his whip.

Andy Campbell already had the stock running in the direction of the tree, and the wagons followed, with Carl's bringing up the rear. He whooped for joy when he saw Rand's team drop from view into a valley. Then Angus and Tom and their wagons and teams also disappeared, and Carl cracked his whip once more to drive his team over the lip of the declivity.

In a second, it seemed, Carl took in the entire scene. Flowing water gleamed in the bottom of the cut, reflecting the billowing tops of three wagons parked on the stream's bank. A fourth wagon stood jacked up in the water with goods scattered on both banks, and both rear wheels lay on the ground alongside a shattered axle. The wagons of the second party still careered down the slope.

Recognition flamed in him. Carl heard a voice yell, "Pa!" and from the rawness of his throat, knew it was his own voice. Relief washed over him as his father's bearded face appeared next to the freight wagon.

"Prairie fire, Pa!" Carl picked up Ida and handed her down to his father, then dangled Eliza to him also. Julia hurried over and took the frightened girls to the stream.

Rod quickly glanced at Carl's smoke-blackened face, then turned to shout, "Ed, Chester, boys, get those wagons into the crick. Grab your shovels and buckets. Fire's coming."

Mary Owen cried out, "Fire! My bed! My food!" and Marie and Julia ran to help her gather up as many of the goods on the near bank as they could handle, and piled them at the edge of the creek.

Tom and Parley Morgan and the Campbell boys helped Chester Bates push the parked wagons into the water as Ed Morgan showed the latecomers where to drive into the stream.

Elizabeth Morgan and Muriel Bates set the girls to wetting quilts and blankets in the water, and Molly Campbell passed them to the men to carry to the top of the slope where they would use them to beat out the rapidly approaching fire.

"Julianna," called out her mother. "You take the babies and little ones to the other side of the creek out of harm's way. Keep them happy, daughter, so they won't take a fright."

The girl ran to scoop up Delia Campbell and her two brothers, their cousin Joshua O'Connor, and her own nephew Roddy, and herded them into the stream. "Let's play a game," she said, trying to keep her voice calm. "Come over here, children. I know a story."

Rida O'Connor followed her, calling out, "I can tend the young'uns, too."

Rulon hurried over to consult with his father. "Pa, let's set a back fire and burn off the grass up there on the rim. It might help us turn the fire away."

Rod nodded. "Take James and Clay. The women'll keep the grass and the wagons wet down here. Carl, show them how to wet down the wagons." Rod grabbed a shovel and ran up the slope, shouting for more assistance.

Once he had driven the freight wagon into the water, Carl started to climb down, but his tensed muscles gave out, and he collapsed into the stream. Wiping the water out of his eyes, he arose, dripping, and grabbed the bucket tied to the side of the wagon. He dipped it into the river and pitched the water over the canvas covering of the freight.

Rand Hilbrands saw what Carl was doing, and cried out, "Stop! You can't wet my cargo."

Carl looked wearily up at him from the stream.

"I can let it burn, if you'd druther."

Rand waved his hand in concession, and his shoulders slumped from exhaustion. Amanda pressed a bucket into his grasp.

"Forget about the store goods," she shrilled. "Look out for our own things."

The wind carried thick, black smoke and sparks down into the valley, as Rulon's fire caught hold ten yards past the rim. He and his brothers nursed the flames in the direction of the rim, scuffing the earth behind the burned section with their shovels to make their firebreak. Ed Morgan sent his sons with filled buckets to help control the burn. "Wet the sides of the bank up there at the top," he called. "Keep the slope soaking wet."

Ida shivered in the stream, wrapped in a drenched blanket. Her sister Eliza, busy splashing water from a bucket onto the family wagon, looked over at her and sniffed.

"Ida ain't working, Mama."

"Pay her no mind, 'Liza," her mother called. "She's no use to us now. Keep the wagon wet!"

"Here it comes," James yelled, tumbling over the rim as he retreated from the extreme heat, with Clay and Rulon hard on his heels. The Owen brothers, faces streaked with sweat and grime, came down to the water, wiping the gritty smoke out of their eyes.

"All that smoke puts me in mind of a battleground," grunted Rulon as he sluiced water up the hill. He paused to rub the back of his neck. "It sure brings back bad memories." Then he bent to the water again.

Nobody but Ida had time to sit and listen to the crackle of the burning vegetation and the roar of the flames. Nobody but Ida noticed the change in volume of sound of the fire as it veered away to the south. Nobody spoke to Ida, so Ida told no one.

Then Carl saw that the smoke had thinned out, and he straightened his back to look up at the rim. The towering clouds of smoke were gone, and he dropped his bucket and scrambled up the bank of the creek to the top of the slope.

"Pa," he shouted. "The fire's gone off to the south. Looks like Rulon's back fire did the trick!"

His older brother climbed the hill to join him, and Carl glanced back to watch him come. Rulon had discarded his sooty shirt, and for the first time, Carl saw the angry purple scars of his brother's war wounds.

"It's a wonder you made it home, Rule," Carl said gravely. "What did you run into that made so many holes?"

Rulon stopped on the edge of the valley. "You ever hear of a mortar shell? Them things explode into a right smart number of pieces when they hit. Shrapnel, they call 'em." He fingered the largest scar. "I was too close to one that last day, and caught a bunch of shrapnel."

"Whatever they are, they didn't do you no good. Mary's lucky she ever saw you again."

"Most of 'em are still in there. The surgeon figured I'd die, so he didn't bother to dig the iron out," Rulon added, and rubbed the scar.

Carl turned and surveyed the blackened east, wiping his hands on his shirtfront. "Makes me ache inside to see all that grass gone. What a ruin!" He hung his forearm over his shorter brother's shoulder. "Did you come across any surprises out this way?"

Rulon's head snapped around to look at Carl. "You mean like that Acosta scum attacking us in this valley? Yeah. We had some surprises." He spat into the ashes at his feet. "We buried Ed Morgan's little girl, and put her brother Harry into the wagon with a bullet through his thigh. Real nice surprise for a ten-year-old."

Carl dropped his arm from Rulon's shoulder, clenched his fists, closed his eyes, and swore. He stabbed his shovel into the earth several times. "Anybody else hurt?"

"Couple of near hits, but the Morgans got the worst of it because they was out wood-gathering when the men rode down on us." He paused for a moment, wiping the sweat from his dripping forehead with the back of his hand.

"How'd it happen?"

"Ed sent Tom out with the kids. The gang rode in from over that rise." Rulon gestured with his hand. "We heard the shots and came a-running with our rifles. We dropped about half of them outlaws before they pulled out for good. Rode on south."

"Gone to Texas?"

"Likely. Good riddance. We'd been here a day when they attacked, on account of my axle."

"How'd that happen?"

"Went off the bank wrong, hit a boulder in the creek. I had a feeling about that axle being flawed when I got the wagon, but I didn't have much choice."

"Where did you get it?"

Rulon smiled crookedly. "I stole it off the Yankee who bought the livery for taxes. Clay helped, but he wasn't real happy about it."

"I guess nobody's happy lately. I'm sorry about the Morgans' loss."

They stood for a moment, looking and thinking, then Carl spoke up slowly, still looking off into the distance.

"Is Mary Hilbrands a good wife to you? Does she make you . . . feel like . . . a man?"

Startled, Rulon raised his eyes to look at Carl's face. After a time, he said, "That's a mighty strange question, brother, but since you make bold to ask, I'll answer best I can."

He paused, evidently searching for words. "Mary was barely scratching at fifteen years old when we wed. I was such a—" He closed his eyes briefly, then shook his head before continuing. "I reckon I was in a hurry to marry her, leaving soon to join the cavalry as I was. We didn't have time to learn much about each other as married folk before I rode away." He clicked his tongue. "Then I didn't see her again for four long years, not 'til I woke up in a strange bed with a mess of holes in me, with Mary's dear face—" He stopped and looked at Carl. "You sure you want to know all this?"

"Yep."

Rulon sighed and squinted and made a little scoffing sound, but continued. "Mary's a good wife, a dutiful wife. After I got home, all shot up and obliged to lie in bed day and night, she kept the house and cooked the meals and tended Roddy, as well as bringing me through the pain and the nightmares and back to living." He paused again, his face working. "She tended to my needs, all of 'em, Carl, and yes, I know I'm a man."

He cuffed Carl on the jaw with a gentle fist. "Now you know more'n you should about Mary'n' me. Mind you, keep it silent."

Carl nodded and swallowed hard. "Do you reckon you love her?"

"I have no doubt on that score, no doubt at all. Despite all our troubles, I'm confident she feels the same."

"Like Pa and Ma?"

Rulon nodded. "Like Pa and Ma."

Carl turned to look down the grade. Ida seemed so tiny and forlorn, standing on the side of the stream, and his throat pinched to see her clutch the damp blanket around her shoulders. "No more questions," he said, and started down the slope.

ఴ

Carl gently took the damp blanket from Ida's stiff fingers. "You'll take a chill, wrapped in that thing," he said.

She hung her head, turning away from his gaze. "Don't look at me," she cried. "I'm all dirty and wet."

"Well, I'm liable to break a looking glass myself. Let's go set in that patch of sun up the crick a ways. We both need to get dry." Carl took her arm and firmly led her away from the wagons.

He sat her down in the full sun, on a rock that jutted out over the bank of the stream, then collapsed into the grass at her feet, spreading full-length on the soft green sod.

"We've had us a time lately, girl. Near calamitous for us all," he said, staring at the sky. "Especially for the Morgans. Did you hear what happened? They lost their little girl to them unholy ruffians from back down the trail." Carl gazed into the sky, blue and white with wispy clouds drifting overhead. "Now, I don't blame your pa for having his own opinion, but that ain't any comfort to Mrs. Morgan, I reckon. Your pa came near ruining our whole enterprise with his notions. We all got to stick together and listen to the leader, and that's my pa. We can't take any more bickering, if we're to get to the Territory before winter sets in."

Carl looked up and saw great tears flooding silently from Ida's blue eyes. He sat upright, got to his knees in front of her, and took her into his arms.

"Hush now, darlin'. I didn't mean to go on so about your pa. You had a mighty hard time out there today, and here I'm just rambling on with a mess of foolish words."

Ida broke into sobs.

"Ah, don't cry on me, sweetie-pie," Carl pleaded with her, alarmed at her tears. "I ain't had much practice with crying women." In his discomfort, Carl began to smooth her hair and wipe the tears from her eyes. He felt clumsy and bumbling, and tried to kiss her forehead in apology.

Ida shut her eyes and tipped back her head, a little shudder moving her body. With her motion, Carl's lips accidentally met hers, and he kissed her gently. She responded with fiery hunger, and a shock went through Carl's system as he realized that she had led him into a trap.

He rose to his feet and pulled her to hers, alarm battling with the stirring in his blood. "We have to go back," he insisted firmly. "I should have looked after the team by now."

Ida picked up a rock and flung it into the water, then stiffly followed him to camp.

Chapter 10

"Rule, let James do that lifting," Rod instructed. "You don't want to tear nothing loose." The two brothers splashed through the water to change places at the rear of the wagon. "Get set with that wheel, son. On the count of three."

James and Carl gathered their limbs beneath them, and at the count, they lifted the wagon atop their backs and Rulon added the wheel to the new axle. Rod placed the pin in the hub and secured it, and the younger men eased the wagon down.

"Glad that's done, Pa," James wheezed. "It must be supper time."

Rod laughed. "Likely. You boys put the tools away and load the wagon, and I'll go see if your ma is ready to feed a bunch of hungry wolves. We'll be on our way first thing tomorrow morning."

"Thanks, Pa," Rulon rubbed raw knuckles. "Next time I cross the country, I'll make sure I have a prime wagon."

"Or bring a spare axle," Carl added.

Soon the men had the tools and the waterlogged wagon out of the creek, then set about gathering Mary's wide-strewn belongings and restoring them to the vehicle. Afterward, they scattered to prepare for supper.

"Mary," Rulon called to his wife from the far side of the stream. "Look here. Our things are back together."

Mary picked her way over a path of rocks that Albert had put in the stream for the use of the ladies and the children. "Oh," she sighed. "That's better. And Ma and Pa are back with us. I reckon I can rest peaceful this night."

Rulon drew her to his side and walked her behind the wagon when they could speak in private. "Are you feeling poorly?" he asked, his voice low.

"No. I've been so worried about my folks and about our wagon. Now at least those cares are swept away." She took his arm. "Rulon?"

"Yes?"

"Are we close to where we're going?"

He sat her down on a barrel that had been left beside the wagon, got his shirt from the wagon seat, and slowly put it on. "I'm sorry, Mary. We have a fair piece yet to travel."

Mary placed her hands on the middle of her bulging abdomen and smoothed her apron over the roundness. "I can't keep doing this, going, and stopping, and traveling on, every day of my life, Rulon. We've got to find a place to stop and stay."

He caught one of her hands and lifted it to his lips. "I know it's hard on you, but it can't be helped. This place ain't Colorado yet. We must keep going." He put her hand on his chest, over his heart, and held it there.

"Does it have to be Colorado?" She took back her hand.

"It does if we're going to settle around our kin, Mary." He leaned over and stroked her cheek. "Isn't that worth a little discomfort?"

She inhaled. "Yes, but will I have a home before I bear this child?"

Rulon's forehead furrowed and he stooped over her. "Are you feeling pains?"

"No, no. That won't happen for a while, but will we be there before the time comes?"

He patted her shoulder. "Pa thinks another four weeks should see us into the Territory. You can hold out that long, can't you, Sugar?"

"I don't know. I yearn for a bed to lie in, a place to rest this heavy body." She caught Rulon's hand under hers. A flicker of a smile touched her lips. "It appears you want the same." The smile retreated. "Will this journey ever end?"

He cringed at the pain in her voice. "Oh, my Mary," he said. He pulled her gently to her feet and enfolded her in his arms, slowly stroked her hair. "You'll feel better after you eat. That'll put spunk into you."

Mary closed her eyes and snuggled her head under his chin. "I want a home of our own," she whispered.

හ

Several days after the fire, Rod directed the weary travelers to set up camp beside Diamond Springs, where water flowed from a hollow rock.

When the evening meal was done and they lay in their blankets beneath the wagon, Julia asked Rod, "When are you going to make your peace with Rand Hilbrands?"

"He owes me the first word of apology," he mumbled.

"The way I see it, both of you were wrong. He divided us, but you didn't see the attack coming."

"But I did, Julia. If I'd had the man-power, the sentries, we wouldn't have been surprised."

"So you keep thinking that, and put off healing this wound in our people?"

"Julie. It's not that way."

"You're a fine, strong man, Rod, and you served well in the war, but you can't court martial your friends because they make mistakes." She sought his hand with hers, and squeezed it. "Rand is a good man. Make peace with him."

"You're a wonder, woman. What do you know of court martial?"

"Being a woman doesn't make me stupid, Rod."

"I didn't say that."

"Well, I'm not ignorant, either, but that's beside the point. I want your promise."

"Julie!"

"Rod, I mean it."

"I reckon you're in the right," he muttered a minute or two later, giving in. "We ought to live in harmony . . . for the next month, at least." He snorted. "To keep the peace, I'll do it."

"Thank you." She squeezed his hand again.

He turned over and looked at her in the quavering light of the dying fire. "I missed you." He carried her hand to his lips.

"What?"

"All that time I was gone. I missed my woman, my helpmeet, my wife."

She stirred in the blankets, moving against him. "Times were hard," she replied.

"Not anymore." His arm slipped around her waist. "Do you love me?"

"Forever and always, Rod Owen."

"That's a long time."

"Even when you're a stubborn, mule-headed man," she whispered, then laughed softly, deep in her throat. "Who would've known this quilt would cover us twenty-five years."

He kissed her, then growled, "Shut up, woman."

Julia laughed again.

୧

At Turkey Creek they ran out of firewood.

"Jonathan Helm warned me this day would come," Rod chuckled when the women brought the lack to his attention. "From here on we gather these here things." He turned over a dry, flattened circle of matter with his boot-tip. "It's called a buffalo chip, and it'll burn quick and hot. But you'll need plenty, for they ain't much more than grass."

Amanda Hilbrands protested. "Why, that's just— It's not fitting for fuel," she finished. Robert Campbell and Joshua O'Connor laughed, and Amanda turned to glare at them. "And you'll be the first to gather them," she declared.

The "gather" was made, gingerly, that first day, but continued without further thought as time went on. Then after days of travel, the party reached the Great Bend of the Arkansas River. Ed Morgan lost the frown he'd carried since the skirmish at the creek, whooped, and threw his hat into the air at the sight of the river after so much dry land.

"Look at them trees." Little Catherine Campbell gave a great sigh. "No buffalo chips tonight."

Cottonwood trees grew in profusion on the little islands in the middle of the river, so Rod sent several of the men and older boys wading over to the nearest island to chop enough wood for a two-night stay.

"All this wood and water does my heart good," he told them all before the supper began. "We'll have singing and dancing tonight."

They set up camp on a sandy yellow ridge several hundred yards from the river. Swarms of small bugs filled the air and bit whatever exposed flesh they landed on, and snakes rustled in the grass around the camp, but the abundance of water made these nuisances bearable.

Albert Owen and Andy Campbell beat the brush with long sticks and shot all the snakes they could find. They took their trophies home. Their mothers, gritting their teeth, took the reptiles, skinned them, cut them up, and threw them into the supper-pots.

After the dishes had been washed and put away, out came the instruments. Edward Morgan's fiddle lacked the low G-string, but he played a merry tune, his fingers flying up and down the remaining three strings.

James produced a small metal object. "This here's a jaws-harp my buddy taught me to play. I was obliged to take it from his pocket before the fall of Richmond." He stopped for a moment. "He had no further use for it." He ducked his head and wiped his nose.

Andy Campbell polished up an old harmonica and introduced the travelers to some of the songs he used to entertain the stock as he drove it along.

"Let's dance with everybody tonight," Rod exhorted. "Have a good time, and don't let any girl sit too long."

The music was lively, and Carl was right in the middle of the crowd, trying to get to Ida, but enjoying a dance with his sister Marie. He claimed Ida for the next dance, but at one point, Tom Morgan, Edward's eldest son, swept by and caught Ida in the exchange of partners, and Carl found himself dancing with Ellen Bates.

Carl grinned at the redheaded girl, relaxed, and forgot Ida for a while. Recalling the last time they had spoken, he bent and whispered in Ellen's ear. "How was that bit of candy I brought you?

She smiled up at him. "It was wondrous sweet." Then she fell silent once more as Carl led her into the next step.

The music died, and Ellen smiled again. "I saved some candy to share with you. It's over in the wagon."

"Lead the way," he said, laughing. Carl went to the big campfire, took a long stick that was blazing at one end, and used it to light their path to the Bates' wagon as the dancing resumed behind them.

Ida saw him go, stamped her foot, and glared after his departing back, but he didn't catch any of the reproach sent his way.

Ellen went around to the dark side of the wagon and stepped up onto the wagon tongue. "I need a little boost," she said.

Carl lifted her up, and she climbed over the seat, then disappeared into the darkness under the wagon cover. He heard her moving around, and soon she poked her head out of the opening and smiled.

"I have it." She held up the small twist of paper, then slipped it into her skirt pocket. Climbing once more over the seat, she stepped to the edge of the wagon box.

Before he could reach out to help her down, Ellen tripped, and dropping the torch into the sand, Carl caught her, going down on his back to break her fall. For a brief moment he held her to him, feeling the quick, hard beating of her heart against his chest.

"Oh! Please . . . I," she stammered, blushing in the wavering torchlight. She struggled out of his arms, whispering, "I'm sorry, I had no thought to— Oh lawsy!" Then she would have fled into the sand hills, but Carl grabbed her hand as he got to his feet.

"Wait." He stopped her flight. "It was an accident. No harm done." Taking her by the shoulders, he sensed the fluttering of her heart as she shivered with embarrassment. "Don't go." He reached out to pull a leaf from her hair. Brushing the red gold strands with his fingertips caused a hot sensation to rush through his blood.

"What about the candy?" He felt the sand, the bank, the earth shift under his feet, and wondered if her lips were as soft as they looked. Longing to touch them, he fought for control as she recovered the sweets from the depths of her pocket. With a shaking hand she held out a piece of the candy, and he took it and bit off a small chunk.

Chewing slowly, he watched the shadows flicker over her grave face. The torch sputtered out in the sand, and she shivered in the darkness.

"It seems you're always saving my life." Her voice sounded thin and shaky, as though someone were squeezing her throat and shaking her by the shoulders at the same time. She shivered again. "Thank you."

The music started up and Ellen turned to listen. "We best go back to the fire."

"Stay a minute. We've missed a dance or two already." He took her hand.

"No!" She pulled loose, and turning, left him.

"Ellen," he whispered, but she was gone, and her leaving brought a sharp ache to his soul. He followed, stomach churning in turmoil, and as he stepped into the firelight, he glanced around. Ellen was nowhere to be seen. At the far side of the party, Ida laughed merrily at James and Tom Morgan. The latter young man took her hand and led her off to dance.

Carl walked over to Marie and startled her by whirling her off balance into his arms. She stumbled a little as he moved her into the dance, but he helped her to recover, and gripped her hands tightly in his, fighting both anger and guilt that rose in him.

"Carl!" Marie tried to free her hands. "What ails you? You're hurting my hands."

Surprised, he loosened his grip. "Sorry," he mumbled.

ဢ

Later, as Carl sat on a stool someone had placed in the shadows by a wagon, resting his feet from the unaccustomed labor of the dance, he sensed someone beside him, and he turned his head, whispering, "Ellen?"

"Not hardly," replied James, speaking low. The younger man massaged his left shoulder with his right hand.

"Are you weary?" Carl got up from the stool and motioned for James to sit.

"I don't need that. I want to talk to you, brother." James paused and flexed his left arm.

"Shoulder bothering you?"

"Not nearly as much as it might later," James said, and Carl shivered a bit at the menace in his voice.

"You said you wanted to talk. Do it."

"I saw Miss Ellen a piece back, and she didn't look very happy. Fact is, she looked like a mule run over her, she was that white and fearful looking." James stopped talking and moved closer to Carl. "That was just after you took her out back of the wagons, brother."

Carl turned to face James. "Meaning?"

"What did you do to put that face on her?" He held his crumpled fist in front of Carl's face.

Carl flushed, remembering. "It ain't your business, James."

"I'm here to remind you it is. You have you a girl you're going to marry— Miss Ida Hilbrands. Miss Ellen is betrothed to me. Stay clear of her." James jabbed Carl's chest lightly with his fist every few words. His face blazed red in the glow from the campfire.

"What do you want with Ellen? You don't love her." Carl sneered.

James hit him in the belly, hard enough to double him over. "That's 'Miss Ellen' to you," his low voice continued, harshly, as Carl remained curled over, guilt constraining him from throwing a punch of his own. "Pa set up the match against my will, but you don't have my leave to break it. Keep your distance."

James turned and stalked away, and Carl took a huge breath. "He means it," he said to himself, and gritted his teeth.

ဆ

The party lasted until very late. Carl could not sleep, and he lay staring into the dying coals of the fire. Ida had not danced with him for the remainder of the night, though she smiled and claimed it was not her fault, but that "the boys" wouldn't let her go for even a minute. Carl made a show of bowing to the superior numbers of "the boys," and did not press her. Once he turned his head suddenly and caught her staring petulantly at him, but usually she kept a smile on her face.

Ellen had appeared toward the end of the party, but she didn't speak to Carl. One time he walked toward her to ask her to dance, but she turned her back and he pretended to be on another errand.

Now Carl rolled onto his back and saw by the left-hand position of the Big Dipper that it was past midnight. The air was warm and still he could not sleep, though he turned in his blankets and shut his eyes.

Half an hour later, Carl tossed the blankets aside and reached for his boots. He shook them upside down in case anything had crawled inside, then pulled them on. Grabbing his gun belt, he stood and strapped the weapon around his hips as he walked toward the edge of camp.

Edward Morgan was on guard, and turned as Carl came up to him. "I thought young Tom was going to take the next watch." Ed yawned and rubbed his neck, then squinted at the stars. "You're an hour early, Carl."

"It isn't my watch, Mr. Morgan. I can't sleep. I reckon I'll go down to the riverbank for a spell. Maybe take a swim."

"It's a nice night for swimming, being so warm." Ed sounded sleepy. "Keep a watch for them snakes."

"I brought my shooter," Carl replied, walking down the sandy slope in the darkness.

The closer he got to the river, the louder he could hear the rush of the water over the sandy bottom. The continuous sound felt easy to his ears, and he sat on the bank watching the stars' reflection in the endlessly rolling water.

Carl gazed at the ripples before him, and thought of Ida and her laughing eyes, how they sparkled when she was happy, and the curve of her lips when they entertained a smile. Then he recalled her shocked state while he fought the fire, her lack of help, and fear of getting scarred. Remembering her panic brought back the feeling of protectiveness.

I don't wonder she didn't want no scars, he mused. *A pretty-looking young thing like her don't care to be disfigured.*

He thought of her lips, and how soft they had been back on the meadow outside Kansas town. Carl stretched out on the sandy bank, arms behind his neck, and closed his eyes and recalled how it had been, holding her in his arms, feeling her heart pounding against his chest. He felt again the sting of fire leaping through his veins as he touched her flame-like hair. He remembered her trembling perplexity, her flight back to the safety of the dance, and he opened his eyes, confused at the vision.

Suddenly he sat up, realizing he dreamed of Ellen in his arms. He groaned, then said aloud, "No! I'm bound to marry Ida!"

He got to his feet. Blood pounded through his temples as he stared into the sky. "Pa arranged it, but we both agreed," he shouted into the void. "I've said my piece to her, and she agreed to be my wife. I won't go back on my word." He shook both his fists at the stars. "I can't betray my brother," he added, his voice dying away to a whisper.

Carl's arms fell to his sides, and for a long time he stood there—the pulse of his pounding heart moving his torso slightly—listening to the water surging past him. He half expected Ed Morgan to come investigate his outcry, then realized his words had been covered by the sound of the waters.

At last, disquiet seeping out of his veins and his resolve firmed by the regular rhythm of the river, he turned and went back to camp.

ॐ

Carl avoided Ida during the next two days that the travelers spent alongside the big river. He spent his time caring for the team and riding Sherando out into the Great American Desert, a place of wind-whipped plain and short buffalo grass. There was no more tall, waving, blue-stemmed grass, no brilliant wild flowers, no escaping the eternally blowing wind. At the end of the second day, Carl returned from his hours of solitary riding ready to accept responsibility for his actions, willing to make the best of his future with Ida.

He went to Ida that evening, quietly insisting that she walk with him along the river. She followed him reluctantly, and he sensed her resentment toward him.

Carl walked along with his hands in his pockets, thinking over his words. Finally he stopped walking and turned to face the silent girl.

"I reckon you're unhappy with me, and I figure you've got a right. I left the dance the other night with another girl, and I owe you a mite of explaining. Ellen Bates went to get something for me from her wagon, and I tagged along."

He stopped, leaving the telling at the bare bones, deciding to spare her the shame and the pain of his struggle, his turmoil over divided loyalty.

She stood with arms akimbo, head thrown back to fully see his face. "Well, I reckon I am a mite peeved with you, Carl. I know we're not wed yet, but folks know it will happen sometime. I expect you to burn your bridges."

Her words hit a guilty spot in his soul, boring into it, and a cloud passed over his lean brown face. "We've both got some making up to do, Ida. You were having an almighty fine time with the boys, seemed like."

"It just looked like it to you," she said, tossing her head, making her curls bounce. "My heart was a-sorrowing something pitiful."

"Well, my heart is turned to you, Ida. I have a powerful liking for you, and I still want you for my wife, if you're willing." He held his breath.

Ida looked at her feet for a moment. She looked up. "My heart's feeling some better. I reckon I'm still betrothed to you." She beamed her most brilliant smile upon Carl.

He sighed, then took her arm to escort her back to the wagons.

℘

The next morning, Rod Owen got his party moving again. The wagons toiled along the sandy valley of the Arkansas, day after day. From time to time Rod sent two or three men to hunt for fresh meat. Often they were gone for several days, returning with heavily laden pack horses.

One day toward the middle of September, James came tearing back from the hunt, riding a lathered horse, with Albert and Clay hard on his heels.

"Pa," James yelled. "Hold up them wagons. There's a herd of buffalo headed this way." He stopped his horse and jumped off, then caught the alarm in his mother's eyes. "Great snakes of the sandy hills, I didn't mean to scare you. They ain't stampeding or nothing like that. They're just moving along, grazing, but there's a powerful lot of them, and it makes an awesome sight."

"Well, Julianna," Rod said over his shoulder to his youngest. "Here's your chance to see a buffalo up close." He took off his hat and scratched his head. "I reckon we'll make camp here, for I been told a buffalo herd can hold up a train for days."

Julianna shook her head. "Papa, I don't want to see no buffaler. Clay says they're 'most as big as monsters, and have long hairy claws coming out of their feet. He says they got a humpback, and make a screeching sound that'll raise the hair off my head as good as any red Indian might. I don't want to see 'em."

"Clay is teasing you, daughter. I heard some of them stories he told you that night, and he's put a mighty lot of nonsense into your pretty little head. Buffalo isn't nothing to go having a fit over. Calm down and enjoy the sight."

The great, hairy, humpbacked creatures came from the north, and browsed slowly along, crossing the trail and the river as though nothing was in their way. For the next two days the women camped, washing clothes and baking. The men stood with their rifles at the edge of the passing herd, shooting any buffalo that strayed too close to the camp. The gunfire only disturbed a few of the shaggy creatures, and they loped off deeper into the herd. After the dead animals were butchered, the women gratefully added the meat to their larders.

On the third day the trail cleared, and Rod gave the order to break camp. The days slowly blended into dusty sunsets as they followed the river through western Kansas, until on the last day of September they crossed the border into Colorado Territory.

When given the news, Ida looked around at the same flat, endless plains and asked, "Is this all there is? It's so empty, and there ain't no hills, neither. I don't think I like Colorado." She crossed her arms and leaned back against the seat of the freight wagon.

"Let's see what comes up ahead. I heard there are mountains a large sight grander than those we left behind, Ida. You won't lack for hills." Carl glanced over at her, and saw that she wore a petulant look on her face. "You got no call to frown yet. We ain't stopping here."

"Carl, I am so tired of traveling that I could fairly scream. I want to find a pretty place to live, where you won't be always toting your rifle and your gun belt against those Indians your pa worries about. I'd favor a nice town, or even a little city."

"I promise you, you'll have a pretty place by and by, but it won't be in no town, nor city neither. We can't raise cattle in the city."

Ida sighed and gave Carl a long look. "You're sure about the cattle? You're bound to raise cattle?"

"Yup." His tone left no chance of argument.

She sighed. "Then I guess I'm bound to live where you raise your cows. But you will take me to see Denver City, won't you, once the cattle get sold?" Ida turned on the seat, using her most winsome smile.

Carl laughed. "Yes, we'll go see the sights. I reckon we'll go hunt up my Uncle Jonathan 'fore too long." He looked at her eager face. "If our house is up by then, likely we can go there on a wedding trip." The delight he saw in her eyes made him laugh again. "You surely do sparkle when you're happy."

"I declare! You do bring out the best in me, Carl Owen." Ida beamed. "I'll really sparkle some once we're wed, and away from all these prying eyes," she finished, looking around at the men, boys, and children on horseback.

Carl's blood pulsed harder in his veins, and he flicked the whip over the heads of the mules to cover the creeping red blush he felt moving up his face. He swallowed once, then matched her boldness with candor of his own.

"I don't reckon I'll be a shy feller, once we're in our own place and you're in my arms. There's going to be no campfire betwixt you and me, nor anything else."

Ida clasped her hands tightly together. "I reckon I'm having a mighty hard time waiting for that day."

"You'll wait." Carl nodded once, firmly. "I'll do you no wrong."

Ida dropped her hands into her lap and shrugged her shoulders. "Carl, what do you aim to use to build our house? I suppose brick ain't very plentiful hereabouts?"

"I'll have to see what's close to hand, Ida. Depends mostly on where we settle, I reckon. If Pa picks a spot this side of the mountains, there won't be logs nor lumber around. I heard tell of something called a soddy, though."

"That's a curious name. What's it mean?"

"It's sort of a cabin built of chunks of sod and earth."

"Sod? You mean dirt and grass? Carl," she cried out, appalled. "That ain't no better than a slave shanty!"

" 'Tain't forever, Ida. I aim to build us a nice home once the beef starts selling."

"That'll take years," she wailed.

Chapter 11

Fort Lyon began life as William Bent's second trading post, but by the time Rod Owen's group reached the fort, the Army had acquired it, changed the name three times, fortified it, and installed a small company of troops. Rod called on the commandant and found that the Indians were busy up north along the Platte.

"That's a mighty relief to us all, I reckon," Rod said. "We been expecting to have a fight on our hands any day."

"Well, it's safe enough right now. If you're going to take up land hereabouts, you'd best get on with it," the Major advised. "Winter's not far off, and you'll need shelter. When those freezing winds hit, you'll wish you were back in the States."

"Thank you kindly for the advice, but we're going on. I promised my wife she'd have trees." Rod tipped his hat and turned to leave, but the major spoke again.

"In another day or two you should catch sight of the mountains. Keep heading west, and you'll run into plenty of trees."

Two days later, before the travelers broke camp for the day's journey, Ellen walked over to Marie and pointed to the cloudy far-western horizon.

"Marie, I been looking at those clouds, and ever so often there's something that looks like a blue cloud amongst the rest. Do you reckon it could be one of them mountains your pa keeps talking about?"

Marie's eyes followed Ellen's finger. The sun had risen enough to sparsely light the brown prairie around them, and a hint of chill pervaded the breeze that tugged at the girls' skirts. Marie shivered as she stared toward the west.

"I don't see anything." Then the clouds parted, revealing a far distant peak thrusting up into the sky. "Oh, Ellen, that's a real mountain. I ain't never seen anything so beautiful! Let's go tell my pa."

The girls found Rod hitching his team to the wagon. Marie tugged on his arm, trying to get him to go with her to see the mountain, but in her excitement, her words spilled out faster than she could arrange them into sentences.

"Whoa, daughter. What's your hurry?" he exclaimed.

Marie pulled him out from between the wagons to where he had a clear view to the west.

"It's them, Pa, it's really them. They're right back of those clouds."

"What do you mean, daughter?"

"The mountains, Pa. Ellen found the mountains!"

Again the clouds dispersed briefly, allowing Rod a glimpse of the peak.

"That must be Zebulon Pike's Peak. You remember, daughter, 'Pike's Peak or Bust'. Your Uncle Jonathan came out here then. Fifty-eight or Fifty-nine, it was. Hush, I never thought to see it." Rod gazed on the sight for a while, then called to his neighbor at the next wagon.

"Chester. Take a look at that. Your girl got the first sight of the mountains. They're just grand."

Chester stepped out from hitching up and looked toward the west. "There's nothing to be seen, Rod."

"Wait a spell. The clouds will clear, I reckon."

"Why, they're so *blue*," Chester cried, as the clouds parted again. "Muriel, look at this."

The word spread through the camp, and all the travelers stood and stared, relief etched on their faces. After a time, Rod called out, "Hitch 'em up. Let's get rolling, or they'll stay as far distant as you see them."

The girls stood together a moment longer, looking at the cloud-covered horizon, their hands tightly clasped in friendship.

"It's beautiful," Ellen whispered. "So wild and untamed. And the wind—I love the wind!"

Marie squeezed her hand. "You're like that, too, Ellen."

Ellen turned to her friend. "How do you mean?"

"You're beautiful and untamed yourself. Under that shy face you show the world, you're a wild, free woman, and I reckon I'm the only one as knows it. Don't I wish Carl did. He needs you, if he could only see it."

Ellen gasped and turned away to hide the red that she felt flaming her face. She had not told Marie about Carl's response to her fall from the wagon. That night she had felt his emotion flowing into her from his hands, almost like fire, and she knew that he had been badly shaken by his unsuspected passion. Still, he had gone back to Ida. Ellen had seen them walking out of the camp on the last night at Great Bend, and had seen Ida's face when they returned, and she knew that Ida was still Carl's intended.

"Don't you give up!" Marie's words pulled Ellen back from the verge of despair. "You can't give up till the preacher says the words over them. She ain't right for him, and I reckon he knows it. His soul is a-raging, and he don't get much sleep, pacing around all the night long."

Ellen pressed two hands against her chest. "It can't be on account of me."

Marie pounced on the comment. "What do you mean? What's happened?"

"Nothing! That's why it can't be on my account. You know I say dumb things sometimes," Ellen mumbled.

"You never do. You always make perfect sense. You're the most sensible girl I know, and you never could tell a lie."

Ellen shut her eyes against the daylight for a moment, then opened them wide. "There ain't nothing I can tell you," she blurted out, and ran blindly back to her wagon.

⁊⊙

Near the junction of the Huerfano and Arkansas Rivers, Autobees' Plaza sat in the sun. Set back from the cabins along the bluffs, the stockade lay with the gate cautiously open, surrounded by corrals and baking ovens. The settlement was a welcome sight, and Rod took Chester Bates with him when he went to collect news.

Hailing the gatekeeper, an old Mexican man with shrewd eyes, Rod and Chester gained entrance to the stockade, and halted their horses by a post outside the main building. They dismounted and tied their animals, then entered the trading room.

A bar of planks laid on two barrels occupied one side of the interior; store goods filled the other walls. A rough wooden box on the counter was labeled "U. S. Mail" in black paint. There were three letters in the box.

Seated behind the bar planks, a slight, clean-shaven man drank milk from a whiskey glass while he munched on a sandwich and read a folded newspaper. He looked up at the approach of the men.

"You the owner?" Rod asked.

The man nodded his head, his cheeks full of bread and meat.

Rod hitched up his belt. "I'm Rod Owen. This here is Chester Bates. We aim to take up land on the Homestead Act. What can you tell us about this country?"

The man swallowed his food and smiled, putting out his large, square hand. "I'm Charlie Autobees, Justice of the Peace for Huerfano County, so I'm the man to ask. What kind of land are you seeking?"

"I aim to graze cattle, but my wife favors trees. Where can I find good pasture land and trees, both?"

Charlie Autobees spread both arms outward. "There's plenty of land in the County, so you got a powerful mite to choose from." He walked over to a map hung on one wall. "We take in pretty near all the corner of the Territory, from here to Kansas, but if I was to hanker after trees, I'd keep on southwest of here and hit for the Wet Mountains." He tapped the spot on the map. "They're plum full of pasture land, and they's a-plenty of water, and about now I 'spect the leaves are bound to be a-turning. Makes a right purty sight for the women folks to take joy in."

"You got any towns around here? We got a storekeep with goods and a blacksmith along with us."

"If it's towns you want, just follow the Arkansas. We ain't too far removed from Pueblo City. Down south there's a Mexican settlement to two. One called Leones ain't far down the Huerfano and the Cuchara. 'Course, down along the Santa Fe road, there's the settlements at Raton Pass, but they ain't a place for the ladies. They got a name for being tough towns." As he mentioned each place, Autobees traced the route on the map.

"How about farming?" Chester asked. "You got any place that'll grow wheat?"

"That'd be down along the Cuchara. You take the Huerfano down to the fork, then head up the left branch. There's folk settling in there growing beans, wheat, hay, and corn. You name it, and it grows down there. For your smith, now, I recollect they was needing one down to Leones. He'd get a warm welcome down that way."

"Rod, looks like I've found the place I'm looking for." Chester hitched up his own belt.

Rod looked closely at the map. "There's a choice of towns for Rand to set up shop in, and Tom's likely to find work down south." Rod turned to Autobees and put out his hand. The man took it and they shook. "We're obliged to you for your help. I reckon we file homestead claims here?"

"Yup."

They took their leave, and Rod looked back at the distance-shrunken stockade as they approached the wagons.

"Looks like our trails are separating, Chester. You're a steady man, and I've valued our friendship."

"This surely ain't good-bye forever, Rod. The women folk will want to see each other, not to mention the unfinished business with the young folks. We'll be a-visiting, I reckon."

"I'll be handy for house-raising and such, Chester. You can count on me and my boys for help when you need it."

"I know it, Rod."

଼

The travelers gathered around Rod and Chester as they dismounted and walked into camp. Rod spoke first.

"Pueblo City is close by, on the Arkansas. Rand, you could set up your store there, or go further south where some farmers have a settlement."

"I'd just as lief settle near the mining activities," said Rand. "I'll take a look at Pueblo City."

"I'm ready to follow the river south," announced Chester. "There's good land for crops down there. Who'll go with me?"

"I will," said Ed Morgan. "Elizabeth is of a mind to settle near Muriel."

"Molly and me will join you," added Angus Campbell.

"There's a town down there needing a smith, Tom. Come along, settle near your kin," Chester urged.

Tom O'Connor flexed his heavy shoulders. "All this traveling has me hankering after the fire and the forge. Next to the fire is a pleasant spot to be, come wintertime."

"I'll go in with Rand to Pueblo City and pick up Carl, then head south for the Wet Mountains," Rod said. "If I picture it right, we'll be about forty miles northwest of you folks."

"Then this is our last camp together?" asked Carl.

"We go our own ways after the nooning," his father answered.

Carl glanced around the circle. A bond of strength gained from trials overcome joined him to these men: Chester Bates, strong and solid, quietly going about doing the right thing; Edward Morgan, thin and dark, his quick grin and friendly ways starting to return after the blow of his little girl's death; Angus Campbell, with piercing blue eyes and sandy hair; Tom O'Connor, brawny and restless, still mourning for his long-dead wife; and Rand Hilbrands, tall and fleshy, with a somber air. Now they were parting, and pain squeezed his stomach.

James had brought in an antelope the previous night, and Julia cut up what remained of it for dinner. Marie invited Ellen to eat, and the girls huddled together, dreading their separation.

Ellen looked at Marie, whose eyelashes were jeweled with tears.

"Don't cry or you'll start me off. You heard your pa. We won't be that far away from you. Only forty miles."

"Forty miles! Ellen Bates, that's as far away as Staunton or Winchester is from Mount Jackson. How often did you get to go that far away from home?"

"I think it's different out here, Marie. A body has to go far to get to any place from another. We'll visit back and forth. I just feel it in my bones."

Chester Bates arrived with Rand Hilbrands right behind him. "It's time to be off, Ellen. We'll see you, Mistress Owen, Miss Marie." Chester nodded to them.

"Before you go, Chester, listen a minute," Rand said. "I plan to have a little Christmas party for everyone come the holidays. You'll pass the word to your group?"

"I will."

"Then come look me up in Pueblo City on Christmas Eve, and we'll make merry in our new home."

Julia smiled. "Thank you for the invitation, Mr. Hilbrands. It'll be like long-ago times."

"Let's be off, miss," Chester said, taking Ellen's arm. She walked off with her father, looking back at Marie as long as she could. Then she got in the wagon, and it rumbled away with the others, heading southwest along the Huerfano River.

છ

There was one more fort to pass before they arrived at the town, and Rod spotted it at noon on the following day.

"Fort Reynolds," he told Julia. "We'll stop to eat here, then get on the road again. We should reach Pueblo City before dark."

"It will be nice to see a town, and I know Amanda will be happy to settle here, but I'm not a city girl, Rod. One night will be enough for me."

Dusk turned the sky to lead when the party first glimpsed the lights of Pueblo City. Small adobe buildings and timbered shacks abounded on the outskirts. In the center of commerce stood a hotel, a squat affair of Spanish styling, short on grace, but long on hospitality. Even before they approached the front of the hotel, they could hear a fiddle squawking and a loud voice attempting to sing:

"I got a mule, her name is Sal, fifteen miles on the Erie Canal. She's a good ol' worker and a good ol' gal; fifteen miles on the Erie Canal."

Carl grinned at the sound. "He sings worse than me, Ida, but it's Friday night, and I reckon nobody minds much."

"I mind. I hope he don't think to go on all night. I was planning to sleep sound, in a real bed."

"That sounds mighty nice. If your pa pays me off tonight, I'll have the price of a bed, too." He blushed as his thoughts wandered back over his words.

"Oh, pooh," Ida said, flicking her fingertip across his nose. She sighed deeply. "How soon till we can wed, Carl?"

"Soon as the house is built, I'll come after you. Surely there's somebody in town that can marry us." Ida laid her hand on his arm and turned to look at him. Carl squirmed on the seat. "It won't be long now, girl. I'll come visit you if I can get away." He turned to look into her blue eyes.

"That'll be grand, Carl." She smoothed her dress across her knees, then brushed a speck of dust from her bodice. "I'll look forward to your visits."

Carl turned his eyes front in time to pull the team to a halt before the mules ran into the back of the Hilbrands' family wagon. He jumped off the high seat, went around the wagon, and scooped up Eliza, who was in danger of falling asleep, and as a consequence, of falling off the wagon.

He settled the little girl in his arms and carried her toward the front of the next wagon, where Rand met him with a canvas sack in his hand.

"Put Eliza up there on the seat. Thank you, boy. Here. I'll pay you now, in case your pa decides to take off in the night." He handed Carl the sack. "One hundred and fifty dollars."

Carl hefted the sack. "Seems a mite much just for driving a wagon."

"Take it, boy. I promised you a good wage. I'll make plenty off the goods."

Carl thanked him and went to the wagon to help Ida. He stood on a wheel spoke and took her hand. "Your pa paid me a hundred and fifty dollars, girl! I'm going to build us a fine house."

"With a fine feather bed?" She arched her brows and stood up.

"Don't tease me. A man's got only so much he can stand." He dropped to the ground from the wheel.

"I know," she answered. "Get me down from here."

"I don't know as I dare."

"Silly boy. I won't hurt you."

"I don't reckon you will. It's your pa I worry about."

"Papa?"

"If he sees me hugging you, I'll be in a fine jam."

"Will that get us wed sooner?"

"Ida! We need a house first. Now, are you going to behave yourself, or do I leave you up there all night?"

She looked from side to side, bent her head and closed her eyes, then opened her eyes and gazed at Carl. "I really can get down by myself, you know."

"I know. You done it before when you was mad at me."

She wiggled her shoulders at him. "But it's nicer when you lift me down."

He groaned. "Is this the good-bye you want?"

"Just a little peck, so I'll know you're coming back to visit."

"One little peck then." He stuffed the sack into his trousers pocket, reached up his arms for her, and she extended hers, laying her hands on his shoulders.

"You've got such a nice frame, Carl Owen," she murmured as he set her on the ground. "So strong. And you're so fine looking, too." She passed her fingers over his cheek. "Now, where's my peck?" She put back her head, lifting her lips to where he could reach them.

He gave her a chaste kiss, but it wasn't enough, not for Ida. "Please, show me you'll come for me," she breathed, and he took her into his arms.

He didn't mean to linger, but she was so warm in his arms, and so eager, so willing to receive his embrace. His lips covered hers again, and he pretended it was auburn hair slipping through his fingers.

"Doggone you, girl," he muttered when he finally broke free. "I'll visit when I can. Your pa will come looking for you in a minute. Good-bye." He loosed her and stepped back. *And you ain't Ellen Bates*, he thought, wondering if she would always be in his thoughts when he kissed Ida. Carl turned away and went to find his family, trying to shake the mood.

"Pa," he said when he saw Rod. "Rand Hilbrands paid me. I'll buy supper for us tonight."

"Sure. Let's see what Colorado folks eat."

Rod and Carl led the Owen family into the lobby and common room of the hotel. The appearance of the inn was rustic, for the chairs and stools were made of unpeeled pine logs and rawhide. A door led off to the right, where the aroma of meat drifted on the air. Another door, to the left, opened into the barroom, already crowded in the first hours of weekend freedom.

As Carl glanced around the lobby, Rand brought his family into the hotel. The Owens and the Hilbrands filled the lobby, and the dark-haired man at the desk looked angrily over at them.

"I can't put ye all up for the night," he growled. "I've got lots of folks in for the weekend, and I'm nearly full up."

Rand approached the desk. "I'll be wanting a room for my girls and a room for the wife and me."

"The best I can do ye is one room, but it's big and has plenty of room for spreading quilts and such. Ye can all fit in."

"This seems a poor excuse for a hotel, if you can't find rooms for your guests," Rand blustered.

The proprietor planted his feet on the floor and placed his fists on his hips. "This ain't your Grand Hotel, mister, and I don't believe ye made arrangements beforehand, neither. I gives ye what I has to give. If ye can do better than that, buy me out and I'll be off to the gold fields!"

Chapter 12

Rand looked at Amanda. She nodded her head. He scratched his ear, looked over at Rod, and shrugged his shoulders.

"I'll give you fifty dollars and a hundred pounds of flour. If you're anxious to be off, I'll be happy to help you pack your bags."

The dark-haired owner laughed and slapped his chest. "Ye can keep the flour. I'll take the cash and leave in the morning. My brother's holding a claim for me that shows signs of being the biggest strike in Colorado history. Ye won't see me keeping no flea-bitten hotel no more after tonight. I've got a fortune waiting for me over yonder."

Rand turned to his wife. "I reckon we've got a hotel to run, Mandy. We'll see if there's a place to set up the store." He glanced at Rod. "You won't have to look far to find us come Christmas time, Rod."

"You've a lucky streak in you, Rand. Ten minutes in town and already you're a leading citizen. We'll just eat and be on our way."

Rand gestured toward the dining room. "Go find a table and eat up."

Ten members of the Owen family followed Rod into the dining room, Roddy in his father's arms. The lighting—coming from six candles in wall holders—was dim, and Carl stopped to let his eyes adjust. He noticed that the tables, jammed with avidly eating men, were made of rough planks of wood, splintered along the edges, while the men sat on benches made of half-logs.

"Do you bring your own lamp to see by, Papa?" Julianna looked around curiously.

"It would make an improvement, I reckon, daughter." Rod laughed.

"Look, Rod." Julia pointed. "Those men are getting up. I figure there's room for us at that table."

Seven big men filed past the family, one holding his full belly and burping loudly. Another nodded to Julia and said, "Eat fast, ma'am. They clear the room at seven for the dance."

"A dance, Pa?" Marie's eyes sparkled.

"Not tonight, daughter. We have to be on our way early tomorrow. We'll be in at Christmas time, and there'll be plenty of dancing then." Rod sat down, and the rest of the group squeezed onto the benches.

A sturdy matron came over to the table and cocked her head to one side. "Buffalo steaks, beans and sourdough bread are what we serve. Butter and peach preserves is extra."

Rod pointed to Carl. "He gives the orders tonight."

"There's ten of us can do justice to that fare," Carl said, turning to Mary. "What's the young'un eat, Mistress Mary?"

"Bread and butter and peach preserves. And half a helping of beans."

"Bring what she said for the young'un," ordered Carl. "And bring all the rest of us butter and preserves."

಄

First light saw the Owen wagons already on the prairie heading southwest for the mountains. A constant wind blew over the small hills and rocky outcroppings of the desolate countryside. Ahead lay the Wet Mountains, their wooded green flanks topped by moisture-laden clouds.

"That sight over yonder gives me a real peace, Rod. I don't mind traversing this arid land if I can live snuggled up against them sweet green hills." Julia gave a sigh of contentment. "I reckon if we get a nice piece of property up there, I'll say you kept your promise of trees, and right handsomely, too."

"With those rain clouds, there's bound to be water a-plenty in this country. We need to look for a spring or a creek coming off those mountains, and there we'll build."

The next day, Rod stopped the team in a secluded meadow through which a creek flowed from the side of Greenhorn Mountain. Juniper and piñon trees surrounded the grassy field, and on the bench below them, bands of color showed where aspen and oak trees lived. Up the mountain, pine, fir, and spruce promised an evergreen world.

As he helped Julia to the ground, Rod asked, "How does this place suit you?"

Julia ran out on the thick carpet of grass. She whirled around, laughing. "This is home, Rod. This is our home!" She ran back and stopped, breathless, in front of him. "This is better than back in the Valley. We have all of this to ourselves." The motion of her arm took in the entire mountain and the valley of the creek below. "And no Yankees to drive us out. Oh, Rod, it's well-nigh perfect!"

"You've got a sparkle to you like a dozen gems, Julie. My heart leaps to know you're mine." He took her in his arms and looked around at his grinning sons. "Well, she *is* mine," he declared, and kissed their mother.

Julianna giggled and hid her face in her hands. "Why's Papa acting so silly, Marie?" she asked from between her fingers.

"He's so glad to be home, Jule," answered her sister, eyeing the rolling tops of the mountains before them. "You know, these mountains look like the ones we left in Virginia. I feel like I'm home, too."

"Well, if we're home, where is our house?"

"Julianna! Pa and the boys have to build it. You can't expect it to be here waiting for us." Marie turned and walked away.

Her sister followed, tugging on her skirt. "You mean we have to make everything, just like we done all across the country?"

"I bet you thought it'd all be here like back in Virginia, didn't you?"

"This is sure different than I expected. Marie, I'm scared of critters. I want a proper house."

"Who you been talking to, Ida Hilbrands? We'll have a house by and by, Jule, and Pa won't let anything get you; so don't go to crying on me. I want to go see that crick."

Rod sent Clay and Albert to water the stock and the teams, then turned to his older sons. "Well boys, it's time to sharpen the axes. I'll stake out my homestead on the south side of the creek, and Rulon, you can have the north side, if you like. We could put the cabins right opposite each other, and build a little bridge over the creek for sociability. We'll put a half-shelter behind the house for the horses and mules, and the cattle pens right out there, in the meadow. They'll have plenty of grass down there."

Carl scratched his shoulder. "I'm going to need me a homestead, too, Pa. I like that little bench land we passed just north of here."

Rod nodded. "That looked like a fine place for a cabin."

"I'm hoping there's a sweet water creek south of here," James said, eyeing the trees in that direction.

"As soon as we set up camp here, you can ride over and find a place you like," Rod said. "Pick your spot and drive your stakes." He looked around the sweep of the horizon. "We'll work on cabins for your wives as soon as your ma and Mary have theirs."

The men cut small saplings and made temporary shelters with the wagon covers until cabins could be raised. Julia arranged her kitchen goods on a pile of boxes, and set about fixing a fire ring for the Dutch ovens and iron skillets. Mary joined her while Marie and Julianna took Roddy for a walk to gather firewood.

"Here now, don't you go to lifting that heavy oven, girl," Julia cautioned, looking at Mary's flushed face with a critical eye. "You need to set and rest a mite. Just take a seat on that stool, yes, draw it over here and put your feet up a while. There's no hurry to make the fire. We don't need to start on supper for an hour yet."

Mary sat down heavily, and slowly swung her feet up to rest on a wooden box. "I'm fine, Mother Owen. Just worn out from traveling. It's so good to stop at last."

"Mary, you ought to be blooming right now, but most of the time you do look all tuckered out. What can I do to bring a mite of sparkle to those pretty eyes?"

Mary stared down at her hands. "I suppose I am an ungrateful ninny. I wanted Rulon back from the war for so long, and then he— It was hard."

"You did your duty and then some," Julia murmured.

"It wasn't only duty. Then, when he'd mostly healed, and I, well . . ." She laid her hand atop the swell of her abdomen and sighed. "Father Owen proposed that we make this journey. It's been so much longer than I thought. All along the way, I've been yearning for a home of my own. Now we've finally arrived. I must be grateful for that."

"We're all grateful to stop," Julia said, nodding. "Mr. Owen has a forceful attitude, but he wants the best for us all."

"I used to be frightened of him," Mary admitted.

"You haven't seen his tender heart."

"No."

"If you'd come to live with us after you wed Rulon, you'd have been bossing him around by now."

"Oh, I can't think so." She rubbed the bulge beneath her skirt. "That's not my place."

"Well, I suppose not. It's mine to keep him upright and flush the conceit out of his soul."

"Conceit? Surely not."

Julia laughed. "Mr. Owen needs a daily dose of reality and humility, else his opinion of himself will grow too large."

"Mother Owen!"

"You should have come to us, girl, then you'd know it. But during the war times, unsettled as they was, you probably got more food to eat from the store, living with your pa. I see now it was best."

Mary shook her head. "I wish I had been on the farm. You know how prickly Mama was."

"That's water under the bridge, Mary. You were a real help to her, even if she didn't reckon it at the time." Julia sat quietly for a few moments. "Thank goodness she's recovered her true self. I didn't like being at odds with her. Now you have the chance to live nearby and get to know us better. I hope you won't miss your folks too much."

"I want to make a family with Rulon at last, and not wish for my Mama."

"You've got a good start on that family. Rulon is a gentle man, but he's got plenty of strength for you to rely on. He won't let you down." Julia patted Mary's shoulder. "I now know what's wanted. I'll speak to Mr. Owen about building you the first cabin. You have more need than I do."

After several days of logging, enough trees had been cut, and the men raised Rulon's cabin. When the last shingle was finally bound into place, Rulon took his wife inside, shut the door, and remained there for a long time.

Julia hummed a song as she went about making supper, skinning a squirrel that Albert had brought her. She turned toward the snug little house, nodding approvingly at the smoke that puffed out of the chimney.

"I knew Rulon would make a good husband, given the proper chance," she said under her breath.

A long time later, Mary opened the door and stepped over the log doorsill, her eyes bright. She looked back into the cabin with her mouth curved into a smile, carefully shut the door, then hurried over to Julia and hugged her.

"Mother Owen, you're a dear sweet lady to let me have the first home." She laughed, the first time in months. "I'm mighty obliged." Mary shivered in the chill wind that suddenly came through the trees. "Rulon laid a fire. You'd best come inside."

"Does he know you're giving this invite?"

Mary clapped a hand over her mouth and giggled. "No. I'd best warn him you're coming."

Julia laid her hand on Mary's arm. "Never mind, then. I'll have my own hearth in a few days. You run along and get warm." She shooed her toward the little house, thinking, *Cleaving to your husband is the best way to make a family, Mary-girl.*

When the week was up, Julia had her cabin, larger than Mary's, with a lean-to kitchen alongside the large fireplace, and a loft divided into two portions.

Marie and Julianna tugged their big feather bed into the smaller of the rooms, spread it with sheets and a quilt, and then snuggled down into its warmth.

"Oh-h-h, that feels so good," said Julianna, shivering her chills away.

"It's getting right cold at night," agreed Marie, pulling the quilt over her head. Then she sat up. "I guess Carl's going to start on his cabin tomorrow," she added mournfully.

"Carl's getting married. Carl's getting married," Julianna sang out, then collapsed in giggles.

"Hush you," came her brother's voice through the wall.

"Save the noise for the shiveree," called out James.

"Quiet up there!" thundered Rod Owen from below.

The weather grew steadily colder as the men continued with the logging. James found his creek, and started cutting logs for a cabin for Ellen. Carl chose the wooded bench with a natural clearing in the center for his home site. An artesian spring rose just below the clearing, which became the headwaters of a little stream that ran to join the creek far below his father's home. Carl had staked out a homestead that took in both sides of the stream and down into the valley. Ida would favor the cabin being surrounded by trees, snugly tucked into the forest.

The walls of both cabins were half way to the top, and the Christmas party was ten days away when the good weather broke in late afternoon. White clouds laden with snow rolled down from the mountain summits. A freezing wind blew from the north, forcing Carl, working alone at the cabin, to pull his gray coat collar up around his chin. He saddled Sherando, headed him south, and told the gray gelding, "Take me to Pa's, boy."

The horse started off into the driven needles of snow. Carl hunched his back against the wind, crossed his arms, and stuck his hands beneath them. After a while, the trail lay through the sheltering trees between his cabin site and Rulon's, but at the end, there was still the meadow to cross.

Carl halted Sherando before he left the trees to let the horse rest. He dismounted and stamped his feet to restore circulation, beating his hands together to warm them.

"Sherando boy, this storm can't last long. I've got to get that cabin built before Christmas." Climbing into the saddle once more, Carl urged the gray into the biting wind. "It's only a quarter mile," he told the animal. "It's mighty cold, but you're tough, horse."

The moaning wind blew his words away as the icy blast hit them. On every side, Carl could see only swirling white ice crystals. He gave the horse its head, trusting its instinct to reach the cabin.

Sherando moved slowly, fighting the cross wind as it headed west up the meadow. The wind increased and tugged at Carl, almost dislodging him from the horse's back. Ice caked his hair and snow sifted down into his collar. Then they passed the bulk of Rulon's cabin on the right, and Sherando changed direction to cross the creek.

The horse paused at the log bridge spanning the water, and Carl saw that ice was forming at the sides of the stream. He shivered, and urged the tired horse to step onto the bridge.

"Come on, boy," he shouted over the keening of the wind. "Them logs are set solid."

The gray stepped tentatively onto the slippery surface of the logs, then skittered hurriedly across.

"That's a boy," Carl shouted triumphantly.

Snatched by the wind, his voice carried to his father's cabin, and a light shined out into the white yard as the door opened.

James blocked out the light as he came through the door and caught Carl, who was sliding off the gray's back.

James called out, "Clay, grab them reins and take care of the horse. I'll get Carl into the house."

"You're well-nigh froze, son." His father helped James assist Carl across the doorsill. "That blow came up mighty sudden. It's a wonder you made it back here."

Carl shivered, then said, "It's my fault I got caught. I want that cabin up and finished so bad, I let the storm take me by surprise."

∞

Morning came without a change in the weather, and Clay had to lean heavily against the door to crack loose the ice binding it to the jamb.

"Pa, that storm's still a-blowing, and the snow's piled up next to the door. How am I going to get out to feed the stock?"

"There's always a way for a man to feed his animals." Rod went over to the door. He tugged it open and faced a wall of white. "Fetch me a stick," he told Clay. "Maybe it ain't packed down tight."

Reaching as high as he could through the doorway, he flailed the stick into the snow. "It's still loose. Get some pails, boys."

Rod buttoned on his coat while Clay and Carl brought the buckets. "Clay, keep that second pail until I need it. Carl, you empty the full ones into the washtub."

Rod scooped out a pail full of snow at the top of the doorway and handed it over his shoulder to Clay. Taking the other bucket, he scooped again. Repeating the process until he had a hole big enough to crawl into, Rod then wiggled his way out the door and entered the icy cavern. "Clay, give me that stick again." His voice boomed in the confined space. "We'll see how deep this drift is."

Thrusting the stick into the snow above him, Rod felt a light resistance. He coughed as a load of snow fell into his upturned face. "Get me a longer stick," he commanded, angry at the elements.

Carl handed him Julia's broom, and Rod took it with a jerk. He stabbed it upward and broke through into the howling morning. New snow burst into his cavern, blinding him for a moment. Then he broke loose more of the crusty roof, and packed the snow down on one side to make a ramp to exit the hole. Triumphantly, he pulled himself out into the storm, floundering in the cabin-high drift.

"By gum, Colorado does everything in a big way," he shouted down to his family. "I have never seen a blow like this before."

Rod slid down the side of the drift and felt his way around the cabin, stomping down a path as he went, and found the horses cold, but snow-free in their shelter. The animals stood nose to tail, huddling together for warmth. Carl soon joined Rod, stamping his own feet as he came.

"Pa, we better run a rope from here to the stock pens, or we'll never get there and back every day."

"Good idea, son." Rod took down a rope from the side of the shelter. It was stiff in the cold, so he held it under his coat for a moment. Carl did the same with a second coil of rope, then they tied the ends together. Rod fastened one end of his double coil to a pine log that jutted from the side of the shelter and stepped into the storm.

Clay joined Carl as their father disappeared into a white swirl. "I wish we'd built the pens right alongside the house, 'stead of out in the meadow." Clay blew on his hands, then pulled gloves from his pocket and worked his hands into them.

"You'll be glad we did, come summertime and the flies gather. Grab the rope. We'd best follow Pa close." Carl moved off into the blizzard.

The rope was tight and easy to follow, for Rod was leaning against the wind, fighting to reach the cattle pens. Carl and Clay caught up with him, and presently, Rod stumbled against a pine pole.

"I reckon we're here," he shouted into the storm, tying off the rope and climbing into the enclosure.

Carl and Clay followed behind him, spreading out a little to search the inside of the fence for the cattle.

"Shoot, they got to be here somewhere," Rod growled. "They can't get out of this pen." He let go of the fence rail and pushed out into the middle of the pen, and the wind bowled him over.

Carl stooped to help his father to his feet, then Rod continued to fight through the drifts, only to fall again. He got up, brushing the snow from a large black and white object in his path.

"Well, I found the cattle," he muttered. "That there Brindle cow won't be knocking you into the mud ever again."

Chapter 13

Rod Owen said nothing more once he and his sons checked the carcasses of the cattle for any chance survivors. He returned in silence to the cabin, where Julia read disaster in his face. She glanced questioningly at him, but received only a shake of the head in reply.

Julia turned to Carl, who enlightened her in somber whispers.

"Not one?" she asked.

"No," he said, shaking his head. "Not one."

Julia sat down and rubbed her forehead with one hand, feeling the weight of the news upon her brow. "Lord God, don't desert us now," she breathed in prayer.

Marie and Julianna wept openly about the loss of the cattle, while the storm raged on for three days. Finally, the sun came out bright and strong, and melted down a portion of the drift around the cabin.

Rod and Carl stamped down a path to Rulon's cabin and found his family snug and warm.

"The cattle froze, son," Rod told Rulon, speaking of it for the first time since leaving the stock pen. "I reckon we'd best make use of this sunshine, and drag them carcasses into the woods. I don't favor them bringing wolves and such down by the cabins."

"Can we get the hides off them?" Rulon asked.

"Maybe a few," Rod answered with a shrug. "It may be too cold to salvage them."

"Well, what are we standing around here for?" Rulon asked, pulling on his coat. "Let's get on with it. The day ain't getting any longer."

The men found the mules frisky and eager to work after their long and idle confinement. Hitching the animals to one of the dead cows, they hauled the animal into the forest. James and the younger boys joined them, and they worked throughout the morning, dragging the carcasses into the woods. Rulon and Carl skinned a few head of cattle before they found the task too difficult in the cold, but they were able to butcher the remains with axes and the two-man saw.

Returning to the house for dinner at noon, they stood in a bunch before the fireplace, warming their stiff fingers.

"Shore feels good, Ma," said a shivering James. "You can't imagine how cold it is out there. We dasn't stand around, for fear of turning into ice cakes, like Lot's wife."

Julia laughed. "That was a pillar of salt, boy. You need some study in the Good Book."

"I meant shaped like Lot's wife, Ma."

Carl looked gravely at James. "I reckon I ain't going to claim to be shaped like Lot's wife, little brother. Speak for yourself. Me, I'm a man grown." He hooted at James's affronted expression.

James threw up his hands. "Chiggers and fleas! It's mighty bad times when a body can't speak his piece around here without a lot of idle comment. You know I mean ice cakes in human form, not female form. I reckon I can tell what you got on your mind. You're just chafing to get that cabin of yours built, ain't you?"

Carl's face flushed red, and his brothers cackled and roared at his discomfort. "Hush," he drawled, "the only thing keeping me single right now is this dad blamed storm and a half-made house."

James's grin was crooked, then his face went somber. "The sooner you marry Miss Ida Hilbrands, the better I'll like it."

∞

That night it froze. The snowmelt at the bottom of the drifts glazed into sheets of ice, and icicles hung from the eaves of the cabins.

Carl lay in his bed and listened to the sounds of the night. The roof boards above him crackled as they shrank in the dropping temperature, and somewhere in the forest, a tree split open with a pop, as ice formed in its heart.

Here in the loft he could see his breath, and when the hairs in his nose stiffened and froze, he knew the fire was out downstairs. He pulled the quilt over his face, and yearned for his own cabin, where he would keep the fire roaring all night, even if he had to chop wood all summer to fuel it.

He dreamed of a warm, sweet-smelling girl beside him in the bed, but could not see her face, for her back was to him. When he tried to turn her over, she became a lost cow, frozen in the storm. He cried out, "Ellen!" and awoke.

Sitting up in his bed, he anxiously looked over at James, and noted with relief that he still slept. He lay down again, chest heaving for a time, but sleep soon took him.

∞

On the far side of the partition, Marie heard the cry, and bit her knuckle in frustration. *He'll still marry Ida*, she thought bitterly. *He's said he will.* She closed her eyes, praying for her friend, then fell into a restless sleep.

∞

Two days were shrouded in cloud and freezing weather, but no more snow fell. Then two days of thaw lifted the hopes of the Owens in anticipation of the

Christmas party in Pueblo City. The morning of the twenty-third, however, came without sun. A furious ice storm blew for four days, canceling any thought of leaving the cabin for travel.

Then Nature turned capricious, and brought along warm, fall-like days, and the men worked fast to finish Carl's cabin. On the third morning, a messenger rode through, bringing a note from Rand Hilbrands that the party was set for New Year's Eve, if the weather held. "Even if it snows again, come on in. I've got plenty of room, and some wonderful news," the note concluded.

"Mary and I ain't going anywhere," Rulon announced. "Her time is too near for traveling."

"Don't she lack a month yet, Rule?" asked Julia.

"That's right, but she ain't up to the trip. Go ahead, and I'll stay here with her."

Rod and the family left the next day, except for Carl, who wanted to put some finishing touches on the cabin before he left. "I'll be through by tomorrow morning," he said. "Sherando and me'll get there late tomorrow."

"Looks like we're going to a wedding as well as a dance, Rod," Julia said as they left in the wagon.

Yep, I reckon you'll have new kin before the week's up."

"I wish Ida had some cattle to bring with her," Julia murmured.

"Now don't fret, woman. I've been contemplating on what to do about getting us new stock. I'll take a few of the boys up to Denver City to look up Jonathan. If he can't put us to work, I'm sure he'll know of miners we can work for until we have some money. Then I reckon we'll ride to Texas and pick up some of them long-horned cows. I heard tell at Fort Lyon they're selling at three dollars a head."

"That's sure a fancy plan, Rod Owen. Don't forget to tote that strong box back to Jonathan."

Rod laughed at her easy acceptance of his scheme. "You're a surprising woman, Julia Owen."

"I reckon. And don't you forget it."

∞

On the morning of December thirty-first, Carl awoke for the first time in his new cabin. He glanced around the dim room, satisfaction stealing over his face. He had built well, and he hoped Ida would appreciate the solidness and hard work that had gone into its creation. Looking up at the loft above him, he thought ahead to the children who would fill it, and smiled as he imagined himself roaring out, "Quiet up there!" echoing his father.

He sat up in the rope bed he had constructed against the end of the room. Fir boughs beneath him creaked with his shifting weight, and he recalled the comfort of the springy branches during the night.

Carl bent over and picked up his jean trousers from the stool near the bed. They were the pants he had bought in Kansas town, his newest clothes. They would have to do for the party, and for the wedding, and for many months of hard work to follow. He stooped and pulled them on, then finished dressing and went outside to the washstand.

The water in the bucket was clear of ice, and Carl felt good about the day. He washed, and shaved carefully with Rulon's razor, remembering that he must ride back to Rulon's cabin with it this morning before he left. He would buy a razor and such gear in Pueblo City when he arrived.

He stepped back into the doorway of the new house, and smelled the pungent odor of the newly cut wood in the box beside the fireplace. Ida would love this place, nestled into the clearing like it had grown there. Everything was ready for her to step into the room and take over the cabin to make it a home.

Some primitive caution, born of the howling storms he had undergone, made Carl roll a blanket and tie it to his saddle before he left the cabin. Then he tucked a double handful of jerky made from one of the frozen cows into a sack and tied that on the saddle, too. The same feeling urged him to belt on his pistol. He thought twice over that, telling himself a man didn't go armed to his wedding. He ignored the thought, and slung the gun around his hips. "I got a ways to go before Pueblo City," he muttered aloud.

&

Carl rode into Rulon's dooryard just as Chester Bates and his family broke into the clearing from the south.

"Company coming, Rulon," Carl pointed out as his brother stopped chopping wood to accept the razor. Carl cantered his horse over to meet the new arrivals in front of Rod's cabin, as Rulon followed on foot. "All y'all light and set," he called to the Bates family.

Chester dismounted from a tall brown horse and helped his wife dismount from her bay. Carl dropped off Sherando and ran to help Ellen swing off her dun mare as Rulon arrived to greet the Bates.

Carl grinned at the girl and teased, "You go astride now, Miss Ellen?"

She grinned back. "The wagon broke a wheel, and pa only had one sidesaddle, so Ma got it. I like to ride astride," she insisted. "I can tell what Dun Baby's going to do next. She likes to try to throw folks," she finished in a whisper.

Carl rubbed the frisky animal's cheek. "Where'd you get her?"

"Pa made up some furniture and traded to a Spanish gentleman for a string of horses. I think they're only half-broke, but I like that." Her eyes shone with excitement. "There's just lots of Spanish folks down where we live, and I'm learning some words already." She turned toward the stock pens. "Like, 'corral' means 'stock pen'." She paused. "Where's your cattle?"

"Up in the woods a piece. We had a little storm up here. Froze 'em solid as ice cakes, to quote James."

"Oh. I'm sorry," she said in a small voice. Her brow furrowed with pain. "That must be a big blow to your pa."

"He didn't say a word about it for three days, but you know Pa, nothing keeps him down for long. By now he's hatching a plan to get us out of this fix."

Chester came over to Carl and Ellen. "I'm sorry to hear about your cattle. And it looks like we missed your folks. Rulon tells me you're not going in to the party. I reckon we made this detour for nothing."

"No, sir. Rulon's the one not going. I am, and I'd be pleased to ride along with you. How are the rest of the folks? Are any of them coming?"

"The Campbells and the Morgans are back a ways in a wagon, but Tom O'Connor stayed to tend the stock. He says his kids are too young for a dance, anyhow."

Ellen laughed. "Tom O'Connor is courting a pretty little Spanish girl down in Leones. No dance in Pueblo City could drag him away."

"You don't say! I reckon there's something about this Colorado air."

Ellen looked puzzled at his remark. He offered no enlightenment, and she looked away, a little sigh moving her shoulders.

"Well, we'd better get, if we're going to make Pueblo by nightfall," Chester said. He helped his wife into her saddle and swung into his. "Carl, you young people have frisky horses, so why don't you take the lead for a while?"

"Suits me," Carl said, and locked his fingers to give Ellen a boost onto her dun. Ellen held onto the high horn of the saddle and accepted his help by placing her boot into his hands. Then she was astride the horse, her long skirt flaring out over the cantle and down Dun Baby's haunches. The dun mare danced around, eager to be off again. Carl laughed in pleasure at the sight, then mounted Sherando.

"That's a funny looking saddle," he said, grinning, as they started off. "What's that high thing in front for?"

Ellen patted the horn. "This here thing is for wrapping a rope around after you get it on a cow. I watched some Mexicans tending cattle down to home, and it's so exciting what they can do with a rope and a good cow pony. I've been practicing throwing a rope, but only when Pa's not around," she admitted, wrinkling her nose as she grinned. "He thinks a girl should stick to kitchen chores, but he could use some help when inside work is done."

"Sounds like you have your house all built."

"Pa put up the cutest little sod house. It ain't very big, but it's enough for the three of us for now." A lock of red-gold hair got loose from the rest and Ellen pushed it back into place. "Lawsy, I'm going to look a sight when we get to the dance."

Carl looked at her a long time. "I reckon you'll do," he said. "You look kind of carefree and happy, and full of fire."

Ellen blushed. "I never knew you had a silver tongue, Carl Owen," she exclaimed.

"I don't. You look so excited. You'll be the most fetching girl at the dance. I surely hope you'll save me a right smart lot of dances."

"Well," she said, looking down at the ground. "I'll think about it."

The trail they followed dipped into a stream bed, and Ellen slowed her horse to cross it. Dun Baby suddenly stopped and lowered her head to drink. Ellen kept her seat and laughed, then looked around her.

"She won't move till she's had her fill," she called to Carl, who turned Sherando and came back to the stream. "What a pretty valley," she said, smiling. "And that bench up there, with all those trees. I can almost imagine a cabin built in there. Why, I believe I do see a cabin up there!"

"You do," Carl said, grinning. "It's mine. Ain't it a purty place?"

"It's right lovely." Ellen eyed him closely. "Are you bringing Ida back, now that the cabin's built?"

Before he could answer, Chester Bates and his wife caught up with them.

"I reckon you're stuck there till she drinks the stream dry, daughter," Chester mused as he came alongside. "We'll go on ahead." He and Muriel trotted their horses out of sight toward the north.

Carl turned to watch them go, his heart pounding. He had almost forgotten Ida in his pleasure at Ellen's company. Slowly he faced the girl in the stream, setting his teeth and flexing the muscles of his jaw. "Yes," he said slowly. "She's expecting me."

Dun Baby quit drinking, continued across the stream and ascended the bank. Ellen pulled up alongside Carl. Her face was white, and she lifted her chin before she spoke. "I thought you had more sense than to ask one girl to dance while on the way to wed another, Carl Owen." Her green eyes seemed to be filled with brown sparks as she sat erect on her mare. Then she kneed the dun and started off across the rising valley slope after her parents.

"A man can dance with any girl until he's wed," he shouted, urging Sherando to follow her.

The rest of the journey was a misery for Carl. Ellen answered when spoken to, but the ease of their conversation had vanished. She rode beside him, but her excitement and joy were gone, and he shrank from the knowledge that he had robbed her of them. The bright, crisp day seemed gloomy and overcast to him. Finally, he rode silently through the tedious miles across the prairie.

Chester called a halt at noon, on the sandy bank of a waterhole. After the horses drank their fill, he allowed them to crop the brown buffalo grass on the plain surrounding the water. When the travelers had eaten and the horses were rested, they resumed their trip.

∞

Five o'clock had come and gone before Chester Bates and his party rode into Pueblo. Rand Hilbrands' hotel was well lit for the festivities. Candles burned on every wall inside, and they found that the formerly dim dining room was ablaze with light. The tables and benches had been cleared away, and the space was reserved for dancing. Three musicians tuned their instruments for the next dance set.

Carl glanced around the room, excitement building in him in spite of his miserable trip. He did not see Ida, and turned to Ellen with fierce determination.

"I've seen you this far, and I'm claiming the first dance," he told her, and before she could deny him, he took her hands and pulled her onto the dance floor. Ellen allowed him to lead her into the gaiety, but her stiff movements betrayed her reluctance to dance with him.

"This ain't fair, Carl Owen," she whispered grimly, as he held her hands firmly in his.

"Nobody promised you life was fair," he grunted back.

When the music finished, Ellen removed her hands from Carl's and fled. He turned to watch her go, and saw Ida coming into the room from the kitchen. She wore a pale yellow dress, the same color as her hair, which was piled upon her head in a new style.

She seemed to see him, then her eyes slid past his in an embarrassed manner, as she continued her advance into the room. Carl felt his heart leap as he made his way through the press of people. She was as pretty as ever, and soon she would be his.

Ida stopped in front of a group of strangers, three young men and two ladies of expensive foreign dress. She greeted them warmly as Carl came up beside her. The strangers replied, and Carl heard the unfamiliar cadences of the King's English for the first time. He strained to understand the odd phrases and inflections they used as he nervously waited for Ida to break off her chatter and acknowledge his presence. Carl sensed a tensing in her, a strain in her voice as she continued her conversation with the people in the group.

Becoming impatient, and feeling a slow heat creeping up his neck at her continued snub, Carl placed his hand on her elbow to draw her attention. She stiffened, and glanced at him uneasily.

"Hello, Carl," she said coldly. "Can't you see that I am talking to my friends?"

A dark-haired young man detached himself from the group and came to Ida's other side, an air of protectiveness hovering over him. He glanced sharply at Carl and said in an aggrieved voice, "I say, what's the meaning of this? Take your hand off her arm, your boorish fellow."

Carl tightened his grip and turned to face this challenge. He looked closely at the Englishman, and saw that the young man was a few years older than himself, slight, and had a long, straight nose, a thin mouth, and a jutting chin. His swaggering manner suited his expensive clothes. Reading disdain in the man's pale eyes, Carl turned a questioning look on Ida, who avoided his eyes.

"I reckon I have a right to speak to the lady," he said, trying to get her to look at him. "I have to speak to you, Ida, and we'd best be alone."

"Say your piece here, Carl. Whatever it is, my friends can hear it, too." She finally looked at him, then away again, her eyes resting on the young Englishman and his party.

Amazed at her treatment of him, Carl dropped his hands and shifted his weight. "I reckon this has to be private, Ida." Then realizing the import of his message, he continued. "Hush, if you want your new friends to hear, that's proper. The whole town will know soon enough."

He grabbed Ida's hands, turned her to face him, and looked down at her lowered eyes. "I've come for you, Ida. The cabin's done."

Ida jerked up her chin and looked at him, then her eyes slipped sideways to look around the room, as though in a panic.

Carl spoke again. "We'll find a preacher and get wed, enjoy the party, and then we can go home."

Ida looked directly at him then, a strange light burning through her eyes. "No, Carl," she whispered, and pulled her hands from his grasp.

Pale Eyes stepped forward, muttering, "This is a muddle. Who is this chap, Ida?"

She waved a hand at the Englishman, stopping him in his tracks.

"Wait, Cecil. I have to tell him."

Carl focused his attention on Ida's eyes, trying to read her expression. "Who is this feller, Ida?" he echoed, his voice barely above a whisper. "Why's he acting so familiar with you?"

Ida flew to the offensive, stamping her foot and fisting her hands. "He has more right than you, Carl Owen. You said you'd visit, and I waited for you ever so long. You never came, Carl Owen, so you gave up any rights to me. Mr. Gilbert, here, came along and asked for my hand, and I figured it was mine to give. I'm getting wed, all right, but to him!"

Chapter 14

Carl staggered backward, as though Ida had buried her small fists in his belly. His jaw dropped, and he took a long shuddering breath.

"What's this man got that I ain't?" he shouted, his voice hoarse. Then he read his answer in her hard, glittering eyes, as she looked from him down to the gems sparkling on her finger. "He bought you from me," Carl grunted. "He bought you with pretty things, and you was fool enough to let him."

He bunched his fists to swing at the sneering stranger who had put his arm around Ida's waist, but two pairs of arms caught him from behind, and his father and James hustled him away from Ida and her beau.

"I'll be a pinch-toed son of a red-wattled turkey buzzard!" James exclaimed when he and Rod deposited a struggling Carl in the hotel lobby. "You've been double-damn-crossed, big brother." James scowled, looking as angry as Carl.

"Rand told us when we got into town, son. Ida convinced him she was free to marry," Rod said, scratching his head. He looked at Carl, then plunged ahead with the story. "This Englishman came into town and stayed. After a while, he asked Ida to marry him, and she went ahead and accepted him."

Carl paced the lobby, alternately gripping his hands tightly together and driving one fist into his other hand. He cursed Ida, her love of money, and her shabby treatment of him. Then his voice lowered as he cursed himself for falling prey to her charms. James retreated to the dining room, leaving Rod to deal with Carl.

"Why, Pa?" Carl turned to his father, his voice rasping. "I was good enough for her in Virginia. Why ain't I good enough for her now?"

"I don't have an answer to that, Carl. You cool off, and if you feel like you can keep your temper in check, you can stay and try to salvage this party. There are plenty of pretty girls here. But if you feel like making trouble, you go on home." He waited for a moment, then added, "I know you'll be angry at me for saying this, since I arranged your marriage in the first place, but now I think you got off luckier than Mr. Cecil Gilbert over yonder."

Carl glared at his father. His father stared back, waiting. Carl breathed hard, resumed his pacing, then after several minutes had passed, he stopped in front of his father and nodded his head. "I've come this far, so I'll take hold of Rand

Hilbrands' party with both hands." He shook his fists in illustration. "That two-faced little fox won't get the best of me."

"If you can't hold your tongue, you'd best leave right now," Rod warned.

Carl slumped into a nearby chair. His body shook with released tension. After a few minutes he said, "I'll mind my manners, and I'll hold my tongue, but you can't expect me to smile."

"No man will ask that of you, son" Rod answered gently. "Come in and find a pretty-looking gal to dance with. The night is plenty young."

Carl nodded grimly and followed his father into the dining room. A dance was in progress, a waltz, and his eyes glanced over the swirling couples to find Ida. They found Ellen, encircled by James's arms, gracefully moving in three-quarter time around the room. She was smiling, then laughing at James's joke, then her eyes met Carl's and she looked away, face gone white.

He tore his gaze from her face, disgruntled that she was occupied when he wanted her company. But he could not keep from watching her, and when the waltz ended and James went to get refreshments, he was ready.

He came up behind her in the corner where she stood, apart from the rest of the party-goers, and placed his hands on her shoulders. She stiffened, and he bent over to whisper in her ear.

"I reckon I can ask you to dance now, and have no anger betwixt us."

Something in his shaky whisper made Ellen whirl around and stare up at him. Her eyes searched his face. "What do you mean?"

Carl closed his eyes for a moment, then opened them and looked straight into Ellen's. "I'm a free man, Ellen. Ida found somebody more moneyed than me, and she kicked me loose."

Carl saw the flame of joy that leaped into her eyes before she could lower her head. He said, "Pa said I should come in here and find a pretty girl to dance with. You're the prettiest one I know. Will you take a whirl with me?"

"James went—"

"Forget James. He'll be gone a while. Dance with me."

A shadow crossed her face, then she straightened and smiled a bit. "I'll do it."

"Thank you," he said.

୫୬

Carl was able to dance with Ellen one more time before he came across Ida in a corner kissing Cecil. Anger rose up in his throat, threatening to choke him, and he knew the time had come for him to leave. He shook as he turned his back on all that he had worked for, and walked slowly toward the lobby door, his eyes glazed, fists clenched.

Someone reached out and touched his arm, and he started to shake off the hand, then realized that Ellen was standing there, trembling at the sight of his glowering face.

"Carl?"

"I've got to get out of this place. I can't mind my manners any longer." He turned his red-rimmed eyes on her, and she gave a little cry at the wildness in his face. "Come with me," he pleaded. "Come help me ride the meanness away." Then he turned and bolted through the door.

Ellen, shaken, jumped at the touch of a hand on her arm. She turned to see Marie standing next to her, smiling.

"I told you a time would come. Go with him. It's just his pride that's wounded. He calls your name in his sleep."

"Oh," Ellen gasped, and ran out the door.

The lobby was empty. Ellen grabbed a cloak from a coat rack beside the dining room door, and swirled it around her as she walked out into the darkness of the street.

Pausing to get her bearings, she looked down the street toward the livery stable. A lantern burned beside the big front doors, and she stepped off the hotel porch and hurried toward the light. The stable boy was asleep beside the open door, and she ran past him into the barn.

Carl stood beside Sherando, saddling the gray gelding by the light of another lantern. His face was gaunt in the lamplight. She walked toward him, and he looked up, surprising her with a wan smile.

"Good girl. I figured you'd come."

"What?"

"You're a stayer."

"Is that something good?"

"Means you stick to a task."

Ellen shivered. "It's cold tonight."

"We can leave right now," Carl said, ducking under Sherando's neck and going into the next stall. His voice floated back over the side of the wooden enclosure. "We'll get some exercise and warm you right up."

He returned, leading Dun Baby, already saddled. A grin spread over his face. "I took a chance on being ready, but I wasn't wrong about you."

so

The horses were rested and willing to run. Carl gave Sherando his head as soon as they were clear of the town, and the gray galloped off into the prairie. Dun Baby did her best to catch the bigger horse. After two miles, Carl pulled the horse up and let him breathe. He looked up into the night sky, and figured it was about ten o'clock.

Ellen reined in her horse when she caught up, and slid off onto the ground. She stood with her arms outstretched and turned slowly around, as if embracing the whole sky.

The moon slid out from behind a cloud and shed silver light on the radiant girl. Carl noticed the joy in her as she lifted her arms to the moon.

"I love you," she cried out. "Colorado, you're beautiful."

So are you, girl, he thought, and swallowed hard. *She looks like Ma did the day we came into the meadow. So different from Ida.* He scowled and said, "You'd best get in the saddle. It's a long ride to the Greenhorn."

"The Greenhorn? Ain't we going back to the dance?"

"No. I thought getting out into the air would help, but I can't abide seeing that double-dealing fox again." He stopped, and set his teeth for a moment. "Pa told me to go home if I couldn't mind my manners. I reckon I'm heading back home."

Ellen walked over to Sherando and looked up at Carl. "It's beautiful out here, but I don't favor being left alone in the prairie."

"I don't figure to leave you. Come along and keep me company."

He watched her face as she took a step backward, concern in her eyes. "That ain't fitting, Carl. I can't go that far alone with you."

"I don't aim to do you no harm," he said firmly. "It ain't in me to punish you for what she did to me."

She put a hand over her mouth and gasped. "What about my folks? What about James?"

He gritted his teeth. "James! You don't love James."

"I owe him my hand."

"You owe me your life!"

She sighed and backed away. He dismounted and caught her by the shoulders.

"Your folks will be along when the party is over. You can stay with Mary and Rulon. She'll be pleased at your company."

"Marie knows I came with you," Ellen said. "She'll know what to say to Ma and Pa." She pursed her lips and blew out a breath. "Folk'll talk, but I don't care. I would just be a mound of earth in the graveyard if you hadn't plucked me out of the way of those Yankees in Mount Jackson. I'll go with you."

Carl dropped his hands to his sides. "Thank you."

He went after Dun Baby, grazing on dry buffalo grass on a nearby hillock, and brought the mare to Ellen. He bent and made a stirrup with his hand for her and she swung into the saddle. Her frisky horse sidestepped, and Ellen pulled her up short.

"She'll run for me now, and you can't catch me!" she challenged. Then she was racing over the moonlit plain, and Carl scrambled for Sherando.

It seemed vastly important to catch her, to draw up even with her. Carl flung himself onto the gelding's back, and urged the horse forward with little grunts and mutters, as though all his energy was focused on the fleeing girl before him, leaving him with few words.

She had a good head start on him and held onto the lead for a half-mile, then the big gray started to catch up with the mare. Ellen turned to look back at Carl, her face alive with excitement as she drove her horse to keep up the pace.

Carl ducked lower over his horse's neck, willing Sherando to catch the mare. Then he was alongside, and stole a glance at Ellen.

She was grinning, and looked at him in triumph, hair streaming back from her face. She reined Dun Baby down to a trot, then cooled her off at a walk. Carl kept pace with her horse, patting the lathered Sherando.

"You act like you won," he chuckled, when he had caught his breath.

"Maybe I did," she answered, running her fingers through her tangled locks.

A snowflake drifted down from the sky and landed on Ellen's hair. It melted, leaving a drop of water sparkling in its place, then the moon disappeared behind a thick cloud as other flakes swirled toward the ground. Ellen pulled the hood of the cloak over her head and snuggled into the folds of the cape.

"I grabbed this cloak and ran. I don't know whose it is, but it's good and warm," she shouted in Carl's direction.

Carl looked around at the eddying flakes, and noticed that the wind was moaning and whining in his ears. It blew the thick flakes into his eyes, and he shut them for a moment. When he reopened them, Ellen was gone!

Chapter 15

"Ellen!" he yelled into the white blanket before his eyes. "Ellen, where are you?"

No voice answered him, no cry cut through the keen of the wind. "Where are you, girl?" he shouted against the wind's shriek. Still no human sound reached his ears, and he strained to see through the frozen curtain enveloping him.

Panic seized him. Ellen was lost; Ellen, who just moments before was glorious, wild, free. He turned Sherando this way and that, calling her name, trying to see through the storm. As he whipped his body from side to side in the saddle in his attempt to catch her voice in his ears, his arm brushed against his holstered pistol. He tugged on the binding loop and yanked the gun free, then fired it into the ground.

"Carl," he heard Ellen cry, her voice whipped in all directions by the wind.

He glanced wildly about. "Ellen," he bellowed, and this time heard her reply off to his left. He turned Sherando in the direction of her voice and called for her to stay in one place. Blindly, he followed her calls, hoping panic would not make her mute before he could reach her.

The wind puffed away a sheet of snowflakes, and he saw the dark cloak just ahead. He cried out "Ellen," as he reached her side.

She turned, clutching the cloak around her. "Oh, Carl," she breathed, and gave a great sigh of relief.

"We can't stay here in the open or we'll freeze," he told her, voice raised over the storm. "I wish I knew what direction I'm headed. With all this snow blowing around, I've lost my bearings." He reached over for her reins and looped them around his left hand. "If we're heading south, we'll reach the St. Charles before too long, and we can hole up on the bank."

"Dun Baby should be headed south. I never turned her. I pulled up soon as I lost sight of you."

"We'll go that way, then," he agreed, thankful for her good sense. "I reckon we can't miss the river."

Carl turned Sherando and started him off at a walk, wondering which was worse, to trot forward into the uncertain footing of the unfamiliar ground ahead, or to go at a walking pace and slowly freeze. He wished he'd paid better attention to the country as they had traveled through it, and he hoped the river wasn't as far as he thought it was.

He heard Ellen behind him, shifting in her saddle. The leather groaned in the frigid air, crackling louder for a moment than the wind could moan. Carl gritted his teeth and pulled his hat down lower over his ears, and hoped that Ellen was warmer than he.

The horses plodded along, stumbling from time to time on the uneven ground. Occasionally, Carl dismounted and led the way, stamping a path through belly-high drifts, but the cold crept up his legs, and even when he rubbed his ankles, the loss of feeling persisted while he walked, and he had to remount.

To his frozen senses, it seemed hours later that the horses nosed downward into a gully, and the sound of the wind died abruptly. Carl pulled Sherando to a stop and peered through his ice-encrusted lashes.

The horses had brought them to a narrow ravine, an ancient waterway, protected from the driving wind by an overhang of sandstone. Carl climbed swiftly out of the saddle, gripping both sets of reins in his left hand. He ducked under Sherando's neck, and stamping his feet as he walked, led the horses further under the overhang. Tying the reins to a creosote bush, he limped over to Ellen's side, his cold muscles cramping as he used them.

Ellen awkwardly dismounted and rubbed her hands together to move the blood into her fingers.

"I'm glad we're out of the wind," she said, her voice quivering as she shook with cold. "I reckon I'm near froze."

Carl helped her walk to a little cup-like depression in the wall of the stream bed and sat her down out of the storm. Returning to the horses, he unsaddled Dun Baby, patting her affectionately. "You're a good horse," he muttered. "A stayer like your rider."

He turned to Sherando and rubbed the gelding's muzzle and neck. "Let me get your saddle off, boy," he said.

His hand brushed against the blanket rolled behind the saddle, and he remembered the prompting to bring it along. Untying the blanket and the bag of jerky, Carl unsaddled the gray, and did his best to make the horses comfortable before he returned to Ellen's side.

"Sometimes I get smart," he told her. "Put this blanket around you while I see if these bushes will burn. And help yourself to the jerky."

Carl left the overhang and went out into the ravine to collect brush. Snow fell steadily into the little valley but the wind was cut off, and he could walk up the gully without fighting his way through high-piled drifts. The sky glowed with diffused moonlight, scattered by the clouds and the million snowflakes, and Carl could see where he was going, although he knew it was midnight or later.

Under one bank of the ravine he found an animal burrow lined with dry twigs and soft leaves. He cleaned it out and stuffed it all into his pockets for tinder. A few yards farther on, he came to an old scrub oak with several dead lower limbs that would be dry on the inside. He broke off as many of the dead branches as he could carry, then turned back to the overhang.

"Wish I had an ax," he told Ellen. "There's a big oak up the gully a ways. It would keep us in wood for a couple of days, if need be. Hush, the way these Colorado storms blow, we might need it."

He set to work building the fire, keeping it small, but big enough to warm them, then struck his knife against an old piece of flint he had brought home from the war. When the sparks landed in the tinder, he blew them gently to life, nursing the baby flames with bits of dry grass and leaves, then twigs and finger-sized branches.

When the blaze had a strength of its own, he got up and stepped back to join Ellen. As he let himself collapse beside her, Ellen offered him a piece of jerky. He took it and held it up.

"Seems a shame to eat this critter after it walked all the way across the U-nited States. A hungry man ain't got much choice, I reckon." He tossed the jerky into the air and caught it.

"Eat it, Carl. It'll give you strength." Ellen shrugged the blanket off her shoulders and threw it around him. "You look froze, so you'd best take the blanket. I'll get close to the fire."

"Ellen, I ain't going to get warm and leave you out in the cold. You take the blanket and get some sleep. I'm going to be fine." He held out the woven wool.

"You're *loco*, Carl Owen! I ain't about to let you freeze yourself on my account. Get over here and we'll share the blanket."

"You ain't afraid of what folks will say?" He took a bite of meat.

"In the middle of a blizzard? Not anymore. I reckon this storm in this country makes the rules a mite different." She eyed him sideways. "Besides, I have your word."

Carl smiled, then yawned as fatigue swept over him. "And I'm a man of my word." He scooted over next to the girl and enveloped both of them in the blanket. "My brother Peter used to tell me I snored louder 'n a mess of locusts. I never believed him, but I best warn you, just in case he wasn't lying."

She laughed. "That's silly, to worry about snoring. I always felt like my pa had a right pleasing kind of snore. I missed it all the time he was gone to the fighting. When he got back, even the tool shed was home, once he got to snoring away at night."

Carl lay back against the rock and earth wall. "Strange what little things will bring a body comfort, ain't it?" He chewed on the jerky. "A fire goes a long way to help a man forget his troubles." He took another bite. "You feel the same?"

There was no response from Ellen, and Carl turned to look. Her head nodded downward, her eyes closed. Carl put his arm around her and eased her head back onto his shoulder. "You're all tuckered out," he whispered. "It's good you sleep."

∽

Ellen woke to the touch of pale sunrise on her cheek, which rose and fell with the motion of Carl's chest beneath her head. Something held her from moving out of the warmth of the blanket, and she discovered his arm around her shoulders.

She stiffened, then relaxed as she recalled her invitation to Carl to share the blanket. *I ain't never been this close to him before,* she thought, and remembered with a start the night she had tripped from the wagon and landed in his arms. But he had been another woman's man then, and now he was free, at least he would be once his injured pride healed over. She bit her lip and eased her head off Carl's chest. She wasn't free.

I ain't been free since the day Rod Owen said he'd give us food and a wagon if we'd go west with his family, Ellen thought, a sour taste rising in her mouth. She closed her eyes. *Pa and Ma didn't tell me I was part of the bargain.* But she knew, when they said, "We've picked out a husband for you," that Rod Owen had required her hand in marriage to his son as payment in full.

James ain't free, neither. The thought brought Ellen's eyes wide open. She'd heard he was courting Jessica Bingham, and wasn't happy that his pa had made a match for him. *He don't hate me, nor dislike me*, she reminded herself, swallowing her bitterness. *I simply ain't Jessie Bingham.*

She caught her breath, and held it so she wouldn't cry out. When she thought of James, no stir of passion tightened her body, no urgency bid her hold him in her arms. There was affection all right, like for a brother or a good friend, but no strong heartbeat or racing, heated blood that would melt her natural, modest barriers in their marriage bed.

Who could not love James? All the girls in Mount Jackson said he was handsome, with his crisp black hair and strong mouth. He was respectful, kind, and willing to work long, wretched hours to advance a good cause. Over time he had seemed resigned to the fact that they would wed sooner or later. Who would not love James? *I would not.*

Ellen turned her head, slowly, carefully, breathlessly, so as not to wake Carl. She gazed at his stubbled cheek and jaw line, which filled her vision. She took a shallow breath, and looked for signs of hurt or suffering. His sleep seemed peaceful, undisturbed. All she could see of his unlined face convinced her that there was no pain today. He slept deeply, looking younger than his twenty years.

She inched her face back until she could see his eyes, finely chiseled lids rimmed with light lashes closed over eyes as blue as a Colorado afternoon sky. There was no pain in the hair-shadowed forehead, in the molded ears, in the sculpted nose, or in the slightly parted lips, full and chapped from the cold. There was no pain in his countenance.

Carl ain't James, she thought, *and James ain't Carl. I would love this man.* Ellen suddenly felt overwhelming peace come over her, and she allowed her hand to sneak up to cuddle his cheek. The stubble of his beard, which blurred the strong line of his jaw, was soft under her fingertips. His eyelids flickered, then opened. He was instantly awake, and his hand trapped hers against his cheek.

"Good morning, Ellen. You've a mighty gentle way of waking a man. Was I snoring?"

"No." He had hard calluses on his hand. "The sun is up. We'd best travel while the weather holds." She pulled at her hand and he released it. Her face coloring, she sat up. "It's still cloudy, and we've got a long ride." She shook off Carl's arm and stood up, brushing the wrinkles out of her skirt.

He grinned, looking up at her. "I reckon I'm rumpled and crushed, but you look like a bouquet of fall flowers, rich and red and full of spunk." Carl got to his feet. "I'll see to the horses."

஧

The clouds hovered low and dark, but the sun shone through enough for Carl to get his bearings as they started off. The plain shimmered white in the weak sunlight, the glare broken only by the dusky tips of sagebrush poking through the snow.

Sherando and Dun Baby struggled in the drifts, tiring easily from the exposure and lack of feed. Carl stopped often, rubbing the horses' legs to warm them.

They passed Carl's cabin in the late afternoon, and Carl saw Ellen's stealthy look at the house as they passed. *I'd give a nickel to know her mind*, he thought. *What does she think of me, after all I done that's hurt her feelings?*

The creek was slushy as they rode through, and Carl dismounted to wipe the horses' legs once more.

"It's a mile, mile-and-a-half to Rulon's" he said. He looked around at the darkening sky, mounted, and reached for Ellen's reins. "I reckon it's going to blow again. This time I ain't going to lose you."

Carl kicked Sherando up the side of the creek of the creek bed and onto the flat. He headed for the trees, pulling Dun Baby and Ellen along with him. The mare tossed her head and fought the lead, but settled down as she came into the shelter of the oaks.

Ellen tossed her own head. "It ain't even begun to snow. I could've ridden all by myself up to here."

Carl turned Sherando and eased him up to Ellen's side. "I ain't willing to take a chance on losing you to the storm again. I asked you to come out here with me, and I'm responsible for your safety. I don't take that lightly." He handed her back the reins. "There's a path through the trees. We can make it to Rulon's in a few minutes. I reckon Mary won't mind some company for supper."

"I'll be glad for a home-cooked meal. We didn't come prepared for camping-out."

Rulon's cabin looked solid and comforting when Carl and Ellen rode into the open a short time later. Smoke rose from the chimney, curling up into lazy snowflakes that now drifted down into the meadow from the leaden sky. Rod's cabin lay cold and frozen across the creek, snowdrifts halfway up the sides. Carl was glad of the welcome Rulon's home promised.

As they approached the cabin, a shriek sliced through the frozen air, and Carl drew his pistol.

"You wait here," he cautioned Ellen. "That sounds like a big cat, and it's inside the cabin." Carl dismounted, threw his reins to Ellen, and pushed through the snow toward the cabin.

A throat-rending scream came from the house, followed by Rulon's panicky voice.

"No, Mary! You can't! Not till Ma gets back."

Ellen flung herself from the horse. "Put up your gun, Carl. Mary's baby is coming." She floundered through the snow and pounded on the door. "Rulon, let me in. It's Ellen Bates."

Rulon opened the door and hustled Ellen into the room. "Thank God you're here. Tell her she can't have the baby yet, please, Ellen."

"Shush, Rulon. You're scaring her." She looked around and saw Roddy's big eyes peering from under the bedcovers where Mary lay, alternately moaning and shrieking. "Mr. Owen," Ellen exclaimed, "dress that boy and take him outside. He's big enough to help his Uncle Carl with the horses. You start a fire to warm your pa's cabin and stay over there. Send Carl back when he's done with the animals. I'll need his help."

Rulon followed her orders as Ellen approached the bed. "Hello, Mary. I've come to visit you. I reckon you need a mite of help."

Mary stared wild-eyed at Ellen, moaning as pain shot through her. "Ida? Where's Rulon?"

"Your man's gone on a little errand to the Owen's cabin," Ellen said, her voice soothing. "He'll be gone for a spell, but I'll be here, and I'll help you. I'm going to have a look around for some things I'll need. You rest easy, 'cause I'm right here." She took off the cloak.

You're Ellen Bates," Mary moaned. "That's Ida's cloak. I thought you was her." Mary took a ragged breath. "I can't last much longer. Two days I been a-laboring, and Rulon no help." She stopped to wheeze and pant, squeezing her eyes shut against the light of the fire. "He keeps bidding me to wait for his ma to come. Ellen, there ain't no waiting when the babe wants to come."

Ellen rummaged through Mary's trunk and found clean linens. She tore a sheet into pieces and brought the rags to the bed.

"I'll get water to wipe off your brow. I reckon you're thirsty, too."

"I ain't got time for being thirsty," Mary panted. "I can't hold back this baby no longer." Her voice rose in a wail of anguish.

"Mary, don't hold back. Let that child come." Ellen returned with the water, as Carl opened the door and stood in the opening.

"Rulon took over tending the horses. Said you wanted me here." He looked as though he'd rather be out in the storm.

"Carl Owen, you shut that door and come over here!" Ellen's voice was stern. She shoved the basin of water into Carl's hands as he tiptoed forward. "Wipe off her face, then sit behind her and hold her up."

Carl's chin jerked up, and he shot Ellen a look of pure horror. "I ain't climbing into that bed with my brother's wife," he whispered hoarsely.

"You hush and do what I tell you. I reckon she won't mind you more than a great lump of bedclothes. Get her onto the side of the bed. She should sit up to push that baby out." Ellen pulled back the bedcovers.

"You ever done this before?"

"I've helped my pa birth calves. I reckon it's the same, only smaller."

"Ellen Bates, I been through a war and across the country, but I never seen the likes of you before."

"I hope not," she muttered as Carl tended to Mary's dripping face. "Mary, before the next pain comes, try to get to the side of the bed."

Mary panted. "Ain't no time without pain." She inhaled, then stiffened and screamed into the ache and the agony. Carl flinched, set aside the basin, and turned to Ellen.

"Can you draw her forward?"

Carl nodded, his face blanched, lips pressed tightly together.

"Put her here onto the edge, get on the bed, and hold her up."

He gathered Mary up in his arms and lifted her to the side of the bed. Mary moaned. Carl let out his breath with a shudder and got behind her on the bed.

Ellen pulled Mary's bed gown up over her legs, and tugged it up around her waist. Carl squeezed his eyes shut. "Rulon's gonna kill me," he groaned.

"Hush up, Carl. Hold her tight." Ellen spread a towel on the floor below Mary's dangling legs. Carl held Mary by the shoulders, and she hunched forward, grunting. "You help, Mary," Ellen urged, holding Mary's legs apart. "Push that babe out. Don't give up yet!"

"I'm dying," Mary shrieked, pushing.

"No you're not," Ellen answered, kneeling on the floor. "You're giving life. Push again, Mary. I can see the head."

Mary obliged, her scream high-pitched and keening.

"Oh good. The head's out. Hold on, Mary, let me get the shoulders straight. Don't push!"

Mary panted, "I have to push."

"Wait, wait. Now, go ahead."

"Ohhh!" Mary gave a great push, bearing down with all her strength.

"Ah! Here's the babe." Ellen sighed. "You've done good, Mary." She wrapped the child in a piece of sheeting. "Carl, I need your knife."

Carl opened his eyes and dug into his pocket. He handed Ellen his clasp knife, which she opened and used to cut the baby's cord. She tied it off, then laid the child at the head of the bed. "Now one more push," she told Mary. "You've got to get the afterbirth out."

∞

Ellen looked up from washing the struggling infant. "You can go get Rulon now," she said to Carl.

He wiped his sweating face with his shirtsleeve. "Good. I need some air."

Ellen laughed. "You look like you think you did all the work. Look at Mary. She's wore out from two days of struggle with this lively little one. It's sure full of ginger."

Ellen dried the child, wrapped it up in fresh cloths, and carried it to Mary, who cuddled the baby and held it close as Ellen walked Carl to the door.

He put on his coat and looked down at the girl beside him.

"You're full of ginger yourself." He held out his hand to see if it still shook. It did. "Look at that. I'm all undone, and you're going strong." His voice filled with awe as he continued. "I reckon Marie couldn't do what you just done, and I'm almighty sure *she*... Ida couldn't. You stand mighty tall in my eyes, Ellen Bates." Then he bolted through the door.

∞

"It's a girl, Rulon," Mary whispered a few minutes later. "Look at all that hair. She's real lively, too."

"Ah, she's sure a pretty little thing. You give her a name?"

"I favor naming her 'Ellen'." Mary smiled.

"'Ellen Owen.' It sounds mighty fine, Mary. We'll do it."

Ellen got up from the fire where she was cooking supper. "No. Name the baby for your ma, or for Rulon's, but not for me. I ain't kin."

"You should be," Mary sighed. "Without your doing, I'd likely be cold and stiff by now."

"I just happened by. Name the baby for your ma or your sister."

"You can't deny me, Ellen. I can put your name to my child, and you can't do anything to prevent me. 'Juliellen Amanda Owen'. That's her name. It's right and fitting." Mary sank back on the bed.

"As long as you don't put my name up front, I guess I can't complain." Ellen shrugged and returned to stirring the pot.

Carl eased in from the night, accompanied by young Roddy. He beat his hands together and stamped his feet, sending a shower of snow onto the floor. The youngster mimicked him, then shed his coat on the floor and ran to his mother's bedside.

"It's snowing steady, but the wind ain't come up yet," Carl announced, bending to pick up the abandoned wrap. "I made us a bed up to the other house, Rulon. Best we leave the ladies here after supper. Is that agreeable?"

"That's fine, just fine." Rulon pulled Carl over to the side of the bed. "Come see my daughter. Ain't she a sight? We named her after Ma and Ellen, and Mary's ma."

Carl rubbed one boot behind the heel of the other. "You give her three names? Ain't that a lot for such a tiny girl?"

"We think Juliellen Amanda suits her just fine. Ain't she a pretty thing?" Rulon lifted the baby and turned to his son. "Roddy, look at them tiny hands."

"Pa, was I that puny?" Roddy ventured to put out a finger to stroke the baby's hand.

Rulon laughed. "I wasn't around when you arrived, youngster. I was off fighting for Jeff Davis and the Confederacy, so I got limited knowledge in that line. Ask your ma."

"Was I puny like that, Ma?"

"You were strong and fat, Roddy. But all babies start small."

"Why, Ma?"

"They start out little so they can grow, Roddy, just like you." Carl scooped up the boy and planted him on his shoulders. "See how tall you'll be one day? 'Course you got to eat all your supper to grow this tall." He carried the boy over to the table. "Let's help Miss Ellen lay the table, then you can start in on all that good food she's a-fixing."

Ellen turned and hid a smile behind her hand. "If you set that silver tongue to wagging, Carl Owen, you won't have no place in your mouth to put the food. Set the boy down and find the plates. I'll dish up from here."

"Yes, Miss Ellen."

She gave him a quizzical look, then turned back to the fire. Carl put Roddy off his shoulders and looked at Ellen's back.

The blaze of the fire backlighted her auburn hair, giving it the effect of a crown of flames. Silhouetted against the light, her slim form, moving with the rhythm of her arm, stirred up an excitement in his blood.

As if a burning coal had escaped from the fire and hit him in the pit of his stomach, fire spread up his chest and down his arms, leaving his fingers tingling, shaking. He tried to shrug off the feeling of burning that flowed through his blood, but he only remembered another time when he had felt this same excitement, at the bend of the river, where she had fallen into his arms.

The feeling built in him as he walked unsteadily to the shelf to get the plates, and lifted his feet as he walked the few steps to the fireplace. He put the plates on the hearth, not daring to risk touching Ellen's hand, and backed away to the table.

"Here, Roddy. Take the plates to the table when I fill them." Ellen looked at Carl. "I reckon your uncle's feeling faint. You'd best give him this first one. Rulon, come eat. Don't worry about Mary. I'll feed her while you men partake." She turned her attention back to Carl. "Are you feeling poorly? You look a mite strange."

"I feel . . . a mite strange," he stammered. Carl turned his head back toward his plate. "This food looks good. I didn't know I was so hungry."

"Well, you been through a mighty rough time for a man. I needed your help, or I wouldn't have put you through it." Ellen came to the table with Mary's plate. "I reckon I own you a right smart lot of thanks." She touched Carl's shoulder lightly as she walked to the bed.

He grabbed his shoulder where she had touched him, then let his hand fall to his side. "Let's eat, Rulon, before I lose all my strength."

"I'm going to say grace first. I got a lot to say thanks over."

୬

"Ellen?" Mary whispered in the darkness as Ellen slipped into the bed beside mother and baby.

"It's me, Mary," she soothed. "Try to get some sleep. You're all wore out."

"I just remembered something. Rulon told me Carl was going in to my pa's party specially to marry Ida." Her voice was sleepy.

"I guess that was his plan."

"Well, you ain't Ida."

"I ain't Ida."

"Are you two wed?"

"No."

"How come you to be here, and where's my sister?"

"She's still in town, fixing to wed some English fellow. Right in the midst of the party she broke the news to Carl, and he took it powerful hard. He asked me to go for a ride, and we got caught in the storm. That's what happened."

"He didn't seem to be pining any."

"He didn't get a chance today. He helped me birth your baby."

"Did he act better than Rulon?"

Ellen chuckled. "Some better, but not much. He was scared. I ain't ever seen a man so white in the face. But he stayed in here, and he did what I bid him."

"I'm glad it was you came with him. Ida wouldn't have been any help. She ran into a corner and hid when Roddy came along. I'm glad James let you come back with Carl."

"You go to sleep now, Mary." Ellen patted Mary's arm, frowning. "Good night."

"Good night, Ellen. Thank you."

Chapter 16

Chester Bates rode into the clearing at noon the next day.

"Ellen!" he hollered out. "Ellen Bates, where are you?"

Ellen's heart quaked as she opened the door of Rulon's cabin. "Pa!" she called. "Pa. It's good to see you."

"Daughter!" he yelled as he hit the ground. "Where is that young hellion? I'll shoot him. I swear it! If he harmed a hair of your head—" He craned his neck, looking around for Carl.

"Pa, shush now. Calm down. Stop shouting. Carl didn't lay a hand on me." She took his arm. "Please, Pa. Don't go to shouting again. There's a new baby trying to sleep."

"A baby? What're you saying? Who's got a baby?"

"Mary Owen had her baby. I birthed it for her. No, don't you yell none. Rulon wasn't any kind of help. I had it to do, Pa."

Carl came out of the woods behind Rulon's cabin with an armload of deadwood. He dropped it on the woodpile and strolled over toward the visitor. Ellen looked wild-eyed in his direction and took hold of her father's other arm.

"There he is!" Chester cried, struggling with Ellen. "I'll wring his scrawny neck, taking you off like that, without a 'by your leave'. Carl Owen, I'm calling you out!"

"Pa, listen to me. Carl, get away! Don't you come over here. Pa, don't you dare touch him! I went with him willing. He gave his word I'd come to no harm, and he's kept it. Pa, listen to me!"

Chester struggled again as Carl strode up and came to a halt before them, crossing his arms.

"You piece of trash. You ruined my daughter," Chester bellowed, spitting on the ground. He tried to reach his gun, but Ellen held him fast, desperation strengthening her arms.

"Mr. Bates, I ain't touched Miss Ellen. I own I acted a mite foolish to ask her to ride with me on such a stormy night, but I was awful muddleheaded then. You got a right to take a poke at me for being a fool, but I don't reckon you should shoot me. I wouldn't harm Miss Ellen to spite Ida Hilbrands."

Chester swore, then went limp. Ellen realized that the heat had gone out of her father and released him. He went over to lean on his horse, taking several deep breaths, then turned back to Carl.

"I been so mad at you, I even took a poke at your pa. I 'spect I lost my best friend, and my wife ain't so pleased with me, neither. Ellen, you ma says you have good sense. I hope you ain't let her down."

"Pa, I told you, Carl gave me his word of honor. He's a gentleman. You know all Rod Owen's sons are gentlemen. You told me so yourself."

Chester swore again. "You're the only child I got, Ellen. I reckon I worry overmuch about you, but daughter, this ain't your ordinary turn of events. Things are new and different out here, I give you that, but some things never change. A girl don't go alone with a man, not overnight. He done damage to your name, and it ain't going to be easy to wash it clean. I'm taking you home, now."

"I ain't going, Pa. I promised to stay with Mary till she's up and about. It's a duty I have, and I won't leave her."

Chester looked helplessly at his big, hard hands. "You got me between a rock and a hard place, daughter. I can't fault you wanting to do your duty, for I taught you myself to carry through on a task, but you got a duty to your own self, too."

"Pa, when I rode off with Carl, that was a task I was carrying through. He was hurting real bad, and he needed a friend." She stood in front of Carl, facing her father.

"That's my point, daughter. There's some will say he needed you to take advantage of. This is a compromising situation you got yourself into, right compromising, and no man'll want a wife with a smear on her name."

"That ain't rightly so, sir," Carl broke in. "I seen the pluck of your daughter, and what she can turn her hand to. I know she ain't done anything wrong, and I don't have to think twice."

He stopped short, face flaming. Looking down, he kicked a clump of grass that was poking through the melting snow. Then he shoved his thumbs into his trousers pockets, rocked back on his heels, and looked at the sky.

Chester and Ellen watched him, clearly fascinated, waiting for Carl's next words. Carl took his hands from his pockets and clasped them behind his back, then he spoke.

"I reckon if I've hurt Miss Ellen's name, I'm sorry for it. I don't know what James'll say in the matter, but I should have said this a long time ago. Mr. Bates, I'm seeking permission to court your daughter."

෪

Rod Owen was back, bringing his wife, his daughters, and Muriel Bates. As he passed Rulon's cabin, Rod spotted his runaway son chopping wood with a red, scowling face. Then, driving up to the front of his own house, he saw Chester Bates sitting on the bench outside the cabin, back to the log wall, smoking his pipe.

Rod pulled the horses to a halt and helped the women and girls down from the wagon box. They went into the house, after glancing at Rod and Chester. Rod let the animals blow a bit, while he looked the situation over. Rubbing his cheek, which bore a new bruise, he looked at his friend. "Well, Chester?"

"Well, Rod," the other man answered. He paused to puff the smoke from his cheeks. "You had the right of it. He laid no hand on her."

"He seems powerful vexed about something."

"He is."

"Well?"

Chester exhaled. "He wants my permission to court her. I told him nay."

"James will be along in a bit."

Chester squinted at Rod. "I figured he has a say in this affair." He hoisted one leg over the other. "Has he spoke his mind yet?"

"No, but his glower is as black as his hair."

"Well then, we'll have to wait to see if he still wants to marry her. If not, I can't just give Carl free rein, what with Ellen staying here and all."

"Hold on. Who says Ellen's staying here?"

"She does. She won't go home with me. Claims she owes a duty to stay here with Mary and the baby, to help her get back on her feet."

"Mary? Baby? What are you telling me, man?"

"She brought forth a girl."

"Julia!" Rod hollered, poking his head into the doorway. "Julia, we got a granddaughter! Wife! Come out here. Chester, who helped her along?"

"Ellen says she did. It appears she and Carl came along just in time to ease the child into the world. Evening, Julia." He nodded as she stepped through the door.

"Rod, I could hear you bellowing your lungs out, but I missed your message. What's the trouble?"

"Mary went and had her child whilst we was gone. Ellen played midwife. It's a girl-baby."

"Well!" Julia sat down on the bench beside Chester. "I never heard the like! Chester Bates, don't you go too hard on that girl. I say the Good Lord sent her along with Carl, to help out Rulon's wife."

"Seems she's a blessing to everyone but herself," he grumbled.

Three riders came from the trees. James was in the front, his horse lathered, followed by Clay and Albert.

"Rod Owen, I'm fairly burning to go see that grandbaby of ours." Julia rose to her feet and saw the young men approaching. "I'll set Marie to stirring up supper. You get the boys to put up them horses, so you can come over with me, if you've a mind to do so."

"Of course I'll come. You'd think I was a lump of clay." He winked at Chester.

⅏

James gave his horse the minimum of care before he loped across the bridge toward Rulon's house. Carl saw him coming, and swung the ax into the chopping block. He dusted his hands together and waited.

"You double-dyed yellow-back sneak thief!" James yelled. "I ought to thrash you right here."

"You and who else?" Carl returned, his face hardening. He fisted his hands, and stood waiting in a crouch.

"Just me!" James didn't waste time, but swung at Carl, who dodged away and jabbed at James's face. Neither man connected, and they circled in the yard, trading loud insults.

Julia stepped out of the door. "Carl! James! What's got into the two of you? Hush, now. There's a baby here."

The young men straightened from their crouches.

"What's this about?" Julia demanded.

"He sullied Ellen's name!"

"I ain't! Nothing happened between us."

"Worse, he wants to steal her from me."

"I want to marry her, yes I do."

"She ain't yours to marry. Find yourself another girl."

Piercing wails from the vicinity of Rulon's cabin interrupted the argument.

"Boys!" Julia was between them now, her hands gripping their arms. "This ain't the time or place to have a ruckus. Shame on the both of you. The baby was asleep until you woke her up!"

"Sorry, Ma." James bowed his head and compressed his lips. Then he turned to Carl with narrowed eyes. "This ain't over yet." His chest heaved.

"No, it surely ain't," Carl agreed in a growl.

∞

When Julia and Rod returned to their cabin, Marie was dishing up supper to the guests. James and Carl sat as far apart as possible at the table, apparently holding on to their tempers until they had eaten. Rod pulled Chester aside and asked, "Has James declared his mind to you yet?"

"No. He's eating first."

"The two of them was fighting up yonder." Rod nodded toward Rulon's place. "I been thinking, and I figure I've solved a problem or two. I'm going up Denver City way to find my brother-in-law and work in the mines. I'll take Carl and James along with me. Ellen can stay here as long as she needs to. Suit you?"

"That sounds fine. If they're away from Ellen, maybe they won't come to blows over her."

"Oh, I don't know about that," Rod said. He picked up a plate and approached the fireplace, and Chester followed. Marie ladled beef stew into their plates while Rod looked around the crowded room for a place to sit. Seeing none, he leaned up against the wall. "But at least Ellen will have some peace whilst she tends to Mary."

"Yes." Chester leaned on the wall beside Rod. "Maybe while she's during her duty by Mary her mind will settle on doing her duty by James."

Rod shrugged. "Time will tell. By the way, I asked Carl to let the men sleep in his cabin tonight."

"We'll be a sight different company than he expected to have tonight. Ida surely played him false."

Rod dug into his food with his knife before answering. "I knew she was flighty, but I thought he could handle her." He poked a chunk of meat into his mouth and chewed it before continuing. "I reckon it was more than he could do, from down here. That stormy weather was back luck all around." He shook his knife at Chester. "Mayhap the best thing Ida ever did for Carl was to throw him over for that stuffy peacock she's set to wed."

"We'll see," Chester said, shaking his head. "When James speaks to me, we'll know which way the wind blows."

"I don't think he'll have the chance. We're leaving in the morning."

∞

Denver City lay spread out between Cherry Creek and the South Platte, treeless and bustling. Log and mud buildings, some half completed, lined Blake Street where the business of the camp was concentrated. Some of the buildings were so hastily built that they seemed ready to fall down around the ears of the users.

Carl rode into town behind his father and two of his brothers. Rod dodged a freight wagon and edged his horse to the side of the road in front of a hotel. Rulon and James followed him, and Carl cut behind the stage once it had gone down the street. The men dismounted and tied their horses.

Pointing up the street, Rod wiped his face. "Rulon, you and James take that end of the street and Carl and me'll work this end. Ask after Jonathan Helm. Somebody's sure to have word of him. We'll meet back here for dinner." Then Rod entered the hotel and was gone.

Carl walked past the hotel front and ducked into the low doorway of a freight office. The clerk looked up at Carl's question and shook his head. "Jonathan Helm? No, but I ain't been here long. You'll have to ask the boss. He's out, gone up to the camps for the week. Sorry."

"Much obliged." Carl returned to the street and let his eyes roam down it, then strode into the next business.

"If he's been here since Fifty-nine, likely he's at the diggings west of here. I ain't heard of no man named Helm here in town," said the merchant.

The banker squinted at Carl over his spectacles. "Helm? No, that's not a name I recall. Try up the street at the assayer's place. Maybe Upshaw knows of him."

"Jonathan Helm? Wait a minute. Let me look in the records," said the assayer. He rummaged through some cards in a box, humming a tune to himself. "Was he a big man, with heavy shoulders and a black beard?"

Carl felt excitement stirring in him. "That's him. Ma last heard from him about Sixty-two, I reckon."

"Well, here it is." The man pulled a card from the box." I did this assay for him in Sixty-four. A mighty good one, it turned out. Yes, Jonathan Helm struck it rich up to Gregory Gulch. That's Central City, you know, the richest square mile in the world. But I haven't heard from him nor done another assay since this one. Likely there's plenty of back door rock-crushers who call themselves assayers up there, telling him what he's got."

"I'm mighty grateful for the information, Mr. Upshaw. We been following after Uncle Jonathan now for nigh on to a year."

"Well, good luck, young man. Just go on up to the north fork of Clear Creek. Somebody up there can set you back on his trail, I figure."

Carl dashed back up the street, looking for his father. He ran from door to door, poking his head in each one, dodging passers-by on the street until he located Rod.

"Pa!" Carl called into the dimness of a saloon. He started through the door in a rush, then remembered his manners and settled down to a walk to approach the table where his father sat with a small bald-headed man.

"Son, your feet will arrive ahead of your brains, if you don't have a care. I reckon you found out something?" Rod grinned over his hat, which sat on the table in front of him. "Sam Whitney here gave me a good lead, too. Sit down and we'll swap our news."

Carl pulled back a chair and sat on the edge of it. "The assayer says Uncle Jonathan's got a claim up to Central City, Pa."

"I reckon that's where we'll head after we noon, boy. Sam, this is my son Carl. Carl, Sam Whitney from the mint. He says Jonathan has been a steady supplier for a brace of years now. At least, the stuff Sam's been working with has come out of Jonathan's claim."

Carl took off his hat and nodded to the man. He turned to his father and said in a rush, "Shoot, Pa, can't we leave now? We ain't seen him for a long spell."

Rod chuckled. "My brother-in-law was a favorite with the young'uns back home," he told Sam. "I reckon that's the way it'll be out here, too. Boy, we got to gather up your brothers and have us some dinner. Go poke your head out into the street and see if you can spot 'em. The sooner we eat, the sooner we'll be on the road." Rod adjusted his chair. "And Carl, no—"

"I know, Pa." Carl cut him off and rose from the table. When he pushed through the door of the saloon, the light and uproar of the street engulfed him, and he looked around for Rulon and James.

After a moment, Rulon came out of a door two buildings down on the other side of the street. He saw Carl and waved to him, beckoning him to join him.

Carl stepped off the walk and waited on the edge of the street for a chance to safely cross. A party of horsemen trotted their mounts through the business district, leading pack mules loaded with supplies, presumably for their mining camp. Carl crossed after the mules had passed, and soon was at Rulon's side.

"Carl, you know them cartridges you shoot in your Spencer? They got a pistol in here that uses them same things instead of cap and ball. You load them in the back of the pistol cylinder, fire 'em off, then push out the casings and whang in another set of cartridges. Fastest reloading I ever seen in my life."

Carl grinned. "I had one in my hands, once. It's a marvel, all right."

"The gun is for sale, little brother. You got any of that money Rand paid you? I mean just kinda burning away in your pocket?"

"I was saving it to get a load of goods for when Ida and I—" He stopped, scowling. "Let's take a look."

Rulon led the way into the dark store. The pistols were on display in a glass case under the hardware counter. Rulon pointed to the Smith and Wesson at the back, and addressed the clerk. "Show my brother the cartridge pistol," he requested.

The clerk, a brown-haired man with an eyeshade, brought out the blued steel revolver and placed it into Carl's palm. "This is a mighty fine gun," he began.

Carl sighted down the octagonal barrel.

"You have six chambers, .32 caliber cartridges is what you use, and you can be sure it's a mighty fine gun for a man to have out here," the clerk continued.

Carl considered. "You got the cartridges?"

"Plenty. I figure to have a steady supply, now that the Army's fixing to clear up the Indian problem. I'm an Army supplier, you know."

"I didn't, but I reckon I'll take the gun." Carl looked at Rulon. "Maybe if you treat me right, I'll let you try it out from time to time." A slow grin cracked his face. He paid, shoved the pistol down into his waistband, scooped up several boxes of cartridges, and whistled his way to the door. When he stepped through, he stopped with one foot in midair and froze.

He swore gently. "I bet I'm in trouble with Pa," he said, slowly putting down his foot. "I just now recollected why I came out to get you. Pa's waiting back at the Blue Belle Saloon." He gestured with his head. "Could you—nah, I'd best look for James right quick, and you'd best scurry over and get washed up for dinner. Pa's anxious to ride soon as we get our bellies full." Carl walked down the street beside Rulon.

"What's the hurry?"

"That's what I forgot to tell you. Him and me both got word on Uncle Jonathan." Carl stopped in front of the saloon. "You go on in. I'll look for James."

Carl walked down the street toward the hotel, where he pushed his way next to his horse and loaded the shell boxes into his saddlebags. He patted Sherando, then continued down the dusty road.

He caught up with James on the outskirts of the town, where he was asking after Jonathan at the livery stable.

"Come on," he told James, his voice rough and his face set. "Pa's raring to get on the road. We got word about Jonathan. He's up north a piece, has some workings at Central City."

"Where's Central City?" James asked gruffly, waving his thanks to the stableman. He followed Carl back up the street.

"Northwest of here, at a place called Gregory Gulch. It's on the north branch of Clear Creek."

The brothers stepped around opposite sides of a wagon and entered the saloon, maintaining a polite distance from each other. Rod and Rulon sat at the table with Sam Whitney. As Carl and James came up, the man stood.

"I'll be going along, Mr. Owen. It's been a pleasure to meet you." He shook hands with Rod. "I hope you find Jonathan doing well. So long, boys." Sam retrieved his hat from the table, put it on, and nodding to the barkeeper, left the saloon.

Carl and James pulled out chairs on opposite sides of Rulon and sat. Rod looked at Carl, and a grin creased his beard. "Rulon says you got you a gun that shoots cartridges, same as a rifle. He says it's the coming thing."

Carl chuckled. "Up to date, Pa. A sure-thing, modern invention."

"Well, I reckon it's fine to keep up with the times, if you can afford it. Just now, I figure we should put something besides a pistol under that belt of yours. How about it?"

"Let's go eat!" Carl said.

∞

Central City was a raw, wide-open town set in the midst of scarred earth and muddy water. Devotion was offered to only one god here: gold was the ruler, and the offerings were single-minded efforts to acquire possession of it. Some of the worshippers spent their days wresting it from the soil; others made their prayers on the altars of whiskey-soaked bars in tents along the creek.

Here was a town built in haste. Tents and half-shelters answered the need for basic housing, with only an occasional log house thrown up by a miner with vision. Every man's energy was directed to his particular rectangle of ravaged earth. None was spared to build beyond a primitive level.

"Can you imagine Ma in a pesthole like this?" James wrinkled his nose in disgust. "I'm a dad-blamed fool if I ever take up mining as regular work. 'Taint fit labor for a horseman."

"Where do you reckon we should start looking for Uncle Jonathan?" Rulon craned his neck to take in all the sights of the miserable camp.

"Assay office ought to do it, I reckon," Rod said. He took off his hat and reseated it on his head. "Carl, see if yonder gent can direct us to the assayer."

Carl pulled Sherando off the trail and walked him up to a miner hurrying along in the same direction. "Begging your pardon, can you direct us to the assay office?"

The man stopped and pointed to a trail leading up the hill to the left. "Ye can't miss it. Last tent on the path, or so it was last week."

"Still lots of folks coming in?"

"Every day some new Cousin Jack comes over the hill." He spat into the dirt. "Ye haven't the look of miners."

"We're fixing to visit kin."

The miner laughed, expelling a hoarse, croaking sound. "That's a new story. Mighty original. Good luck." He hurried off, glancing over his shoulder at the four horsemen, as if he expected them to follow him with ill intent.

"Obliging fellow, but almighty suspicious," Carl reported. "The office is up the trail."

Rod kneed his horse up the path and the others followed. When the way became too steep for riding, they dismounted and led the horses, and Carl took the position of guide.

Another fifty yards up the path, they came upon the assay office, half dugout, half tent, burrowed into the hill at the trail's end. A mild breeze stirred the door flap as they walked up to it.

Rod called out, "Hello. Anybody inside?"

"Raise the flap and dump your sample. I can't get to it tonight," a raspy voice answered.

"No samples here. We want information. Do you have a minute to spare?"

A sandy-haired man with mutton-chop whiskers and a black vest over his shirtsleeves opened the tent flap. He looked around at the four men, then fixed his gaze on Rod. "Well?" he challenged.

"I'm Roderick Owen from down south of Pueblo City. These here are my sons. We've come inquiring for my wife's brother, and figured you'd be the likely man to know his whereabouts. His name is Jonathan Helm."

The man's face darkened. He put his hands on his waist. "You come a long way, but you're a week too late. His shaft fell in last Tuesday. They dug him out and replanted him in the graveyard yonder."

Chapter 17

Julia caught sight of the men just as they entered the meadow. They were leading a mule loaded with mining gear, and her heart began to flutter. Even at a distance, she could sense an air of dejection and pain in the slump of her husband's shoulders. Something was terrible wrong, and she counted the horsemen over and over to be sure there were four, all sitting their saddles. Her body steeled itself, back straightening, shoulders stiffening, as the men came nearer and she recognized Jonathan's leather strongbox strapped to the mule's back.

Then she ran toward the riders, clutching the over-sized wooden paddle she'd been using to stir boiling clothes. Her washing-day apron flapped in the wind of her hurry, making a whit-whit noise that momentarily distracted her from her goal. She stopped and glanced around for the source of the noise, then looked to where Rod was stepping wearily down from his horse.

She inhaled, sharp and short, dropped the paddle, and ran again toward the men, confused by how old her husband looked. Their sons drew the animals up beside Rod, shutting off the world with a semi-circle of horseflesh.

She was gathered into the strong arms she had missed this last month, and his beard scratched her neck as he engulfed her, burying his face in the hollow between chin and shoulder.

"Oh, Julie," he sighed.

"He's dead?" Soft, and low, and horror-struck.

"Oh, my girl." Rod turned, and with a look dismissed the boys, and they gigged their horses toward the house.

"It's not possible," she said.

Rod nodded.

"No!" she cried, and he held her, soothed her in the meadow as she sobbed.

She couldn't bear to look at the box, not for several days. Then Rod gently reminded her that it was hers, and that she should open it.

"I don't have the key. I left it on the mantle."

He carried it out into the yard and put in on the chopping block. Two shots from his .44 mangled the lock enough to pry it loose. Setting it before her at the table, he stepped back and waited.

Julia looked up at Rod. "He always took care of me, especially after Pa died." Her eyes brightened with tears, but she blinked them back and looked upon the box once more. "Ain't it strange? In all the years I didn't see him, I never missed him. I knew he was doing fine. Now he's gone, the hurt is powerful. Powerful." She sighed and gazed at the box, then lifted the lid.

A letter lay on a cloth, which covered the other contents of the box. Julia sighed again and picked up the letter. She glanced around at her family, took a deep breath, let it out, and broke the seal of wax that closed the flap of the envelope. The brittle wax shattered, falling onto the tabletop and into her lap. She paused for a moment, then removed the folded sheet.

"Dear Julia," she read aloud. "When Pa died, I worried myself sick about taking proper care of you, because you was such a dear little sister and I didn't want to go wrong. Then you went south for your cousin's wedding, which I thought was only for the summer, and somehow, overnight it seemed, you grew into a woman. Then you up and tied the knot with a fellow from down there in Virginia named Rod Owen. That was a shock to me." She paused to wipe her eyes with the corner of her apron.

"I had my reservations, but Mr. Owen's been good to you. However, I am still your big brother, so I'm leaving you a little something to remember me by. Lady Colorado yielded up her secrets to me, and I'm passing them on to you. The contents of this box are from my first strike, and it's all yours. Here's the deed and all, so whatever I leave in the hole is yours after I'm gone. Your loving big brother, Jonathan."

Julia removed the cloth from the box. Inside lay five leather pouches, tied up with rawhide laces. She lifted one of them, surprised at its weight, and put it before her on the table. With shaking hands she untied the laces and opened the mouth of the bag.

"Oh," she exclaimed. "I been complaining about toting this heavy box around with us. It's gold, Rod, and a right smart lot of it." She sat back in the chair, pulling the strings tight on the bag. She looked at it for a moment, then replaced it in the box. Looking up, she caught Rod's eye, and she gazed at him for a long time.

"I tell you what, Roderick Owen," she finally said. "You take this here gold, and you ride down to Texas and fetch you a herd of them long-horned cows. You drive 'em up here and learn how to take proper care of 'em in this new land, and you build you a cattle outfit. I ain't likely to miss the treasure, seeing as how I never knew I had one." She saw he was set to protest, and raised her hand. "That's my wish, and if I die tomorrow, I want it carried out."

8✺

Rod took a week to get ready, making doubly sure that Julia was serious about parting with the gold. She only said, "The Lord moves in mysterious ways," and refused to discuss it further, so he plunged into preparations.

Rulon, Carl and James were sent out hunting, while Clay and Albert chopped firewood and helped their father butcher the game and dry the meat.

"I ain't going to leave you here needing food," he told Julia. "I feel bad enough leaving y'all without a man for protection."

Julia smiled and patted her Sharps rifle. "I reckon I can still shoot well enough to discourage any prowler."

"That's so, but you keep a wary eye open. We ain't seen any of them Ute Indians I was told hunt up in these hills. Stay around close to the cabins whilst we're gone."

At the end of the week, early in the morning, Rod gathered his family for final instructions. He looked at the pile of firewood that Albert and Clay had split.

"I reckon we've provided for your needs, at least for a couple of months, but I'm nervous as a spring colt about leaving y'all alone. I can't say for sure how long we'll be gone."

He turned to his wife. "Take care to keep sight of the girls, and don't let Roddy wander into the woods alone. That boy's taken to straying like a pumpkin vine." He shook his head. "Check up regular on Mary and Ellen. I wish I could leave Rulon, but I need all the hands I have to move a herd the size I plan to buy."

"We'll be just fine, Rod. Don't you worry none about us. Get them cows up here safe and sound." Julia moved into Rod's arms for an embrace. He nuzzled her neck, then kissed her.

"I aim to go and come safely, woman. I know I got a lot to learn, but I ain't too old to acquire knowledge." Rod released Julia and stepped into his saddle, and his sons mounted up. Lifting his hand in farewell, Rod turned his horse and rode at a jog toward the south.

℘

Ellen watched the Owen men leave, then turned from the door of the cabin, hoping the dim light of the room was not sufficient to show her face. Mary had begged her to stay for company while Rulon was away, and Ellen had agreed, even though Mary was doing better, healthy enough to get up and share the work. Now Ellen knew that the days ahead would be lonely ones; she would not have all the work to keep her mind occupied.

She picked up the hairbrush her mother had brought with her things from Pueblo City, and began to arrange her hair for the day. The breakfast fire reflected off her locks as she brushed out the tangles, then twisted her hair into a coil atop her head. As she placed the last hairpin, she thought back to last evening, and the fierce light in Carl's eye as he insisted that Ellen walk with him to the creek.

"I've stayed away from you since I got back from Denver, not because I wanted to, but because I knew it was your pa's will," he said, face twisted and uncertain. "I'm going away again, and I got to say something to you. Please come."

"We'll need water for the morning anyway, so you just take the buckets and help me. Pa could not object to that."

She smiled to herself as a light leaped to Carl's eyes, and a grin spread over his face as he followed her in the near-twilight. She heard Carl whistling to himself as she approached the creek and sat down on a rocky ledge that formed part of the bank.

Carl hunkered down on the edge of the creek and dipped the buckets into the water. He set them out of harm's way, then settled down to watch the ripples in the creek as the water flowed over the pebbly bottom.

Ellen watched him from the corner of her eye. He looked determined, pursing his lips in thought as he gazed into the stream, apparently studying out what he had to say. He tossed a stone into the flow, glanced quickly at her, and directed his gaze again to the water.

When he began to talk, his voice was so low that Ellen had to strain to listen, leaning forward a little to catch every word.

"I ain't got much time, and I've got a lot to say. Reckon I'd best start." He looked around once more, then looked her in the eyes. "Ever since that night we had the dance on the river, and you fell into my arms off that wagon, I been mighty unrestful in my soul. I thought I had a girl to share my life. I was wrong."

He gulped once, then continued. "When I held you against me, and felt your heart a-pounding away, I knew I was a ring-tailed double fool for sticking with Ida. But I'd given my word, and I was stuck with Pa's choice."

He stopped a moment and shifted his weight. "After we went our ways to settle, I figured things would get better for me. I hoped I'd get some sleep, not have nightmares, what with all the hard work I was doing. I made my plans and built my house, and I got excited about getting wed. Then Ida took me by the tail and threw me out the door. I thought I was going to die, I was that prideful. But you were there, like a ray of light on a foggy morning."

He looked at her face, and she could see sweat beading his forehead, even in the chill of twilight.

"Shoot, I'm just going on and on. The important thing is, I got to see what a man rarely finds out before he's wed. You got a backbone of pure steel inside that soft form of yours."

Ellen felt her face burning in the evening darkness. She put a hand to her cheek. It was warm, and she knew she was blushing. Peeking back at Carl, she saw that he had stretched out on the ground on his side, with his elbow supporting his cheek, as though he were exhausted from the effort of talking.

"I ain't done," he whispered, and sat upright again, in one quick motion. "Now I got the freedom from Ida I need to court you, your pa says I can't call. He says only James has that right, and he ain't made it clear to your pa what his mind is. What I want to know before I go away for a couple of months is, do I have anything to look forward to on your account? If I can talk James into thinking he don't really want you after all, and then do whatever task your pa sets for me, are you willing for me to call?"

Ellen sat with her hands on her cheeks, wondering what to reply. Then she softly opened her heart to him as frankly as he had to her.

"Carl, I reckon I been willing for you to call from the day you plucked me out of the muddy street in Mount Jackson and cussed me from head to toe. I'll pray you can use that silver tongue for some good on James, and that my pa comes around to my way of thinking."

The last light faded, but Ellen knew Carl was still nearby from the deep breathing she could hear. Then she heard him stand up.

"I reckon that'll hold me for a couple of months," Carl said. "I'll carry your water to Rulon's."

She followed in the darkness, and he waited for her at the door, setting the pails on the bench. Then she was enfolded in his arms, and he embraced her tenderly as he whispered in her ear, "Ellen Bates, I love you!"

Then he was gone, his footsteps fading into the satin darkness.

Ellen shook herself free from the memory, then washed her face with the water Carl had dipped up the night before. Tying on her apron, she went to the fireplace and thrust another chunk of wood into the flames, for today he was truly gone, and the air in the cabin felt cold and damp.

The grizzled old man in the wide-brimmed hat shook his head. "I cain't figure how you aim to get them cows past the Comanches and Kiowas in the Panhandle. They'll grab up them cattle soon as they see you coming. You're a crazy man to try trailing cattle with the Indians all stirred up."

"I reckon that's my gamble. All I want is some hands willing to make the trip." Rod slapped his hand down on his thigh. "I always heard a Texas man was full of courage. I only need five or six fellers to prove me right."

The old man removed his hat and scratched his head, reseated his hat, and took a swig from the glass on the table. He looked Rod over once more, then nodded. "Then I reckon you need to see Bill Henry. He's got him an outfit looking to hire out, but work's mighty scarce around here. Well," he shook his head again, "work ain't scarce, but money sure is."

"What's his experience with these longhorn critters?"

"He's trailed them a good mite, and he's a hard worker. I'd say his bad luck is your good fortune."

"Where do I find him?"

"Ask after him down at the livery stable. His cousin will know how to get a-hold of him." Sucking on his yellowed teeth, the man looked once more at Rod. "Well, I wish you luck. And keep your eyes open for the Carpetbaggers. They come down here with some new law called 'Reconstruction', and they're 'reconstructing' the whole countryside into their own pockets. They's made laws agin any man who fit for Davis and the Cause. You tread light here in town."

"I thank you for the warning."

Rod took his leave and sought out the information he needed from the stable hand.

The quiet young man in the patched shirt shifted his feet. "Bill Henry? You say you got work for him? He'll be mighty tickled to hear it. Things ain't gone so well for him of late. He's coming in to town tonight, and I'll bring him up to the hotel about suppertime. We'll meet you in the dining room."

That evening, Rod and Rulon took a table in the back of the dining room and ordered steak and beans. Carl and Albert occupied the table beside the outer door, while James and Clay sat in a corner against the window wall, where they could see everyone who entered from the hotel lobby.

"Why does Pa want us all spread out like this?" Albert asked Carl before he wolfed down a bite of steak.

"He's a mite cautious, as usual. That old codger warned him about the laws down here. The sooner we hire on a crew of herders and light a shuck for home, the better I'll feel." Carl paused to spear a chunk of steak. "I hope this Henry feller can take the job. Being in a state where a man's got no rights makes me a mite cautious, too."

"Can them Unionists stop us from taking our cattle out of here?"

Carl spoke low. "I reckon them low-life carpetbaggers make up the rules as they go along, especially if they see a profit in doing it."

"I favor that Henry feller getting here with a powerful yearning to travel on with us. We come too far with Ma's gold to see any Yankees make off with the cows she bought." Albert sat up straight. "That there's the stable hand coming up the walk, and he's got another feller with him."

Bob and Bill Henry came through the door of the dining room, Bill brushing the dust of the road from his sleeves. He had light brown hair that curled over his shirt collar, and blue eyes that flicked around the room and settled on Rod, at the rear table.

From his seat two feet away, Carl looked over the powerfully built Texan. He wore a moustache that drooped over the sides of his mouth. His face, shaded by a hat with a wide brim, was brown and unseamed, and Carl guessed he was at least two years older than himself. Judging from the bulge of muscles in his thighs, he had spent most of those years on a horse.

The man spoke to his cousin in a low voice, "I reckon that's the fellow with the cows and no savvy on moving them. Let's go see what he has in mind."

∞

Bill Henry swaggered across the room like he owned the whole of West Texas. His cousin Bob followed after, and came up to the table as Rod rose to his feet.

Bob nodded to Rod. "Mr. Owen, this here's my cousin, Bill Henry."

"Sit down, gentlemen. Can I offer you supper?" At the nod of the young man before him, Rod waved in the direction of the kitchen. "Two more places at this table," he called out.

Bill Henry sat down, and leaned back in his chair. "I heard you're looking for a trail boss and some hands to move cattle." His blue eyes never looked over at Rulon, but gazed straight into Rod's.

"I bought a herd, something over fourteen hundred cows. I reckon I need help to get it to the Colorado Territory. I've raised dairy cattle all my life, but these longhorns are a different breed. I need a good man to show me and my five boys the proper handling of this herd. If that man was willing to stay up in Colorado and show us the rest of the beef cattle business, I reckon he'd be the right man for the job."

"You say there's six of you?" Bill tipped back his hat with one finger. "I know cattle trailing as good as any other man, and I know the rest of the business, but I ain't so sure about leaving Texas for good. I'm a Texas man born and bred."

"Well, I'm offering twenty-five dollars a month and room and board for the man who'll come with me and stay on to settle nearby. We got us a place of trees and meadows, grass a plenty, and water enough for all the cattle we can bring. You look like a canny man, and if what you tell me about yourself is true, you're the man for me."

Bill Henry frowned and sat up in his chair. "Seeing as how you're just come to Texas, I won't take that for insult. Out here we don't question what a man says he can do. A man's word is all he has, sometimes, and if he can't tell the truth about his abilities, he won't last long."

Rod grinned. "I thank you for not taking offense at my mistake. I reckon I'm still a little green around the edges, in spite of my gray hairs."

Bill cracked a thin smile. "You're a fair man to admit it. I figure you'll do. If your place is as green as you say, no offense meant, I could settle there while you learn the business."

"No offense taken. Do we have a deal?"

"Thirty dollars a month for me as trail boss, and twenty-five for the rest of the hands." Bill sat back in his chair and waited.

"Thirty for you?" Rod considered the matter for a moment, then shrugged one shoulder. "Deal."

"I reckon you bought horses? We'll take my cousin here as horse wrangler. I've got another prime hand in my outfit—Chico Henderson—and Sourdough Smith, who is a mighty fine cook, even if he is a little long in the tooth. Sourdough used to trap up in Colorado Territory, and he said he wouldn't mind seeing it again. We could use a couple more men, but if you're in a hurry, we can do it shorthanded."

"My boys are steady workers and fast learners, but if you think we need more men, hire them. We have to pick up the herd on Tuesday. Oh yes, I bought a hundred horses with the herd. I figure that should keep us mounted across West Texas and up the Pecos."

"You're not going through the Panhandle?"

"Too many Indians driving off stock up that way. We'll go the same way we came, through West Texas and up the Pecos in the New Mexico Territory."

"You remember coming through the Staked Plains? How do you figure to get cows across that desert?"

"As fast as I can. I figure we'll lose some there, but it's better than losing the whole herd to the Indians in the Panhandle."

"You're the boss, but I have my doubts about your choice of trails."

Rod's grin split his beard. A waitress brought two more platters to the table. "Like you said, I'm the boss. Get your crew and meet me at the Davis ranch early on Tuesday. Here's your food, boys. Eat hearty." Rod settled back in his chair and resumed eating.

℘

"I tell you, Berto, it's them same tenderfeet we laid for out of Kansas City, them as drove us off from that little camp in the crick. I'd know that old man anywhere." Willy took a long slug of water from the canteen. "'Course he didn't see me in the back of the room, but now that I shaved my beard, he ain't likely to know me anyhow."

"And this man wants to hire cowhands, you say?" Berto Acosta looked around at his henchmen and tossed his cigar into the fire.

"Jellico told him to look up Bill Henry, but he's only got that old cook and Henderson with him, and maybe his cousin. The tenderfoot's going to need more hands than that."

"Are the sons with him?" Acosta asked, stroking his scarred right cheekbone with his forefinger.

"I counted five."

"And the hot-head, he is one of them?" The Mexican's grin chilled Willy's heart.

"He's there."

"I wonder where is that girl he fought for?"

"I asked around. They came down from Colorado."

Acosta stood up and looked around the group. "*Amigos*, we have to make a little trip to Colorado, a business trip. Tilden, Dawes, you will go into town tomorrow and hire on with this man. You will get word to Willy at the saloon of when you leave and what route you will take. We will follow behind, and when the work is done, we will take the herd and have our revenge. And *amigos*," he threw back his head and laughed. "There is such a girl as you have never seen, a white goddess to enjoy, when the job is completed. It will be worth every mile!"

"That little dark-haired one is the filly I fancy," leered Rankin.

"I got first call on the one with the fight, that red-headed gal." Willy rubbed his chin. "I figure to tame her."

"If I got to eat trail dust and smell longhorns, I reckon I'll take a share," mumbled Frank Tilden, wolfing down his beans.

Pete Dawes ate a biscuit, his piercing blue eyes staring into the fire. When he had swallowed, he turned to Acosta. "Colorado's a far piece. You aim to get more than revenge out of this drive?"

"We will sell the herd after we take it from those tenderfeet. The cows will bring much money. There is more than pleasure to be had." Berto frowned. "You must gain their confidence. You must be trusted. Work hard, and do not complain. You will get a just reward, I promise you."

Chapter 18

Carl decided that riding drag on a herd of ornery, mean-minded, long-legged, slab-sided cows was the most punishing and dangerous job he'd ever attempted. Getting the long-horned critters used to the idea of grazing all in one direction took every bit of his concentration, and a good deal of muscle, besides. He saw why Bill Henry rotated the cowhands to different positions every day.

As they crossed the great dry desert west of Centralia Draw, the bitter alkali dust stirred up by thousands of hooves rose in clouds to choke the men and coat their bodies with briny white powder. Water barrels ran low, canteens were sucked dry, and thirst added to the cowhands' misery as they fought to keep the weaker cattle moving with the rest.

Bill Henry rode back from the head of the herd to speak with Rod.

"We won't bed the cattle down tonight. We've got to keep them moving toward the Pecos."

"The men are tired."

"It can't be helped. There's no water until we hit the river, and if you want to save your herd, you've got to keep them on their feet."

Rod let his breath out in a rush. "I'll tell the men back here."

"I'm headed up the other side to spread the word." Bill rode off, white dust following his trail.

ം

Later on in the day, the cows bawled and moaned for water. Their tongues, coated with the roiling alkali dust, lolled from their mouths. Their ribs began to protrude from sunken sides like the bars of a wrought-iron window grill, and the suffering of the animals caused friction to surface among the men.

"Hey, you're letting one get by you!" warned Clay, as a wild-eyed cow attempted to slip past Carl into the freedom of the desert.

Carl's nerves rebounded, and he drew his gun halfway from its holster. "That's my lookout, you half-grown busybody. Get along, or I'll clip your tail feathers for you," he shouted.

Clay's face blanched beneath the coating of alkali already whitening his features, and he wheeled his horse away around the herd.

Horrified at his demented action, Carl dropped the pistol into its sheath and reined in to remove his hat and knead the back of his neck. "Hush, them cows give me such a pain, I came mighty near shooting my own brother. And now I'm talking to myself."

He slapped his hat against his thigh, raising a billow of white. "I surely do wish I was back in Colorado, paying court to Miss Ellen, instead of pushing a bunch of cow critters down the trail."

ം

"Clay says he won't ride near you until we get over to the Pecos, son. What happened?" Rod's eyes skewered Carl's as they rode side by side at drag position that afternoon.

Carl took a small sip from his almost-empty canteen. "I don't reckon I blame him. If there's one man on the crew who's worse off than these cows, it's me."

Rod remained silent, and waited for more explanation.

"He was riding me about letting a cow through. I pulled my pistol and yelled at him. I reckon he worried I was gonna shoot him."

"We can't get our work done if we're fighting, Carl. You go—"

"I know, apologize to him." He bit his lip, then regretted the action as alkali hit his tongue. He spat, then took off his hat, smoothed back his hair with his forearm, and reseated his hat. "I suppose you want me to apologize to James, too."

"That would go a long way toward making peace in the family." Rod rode off a short distance and slapped the rear of a weary cow with a rope coil he held in his hand. "Hi-yup, there," he called, getting the animal started on the trail again before he returned to Carl's side. "I've found that a man's family needs to be peaceful to work well."

"Pa, I can't help that I fell in love with James's girl."

"Maybe not, but you can give her up with the same grace James showed about the Bingham girl."

"He carried on something fierce, as I recall." Carl attempted a grin, but noted that it didn't go over well with Rod.

"He got used to the situation and did his duty to court her."

"Pa, a girl don't want duty from her husband. She wants romance, devotion."

Rod's glare was chilling. "You mend your fences with your brothers, both of them."

Carl spat again. "Yes, Pa," he grunted, and hurried out after a steer, thinking, *I'll say I'm sorry, but I won't give up Ellen!*

∞

After three grueling days and three sleepless nights, the herd neared the Pecos, and the cattle, smelling water, stampeded. Bill Henry and the hands riding at point and flank tried to turn the lead animals in on the herd to circle them. By this time, though, the exhausted cows were unmanageable, and they broke through the shouting, cursing cowhands and continued toward the river. As they ran, their horns banged together, creating a din of clack and clatter. Then the drumming of their hooves crowded out any other sound, even the futile gunshots the cowhands fired off in hopes of turning the herd.

Carl watched in disbelief as the lead cattle disappeared from sight, bawling in fright as they galloped off a cliff.

"Owen!" Bill yelled at him from ahead. "Get down that bank! Use your rope. Don't let them pile up and drown!"

Carl was halfway down the slope before he realized it, yelling, whooping, driving his horse down the steep incline. He hit the water with a great splash, and gasped for air as it cascaded on top of him. Grinning at the liberation from dust, he whirled his rope and snared a cow thrashing on top of a yearling in the water. "Hiy-hiy-hiy," he hollered, dragging the cow off the other animal.

"Keep 'em moving to the other side," Bill called. "There's quicksand yonder."

Carl rode back and forth in the water with the others, yanking struggling cattle to their feet and hazing them to the other bank of the river. By nightfall, most of the cows had crossed the river.

Bill Henry called to Rod from the water. "Mr. Owen, hold up and wait for me!" He rode out of the river, then climbed off his mount and strode over to Rod. "Six cows are bogged down in the quicksand and they're likely goners, and about twelve drowned at the start, but that's a small loss, considering."

"Considering what?" Rod growled.

"Considering they stampeded in."

"Am I to be happy I lost any?" Rod stared down at his trail boss.

"You're to be happy your crew is safe and you lost so few cows. You will lose cows, Mr. Owen." Bill widened his stance. "I can guarantee that. My job is to keep the numbers low and try to keep the hands alive and well."

"Then you're doing your job," Rod slowly agreed. He nodded at the Texan and rode away onto the flat, where the cattle were finally bedding down for the night.

∞

Bill Henry held the herd in camp for a day, watering the cows until they'd had their fill before he gave the word to move them out again.

Two nights later, Carl rode slowly out to the herd, chewing on the last of his biscuit. He was to relieve James on night guard, and his nerves were taut. Earlier in the day, he had tried to speak to James, but his brother shrugged off the hand he'd placed on his shoulder, and walked away. Now he hoped James's weariness would work in his favor.

As he approached, he heard the twang of the jaw's harp as James played a song for the cattle. Carl made sure James saw him coming, and halted his horse in front of him. James continued to play until he came to the end of the song, then he lowered the instrument and blinked Carl's dust out of his eyes.

"Are they quiet?" Carl asked.

"All bedded down. They like the music." James sounded defensive.

Carl put out his hand. "Will you teach me to play that harp?"

James slowly raised his chin and stared long at his brother. He finally put the instrument into his shirt pocket. "I keep what's mine."

"I'm sorry things ain't smooth between us, brother." Carl dropped his hand, and brushed at his trousers.

"That's not my doing."

"I know, I know. I reckon I should have left Miss Ellen at the dance. I didn't, though, and James, I can't change that."

"You can leave her be." James's voice was husky.

Carl shook his head slightly. "It ain't as simple as that, brother."

"Sure it is. You just pull your heart out, cut it into strips, stomp it into the dust, and do your duty. I done it." James took off his hat and slapped it against his thigh.

"I don't want to do that."

James swore. "Then don't come to me with that thin excuse for an apology. You just tell Pa I didn't accept it."

"She wants me, James."

James swore again, kicked his horse away from Carl, and headed toward the campfire.

☙

By the time Rod Owen's slightly diminished herd of cattle came through Raton Pass and entered Colorado Territory, Carl had a collection of sixty-three rattles from snakes he'd shot along the Pecos, a wild mustang, and a healthy respect for Bill Henry and his instructions.

"That Texan knows his business," he told Albert, as the two brothers rode along at the drag position. "Who would have thought he could teach us to twirl a rope and grab a cow with it?"

"I reckon," the youngest Owen son answered. "I'm just glad to be back in the Territory." He raked at his tousled hair. "I want a good, long, hot bath." Albert looked at the dirty blond locks spilling over the neck of Carl's shirt, and the red-gold beard masking the front of his visage, and a slow grin stole across his mouth. "From the looks of you, you'd better hunt up a razor when we get back. You smell scruffy as a mossy horn steer, too."

Carl rubbed his bushy beard and grinned back. "I reckon when a man's busy night and day, he has a right to grow himself a little face hair. As to smell, you don't take no first prize, little brother. When Ma catches a whiff of you, she'll plunge you into the wash kettle so fast you won't have a chance to get your clothes off first. 'Course, that'll save her some time and labor, having you wash your own filthy clothes at the same time you scrub your hide."

Albert's tanned face reddened. Grasping at a straw, he countered, "Well, you better have yourself a bath before you go a-visiting, or Miss Ellen will catch the first freight wagon back to civilization and take her chances with them rowdies we scared off back on the plains."

Now Carl colored, and rode off after a lagging cow, thankful for the action to divert his mind. He'd tried not to spend much time thinking about Ellen, because the memory of her face brought up the remembrance of Chester Bates refusing his proposal.

"James has the right to say yeah or nay whether he'll marry Ellen. You don't hold any cards there. You're not to speak to her, nor come near her in any fashion, until he plays his hand. If he won't marry her, you still have to wipe clean the blot you've set against her name," Chester had said, blue eyes drilling into Carl's. "You prove to me that you're a man of honor, then I'll consider giving my leave for you to court her."

As he swung around the heels of the cow he'd set after, Carl acknowledged to himself that he'd been a bit callous in observing that ban when he spoke to Ellen the night before he left, but now a great joy surged through him as he remembered her reply to his frenzied speech.

"Ha, ha, ha, ha-a-a!" he cried out, throwing his hat into the air. The cow he'd been following shied away and started toward the herd at a lope. Carl laughed again and trotted the horse back to retrieve his hat, bending far down to pick it out of a patch of Spanish bayonet. "Ellen wants me to call," he shouted to the hills. "**Ellen wants me to call!**" He gave another great whoop, then started after the moving herd.

℀

"I heard quite a commotion back in your neck of the woods today," Bill Henry remarked around the fire that night. "Did you happen across some loco weed out there?"

Carl grinned and shook his head. "Uh-uh," was all he said.

Clay looked up from his plate, chewing his food. "I reckon he's fired up about us being back in Colorado. He thinks he's got a girl waiting for him." His voice was light and bantering. "I think she'll take one look at that set of fox tails he's got stuck on his cheeks, and she'll walk right into my arms." He ducked his head as the men around the fire laughed.

Carl wiped his knife blade on his jean trousers leg and stood up. "I reckon there ain't nothing wrong with a red beard, 'specially since it matches the color of her hair so nice."

Rulon looked up from scraping his plate. "It's a good thing James is out with the herd, Carl." He stood up and dumped the plate into the cook's washtub.

"James don't scare me," Carl retorted. "He'll come to see things my way, by and by."

"I don't think you should sell James short, brother." Rulon wiped his hands on his trousers. "He still claims Miss Ellen's hand."

"Well, I claim Miss Ellen's heart!"

∞

Frank Tilden rose and put his dinnerware in the tub. Nodding to the others, he strolled over to his horse and mounted it, then moved off in the direction of the herd. After a few minutes' ride, he came alongside Pete Dawes, who—with James on the far side of the herd—was holding the cattle while the others ate.

"Go in and eat, Pete. No, wait a minute." Tilden took out a tobacco pouch and prepared to roll a cigarette. "They're all joshing Carl back there about his red beard. He says it's the same color as his girl's hair. She, I gather, is also under the claim of the black-haired brother. I thought the boss was going after some yellow-haired dame that's supposed to be Carl's girl." He licked the cigarette paper and carefully pinched it together. "I get a piece of that red-head when we've finished off the men, if I recollect rightly."

"I do recall your saying so." Pete's voice was quiet in the darkness. "There's a dark-haired one, too, ain't there?"

"That's Marie, the old man's daughter." The cigarette between his lips muffled Tilden's voice. A match flared in the night.

"I'm partial to dark hair," Pete said, sniffing. "I earned it, too. Trailing cattle ain't my favorite occupation."

"You'd rather plug Rebels full of holes, eh, Pete?" Frank laughed.

"Don't even have to be Rebels." Pete sat his horse in silence for a long time. "Just anybody I don't like." His saddle creaked as he shifted weight.

Frank felt a chill scurrying along his backbone, raising goose bumps. He hurried to change the subject. "You figure Berto's out there behind us?"

"He said he'd be there, didn't he? Berto don't tell no lies. I reckon he's going to close the noose pretty quick now. You look sharp, and don't get caught sleeping when he comes down on this bunch of high-thinking Rebels." Pete rode off toward the campfire.

∞

When they had driven the herd past Edward Morgan's farm down on the Cuchara River, Ed and his sons had come out to meet them, and to keep the cattle out of the young corn crop. Tom Morgan told Rulon that Ellen was still up at the Owen's place, and Rulon passed on the information to Carl.

"I ain't seen her for such a long spell," he said, coughing on the dust the cattle raised from the prairie. "I'm almighty scared I'm going to take her right into my arms and hug her to pieces without asking her pa's leave."

"Not to mention, James's," Rulon said wryly.

Carl shrugged, and spurred his horse after a hungry cow trotting off toward Ed Morgan's field.

∞

"I have a meadow picked out on the flank of the mountain," Rod said at dawn in the final camp near the homesteads. "It connects to another one higher up, and there's plenty of grass and water. We'll drive the cattle back in there and they'll pretty near take care of themselves all summer. That's good, because we've got plenty of work and lots of building to do down at headquarters."

Rulon nudged Carl. "Pa likes that word, 'headquarters'. He ain't called the cabins anything but that since we got back this side of the Colorado line. I reckon he's got a dream again."

Carl laughed. "He can dream all he wants as long as we got the muscle to bring it to life. I don't take no offense. I reckon I dream a mite myself."

Rod took the lead and showed where a game trail led through the trees toward the meadow he had in mind. All hands fell back into position around the herd, driving it along the narrow trail and preventing cows from breaking loose into the brush and trees.

Riding at flank position well back along the side of the herd, Carl found that keeping the cattle from wandering into the trees was hard work, and it left him little time for thinking how close by Ellen was. He turned the brown gelding he was using that day toward a cow bent on escaping through the underbrush. The horse cut off its route, and the cow loped back to the herd, bawling in protest.

"Brownie, you're one good cow pony." Carl patted his mount. "Let's get that steer up there."

Ducking under the overhanging limb of a juniper, Carl and the brown horse went after yet another errant steer.

๛

Marie looked around, peering through the berry-laden bushes as she popped a blackberry into her mouth. "Where's Julianna? " she asked Ellen Bates. "Has that girl wandered off again?"

"I haven't seen her since we moved into this gully. I reckon we'd best go back and find her." Ellen craned her neck to examine the brambles through which they had come.

"Oh, let her find us. I'm tired of coaxing her to keep up."

"Marie, what if the Indians get her? Your ma will have our hides. Besides, we've got enough berries for the pies."

"Well, we have come pretty far today. You're right. We'd better go back." Marie turned to un-snag her apron from a bramble, and smoothed it down over her skirt. She straightened up and tugged her sunbonnet into place, then turned again and looked toward her friend.

Ellen stood in front of a big black horse, her hands pinioned behind her back. The scruffy, thickset man who held her covered her mouth with his massive hand. Ellen struggled, and her abductor laughed as the berries in her pail scattered on the ground.

Marie screamed, and the cry echoed back, bouncing on the walls of the canyon. A heavy hand clamped over her own mouth, and she tried to bite it, but the man only let go and slapped her across the mouth. She fell, scraping her arm on a rock as she went down. She screamed again, and the man reached down and yanked her to her feet. He turned her roughly around and tied her hands, laughing.

"Go ahead and scream till you're blue in the face, girlie. Ain't nobody out here to give a listen. 'Course, if your noise gets on my nerves, I'll slug you again." He tested the security of his knots, then whipped her around and leered at her, sunken blue eyes beneath shaggy eyebrows looking her up and down. His dirty brown hair hung to his shoulders, matted and tangled, and his beard was stained with tobacco juice and old bits of food.

Marie choked back her next scream, almost retching at the sight of her attacker.

"Rankin, you gag her up. No telling how far those cries will carry in this still air. We ain't far enough behind them riders to take a chance." Willy held his hand over Ellen's mouth, and he grinned at her as he let go. "You cry out and you'll get the same treatment as your friend. I ain't opposed to taming you good and proper, you little wildcat."

He tied Ellen's hands, then stuffed a dirty neckerchief into her mouth and shoved her toward his horse.

"We're going to take a little ride," he chortled. He mounted his horse and hauled Ellen up into the saddle in front of him. Rankin pushed Marie over to his horse and stepped into his saddle.

"You let loose a peep and I'll yank out your hair," he threatened the terrified girl. Then he bent down and jerked her up into his filthy arms.

Julianna scrambled behind a boulder as the men rode out of the ravine with their captives. She watched, breathless, as they passed three feet in front of her hiding place, saddle leather creaking with the added weight of the two girls. In silence she waited, long agonizing minutes until she was sure the men were gone, then she crept out from behind the rock and set off for home, running as best she could down the hills that lay in her path, heart thumping, pounding, choking up into her throat.

She heard riders coming behind her, and she darted into a clump of trees, hoping they hadn't seen her yet. Trying not to breathe aloud, she gulped air, waiting for them to capture her. Then, as they came alongside her place of concealment, she recognized the men, and cried out, "Papa, Papa! Help them! They been carried off!"

Chapter 19

"Julianna! Daughter, you're a welcome sight." Rod reined in his horse as his youngest child dashed from behind the tree. "You're not out here alone, are you?" He dismounted, and Julianna flung herself into his arms, sobbing.

"Oh Papa, they been took away." She burrowed her face into his chest. "We was picking blackberries, and two mangy old men came up and grabbed 'em. I heard 'em screaming and I hid when they went by. Oh Papa, you got to go after 'em!"

"Whoa there, Jule. Who got took?" Rod tried to calm the hysterical child.

"Marie and Ellen. They took 'em up toward the mountain." She waved her hand toward the looming Greenhorn.

Carl blanched and wheeled his horse back the way they had come, and James followed closely behind him.

Rod boosted Julianna up onto Albert's horse. "Clay, Albert, take your sister home. If there are only two of them acting so bold this close to the headquarters, there's likely more around somewhere. You stay there and see that your ma's safe."

Rod mounted his horse as his two younger sons rode down the mountain with their sister. He motioned up the trail with his head, and spoke to the others. "We'd best catch up to the boys, or they'll have the whole situation arranged without our help." Rod rode off in the direction Carl and James had taken.

Tilden looked at Dawes. Pete nodded his head in the same direction. "Let's go." They followed Rod and the other riders up the trail.

છ

Carl drew rein in the blackberry canyon. Ellen's pail lay in the path, contents scattered and mashed into the dirt.

"They took them here, but they didn't linger," he told James through tight lips.

"We'd best wait for Rulon. He's the best tracker of us all."

"I'm good enough to follow these hair-bellied four-flushers. I ain't waiting for Rulon. They've got Ellen."

Carl alighted from his horse and fingered the hoof marks left by the kidnappers' horses. "Only one bug has scooted through here. They ain't been gone long." He stepped into the saddle. "Come on, James. Let's get them scoundrels."

James checked his pistol load, and made sure the rifle was secure in the saddle scabbard. "How are your firearms?" he asked Carl.

His brother drew his pistol and spun the cylinder. "It's full but for one chamber." Turning in the saddle, he loosened the flap of a saddlebag and removed the Smith and Wesson. "This one's ready to go. I keep all six chambers loaded, just for varmints." He tucked it down behind his waistband, then checked the rifle in his scabbard. "We'd best get a move on," he said, frowning. "Every minute their lead gets longer." He put spurs to the horse's flanks and followed the trail out of the canyon.

Heading south, he skirted the boulder Julianna had used for cover and picked up the tracks of the abductors. James came behind, and they took the trail leading upward, into the pine forest, then past a deep canyon that reached back up the mountain. The trail forked, and Carl took the branch that stretched into the forest, where the path soon lay under a thick layer of pine needles.

"I lost 'em," he sputtered, and circled his horse back to cast around for the tracks. He glanced up and saw his father and the other riders coming through the trees. "Well, here's Rulon's chance to go to work," he muttered.

When Rulon was in hailing distance, Carl called out to him. "I lost the trail. You been tracking?"

Rulon grinned. "Does a red hound have fleas? You missed a turn back yonder. They headed straight into the canyon. I reckon they know you're following them now."

"Where they going? We ain't been on this section of the mountain."

Sourdough Smith, the cook Bill Henry had brought along, turned over the lump of plug tobacco in his cheek. "I reckon they're heading for an old cabin up there, below the crest of the ridge. I done some trapping through here, years ago." He spit a stream of tobacco juice into the brush. "I reckon I can still find it, if you want me to take you there."

"You find it," Carl said. "I'll be right behind you. Nobody but a lowdown snake abuses a woman where I come from."

Rod looked around at the riders. "I know I'm not paying soldier's wages, but who will stand with me and my boys to get those girls back?"

Bill Henry said, "Down in Texas, we go after scum like that for free." He turned to the others. "Any of you want to stay behind, you're declaring yourselves in favor of snakes and lowlifes."

Pete Dawes looked around at the sober-eyed Owen men. "Well, I shoot any snakes I come across," he said, spreading his lips open across his teeth.

"I ain't in favor of no lowlifes," grunted Frank Tilden.

Chico Henderson checked his revolver. "Let's go."

"You got my gun," added Bob Henry.

Sourdough led off, up the canyon on the left side, the rest of the riders following him on the dim trail, one by one, riding with their rifles loose in their scabbards and their eyes scanning the way ahead.

Carl felt a prickle in the hairs on the back of his neck. As he changed directions on a switchback in the trail, he muttered to Rulon, "I don't like this. We're all exposed on the face of this wall. If they're laying for us, they can pick us off one at a time, and us with no cover."

Rulon nodded. "Keep your eyes peeled when we top that ridge."

The canyon wall was steep, and the horses were winded by the climb as they approached the lip of the cut. The ten riders edged cautiously into the open on top, and moved quickly into the shelter of the forest.

Sourdough pointed through the trees in the direction of the summit. "We've got a right smart way yet to go. Best we let the horses rest a while." He dismounted, and his horse shied against Frank Tilden's mount.

Tilden's horse reared, but the man kept his seat, cursing the cook. "I don't ride with rum-soaked, broken-down old codgers. Here's yours."

He drew and fired at Sourdough, but the horse turned as he pulled the trigger, and his bullet struck Bob Henry in the chest, knocking him off his horse.

"You stupid oaf," cried Pete Dawes. "Can't you do anything right?" His gun was out, and he shot Chico through the left shoulder. "Damn, you got me doing it now," he shouted, firing at Rod as he turned his horse to flee. His last shot also went high, and opened a furrow across Rod's skull. Then he was gone, and Tilden with him, and three men were down, their blood soaking into the pine needles.

Carl and Bill Henry started to ride after them, but Rulon called them back.

"Let them go. I reckon I'd druther have them in front of me than behind, now that we know the set of their minds."

James and Sourdough bent over the injured men. Bob was the worst hit, struggling to breathe, fighting the pain of his shattered chest.

Bill went to his knees and looked at the gaping hole in his cousin's body. "Lie still," he growled, his face working. "You're going to pull through."

"Ah, Bill," Bob coughed, choking on his own blood. "Be sure they bury me in a patch of green. I never could abide the dust in Texas."

"Don't you go!" his cousin cried out, but Bob never heard him.

James stuffed moss into the hole in Chico's shoulder. "It missed the bone, tore up the muscle, then came out the back, so you won't die of lead poisoning," He untied Chico's neckerchief and used it to bind the wound. "We got to get you off this mountain and down to Ma. She can clean you up better." James looked around at Rulon and Carl, who were tending to Rod's wound. "How's Pa? Can he ride?"

"It's deeper than I first thought, but if he don't pass out, he's tough enough to make it." Rulon helped his father to his feet. "Dizzy, Pa? This fight's over for you. You need to get Chico down where Ma can put him and you to rights."

Rod shook his head to clear it. "I got to what?" he asked, obviously confused by the bullet crease on his head.

"Go home, Pa. We lost Bob. Take his body down home. Ma will patch you up."

"I should have had more sense," Rod muttered, seemingly getting his thoughts straight at last. "Them eyes always had something in them I didn't like." Drying blood covered one side of his face.

Rulon brought Rod's horse over to him and helped him to mount. James had Chico in the saddle and handed the reins to Rod, then patted the neck of Chico's horse. Carl tied the reins of Bob's horse onto Chico's saddle while Sourdough and Bill secured the blanket-wrapped burden of Bob's body across his horse.

"Don't stop until you get home, Pa," said Rulon, slapping Rod's horse on the rump. The animal started down the trail.

"I hope Chico can stay on that horse," James said. "He's lost a passel of blood."

"He'll do," said Bill. "He's got sand in his craw."

Sourdough was up on his horse. "That cabin's still a good piece distant," he reminded them. "We need to ride to catch them fellers before nightfall."

Carl's blood boiled him up into his saddle as he remembered that Ellen was in the hands of men like Dawes and Tilden. "I reckon the odds are getting well-nigh even now," he shouted. "They got four, and we got five."

"We know about four," Rulon corrected. "The way Dawes and Tilden chewed up the trail, I can't tell if anybody else has been along this way."

Sourdough led off again, Rulon beside him to check the trail, and the other three came in a bunch behind. The horses were rested, and they made good time, climbing the gentle slope of the mountain through the pines and firs that girdled its higher reaches.

Three hours before nightfall, Sourdough called a halt.

"That cabin ain't but a half mile or less through them trees," he said. "It's partly a dugout into the side of the mountain. We'll surround it easy, for there ain't but one way in, but they've got them girls, so they have a fair hand of cards, too. What you might call a Mexican standoff. When dark falls, we can get in real close, but if we go to shooting, we might hit them girls."

"Best we sneak on up there and have a good look," Bill said. "Can't harm nothing to know how the ground lies."

Dismounting, they picketed their horses in a protected hollow where they could graze, took their rifles, and set out on foot.

Rulon saw the cabin first, its log front protruding from the side of the mountain, and reached out to tap Carl on the shoulder.

"Yep," whispered Carl, crouching behind a pine trunk.

James came silently behind them, and whispered, "Where do you think they put their horses? I went a piece to the right, and there's no cover close in big enough to hide four horses. They ain't in the woods, or we would have heard them."

"I reckon if I was them, I'd want my horse close by," Rulon reasoned. "We'll circle to the left and check. The mountain ain't swallowed them up."

Sourdough appeared behind a neighboring pine. He glided over to join the three brothers.

"That cabin's weathered some since I was last here. The roof's in bad shape. Another storm will knock it down, and then the front wall will fall in." He looked back toward the cabin and spotted a rifle barrel poking through the front window. "I reckon they know we arrived."

A bullet whanged into a tree behind them, and the four men ducked into the brush, spreading out to cover the entire front of the cabin.

"Ah ha!" rang out a cry. "We have meet again. And this time you will not have the good luck."

Carl's stomach churned. "It's Acosta," he exclaimed. "I should have finished him off back in Kansas City."

"We should have ground his bones on the prairie," James responded, gritting his teeth.

"I must thank you for the gift of these lovely young *muchachas*, but where is the other one, the *diosa blanca*? I have been yearning to pay my respects to her."

"Yearn away. She couldn't make the trip," Carl yelled, and moved back from his position.

Another slug whipped through the air, barking the tree where Carl had stood. "He can shoot," Carl whispered from his new bush.

A twig snapped off to the left, and Carl swung his rifle to cover whoever was approaching. After a moment, Bill's head moved into view, and he hissed, "Stand easy. It's me."

He motioned for the men to join him, and they all moved out of rifle range to confer. "I been scouting on the left, and there's no sign of their horses." He paused a moment, puzzlement twisting his face. "I heard a whinny once, but I'll be switched if I could locate them." He glanced around at the other men. "Any luck on the right?"

"Nothing," James answered. "But we know who's in there now. Feller by the name of Berto Acosta. We tussled with him back in Kansas City on our way out here."

"Berto Acosta? He's got a black name in Texas," said Bill. "Cattle thief, stage robber, murderer: he's done it all. I wondered where Dawes and Tilden blew in from. It pains me to find I hired a pair of spies and murderers." Bill scowled and looked fiercely at the old trapper and the brothers. "I got a bullet with Tilden's name on it. Don't you forget that. When the time comes, he's all mine."

Rulon rubbed his cheek with his left hand. "Sourdough, you stay in that cabin long? When you was trapping?"

"Two winters I holed up there. But I didn't just trap. When I had nothing to do, I'd take a pick and do some hacking against the back wall. I'd heard tell there was a vein somewheres, but I never found it. I must have moved three ton of rock out of there for my trouble, but nary an ounce of gold did I find."

"And folks stayed in there since then?"

"Before and since. Folks have been moving up and down through these hills for centuries: Indians, Spanish, trappers, and prospectors. I don't know how old the cabin is, but over the years, many a body's bound to have stumbled onto it and put it to use."

Rulon could barely contain his excitement. "You reckon one of those bodies could have dug clear through the hill? Made a back door?"

"There was a bear's den over yonder. I left the old she and her cubs alone." He ran his fingers through his white thatch of hair. "If some feller with more brawn than brain camped in here long enough, he could have tunneled through to the den. They could keep horses in such a tunnel."

"It's coming on dark in an hour or so. Now's the time to find that den, or cave, or tunnel." Rulon turned to Bill. "Take me over to where you heard the whinny. If there's an opening, we'll find it and see if it connects with the house. Carl, you and James go to shooting from different positions, to make them think we're all out here. Sourdough, you go to the right and give them a cross fire. If Bill and me find a back way in, you'll know it by the commotion. Give them a rush when you hear us blast our way in."

"I thought this was my fight," Carl growled.

Rulon thumbed his nose with his knuckle, and put his other hand on James's arm to keep him still. "I figure we three got equal shares in it, seeing as how it's our sister over yonder. And Bill has a stake because of Bob. Sourdough knows this place." Rulon looked around at all the men, then addressed Carl again. "Your job is to get in there with these two and fetch the girls out when Bill and me stir up a ruckus."

ℂ

Waiting was pure agony. Carl bellied down in the pine needles and crawled to a fresh position from time to time before he sent a bullet singing into the hill above the cabin roof, but the time he spent waiting for return fire and for Rulon's diversion was time spent chewing his cheeks in frustration.

James scooted around in the woods to his left, shooting above the roof each time he moved. Carl wasn't sure where Sourdough was, but he knew the old man was somewhere on the right, shooting occasionally, and waiting for the ruckus Rulon had promised.

After his third shot at a dead branch overhanging the roof, Carl noticed that the debris knocked off by his bullets wasn't collecting on the shingles. It disappeared each time, dropping into the cabin.

"James," he hissed, when next James came close. "Look at this." Carl threw lead into the dead branch, and a chunk dropped into the hole. "I'll wager I can get up above there and drop through that hole into the cabin."

"Yup, and wind up looking like a piece of Irish lace. That's a sure way to an early grave. You keep down here and do what Rulon told you."

"But if I'm up there, I can see down into the house, and find the girls. Then we won't go in blind. It's a good plan, James, and I aim to try it."

"Where am I supposed to shoot if you're in my sights?"

Carl pursed his lips for a moment. "Sometimes I get the idea you would favor putting lead into me," he said, and compressed his jaw. "We don't see eye to eye anymore."

"I don't stoop to murder," his brother growled.

Carl nodded. "I'm mighty thankful for that," he said, then slipped into the forest to circle around.

Moving warily, in case there was a guard in the forest, Carl crept through the pines, avoiding the sticks that littered the brown pine-needle carpet beneath his feet. Turning south, he walked toward James's left, edging toward an arc of brush that might afford cover to his scramble up the slope.

He stopped at the edge of the clearing and glanced back at the cabin. The window on this side would show a fine view of him when he dashed into the open. He hesitated, and then James fired a volley of shots above the roofline.

"Thanks, little brother," Carl muttered, and ran, doubled over, into the clearing as answering shots thudded around James's position.

Carl hit the rise of the mountain going full blast, and his momentum carried him up the first ten feet. Then he flattened out on his belly, scooting the Spencer ahead of him, aware that his movements could be sensed through the thin brush between him and the cabin window. Being careful not to scrape the barrel and action along the rocks, Carl moved first the rifle, then himself, up the steep, rocky hill.

To get above the cabin, Carl saw that he would have to swing out onto a crumbling ledge above a sharp drop. The ledge gradually rose about fifteen feet before it angled down toward the roofline. There was one spot where he could probably be seen from the window, before he got high enough to be out of view, but there he would be on his own. James could not risk shooting then, for fear of hitting him.

Holding his breath, Carl eased out onto the ledge, praying that it would hold his weight. He clung to the rock face, slowly letting the air out of his lungs. One shard of rock tumbled off the ledge, but the rest held, and he moved, inch by inch, along the rising shelf of rotten rock.

Then he was at the spot where anybody looking through the window and glancing upward could see him plain as the wattles on a tom turkey. He stopped, feeling the skin of his exposed back crawling with raw nerves. One pebble, bounding down the face of the hill, might alert the inhabitants of the cabin and send a bullet into his back. One misstep, and he'd plunge down the sheer cliff face to his death.

There was no sound from the cabin, no gunfire and no voices, and the stillness made Carl's palms clammy. He could feel drops of sweat trickling along the valley of his spine. Rulon had had plenty of time to find the mouth of the bear's den and make his way with Bill through the tunnel.

The silence below was worrisome. *Maybe there is no tunnel after all*, he thought. *I'm up here, set for disaster, with no remedy close at hand.*

Carl scrunched up his face, tight as he could, then let it go slack, hoping to slow his breathing. His left arm ached from the effort of keeping the rifle free of the rocks, safe from striking with the telltale clang of metal against stone. He elected to move now in short, deliberate progressions, and it seemed to him that eternity could not be as long as this trip across the field of fire from the cabin.

Slowly, Carl inched his way up the ledge. He thought his heart must be beating loud enough to alarm the ruffians below him. Then, slowly he turned his head and looked over his shoulder toward the cabin. He could no longer see the window, and knew that he was safe from view.

Now was the time for speed, and his bunched muscles cried out in agony as he took hurried steps down the ledge to the place where he had aimed his rifle so many times. He fingered the dead branch where the bullets had stripped off the back, then looked down, into the dark interior of the cabin.

There was not just a single breach spreading between two roof beams, but a large hole that gaped open to the sky where several of the beams had rotted away. Carl looked up and signaled to James the size of the hole, framing a circle in the air, then he peered down again, hoping to locate the girls.

The ruckus began with a mighty concussion beneath him, and Carl felt himself slipping into space, caught off guard as he tumbled into the void. He fell heavily on his left leg and collapsed. Debris from the rotted roof struck his head and shoulders, and when he tried to get up and back himself into the corner of the room, he knew by the way his leg folded up under him that it was broken.

Using his Spencer as a crutch, he crouched in the dim room and pulled the Smith and Wesson from his waistband, aware of the terrific din coming from the rear of the cabin. Rulon and Bill must have got through, for bullets were whanging and spattering behind a hanging blanket. A man yelled in pain, and the sound filled the hollow with echoes.

Then he saw the girls, tied together behind the overturned table by the front door, and heard them shrieking a warning to him. He half-turned, his pistol feeling like a living part of his hand, and heard Pete Dawes exclaim, "How'd that tenderfoot get in here?"

Carl shot across his body, and heard the thunk of his bullet entering Dawes' chest. He recognized his own voice saying, "That's for Chico, and this here's for my pa," as he fired again, his slug going into the bridge of Dawes' nose.

Carl felt the jolt of the lead from Dawes' last shot as it hit his left hipbone, and thought, *That leg's gone*, as he spun around with the blow.

He landed up against the window that had worried him, while he was out there on the mountain. His rifle was gone from his hand, laying several feet from him on the floor. Knowing he couldn't reach it, he shifted the Smith and Wesson to his left hand and drew the Colt from his holster.

Willy thrust away the blanket and threw himself across the room, trying to get behind the girls, but Carl's shots stopped him, and Willy fell, sprawling on the dirt floor.

Now he had to find Acosta, but Carl couldn't see him in the gloom of the fading light. Powder smoke hung heavy in the room, choking off the oxygen and blurring his vision. Shots still rang out from time to time in the tunnel, and the pounding of boots on the hardpan outside let him know James and Sourdough were on the way in.

Where was Berto Acosta? All the revulsion he had ever felt for the man rose in his chest, squeezing the breath out of him. He inhaled the putrid air of the cabin, shuddering as the numbness from his leg wounds wore off. His head felt like it was floating, and each time he moved, the bullet hole opened, gushing blood. He knew he had to find Acosta now, before he passed out.

The door splintered under the butt of James's rifle, and fresh air moved into the room as he enlarged the hole. James wiggled through, lifted the bar, and swung open the shattered door. "Where are they?" he hissed, then grunted as he located the girls.

"Get them out!" Carl yelled, and heard his brother hustle the girls through the doorway. Now he had to find Acosta and make an end to the man's corruption.

Carl holstered his Colt and, dragging his leg, using the rough furniture as props, he crossed the room and stumbled over Willy's body. He avoided Dawes, whose surprised eyes would never take the measure of another man, and hesitated before the blanket that marked the entrance to the tunnel. The hair rose on the back of his neck. He drew his Colt again, then swept the blanket aside with the pistol in his left hand, and froze.

Berto Acosta stood beyond the blanket, the fingers of his left hand caressing the scar where Carl had split his cheekbone. His gun was leveled at Carl's heart.

"You!" the man hissed. "You are just a *muchacho*, but you have spoiled the face of Berto Acosta, and kept from him the delights of the yellow-haired girl. No one, no one keeps me from having my way. Now you die."

Carl saw the furious black eyes narrow and he brought down his left arm just before Berto fired, turning it to knock aside the barrel of the gun, and the bullet whizzed by under Carl's arm.

Grunting, "I don't die so easy as that," Carl half tackled, half fell on the big Mexican, and felt the concussion of Berto's second shot going off next to his head. Carl landed with the barrel of his right-hand gun tucked into the soft flesh of Berto's throat, just where it jutted out to form the floor of his mouth, but he didn't hear the shot. He knew he fired by the jump of the Colt in his hand, and by the sudden slackness of the Mexican's body.

Rulon's legs came into sight as Carl brushed the back of his left hand alongside his head. His hand came away from his head warm and sticky with his own blood. Then the gloom of the tunnel gathered around him, and he slumped into the darkness.

Chapter 20

Carl opened his eyes to a blinding light and a fuzzy, isolated feeling. The side of his head throbbed with pain, and when he shifted his weight to get out of bed, his left hip and thigh answered the motion with a jolt and ache of agony that threatened to send him back into blackness. Catching his breath, resting a moment, he recognized his father's house, and knew he was in his father's bed. No one seemed to be in the room, and Carl lay back and drifted into the welcoming darkness.

When next he woke, it was night, and he was in his own bed, in his own cabin, with the same pain and fuzzy, cottony feeling inside his head. He became aware of a restraint on his left leg, and looked down over his beard to investigate. Someone had bound a set of narrow, thinly split cedar shakes to his thigh, from hip to knee, and his pants and shirt were gone.

The ache in his thigh told him that he had not been mistaken about breaking his leg. He tried not to shift his weight as he reached down to probe the sorest part. The leg was swollen and tender, and hot to the touch.

As he reached over to retrieve the comforter that had slipped off to one side, his elbow brushed against a bandage on his hip, and he gasped with the pain that came awake, brutalizing his nerves. Taking long, shuddering breaths to fight back the agony, he remembered the last bullet from Pete Dawes' gun.

Gritting his teeth against the torment, squeezing his eyes shut to blot out the pain, Carl waited until the nerves he had awakened slipped off into a place filled with dull, scraping razors, and he could bear to open his eyes again.

James stood over him, candle in hand, face clean-shaven. His mouth moved, but no sound reached Carl's ears.

"You don't got to whisper just because it's night," Carl said, then frowned. "Am I talking out loud?" he asked.

James nodded and moved his mouth once more.

Carl put a finger into his ear and wiggled it, unsuccessfully, for there was nothing save the fuzzy, stuffed sensation. His head ached, and he raised his hand to find another bandage, bound on by a cloth wrapped around his head.

"Hush, I can't hear my own voice. What happened to me?"

James frowned and put the candle on the floor. In the eerily flickering light, he pantomimed drawing a gun, aiming it and pulling the trigger. Then he put the pretended weapon alongside his own head, just above the left ear, and made his hand move as though it held a bucking pistol. Then he fell to the floor.

Carl recalled the struggle with Berto Acosta. "Did I kill him?"

James's face appeared over the side of the bed, and he nodded emphatically, looking grim. He started to speak, then shrugged his shoulders and pointed to his throat with the imaginary Colt

Carl heaved a sigh, and closing his eyes, went to sleep.

₮

Daylight brightened the room, and Carl sat up. Then he wished he hadn't and he lay down again to wait for the pain to subside. A buzzing filled his head, and he shook it to clear away the annoyance, but it stayed with him.

"Shoot!" he said aloud, and thought he heard the word echoing faintly back to his right ear. He sat up again, ignoring the pain that jolted through him, and shouted, "Hey!" Again he heard a faint version of his voice. "Hallelujah, I ain't completely deaf," he chortled. Then he became very still, holding his breath and straining to hear any sounds through the cotton in his head. A thudding sound came through the window, and after a bit, he identified it as someone chopping wood.

"Glory be, glory be!" he whispered, sinking back into the feather tick.

A bird sat outside the cabin on a roof pole, twittering its morning adoration of the sun, and Carl thought there wasn't a sweeter sound on earth than that muffled bird song.

James came clumping into the room and dumped a load of fireplace logs into the fuel box. "That sounds wonderful," Carl called from the bed.

James whirled around. "What?"

"I heard the logs drop. I reckon I got a mite of hearing back."

His brother came over to the bed and pulled up a stool. He sat on it and peered at Carl. "It's about time you came back to join us. It ain't fun playing nursemaid to a feller who won't even say 'Thank you kindly, sir'."

Carl fingered his quilt. "How long have I been out?" He turned his good ear to catch James's reply.

"Eight days. You got a right smart furrow alongside your noggin. You and Pa, you're a pair." James laughed, and Carl smiled to hear it. "How in six little beans did you stay on your feet to finish off Berto Acosta? You got you a hole in your hip big enough to stick a fist inside, not to mention your leg's broke."

Carl sorted through the muffled sounds for a moment, piecing them together into words. When he figured he had the sense of them, he grinned. "Just ornery." He peered around the orderly room, and spotted the bedroll James had used during the night. "You been keeping this place clean?"

"No." James's voice held a hint of rancor. "You got a day girl comes in and cleans up and changes your bandages."

"What?" Carl clutched the comforter up over his chest.

James smile didn't reach his eyes. "She only tends to your head. You ain't got cause for alarm. Besides, her pa heard about our little fracas, and he's coming to take her home to the Cuchara."

"How soon?"

"Tomorrow. Not soon enough for me." James scowled and turned his back, then muttered, "You want anything to eat?"

"What's that?"

James turned around, his face once again smooth. "I said, do you want something to eat?"

Carl weighed the matter, wondering if the hollowness in his belly came from hunger or sorrow at the news that Ellen was leaving. He looked up at James. "I'll try something. James, I got to see her before she goes."

"You want me to carry that message?"

"I'd take it as a favor."

"I won't do that, but it don't make no difference. She'll bring breakfast by before too long." He went to the row of pegs against the wall. "Seeing as how you're going to have company and you awake to know it, I'll rustle up a shirt to cover your nakedness." He fingered a few pieces of clothing hung on the makeshift dowels. "You ain't got a big selection here, but I reckon this one'll do." James brought back an old shirt of Peter's that their mother had passed on to Carl.

Carl shrugged in on, finding it a tight fit, and trying to ignore the pain from his hip. "How long you figure I'm going to be laid up?"

"Oh, Ma calculates about a month of loafing will cure you or kill you. She says you snapped that bone clean in two, and your leg swelled up twice its size before we got you off the mountain. It took the whole bunch of us to set it, and you cussing and hollering the whole time. My, you about made me blush to hear it."

"What's that? Blush, you say? You ain't never blushed in your life, you're that brazen. Besides, I don't recall any such a thing."

"That don't mean it ain't so. I reckon I didn't even know some of them colorful words you was spouting. Pa was fit to be tied at the words you used."

Carl tried to sit up. "I never. James, you're pulling my leg."

"I don't think you'd allow that now that you're conscious. That leg pains you a mite, I can tell. Here, let me help you sit up."

Carl stiffened as James raised him to a sitting position. He felt dizzy with the shock of the movement.

"Shoot! That hurt you. I'm sorry, Carl."

Carl shook his head. "Nothing you could help, but I don't want to get in the way of no flying lead again for a long spell." His head still whirling, he eased himself back on the pillow James had propped against the wall behind him. "Did you get the bullet out?"

"Not me. Ellen fished it out." At the look on Carl's face, James added, "It wasn't a time for modesty, big brother. You was pumping blood all over the floor, white as a ghost, and she dived in and ripped a hunk off her skirt to keep you from dying right then and there." He shook his head. "She's one level-headed gal."

Carl groaned. "That's throwing powder on the fire. When her pa finds out I was uncovered in her sight, I ain't never going to win that girl's hand."

"Suits me just fine, since she's my girl,' James growled. "Don't you worry none, though. You was covered decent the whole time. We didn't pause to pull your britches off, or it would have been all over for you."

"You can drive a body crazy, you know that, James? Half the time I ain't sure I'm hearing you clear, and the other half I reckon you're standing there making up the whole thing out of your head."

"I ain't. Miss Ellen is a remarkable girl. Pa claims our betrothal is broken off, but I still count her my own." His face was set in determined lines. "You ain't won her hand, big brother. Nor have you won over Chester Bates."

"You get out of here before I rise off this bed and whup you," Carl threatened, his face gray and drawn. "I snuffed out the breath of three men who aimed to keep Ellen from me. I ain't proud of it, but I had it to do. I'm going to win her hand, even from you, little brother."

"We'll see about that." James turned on his heel and went out the door.

୫

Carl dozed for a while, and then awakened as a hand touched him on the shoulder. He opened his eyes, hearing the buzz in his ears again. Ellen sat on the stool, smiling at him, a bowl of porridge in her hand.

"James says you've been awake. I allow I'm right thankful to see it."

"You'll have to come around to this side of the bed," he said. "I don't hear so good on that side." His heart pounded at the sight of her, sitting there in a faded green dress that couldn't detract from her fresh, alive face.

"I reckon you're hungry," she said once she stood at his right side. She looked around for a chair.

"Take a seat on the bed," Carl said, patting the place. "I'm a mite shy of strength to lift a spoon."

"You poor thing," she murmured, sitting gingerly on the edge. "I reckon I should have brought broth."

Carl smiled. "No, I need something to give me meat on my bones. Look how thin I got."

Ellen looked at him, noting the tightness of the shirt over his chest. "You appear to have filled out some."

Carl looked down. "Shoot, this shirt belonged to Peter when he was a young'un. I don't know what become of my shirt."

"I've got it over to Mary's. You bled a fierce lot all over it. I didn't know you were ready to get up and dress, or I would have fetched it along." She smiled.

"I ain't ready to dance a reel, but I reckon I need something to cover my body."

Ellen looked down at the bowl. "I don't mind," she whispered. "You got a right nice looking chest." She glanced up at Carl then, challenge in her eyes. "You have been so close to dying on me. I don't want to take the chance of losing you now." She bit her lip. "I aim to tell Pa it's time he let me wed the man of my choosing. I'm going down to the Cuchara and bring back the Spanish mission priest. It don't matter to me what words he uses, so long as they mean I'm your wife." She picked up the bowl. "Eat, now. I don't figure to give you more than three, four weeks to get well before I come back, so you be ready, you hear?" She blushed, rosy red in the light from the window, thrust the bowl into Carl's hands, and ran out the cabin door.

Carl grinned, and lifted a spoonful of mush to his lips. "Well, I'll be switched," he said, and shoveled the food into his mouth.

୫

Soon after he arrived from his farm the next day, Chester Bates knocked on the door of Carl's cabin. Carl bade him enter, and Chester came around the doorjamb, his face flushed red.

Carl lay back on the bed, trying to quiet his quick breathing, steeling himself for Chester's harsh words.

The man came to the bedside, took off his hat and gripped it hard, his knuckles blanching white from the effort.

"I reckon I owe you my daughter's life, boy. I'm mighty sorry you got shot up that way. Your pa tells me Rulon despaired for your life before he got you home."

Carl let out a long breath. "I didn't know that, but I ain't sorry. I'd do it again to prove what that girl means to me." He felt drops of sweat forming on his forehead, threatening to trickle down to sting his eyes and betray his nervousness.

"I ain't an unreasonable man. Ellen's my only child, and I set great store by her." Chester's voice shook a bit. "I always wanted the best for her. I reckon she and her ma got the worst during the fighting, being left with a tool shed for shelter." Chester's voice took on a hard edge. "A tool shed! I swore they'd have a chance to forget all that. Your pa helped considerable that day when he rode up with his plan to come out here." He looked at his white knuckles.

"Pa needed all y'all to make a big enough party for traveling safe."

"He cared about us, too. A lot of water has gone by since that day. James—" He paused uncertainly. "And now it appears Ellen wants someone else to give her the best of this world. She spoke me quite a speech this morning." Chester paused again and sank down on the stool.

"She did?"

"She did. I reckon this is the day a father hopes will never come, but it always does. This is the day I take that little hand that's been in mine for these few years and place it into yours."

Carl's head came off the pillow an inch or two, but he didn't say anything.

"You proved you're a man who will lay your life down to save hers, and a father can't ask more than that." Chester rose to his feet.

"Are you giving your consent for me to call on her?" Carl whispered.

"Boy, I don't think you get my meaning. With feelings like you got, I'm playing it safe. I brought Mrs. Bates along, and a friend of ours. His name is Padre Gallegos, he's a priest, and he's here to marry you."

Carl sat bolt upright, disregarding the stabbing pain from his leg. A burning filled his chest, rushed into his throat. His arms shook as he supported himself in the bed. "My ears have been playing tricks on me the last couple of days, but I swear I heard you say you brought a priest along to marry me." He cracked a grin through his beard. "Hush, I don't want to marry no priest. I want to marry Ellen."

Chester stared at him, then clapped his hat on his head and roared into laughter. "Ellen's going to have a bit of humor in her life, I see. That's good. That's mighty good," he chortled, and strode through the open door.

Carl turned and looked out the window. Ellen stood in the dooryard, holding her hands clasped together. Joy flashed over her face when her father spoke to her. She threw her arms around him and hugged him tightly.

Lying back on his pillow, his heart pounding, Carl looked around at the room he had built with his own labor. This was a home worth the sweat and effort, and here he would build his life and work toward his dreams.

And Ellen would stand tall beside him.

: : : : :

Spinster's Folly
Author's Note

The terms "making love to" and "lover" had a different meaning in the 1860s than they do today. They equate to "wooing" and "suitor," so don't let your imagination run away.

Chapter 1

Marie Owen pressed forward through the crowd that surrounded her brother Carl and his new bride. She pushed her way across the patch of trampled grass in the Colorado meadow, trying to get closer to the bridal pair. She could barely see Ma hugging on Ellen. Mrs. Bates dabbed at her eyes. Mr. Bates stood alongside them, looking stern. Pa stood back a bit, looking pleased with himself.

Someone in a great hurry to leave the site of the makeshift altar bumped Marie's shoulder hard, and a flailing hand knocked her bonnet askew. She cried out, "Have a care!" as she turned to see who had been so heedless, then shook her head as she realized it was only her next older brother, James, fleeing from Carl's triumphant grin.

"You behave, James," she muttered, loosening the strings beneath her chin so she could straighten her headgear. When she was satisfied that it was once again firmly in place, she returned to her purpose of reaching her best friend.

Her youngest brother, Albert, was her last obstacle. He had wormed his way to the front of the crowd, and was enthusiastically engaged in kissing Ellen's cheek. Marie elbowed the youth aside, reached her friend, and threw her arms around her.

"Lawsy," Marie whispered in Ellen's ear as she hugged her tight. "I'd begun to fear this day was never coming. Now you're truly my sister!"

Ellen pushed back from the embrace slightly, her green eyes shining like dewdrops above her freckled cheeks. "It was so sudden. I didn't figure Pa would bring the priest with him." Her voice quivered. "Who would have thought . . ." She scanned the meadow, craning her neck as she looked back and forth. "Where is James?"

Marie squeezed Ellen's arm. "Now don't you fret about him on your wedding day. He'll get over his disappointment."

"I want to tell him I am sorry."

"Don't you bother. He's been acting like such a ninny. It was plain as the nose on your face that you loved Carl and not him."

Ellen ducked her head, but when she raised it a moment later, her radiant smile bespoke her happiness.

Marie couldn't help kissing her cheek. "I'm thrilled for you," she murmured, and gave Ellen another hug.

"I cannot believe this happened so fast," Ellen whispered. She took a deep breath, then turned to look at Carl, who was sitting himself down on a chair, his face white.

Ellen's smile disappeared, and she turned back to Marie as people shoved against them. "Carl's bleeding. I must get him to the cabin." She gripped Marie's shoulder. "You'll be next to marry," she said in a rush. "I see the way Bill Henry looks at you."

"What?" Marie protested, but Ellen had slipped away, entreating Rulon and Clay Owen to haul up the chair and carry Carl to the house.

Marie stood rooted in place by her friend's astonishing words. She watched a crimson stain spread across the hip of Carl's trousers, and a shiver of fear coursed down her spine. Carl had been wounded in a shootout with kidnappers. Surely he wouldn't bleed to death because he got out of bed to marry. Ellen was as good a nurse as anyone hereabouts. She would take ample care of Carl and pull him through this bad spell.

"James!" Ma's sharp call cut through the babble of voices.

Marie turned to see what had alarmed her mother, and saw James loping into the forest. She breathed out in exasperation. He had been so temperamental lately, stumping around like a bear with a hangnail.

"Rod, go see—"

Marie went to her mother's side. "He's fine, Ma. Give him a fortnight to clear his mind, and he'll be the light of your eyes again."

Ma grasped Marie's wrist without looking at her. She spoke low. "Daughter, he's not fine. Make your pa go after him." She glanced down at her clenched hand, opened it, and let Marie go free. "Tell your pa—"

"James is man-grown, Ma."

Her mother seemed not to hear her. "Good, Rod is going." She called out, "Bring him back," sighed, gave herself a shake, then turned her attention to the departing newlyweds.

Marie shrugged her shoulders and followed her mother's gaze. Ellen walked beside Carl, fussing a little, patting his hand. His brothers carried his chair toward the little log house Carl had built with his own hands to receive his bride. No matter that his wife wasn't the one Pa had intended for him. It seemed such an age since Pa had connived to arrange marriages for two of his sons before they'd all fled the ruins of the Shenandoah Valley and headed out here to Colorado Territory. Carl's betrothed, Ida Hilbrands, was long gone.

"Good riddance," Marie said aloud.

"Good riddance to what?" a young female voice asked behind her.

Marie jumped and whirled to face her younger sister. "Julianna! Don't creep up on me like that. It's not ladylike."

"What do you know about being a lady? More like a spinster, if you ask me."

"Spinster? Don't you call me names!"

"I will if I want to. You're getting awful long in the tooth, Marie. You've got no beaus in sight, but I do. I'll be married soon."

"You're lying to make me feel bad. You're only thirteen!"

"I'll be fourteen soon," she simpered. "Mama wasn't much older'n that when she and Papa wed."

"You're ridiculous, Jule. Nobody marries so young anymore."

"And you're an old maid, 'cause you're overripe. Papa surely wasn't thinking when he left you off his marrying list." She swished her skirt with both hands and stuck out her tongue.

Marie felt warm blood rising into her neck and face at her sister's insolence. "Leave Pa out of this," she barked. "You see how well his plans turned out." She gestured toward the departing couple. "True affection conquered his meddlesome—" She fumbled for a word, then spat out, "meddling. Ellen is happy, and so am I."

Julianna smirked, pointing toward the forest. "James ain't happy. He stomped off. Papa went after him, glowering almost as much as James."

Marie balled her fists, glaring at her sister. "Thank you for telling me something I already know, Miss Snippety Nose. James'll mend, given enough time."

"But in no time at all, Papa will have to put you on the shelf. Nobody will even look at you by Christmas, old maid!"

৩

Marie turned and stalked off toward the plank tables set out under the oak trees nearby. When Ma had found out Carl was rising from his bed to get married, she had bustled about—with the aid of Rulon's Mary—and put together a special wedding dinner. Well, special, if you count honey drizzled on corn cakes as special. Add the meat pulled from the bones of a few roasted chickens, gallons of milk, cold from sitting in stone crocks in the spring, and the meal could pass as special.

No matter what irritating things Julianna may say, Marie couldn't take the time to tussle with her. There was aplenty of work to do today. Even so, she felt burgeoning anger consuming her good sense as she eyed a washtub full of tableware sitting on the grass beside the table. Which of her brothers had left the dishes on the ground instead of putting them on the table? *Inconsiderate clod!* She bent over, pulled a stack of tin plates from the tub, and slammed them onto the table. Her ears rang with the cacophonous sound. She retrieved a second bunch of plates, dropped them onto the first pile, then grabbed a double handful of tin cups, which she banged down on the planks, not caring if she dented them.

After a few moments of rebellion, reveling in the clinks and clanks of the tin ware, she straightened up, put her hands at her waist and stretched her back. Then she blew an escaping lock of hair out of her eyes and twisted the kinks out of her neck. Remembering that—despite Carl and Ellen's hasty withdrawal—there were still plenty of folks to feed, served to pull her out of her misery and helped her transform back into sensible, responsible Marie.

The Spanish priest robed in brown was the first to enter the shade under the oak trees, wiping sweat from his forehead with his sleeve. The Texas cowboys followed, discussing the possibility of a shiveree that night. Mr. and Mrs. Bates came along with Ma. Pa was nowhere to be seen, but the rest of the family pressed forward, intent upon taking nourishment after the arduous work of getting Carl wed.

Marie hurried to get behind the food-laden table to serve as her younger brothers pushed and shoved to position themselves at the head of the line in order to grab generous portions. Marie smacked the backs of their hands with the bowl of the honey spoon.

"Ow!" howled Albert. "There's no call to beat me."

"Guests first," she replied, pointing with the spoon. "Get yourselves to the back of the line."

Clay licked honey off the back of his hand and glared at Marie, but obeyed without a word.

Mr. Bates escorted the priest to the head of the now-orderly line, accompanied by many polite gestures on the part of both men. Marie smiled at the priest, racking her brain for something to say, then, as she heaped his plate, remembered a Spanish word she'd heard recently. "*Señor*," she said, and made a bobbing sort of curtsey.

"*Muchas gracias, muy amable*," he said, smiling back at her and making little crosses in the air over the food table.

"Muchas grachius," she parroted back, wondering what she'd just said as the priest moved on.

By and by, everyone who had crowded around the table had their plates full, and all were engaged in seeking places to sit to devour the comestibles. After consolidating the leftovers, Marie picked up a plate and fork.

Just then, an excited voice called from the woods, "Hey, James is riding the mustang!" The Owen brothers and the cowboys abandoned their plates and cups on the grass and hurried off to see the spectacle.

Marie watched them go, then forked up a bit of chicken, put a corn cake on her plate, and drenched it with honey. She found a place to sit by herself on the grass, and bit into the sweetened breadstuff. The bland corn cake reminded her of all such dry mouthfuls she'd endured in the years since Lincoln's Northern soldiers had come marching into Virginia. As she chewed, she wished she'd thought to get a cupful of milk. Eventually, the honey helped ease the ground corn down her throat. She dearly hoped Pa would trade a beef cow or two for part of Mr. Bates's wheat crop after harvest time. Wheat bread would be such a welcome change.

Young Roddy, Rulon's boy, came galloping under the oaks astride a stick Pa had fitted with a stuffed horse head made of burlap. "The horsie bucked," he announced in a high, shrill voice. "Unca James fell off." He pranced around his mother. "Mama, he said bad words."

Marie didn't fight the chortle the boy's comment brought upon her. *I reckon he did*, she thought, covering her mouth. *James don't like blemishes on his reputation as a horseman.* She watched Mary bend over and exhort her son about sticking close to her. *That baby's growing up. Good thing Mary's got a new wee one to dote on.*

Her good humor faded as her heart constricted. She had empty arms and no prospects for a man to help her fill them with a babe of her own. She wondered if Julianna's words about her being an old maid had any truth. She was eighteen years old, after all. She closed her eyes and felt a chill move up her spine.

Rulon had taken Mary to wife years ago, just before he went to the war. Roddy had come along in the due course of time. Now Carl had wed Ellen. When was her time to marry and have a family? Had it passed her by when Virginia got tangled up in that cursed fight? Marie shivered as the chill enveloped the rest of her body. So many young men had gone for soldiers. So many hadn't returned home once the fighting was done. Now she was way out here in Colorado

Territory. Her chances for finding a suitor weren't showing any more promise than they had during the Unpleasantness.

Marie opened her eyes as she heard a murmur of male voices and a few laughs. Evidently the show at the corral was over. The cowboys drifted back to the serving table and piled their plates a second time.

She shook off her somber thoughts and wondered if she should take Carl and Ellen a bite of dinner. Surely, with Carl so sorely wounded, the two of them wouldn't be in a romantic frame of mind.

But what if they were? She wouldn't dare interrupt their honeymoon.

"Oh claptrap," she muttered. "If Carl's hungry, Ellen will fetch something to feed him."

"I reckon that's so," a male voice said. "May I refill your plate, Miss Marie?"

Drawing in a gasp of air and jerking to attention, Marie almost spilled the food remaining on her plate to the ground. *Bill Henry!*

It took her a moment to recover from her surprise at his overture, but she eventually replied, "I . . . reckon I have plenty to eat here, thank you, Mr. Henry. You're most obliging to ask."

"Not even a cup of milk?"

"No. No, I'm real content." She smoothed her woolen skirt, brushing at a wrinkle.

"Well then, would it be amiss if I joined you here while I ate?"

"Ma might need me," she said, trying unsuccessfully to figure out how to get to her feet in a ladylike manner.

"I reckon she's otherwise occupied, bidding folks good-bye," Mr. Henry said, looking in Mrs. Owen's direction. She stood near a cluster of horses, talking to Mrs. Bates.

"Suit yourself," Marie murmured, wishing she didn't feel so flustered. Bill Henry was a mighty good-looking man, with those deep blue eyes sparkling in his broad, tanned face. But if he had courtship in mind, he was wasting his time talking her. Pa wasn't likely to give his consent to a match of his daughter with a cowhand. *Except it's very likely Pa hasn't given me much thought at all. He has always worried first about setting his boys up in life.* Be that as it may, all the world knew that sooner or later, Mr. Henry was heading back to Texas. Marie's stomach began to ache.

Now he sat beside her in one smooth movement and tucked into his food. After chewing up a bite of dark chicken meat, he swallowed and looked at her. "Surprising doings today." He gestured in the direction of Carl's cabin. "Your brother's got pluck to stand up on that leg and get married."

"There's no shortness of pluck amongst my brothers, Mr. Henry," Marie said, measuring her words. "Every single one of them is stuffed full of it. You'd think it would run out their ears, they're so plucky." The last word almost exploded from her lips. Exasperation unexpectedly rose up like gall in her throat. "Pa built it into them from the time they were in short pants."

"Whoa there." Mr. Henry held up his hands. "What did I say to cause you hurt, miss?"

She picked at a stem of grass beside her skirt, pulling it to pieces, playing for time to settle her voice into more suitable tones. She glanced up, saw that the Bates family was riding off with the Spanish preacher in tow. "Nothing, sir," she finally said after taking a deep breath. "I'm right pleased to see my brother wed. Nothing gives me more joy than the happiness of Miss Ellen, my good friend." She knew she was enunciating her words carefully, but she couldn't help the brusque note that had crept into her voice. Somehow, it went well with her stomachache.

"Is it your brothers' pluck or your pa's heavy-handedness that has you in a dither, miss?" Mr. Henry softened his critical words with a quick smile that briefly lifted the corners of his moustache.

"My pa? Heavy-handed? Oh, yes," she said, her voice sounding sarcastic to her ears. She gave a little shudder, and tried to remember herself, tried to beat back the great ache cramping her midsection. She finally managed a more moderate tone, saying, "I'm speaking out of turn, Mr. Henry. My pa is an honorable man."

"He is that," he agreed. "He's also a commanding figure of a man who wants every soul to do his will."

She didn't reply. There was nothing to debate in his words.

"Aside from that," he said, a muffled snort escaping his throat, "he's my boss, so I reckon *I'm* speaking out of turn, as well." He lifted his hat and smoothed back his light brown hair before he carefully replaced the hat. "Begging your pardon, miss, I'd best get back to my work."

Marie looked around. The cowboys had drifted away and the glade was empty of guests. Only Albert remained, still stuffing food into his apparently bottomless maw. "It appears our wedding party has come to an end," she said, rearranging the utensils on her plate. "I reckon it's time for me to gather the dishes and such."

He helped her to her feet without further comment, and walked her over to the tables. "I'm grateful for our talk, Miss Marie, even if I am a fair lummox at conversating."

"You have no fault in speaking," she said, a bit too forcefully. She looked downward. "I must beg your pardon for putting you ill at ease. I haven't been the best company." She looked up again, right into soft blue eyes that seemed to see into her soul. "I fear I've been a bit, um, cranky."

He bent his head, accepting her apology. "Next time, I'll not come up and surprise you, miss."

She nodded, and he went away, leaving his plate behind on the table. She picked it up and ran her fingers slowly around the smooth rim as she watched him go, her attention fixed on the power in his easy stride. When she realized what her fingers were doing, she hastily set down the plate, pulled her attention back to her chore and made piles of the remains of the meal. Her thoughts buzzed in disarray, crossing one upon the other as she worked.

That Bill Henry! Is he toying with me? Jule thinks I'm ugly. Am I, truly? All the county boys said I was pretty. Why didn't Pa set me up with a husband when he arranged matches for the boys? I was plenty old enough to get wed. There's hardly anybody out here. Why did Mr. Henry come to sit with me? He is surely going back to Texas. Is Jule right and I'm ripe for the shelf? Why did the county boys go to war? They left me behind to wither away. What does a handsome devil like Mr. Henry want with a homely spinster? He likely left a sweetheart waiting for him. Who is there left to hold his nose and marry me? A Mexican? Tom Morgan? He never played up to me. Tom always hankered after Ellen more than James did. I'll wager Bill kissed a pretty young thing farewell when Pa hired him on. Why didn't Pa think of me?

Afraid she might dissolve into tears and betray her fragile state of mind to her brother, Marie dumped the dirty dishes into the washtub and fled with it toward the house.

୫

Pa burst into the cabin, flinging the door open so hard that it banged against the wall. Marie, placing a stack of washed plates on the shelf beside the fireplace, felt the shaved boards vibrate from the concussion.

"Pa!" She let go of the plates and steadied the pair of kerosene lamps teetering on the shelf. "Mind the lamps."

"He's left! He didn't even come say goodbye to his ma."

"What do you mean? Who's left?" Marie went to close the door, a sick premonition washing through her.

"Your brother. He has no more sense than a beetle, pining over a girl who doesn't care for him." He paced around the room, angrily pounding a fist into his open hand.

She crossed the distance between them and laid her fingers on her father's arm. The queasiness settled in her stomach. "James? Where's he gone to?"

"North. He has an idea of working your uncle's mine. Darn fool boy." He left Marie's grasp and sank into his chair. "He wouldn't even take my coin."

She hesitated, but couldn't keep her question back. "Did you tell Ma? She'll be heartsick."

"Don't I know it!" He shook his head. "She wasn't in sight. I figured she was here in the house."

"She's around back washing the stew kettle. I'll go fetch her." She started towards the door.

"Missy Marie?" Pa's voice sounded worn out, but he got to his feet as she turned around. "I'll do it. You go find the family. Bring 'em all," he said, then paused, gently probing the healing furrow on his scalp where a bullet had grazed him recently, as though it would aid his thought process. "No, leave Carl be. We'll tell him later."

She stood in the open doorway gazing at her father. "Pa," she started, then stopped, uncertainty flooding over her. Her throat tightened, but she finally croaked, "How did James look?"

He snorted. "Full of ire and pride. I reckon he won't be back for a spell."

୫

Marie shuddered as she left the cabin. She'd surely misjudged James's hurt. Her thoughts raced, full of foreboding at James's lonely flight. *What if he never comes back? What if a mineshaft falls in on him? What if a mountain lion eats him? What if he falls off a cliff? What if a lowlife sticks a knife in him? What if he dies alone in the mountains?* She looked around the compound as though unsure where to start her search, then set off on her task. Where were her brothers? Where was that scamp, Jule?

She found Albert feeding the horses, and told him to get home as soon as he had finished. Clay labored in the shade of the oaks, taking apart the tables and bundling the planks together so he could cart them to the shed.

"Pa wants us at home," she said. "Soon as you can get there. Have you seen Jule?"

Clay glanced up, blowing a lock of his hair out of an eye. "Can't say that I have. Tell Pa I'll be there when I can." He looked hard at Marie. "Something's amiss?"

She bit her lip. "That's for Pa to recount. Hurry."

When Clay nodded, she turned away, thinking about where her sister could have taken herself. Then she remembered the girl's preoccupation with marriage and ran toward Carl's cabin tucked into the woods.

As she rounded the final bend in the path, she was horrified to see her sister with her back pressed against the log wall of the cabin, listening at the window. Marie darted forward, grabbed her wrist, and hauled her away from the cabin.

"Leave me be!" Julianna shrieked. "Turn me loose!"

Ellen put her head out of the window, a startled look on her face, and pulled the shutters closed.

"See there, now I won't hear anything," the younger girl ranted, struggling against Marie's restraining hand. "You're so mean."

"What a despicable thing to do, spying on the newlyweds like that. For shame!" Marie said, tightening her hold and wrapping her other arm around Julianna in a further effort to get her away from the scene. "Whatever possessed you?"

"I need to know about things," Julianna shouted, wriggling in Marie's embrace. "Ma won't tell me what folks do when they're married. I've got to know."

"It's none of your business. You're not married, and won't be for a long spell." Since they were now a suitable distance from the cabin, Marie stopped dragging Julianna away, and stood blocking the path so she couldn't return.

The girl shrugged off Marie's arms and spat out, "I'll be wed before you. Parley Morgan's sweet on me. I wager we'll get married by next spring."

"Parley? That's preposterous! He's ages older than you! Get to the house." Marie pointed to the cabin and shook her finger in emphasis.

Julianna stood upright, thin chest thrust forward, arms akimbo, and spewed out venomous words. "You're jealous. You don't have a beau. You won't ever have a beau. You're too old to catch one!"

Marie felt her cheeks burn. Her hand swung in a short arc and caught Julianna on *her* cheek. "You little vixen," she yelled. "You mind your tongue. Ma's going to hear of this, but not today. She's got enough grief to bear. Get home!"

Julianna turned and stormed off down the path toward the main cabin, muttering imprecations beneath her breath. Marie followed, trying to calm down. It infuriated her that Jule had such power over her. In a few words, she'd managed to throw Marie's world into a blazing, furious uproar, and she didn't like the feeling.

Ma would be beside herself when she learned James took off. She'd only recently got over a measure of her grief from losing Peter, then Ben in the fighting. How could she stand the thought of losing another son to anger? "Pa won't be much use to comfort her," she mumbled out loud in the direction of Jule's retreating back. "He's madder'n a cat caught in a rain barrel."

ॐ

Marie shooed Jule into the cabin, and saw that someone had informed Rulon and Mary of the family meeting. They must barely have arrived ahead of herself and her sister. They still huddled together on the periphery of the family gathered around the table.

Rulon had a protective arm around his wife's shoulders as she bounced their infant daughter in her arms. Roddy, still riding his stick horse, galloped around the room. Marie wondered which of her younger brothers would remember to be a gentleman and allow Mary to sit in his chair.

Ma sat in a chair at the head of the table, her face pinched and white as though she knew something horrible was in the air. Pa stood behind her, his forehead drawn into severe lines above his gray eyes. He waved Marie and Julianna into the room, then waited silently while they approached the table.

Clay remembered his manners, quit his chair, drew up a bench, and shoved Albert's shoulder so he would give up his seat. Rulon helped Mary into the chair Albert had abandoned, and Marie perched on the other. The three younger siblings arranged themselves on the bench and fell silent.

Pa took one deep breath, then another. His inhalations and exhalations filled the quiet in the cabin. Marie held her own breath while her father spoke.

"I have hard news. Your brother has taken it into his head that he's not welcome here, so he rode out. He said he'd try his hand at mining. Mining! He's not cut out for going into a hole in the ground." He punctuated his words by smacking his fist into his open hand. In the stillness, the act made a surprising amount of noise.

As Pa's voice died away, a hush moved in to replace it, lasting for perhaps three seconds, stretching and pulling the air until it seemed thin and suffocating. No one moved. Then Rulon leaned forward and said, "You can't be serious, Pa. I reckon he'll ride around a while and come back home, leaving his troubles in the wind."

At the same time, Albert asked, "Can I have his cabin?" at which Clay cuffed him on the side of the head, yelling, "You ornery son of a—" then bit his lip before he got his own cuffing from Pa for swearing.

Julianna had burst into tears when Rulon spoke. She cried out, "That's not fair! James said he'd take me rabbit hunting."

<hr>

The Complete Owen Family Saga

"Hush, Jule!" Ma said sharply, then dissolved into tears herself, throwing her apron over her head, which served to muffle her sobs a bit.

Albert threw his own punch, then launched himself at Clay, at which the bench went over backwards. Julianna screamed, rubbing her head where it had hit the floor.

Marie finally exhaled, then repeatedly tried to draw air into her protesting lungs, listening to the hubbub without adding more than her gasps to it as she clenched her hands into balls in her lap.

Pa bent over Ma, awkwardly patting her shoulder and making shushing sounds. He looked up and glared at Albert and Clay, who were rolling on the floor, trading blows. Then he included Julianna in his entreaties, trying to quiet her sobs.

Marie hid her face in her hands, overcome with the selfishness of her younger siblings . . . and herself. *Oh James,* she thought, *will I ever see you again? It was wrong of me to think only of Ellen's happiness and not see your side of the hill. I didn't know you cared so much.*

Then Pa cleared his throat and Marie spread her fingers so she could look at him. He drew himself up to his full height. Marie saw a change in his aspect that meant he had gone from comforter to patriarch. "Silence!" he shouted into the noise.

The family members slowly lapsed into silence, Clay and Albert sprawled on the floor, giving each other hard looks. Rulon leaned down, extended a hand to each boy, and hauled them to their feet, giving them quiet words of brotherly admonition.

Pa's brow remained crinkled, and Marie wondered if his worried countenance reflected concern for his son or astonishment that James had defied his father's will.

When he spoke, Pa's tone was commanding. "James is still part of this family, no matter how long he's gone, so we will not be parceling off his belongings just yet. If he's gone more than a year, we'll think about what that means at that time."

Ma let out a moan at Pa's words, and he patted her shoulder again, but followed up the action with a crisper note in his voice. "There now, Julie, don't borrow trouble. He's going to find himself by and by and return home a wiser man."

Ma grabbed Pa's hand and said, "Oh Rod," in a mournful tone.

Marie couldn't look at the naked grief in her mother's face any longer, and turned her eyes away. *Godspeed, James,* she thought. *Come back soon.*

"But Pa," Albert said, "if James don't come back in a hurry, we'll lose his homestead. I reckon I should prove up what he's started."

"You're not old enough," Clay said with a glare at his younger brother. "If anyone can do it, I can."

"You're not old enough, either," Rulon put in. He stroked his chin, then looked at his fingers and rubbed them together. "What if Marie takes the cabin? She's nearly of age."

"It hardly matters if she's of age or not," Pa said. "We bore arms against the Union. None of us can expect to hold our homestead claims, if any should want them."

Rulon's face went white. "We're squatters? I didn't know that."

"I didn't see fit to tell you, once I learned the way of the homestead law. When the time comes to apply for the land rights, we're God-fearing Yankees from West Virginia, you hear?"

Ma was no longer crying. She looked at Pa, her mouth working for a moment before any words came out. "You wouldn't say that." Her tone was low and her words clipped.

"I would say I was a black-skinned slave man if it would get us title to the land!"

"I didn't bear arms," Marie cut in, as she stood up and planted her hands, palms down, on the table. "I can get land on my own, and it will be done honestly." She raised her chin, knowing her defiant words would hurt her father. What did that matter? He had hurt her, putting her welfare last on his list. She looked over at Rulon, whose face was now pinched with worry. "Rule, I would not be a squatter. I can file for your land and sell it to you in exchange for a," she paused and thought, then continued, "a cow."

"There'll be no more talk of this sort," Pa declared, his face working as though he were suffering a fit. "No one is going to do us out of the land. We'll get title to it one way or another. We're here, and it's ours." He brought his fist down on the table, and Marie knew the discussion of James's departure and the status of their homesteads was over. She let out a breath. *Be safe, James, wherever you go.*

Chapter 2

He's gone and done it, Bill Henry thought as he saddled a horse the next morning. Defied his pa and gone off. He's got more gumption than I thought he did.

Bill swung into the saddle, gathered the reins, and clucked to his mount, a frisky dun mustang, one of the horses Mr. Owen had bought in Texas. The animal frog-jumped and bucked for a few minutes, but Bill stuck tight and waited out the horse's temper tantrum. The dun would settle down soon and carry him through the morning without further complaint.

Yes, James Owen had sand, he had to give him that. Who else around here was willing to go toe-to-toe and have it out with the fearsome Rod Owen? Nobody else he could name, including himself.

The dun gave a final crow-hop, then stood quiet, waiting for guidance. Bill crossed his wrists, rested them on the saddle horn, and gave himself up to a moment of reverie.

He was no coward, but he had no reason to butt heads with the Old Man, because he didn't hanker to leave Colorado Territory at this time. He'd given his word that he'd teach the Owen men the cattle business. Even though he was without kin in this place, it suited him fine to light here a while, there being no work for him in Texas.

Besides, if I head back now, I'll never see Miss Marie again.

There it was, finally, the hitherto unspoken reason for staying. He smoothed his moustache as he contemplated his situation. The Owen boys had caught on to every cattle-handling trick he'd taught them much faster than he'd supposed they would. Nothing kept him here beyond that obligation. Except . . . *I don't want to leave her.*

Bill exhaled. Now the big bear had been flushed into the open, so to speak, and he had to face it or turn tail and run. He'd not ever admitted to himself that in the few short weeks since he'd arrived in Colorado Territory, he had grown mighty fond of the pretty, dark-haired daughter of his boss. Now he let himself acknowledge that he had grown serious feelings for the sprightly miss. Truth was, he'd taken to being on hand when she rode out each morning to exercise her horse. That way he had a glimpse of her to carry in his thoughts throughout the long hours he spent dealing with slab-sided cattle.

No point in avoiding reality. Marie Owen was the reason he was willing to stay on in this unnaturally green land beneath the mountain.

He whispered her name and smiled so broadly that his moustache tickled his cheeks. The very sound, Marie, had a sort of music in it.

Finally realizing that daylight was a-burning, Bill clucked and put his heels into the dun's flanks, turning it toward the uphill path.

He wondered if there was any chance he could woo Miss Marie, any chance of persuading her to marry him. She was prettier than any girl he'd seen before. Feeling as he did about her, he had to try. She was worth every effort to win her.

How could he forget the day he'd met the girl? He'd ramrodded Old Man Owen's cattle drive from Texas. As he, his cowhands, and the Owen men drove the livestock up this same mountain, they encountered the little sister, half paralyzed with fear. She'd barely missed being taken off by an outlaw band. She was safe, but the varmints had kidnapped Marie and the Bates girl.

The whole bunch of them left the beeves behind and tracked the outlaws to a cave, where they managed to recover the girls. That victory came at great cost. His own cousin had paid the ultimate price.

For a moment, Bill let the barely abated grief of losing Bob wash over him, but his cheerful mood didn't want to go toward darkness just now. He shook it off and went back to more pleasant memories of that day.

On the way down the mountain after the shooting affair, they'd stumbled across a deep pool of water surrounded by protective boulders, and so shaded by trees that the water appeared black. Rulon Owen called a brief halt to better bind up Carl's wounds so he wouldn't expire from loss of blood.

Marie rested beside the pool, clearly anxious over Carl's dire condition and desirous of reaching the safety of home. He gave her a tin cup to dip into the water. She looked up at him, gratitude in her eyes as she thanked him for being in the rescue party.

That was the moment she had captured his interest. Even bedraggled as she was, with her shoulders and sleeves covered with dirt and her hair tangled and bedecked with twigs and leaves, she was the most beautiful creature he had ever seen.

Since that day, he had thought of the pool as *their* special spot. Not that they'd ever been back to it, but they would, someday. Maybe when he asked—

The sound of rapid hoof beats brought him out of his reverie. Who was riding a horse hard this early in the morning? Was James Owen coming back?

He looked around for the horse. When he located it, he saw a skirt billowing behind and knew it was Marie. Irritation washed over him. She knew better than to treat horseflesh so harshly. Then concern for her welfare crowded out the negative thought. Had the horse run away with her? Was someone chasing her? He didn't know the state of affairs with the Indian tribes in the area. Maybe she'd had a run in with a party of hostiles.

Bill rode toward the girl, gigging the dun into a gallop, his heart beating as fast as the hooves on the earth. Then he was choking, trying to swallow his fear as he saw her terrified face. Something was horribly wrong.

When he came near, he swung his horse around and caught up to hers. She held only one rein. The other hung loose, dragging on the ground. He leaned over and tried to grab it. She resisted, fending off his hand, shoving it away.

He called out sharply to her, "Don't run the horse," then wished he'd kept his mouth shut. For one thing, it filled with dust, and for another, she looked sideways at him with such wide eyes and such a grimness on her face that she looked as though he'd slapped her.

"Foolish," he muttered, half under his breath.

He chased Marie back to the stable, wishing he'd let her run the horse towards him in the first place. He berated himself the whole time until he pulled up his mount, kicked free of the stirrups, and launched himself out of the saddle.

By this time, Marie's horse had stopped in front of the stable, sides heaving and lathered. The girl slipped off and would have collapsed in a heap if Bill hadn't caught her. She breathed in concert with the laboring horse for a moment, then drew herself up and stepped out of Bill's arms.

"Don't touch me, Mr. Henry," she snapped, and the coldness of her tone brought Bill up short, rocking back on his heels as though she had slapped him.

"What happened?" he asked. His voice sounded harsh in his ears.

"What does it matter? I'm not foolish."

Bill inhaled sharply. She must have thought his muttered, self-deprecating remark had been aimed at her.

"I didn't mean you." The explanation came too late. Marie's scathing gaze lingered on him for a moment, then she stalked off, jerking on the reins to pull her horse along behind her into the stable.

"Henry." He turned and met the stern eyes of the Old Man. "Get about your work," he commanded, motioning with his head toward the mountain.

Bill nodded and remounted, regret flooding his thoughts. *Not a good start to the day.*

What power on earth or heaven gives him the right to speak to me like that? Marie fumed as she tromped into the stable. *What an inconsiderate clod, thinking I was foolish to run the horse.* She shook herself, her body still encased in the terror she'd felt as her mount shied to get away from the striking snake and then ran away with her. She'd lost the reins and the stirrups, and almost fell off when the animal had begun to race back toward home.

She'd finally calmed down enough to get her feet back in the stirrups and one rein in her hand when Mr. Heroic Henry had caught up to her. But when he'd leaned over to grab the trailing rein and she'd felt the horse gathering itself to jump away, her sheer terror had returned. Hadn't he seen her predicament? Didn't he care that she was about to be thrown off? What a lout he must be, uncaring and thoughtless of her well-being! Why did men always want to be the heroes?

Marie slid the saddle off the horse and, despite its sidestepping, managed to remove the bit and bridle. Thank goodness she had been riding astride a Western-style saddle with an upright horn. Otherwise she would've had nothing to hang onto. *What if I'd been riding sidesaddle?*

As Marie brushed down her horse, her opinion of Mr. Henry did not improve. *Selfish oaf!* Her brushing increased in both speed and depth.

"Daughter, the horse won't have any coat if you don't lighten your touch."

Marie turned at her father's voice, and almost flung the brush at him. "Imagine that," she said in a strident tone. "You care more for your animals than you do for me." She threw the brush into the corner and flounced toward the door.

"Hold up, there!" Pa said, catching her by the shoulders and turning her to face him. "What's distressing you? Did that Texas cowhand give you an insult? I'll whip his hide back to the Staked Plains if he did."

Marie held herself stiff against her father's hands. "Pa." Her words were clipped. "It's not him. No. You might say it's him. No. It's mainly you. You don't care a fig for me." She ducked her head, gulped air, then raised her chin, and her words flowed more freely. "You're worked up at James and his leaving. It hardly matters to you that I've got no prospects, no future here."

"Now girl, that's not so." Pa's face burned red. "You've got everything to look forward to. A nice house by and by, plenty of chickens, a kitchen garden. This land will grow a passel of greens, I'll wager."

"Greens!" Marie endeavored to lean away from him, feeling trapped within his confining grip. "You think this is about gardens and eggs and living out my life in a fine house with you and Ma? You're wrong." She paused and drew a deep breath, then spit out her words. "I'm upset because there's no one hereabouts for me to marry. No one to cherish me and care about my dreams and wishes."

He dropped his hold on Marie and stood bolt upright, looking like he'd been whacked upside the head with a cast iron skillet.

She continued, feeling as though her insides were squeezed together from the anger that ballooned against her ribs. "You didn't think of that, did you?" Her voice rose. "You were so set on fixing things up with the neighbors and arranging marriages for the boys." She was shouting now. "You didn't give me a single thought."

He seemed to recover himself, then said, "You have it wrong, daughter. I've had it in mind for you and Tom Morgan to wed bye and bye. You're both a bit young yet."

"Young!" Marie almost stamped her foot, but instead brought her bunched fists up to her chin. "Pa, how old do you figure I am? How old do you reckon he is?"

He scratched his head. "Ain't you about fifteen? Tom needs to get set up, grow his crops and sell them, build you a house. There's plenty of time."

Marie felt her heart shrivel in her chest. This was worse than she'd thought. "I'm eighteen," she whispered, her words measured. "Tom is twenty." Her voice rose again. "We're not babies, but at this rate, I won't ever *have* any of those."

He narrowed his eyes. "Eighteen? When did you get to be that age?"

She looked at the floor, anger shaking her body, then looked at her father. Her emotion drained away as she watched his shoulders slump. "How old are you, Pa? Didn't you gain any years while you were away fighting a war?"

He let out his breath in a great gusty sigh. After a few moments of silence, he spoke in a voice tinged with regret. "I didn't do right by you, daughter. I should have been thinking that you were growing up alongside your brothers. I reckon I thought you'd always be my little girl."

Marie's anger boiled anew. She snapped, "I'm not so little now, Pa. I've grown old and lonely on account of the Unpleasantness. Where's my chance for happiness?" She gestured out the door. "This place is nothing but a nice-looking graveyard for me."

"That's not so, girl. The countryside is full of young men. Why, there's . . ." He scratched his head again. "Tom, of course, and well, Parley—"

"Who's younger'n me," she interrupted.

"How about one of those young boys I brought back from Texas? That Henry fellow's not so bad, I reckon."

"You were going to whip his hide back to where he came from."

"He's a stout lad, and he knows his business."

"He's bound to go home soon." Marie swallowed hard. "Probably left a girl behind he's anxious to wed." She kicked at a clump of straw, gathering courage to make an outrageous suggestion. "I suppose the Dominguez boys are out of the question?"

Pa looked startled. "They're Mexicans, girl."

"They've been in this territory longer'n we have." Marie twitched her skirt. "They're citizens now. And landowners. Land owners. That's more than we can say."

"But they're not our kind." He brushed the back of his fist across his chin.

Her eyes closed. "Of course. So I have few choices for suitors and little time to marry before I'm truly an old maid, as Jule claims." She opened her eyes, turned away and headed for the door.

He called out before she could leave the stable, "Daughter. Chester Bates says he'll have done harvesting his wheat in a few weeks. I plan to drive a few head of beef steers down to trade for grain. Why don't you come along?"

He paused, and she looked back to see if he expected an answer.

Pa continued, "I'll take a look at Tom and see if he's ready to make a match." He was silent for a moment, then frowned and said, "We'll go on Thursday. Mr. Bates will be good for the wheat after harvest."

Marie didn't reply aloud. She swept a trailing lock of hair from her forehead and thought as she turned away, *At least Pa's finally thinking about me. I only hope Tom's ready to settle down.*

৪৩

As he rode toward the group of cowboys gathered at the foot of the trail, Bill wondered if his job was in jeopardy. Mr. Owen hadn't been pleased when he'd caught Bill loitering around the stable talking to his daughter.

I wasn't harming her, even if she tells her pappy what a dunderhead I am, he thought. *My lands, she's pretty when her eyes snap fire!*

Bill arrived at the trailhead where the cowboys awaited him, and one of them, Chico Henderson, laughed.

He said, "You got you a woebegone visage, Henry. What's eating you?" The cowhand circled his horse around Bill, then drew up in front of him and laughed again. "Saw the daughter out early. Did she waylay you? Is that why you're late?"

"Cut out the palaver, Chico. There's work to be done." Bill pulled the dun's head to the side so he could pass his fellow Texan, and kicked it into motion.

"Don't put your eggs in that basket," Chico said, then laughed a third time.

Bill gritted his teeth. He already felt discombobulated from his encounter with Miss Marie. Tangling with Chico would only put his mood more off-kilter, so he gigged his horse up the trail toward the herd.

Maybe Chico was right. Maybe he shouldn't set his sights on a dubious dream. Mr. Owen would never let his daughter marry the likes of him—a dusty cowhand with nothing to his name but a horse, a saddle, and a lariat. Well, there was the ranch down in Texas, if it hadn't already been claimed by one mangy, tweed-backed carpetbagger or another for taxes due. He'd better keep his dreams within reason. He could never take Old Man Owen's pride and joy a thousand miles away to live.

Humph! It would serve the Old Man right if Miss Marie left hearth and home and went off to live her own life, far away from pappy. Wouldn't he rant and rave if his daughter showed her own mind and joined her brother in setting him back on his heels? Bill grinned.

The grin dropped to the ground in the next moment, when he remembered the state Miss Marie had been in when he'd taken his leave of her. Not only was it a poor bet that he could go home with a bride, the chance that he'd have a job much longer was between slim and none.

"I didn't mean no disrespect," he muttered aloud.

"Who you been disrespecting?" came a voice from a foot or so behind him. "Not the beauteous Miss Owen?"

Chico again! "Mind your business, Henderson," Bill snapped. "We got steers to brand."

"I don't use my mouth to brand. It's free to speak my mind." Chico rode up even with Bill, wearing a wide grin.

"You're useless," Bill said.

"I'm your conscience. I keep you from flying off to the moon when you should be roping a yearling calf."

"You're imagining things. I'm levelheaded and lucid."

"Not lately. I reckon you're in luuuv." Chico drew out the vowel, letting his bottom lip hang away from his mouth. "You're so in luuuv you can't see a painter creeping up on you in broad daylight. You're so in luuuv—"

Bill shoved hard against Chico's shoulder, and the cowboy winced. "Hey! Leave off, Henry. That wound ain't healed up yet."

"You're a fraud. You got shot in the left side. Don't carry on about your right wing, or I'll shoot you again myself."

"Ah, you wouldn't do that. I'm too good a roper, even with a bad arm."

"You can be replaced with a Mexican," Bill growled. "They're all better ropers than you."

The old trail cook, Sourdough, doubling as a cowhand these days, called out, "Boss a-coming. Mind your tongues."

Bill glanced over his shoulder. Old Man Owen and his sons were indeed approaching, and he had a serious set to his face. *Uh-oh*, he thought. *I reckon I'm in trouble.*

He pulled up his horse, letting the others get ahead of him while he waited at the side of the trail. Mr. Owen waved his sons ahead and stopped to confer with Bill.

"Leave off branding and cut out a dozen steers for sale. I'm taking 'em down to the Cuchara."

"Want branded stock?"

"Not especially. They're going to be butchered soon. It don't matter what the hides say."

"How many hands you want to go with you?"

"Just my boys. They're plenty and to spare to handle that small a herd. The rest of you can get on with the branding once you get the dozen separated out."

"Yes, sir. How soon you need them?"

"We'll head out on Thursday morning," he said. "Bring them down to the lower corral Wednesday night."

Bill agreed, relieved that he yet had a job, and even more elated that he would have an opportunity to seek out Marie in her father's absence.

The Old Man cleared his throat, then spoke again. "I'm taking my daughter with me, Henry. You won't make free with her feelings again." He clucked to his horse and moved away.

He saw right through me. My poker face needs work. Bill's disappointment stung, but the girl would be back soon.

Rod Owen turned his horse and tossed Bill a bit more news. "I'm matching my girl up with a Virginia boy. Tom Morgan is known blood."

Bill caught himself in mid-nod. Strong chills washed over him as though he'd been caught in a freezing rain. *Tom Morgan? The corn farmer's son?*

∽

Marie headed toward the creek, intent on dipping up a handful of water to cool her face. Her cheeks still burned from the encounter with her pa, and she didn't want Ma asking uncomfortable questions.

"Drat Pa anyway," she muttered, head down as she tromped along the bank to her favorite place. "Why does he meddle so?" She started to gather her skirts to kneel in the grass.

"Marie. Good morning to you."

Marie dropped the fabric and looked around for the origin of the familiar voice. It was Ellen, as she had supposed, coming toward her from the opposite side of the creek. What was she doing here? She should be in her cabin, tending to Carl.

"I—" She brushed at one cheek, feeling for heat, hoping Ellen hadn't noticed her discomposure. Perhaps her flush had faded. "I've been out riding," she said, in case it hadn't. "I thought you'd be up yonder." She gestured toward the forested bench where Carl had built his new home.

Ellen's chuckle surprised Marie, but she tried to hide her expression by rubbing her forehead.

"I can't be there all day and all night. We needed water, and besides, I wanted to take the air." She lowered a bucket to the grass.

"Ain't newlyweds supposed to stay indoors? Most all the ones I've known went away and I didn't see them for a long time after the wedding."

"It's a tiny mite different when the groom is laid up with a horrible wound," Ellen, said, but there was no hint of self-pity in her tone.

In fact, Marie detected laughter underneath the grim words. "What's funny?" she demanded to know. "You're all sunshiny for a bride in such a circumstance."

Ellen laughed out loud. "I like being married," she said, once she had regained composure. "I like being Carl's wife. He's cheerful, despite being laid up, and he's funny, and he loves me to pieces." She wrapped her arms around herself, smiling.

Marie frowned, and thought, *Will Tom Morgan ever make me feel that way?* A shiver ran through her body, top to toe. *Not if he's still mooning after Ellen, he won't.* She hugged herself then, feeling alienated from her friend by her discouragement.

Ellen noticed Marie's movement and laughed again. "Look at us," she said, "a pair of sillies a-hugging on ourselves." She broke her stance and shook her finger in Marie's direction. "Marie? Something's amiss. You're off woolgathering in a dark place."

Marie bent her head forward, hiding her face with her hands, ashamed of the tears gathering behind her eyelids.

"Oh no!" Ellen cried out, and jumped across the water. "There is something wrong." She put her arms around Marie's shoulders and rocked slightly. "You let yourself have a good cry, then you can tell me all about it."

Marie sank against Ellen and surprised herself by bursting into tears. They spilled from between her closed lids, hot and stinging, accompanied by sobs that shook her shoulders and tore at her throat. Shame suffused her body, shame at losing control of her emotions, shame at caring so deeply about her father's ongoing slight, shame at her actions toward Bill Henry, who had only been trying to help her, after all.

She sobbed on, despite Ellen's comforting embrace, despite her father's claim that he would see to her wants and needs, knowing that marriage to a reluctant Tom would never bring her the happiness Ellen enjoyed. Then she sobbed because she was a hypocrite, begrudging Ellen her joy because she herself was miserable.

Finally, she sobbed because James was gone. James had left them, and she didn't know if she would ever see him again. Her last exchange with him had been to belittle his pain, to berate him for his heedless flight from grief. She had not said goodbye.

After a bit, Marie's sobs abated enough that she realized Ellen was rocking her, crooning soothing sounds into her ear, stroking her hair with gentle hands. Ellen's hands. James could never again clasp them in his, nor ever again tuck one into the crook of his arm, even though she had been betrothed to him. Ellen was married. James was gone. She took a long, shuddering breath and let it out slowly. Ellen did not know of his departure.

Marie opened her eyes. Ellen's stared back at her, warm with concern and regard.

"He's gone," Marie said in a high, tight voice.

"Who?"

"James. He's left us."

Ellen inhaled sharply. "Ah!" She let Marie go and put a hand to her mouth. "I drove him away!"

"No. No!" Marie said. "He and Pa had words." She put a hand on Ellen's hair. It was her turn to comfort. "If anybody drove him away, it was Pa."

"I knew I was too happy by half."

"You can't say that. James is prideful. He can't abide losing. Not after. . . . Never mind that. I didn't tell you he'd gone to heap blame on you, or on Carl. James'll work it out. He'll come back."

"You're talking about him losing Jessie? Leaving her behind?" At Marie's nod, Ellen spoke hesitantly. "At first, being betrothed to me was a heavy cross for him to bear." She began to shake her head. "After he resigned himself to the match your pa made, and knowing Jessie was lost to him, he worked so hard . . . so hard to accept me, to acknowledge me." Her eyes darted around, unfocused, and when she spoke again, her voice was husky with emotion. "But I couldn't love him, Marie. I couldn't come to care for him. Carl was always the one I loved."

"There, there."

The girls clung together in mutual pain, until Ellen said softly, "Carl needs to know about his brother leaving. I have to tell him."

"Yes." Marie sniffed and swiped the back of her hand across her eyes. "I reckon you should. Now I've got to be doing my chores." She gave Ellen another squeeze and turned away.

೮ა

Feeling the overwhelming fatigue brought on by two days of mourning, Julia Owen only half listened to her husband tell her his plan to leave early Thursday morning on a three-day journey to sell beeves. Getting to sleep was of higher importance to her than staying awake until Rod ran out of steam, turned on his side, and began to snore.

She hoped this was not a night when he felt amorous. She had barely been able to go through the motions of her chores today, and had no strength left to spare for her husband's needs.

Then a question worked its way into the forefront of her mind. She opened one eye, waited for Rod to take a breath, and asked, "Why are you herding cows down to Chester Bates this week? I recall his letter made an offer to trade them for part of his wheat crop. He won't be harvesting yet."

"Steers. I'm taking steers."

She refused to be distracted. "They're all cows to me. Why are you going before harvest?"

"I have a pressing matter to take up in that country. I reckon it won't wait until then." He scratched his chest above the neck of his nightshirt. "I figure I may as well make one trip as two. Chester will bring us the wheat."

She whispered, "If you're going after James, that's entirely the wrong direction." Pain at the unexpected loss of her son made her body quiver.

"I know that, woman." His voice had taken on the soft gruff tone he used in tender moments when he felt vulnerable.

Annoyance that he hadn't expanded his answer sufficiently to tell her his business drove Julia to shift her weight, rise on her elbow, and open both eyes to stare down at him. "What ain't you telling me?"

After a long moment, he turned his own eyes away and said, "I have an errand."

"Roderick Owen, don't you be speaking nonsense to me. What errand takes you away from chores at this season?"

When his hand flew to his head, she barked at him, "Don't be a-worrying that scab or it won't never heal. What's the truth?"

"It's a little errand for Marie," he admitted, tucking his hand under the covers.

"Marie?" Surprised, she almost missed his failure to explain himself further. When she had gathered her wits sufficiently to notice his silence, she poked him in the ribs. "What business does the girl have in the Cuchara country?"

He sighed. "She accused me of neglecting her welfare. She wants a husband."

"No!" Julia sat up.

"She made it plain she's woman-grown and expects me to get her one."

She looked at him. "You're not—"

He cut her off. "She said young Tom Morgan is twenty. I had no notion he'd got to that age."

She shook her head and sighed in turn. "Your matchmaking has an ill reputation." She sank back onto the bed. "Does she have her cap set for Tom?"

He shifted one of his legs. "I've had him in mind for years."

"I asked does Marie want him."

He shifted the other leg. "She didn't say me nay." After another long pause, he continued, "I'll know more when I get the two in the same room."

"What?" She sat up again, her back stiff.

"Julie, shh."

"You're taking my daughter down country with a passel of cows?"

"Shh. I can best see if Tom is willing to step up to the mark when he encounters the girl face to face."

"Well, which of the hands will you take to drive the wagon? You dasn't let Albert have the lines when he's got his sister in his care. He's too reckless."

He shifted his leg. "There's no need of a wagon, nor of a crew. Marie rides well, and the boys can handle twelve beeves."

She recognized his blustery tone.

"You're justifying using my daughter as a cattle drover because she sits a horse well?"

"No. No. She'll be along for the journey, not driving steers. She'll take charge of the camp chores."

"She'll drive cattle and then cook for y'all, besides?"

"Julie, lie back and go to sleep." He sat up and pressed her shoulders backward with gentle hands. "Marie agreed to go along. I reckon she's eager to make a match."

"Humph," she snorted, but she allowed him to make a fuss for a few moments until she let her body relax and her eyes close again.

Although she knew she appeared at rest, her mind zipped to and fro with anxiety. What was the world coming to? Girls chasing around the country looking for husbands? That was not the way things had been done in her youth. No indeed. A proper courtship took time, and wooing, and discreet meetings at county gatherings. She exhaled. *Not that Rod courted me in the proper manner.* Be that as it may, The Unpleasantness had changed the world for Marie. That was mighty clear.

Chapter 3

The night before Pa trailed his beef cows to the Cuchara, Marie tossed and turned. Jule elbowed her once, then went back into slumber land, but Marie's mind seemed to bubble with imaginings like a pot boiling over on a too-hot stove. It wouldn't allow her the relief of sleep.

She wondered whether she dreaded or anticipated the next few days. If Pa liked Tom's prospects and proposed to add him to the family, the young man's reaction would play a big part in Marie's future. He might have given up thinking about Ellen by now. He might accept Pa's suggestion with enthusiasm. He might jump into making and carrying out plans for a wedding and a life together. On the other hand, he might have no notion of marrying her, and his disinclination could doom her to spinsterhood.

Who else was there for her to marry? She lay very still, searching every nook and cranny of her brain for prospects. She'd seen the Dominguez brothers several times when they stopped by to water their horses on their way to Pueblo Town or back. Patricio and Enrique Dominguez cut blazingly romantic figures, with their wide-brimmed hats and differently-styled clothes, their teeth-flashing smiles and flirtatious comments. She thought the pair of them was tremendously exciting. Given the chance, which one would she choose to wed?

After thinking on the exotic brothers for a time, she sighed and discarded the wild idea of being courted by such a man, knowing Pa was dead set against any marriage in that direction. That left her with a suitor pool made up of Tom Morgan, grubby freighters from Pueblo Town, hard rock miners from the north and the west, or her father's cowhands.

Tom had his distinctions. Despite being a farmer, he washed his hands before eating and wore fresh clothing to social events. He kept his medium brown hair trimmed above his collar, and it was never greasy. He had his moments of merriment, but he'd always treated her with respect. Or maybe it was diffidence.

Marie turned on her side, and let her mind examine that topic. Tom had never sought her out as an object of courtship, although she now suspected his pa and her own had intended for some years for them to marry one day. She and Tom, though, had never discussed marrying. Never once.

During their journey to the West, Tom had acted the same way toward her as he had towards Carl's then-fiancée, Ida Hilbrands, or to Ida's younger sisters. He had turned on the charm with Ellen, but she had given him little chance to make inroads into her heart. Marie alone had known of Ellen's secret yearning for Carl, although she was betrothed to James. Yes, Tom could be witty, but he could be mighty boring, as well.

Patricio Dominguez would never be boring. She didn't know how much English he spoke or understood, but it would certainly be interesting, no, it would be tremendously exciting, to live in his house, learning a new language, having servants, being married . . ..

She inhaled sharply and pulled the quilt over her head. What was she thinking? She was as bad as Jule, trying to picture what goes on behind a couple's closed door. She'd seen horses mating, and a human encounter must involve the same elements. That wasn't her business yet. She'd learn all about it first hand, once she married Bill.

Bill? The hot flush of burning cheeks drove her out from under the covers. *I don't mean Bill. I mean Tom. Lawsy! What am I thinking?* She squeezed her eyes tight, trying to banish the errant image that persisted in her brain of Bill Henry's contrite face when she'd lashed out at him in anger the morning her horse had bolted.

The image lingered, however. She could not banish it in favor of Tom's bland visage. Then a series of Bills lined up before her inner eye: Bill, looking stricken as she berated him, the color of his eyes deepening almost to black, as though he willed them to shelter his soul. Bill, saying, "I didn't mean you." Bill, his moustache twitching on the left side of his mouth as she turned away from him.

Marie shook her head, trying to drive the specters away. Bill Henry should not be in her mind when she was, in all likelihood, going to end up in Tom Morgan's marriage bed.

℘

When Pa called Marie to rise, she opened her eyes, surprised that she had, at last, slept. Her last memory was of Bill Henry's face, and her cheeks flushed again as she flipped the quilt aside, swung her legs out of the bed, and drew her nightgown down over her knees.

Jule lay still, her breath rattling a bit in her nose.

Disgusting! Marie thought. *She's snoring. Thinks she's so high and mighty.*

After feeling her way to the clothes she'd laid out the previous night, she dressed in the dark. Dawn hadn't broken yet; it wasn't due for another hour. She yawned, shivered a bit, then fastened her shoes. She didn't want to take the trouble or the time to dress her hair in the dark, so she threw it back over her shoulders as she climbed down the ladder from the loft.

Pa had left a lantern on the floor beside the outside door. Marie picked it up, opened the door, and hurried through the dooryard.

As she arrived at the stable, Marie saw that Albert held three saddled horses just past the corner of the building. Pa had already mounted his horse, a crow-hopping dun mustang she remembered from the day her horse ran away. Her face warmed. Bill Henry had been in the mustang's saddle that day. *Is he coming with us?* she wondered, looking around to see if the Texan was hiding outside the reach of her light. *Evidently not.* Her disappointment surprised her.

"There you are," Pa said, catching sight of Marie as the nervous horse turned him around. He sounded impatient.

"I came straight away," she said, lifting her chin.

"Well, find your horse. We must get on the trail." He clicked his tongue at the mustang and moved off into the darkness.

Rulon approached and took the lantern from Marie. He hung it on a peg driven into the wall of the stable, then boosted her into the saddle cinched onto the back of a docile brown mare she hadn't ridden before. "Take heart, sis," he said, making a rueful face she could barely see in the lamplight. "He's always grouchy when his horse won't obey, but that one settles down, and Pa will, too."

Marie made her own face back, and adjusted her seat in the saddle. This animal was the one usually ridden by Jule, and she wasn't sure if it would keep up with the others.

As though reading her mind, Rulon patted the horse's neck. "Bess is a traveler," he said. "Good tempered she may be, but she's got heart, as well, and a good gait. You'll like the ride."

"Did you pick her out for me?"

Rulon's smile crinkled the corners of his eyes. "Nope. Pa did that." He nodded in the direction their father had gone. "We'll have a long day's journey, and he looked to your comfort."

Just then, Albert blew out the lamp, and Marie was grateful for the darkness that rushed in to replace the light. She was glad Rulon couldn't see what she felt: her cheeks were burning as they colored. She listened to the twin creaks of leather as her brothers swung onto their horses. Rulon said "Hiyah!" and slapped the free ends of his reins against his horse's side to get it underway. The tinkle of spurs told her Albert used his heels. She clucked Bess into motion to follow them. The warmth of her cheeks spread into her bosom. Her pa did take notice of her well-being.

❧

As the first suggestions of light brightened the eastern sky, Marie let her horse follow Rulon's toward the corral. They drew up in a bunch behind Pa on the side of the trail.

The cowboys had driven the chosen longhorn steers down from the mountain the previous afternoon. Now they bawled and moved around in the enclosure, as Clay went to unlatch the gate and let them out. The moment he swung the gate open, a fat steer burst through the hole, and Albert, on one side, and Pa, on the other, headed the animal toward the trail south. The other eleven steers followed.

Clay mounted his horse and caught up to Albert, while Marie let Rulon follow their father. She lagged to the rear, as she had been told to do the previous day. She didn't expect to do any work, but found that she occasionally needed to urge a steer forward. Bess seemed to know what to do, so she eased up on the reins and let the horse have its head. Marie merely hung on for the ride.

After a while, Marie began to enjoy chasing the errant steers. One took off to the left, and Marie leaned forward in the saddle, put her heels into Bess's sides and yelled "Hi there!" The horse jumped forward and set out after the steer. With Marie's vocal encouragement, Bess drove the animal back to the little herd.

Pa looked around, and rode back to where Marie followed the herd. "I don't mean for you to work the cattle, daughter. Follow along, and if a steer escapes, call out for one of your brothers."

"I can do the job," she answered back.

He scowled. "You mind. Those horns can catch you quick as a wink."

"I'm watching out for them." She raised her chin a bit, but kept her face smooth, expecting a dressing-down.

He gave her a disapproving look, but said nothing else before returning to his position at the side of the herd.

"Hmm," Marie said. "He's going to allow it." She didn't dare give vent to the yell she wanted to launch. Instead, she whispered, "Yippee."

After a while, the steers behaved better, docilely following the lead steer down the trail. Marie, left to her own devices, found herself enjoying the view. Although it wasn't as green as Virginia, the undulating nature of the mostly bare landscape, coupled with occasional buttes poking up like thumbs, intrigued her. At a distance of several miles, she saw a few buildings built in the shade of trees along a watercourse, and others against a hilly up cropping. Where did the Dominguez family live? Was that their homestead tucked beneath one of those worn earthen hills?

She mused on her own wonderings. Pa's stand against her offhand suggestion of a match with a Mexican had left no question in her mind that no such marriage would take place while Roderick Owen lived. She shrugged. She had only tossed the notion into their altercation as a challenge to his authority. She had been angry, true enough. No one likes to feel they've been ignored, or even worse, slighted on purpose. The gentle gait of her horse, Bess, was a testament that Pa did care about her, or at the very least, he was thinking about her now.

Her mind leaped to her uncertainty about Tom. He'd run with a bunch of the county boys who were a tad younger than Carl, always around since she could remember. Yes, he'd gone away when he'd been called up to the infantry, but had managed to come through all the fighting without any major wounds. When he returned, she heard his intention was to go halves with his father on the farm. But the fields had been burned—scorched black—by Sheridan's army, and the ground had not recovered. Mr. Morgan had jumped at Pa's offer to bring them west, and that had been that.

Marie wondered why Pa hadn't arranged a marriage for her with Tom from the outset. Hadn't he seen that she was woman-grown? If they'd been promised, he wouldn't have chased after Ellen.

Not wanting to fall back into her former despair, Marie shook back her wind-whipped hair and started looking around at the countryside again. Far to the south, two mounded peaks thrust up from the prairie, a pair of mountains that looked like, well, very like her own bosom. She blushed at the thought. Ma would be mortified to know her daughter was thinking about body parts. That was unseemly.

She focused again on the steers slowly moving forward before her. Albert and Clay had switched places, and her youngest brother was off chasing a critter. He whooped with great gusto, his high yells filling the air. She thought of telling him to be quiet, that he was scaring the poor animal, but what did she know about how steers reacted to noise? Maybe they liked being chased and harassed by young boys.

I don't think I would like it, she thought. *Bertie can be an awful pest. He would drive me wild, if I was a steer, chasing me and yelluping that way.*

A steer bawled to her left, running toward a scrubby cedar tree, and after no one dropped back to head it off, Marie went after it.

Wishing she had a rope like her brothers, she yelled at the animal. Bess got to the far side of the steer and moved to block its progress.

"Get over there," Marie whooped, "scat, go on!" She waved her free arm and the steer turned, showed the whites of its wild eyes, and ran back to the rest of the herd.

Ha! she thought. *I'm just as good a cow driver as Bertie.*

Marie looked up to see Rulon riding back toward her. She steeled herself for a confrontation, but saw he was grinning at her.

"Well done, sis," he said.

"I thought Pa sent you to scold me."

Rulon chuckled. "That he did. That he did. You don't have to tell him I reckon you're doing a fine job of work." He winked at her, then raised his voice. "What do you think you're doing, girl?"

Marie put on a contrite face in case Pa was watching, and bowed her head in submission, but she could scarcely keep her giggles in check. Rulon shook his finger in her face for good measure, then winked again, turned his horse around, and rode away. Knowing Pa could see her if he took a notion, Marie compressed her lips to stifle a smile or a laugh, then rode back to the rear of the cavalcade.

The day grew warmer as the sun rose higher in the slate blue sky. Dust arose in abundance behind the steers, hanging in the air in their wake. A swarm of flies happened by, attacking the steers, who switched their tails to drive off the pests.

Marie batted away a few of the biting flies, and wished she had a canteen filled with water to sooth her dry throat. Or maybe, since they were moving through land that had been settled by Mexican folks, she should carry the kind of skin bottle she had seen the Dominguez brothers filling up at Pa's creek. Lacking either one, she'd have to ask one of her brothers for a drink.

Clay was closest to her, so she hurried Bess in his direction. When she caught up to him, she asked for his canteen.

"Where's yours, sis?"

"I don't own a canteen. I'm thirsty, so I'm asking you for water."

Clay held his up. "This is Carl's. He don't need it these days." He held it beside his ear and shook it.

"Clay!" Marie held out her hand so Clay would give her the water container.

He handed it over, and watched as Marie tipped it up and greedily slaked her thirst.

"Huh! I thought girls drank a mite more dainty-like," Clay said.

She swallowed again, then lowered the canteen. "Maybe I would if I wasn't doing a boy's job. It's dusty back there." She handed it back, then flipped her hair forward over her shoulders, and beat some of the dirt out of it.

Clay shook the canteen, anxiety clouding his countenance. "Sounds like you drank it dry, sister."

Marie lifted her hair in both hands and shook it. "I left you at least one swallow."

"Barely that," Clay protested.

"It's nearly noontime. Pa should call a halt for dinner soon. You can fill it then." She reined Bess around and rode away.

୧୦

As Marie drove the steers closer to the Southerners' settlement on the Cuchara River, her good humor abandoned her. Nervous foreboding rushed in to take its place.

Bess must have sensed her unease, for she stopped moving forward, turned her head, and looked inquiringly at Marie. Marie looked back at the mare, her stomach flip-flopping with anxiety. Bess shook her head and whinnied. The herd disappeared into a draw, tails flicking the flies away. Marie sighed.

"Let's keep up, good horse," she said, reaching forward to pat the animal on the neck. "I'm nervy enough without getting left behind." She bumped her heels on Bess's flanks, and finally persuaded her to move forward after the steers again.

Rulon's head came up out of the draw, followed by his body, then his mount. When the entirety of him came into view, Marie could see the relief spreading over his tanned face. He waved, and beckoned to her in a "come along" gesture. She waved back, and urged Bess into a lope.

"Trouble?" Rulon asked once they were riding together down the slope of the draw.

"No. Bess took a notion that I needed a rest." She laughed, then reflected on the thinness of the sound. It would not convince a careful listener that she had merriment in her soul. "No matter," she added.

Rulon glanced over at her, studied her face for a moment. "You do look a mite peaked, sis, not to mention sunburnt." He cocked an eyebrow. "Pa says by and by we'll be nooning for a bite to eat and a rest." He nodded at her then. "You keep up, you hear?"

When she nodded in reply, he clucked to his horse, and it jumped forward across the bottom of the draw and up the other side.

The noon stop couldn't come fast enough to suit her. It would be a welcome relief from the sun and the dust and the flies. Marie wiped her sweaty, dusty forehead with the back of her hand, then realized her face was tender to the touch. *Sunburnt indeed*, she thought. *That's my own folly.* She sent Bess into a bit more speed to rejoin the herd, wishing she'd thought to borrow a hat, or at least, to bring her sunbonnet.

An hour later, Pa did call a halt for dinner when the company came upon a stream with a pebbled bottom. After the boys watered the steers in the stream, they drove them up the southern bank and onto a grassy area. Then they watered all the horses and picketed them nearby on the grass.

Marie opened the saddlebags, spread a cloth on the bank, and put out tin plates and cups for her father, her brothers, and herself. She unwrapped the cornbread and beef she and Ma had prepared and put a portion of each on the plates. Then she went to the creek, upstream from the place they'd crossed, and dipped a bucket into the water.

She had almost carried it back to the eating area when Albert swooped in, snatched the bucket, and poured the water over himself.

As he wiped the water from his eyes, Marie cried out, "You oaf! That's drinking water!"

"Works just as well to cool me off," he said in a sneering tone, shaking himself like a dog to make Marie wet.

"Bertie, I'll get you," she cried, and picked up the bucket to hurl at him.

Rulon restrained her arm, and thrust the container into Albert's stomach. "Fetch clean water," he barked. "Now."

"Ah, you're no fun." Albert rubbed his abused belly. "You sound just like Pa, ordering me about."

"That's enough," Pa said, coming onto the scene. "Do as your brother says. Fetch fresh water."

Albert scowled and muttered, but did as he was bidden, stalking to the creek and back with ill humor.

Marie's hand trembled as she ate her meal. Although she was in good health, the sun, wind, dust, and insects all had combined to sap her strength during the morning's drive. Her muscles ached from unfamiliar use. She wondered how she would fare for the rest of the day, and the morrow's trek, as well. *However did I forget to bring my bonnet?* She regretted that she'd been in so great a haste to leave this morning that she gave no thought to effects of the sun.

She scratched surreptitiously at a fly bite on her neck. Her cheeks burned from sun exposure, and her throat was dry and scratchy, no matter how much water she drank. She raked her fingers through her tangled hair, with little success at smoothing it. Then she sighed.

I'm surely going to make an impression on Tom Morgan, and not for the better!

∞

When Pa called, "Mount up," at the end of their noon rest, Marie hauled herself up into the saddle with shaky arms. The noon break hadn't been long enough to restore the strength she'd lost as the morning waned. How she would keep up with the steers for the rest of the day was uncertain to her mind, but she surely wasn't going to voice her doubts in this company.

Fortunately, Pa's next words were to Albert. "You take drag this afternoon. Marie can ride in your place."

Mentally thanking her father, Marie rode to where the steers had been grazing as she rested. *How do I get them started?* she wondered, but Clay came along and answered that question by riding up to the rump of the nearest animal and prodding it into motion with his foot. "Get 'em moving. You don't have a rope, so twist a stick off a tree to poke 'em with, or use your foot. They'll follow this critter, once he's going down the trail."

"Is he the leader? The spotted one?" She gestured toward Clay's steer.

"Yep." Satisfied with his efforts with the first steer, he started in the direction of another, then wheeled his mount and returned to Marie's side. "Do you want me to get you a stick?"

"Might as well," she answered, heading toward a brown animal. "Could be my feet won't work as well, being smaller'n yours, by far."

Clay twisted a branch off a nearby willow and stripped off the leaves with his pocket knife. He brought it over to her, and gave it to her with a smirk. "It's going to bend a bit, but should serve the purpose."

"You think this will serve?" she exclaimed, bowing the branch nearly double.

"Whip 'em on the rear, if they won't get moving fast enough," he said, laughing.

"Oh bother," she said, and shrugged her shoulders. "Men and boys will be the ruination of me yet!"

"We're meant to torment the female of the species," Clay said, and rode off to his position.

"You do a right good job of it," she mumbled, and used the willow slip to good effect.

After what seemed to be hours of riding along the road, they approached another creek, and Pa called out, "We'll stop here for the night. Water 'em and bed 'em down, boys. Daughter, get supper ready."

Marie blew out a breath of air and climbed off Bess. Rulon came and got the mare while Marie set about getting the evening meal together.

After she had eaten and cleaned up, Marie prepared her bed at the foot of a tree, and then sat on her quilt for a while, her back against the trunk. Rulon strolled over and squatted beside her.

"You all set here?" He picked at his teeth with a flayed willow twig.

"Yes sir. Almost as comfy as my bed at home." She hugged herself. "I reckon I'll sleep after a bit, but I can't bring myself to close my eyes yet."

"It's a pretty night," he said, looking at the stars. When he looked at her again, he tilted his head to one side. "Are you sore, sis? You've been in the saddle for a long stretch, and you're not used to the sort of work you've been doing today."

She smiled wryly. "You caught me out, didn't you? I'm also burned and windblown and fly-bitten. I'll make a handsome prize for Tom Morgan."

"No, sis," Rulon said, drawing out the initial vowel as he shook his head. "You're a beauty despite a tad bit of sunburn. Tom Morgan's a fool if he don't see that tomorrow."

She rolled her eyes. "Big brothers always say such dainty things."

"The truth ain't a dainty thing." Rulon smiled. "Granted, I'm your big brother, and I may be a tad bit partial to you, but there's no denying you're a comely woman. You stand the competition on their noses."

Marie couldn't help but laugh.

"There now." He patted her hand. "That's what I like to hear."

"Rulon, who do you reckon is my competition?"

"Just a figure of speech, sis. There is no competition that stands up to you."

"There is no competition at all. I'm the only girl left single hereabouts." She ducked her head so Rulon wouldn't see hopelessness in her eyes.

He put two fingers under her chin, raised her face, and looked at her for a long time. "That is an unfortunate circumstance. You are worth more than any three girls back home. Don't forget that. Not ever."

She hoped the deepening darkness prevented Rulon from seeing the tears that suddenly caused her vision to swim. "That's sweet of you to say," she whispered, catching his hand. "No wonder Mary thinks the sun rises and sets on you."

Now Rulon ducked his head. "Go on!"

"I reckon I think that, too, big brother." She pushed him on the shoulder. "I'm sleepy now. You needn't watch over me tonight."

He touched her on the tip of her nose. "That's what big brothers are for." He got to his feet. "Good night, sis."

"Good night, Rulon."

Chapter 4

Although Chester Bates was obviously surprised to see a dozen steers being driven into his door yard several weeks before he'd planned for them to arrive, Marie thought he masked it well when he greeted Pa the next day.

"They look hale and hearty," Mr. Bates said, gesturing to the cattle.

"The pick of the lot."

"You're early."

"I need to see Ed Morgan right away. No sense making two trips when one will do."

Mr. Bates nodded slowly. "You may as well 'light, then. Rest your bones. Let your boys drive the beeves into the pen." He counted the crew members with a glance, his eyes widening when he saw Marie. "You brought the girl?"

"I have business that concerns her." Pa dismounted.

Mr. Bates's brow creased. "Are you brokering another marriage?"

Marie thought she would die as her father nodded. She hoped he would not begin to talk about her while she was still in earshot. She slipped off Bess and led her toward a tie post.

Mrs. Bates came from the house to join her, beaming as Marie looped the reins around the post. "Marie Owen! It is a blessed day when I get a caller." She hugged her, then, beckoning to a brown-skinned lad who was working nearby, called out in Spanish. "Ven aqui, joven."

The boy dropped his pitchfork and came running to see what Mrs. Bates needed.

"Quida al caballo," she said, giving the lad a few more instructions as to the comfort of the mare.

Marie marveled at the woman's command of the foreign language as the boy left with Bess in tow. "I didn't know you spoke Spanish, ma'am."

Laughing, Mrs. Bates drew her toward the house. "Why girl, a body has to know how to speak it hereabouts if you want to get the work done. It's a pretty tongue." Patting Marie's tangled hair, she said, "Now, we'll just take a brush to that mess of locks, and put buttermilk on your face to take the sting out of the sunburn."

In no more than five minutes, Marie sat on a chair in the kitchen, holding a buttermilk-soaked cloth to her face. She felt the heat lifting from her skin.

Mrs. Bates ran the brush through Marie's hair, stroke after stroke, patiently working out the knots. "Tell me the news, girl. How is your ma? Is Ellen well? How is that husband of hers? Is he on the mend?"

Marie spoke through the wet cloth. "Ma is doing as well as a body might expect. Carl is still mostly down in bed, but Ellen says he's making progress." She paused to remove the cloth and turn it over to the cool side. "Ellen is well, and she is happy. I ain't never seen a body so content."

"That's right gratifying to hear." Mrs. Bates worked at a particularly stubborn tangle for a moment, then asked, "Did your brother come back yet? Mr. Bates said your pa was right vexed that he left."

"No," Marie mumbled. "He's still gone. Ma grieves."

"I imagine so," Mrs. Bates said. "I imagine so." She lapsed into silence as she tackled another matted spot in Marie's hair.

Marie squeaked as the hairbrush pulled tight against her tender scalp.

"Oh, oh, oh, I'm sorry, girl," Mrs. Bates crooned. "Let me finger comb through that one." She put down the brush and used her fingers to coax the hair to separate. "You didn't bring any pins to put up your hair?"

"No. Pa was in such a hurry to leave, and I didn't have time to dress my hair. I didn't think to bring my bonnet, either. I'm paying the price now." She sighed.

"Let me wet that cloth again. I have plenty of buttermilk today." Mrs. Bates took the cloth from her, dipped it in a bowl, and wrung out the excess. "The butter specks look like yellow freckles, but I reckon they'll wash off." She gave the cloth back, and started in on the last tangle. "I don't have no spare hairpins. I can try something new, though, a little trick I learned from Paco's mama. She's the one teaching me the Spanish tongue," she continued. "She helps out here and there when I need her."

Once Marie's hair flowed freely down her back, Mrs. Bates went to a box shelf hanging next to the bed in the corner. She ran her fingers along the tops of the items stored there, then picked something up. She brought back a rectangle of embossed leather and showed it to Marie.

"Oh my, that's pretty," she said, fingering the design in the leather and the carving on a wooden pin that ran through a hole punched in one end and out a corresponding hole in the other. "What's it for?"

"You'll see," Mrs. Bates said, taking the item back and setting it on the table. She twisted Marie's hair into a bunch at the back of her head. "This won't hurt a bit," she murmured, as she fitted the leather piece to curve over the top of the hair. She thrust the wooden spike into one hole, worked it gently through Marie's hair, then poked it out the other. "There now," she said, making sure the clasp was secure. "That's right pretty, and will keep the tangles away, for sure." She handed Marie a bit of mirror. "If you don't like this, I can braid your hair."

Marie caught her breath at the tidy reflection. "I never thought of braids, being so old and all."

"Old!" Mrs. Bates laughed. "When did you get to be old? You're just now at your best, girl."

"My sister tells me I'm old."

"Julianna? That girl has no sense. Get the notion of being old out of your head. It will only give you the vapors. You're as lovely as can be, and don't you forget it."

Pa swung open the door and poked his head into the kitchen. "Time to leave, daughter."

"I'm coming," she said, and removed the cloth from her face as he pulled his head back through the opening and shut the door. "I thank you for the buttermilk cure, Mrs. Bates, and for pulling the snarls out of my hair." She touched the leather clasp. "May I use this while I'm down hereabouts? I reckon Pa will let me bring it to you when we come back through on the way home."

"You keep it, girl. I'll have Mr. Bates make me another."

"Thank you, ma'am!" Marie almost squealed in her delight.

Mrs. Bates poured the buttermilk from the bowl into a small crockery container. "You take this crock of buttermilk, now. Keep putting it on your face when you get a moment. It will help that burn heal up."

"You're so kind, ma'am."

"Now girl, don't you be 'ma'aming' me anymore. You'll be a married lady one of these days. You need to get used to naming me 'Muriel'."

"Oh, no, ma'am, I couldn't. It wouldn't be fitting."

Mrs. Bates put the crock and the cloth into Marie's hands. "Nonsense. You'll be a-calling me 'Muriel' before you know it."

"Perhaps, once I've wed. I'll try it on for size when that time comes."

Mrs. Bates hugged her and started to see her to the door. She stopped and said, "Hold on now. I have something else you can use." She went to a trunk and raised the lid. Rummaging around among the clothes inside, she lifted out a yellow sunbonnet. She dropped the lid, brought the bonnet to Marie, and tied it on her. "There now. That's Ellen's. When you get home, return it to her."

"Thank you, ma'am," Marie said on a gusty sigh. "That will be a relief to my woes."

Even though she looked and felt more presentable now, Marie climbed on Bess's back with dread beginning to curdle her stomach. Inside of a few miles, all the Owens would get off their horses at the Morgan homestead, and Marie would face her future.

∞

Without any steers to chase, Marie rode beside Rulon along the bank of the Cuchara River. Clay and Albert loped their horses in the distance, and Pa's dust lingered in the air ahead.

"Calm yourself, sis," he said.

"I'm trying to. Truly I am." She felt like a baby kitten, too weak to open its eyes or walk proper.

"Mrs. Bates did a fine job of fixing you up right nice," he said as he appraised her. "A fine job."

"She has a kind heart," she said, then put her hand to her face. "Did I wipe off all the yellow specks? I don't want to look like a bowl of buttermilk."

He laughed and inspected her closely. "Yep, you're free of specks. You'll pass Mrs. Morgan's muster."

"I can only hope for such good fortune." She rode in silence for a hundred yards, then said, her voice shaking, "Rulon, I'm scared."

"What's got you in a dither, sis?"

"Tom."

"Tom?"

"He's never made any fuss over me. What's to change that now?"

Rulon held his peace for a long time. "There's nothing about you to dislike," he finally said, his voice rumbling, seeming to come from his chest. "Everybody who knows you values your good sense. You're a hard worker. You're a fine looking girl. Once Tom sees his future clear, he's bound to strive to make a good life for you. If he doesn't . . .." He let his voice trail off.

"If he doesn't, what could you do, Rulon?"

He thought for a moment. "If Tom mistreated you, Pa would have the first right to act, but if he didn't, I would come and fetch you back home."

"Ah," she cried out. "That would be worse than being on the shelf. I'd be the pity of the neighborhood, a rejected wife!"

"There now. I didn't mean to send you off into a state. There now, Marie. That's not so. We'd be . . . We would . . ." He lapsed into silence.

Marie sniffed several times.

"Don't you go to cryin'! You'll make streaks down your face," Rulon said, clearly alarmed.

"Well, we can't have that," she said, and sniffed again, swiping her eyes with her sleeve. "Are we close to the place?"

"I see a barn ahead, a half mile or so off."

"I can't—"

"Yes you can. Raise up your chin, sis. You're an Owen, and no better stock is to be found hereabouts."

"Stock!" she exclaimed. "Yes, as good as any Owen heifer," but she gave herself a little shake and sat upright in the saddle.

The pair rode on without a word until they reached the Morgan farm, when Rulon caught hold of Bess's bridle and murmured to Marie, "Remember, sis, chin up. Tom's a fool if he don't come to care for you."

More fool me if he doesn't, she thought, but gave her brother a ghost of a smile.

༄

Rod encountered Edward Morgan in his corn field, where he was engaged in chopping weeds. "Rough work on a warm day," he said.

Ed looked up, straightened his back until it creaked, then leaned on the hoe, pursing his lips before he spoke. "Yep."

"You're looking a mite down in the mouth. What's ailing you?"

The farmer rubbed his upper lip with a knuckle, then dropped his hand and rubbed his thigh.

At length he said, "It's the missus," and shook his head. "She's bothered, so she shares with me."

"Humph," Rod commiserated. "Womenfolk." He doffed his hat and began to feel along the scab above his ear, then let his own hand descend as he re-seated his hat. "What's she bothered about?"

"Lizzie don't much like it out here. She says it's too dusty. Then the wind comes up, blows the dust away, and she complains it's too windy."

"What are you doing about it?"

Ed humphed on his own accord. "Mostly staying out of her way! She'll hunt me down, though, time to time. I got cornered last week, and ended up promising to dig her a well." He flung his hand outward. "She's got a perfectly good river just yards away, and she wants a well!"

Rod tugged on his earlobe. "That does make a man weary. You've got a fair piece of work ahead of you."

Ed nodded. "Your woman minding her manners?"

"Mostly," Rod said, nodding in concert with Ed. "I reckon she's worried some about the girl."

"Which one?"

"The older one. To tell you the truth, that's why I come a calling." Rod drew himself to his full height. "That Tom of yours. Does he have plans?"

৯৩

Elizabeth Morgan bustled up, followed by her two daughters, Louisa and Melissa. "Just look who is here," Mrs. Morgan crooned. "It is Miss Marie, come for company. Now you get yourself down off that horse, missy, and come along into the house. Is that sunburn I spy? However did you come to be sunburned?"

She looked to Rulon for support, but he raised his eyebrows and shrugged as though to say, "You're on your own with the women folk," and heeled his horse toward the knot of men at the barn.

She slid off Bess, and Mrs. Morgan bundled her along toward the house, despite Marie's intense desire to know what Pa was saying to Mr. Morgan about his errand.

Mrs. Morgan asked, "Whatever are you doing, riding astride that horse? Why ever are you here with your papa and the boys?"

"You're all sunburnt," Louisa exclaimed, echoing her mother's tone. "Come out of this heat. You're fixing to grow freckles on that burnt skin."

"We brought steers down to Mr. Bates," Marie managed to say, removing her sunbonnet in between the fuss Mrs. Morgan and her daughters made over her.

"But your papa didn't need you to shoo them cow critters down the trail, surely?" Mrs. Morgan protested.

"Why were you forking a horse'?" Melissa asked. "Don't your pa have a proper saddle for you?"

"I forgot my bonnet," she said. She tried to answer all the questions, first turning to Mrs. Morgan. "It was dark when we left, and I simply forgot to fetch it along." She held up the yellow bonnet. "Mrs. Bates gave me this one." She turned to Melissa. "No, we don't have a sidesaddle. I don't mind. Riding astride a horse is simpler than riding sidesaddle. Safer, I reckon." She felt a touch faint. So much attention at one time overwhelmed her, and she wondered if she'd forgotten any important questions. The matter of her being along for the cattle drive remained unaddressed, however, even under further prodding by Mrs. Morgan.

Once inside the house, Mrs. Morgan and her coterie swept her into a small side room that served as a parlor.

"You set down, now," Mrs. Morgan proclaimed. "Tell us all the news. Is it a fact Ellen Bates got herself married to your brother Carl? Ain't he the wrong brother? Weren't she meant to marry James?"

Marie took a seat as Louisa put in her query, "Is it true James took himself off to work in the mines?"

Melissa added, "Did he sock your pa?"

Horrified at the thought, she shook her head repeatedly. "No! He wouldn't. He never. I mean—"

"There now. Drink a cup of tea," Mrs. Morgan said, handing her one. "I made it up this morning, so now it's cool and refreshing."

Marie sipped the cold tea, her mouth puckering at the slightly bitter taste while her mind whirled at the notion of her brother doing violence on her father. James couldn't have been that angry! He was prideful, yes, but not violent. Her hand shook and she lowered the cup to its saucer to keep it from spilling. Mrs. Morgan must not have any sweetener. That surely wasn't sweet tea.

When she heard the tread of men's boots in the kitchen, her stomach quaked. The time of reckoning had come.

Even Rulon's recent exhortation couldn't make her raise her head to seek out Tom Morgan's eyes as the men folk trooped into the room.

"Make yourself comfortable, Rod," Mr. Morgan said.

She heard Pa sit down, but Mr. Morgan remained on his feet. "Mrs. Morgan, our neighbor has a proposition," he said.

She wanted to flee. She bent forward to place the rattling cup and saucer on a table that was barely within her reach, as she didn't want to dump the tea onto the floor. Where was Tom? Had he accompanied the two men into the parlor? A hand clasped her shoulder and she jumped.

"Steady," came a whisper.

Rulon.

"Chin up."

She tried, but couldn't achieve the task.

"You girls go sweep out the kitchen and wash up the dishes," Mr. Morgan continued.

Marie heard the footfalls as Louisa and Melissa scurried out of the room without saying a word.

"Rod Owen thinks it's time Tom took a wife."

Marie inhaled so violently that she squeaked, but the sound was masked by Mrs. Morgan blurting, "Oh my! That's a bit . . . sudden."

"I understand he's twenty years of age," Pa said. "It's high time he got hitched in double harness."

"He's proposing that Tom ask Miss Marie for her hand," Mr. Morgan said.

When Mrs. Morgan made no response, and no one else ventured to speak, Marie felt as though she could not breathe. The silence continued, except for inhalations. Exhalations. All but hers.

When she could not bear to hear the breathing of the others in the room while she suffocated, she glanced up at last. Tom leaned against the wall, his arms folded, staring at her. His frown was an arrow to her heart.

"He's only a boy," Mrs. Morgan finally said.

"He's old enough," Mr. Morgan answered. "What do you say to that, Thomas?"

"I ain't got a choice?" Tom asked in a clipped tone, glancing at Mr. Morgan.

Marie looked at the man, and seeing his pursed lips, looked back at Tom.

He turned his stony glare in her direction. "It appears to be decided," he said. Ice dripped from his voice. "We're to make a couple, Marie."

Marie's heart sank at the stark statement. Was that how a man asked for a girl's hand? He'd even left off the customary "Miss," as though he spoke to an inferior soul. *He won't love me,* she thought, panic filling her chest. *He'll never love me.* She wanted to melt down into the horsehair seat cover. She wanted to scream, "Rulon, take me home and hide me away." But she didn't. She had no breath for words.

Pa said, "Good. We'll make plans, then. How about . . ."

Marie shut her eyes and finally sucked in a burning lungful of air as others in the room took control of her future.

෨

As soon as she could manage it, Marie got out of the parlor and left the house. She wanted to find Bess, climb on the mare's back, and gallop back home.

Before she could accomplish her desires, Tom came out and joined her in the dooryard. "How about that?" he said. "Me pairing up with you."

His distant tone filled her with rage, and she wanted to lash out at him, but knew it would be futile.

"Yes sir," she muttered instead. "You and me."

Tom narrowed his eyes and put an arm across her shoulders. "They're planning to see us wed this fall, after the harvest."

"That soon?" Marie voice rose in a squeak. Feeling Tom's arm heavy on her, she fidgeted, wondering how best to remove it.

"Don't be nervous, girl. I'm disposed to treat you kindly." He began to walk, and she could do nothing but walk along beside him.

His path took them out behind the barn and into a field of corn. The row was too narrow for them to walk abreast, so Tom dropped his arm from Marie's shoulders and took her hand to draw her along behind him. She followed woodenly, stumbling occasionally on a clod of earth.

"Careful now," he said, turning to her and grabbing her other hand. "Don't be clumsy and knock down the stocks."

He cares for the corn more than for me.

"You may like it here," he said offhandedly. "That river runs cold. It comes from the high mountains behind the Spanish Peaks over yonder. I reckon the water's snow melt." He let go of her hands and grasped her by the shoulders, rubbing his thumbs along the fabric above her collarbones in a proprietary manner. "It's a hot day. Let's take a wade in the water."

"What are you talking about? Right now?" Marie felt her brows drawing together. She wished he'd remove his hands from her.

"You seem a mite warm from your journey. Could be you need a dip in that stream."

"I don't know. I think I hear Pa calling."

He snorted. "No. He'll be busy for quite a spell. We'll go wade in that water." He took her hand again and yanked her into a run down the row. She passed through the stiff stalks, getting silk and pollen all down her sleeves and skirt, and felt her nose twitching. Just as a sneeze gathered, ready to burst out, they broke into the open, on the bank of the river.

Tom didn't stop, but kept pulling Marie behind him down the bank and into the water.

"My shoes," she cried out, stumbling, losing her footing, falling, trying to catch herself against Tom. But he was deep in the stream, too, and there was nothing to keep her from plunging into the chilly water.

Panicked, she flailed against the drag of her clothes pulling her under. Thrashing around, she broke the surface and gasped for air, trying to remember what James had taught her so long ago about moving around in water. *I won't drown*, she thought. *If Tom's trying to drown me out of spite, I won't oblige him.*

Something caught her hand, and suddenly Tom was there, pulling her toward the edge of the river.

"I didn't figure you'd sink like that. Parley and Harry never do."

"Parley likely knows where he's going," she shouted, anger finally overcoming her panic as she made it to dry land. "Harry likely doesn't trip on the stones." She fell onto the grass, struggling to arrange her sodden clothing into order, then looked at her soaked shoes. "They likely don't ruin their only shoes."

"You're right. We don't wear shoes in the river. Nor nothing else," he said, looking her over with bold eyes. "I should have let you shuck your clothes."

"Shuck my—" Marie got to her feet and stormed toward the corn field. "You are a thoroughly crazy man, Thomas Morgan." She stomped away, muttering to herself, "He has his nerve. 'Shuck my clothes!' The idea!"

Tom followed her. "Don't go getting upset. We go dipping all the time with no clothes on."

"You and your brothers do! I ain't your brother." She wouldn't give him the satisfaction of seeing her red face, so she didn't turn to look at him as she flailed him with her words. "My pa means for me to be your wife." She couldn't bare the shame of his suggestion anymore, so she started to run through the corn stalks.

"What's the harm?" he asked, catching up to her, grabbing her hand and swinging her around to face him. "Once we're married, I reckon we'll see each other with no clothes quite regular."

Rattled by her abrupt spinning halt, but even more by Tom's unseemly words, Marie tried to get the picture of herself lying naked with the young man out of her head. Shame transformed to anger. She breathed hard two times, her breath coming and going with a rasp, then raised her chin and looked him in the eye while she shook her hand out of his grasp with one strong downward swing of her arm. "That time hasn't come. You leave me alone until it does, you hear? My pa won't stand for you fooling with me, no matter how anxious he is to see us wed."

She stared him down, and he had the good grace to lower his eyes.

"If you reckon he's not man enough to keep you honest, Rulon will back him up."

"Humph," Tom snorted, but didn't object further.

Marie turned and left him, almost frantic to seek shelter until her clothing dried and she could make herself presentable.

ဢ

Pa selected a campsite along the river, in a spot that lay between two fields of Mr. Morgan's corn.

Marie didn't particularly want to speak to anyone while the bitter memory of Tom's behavior sat in the front parlor of her mind. She busied herself with the camp chores, building a fire, cooking a meal, and preparing a pot of beans for their dinner on the journey home.

She thought work was enough of a barrier to keep her family from talking to her, but Pa sat himself beside her while she cleaned the dishes.

"Daughter," he began. "Did you and young Tom get your plans laid out?" He ran his hand through his beard for a moment, then added, "You were gone a long spell, so I went to seek you out. I found only the boy down at the river, chucking stones into the water."

She swiped the tin plate in her hand with her dishrag, watching it go around and around, until she almost felt dizzy. Words had abandoned her. What could she dare tell Pa about Tom's actions and words, his impious suggestions? Although Pa was her father, he was also a man. From the nighttime giggles she'd heard coming from below the loft, she guessed that he and Ma still had carnal relations, even though it was unlikely they wanted more children.

When she realized her father's gaze upon her had lingered long enough to turn into an inspection, she swallowed a couple of times to raise a bit of moisture in her dry throat, but her voice still sounded like a strangled cat when she said, "We had some talk, then I went to tend to Bess."

"Tom was a mite closemouthed. You and he didn't flaunt the conventions, did you?"

"No!" she denied, a bit more sharply than she would have wished. "I'm a proper girl."

Pa looked at her a long time, his gray eyes seeming to read her soul. Then he nodded and got to his feet. "I reckon your ma brought you up right." He reached out and patted her on the shoulder. "Get to sleep. We have a long trip home."

Chapter 5

The next morning, preparations for the journey home were a misery to Marie. She had no desire to talk to Rulon or anyone else, but went through the motions of making breakfast in the half-light before sunrise. After she packed up the remains of the meal, she went to arrange herself for the day. She looked for the hair clasp Mrs. Bates had given her so she could twist up her hair. Failing to locate it in the time she had available, she threw together one long braid to keep her hair in order, and then saddled Bess for the long ride.

For reasons known only to himself, Pa went back to the Bates homestead and stood in the barnyard to chat with Mr. Bates. Realizing that the farmer's kind wife would immediately sense her despair if she came out to talk, Marie forestalled an encounter with Mrs. Bates by fleeing into the wheat field behind the barn. She stood for a long time gazing toward the north. Although she had said her home felt like a prison, she acknowledged that it actually represented her sanctuary after their dreadful trek from Shenandoah County. Melancholy descended upon her like a heavy cloak as she thought of departing that home after the harvest. She scarcely moved until the sun climbed into the sky and Pa called that it was time to leave.

During their brief noon pause for dinner, Marie maintained her silence, spooning out beans and distributing the last of the corn bread, and then packing away the pot and utensils until their arrival home. Even when her younger brothers sought to tease her into joining them in splashing in the creek, she resisted their rambunctious delight.

❧

Without the need to herd cattle, the homeward trek lasted only until sundown. When Rulon peeled her off her horse in the twilight, Marie stubbornly took charge of her horse's care, then hauled the cooking gear into the house. Pleading fatigue, she retired without supper to the loft to be alone. She wrapped her arms around herself as she lay curled on the bed, wishing she could make the nightmare go away.

Her solitude was interrupted a half hour later when Jule climbed partway up the ladder and called out importantly, "Papa wants you. Come down right away." She disappeared before Marie could reply or uncoil herself to throw her pillow at her sister's insolent expression.

Knowing there was no remedy but to go see what was wanted, Marie backed down the ladder and turned to find the entire family still gathered around the supper table.

Pa arose from his chair and said, "Come, come, daughter. Don't keep us waiting longer," and indicated that she was to sit in his seat at the head of the table.

Marie sat, hanging her head.

"There now," her father exclaimed, "what aspect is this?"

She raised her chin and threw back her shoulders. *It's to be an announcement,* she thought. *Pa wants to preen himself.*

"This is a happy occasion," he began. "Tom Morgan has offered for the hand of our Marie, and they will be wed when the harvest has been gathered in." He patted her shoulder. "We'll make the word known at our barn raising."

She turned her head and stared at Pa. *Barn raising? He does like his surprises.*

Throughout the hubbub that ensued, Pa smiled, holding up a hand that called for silence. When the noise had died, he said, "We had a successful journey. I delivered the cattle, and made arrangements with Ed Morgan and his missus for Marie's marriage to Tom. Then I stopped back by and asked Mr. Bates to spread the news down along the Cuchara that I'm planning to build a barn. We'll have a great gathering of neighbors, and construct the barn on Saturday one month hence."

That's what Pa and he were jawing about. A barn raising.

Her father addressed himself to the boys. "We have half enough logs cut for a comfortable building for stock and tack. In the next month we'll finish logging, and then set up the foundation. You won't do it alone. I'll tell Henry to leave off branding, and enlist the hands to cut and haul the timbers."

I wonder what Bill Henry will think of that? Marie looked at her hands, gripped together. *Are there trees in Texas? Has he ever cut down a log? Does he even own an ax?* Then she remembered that Bill Henry was not her concern, and Pa was still talking, so she wrenched her mind over to the matter at hand.

"On Sunday, following all the work, we'll hold a Sabbath service. Randolph Hilbrands has come across a preacher in Pueblo Town who is amenable to traveling here from time to time to give us a good sermon. I'll send for him, for I believe we're all in need of a bit of worship."

Ma nodded her head, her hands tightly clasped on the table.

"Our neighbors will bring victuals to feed the workers, but you girls will need to help your ma prepare our share before they come." He looked at the boys. "Let's put in the work, and we'll have a sturdy building before snow flies. Now, prayers and to bed. Tomorrow will be a long day."

Marie went through the motions of participating in the nighttime devotions, but her mind was on the thought of the neighbors who would come to help raise the barn. Within a month, all the world would know she was going to wed Thomas Morgan, farmer. What they wouldn't know was that she would be trapped in an ugly situation for the rest of her life.

∞

Julia drew her shift over her head again, smoothing it down over her body as she glanced sidelong at Rod. He lay beside her, his eyelids only half open as his breathing slowed.

"You're a caution, you know that?" she murmured, wanting to snuggle against his bare chest, but resisting the impulse. The night wasn't as long as it needed to be, and they had best get to sleep.

He took a long lungful of air before replying. "I missed you. I missed my Julie-girl." He slid his arm under her neck and, turning to her, exhaled softly into her ear.

"There now, don't you begin again," she remonstrated, chuckling in a low tone. "We're getting too old for that business."

"What do you mean, woman? I can still love you 'til the day breaks."

She wanted to tell him that was nonsense, but knew he would take it as a challenge and that would be that for a good night's sleep. Instead, she gave him his nightshirt and asked, "Did you encounter any difficulties in making your arrangements with Ed Morgan?" She waited until he'd put the nightshirt onto his head before she let her fingers explore the red spot at the base of her throat where his enthusiasm had gotten out of hand.

"I did not," he said, his voice muffled by the soft cloth descending over his face. "I believe he took to the notion of joining our families."

She dropped her hand to the bed. "And Lizzie?" She felt a tingle of perversity at calling the woman by the nickname she so detested.

"I've no doubt she'll go along with it. Ed knows how to manage her."

She chuckled. "I daresay she manages him."

He inclined his head. "That may be," he acknowledged. "They're a pair, but good folks deep down."

"Just so she treats my daughter right."

"I reckon she won't hold a grudge against her because of your old quarrel."

"After all these years, you'd think she'd forget an apple pie prize at the county fair."

"You scratched her dignity, winning the ribbon when she'd prepared a place on the mantelpiece for it."

"I couldn't help that my apple crop turned out better that year. You'd think she could be content that she'd won half a dozen ribbons up until then."

"She is a mite prideful, that's true, but I don't see why she would harm Marie. It's not a blood feud between you two."

"I don't count it as such." She yawned. "I can't let that be a-preying on my spirits when it's after dark, husband. We've lost enough sleep as it is." Her words may have been sharp, but she smiled to think that her man still craved her favors after twenty five years.

He rested his hand on her arm, then patted it. "I know you're a-smiling over there, woman. You delight in me. Admit it."

She reached across her body and squeezed his hand. "Good night, husband."

He laughed, and she finally gave in to the desire to nestle against him, just for a moment, but not quite long enough to give his body any ideas.

Chapter 6

Bill had one leg raised with a foot in the stirrup, about to step into the saddle, when Mr. Owen hailed him.

"Henry!"

Bill had to extract his foot in a hurry. The Old Man's strident tone had upset his mount and it took to bucking, almost getting its chance to drag Bill.

Once he'd got two feet on solid ground, he turned to his employer, hoping the anger he felt wasn't showing on his visage.

"Glad I caught you," the boss said. "I have a new task for you and the hands. I'm building a barn come a month, and we all need to cut timber for the sides. Pine logs. Cut 'em to size, too. Twelve foot, I reckon. Here's the plan." He handed Bill a sheet of paper with figures written on one side and a drawing on the other. "We'll drag the logs out of the woods and stack them there." He gestured toward his chosen spot. "When folks gather to help us with the raising, I want the logs right at hand."

"Lots of folks?"

"I'm spreading the word through the country."

Bill looked at the paper. "Plan for Logging," it said. *Logging? I have no experience of that task.*

His doubts must have shown on his face because the Old Man asked, "All y'all have cut trees before?"

"In Texas? We was lucky when we had mesquite and cedar. Some live oak. There's nothing like pine in my part of the country."

Rod shrugged. "The same principle applies to cutting one tree as another. Rulon will show you where to begin."

Bill shook his head as the Old Man walked away. The cattle needed tending to, but that didn't seem to matter. Logging seemed to be number one on Rod Owen's chore list.

Bill put on speed to get to where Chico and Sourdough were saddling up. He explained the change in plans, tapping the paper he still held.

"What's that? You want us a-chopping down trees?"

Bill watched as Chico rolled his eyes and groaned at the news. He felt the same, but wasn't going to mention that fact to the cowhand. "It won't last long. We'll be done in a month."

"A month? Thirty days of hard labor on our feet?"

"We'll take Sundays off."

"They won't come near fast enough. I'll get calluses on my feet, never you mind the blisters I'll raise on my pretty hands. Have to soak 'em every night."

"You have a *queja*, take it to the Boss."

"Not me. That's your job. I signed on to work cattle, not make my complaint to the Old Man."

"Shut your mouth and get an ax. Rulon's in charge of the tree felling."

Chico swore mildly. "What's Old Man Owen want with a bunch of logs?"

Bill snorted. "The paper says he's fixing to build a barn. I reckon he's throwing a regular party to get it done. Inviting the whole countryside to pitch in." He chewed on a loose bit of dry skin hanging from his lip. "You reckon he'll farm us out for laborers come harvest time? He'll need to pay back a lot of favors."

"You're the one with the inside word, Henry. You ask him!"

∽

"Daughter, it's time you gave thought to your hope chest."

Hope chest? Without hope? Marie thrust aside the bitter qualms and answered, "Pa was too busy going to war to make me one, Ma."

Jule began chanting, "Marie don't have a hope chest. Marie don't have a hope chest."

"Stop up your mouth or I'll put a rag in it," Marie countered, lifting the dripping dish cloth from the tub. "I'll make sure it's slimy with soap."

Jule stuck out her tongue and fled outside, with one last jibing whisper trailing behind her, "Marie don't have a hope chest."

"She's a caution," Ma said, shaking her head. "I don't know what's got into the girl."

"Spite," she answered, biting off the word. "Jealousy. Woman's curse."

"I've never seen it come so early," Ma mused, putting dried plates on the kitchen shelf. "Be that as it may, we've got to find you the necessaries for wedded life." She scratched the base of her neck under her collar. "Linens. Where will we get linens?"

Marie saw the action. "Poison oak, Ma?"

A pink blush rose into her mother's cheeks. "No. An irritation. I'll put a bit of tallow on it."

Whisker burn, I reckon, Marie thought. *Pa's been after her again.* Then she felt shame that she was being disrespectful of her mother, and regretted that the notion had passed through her mind. It was no fault of her ma's that Pa had a mysterious, powerful drive to know her. *Know her. Like in the Bible. 'And Adam knew Eve his wife; and she conceived, and bare Cain.' Along with the knowing comes the begetting. I don't want to know Tom. I don't want to conceive and bare his sons! I want— I don't know what I want, but he don't have a willing spirit to want me, so I don't want him.* But she was trapped now, bound to marry Tom. Bound to be his wife. *What folly have I done? I should never have cast Pa's failings up to him.*

Ma was watching her, the high color draining out of her face now, watching her like she knew what Marie had been thinking about.

"You've seen the horses breed," Ma said, after she'd stared at Marie long enough to make her squirm. "And the cattle."

Marie's suspicions were confirmed. Ma had read her mind. Hands of guilt clamped around her throat so tightly that she couldn't speak. After a lengthy pause, she nodded, feeling her own blush suffusing her face.

"Human folks do the same to breed children." Ma's voice scarcely reached above a whisper. "It's needful, so as to keep the race of man alive."

Marie nodded again, mortified that she'd been caught with her mind fixed upon carnal thoughts.

"Time to time they do it for . . . for pleasure, for enjoyment." Her voice was even lower now. "They do it to show they care, one for another. I don't hold that a sin, like some folks do."

Marie's mind took hold of a dreadful notion. "Is Mrs. Morgan of that persuasion?"

Ma nodded. "I reckon she is."

The two of them merely breathed in concert for a while.

"Most men ain't persuaded of that idea," said Ma. "They have a need in them that makes them fairly fools from time to time. It takes hold of them, deep down, and there's no denying that . . . desire." She whispered the word as though it burned her lips. She licked them.

Marie felt like she was caught in a whirlpool, listening to her mother give voice to the forbidden subject. Her head swam.

"Some women feel it too. Strong." Ma bit her lip as though she didn't want to let out more of these searing words.

"You?" Marie wasn't sure she had actually asked that, for it felt more like she'd only breathed out.

Ma turned her head away, then after the air in the room felt thick as syrup as it entered her chest, Marie saw her look back.

"Yes," she said. Then she did a surprising thing. She smiled. "Call me a fool. Call me a sinner. Your pa can turn me to liquid butter with a touch. The yearning to join with him is." She stopped talking and bent her head to the side. She sighed. "There ain't no words, daughter. There ain't no more words to tell you." She shut her eyes. "I'm hoping Tom can bring that gift to you."

ℬ

Several days went by, as the cowhands engaged in their unfamiliar logging task. It wasn't like they were alone doing the chore, Bill reflected. The Owen brothers matched the hands tree for tree. Even the Old Man pitched in, with an air of nervous excitement. The only Owens not turning up for the work were Carl, who was taking his ease with a new bride while he recovered his health, and James, who had quit the place just in time to avoid this spate of labor.

Well now, that's not fair of me. Mining's no easy task. His ax thumped solidly into the pine trunk he was undercutting. As he worked, he likened his own situation with the fairer sex to that of James, whose fiancée had married another man, and worse still, his own brother. Bill had heard tell the Old Man had pressed the betrothal on James against his will in the first place. The whole business had gone bad for James. He wondered if the young man would ever come back and reconcile himself with his father. *I don't reckon he will. Rod Owen can be a hard man.*

It was that hard man's words that haunted him now. *I'm matching my girl up with a Virginia boy.* Bill wondered if the match had indeed been made down country, for Miss Marie had come home in a mighty sour mood, and she hadn't yet shook it off. Had the Old Man's matchmaking gone awry? All the family members did seem exercised about something.

He loosed his ax from the tree and stood it upright, leaning on the end of the handle for a brief respite.

"Hey, Henry. Hey! You sleeping? Shake your tail!"

Bill looked up to see a tree falling toward him, and he turned and ran from death.

The pine hit the earth where he'd been standing—limbs crashing and tearing—and bounced once before it settled amid a cloud of dust and pine needles.

He bent over, hands on his knees, and panted, trying to catch a breath, coughing out the dust he inhaled along with the air, shaken by the close call. With the pounding of his heart filling his ears, he could barely hear Chico razzing him, Rulon's concerned voice, and Albert's cat calls.

Chico sprinted to his side, his pale face belying the curses he let fall upon Bill's head.

"You got a death wish, *hombre*? Git your head outta the clouds and pay heed!"

An exhaled "Yeah," was all Bill could respond as he tried to will his heart to slow to a normal rate. He still felt the evil swish of a branch clipping his rear as he tried to get out of the way.

"Close," came Rulon's voice above him. It had a slight quiver to it.

"Yeah," Bill said again, not able or willing to speak more for fear of hearing his own voice break.

He raised himself up, feeling Rulon's light touch on one shoulder at the same time as Chico belted him on the opposite arm.

"Ow! I got clear of the tree, and you want to make me dead?" Anger firmed up his voice, and as he fended off Chico's next punch, Rulon walked away to continue felling his tree.

"Oh, git over there and pick up your ax," Chico countered.

"You the *segundo* now?"

"If you're dead, I'm the next man for the job."

"That's a likely tale," Bill muttered, but picked up the tool and went back to work.

଼

Late that afternoon, after Bill had stripped his upper body to the skin to remove chips of wood and pine sap with a good scrubbing, he stood beside the door of the bunkhouse, drying his chest with a piece of Turkish towel. He heard the jingle of spurs and the thud of hooves on the path behind him, so he looked around to see the Dominguez brothers ride into the clearing. He found his clothing and covered himself. Waiting until they were within earshot, he stepped forward and greeted the pair with, "*Buenas tardes.*"

Patricio responded in kind, and sat his horse until Enrique drew up beside him.

Bill told them to alight and care for their horses, and the brothers took to that business. When they had finished, they tied their mounts to a tree nearby and walked back to the creek to freshen themselves.

Squinting at the sun sliding behind the mountain, Bill buttoned his shirt and tucked it into his trousers while he tossed the idea of inviting the brothers to stop over for the night from one side of his mind to the other. He concluded that it was the polite thing to do, despite his reservations about the men's moral character, and waited until Patricio returned from filling his skin canteen with fresh water from the creek.

Bill extended the invitation, and the man accepted with a big smile and effusive thanks.

Then Enrique came up, bearing his own water container. Patricio let him in on the plan, and Enrique joined in the "gracias" giving.

"*Que Dios te bendiga.*" Enrique added a wish for heavenly blessings on Bill.

"*Muy amable,*" Bill thanked him, and bid the brothers come inside for supper.

After Sourdough's filling meal of beans and cornbread, Enrique piled his utensils on his plate and looked at his brother, who grinned back at him.

Enrique turned his eyes upon Bill. "You desire to have a leetle game?" He pulled a deck of worn cards from the inner pocket of his vest and wiggled them enticingly in front of the cowhands. "We play for esmall ante, *sí*? A penny only."

"That's about all I have left," said Chico. "Payday don't come around 'til the end of the month."

"I sure you have the luck," Enrique encouraged him. "Eet ees your time, no?"

"*Seguramente,*" added Patricio, nodding and smiling. "*Nosotros,* we have the luck turning, *este,*" he turned to Bill for help. "How you say '*mala suerte*'?"

"Bad luck. Taking a turn for the worse. Turning sour." He got up with his utensils and plate and carried them to the washtub, then headed for his bunk, thinking to get a full night's sleep.

"Ah, *gracias* señor," Patricio said to Bill's back. "We, eh, our luck ees taking a toorn for thee worse. That mean your *suerte* ees turning *buena*, good." Patricio's brows knit as he struggled with the language barrier, but he ended his inducement speech beaming broadly at Chico.

The cowhand pursed his mouth to the side, then arose, picked up his and Sourdough's plates, and nodded. "I ain't got but a little coin, but on the other hand, I ain't got no place to spend it this minute. Go ahead and set up the game while I wash up."

After the supper dishes were washed and put away, Bill changed his mind, dug into his saddlebag for a couple of dollars in coins, and drew up a chair to the table. The other men pulled out what little money they possessed and put it before them.

"Go easy on me," Sourdough said. "I ain't held pasteboards for longer'n I can remember."

"We play a friendly game," Patricio assured him. "The esmall ante, *sí?*"

The game commenced, and Bill found himself winning a hand, then losing a pot. He was about to quit the game in favor of sleep when a voice spoke from the doorway.

"Kin I play?"

Bill turned, irritated from his recent loss. Bertie Owen stood inside the half opened door.

"Ain't you supposed to be in your cradle by this hour?"

The boy hunched forward at the reply, his face pinking up a bit.

Bill knew he was being unkind, but sometimes the kid rubbed his fur wrong, and this was one of those occasions.

But Bertie wasn't through. He unfolded his shoulders and glared at Bill. "I've got cash and I know how to play."

"This is a man's game," Bill replied. Then he repented of his hard stance and said, "I suppose you can watch, if you don't interfere." He looked to the other players for backup.

They all nodded, and Bertie seemed to accept the decision. He hung an elbow over the spindle back of Chico's chair and settled himself to observe.

Bill played what he thought would be his final hand, but Lady Luck seemed to favor him at last. He won the pot, kept playing, and soon began building up a little pile of coins on the table before him.

When the hour had advanced beyond a time later than he was accustomed to being awake, sleep threatened to overcome him. He yawned as Chico folded, leaving Patricio as the only other player. With two aces and two kings, Bill figured this pot was a sure win, but to his chagrin, he lost it when Patricio displayed three twos that beat his two pair. He shrugged, pushed the money over to the man, and chalked it up to carelessness brought on by exhaustion and '*mala suerte.*' He'd sure enough had plenty of that lately.

Patricio and Enrique had almost reached the bunkhouse with their bedrolls when Albert stepped into their path. He looked back over his shoulder to make sure none of the hands were in sight, and said, "I saw what you did. Teach me that trick."

The brothers looked at each other, shrugged their shoulders, and made as though they would walk around Albert, but he forestalled them by acting out his demand.

"I saw you," he said, pointing to himself and then to his eye. Then he pulled on his shirt sleeve and appeared to be putting something into it. "I saw the trick," he repeated. "I want to know how you done it."

"No, *muchacho*," said Patricio in a patronizing voice. "*No hize nada.*" He tried again, in his muddled English this time, but his tone was still superior. "I do nothing."

"Don't you go lying to me. I saw that two card drop. You're a card sharp."

"*No soy trampista*," Patricio declared. "I no cheet."

"Yes you did. Teach me, en-sen-yar-meh, or I'll tell Mr. Henry you're a crook."

Patricio looked at his brother and shrugged, then addressed himself to Albert. "Come leetle boy. I teech."

Chapter 7

When Monday rolled around, Bill had scarcely set foot out of the bunkhouse when Albert Owen approached him.

"Nice day," he said. "You got a hankering for trading a chore with me?"

"Depends," said Bill. "What you trying to pawn off, Bertie?"

"Just a little light work carrying a bucket or two of water for my Ma. She says it's wash day. I'd druther chop and haul trees than spend my time listening to my sisters jaw at me. How about it?"

Bill's heart rose tight against his throat. He harumphed a time or two to get his voice back, then asked, "A bucket or two of water, you say?"

"Maybe four or five." He looked around, then spoke again. "Ma's not bad. It's Marie bossing me around that raises my hackles. I reckon she'd speak softer to someone besides me."

Bill tried to keep his face smooth. "I could use a break from stinking up my clothes with sweat." He put out his hand and shook the boy's. "I'll do it. Let Rulon know I switched with you so he doesn't think I'm sick in my bunk, or playing hooky."

The lad's got a future in wheedling folks to his will, Bill thought as he walked toward the Owen cabin to present himself for work. *Not that I mind one bit. This is a prime chance to talk to Miss Marie.*

Since the Old Man had rearranged the chore schedule, Bill had not been able to get close to the girl to find out what had her upset. She no longer took her horse out early for exercise, but stuck close to the main house, involved in a multitude of chores he could only guess at. Now, if he could get a minute alone with her, he might be able to discover if she was spoken for, or if he still had a chance to woo and win her.

By the time he'd come upon Mrs. Owen at the back of the cabin, his heart had worked itself up into his mouth. It took a fair bit of swallowing to do more than croak when she smiled briefly at him, raised her eyebrow, and said, "Morning, Mr. Henry. How can I help you?"

"It's my chore to bring you water, ma'am. I traded the job with Bert— Albert."

"Hmm," she said. "That young'un will do anything rather than carry water. I hope he's in for a good lot of work." She sighed, nodded toward the door, and said, "Yonder's the buckets. First, hang the wash kettle over the fire, then you can fill it 'bout midway. After that, bring up water for the rinse kettle. I haven't built the fire for that yet, but by the time the wash is boiling, I'll have it ready."

"Do you need help with the fire, ma'am?"

"No. Marie can help me with that task."

Bill glanced around, but Marie was nowhere in sight. As he drew near to where the buckets sat alongside the open door, he heard her speaking sharply to her sister.

"Pick that up, Jule. We can't waste it."

Julianna protested, but Marie continued, "Oh, brush it off. No, use this cloth. It's damp."

Bill caught up the buckets and headed for the creek, wondering what fair tidbit of food had fallen on the floor.

On the return trip, he saw Marie come out of the door and speak to her ma. Before he reached the kettles, she had gone back into the house.

That seemed to be the pattern for the day. He would go to the creek to fill another pair of buckets with water, and Marie would come outside. Before he returned, she had retreated.

A body would think she's avoiding me, he thought.

When Mrs. Owen bid him rest for a bit, Marie had gone up into the woods on an errand. When he went back to work, she came back to the house, but made no eye contact with him before entering and going about her own tasks.

Mrs. Owen added to his duties by giving him a long stick. "Stir the clothes around a bit, if you would. The water's boiling right nice, but the soap works better if it gets to all parts of the batch."

"Yes, ma'am." Bill stood over the kettle, stirring according to her directions until she put him to work rinsing the soap out of a batch of clothes.

When noon came, Mrs. Owen told him to go into the house and eat. Marie was alone.

Bill doffed his hat and held it in two hands. "Miss Marie," he said, feeling his heart thumping so hard he feared she could hear it. "Your ma sent me to eat."

She looked surprised, but recovered enough to point out the chair he could use. "Take Pa's seat, Mr. Henry. He won't be back for dinner."

He hung his hat on the back of the chair and seated himself. Marie brought him a plate of beans and cornbread, put a tin cup beside it, and indicated the milk jug on the table.

"Thank you kindly," he offered, but she didn't reply.

Before the silence got too awkward, Mrs. Owen and the younger sister joined them, and Marie finally sat opposite him to eat.

As he ate, he glanced at her from time to time, hoping he didn't seem overly-occupied with doing so. Mrs. Owen inquired about the progress of the logging operation, and he took care to answer as much as he knew.

One of her questions caught him off guard.

"Is Mr. Owen treating you well?"

"Ma'am?"

"He can seem harsh, time to time, but he knows you're a good worker. He values that in a man."

He swallowed his food before he could answer, "Thank you, ma'am. I appreciate the sentiment."

She laughed, a muffled sound from her throat. "He got bossy during the Hard Time. Some of his men were out 'n' out scallywags, and he was obliged to speak to them rough to get the lines to advance."

Bill made agreeable noises, chewing his beans and musing that having been an officer accounted for Rod Owen's commanding attitude. That kind of experience had to change a man.

After that, the meal limped along to an unsatisfactory end, to Bill's mind, as he found no moment to speak privately with the girl.

Back at work, wringing out clothes for Mrs. Owen, Bill thought a private time had come when he was paired with Marie to twist the water out of a load of sheets. They were never alone, though, and Bill found no opportunity to engage her in conversation. He finished the day's work with a frustrated spirit.

෫

Marie climbed off the stool that stood in front of the kitchen shelf and turned to see Ma through the open door, shading her eyes and gazing into the distance.

What's she looking at? she wondered, and called to her sister in the loft. "Jule, go find out what's got Ma standing like a tree in the dooryard."

"Go see for yourself," her sister refused. "I'm busy. These towels are all tangled. Mr. Henry didn't fold them right."

"He's a man. A body can't expect him to know how." She abandoned her attempt to cajole her sister into running her own errand, picked up the washtub and stepped to the door.

She flung the water onto the dusty soil, then put down the tub and approached her mother.

"Someone's a-coming," Ma told Marie, as though she had eyes in the back of her head to see her. "Driving a wagon."

"Settlers?" There was still land to be had south of here. Perhaps they would have new neighbors.

"I don't reckon. I only see the one soul on the seat."

"Hmm," Marie replied. "There's something shiny hanging on the side."

"I see it. Copper?"

"Might be."

"Is that a pot?"

Marie shaded her own eyes, then said, "That it would appear."

The person on the wagon seat drew near enough they could make out that it was a man with a dark, swarthy face and felt hat pulled over his brow. As he come closer, he began to sing a song about the goods he had to sell.

"A peddler? We've got a peddler coming! Girl, we'll get you the necessaries for your marriage after all." Ma's smiled brightened her face.

"That's . . . good," Marie said, and hoped her voice didn't sound as disheartened as she felt.

The man came on, driving his wagon and singing his song, until he halted the horse, and pots and pans covering the outside of the vehicle clattered and clanged as they settled to a stop.

Jule came out of the house and joined them. Ma put her arm around her shoulders and gave her a squeeze. "Welcome," she said to the man, her voice reflecting her good cheer. "Climb down and take a rest."

"I do not mind if I do," the man replied, suiting his actions to his words, and tipping his hat to Marie and Ma once he was on the ground. His lean face cracked a wide smile. "I am Raphael, ladies, and I wish you good morning."

"And a good morning to you, sir," Ma said, her smile rivaling that of the peddler man. "Can I get you breakfast?"

"No, no, I've feasted long since, madam." He looked around. "A tidy homestead you have here."

"This is Rod Owen's land. You'll never see another man work so hard as he."

"Indeed. Indeed," said the peddler with one name. "I have wares to sell today. Pots, both copper and iron. Muslin and linsey-woolsey by the bolt or by the yard. Scissors, needles, and pins. Foodstuffs in tinned vessels. Beans and bacon. Sacks of salt and vials of spices. Knives and flatware and tableware. Sharpening stones, grinding stones, and stones for the chickens' gizzards. Chickens and rabbits, if you have none. Liniment and ointment and salves to soften your skin and draw your splinters. And trinkets. Mirrors and ribbons and lace. Bonnets and feathers and lockets and rings. Cushions for your chairs or for your footstools. What do you need to buy?"

"I'll be trading for a beef cow, butchered or on the hoof."

"I will trade for beef," the man agreed. "Live on the hoof will suffice."

"Good." She turned to Julianna. "Daughter, go up where your pa is working. Tell him a trader's come, and I need a cow."

"Yes ma'am," she said, and ran toward the mountain.

"Now then, tell me when I've reached the worth of a good beef cow. I need sharp kitchen knives. Utensils. Tableware for two. A pot and a spider, both iron. Bed linens. Ticking for pillows." Ma continued with a list of necessaries, and the peddler pulled out a note pad and pencil to jot down her wants. Then he began to fill her order, making a pile beside the door. Marie slipped into the house and put the washtub away, her mind unsettled by the tangible evidence of her coming change of circumstances.

When Marie left the cabin again, Ma was still piling up a passel of goods. Marie headed toward the chosen items, thinking if she had to marry Tom, she might as well have a say in the everyday necessities of life. She would be using them for a long time.

The first thing she spotted was the enormous fry pan among the chosen implements.

"Ma, why did you pick such a big spider?"

Her mother looked her way, puzzlement evident on her face. "You'll be needing one to cook your meals."

Marie lifted it out of the stack. "I don't aim to do for the entire Morgan family. It'll be just me and Tom to make a beginning." *I may as well accept it. Tom and me.* She pushed away the dark reality and let the power of Ma's excitement catch her for the moment.

"Hmm." Ma appeared to contemplate. Then she nodded. "Go ahead and change it," she agreed. "I had my mind fixed on my heap of young'uns." She gestured to the amassed treasures. "You'd best check over what I picked for you."

"I will, Ma."

Marie dug around and found another few items she thought too big. As she was returning them to the peddler's vehicle, she noticed an array of kitchen cutlery. Among them were several knives in leather sheaths. She picked one up and slid it free of the covering. *How odd. Ma has one just like it in the house. With such a protection, I thought it would be a fighting knife.*

"Mr. Raphael," she said to get the man's attention. "Are these ordinary kitchen knives? I've not seen the likes of this sheath on a trimming or cutting blade for kitchen use."

The peddler smiled and nodded. "That is my own improvement, miss. With so many folks traveling about the country these days, they find there's danger to the small ones if a knife is laying loose. The leather also keeps the blades sharp and free of nicks." He chuckled. "I do sharpen knives, so you might think I'm cutting down my own income, but when I came across a poor little child all cut up from an accident, I got the idea for the leather encasement."

"Who would have thought?" Marie mused. "Is the price much higher?"

"I make the covers myself, miss, so the cost is low."

She picked through the knives and chose one of medium size. She showed it to the man. "I would like this one."

"A wise choice," he said, making a notation on the paper.

On Saturday evening, after a hard week of cutting logs, and with another such week in prospect before the day set for the barn raising, Bill felt ready to cut loose or bust. He started off toward the tool shed, carrying his ax in one hand and a two-man saw over his shoulder. Bertie Owen came up alongside him, matching his stride to Bill's.

"Mr. Henry. You going to get up a card game after dinner?"

Not having the patience to fend off the boy, Bill sighed and keep walking.

"Will you?"

Bill shook his head. Maybe he needed a good run on a fast horse to relieve his tension.

"Ah, come on. I still have my cash, and if you don't have any, I'll lend you some."

The idea of taking Bertie's money and then winning the rest of it had a fair measure of appeal. Bill nodded.

Bertie grinned. "I'll bring my cards."

"We have a deck."

The boy's face lost the grin, but he recovered quickly and said, "I'll bring the money."

When he showed up at the bunkhouse after dinner, he had indeed brought money, as the sack he tossed onto the table jingled enticingly.

Sourdough had a few coins, and the previous game having whetted his appetite for gambling, he joined in. Chico went to bed, claiming a toothache.

Bill wondered if he'd get in trouble letting the boy participate and gamble away his money. However, it soon became clear that this wasn't Bertie's first time playing poker. The boy knew the rules. Soon Bill was engrossed in planning his strategy and forgot the boy's age.

When ten o'clock came and Bill had five excellent cards in his hand, he felt comfortable that he would cap off the night with a win. But then Bertie let three cards fall out of his sleeve into his lap, palmed them, and exchanged them for three from his hand that he slipped between his legs.

Bill pretended he hadn't seen the exchange, wondering where the boy had picked up the trick. Then young Mr. Owen's trio of fours beat his own double pair of high cards, and he knew. Patricio Dominguez had to have used the same sleight of hand on him two weeks ago.

How'd the young'un convince the man to show him the trick?

Chapter 8

Bill watched from his post at the log pile as neighbors gathered late on a Friday afternoon. He and the hands had barely finished their labors at the unfamiliar tasks: felling trees, lopping off branches, dragging the trunks to a spot on the meadow, and stacking them side-by-side and then cross hatched, all in preparation for the barn raising.

During the past month, he had sensed an undercurrent of excitement from family members, and it piqued his curiosity. Overlaying his intellectual interest, a feeling of anxiety accompanied him each day as he reflected that more than a barn raising was in the offing. Had Old Man Owen succeeded in his matchmaking quest? Not knowing the answer played hob with Bill's mind.

He tried sounding out Rulon, but he was always too busy directing the logging operation for small talk. His stint with the water buckets on that wash day hadn't resulted in a talk with Marie. Bill remained in the dark as to the reason for the heightened emotion about the place. Something new, something different was in the wind, and constructing a new barn should not create such a lot of activity and fervor.

And then, that peddler had come.

The boss had been mighty pleased with himself when he'd put a rope on a fat steer and took it off the mountain to the missus. What lot of goods merited giving a steer in trade?

As he worried on the meaning of the enthusiasm he'd seen in the Old Man after that occasion, he saw Marie leading her saddled horse from the stable. She mounted at the block and rode away, up toward the tree line. He ached to join her, but he was obliged to stay where he was, stacking the last of the logs alongside of Chico Henderson.

"Don't you wish you could fork a horse and follow Miss Marie?" Chico asked in an undertone, his grin almost splitting his face.

Bill knocked hard against Chico's shoulder, the one that had been wounded.

"Ow! There's no call for that, Henry."

"Keep your mouth buttoned. I don't want to hear your palaver."

"Where'd you get that burr under your blanket?" Chico taunted. "Ain't she makin eyes at you these days?"

"I told you to shut up."

"Ohhhh." Chico made his voice scary. "Is she in love with someone else?"

"Get back to work. These logs don't get stacked by magic." He gave a heave and settled another log onto the stack as Chico chuckled. The sound rankled. Bill looked hard at his comrade, then walked away, unwilling to let his temper flare out of control with so many folks about.

A wagon came toward him from the south. Bill recognized the man driving as Ed Morgan, whose corn crop had almost been trampled by the Owen cattle a while back.

His prissy-faced wife sat beside him on the seat, and several children crowded in the back along with assorted baskets and crates. Two young men rode horses behind the wagon. One, the elder of the two, had his face turned about, watching something.

Bill looked in the same direction as the young man. Marie was coming out of the stable. The wagon must have caught her eye. She glanced their way and stopped in her tracks.

She wasn't looking at Bill, hope as he would that she'd take notice of him. Her eyes had landed on the young man riding behind the wagon.

Her head went down, and she made for the house with all speed.

She don't want him to give her a greeting.

At that moment, he realized the young man was Tom Morgan. Tom, the Virginia boy Old Man Owen had spoken about. The "known blood." Tom Morgan, whose rapt attention announced him as the bridegroom.

The bridegroom. Miss Marie's intended husband.

A white flame of jealousy leaped into his chest as he imagined the girl in that man's house, in his arms, in his bed.

He turned away, icy fingers of despair dumping ashes over the flame. The deed was done, the match made. He was out in the cold.

As he paced heedlessly about the meadow, more clumps of people arrived from the north, on horseback or in wagons, some dressed in sturdy clothing, others in more showy garb. Among the latter, he recognized the Dominguez brothers in their best get-up. *They must have been on another of their errands to Pueblo Town*, he thought. *Gambling again.* With them rode a man dressed in a suit, but he didn't look like the preacher Old Man Owen had said was coming. This man sported a silver chain across the front of his vest and tucked into the pocket. No doubt there was a fine silver watch on the end of it. His moustache was finely groomed into points. *Uses wax on it, I'll wager*, Bill scoffed, stroking his own full facial adornment. *He's a town man. Likely not given to honest labor.*

He shrugged off the disdain he felt toward the stranger and turned toward the shed as he remembered where he was supposed to be now. Mrs. Owen wanted plank tables built for the doings tomorrow, and he'd best get to work.

⁊

Marie hurried into the house. Melancholy, almost despair, had taken her in its grip today of all days. She needed to wash her face before anyone noticed that it was streaked with tears. How unseemly it would be if the prospective bride didn't have a cheerful countenance when mention was made of her coming happy day.

Happy day! she thought, and shivered. *I'd best have my happy days while I can. I reckon there's few ahead for me.*

Why had she badgered Pa so strenuously about her single state? She might have chanced upon a beau on her own account. Perhaps.

She climbed the ladder to the loft, poured a bit of water onto a rag, and scrubbed her face until it glowed pink. At least the dead skin from her sunburn had stopped peeling off weeks ago. She could be thankful for that. There was nothing so unappealing as peeling skin.

Marie tried to laugh at her silent word play, but nothing came from her throat but a strangled sound. Tom Morgan had made it plain that he would not have chosen her for his bride. Then he had put his hands on her, caused her misadventure at the river, laughed at her, and made uncouth comments. Remembering the occasion disheartened her anew. What new disrespect would she be obliged to endure this weekend?

"Marie?"

Ma wants me. Have the Morgans come? Marie hugged herself in dismay, her shoulders hunching nearly to her ears. *Rulon would say to keep my chin up. How can I do that when my heart is so low?* Marie dropped her arms from around herself, lowered her shoulders and descended the ladder.

"We'll need to begin serving supper before long," Ma said. "Folks are coming in droves."

"I hope they brought plenty of provisions," Marie answered, attempting to put a lighthearted lilt in her voice, and failing miserably. "Has anyone in particular— have the Morgans arrived yet?"

"If they have, they've not come to the house." Ma's voice lacked its usual sparkle.

Is she still pining for James? Marie wondered, and gathered herself out of her own misery to try to lift her mother's spirits.

"Ma, James can take care of himself. I reckon he won't be gone long." She wondered if what she said were true. She might never see her brother again.

Ma laid her hand on Marie's arm. "I wish I could be as certain as you, sweet daughter." She looked searchingly at her, then drew her into a tight embrace. "You miss him too, I reckon. You always thought he hung the moon."

Surprised at the action, Marie patted her mother's back a trifle hesitantly. She wished she could share her thoughts, talk with her about all of them, from guilt over not seeing James's pain, to worry about Tom's attitude and his unseemly advances, and concern that marrying him would not bring her the happiness she sought.

But something now constrained her from sharing such secrets with Ma. Ma had the notion she and Tom were a good match. She couldn't blight her confidence. Not after their talk about—Not now. *I want to confide in her, but there's a gulf between us as wide as the prairie.*

∽

When she heard the creak of wagon wheels, Marie disengaged herself from her mother's grasp and straightened her skirt. "Someone's coming, Ma."

"I reckon they'll be needing my attention," Ma said, nodding, and patting her own self into a presentable state.

Marie hesitated at the door, then drew it open and stepped outside, Ma right behind her.

Mr. Morgan halted his team of horses in the dooryard of the cabin, set the brake, and looped the lines around the handle. Tom and Parley sat their horses behind the wagon, Parley craning his neck looking around the homestead as though searching for someone. Tom looked her way, displaying a stern expression. Marie decided she would ignore him.

"Lizzie, don't fret," Mr. Morgan said in an undertone, but loud enough that Marie heard it.

Lizzie? I'd not like to be called that, Marie thought, biting her lip to prevent herself from smiling. *Good thing my name is plain enough that Tom can't shorten it.*

"Elizabeth," Ma said. "Mr. Morgan."

"Julia, you picked a pretty place to settle," Mrs. Morgan said, climbing over her husband's feet as she got down from the wagon. "Look at this meadow, and you have your own creek!"

"We have a river," Ed Morgan muttered, but his wife ignored him. Parley smirked and Tom forgot himself enough to snicker.

Mrs. Morgan turned to give the house a good looking over, shading her eyes from the rays of the lowering sun. "Your cabin is so sweet, just like your house back home."

"This is my home," Ma said, a trifle stiffly.

Why's Miz Morgan taking that snippity tone with Ma? Marie wondered, then turned her attention to her mother. Her voice wasn't exactly cold, Marie judged, but she seemed a mite restrained instead of being her usual affable self.

"Yes, yes, of course. It's so quaintly situated. Did Mr. Owen pick the location?" She went on, seeming to have no expectation of being answered. "Of course he did. Only a man would put such a distance between the house and the water." She turned on a smile.

"I picked the location," Ma said, and this time, frost crept into her response. "I'm putting in a garden next spring between the creek and the house. Being close there, I won't have to haul the water so far to the plants."

"Well, I never! You're going to have to bring up the water? Your man won't see to it that the boys water the vegetables?" She turned a circle and faced Ma, her smile broadening. "My man is digging me a well, right there in the yard beside the house."

Ma squared her shoulders. "Come in and quench your thirst, Elizabeth. We have water enough here for that."

"Oh, we couldn't wear out our welcome as soon as we've arrived," Mrs. Morgan answered. "Besides, I can't leave my pies in the wagon for the crows to pick over."

Marie heard her mother's quick inward breath.

The woman continued, "Simply tell us where to pitch our camp, and we'll settle in. Mr. Morgan and the boys need a good night's rest so they can do a good day's work on your barn."

"Suit yourself," Ma said, and waved her hand toward the south. "Pick out any spot." Her voice sounded for all the world as though she spoke through clenched teeth.

Miz Morgan refused our hospitality! No wonder Ma's cross with her. What sort of family am I obliged to join?

Chapter 9

Bill kept his face smooth as Chico threw down his playing cards. It would be unseemly to chortle over his good fortune tonight. Admittedly, he had helped Lady Luck along a trifle, but he didn't want to share that fact with Chico or the other players in the bunkhouse.

Maybe I'm just an ornery cuss, he thought. He dropped his hand, took the cards out of his lap, and slid them into his boot top. *I only hankered to know if I could pull off that trick.* He'd find a way to return Chico's cash to him later. He never had intended this game to be like the one when that little scoundrel, Bertie Owen, had cleaned him out. *He* hadn't felt any impulse to turn over his ill-gotten gains.

Chico pushed back his chair, the lamplight flickering over his scowl. "Hang it all, Henry! Where'd you get so lucky? Miss Marie ain't here to plant a kiss on your cards."

Bill raised a finger and tilted back his hat so he could see Chico. "Don't go mixing the lady into our game, Chico. She ain't a factor in your bad luck."

Chico took off his own hat and slammed it onto the floor. "Damn you, Bill Henry! That was my last three dollars! Now I can't—"

He cut off the diatribe by saying, "Have it back, friend, with interest. I don't want a five spot standing between us." He extracted a five-dollar note from the pile of bills before him and slid it across the table toward Chico.

Chico snatched up the bill, his face relaxing just a mite. "Someday you'll go too far, *friend.*"

Allowing a grin, Bill retorted, "You came all the way from Texas with me, Henderson. You know I'm the best *friend* you have."

"Humph," Chico grunted, picked up his hat, and strode toward the bunkhouse door, stuffing the money into his shirt pocket with one hand and his hat onto his head with the other.

"Have you gentlemen had enough?" Bill asked the other players.

A chorus of agreement met his question, and he took a few greenbacks off the pile and pocketed them as he arose. "Split it up, boys," he said, indicated the remainder. "Be fair." Then he made an exit amidst the cacophony he left in his wake.

He walked out into the softness of the night, the stars overhead shining brilliantly before the moon elbowed its way into the sky. He strolled among the campfires, greeting folks he'd met that day and others he already knew. The Mexican brothers and their compañero from Pueblo town played cards on a barrel fitted with a couple of planks on top for a table, swigging from a bottle passed between them. He felt his moustache twitch against his cheeks as he scowled and passed them by without a word, unwilling to meet the dandified man with the thin, pointy moustache.

ॐ

Shortly after supper, Marie accompanied her mother as she walked from one camp to another to greet her guests and be sure they had all they required for their comfort.

Ma carried a lantern to light their way. Her steps slowed as they approached a bit of brush that marked the Morgan family's camp, and Marie put a hand on her arm.

"I'll see to their needs, Ma. You go have a good visit with Mrs. Bates."

Ma's shoulders relaxed. She gave Marie a wan smile, and as she patted her hand, said, "Thank you, daughter. Lizzie Morgan got my back up this afternoon."

"I could see that."

Ma sighed. "We had a bit of a misunderstanding years ago that she don't want to leave go of. One year I happened to bake a better apple pie than she did, and took home the county prize she'd counted on winning. She didn't take kindly to that. She always thought herself a notch above everybody else in the county, especially when it came to baking apple pies." She snorted and wagged her head. "Do you want the lantern?"

"No. You take it. I have young eyes. Don't you worry none, Ma. There's aplenty of campfires to light my way."

"Bless you, daughter."

Marie watched as her mother hurried off. She steeled her courage, then turned and approached the Morgan's fire.

"Marie," said Tom, stepping into her path from behind the brush. "What a pleasure."

Startled at his sudden appearance, Marie laid her hand over her heart. "I didn't see you standing there." With his back to the fire, Tom's figure was outlined with light, and she couldn't see his face clearly. His tone had not been welcoming, despite his words. She almost abandoned her task.

"I saw you a-coming. Thought as I'd greet you ahead of the folks." He leaned in toward her.

She took a step backwards. "How nice of you. I come to ask after your comfort."

Tom was silent for a moment, then said, "I believe we're set." He moved forward and took her arm, fitting it through the crook of his. "Come to the fire and say hello to the folks."

Unable to think of a polite refusal, Marie let him lead her into the circle of light.

Mrs. Morgan glanced up from her seat on a log. "Well, look who's here. Mr. Morgan. It's Miss Marie, come to call on us."

"Miss Marie," Ed Morgan said, then stepped away from the fire and into the darkness.

Stung at his abrupt departure, Marie blurted out, "Tom says you're set for the night." The look on Mrs. Morgan's face made her regret that she hadn't started out with pleasantries. Then Louisa and Melissa crowded around, asking questions and diverting her attention as she tried to make up for her mistake with Mrs. Morgan.

"It's a nice evening," she began again. "I trust your journey wasn't taxing?"

"Uneventful," Mrs. Morgan murmured, nodding. "Uneventful, but warm."

"It has been a warm day," Marie agreed. "It's fixing to cool off, I believe."

"I can only hope it don't get too chilly."

"No, ma'am. It should be pleasant tonight."

Mrs. Morgan didn't reply, but instead examined the hand work in her lap.

Louisa and Melissa went back to their chores, and Marie stood awkwardly beside Tom, her hand trapped between his arm and his body. The rhythm of his breathing pressed against the back of her arm, and his warmth seeped into her skin. Her throat constricted.

After several long minutes of silence, it became apparent that Mrs. Morgan had finished with her. Marie cleared her throat and said, "Well, good evening to you. I must be going." She tried to remove her arm from Tom's grasp, but he kept it tightly bound, even placing his other hand over hers to maintain his mastery of it.

"I'll walk Miss Marie home, Ma."

"Don't be gone all night," Mrs. Morgan said, without looking up.

What does she mean by that remark? Marie wondered as she walked away from the fire, Tom moving along with her. Trying to quit his company, she said, "I have to see to the other visitors, Tom. I'll be just fine, walking about by myself."

"It's too dark for you to stumble around," Tom answered. "I'll keep you company."

"There's no need." She tried to disentangle her hand again, and Tom let her slip it from his arm, but grasped her hand as it came free.

"That's a piece of my obligation now," he said, his voice a trifle bitter sounding. "I'll see to your safety." He started off, and Marie, unable to shake off his hold on her, followed along.

"We're practically in my own door yard," she protested. "I dare say no harm will come to me between here and my house."

"This appears to be a rough crowd," he answered. "When folks gather, you can't ever tell who they brought with them."

"Don't be a silly." As soon as she finished speaking, she wished she could take back the words, and threw a guilty glance up at Tom.

He glared down at her, pursing his lips. She'd seen that same expression on his father's face. After a few more steps he said, "I saw strangers over yonder."

"I'm sure they're known to my pa."

"I mistrust the look of them, especially those dark folks." Tom motioned to a fire where several men sat around a makeshift table, playing cards.

Marie looked where Tom gestured, and recognized the Dominguez brothers. "I know who they are. They have a place south of here. They stop to water their horses at our creek."

"You can't trust Mexicans. Always taking what's not theirs."

"Do you have experience of that?" Marie asked, looking sideways up at Tom.

"I've heard about them." He turned his head, glanced at her, and laid his finger alongside his nose as if to imply he had vast knowledge of such things.

"That's foolishness. They're like any other folks."

Tom stopped in the dark shelter of the clump of brush and pulled Marie close to him. "You won't talk like that around me. I know better." His voice dropped an octave. "Keep your place."

"Keep my place?" She pulled free of his restraining hand. "Don't dare speak to me like that."

Tom grabbed her arms, though she tried to beat off his hands, and he put his face close to hers. "I'm your man now. You'll do as I say."

"Who commands me so?" She struggled against the hold of his rough hands. "You're not my man until the preacher speaks the words."

"Your pa gave you to me."

"Not yet, he didn't."

"You've nothing to gain being difficult," he grunted, pulling her closer to him. "Heed my words, and I'll treat you well."

"I won't be bullied," she muttered, straining against his grasp, panic squeezing her chest. "Let me go!"

"No. You're not going anywhere." He wrapped his muscular arms around her and lowered his face to hers again. "I didn't choose it, but you're bound to me, and you'll obey." He put his mouth on hers, hot and wet, and kissed her repeatedly, the stiff evening stubble above and below his lips scratching her face.

"No," she cried, although the sound didn't escape her dry throat. She twisted against him, thrashing, her arms thrusting against his chest, until she remembered a bit of advice James had once told her, half-jokingly, about how to fight off a Yankee. She bent her knee and brought it up quickly, connecting with Tom's groin, and as he bent double, moaning and covering the stricken area, she fled, straight into the camp of the card players.

৯৹

She brought her headlong rush to a stop, working to keep upright as she teetered before three men seated around a barrel. Laying on top of it were two planks that formed a rough table, which was littered with cards and poker markers that shook and bounced as the men scrambled to their feet. Marie blinked back her indignant tears. Enrique Dominguez reached forward and snatched a bottle of liquor off the table and hid it behind his back. His brother Patricio removed a cigarillo from his lips and palmed it.

"Señorita Maria, ¿que le pasó? Ah, I say, what ees happen weeth you?" Patricio used a mixture of Spanish and English, his voice raspy with concern.

Marie shook her head, more to clear it than to indicate a negative response. "I— Nothing of— It was a momentary trifle," she ended, flustered more than she would have wished. *That Tom!* She must speak with Pa, as soon as could be done.

"If there's something we can do, miss?" a man asked, his voice low and melodious. He was unknown to her. "We would be happy to assist you in any way." He removed his hat and inclined his head.

She noticed that his hair appeared to be black and wavy in the firelight, not unlike that of her brother James. She put the back of her hand to her nose to mask a snuffle. "Thank you, sir. There's nothing of importance to be done. I thank y'all for your concern." She nodded toward the men and turned to go, but the black-haired man grasped her elbow and stopped her.

"Miss. I beg you to sit and compose yourself." He motioned to his recently-abandoned chair as he spoke to Patricio. "Tráigame un vaso de agua." He again addressed Marie. "Will you take a glass of water? You seem uncomfortable."

"I—I thank you, sir. And you are?"

"C. G. Thorne, at your service." He bowed as he made his hat cut a figure through the air.

Marie imagined the hat would look quite at home if it had a feather sweeping from the side of the crown. Oddly, the thought did not strike her as ridiculous, but as courtly and comforting. The man seemed genuinely concerned for her welfare. With that, Marie took the chair offered by Mr. Thorne.

Enrique Dominguez brought her a tin cup of water, and Marie accepted it, wondering when Patricio had delegated the task to his brother. She put the cup to her lips, sighed, and took a sip. What did it matter who fetched the water? Her life had shattered into shards around her ears.

"Miss, you truly must allow us to help you if you have trouble to be mended."

It was the same man speaking, Mr. Thorne.

"Sí, señorita," chimed in Enrique. "Queremos— We want to ayud—help you si es posible." He looked at Patricio, as though he were seeking affirmation that his speech was in proper form.

"It was nothing," she repeated. "A slight disagreement."

"Who would offer you such an affront?" Mr. Thorne seemed taken aback at the temerity of anyone to annoy her. "You have but to mention his name." An unspoken threat to the malefactor hung in the air.

"*His* name?" Marie felt a small smile lifting her lips. "You are sure a man wronged me?" Her tears had gone.

Thorne hung his head. "Dear lady, I beg your pardon at making any false assumption." He raised his head again and looked her straight in the eye, one eyebrow raised. "It is the highest dishonor imaginable to distress such a fair creature as yourself. That is my only defense, that I imagined a scoundrel of the male persuasion gave you an insult. Was I not right, dear lady?"

"Sir, you were not wrong, but I doubt the offense will reoccur." Marie heard herself using formal language, and cast her eyes down to mask any delight that might be showing in them at the opportunity. "Once my father takes a hand—" She stopped herself. It was likely that her father would disregard any misgivings she had over marrying Tom at this late date. "That is to say . . ." Again, she felt at a loss for words. What could she say, not knowing where this weekend's events would lead her? Pa was entirely likely to go through with his scheme to announce her engagement to that odious man. Her mouth went dry.

"You are distressed anew," Mr. Thorne stated. "Would a sip of spirits fortify you?" He held up the liquor bottle that had somehow gotten from behind Enrique Dominguez's back into his hand.

Marie first felt shocked by his suggestion, then, as the feeling faded, reconsidered. *Why not? It works for men.* She nodded, not trusting herself to speak.

Somehow, she found herself steadying the bottle that Mr. Thorne had uncorked, wiped on his sleeve and lifted to her mouth. She took a tentative sip. White fire burned down her throat and she almost gagged. Then Mr. Thorne raised the container slightly, and the liquid flowed into her mouth, filling it. Reflexively, Marie swallowed once, then was obliged to do so in vast gulps, twice, three times, before she could thrust the bottle away. She almost choked as she swallowed the liquor remaining in her mouth.

"There." Mr. Thorne said, stopping up the container with a hard thrust of his palm upon the cork. "That should hearten you."

Marie felt herself shudder at the strong taste of the liquor. She licked her lips to cleanse them of a lingering drop. It burned her tongue. She sensed, rather than saw Mr. Thorne tilt his head at the Dominguez brothers, who melted away from the table and left her alone with him.

He placed the bottle on the table and seated himself beside her. He drew the chair close, momentarily bumping his knee against hers. "You must tell me your troubles, my dear," he said.

∽

Marie drew her skirt together at the knees, hands gripping the fabric. "Sir, I don't know what you mean."

Mr. Thorne tilted his head and the corner of his mouth twitched ever so slightly. "Why, Miss Marie, you seem quite vexed with troubles. Won't you allow me to share your burden, even only a tiny bit?" He held his thumb and forefinger together, almost touching.

The fire from the swallows of liquor seemed to be spreading from Marie's stomach to her limbs. She brought a finger to her lips to bite the nail, then thought better of it, and dropped her hand back into her lap. "You are a stranger, sir. How odd, that you wish to be my confidant."

The man drew back a trifle, pressed his lips together, then blurted out, "I beg your pardon for moving beyond my place, Miss Marie. Your beauty overwhelms me." He sucked in a breath through pursed lips, and hung his head. His voice sounded hollow as he said, "I do beg your pardon, very humbly, Miss. Please forgive me."

Marie felt in a forgiving mood. The skin of her hands felt soft enough to run off her fingers like melted butter. *Ma talked . . . 'bout melting. Butter, wasn't it?* "I . . ." she began, but her voice faded. "It's not . . . Usually I would not . . ." She shook her head gently, feeling as though her brains would collide with the bones of her skull if she exerted herself overmuch. "You are forgiven, Mr. Thorne," she said in a rush, before her voice failed her again. "Forgiven," she repeated for emphasis. The consonants ran together.

Mr. Thorne raised his head and stared into her eyes. "You are quite magnificent," he said slowly. "Magnificent and magnanimous, together in one generous soul. I feel as though I were in the presence of a royal personage. Such grace. Such charm." He took her hand in both of his, and lifted it toward his lips. He stopped midway and murmured, "I am quite overcome with emotion, Miss Marie. Will you permit . . .?" and he kissed the inside of her wrist.

Looking at the man's bent head, Marie wondered that his moustache did not tickle her skin. Instead, it felt stiff, yet flexible and yielding at the same time, and his warm lips spread the heat from the alcohol up her arm. She knew she must remove her hand from his grasp, but her strength failed her just as her voice had, and the lethargy caused her head to tilt toward her shoulder.

He made circles on her wrist with the back of one finger, his nail smooth, not catching her skin with jagged edges or nicks, but sliding over her flesh like it rode on a film of sweet oil.

"Sir," she protested, her voice little more than an echo, as he began to place gentle kisses on the heel of her hand. Kisses like the brief touch of a moth's wing. Kisses that progressed slowly onto the sensitive flesh of her palm. Such light kisses, that nonetheless stirred her blood and drove her inhibitions far away, far up the mountain, diving into the depths of a dark pool of water where she had sat once in time, a man bending over her, offering her a cup to dip into the black water. Who had that been? Her head swam as memory eluded her, and she swallowed, no longer fighting the wild pulse of blood that throbbed in her temples.

She raised her head with an effort. The camp fire had gone to embers, no longer lighting the table before her. The man beside her murmured, "So lovely," and placed his hand on her knee.

An internal alarm roused her senses. *This is wrong. I did not tolerate Tom's hands on me. This man is a stranger. He has less right.* She shifted her body so that her limbs slid out from under the man's hand. "I . . . must go," she said, grateful that her voice seemed steady. She pushed herself to her feet against the man's protests. "You must forebear, sir," she added, tugging her hand free. "Goodnight."

Steering herself toward the light of the distant lantern hanging from the door post of her father's house, Marie splashed through the creek and felt the shock of the cold water bring her wits into sharper focus. She grimaced against the headache starting behind her eyes, but made it through the front door and into the loft before anyone greeted her or made note of her wet shoes and hem.

I'm shameless, she told herself. *A shameless spinster, acting like a brazen hussy.* And yet, part of the warmth from the man's moth-like kisses had not faded from her body, and she wrapped herself in that warmth as she fell asleep.

Chapter 10

Marie awoke, her head pounding and her eyes sensitive to light. *What happened to me?* she wondered, trying to think back to last night as she dashed cold water onto her face. *Ma and I. We visited . . . Tom! Blast him! Where's Pa?* She hastily dried her face, dressed, bundled up her hair in the leather clasp Mrs. Bates had given her, and dropped down into the cabin. No Pa in sight.

"Mighty late coming in last night," Julianna jeered at her. "Made you a slug-a-bed." She raised her chin and sniffed, then swiped at the tin plate in her hands with an old flour sacking towel.

"Leave her be, Jule," Ma said sharply from where she knelt at the fireplace, pouring batter into a heavy iron oven.

"I may, or I may not."

"Don't sass Ma," Marie said. Her voice hardly made it past her lips, and horrors! It sounded like a frog's croak! She cleared her throat and tried again. "You're impertinent, Jule."

"Better'n being a slug-a-bed!" She stuck out her tongue.

Marie reciprocated, feeling foolish but justified.

Ma turned her head away from the fire. "I saved your breakfast, daughter." She gestured with a spoon toward the table. "Under the cloth."

Marie lifted the dish towel, drew up a chair, and sat before a plate of one fried egg, a slice of beef, and a slice of corn bread. The honey pot also sat on the table beside a cup of milk, and she spilled a bit of sweetener onto the bread. "Thank you, Ma," she said after she'd swallowed a mouthful. "I'm sorry to be a slug-a-bed."

"See?" Jule dried another plate and smirked.

"I heard you come in late. Is all well with you and Tom Morgan?"

Marie hastily filled her mouth so she would have an excuse for a delayed answer. She didn't want to talk about the revulsion Tom had raised in her. She chewed. Good thing she'd gotten away . . . from . . . him. . . . "Oh!" She drew in a breath, then choked and coughed out the piece of corn bread that had gone down the wrong pipe.

Jule came and pounded on her back, much harder than was necessary.

When she'd regained her breath, Marie turned around and slapped at her sister's hand, then huddled over her plate, remembering the soft kisses on her wrist and palm that had sent her senses shivering into oblivion. That man, Mr. Thorne, had been making love to her. Had he meant what he'd said about being overcome by her charms? Warmth spread through her body. The man certainly had seemed sincere.

"Marie?" Ma's voice came from close behind Marie.

She looked up, hoping she wasn't blushing.

"Hmm." Ma nodded. "I can see you have pleasant thoughts about your evening."

Marie said nothing, grateful for once that she *was* blushing. Since the coloring spoke for her, she would have no need to comment or to speak a lie.

Ma laid a hand on Marie's shoulder. "Go slow, daughter. Harvest time will come soon enough."

A lump rose in Marie's throat, choking her just as effectively as had the bit of corn cake before. She couldn't make a sound, but reached up and patted her mother's hand as she swallowed hard. She couldn't speak of Tom to Ma. She seemed so sure that Marie was pleased with the recent turn of events. But with Pa it was a different matter. Pa would get an earful . . . just as soon as she could catch up to him!

∞

Bill hadn't seen Marie all morning. The fact that he'd been busy lifting logs and pegging them into place hadn't kept his eyes from scanning the female figures that brought water to the crew. Not one had the dark, waving hair, the winsome smile, the light step of Marie. Not one made his heart swell in his chest. Not one made him ache to converse with her, to touch her arm. Where was she keeping herself?

"Henry!" Mr. Owen bellowed.

Bill looked down at the boss standing at the foot of the ladder and waving for him to descend.

"Yes, sir?"

"Come down."

He went down. Once on the ground, he took off his hat and wiped the sweat out of his eyes with his sleeve. "Yes, sir?"

"Where's that bale of leather thongs you had Carl cut?"

"I wrapped them strings in a piece of holey hide and put 'em on a shelf in the stable. Want me to fetch 'em?"

"No, I'll send Albert. Return to your work up there."

Bill swept his hair back with his fingers and put his hat on his head. He nodded, climbed to his previous position, and grasped the log that was being levered atop the last. He got it on his shoulder and heaved. He still hadn't seen Marie.

The man next to him grunted and swore as he dropped his end of the log onto his own fingers.

"Careful," Bill said automatically.

The man swore again, berating Bill for not catching the log when he had dropped it.

"Beg pardon, friend. I'll do better next time." He gritted his teeth. How was he supposed to know when a man was going to fumble his load?

Although his neighbor groused for quite a spell, Bill tried to ignore the man and deal with the unfamiliar work. Give him adobe blocks for a building material any day. This business of constructing with logs was out of his experience.

※

The girl. Where is the girl?

C. G. Thorne sipped from the dipper, wiped a drop of water from the corner of his mouth with his handkerchief, and looked around the meadow again. It was becoming quite a chore, moving from spot to spot to avoid being assigned to a work crew. He continued to walk about as though he had a purpose, and came upon Enrique Dominguez, who was engaged in trimming the end of a log with an adz.

"Oye, hombre," Thorne said as he drew near. "¿Dónde está la chica de anoche?"

Enrique looked up and surveyed the crowd. "No sé, señor. No la he visto. She no work here."

"¿Sabes quién es?"

"Sí, señor. Ella es la hija del patrón Owen, el gran dueño en estos lugares." Enrique raised his eyebrows and waggled them.

Thorne swore. *Old Man Owen's daughter.* "¡No me digas!" He preened his moustache. "¿El Viejo tiene dinero?" He rubbed his fingers together in the age-old sign for money.

"No sé. El patrón vino aquí el año pasado. Pero yo sé que él compró mucho ganado en Tejas." Enrique shrugged. "Tal vez todavía tiene dinero. Es seguro que él tiene que pagar a los vaqueros."

So the old man has money. Thorne rubbed his chin. *Enough to get himself a herd in Texas and pay the help. Those cowhands wouldn't stick if he didn't pay them.* "Gracias, amigo," he said, clapped Enrique on the shoulder, and moved off.

※

Engaged as she was in helping Ma cook for the noon meal, Marie didn't get out to locate her father until it was nearly time for dinner. However, a need to visit the outhouse finally took her outside, and she ran up the trail into the woods.

As she did her business, she heard voices, low-pitched voices, accompanied by long pauses and suspicious noises. Fearing what she would find, she carefully closed the door, rounded the wooden structure, and followed the sounds.

Her ears led her toward a nearby copse of oak trees. When she got closer, she identified one male and one female voice, and inwardly groaned as she hurried toward the source.

Parley Morgan! He was crooning to her sister, "Come on, girl. No one's going to know. I can't stand being so far away when I love you so much."

Kissing noises. Rustling of fabric. Halfhearted protests.

Marie burst into the clearing, yelling, "Oh, no, you don't!" She skidded to a halt beside Jule. Her sister's bodice was open, and Parley had one hand where it had no right to be.

Jule looked up, saw Marie, and her face went pale. She began to scream and Parley swore and jumped away from her. Then he high-tailed it down the trail.

Before Marie could grab Jule's arm, the girl fled in another direction, sobbing and clutching her bodice together. Marie stood in the clearing, panting, wishing she were a man so she could swear as Parley had done. What was her sister thinking? Had she no shame, no pride, no sense of decorum?

Feeling her strength leave her, she sank down on the dense carpet of decaying leaves and fallen pine needles, holding herself and weeping.

She didn't know if she wept because Jule was shaming the family, or for her own pain in knowing Tom wanted to do those same things to her, as soon as he could, and without benefit of marriage words and vows. *What makes men such beasts?* she wondered, and cried harder, rocking, barely feeling the beetles that crawled up her limbs and into her stockings.

When she had cried out her anger and sorrow and her focus widened to include the world around her, she finally felt the scurrying on her flesh. Shuddering as she leapt to her feet, she yanked down her stockings and swept the insects into the leaves.

Marie straightened, breathing heavily, and looked around. Jule was long gone and she couldn't berate her, so the next order of business was to find Pa and tell him what his younger daughter was up to. Pa would put a stop to that!

Chapter 11

Time and again, Marie missed finding Pa. *Where is he?* she asked herself as she looked into the stable. Then she ran to the house and put her head inside the door, but Ma was the only one in the room. She had expected to see Jule clinging to Ma, making her complaints, but evidently the girl had felt some shame and hadn't come here.

"Have you seen Pa?" she barked more than asked, but Ma only shook her head as she lifted a kettle off the andiron at the fire. Fearing she would ask her to stay and help, Marie shut the door and ran toward the crowd raising the barn.

The first person she encountered was Patricio Dominguez, who swept off his hat and nodded to her. "Señorita. Cómo le va? How you do this fine day?"

"Hello," she said, looking about. "Have you seen my father?"

"El patrón?" The man also looked around. "No sé dónde—I don know where he be, Mees Maria. Perhaps . . . at . . . thee . . ." Struggling with his English, he described the log pile with his hands.

"Thank you, sir. You are most kind." She dashed in the direction of the logs, but Mr. Thorne, the man she had met the night before, stepped into her path and she had to stop short to keep herself from ramming into him.

"My dear Miss Marie," he exclaimed. "Where can you be off to in such a hurry? May I assist?"

His eyes were so expressive, so keenly trained on her, that she almost squirmed with unease at the attention, but she kept herself from being impolite, and nodded her head at him in greeting. "Mr. Thorne. I seek my father. I can't seem to find him anywhere."

"There, there," he said, taking her hand and fitting it into the crook of his arm. "He must be somewhere about. We'll find him in short order."

Hesitating to be burdened by a companion when she was in such a hurry and on such a delicate errand, Marie tried to pull her hand free, but Mr. Thorne's grip was firm, and she finally ceased resisting. "Thank you, sir," she forced herself to say. "I have urgent business with him. The sooner we can find him, the sooner my errand will be accomplished."

"Well then," he said, looking around again. "Perhaps he's off under the trees seeking shade. It's been a hot morning." He started to walk toward the edge of the forest.

Not able to feature her father taking his ease when everyone else was engaged in a task, Marie started to shake her head, but Thorne's grip on her hand persuaded her to accompany him, and they soon gained the shadows under a stand of pines.

"Hmm," Mr. Thorne grunted. "He doesn't seem to be here. I was sure I had seen him walking in this direction." He stroked his moustache. "I must have been mistaken, or he returned to the building enterprise while I was otherwise engaged."

Marie tugged Thorne in the direction of the meadow. "I must find him, sir," she said, but the man touched her hand briefly, as though he meant to further restrain her. He ending up pausing, then patting the back of her hand.

"Wait a bit, Miss Marie. The sun is hot. You will burn your lovely face." He left off patting, and reached up to touch her cheek with the backs of his fingers. "You must not ruin such beauty."

Thinking of the dreadful molting process she's undergone after the journey to the Cuchara, Marie felt herself blushing.

"Ah, there. Have I said something rash? My dear, you are such a marvel. Stay and cool yourself." He let go of her hand and drew a flask from his pocket. "Would you care for a bit of lemonade? I only just filled up my flask." He handed the container to her, and she took it automatically.

"I don't know—" she began, but he cut her off.

"You are flushed, dear Miss Marie. The drink will cool you."

"Perhaps a little taste," she conceded, and unscrewed the lid. She took a hesitant sip, but the fluid was clearly lemonade, and would not compromise her thinking as the liquor had done. She took a large swallow, then another, then removed the flask from her lips, secured the lid upon it, and returned it to its owner.

"That is good," he said, then reached out and removed a lingering drop of lemonade from her lip with a light touch. He put his finger into his mouth and drew it out in a long motion. "Sweet," he said, drawling the word into several syllables.

Marie watched him, fascinated by his action. Again, his touch had been light as the wing of a fluttering moth. Certainly a too-familiar gesture, much more familiar than the length of their acquaintance warranted, but certainly it reflected care of her feelings, and tenderness.

"You quite take my breath away," he murmured, closing his eyes, and sighing heavily.

Not sure how to react, Marie stood frozen, awaiting she knew not what.

He opened his eyes and looked at her, longingly, it seemed. "I think I've fallen in love with you," he whispered. "Is it possible?"

Marie looked down, a bit frightened to have glimpsed naked yearning in his eyes, and fearing what might be showing in her own. Had she imagined he said that, that he loved her? The growing warmth in her body belied the thought that she had dreamed up his words. He *had* professed his love. Her mind churned. How did she feel about Mr. Thorne? Was it within the realm of reason to suppose that she was falling in love with him, as well?

"Would you permit—" He stopped, hung his head. "I feel it is a great liberty I'm asking. Oh, dear Miss Marie. May I call you 'Marie'?" He looked up again, a smitten expression on his face. "I feel I have known you forever. May I, would you permit me to kiss you, dear Marie?"

She took in a sharp breath of air, but before she could say yea or nay, Mr. Thorne's lips were on hers, soft and gentle, and pressed hers briefly, then released.

Marie breathed out. That hadn't been distressing. Indeed, she felt a longing to repeat the experience, and when he gently cupped her face between his hands, she permitted a second kiss.

This one was a trifle longer, more heartfelt, and caused her knees to quake. She put her hands on his shoulders to steady herself, and he wrapped his arms around her, pulled her against him, and kissed her again, with mounting fervor.

She halfheartedly pushed against him, at the same time as she reveled in the heady sensation of being wrapped in the comforting circle of his arms. Yet, at the same time, she struggled against the enchantment, a part of her not wanting to escape so quickly into the bubble of unrestrained joy.

When she at last broke away from the embrace, Thorne seemed repentant, a little shamefaced. "I—I beg your pardon, my dearest Marie. I became carried away. Your loveliness is as attractive as nectar to the honeybee. I could not resist your charms."

Marie tried to moderate her heavy breathing as she realize that he had dropped the construction of "Miss Marie" and was using her Christian name alone. She hadn't given him leave, but she didn't mind, not a whit. She felt ready to float away from beneath the trees. It appeared that they both were carried away on the wings of emotion.

He sighed and shook his head. "We must return to the building enterprise at once. I believe you were seeking out your father?"

"Ah, yes," she replied, remembering that she *had* indeed been looking for him, but searched her mind unsuccessfully for the reason why. The spread of the warmth that rose into her bosom almost persuaded her that her errand no longer was of any significance. What mattered most to her at that moment was that this man cared for her. She was sure of that. Didn't his manner, his actions speak of it?

Thorne shifted from foot to foot for a spell, then said, "My darling Marie, it would be best if you preceded me alone. If your father—" He left the thought unsaid.

"But—" she began to protest, but he shushed her with a quick kiss.

"It will appear better, my dear. Our acquaintance is a bit tenuous, as yet. I will follow you in a moment." He looked quite crestfallen at the notion that they should not be seen together.

She gave him a questioning glance, but his forlorn expression convinced her that he meant to compose himself before again being seen among the people working on the barn, so she left without him, looking back once at his dear face before she walked out into the sunshine.

∞

Bill looked up from the log he was trimming square and almost cut off his foot with the adz. Marie came toward him, out of the shadows of the trees on the hill above him. She had a faraway look in her eyes, then she glanced over her shoulder toward the forest, and he caught a glimpse of a man standing next to a pine. His stomach clenched. It was the town man he'd seen riding in with the Dominguez brothers. What had she been doing in *his* company? Alone?

He put down the implement and wiped the sweat from his face, lifted his hat, and raked his hair back with his fingers. *Marie Owen, off in the trees with that man?* He swore softly as he jammed his hat on his head. *He's up to no good.*

Marie walked right by him as though he weren't standing there, prepared to speak to her. He pivoted to follow her with his gaze. She seemed almost to walk in a dream state, and he determined to catch up to her to find out why.

Leaving his work, he angled to where their paths would meet, and put on a bit of speed to encounter her.

"Miss Owen," he said when he was near enough for her to hear him. Not knowing what next to say, he ventured, "Have you any water?" Then he felt a fool, for she clearly wasn't carrying anything with her.

She seemed startled at his voice, stopping and looking around as though coming out of a daze. Then she smiled and said, "Oh, hello, Mr. Henry. Water? No. I don't have any with me. I can fetch you a bucket, though."

"Don't go to any trouble," he said. "I reckon I wanted mostly to say 'hello'."

"Hello, then," she said, and walked away.

"You're a fool, Bill Henry," he berated himself in a low tone. "She wants nothing to do with you." He glanced back at the trees. The man who he'd seen a few moments ago was now halfway to the barn site, preening his moustache as he walked.

"Dandy!" Bill muttered, and got his feet moving toward the log he'd abandoned. He would dearly love to put his fist into the man's face, but what would be the point? The dandy had been the one consorting with Miss Marie under the shade of the trees, not him. What would a fight gain him? Exile, most likely. He picked up the adz and began chopping it into the log, thinking dire thoughts about the town man who passed by with clean hands and not a speck of dust on him. Had the man done a lick of work today? It seemed unlikely.

&

"Pa. I need to speak to Pa," Marie reminded herself as she left Bill Henry. "I need to tell him—" Why couldn't she remember what had been so important this morning? Something had occurred. It upset her, she remembered, but what had it been?

She decided to think back through her day. *I was late rising,* she remembered. *Jule called me a slug-a-bed. Then Ma had me help her all morning. Then I had to use—*

She stopped so abruptly that she almost toppled over. Her memory had returned, with a picture clear as if it were reflected in a good looking glass. *Jule's scandalous behavior with Tom's brother! And Tom!* She recalled the struggle with him from the night before. She couldn't marry Tom. "Where's Pa?" she said aloud, now frantic to speak to him.

People moved by her, jostling her one way, then the other. "Let me through," she pleaded, pushing, shoving, trying to get to the front of the crowd before Pa ruined her life. Then she wriggled herself free of those who had bumped into her, preventing her passage, and she stood on her toes in a vain attempt to gain a better view. She resorted to jumping, but still couldn't see him.

Then she heard her father's voice, and her heart seemed to stop.

"Gather 'round here. I have a grand announcement to make. Attention, folks. Come along over here. I have a few words to speak to all," he was saying, in a voice so loud it broke her heart free from its temporary failure.

Pa had already launched into his speech, and now the crowd shifted, so she saw him, talking from where he stood in the bed of a wagon, one foot perched on the seat.

"When I arrived in this place, I brought with me a host of fine folks. Among them was my good neighbor, Ed Morgan, who settled down the country to grow crops along the river. Now Ed has a strapping son, Tom. He's a fine lad, sturdy and a hard worker, good as the day is long."

No! Marie thought, her chest thudding with the renewed pounding of her heart. She threw herself into the press of the crowd. She struggled to get to Pa's side, to gain his attention, to forestall the rest of his words, but folks had again jammed themselves so tightly together that her progress was slow and uneven.

Pa's voice continued to ring out over the heads of the people gathered in his meadow. "I have a comely daughter," he said. "In normal times, she would've been the first of her age to marry. But times were hard in our neighborhood a few years ago, and that chance didn't come her way. It's high time she became a bride."

What is he saying? Why is he pouring shame over my head? Marie's soul cringed.

" . . .so it is my great pleasure to make known my daughter Marie's upcoming nuptials to the son of—"

No! She was too late. And Pa had caught sight of her, was beckoning her up to his side.

All at once, she found herself staring up at her father, and didn't know how she had arrived there, standing below his high perch. Perhaps the hands she had sensed on her arms and body had something to do with her rapid forward movement. Then she was standing beside him in the wagon, stunned as she heard him conclude his announcement, and again, knew not how she came to be there. She felt as though she'd been drenched in icy water. The people below her, clapping and making joyful gestures, had no distinguishable faces, only blurs of pink or brown. A buzzing filled her head from ear to ear, sounding like a giant swarm of bees intent on traveling through her brain. She pulled on Pa's arm, struggled to get out a few words, important words about Tom, as he leaned over to receive them. Then she was falling, and the last thing she knew was a sharp pain when her cheek met the boards of the wagon bed with a thunk.

Chapter 12

Bill watched as Marie toppled to the bed of the wagon and heard the sickening thud when she landed. Then he began to push through the crowd, trying to get to her, shoving the milling, gawking onlookers, who shoved back with many a curt comment.

"Watch it, buddy. Don't be pushing on me."

"Hey! Keep your hands to yourself!"

A blow landed on the side of his neck, but he pressed on, frantic to see if Marie was all right. He reached the wagon just as Tom Morgan vaulted into it ahead of him. Then he could do nothing as the young man gathered up the girl and began to pat her cheeks, a bit too roughly for his liking.

An awful truth engulfed Bill, and he shrank into himself, feeling bereft, empty. Tom Morgan had the right to be up there in the wagon, holding Marie Owen in his arms, and he didn't. Hadn't her father just announced the couple's betrothal?

The Morgan youth was shaking Marie now, and Bill couldn't help himself. He leaped onto the wagon tongue, over the seat, and into the wagon, then began to pry the boy's fingers off Marie's shoulders.

Mr. Owen said, "Here now!" and grabbed Bill's arm. He shook off the man's grasp, and kept trying to get Marie out of Morgan's hands.

"Leave her be!" he cried out. "You'll hurt her."

Tom blustered, "She's mine," and struggled against Bill's intrusion.

Old Man Owen leaned in and tried to intervene, but Tom's elbow found his stomach, and he backed away, clutching his middle.

Then Mrs. Owen fired a shotgun into the ground, which got everyone's attention. She stood enveloped in a cloud of dust while silence fell over the crowd. Finally, she broke the stillness, speaking in a quiet but intense voice that throbbed with anger.

"You men unhand my daughter," she said. She lifted the firearm, put it in the wagon box, and climbed up.

Bill backed away and over the wagon side, giving her room as he recognized that his dog was no longer in the fight. At least Marie was in good hands, with her mother taking over the situation.

Tom attempted a protest, but the missus turned on him.

"You was shaking her," she said, glaring at Tom, her eyes fierce as fire. "Do you have a brain in that head of yours, boy? She's passed out cold, and you was likely doing more damage than good. Get out of here." She waved her hand, and Tom got.

𝕰𝕺

Julia glared up at her husband, who looked down at her and Marie, furrowed eyebrows topping his puzzled countenance.

"You and me are goin' to have a conversation," she said in an undertone, mindful of the crowd surrounding the wagon. Her face felt as though it were setting into stone as she continued her baleful glare. She watched his reactions flickering in his eyes: first shock, then dawning comprehension, and finally, defensiveness and bluster. She held up a hand in a shushing motion before he could propel himself into speech and murmured, "Later. We'll talk on this later, you may be sure."

𝕰𝕺

Bill watched Tom descend from the wagon. The farmer glanced around the crowd, and when he had found Bill, he locked eyes with him. He stalked closer, and as soon as he had his face up next to Bill's, he growled, "You keep away from my woman. You ain't got any claim on her, filthy cowhand."

He wanted to deck the man, but balled his fists tightly at his sides instead, to keep from flinging himself into a fight. Brawling wouldn't help Miss Marie, and it might upset her if she came to herself to hear a ruckus going on. He compressed his lips over clenched teeth.

Tom, evidently thinking him a coward, made a derisive noise, roughly barged into Bill's shoulder as he passed him, and started off through the crowd.

He let him go on his way without a word, but moved up toward the wagon again, kneading his arm to release the pain. It was much less than the pain in his heart, knowing Marie was lost to him, but neither one could match the anxiety he felt for her welfare now. He reached the wagon and saw that Marie lay—still and pale—on the floor of the wagon box. A wash of nausea attacked his stomach. Then he saw that her chest moved slightly, and he let out the breath he didn't know he was holding. She lived!

Mrs. Owen sat herself beside Marie and gently lifted the girl's head into her lap, talking softly to her all the while. She pulled a small vial from her apron pocket, removed the cork from the neck, and held it in front of Marie's nose.

After a short pause, the girl reacted, pulling away from the strong odor of ammonia that he could smell from where he was standing. Marie's hand came up, futilely batting at the vial.

"There now, easy, girl. Come back to us," Mrs. Owen crooned.

Marie opened her eyes and said, "Ma?"

Bill's heart stopped beating for a moment, then lurched back into rhythm. She knew her mother. Mayhap she would recover.

೫

Marie's throbbing cheek brought her to awareness, but the pain was second on her list of importance once she gained consciousness. The first item was the awful stink filling her nose, and she turned her head aside to avoid it, batting at the source to get it away from her. The odor faded, and Marie opened her eyes to see Ma removing a vial from underneath her nose and corking it.

"Ma?" she asked, and touched her cheek, but it was too tender to permit exploration, and she couldn't restrain a small moan.

"Daughter."

Marie began to shake her head to drive away the pain, but stopped after one movement when it felt like her brains might spill out onto the wagon bed. Her cheek hurt, but so did her head. She wondered if she were concussed. That was the least of her worries, she decided, trying to pull her random thoughts into order. Why was she lying here in a wagon? The sun was high overhead in the bright bowl of heaven, so it was time for dinner, and Ma should have been presiding over the victuals, with Marie at her side with a utensil in hand, ready to threaten her younger brothers into going to the back of the line. *Like I did when Carl wed Ellen.*

Then her father asked, "Is she waking?"

Marie went still as memory sharpened.

Pa had only just made his horrible announcement, binding her to that loutish Tom Morgan. She remembered coming out of the crowd and climbing into the box of the wagon, intent upon lighting into her father, then she had collapsed. Why? She didn't have a tendency toward fainting. However, she had felt strange, a bit lightheaded. Was that due to her distaste toward Tom? It didn't seem logical.

Ma and Pa were discussing her in low voices. Marie sat up. Her cheek still throbbed, but her senses were clearing, probably because the headache pain had lessened a bit. Now annoyance at the hubbub and the attention on her took its place alongside of the pain.

"Are all these folks to be kept waiting for their meal?" she asked, gesturing to the people beyond the sides of the wagon, and made a move to get to her feet. Pa took her hand and helped her up, his face a study in confusion.

"Daughter?" he said, his voice raising a question, but since she didn't know what it was, she didn't answer him.

Before she could scramble down the spokes of the wagon wheel, Pa found his question.

"What of the celebration I planned?" he asked. "We owe these folks that."

Marie looked over at her father. "Celebration?" she asked in her turn. *More like a wake*, she told herself, but then spoke in a soft but firm voice, "Pa, I'll not be marrying Tom Morgan." Before he could respond with the full force of blustering fury, she was off the wagon wheel and hurrying away toward the food tables.

☙

C. G. Thorne pretended to examine his fingernails. The action kept his head down so the satisfaction he felt would not be plainly visible for all to see. He had gotten as close to the wagon as he could to find out what was important to the old man to make such a fuss. This engagement uproar would play nicely into his hands. He must get the girl alone again to talk. Ten minutes should do the job. He'd have to keep a sharp eye out for an opportunity. He didn't want the farmer to interrupt his plans, but the mother had helped by sending *him* scurrying away. *While the boy licks his wounds, a man will step in and gather up the prize.*

C. G. felt like laughing, but resisted the urge. Instead, he surreptitiously scrubbed his lips with his handkerchief. It was good to know the drug worked as well as he'd been told. It appeared there were plenty of rich pickings to be had here, if the Mexican was right about the money. The girl was nice enough looking. Pleasing figure. Clear skin. Seemed to be clean. He lifted his head and surveyed the meadow until he caught sight of her. *Nice walk*, he thought, and let himself go into imaginings that would have horrified her and sent her mother into a fit of vapors. After a few moments of musing on the possibilities, he thought, *I'll spend a few dollars of her old man's money on making her fancy. Time I got back in the game.*

Chapter 13

At the beginning of the dinner break, Bill looked for Marie to find out how she fared. When he located her, he was surprised that she stood alongside her mother at the plank table under the oaks, serving up the victuals. He had thought she'd be resting in a chair under the oaks.

Her cheek hadn't turned black from the fall yet, but the bruise was a deep red color, and must be giving her a deal of pain. His stomach lurched in sympathy and began to ache.

He got into the line and moved forward toward the table. He wondered if he would even be able to eat with his gut acting up in such a treacherous way. Then Miss Marie asked, "What's your pleasure?" and gestured toward the array of dishes on the table. He stopped looking at her and took a look at the food. It didn't much matter what he picked, as anything he put in his mouth would surely taste like ashes.

He frowned, studying the choices, then pointed toward a hot dish the likes of which he'd never seen before. Through the sinkhole of previously-removed food, he could see it was brown in the interior, with layers of something that was not quite white, covered with what appeared to be white cheese. Miss Marie dug into the cheese with her spoon and plopped a hearty portion on his plate. Mrs. Owen added one or two other bits of food, then he was through the line, his heart aching as much as his stomach.

Marie Owen was pledged to another man. Her pa had made the public announcement, speaking words that scourged Bill's soul. "What was his pleasure?" she had asked. He gritted his teeth. His pleasure would be to scoop up the girl and take her home with him to Texas. They could find that priest who did the marrying for Carl and Miss Ellen and get the holy words said over them.

He mumbled an unholy word. That option was as far distant as the moon. Miss Marie would marry the farmer when the upcoming harvest was done.

℅

Despite the throbbing ache in her cheek, Marie stood beside her mother and handed out chicken, spooned up hot dishes made of the most amazing ingredients, and felt her nose twitch as she served highly spiced dishes brought by the Mexican families who had come to help. As the parade of strangers from around about passed before her, her stomach began to greet them, and she bit her lip for the shame of it.

Then the line dwindled to nothing. Ma wiped her hands on her apron, smiled at Marie, and said, "I appreciate your help. You're a good worker." She looked Marie over, then continued. "You don't appear to suffer lasting damage from your fall. God is gracious."

"Yes, Ma. You need to eat now."

"We both do."

"Oh drat," Marie said.

Ma laughed. "Nothing can control those noises but a bite to eat, girl." Her face went sober. "How's that cheek faring? Can you chew?"

"It hurts some, but I can talk fine, so I don't reckon any bones are broke." She touched the area carefully, then grimaced. "I will have a nasty bruise."

"It's forming up now. Put a cold cloth on it when you can."

Marie dished up a plate of food for her mother and then one for herself, and found a seat against a tree. She was just biting into a chicken leg when Mr. Thorne spread a handkerchief on the ground and sat beside her, his face crestfallen. Her brow furrowed. He'd caught her with her mouth full.

"My darling," he whispered, looking around furtively. "My sweet Marie. I am gratified that you are well. However, I cannot believe what your father said. You are marrying that farm boy?" He gulped convulsively. "I had such hopes of a future with you."

Marie choked. Thorne gently patted her on the back until she recovered. She drew a deep breath, and finding her voice unimpaired by the passage of the chicken, said, "I won't marry him. Pa has put me in an impossible situation." She lowered her voice and hung her head. "I own a mite of fault in the matter. I pressed Pa to think about my need for prospects."

Thorne screwed up his face in obvious agony. "What will you do, my darling? The wedding has been announced. The farmer's parents will expect—"

"I don't know, but I can't marry him. He's vile."

Thorne sat back.

Marie stole a look in his direction. He seemed to be gathering his thoughts. She waited.

"It was he you were fleeing. It was he who caused you grief." He paused again, then said with some heat, "That simply will not do, my darling. It will not do!"

Marie shivered. No light dawned to brighten her path. Without a doubt Pa would bring pressure on her to fulfill his commitment to the Morgans. Her head began to ache again.

"Oh," said Mr. Thorne, a long sighing vowel. "I have it, my dear. A plan."

Marie hardly dared breathe, waiting for him to enlighten her.

"We will go away. We will ride to Denver and be married there. I have a lovely home in the foothills." He spoke rapidly, breathing hard. "My dear aunt died recently and left me the house. There will be quite a bit of money, by and by. We will be well situated, my love." He took her hand. "Say you will do it. Say you will come away with me!"

Marie's breath was shaky as she inhaled. She hardly knew this man, but he seemed to be over the moon in love with her. Surely this was her salvation. She would not need to marry Tom if she went away with Mr. Thorne.

She looked at him closely. He was well groomed. There were no bits of food in his moustache. His clothing was clean and well kept. His fingernails were trimmed and clean. His breath was sweet. His hands were soft and gentle, and not at all sweaty. She remembered that merely being in his presence often caused her bones to melt. Surely that was a sign she loved him.

She let out the breath. "Yes," she said. "When can we leave?"

Thorne looked around again. Then his gaze returned and he lowered his voice, almost to a whisper. "Tonight. We will make our escape when everyone is asleep." His face looked pained for an instant, then it cleared as he obviously made an effort to shake off a doubt.

"What's amiss, dear Mr. Thorne?" Her voice shook as she tried out the endearment.

"I am ashamed to say that I have no money for our expenses. I was foolish and played poker with the Dominguez boys. They are sharper players than I." He looked down.

"Pa has a bit of money." She clapped her hand over her mouth, horrified that those words had escaped her lips.

Mr. Thorne gently removed her hand and patted it between his. "That is a fortunate happenstance. You can bring it along tonight."

"I cannot simply take it." Marie's head swam at the thought of stealing the remaining gold dust in Uncle Jonathan's box.

Mr. Thorne's chin came up. His eyes narrowed. "Does not your father owe you a dower price?"

The words hung in the air between them for a long moment.

Marie thought of all the grief she'd had to bear in the last year. She thought of her father's lack of concern for her needs. She thought of the pain of becoming a woman without a future. She thought of Jule's taunting words and scandalous behavior.

"Yes," she said in a burst of emotion. "He does, and much more. He owes me respect, and he doesn't give me any."

Thorne shook his head. "A dowry doesn't make up for a father's lack of affection, but it goes a long way in soothing hurt feelings."

Marie began to protest, but Thorne shushed her with a lingering kiss, hidden behind his hat.

"We haven't more time to plan. Put a bundle together, bring food and cooking tools, and get the money. Meet me at that lightning-struck oak on the north side of the clearing at ten o'clock. Bring a good horse." He finished his instructions and rose easily to his feet, bending down to retrieve his handkerchief. "Until then, my sweet Marie." He gave her a wistful look, gently squeezed her hand, and left.

When Mr. Thorne had gone, Marie's head swirled with details, the warmth of his kiss spreading through her body. *This is right*, she thought. *He loves me. He will treat me gently. Yes, this is the right thing to do.*

જી

This time when Thorne had slipped deep into the forest, he gave himself up to great peals of mirth. *That was easy as eating pie,* he thought, wiping his eyes when he had recovered his equanimity. *The girl is sitting in the palm of my hand.*

He composed his face, straightened his waistcoat, and strode off in search of the Dominguez brothers.

Chapter 14

With dinner out of the way, Marie was gratified that Ma sent her back to the cabin with a load of dishes to wash.

"If you don't mind, daughter, start the fire under the wash water. I'll be along by and by, after I visit with Mrs. Bates. I won't tarry long."

Here's a blessing, Marie thought. *I'll put together the things I want to take. Just a change of clothes. A pot and the spider, will do, I reckon. Food will have to wait until Ma brings back the leftovers.*

She hesitated, not wanting to think yet on the other item she must put in her bundle of necessities. Mr. Thorne had the right of it. Pa owed her a dowry. Even though he had put the gold aside to pay the cowhands and purchase supplies, she surely wasn't stealing if she took the portion that he would have used to marry her to a proper suitor back in the county.

And yet, the thought of carrying a sack of gold dust away with her, even a part of a sack, squeezed her chest, leaving her without breath.

How would Pa react? Would he be sorrowful? Angry? Bluster about for days, castigating her name and memory? Disown her?

Ma would bite her lip, then mourn silently for weeks. At least four. Maybe five. How many weeks had it been since James had left?

The thought of causing her mother to mourn threw Marie into a frenzy of activity to fend off dwelling on it. She found a gunnysack and put her new fry pan and stew pot into the bottom. Then she put half a sack of cornmeal into the pot, and a sack of beef jerky beside it. She moved about the kitchen corner mechanically, gathering a few of the cooking implements that Ma had gotten for her from the peddler. She smiled as she included the sharp new knife in the leather sheath. That covering was going to be handy. Into the sack the knife went, along with a spoon and fork from her new flatware set. She assumed Mr. Thorne had his own utensils, so she limited herself to one set. When he and she were established in their new home, she would send for the other items that made up her hope chest.

Marie steeled herself and went to the mantel. Uncle Jonathan's small, but heavy leather-bound box had sat for years on the mantelpiece of their home in the Shenandoah Valley of Virginia. Marie had dusted it a thousand, thousand times. Only after his death had Ma opened it to find a cache of gold nuggets and dust. Now the box occupied the same place of honor upon their Colorado mantel, although it was somewhat lighter in weight.

For several moments, she stared at the box. Pa had shot off the lock, since Ma accidentally left the key to it behind. It had taken a few bullets to sever the steel, so chips and slivers of wood were missing from the front. She finally lifted the box down and put it on the floor before the fireplace. She opened it and looked for the smallest poke. She didn't want to leave her family destitute and unable to pay its obligations. At the same time, resentment surged through her chest.

"Pa owes me something," she said hotly. "There must be a price for having Tom Morgan's hands wandering over my body." She paused a moment, cringing at the thought of taking Pa's money in exchange for serving as the young man's plaything. She wondered if that made her a wanton woman.

"No," she decided aloud, "not now, nor ever!"

৪১

Once she'd sent Marie on her way, Julia didn't seek out Muriel Bates, but instead went hunting her husband. She found him walking around the far side of the half built barn, inspecting the sheathing timbers. Chester Bates strode beside him, looking skyward while engaging him in talk.

Julia approached the men at a fast walk to catch up to them. "Mr. Bates, Mrs. Bates needs you over to the horses," she lied.

The men halted in their tracks.

"Well, that's a caution—" Chester began.

"Now!" Julia barked.

Chester looked at her in surprise, but after nodding a goodbye to Rod, he hurried off.

When they were alone, Julia turned on her husband.

"What were you thinking, making a grand public announcement thataway? Did you see the look on my daughter's face?"

She paused to draw a breath, and Rod found his voice.

"Wife, I did what seemed the right thing at the time. There's no harm in spreading the news so folks can give thought to coming for the wedding." He pulled at his collar and cleared his throat.

"I reckon she don't want a big gathering." She set her hands on her hips and glared at him. "I reckon she's simply pleased to make a match and get on with living."

He squirmed. "She said something different before she tumbled over."

"What did she say? She does seek a crowd?"

He shook his head, pursing his lips before he spoke. "She said she won't marry Tom Morgan."

She felt her face slacken as her jaw dropped, her mouth falling open. For a moment, she couldn't even move, let alone respond to her husband's astounding news. She finally got her mouth closed and swallowed, cleared her throat and asked, "You heard her right?"

"There's no question, Julie. She said it to me again after she come to herself. Something's gone awry."

"Land a mercy! She won't have Tom? What is in that girl's mind?"

"I reckon it's your job to find out, woman. I've got fences to mend."

She turned her back and stared toward the mountain. "I fear I told her why Lizzie and me don't see eye to eye." She bit her lip. "Is she scared that woman will mistreat her?"

He put his hand on her shoulder, hesitantly, she thought, and she covered it with her own.

"I don't reckon the fault lies with you," he said quietly, his voice a bit rough around the edges, as though he had forgotten how to use it to express tenderness. "The girl's been acting a tad off ever since we come back from down south. It would appear something went amiss there. I should have asked her straight out what was plaguing her mind."

She turned, still holding his hand under hers as she pivoted to face him. His countenance twisted.

"She bears an air of," he paused, considering. "Dread," he said at a low volume. "She's a strong girl, but something has her spooked." He paused, but then merely exhaled and pressed his lips together, his jaw thrust forward.

She patted his hand, squeezed it once, then released it. "I noticed she and Jule have been squabbling more than usual. The girl's in a dither." She turned and took three steps away from him, then retraced her path. "She don't confide in me, Rod. Not for quite a spell now." She left him again to pace. When she drew near again, she wiped an eye. "I miss talking secrets with my girl."

"She and I had quite a lengthy talk back when she dressed me down for not fixing her up with a husband." He shook his head. "How'd she get to be woman-grown?"

"That war took the years," she said, and heard her voice break. "It stole a piece of our lives and our young'uns lost their childhood." By the time she finished speaking, it was all she could do to hold the tears in check.

He put his arms around her. "Woman, don't you cry." He nuzzled the top of her head. "You'll unman me, here in front of the folks."

"I don't care," she snuffled. "I'm worried about my girl."

❦

Rod held Julia close as long as he dared, knowing that at any time, Chester would be back to help him inspect the construction work accomplished during the morning hours. Just as he was fixing to go about the process of getting his wife back on track with the chores of the day, he noticed a movement at the barn's corner. A head popped around it, then disappeared again. When this had happened for the third time, he patted Julia on the back and, sidestepping around her, strode to the corner, reached around it, and seized the collar of his youngest son, Albert.

"Confound it, what's the problem?" he asked, dragging the youth around the corner.

"I gotta talk to you." Albert shuffled his feet as Rod pulled on him, finally digging in his heels against any further movement.

Rod tugged again on the back of Albert's shirt. "Come along here and talk."

"Not to Ma. To you."

"Humph," he grunted, and stopped trying to haul the boy toward Julia. "Speak up."

"She'll hear me."

Rod pivoted. "Julie, are we talked out?"

She looked steadily at him for a moment, nodded once, then turned and left.

He watched until she turned the far corner of the barn, then gave his attention back to Albert. "She's gone. Speak your piece."

Albert looked at his toes, breathing noisily for a few moments as he fidgeted, then looked up and sighed.

"Sister's been fooling around with Parley Morgan."

"What?" His hand tightened on Albert's shoulder. "Why would Marie—"

"Nooo," Albert said, drawing out the word as he shook his head with vigor. "Not Marie." He clasped his hands together, moving one within the other. "It's Jule. I caught her half dressed, kissing Par—"

"Where is she?" Rod started to shake Albert by the shoulders.

"Pa! Leave off! Let me go!" Albert's voice rose until it cracked.

"Where's your sister?"

"She's hiding in the stable."

Rod let the boy go and stalked away, feeling cold rage swelling up through his chest and into his throat. What was the girl thinking? She was just a baby. *I won't stand for outrageous fiddling of that sort. Parley Morgan is going to pay the piper.*

಄

Marie cut a length of string from the ball Ma kept, threaded one end through the two drawstrings holding the small, but heavy leather bag closed, and tied it to the other end. She slipped the string over her head, lifted her hair to hide it, opened the top button of her bodice, and guided the poke underneath her camisole so that it lay between her breasts. She had just replaced the strong box on the mantelpiece and turned away, when Jule threw open the door and stomped into the room.

She looked a sight, her eyes red and puffy as she screamed, "You told Papa! You told him about Parley." She rushed at Marie, and began to pummel her on the shoulders.

Startled, Marie grabbed at her sister's fists and held them fast. "I didn't," she grunted, struggling with the girl. "I would have, but didn't get a chance."

"You're lying!"

"No." Marie lost one of Julianna's hands, and took a fist on her sore cheek. "Ow! Stop it, Jule!"

"Papa's angry at me 'n' Parley, so you must have told him." The girl flailed about, hitting Marie wherever she could.

Marie caught the errant hand again, and held it away from her face. She said, "Hear me. I didn't have a chance to tell tales. Ma's had me working the skin off my bones. Besides, I don't want to talk to Pa just now. I'm plenty annoyed with him."

Jule stopped carrying on, seeming to realize at last that Marie was speaking the truth. "Humph," she snorted. "What do you have to be annoyed about? Papa made known your betrothal and I reckon you should be dancing a jig. You won't be an old maid after all."

Marie realized that the gunnysack lay on the floor next to the table. She had to keep Jule from seeing it. She racked her brain to find an answer that would turn away her question, and an errand to send her on.

She finally arrived on a plausible answer and said, "He cast a heap of shame on my head the way he did it, before all and sundry, making it sound like I was already ripe for the shelf. He could have been more closemouthed about my affairs."

Jule's eye grew huge. "Do you reckon he'll stand up tomorrow and make me a laughingstock with another announcement?" Then she mumbled, "He says if I'm going to pretend at being a wife, I ought to get married when you do. He's awful mad. He says he's going to cut Parley." She furrowed her brow, scowling. "I don't know what he means, but I reckon I shouldn't marry Parley after all. He did disgusting things to me." She stopped and hung her head. "I thought getting married meant going on picnics and kissing and holding hands."

Marie almost let pity curb her indignation. "When did you ever see Ma and Pa going on a picnic? I swear I don't know where you acquire such notions." She let loose of Jule's hands and continued in a softer tone. "I reckon there's a long sight more involved, like the disgusting things Parley wants to do to you. Tom has those same notions in his head." She gave a shudder.

"Sister." Julianna's voice took on a whining characteristic. "Please talk to Papa. Tell him I'm too young to make a marriage. Tell him I don't hanker to carry on with Parley anymore. He'll listen to you."

Marie wondered why Jule had that idea. To her great chagrin, Pa had never much listened to her until just lately. It was a fine thing that she was getting out from under his thumb tonight. Before she could build a head of steam at the thought of his overbearing nature, the remembrance of Mr. Thorne's kiss warmed her, steadied her.

"Please talk to him for me," her sister begged.

She blinked, remembering that she was conversing with Jule and needed to get her out of the cabin.

"I got chores to do and don't have time to find Pa this minute. I got a blinding headache, besides." She touched her cheek. "I'll try to get Pa to see things your way later on, but I swear I didn't tell him about your little escapade."

Jule's face wore a scowl once more. "Wait a minute. If you didn't tell Papa about Parley 'n' me, who did?"

Marie let loose her own "humph," then added, "I reckon you can lay that to Albert's door. He's always sneaking around, getting secrets, and working blackmail on folks. Why don't you go pull his nose for being a pest?"

Jule appeared to be letting her anger come back in full measure, for her face grew red and blotchy. "I will do that," she said, and stormed out of the door as upset as when she'd come into it.

Marie grabbed the gunnysack and hid it behind the wood box. Only then did she begin the task of getting a kettle of water hot for cleaning up.

ဆ

Marie finished washing the dishes, curious and a bit concerned that Ma still had not returned. After she had worked herself into a fret, she set off to find her.

That task wasn't hard. Suddenly hearing a wail that could only have come from her mother's throat, Marie broke into a run. The continuing anguished sound came from the meadow, and as soon as she could, Marie arrived and found the source.

Ma would have crumpled in a heap, save that Pa was holding her up, his arms wrapped around her in a tight embrace. Mr. and Mrs. Hilbrands from Pueblo Town were standing nearby, Mrs. Hilbrands wringing her hands, and Mr. Hilbrands stroking his chin and muttering, "I didn't think she'd take it so hard," over and over.

Another man stood behind Mrs. Hilbrands, patting her shoulder and crinkling his eyebrows.

Pa caught sight of Marie and motioned her over with his head.

Does he think I won't come near because she's crying? Marie thought, still regarding her father in a poor light. She looked a question at Mr. Hilbrands, and stroked her mother's cheeks, saying, "There now, Ma. It can't be that bad."

Ma answered in a high, thin voice, "He's been shot, daughter."

"Who, Ma?" she asked. A chill passed through her body, and she knew full well the commotion must have something to do with her missing brother.

"It's James."

The chill settled in her stomach. "What about him, Ma?"

"He's been boarding with the Hilbrands, but he's shot to pieces."

Marie looked at the Hilbrands, and then at the stranger, gauging which of them would tell the clearer story, and decided to query the missus.

"Ma'am, is it all that bad?" She looked toward the Hilbrands's wagon. "Did you bring him with you?"

Mrs. Hilbrands quit the hand-wringing and seemed to pull herself together. "He was hurt some bad, with two wounds that I stitched up, but he is not in danger of death. Mr. Hilbrands wanted to inform your folks, but James refused to let him write a note. He left a few days ago, and I do not know for sure where he went."

"He was much improved when he left after a few weeks with us," Mr. Hilbrands chimed in. "He sat the saddle fine."

"Julie," Pa murmured. "You hear that? He could ride when he left Pueblo Town."

Mr. Hilbrands continued. "A week ago he decided he'd had enough of bed rest. Mandy said the daughter told her he was fit enough to stretch and turn without showing any pain. He seemed fine when he drove a mule team for me before he took out. Well, maybe not in the best of spirits, but not favoring any of his parts. I reckon he's on the mend, Miz Owen."

Ma wiped her eyes and straightened in Pa's arms. Marie stepped back, glancing at the stranger again and wondering who he could be.

"I regret fussing so much," Ma said, her voice still thin and whispery. "It came as a great shock to learn he had been doing so poorly and I didn't know of it." She took a gulp of air and continued. "I should have felt his wounds in my body."

"Julie, you can't sense everything," Pa protested.

"I should have known," she insisted. "I've felt your pains."

"Ma, Mr. Hilbrands says he's on the mend now," Marie said. "Take comfort in that."

Ma stood still, breathing deeply. "It appears he's not going to come home soon as I'd hoped."

"No, Mrs. Owen," the stranger said, speaking for the first time. "He seemed intent upon a journey, perhaps a spiritual progress of sorts."

This is Pa's preacher man. I wonder what sermon he'll preach tomorrow when they know I'm gone?

"He did ask about a job with Angus Campbell," Mr. Hilbrands said. "I figured he came south. He didn't stop in to give you greetings on his way?"

Ma shook her head. "He did not," she said, with a return to a moaning sound.

"There now, Ma," Marie said, stepping up to touch her cheek. "He'll come back when he's calmed down some. A body must be a tad bit angry when he's been shot up."

"It was a drunk Irish did it, I was told," the preacher put forth.

No one had anything to say in reply to that, but Mr. Hilbrands spoke up after a pause. "I think the worst of it was over when young James left town."

"The worst of what?" asked Marie.

Mr. Hilbrands shook his head. "There's still sentiment against those of us who, ahem, who took sides against the Union," he said with a shake of his head. "There are saloons in the town that cater to Unionists, and others who serve Southerners. The folks don't mix freely."

"Oh dear," Marie said, mostly to herself. She'd have to pass through the town on the way to Denver City. Then she spoke up in a firm voice. "Ma, he's out of the town, and it's good and proper that he left. We will hear from him by and by, I know it."

Ma gave a moaning sigh, then drew herself up and shook off Pa's arms. "We will pray fervently for that," she said. "The Reverend will surely help us in that respect." She turned to Mrs. Hilbrands. "Amanda, despite the news you bring, you're welcome to our homestead. Rod, help Mr. Hilbrands unload his wagon."

Chapter 15

Marie's stomach roiled with nerves as she backed down the loft ladder. Clay's canteen hung by its strap from the shoulder of her coat, and she carried her shoes in her hand, hoping her stocking feet would make less noise on the floor. There was one plank to be avoided at all costs. It would simply shriek if she stepped on it. Although she could hear Pa's regular snores now, if he heard that plank! Well, she'd be discovered, and all her plans would be for naught.

She had traversed halfway to the door in safety when she remembered she needed her sunbonnet. Without it, her face would surely suffer a recurrence of the burn it received on her trip to the Cuchara land. Even though Mrs. Bates's strong leather clasp would keep her hair in order, it would not help with the sun.

Restraining a sigh, Marie finished her trek to the door and placed her shoes beside the wall. She unlimbered the canteen and put it atop her shoes, taking care that it did not bang the wall. Then she retraced her steps across the room and up the ladder. Feeling her way in the darkness blacker than stove soot, she found the article and put it on her head, tying the strings under her chin. This severely restricted her sight to the sides, but at least she would have the bonnet when she needed it tomorrow.

In her haste to get back to the door, she almost stepped on the squeaking floorboard, but stopped herself in time, rocking in her abrupt halt, and holding her breath as Pa snorted in his sleep.

Would he wake? Was her escape to be thwarted? She didn't dare breathe until the sonorous exhalations became regular again. Then she let out her breath slowly, sidestepped to avoid the villainous board, and resumed her trip across the room.

Now she had to get out the door. The hinges sometimes made noise, but Marie hoped the oil she had put on the leather that afternoon would keep that from happening. She picked up her shoes and canteen, took a shuddering breath, and pulled the latch.

The wooden stop lifted, the door opened soundlessly at her touch, and then she was free.

Pausing only long enough to sit on the bench beside the door to put on her shoes and fasten them, Marie hurried across the yard toward the creek. She tiptoed across the plank bridge toward the stable, her mind whirling with a mixture of relief and concern. She still hadn't decided whether to take her black riding horse or Bess, the gentle mare she'd ridden on the Cuchara expedition. Both were good mounts, but the remembrance of Bess's easy gait and comfortable ride weighed heavily in her favor. Besides, the black could be uppity of a morning, and Bess never had been.

In the end, Marie woke the more comfortable horse, took the tack she needed, then put it all on Bess, arranging her bundle and supplies on the mare.

Do I have all I'll need? she questioned herself before she mounted. She'd brought no trinkets or baubles, but only a change of clothes, the cooking utensils, the poke of gold dust around her neck, a bit of grain for the mare, and food and water for the first few days of the journey. She left behind a letter she'd written on the sly upon the last piece of the pink stationery she'd hoarded since the war. She simply said she was heading north with her own true love, and that the next time anyone from the homestead saw her, she would "be a married woman."

Once in the saddle atop Bess's broad back, she surveyed the meadow with the embers of all the campfires scattered across it, looking for the surest route through them. If she bent her way south around the Bates's camp, then between the Campbells and the Hilbrands, she should soon be out of harm's way.

Gently putting her heels to the horse's sides, she sat forward, and Bess moved out into the vastness of the night at a walk, nickering softly.

"Oh hush, Bess," Marie whispered. Perhaps she should have blindfolded the mare and led her? *It's too late for that,* she acknowledged, and resorted to patting the mare's neck and whispering soft encouragement instead.

Once she heard voices and froze, reining Bess to a halt. She listened, and located the sounds as coming from the far side of the meadow. *A couple up late, romancing?* She couldn't tell, as no clear words came to her ears. Finally judging the late-night chatterers to be no threat to her, she clicked her tongue at Bess and got the animal moving again. In only a few moments more, she would be through the visitors' camps, and well away.

Although she didn't actually hold her breath as she guided the mare between the intervening campsites, when she reached the appointed spot beside the lightning-blasted oak near the road to Pueblo Town, Marie felt as though she'd gone far too long without air. She slid from the saddle into Mr. Thorne's arms, stumbling a bit, but with his aid, she recovered herself.

Mr. Thorne then clasped her tightly, pressing kisses on her brow, her cheeks, then finally, on her lips. Marie responded, relief at getting away clean feeding her fervor. At last, they broke apart and looked at each other.

"I am so gratified that you came," Mr. Thorne murmured, holding her face between his palms. "Yes. Most gratified." He dropped his hands and looked her up and down. Drawing a deep breath, he said, "We really should be on our way." He hugged Marie again, then whispered, "My companions may miss me. I'm not sure they were asleep when I left the camp."

A tingle of fear swept down Marie's spine. "Let us leave now," she agreed, shivering.

She remounted with a boost from her swain, then Mr. Thorne got up on his horse, signaled with his head the direction they would take, and they left the meadow for a path through the trees and out of the Owen claims. Soon they arrived at the well-traveled road, and started their journey north.

಄

Within an hour, Marie was thirsty, and leaned over the pommel to retrieve her canteen. Not knowing how long Mr. Thorne had it in mind to travel that night, she took only a shallow sip of water. That served to refresh her though, and she continued to follow the man ahead of her on the moonlit road.

Finding herself yawning, Marie closed her eyes for a moment and let Bess follow the other horse. The gentle gait of her mount soon had her fighting to stay awake.

She must have slept, because the next time she opened her eyes, the moon had risen higher in the sky than it had been before. The flat landscape, broken by the occasional stream bed and butte, glistened here and there where minerals lay exposed on the earth. Marie gave herself a little shake as she endeavored to awaken, but soon, she was nodding in concert with the horse's easy movement.

Bill Henry soon joined her, in a dream so vivid that she might have said his name in her surprise. He talked of her Pa's heavy-handed ways, and Marie could only nod vigorously, given the recent events that had caused her such grief. He lifted his hat and raked back his hair, and then reseated the head gear. Suddenly, she was rebuking him for calling her foolish. The light in his eyes faded and his expression grew guarded. His grave voice echoed in her mind, "I didn't mean you, I didn't mean you, I didn't mean you."

The next thing she knew, Marie opened her eyes to find Mr. Thorne standing beside her stirrup, shaking her shoulder and muttering her name.

"Come on, wake up. I don't have all night to stand here."

Marie pulled away at the frank irritation in her lover's voice, straightening her torso from her sleepy crouch. Guilt at dreaming of another man at the very onset of her elopement made her cautious, and she replied tersely, "I'm awake. Are we camping here?" *Did I speak his name aloud? Did Mr. Thorne hear? Did I upset him?*

"No. We'll rest the horses for a spell, then travel along for a while longer." The irritation had left his voice, and he smiled at Marie. "I apologize for being short with you. I fear I'm not at my best tonight. It must be nerves from the anticipation of having trouble getting away." He helped her dismount, then continued. "I must say, I'm vastly relieved that no one was about to stop us from leaving."

Marie nodded, feeling a release of her anxiety, and smiled back. "I reckon I'm a bit unsettled myself. It was quite unnerving riding between the camps. I feared a dog would bark and set up an alarm."

"We've had luck on our side tonight. That is sure." He kissed her on the brow, gently, tenderly, briefly.

Marie yearned for a further expression of affection from the man, but Mr. Thorne took himself away to tend to the horses. She found a suitable place on the ground to sit and rest, a hummock of earth crowned by a sparse grassy growth, and lowered herself onto it. She reminded herself that she must bridle her passions, as the Bible counseled, until she was a married woman. When that moment came, she could enjoy all the expressions of affection with which Mr. Thorne chose to favor her.

Marie sipped from her canteen, trying to cool the rising warmth of her body. This ardor would never do. It was unseemly. Even though she had run off with a man she barely knew, she must uphold the standards Ma had drummed into her from childhood. *I can wait a bit longer for married life*, she told herself, reluctance tingeing her thought. *We'll be in Denver inside of a week.*

Once the horses were sufficiently rested, Mr. Thorne prepared them to get on the move again. He first saddled Bess and brought the mare to Marie's side. Then, as he tacked up his own horse, Marie noticed for the first time a coil of rope that he tied onto the right side in front of the stirrup, and she idly wondered if he had worked cattle sometime in his past. She mounted, clucked Bess into movement, and followed behind the man into whose hands she was entrusting her future. She had left her past behind. She had all the time in the world ahead of her to study Mr. Thorne's many sterling qualities and savor stories from his youth. A fascinating new life opened before her.

She'd never seen much of how others lived, spending all her formative years on a farm and interacting with the small community in Shenandoah County. Her journey across the Great Plains had been cautious, as her pa hadn't wanted to draw attention to their party. Not much had happened to her personally in Colorado, beyond that horrid outlaw encounter and Tom's outrageous behavior. One thing she did know. She looked forward to the adventures ahead.

For the moment, however, nothing much was occurring, beyond sitting her horse and fighting off her tendency to yawn and close her eyes. From time to time, Mr. Thorne glanced at her over his shoulder, and she endeavored to smile reassuringly at him. Her fatigue was stronger than her resolve, however, and again, she slept.

Bill slipped back into her dreams, and for a spell she enjoyed watching the way his moustache turned up on the left side of his mouth when he smiled. Then her inner self realized she should be leaving Mr. Henry behind to do his chores with her father's cattle, and not tug him along on what would soon become her honeymoon. She struggled to cast him out of her mind, and finally slept deeply and alone.

When she next awoke, Marie noticed that the moon was in the wrong section of the sky. The trail beneath them had disappeared, and it looked as though they were traveling overland.

Marie urged Bess to greater speed to overtake Mr. Thorne. When she had come alongside him, she said, "We're off the road, and we're not going north."

Thorne drew up his horse and smiled at her. "No, my love. I've been pondering. I heard talk of a priest living in a town south of here. It occurred to me that you might prefer being a married lady for the rest of our journey."

Marie drew in a sharp breath. She hadn't given the timing or location of her marriage much thought, beyond having a lovely wedding somewhere in Denver City once they had arrived and made arrangements. "We won't wait until Denver?"

Mr. Thorne seemed unsettled. "My love, I can scarcely hold my ardor in check. It would be much better to marry soon. A day or two more, and we'll be man and wife."

"We're not going back through the homestead, are we?" she asked. The thought of encountering Pa dried her throat. The thought of encountering Bill Henry raised gooseflesh on her skin.

"No. We'll swing wide to avoid it. Showing ourselves there at this time would perhaps be unpleasant."

And yet, there was a preacher already at hand, if Mr. Thorne was in such a hurry to wed. After only a second of reflection, she knew she'd make no mention of the reverend. There was little chance he would be willing to fly in the face of her father's agreement with the Morgans and marry her to someone else. Besides, she was not ready to face her father's wrath, even with her beloved Mr. Thorne at her side to bolster her courage. *And Bill Henry's eyes would go dark as midnight.*

Marie swallowed hard and nodded her agreement with the plan, so they resumed their journey.

₭

It seemed to Marie to be a shameful thing that she kept nodding off, especially when she began to dream again, but she couldn't help it. Bess's gait was most easy, and she was so tired. The strain of the day's events, not to mention the aftereffect of the blow to her face when she fell, had built up a great lethargy, and she kept giving in to the need to sleep.

She awoke with a jolt when a chill wind hit her cheek. She shivered. The moon's light had diminished due to an obscuring bank of clouds. With the wind blowing stronger each moment, she feared it would soon rain, so she urged Bess to overtake Mr. Thorne once more.

"Will we camp before the storm comes?" she asked him, a note of anxiety making her voice sound high and thin to her ears.

Mr. Thorne looked up and tilted his head. "I imagine we do need to seek shelter. Look for any trees, or a butte we can camp beside." He patted her hand. "We'll be safe. Don't worry."

"I can't help a bit of nerves."

"So you cannot. Let me relieve your mind. I'll do the worrying from now on." He smiled in the dim light and gave her hand a final pat before turning away.

Marie heaved a sigh and let Mr. Thorne take the lead again. It made good sense that all would be well with Mr. Thorne doing the thinking. She had cast her lot with him, and looked forward to their future together, did she not? She felt a bit of her burden lifting from her shoulders. *Yes, all will be well.*

After a while, she heard Mr. Thorne laugh from ahead.

"See there? I believe we've come upon a stream. We will have good shelter there."

Soon they were dismounting near the bank, and discovered that the stand of oak trees lining the creek served somewhat to cut the wind.

"I'll water the horses. You find wood and build a fire," Mr. Thorne said.

Marie nodded, grateful that the rain hadn't yet started. She'd still be able to find dry kindling and branches for her fire. She hurried to her task, and within ten minutes had gathered enough fuel to start a small fire. Mr. Thorne could search out more wood later, if they needed to keep the fire going for long. She hoped he had a hand ax in one of his saddlebags, in case he needed to cut a large branch. Then she thought that if the trees were dry enough, he could pull off a branch with his rope.

She scraped a patch of earth until it lay bare, and arranged the tinder and kindling to her satisfaction. She put a piece of cotton wool underneath, and struck flint and steel together until the resultant sparks set the tinder to smoldering in a couple of places. She carefully blew on the best spots, then pulled back when they burst into flame. She pushed the tinder together so the flames would intensify, and soon the kindling was ablaze. It didn't take long until the sticks she had found were also afire, and she rocked back on her heels to admire her work.

Mr. Thorne came up and laid his hands on her shoulders. "That's a fine fire," he said, his fingers squeezing.

"We'll need more wood if we're to stay here for a while," Marie answered. "Would you fetch a few larger branches?"

"Isn't that your task?"

"Not if we need a quantity of logs."

Mr. Thorne made a sound that Marie thought expressed dissatisfaction, and she frowned. She didn't want him to think ill of her. She moderated her voice to be soothing as she said, "I can gather a few more fallen limbs, but if wood must be cut, it's a task I can't accomplish."

"I'll do it if I must," he said in a surly tone, his fingers digging into Marie's shoulders. "Put food together. I'm hungry." Then he released her and stalked off.

Marie hunched her shoulders, rubbing the abused muscles alternately to ease the pain he had left behind. *What have I done to make him angry?* she wondered. *I hope he doesn't know I've been having scandalous dreams. Aside from that, in my family it's a man's job to cut wood.* She got to her feet and moved toward the bundles she'd brought. *Perhaps his mother and sisters did that chore? I will have to be more careful from now on not to cause him grief.*

Chapter 16

Bill awoke before dawn with an uneasy feeling. As he sat on the edge of his bunk, he paused before pulling on his second boot. What was bothering him? It didn't take much pondering to know that the path he had planned for his life had gone terribly wrong. Marie Owen was promised to that wretched farmer, Tom Morgan. That was enough to bother anyone.

"Tom," he growled, yanking on his boot. "What a puny excuse for a man!"

He rose and slammed his hat onto his head. *Why did she choose Tom Morgan? Doesn't she know how I feel about her?* Anger battled grief in his body, his heart pounding like galloping hooves on a hardpan road. He took several deep breaths, trying to get the emotions under control so he could get about his day, but the sense of wrong, the sense of foreboding wouldn't leave him. Maybe something else was gnawing at him.

Try as he would to shake off the feeling of disaster that lingered like a bitter aftertaste in the mouth, Bill went to breakfast without any relief from the sensation. Even three spoonfuls of sugar mixed into his coffee didn't take away the dread.

A heavy hand came down on his shoulder from behind, startling him. Immediately the hoarse sound of Chico Henderson's morning voice cut through what remained of his reflective fog.

"Sorry I was a porcupine the other evening," Chico said. "You don't usually take my money so handily."

Bill attempted to add a light tone to his reply. "You're a sore loser, Henderson." He failed. His voice grated in his ears as though he were drawing a rasp over a tin washboard. He clamped his jaw shut.

"I ain't so much, old son. You were on a winning streak the likes of which I ain't seen before." Chico sat in the chair next to Bill's and lifted his mug toward his mouth. "It took me by surprise, I got to say." After a slurp or two, he cut his eyes toward Bill. "What's tugging on your brainpan?"

Bill shrugged.

"Something has you befogged. Out with it."

"I can't say." He shrugged again. "I don't know." He chewed on his lip for a moment, then blurted out, "How could she up and get herself promised to that lump?"

Chico wiped the last sip of coffee from his moustache. "Was you makin' plans with her?"

Bill hesitated. Then, remembering that Chico Henderson had saved his life on several occasions, he acknowledged that the man was indeed the closest thing to a good friend that he had. He spoke in the direction of his coffee cup, "It didn't get that far along. I was hoping, but—" He stopped short when the cook, Sourdough Smith, slapped a plate of eggs and beans onto the table before him.

Chico waited until Sourdough stepped back to the stove before he spoke again. "Uh-huh?"

"I had no chance to speak to the girl."

"Why's that?"

"She went on that little expedition with her pa and the boys."

"She come back."

"Maybe so, but she's mighty changed. She's put up a wall betwixt us the size of the Guadalupes."

"You saying you ain't much of a mountain climber?"

Bill snorted derisively. "Chico, you trying to make me smile? I'm not in a cheerful mood."

"I'll say you ain't!" Chico took a plate from Sourdough's hand and shoveled a mouthful of eggs beneath his moustache. Then he mumbled through the food, "You oughta talk to her. Speak your mind."

"You think Rod Owen would stand for that?"

"The ol' man don't got to know."

"Humph."

"You got to gather the reins and use the spurs to make the horse run, Henry. I know you ain't afeared of a little slip of a gal, nor her pappy, neither. Speak at her."

Bill chewed a mouthful of beans. "I ain't usually a coward, Chico," he said once he'd swallowed it.

"No, you ain't. Not in my experience of you."

"I'm unmanned by the cold she breathes out."

Chico stared at Bill for a while, then swallowed his own mouthful. "It happens. A girl has the power. Howsomever, you know you're a better man for her then any mule-eared farmer boy, and mayhap she knows it, as well. Tell her you got feelings. Show her you got the grit to be tender."

Bill exhaled a long breath. "It's got to be done. Today's as good as tomorrow." He arose and gripped Chico's shoulder, then left the bunkhouse with long strides.

☙

Marie rose shortly after dawn to build a fire. Thank the Lord she hadn't had any more of those disturbing dreams! She hauled half a potful of water from the creek, which she set beside the fire to boil. After that, she dug into the gunnysack for the cornmeal, and salt to add to the water to make it boil sooner and season the mush so the taste would be appealing to Mr. Thorne.

She readily found the cornmeal and set the sack to the side, but couldn't locate the packet of salt.

Drat, she thought, feeling around in every corner of the sack. *Why can't I find it? I surely remem—* That thought dried up as she froze. Slowly, she withdrew her hand from the depths of the sack. *I forgot to bring salt. I'm a silly goose. How can I make a decent pot of breakfast without salt?* Anxiety crowded through her breast and tightened her throat. *Mr. Thorne will think I don't take care for his comfort.*

She went back to her exploration of the sack. Had she brought an onion? That would add savor. But after checking every possible cranny of the provision sack, she discovered she had not put an onion into it. Just as exasperation threatened to overtake her, she had a welcome thought. *I did bring jerky. I'll cut it into pieces and mix it into the mush.*

Feeling among the utensils in the gunnysack, Marie located the knife and slipped it into her pocket. As she searched for the bag of jerky, she heard a rustle from behind her, then a loud voice startled her.

"Marie!"

After her initial jolt from hearing Mr. Thorne call her when she thought she was the only one awake, Marie answered, "Yes?" thinking his voice sounded unusually stern this morning. Perhaps he hadn't slept well on the stony ground.

"What's the delay in getting food together? We have to be off soon."

Marie looked over her shoulder. Mr. Thorne was still abed. Irritation at his brusque manner warred with the anxiety she already had to deal with. *Goodness sakes! He should be up and feeding the livestock.* "I'll have breakfast very soon," she told him. "It will be ready after you tend to the animals."

"You will do that," he replied, lying down again.

"I have this chore to do," she said, not very loudly.

"What's that? Speak up when you address me. I can't come over there merely to listen to you prattle on."

Marie felt her eyebrows draw together. She turned her face away so he wouldn't see her expression of dismay. Mr. Thorne really must have slept ill to be so out of sorts with her today. Their elopement wasn't starting off very smoothly. Her shoulders tightened and drew forward, but she stopped herself from crossing her arms in front of herself with a conscious thought. *I must make a better effort to be pleasant to him when he's tired. He had such a long night, guiding us overland, and he wasn't able to sleep in the saddle like I did. No wonder he's a grump today.*

"Marie!"

She jumped at the urgency in his tone, then calmed herself and spoke up in a more or less steady voice. "What is it, my darling?" At least her voice was audible this time; she felt sure of that.

"Roll up your bed!"

"What? You see I'm busy with the meal."

"That doesn't concern me. This mess offends me. Take it out of my sight."

The unreasonableness of his request puzzled her. "Ain't you hungry? You spoke up for a meal."

"Leave it! I can see you are not competent to boil up a simple pot of mush in time to eat and be gone."

"I'm sorry," she said with a conciliatory tone, feeling her shoulders hunching. "It won't take much longer. See? The water is boiling now."

"Pour it on the fire," he demanded. "Get up and do as I told you."

She did so, racking her brain to determine what she had done so poorly as to make him unhappy and so stern with her. Steam enveloped her as the water doused the flames she had so carefully coaxed to life just minutes before.

"I don't understand," she ventured, but regretted it a moment afterward when Mr. Thorne jumped to his feet, shedding bedclothes in his wake as he ran upon her and gave her a sharp slap across the cheek.

"Don't answer back," he thundered. "My wife must be meek and compliant."

"Yes sir," she whispered, trying to swallow a sob.

"Stop your sniveling. I can't abide sniveling."

"Yes sir. I won't snivel, sir." She held herself very still, not daring to cross him again.

"Put those things away, then tend to your bed. You have the horses to saddle, and it's almost daylight."

She hastened to restore the cooking utensils and meal to the gunnysack, tie the neck, and hoist it toward the animals, then ran to scoop up her bedding before he had time to think of another chore.

As she rolled up her blanket, she craned her neck to see what was occupying the man in silence. He sat astride his saddle on the ground, smoking a cigar.

∞

Bill's long strides took him within earshot of the Owen's cabin before he paused and took off his hat. In the half light, he noticed that his hand was shaking, making his hat shiver like a giant aspen leaf. He ran his other hand through his hair, re-seated the hat, and took several deep breaths to steady himself.

As he was about to move toward the cabin to have conversation with Marie, he heard a cry that reminded him of those of the panthers he hunted in Texas as a boy. Even as he squinted towards the woods behind him, he realized the sound hadn't come from that location. It had come from the cabin, and it continued as he gathered his wits and sprinted across the meadow, leaping the creek to arrive in the yard.

Bill barely knocked before he threw caution to the wind and hauled on the latchstring to open the door. He put his shoulder against the wood and, as it swung open, abruptly stopped himself from falling into the room.

Mrs. Owen stood nearly in the fireplace, her head bowed over a piece of rosy-colored paper. All her energy seemed absorbed in making a keening wail. The younger Owen girl knelt beside her, face in her hands, sobbing. Mr. Owen bent over his wife, his brows drawn together, strong emotions chasing themselves across his face. The two younger sons, Clay and Albert, stood frozen at their places at the table, breakfast abandoned. Then Clay broke the tableau when he bent to right the chair he must have overturned just moments before.

The Old Man looked up at Bill's intrusion, blinked, then barked an order at him. "Take Clay. See if that blasted Tom Morgan has lit out with my daughter!"

He felt the blood drain from his face and arms, chilling his skin. "What?" The strangled word sounded like a groan.

The man snatched the paper from Mrs. Owen's grasp, crossed the room, and thrust it into Bill's hand. "Read it. She's run off. If that young pup took her for his pleasure, I'll hound him to Hell and back."

Bill almost dropped the sheet, but got his fingers pressed onto it in time to keep it in his grasp. He brought it up where he could scan it.

Dear Ma and Pa,
I cain't bear the thought you would stop me, so I have stealed away with my own true love. We aire going North to Denver, where we will be wed. The next time you see me, I will be a married woman.
Always your loving dauter,
Marie

He stared at the paper until the lines of script began to wiggle before his eyes, pain surging throughout his body, from the part of his hair to his toenails. He knew he looked a fool with his mouth open, but if he was going to breathe again, the happenstance of his jaw having gone slack might help him drag in a little air, if only he could remember how that was done.

Bill shook his head and read the note again. Then he crumpled the paper and shoved it into his pocket. He turned and left the house, his heart pounding as though it would escape his chest.

℘

Bill could hear footsteps behind him, and supposed they were Clay's, but he couldn't stop to talk to the boy with the wind knocked out of his body by the grim news. He struggled to inhale, then to get that lungful of air back out and suck another one in. Did it matter to keep breathing? Marie was gone. Life didn't seem worth the struggle. Then he thought if Tom Morgan was to blame, yes, he'd need all his faculties to find the kid and beat him into the ground before Rod Owen did.

Now Bill's breath came easier as deadly resolve took hold. He'd catch the scoundrel and bring Marie back home. He had to get her back. The phrase repeated in his brain, pushing against his skull, crying from every corner of his soul to be screamed aloud: *got to get her back, got to get her back, got to get her back.*

Clay shouted, "Hold up."

Bill slowed his pace a fraction to allow the youth to join him. Without a word, he began to run in the direction of the Morgan family's camp, Clay beside him.

When they skidded to a stop beside the Morgan's wagon, the family seemed barely to have risen. Bill looked at the figures in front of him: Mr. Morgan yawning and stretching his arms above his head, Mrs. Morgan bent over the fire, the two girls looking at him with wide eyes, the boys . . . he counted. The youngest one with the limp, Parley . . . and Tom.

"Where is she?" Bill shouted at Tom, drawing near enough to yell the question again into his face.

"Who the hell you talking about?" Tom blustered.

"The Owen girl. Marie. What've you done with her?"

Tom gave no quarter. His body arranged itself into a crouch and he spit his words back at Bill. "I ain't done nothing with her."

Tom's fists were coming up quickly, guarding his face, poised to strike, and Bill backed off a pace, puzzled at this outcome. "You ain't seen her today?"

"It's none of your affair had I done so, but no. I ain't seen her."

An odd wash of disappointment enveloped him, primed as he was for battle, hating Tom for being Marie's betrothed, hating him in this moment because he was here instead of being the proper object of Bill's wrath, that man who was absent with Marie.

Voices surrounded him then, buzzing in his head: angry, concerned, shushing, petulant.

"My boy was here all night," Mr. Morgan said, a brittle edge to his speech. "When I arose to . . ." His words drifted into an uncomfortable silence. Then he spoke again. "He was here."

Bill flung himself in a circle, taking in all the eyes staring at him. "Well, Miss Marie ain't. She's . . . gone." His voice sounded tinny in the silence of dawn.

Then the uproar began again, but sounded different this time, more muted, cautious.

"What you mean, gone? Not dead?" Mrs. Morgan's voice quavered through an ascending octave.

"If it's not Tom—" Clay began in a strident tone, then looked at Bill and shut up.

"Here now," Tom started, then his face went dead white. He gasped out, "Check the Mexican's camp." He took a harsh breath. "She was having some truck with them."

"Mexicans?" Bill could scarcely get the word out.

"Them Dominguez dandies. I don't trust 'em."

Bill remembered the brothers and the town man who had ridden in with them, the man he'd seen lurking in the forest on the occasion when he'd made a fool of himself asking Marie for water when she'd not been carrying any. The idler. The smooth, soft-handed man who'd been consorting with Marie in the shade. Was he a seducer as well as a lay-about? Had he convinced her to leave with him on such a vile pretext as being her "true love?" Bill's stomach clenched over his breakfast, and he had to take a moment to will it into submission.

Conviction growing that he was on the right scent, Bill lowered his chin and spoke softly. "It's not the brothers. I reckon it's their *compadre*, that man playing cards with them the first night. He must of took her."

"Thorne. His name is Thorne," Clay murmured. "Pa asked."

Bill swore softly. The name fit. He was surely the wily beast who had stolen the girl away. He looked around at the Morgans again, then asked, his voice barely above a whisper, "Who'll join a search party?"

Mr. Morgan tilted his head. "Tom and me will come."

Parley tried to speak up to go along with his pa and brother, but was shushed by Mrs. Morgan with a single "No!"

Mr. Morgan added, "We ought to check if Thorne is here. Mayhap he's not the one."

Bill said, "I'll go find out." A curious calm settled over him now that he had a clear task. "You and the older son gather your gear and go down to the main house." Even nestled within the calm, he couldn't bear to speak the young man's name just now. "I reckon Mr. Owen will want to set off as soon as may be." He focused on Clay and motioned with his chin. "You go report to your pa."

Clay absorbed Bill's look and hunched into himself. Then he turned and ran toward the Owen's cabin.

✂

Bill set off for the last place he'd seen the town dandy, the camp where the man had been playing cards with the Dominguez brothers. The fire lay dormant, ashes and half-burned sticks in a circle. Beside it, two bedrolls manifested by their lumpy appearance that the brothers favored sleeping late. He nudged one of them with his toe, just forcefully enough to show that he meant business.

"¡Maldito seas, hombre!" came from the folds of the quilt. "¡Déjame dormir en paz!"

Bill ran off a string of border Spanish, and the bedroll creased into an "L" shape as the occupant sat up, flinging out new curses.

"Where is the man?" Bill asked again, his foot in action once more, a bit more urgency in the nudge this time.

"¿Quien?"

"El hombre feo que no está aquí," Bill replied. "Where is he?"

"No sé. ¡Déjame solo!" A face appeared, and Patricio Dominguez didn't carry a smile.

Continuing his conversation as he rousted the other man from his bedroll, Bill discovered that neither the elder nor the younger brother could remember a thing about the previous night's events.

"Tomé mucho anoche," Enrique complained, holding his head and almost whimpering. "¡Ay, que dolor de cabeza!"

"Your hangover is your concern. How do you know the man Thorne?" Bill demanded. "Where is he heading?"

This time, Enrique screwed up his face and appeared to be attempting thought. After carefully managing a headshake, he replied, "Thees man Thorne, Geraldo Thorne, I theenk he say, he come to town a while ago."

"¡Basta ya!" cautioned his brother. "Say no more."

Bill hauled Patricio out of his bed and held him by the front of his shirt. "Where is he heading?"

"Cálmate, hombre. No sé. He ees an estranger to we . . . us."

"Not last night, he wasn't. You know him well. I saw you ride in together."

"We solamente ride in at thee same time," Patricio insisted. "He no ees un amigo."

Bill dropped his grip on the man's shirt, but gave him a little shove to distance him. He didn't want to breath the same air as a liar.

"Get your gear and clear out," he growled. "We don't want you around here."

The two men cast dark glances at him, but began to gather their belongings. He watched for a moment to be sure they had a good start on packing up, then turned and hustled toward the bunkhouse.

Chapter 17

Although he spent several minutes comforting Julia and their daughter, as soon as Clay brought the news that Tom Morgan was not involved in Marie's disappearance, Rod became the commander.

"It was Thorne, you say?"

"Mr. Henry's making sure of that. He headed for the Dominguez brothers' camp."

Rod scowled and took a few paces toward the fireplace, then returned to where his sons stood. "The man don't have that much of a head start, maybe six or seven hours. We need to raise a party to get Marie away from him. Are any of the Morgans with us?" He massaged his chin.

Clay nodded. "The mister and Tom will join us. Miz Morgan wouldn't let Parley come along."

Rod's mouth tightened, and he grunted, "Not surprising, but I won't allow him to hang around here to—" He broke his sentence off sharply, and narrowing his eyes, nodded toward Clay. "Go inform Mr. Bates of the situation. Ask him if he'll accompany us. If he will, he'll know what to bring along. I'll deal with Parley Morgan."

Clay nodded and then bolted out the door. Rod turned to his youngest son. "Albert."

"Yes sir?"

"Tell Mr. Hilbrands he's wanted. Tell him to bring a pistol and provisions. Tell him it's a manhunt. That should excite his blood."

"Yes, Pa."

"Tell him Mrs. Hilbrands can stay with your ma until we get back. Tell him to invite the preacher along." He rubbed his whiskers again, then continued, "I wager Muriel Bates will stay over to help out. She'll be a comfort, and she can visit with the daughter a mite longer." He nodded once, dismissing the boy.

"Yes, Pa." Albert scurried off on his errand. Rod looked over at Julia. She huddled into herself, one arm around Jule and the other raised, with the back of her hand covering her mouth. Her face looked as gray as though she had scooped up a handful of ashes from the hearth and rubbed them into her skin. If only he had time to enfold her in an embrace and give her a mite of comfort.

"Woman," he said in his gruff voice, rubbing his finger against his thumb, "we'll find her. By all that's holy, I vow he won't have her long."

∞

When Bill arrived at the Owen cabin with his horse, his gear, and the cowhands in tow, it appeared that Old Man Owen had affairs well in hand. The Morgans had shown up, including a surly-looking Parley; Mr. Bates stood in the yard tightening his cinch; Mr. Hilbrands stroked his chin and decided to mimic Mr. Bates' actions; and two other men who had volunteered for the search party sat their horses nearby.

Bertie Owen led up three horses from the stable and threw himself aboard a buckskin. Mr. Owen came out of the house, followed by his son Clay, Mrs. Owen, and the little girl. Carl hobbled after them with the aid by a hand fashioned crutch and stood in the doorway, grasping hold of the frame. He had gumption to come down from his cabin to see them off. His red-headed wife appeared to have a firm grip under his elbow as she shielded her eyes from the rising sun with her other hand.

One of the Morgan's horses raised its tail and did its business, forcing Mr. Morgan to dance out of the way. Chico's rude comment resulted in a retort from Tom.

We're off to a good start, Bill thought, his mood as dark as the droppings.

Old Man Owen held up his hands to quiet the hubbub. "Hilbrands, is the reverend accompanying us?"

Mr. Hilbrands looked startled at the notion. "No. He said he'd stay behind to lend comfort to the women."

The boss made a face, then continued talking. "We'll head north along the road. The man strikes me as a townie. I don't reckon he'd head off across the country, so it's most likely they took the road." He looked up as Rulon rode into the yard. "Good. Rulon is our best tracker. Son, you take the lead."

Rulon nodded. "Ready to go?"

"Soon as we're all in the saddle."

As the remainder of the men got on their horses, Mr. Owen gave his wife a quick embrace, rested his hand briefly on the young girl's head, and strode to his horse. Once mounted, he looked around at the searchers, his mouth a grim slash across the bottom of his face.

Rulon led off, his father right behind him. The rest of the searchers followed.

Bill clucked to the horse he'd chosen, and it responded smoothly without the use of spurs on its flanks. *At least one thing is going well*, he thought, trying not to gnash his teeth at the delay occasioned by rounding up the men. *I should have taken out after that gambling lay-about an hour ago.*

Before too long, the horses and riders began to string out along the road according to the swiftness of each mount. Bill soon surged to the front, just behind Rulon, his gut seething with anger as well as the dread he'd felt upon awakening. Maybe his place in Marie's future wasn't as secure as Tom Morgan's, but if he could bring the girl back home, that surely should count for something.

He shook his head, despairing of his chances. On the other hand, the girl hadn't liked the arrangement enough to stick with Tom. She'd lit out with Thorne, even though she'd only known him for a day. He sighed, sucking part of a bean from where it had stuck to his back tooth.

His see-sawing emotions caused an about-face. Evil intent wasn't in her. He was sure of it. More likely, Thorne had seduced her into fleeing with him, probably telling her a pack of lies to achieve his ends.

His ends. Whatever were the man's ends? What advantage had Thorne gained from stealing off with Marie Owen? He had no feelings for her. Of that, he was sure.

The man is a bloodsucking leech.

Bill looked back at Tom, riding at the rear of the pack, a scowl firmly in place on his visage. Without a doubt, the farmer was not happy with the situation. *I reckon he's irked that Miss Marie spurned him in so public a fashion.* Out of the blue he chuckled, relishing the man's discomfort. The humor didn't last. His mind turned again to puzzling out what end Thorne had sought.

After a few miles, Rulon called a halt, and everyone dismounted to rest their animals. Rulon knelt on the ground, touched a hoof print, and contemplated it for a time. Then he raised his head to scan the area.

Tom led his horse around the outside of the group, cooling it down.

"Stop!" Rulon thundered, getting to his feet, and Tom jumped backwards, scuffing the earth as he landed on his backside underneath his mount.

Bill watched Rulon bow his head and gnaw his lip, seemingly trying to keep his temper. But then the man's teeth released his lips and they moved silently. Not in prayer.

Tom frantically tried to get out from under his horse before it panicked and trampled him. When a hind hoof clipped his shoulder, he swore and batted at the animal's legs.

Rulon ran over, bent down, and hauled Tom to his feet. He spoke to him quietly, but anger was clearly upon Rulon, even when he kept the rest of the men out of his quarrel with Tom.

The farmer raised his shoulders in denial of his wrongdoing, whatever it was, but Bill was able to approach the two before Rulon had made an end to it, and overheard his forceful complaint.

Bill let out a slow breath. The farmer had wiped out the tracks Rulon had found, tracks he evidently thought were vital in discovering the route the couple had taken.

Rulon left Tom and stalked over to Mr. Owen. Bill was too far away to hear their talk, but after a heated discussion, Rulon stamped over to his horse, got aboard, and led off, following the road as before.

∞

Hours later, Marie sighed with relief when Mr. Thorne called a halt. She had followed his horse across a very broken land with her saddle slipping back and forth because she had not had the time to cinch it securely before Mr. Thorne had thrown her on top of it and started off at a trot, holding onto a lead rope attached to Bess's bridle.

Now he approached her horse, and she shrank away from him as he put up his hands and smiled.

"There now, my love. Why the curdled expression? Let me help you alight. You need to rest yourself." He wiggled his hands in a fashion designed to draw her near so he could get her off the horse. "Look around. There's a brook just over there, and a lovely stand of shade trees beside it. You must come off the horse and take rest."

Not knowing what to expect from the man at this moment, Marie slid from Bess's back, feeling as though spiders crawled on her flesh as he solicitously took her elbow to guide her.

"There now. Sit yourself down and take delight in the shade. I'll draw you a cup of cool water." He took a collapsible silver cup from an inside pocket, pushed it into shape, and smiled over his shoulder at Marie as he approached the bank of the stream.

She sat.

He sloshed the cup around in the water for a few seconds, then pointed off to the side, where the horses had gathered in the water, muzzles down, attempting to drink. "The gait of your mare is quite comfortable?"

Marie looked at Bess, the gentle Bess her father had picked for her to ride on the journey to the Cuchara. "Yes, she is a good horse with a good gait." She glanced back at Thorne, who finally seemed satisfied with the cupful of water he had acquired.

He lifted the cup, got to his feet, shook out the handkerchief he pulled from a pocket, and laid it over the cup. "That is good. Yes, that is very good," he crooned, coming toward her with careful steps, as though the water he bore were precious mead instead of the most common of liquids. "Now you must slake your thirst, my dearest heart. See, I have kept any insects or leaves from falling into the cup." He knelt beside Marie and proffered the drink, bringing it close to her mouth before he whisked the fabric off.

Marie closed her eyes and sipped. The water was cool. That was a help. It tasted slightly alkali, and she hoped it didn't contain an overabundance of the stuff. She surely did not need any stomach aches or worse maladies on this journey.

℘

Julia stopped stirring the pot hanging over the fire and returned to her seat. Gripping one hand with the other, she set her mouth and waited, her head inclined so she could see an area on the floor about fifteen inches in front of her shoes.

"It won't do to fret, Julia," Elizabeth said. "If Mr. Morgan catches up to them today, we'll know by nightfall."

"Leave her be, Lizzie." Muriel Bates stood from her chair and went to Julia's side, gave her a pat on the shoulder, then turned to remonstrate with Elizabeth, whose face had turned ashen. "Yes, you know I call you 'Lizzie' whenever I've a mind to. This is one of those times when a body ought to be allowed to fret all she wants, and I'll stand here and tell you so to your face."

"Well! I never heard the like in all my days! I've a mind to get in my wagon and go home, if this is the treatment I can expect hereabouts."

"You know you're blowing hot air, dearie. You've never hitched up a team in your life. Mind your manners and leave Julia to have as many dark thoughts as she's willing to bear."

"You really are being dreadful to her, Muriel," Julia said, not moving a muscle beyond those necessary to talk. "I grieve in the open. Elizabeth hides her feelings behind charitable acts."

"Charitable acts? Pshaw!" Muriel strode to the fireplace and stirred the pot. Then she rounded on Elizabeth again. "I don't blame the girl for running off when her expectations were wrapped up in living her life under your thumb."

"Stop it, Muriel!" Julia arose and felt her cheeks burning. "I don't reckon quarreling will help me or you or Elizabeth abide the waiting with any hope of decorum or calm. It's not your dog in this fight, much as I value your friendship and good sense." Seeing Muriel's crestfallen countenance, she took two steps and folded her in a tight embrace. "Oh, you know I mean you no ill will. I do need all the peace I can muster." As the gravity of the night's events overcame her again, she dropped her arms from around her friend and moaned, her voice breaking, "My girl. My girl! Will I ever see you again?" Her shoulders slumped and her head hung forward. "Please, pray with me."

A voice came from the doorway. "I will join you. It is but the least thing I can do for you, Julia."

Julia turned and saw Amanda Hilbrands coming toward her, and she swiped at her eyes. "Yes. Thank you. Ladies, please pray for my girl, and for my wounded boy, for that matter. And for Lizzie's boy. His feelings must be mighty raw, Marie treating him thataway."

After an extended time spent beside the creek drinking several cups of water borne to her by an exceedingly attentive Mr. Thorne, Marie wondered if he expected her to make a meal for them, since it was drawing close to noon. It only made sense. There was good grass for the animals and a water source. *But please,* she thought, *no more water to drink!* She had but to get the necessaries sack off the back of her horse to begin. But before she could even think about approaching Mr. Thorne with the idea, he lifted her bodily from the ground and threw her into Bess's saddle. While she was getting back her breath, he tied a length of rope around one of her ankles, then ran it under the horse's belly to wrap around her other leg, and knotted the end of it to the stirrup. Then he mounted his own horse.

Without a word, he set off at a rapid pace, whipping the free ends of his reins against the neck of his horse.

I must have said something wrong, Marie thought, alarmed by his odd actions. *I didn't mean to. Did I complain to him that I was getting over full of water? What did I say?*

When Mr. Thorne suddenly slowed to a trot, Marie found herself leaning forward so she could grasp Bess's neck in order to stay on the horse. With the cinch still loose, the saddle had canted precariously to the off side. Although her left leg was encircled with a rope loop, her right leg was tied in place, and it was all she could do to keep her body weight from dragging her to the side and underneath the horse.

Her arms soon ached from encircling the thick neck of the old mare. Her right leg felt like it was tearing from her hip socket. The rope chafed the skin of her ankles. She also had an urgent need to dismount and seek the shelter of a large bush to perform personal business.

Dear God, tell me how to make amends! I'm so sorry! I didn't mean to offend him.

Resorting to prayer gave her comfort, but no immediate physical relief. Her position caught the saddle horn between herself and safety. She dared not release her hold around Bess's neck. The horn pressed upon her intimate reservoir, which seemed to continue filling with fluid as each minute passed. "I'm sorry," she sobbed, and knew she had said that aloud. Ashamed, she gritted her teeth to keep from crying out again, but pain welled up with another bounce, and she could no longer maintain control of all her muscles.

Warm liquid flooded from her body. *He will beat me for ruining the saddle*, she mourned, and almost let go so she would be trampled, rather than endure Mr. Thorne's wrath. But just as she was willing her arms to loose themselves from their frozen encirclement, he pulled his horse to a halt.

Chapter 18

After the search party had ridden for several hours under an increasingly somber sky, Rulon called a halt to rest and eat. The horses badly needed the break.

Bill led his animal to water, but glanced around as his ears picked up the mutter of one man speaking to another in an undertone, complaining about the possibility of being caught out in a storm.

"More fool you if you didn't bring your oilskin," his companion replied. "I knew this hunt might take a day, or two at the most, but I taken a look at the sky and brung my rain gear."

We might lose several days' time if we're on the wrong trail, Bill fretted, remembering Rulon's thunderous voice and stormy aspect, and not at all sharing the speaker's confident assessment. When his horse had begun drinking, he pulled the pink paper out of his pocket and read it over for at least the tenth time. *Miss Marie thought she was headed to Denver. Who knows what that louse planned instead?*

Rulon must have seen the note before Bill jammed it into his pocket again. He came loping over to the stream bank to stand beside Bill, and put out his hand. "Can I take a look?"

"It's spare on clues." Bill retrieved the letter and gave it over, albeit with reluctance.

Rulon studied it out for a time, nodded, and looked up at Bill. "You have that right. She says 'Denver,' but I was almost convinced the tracks turned off the road onto rock before the Morgan kid spoiled 'em."

"Could you be wrong?"

Rulon tipped his head to the side and cocked his brow. "I could be. They might only have rested off the trail for a spell." He lowered his eyes to the note again. "Pa said Marie was clear, so here we are, headed north." He shrugged.

"You think he took her south?"

Rulon shook his head. "The tracks were ruined, so I can't say for sure. There's plenty of traffic on this road, heading both ways, so I can't trail them with any certainty." He spread his hands. "I just don't know. There was nothing left to see."

Bill felt his heart sink into his nether regions. *If Rulon doesn't know . . .* "So we'll go to Denver?"

"All the way. Pa won't quit the hunt until the scent dries up. Even then . . . he can't go home to my ma without something to show for his efforts." Rulon's shoulders slumped and he looked at the stream.

Bill directed his gaze in the same direction for a long moment. The cloudy water burbled over a pebbled bottom for a stretch, then fell, splashing, about a foot into a pool that took shade from a large cottonwood tree. Although he recognized the beauty in the spot, the sight and sound had no power to raise his spirits. Marie was gone, and these men could be on one of the wildest of misdirected chases known to man.

After a time, Bill turned back to Rulon and asked in so low a voice he hardly could hear himself, "Do you mind if I keep the letter?"

Rulon held it out, catching Bill's eye. "You're fond of my sister." He had no hint of a question in his words.

"I am," Bill said, almost whispering the acknowledgment.

"When we retrieve her, make your play, and I'll back you."

Bill took the paper, feeling a flood of emotion coloring his face. "I'm a hired hand. You'd favor me over your pa's chosen 'known blood'?"

"I favor Marie's welfare above all else. I reckon you feel the same."

Bill kept Rulon's eye as he carefully folded the note. Then he nodded in thanks, replaced the paper in his pocket, and walked into the water to get the horse.

සෝ

Thorne wheeled his horse back toward Marie, gathering the slack in his lead rope as he came. She began to shudder from anxiety. With his hat shielding his face, she had no idea of his mood.

Then he lifted his head and drew his horse alongside Bess.

"What's the meaning of this? Your clothing is totally sodden!"

"I'm sorry, I'm sorry." She couldn't keep tears from dripping down her cheeks from her overflowing eyes.

"You're quite askew as well. Straighten up!" He moved his hand as though he would strike her.

"I cannot reach," she whimpered.

He hit her then, once, the back of his hand across her cheek. Thorne spoke in a soft, caressing voice. "You look frightful. Pull yourself together."

The tender voice made Thorne's words doubly frightening, and Marie struggled to haul her torso up onto the horse's neck so her legs would drag the saddle into place. With rubbery arms, she could not achieve her goal, and sank back to her original position, sobbing, and growing chilled as her saturated skirt and petticoat cooled.

Thorne clucked to his horse, and letting the lead rope droop, moved around to Marie's other side, pulling the slack out of the rope so as to catch her around the waist. Then he heaved her back into place. Bess whinnied in protest.

Marie cried out as the rope dug into her flesh. But the movement brought her atop the horse again, and she could finally unclasp her arms from about its neck.

She lay against the mare's warm hide, sobbing from pain and embarrassment. Never had she wet herself with an audience, certainly never in the presence of a member of the male sex. She couldn't fathom any such occasion in her life since childhood, and no one but her mother would have seen her in a similar condition.

"Get off the horse," Thorne directed.

Marie, disbelieving her ears, raised her head and looked at him.

"Don't play dumb. Dismount."

"But the rope . . ."

He bent and fiddled with the knot, then yanked the rope from around her ankle, scraping it through her stocking in the process. "Get off that horse," he shouted.

Marie cowered toward the off side, dragging her free leg over the back of the saddle. She still couldn't dismount with her left foot tied to the stirrup, so she curled her body and clung to the horn, getting as far from Thorne as she could without actually falling to the ground.

"Do you think I'm a fool?" he yelled.

Marie dropped her body lower, her arms aching anew and her legs in pain from the unaccustomed crouch in the air.

He clucked to his horse again, and Bess took a step forward.

"No!" Marie batted at the mare's neck. "Stop!"

Thorne had circled to a spot behind her, and was breathing on her neck, pressing his lips against her ear. "What is this contretemps?" he crooned, leaning over and reaching beneath her.

Marie wondered what he'd done, but then figured he had to have untied the rope, because she felt her foot slip in the stirrup, and knew she was falling.

Thorne's hands remained below Marie's body, as though he was preparing to catch her. "You must trust me, my darling," he whispered. Again his mouth was at her ear, his hands now upraised and supporting her body weight in a fashion that would not bear her mother's scrutiny.

She tried to keep her hold on the horn, but the sweat of her hands had made the leather surface slick. She fell against his chest, onto the neck of his horse, and one of his arms snaked around her, holding her fast.

"There now," he said, his breath like a feather tickling her neck. "You are where you ought to be, my sweet. Safe in my arms." He clasped his other arm around her and rocked her a bit, planting light kisses on her ear lobes, on her jaw, on her neck. "Safe in my arms," he repeated, and then let her slide a bit. "Oh, that won't do." He tightened his embrace around her and drew her up against his chest again.

She stiffened as his fingers brushed against her breast, but then he readjusted his hold, and his hand ceased the brief exploratory movement. Perhaps she had imagined the touch. *Yes. Probably so*, she thought. *Mr. Thorne was merely keeping me from slipping.*

Bess sidestepped away, the saddle again leaning off center, the lead rope dragging the ground. Marie watched the mare move off, and experienced an odd sense of abandonment. She was beginning to feel awkward locked in Thorne's encircling arms, and wished she were safe on her gentle horse's back once more. But of course that would not be possible unless she were given a moment to tighten the cinch. Otherwise, she knew she could not chance mounting Bess.

Thorne moved his head to the other side of her neck and began to nuzzle her again.

Marie closed her eyes and slipped into a sort of trance. *He does love me, but I have been a great trial. I must try harder to please him.*

Her stomach rumbled.

"Thunder!" he cried, and dumped Marie onto the ground.

80

"Is that man joining us for dinner?" Julia asked Muriel as they put plates on the tables set up within the shelter of the new barn. She'd commandeered Parley and his younger brother to construct the tables despite Lizzie Morgan's strenuous objections against working on the Sabbath, and they'd done a credible job of the chore.

"What man?"

"The reverend Amanda brought from town. I'm sure he was hoping to send around a collection plate during a sermon Mr. Hilbrands enticed him to prepare. I've half a mind to send him on home."

"Why would you be inhospitable, Julia?"

Julia stopped her task and gazed at her friend. "He makes me nervous, prattling on about James's spiritual progress and Marie's misdeed, and always patting and touching a body. Gives me the shivers."

Muriel laughed briefly, then her mouth fell into a slight frown. "I reckon he's either freshly embarked upon a new career of ministering, or he hasn't suffered any pain in his life. How do folks go through life skipping along the top of troubles?"

Julia snorted. "I haven't. You haven't. Who do you know who hasn't suffered loss and grief and the like?" Then her voice broke on her next words. "I'm full up, I tell you. Marie going off is such a blow to me, coming on top of James leaving us." She sat down in a heap, as though she had no more strength in her body.

Muriel hastened to her side. "Julie, don't you give up hope. Your man is as good as any hound dog in keeping to the chase. He'll bring her home in good order."

"He'll bring her home, but he'll be shamed. When a child takes a notion to disobey him, he does not take kindly to the slight. No, not at all." She pinched the bridge of her nose between two fingers, eyes closed tightly. "He'll drown the girl in cascades of silent reproach."

Muriel kept quiet.

"On the occasion that Carl enlisted, I thought Rod would never get over it. 'Course he was off fighting most of the time, but he wrote home, and I could hear his voice as I read each letter. Bitter. Yes, downright impolite, he was." She shook her head and dabbed at her eyes with her apron. "Then we thought we had lost the boy. That cured Rod of his pique mighty quick."

"I remember Carl's homecoming. All the excitement, then getting fixed up to come west in such a hurry."

"I hope to goodness Rod's learned a lesson from that time. We'll see, we'll see." Julia got up and resumed setting the places, then stopped again, holding a plate in the air. "Lawsy me, I hope he's learned something," she said, shaking her head and swiping her eyes again with her other hand.

ಬಿ

Marie landed hard on her side, and the pain radiating to every part of her being seared away any action but to curl into as near to a ball as was possible and lie still. Her head swam. Her breath had escaped her. She felt as though she would surely suffocate before she could draw another one into her lungs.

Thorne kicked his horse into moving over to where Bess was standing, shaking herself to get rid of the unbalanced load. He leaned down and caught the dragging rope, then led the mare back to where Marie lay. Bess quit trying to shake off the saddle and stood still, but seemed to quiver.

"My darling, your wicked horse threw you. That cinch is a menace. Get up and tighten it so you can ride in security."

Marie remained where she was, struggling to get air, trying to block the pain.

"Did not you hear me? Arise and commence the task. We must be on our way."

She didn't move, although the thought that she should make haste to do so niggled at the margins of her battered mind.

Thorne started to dismount, throwing his right leg over the back of his saddle. Before he could finish the action, Marie whimpered and rolled onto her knees. She heard him settle back into the seat as she reached upward to get her hand through the stirrup that dangled nearby.

"That's my good love," she heard him croon, and she hauled herself to her feet with all speed.

Clinging to the horse, trying to will her hands to tug the saddle into position and find the buckle on the cinch, she wondered why Thorne had blamed Bess for throwing her. Hadn't the man been clutching her? Hadn't she been sitting atop his own horse? Marie's head refused to offer up the correct answer.

"We're late," Thorne barked. "Hurry it up."

She gained a purchase on the saddle and yanked on it, again and again, her arms burning and her ribs hurting her so badly that she wanted to scream. Her legs felt like rolls of muslin, and she struggled to stay upright on them. Finally, the leather sat upon Bess's back in the correct position. She slumped against the mare, catching her breath, but a movement she sensed behind her drove her to reach for the buckle.

"Bess," she whispered as she loosened the strap, "Let me draw this tight. Don't, no don't fill your belly."

The horse rolled her eye to look back at Marie, who patted her and encouraged her to stand still and exhale. Her own stomach cramped, adding to her anxiety.

"This must be tight. I can't slip again." Marie's crumpled voice sounded to her ears as though it came from someone else, some cowed, whimpering soul in dire straits. She pulled the cinch strap as far as her straining muscles would allow, then fought the tongue into the buckle and secured the end.

The second she had done so, arms snatched her up and flung her toward the saddle. Terrified at the consequences if she landed in it on her side, she managed to kick her legs apart against the mass of her skirt. The arms released her above the horse, and she fell, hitting the seat awkwardly, but at least she was astride. Before she had gained a good seat, they were moving again, Thorne dragging Bess forward by the lead rope.

Marie hung on to the mare's mane with a frantic grip as they picked up speed. She gasped at the jolting ride, racked with pain from her head to her toe. But before they had gone too much farther, she finally got herself properly adjusted in the saddle, with her feet shoved firmly into the stirrups.

Rain began to hit her back with soft drops, then hard pebbles, then stinging nettles.

℠

Nigh onto dusk, the search party reached Pueblo Town with not a moment to spare. As soon as the men had crowded their way into the livery barn, the skies opened and let fall a torrent of rain.

Bill dismounted and strode to the open door. Rulon and Chico joined him, and Bill looked over to see a forlorn countenance steal upon the former man's face.

"Still been trying to track?"

"Some. All sign is gone now."

Bill looked at the sky. He sighed. "I reckon it's fixin' to snow at the homestead."

"Maybe here, in an hour or so," Chico said. He turned up his collar and moved away from the incoming wind.

Bill gripped the door jamb. "Think we're bunking here overnight?"

"Likely," said Rulon. "I don't reckon Pa's going to stand us to hotel rooms."

"Ain't Hilbrands your father-in-law?"

Rulon put a shushing finger to his lips, looked around, and craned his neck until he located Randolph Hilbrands. He turned back and lowered his voice. "Yes, and tighter'n a Yankee drumhead. You won't catch me asking him for a favor."

Bill chuckled. "I knew a man like that once. He'd squeeze a penny 'til it barked, then save the sound to chase away thieves."

Rulon cracked a smile. "Good story, Henry." He cuffed Bill on the upper arm.

"I keep it in my vest pocket for use. Sometimes it's worth a drink in the right saloon."

Once the conversation with Rulon had run its course, Bill turned to the interior of the barn to care for his mount. The Old Man and Mr. Hilbrands moved toward the door, speaking with a tad bit of agitation. Bill got out of their way.

"They should know of the man." Mr. Owen turned up his collar.

"But they don't like to meet unless it's town business," Mr. Hilbrands protested. "I doubt the mayor will summon them."

"Time is running on. What's the quickest way to get answers?"

Mr. Hilbrands wiped under his nose with the back of his hand. "The saloons. If he's a gambler, he'll be known there."

Chapter 19

When Old Man Owen and Mr. Hilbrands returned from their foray into the rain, Bill couldn't help noticing the sour expression shared by both men. Mr. Hilbrands carried a pot smelling of beans and pork, which he apportioned out to the men.

Bill sat cross-legged on the floor beside Rulon, Chico, and Sourdough. They ate plates of beans and hunks of bread from a loaf Mr. Hilbrands had taken from inside his coat. He'd said the food came from his hotel restaurant.

Chico looked up, his mouth full of half-chewed beans. "You reckon Hilbrands will pass a cup for us to pay for this here grub?" he mumbled over the food.

"Humph," Sourdough grunted, sopping bean juice with a crust of the bread. "The bread's stale. I wouldn't pay a penny for it."

"It's wheat bread," Bill observed.

"It ain't decent wheat bread," Sourdough claimed.

Bill managed half a smile at the outrage in the cook's voice.

After the meal, he stood beside the open door, watching the clouds to the west brightening a bit just before the sun went down. He turned away. Mr. Bates and the stable hand were lighting lanterns.

Rulon, who was sitting against a wooden upright in the open alleyway between the two rows of stalls, beckoned to him, and he walked over to join him.

"Thorne ain't anywhere in the town," Rulon said as Bill took his seat on the floor. "Nobody has seen him since he left here in the company of the Dominguez boys a couple of days ago." Rulon rubbed his thigh. "Pa says there's some talk he was forced out of town."

"Any idea why?" Fear clutched at Bill's throat, and he swallowed a couple of times, trying to clear it off as he waited for the answer.

Rulon's face had darkened in the lamplight. "Something about mistreating a girl."

A thick chill swept over Bill. "We should leave tonight," he muttered.

He started to get to his feet, but Rulon put a hand on his arm and pulled him back down.

"There's no sense freezing yourself in that rain. You'll be cold enough tomorrow when we head out for Denver City."

"Early?" Bill heard in the pitch of his voice the fear, the anger he was trying to hold back.

"I reckon. Pa will leave plenty early. Bunk down and sleep."

Bill shook his head, meaning to reject the advice after all, but Rulon persisted, and he finally agreed.

As Bill wrapped his blanket around himself and began to wiggle a space for himself between Chico and Sourdough on the floor of a stall, raised voices attracted his attention.

Old Man Owen and Mr. Hilbrands sat in a stall across the alleyway, consulting with their Virginia comrade, Mr. Bates. They spent the next half hour in a discussion that frequently escalated toward an argument.

Bill tried to block out their voices by tying his neck scarf around his ears and pulling his hat further down onto his head. Then he attempted to find a bit of sleep atop the dusty hay, jammed in among other men trying to achieve the same goal.

When the search party mounted up early the next morning, it was evident that Mr. Hilbrands had no plans to continue onward. He and Mr. Owen exchanged a few heated words, then they parted ways as the mounted men rode into the teeth of the wind-swept rain.

The initial rainfall let up toward midday, but began to came down again in fits and starts during the afternoon. Riding in the wet was pure misery to Bill. The only things keeping him going despite his sodden exhaustion were recovering the girl and taking vengeance on the man.

He found himself riding alongside the boss a few minutes later, and was surprised to recognize the same ends reflected in his haggard, tightly set expression.

He is *her pa. If Marie was my daughter, I reckon I'd take it mighty hard to have her stolen away.*

The possibility that the vile scoundrel had taken the girl's virtue crossed his mind. Anger flashed with the power of lightning through his veins at the repugnant thought of another man, especially *that* man, possessing Marie against her will. He knew he'd been avoiding letting the idea out into the open, realizing that rage would paralyze him. As he struggled to concentrate on the obscure trail ahead, he thrust the fury down into his gut where he could bring it out later for examination.

The rain ceased again late in the day, about the time they found a wide spot in the road that consisted of a pair of saloons, a couple of bathhouses, and a few outbuildings. The Old Man called a halt.

As Bill climbed off his horse, he noticed a peculiar rumbling sound. It was not loud, but continuous, like a chorus of men humming at a low pitch.

Rulon and Mr. Bates accompanied the boss into one of the establishments while he and the other men looked around for accommodations for the night. Quiet, persuasive Clay got them the use of a stable behind a bathhouse, and found Bill and Chico together near one of the saloons.

Clay imparted the news, then added over the low rumble behind him, "They call this Boiling Springs, on account of the noise the gas makes rising up through the water. Folks come here to sooth themselves and drink the water. It is plenty tasty." His morose expression didn't harmonize with the good cheer in his words. He showed them the way to their lodgings.

Rulon came later, and drew Bill out of the stable where they could talk in private. He bore a visage carved from equal parts of anger and despair.

Bill's limbs began to quiver as he eyed Rulon. "What did you learn?"

Rulon's voice came slow and steady, but with an edge of steel. "He called himself Thornecroft hereabouts. Set up a poker table in one of the saloons for a spell."

Bill sensed there was more, and waited for it with a feeling of dread.

"They say he's cold, not right in the head." He paused, gazed at his toes, then raised his chin and looked Bill in the eye. "He abused a girl so bad it killed her."

Bill reached behind him, feeling for the stable timbers to hold him up as his legs threatened to fold.

"They was fixing to string him up, but he got away clean and headed south. I don't reckon he'd come back this way, nor head to Denver."

"You argued that to your pa?"

"I did. He's seen the error of his ways."

Bill sucked in air through clenched teeth.

Rulon gestured toward a stall. "Rest up. We're turning south at first light."

&

Marie awoke to half-light with hunger clawing at her innards. She clutched her abdomen, her head feeling as though her thoughts were wrapped in cotton wool, and her body shouting against any movement that would stir up more pain.

Where was she? Why did she have a rank barnyard odor clinging to her clothing? She looked around at the gray surroundings, hesitant, frightened, but not even sure why she was fearful. Why was she lying in the open, the ashes of a campfire beside her? Who was that wrapped in a blanket, snoring softly?

Why can't I think?

She strained to bring back any memory, and grabbed at a passing notion that she was camped with her father and brothers. Something about cattle brushed against her mind.

She lay still and listened for a moment. No. There was no sound of cattle bedded down nearby. She could see only two horses standing hobbled, each one nose to tail with the other. As she continued to listen to the noise coming from the blanket, she became convinced that the sound was unlike that which her father made at night.

Who kept her company? Why were they alone?

She lay still, letting her mind do its best to clear through the pain and the fog and the fear.

Slowly, slowly she walled the pain into a tidy compartment of her brain, straining to keep it intact with mental arms encircling it. Then she felt a light memory touch, very like a feather, stroking the back of her hand: a man with a waxed moustache bending over her hand, kissing it. The dream image faded as stark terror chased it away. She was bouncing crazily on a horse's overset saddle, and she couldn't draw rein to make the animal halt.

A tiny moan escaped her throat. Her stomach burned with acid. Her arms flailed as she fell from the horse, trapped in soaked skirts. A man reviled her for wetting herself.

She no longer wanted any part of memory, and retreated inside the pain, letting it flood over her until she had no more thoughts.

She didn't know how long she lay encased in pulsing agony, welcoming it to overwhelm her. But when she could no longer bear it, at the point where she knew she must die, her mind cleared and she could think again.

She had chosen to run away with a man who said he loved her. She swallowed down the mouthful of gall that rose to choke her. Doubt grated her thoughts as surely as though a rasp had been applied to her brain. The man who called himself C. G. Thorne lay just beyond her, snoring. She didn't even know what those initials signified, yet she had entrusted her life to him.

She turned on her side and threw up bitter acid.

When she had passed through the vomiting to dry heaves, she lay back on her bedding, taking in rapid, shallow breaths. Last night was very clear to her now. Last night, after riding for hours without a break, Mr. Thorne had finally stopped to make camp. When he insisted that she put together a meal, she had felt heartened. But when she had finished preparing the food, Thorne took it away and consumed the whole of it. He had only allowed her a sip of water that he tipped from his flask into a cup. She had grasped it tightly, shaking in her eagerness to ease the dryness of her mouth.

Drugged! She was sure he had drugged her. What poison was in that flask of water? She realized the man never drank from it now. On one occasion, it had contained lemonade. She wondered if that had been drugged, as well. Had she taken that unexplained fall in the wagon because Thorne had poisoned her?

What a fool I am! she thought. *He has no plan to marry me.* A chill swept through her. If not that, what base scheme had he devised? *A man this foul will sink to any depths. He wants to sell my body.*

The blinding conviction that her thought was the true case made her want to vomit again. But when she tried, she had nothing to expel. Nothing but foolishness. Nothing but folly. She berated herself for trusting a man with such vile intentions.

When she sank again onto the bedding, her hand flopped against her skirt and it struck a hard object. Puzzled, she untangled the fabric until she could put her fingers into her pocket to investigate.

Leather. Wood. She froze. She had the sheathed knife in her pocket.

೫

Old Man Owen was as good as Rulon's word, Bill reflected as he saddled up by lantern light. He had no pocket watch, and could only guess at the hour, but from the aching in his limbs, he figured he hadn't slept very long. *Midnight, maybe?* It could be later, but he was sure it wasn't nigh on to dawn.

His horse was just about played out, as were the other mounts. The thought that they couldn't go at the speed he would have liked galled him. There was nothing he could do about the situation. Thorne was getting away from them.

"Steady there," Sourdough spoke from behind him.

Bill thought he was talking to his horse, but when the man's hand settled on his shoulder, he knew the advice was for him.

He glanced around, and yes, the old-timer was looking at him.

"I know you're in a rough spot, Henry. Keep in mind, the girl has spunk."

"Thorne's pulled the wool over her eyes."

"It won't take long for her to see through it. Them swindlers can only run a confidence game on a body for so long before their victim's good sense kicks in."

"What day is it now?" Bill tried hard to keep desperation out of his voice, and nearly succeeded.

"What does that matter? I didn't know what day it was yesterday. If this ain't still yesterday," he muttered.

Bill doffed his hat and had a try at hand-combing his hair. "My brain's a muddle. How many days since he took her?"

"Well now," Sourdough ticked them off on his fingers. "This is the third day." He pursed his lips. "Don't give in to despair, boy."

Tom Morgan let go of his mount's bridle and pushed his way between Bill's and Sourdough's horses, glaring at Bill. "I told you. Marie is my woman. You ain't got any claim to plow that field." He shoved Bill on one shoulder for emphasis.

"Keep a civil tongue," Bill growled, and shoved back. "She surely don't want you. She left with Thorne."

Tom went after him, fists flying, howling curses.

"Boys, boys!" Sourdough shouted, but stepped back out of the way, pushing on his animal's rump to clear more room.

Before the Old Man and Mr. Morgan could stop the scuffle, Bill landed a few good blows, but received five or six himself. He backed up, one ear ringing from Tom's strike as the farmer's father pulled him off and muttered warnings at his offspring.

"We have business!" Mr. Owen barked, his furious face not two inches from Bill's. "Get mounted!" He spun about and stomped away to take his own advice.

Bill swiped at his trickling nose, then yanked at an edge of his neckerchief to sop up the blood. "Damned corn farmer!"

The ride back to Pueblo Town commenced without further incident, but Bill avoided the spurned farmer as they traveled, hunching himself against the wind and rain that persisted to torment them.

Chico approached him as he leaned against his horse when the party rested at noon.

"Why you want to tussle with the farm boy?"

"He threw the first punch. I had to defend against it."

"Keep your head clear, Henry. He's a thin reed, easy to break. The big stick is the con man."

Bill heaved a sigh. "I reckon you have the right of it."

"We'll catch up and break him over our knees."

Bill nodded. Then as he caught sight of Old Man Owen's example, he swung into his saddle. "He's got a long lead on us. We've wasted good horseflesh on a false trail." His belly ached at the misuse of their resources.

"Yep," Chico agreed, his mouth twisting down as he got his own foot in the stirrup.

They entered Pueblo Town after dark, to discover that Mr. Hilbrands had gone south to retrieve his wife.

"No fine food tonight, boys," Rulon announced in a rueful tone. He handed around two loaves of brown bread.

Sourdough yelped, "Weevils," in high indignation when he tore himself a chunk.

"Hand it here," Chico said, chuckling. "Extra meat."

"I fancy my meat on the hoof," the old cook replied, digging into the bread with the tip of his knife and flicking out the insects. "Catch 'em, if you want 'em so bad."

☙

At noon the next day, Marie huddled beside a fire sheltered under an overhanging rock, stirring gruel. The never-ending rain dripped off her sunbonnet onto her shoulders. Thorne sat wrapped in his blanket, watching her, the once-elegant hat atop his head now drooping and sodden. Yesterday, he had allowed her to saddle Bess properly, but once again tied her ankles to her stirrups for the cold, wet ride. He'd also persisted in denying her nourishment, and her stomach felt as though it must be grinding against itself. Other than that, the journey had been unremarkable.

Except for the daydreams. She couldn't get Bill Henry's harrowed countenance to leave her alone.

Then, at day's end, she had discovered large holes in her stockings from binding against the rope, and despairing of any chance to repair them, removed them and tossed them behind a bush.

Today her muscles trembled from fatigue and weakness, and her legs felt the cold more intensely due to her hasty action. She wasn't used to so much horseback travel, and she certainly wasn't used to starving.

Thinking she must do something to preserve her strength, she plunged her hand into the sack lying beside her leg and took a bit of cornmeal between her fingers. She crammed it into her mouth on the sly, holding the lump in her cheek, hoping it would soften enough to chew, terrified that Thorne would discover what she had done.

The gruel had thickened, so Marie removed the pot from the fire and glanced at the man. He got to his feet, came to the fire, grabbed the pot, and carried it away.

She remained beside the fire, trying to raise saliva in her dry mouth so the cornmeal could soften. She had drained her canteen long since, but didn't trust the contents of Thorne's flask. Perhaps she should spend the afternoon's ride holding the canteen to collect rainwater.

Idleness brought back her daydream, strong and almost tangible. Bill Henry sat beside her at Ellen's wedding dinner, smiling and chatting at her, pausing from time to time to take a bite of chicken or cornbread.

Marie fought the temptation to put out her hand, to see if she could touch the image of Bill's face. *He's just a fancy, my tired mind playing tricks.*

She'd had plenty of the dreams, waking or sleeping. They must have a meaning. Surely she wasn't conjuring them herself.

When Thorne had eaten, with much slurping and lip-smacking, he grunted at Marie and made a gesture toward her horse. She got up to make ready for the journey, chagrined that she had been caught idle. It was a wonder that the man hadn't got up and backhanded her.

Carefully, whenever her back was turned to Thorne, she ventured to chew the corn, one motion at a time, as she packed away the implements and sack of cornmeal. Then she saddled Bess, taking care to tighten the cinch.

She held her breath when he wrapped her bare ankles with the prickly rope and secured her on the horse, fearful of what new indignity he might visit upon her. His imagination seemed to have failed him, however, and he did nothing more to add to her present uncomfortable state.

As they rode, Marie stared at the deep hoof prints made by Thorne's horse in the mud through which they rode. How much longer would it rain? She swallowed the corn meal. It seemed to form a lump in her stomach, but at least it was there to give her the power to sit the saddle.

After several hours of travel, Marie wondered if they were going in circles. With no sight of the sun behind the constantly weeping clouds and no road to follow, it was highly likely that they were lost. One scrawny creosote bush passing beside her foot looked like another. Even the tracks looked the same, chewed up by the horse ahead of her.

She asked herself why she stayed with Thorne. Couldn't she escape? Couldn't she whip Bess into a run and outdistance the other horse?

Her spirits sank as she looked at her horse's lowered neck. Bess had no more reserve than she. The mare's strength was near to failing.

As the miles piled up through the day, miles that she was almost certain they were traversing over and over, Marie began to lose any hope that her world would ever consist of anything but riding in circles in the rain, soaked to the skin, with a madman holding the upper hand. The thought wore on her soul, chafing her spirit as much as the rope running beneath the horse's belly chafed her skin.

Late in the afternoon, she could bear no more of the endless plodding, and she kicked her heels against Bess's flanks, yelling to the horse to "Giddyup."

The startled mare leaped a foot forward, and Marie rejoiced in finally getting away from the man.

She made no great progress in her attempt to escape. Thorne still had control of the lead rope, and he'd dallied it around his saddle horn. Although Bess's yank caused him to lean precariously to one side and cry out, he regained his balance, hauled on the rope, and pulled Marie to his side.

"You can't get away from me," he yelled, slapping her until she covered her face with her arms. He flung himself off his horse, dug in a saddle bag, and pulled out another length of rope. Then he snatched one of Marie's wrists. She struggled with him, shrieking with rage and fear, but he soon overpowered her and immobilized her arms, tying them to her own saddle horn.

છ

Marie lay on her side in the brightening morning light. She could see well enough to realize that the clouds had moved off during the night. Sunshine at last! Perhaps she would be able to gain her bearings and make another attempt to escape from Thorne. This time, she would take care to slash the lead rope just before kicking Bess into flight.

Thorne had tied her wrists and her ankles last night. He'd told her she had been a naughty maiden to try to get away, and then roughly shoved her onto her blankets.

If it hadn't been for yesterday's rain that left the ground a quagmire, Marie would have cut her bindings and left under cover of the night's darkness. She had only resisted the notion because she knew he would have no problem finding her tracks in the mud when he awoke and found her gone. A sense of despair chilled her heart. Until she could find a way to make good her flight, the constant belittling mixed with the sudden bursts of strange behavior that so frightened her would continue.

Her heart sank at the predicament in which she had put herself. Why had she listened to the man's silver words, trusted that he cared for her? The immensity of her folly loomed over her, further diminishing any sense of her own worth. What a fool she was!

Thorne moved in his sleep, and Marie froze. The man finally lay still again, and Marie relaxed her tightened muscles. There was little point in trying to cut her way out of the knotted rope restraints with escape so fruitless.

She realized what little esteem she retained, and the thought rankled her. That lack of gumption had enabled Thorne to keep her captive. His prisoner! And yet . . . She felt the return of her resolve like little iron bars slipping into place within her spine. The time would come. She would get free of him and his despicable plans.

This time when Thorne stirred, his eyes opened, and he raised his head and looked at her.

"Don't think it, little Miss Owen." His voice was rough with sleep, but well conveyed his power over her. He closed his eyes, and seemed to sink into slumber once more.

She quaked at the chilly threat in his voice. Would she never get free of the man?

She started to imagine ways to disable his horse so he couldn't follow her. It pained her to think about hurting an animal, but if it were necessary—

He was on her in an instant, his knees astride her body. She began to scream as he tore at the neck of her dress. She struggled with the man, frantic that she hadn't wiggled the knife out of her pocket and cut her bonds. Her screams diminished to sobs. She would lose her virtue today. She renewed her fight against him. Better she should lose her life.

When Thorne had gotten her bodice open, he reached down between her breasts and grasped the sack containing the gold dust. "I thought so," he growled, and yanked the string until it broke, leaving a welt on the back of her neck.

He got off her, thrust the poke into his pocket, and went off beyond the boundaries of the camp to perform his morning business.

Marie lay as he left her, sobbing into her bound hands, relieved that after so long a forbearance, he hadn't attacked her virtue, but distraught that he had robbed her of Pa's gold.

❧

Rod arrived home Wednesday night in the forefront of a footsore party of complaining men leading played-out horses. The situation he found was no less grim.

Rand Hilbrands, having deserted him in his hour of need, had fetched Amanda and the preacher back to town, upsetting the remaining women.

Julia, who he'd always counted on to be levelheaded when he flew into pieces, clung to him, weeping.

Lizzie Morgan jumped up and demanded of her husband to be taken home as soon as horses could be hitched to the wagon. Ed refused her, showing either exhaustion or a surprising rise of gumption. Their quarrel could be heard across the meadow for what seemed to Rod to be hours.

Chester Bates got pulled off to one side by his wife, and they conversed for quite a time until Chester returned and made the excuse that Muriel was worried for the wheat crop. He said he was heartsick about the whole affair, but he owed harvested wheat to quite a number of folks, Rod included, and had best get home tomorrow.

And Mary was sick. Rod had no more than put Julia to bed after dosing her with laudanum when Rulon, looking more peaked than he had since healing from his war wounds, came to the big cabin. He paced back and forth outside until he poked his head in the door and blurted out that he couldn't ride on the morrow.

"We need to fetch your sister back." Rod slammed his hand into his fist, catching himself before he let a curse escape his lips.

Rulon stood in the doorway and appeared about to collapse. "I'm feeling mighty low about turning you down." His voice was so cowed Rod could barely hear it. "I'm obliged to choose my wife and young'uns."

"What ails her? It can't be more than your ma can deal with." Then he realized that his own wife was unlikely to be of any assistance, given her present state of emotional disarray.

Rulon crossed his arms, pressed his lips together and lowered his head. He gazed at his toes for quite a spell, then shrugged his shoulders and let them fall.

From his discomfiture, Rod guessed the problem. "She's increasing?" He turned and paced across the room to the fireplace, and then turned back to stand in front of Rulon. Then, before he spoke in haste and blundered into the middle of his son's private affair, he took another circuit.

Rulon was ready for him now, and said merely, "Yes, Pa."

"She's not feeding the babe? Preventing another?"

"She is." Rulon shook his head ruefully.

"Well, I'm gratified the mumps didn't steal your vigor." He took another walk across the room, an undercurrent of pride in his son swelling from his toes, but uppermost in his feelings was slashing anguish that his daughter was still in the clutches of a dangerous man.

Rulon left to return to Mary's side, and Rod was halfway across the room when he heard him speak out in the yard. "Henry." And a second later, surprise in his voice, "Morgan?"

Rod steeled himself to break up another row. One of the men knocked on the door, and at his invitation, Henry opened it and stood on the doorstep. He removed his hat.

Rod beckoned him in, and the man looked over his shoulder, then took a step inside the door, holding his hat at his side by the brim. "There's one horse fit to travel tomorrow," he reported.

Rod inhaled sharply. *As bad as that?*

Tom Morgan pushed his way into the house, knocking sideways into Henry.

The cowman straightened his shoulders and stepped back out of the way, but his dislike for Morgan showed plainly in his glower.

The boy had wrath written up one side of his face and down the other. "I've come to call off the wedding," he said in a voice louder than the location warranted.

Rod looked over his shoulder to see if his strident voice had awakened Julia. Not seeing her face peering from behind the curtains that enclosed their bed, he turned back to Tom, an angry retort on his lips.

Cutting him off, Tom declared, "Thorne's had her too long. She's damaged goods, not fit to be my wife."

Henry stirred behind him, and Rod barked at him, "No!" Then he directed his anger and frustration toward spoiled Lizzie Morgan's spoiled son. "You pompous, craven, dog hearted lout! If General Lee himself sent orders my daughter was to marry you, I'd tell him no to his face." He took a raspy breath. "My daughter is worth any ten Morgans, and you can tell your mama I said so. Get out of my house! Be off my land by sunup!"

Tom's face blanched, and he balled his fists, but he took his leave in haste, slamming the door behind him.

Rod felt the anger draining from him, leaving him feeling slightly lightheaded.

Henry cleared his throat. "Sir?"

He looked at the man and nodded for him to speak.

"I'm asking to draw my pay. I beg leave to take that sound horse at first light and track down Miss Marie. If I can't . . ." He paused for a moment to clear his throat again. "If I can't recover her, I'll light out for Texas. I reckon I . . ." He couldn't finish his thought.

Rod's own throat tightened. He'd judged the man a poor match for his daughter, dazzled by pride in his own connections, yet as narrow-sighted as though he'd donned horse blinders. If he'd only seen the man's affection for Marie before now— Rod abandoned that train of thought. Fact was, he had seen it, and discarded it as a matter of little weight.

He drew himself up, filling his lungs with air. *I can't dwell on my past sins,* he thought. *I'll send Henry after my girl. If he can't bring her back, nobody can.*

Chapter 20

The last thing Bill packed into a saddlebag the next morning was the deed to the Texas ranch that he'd hidden away under the mattress of his bunk. The action brought a wave of melancholy flooding over his churning thoughts. That paper represented failure, his failure in the past to get enough work to keep the place going, and a pending failure if he did not succeed in his quest to find the girl, wrench her out of Thorne's hands, and bring her home. Not for a second did he contemplate leaving the deed behind. He couldn't be sure he would return to this place. If he didn't, he'd battle all the carpetbaggers in Texas to get the ranch back. Henry blood had been shed to gain it. His folks now lay beneath its earth. It belonged to him.

After eating a hurried meal, he embraced Chico silently. Choked up as he was, he dared not risk saying a word. Then he departed from the bunkhouse and mounted, feeling the weight of his revolver in one coat pocket, and the heft of his wages in the other.

Rod Owen had paid him off with a mixture of bills, coins, and gold dust. When the man had opened the box in which he kept the gold, he'd turned back from it with a grim set to his mouth. "It appears the scoundrel talked my girl into helping herself to a small poke I had in here. As you ask after them, it might aid you to know that. He'll leave a trail if he's spending my dust."

The wages had to last him for a good length of time, either on his desperate manhunt, or on a long journey home to Texas.

೫

Marie had not yet seen a chance to get away from Thorne, but he had finally led them back to the road that ran south. During the early afternoon, he stopped at a farm to buy food. That night, Marie devised a soup by boiling a handful of the beef he had bought, along with a turnip and a potato, which she cut into the broth. Afterward, she took care to sheath the knife and furtively place it back in her pocket.

The man surprised her greatly when he left soup in the pot and bid her eat it.

"You're losing flesh," he said. "That won't do. You're of no use to me if you're skin and bones."

She took the pot and spoon, wiped the utensil on her skirt, and ate the soup, trying not to gulp it down. As she savored the hot liquid, she pondered on his choice of words. She had escaped what she had thought were his advances earlier in the week. However, his comment supported her fear. It appeared he intended to make his livelihood by offering her to be used for men's carnal pleasures. She shuddered. It was entirely likely he would yet take it into his head to use her himself as a prelude to the degrading life he had chosen for her.

When he tied her wrists that night, Marie followed the pattern she'd set at their previous night's encampment of making sure there was slack in the bindings so she could free her hands during the hours of darkness. This time, she distracted him from the task by asking him annoying questions about the people at the farm, and managed to keep her wrists slightly apart as he secured them.

She didn't fancy being helpless if this was the night he tried to assault her. She had to have her hands free to wield her only weapon.

She had almost dozed off when a slight noise alerted her that Thorne was awake. She strained to see into the darkness as she slipped the blade free of the leather. He would not catch her vulnerable.

He tried, clasping his hand over her mouth to silence her. But she didn't want to scream. She wanted to cut him, hurt him, cause him great discomfort.

And she did. The faint contrast of his grotesque white appendage against the dark fabric of his trousers was a good target, and she poked and slashed at it, sending him howling away. She hurriedly got up from the bed, trying to locate Bess so she could haul herself on the mare's back and flee.

But he must have seen her intentions for, despite his wounds, he came back and hit her with his fist, and she fell into blackness.

ℒ

Bill continued south, keeping the horse to a lope where it could, and going forward at a trot when it couldn't. He stopped at every farmhouse, every hacienda, every settlement, asking after a man dressed in fancy duds and a young woman riding a brown mare. He didn't get any news of them until after he'd left the Spanish settlement on the Cuchara. But while asking around in Leones, he had picked up the intriguing information that James Owen had up and got himself married, and might still be in the country.

I can't stop to locate but one Owen, he reminded himself, and pressed on south toward the Apishapa River.

At a farmhouse set back off the road in the midst of a field of wheat, he got the first encouraging report.

"I did see such a man yestiddy," said the woman of the household when Bill had roused her from pulling weeds in the kitchen garden. "I sold 'im a cut of beef and a few root vegetables." She wiped her hands on the apron covering the front of her drab dress. "It's handy to have a bit a dust in the house." She closed one eye against the sun and squinted down the lane. "I didn't see no girl." She pointed with her chin. "She may've waited down to the road."

Bill took his leave with thanks, his heart lighter for having the information that Thorne had gold. Then it skipped a beat. *Where is Marie?*

ℒ

Thorne had spent the day before alternating between railing at Marie and dismounting every other mile to open his pants and check the bandages he'd applied to his wounds. He swore mightily each time he reseated himself atop his saddle. She was glad she'd cut him there, although she would have preferred to have made a thrust into his black heart. At least he would not be coming at her anytime soon.

Today, their progress was as before. Thorne kept the horses at a slow, easy walk to prevent any jolting of his private parts. That suited Marie. The walking gait prevented any unnecessary jolt to her aching head.

Across a field of maturing corn, Marie glimpsed a couple of enclosures, rough corrals, with several horses divided among them. One small ring, where six or seven idlers lined the fence, detained a buckskin colt, kicking for all it was worth, desperately trying to rid itself of a puny human male who was sprawled halfway in the saddle and halfway out. His feet had no firm foundation, out of the stirrups as they were. The man gripped the colt's mane with one hand while the other grabbed naught but air. Yet he clearly endeavored to find a stable lodging upon the animal.

Bess continued her slow walk behind Thorne's mount. The distant colt spun ferociously, its hooves throwing dirt into the air, which then hung suspended in a half-obscuring cloud. Marie's detached observation turned to fascination with the age-old struggle between man and beast that was taking place in the corral.

I need to do that, Marie thought. *Get shed of this evil man trying to break my spirit.*

Just when it seemed the man would attain his desired seat, the horse leaped into the air and landed with its head down, all four legs closely bunched, then paused but a second, gathering strength for another burst of cyclonic activity. Jarred by the harshness of the landing, the wrangler lost his tenuous grip, left the animal entirely, and cartwheeled in the air a couple of times before he met the ground.

Marie drew in a sharp breath and peered through the murky cloud, watching for the figure to get up and try again, but he didn't rise. As the colt bucked and kicked, jumping closer to where the man had fallen, she bit her lip, her loyalty shifting in the moment to the human in mortal danger. The folks around the corral grew increasingly agitated, and she imagined there must be quite a noise being raised, although at this distance, she didn't hear much of it.

Then a figure wearing a dress and apron flew from the fence into the dust cloud, flapping her apron and swirling her skirt at the colt, driving it away from the horseman, who still lay prone in the ring.

She knelt alongside him, and for a moment, Marie thought the girl's skin was brown, but she discounted the idea, marking it up to imperfect vision through the opaque air swirling above the enclosure.

Although Bess's progress had slowed almost to a stop, Marie had just about passed the farm before the man got to his feet. As she looked back over her shoulder, Marie thought there was something familiar in the way he bent to pick up his hat, then used it to swat the dirt from his clothing. Her brothers used their hats in a similar fashion to beat dust off their shirts and trousers, but perhaps other men did the same thing.

Thorne growled something at her, and Marie reluctantly gave up watching the spectacle, turned toward him, and asked in a voice devoid of light, "What did you say?"

"I said we'll camp against that farthest hill." His face set in angry lines as he gestured ahead. "Pay attention. Those people can't help you."

"No one can help me," she agreed in an undertone. She gazed at her bound wrists as the raw umber cloud from the farm seemed to encompass her soul.

Chapter 21

After traveling for several hours the next day, Thorne and Marie came upon a curious sight. A red buggy with gold fringe fluttering from the top occupied the road before them.

The vicious set of Thorne's face disappeared in an instant. He laughed heartily. "You don't see that every day. The rig belongs to a former colleague of mine." He turned his horse and circled it back toward Marie. "You behave properly, and I'll make it worth your while."

She nodded, wondering what Mr. Thorne's 'gift' would be. Anything was better than how she'd lived the last few days.

"Your nod better be as good as your word. I'll hold you to it," he said, released the rope binding her wrists, and slung the lead rope around Bess's neck. Then he put spurs to his horse's flanks, and Marie urged Bess into a trot to keep up.

As soon as they came alongside the buggy, Marie kept her head down to hide the bruises on her face. The one she got falling in the wagon was bad enough, although the color had faded to yellow. The newer ones from Thorne's mistreatment hadn't had time to heal. The best thing was to hope her bonnet cast enough shadow to conceal the worst of the color.

Mr. Thorne took Marie by the wrist and held it firmly. "Rallison!" he saluted the buggy as they trotted alongside. His cheerful voice gave little indication that he was aware that the male occupant of the rig had a pistol trained upon him. "Put that away. It's me."

The man reined in the buggy horse with one hand while he gave the gun to his female companion. Then he said, "I thought you were up north, Thornecroft. What are you doing in my neck of the woods?"

"The north is too hot for my taste, so I determined to have a bit of an adventure. I've acquired a new girl, name of Marie." He motioned with his head toward her, then inclined it in the opposite direction. "Here's my old friend, Guy Rallison. We worked together on the Mississippi riverboats."

Marie didn't dare look up, afraid disgust would show in her face, so she merely nodded. Here was proof that everything the man had told her was a lie, even down to his own name. She had been so blinded by fancy manners and cunning words that she'd believed the whole mess of falsehoods.

"Who is that with you, Rallison?"

The man chuckled. "I married, or didn't you hear? This is the wife, Madame Janette."

Clearly irritated, the woman spoke her name again, but she said it differently, and with great emphasis, "Jhah-net!"

Marie looked up briefly, only enough to catch sight of a beautiful brown-haired woman dressed in a deep yellow gown with a be-feathered hat to match.

"I beg your pardon, my sweet. Madame Jhah-net it is." He laughed. "Saucy, is she not?"

"The French often are. Are you stopping nearby?" Thorne asked. "I need to acquire proper duds for the girl."

He's even changed the style of his words. There's no fanciness in his talk now.

"You're in luck, Thornecroft. The little lady decided she doesn't care for blue anymore. I have her cast-offs in my trunk." He gestured toward the rear of the buggy, where a leather-bound wooden truck was affixed with ropes to the chassis. "Ten dollars, if you want the outfit." He climbed out of the rig, knocking off his hat against the buggy's top. He retrieved it from the floor of the buggy and put it on again, but not before the sun brightened the man's fair hair. He was quite tall, and strode on long legs toward the rear. He bent over to open the luggage and rummage inside.

Thorne dismounted and hauled Marie off Bess, whispering threats in a mild voice as he did so. They joined Rallison, and Thorne pawed through the clothes as well.

Rallison pulled out a short, dark blue dress. "Here it is." He held it up in front of Marie, pursing his lips. "It will fit. Ten dollars."

Thorne took the garment and fingered the material. "That's steep for used clothing. I'll give you three."

"Eight."

"Five."

"Six, and that's as low as I'll go."

Thorne raised his chin. "I'll bet you paid no more than five for new."

"All right. I'll take five-fifty. That's a fair price, mind you. The corset, petticoat, stockings, and hat go with it."

"Humph," Thorne snorted. "You drive a hard bargain. Five-fifty it is."

Mr. Thorne gathered up the outfit and turned to Marie.

Who was he? Thorne, or was he really named Thornecroft? Marie shook her aching head.

"Yes, you will wear it," he said, probably taking her headshake for refusal. "I didn't buy it to decorate my horse." He turned to Rallison. "Where are you bound?"

Mr. Rallison stopped in the act of climbing into the rig. "I have a place down the country a piece, near the Apishapa."

"What's that? A mountain?"

Rallison chuckled. "It's a stream. If you're looking for employment, Madame could use your girl. I already have one gambler working a table. If you want to set up another, you'll have to share your winnings with the house, seventy-five, twenty-five."

Thorne snorted. "Not too bad. I like seventy-five percent."

Rallison shook his head. "Seventy-five is my take."

"That's robbery!"

"It's my house. Take it or leave it." He gathered up the lines and prepared to slap the horse into action.

"Wait! I'll take it. Where is your establishment?"

Rallison furnished directions while Marie stood in the road, shivering. She was about to become a fallen woman.

Bill rode into another farmstead just like the one before and the one before that. This one sat on the banks of a stream so sand-choked that he'd nearly been able to walk the horse over the top of the water when he crossed it.

He hailed the farmer in his field, left his horse ground tied, and waded his way down a crooked row through the crop.

"Good day," the man said, eying him suspiciously.

"Good day to you, sir," Bill said, taking off his hat and letting it dangle at his arm's length.

Evidently satisfied with what he saw, the farmer replied, "I'll have work for you next week."

Bill hurried into his question. "I'm not here about your harvest, sir. I'm inquiring if you've seen a man and a young woman pass by. The man was outfitted in fancy clothes, vest, big hat, watch chain across his middle. The girl wore a plain stuff dress with a black coat, bonnet, and rode a brown mare. I don't recall the color of the bonnet, but her hair is dark colored."

The man considered for a time, then shook his head. "I might have been up to the house," he said. "I had chores thereabouts part of the day."

Disappointment tasted like moldy bread in Bill's mouth. "I thank you, sir, for your time." He turned away and started to traverse the field toward where he'd left the horse.

"Run away with him, did she?" the farmer called.

His words felt like an ax striking Bill between the shoulder blades, and he stopped and began to turn.

"I hope you do find her soon. He'll likely put her to work in that new house."

"House?" Bill swallowed at the lump building inside his craw.

"Tall fellow and his pretty wife built them a saloon down the country a piece in one of them Mexican towns. Plaza this or that. The wife runs the entertainment."

Bill waited until his voice might be steady, then asked, "Do you recall what name they put to the place?"

"Nah. Something furren-sounding, but not the Spanish." He paused. "If she's your gal, get 'er back afore she's soiled. Then whip 'er good for sloping off thataway."

Gall rising in his throat, Bill fled the man's presence.

The sun had almost slid behind one of the Spanish Peaks to the west. Thorne was still nursing his wounds and had exhibited his ill temper the afternoon long by threatening her over his shoulder in all manner of disrespectful language.

That behavior hadn't raised Marie's spirits. Her head still felt fuzzy from Thorne's blow that had made the world go dark. *I'm sure to have a black eye.* She wondered if they would arrive in the town before darkness fell.

The bristly end of a rope fiber dug into a raw welt in her flesh, and she moved her wrists slightly, trying to ease it out of its position. How could Thorne think the injuries from this mistreatment would be attractive? The man's mind had to be off plumb. She mourned the confiscation of her knife. If she'd had it in hand, Thorne would surely rue the day they'd met.

Presently, a town of the Spanish pattern appeared as they came in sight of a river valley. Thorne grunted and spurred his horse to a trot. The increased pace didn't seem to please him, as he soon reduced it to the previous placid walk. Even though Marie had no desire to get to their destination, her misused body told her that an end to the riding within a reasonable time would be well received.

Lights twinkled on ahead of them as inhabitants of the houses lit lamps against the coming night. A great many lights came on, one by one, in a building on the outskirts of town. Marie thought the structure would have been more suitably placed in Pueblo Town than here. *Or maybe Hell.* It was constructed of lumber, not mud-smoothed adobe blocks. Marie wondered how far the milled boards had traveled to be used there. *The shipping must have cost a pretty penny. Someone expects to make money.*

She shuddered, realizing it was Rallison's place of business. Once she passed through the doors, she would have little chance of exiting them whole.

Thorne took a path right through the center of the town, skirting the plaza. They passed a store whose proprietor bent to gather up goods that had likely sat in the sun in front of the shop all day. He straightened and gazed at them as they went by. Marie imagined his eyes drilling holes of disapproval into her back as he followed their progress.

At length they stopped in front of Rallison's saloon. While Thorne dismounted and came around his horse to remove her fetters, Marie looked at the gaudy sign hanging above the door. "Lay May-ee-sohn des Low-ee-sirs," she mouthed slowly as she worked out the foreign phrase. It had no meaning to her. But frothing mugs and bottles and face cards and wicked women in various states of undress decorated the margins around the words. They seemed to dance and sway, or maybe it was herself moving erratically as Thorne tugged on the fraying rope. She bit her lip to block out the other pain. Why had the inhabitants hereabouts let this monstrosity be erected? Didn't they know how it sullied their town? *It will surely sully me.*

She didn't know whether to sob or scream. Then Thorne untied the last knot around her ankle, and she hastened to dismount before he took a notion to topple her out of the saddle.

She stood beside Bess, shivering, unwilling to put her foot onto the steps leading to perdition. Thorne solved her inability to move with a jolting pull on her wrist, and she stumbled up the steps and through the doors in his wake.

What a picture she must make! Dirty, drooping bonnet sitting awry atop filthy locks of hair. Bruises of all colors marking her face and one eye. A welt on her neck. A sodden coat hanging limply from her shoulders. Missing bodice buttons that permitted her dress to gape open at the top. Raw welts about her wrists and bare ankles. Skirt and underclothing that reeked of urine.

What a bundle of shame she had brought upon herself! And Ma. And Pa. He would never forgive her for blackening the Owen name with her foolishness. All hope drained from her bosom as Thorne called out, "Here she is. The new girl."

Eyes turned toward her. Eyes from all corners of the room. Eyes of farmers. Eyes of drovers. Eyes of teamsters. Eyes of men with brown faces. She shuddered anew, sick with fear.

The brown-haired woman she had encountered on the road descended the last few treads of a stairway that clung to the far wall of the room and came toward her.

"What you doing to her? Why you make this spectacle?" she asked Thorne, her voice evincing strong disapproval. She approached Marie and laid her hand on her arm. In a more soothing tone she said, "Come with me, *ma cherie*. Madame Janette will take the *bon* care of you." Turning on Thorne, she raised her voice again. "Where is the dress, my fine azure dress?"

He produced the dress and its accompanying articles of clothing in a hurry. The woman turned away from him, scorn covering her countenance as she took Marie by the hand.

Madame Janette led her upstairs to a quiet suite of rooms, then left her in private to bathe herself and put on the unfamiliar clothing.

The woman returned just as Marie had figured out how to hold the stockings up.

"There," she said. "It is well. You are veree pretty girl. Eh, the bruises, the cuts, they heal soon. Then I will teach you the best ways to earn the money. More money than you think you see all your life."

Marie made a croaking sound, and the woman patted one of her barely covered shoulders.

"Come, come. It is not so bad as you think, *ma cherie*. You will see."

Marie crossed her arms over her chest, fists clenched, and bent over to hide her weeping soul.

"*Non non non, ma cherie*. Stand erect." She pushed back Marie's shoulders. "You sell more drinks if you smile big. Come, dry the eyes and we go down the stairs. You begin with get the men to buy the drinks. We save the rest for later, *non*?"

⁊

Another little town, Bill thought as he rode in, half dozing from fatigue. *Another box canyon.* He looked at the one o'clock sun and mentally ticked off the days since Marie had left with Thorne. *This is the tenth day.* Ten days she'd been gone! Four days ago Thorne bought food. He'd been alone. Bill's stomach twisted. Was Marie dead?

How could she be dead? His mind couldn't make the leap to thinking that. But if she was alive, was she whole? The encounter with the farmer had shaken him, more than he'd imagined was possible. He had to take several long breaths and let the air leave him slowly, slowly, before he could pull out that awful thought and take a look at it. Had that cold, dangerous man used her? He bowed his head in grief at the notion. Grief for Marie, for her suffering at Thorne's hands. Not grief on his own account.

His thoughts whirled. The corn farmer had spurned her, reasoning that the act had been done. He didn't know that with any speck of surety. *I don't know it.* He sucked in another lungful of air and held it until he grew faint before blowing it out. *I don't care. I don't care.* The thought echoed with such strength that his body vibrated. *If she's alive, it don't matter. I'll get her free from that filthy man and offer my name. If she'll have it. If she'll have me.*

His mind cleared with his resolve and he dismounted in front of an adobe store. Merchandise was laid out on blankets placed on the hard-packed earth. He shook his canteen, then took a sip of the brackish water. *Ten days.*

He entered the store and spoke to the proprietor in his border Spanish, stumbling over the descriptive words. *How the Sam Hill do you say 'sunbonnet' in Mex?* He decided to try 'hat against the sun.' *Sombrero contra el sol.*

The man's eyes grew wary and he took a step backward.

Bill put on an even more concerned expression and leaned his head forward slightly in encouragement.

The storekeeper finally decided to share his knowledge. "Ella pasó por aquí ayer con ese hombre." He motioned in the direction they had gone.

"They went by yesterday?" Bill confirmed in the same tongue.

"Sí, señor. Ayer por la tarde."

Bill cast his eyes upward and whispered, "Dear God, thank you. She's alive." At least she was yesterday afternoon.

The man crossed himself, then shook his head a bit. "Ella parece un poco maltratada." His voice held a sad note.

"Mistreated," Bill murmured, anger rising from his belly. He'd like to get his hands around Thorne's throat and mistreat him plenty. Batting down the emotion, he said, "Mil gracias, señor," and left the store, his heart seeming to throb in his throat.

She's alive! Beaten down, but living still.

He threw himself into the saddle and looked down the path in the direction the man had indicated. A large building stood a ways apart from the town, aloof in its separateness. An American-style building, with a sign board beckoning him. That had to be the house with the foreign name, the new house the farmer had told him about. The house of entertainment.

Bill leaned forward and slapped the horse with his heels. *That's where Thorne took Marie.*

The horse responded to Bill's urging and lunged down the street. Moments later, he pulled it to a stop in front of the garish edifice. Yep. Those were foreign words splayed across the sign. Maybe French. He took a deep breath to steady himself. *If she's here, how do I get her out?*

A boy ran up and asked in passable English, "You want me to take care of your horse, sir?"

Bill pulled his mind around to the situation in front of him and asked the price, which the boy named. He dug in his pocket and paid the lad, then removed his saddlebags. But as the youngster led the horse off, he called out, "Where you taking it?"

"To the stable in back."

Bill nodded. Good the horse was under care. He might be here for a spell, until he could figure out the dilemma that pounded through his brain. *If she's here, how do I get her out?*

He'd better make a start by entering the place, he decided, and took the steps to the porch. A deep breath before the flap doors, a shove against them, and he was inside. A quick look around and disappointment soured his stomach. *She ain't here.*

Steady, he thought. *Considered precisely, she ain't in this room.* He glanced upward, and hoped she wasn't above stairs. He walked on wooden legs to the bar and ordered a bottle and a glass to be brought to a table. *A table close to the door*, he told himself, then remembered his horse was not just beyond the veranda. He'd have to figure a plan for escape, as soon as he'd confirmed that she was in the place.

He choose an empty table, as near to the door as he could find, even if the horse was absent, dumped his gear on the floor and took a seat, pulling his hat low to mask his eyes. He scanned the interior, slower this time, taking in the details of the inhabitants. Three men standing easy at the bar. One barkeep. Two girls working the men. Marie was not among them. Four other men, two to a table, on his left. A gambler engrossed in dealing faro, but he wasn't Thorne. A girl hovering over one of the players. Not Marie. Three more men, teamsters maybe, drinking at a table on his right. A table with a poker game in progress, but the man running it had his back to Bill. He couldn't tell if that was Thorne or not. The coat was different. No girls there. Light footsteps to his left, approaching. He stiffened, then swung his head to assess the danger, and looked up into the saloon girl's eyes.

Chapter 22

Marie stretched her arms out in front of her as far as they would reach, reluctant to get close enough to place the bottle and glass on the table. The trail-worn cowboy seated there might take it into his head to grab at her. Then he looked up and she saw his face. She inhaled sharply. *Bill! He came for me!* Panic seized her as she realized the danger this place held for him, but she got a tight hold on her sense, lowered her eyes and whispered, "Your bottle, sir."

Her heart felt as though it had frozen in her bosom. *He's seen me, looking like this. Now he'll do something foolish and get killed.* She turned to skedaddle, but he grasped her hand. She turned back, shaking her head with tiny movements. "You want something else, mister?" *Surely he can tell I don't want to acknowledge him.* He relaxed his grip. *He's puzzled. Please, God, he's got to play along.*

"Something else for you, mister? I have to get back to my work."

He stared at her with such intensity that she thought her face would melt. *Please, please, Mr. Henry. Follow my lead.* "Enjoy your bottle," she said, and shook her hand free. She took two steps away and heard him clear his throat. *Don't call my name!*

"Miss," he said, instead.

She closed her eyes on a sigh, opened them, and turned back to his table. "Yes, sir?"

He nodded towards Thorne's back. "Does your dealer have an open seat at his table?"

She hesitated. Was he seeking information about Thorne? Of course he was. She took another moment to clear her own throat. "I believe Mr. Thorne, er, croft, Thornecroft will let you buy into the game." *No. Don't get close to him.*

"Thank you, miss."

She scurried back behind the bar and into the small room behind it, picked up her dishrag and resumed washing glasses, choking as black fear closed her throat. *Bill came to get me, but Thorne will kill him.*

Ⅎ

Bill watched her go, so relieved to see her, missing her already. He swore under his breath, cursing Thorne for putting her into such a state of injury and indignity. *That dress!* He wished he dared throw a tablecloth about her and quit the country. *Those bruises! He's been beating on her.*

He uncorked the bottle and poured a drink with a shaking hand. He took a sip. Frowned. Rotgut whiskey. Didn't matter. The whiskey was for show. *I dasn't get drunk.* He took the time between several slight sips to try to calm himself, but his anxiety persisted. *How do I get her out of here?*

He pushed back his chair as though he would rise, paused as though changing his mind, then drew it forward again, but turned a bit so he could watch the poker table.

Thorne don't know me. Mayhap getting in the game is a good choice. I can read him better up close. He scoffed at the thought. Thorne was a gambler. An unreadable face would be part of his stock in trade. *It's worth a try anyhow.*

Someone at the table raised his voice. The young man on the left. Farmer's clothing. Thorne replied, his voice cold. The young man rose to his feet and protested. Thorne brought a revolver out of his lap and shot him.

Bill inhaled sharply as the pistol boomed. The farm boy went over backwards and down onto the floor. Thorne didn't seem concerned. He'd pushed back his chair a bit, crossed his legs, pulled out a cigar and now leaned over a match, sucking air to light the cigar. The round was over.

Bill let out his breath and downed the whiskey. Maybe it wouldn't hurt to be a bit numb.

He let several minutes go by as the saloon sounds returned to normal. A new hand began. No one came to remove the boy's body. It lay crumpled, an empty shell made so by a callous hand, a twisted mind. Not right in the head, Rulon had said.

Thorne started gathering the cards, preparing to deal.

Well, Bill thought, *if there wasn't a seat at the table before, there surely is one now. I'd best get in the game.*

He steeled himself, got up and snatched the bags from the floor and slung them over his shoulder. He picked up the bottle and the glass, and made himself walk over to the table, keeping where Thorne could see him.

"What's your buy in?" he asked as he set the bottle and glass on the table.

Thorne looked up and squinted through his cigar smoke. "A hundred."

Bill swallowed and dug in his pocket for enough Federal coins to buy the chips. He unslung the bags and put them out of the way of the pool of blood. Then he sat, and pulled up the chair so lately pushed backwards by a callow youth with not enough experience to survive in Thorne's game. Did *he* have any better sense, willingly stepping to the brink of the man's dark pit?

Thorne dealt the cards, and Bill folded his first hand. Out of the action, he had a mite of time to study Thorne's bland face. The man was good at masking his thoughts, but Bill noticed that he puffed on his cigar twice after he drew new cards. Sign of a good or bad hand?

Thorne lost the hand. Two puffs. Poor cards.

Bill checked on the next hand, watching his opponent, who drew two cards after the betting round and shifted in his seat. Was that a telling action?

Thorne lost on a showdown. The cards hadn't been bad, but the man seated opposite Bill had a stronger hand and took the chips.

Third hand. Thorne leaned backwards ever so slightly when he looked at his dealt hand. Didn't draw cards. The hand must be good. Bill noted the movement in the part of his mind he'd set aside for listing any of the gambler's actions that might reveal what his face concealed. Thorne won.

Bill looked up when the barkeep came around and lit a lantern overhead with a long punk stick. The windows looked out onto a black night. How long had he been playing? Hours. He thought he knew one or two of Thorne's "tells" now. Maybe three. Did the man even know he gave signs? Bill wondered what his own were.

The hand ended, and Bill won the pot. He stacked his chips, then rose and asked, "Privy out back?" At Thorne's confirming nod, he said, "I'll be back," and picked up his saddlebags. No sense leaving valuables about.

He borrowed a lantern from the barkeep and asked the way to the rear door. He might as well learn the layout of the place.

He stood in the outhouse, wondering once more how he could get Marie out of the place. Her work seemed to be confined to fetching drinks and whatever she did in the room behind the bar, but that could change at any time. Any of the men in the saloon might insist on a trip up the stairs. He knew he couldn't bear to see that happen. *How do I get her out?*

He couldn't stay much longer in the privy while he pondered on the matter. What advantage did he have? He buttoned up while he thought about the situation.

The man seated across from him had been winning steadily. Bill had amassed a pile of chips, and Thorne's piles were decreasing. Could he force bets higher and clean out the gambler? He'd heard of high stakes games where men risked personal property against a big win. He'd done a fair amount of gambling with a saddle or a pistol as stakes. Could he— He swallowed hard. Could he drive Thorne into wagering Marie?

The man seemed reckless enough. Marie might have been troublesome to him. He didn't know that. Did he dare take a risk on her spunky nature? Did he have enough luck and skill to pull off such a scheme?

He'd need an extra bit of luck. Could he get Marie to kiss the cards? He scoffed at that notion. He needed something real. A remembrance flashed through his mind. Chico had said something about Marie kissing his cards the night he'd tried out the card trick Bertie had used on him. The one and only time he'd tried it. It had worked, hadn't it? Could he give himself four of a kind?

He scrambled to fish out his old worn card deck from one of the bags. His fingers touched the ranch deed. He hauled it out, too, and stuffed it into his coat pocket. Riffling the deck, he extracted all of the three cards and put them in his pocket, but he'd have to get them out of his pocket and into his lap as he sat down. Yes, he could do that. He put the rest of the deck back in the bag and abandoned the privy.

𝔰𝔬

Bill placed his hand of cards carefully on the table, face up, one by one, and grinned at Thorne in his best imitation of bleary-eyed drunkenness. Thorne huffed a stream of smoke around his new cigar and pushed the chips over to him.

So far, he hadn't used the trick, but his cards sat in his lap, awaiting need. Luck had been with him. The pattern on their back sides was the same as the cards used in Thorne's game. It was likely the only brand available hereabouts. His cards were a bit more worn, but he had to take the chance no one would notice if he was forced to use them.

The man opposite Bill had taken his winnings and departed two hands ago. The man on his left didn't have the sense to stop losing and go home. The seat between those two had been filled twice, but now sat empty. Thorne's chips had diminished significantly in the last hour. This was likely the time to start raising the bets.

Bill raised the bottle to his lips and took a swig. Then he managed to drop it to the floor, where it rolled until he heard it stop. Mayhap it fetched up against that poor boy's body.

"Barkeep, bring me a bottle," he roared, continuing the role of tipsy cowman.

The man sent Marie, and as she placed the bottle before him he grabbed her wrist to pull her down toward him. He planted a sloppy kiss as near as he could get to her lips, then whispered "Get your parcel," as he pretended to nibble on her ear.

Her eyes became aware, and she drew aside and slapped him. Then she dashed up the stairs. He watched her go through slitted eyes, enjoying the performance, hoping she had a clue what he was up to, hoping Thorne had none.

He raised a reckless amount on the next hand, driving the loser to quit the game. Thorne's eyes seemed like balls of ice as he gave Bill the chips. Those left in front of Thorne were a mere handful.

Behind Thorne, Marie came back down to the saloon. Bill took a gamble and slurred, "Whassa matter, dealer? Too rich for your blood?" He leaned forward and cupped his arms around his chips. "I've got all this to put in the next pot, an' the ranch, too." He blinked and looked around the room, then tried to focus on

Thorne. "What you got to put up?" He leaned back. "How about a girl?" He leered lopsidedly.

"You're drunk," Thorne sneered.

"Yeah," Bill drawled, making his voice raspy and slow, "but I got all the chips." He clipped the last word and grinned again. "One more hand, dealer. One more." He pulled out the deed and put it on top of his stack.

A well-dressed tall man, who Bill took to be the proprietor, and a nice-looking, showy woman had come over to stand behind Thorne. She clung to the man's arm, and deigned to smile at Bill.

"This should be amusing," the owner said to the gambler. "Let him play one more hand." He arched an eyebrow. "What *will* you wager, Thornecroft?"

The gambler turned his head, searching, and when his eyes stopped on Marie, he beckoned to her. "Get over here! You've given me a lot of sass. It would serve you right if he won." He reseated himself facing Bill as Marie came to stand beside his chair. "Consider her among my assets."

Bill put a one dollar chip in the center of the table. Thorne put in his ante. He had a few chips left. Then he dealt.

Bill picked up his cards, and without looking at them, said to Marie, "Girl, come kiss 'em. I need a li'l more luck." Again, he clipped the last word.

Thorne had picked up his cards, looked at them, and leaned back in his chair.

Marie stared at Bill, her eyes fearful.

"Come on. I won't bite. Just put a li'l kiss on 'em." He held out the hand, grinning, despite his mouth having gone dry at seeing the gambler's tell.

She approached and bent to kiss the cards, her eyes holding his.

Even in that ridiculous get-up, she looked beautiful to him. He touched the kissed cards to his lips and finally looked at them.

He held a full house, eights on deuces. A strong hand. Thorne's tell said he also had good cards. Bill kept breathing as he had before, fighting to stay steady. He glanced down. His hands were shaking too much to substitute cards for any better hand. These would have to do.

"I bet two dollars," he said, putting the chips in the pot. "Two dollars," he repeated, remembering almost too late to slur his words.

"Call," responded Thorne, adding his two chips. "How many cards?"

Bill thought about his cards, not knowing if Thorne would draw new ones. How good was Thorne's hand?

Lord, he thought, *You know I ain't much of a praying man, but my mam taught me You're up there. You surely love Miss Marie. Lord God, for her sake, let me get her out of this mess.*

He reached for his glass and pretended to drink, playing for time to make his decision. He put the glass down with careful precision, although it quivered in a circle before it hit the table top. "None," he said, and inhaled gustily. "Not a single one." He weaved a little in his chair, sweat beginning to drip off the tip of his nose.

Thorne also declined to draw new cards.

Bill heard Marie's breath hiss out. She hadn't looked at his hand, but she knew what Thorne was holding, and she was scared. *I am too.*

Bill laid the cards on the table, backs up, and moved all his chips to the pot, stack by careful stack. Then he put the ranch deed on the top, allowing it to teeter and fall between two of the stacks.

"I bet a hunnert an' fifty-six dollars an' the ranch," he said, and weaved again.

Thorne looked at the proprietor.

He came forward and took the deed, unfolded the paper. "Texas, huh?" He looked a question at Thorne.

Thorne gave his assent to the property, then asked in a raspy voice, "Does the girl and six dollars equal his bet?"

The owner considered, quirking his eyebrow. Then he said, "A ranch is work. The girl is pleasure. That's equal."

Thorne said, "Call," and moved his chips to the pot. He narrowed his eyes and barked at Bill, "Do you want her atop the table?"

"No," Bill said, closing his eyes, and opening them with great effort. "S-she can sit in a chair." He pointed to one on his left between the other two vacant seats.

The tall man nodded, and Marie hurried around the table to sit.

"Show your hand, Thornecroft," said the proprietor.

The gambler laid down his cards. Three sevens. Two tens. A full house.

Bill stared at them. He wobbled as though he would fall face down onto the pot, then straightened and turned over his eights and twos.

He'd won.

Chapter 23

When Thorne moved as though he would pull his gun, Bill was ready for him, his revolver already out of his pocket, and his left fist connecting with the man's chin. He went down without a sound, and Bill yelled to Marie, "Get the deed." He kept his pistol trained on the saloon's owner, who bore a curious expression, almost of satisfaction.

The woman said to Bill, "You have the luck," and tugged the man back away from Thorne.

"Hands high," Bill told the barkeeper, his eyes darting briefly to Marie to see what was holding her up. She held a sack in one hand and scooped chips into it with the other. "Worthless," he growled. "Leave 'em. Get my bags. Go out the back door. Now!" he barked.

She dropped the sack like it burned her fingers, hauled up his saddlebags and fled. Bill followed her, facing the saloon.

When he'd backed out the door and closed it, he jammed the bench beside the door under the latch. "That won't hold them long," he grunted, turning and relieving Marie of his saddlebags. She ran to a place along the back wall where she picked up a bundle. "Good girl," he said, and grabbed her free hand to run with her to the stable.

"Are you truly drunk?" she whispered as he slapped the saddle on Bess.

"Not so much," he replied, drawing the cinch tight and boosting Marie aboard.

He tacked up his own horse in a great hurry, and got into the saddle, then put his heels hard into the animal's sides.

They left at a run, the echo of the drum of their horses' hooves beating back at them as they fled past the town's adobe walls.

Bill pulled up a couple of miles outside the town to let the winded horses breathe. He swung down and went to assist Marie.

"He didn't follow us," Marie observed in a shaky voice as she dismounted. She look back the way they'd come. "It appears no one did."

"I put him out pretty solid," Bill said, shaking his hand. "Might have broke something." He flexed it with care, then asked, "How well liked was the man?"

She began to walk the mare. "Not at all. I reckon Miz Janette hated his lights and liver. For all Thorne's big talk of them being friends, I suspect Mr. Guy wasn't far behind that." She made a noise that appeared to be a muffled sob. "He'll come after us when he has revived."

"He'll come alone." He yearned to gather Marie up in his arms and make that haunted look in her eyes disappear. He didn't dare. Not yet. Not while they were still here on the road. "I passed a place up yonder. We can hide there for a spell. Leastwise until morning."

₮

The night was black as soot. Black as ink. Black as shoe blacking. A chill breeze scurried along the road from the direction of the town. Marie sat on Bess's back, wondering if it would rain again, as Bill led their horses forward, trying to locate the hiding place. She began to shiver violently.

After a long while, she heard a sustained sigh from Bill, then felt the direction of the wind change. They must be off the road. She tried to keep her teeth from chattering. Presently, she noticed a deeper blackness to the right, and he stopped the horses, speaking to them in a low tone. Then she heard his boots crunching on the earth, no, a gravelly surface, as he came to her side.

"Slip your feet free," he said. When she had removed her shoes from the stirrups, strong, careful hands grasped her on each side of her waist, lifted her from the saddle and placed her on the ground.

He must have felt her quaking. "We've got to risk a fire, get you warm," he said, and began to kick the ground.

"What are you doing?" She sat down and tried to make herself stop shaking.

"Clearing a spot."

She heard crackling. He grunted, then said, "Good. Here's a tree. Or a bush, perhaps." He must have kicked at it, from the increased sound of crackling branches. "This should serve."

He built a small fire close to her, using the old-fashioned method of flint and knife blade. By the flickering light, Marie watch him put a handful of coffee makings into his coffeepot, then empty his canteen into it and put it to heat.

"It's foolish—" He stumbled over the word and began again. "It's not canny to put the smell in the air, but I must be sober."

She nodded, pondering the word foolish.

"We'll drink it down before he comes."

She nodded again, feeling the weight of every action she'd taken lately. The heaping pile of her follies. She wanted to cry. She didn't dare make such noise, but put her face in her hands, just in case.

She heard him taking the tack off the horses outside the circle of firelight, the crunch of gravel when he brought his saddle to the fireside, and a small grunt when he sat down upon it. After a while, she heard him stir.

"I reckon I love you," Bill said.

His voice was low, and she thought she'd misheard him. She brought her hands down into her lap and looked towards him.

He began to talk again, fast, like his mouth was overflowing with words and he had to spill out the excess.

"I reckon my affection for you began to growing that first day we met, with you all shocked and discombobulated, with leaves and dirt and such on your dress. Despite your disarray, I knew, I knew for sure, you were the most beautiful girl in the world."

She cringed. "Don't mock me!"

"I'd never do that."

Marie bent her shoulders forward and hugged herself. "I don't want your pity." Even in her distress, she couldn't take her eyes from his face.

He sat for a long time, looking down at the hatful of fire. Finally he lifted his head and gazed at her. He swallowed, then spoke, his voice steady, but holding a marked gentleness. "I bear you no pity. I have naught to give you but the devotion of a revived man." He paused for a moment, seeming to need courage to continue. "When your pa told me he was marrying you off to the farmer, that bruised and battered my soul. When you left with Thorne, my heart shattered to pieces. I thought never to see you again."

She turned her head aside, unwilling to see the hurt in his eyes. "Going off with that wicked man was a terrible folly," she said, her voice bitter. "He bore me no love, as he had led me to believe."

"He's nothing but a confidence man, a very practiced, cruel confidence man."

Marie wanted so badly to cry, to give vent to her rage and her sorrow and her relief, but she simply couldn't show weakness in front of Bill. With all good intentions, he might smother her feelings, take charge, and reduce her to the state of vulnerability that she had lived in under Thorne's influence. She wanted never be that frail again.

He spoke again, his voice soft this time, and she had to lean forward to hear him.

"Having you here, my heart is whole again." He stopped talking.

She wished to goodness he was done talking about his heart when hers felt like a lead brick in her bosom.

When he commenced to speak again, his voice had changed. "The way I see it, we have two choices," he said in a more practical tone. "We could go to Texas. Life is mighty hard there with the carpetbaggers in control, but you would be spared any words of shame coming from your folks." He stopped briefly. His next words came out forcefully. "We'd have to be wed. I won't take you that far without a ring on your finger."

She took a sharp breath and held it for two seconds. "What's your second notion?" She tried to keep her voice neutral, but failed. Bitterness crept into it again. A marriage based on Bill's pity would be worse than one built on Tom's lust.

"We could go back to your folks." He fell silent for a moment, and evidently, from the creaking sound the leather of his saddle made, he shifted around on his seat.

She glanced his way and noticed he held a much-wrinkled piece of paper that he was smoothing out with great care. Pink paper. Stationery. He had her letter.

He looked up, his eyes holding hers. "You told them the next time they saw you, you'd be a married woman. Thorne didn't live up to his word. I fancy replacing him. In your life." He swallowed hard. "In your heart."

She shook her head, breaking eye contact, and cut him off before he could say binding words. "There's another path." Her voice sounded to her ears hollow and beaten, as she motioned to her extravagant clothing. "I could become the wanton woman Thorne had in mind for me. I'm dressed for that life."

Her words brought Bill up from his seat and across the fire. "No! You can't consider that." He'd pulled her to her feet, and he gripped her arms, the pressure of his hands telling of his fury at the thought. "He tried to do you damage. Did he—"

"No. He never had his way with me. He tried, but I had a knife. He had to back down after I used it."

Bill relaxed his grip and sighed, a heavy exhalation. "It wouldn't matter to me if he had. It wouldn't matter one tad bit. Marry me, girl. I can't bear it one minute more." His hands tightened a fraction and his voice throbbed, as though he were losing control of it.

Marie meant to say, "I can't," but an explosion ripped the air, and turning loose of her arms, Bill fell over backward, onto the fire.

Struggling to move, he finally rolled off it, but the back of his coat glowed with tiny live embers. Another shot came from the darkness, and Marie grabbed the coffeepot and extinguished what was left of the fire. She fell upon Bill, beating the embers off with her bare hands, then dragged him away from the spot, inch by inch.

"I know I hit him," came a voice, the hated, disgusting voice of C. G. Thorne. "You get over here. I don't take kindly to uppity women."

Marie froze. Then she took a breath and held it. If she maintained silence, he couldn't know where she was. The darkness was too complete . . . except for one lone ember that she surreptitiously crushed with her foot.

Thorne swore. "Did you think you could get away from me?" He dismounted, his saddle leather creaking in the still air. "That cowboy can't shield you. He's worthless to you."

As Thorne kept up a string of demeaning invective, Marie's hands searched Bill's body for his gun. She found it at last in his coat pocket, and eased it out of confinement, fighting down panic and her rising conviction that Bill was dead or mortally wounded. *Not my Bill!*

From the sound of his voice, Thorne moved slowly, probably taking caution for his footing on the uneven ground. Marie got herself between Bill and Thorne, and hunched as low to the ground as she could.

"I don't know why I bother," Thorne spat. "You're a worthless piece of dog meat, but you're wearing my investment."

From Pa's gold.

"I won't give that up. I'll take it from your dead body, once I'm through with you," he said, a step closer this time.

The menace in his voice nearly sent Marie into flight, but she resisted her impulse. *I can't leave Bill to his wrath.*

Thorne swore again, another step closer to where the fire had burned.

Bill moaned, and Marie's heart leapt in her bosom. *He's alive!* She put a hand behind her and found his face, his mouth, and patted his lips to urge him to silence.

"Ah, you're over there, cowboy," Thorne chortled. "This time I'll finish you."

Marie heard the click of the pistol being cocked as Thorne made ready for his killing shot. The sound was very close by. Another step. Gravel crunched. Another. He kicked a rock aside and it rolled a ways off. Another. He was standing not five feet off.

Marie thrust herself to her feet before he could advance any closer. "You won't do any of those things," she said softly, cocking her own pistol as she raised it, holding its weight in two hands before her as she stepped silently to her right.

Thorne's shot whizzed by her ear as he swore at her again. She angled the gun toward where the man must be and pulled the trigger, then kept cocking and pulling and cocking and pulling until all the bullets had been expended and only a dry click met her ears.

Thorne was down, lying with his weapon resting on her shoes, the heat of the barrel seeping through the thin leather. She tugged it out of his hand and stepped backward, almost stumbling when she fetched up against Bill.

He caught her in his arms. He was alive, and standing, and holding her . . . and she was melting.

"Give me his gun," he said, letting her go. "I have to check—"

"He must be dead." *You're alive!* Waves of emotion swept through her as she handed over the pistol. Relief. Revulsion. Disappointment at not being enwrapped in Bill's arms. Love. *Love?*

As Bill bent to his task, the moon peeked through the clouds, as though it came out especially to aid him. He lifted one lapel of Thorne's coat aside and felt for a heartbeat, then shook his head. Thorne was gone. But there was something about the way his coat had landed.

Marie flew at the man and dug in his coat pockets, inside and out. She came up with a small leather pouch and held it for Bill to see.

He snorted. "I didn't clean him out after all."

The high emotion that had sustained her through the past few minutes suddenly drained from her body, and Marie turned and retched on the ground. Bill was with her in an instant, holding her hair aside as vomit flooded through her mouth.

When she had finished, he gently wiped her lips with his handkerchief.

She spit out one last clot of bitterness, then whispered in a shaky voice, "I killed him." A cramp gripped her abdomen, but it wasn't the prelude to another bout of nausea. It was fear for her soul, cold and stark and threatening.

"Yes. You saved me."

She could see Bill's smile. The clouds seemed to be dissipating, and the moon cast a warm light over the earth. "I saved you?"

"He meant to kill us both. You prevented that happening."

The smile was gone, replaced by a soberness that calmed Marie a bit. "I did? I'm not bound for Hell?"

"No, no. Never." He shook his head and held her face in his hands. His left palm was sticky.

She lifted it off her face and examined it through eyes full of moisture. "That's blood." She saw a wet patch on the sleeve of his coat.

"Ball went through my arm. Don't hurt much." He raised his hand to his head. "This one put me out for a spell." He ran a finger through a groove in his scalp. "I match your pa."

"Hmm," came softly from her throat. *Indeed.* She blinked rapidly, surprised at the strong emotion welling in her heart, tightening her throat. Then she forced practicality to take control and said, "Shuck your coat. I'll bind up your wounds."

As he did so, she turned aside and lifted the hem of the horrid dress. She ripped a couple of strips off the fancy petticoat, and set to work dressing Bill's arm and head.

When she had finished, he motioned in the direction of Thorne's still form lying on the ground. "I'll bury him come sunup. Don't want critters to get a bad taste in their craws."

Marie nodded, now unable to speak.

"Whither are we bound?" he asked as he got to his feet. "Texas, or your place?" He didn't touch her, but stood apart, evidently waiting for her decision.

The tightness in her chest loosened a fraction so she could speak. "I want to go home."

"Where is home?" Bill's voice came out hushed, as though he were holding his breath and talking at the same time.

"Back."

He started to speak, but instead, hung his head and looked at the ground. She watched him struggle, something deep down causing him hesitation.

Presently, he raised his head and stared into her eyes. "Are you going to marry me?"

Marie stood still, rooted, it seemed, to the earth beneath her feet. All the dreams she'd had over the past weeks flashed through her mind, all the moments when she'd thought of no one but Bill Henry. At once, she realized there was no one else she wanted for her husband, no one who could suit her better than the sturdy cowman who stood before her, his blue eyes cautious, hooded, going dark. She wished for nothing more than to brighten those eyes, bring gladness and light to them, and to feel his strong arms around her, sheltering her from harm, his touch turning her to liquid butter.

"Yes," she whispered. Then she said it louder. "Yes. Yes, I will." She heard her voice tremble. "I will be your wife."

Bill's eyes glowed, happiness shining through them, revealing the joy in his heart. His arms came around her. "We'll make a pretty pair before the priest," he murmured. "Me wrapped in bandages, and you in—" He broke off. "No. We'll get you clothes suitable for a lady before we seek him out."

She shook her head. "The ordinary clothes in my bundle will suit me fine," she said. "Once they're washed." She quivered in his arms. She knew that he loved her at least a little, knew that she cherished him. "You're a good man, never mind your head is bandaged." She touched his cheek and closed her eyes for a moment. When she opened them, she said in a rush, "Can you forgive my horrible folly?" She held her breath, anxious for his reply.

"With all my soul," Bill said. His blue eyes seemed to burn with light.

Marie swallowed hard, then she kissed him, not with maidenly reserve, but with a lover's passion and desire and fervor. It must have caught him off guard, all wooden in her arms for a moment, but he warmed to the notion of taking part in no time at all.

When they broke apart for air, she gasped, "Where does that priest dwell?" After she'd filled her lungs, she added, "I'll ride all night to get there. I do not fancy being a spinster one moment longer."

: : : : :

Ride to Raton

Chapter 1

As soon as James Owen heard the Spanish priest's final amen, he stepped back from the makeshift altar in the Colorado meadow and made his legs carry him to the edge of the forest. Behind him he knew Ma, Pa, and the rest of the family and guests were crowding around to congratulate the bride and groom.

The bride was Ellen Bates—who'd been *his* fiancée.

And the groom was his brother, Carl.

His own brother . . .

James gagged.

When his stomach had emptied itself over the pine needles and columbines, he straightened up, chest heaving, and gripped a sapling until the quivering left his legs. He yanked his high, stiff collar loose and threw it on the ground, wiped his mouth with the back of his shirt sleeve, then threw a quick glance behind him.

Carl now sat down on the chair his brothers had used to bring him to the meadow. The bridegroom's gunshot wound was bleeding; a crimson stain spread across the hip of his trousers. Ellen fussed around, pointing at his brothers, Rulon and Clay. She shooed off the other cowboys, who seemed eager to put her on their shoulders for a shiveree.

Ma was looking toward James, her forehead furrowed with worry. She took two steps toward him, then stopped. He cleared his throat and spat, straightened his shoulders—which ached from the strain of keeping himself tightly under control—and took the path that led through the forest to the ranch headquarters.

He heard Ma call out, "James!" then "Rod, go see—"

"Leave Pa out of it," James grunted so low that she couldn't possibly hear him, and kept moving. He stamped through the trees, pounding his fist into his open hand and wishing it was Carl's face. He approached a holding pen, where a wild horse wheeled and snorted, upset by the noise James made.

James swore at his brother for getting injured. *When he gets well—* He pressed his lips tightly together, as though to restrain his vengeful thoughts.

The black horse watched every move James made, its wary eyes following him as he approached. It snorted, sniffed the air, then whirled around to track his progress along the fence line. James looked at the beast that Carl had caught as the Owen men returned from Texas with a herd of cattle and a crew of cowboys. When a gang of ruffians had kidnapped two young ladies, the Owen crew had confronted them in a gun battle. Carl had been sorely wounded.

A harsh sound escaped James's throat. It wasn't quite a laugh. *He took Miss Ellen. I'll take the mustang.*

James stalked into the shed, snatched a rope from where it hung on a peg pounded into the wall, and stalked out again. Entering the enclosure, he leaned against the gate and built a loop in his rope. *Let's see if the Texan's roping trick works.* He looked up.

The black snorted and moved off as far as it could get in the pen. James stepped toward the horse, holding the rope behind him. He crowded the animal to one side of the corral, then flipped the loop up from the ground and around the horse's neck.

Gripping the rope with one hand, he ran to the horse, grabbed a handful of mane, and hauled himself up. The horse tried to shake him off, but he got his right leg over its back just as the animal reared on its hind legs, bellowing. James stayed on, clamping his knees against the rough hair and bending low over the neck.

You're not so easily rid of me.

The black met the ground stiff legged, screaming, and James felt his stomach crowding his throat. He swallowed hard, digging his boots into the barrel of the animal as it whipped up its heels, tucking its head toward the earth. Then the two of them were airborne, and James braced for the shock of landing against the black's spine. His teeth jarred together, then again and again and again as, pitching, bucking, whirling, the beast tried to get James's weight off its back.

"Blasted devil horse," he muttered as he came down hard, a little off center, and grabbed for a new fistful of the stiff black mane hairs. But the horse was in the air again—head and heels together, back arched—and James lost his grasp on the mane and the rope. Flying off, he landed on his left shoulder in the center of the ring.

"You fool, you're like to be killed!"

James shook his head to clear away his father's strident voice, looked for the horse, then rolled clear when it dove at him with stiff front legs. Rising from the dust, he ran after the animal, grabbing for the trailing rope with his left hand as he kneaded his sore shoulder with his right.

"Don't you know when you've had enough?" yelled his father as he opened the gate. "Get out of there, you—"

James had the rope in his hands and wrapped it around his left arm. Then he dug in his heels to bring the horse under control.

"You're crazy," Roderick Owen shouted, shutting the gate and lending his weight to the end of the lariat whipping free behind his son.

"Get off my rope!"

"You're double dumb crazy." Rod held on, hauling backward.

"Get off! You're cutting my arm!"

Rod let go of the rope, and James was jerked forward, scrambling to keep his feet under him. Suddenly the animal quit fighting, its head drooping. It stood against the fence, quivering, its slick black sides heaving as it filled its lungs.

James flipped the noose off the animal's neck and dropped it in the dust, to the accompaniment of catcalls from a line of spectators along the fence. Doubled over, hands on his knees, his gasping matched the horse's. When he finally got his breath, he spat the grit from his mouth, surveyed the men peering through the fence, and waved his arms at them.

"This ain't a free show," he yelled. "All y'all get away from here!"

The crowd broke up, each man muttering his displeasure as he drifted back toward the meadow. James watched them go as he kneaded his shoulder again. He turned on his father.

"Why'd you butt in on my business?"

"You were next to getting killed, trying to ride that outlaw horse."

"I'm not talking about the horse. I'm talking about Miss Ellen. And Miss Jessica! You forced me to leave her behind in the Shenandoah and hatched a scheme to marry Miss Ellen to me. You got her pa to agree for a few sacks of provisions and a wagon!" James spat on the ground.

"It wasn't quite like that."

James ignored his father's response as his words rushed on. "You dragged me across the country, preaching duty every day. I obeyed you. I put off Miss Jessica to court Miss Ellen. I did my duty, Pa, and I even grew fond of her. I looked forward to settling down, having a little house, raising up young—"

"Stop it!" Rod's eyes narrowed. He squinted at his son's left sleeve, watching a line of blood seep through the fabric. "You're hurt, boy."

James glanced at the sleeve, then shook his arm, wincing as pain lanced through the shoulder. He looked up, glaring. "Carl had no claim to Ellen, yet you let him take her from me. Did you think I wouldn't mind?"

Rod Owen's face resembled a limestone outcrop bristling with fire blackened buffalo grass stubble. His voice came out in a whisper. "It was Ellen's choice, James. She loves Carl."

"No!" James sucked in a ragged breath. "She wouldn't gainsay her pa's pledge."

"James, there's no telling what's in the mind of a woman. Maybe Miss Ellen didn't cotton to the idea of being traded for a wagon. I thought it was a good deal for both her and her folks. Somehow she didn't come to care for you."

"That didn't matter to me!" James shouted.

"She came to love your brother, and when he saved her life, that was good enough for her pa." Rod shifted his weight from one leg to the other. "Set your mind to keeping peace, now, and we'll get back to ranching."

James's breathing tore at his throat, and pain seared through his belly. "Peace?" He looked square at his father, then fury rose up and he jabbed the man's chest with his forefinger. "My pride and my affection for that girl is stomped into the ground, and now you call for peace?" He swore, his voice venomous, and his finger jabbed harder.

Rod knocked down James's hand. His voice was quiet, yet rumbled around the corral when he spoke. "Keep your place, son."

James reared back, gathered himself, then spat on the ground. "There *is* no place for me here."

Silence stretched like silver cobwebs between the peeled logs surrounding the two men. Even the horse was quiet. A bushy tailed squirrel rushed up a nearby pine tree, found a limb, and held its breath. Suddenly it chattered, scolding the frozen humans, then flicked its tail as it scuttled away up the tree trunk.

"Once you leave go of that anger, your place will be as large as your brother's. We got a big job of work ahead, son. Now settle down and let's get back to the party."

James stood still, his head thrown back. He was silent.

Rod scowled. "I've preached peace amongst my sons as long as I've had them. It makes the work go smoother." He rubbed his beard. "I need you here, James, but if you can't keep . . ." His voice trailed off to silence.

James squinted at his father.

Rod pulled in a breath and held it a long time before he let it go. His words came out soft as a breeze down the mountain. "Son, I reckon you're too prideful and angry right now to keep peace. Until you get free of that, the best thing is for you to light a shuck for someplace else."

Chapter 2

As Amparo Garcés y Martinez wrung another rivulet of soapy water from the twisted white blouse she held in her brown hands, she gazed above the roofline of her home toward the sun-bathed mountains notching the horizon beyond Santa Fe. Puffy white clouds hung above the hills as though they were pinned on a clothesline stretched across the brilliant blue sky. Vegetation painted the slopes in variegated hues of greens and browns.

This is beauty, she thought, sighing, and glanced toward the shrine tucked into a niche in the corner of the courtyard. *María Santísima, is Heaven so lovely a place as Santa Fe? Is my dear papá there? Tell me it is so, Holy Mother. If I know he is happy, I can bear to live without him.*

Amparo wiped one eye with the back of her hand, then gave the blouse another twist. *I miss him so much, Little Beloved Mother. I never got to tell him goodbye.*

She took a deep breath and let it escape slowly from between her full lips. *Oh, Madre de Dios, give me a little of your strength. Help me to bear my burdens with a light heart.*

Amparo remembered the blouse clasped in her slim hands, shook it gently to uncoil it, then thrust the garment into the rinsing pool of the stone laundry basin. A few drops of water splashed onto her richly embroidered green satin skirt. She frowned, exclaimed, *"¡Vaya!"* and grabbed for a dry rag to sop up the liquid before it spotted the stiff cloth. She dropped the rag to the flagstone beneath her soft slippers and raised her arm to her head to push back the fringe of soft black hair clinging to her damp forehead.

I am sorry, Virgen Santa. I became distracted. I know it is absurd to wear my best clothes for this task. But they are the only clean clothes I have left, and if I am to have anything else to wear, I must do the laundry myself. You see, the woman came home from her errand this morning and dismissed the maid before she could even begin the washing.

"¡Chica!" cried a disapproving voice from a doorway. Amparo jumped. The voice continued. "Why do you wear your good clothes to do the wash? You will

ruin them, and I cannot buy you any more fine things."

"*Señora* Catarina, you startled me!" The girl turned from the washtub and snatched up another blouse from a woven basket at her feet. "I could not help but wear these clothes. They were all I had to wear when you sent Lupe away." She rubbed the blouse with a bar of soap smelling strongly of lye, then began to scrub the garment against the stone washboard in front of her.

A slender woman with thin red lips and wide eyes fringed with spiky black lashes stepped into the courtyard, her long black taffeta skirt swishing with the motion of her hips. She approached a pot of geraniums hanging from a bracket against the kitchen wall and, plucking a blossom, inserted it into the black knot of hair coiled at the back of her head.

"You forgot to call me '*Mamá*'," said the woman, hiding a yawn behind her hand. "Until I met with the lawyer, I did not realize we were so poor that we could not afford to keep Lupe," she added, arching her dark brows. "We will have to conserve until matters improve, so for the time being, you will wash the clothes and linen, and I will watch that Rafaela does not waste any food as she cooks."

"My papá would not want me to do the wash always," the girl protested, shaking her shoulder to dislodge a thick braid of black hair that rested upon it. "He said I must learn to keep a household, but I also must remember to be a lady."

"Then your papá should have left more money to me and not so much to the beggars on the street," the woman answered in a sharp tone. "You will do as you are told, chica."

Amparo drew herself up proudly, rapidly blinking her dark brown eyes. "My papá was a great man to give money to the poor. He said we did not need much, and he was looking forward to receiving his reward for good deeds in Heaven, once he arrived there."

"And for his stupid deeds, I have to suffer." Catarina folded her arms across the front of her white blouse.

Amparo bit her lip. "My papá was not stupid. And it will not injure us to suffer in life." She looked at the woman for a moment, then resumed her labors.

The woman drew in a noisy breath. "If you like to suffer, then we will do so," she said, putting her hands on her hips. "We will not buy cream for the coffee, and no more sugar."

Before Amparo could protest, the iron knocker boomed against the front door six times. The sound filled the courtyard with echoes. The girl stopped scrubbing and looked up. "Shall I see who is at the door?"

Catarina shook her head. "Keep working. I will go." The woman moved in the direction of the front hallway, and Amparo went back to her work.

As she worked, she heard a murmur of voices at the front door. When it stopped, Catarina came back across the courtyard toward the laundry basin. Her mouth was brittle with a smile of satisfaction as she slowly fanned a folded sheet of paper before her face.

"Well, chica, perhaps I will have cream and sugar after all."

Amparo raised her arms from the washbasin and dropped a skirt into the rinse tub. "What is that?"

Catarina regarded the girl with a cold look in her narrowed eyes. She tapped the paper against the open palm of one hand.

Why does she hate me so much, Holy Mother? Amparo asked silently.

Presently the woman spoke. "It is a way out of our difficulties, chica." She turned away.

"What do you mean?"

Catarina cocked her head, then slowly pivoted on her high-heeled shoes. The smile on her lips sent a chill up Amparo's neck, and she felt a prickle at her scalp. The woman held the paper high. "If you must know, this is your salvation."

The girl took two steps forward, then stood stiffly beside the washbasin as Catarina came toward her, looked her over, then circled behind Amparo, trailing her free hand along the girl's shoulders.

Amparo shuddered at her touch.

"When your papá had the poor taste to die, I asked my friend *Señor* Fuentes for his assistance." Now Catarina was again in front of Amparo, her carefully rouged upper lip curling as she tilted Amparo's chin upward with two fingers. "He saw you in the marketplace one day, and suggested that there is one good solution to my struggles."

The woman turned Amparo's head from side to side with her hand. "I am sure now that he was right." Catarina loosed the girl's face and tapped the paper. "Señor Fuentes received this communication yesterday. There is a man, a young man, who lives in the Territory of Colorado." She paused, again arching a brow. "He is seeking a wife."

"You are going to remarry?"

"No. It is not I who shall be a bride." Her thin lips twisted toward a smile, and her eyes went hard as she gloated.

"¡Ave María, Madre de Dios!" Amparo whispered as comprehension froze her face. Her body went rigid, her hands in midair.

"You are to meet him in a small village known as *Leones* on the twenty-sixth day of October. Señor Fuentes is making arrangements for your *jornada*."

"My journey?" Amparo's hands dropped to her sides.

"Yes." Catarina consulted the paper. "In the mission church you will marry the man, one Julio Rodríguez y Guzmán. In a few days, he will make a fine settlement on you. I, of course, will see to the disposition of the money."

"Vaya, mi mamá," said the girl, almost whispering. She swallowed, trying to wet her arid throat. "It is too soon to talk of marriage. I am not seventeen for two more weeks. I know nothing of men." *Virgen Santísima, intercede for me now in this time of trial.*

"You've gone pale, chica. You do not appreciate our wonderful news?"

Amparo shook her head to clear it, then took a deep breath to settle herself.

"I suppose you do not want to go to the man? You would rather stay here and starve?" The woman laughed as Amparo shook her head again. "You need not worry, chica. It is very simple to please a man."

Catarina approached Amparo and, taking her by the hand, drew her out into the middle of the courtyard. She tilted her head and looked at the girl.

"First, you will undress, so that he may appreciate your charms." Catarina's voice was low, seductive. "Do not look so shocked, chica. After all, you will be married. He will touch you." The woman caressed Amparo's cheek, and the girl shrank from her. Catarina laughed and drew her handkerchief from her pocket. "He will probably kiss you. Then he will take you to the bed, and you will lie down, perhaps upon silken sheets and pillows." The woman trailed the scrap of silk across Amparo's hand. "That will be pleasant upon your skin." Catarina gave a bark of a laugh, and waved one hand in the air matter-of-factly. "Then he will do what he will do. You will pretend that you like it."

Amparo lowered her head, attempting to hide her horrified face. After a moment, she looked up to find the woman appraising her.

"Will you like it?" Catarina smiled on one side of her mouth. "Will you like it when he touches you, strokes you, when he makes you a woman?" She laughed. "No, I do not suppose that a timorous child like you will appreciate the pleasures your bridegroom will bring to you." She shrugged her shoulders. "Of course, it is possible that he will not be gentle. No matter. I will have cream in my coffee, and you will be the mistress of a large *rancho*. Make an heir for the man quickly, chica." She turned away dismissively.

Amparo drew a quick breath. She took another, then angry words burst from her mouth. "You are selling me to this stranger! You are selling me like a . . . whore!"

Catarina gasped, turned, and struck Amparo across the face. The girl fell to the tile floor, hitting her arm against a large carved chest. She hunched her shoulders, clasped the injured arm against her chest with her other hand. Her eyes were tearless. *Santa María, I will not cry.*

"It is impossible to help you, chica. You appreciate nothing. Nothing!"

"You cannot make me do this hateful thing," Amparo cried out, her back braced against the chest.

"Evil, willful girl, if it takes a stick to teach you, that is how you will learn to be obedient."

"I will not do this," Amparo whispered.

"Ungrateful child! Because of your thoughtless, selfish deviltry, your papá will weep in Purgatory forevermore!" The woman swept from the room, skirts rustling.

Forever in Purgatory? It cannot be so! Amparo fell forward onto the cold floor before the shrine. *Blessed Virgin, tell me my papá is safely in Heaven!*

৯৩

Sunset blazed orange and gold across the pale blue rim of the western sky as Amparo paused at the edge of the plaza. She adjusted her white lace shawl to cover her black hair before she ascended the stone steps leading to the portals of the whitewashed church. Waves of heat rising from the stonework shimmered in the air like silken veils barring the way between her and sanctuary. Her feet, girdled by leather sandals, felt shriveled and gritty, as though they were baked by the afternoon air. The oppression of the day's oven-like temperature would soon abate with the coming of the night, but what could relieve the oppression in her heart?

O mi papá. What have I done? Have I truly kept your soul in Purgatory? It must not be! Holy Virgin, show me how to send my papá to heaven!

The girl climbed the steps, passed through the large open doors of the church and stopped in the welcome cool of the hall to dip her finger into the waiting font of holy water. The moisture caressed her finger as she made the sign of the cross, whispering the words that accompanied the action. She moved forward between the rows of wooden pews into the church, trying to gather peace to her from under the vaulted ceiling above her head. She put out her left hand and grasped the back of the nearest pew, sank to her right knee before the Host, then arose and slipped into a pew on her right.

Her knees found depressions in the hard leather cushion of the kneeler as she bowed her head, pulled her mother's rosary from her pocket, and whispered the "Our Father." At the end of her prayer, as the hush of the place surrounded her, her soul cried out: *Blessed Mary, my papá was so good, so kind to all. Surely his soul will have ascended to Heaven by now? Oh, Holy Mother, can my little wish to stay in Santa Fe be so evil?*

Half a dozen people knelt in the half-light of the church, although evening mass would not be celebrated for another hour. Amparo leaned back into the pew, worn smooth by the sliding action of hundreds of worshipers over the years. She pulled the ends of her shawl tightly across her chest, as though she was attempting to draw a cloak of privacy around herself.

After a while, her hands began to twitch from tension, and she stretched them out in front of her, opening wide. Her beads clicked against the missal box attached to the back of the pew, and her hand closed on the nearest book. She drew it toward her, enfolded it against her breast. Her head bowed, she sank forward onto her knees once more.

Then the idea came, the offering she must make, the sacrifice she must suffer to show God her intention.

Amparo rose and placed the missal back in the box. She moved quickly across the center aisle and into the left-hand row of pews, heading toward the side aisle. Her sandaled feet slip slapped on the bare stone walkway as she moved past the confession boxes toward the front of the church where a small chapel branched off to the left.

She stopped before a large wrought iron stand containing both lit and unlit vigil candles, and dropped a small coin into the offering box before she lighted the wick of a candle on the front row. As its light flickered heavenward she slipped into the side chapel to kneel at a rail before which a metal latticework grille protected the painted plaster statue of the Virgin Mother.

"Hail Mary, full of grace, the Lord is with Thee," she said, gazing up at the haunting sadness on the face of the Madonna and wondering if the same sadness was reflected on her own. "Blessed art thou among women, and blessed is the fruit of thy womb, Jesus. Holy Mary, Mother of God, pray for us sinners now and at the hour of our death, Amen."

Amparo looked at her hands, tightly woven around the rosary and resting on the rail. Then she looked upon the Lady's face once more. The moment had come. The vow must be spoken.

"Holy Mary, Mother of God, I have no money to buy an indulgence so that my dear papá may ascend from Purgatory into Heaven," she whispered. "To show Our Lord how much I love Him, to show my complete devotion, dearest Lady, I offer up a vow. It is this: I will obey the woman in her plan. I will go to the Territory of Colorado, and I will marry the stranger."

Amparo paused to take a shuddering breath. Then she continued. "This is my intention, the desire of my heart, to please Our Lord Jesus enough that He will take my papá to His bosom." Her head bowed until it touched her thumbs, and she waited for a moment, hearing the pounding of her pulse in her ears. "Blessed Virgin, let your prayers ascend to God that He may hear my petition."

Amparo stretched out her arms in supplication to the figure of Our Lady, and she remained in that position, listening to the rustle of the wax candles burning behind her, to the click of rosary beads being told among the pews.

It seemed a very long time later that her soul found strength enough to raise her body from her knees.

Blessed Mother, I must go now. There is much to do. The woman says it is arranged that I leave in two days. Do not forget me, Blessed Virgin! Do not forget my petition, and my sacrifice!

Amparo crept with slow steps from the church, harboring a small joy in one corner of her heart because she was leaving obedience as a sacrifice upon the altar. The rest of her heart was full of unease at the thought of going into a world of strangers, like the one awaiting her in Colorado.

Chapter 3

James felt a shudder cross his frame. Pa was still talking. "Are you of a mind to tell me where you're bound?"

Bound? Pa's words kicked dirt over some of the fire of James's rage, and he swallowed hard. Where was he bound? What could he do? A list of his skills ran past his mind—farmer, stock raiser, horse breaker, soldier—

"I don't reckon there's call for an infantryman anywhere about." James bit his lip at voicing his absurd thought.

"Not likely." Rod waited for a moment before he continued. "What's your plan?"

"I'll . . ." James looked around the enclosure, then raised his chin and exhaled. "I'll dig out Uncle Jonathan's mine."

Rod was silent again for a time. He sniffed once. "It was a rich hole before it fell in on him." He rubbed his beard again. "I'll lend you a dollar or two to get you on your way. Take the sorrel and the mule and the mining gear."

James looked at his hands. The nineteen-year-old palms were callused from years of work. The fingers were large and squared off at the tips. *Worker's hands.*

Hard work would help. He curled the hands into fists. "I'll take the animals and the gear, but I won't take your coin. I'll work my way north." James glanced up. *Pa looks like I took a strap to him*. He swallowed again. "Tell Ma I'll miss her." His voice seemed caught in his throat.

"Say your own good byes," Rod said in a voice that was tight with emotion.

"No. It'll spoil the party for her."

James bent, picked up his rope, and coiled it. Then he turned his back on his father, pushed the gate open, and started for the log corral beyond the main cabin, bleakness filling his belly. Ellen was gone, yoked to Carl. Ellen, with her blooming red hair and the dusting of freckles on her nose; with her crooked smile and merry laugh—ripped from him like a piece of flesh by the foreign words of a Spanish priest. The world lost its brightness as he trudged through the dust.

To his left across a creek was a small cabin—home to his oldest brother Rulon, his wife Mary, and their two babies—and to his right stood the main cabin that housed his father and mother and the children younger than himself. He went behind the bigger log house to the corral, and stooped to get under the top pole of the fence that enclosed several grazing horses.

James whistled to a light reddish brown colored horse. It continued to crop grass, although its ears swiveled in his direction. He glanced at the sun; its rays shed no warmth on him today, and he shivered as he made a loop in his rope and pitched it toward the neck of the sorrel horse.

The loop soared over the horse's head and settled squarely on its shoulders. James walked up the rope toward the animal, talking to it in a soothing tone. He led it through the gate to the nearby shed and saddled up. When James mounted, the sorrel bucked a few times, but he rode out the kinks in the animal, then turned it toward the big shed his father called the stable.

He roused the mule from its slumber and put a pack frame on its back. In one corner of the shed lay the mining equipment four of the Owen men had brought back from a rubble filled hole at Central City that had claimed the life of Ma's brother.

I never had no mind to go digging in the earth, James thought, squinting at the pick, shovel, and pans. *Mining sure wasn't lucky for Uncle Jonathan*. He approached the pile of equipment and gave it a kick. *But then, I reckon my luck ran out today*. He blew out his breath between pursed lips.

James kicked the equipment again, and figured it would take two weeks of hard riding—no, it would be more like a month, working his way—to get to Central City, northwest of Denver City. And when he got there . . . *I'll have to hire out to a miner until I get a grubstake together*.

James loaded the tools onto the pack saddle and tied them in place. He raided the cook shack for a handful of dried meat strips and a few hard corn dodgers. With the mule's lead rope in his hand, he mounted, and kicked the horse toward his unfinished cabin.

A few moments later, the sight of two log walls standing head high, and two others up to his hip deepened James's gloom. After working full days at his father's place, he had labored by lantern light to fashion a home for Ellen Bates, but she had slipped from his grasp like quicksilver chased across a tabletop.

"Tarnation!" he growled as he looked at the shell of the house that now represented a future that would not be. He slid from the saddle, tied the horse and mule, and ducked under the suspended wagon sheet that roofed his bed and belongings.

James changed his clothes, rolled his bedding, and packed his personal goods into the leather carryall he'd toted during the war. He stepped through the doorway, carrying the war bag and bedding. He stopped beside a mound of logs piled up against the wall and ran his hand over the length of one he'd peeled for use inside the house. Even though the color of the wood was bleaching from bright yellow tan to gray, the piece still had a silky smooth surface that reminded him of the one time he had held Ellen in his arms and kissed her.

She had stood alone on the prairie early one morning near the end of their journey, staring as the first light of dawn revealed a mountain peak in the distant west. Pike's Peak, it was called, and Ellen was first to spot it as she stood apart from the wagons, the wind whipping her skirt, and her hair streaming loose over her shoulder. She stretched out her arms to the mountain as though she meant to embrace it.

James had felt a quickening of his pulse at the sight of her, a dryness of the throat, a quivering of the sinews that surprised him, as he hadn't to then felt more than fondness for her. With swift, light strides he went to her and stepped into the circle of her arms. A peculiar look widened her eyes as his mouth came down toward hers, but her lashes descended and shut it away from his view.

Wondrous sensations warmed his veins as James kissed the trembling girl. His arms enfolded her. His hands crept across her shoulders and through her hair until he held her face between them. Only then did he notice her hands pushing gently against his chest. She rolled her head out of his grasp and opened her green, green eyes.

"No, James. Please don't," she whispered, and was gone from his arms.

She's modest, he thought. *That's good and proper.* Then he chastised himself. *Do your wooing in private, James.*

Since that day, he'd kept the memory of the feel of her cheeks in his fingertips, marveling at the softness of a woman's skin. Now he would never touch her again, and cold flowed down his body as though he had stepped naked under an icy waterfall.

James pressed his lips together and drew his knife, looking at the keen edge of the blade, the finely-honed point. He drew the blade along the meat of the edge of his palm. It was sharp, as always, leaving a thin bead of crimson. A dark thought fluttered in his mind, but he pushed it away and cut the wagon sheet free of the thongs that held it in place above the log walls. He spread the canvas cloth on the packed earth, wrapped all the gear inside, and tied it atop the mule's packsaddle. Then he mounted up and put the horse onto the trail.

North. Up through Pueblo to Denver City. Then to Central City. I got to put distance between me and Ellen's eyes.

James settled the horse into a trot for a bit over a mile, then reined in to cross the stream that ran slowly down from behind Carl's cabin. As he rode through the water without stopping, not looking toward the house on the wooded bench of land to his left, he glanced at his fists. They were balled tight as caterpillar cocoons.

Eyes green as the spring grass, filled with flecks of gold and maidenly modesty. Eyes to lose my soul in.

The horse scrambled up the slope of the bank, the saddle lurched back onto the horse's croup, and James halted to check the front cinch. He dismounted, raised the stirrup leather, and adjusted the knot on the latigo, but the work didn't quiet a rage that burned like a prairie fire within: rage against Carl, and against Pa. He cursed his father and brother. If he never set eyes on this range again, he would rest easy. But the horse wheeled when James climbed into the saddle, and his gaze caught Carl's little house tucked in among the trees.

A chill rose up his spine, lifting the hair on the back of his neck. *I am a blind fool*, he berated himself, then shouted, "Girl, I would've loved you!"

He gigged the horse into a lope through the broken countryside. The mule followed, braying in protest. James merely tightened his grip on the lead rope and lowered his head over the horse's mane.

James stopped twice to let the animals breathe, cool down, and drink. Other than that, he pushed forward, heedless of the approaching dusk. A last gleam of light streaked the sky, and night lay in wait to engulf the three of them when he finally turned off the trail.

He found a flat area covered with buffalo grass that lay next to a stream of water. His raw anger had abated somewhat, and he tended the animals carefully, removing saddles, packs and head gear. He checked hooves for stones, and led the animals down to the water. While he waited for them to drink, he dabbed at the dried blood on his arm with a water soaked bit of handkerchief. After he hobbled them, he turned them out to graze. When he'd eaten his handful of supper, he lay down with his hat over his eyes and fought his nightmares for an hour's worth of sleep.

∽

The sun climbed overhead into a cloudless, burnished bowl of a sky. By mid-morning, a tiny hammer pounded against a miniature anvil in James's skull. As he rode through the broken hills and undulating plains toward the first big town on the trail—Pueblo City—the size of the anvil and the hammer increased until he felt sure the thud was ringing clear to Kansas.

When James at last noticed outbuildings around him, he had to force his eyes open from the squint they'd taken on to shut out the sun's glare radiating upward from the parched earth. He rode into the welcomed darkness of the runway of a livery barn, rubbed his burning eyes, and dismounted.

"How much to put up my horse and mule?" he asked a tow headed youth lounging on a bale of hay beside the door, just out of the sun's reach.

"Two bits," said the boy, poking at his broken front teeth with a sliver of wood. "That includes grain."

James put his hand into his pants pocket and pulled out his money. "Humph," he said, rubbing the two quarters in his hand. He gave one to the boy, then stared at the remaining coin before he slid it down into his pocket again. "Can I get a meal cheap around here?"

"The saloon down the street puts out a free lunch . . . for customers."

"That'll have to do. Where can I throw my saddles?"

The boy raised his chin toward the rear of the barn. "Tack room's got an empty corner. I won't charge if you haul the gear yourself."

"I'm obliged," James muttered. "See to it the animals get the grain." He turned to lead them away.

"Wait a minute, mister," called out the boy.

James looked back, raising one eyebrow.

"If you could use some work, ask the bartender for Len Strummond. I hear he's got a job open."

"Thanks." James began to ask what sort of work it was, then clamped his mouth shut. What did it matter, so long as it was hard work, good and hard, and didn't give him time to think?

He tugged on the reins, and the horse and mule shuffled forward and entered a pair of stalls. When James had stripped the saddles and packs from the animals, and carried the gear into the tack room, he picked up his war bag—the ancient brown catchall with the leather crazed like old china from the neglect the urgency of war had imposed—and walked down the runway toward the sunshine. He took four or five steps along the street in the powdery dust, then heard the youth calling him.

"Mister, wait. I forgot that saloon's full of Yankees. You can't go in there."

James turned half around, anger narrowing his eyes. "That squabble's done with," he said, his voice gravelly. Then he spun around and continued down the street.

"It isn't over in this town," the boy yelled. James didn't stop. The boy shrugged his shoulders and turned back to the barn to do his work. "Oh well, what can they do, shoot you?"

James kept walking, watching for the saloon. It loomed ahead in the middle of the block, a free-standing, unpainted lumber building, narrow in width, but standing two stories tall. Noise from the dinnertime crowd poured through two small windows in the front wall.

James shut his eyes for a moment in an attempt to ease the pain throbbing in his head. Then he pushed through the batwing doors and eased to one side of the opening, pausing to look down the long room. After a while his eyes adjusted to the dimness of the saloon, lit only by the windows and a trio of lamps hanging behind the bar.

Seven tables filled the open space of the room. Around them, diners sat in barrel and ladder backed chairs; not a seat was empty. Three or four sturdy men stood along the mahogany bar, drinking their dinner and tucking up their tails, for the crowded tables seemed to push the men against the wooden barrier. Laughter came from a door at the right of the room behind the bar, accompanied by the clink of dishware and the clatter of cutlery dropped to the floor.

The aroma of fresh baked bread teased James's nose, and he moved into the room and threaded himself between the bar and the tables, brushing the leg of one of the drinkers with his war bag as he passed.

"Yeow!" the man yelled, gripping a half empty whiskey bottle. "That's me sore leg."

"I'm almighty sorry, friend. I beg your pardon," James drawled, trying to squeeze past the man and his neighbor at the bar, who stepped into James's path. James half-turned and backed a step into the room, facing the bar.

The first man swore, turning from the bar with a lurch. He looked at James, his eyes traveling from his hat to his boots. He spat on the floor. "Ye're one of them 'Suth-ren' butternut rebels come to stink up tha place. This be a Union bar, Johnny Reb. Ye don't come in here."

Something cold as a chunk of river ice congealed in James's belly as he listened to the Irish brogue that was neither pleasant nor lilting coming from the older man. As he turned to face the man's outraged face, a chill seeped from that icy lump into every empty space in his gut, spread into his chest, then bubbled up into his shoulders and ran down inside his arms to tingle his fingertips. "The war's over, friend." There was a hard edge to his voice.

The man's partner grabbed James's shoulder. "'Twon't never be for Danny O'Brien," he said, his voice whining. "He's got a crook leg from that war, and it pains him night and day, Rebel."

"That's not my doing." Irritated, James shook himself loose from the man's grasp and backed as far as he could into the room, sensing that danger came chiefly from the man called Danny.

"Liar! Ye're the man thet just now set it off agin," Danny shouted, bending over to rub his injured thigh. He started to pour himself a drink with his free hand, but it shook so badly that he raised the bottle to his lips, instead, and took a deep swig of the liquor.

The tingling and the sense of danger left James, and he shrugged his shoulders. "It was an unhappy accident. I already begged pardon. Now I'll be about my business." He turned toward the man's friend. "Let me pass," he said in a curt tone of voice.

The second man backed up a step, then his eyes widened as he looked over James's shoulder.

"No, Danny! You canna do that!"

James whirled to face the Irishman, who held the bottle in his left hand, and a revolver in his right. The blued barrel wavered, describing circles in the air between the two men.

"Ye're going to be a'paying me back for my pain, Reb," Danny growled.

James put out his hand, palm in front of him. "Friend, you picked the wrong man to rob. I've only two bits to my name."

"I've no need a' yer money. It's yer blood I want, and that spilled!"

Danny twisted to his right to set the bottle on the bar. It teetered on the turned edge for a moment, then fell to the floor, the sound shattering the bustle in the room as effectively as the wood planks shattered the glass.

Silence spread in the room like ripples on the still surface of a pond, widening in circles that soon lapped against the farthest reaches of the room. Then the silence fled as men scattered, scrambling from the chairs nearest the bar to huddle against the walls.

"I'm unarmed," James said, lifting his war bag slightly in his left hand and trying to raise saliva in his mouth. The cold and the tingle were back. He silently belabored himself for not buckling his Army model Colt around his hips when he left the cabin. Icy fingers throbbed to feel the weight of the .44 caliber weapon, which was buckled away out of reach in the carryall.

"Ye canna shoot him down like a dog, Danny," said a cracking voice behind James. "He has no gun, man."

"I can and I will, Liam. He's a dog of a Rebel, and deserves no better."

"Danny—"

"Quiet, Liam." Danny laughed. "He's got his stinking Rebel pride. That's weapon enough," he hissed.

James considered if the man was drunk enough that he would miss his shot. *He's holding pretty steady*, he thought. A draining sensation sucked at his belly. *This fellow wants to plow a furrow through my chest.* The cold gathered in from James's arms and shrank into a frozen lump that lodged just under his ribs. *Ma, this is not the way I want to die.*

Danny's laughter was a raw sound as he drew back the hammer of the pistol. James heard the click of the action, and the snick of the cylinder moving into place.

"That's right, Reb," Danny whispered. "Ye're going to pay for this leg, and all the nights I lay crying out in pain, and all the shame it brung me." His voice rose with his fury. "And then ye're going to pay for the wife that left me for a whole man."

"You're crazy," muttered James, and his belly twisted in agony because of a girl who had left him for a broken man. *Ellen. No! I can't think of her now.* He wrenched his thoughts away from the girl with the laughing green eyes. The gun stopped moving, pointed at his chest, and James whispered, "Don't do anything foolish, Danny." Then the muscles of his upper arms bunched as his mind rehearsed the motion of releasing the catch to the war bag.

Danny replied with a yell. He squeezed the trigger and a bullet whined over James's left shoulder and struck the back wall of the saloon. James heard a wild cry of "No, Danny, no!" As he ducked, crouching over the war bag, tearing at the buckle, the man to his left dropped to the floor and huddled against the bar, whimpering, "Don't do it, Danny boy."

"He's a damnable Rebel, Liam. This is war!" the man howled, re-cocking the pistol.

Still crouched forward, James managed to open the buckle to the bag as Danny got off another shot, yelling all the while. The lead ball caught the flesh of James's left arm and slammed him to the floor as he yanked his pistol free.

James raised his arm, gritted his teeth, pulled back the hammer, and aimed toward the man as Danny's third bullet struck him in the right side. He jerked the trigger. The clap of the shot smote his ears.

Danny fell against the bar, screaming, and dropped his gun as a cherry colored stain spread across his left shoulder. The man slid inch by inch down the bar to plop onto the floor as blue powder smoke swirled in the open space. James raised and cocked his gun again as several men stepped forward, muttering. Danny's friend scuttled across the floor and bent over his fallen comrade.

"You didn't have to shoot him, mister," he complained. "Danny was a good man, up until Rosie left him." He pulled out a grimy handkerchief and pressed it to the Irishman's wound.

"He didn't give me a choice." Breath was coming hard against a shattered rib, and James fought to keep his wavering gun trained on the unfriendly group as he tried to sit up.

"What's going on here?" A brawny man wearing a pistol in a belt holster and a tin star on a leather vest came through the crowd. "Drop your weapon, boy," he said, not even bothering to draw his own gun. "I'm the law in this town."

"The kid shot Danny," shouted the friend.

"Is he dead?"

"No, but he's pretty bad off."

"I don't think he's dying, Connolly. I'd say the boy just clipped his shoulder. Get him down to Doc's place."

The marshal watched as the man's friends carried him away, then stooped and plucked the gun from James's hand. Blood gushed from James's wounded side, and the man plugged his own handkerchief into the hole. "There," he said, "That should hold you. Got a name, boy?"

"I'm James Owen," he said, struggling against a darkness that flitted across his mind like a thousand bats' wings brushing against his face.

"Well, James Owen, you'd best come with me," the marshal said. "Watch it now! Looks like you're fainting. A couple of you fellows hoist him to his feet and bring him along. Chancy, get the doc when he's through with Danny. Tell him to meet me over to the office."

Two men dragged James to his feet as he strained to keep his eyes open. "Where're you taking me?" he muttered.

"Guess he's still alive, boys. Haul him up a bit there. He's unsteady on his feet." The marshal yawned, then glanced at James. "We've got a nice jail to keep you snug until we find out if you're a wanted man or just a gun brawler, boy."

The man took a step toward the door, then turned back to look at James.

"Doc'll be along by and by to patch you up. He don't mind calling on his patients in a jail cell, as long as they pay him." Then the marshal turned his back and banged his way through the doors of the saloon.

Chapter 4

James came to consciousness with a jerk and a yelp. A long, hard, cold object had entered his side, bringing agony with it. Strong hands pulled his naked shoulders back onto a mattress that crackled with each buck of his body, and the sweet odor of fresh blood filled his nostrils. The hands gripped him tighter than before, inhibiting his struggles, until he sank back, exhausted, on the mattress, his eyes opening slightly. He could see nothing for a red fog that seemed to hang inside his eyes.

The cold probe brushed a piece of splintered rib and drove it into his flesh, and he cried out, sending echoes around the room.

"Lie still, lad," muttered a man leaning over the cot. "I'm coming up on the bullet now." The probe lunged again into the hole, side by side with another, larger instrument, then James ground his teeth as the two metal objects pushed pieces of his shattered rib into the margins of the wound.

"Ahhh. There it is." A lump of metal clanged dully against the bottom of an enamel basin. "I'd best clear out one or two of these chunks of bone. They won't do him any good, and they will just end up making misery," the voice went on.

"Can you work them loose, Doc?" asked someone standing at James's head. James recognized his voice. It was the lawman from the saloon.

"I'll manage," replied the doctor. Then instruments nipped and tore at James's flesh, nudging and cutting loose and removing bone fragments to drop into the basin, where they fell with muted clinks.

"I guess that's about all of them," said the doctor, as he slipped the instruments from the wound. Striving to see through the ruddy haze, James blew out his breath in a long, ragged sigh. The enemy had withdrawn.

"I didn't know Danny was so poor a shot," added the doctor.

James inhaled sharply as liquid flame bubbled into the wound. Then he gasped as it transmuted to ice, and spread down his side onto his back. The doctor dabbed at the spillage with a rough towel. From the fumes that struck his nostrils, James figured the man was cleaning the hole with whiskey.

"Well, he was drunk. This boy shot true enough. Liam Connolly thinks Danny's in a sorry state and like to die. Is that so?" asked the lawman.

James concentrated on forcing a breath into his lungs past the incessantly throbbing pain, expelling air, then taking another lungful as the doctor began to wrap his chest and side with strips of soft cloth.

"No. All that ails Danny is a bloody flesh wound and a snortful of whiskey. The hangover will pain him more than the shoulder, I wager. This lad's arm will be fine in a day or two," the doctor added. "The lead went clean through, just under the skin, and didn't touch the bone. You know, Danny should have tried a knife if he'd wanted to bag him a rebel. I hear he is skilled with a blade. How many shots did he fire, anyway?"

"The barkeep said three. Harvey dug one slug out of the back wall. The boy shot once, after Danny'd had his chance."

"The lad is lucky. He'll pull through if he doesn't take a fever or get infection in the side wound."

"You didn't sew it up."

"No. I already have it bandaged. The wound will heal closed if he don't move around much."

The haze before James's eyes cleared as he blinked, and he glanced around the cramped cell. He was lying on a metal bunk topped with a striped mattress tick. The only other object belonging in the cell was a bucket in the corner for slops. The floor of the room was made of uneven gray granite chunks mortared together, as were two of the walls, and iron bars guarded the window opening. On the inside of the room, one entire wall was fashioned of iron bars set in the floor and ceiling six inches apart, with the exception of a metal plate that framed an opening about a foot wide in the swinging section that marked the door. A wall behind the bars, made of heavy planks, held a wooden door and formed a corridor between the wall and the bars. The fourth wall of the cell was also constructed of bars, dividing it from an identical cell.

James rolled his eyes upward and saw the lawman standing at the head of the bunk, arms crossed in front of his chest. The doctor sat on a stool, fastening the last bandage around James's ribs.

"I see you've come to yourself," said the doctor, and gave him a pat on the shoulder, then stood up, wiped his instruments, and put them away. "That's a dollar, lad. I'm charging extra for digging out the bone."

"You should pay me for holding still," James whispered, patting his right pocket. It was empty, so he crossed his arm in front to get to the left pocket and winced at the pain the motion sent tearing up his side. He tried to reach the money with his left arm, but that one was bound against his chest, and when he flexed the muscles, he found he didn't want to move the arm anyway, for pain stabbed sharply under the skin.

The doctor frowned. "I'll get it from you later."

"I don't have a dollar," James said. He looked at the lawman. "All I have is a quarter, Federal."

"That's a pity. I guess I'll have to add vagrancy to the charges against you, boy." The marshal crossed his arms.

"Huh." James tried to rise up on his elbow, but the attempt brought nausea, and he lay back, gasping. As the mattress crackled underneath him, he asked, "What are you holding me for?"

"Liam Connolly wants Danny to press a charge of attempted murder, but that's nonsense. The barkeep says you defended yourself fair and square. That leaves the offenses of discharging your weapon inside the town limits, and gun brawling. Then too, you've got to pay off your bill to the doc or face the vagrancy charge."

James closed his eyes. The hammer was at work again in his head, striking sparks behind his eyes as it hit the anvil in monotonous rhythm, pounding until he was sure his body shook with the thunder of it. "I had to disarm him or be killed. He kept firing at me," he said.

"Well now, that's what I figured, but we got the ordinance against gun play."

"There was nothing playful about it. I'm not guilty."

"Then you'll have to stand trial."

"I'll work off the doctor bill," James said through the pounding of his head.

The lawman laughed. "Was you able bodied, I'd consider it, a strong young man like yourself, but you'll be laid up for quite a spell now. How long do you figure, Doc?"

"Anywhere from one week to six. It depends on how that side mends, and like I said before, if he gets infection or fever." The doctor swirled the whiskey around in the bottle.

The liquid sounded to James like the whisper made by Ma's silk petticoats as she walked. But that was long ago, and in another place. He shook his head to clear away the illusion.

"Will you be back later to tend him, Doc?"

"He can't pay me for the work I done just now! Get one of them Southern gals from over to the hotel to change his dressings once a day, and he ought to heal up, if he don't—"

"I know, get a fever or infection," the lawman interrupted, nodding his head. "Thanks for coming by." He opened the cell door and ushered the doctor to the inner door, then turned back into the cell, his teeth worrying his lip, and frowned down at James.

"I'm Marshal Tate. I like you, boy. It pains me to see you in such a fix. Now tell me, don't you have kin close about who can bail you out?"

James shut his eyes for a moment and lay quietly, breathing slowly. When he looked up again, he rasped, "No."

"That's a pity. I thought you might be kin of that fellow Rod Owen down the country a piece that folks are talking about. They say he trailed a herd of cattle in from Texas. Is that true?"

James held his breath. To lie wrenched his soul, but hadn't Pa sent him off, as much as thrown him out? And hadn't he left the place and the people willingly? He felt only bitterness in the portion of his gut that should swell with Owen pride for Pa's vision, and a difficult job well done by him and his brothers. Darkness swept through his mind, and he answered, "I don't know the man."

The marshal cleared his throat and paced the cell. "Well, that's a pity," he said as he walked. "A deed like that is something to hold pride in." Soon the marshal came over to the cot and looked down at James. "Can you play poker? Maybe if you're good enough, when you're up to it, you can get some cash out of my deputy, Harvey. He purely loves a hand, but can't play worth beans."

James shook his head against the rustling tick and closed his eyes again. The afternoon sun flooding through the barred window lit up the room beyond his ability to bear the strong light. Foul odors invaded his nose from the bucket in the corner. The hammer continued to strike the anvil. Pain from his side and from his soul lapped at the borders of his brain. "I never had much time to learn the game," he said.

"Well, now you've got an opportunity to learn. You've got nothing but time here, boy. The circuit judge ought to come through here for your trial about the time you get on your feet. If you could win some cash and clear up the doctor bill, that would be one less charge for him to bang his gavel about."

James made no answer, and the man shrugged his shoulders and backed out of the cell. The clang of metal on metal bruised James's brain.

ജ

James opened his eyes and lay still. The pounding in his head had retreated with the few hours of rest he'd gained, and at present the pain in his side and left arm had receded to a dull throb, so it wasn't pain that had awakened him.

He blinked, wondering what had snatched him from the depths of sleep. Then he closed his eyes and tried to sink back into oblivion. But though the room was dark, he couldn't find sleep as his brain replayed the sight of Danny's shoulder blossoming crimson like a giant spray of honeysuckle flowers. He opened his eyes again and stared at the ceiling. If his shot had gone five inches lower when Danny's bullet smashed his rib, he would have snuffed out the life of the drunken man as easily as a man would smash a bedbug. James closed his eyes and sighed.

Then he heard a distinct, though muted, sound and came wide awake, holding his breath in the night darkened cell as he listened for a repetition.

After long moments, his body began quivering from tension, and he struggled to relax, exhaled, then took another breath and held it.

Finally it came: a scraping noise in the alley outside the barred window above his cot. Then came the sound of bits of gravel turning under a carelessly placed boot, accompanied by a shushing noise. Someone was outside the jail, attempting to be silent, and a chill raised the hair on James' scalp. Whoever they were, they were up to no good.

"Watch it! Stay out of the light!"

James went rigid, and waves of pain assaulted his brain. The man's whisper had come from just outside the window.

"Quiet!" hissed the second man. "Harvey'll hear us."

"He snuck out to get a drink."

"Then hurry up about it. You want the whole town to see us?"

A gun barrel appeared between the bars of the window. James rolled onto his side and hugged the wall. *Ma, these yahoos aren't giving up—*

An explosion echoed and re echoed around the cell. Chips of stone from the ceiling above James's head rained down over him.

More explosions—one, two—he lost count.

Silence.

"Did you get him?"

"How should I know—"

"Somebody's coming."

"Run, you jackass! Run!"

Footsteps crunched in the gravel and faded away with the echoes of the voices. The office door was flung back. James turned and looked up as Marshal Tate peered into the cellblock, holding a lantern high.

"You hit, boy?"

James tried to sit up, but the pain stabbed through his stomach and he fell back. His head was spinning. "Who was that taking target practice?"

The man came toward the cell bars. "You're a cool youngster. You remind me of a man I once knew." He unlocked the cell and stepped inside, crossed to the window, and peered into the alley. "Some of Danny's misguided friends, I imagine. I'll check their stories in the morning." Tate glanced at James again, then backed out of the cell, locked the door, and left the room.

They want to murder me, Ma. Why? 'Cause I fought under the Stars and Bars? Ain't it enough we lost everything, including Ben and Peter? Bile burned into his mouth at the thought of his brothers lying lifeless on a bloody battleground. He twisted swiftly on his side to vomit on the floor. Then he lay back on the bunk, body racked with agony from all the twisting motions. Only much later did sleep lay a quilt of blackness over his exhausted body.

℘

When James next opened his eyes, two things caught his notice. Coming day was gradually brightening the jail, and a small, bearded man dressed in buckskin shook the bars of the door in the cell next to his, making them rattle and clank.

The man shouted at the top of his voice, "Harvey, you made a mistake. Get me out of here. Har vee! Tate! Open this door."

Irritation flooded James's chest at the stranger's noisy demonstration. "Shut up, man," he growled. "Can't a body sleep in this jail?"

The stranger turned on James, jabbing his finger toward a spot alongside the cot. "How can you rest with all that puke stinking up the floor? Har vee! Let me out!"

The door to the outer office was swept back on its hinges to bang against the wall, and a potbellied deputy stormed into the cell corridor.

"What's the matter with you, Brenner? Can't you sleep off a drunk quiet like no more?" the man sputtered. "Tate said to lock you up all night this time. You gave him a fine case of the wearies."

"It's morning now, Harvey," the man complained. "I can't draw breath in here. This fellow spent the night puking on the floor, and I got me a sensitive nose."

Harvey sniffed the air, then turned and spat on the stones.

"Augh," he said, and unlocked Brenner's cell door. The man stumbled through the opening, and Harvey gave him a shove in the direction of the outer office. "Get out of here. Tate's fed up with you, and so am I."

"I won't set foot in here again if you can't keep the place clean," the man muttered as he disappeared.

Harvey approached James's cell, face twisted in disgust.

"You'd better get that stinking vomit cleaned up, boy. Tate'll hit the roof." Then the man stopped and stared at James's bandages. He swore slowly. "You don't need a cell to keep you captive, do you? Danny did a fine job on you, Rebel Boy. You look like one of them mummies they got in a museum back home." Harvey wiped his nose with the back of his hand and swore mildly. "I ain't cleaning up that mess," he continued. "I'll get one of them fine suth-ren belles from over to the hotel to scrub it up, seeing as how one of their own kind made it."

"Much obliged, I'm sure," James growled.

"Yep, them Hilbrands gals think they're so fine. Wait till they come over and smell the stink one of their heroes threw up. That'll be a fine sight to see."

While Harvey cackled at his joke, James lay stiffly on the bunk, his mind thrashing through a bog of fury.

Hilbrands? Ida Hilbrands! He silently swore at the girl. *If she'd kept her heart set upon Carl instead of running after that fancy Dan Englishman, my brother wouldn't have ended up with my girl.*

James gritted his teeth and squinted his eyes. *Ellen! I was learning to love you by following duty, and all the time, Carl was turning your heart away from me.* He swore bitterly at his brother, at Ida, then at himself for being a fool.

Darkness came upon his soul, accompanied by a fiery rage. James turned his face to the wall and refused to eat the breakfast Harvey brought.

∞

"Faugh!"

James's body jumped on the rustling mattress as a sudden booming voice sent echoes around the marshal's office.

"Can't you keep your jail clean, Tate?" the voice continued. "The odor in here would founder a hog."

"It's one of your Southern boys did the deed," the marshal answered in a softer voice. "His stomach turned inside out during the night."

James grimaced, squeezing his hands into fists, although the action caused him such pain that he saw dots of yellow dancing behind his eyelids. "Ma," he groaned aloud. "It's Randolph Hilbrands. Hearing him is worse'n being shot."

"What is he, drunk?" the man asked. "I can't bail out every Southern tippler you lock up."

"I want you to take a look at him. I've an idea you might know the boy."

"Show him to me, then. I haven't got all day."

"Tarnation, tarnation! Double and double again!" James whispered.

"By the way, I need someone to clean up the mess."

"What? Haven't you got Harvey?"

"He's being a sluggard about it. Will you send over one of your girls?" As he spoke, Tate opened the door between the office and the cells and Hilbrands moved into the corridor.

"They're my daughters, man!" he snapped. "I don't throw them in a cell with a stranger to wipe up his puke." He went to the bars and peered in. "How can I tell anything from a man in shadow?"

Tate unlocked the cell, and the two men crossed to the cot. The marshal chuckled. He grabbed James's head with two hands and twisted it to the light. "Take a good look. Do you know him?"

James struggled free of the marshal's grasp, and lay panting on the cot as Hilbrands swore fervently and stroked his thin black moustache.

"This is Rod Owen's boy, James! What's happened to him?"

The marshal chuckled again and nodded. "I thought as much. He acted mighty strange when I mentioned his pa."

"How'd he get hurt?" Hilbrands asked.

"He got mixed up in a little gunfight. Danny O'Brien shot first, three times. Then this boy stopped him with one bullet."

"He always had a keen eye. James, my boy, you lie still. I'll have you out of here in a trice."

"He's done nothing but lie still since this morning. Harvey says he won't take nourishment."

"No matter. Mandy'll have him eating in no time at all. What's his fine?"

"Well now. If you pay for him, he won't have to stand trial. Let's see." Tate ticked off the amounts on his fingers. "Gun brawling, first of all, that's five dollars. Discharging his weapon is another five. Then there's the doctor's bill. That's one dollar. And four to pay Harvey to clean up. That makes fifteen to get the boy out."

Hilbrands took out his wallet and laid the money in the lawman's palm. "You say Danny O'Brien fired three times. I hope you collect your twenty from him before he blows it all on whiskey."

"Now that's what I like, Hilbrands, a man who pays up with a touch of wit. You Southern folk have made a study of humor, I think."

Hilbrands scowled. "I don't know what you're talking about. Now let this boy out of the cell."

James struggled onto his elbow. "Give the man back his money, Mr. Tate. I won't go with him."

"Nonsense, boy. He's your own kind," said the marshal.

"He and his kind are a jinx to me," James replied.

Hilbrands leaned one hand against the wall and stared down at James. "You wound me to the core, my boy. How many years have you known me? I used to give you candy at my store in Mount Jackson."

"You raised a viperous woman on your hearth!"

Hilbrands stepped back and said nothing. He ran one hand slowly down the front of his black broadcloth coat. The fingers came to rest where a slight paunch stretched the fabric.

"What does the boy mean, Hilbrands?" asked Tate.

Hilbrands sighed. "My daughter caused a problem in his house. I reckon his family is slow to forgive."

The marshal pushed open the cell door. "That's a pity, but you've paid your money down. Take him out of here."

"How? Over my shoulder?"

"If you have to. Maybe he'll pass out from pain until you get him to your place."

Hilbrands strode through the doorway and pushed the barred door closed. "I'll be back with a litter, Tate."

⁊

Three men followed Randolph Hilbrands into the cell, two of them carrying a stretcher made of canvas with wooden support poles. "Load him up, men," said Hilbrands. "I haven't got all day."

A tall man with yellow hair put his hands under James's shoulders. James shrugged the man's hands off his body. "I'm not going with you, Randolph Hilbrands."

"Pay no mind, Freddie," Hilbrands said to the man with the yellow hair. "He's hurt and weak—he can't do anything about this." Hilbrands laughed. "First time I ever got me an Owen by paying for him."

"You haven't got this Owen," James declared, struggling to grab hold of the cot as Freddie tried again to lift him.

Hilbrands chuckled. "See? He can't hardly move. Give Freddie a hand, Joshua. I'll hold the litter." Hilbrands took the handles at the foot of the litter from a beefy man dressed in a frock coat. "Hurry. I got a lot to do today."

Joshua bent over to pick up James's feet, and James kicked him a glancing blow to the belly.

The man backed up. "He's pretty strong for a sick man, Hilbrands," he puffed, holding his stomach.

"Grab his legs. Swing him over here. He ain't got any reserves, bunged up as he is."

Freddie and Joshua grabbed what they could hold on to and tried again to move James to the stretcher. He kicked and bucked and doubled up, and they dropped him onto the floor.

James grunted as he hit the granite, and lay still, momentarily stunned.

"Quick, men. Roll him over while the pain's upon him." Hilbrands lowered the litter to the uneven floor, and the man at the other end followed suit. Joshua dragged James's legs out of the muck beside the bed.

"He stinks, Hilbrands," he protested.

"Let me worry about that. He's going to my house, not yours. Get his shoulders, Freddie."

"I'm getting, I'm getting," the man replied, pulling James onto the canvas.

"He's catching his breath, Randolph," warned the third man, who knelt at the head of the stretcher.

"Lift him up, Elias! Freddie, Joshua, get your cord and tie him on." Hilbrands raised his end of the stretcher a few inches off the floor, and Elias followed suit.

Freddie and Joshua pulled short lengths of rope out of their pockets and bound James to the litter. As they tested the knots, James started struggling again, but the restraints were secure, and he finally lay quiet, his chest heaving, watching Hilbrands with narrowed eyes.

"Here, Freddie. Take this end. Let's be on our way." Hilbrands set the handles on the stone floor, and the man took his place at James's feet.

"Together, Elias," Freddie said. "One, two, lift."

As they hoisted James into the air, Hilbrands fingered the bandage on James's side, which was seeping blood. "It don't seem worthwhile to open your wounds again, my boy. Oh, stop your glaring. I'm taking you out of this stinking cell. You could at least be grateful for that."

"It's more welcome than living in the same house with your fickle daughter and her Johnny English husband," James growled.

Hilbrands hooted with laughter. "If that's what troubles you, rest easy, my boy. She's long gone to San Francisco with that jackanapes she married. I will say this: you Owen boys stick together. You're mad enough for you and Carl both."

James closed his eyes and swallowed. His body started to shake. Hilbrands put out a hand and gripped his good shoulder.

"We'll have you cleaned up and in a real bed soon. Come on, let's move him."

Joshua went in front and opened doors. Elias and Freddie carried James out of the cell, through the inner doorway, then across the jail office and out to the sunshine of the street. Several men lounged on a bench in front of the general store next door to the jail. As the procession passed, they sat up and commented on the sight.

James gritted his teeth and glared at Hilbrands. "You could have moved me at night," he hissed.

"No. It couldn't wait. Besides, you would have had a bigger audience after dark. That's when the whole town comes alive."

"Randolph, I swear—"

"Repay me once you're up and about, my boy." The man chuckled, walking along beside the swaying stretcher.

James narrowed his eyes. "That wasn't on my mind. Besides, one quarter won't stretch to cover fifteen dollars."

"You can work off your debt. I've plenty a boy of your talents can do."

"Then you may as well tell your men to trot. The sooner I get shed of these bindings, the sooner you'll have your money's worth."

"Oh no, my boy. You're going to lie flat for some days yet. You've got a powerful lot of mending to do. Doc says Danny shot you up pretty bad. And you struggling back there didn't help any."

James growled something deep in his throat.

Hilbrands laughed again. "Fretting won't help, James, my boy. Maybe you think you've got better things to do than stay abed with a houseful of pretty girls to wait on you, hand and foot. But I tell you, that's a sight more comfy than laying on a hard cot in a stinking jail cell waiting for the judge to sentence you to more time doing the same."

"I prefer it to being in your debt."

"Watch the steps, Freddie. Sorry if you feel a mite inconvenienced, James. We're here."

Joshua held open the hotel door and Elias and Freddie carried the litter into the lobby. James looked around at what Hilbrands had wrought since buying the place a year ago. The lobby was furnished with hand sawn log chairs and settees covered with cowhide, and since the last time James had seen the hotel, one corner of the open area had been stripped of furniture to allow room for the mercantile goods that the man had brought across the continent in a freight wagon.

"Mandy!" Hilbrands called out. "We're back." He turned to James. "My wife is fixing up a room for you on this floor. It's not big, but it'll be more handy for the girls when they tend you."

"I'm not an invalid," James snarled.

"Faugh," Hilbrands barked. "That's not what the doctor said. You're going to bed, my boy!"

Chapter 5

At her husband's call, Amanda Hilbrands swept into the hotel lobby from the back corridor, wiping her hands on the full white apron that covered the front of her gray dress. She patted her tumbling blonde curls back into place at the top of her head, then came and looked down at James with a smile playing about her strong, wide mouth.

"James Owen, your ma will have your hide for getting into a gun fight."

James stiffened, his shoulders pressing back onto the stretcher. "Good afternoon, Mrs. H. I'm hoping you won't tell her."

She laughed. "You Owen boys always were fools for getting into scrapes. I am just glad Mr. Hilbrands is here to bail you out." She straightened up and motioned toward the back of the hotel. "The room is ready now, if you men will carry him in. Put the litter on the bed and loose his bonds, and I will be there in a few minutes." Freddie and Elias carried James into the corridor as Amanda stopped her husband from going into the office with a hand on his forearm. "Mr. Hilbrands, a word with you, please."

The man looked down at her, a faint frown creasing his cheeks. Amanda took a deep breath. "The water is hot in the tub, Randolph. You must hurry him into it before it cools. He dearly needs that bath, but be careful. The boy looks peaked as a new birthed colt."

Hilbrands stroked his moustache. "You'll have to manage it, Mandy. I have the shipment to the mines to take care of. You know I put it off to get the boy out of that stink hole of a jail."

She stood silent, her shoulders stiff. "Dear Lord! You expect me to bathe the boy!"

Hilbrands grunted, then said, "Don't be foolish. Pretend he's the son we buried in a hand basket."

Amanda's eyes closed and she saw the tiny, two-months-from-perfect body wrapped in a blue woolen blanket against the elements. Three days were all the time she had had with the baby, three short days to hold him as he struggled to breath with seven month old lungs. *I will mourn him forever. Julia Owen is blessed, with sons on every hand, growing tall and straight.* She blinked open her eyes, remembering James.

"He is a grown man, Randolph!"

"Then pretend he's our son, all grown up." He shrugged his shoulders and took a step into the office. "You'd tend him without a second thought if he was our son."

She shook off the image of her lost child's carefully tended grave in the apple orchard behind her Virginia home. *Yes, I would do that.* She breathed deeply. *I shall see no evil in doing a good deed.* She straightened her shoulders. "I have one question. Why is James traveling? I thought he and the Bates girl were getting married soon."

Hilbrands' black eyebrows arched upward. "He's powerfully angry about something, but he didn't confide in me. Give him time to tell us what's happening."

"From what you have said, he will have plenty of time as he heals." Amanda turned and hurried down the corridor toward the back room, hesitating only a second before opening the door and entering the room.

"Thank you, men. I will take charge of the boy now." She hustled them to the door and closed it, then leaned on the smooth wood for a moment, looking at James, willing herself to imagine that he was her son.

Lord God, why did you leave me five daughters and take my only son? Three of those girls need husbands. Where can I find good men in this uncouth place? If only this boy was not spoken for . . ..

James lay on the litter, his face white. The bandage at his side was dark red from absorbed blood. *He will bleed to death if I do not tend him now.* Amanda sighed, then pushed herself away from the door and went to stand beside the young man lying on the bed.

"There is a tub beyond the bed, James," she said. "If you are not strong enough to get into it, I will give you a sponge bath."

"Oh no, ma'am. I can manage."

"That is good. Let us remove the bandage and free your left arm." Amanda helped him to a sitting position, then unwound the bloody cloth above the wound, clucking at the crusted gash in his side as she gently uncovered it. "Oh, my dear boy! Are you in pain?"

"No."

She looked at him, sitting rigidly on the bed, trying to smile, and decided he was lying to spare her. "A hot bath will clean away much of the blood and any putrefaction. Then I will see what is to be done," said Amanda. Her fingers went to examine his arm. "Can you move your hand?"

James tried. "The muscles are stiff," he said, but slowly opened the hand, then closed it again.

Amanda saw that the skin had grown closed over the spot where the bullet had entered James's arm, but the skin around the hole where it had exited—although clean—still gaped open.

"It is not too bad, after all. When you have finished with your bath, I will stitch the flaps closed."

James drew in a sharp breath.

"Yes, it will hurt, but it is necessary if you would use your arm soon. Now I will remove your boots and stockings."

James moved slightly as though he would pull off the boots himself. "I do not think you should double up with that wound bleeding so much, young man." Amanda bent over and soon had the footgear on the floor. "However, I will let you remove your own trousers."

"I—"

"What is it?"

James looked away. "I'm not wearing underclothes, ma'am."

Amanda fought the feeling of blood rushing to her cheeks, knowing the boy could see her embarrassment if he turned his head. "I see." She stood up, gently pulling at his good arm. "Get up, James, and I will walk you to the tub. Lean on me. 'Twill make the going easier for you."

James eased his feet off the edge of the bed and stood on unsteady legs, and they slowly crossed the short distance separating the bed from the bath. "Now I will turn my back while you undress and get into the water," Amanda said, carrying out the actions. "Can you manage it?" A moment later a splash answered her, and she bit her lip and turned to see if he had fallen.

James sat—face blanched as white as his shoulders—in the upright copper tub, clutching the rolled rim with both hands.

"There, now. Will you be all right alone for a few minutes?" At his nod, she picked up his pants and the soiled bandages and wrapped them up in the litter. "I will return in a few minutes. Mind you, I will want to check behind your ears."

Amanda swept around the bed and toward the door, and heard James expel a long, shuddering breath.

ଜ

James slid as far as he could beneath the water as Mrs. Hilbrands left the room. "Six little beans!" he exclaimed, and let his arms float on the water, then sink to his sides. "That woman is near as strong willed as Ma!"

For a moment he sat quietly, letting the heat of the water soothe him as it lapped gently against his chest. Then he tilted back his head and splashed a handful of water across his neck and chin. The movement brought sharp flashes of pain from his side, and he sat still for a while.

Finally the pain subsided, and he bent forward, cupped his hands, and wet his head. Rivulets of water ran through his black hair and the stubble on his cheeks, then onto his back and chest. At his right side the liquid began to take on a reddish tinge as blood seeped from the wound, hanging suspended in twisting tendrils before blending with the water.

A bar of soap lay on a wooden rack that hung at the front of the tub, and beside it lay a washrag. James thrust one hand out of the water to get the soap, and an outflow of blood deepened the color of the water. He hastened to return his arm to his side, and the soap slipped from his hand. Beads of sweat stood on his forehead.

"Whew!" He expelled a lungful of air, and wondered how long he'd have to put up with the pain and the weakness. "I got to pay off that debt," he muttered, craning his head to get a look at the gash.

"Tarnation," he said, gingerly prodding the white, swollen flesh around the oozing wound with his fingertips. Beside the swelling he walked his fingers across the sunken area where the doctor had removed his shattered rib. The opening bled still.

"I reckon Mrs. H. better take a stitch down there," he grumbled, then gently fished the soap from the bottom of the tub, took up the rag, and started to scrub.

ଜ

Amanda returned to the room, bearing a large Turkish towel, a bottle of whiskey, and a sewing kit. She placed the items on the bed as she came around it to the tub.

"Have you finished?" she asked.

"Yes, ma'am," James said, looking at his fingertips. "I reckon I'm becoming a prune, too."

"I will turn my back while you climb out of the tub. Here is the towel. Wrap it around you and sit on the bed. I want to stitch that arm before you rest."

Amanda moved away with her back to the tub, and picked up a glass tumbler that was sitting on the washstand. James held the towel in one hand as he rose unsteadily to his feet and climbed out, trying to envelop himself in the fleecy folds. Hampered by the weakness in his left arm, he finally got the towel wrapped about his hips and sat on the edge of the gray coverlet.

"I'm ready, Mrs. H. While you're at it, I reckon you'd best put a bit of thread into my side. I don't hanker after the pain, but I'm not willing to bleed to death, neither, and this hole keeps seeping like a broken ragweed stem."

Amanda turned, came around the bed to look at the clean wound, and bit her lip so hard that warm, salty blood flooded the space between her lip and her teeth. "I cannot imagine why the doctor did not do that job in the first place," she exclaimed. "The fellow is not competent, James. I do not want him to treat you ever again." She threaded a large needle with a double strand of heavy thread.

James took a full breath and averted his eyes. "Don't worry. He doesn't want to treat me, neither, since I couldn't pay his bill."

"The man thinks of nothing but his fee!" Amanda tipped some whiskey into the tumbler and offered it to James.

He made a face and drank it down. "No. He got the lead out of me without asking first was I rich enough to pay. I'll give him credit for that." He looked around for a place to put the tumbler, then set it on the coverlet.

"He is an insufferable drunk. Now, please sit sideways," Amanda requested, sat behind him on the bed, and took a stitch in the meat of his arm.

"Ah!" he gasped. "That smarts, ma'am."

"Bite this," she commanded, grabbing the washrag and thrusting it between his teeth.

He spit out the cloth. "Tastes of lye soap," he said.

"Nevertheless, James, it will help the pain until the alcohol has taken effect."

He sighed, and accepted the rag. Amanda glanced at his twitching face as she stitched as quickly as she could. She knew he was fighting to stay conscious.

"You will need to lie down for me to work on the wound in your side," she said as she snipped the thread behind his arm. "I do not imagine you can bear the pain, even with the spirits, and I will not have you falling on the floor."

Half a grin moved James's mouth. "Tarnation!" he exclaimed.

"What is it?"

"Too many spots," he replied, levering himself down to the coverlet and tightening his gut against the gouge of the needle.

Amanda took several hesitant stitches—pulling the thread through the flesh as rapidly as she dared—before James's body relaxed in unconsciousness. Then she took her time to finish the job properly, fighting the rise of bile in her throat. After she tied off the thread, she went to the washstand, opened a drawer, and brought out several rolls of white bandage material.

"My poor boy," she murmured as she approached the bed. "What pain you must be suffering." She removed the cloth from his mouth and threw it into the tub. James didn't move, neither at the sound of the splash, nor while Amanda bandaged his arm. With shaking hands, she rolled him from side to side to bind the cloth around his chest.

Before she gathered up her things, Amanda pulled the coverlet loose from the far side of the bed and threw it over James's recumbent form. Then she gave the young man a pat on the shoulder, and hurried from the room.

ဢ

"Mister James, Mister James, wake up, please? You must be hungry."

Surprised to hear his name, James rolled over, grinning at the soothing touch of the water on his naked body, and swam upward from exploring the bottom of the pond behind the flour mill on a creek feeding the Shenandoah River. He tried to shrug off the hand that gently touched his right shoulder, but the movement brought such a flood of pain to his side that he moaned before he could catch himself.

"Please, Mister James. Ma said I wasn't to come back to the kitchen without feeding you. If you don't wake up soon, your food'll be stone cold."

He thrust his head and shoulders above the water, opened one eye, then immediately shut it against the sunlight that streamed through an open window between muslin drapes and hit his face. His body felt bloated, invaded by aches and twitches. And although he was still naked, he seemed to be lying half covered by a sheet and quilt on a bed inside a room, instead of treading water in the millpond.

Someone besides himself was in the room. "Six little beans!" he grunted, trying to shade his eyes with his left hand, remembering that a girl's voice had addressed him. "It's brighter than noon day in here. Can you shut them curtains?"

A young girl put the tray of food on the washstand and ran to the window to pull the drapes together. She returned to stand beside the bed, and James blinked his eyes as she drew near.

The girl was about fifteen, he judged, slender and blonde. She wore a white bib apron with a full skirt over a light weight gingham gown patterned with sprigs of lilacs on a white background. Her wavy hair hung below her shoulders, tied back with a white ribbon. The girl smiled, tentatively, and one dimple appeared in her cheek.

"Who're you?" he asked, wondering how he came to be between the sheets. The last thing he remembered, he had been lying atop the coverlet, enduring the sting of a thousand hornets as Amanda Hilbrands' needle pierced the flesh of his side. Now he looked around. The tub was gone from the room, and the towel had disappeared from around his hips. James blinked twice, and reached down to draw the sheet over his chest, grateful that the quilt masked his nakedness from the girl.

"I'm Sylvia. My pa runs the hotel. Don't you recall he brought you here?"

James shut his eyes for a moment, less to remember his arrival than to recall where he had heard the girl's voice before. He gave his head a shake, then opened his eyes.

"Yeah," he sighed, a long drawn out sound, and fingered the bandage around his chest. "Your ma put this thread into me a couple of hours ago."

"That was two days back!" the girl exclaimed. "You've been asleep since then."

"Six little beans! Did I take a fever?" James got himself onto his elbows, and the girl bent forward to put a pillow behind his back so he could sit partway up. As the sheet slipped and gathered in creases about his waist, the girl's hair brushed his shoulder.

The blonde hair—he could see it on another head, arranged in tumbling ringlets behind a face twisted with fury. A voice—with the same timbre as this girl's voice—batted at his ears: "You never came around, Carl Owen. Cecil was here. I have a right to marry a man I can trust!"

James shuddered.

"No." A frown furrowed Sylvia's forehead. "I reckon you're just wore out. You been through a lot of woe since you came to Pueblo City." She turned away to bring the food tray, then sat gingerly on the edge of the bed with the tray on her lap. "This is a good room, though. Pa let Ida use it for her wedding night."

A wrenching pain invaded James's gut. Ida Hilbrands had breathed this air, her body had lain on this bed. The body that should have quieted Carl's lusts was given to an English dandy—on this bed, beneath this quilt. James swallowed. His throat closed on cotton.

The girl touched his wrist. James's arm twitched under the cool fingers.

"Are you all right, Mister James?"

He cleared his throat. "You sound like your . . . older sister."

"You mean Mary?" The girl's face brightened. "How is her little baby doing? We all want to see her." Sylvia picked up a spoon and a bowl and stirred the contents.

James eased the sheet up to cover his chest. "The little gal's growing, but no, I wasn't speaking of Mary." The sheet bunched in his lap again, and James jerked it upward and pinned it underneath his arm.

"Oh. You mean—"

"Ida! I mean Ida." His voice rasped in his throat as he said the name.

The girl looked puzzled. "Are you angry with Ida?"

James felt his face settling into ridges as he scowled. Angry? The word was wrong. Wrong and far too weak. *I hate her. I despise her wide blue eyes and her lying, cheating heart.* He cleared his throat again. "I have reason." His breath left his lungs in a lengthy shudder.

Sylvia looked at him for a moment, puzzlement crinkling the skin around her eyes. Then she picked up a spoon.

"Here, have a taste of porridge. Ma made it fresh for you today." Sylvia held the spoon to James's lips, and he accepted the morsel. "What did Ida do to you? I thought it was Carl she threw over."

For a moment, he could only chew, then swallow. He sensed no taste, no savor. Before he had a chance to speak, Sylvia put another spoonful of mush into his mouth. He swallowed that down, then, as Sylvia brought up another bite, James shook his head.

They'll know sooner or later. Pa will come in for supplies, or Ma will send a note to Mrs. H. by a passing stranger. He turned his head to look at the doorway. *Will I be gone, first? Or will Danny O'Brien shoot me in the back?* He looked at the girl and squeezed his hands into fists. The pain forced his mouth open.

"You didn't hear, I reckon. Carl got over being mad at Ida. He wed Ellen Bates about a week past."

"Oh, Mister James! She was pledged to you!" Sylvia dropped the spoon into the bowl, and it clanked against the side.

Instantly, he repented of his burst of words. "Forget I said that. Just forget it!"

"I'm sorry." Sylvia held her hands tightly together in front of her mouth.

James snorted. "It's done and over."

"How could that happen?" The girl moved the tray from her lap to the bed and leaned forward.

Bitterness rose in James's throat, and he turned his head to swallow it down.

Sylvia bounced once on the bed. "Ida caused it. She sure is mean."

James shuddered, slumping against the pillow. "Go away," he said.

"What?"

"Take your gruel and leave me be. I'm weary."

"But you didn't finish."

"Tell your Ma I fell asleep again. It won't be a lie. Look. I'm nodding off now." James shut his eyes.

He heard her get to her feet and pick up the tray. "I reckon I tired you out, talking so much."

"It's not you. I'm wore out, like you said." James twitched the quilt higher on his chest. Suddenly he bolted upright, winced, then lay down again. "You'd better get your papa, girl. I got to put myself deeper in his debt."

🙰

James sat up, craning his neck toward the doorway when Hilbrands sauntered into the room.

"It's good to see you awake, my boy," the man said, his voice booming in the small room. "Mandy was mighty concerned that you slept so long."

"Tarnation, Randolph, I'm not on my deathbed. I'm sorry Mrs. H. took a notion to worry, but I'm almost ready to get up."

The man chuckled. "You were so dead to the world a day or so ago, I wondered if it was worth the effort to tuck you in. Take your time and heal up right, my boy." Hilbrands sat on the bed. "What do you want me for?"

James shifted his weight. "It rankles me to put you to further trouble, but I got a horse and mule boarding over at the livery stable, eating grain I haven't got cash to pay for. My saddles are taking up space in the tack room, to boot. I also brung a war bag and a pistol I ain't seen since the Irishman shot holes in me. I'd take it kindly if you would see to my animals and bring me my gear."

Hilbrands laughed. "Seen to and done, my boy. That's your bag tucked into the corner, and your animals are eating my hay out back."

James made a fist and thumped it against the coverlet over his thigh. "When you kidnap a man, you do a thorough job of work," he said, sighing.

"That I do. I figure once you're up and about, you will owe me a couple of weeks' worth of labor, my boy." He laughed again. "That is, if we can keep you out of harm's way. Danny O'Brien's friends have been boasting about how they'll turn your hide into a sieve the day you walk out the door. But that's mostly talk, my boy, big talk and mighty little action. After all, them's the same brave ruffians that shot up the jail in the dark of night."

Hilbrands got up and stepped toward the doorway, passed through it and pulled the door almost closed behind him. Then he poked his head back into the room to grin at James. "I've got guards posted upstairs, my boy. I'm not going to let them shoot a man I don't have to pay."

"I'll be up, work off those two weeks, then be gone before you can wipe your mouth, Randolph Hilbrands," James declared, glowering from the bed at the departing man.

ဢ

Two nights later, James asked Sylvia to bring him underclothes from his war bag. He awoke before first light the next morning to struggle into the garments by himself, then lay on the bed, breathing hard, until the pain from his side abated enough that he could sit upright. He rested on the edge of the bed, gathering strength and courage to rise and walk to the window.

He lurched to his feet, arms outstretched as much as he could lift them to balance himself, and took one step away from the bed. His legs quaked and shivered, but he forced a foot to shuffle forward for another step. Then his knees buckled, and he grabbed for the washstand to break his fall. Sylvia came running to pick him out of the shattered remnants of the washbasin he pulled down. Every morning and afternoon from that time on, the girl insisted on standing beside James, with his arm over her shoulders as he took halting steps across the room.

After several days, he no longer needed assistance, and when Sylvia came to his quarters to help him take his afternoon stroll about the room, she found James dressed and booted, with his gun belt buckled about his hips, looking for his hat.

"Land of Goshen! Where do you think you're bound, Mister James?" she demanded.

"Where did you put my hat, Miss Sylvia?"

"It's in the cupboard on the high shelf. Where're you going?"

James went to the armoire, retrieved his hat, and jammed it on his head. "It's time I worked off the debt to your pa. I've had enough of lying around in bed."

"But your side isn't healed!"

For answer, he stretched his arms above his head, without wincing. "I told myself when I could do that, I was ready to work. Move away from the door, Miss Sylvia."

The girl stood with her arms spread in front of the portal. "I'll get my mother. She'll make you stay put."

James shook his head.

"Pa will make you."

"He'll welcome the help." He bent to take her by the arms and put her aside, but she evaded his grasp by stepping closer to him. James retreated backward, arms flung wide, until his knees buckled as they hit the bed. He sprawled back, clutching at Sylvia in a vain attempt to balance.

"Oof," he gasped as the girl fell atop him.

She scrambled up and stood glaring down at James. "You're going to get yourself shot by those horrid men!"

"Tar nation!" he grumbled, panting. "Don't you think I know that? They won't expect me to be up and around so soon. Now get out of my way, Miss. I've wasted enough time." James got to his feet.

Sylvia put out her hands and shoved James hard in the belly. He doubled up and fell once more on the bed, twisted as he fell, and caught his spurs in the quilt. The girl cried out, "I worked my hands to the bone helping you mend, and now you want to get up and get shot again by those bullies. Get back in that bed, James Owen. I'm not through with you!"

He looked up, gasping for a breath. "Miss Sylvia . . . you're a caution. I own you been . . . almighty kind. But that don't give you . . . the right to boss me around."

The girl was looking round eyed at him. "Pa said different. Pa said he would arrange things for me."

"What're you talking about?" Now that he had caught some air, he sat up, trying to get his spurs clear of the coverlet. "What did your pa tell you?"

"He said he would fix it so you'd stay on. He said . . ." She caught her breath in a gasp, her face blushed pink, and she stood still for a moment, as though frozen. "Oh, never mind," she blurted out, then whirled about and ran from the room. James struggled once more to his feet.

"Hush, that girl acts like she owns me," he complained out loud, and followed her through the door.

℅

"Well, you look fit, James. Must be that good food Sylvia hand fed you, heh? Except for your faded color, I'd say you was just in from off the range." Hilbrands chuckled as he sat back in the leather chair he shoved away from a roll top desk in the hotel office. "Sit down. Are you ready to work?"

James wondered if his face looked as taut as it felt. He perched on a chair made of peeled saplings. "I'm ready," he answered. "The sooner I work off this debt, the sooner I can get shed of this place."

"As you say." Hilbrands chuckled, leaned back in his chair and put his feet up on the desk. "Now, I've got contracts to deliver dry goods, explosives and machine parts, when they come in, to several mines in the area," he said. "I also order all the goods, so I've really got two hands in the pie."

"But what do you want me to do?"

"I've built up a stable of mules to haul my big freight wagon up to the mines, and I need someone to take care of them. Up to now, I been doing all the driving and all the handling and swamping myself, my boy, and I can't attend to business when I'm out back or up in the hills."

"Hard work never hurt a man."

"I know that, my boy, but I can't expand the business if I don't have time to do the paper work. I want you to take on the stable for a week or so, until you get strength enough to do the hauling. I'll get a boy for the swamping once you start driving."

"Suits me." James stood to go. "'Til my time is up."

"Fine. Fine. The stable is right out the back door, across the alley." Hilbrands' feet came down to hit the floor with a thud. "Just one more thing, my boy."

"What is it?"

"Sylvia came rushing out of your room a while ago, crying like she was mighty upset by something. You haven't been trifling with her, have you?"

James looked hard at the man, squinting his eyes. He took a deep breath, and knew why he'd never much liked Randolph Hilbrands. "I'm not the sort that takes a woman's favors where they ain't offered. On the other hand, I don't sell myself cheap, either."

Hilbrands bounded to his feet. "What kind of answer is that?"

"You bailed me out of jail against my will and named a fair price for your good deed. I owe you two weeks of work. That's all. Nothing beyond that. Surely not my future."

The man's slack face scrunched up as he took a step forward, and James wondered if he was angry, but even if he was, it didn't matter. All that mattered was paying off the debt and leaving Pueblo City in one piece. James drew himself up to his full height.

Hilbrands stopped and glared at James. "Then get to it," he sputtered, his face brick red.

James obliged the man by turning away and stalking out of the room and down the corridor to the back door.

Chapter 6

By the time three o'clock rolled around, James thought evening would never come. Although he felt stiff and sore, he stuck to his job, cleaning out the stalls, shoveling manure into a pile behind the stable, and rubbing down the mules when Randolph drove them back from the day's short haul. When the supper bell finally rang out from the kitchen, James looked up, wiped his sleeve across his dripping face, and hung the scoop shovel in its place against the wall.

After a cautious glance around the alley, he washed at a bench behind the kitchen where a bar of yellow soap lay in a pool of suds beside a basin of gray water. A towel, gray as the water, was nailed above the basin. James shook the water off his hands and arms and hoped his face would pass Amanda's inspection without washing it. Then he stepped into the back hallway and went toward the hotel lobby.

As he came past the desk, James paused, his hand near the grip of his pistol, and glanced into the room at his right. He remembered it as a bar, and a bar it remained, full of silent men and clinking glass. No one looked in his direction as he passed the door, and he figured Danny's cronies would not be drinking in Randolph Hilbrands' bar.

The dining room lay beyond a closed door to the left. Through the barrier he heard a man suddenly laugh and a woman join in. James pushed open the door and looked for a place to sit at the trestle tables fronted by benches and the occasional chair. Near the entrance was an empty table. James walked to it and sat on a bench with his back to the kitchen.

Unbidden, the vision came: Ellen, light in his arms and his heart as he and she danced in the furniture free dining room, her shy smile and half veiled eyes masking emotion. Ida Hilbrands' scream. Pa tapping his shoulder and waving to him to follow. Then he and Pa grabbing Carl's arms before he could knock Cecil Gilbert flat. Hauling Carl kicking and struggling out of the dance and into the hotel lobby.

That was the night Ida broke her engagement to Carl to marry that English fellow. The night Carl played on Ellen's sympathy to lure her from her rightful place. *The night I lost everything that means anything to a man.* Bitter gall rose in James's throat, and he shoved himself to his feet and fled to his room, chased all the way down the hall by memories.

ೕ

Determined to survive any further trouble with Danny, James buckled on his heavy gun belt every morning and lay the big Colt close to his hand each night. But he wasn't looking for a fight. He kept to the shadows in the mule shed as he shoveled manure and pitched new straw down from the loft. Grooming each mule kept him behind the partitions that formed the stalls. His life revolved around the hotel and the stables, and when he set foot between them, it was only after he had looked down the alley both ways and figured the way was safe.

But irritation grew in him like a desert cat claw vine, rubbing at the scabs on his wounded sense of manhood. He couldn't shake off a feeling that he was being guarded.

One noon he stalked into Hilbrands' office. The hotel owner looked up from his paper work.

"What is it, my boy?"

"Pull off your guards, Randolph. It's penny wise and pound foolish to pay men to keep watch over me." He drew the pistol from his holster and held it in both palms. "See this? I can care for my own self." James returned the revolver to its place.

"My boy! I don't know what you—"

"You told me you had guards posted, Randolph. That was fine when I was abed, but I'm up now. Pay off the men and send them home."

Hilbrands worked his mouth, then stood up and laid his hand on James's shoulder. "My boy, I feel duty bound to see that no harm comes to you. Why, if you got hurt any more, or—perish the thought—got killed, your pa would be up here in a minute to put a bullet through my brain."

James shrugged off the hand. "He doesn't know I'm here. If he did know, he would expect me to look out for myself. Tarnation, Rand, I was in the war! As I recall, you stayed home."

Hilbrands' face grew red. "I had a store, daughters to tend to—"

"I'm not judging you, man. I'm stating a fact. Now, call off your guardian angels. If Danny or his friends want a piece of my hide, it's my duty to deny them the pleasure."

James turned on his heel and walked out the door. He paused at the doorway leading outside and looked into the yard. Everything seemed normal. Then he strode toward the stables.

As he entered the dimness of the interior, James stepped to one side of the door and stopped, hand on his pistol butt. This was the time for an attack, while his eyes were adjusting to the half light, so he listened. The scuffling sound he heard sent him into a dive behind a stall partition, trying to draw the revolver as he went down. He fell hard on his left shoulder, landing on scar tissue from a bayonet wound he'd received during the war. He swore softly, rolling to a crouch with his pistol in his hand.

James blinked several times to free his eyes of fragments of straw, but remained otherwise motionless, trying to locate the source of the danger. There was no sound but the pounding of his heart in his ears for long moments, then, the shuffling noise he had first heard came again from the other side of the shed.

From the darkness beyond the door, through the rectangular light, and into the darkness again, scurried a large rat. James holstered his revolver and wiped sweat from his eyes. He got to his feet and started toward where the hayfork hung on the wall.

James heard the report of the pistol at the same moment a lead ball whizzed past his right ear. He hit the straw covered floor again. James rolled to his left, toward the protection of the nearest stall. The shot had come from the direction of the shuttered window near the back of the shed, close to where the harnesses were draped to dry on pegs, looking like so many brown spider webs in the dim light.

Ma, they're at it again. Can't a man pay his debt and leave a place still in one piece? With his revolver in his hand, James waited for what would come next—another shot, a rush of men, or the marshal, Tate. As he waited, a bead of sweat ran out from under his hat, down his temple, and into his beard. His side and shoulder throbbed with pain. *Six little beans! Why'd I ever stop in Pueblo Town?*

No shot came, and James slipped out of the stall and rushed to the doorway. He glanced into the alley. No one was in sight, so he slid through the door and made his way to the back corner of the shed.

Holding his breath, James craned his neck around the corner. One man stood there with a revolver pressed to a crack in the shutter and one eye up to a knothole in the wood. Two steps, and James was behind him. The man reacted to the slight noise of his coming by whispering, "That you, Li—"

James laid the pistol barrel un-gently alongside the man's head and caught his body as he crumpled.

No. It's me, James Owen, and I'm tired of dodging lead for no good reason, he thought as he holstered his gun and laid the limp body on the straw covered dirt. *Tarnation. This can wear a man down.*

As he stretched out the man's tangled limbs, he glanced at the face, but it was no one he'd ever seen before. "One of Danny O'Brien's bunch, I reckon," he muttered.

"I'm another. Rise up and stand still," said a voice close behind James, a voice that was accompanied by an urgent pressure against the small of his back. "I've got me knife ready, man. Don't make a false move, now," the voice continued.

James, back stiff, arms held extended, rose slowly. "Who are you? What is it you want?" He felt a hand slip his revolver from the holster.

"Justice, no more," said the voice.

James half turned.

"No, man! Stand still!" The voice shook, and James recognized it.

"You're Liam Connolly. You were at the saloon," James said. He sighed. "Mr. Connolly, you struck me as one having a voice of reason. I reckon such a man would rather use his knife face to face than stab a man in the back." He waited. He could hear the man's harsh breathing. It seemed to slow, become less ragged. "I'm going to turn around. Then if you can look me in the eye and speak of justice as you spill my blood, so be it."

James turned, slowly, carefully. He took a quick look at the man with the knife. Liam's hair stood out in black, tufted spikes around his blanched face. He clutched the knife in a hand held close to his own body; James's gun dangled from the other hand.

"Can you kill me now, man?" James whispered.

"No! I canna kill ye. Danny said— He said it would be easy to knife you and rid the earth of Rebel vermin."

"Is it easy? Can you kill a man who has no weapon?"

Liam's face fell. "I canna do it. Ye didna cause Danny's troubles." He looked up again. "Truth to tell, he was cruel to Rosie. She couldna take the abuse."

"And now he's passing it along for you to give out? Leave me be, Mr. Connolly. I'll be out of town inside of two weeks."

The man lowered his knife and came out of his guarded position. "Is that the truth? Ye'll go?"

"I'm only here because I owe Mr. Hilbrands two weeks work. Once I have the debt paid, there's nothing to keep me in Pueblo."

"No ties in the town?"

"I was headed north when your friend stopped me."

"Danny ever was a hothead. But now he's lying abed, healing from that wound you gave him, half potted most of the hours of the day. From the looks of him, he plans to stay there as long as he can get us to bring him drink. Here." He laid the pistol on the ground. "Ye have two weeks, no more. If ye're still here thereafter, I'll not answer for Danny's actions."

"That's fair enough."

"Turn around, now, and count to one hundred."

James complied, and while he stood looking away, Liam left, dragging his companion with him.

James figured he'd learned more about mules than he cared to know before the week was out. But he kept working, feeling strength return to his muscles day by day, and near the end of his two weeks' service, Hilbrands stalked out to the stable and hailed him.

"You drive tomorrow, my boy. Think you can handle the team?"

James looked down from the stool on which he perched, hanging a harness on pegs driven into the board wall of the building.

"I been handling 'em for some time, now. Yeah, I can drive 'em, too."

"That's good. You're going up to Cañon City. There's a bunch of mines up there waiting for supplies."

"Is this a regular run or a special?"

"Regular. Once a week. Come over to the office when you're through here, and I'll show you the bills of lading." Hilbrands stepped toward the door of the stable, then turned again to speak to James. "Better yet, I'll go with you on the wagon. I don't want you to lose your way."

James jumped off the stool and walked toward the first stall. "I'm obliged. I've never been up the canyon." He picked up the off rear hoof of the beast in the stall. "Did Silky pull up lame on you today? He came in limping."

"Nah. He stepped on the chain coming up the street. Darn mule does it all the time. He'll be fine tomorrow."

"I'll use Old Cutlip in his place."

"I told you, the mule will mend."

"You made me boss of the stable, Randolph. I'll use Cutlip and let Silky have a day's rest."

"You've a stubborn streak in you, James Owen. It's no wonder you butted heads with your pa."

An icy hand jerked James erect, and he dropped the sore hoof. He let out a rush of breath from his lungs as if he'd been socked in the gut. When he looked up, Hilbrands was eyeing him, but James said nothing.

The man swore softly. "My girl was right. You and Rod did lock horns."

"Yeah." James set his hands astride his hips. "What else did she let slip?"

Hilbrands coughed a bit, worked his mouth, then spat into the straw covering the packed earth floor. "She mentioned Ellen Bates got took to wife by the wrong Owen brother."

The words were like a blow to the chin. James recoiled a step, flinging his arms wide.

Hilbrands looked up. "That's when you 'n Rod tangled?"

James could only nod.

"Rod's a stubborn man, too. Did he throw you out?"

James took in air, held it for a spell, then flushed it out of his lungs. "We agreed I'd best leave." He scuffed the straw with his foot. "Does that mean you're of a mind to fire me?"

"No, no!" Hilbrands looked shocked. "You're here in my employ until you finish the two weeks you owe me."

James grunted, shifting his weight from one leg to the other. He laid his left arm across his chest, then resisted the urge to scratch the healing gash on his side. "I only got one more day, Randolph. I hanker to ride out of this town before I get shot to doll rags again."

Hilbrands sighed. "So you're bound to leave? Can't I offer you something to change your mind?"

"That ain't likely, Randolph. I got a mine tunnel up north to dig out. Weather's turning cold, and I got to raise a grubstake before snow flies."

"You could stay here and work for wages, my boy."

"No, Randolph. My mind's made up. Now, what's for supper?"

Hilbrands scowled, then his face brightened. "Mandy said Sylvia cooked up something special for you." The man winked as he turned away.

"Tarnation!" James said to the man's retreating back.

෨

That evening, James whacked his hat against his thigh before he opened the outside door to the dining room, then he jammed the hat back on his head and left the door undisturbed.

Through the window he saw Sylvia's small figure coming from the kitchen with a tray of food. He stepped backward, wheeled around, and walked down the alley toward the rear of the hotel. Then he stopped and took a long, settling breath.

"Coward," he called himself. "That little girl don't bite as hard as a flea in the blankets. You got your wits. Use them."

He turned and strode back through the alley to the door, grabbed it open, stepped through, pulled the door to, and let out the breath he'd been holding.

James's gut tightened up as he caught sight of the girl, but he got himself over to a table and was reaching for a chair when she hustled over and pulled it out for him.

"Mister James, you look tuckered out tonight. Let me take your hat. You sit right down and rest yourself." The girl put out her hand and James gave her the hat. Sylvia took it and hung it on a peg nearby, then returned and indicated the chair again.

James sat. The girl bustled away to the sideboard and came back with a cup and saucer.

"Here's your coffee, Mister James. Just the way you like it. You rest easy, now, and I'll bring your supper. Ma let me cook it special for you." She beamed at him and touched the blonde curls gathered at the back of her head.

James groaned as she rushed off toward the kitchen. *I got to light a shuck out of here,* he thought, sipping the hot drink. *She's digging in for a siege.*

With the back of his sleeve, he wiped the black moustache he'd been training to droop on either side of his mouth, then turned at the sound of footsteps approaching. Hilbrands spun a chair outward and dropped his fleshy body into it.

"Get to bed early, my boy. We leave at five."

"That suits me."

"Good. Use Cutlip tomorrow, if you'd rather. You have an eye for animals."

James took another sip of his coffee, then let part of his mouth turn up in a grin. "I planned to, Randolph. With or without your say so."

The man rapped his knuckles on the table. "Cheeky young'un, ain't you? You need somebody to put you into double harness, take some of that extra starch out of your veins."

James tipped his chair backward, balancing it on two legs. His grin faded, and his steady stare made Hilbrands squirm in his seat.

"Just a suggestion, you understand. Don't forget to hit the pillow early."

"You can count on that, Randolph."

"Here comes your supper. Eat hearty. The girl worked hard."

"My time's about up."

Hilbrands rose and moved toward the kitchen as Sylvia put a plate on the table. It contained a large slice of boiled buffalo tongue, two boiled potatoes with the jackets on, and a pool of gravy. The girl stood back and looked anxiously at James. He closed his eyes and breathed deeply of the delicate aroma of the tongue.

"Six little beans, girl. How'd you know that was my favorite, next to antelope tongue? I reckon you done yourself proud."

The girl took in a breath, her smile going from tentative to beaming, and headed for the kitchen, calling out, "Ma. Ma, you were right. He likes it!"

Yes, indeed I do. But I ain't staying around, little girl, he thought, cutting a generous bite of the tender meat and bearing it to his mouth. *I won't pay double for Ida's trick.*

Chapter 7

As James got the last mule into harness he looked at the sky. It had changed in color from black to gray since he'd risen and started harnessing the animals. Dawn was coming.

He'd loaded the freight wagon after supper and left it standing overnight in the yard behind the hotel. Now he brought up the team and backed the mules alongside the tongue of the black shadowed wagon. He hooked the doubletree and swing chain into place in front of the axle and gathered the lines, waiting for Randolph Hilbrands to come out the back door.

The chain clinked as one of the animals shifted position. James looked to see if the beast was straddling the iron links, then stooped between the mules to lift a misplaced hoof. The brown odor of warm mule flesh surrounded him, filling his nose, and he sucked the fragrance deep into his lungs, taking pleasure in the smell and the heat given off by the animals.

Light began to work its way into the sky on the prairie side of town. First the gray turned to a peach like glow, then red streaks shot up toward heaven, lighting up the cloud or two that floated on the high up breeze. James leaned back with his elbows propped against the side of the wagon and watched the free show. He couldn't help feeling good with such a glory of a morning shaping up. He pushed aside a sudden pang when he thought how much the sunrise reminded him of Ellen's bright hair, and set his mind to enjoy the upcoming trip.

Hilbrands ambled through the rear door opening with a "Good morning to you, my boy," and climbed into the wagon, stowing a brown paper wrapped parcel and a lunch tin underneath the seat before he sat down.

"Sylvia made a meal for us, my boy. She was up cooking breakfast at three. Insisted on doing it herself."

A shiver ran down James's back under his coat, and he wondered why he felt like somebody just stepped on his grave. Something about the hearty way Hilbrands spoke set the hair to rising on the back of his neck. James shook off the sensation, climbed to the right hand seat, and sorted out the leather ribbons as he seated himself. Then he released the brake and picked up the coiled whip from the wagon seat.

"Ready?"

"Let's go, my boy."

James cracked the whip popper over the ears of the lead team, shouting "Come up there, mules!" and the six animals leaned into their collars. The chain behind the leaders' doubletree snapped taut against its mooring at the axle, and the point and wheel teams pulled the wagon into slow motion, creaking as it began to roll.

The mules hauled the wagon out of the opening to the yard of the hotel and down the alley, where James swung the animals wide at the corner where the alley met the side street. They turned into the main road, and the wagon straightened out for the trip up river to the mining district around Cañon City.

Once they were on the road outside of Pueblo, James looked sideways at Hilbrands. The man's thin black moustache had been freshly trimmed, and one or two small red spots on his throat showed his hurry in shaving this morning. James tweaked his mouth to one side as he faced front again, ashamed of the unkempt condition of the heavy black beard that covered his jaw.

You're not a town boy, James, he reminded himself. *He was born and bred a storekeeper, and he looks it. Mule tails, Randolph Hilbrands has his own style. That don't make it wrong for me to wear a full beard.*

James drove the mules around a curve in the road, taking heed that the point and wheel teams stepped over the chain as it moved into their path. Once they'd made the turn without tangling up, he sat easy on the seat again.

"Good mules, Randolph," he commented, breaking the silence between the men.

"Best in the Territory." The man squinched up his face, then looked over the rolling ground through which they traveled. His voice came slowly. "My boy, I feel real bad about the trouble Ida caused you, throwing over Carl, then him wedding Miss Ellen, and all. I owe you a debt of honor."

James lurched on the seat at the man's words. "No! There's no sense talking like that. What's done is done, and you can't change it." His voice was a file rasping against iron.

"I know that, but maybe I can offer something to make up—"

"I said no! It's best forgot." James wished the man would stop bringing up the subject of Ellen. His enjoyment of the bright morning was slipping down a garbage hole.

"What about Sylvia?"

"What do you mean?"

"I know she's a mite young, but I reckon she's a real nice looking gal, and she takes after her ma in the cooking department."

James half rose on the wagon seat, then sank back, swallowing hard to contain his breakfast. He breathed in great, ragged gulps for a time, then took up the whip and popped it to cover his discomfort. Hilbrands sat quietly, staring into the distance at the canyon walls rising ahead, lit by the sun burning level over the prairie.

Sometime later, Hilbrands turned his face toward James, creases pulling his mouth down. "I spoke out of turn. I hope you bear no ill will."

James compressed his lips, then pushed out a breath between them. "Not toward you, no."

"I reckon the thought of another girl is out of the question right now?"

James gave no answer, and Hilbrands looked away.

The horizon drew up close to the wagon as they entered the gorge of the river. James cracked the whip over the leaders' ears, and the mules put their shoulders into the collars, hauling the wagon up the grade. The sun hadn't warmed up the red rock walls yet, and James shivered a bit in the crisp air.

"Plenty of time later." Hilbrands rubbed his cheek.

"What's that?"

"You'll get over this disappointment. A man like you don't want the girls to keep away for long. You stand six feet in your stockings, I'll wager, and look at them thick shoulders and arms you carry."

James silently granted the point that he was full grown and then some through his shoulders, chest and arms, being that he was farm bred, and used to heavy work all his life. But the way Hilbrands talked about his body, as if he were a horse at auction, made James squirm. He clamped his jaw, waiting for Hilbrands to try to open his mouth and inspect his teeth.

"Good muscle there, and a strong back," the man continued, prodding James in the side. "Why, those bullets Danny put in you hardly slowed you up at all. With a shave and a change of clothes you can have your pick of any woman in the Territory."

James took a deep breath, feeling a mad rising up from his toes. He couldn't keep it in, and he exploded.

"For all the little brown beans! I don't want my pick of women. What I want, I can't have, so leave me be!"

Hilbrands backed down, nodding his head like he wanted no part of James's temper, and fisted his hands together in front of him. His knuckles stood out in white peaks above lumpy veins.

After that, the men spoke only when necessary. At mid day they watered and fed the mules, then the two of them sat a couple of yards apart under a clump of oak trees to eat the ham sandwiches and split pea soup Sylvia had packed. Some of the autumn brushed leaves still clung to the high branches above James, and he chewed and spooned and contemplated the leaves, wondering how soon they were likely to fall and go back to the cycle nature intended.

As long as he sat beneath, the leaves clung there, like they hoped to stave off what must be. James wondered if he'd done the same, clinging to his hard headed belief that Ellen's reserved way when they were together meant maidenly modesty, not reluctance to love him. *Maybe Pa spoke the truth*, he thought. *Maybe she did choose not to have me.* A fear of that had once crossed his mind like a raven's shadow, but he had driven it out, thinking she would not fight her pa's will.

Now, as James sat wrapped in bitterness, hope dead, he felt a kinship to the leaves scattered around him, their glory decaying, as though he, too, was waiting his turn to rot into the earth.

After an hour's pause, James got the mules into harness, and drove the wagon to several mine headquarters Hilbrands pointed out, where they left supplies. James unloaded orders while Hilbrands settled accounts, then he drove the empty wagon into a livery yard in Cañon City as dusk marched down the canyon.

When James had turned the mules into the corral and the men had pushed the wagon into a corner of the yard, Hilbrands took James's elbow and steered him into the darkness of the street. Somewhere ahead a piano player thumped out a tune over the hum of voices and the clink of glasses on a bar. They passed the bright lamplight, the noise, the smell of cheap whiskey, and turned onto a side street, stopping in front of a small dining room tucked into a fold of clapboard wall.

Several men sat at rough tables in the half dark room. None of them looked up from the grub on their plates as Hilbrands and James entered. A pudgy woman with lank, mouse colored hair escaping from the twist at her neck ladled stew onto one man's plate from a blackened pot she held against a grimy apron.

"How do," said the woman. Her voice matched her apron. "We got stew tonight."

"Two," said Hilbrands, and pulled out a chair. "Maybelle, this here's my new teamster, James Owen. Make up a tab for him, and you can take it out in trade."

"They call you Jim?" The woman plunked down two plates and a handful of silverware.

"No. James. From the Bible," he said. Ma would have been scandalized. The Good Lord never called his apostle 'Jim'.

She shrugged. "Fancy handle. You pack a gun?"

"I drive a team." He hadn't seen a need for his gun belt and pistol outside of Pueblo City, so he'd left them tucked into his war bag back at the hotel.

"You'd best pack a gun here with that fancy name." She turned to Hilbrands. "Short of speech, ain't he?"

"He's pining over a girl, plum lovesick," he said, grinning at the waitress.

James sat up straight. He didn't like the jesting way Hilbrands made light of his code of honor. In fact, several things about Randolph Hilbrands rankled him by now.

The woman laughed, a crow's caw. "You take him down the alley. Annie'll cure that."

James raised his eyes from a greasy lump of potato and stared at the waitress.

Ma used to say, 'A man don't slither with the snakes to show backbone'. She was firm set against girling and drunkenness and such, and favored living by the Ten Commandments. He thought he'd only paid as much heed to her words as any high spirited young'un, but here he was in a place he didn't want to be, with a man bound on molding him after his pattern, and the notion galled him. "I want no truck with a strange woman," he said.

Hilbrands chuckled. "Oh, Annie's not strange. She's the best dove in town."

"Six little beans!" James grabbed the edge of the table to stop the anger from lifting him to his feet. He fought to keep his hands from curling into fists to strike Hilbrands. "I don't want your harlot."

Hilbrands' fingers gripped his shoulder. "You're a man, aren't you? Annie'll fix you right up."

"I don't need a whore to know I'm a man." James shrugged the man's hand loose. "Leave me be, Randolph!"

The woman spoke up. "Come on, boy. Loosen up. Enjoy the town."

James took a deep breath and held it. *A man can take only so much nonsense before he makes a stand or caves in*, he thought. He let the air release slowly from between his lips. He had no family and no girl. Pain lanced through him like the devil's own fork was stabbing him when he thought of Ellen encircled in Carl's arms, but he wasn't of a mind to follow the path of Randolph Hilbrands, down the alley to sow wild oats with a strange woman. He shoved away the plate and stood up.

"I'm obliged for the meal, Mr. Hilbrands. If you want me, I'll be at the wagon yard."

₧

At dawn James put the team on the road for Pueblo. He popped the whip and cursed the mules, and said nothing to Hilbrands for miles. The mangy demon was back in his belly, rending and tearing, and he regretted having to be in the employ of a man who would try to force his ways on another.

Hilbrands sat quietly on the seat. Every fifteen minutes his mouth would open as if he were about to say something, but then he would clamp it shut and bite his lip.

About mid morning, he finally asked James, "Were you warm enough under the wagon?"

James swiveled his head to look at the man. "It was about tolerable."

"Do you bear me ill will now?"

James considered. "Some." They went back to silence.

At the nooning James spoke up as they rested under the oaks on the bank of the river. "I reckon I better head for Denver City once I get this team back home."

"You'd leave me after driving only one day?"

"My time's up. Every day I stay on rubs salt in Danny's wound. I don't want to kill the man, but it would come to that if I stayed."

"But James, my boy, I need you. Not just for these two weeks, but for steady work. If you don't like driving the team, why, you can run the office or the store, and I'll do the hauling."

"It isn't the mules I object to."

"I won't push my daughter at you."

"It's no good, Randolph. I've got to dig out that tunnel."

"That's your final word?"

James expelled a lungful of air. Then he nodded. "I'm pressed for time."

Hilbrands subsided, lounging back on the grass.

He spoke again at the middle of the afternoon, as they bounced along in the empty wagon. "Maybe you'd be interested in a letter I got a few days back."

James grunted.

"Angus Campbell has work. He's got some colts he needs broke, and he wondered could you do the job."

"News travels fast for such a far flung country." James squinted toward the sun.

"It does." Hilbrands shifted on the seat.

"Where's he located?"

"Down south on the Cuchara. Nice country, I been told. He sent a map."

"I'll give it thought."

At twilight, as they came into the final bend of the road before they reached Pueblo, James said, "It's late in the season to start mining. I can go north come spring. Will you give me the map?"

"Are you dead set against staying in my employ?"

"Rand—"

"I shouldn't have tried to push Annie on you. She wasn't in a good mood, anyhow. You can have the map."

Hilbrands was silent again until they caught sight of the lights of the town. He cleared his throat. "I'm obliged that you didn't holler at Maybelle. One thing about you Owen boys. Your ma reared you up courteous like. Even when you get temper struck, you're kind to the ladies."

James wanted to tell Randolph Hilbrands how Carl had cursed the man's daughter when his pride got bent, but that was low of him. Hilbrands wouldn't believe it anyway, so he sat on the wagon seat, drove the mules into town, and let the older man speak his piece as he listened to his own bent pride cursing his older brother.

There had not been too many such spells in his life before, but a black, mean mood was on him now, and he said nothing as he put up the animals and stowed away the harness. *This ain't good for your soul*, he told himself, but the meanness stayed, and the pain in his belly twisted and turned all the long night as he lay on the hard bed in the back room of the hotel, remembering the glowing look on Ellen's face when Carl got up from his sick bed to marry her.

The two of them stood in the meadow having the marriage words said over them. James had seen how Ellen's shining eyes spoke of the love she gave to Carl but not to him. Carl—only half a man, with a broken leg, a bullet hole big as a fist in the meat of his hip, and a furrow above one ear—ended up with a grin of triumph and a bride. It hardly seemed like justice that James—victorious, whole, and sound, while the family's battle with the kidnappers had robbed Carl of so much vigor—had no scratch on him, yet he had lost the battle for Ellen's hand.

Hilbrands tried to keep him, but before dawn the next day James strapped on his gun belt, saddled his animals, and took the road south, following Angus Campbell's map. When the way led too close to the homeward path, he headed for open country, breaking his own trail and making a dry camp or two to avoid meeting any of his kin.

Chapter 8

Sunrise fanned golden rays into the eastern sky as the horses ridden by Don Enrique Olmedo y Landa and Amparo Garcés y Martínez cantered into the Cuchara River Valley near Leones. The Don had pushed on through the night to get the girl to the mission priest on this, the twenty sixth day of October. Although the girl was weary, Don Enrique's sense of honor and the memory of his friend, Tomás Garcés y Vega, demanded that he discharge this duty before he continued with his own business.

Covered with dust and chilled to the bone, the girl blinked her eyes to clear them, and a shudder ran through her slender frame as she reined in her horse on a flat section of the river bank. An icy breeze blew, causing the bare branches of the cottonwoods along the river to rub together. Hundreds of birds twittered in the trees, greeting the new day. The river was as dry as Amparo's mouth.

Santa María, we are nearing the place of my sacrifice. Please, Holy Mother, petition your Beloved Son that He will accept my dear papá into His bosom.

Don Enrique wheeled his horse and came back for the girl, a frown drawing his moustache-covered mouth downward into his beard. "*Señorita*, what is the trouble? Why have you stopped?"

Amparo turned her anxious face toward the tall, gaunt man. "Please, señor. Permit me a moment to compose myself. Today this place marks the beginning of my new life. I need a little moment."

The stern face softened. "Poor girl. I understand. However, we must still ride a small distance to arrive at the village. We can stop before we meet the priest, if you like. Be quick, señorita."

"I am now ready." The girl sighed, then took a deep breath and squared her shoulders. "We will continue, Don Enrique." Amparo lifted the reins and clucked to her horse, and it moved up to follow the caballero and his pack mules.

All along the road, dust lay thick upon the brush. The trees thinned out as they went upstream, until, when they entered the village, there were no trees in sight.

Don Enrique led the way through the square to the whitewashed mission. There he dismounted and tethered his horse and the mules to a post embedded in the ground in front of the church. Amparo sat stiffly on her mount, trying to keep wisps of hair loosened from her braid from blowing into her face.

"Wait here, señorita. I will rouse the holy Father." Then he was off, around the back of the church, where Amparo presently heard him pounding the knocker on the door of the priest's lodgings.

The girl shivered as the sound died away. A large flake of whitewash drifted to the ground from the wall alongside the church door. Off to her right a rooster crowed. A barking dog chased a shadow into the square, then retreated to raise its leg against the side of a house.

Blessed Mother, are the people friendly in this village? Is my bridegroom truly a good man? I wonder if he will receive me kindly.

A pair of voices exchanged messages at the rear of the church. Then Don Enrique came around the corner, followed by a round-shouldered priest who carried a large key.

"Is this the señorita?" The priest gestured toward Amparo, then continued talking to Don Enrique. "I know nothing of her plans. The convent you speak of is quite a distance away, and I do not have any connection with the Sisters there."

Don Enrique plucked at his beard. "This is most extraordinary. The señora said I was to bear the girl to you and deliver her upon this date, and that you would have made arrangements for her."

The priest approached Amparo's horse and looked up at her. "Little daughter," he said gently, "I am Father Gallegos. Can you explain? I was expecting that a bride would arrive from Santa Fe by today."

"My Father, this talk of a convent is foreign to me. Señor Fuentes made arrangements to send me here. I am the bride whom you seek." Amparo's hands gripped the reins, yet she could not feel them for the numbness in her fingers from the cold breeze blowing through the square.

Satisfied with her answer, Father Gallegos nodded and reached up to pat her hand. "Good. I look forward to the arrival of Don Julio this afternoon. He is anxious to meet you." He gestured toward the church. "He has had the banns published, and all is in readiness for the ceremony."

"Listen, what is going on?" queried Don Enrique. "You both talk as though this child is going to wed a stranger."

The priest turned his head. "That is the case, my son. You may be at ease. Don Julio is a fine man, and will take good care of the señorita."

"This is incomprehensible! Totally impossible!" Don Enrique's voice rose a notch in both pitch and volume. "The señora told me the girl was to enter holy orders."

"Is there any order holier than matrimony, my son? She will have a fine home, servants at her beck and call, all that she needs or desires."

"I cannot permit it! I was her father's closest friend! ¡Ay! He would not approve of such a ridiculous plan!" he sputtered. "Don Tomás would turn in his—"

"Don Enrique, please," Amparo broke in. "I do this thing of my own free will." She brushed a strand of wind-blown hair from her face and tucked it behind her ear.

"Child, you cannot know what you are doing." Don Enrique's face creased in a frown of solicitude.

Amparo sat up straight in her saddle. "Believe me, señor. It is what I wish. Please do not interfere."

The *caballero* threw his hands into the air. "I see that the girl has made up her mind, but when I return to Santa Fe, the señora will bear the weight of my most strenuous disapproval. The woman misled me!"

Father Gallegos laid his hand on the Don*'s* arm. "We cannot know her mind, my son. You must be guided by charity when you speak to the señora. Peace be unto you."

Don Enrique turned abruptly and strode to Amparo's mount. "In view of your coming marriage, I will leave you the mule that bears your equipage as a gift, señorita. I cannot delay my departure longer." He helped the girl to the ground, then turned to the pack mules and separated one from the bunch. He put the lead rope into Amparo's hand, untethered and mounted his horse, and settled himself into the saddle. "If I had more time, I would not permit this travesty to take place," he said gruffly, then, leaning out of his saddle, said to the priest, "As I am behind times, it must be as the girl wishes." He turned back to Amparo and doffed his great embroidered hat. "*Adiós*, little one. Go with God." Then Don Enrique re-covered his head, wheeled his horse, and rode out of the village in a great amber cloud of dust.

Father Gallegos took the lead rope from Amparo and tied the mule to the hitching post. She got her horse by the bridle, tugged it to the post, and tied it alongside the mule. The priest put his key into the lock of the church door, turned it, and threw wide the portals. "Come with me, my daughter. I will get a boy to care for your animals and bring in your luggage. You can rest in the chapel until Señora Clara arrives. She is my housekeeper, and I have no doubt that she can find you a place to wash and change your clothes." He moved into the darkness of the doorway, then returned when Amparo did not follow him directly into the church. "Come in, little one. The Señora will be here soon. Now I must go prepare for the mass."

"*Gracias*, my Father. Is there a place where I can sleep? The señor was anxious to conclude my journey by today, so we were obliged to ride all night."

"Poor little one. Señora Clara will know such things. I will send her to you the instant she arrives. In the meantime, please sit in the chapel and rest."

The priest escorted Amparo into the little church, and she bent her knee before the Host. Soon she was seated in a dark corner of the chapel, and before long, her head nodded until it touched the enclosed side of the pew, and the girl slept.

&

Amparo awoke with a start as a hand shook her shoulder. She opened her eyes wide, yawned, stretched, and looked around. The church was shrouded in darkness. Only one candle kept away the gloom, and that was carried in the wrinkled hand of the tall old woman who had awakened her.

"Señorita, I am Señora Clara." The voice was soft and gentle. "I tried to awaken you before but could not rouse you, and you have slept for many hours. Come. The Father wishes to speak with you."

Amparo quickly got to her feet. "Is the good Father angry that I missed the mass?"

The old face creased into a smile. "No, *muchacha*. He is a kind man, and you had the look of one who had traveled far. Come, little one. Follow me."

The woman moved toward the rear of the chapel, along a passage, and up the side aisle, and Amparo followed her into a small room where the priest sat at a table.

He rose, smiling, and took her hand. "My daughter. Our Lord looked down on your weariness and smiled, for you dreamed undisturbed."

"You are kind, Father Gallegos. Where are my things? Where may I ready myself for the ceremony? It must be very late."

The holy man's face grew pensive. "My daughter, I fear that something is amiss. Don Julio—Señor Rodríguez—has not yet arrived. Perhaps he was delayed at his rancho, but I thought he would have sent word."

Amparo took a short breath and held herself very still. When she spoke, her voice was low and quivered a fraction. "Then I must wait?"

"Yes, my daughter." The priest frowned. His eyes reflected his concern. "Perhaps you should go ahead with your preparations in case he arrives later tonight. Then we can proceed with the marriage."

Amparo nodded.

"Go with Señora Clara, my daughter. She will assist you."

"*Gracias*, my Father." The girl bent her head, and the priest moved his hand over it.

"Peace be with you, my daughter."

Amparo followed the old woman as she led the way to a small, closet like room opening off the chapel. "You may wash, then change your clothes here, *muchacha*. Armando brought in your valise, and here is a basin of warm water. If Don Julio is delayed much longer, I will have the boy bring in a cot for you to rest upon until the don comes."

"Thank you, Señora. You are very kind." Amparo sighed, and began to untie the ribbons that held her blouse together. "Do you know Don Julio?"

"No, but I have seen him on two occasions, *muchacha*." The woman's black eyes twinkled. "You are curious, *¿no?* I can tell you that he looked like a fine man: prosperous, and with clothes fit for a grandee. And he smiled once, at a joke the good Father told, so he is not without humor, little one. He is older than you, of course, but not much over thirty years. I am sure you are making a fine match."

Amparo sighed again, and gave a little shudder.

"Are you cold, *querida*? No. You are frightened." The old woman smiled. "Marriage is not so bad. You will see."

The girl shut her eyes, then opened them and turned toward Señora Clara. "If only—I mean, I wish—" She lowered her eyes. "It is so hard to wait."

"What do you mean, *muchacha*?"

The girl hugged one arm with the other. "I have come so far to be a bride. Now that I am here, the bridegroom is not. I almost feel sick." She put her hand on her stomach. "In here."

"Yes, you are frightened, and you are anxious to get on with your life. It is understandable that you are nervous, little one, but," the old woman's eyes twinkled, "your nerves will pass by and by."

The girl compressed her lips to still their quiver. She turned to the basin and dipped her hands into the water, then splashed the liquid onto her face.

The woman patted Amparo on the shoulder. "Of course you have some fears, *muchacha*. You are very young, and this is all new to you. God will bless you if you obey your husband." With that, Señora Clara patted Amparo's shoulder once more and left the girl alone in the room.

∞

The wind forced cold air down James's collar as his horse scrambled up the bank of a stream. He'd ridden long, the sun was skidding down the bowl of the sky toward the horizon to the right, and it was time to make camp. James looked for a place to build a fire as the sorrel gelding moved with sure feet along the stream bank with the pack mule following on a lead rope.

Suddenly, the horse's ears flicked forward, and it stopped and set its forelegs in the path, throwing James against its neck.

"Confounded horse," he said, regaining his balance and clucking to the sorrel. It shook its head, sidling and whinnying, then tried to back up.

"Something on the trail, boy? Whoa, settle down. I'll take a look."

As James dismounted, swinging his leg to the ground, he shivered at the chill touch of a wisp of wind that raised the tail of his coat.

It'll frost tonight, he thought, and tied his horse to a scrubby tree beside the trail. *Coming on dark soon.*

James adjusted his gun belt and slipped the loop off the hammer of his revolver as he walked through the fading light toward the place where the sorrel had shied. A twig snapped under his boot, and he started at the sudden sharp noise. Off to the right, across the creek, something scuttled through the underbrush. James stopped, pulled his gun, and swung it in that direction, but nothing menacing appeared.

He peered back into the shadows on the trail to discover what had spooked the horse. There was nothing out of the ordinary in the path, and James started to turn back. Then the wind shifted and he caught a whiff of an overpowering odor.

"Six little beans!" he exclaimed, coughing. He backed up a step, sheathed his gun, and pulled a handkerchief from his pocket. Tying it around his nose and mouth to cut off some of the stench, he advanced again, breathing shallowly through his mouth.

Something lay ahead in the deepening shadows. James drew his gun again and approached slowly. A silver-adorned hat, large-brimmed in the Mexican style, sat beside the trail. James picked it up and took another step. Flung face down against a rocky outcrop at the side of the trail was the body of a richly-dressed man. James put away his pistol, leaned over, and tugged at the man's shoulder to reveal the remains of a brown, decomposing face with prominent cheek bones. The dead man's neck lolled to one side—broken. The Mexican had been dead for several days.

James straightened the body out on the trail. There was no blood, no sign of violence. "Looks like your horse got frisky, *amigo*," he said aloud. "Bucked you off in the wrong place—up against those rocks. I wonder if it galloped all the way home."

The body was dressed in formal clothing. The green satin jacket had a blue serape draped over the shoulder still, and the embroidered hat with the silver adornments was surely not the man's everyday headgear.

James had not met many Mexicans, except journeying to and from Texas with the herd of cattle Rod Owen had bought. He had heard that some of the white settlers in the territory held Mexicans in low esteem, but Ma had always said, "Boys, you hold a man worth his salt until he proves you wrong". That went for whites, Negroes, and Mexicans, too. Even though the Owens had had troubles with a Mexican outlaw, Berto Acosta, James knew the man's brand of evil didn't come from his ancestors. It came out of the blackness of his own soul.

Julia Owen had a clear way of seeing things that didn't always go along with what everybody else believed, but she'd got it right out of the Holy Bible, believed it passionately, and had passed it along to her sons. As a consequence, when James and his brothers went to war, it was to defend Virginia, not to protect slavery.

James searched through the man's pockets. There was nothing to help him identify the man, but tucked into a pocket of his jacket was a new leather pouch and a letter wrapped in a silk scarf. James stuffed them into his own coat and retreated a few steps, gasping for fresh air.

"I'll bury you come first light, *amigo*," he promised. "You'll keep until then, I reckon."

James removed the handkerchief and stood in the trail for a moment, sucking in long drafts of air, then started back to his animals. A low growl came to his ears, and hair stood on end at the back of his neck. He pulled his pistol and turned toward the sound, which came from the underbrush across the creek.

With a rush, a large brown dog darted toward him, through the water, and up the trail. James leaped up into the rocks beside the trail, and scrambled onto a slab-sided boulder. Then he raised the gun barrel toward the sky and whistled in consternation as the animal tried to find a way to attack, barking and growling, its ears laid back flat on its head.

"Hey! Get away! Shoo there!" James flapped his handkerchief in the direction of the rushing animal, and it withdrew a few paces, circled to face James, and barked again. Then it retreated to the dead body, which it sniffed. Whining and whimpering, the dog sank down beside the Mexican's body, its head on its paws.

James warily climbed down out of the rocks and kept his distance from the dog. "Tarnation! You took me by surprise. You must belong to him." He motioned toward the Mexican's body. "Well, I'm planting him tomorrow, old dog. Don't give me grief when I do it."

The dog raised its head and sniffed in James's direction. "I'll bet you're hungry, boy. If you get to feeling starved, come over to my camp and I'll find some scraps for you." The dog sniffed again, then resumed its position.

James cast around for horse sign for a few moments, just in case the Mexican's mount was still in the area, but the light was soon too dim for him to track, so he retraced his steps to his animals, filling his lungs with sweet, sage tinged evening air.

Untying his horse and mule, he led them back up the creek to keep them from running off at the smell of the body. The sorrel followed easily as he moved it and the mule away from the trail onto a wide bench of land above the stream. There he unsaddled the gelding and let it roll in the dusty grass while he removed the pack and saddle from the mule. After watering the animals in the stream and brushing them down a bit, he picketed them to crop at the dry grass.

Afterward, James gathered fuel in the last light and laid wood for a small fire, just enough to heat water for a cup of broth. He struck a flint with the back of his knife and blew gently on the sparks that fell into the dry moss tinder. When it smoked, then flared into flames, he put finger thick sticks into the fire, keeping it small.

James set a tin cup half full of water next to the flames, then rocked back on his heels to wait for it to come to a boil, rubbing his hands together to chase out the chill. When the water bubbled, he fished a piece of jerky out of his pouch and crumbled it into the liquid to make broth.

Like to take my appetite away, coming on that fellow downstream, he thought, then lifted the cup out of the fire with a forked stick. *I'll settle for jerky broth until my belly quiets down.* He set the cup on a flat rock to allow the pieces of beef to soften in the hot water, got to his feet, and strolled over to the animals.

After checking the solidity of the picket pins holding the animals on their grazing ground, James squatted and gathered up a handful of brittle grass. *It'll be buried under snow soon*, he thought, opening his hand and letting the dry blades scatter in the slight breeze. Then he stood and walked into camp.

He unrolled his bedding and reached over to the flat rock beside the fire to fetch his soupy drink. The odor of beef filled his nostrils and he took a sip, sat cross legged on his quilt, and sipped again.

The broth was strong, and warmed him so he didn't notice the nip in the breeze. As James drank with one hand, he took the letter from his pocket, shook it free of the scarf, then flipped it open. The fire had died down enough that he couldn't see to read, so he put down the paper, raised himself to add a few sticks to the fire, then settled down with the letter once more.

Fancy looped words mocked him from the paper, for none of them were in English. Snorting in dismay, he put down his cup to re-wrap the packet and return it to his coat.

"I'd hoped to get word to your folks of what happened to you, *amigo*, but I reckon I got to get somebody to read me that note," he said aloud, his voice regretful.

James fell silent, sitting alone listening to the chirping night. He finished the soup, chewing the last bits of jerky, then placed another small branch on the waning fire and opened the pouch he'd taken from the dead man's jacket. When he shook the upended bag above his hand, a thick, hand worked ring fell onto his palm, followed by a pair of ear ornaments. The ring glinted yellow in the firelight, and he weighed it in his hand.

Gold, from the heft of it. Looks like presents for a lady. He dropped the jewelry back into the pouch, stuffed it in his pocket, removed his boots and trousers, and shucked off his coat. Then he slipped into the blankets, tipped his hat over his face, and breathed leather and sweat.

Whether the chill that swept over him came from the night air or from his conscience, James did not know, but he tossed in his bed for some time. *I should have made peace with Pa before I left*, he thought, and eased himself into a better position in the quilts. *Could be a man's time on this earth turns out to be scant.*

ꙄꙦ

James found a fitting place to lay the Mexican to rest, under a scrub oak tree alongside the stream, where the sandy earth wasn't hard to dig, but far enough from the water that the body wouldn't float away come flood time. He made quick work of the grave digging with a shovel he had brought along in the mining gear when he'd left home.

When James approached the body to carry it to the finished grave, the dog—still lying beside its master's body—whined, then bared its teeth and growled. James went down on one knee and snapped his fingers.

In a low, soothing tone, he spoke to the animal. "Come on, old dog, I've got to put your master to rest. You can see I do it right, but I can't have you nipping at me during the service." He pulled a short length of rope from his pocket and reached out to tie it around the dog's neck for a collar. The animal sprang to its feet and snapped its teeth, and James fell backward and shook a drop of blood from his hand.

"Six little beans!" he exclaimed, scrambling to his feet. "I reckon you're not sure what's going on. If that's the way you're going to be, I'll have to rope you like a cow."

He fetched his catch rope from camp, approached the wary animal, roped it, and dragged it to the scrub oak, where he got the collar rope on it and tied it securely. The dog howled for a time, then began to whine.

"You sit there and watch, dog," James said. "This has to be done."

James went to the body beside the trail, wrapped it in the woolen *serape*, carried it to the hole he had dug, and laid it in the bottom. Considering the decomposing state of the body, it was a noisome task, and James managed to get so rank smelling that he promised himself a soaking bath in the next town he hit. Then he applied himself to covering the body with the sandy soil.

When the dead Mexican was snug in the ground, with rocks laid over the earth, James stood at the head of the grave and removed his hat. The dog stopped whining, and began to howl anew.

"Lord," James said over the ruckus, "I don't know this man's name and I don't know the custom of his people come burying time, but I reckon You know him and take heed of his passing, so I turn his spirit over to You. I reckon I've taken good enough care of his body." He gestured toward the grieving dog. "And Lord, please don't mind the dog's noise. He's the only real mourner here for the man."

Then James recited a couple of Bible verses that seemed to fit: the one in Genesis about man being dust and returning to the ground, and the one about resurrection and though a man be dead, he'll live again if he believes. The dog whimpered and pulled against the rope binding it to the oak.

James tipped his head back and gazed upward. "I don't know if this fellow was a believer, but Lord God, I've said the words anyway. Amen." Ma would have been pleased with the service.

While James had been busy with the digging and burying and reciting, a rising wind had filled the sky with low slung clouds, and by the time he put his hat back on his head, fat flakes of snow drifted around, settling onto the grave like a shroud. The dog pulled at the catch rope, and James turned it loose. The animal ran to the grave, sniffed at the rocks, and looked around at James. It looked back at the rocks, gave one final howl, then turned and trotted to James's side, its head hanging low.

James packed his gear, together with the items he'd found in the Mexican's pockets, and got aboard the sorrel. Then he tried to back track the man, but the snow had blotted out the trail, and the dog ran back and forth making new tracks, so James gave up the task and lit out for a settlement that Angus Campbell had marked on the map he had sent to Randolph Hilbrands—a town called *Leones*.

Chapter 9

James halted the sorrel in front of a low adobe building and dismounted. No trees surrounded this building or any other that he could see. A light brown dust hung in the frosty air, marking his trail into the village. The climate in this place contrasted sharply with that in the higher country he had come through in the past few days.

After he had buried the Mexican, James spent one day trying to make his way through wind whipped, belly deep snow, and another holed up with the dog, waiting for the storm to blow itself out. It was good to be in a town, where he could find shelter for a few days in case the storm headed this way. That didn't seem likely, though. According to the evidence of powdery dust and brown, scant vegetation, this place had not had moisture of any kind for a long time.

James shrugged his shoulders. It mattered little to him. He wasn't looking for a place to settle. He had come to the village to find someone to decipher the letter so he could take the Mexican's pouch to his family or friends. After that, he figured to see Angus Campbell about the colts.

It took just a moment to tie the tether ropes for the animals onto a post set in the ground. Then James looked around the settlement as he loosened the saddle cinches a bit.

Six or seven adobe houses formed three sides of a rough square, backed by a tier of outbuildings, then a second row of homes. A larger building, whitewashed and topped with a carved wooden cross, made up the fourth side of the square.

"That'll be the mission church," he muttered to himself, rubbing his palms on the seat of his pants. He wondered if the priest here could talk English. The one who married Ellen and Carl hadn't. One of the settlers had brought him up and translated for him. Remembering that day brought a black feeling of despair that he didn't have time to deal with, and James thrust it away, deep into the recesses of his mind.

He glanced at the center of the square as he strode toward the church. A well head stood surrounded by several adobe tanks and washbasins. Seven women with shawl covered heads scrubbed and rinsed clothes, and watched his approach with dark and wary eyes. He didn't envy them the work in cold water. He looked up as the dog caught a scent it liked and followed it around the back of a house.

Three little brown girls ranging in age from six to ten played in the mud at the foot of the community well. One looked close at James, then flung a cinnamon braid behind her shoulder with a casual hand.

"Ain't you one of them Owen brothers?" she asked, and he stopped and gave her another look. Although she was dressed in the native style, she was not the Mexican he had first thought, but a white girl, and the bronze color of her skin must have come from playing long hours in the strong sunlight.

"I'm James. Who might you be?"

She straightened up from the mud beside the well. "I am Rida O'Connor. Everybody knows that."

"Is your daddy Tom O'Connor, who was the blacksmith back in Mount Jackson, Virginia?"

"What a silly question," she said. "Of course he is. Now he's the blacksmith here." She wrinkled her nose at him. "You're pretty smelly."

His face curled into a grin. "You ain't so clean yourself." He restrained the impulse to jerk her braid. "Say, where's your pa? Maybe he can help me."

"Rosalinda said I could play. A body can't keep clean all the time."

"I need to see your pa."

"He just got back from a trip. He's over to home."

James looked in the direction of her pointing arm to the second row of houses. "Thank you kindly. I'll go and pay my respects."

"You best stay here a spell. He only just got home, I told you. She sent me'n Josh off to play."

James thought he could have picked up that girl's scorn and cooled a tall drink of water with it. "Who's 'she'?" he asked.

"I already told you." Rida bent over and peeled caked mud off her bare leg. "Rosalinda. She's our new ma."

"Your new ma? Your pa got himself married? You don't say." He spit in the mud. "It's a regular plague going around." Seeing the girl's puzzled expression, he added, "You didn't hear? Some Spanish-talking priest came up a while back and married Ellen Bates to my brother Carl." A flash of fire attacked his belly, but it didn't feel right to double over to nurse the pain in front of this saucy child.

"I heard. That was our priest. *Padre* Gallegos marries everybody around here. That's his work. He married my pa and Rosalinda a while back. We had a party for three days."

It was the priest from here that— No! I've got to find that fellow's family.

James straightened his shoulders against his bitter thoughts. "I'll go now and say hello."

"You better not," she said, shaking her head.

James ignored her and turned to re-cross the square, moving between the houses in the direction the child had indicated. *So Mr. O'Connor took a wife*, he thought. *I reckon I can't blame him. He's been lonely since the missus died.*

He passed the row of outbuildings and rounded the house Rida had pointed out, rubbing his fingertips along the rough adobe blocks as he went. *It's squat and ugly, but warm in winter, I'll bet.* Arriving at the door, James knocked, then backed away a pace and waited. A woman raised her voice in excited Spanish. After a time, someone stomped across the floor.

The plank door opened inward, and Tom O'Connor's thick body filled the space. He was bootless, and his large hands hurriedly hoisted suspenders over bare shoulders. Thrusting his head forward, he blinked in the sunlight, and his black brows drew together as he frowned. The woman's voice coming from deep inside the room kept up the flood of sharp, foreign words.

It was evident that the man had been about some private business. James inhaled noisily and wished he could twist away like a wind spiral he'd seen whipping up snowflakes the day before. Then the scowl on Tom's face changed to resignation, and he crooked his neck to turn his head toward the room.

"*¡Cállate! Tenemos visitante,*" he hollered. "We've got company, so hush up."

"I reckon I come at the wrong time," James muttered.

Tom's face returned to view. "You're Rod Owen's son. James, isn't it? How old are you, boy?"

James felt a creeping flush crossing his jaw, and hoped his beard was full enough by now to hide it. "Old enough to know I ain't a welcome sight. I'll be going."

"No, you come along in. It'll keep." His right eyelid lowered in a slow wink. "But Rosalinda won't like it. I reckon she won't take to you right off. I been away for a while, and she likes my company."

The man stepped back from the door and motioned for James to enter the comfortable room. "Come along in, now. Set down and rest your feet." He walked James to the table and sat down. "Rosalinda, fetch some food. *Comida,*" he said, then turned his head toward James. "I'm teaching her English, now that I got some of her tongue learned. You're hungry?"

"I came to say hello, not to clean out your larder," James said. But he sat anyway—in a chair like any chair, yet foreign to his eyes—and took off his hat, rolled it between his fingers, then hung it on the chair back next to him.

He could see Tom had married a girl from a decent home, because the finish on that table he sat up to was slick enough to mirror every whisker on a body's face. Right then, he looked more scruffy than polished, and shame licked at his gizzard like a flame searching for fuel.

"We've plenty of food." Tom swiveled in his chair and shouted toward the fireplace. "*¡Comida, mujer!* Step lively."

James fished in his pocket to feel the letter as the woman dropped a plate in front of him. *Hush my mouth, she's angry*, he thought, jerking up his chin. As his eyes met hers, he knew he had offended Rosalinda

Of medium height, with eyes black and furious, tucking her white blouse hastily into the waistband of her skirt, Rosalinda backed off and shook untamed hair behind her shoulders. "I no am happy," she declared.

He shook his own head to break contact with those hot eyes. Rosalinda O'Connor was a beauty, and seemed to give off crackles of lightning that sapped his strength. She was like no one he had ever met before.

One deep breath revived him. "Your wife is Spanish?"

"Mexican. Her family owns most of the land between here and the Apishapa River. Ain't she purty?"

"You got to get you a stronger word, Tom O'Connor. I never laid eyes on anybody akin to her before." James's voice sank to a whisper. "Does she get riled like that regular?"

The blacksmith threw his muscled torso backward against his chair, barking out his laugh. "Ain't you a caution. Eat up, James, boy. Your grub's getting cold."

Thinking it polite to eat, James listened with half an ear to Tom's comments about the condition of horse's hooves on the surrounding farms as he tucked into the food. From time to time he glanced up, keeping track of Rosalinda's movements at the fireplace.

He had always thought of his own black hair as ordinary: crisp and curly, yes, but common enough. Rosalinda's hair was straight, black as fireplace soot, and hung to her elbows.

Then a wonderment came upon him, a yearning to know how that hair would feel strung between his fingers like the mane of an unsaddled horse. *Hair to be touched*, he thought, then jerked himself upright in his seat. *Hair to be left alone. She's a woman wed. Like Ellen.* Pain swept from his ears to his toes at the thought, and he felt his face creasing in a grimace.

Rosalinda startled James with laughter. "You no am happy, too." She pulled down the corners of her mouth with her fingers, imitating what she saw on his face. Turning her back to dish up food for her husband, she laughed again.

"Tarnation! Is she poking fun at me?" His hands balled into fists, and he breathed deep for a moment. "First she's riled, then she makes a face and laughs."

Tom chuckled. "You ain't likely to meet up with another woman like mine. She's got some moods, and they change three to the minute, but she can cook mighty fair, and she sure chased off the lonesome." He looked up from his food and pursed his lips. "I reckon I'm a man needs to be married, and I'm right lucky to find her."

James didn't want to believe himself so mean spirited that he would begrudge Tom a bit of happiness after he'd been a widower for a couple of years, but his words touched fire down James's spine. Something Tom had said burned hot into his soul, but the blacksmith went on speaking, and James couldn't sort out his first words and pay mind to the rest at the same time. He decided to listen now and ponder later.

"She's a good ma to the young'uns, too. Look you here." He held out a lock of hair from his temple. "I started going gray trying to handle them two alone. Don't know how I lasted two years without a woman to manage them."

"I reckon you heard Carl got hitched, too?" A searing pain came, and James wondered why he'd brought it on himself by speaking of it.

"Now that surprised me. Ellen's pa Chester Bates stopped by on his way home and gave me the news. I thought you and she—"

"I reckon—I reckon she wanted Carl instead of me."

James sat up straight, his belly tensed, waiting for the shock of hearing those words to batter him like the concussion of an artillery shell blowing up five yards away. It hurt him to say these words, to admit a thing Pa had insisted was so. He stayed still for a long time, running his tongue over his teeth as he mentally tested for damage

There weren't any open wounds. His gut was intact, filled with banked coals. It gave him a turn that the pain hurt less than he expected it to do. After weeks of living with hell's fire in his belly, he was shocked that it had so suddenly died away to mere embers.

"There's no accounting for a woman's taste," Tom said, looking at James. "Eat up now, James, boy. Your grub's going a wasting." He scratched his ear, then dug into a second portion of beans and flat corn patties his wife put before him.

James inhaled the spicy odor of the beans, put aside his thoughts, and finished his meal. Then he brought out the letter.

"What's that you have there, James, boy?"

James recounted his adventure up the country and explained what he intended to do. "This letter was in the man's jacket, and it's writ in a clear hand, but it's writ in Spanish. I can't make it out," he finished.

Tom put out his paw for the paper. "I read a little of the *lingo*, and if I can't make it out, Rosalinda can. Or, we can take it to her pa."

"I'm obliged," James said, handing over the letter. "The fellow was decked out in his best clothes. Carried these, too." He took out the leather sack and emptied the jewelry onto the table. The gold ring spun around on the polished tabletop with a whirring noise, then came to rest, and the ear bobs glittered in a heap nearby.

Rosalinda swooped down on the ring and held it to the light. "*Es un anillo nupcial*," she said.

"It's a wedding ring," Tom explained. "Likely the man was on his way to get married. These here," he lifted the ear bobs, "these here pretties look like the presents men folk around here give their brides." He turned his attention to the letter.

Up to this moment the situation had seemed sad enough, but hadn't overly disturbed James. Of a sudden a great wash of melancholy come upon him. That poor fellow he'd planted was stuck up there in the ground without tasting the happiness he'd planned for, and some little girl was waiting for him, all a flutter, like as not, never even knowing she should be mourning him and their lost life together. Pain came back, a mournful feeling down in James's belly, compassion for two strangers.

Tom looked up from studying the letter. "Listen here. I can make out some of this note. 'I have made arrangements to send Amparo Garcés y Martínez, the daughter of Catarina *viuda* de Garcés of Santa Fe, to be your bride.' There's something about meeting on the twenty sixth. That's near a week past. It's written to Julio Rodríguez y Guzmán—that ain't anyone from town—and it's signed by a lawyer." He tapped a word on the paper. "'*Viuda*' means the mother's a widow woman."

James rubbed his forefinger back and forth over the smoothness of the tabletop next to his plate. "It sounds like the girl doesn't know the fellow. How'd you say her name again?"

"'Ahm-par-o'," said the blacksmith slowly. "I'd say Rodríguez sent for a bride. Packing a daughter off like that is a common enough way out of money problems for a widow. One less mouth to feed, and a marriage payment, besides."

James rubbed so hard at the tabletop that he about wore the polish off that patch of table. "You called him 'Rodríguez.' Ain't he 'Guzmán'?"

"They got a strange way of naming here, carrying both papa and mama's last names. Mexicans set a lot of store by family. Their customs are a mite tangled, but you get used to them."

Miss Amparo Garcés was coming to meet a stranger, and him dead. James's finger moved faster as he wondered what would happen to the girl now. He laid his hand flat down on the table to save the finish, looked at his squared off fingernails, and asked Tom.

The blacksmith shrugged his large shoulders and answered, "The ink is smudged where the note tells their meeting place. Wherever she lands, I reckon the folk'll have to ship her back to Santa Fe to Mama."

James's gut went dead cold as he felt the hair rise behind his neck. "The priest," he whispered. "Your girl Rida said it's his job to marry folks. Miss Amparo's coming here."

Tom sniffed. "I don't recall hearing anything about a new girl hereabouts." He paused and studied the paper, tracing the signature with his finger. "But then, I been away for a spell."

James sat still, recalling the feeling of the bullet Danny O'Brien had shot into his side in Pueblo City. If it had lodged in his belly, he thought it would have felt the same as the cold, cumbersome lump now sitting in his innards. What if the young lady was here in town, waiting and wondering what kind of life she would have with Julio Rodríguez? He had taken upon himself a duty to close down that man's life, a duty to tie up the loose ends left hanging when his horse pitched him into that rocky outcrop of sandstone. That duty, the way James saw it, now included talking to his intended bride, telling her the bad news.

Tom sat silent, working through the letter again. His wife placed the wedding ring beside the ear bobs on the table. Her skirt rustled as she returned to the fireplace and clanked pots together.

James shoved his plate to one side, put his two fists side by side and looked at them. There was dirt under his thumbnails, blisters where Rand's mule team lines had worn against his bare fingers. Something bitter came up his throat, and he swallowed it down.

How can I tell Miss Amparo that no kind of married life awaits her in this town, that she'll have to go back home, likely to poverty, and maybe even starvation?

"Ask your wife if the young lady's here," he said, slow and quiet.

Tom asked, and Rosalinda came back from the fire and answered in staccato fashion. She went on for a long time, sneering a time or two, and James marveled at Tom's knack for sorting the sounds into words. *Tom's got the gift of tongues, I reckon*, James thought. *I've got to learn Spanish, too, if I'm going to live in this country.*

When he turned back to James, Tom had a puzzled look on his face. "I'll be whipped," he snorted. "She's here, all right. Been setting in the church for five days, never saying boo. Some fellow coming through on the way to visit his ailing father in law brought her on horseback, but he left soon as he gave her over to the priest." Tom grinned. "She must be an eyeful, 'cause Rosalinda badmouthed her something awful. My *mujer* can't stand not being the prettiest woman around."

James shook to his toes, and looked around the room, for what, he didn't know. Maybe he was searching out the mournful shadow that pressed upon his soul.

"What am I going to tell her, Tom? How can I march up to a stranger and say 'Go home. There isn't a place for you here'?"

"Best leap right in and get it done," he said.

"You don't reckon she'll cry, do you?"

"Let me get my shirt on, and I'll take you over to the church and you can see for yourself, James, boy."

James let loose a sigh. "I got a bad feeling, Tom. I wish I'd never found that Rodríguez fellow."

Chapter 10

Six little beans! James said to himself when he saw the girl. *She is prettier than Tom's wife.*

Tom engaged the priest in conversation at the front of the mission chapel while James lingered in the side aisle, arms folded, glancing over his shoulder at the girl in a pew toward the middle of the chapel.

His belly felt heavier than ever as he looked at her, sitting so shy and quiet in the corner of a pew, dressed in a simple white blouse and brown skirt, her shoulders covered by a black shawl. She was slight of build compared to Rosalinda, but well proportioned. Because she was sitting, James couldn't easily guess her height. He waited, scuffing his boot toe against a rough hewn bench leg while Tom explained to the priest why James wanted to bother the señorita. Once he understood the problem, Padre Gallegos clucked "*pobrecita*" to himself and led Tom over to meet her. Tom made a "come along" gesture with his hand, and James slowly joined them to stand in the main aisle beside the pew where she sat.

While the girl talked to Tom and the priest, James examined her face. Her skin was smooth, nearly as brown as that of a bay horse, and her hair, black as a bay's mane is black, was slicked back into a heavy coil at the nape of her neck. Her eyes were the outstanding feature, darkest brown, almost black, with long straight lashes, and they sat in the proper place alongside her straight little nose. She had a woman's mouth. The sight of it—so full, and waiting for a husband's kiss that would never come—made him swallow several times.

Between the three of them, they made Miss Amparo Garcés y Martínez understand why Julio Rodríguez y Guzmán was not coming for his bride.

"*¿Muerto? ¿Él está muerto?*"

Her whisper came from deep in her throat. The horror in her pale face made a chill finger run up James's back, and he reached down to pat her hand. It was cold, and he wondered how he could warm it and take that awful look out of her eyes.

"I'm sorry he died," James said, and she looked long at him with those black, deep eyes.

"*¿Y qué de mí?*" She didn't turn away or blink, but asked James straight out, like he was the one with the answer to her question. He wished he knew what she had asked, but doubted that he knew the answer.

Tom came to his rescue. "She wants to know what she's to do."

"What do I say?" James wondered if his wild feeling of helplessness was coming through his eyes.

"Why don't you give her the ear bobs while you think about it?" Tom gestured with his head toward the girl.

James fumbled in his pocket for the jewelry and held all of it out to the girl. She shrank back, shaking her head. "This was meant for you," he said. "Take it." She didn't. James looked at Tom.

"What did I do wrong? Can you find out? Wait. Tell her I'll take her back to her mama in Santa Fe. That's the least thing I can do."

Before Tom said a word, the girl whispered something in Spanish. Tom didn't catch it, but the priest did, and told Tom what she'd said. He turned to James.

"She says it's bad luck for her to have the ring without a husband."

"That's all right. I'll hold onto it until I get her home."

Tom told her she was going home. James watched the look on her face, her little brown face, change from fear to stubbornness. Her hands went white from holding them so tight together, and she said something right out loud. Tom looked shocked as he turned to James.

"She says she came to be a bride, and she ain't leaving without a bridegroom. She won't go a step until she's married."

"Maybe she thinks I'm taking her to my home. Make her clear on that."

Tom and the priest talked to her again, and there were some words repeated over and over.

"She knows you mean Santa Fe, but she ain't budging. She says she has to take a husband." Tom took a piece of linen from his pocket and wiped the sweat from his face.

The girl whispered, "*Hize un convenio sagrado.*"

Tom looked pained, his eyebrows drawn together in a black line. "She says she made a holy vow. That's trouble aplenty, James, boy. These young gals take their religion to heart. She'll never budge now."

James stood next to the pew, looking from time to time at the girl. He rubbed his ear and stroked his chin, feeling how soft his beard was getting with some length to it. He looked at her hands, still white from squeezing them together. *Strong little hands. Chapping a mite from the cold. Is she used to hard work, or was her life in Santa Fe an easy one?*

Tom broke into the quiet. "No two ways about it. She's got to go back where she come from. I got a wife, and the padre ain't looking for one." He stared up at the ceiling.

James looked down at the ring and ear bobs in his hand. He thought back to his recent experience with a wedding: the whole Owen family standing in the meadow before the priest, and James cursing to himself and wishing he was in Carl's place. He thought of Tom, and what he'd said about Rosalinda chasing away the lonesome. *I am lonesome . . ..*

No, he told himself, *I'm more than lonesome. I'm hurting like all the cattle in Texas ran me down and stomped me into the dust, then dragged me through a ten mile patch of prickly pear.*

James's rate of breathing increased to match his agitation, and, uncomfortable, he looked at the girl to distract himself. She held her chin high, looking toward the front of the church. Somehow, the sight of her calmed him, and his breathing slowly returned to normal.

She's just a bit of a thing, he thought. *She's all alone here.*

The girl turned her head, raising it at the same time, and her gaze made contact with his. For a moment he was motionless, staring into the dark brown depths, sensing extreme anguish. After a time, the girl looked away, biting her lip.

Hush my mouth, she's got a load of pain, James thought. *It ain't likely she's mourning that Rodríguez fellow. She never even met him. There's some other grief weighing down her soul.*

James looked at his hands, surprised to see that they were boxed into fists, one tightly curled over the metal ornaments. *Her burden must be mighty heavy*, he thought, *to make her give her word to marry Rodríguez.* He looked at the girl again, and thought, *A little girl pretty as she is should of had six or seven young swains lined up outside her door at home.*

He took a deep breath, suddenly angry. *She should of picked one of them, instead of traveling all the way up here to wed a stranger. Hush, I should of married Ellen Bates before we left Virginia. By now I'd of had my own hearth and home, and maybe some young'uns like Tom's, instead of running around the countryside getting shot to pieces and burying strangers in a creek bed.*

But the chance for him to make that choice had got away from him. Maybe the same thing had happened to this girl.

James put a fist to his belly to press against a sudden sharp pain that joined the leaden lump in his gut. His movement brought the girl's eyes around to his once more, and he wondered if her pain was anything like his.

She took a deep, quick breath, unconsciously drawing James's attention from her face to her form.

Six little beans! A man could forget a multitude of pains if he was cuddled up in a snug cabin next to a girl the likes of this one.

Hold up, James, he told himself, pulling his runaway thoughts down to a trot with a short rein. *Don't you cheat this little girl. She's far from home, and sitting in a mighty worrisome place. Don't you add to her troubles by taking advantage. You said you'd see her home to her mama, and that's where she's going, with a second chance to get a husband from that crowd of young men outside her door.*

James bit his lip, tasting warm blood as his teeth sliced through the smooth inside membrane of his mouth. He stemmed the slightly salty flow with his tongue and swallowed hard.

Then his mouth was open and he was speaking out, and his words surprised himself as much as they surprised Tom. "She came to marry a stranger. I reckon I'm as good a stranger as the next man, and better than some. Tell her I'll stand as her bridegroom."

Tom's face came down in a hurry from gazing at the ceiling, and he looked hard at James, peering into his eyes. James stared back, standing his ground, so Tom turned to the girl and spoke.

James watched her face while Tom talked, and his message seemed to bring peace to her soul. She lowered her tight kept shoulders, and her hands returned to their normal color as she loosened those clenched fingers.

Then James wondered why it worried him to feel the pain leaving and the lump of lead dissolving out of his belly.

&

James walked out of the church toward where he had left his animals. Tom O'Connor stayed behind, talking animatedly to the priest. The Mexican's dog scampered out from between two houses and barked joyfully at finding his new master again. James stopped, went down on one knee and scratched the animal's brown ears.

His thoughts raced as he greeted the dog. He had to get a proper stock of food supplies before he took the girl home. He couldn't feed her jerked beef alone. He'd need beans, at least, and maybe some corn meal, so if she knew how to cook she could make those flat corn cakes like Tom's Rosalinda had given him to eat. Maybe he could take the job working with Angus Campbell's colts, get them rough broke in a week or two, buy supplies, and be on the trail. But did the girl have any warm clothes? It would probably be November before they reached

Ratón Pass, and the weather in the high mountains on the border with New Mexico Territory would likely get cold come wintertime. *Tarnation! What if we hit snow?* he wondered. *I've got an extra blanket for a bedroll, but she's going to freeze in the daytime if that black shawl is all she's got to wrap up in.*

Tom arrived, and James rose to his feet and untied the horse and mule, and the two men started toward the house.

"You won't need the banns," Tom said.

"Banns. What's that mean?"

Tom squinched up his face. "It's an announcement in church, sort of a way of cleaning up any objections to a marriage." He paused to adjust one suspender. "It usually takes several weeks, but the *padre* said since he's already published them for Rodríguez, and you're sort of a replacement, he'll look on it as a special case. He can hitch you up this evening, and after a day or two, you can be on your way to the Greenhorn Valley, James, boy."

James looked at his boot toes for a few steps before answering. "The young lady seems particularly set on having a husband, Tom, *any* husband. I don't know what that's all about. But you said it back in the church: she's got to go back where she came from."

"What do you mean?" Tom asked. He stopped short and grabbed James's arm.

James came to an abrupt halt and turned to face Tom. "If a few words from me in front of the priest can ease the girl's mind, they won't hurt me none. I reckon that's the only way to get her safe back home. Once I turn her over to her ma, that's the end of it."

Tom stared at James, his mouth open. Then he swore. "The good Father won't look on it that way, and neither will the girl. You're taking a vow of marriage here, James, boy."

"Tom—"

"These Mexicans take their vows to heart. Oh, the men folks don't always keep the 'cleave to only one' part, but they stay married. What you're proposing ain't right at all." Tom frowned at James for a moment. "I reckon your ma would want you to think mighty hard about that."

At the mention of his mother, James's face turned red and he threw his hands into the air, startling the horse into neighing and shying into the path of the dog. That animal barked and turned to nip at the heels of the mule, which kicked out at the dog.

As his face grew even redder with embarrassment, James whistled the dog to his side and quieted the animals, then turned again to look at Tom.

"I've parted company with Ma and Pa," he said, resisting the urge to kick the toe of his boot against a tuft of buffalo grass beside the path. "I figure what I do is purely my own business."

Tom looked James up and down, chewing on his cheek.

James continued. "I didn't ride into this town seeking a wife. I figure me burying that fellow makes me responsible to see the girl is safe, though, so the vow I'm taking tonight is to get her back to Santa Fe. That's the honorable thing to do. Once she's home with her mama, that'll be the end of my vow."

Tom moved his head slightly. "Maybe by then you'll be fond of her. She is a mighty comely girl. And that name. *Amparo*. It means shelter, or refuge. You could do worse than to wed a sweet gentle gal like her and gain a shelter place for yourself."

James felt like swearing. "I just want to see the girl home, not start a new life with her." He took a deep breath, ready to curse Tom's meddling, but he got a good whiff of himself, and while he let out the lungful of foul air, his anger cooled.

Tom must have seen that a new thought was upon James, for he came up and clapped his hand on the younger man's shoulder. "You think on it, James, boy. I know you'll do the little lady a justice."

James made a wry face as Tom's hand fell away. "They say Justice is blind, but I reckon she's got a nose. Where can a man get a bath in this town?"

Tom's face split with a grin. "I got a barrel out back you can use, and plenty of cold water in the well. My woman can heat up a couple of buckets, take the chill off. And James, boy, you'd best wear my suit for the marrying. It's bigger'n you are, but it's clean."

₧

When the men had gone, Amparo sat alone in the chapel once more, letting the events of the last half hour flood over her. Her bridegroom was dead—another had taken his place. A shudder shook her frame, and she bit her lip.

Madre de Dios, he is Anglo. He does not speak my language. Amparo fingered the smooth wooden beads of her mother's rosary. *Yet . . . he has a kind aspect. There is strength in the shape of his face, but there is gentleness in his eyes.* She held the cross to her cheek, then brought it to her lips and kissed it. *Beloved Mother, if I must marry a stranger—and that is my vow—can there be some little hope for tenderness? Can he come to care for me?*

The girl clasped her hands under her bowed head, slid forward to kneel on the hard wooden prayer bench, and whispered several "*Ave Marías*". When she had finished, she rose from the bench and left the pew.

Amparo looked for the priest in his room at the back of the chapel. He was not there, but she found him at the front door, looking out into the square with a troubled look on his face. She touched his robe, and he turned to her.

"My Father, the *Anglos* are gone."

"Yes. They will come again later. Little daughter, the young one has agreed to kneel beside you this evening and become your master. I will bless this union with him only if you wish it." Father Gallegos pursed his lips. "There is rebellion in his soul."

Amparo bowed her head so the priest could not see her eyes. *Dearest Mary, I think it is pain.*

The priest lifted her chin. "You do not agree? Tell me your heart, little one."

Amparo looked up into the kind brown eyes of the *padre*. "He seems to be a good man, my Father. Although he is a stranger and an Anglo, he felt obligation to tell me of Señor Rodríguez's death. He does not want me to be alone in a strange place. These things are good."

"I wonder if he will accept the burden of marriage for long, my child."

The girl looked at the priest for a long time. *Without my sacrifice my papá will suffer for eternity*, she thought. She looked out at the dusty square, at the women disappearing into their adobe houses, carrying their clean laundry in baskets on their heads. *They all have homes, husbands, families.* Amparo straightened her shoulders.

"I have come a long distance, my Father. There is nothing for me at home. I will give myself to the Anglo and pray that I will not be a burden to him."

The priest touched Amparo on the forehead. "You are young, my child. He is young. Where there is youth, there is hope. Go now and prepare."

Amparo bent her head and kissed the priest's hand. Then she walked toward the tiny storage room that had become her refuge. She closed the door behind her and leaned on it.

Holy Mother, there is a stirring within me. Almost, I feel happy, almost, I feel at peace. Let this feeling lift me up and sustain me, Blessed Mary, for this night I must go to the Anglo's bed.

ᔥ

James tied the whining dog by the door of the barn, then took a quick look around the space behind Tom's house—between it, the blacksmith shop, and the barn—before he shucked off his winter underwear and climbed into the cold water in the barrel. *Too bad it ain't full dark yet. This isn't my notion of a fit place to bathe, in the open yard in front of all God's angels.* But it was his only chance to get clean, so he got to it, lifting a bucket from the ground and sloshing part of the water in it over his head.

The liquid warmed him as it ran down his face, finding little paths through his beard. A portion of it got into his mouth, and he tasted the bitter alkali of the plains mixed with oil from his hair. James spit sideways, and poured the rest of the water from the bucket over himself.

Rosalinda had provided a new bar of soap. James picked it up, got it wet, and ran it across his body, rubbing it hard into the tangle of black hair that covered his chest. Then he ran the soap block down his arms, ignoring the twinges of pain the action brought on as he passed over the wounds in his left arm. The smell of the lather rose sharply in his nostrils, an odor that seemed as yellow as the bubbles.

All at once the dog began barking, stiff legs planted apart and pulling the rope tight. James ignored the animal.

He was enjoying the slippery feel of getting clean, soaping his neck and face, when a female voice behind him asked, "What happened to your side?"

James almost tipped the barrel over, ducking down so fast behind the staves. "Who's that?" he yelled, feeling the prick of an oak splinter entering his knee. The dog quit barking and wagged its tail, letting its tongue loll out from between its jaws.

All James heard for a moment was footsteps crunching on a patch of gravelly rock as whoever it was came around to the front of the barrel. James hunched over, shivering from the surprise as much as from the cold, until Tom's little girl came into sight, flinging one braid over a shoulder.

"It's me," she said, calm as a freezing night in deep winter. "You look funny, hiding in there."

"Tarnation!" James's inclination was to add a few more words in a harsher vein, but he restrained himself. "Get away from here, Rida!" Soap bubbles flew out from his moustache as he yelled.

The girl's foot twisted back and forth in the dirt. "You're not very polite. You didn't heed me when I told you not to go visiting."

"That's so," he shouted. "I was plainly rude. Now, get along."

"I forgive you." She bent over and snatched at his clothes. "I'll take these to the square and wash them for you."

James lunged for the clothes, but the barrel tipped like it meant to go over, and he rocked back in a hurry. By then, Rida had his shirt, trousers, and underwear behind her back.

"Phew!" She twitched her nose. "You been rolling in the horse stalls? These duds stink something fierce." The girl held her nose with her finger and thumb.

"That's honest sweat," James growled. "Got it burying a dead man."

"Ohhhh," she moaned, shuddering. "Keep your smelly old things." She flung the clothes at him and ran away around the house.

James glared at the dog laying relaxed in the dust. He muttered "Traitor!" then made haste to soap up, wash down, and climb from the barrel. He grabbed a piece of sack towel to wrap around the important parts before anyone came to see what all the yelling was about, then he dashed to Tom's blacksmith shop so he could dress inside the safety of four walls.

Chapter 11

I'm not sure about the rest of it, but this must be the tie that binds.

James knelt before the mission altar with a silken sash wound about his neck and that of the girl, Amparo. It seemed the priest talked on and on, speaking in a tongue James didn't know, saying words he didn't want to hear.

Pretty gold fringe, he thought, tucking down his chin to see the ends of the sash. *Rosalinda's folks must be well off. Good of her to lend the sash to us. I wish this was done with. I need some air.*

Then his chest snapped up straight as James noticed the priest gazing at him. He raised his chin and said, "I resolve to be her bridegroom till I get her home safe."

The good father looked a question at Tom, who shrugged his shoulders and nodded. Then while the priest worked his way through the girl's part, James let his shoulders sag backward, and he looked her over.

Kneeling down, the top of the girl's head came up even with his chin. She wore a little white lace kerchief perched on top of her hair, her black shawl over her shoulders, then a well fitted yellow satin dress with a couple of green bows on the skirt. *Must have cost her mama dearly*, he thought. She twisted her hands together in front of the skirt, then let loose of one hand with the other, and plucked at one of the bows.

She's a mite nervous herself, he thought.

James looked up as the girl began to recite her vows with a great deal of earnestness, and he watched the artificial flowers woven into the twists of hair at the back of her head shake back and forth as she spoke.

This quiet looking gal's got a fire to her, underneath, like a frisky yearling. James's eyes took in the black shawl draped under the sash. Amparo breathed deep and fast as she recited, which made the black stuff rise and fall over her bosom. He felt a prick of excitement and fisted his hands.

Pretty girl, don't go breathing like that, he admonished her silently. *I'm just a country boy, and mighty human.* Then the girl was silent, and turned her face toward James.

Hush my mouth, them eyes are big as doorknobs. James's heart drummed in his chest like horse's hooves on a hardpan road, as he got lost in eyes bright as the moon and dark as the bottom of a dry well. Then he caught a movement with the tail of his eye. It was the priest holding his palm out, and James wondered what he wanted. By and by he remembered the ring in his pocket, so he dug it out and put it in the holy man's hand. The priest held up the ring and said a few words over it, then gave it back to James.

He swallowed four or five times, looking at the designs worked into the gold ring and hefting it in his hand. Then he touched it with the tip of his finger. It was warm, and the edge was as smooth as window glass on a sunny day. He stroked it a couple of times until the girl gave him a nudge with her elbow. Turning to her, James recalled what the ring was for when he looked down at the fingers of one of her hands, spread apart in front of her yellow skirt.

James glanced up at Amparo's eyes, and she looked steadily back at him. The look was so intense that he had to shift his gaze and swallow all over again. He fumbled a bit with the ring, almost dropped it on the piece of red carpet underneath them, but got it on her finger at last. The priest moved his arm over the couple in benediction, saying some more words all the while, then the ceremony was done, and he motioned for them to rise up and stand.

Tom stepped forward, ready to shake hands with James. His hard palm felt cool, and James lost some of the tightness binding his shoulders under the sash.

"There. That didn't hurt at all, James, boy. You're lucky to wed such a fine, pretty woman."

"Just to Santa Fe," he said, as Tom clapped him on the back.

"I don't know if the padre *caught* that or not. He looks a mite glum, James, boy. This should cheer him up." Tom pressed a coin into his hand.

James slipped the money to the priest, who then seemed quite a bit happier. Father Gallegos gave James the wedding license they'd all signed before the ceremony. Then James unwound the sash from his neck and Amparo's, handed it to Tom, and took the girl by the elbow as he wondered on what he'd done.

She's my wife, signed and sealed. What am I to do but get her to Santa Fe as quick as I can?

ᖇ

Blessed Virgin, I am the wife of an Anglo, Amparo thought as she rose to her feet. *He does smell much better than before. I thought he was a trapper, like those my papá told me about so long ago. Holy Mother, I have done my part. I beseech thee, pray that my sacrifice be worthy in the sight of thy Holy Son.*

Amparo cast her eyes sideways and watched James as he shook hands with the other Anglo. *I wonder what he thinks of me? He hardly looks at me. Maybe I am ugly in his sight. Please, let that not be! If he hates me, he will not be gentle!*

℘

James and Amparo walked to Tom's house, where Rosalinda had got together with some of her neighbors to put on a wedding meal and party for the young couple. James stood back, not of a mind to celebrate what seemed an empty thing, but he had no other place to go, so he stayed and played the part of bridegroom, and gave the ear adornments to Amparo when Tom suggested it. That was worth something to him, for the girl gave him a smile, the first he had seen on her face.

She said, "*Gracias,* Señor O-wen," which Tom told him meant 'Thank you, Mr. Owen'.

Tarnation. I'm going to have a hard time of it, traveling alone with this girl, me talking one lingo and her talking another. But James shrugged his shoulders, and ate something called sweet bread, and wished Tom would stop grinning at him.

After the meal, Tom thrust a lamp into James's hand and bid the couple goodnight at the back door. The blacksmith almost snickered as he pronounced the first part of the word. James grunted, and held the light high as he and Amparo stepped into an icy breeze in the yard between the buildings.

When they reached the wide double door to the blacksmith shop, James gave the lamp to Amparo and pulled the right-hand half open far enough for them to slip inside. Then he tugged the planks shut, and looked for a beam or a bar to secure the opening, but there was none.

Well, maybe these Mexican folks don't go in for shiverees. I surely hope Tom's forgot what that is. I don't want to have to fight off a drunken, teasing crowd tonight.

He took the lamp from Amparo and hung it on a hook near the cold forge, where it cast a flickering, crooked halo of light on the floor. Then he made a mound of the fresh hay Tom had provided, and spread the blankets the girl had brought from Santa Fe upon it. His quilts lay nearby, where he would make his bed off to one side. He was determined to leave the girl with the best kind of bait to catch herself a proper husband.

Amparo was up to some errand of her own that set her satin skirt to rustling—almost creaking—behind him, then the sound stopped. Finished with her bed, James rocked back on his heels and rose to his feet, then turned—and stopped like he'd run into the anvil.

She stood, shivering a little in the meager heat of the lamp, wearing only her white linen shift, her arms crossed in front of her breasts. Her thumb, darting out from between fisted fingers, kneaded at the ring James had put on her hand. For a long time she looked for something on the earthen floor, then she raised those great large eyes to his.

He rubbed the back of his neck with his hand and looked at the girl. The lamplight behind made her curves show through the thin cloth, curves that dried his mouth. He swallowed hard.

"Six little beans! You got you a figure like a china doll." He lowered his hand and stared at the palm. It was beaded with fresh sweat. He said, "You got me making my hands all moist," and wiped the palm down the belly of his shirt.

Then he looked into her eyes, soft as brown moss floating on a willow shadowed pond, tender as cat tails sprouting out of black water, eyes that threatened to melt away his resolve, so he put a poker down his spine and tried to get an icy edge to his voice. "I ain't holding you to your vows."

It was no use talking. She stood there, straight and silent, and gazed at him. He sucked in a breath and tried again. "I wish I could make you understand. This isn't a real marriage."

She dropped her arms, placed her hands on her hips, threw back her shoulders, and spouted some Spanish at him, tapping her foot on the hard packed earth and setting her body into motion.

She had his attention. "Six little beans! I heard that word before. What does '*marido*' mean?"

"*Tu . . . eres . . . mi . . .* marido," she said, repeating the words, spacing them out like he was deaf, which maybe he was, he reflected, from her way of seeing it. Then she said the phrase again, pointing first to the ring, then to him.

"That's right. We're married." He licked his parched lips. "But not for long." There was something sticking in his throat, and it took him a time to force a swallow past it. "I'm not taking you to bed. Once you're home you can get a real husband."

It was burdensome talking at that still firmly set, beautiful little face, not knowing how much the girl was taking in, hoping and wishing she was getting some of his meaning. So burdensome it was, thinking of ways to tell her things a man didn't discuss with a girl.

There is a point where a man with a sense of honor knows he's getting onto dangerous ground with a woman. He could clearly see that point, not far ahead, bright and shining and enticing and deadly as the tip of the bayonet that sliced into him in Virginia, and he knew it was time to retreat.

He leaned over and picked up his quilt so he could cover the girl up, and started toward her, trying to concentrate on the top of her head. The light from the lamp wavered across her face, caressed her sweet form, betraying him, and he felt a throb, an ill-omened ache, deep in the base of his belly.

"No," he said, then gritted his teeth and moved to wrap her in the quilt. She tipped her head back to look at him as he stood there in front of her, holding that quilt in his unmoving arms.

He made the mistake of glancing down right then, and her bright eyes caught his as surely as molasses traps an ant.

"*Estamos casados*," she whispered, and reached up to pull his head down to meet her lips. She had strength in those slim brown arms beyond his talent to stand his ground, and he partook of her kiss. Her lips—soft and yielding as rose petals plucked one by one from the bush—tasted of honey and wine. Light from the lamp swirled around the two of them, throwing glints and sparks on the walls as though they were inside a crystal chandelier.

He partook of her kiss, warm as the earth at noontime, forgetting the quilt that slipped from between them to the earth as he put his hands around her back and felt the smoothness of her skin under the linen, rubbing his thumb down the valley of her spine and sensing the quiver of her body under his hand, inhaling the sweet perfume of her waterfall of hair. He hit that danger point and passed it, picked her up, carried her to the bed and let her excite his body, and felt no courage in his spirit to prevent her.

Afterward he rested, trembling, as she lay cradled in the curve of his arm, her heart thumping, thundering against his as she kissed the jagged white scar on his shoulder, and the small round wound in the front of his arm, and the puckered, angry red depression in his side. He felt that her lips, cool on his overheated skin, healed the wounds, sealing the fibers of the muscles together, restoring the lost bone, melting the scar tissue away.

She was still for a moment, breathing as he was breathing, slow and deep. Then she lifted her hand, and moved it so she could touch his mouth with her slim brown finger. He knew a mouth was for eating, and for kissing a girl, but he had never considered it a place for touching, and a wonderment filled his mind as she stroked his lips, slowly, soft as the brush of a spider's web come upon suddenly in the dark. He held his breath, parting his lips as her finger followed the course of them, from the top around to the bottom lip, then down his chin into the beard on his jaw.

A black veil covered his face as her lips came to his. He needed a breath, and he drew in hers, swallowing as she kissed him, swallowing his pride as passion swelled in him. Then, he did not resist the need in her but replied with the hunger in him, and it was nigh to morning when finally they slept.

ᔕᑎ

James awoke with the sun high, and felt shame, both for his late rising and for his weakness in the lamplight. Amparo lay curled beside him, her hand resting heavily on his chest. He touched the dead man's ring on her finger and thought, *I'm a fox in the henhouse.* He sighed, a long shuddering out-breath of air, then wisdom came to his mind: *The girl used a binding knot on me.*

His belly tightened as he remembered the warmth of her, remembered rising from the bed to douse the lamp, then returning to her arms and the laughing triumph of knowing himself full a man alongside a woman full his wife.

Caught up in the memory, he kissed her fingertips, then felt a flush hot as the virgin blood she had shed in coming together with him, and thought, *James, you're a poor excuse for a gentleman, but we still go to Santa Fe.* Then he put her hand carefully from him and rose and hurriedly pulled on his clothes.

ᔕᑎ

When Amparo awoke, she found herself alone, a blanket carefully tucked around her. She gathered her arms in to hug herself, remembering the tickle of the Anglo's moustache on her lips. *Madre de Dios, he is a true caballero. His hands are gentle as . . . as a mother's, no, as a tender lover's hands. Holy Mother, I feel— what is it I feel? Cherished, protected. Señora Catarina was wrong. I like the touch of my husband's hands upon me. His eyes are as sapphires glowing in a precious necklace. His hair is black as nightfall overtaking the day. His breath is sweet as* pan dulce *to the tongue. But María Santa, he is full of pain; not only from the wounds that scar his body, but from a tear in his heart. He called out a name in the night, and it was not my name. Holy Mary, help me to heal him, help me to be a solace to him, for I yearn to hear him call my name.*

Chapter 12

"I came to see about the work."

Angus Campbell stood behind his plow in a field beside a sod built house. James had left Amparo in the road, holding the reins of his horse and the lead line to the pack mules while he tramped across rows of turned under crops to join Angus. The dog licked James's hand, then turned to chase a chicken back toward the coop.

"However," James said, "there's a difficulty."

Angus inclined his head toward the road. "The girl?"

James hadn't planned what to tell Angus, figuring an explanation would come to him when he arrived. "I've been hired to get her over Ratón Pass to her folks before snow flies," he blurted out. "But I need enough work for a grubstake, if you've got something I can handle in the time I have available."

"Well, now, what I have in mind is child's play for you, James. I have some raw three-year-old colts to break for riding. I figured to hire it out, 'cause I don't have time, being so far behind with this fieldwork. Andy is too young to do the job alone."

In Virginia, James had been known as a boy with a knack for gentling horses, and had since picked up the cowboy way of breaking them from his father's Texas foreman, Bill Henry. It pleased him that Angus remembered his skill. "How many you got?" he asked, a slow grin reflecting the lightening of his mood.

"Four. Can you spare a month?"

James squinted at the sky. Today it was bright and blue, with no trace of the snow he had hit on the way down from Pueblo, but there was no way of knowing how long the weather would hold. He scratched his ear and sighed. Time pressed heavy on him, and a frown settled upon his soul again. "Maybe a week is all I got. I can rough break them all now and top off the job when I get back."

"I need one real gentle for the wife. I guess that one'll have to wait until after you get the girl home?"

He nodded. "What are the others for?"

"Riding fence. They only have to get used to a rider on their back."

"I'll have time to break three to saddle. Andy can help me catch them, and watch what I do, but he'll have to ride them enough to train them to rein. I've no time for that."

"Well, do the best you can, and I guess we'll manage. I'll stake you to whatever you need when three are done." Angus looked toward the road. "How did the girl come to be stranded?"

James rubbed his hand across his beard. He didn't want to tell lies about Amparo, but he didn't want to own up to the truth, either. He swallowed hard.

"It's a mighty long story, and if I'm to get those colts started today, I'd best not stand around jawing. One thing, though. The stable is good enough for me, but can you put the young lady up in the house?"

"We'll find a place for her. She has the Mexican look. Does she speak any English?"

"Not a word, as far as I can tell. But she's quiet and won't be any bother, I reckon."

"What's her name?"

"Miss Amparo."

"Pretty name. Well, the colts are in the pasture next to the corral. Plenty of rope in the stable."

They shook hands, and James went back to the road, mounted, and took Amparo to the house to introduce her to Molly Campbell. When he went out the door, leaving the women to sort out a way of communicating, Amparo was putting on an apron, and he figured she was insisting on helping with the noon meal.

Good. She's a worker. She'll fit right in with Molly and her bunch. At least for a week. He wondered how she would stand being in the house with seven young'uns. That made him grin, and he went to work with a light feeling and an even temper.

By the time James chose three colts to break, and he and Andy roped them in the pasture and worked them into the large corral, it was dinnertime and more. James figured Molly would carry on about her boy missing the meal, so he let Andy go to the house to get cleaned up while he dismounted and took care of their horses.

When he got to the house, James was late, and all of the kids but Andy had taken off to do their chores. Molly and Amparo jumped up from their seats when they caught sight of him and bustled about getting his grub together. Angus leaned on his elbows, nursing the last of his coffee, and James figured he wanted a report on the progress.

"Got 'em in the corral," he said as he sat down.

"Good, good," Angus said, nodding his head. "You going to ride them this afternoon?"

Molly added a slice of bread to the food on James's plate and Amparo lowered it in front of him. He took a bite of the bread and looked up at the girl for a fraction of a moment. Then wished he hadn't, because the look she put through those mossy-soft eyes shook him to his boots. It took him a good minute to recover enough to answer Angus.

"No, I think I'm going to work with them a mite. I reckon it will pay in the long run."

"How'll we do that, James?" asked Andy through a mouthful of beans.

"Tie a back leg up to make them less dangerous, then use a gunny sack to mess with them, get them used to humankind."

"When will we ride the colts?" Andy wanted to know, and James laughed at his impatience.

"When they're ready. We'll see how it goes today."

Then he concentrated on his food, trying to forget that sitting across from him was a fetching young woman wearing a ring he had put on her finger, and that he had neglected to tell Angus the truth about him and her. And if truth be known, his blood was pumping fast and hot—maybe from the exercise, maybe from memories of two nights ago, maybe from the glance she just gave him—and he felt mighty uneasy being so close to the girl. He was glad that come nighttime, she would bunk down in the house, and he would make his bed in the stable.

After dinner, James and Andy went back to work at the corral. James snagged a mouse-colored mustang and led it into a smaller corral. He snubbed the lead rope to the fence and began to rub the horse with a gunnysack he had brought along. The colt was a touch fractious, but it was canny, too, and curious to see what James was up to.

He didn't let it know anything more that afternoon, for he had two other horses to work with, so he left it tied to the fence while he repeated the process with a buckskin and the third horse, a brown. When he was through for the day, he and Andy led the horses back to the larger corral and fed and watered them.

Molly's evening meal stuffed James so full he could barely waddle out the door to his bunk. He spent the night dozing and waking, wondering if Amparo was comfortable in the house.

The next morning James put the mousy colt in the small corral, and it stayed calm even when he threw a loop around one of its back feet. It did get a bit worried when Andy pulled the rope through the fence and drew the slack out so its foot was lifted off the ground. Then the colt panicked and fought the rope, and down it went.

When it had struggled onto three feet again, James worked it over—this time with a saddle blanket—letting the colt touch the blanket with its lip and sniff at it, running his hands over its back, and talking it into trusting him. Then he hobbled the horse's back feet and tied the animal to the fence behind it, loosed the halter rope, and let the colt get used to the back hobbles while he took a breather, squatting on his heels in the middle of the corral.

Andy sat on the fence and watched, prodding him to get on with the job.

The colt had its ears laid back and its nostrils flared, so when James was ready to start in again, he hobbled the front feet before he began to pat and rub. The horse strained to look at the awful things James was doing to it, pulling its knotted up tail, cutting some of the rat's nests out of the long strands with his knife, and once in a while, leaning up against the horse's flank to get it used to him putting weight on. He spelled off work on the mousy colt with work on the brown and the buckskin, and by nightfall, he was bone tired.

The next day James grabbed the blanket and his saddle, and started working the colts, letting them smell and touch the things he'd brought to the corral.

He tied the horses by the halter ropes and back hobbled them again. Since the blanket and saddle smelled of his horse, the colts had nothing to fear from them, and before long, he put the blanket on the brown's back and left it there. Then James tied the off side saddle cinches up so they wouldn't bang the colt's side, and slowly set the leather onto its back. The brown nickered a bit but it didn't move, so James went on with the job, slowly cinching the saddle down, just barely snug. He slapped the leather, jiggled the saddle, put his foot into the stirrup and stood up, then got down.

Andy yelled, "Oh boy! James is going to ride the colt!"

"Hold on," he said. "It's not ready yet."

"Whadda you mean, not ready?" the boy asked. "You got the saddle on it, don't you?"

"These horses won't be cowboy broke. I promised your pa you could ride them, and I don't mean for them to buck you off every morning."

"Come on," Andy razzed him. "You ain't afraid, are you?"

James had to ignore Andy for a time.

Then it was up and down, up and down in one stirrup for a long spell, getting the horse used to the feel of weight. Then James put his right leg over, dragging it across the rump a bit, seating himself, all the while talking to the brown and stroking it gentle as a mare's lick. Pretty soon it got over its nerves and stood quiet. James climbed on and off a couple of times, and then decided it was time to ride.

"Hey Andy. You ready for a show?"

The boy had almost gone to sleep on the fence rail, but he came awake when James called, and popped his suspenders with excitement as he ran off to get the rest of the kids. Angus heard the noise and called Molly down to the corral. Amparo figured out something was up, because she was there too, leaning against the top rail, staring at James.

He untied the hobbles, let loose the lead rope from the halter, gathered the reins, and looked toward Amparo. She was still looking at him, and that melted his innards, but he picked his courage up off the ground, stuffed it into his chest, put his foot into the stirrup, and swung aboard.

Nothing happened. The brown horse stood quiet as a tame pony, and James could tell Andy was mighty disappointed by the groan he let out. James got the colt to circle the corral three or four times, then hopped down.

Everybody went away while James played the same up and down game with the buckskin, then with the mousy horse. The buckskin was the more nervous of the two, and he decided to ride it the next day, when he would be rested, but he figured the mouse-colored colt was ready. Andy spread the word, and a crowd built up for his ride on the mouse.

This time the horse bucked a time or two when it found out it was free of the hobbles and ropes, and James had a nice little bouncy ride, but after the colt ran around the corral twice, it settled down and soon he got off.

"Ride the buckskin. You still got plenty of day," said Andy.

James shook his head. "He's fractious, and I'm tired. Tomorrow is soon enough."

"Ah, come on. It's hours till sundown. You can have everything done a day early."

I hadn't better try it, tuckered out as I am, he thought. *But there is that daylight, and I wouldn't mind leaving one day sooner.*

"Young'un," he said to Andy, "you could wear the bark off a tree flapping that tongue of yours. I'll ride the buckskin if your pa has a rope in his hand to catch it if it bucks me off." Then James made ready, knowing all the while it was the wrong thing to do.

The buckskin waited until James's right leg was halfway over its back before inviting him to dance, and right then he should have thrown himself off. But he was stubborn, and wanted to show the colt who was boss, so he grabbed for a handful of mane and stuck with it.

James couldn't get his right foot into the stirrup iron, what with it and him both bouncing in the air. There was more sky between him and the saddle than between the ends of a rainbow. Once James thought he had his boot tip set to shove it home into the stirrup, but the buckskin landed with four feet together, head down, and that was the last jolt he took.

Before James met the ground he cart wheeled twice, and the breath left his lungs with a "whoosh" that could be heard clear back to Tom O'Connor's place. Then the colt turned toward him, snorting and kicking, trying to get rid of the saddle, and James couldn't get his limbs to move him out of the horse's way.

Hush, I'm in trouble.

James lay frozen where he fell, listening to Molly's baby wail. The colt bucked and swirled toward him, shaking its head and blowing clouds of foul smelling breath. Two of the girls screamed.

Andy cried, "Get up, James! Get up outta there!"

Molly started praying out loud. Angus swore at the horse, and started to climb the fence.

James tried to move, but his limbs still wouldn't work. He knew he was about to get hurt bad, or maybe killed.

Five or six puffy clouds scudded around in the sky, white above the dust the colt kicked into the air. James wondered if a body's soul floated through those clouds on the way to heaven.

As he turned his head a bit, he saw that in two more jumps the buckskin would be atop him.

James figured he wasn't going to a saintly reward, what with the lies he'd been telling, the truths he'd not told, the swearing he'd done, and falling into the crack between a couple of other bad sins. He tensed up his belly and closed his eyes, waiting for the colt to stomp him.

James heard a low sound. It wasn't a scream or a cry, but an angry voice getting louder as it came up behind him. He didn't understand a single word, but Amparo wasn't talking to him. She was cussing the colt, and running right toward it, trying to chase it away from James.

"¡Vaya!" she said. "¡Vaya de mi esposo! Maldito caballo, ¡vaya, digo, vaya!"

She came into his view, and there was determination on her face as she flapped her apron and swirled her skirt at the horse. Glory, she had no fear, and she drove that green colt right to the other side of the pen, where Angus got a rope on it and snubbed it up tight to the fence.

Amparo knelt in all that dust and checked him over to see if anything was broken. He quivered from head to toe, as much from her touch upon him as from almighty terror. Her face was white as chalk dust as she ran her hands over his limbs, asking him over and over something he couldn't decipher.

"I'm fine, I'm fine," he said, although he felt like he wanted to lie there and die, now that pain was burning up his spine and down his limbs. That's when she touched under his nose and brought her finger away bright with blood.

"Sangre," she whispered, and chills beat down his back.

"Blood," James said, trying to move his arm up to his nose.

The force of the colt's bucking had started his nose to bleeding, but he had been too busy trying to suck in air to notice. Now that the girl had brought it to his attention, he knew what was making the hairs of his moustache clump together.

Amparo dabbed at his nose with her apron. "Mi pobrecito," she crooned, making little clucking sounds in her throat.

James tried to put on a cheerful face. His arms tingled up and down, like root beer prickling a body's nose, and he let loose a long sigh. Maybe I haven't got any paralyzing damage, he thought. He flexed his fingers, and Amparo took his hand. He held on for a moment, trying to squeeze so she'd know he was sound.

The girl was still clucking and crooning, and James felt a frown creasing his face. "I'm going to live. Don't go worrying over me, girl. Tarnation! How can I let you know not to fuss?"

The best way to tell her was to show her, so James gathered strength, struggled to sit up, and got to his feet. Yellow dust clung to his clothes, so he gingerly bent to pick up his hat and swatted at the dirt. Then he jammed his head into the hat, took Amparo by the elbow, and hauled her back to the fence while she chattered away at him. When she was safely on the far side, he turned away so she couldn't see he was gritting his teeth, and took a careful step or two toward the far side of the corral, intent on showing that colt who was boss.

Amparo called out, "Señor, ¡no!"

James stopped and turned to face her. "Yes," he said, looking into those wide, dark eyes, and breathing hard like someone had let him up after holding his head under water for a long time. Her concern stung him like a swarm of yellow jackets on the prod, but he turned and went to the colt.

"Are you in one piece?" Angus asked from his perch on the top rail of the fence, but James only grunted and fetched a rope.

He had to work the buckskin some more, tying up a foot and putting the hobbles and lead rope on again, then climbing in and out of the saddle eight or ten times before it quit sidestepping. But he did get the animal to quiet down when he sat on its back.

By then, daylight was gone, the crowd had left, a breeze had come over the horizon, and James was stiffening up from the hard landing. Andy had other chores to do, so James sent him off while he left the buckskin in the hobbles, hauled food and water to it, and took care of the other two horses. Then James made for the house and supper.

Amparo was waiting for him beside the back door with a can of hot water and a white towel.

"Is this for me?" James reached out for the water can.

The girl shook her head a bit, and put a corner of the towel into the water. *"Voy a lavar tu cara,"* she said, making scrubbing motions in front of his face with the rag.

"I can do that," he gulped. "Thank you anyway."

"Es mi placer," she said, soft like, and he shivered like she'd stroked his soul with a feather.

James swallowed. He was doing a lot of that, like a green kid at his first dance. Being around this girl he'd vowed to see home safe, then held tight in his arms as if he had no will, this girl who had just saved his life and limb, shamed him as he recalled his weakness.

"It's my face." He put out his hand to take the towel, but Amparo touched it to his upper lip. The wet heat seeped pleasantly into his skin. He was grateful it was dark and nobody was around, for he wasn't sure if he was blushing or not.

The girl kept saying *"mi pobre* marido," and soaking the clots out of his moustache. James swallowed again, not sure how to make his escape, then wondering if he wanted to leave.

Eventually Amparo finished with his face, and he did go. When James sat down at the supper table, Angus said, "That colt scared the living daylights out of me. I thought you were a goner before the girl took a hand. It happened so fast I no more than had my leg over the bar before she had the horse off you and backed against the fence."

James turned his head to look at Angus. "I thought I was out there six or seven minutes before Miss Amparo came up. I'd wondered why you weren't there with the rope."

Ignoring his jibe, Angus continued, "And then I thought you was crippled up for life. I was never so glad when I saw you get up. I thought I'd have to cart you home on a buckboard and face your Ma and Pa."

James grunted and went on eating.

Angus left before James finished his meal. It was just as well, for he didn't want any further conversation just then. But as he approached Molly with his empty plate, she looked sideways at him and said, "Miss Amparo keeps saying *'mi esposo'* and looking at you, James. Are you carrying her away from her husband?"

He blinked four or five times, then said crossly, "Do I look like the sort of man who'd steal another fellow's wife?"

As James said it, pain he thought had gone ripped through his belly as he thought of Ellen and his brother. He frowned, rocking from his toes to his heels and back, then said, "The young lady's had some grief, and I'm taking her home to her ma."

"Oh, the poor little thing!" Molly said, and went about her work. James limped out of the house and off toward the stable, hurting inside and out. The dog trotted up and put its wet, cold nose into James's palm, then turned and ran toward the corrals.

James opened the stable door, closed it behind him, and walked slowly toward his bed in a corner of an empty stall, pulling his shirttail free of his trousers. Then he looked up and stopped short. Amparo sat on a box beside his bed, a bottle of liniment at her feet.

"Where'd you get that stuff?" he asked, and wondered how she told Molly she needed it.

Then he quit wondering and started sweating when she looked him over, demanded *"¡Quita la ropa!"* and made signs for him to shuck his clothes.

"Nooo, girl, you got me at a disadvantage here. Go back to the house and leave me be," he said. The glance of those brown black eyes seemed to burn through to his skin as surely as sitting on a just used poker left carelessly on a hearth.

"¡Quita la ropa!" she repeated, stood up, and started on the buttons of his shirt. He caught her hands, put them aside, and slowly took over the job. When she saw his shirt come off, Amparo picked up a cloth and soaked it in the liniment, then stood tapping her foot and waiting for him to take off the rest of his clothing.

James took his sweet time, but only unbuttoned the top half of his underwear and peeled it down. Amparo clicked her tongue in annoyance, pointed to the box, and said *"¡Siéntate!"*

He sat.

She found the lumps and bruises and scrapes he'd managed to heap up that day, and put that foul-odored stuff on them. The liniment burned, but it lessened the pain. When the aches were eased, she departed. James's body took on a fresh ache at her going, and he went to bed a lonesome man.

Chapter 13

By the end of the week, James had ridden the buckskin fourteen times and proclaimed him ready for Andy to work with. The boy was anxious to start training the colts, Angus was happy with the work, and James had his grubstake. Then he and Amparo were on the trail, with the big brown dog scampering behind their horses, sniffing out every scent that came along.

James rode cautiously that first day. His ribs were still tender from the adventure he and the buckskin had shared. With Amparo riding her horse behind him, he tried to pick the easiest side of the trail so she wouldn't notice how he was favoring his back. He surely did not want her to whip out that vile bottle of liniment he'd seen Molly hand her as she packed the food and supplies.

When he called a halt for the night, he dismounted with an "oof." Amparo looked over at him, but he smiled as he came to help her down, trying to move through the pain as though it did not exist. She narrowed her eyes, then turned and hunted through the packs to put together a meal.

James watched her from the ring of darkness beyond the fire as he rubbed down the animals and grained them. She sang softly as she cooked flat corn patties to go with the beans in the pot, kneeling beside the skillet at the fire, with her brown print skirt tucked up out of the way.

Beneath the white petticoat she wore under the skirt, he could see her knees. He turned away, quaking to his core as he recalled the fine texture of her skin beneath his hands, his fingers twined in the sweet smelling black veil of her hair, the rough places on his skin catching some of the strands. Now those strands of hair were captives in two thick braids tied with bits of cord.

He stroked the sorrel's neck, resting his head against its shoulder, gathering strength from the animal, damping down the yearning that rose in him. When he had won a measure of calm, he returned to the fire.

Amparo gave James a plate, put down a portion of food for the dog, then took up her own plate and settled on her saddle. James ate a few bites, standing in silence, then looked down at her.

"It's good food," he said, his voice a touch gruff. *I wish I could tell her in her own tongue*, he thought, chewing another mouthful. "I'm obliged for the help. My cooking isn't fit for any woman to eat."

Amparo smiled at him. *"Gracias, mi* marido.*"*

"'*Marido*'. You keep saying that." James scooped up beans with one of the corn cakes, in imitation of Amparo's actions.

"Marido." She pointed to him. "*Mujer.*" Her finger turned to herself.

"Mujer. That's woman," he muttered as she pointed to the ring. "More than woman. Wife. So 'marido' must be husband."

"*Sí*. Husban'." She looked thoughtful for a moment, then shook her braids back and pointed to the glints of light at her ears, the adornments Rodríguez had provided. "*Aretes*," she said, and laughed. The dog looked up from its food and barked.

It struck James that Amparo had a pleasant kind of laugh, low and bubbling. *So different from Ellen's laugh, Ma.* He shook off the thought and put his mind to the girl's word game. "You're having fun with this. '*Aretes*' are ear bobs."

Her hand circled over the plate. "*Comida.*"

"I heard that one before. Food." He held up a corn cake. "What's this?"

"*Tortilla. Es una* tortilla."

"Beans. What's that in your tongue?"

She craned her neck to see exactly where James was pointing on his plate, then nodded. "*Frijoles*. Free ho less."

He went over and squatted on his heels beside her. The dog came and lay down, placing its head on its paws beside James's boot. "You're a bright one, that's for sure." He stuffed a piece of tortilla soaked in bean juice into his mouth, then stroked the animal's head.

She scrunched up her face. "Bright?" It sounded funny the way she said it, with a little trill on the r.

"Bright. Smart. Use your noodle," James said, tapping his forehead.

"*Ah. Listo. Por supuesto. ¿Y cuál de nosotros es* listo*?*" Her finger waggled between the two of them.

He caught on and pointed to her. "Listo. You're listo. I reckon you know a little more English than I figured."

Out of the blue James felt a pride for her, almost like it mattered to him that she was a canny woman. And with that pride came back the yearning, filling his belly with a new kind of hurting. He felt a creeping heat going up his body, and hated knowing it wasn't from the fire. "It's sure you know how a woman gets her way," he said. "You had you a proper wedding night."

"*No entiendo.*" She made a face.

James sighed. "I fixed us two beds," he said, holding up two fingers, then putting his palms together and resting his head on them in a sign for sleep. "I'm still taking you to Santa Fe to your ma." He ducked his head and looked at the ground to hide his face in case it showed color. There was a stick near his boot, and he picked it up and fiddled with it to move his mind away from the yearning. Bark flew in all directions as he twisted the dry branch. The dog snuffled, then lay quiet.

"*¿'Ma'? ¿Quieres decir 'mamá'? Ella no es mi mamá. Es mi madrastra.*"

James moved one foot so he could turn and toss the stick into the fire, then faced her again. "I don't take your meaning. I reckon I'm not so listo." He gave her his plate and got to his feet. "But I'm listo enough to keep my britches on for the rest of the trip."

&ombreost;

The trail spread before James like a ribbon laid atop a johnnycake—a smooth path beaten into the uneven earth. Creosote bushes dotted the landscape like orchard plantings, regularly spaced on earth made barren by poison roots that jealously sucked at what little moisture lay beneath the surface.

It was nearly noon, with the November sun pouting on the breast of a hazy sky. A good day for traveling far, James thought. The dog ran off into the creosote to investigate a scent.

With such an easy trail ahead, James half turned in his saddle to take a long look at the girl riding side saddle behind him. Amparo gazed off toward the buttes to the north, a flat brimmed hat shading her eyes as she surveyed the broken prairie. Two thick black braids cuddled the black shawl she wore over a white blouse that was decorated around the scooped neckline with red embroidered flowers.

I've come a long, crooked trail from where I started out to go, James thought. *I should've had Uncle Jonathan's fallen in tunnel half cleared by now. It would've been done if I'd ridden through Pueblo.*

The girl glanced up, and a smile lit her olive toned face. James caught his breath, felt a creeping flow of blood under his beard, and started easing back into his seat.

"Glory, but she's a fine looking woman," he muttered, and stole another glance over his shoulder. The fingers of his left hand twitched with remembrance of fine textures—the silk of her hair, the satin of her skin. His blush deepened.

A high pitched squeal jolted him to reality at the same time he felt himself rising into the air and slipping out of the saddle as his horse reared. He grabbed for the horn, fought to regain his seat, but it was no use; the horse came down stiff legged, then bucked once, twice, and James was off the animal and onto the trail, discovering anew the subtle aches of his recent wounds.

As he landed on his back he heard it behind him—the whirring warning of a rattlesnake in a creosote bush along the trail. He pulled his pistol from the holster at his thigh and cocked it as he rolled to his belly, eyes searching through the multitude of small oval leaves of the bush for the rattler's coiled body. He spotted the head and snapped a shot. The snake died.

The horse, once it was free of James, galloped wildly back the way they had come. The dog barked its way out of the creosote, following the horse in a vain attempt to turn it. The sorrel kicked out its heels, narrowly missed the dog, and fled. The dog followed, yapping.

Amparo dismounted and ran to kneel at James's side. "¡Señor, o señor! ¿Estás herido?" she asked, starting to check his limbs.

"I'm fine, I'm fine," James snapped at her, gathering his legs beneath him and subduing her hands in his. He got to his feet, helped the girl up, and kicked the snake's body away from the road. He loosed Amparo's hands and looked around for his hat. She kept up a steady barrage of questions, and he tried to shush her with a wave of his hand as he bent to retrieve his headgear.

"Where'd that ill-bred horse go?" All that remained of the animal was a cloud of yellow dust hanging in the air above the back trail. James threw down his hat, yelped at the sharp twinges the action brought, then turned back to Amparo, who crooned her concern.

"You stop that cooing, girl. It makes me nervy as a cat caught with cream on its whiskers. Damnation! Oh, I mean— I'm sorry, Miss Amparo. Excuse my foul tongue."

Amparo handed him the hat. He took it with a sigh and a grunted "thanks," and banged it against his thigh to get the dust off.

"Well, miss, I'm in need of your gentle horse. The mules ain't broke for riding. Besides, I'm having about as much luck riding a skittish animal as a blind sparrow has flying. If it gets out that I can't stick on a horse, my reputation will be shot full of holes. I'll never get another job breaking horses."

As he spoke, he put his hat on his head, adjusted it, then stalked over to the mules and stripped off their packsaddles. He hobbled the animals and turned them out beside the trail. Then he approached the black mare and loosened the girth straps. "Can't you just see me riding sideways?" he said, grinning wryly as he heaved the saddle from the horse's back and placed it beside the trail.

"You'll have to stay here alone," he told the girl. "I'm sorry the dog ran off. He would have been company, and protection, besides." He squinted at the far landscape, then looked back at Amparo. "Well, you might as well start some comida while you wait. I don't expect to be gone long, but it'll be something to do."

"*Está bien*," she replied.

James disassembled one of the mule packs and got into his war bag. He brought an object over to Amparo, and knelt beside her where she was pulling foodstuffs out of a sack.

"I'll leave you this pistol. See, you pull back the hammer like this, then squeeze the trigger. Use two hands to hold it out in front of you to aim." He showed her. "I'm afraid I can't leave the rifle." He uncocked the gun and put it in her hands. "The horse carried it off."

"Rye full?" Amparo looked puzzled, then laughed. "Oh. *Rifle*." She pronounced the word "ree flay."

"What's so funny, girl? I don't favor leaving you by your lonesome. Well, I can't sit here jawing. Be careful."

James boosted himself onto the black, clucked it into motion, and headed down the back trail.

✂

Holy Mother, help him find the horse quickly, Amparo pleaded silently as James rode away. She laid the pistol beside the foodstuffs and straightened up, then gathered creosote twigs from the ground around the area and built a small fire, which smoked and gave off a thick odor. She blinked back tears as the smoke billowed toward her, filling her eyes. She gathered her goods and moved to the other side of the fire. Once things were arranged to her satisfaction, she set to work mixing cornmeal, a bit of lard, and water to make tortillas. When the dough reached the consistency she desired, she pinched off a glob of it and began to flatten it between her hands. The circle grew larger as the corn cake got thinner. When it was the right size, she laid it in the bottom of James' skillet, which she had placed on the rocks beside the fire to heat.

While the tortilla baked on the hot iron, Amparo started forming a second one. Before she finished flattening it, she tweaked the tortilla in the skillet onto its other side with her fingers. Soon she had a stack of tortillas wrapped in a white cloth, waiting for James to return with the horse.

The girl moved again to avoid the smoke from the fire. As she did so, she caught sight of the pistol lying beside the sack of cornmeal. Amparo reached over, picked up the heavy gun, and looked at it.

Santa María, it is so weighty. How can a man wear a weapon such as this strapped to his leg all the day? Yet the Anglo carries his pistol with such ease, as though it were a part of him.

Amparo placed the gun on the earth and sighed. *Holy Mother, there is a difficulty. I vowed to give myself freely to the stranger who took me in marriage. While Señor Owen is not the same stranger I had expected, yet I have fulfilled my pledge. But, My Lady of the Conquest, he has somehow found me wanting. The* girl bit her lip. *He rejects me, Blessed Virgin. For so many days he has not come to my bed. I had thought . . .*

Amparo stirred the embers of the dying fire and looked down the back trail. The dust James had raised had long since settled, and there was no sign of his return.

There was a night . . . the first night, Holy Mary, when I thought he was pleased with me. After . . . after I became his wife, he held me tenderly, he kissed me in many places, and I felt almost as though my dear papá had returned to protect me with his love.

Amparo covered her face with her hands. *No. The emotion I felt in my heart was nearly the same, but the action was very different. The embrace of a father is nothing like lying in the arms of a husband. Oh My Lady, I have lost that! What did I do wrong?*

A sound in the brush brought Amparo to her feet, clutching the pistol. Her heart thumped against her chest as she peered into the bushes. After a moment a small furry animal scuttled from under a branch and hurried to another patch of shade.

"*¡Ay de mi!*" Amparo exclaimed, and sank to the ground beside the pile of tortillas. As her breathing returned to normal, she remembered how the Anglo had stirred in his sleep, how he had called a woman's name, then sighed in the darkness.

The girl took a short, sharp breath. *Did I take her place, for one night? Did this bring him shame? Holy Mother of God! Strive with him! I want the Anglo to touch me—Amparo—with gentle fingers, and know that it is I whom he strokes. Cannot this be?*

A drumming noise filled the girl's head, and she thought her heart pounded heavily again, but the sound grew louder, and she looked up.

James, astride the sorrel and leading the black, rode toward her on the trail from Leones. Amparo sprang up.

"*¡Eres tú!*" she cried. "*Gracias a los cielos, eres tú.*"

Pulling the horse to a halt, James grinned down at the girl.

"Don't be waving the pistol at me that a way, Miss Amparo. I'll figure you ain't pleased to see me."

∞

James and Amparo rode south and east through a barren land broken by buttes and gullies, skirting the twin Spanish Peaks that rose out of the country below the *Cuchara* River. James hunted small game to stretch out their beans and tortillas, but he pushed along as fast as he figured Amparo could travel. Hitting deep snow in Ratón Pass still worried him, especially since the girl didn't seem to have much but her black shawl to fend off the wind. At night when the wind blew, her lips took on a bluish cast whenever she worked away from the fire. Without proper clothing, he knew Amparo would never survive a winter storm.

One evening, James sat on his saddle by the side of the fire after supper with one of his quilts and a needle full of thread in his hands. He tucked up a corner of the quilt and jabbed the needle into the cloth, bringing it in and out with the thread following until he had a rough head covering made from the corner. Amparo had been cleaning up the dishes, but now she took notice of his labors and came around the fire to him.

"*¿Qué es esta cosa?*" she asked, wide eyes reflecting disbelief that a man could do needlework.

It wasn't fine needlework. The sewing project was crude looking and ugly, but James hoped it would serve the purpose for which he had started it.

"I'm making you a cloak," he said, and motioned for Amparo to put it over her head. She got it on, and James adjusted some of the stitches he had left loose. Then he used his knife to slash two holes for her arms to come through, and marked places for ties to close the front.

Amparo giggled, and James looked up at the sound. The dog wandered into the firelight from the direction of the horses, saw Amparo, set his feet, and started barking. The girl held her sides and laughed aloud.

"What's so funny, mujer?"

"*Esta capa es tan fea,*" she said, covering her eyes with one hand and making a face. She then slipped the cape off. "*Déjame acabarla,*" she added, putting out her palm for the needle.

James said, "I know it ain't much for looks, but it should keep you warm." Then he gave the needle to her with a wry look. "You want to finish the job, I reckon."

Amparo smiled and started making tiny stitches, binding the edges of the armholes to keep the stuffing inside. When she finished, the cloak looked much more serviceable, and James grinned at her.

"You're a better seamstress than me. I only learned to do patching in the army."

Amparo's lips weren't blue anymore after she started wearing the homemade cloak, and James's mind was relieved on one score. However, he was short a bed covering now.

That night he tried to wrap up in the quilt he had left, but he shivered so much that he woke up—stone cold—in the middle of the night. He got out of bed, tied the quilt around his neck to leave his arms free, hunkered down next to the embers of the fire, and got a blaze built up so that it would warm his chilled body.

The fire must have cast too much light, for Amparo stirred, then sat up and looked around. "*¿Qué pasa?*" she asked.

That means 'what's going on,' James remembered Tom had told him. "I reckon it's a cold night," he replied, shrinking into the quilt so she could not see his long underwear.

She gave him a look like he was a helpless child, and sighed. "Señor Owen, *ven aquí.*"

James tossed another stick into the fire, not knowing what she meant to say. Then she crooked her finger at him and patted her bed.

He took a deep breath. "No, girl," he said. "I can't do that."

"*No seas estúpido,*" she said.

'*Estupido*' sounded so much like 'stupid' that James stiffened, and gave Amparo a hard look. "I made one bad mistake, girl, but I'm not going to repeat it." Then he sighed and softened a bit. "Don't you tempt me, now." As he gazed at her, he realized that the look on her face wasn't a bit tempting. In fact, she stared back at him with a cold air that seemed more like contempt for his stubbornness.

Amparo gave a short sigh and said, "Señor, *tienes frío. Ven aquí o yo tendré que ir allá.*" As she spoke, her hand motions made it clear to him that she intended to join him if he didn't go to her side of the fire, and when he didn't take the hint fast enough, she started to get up.

"Whoa, hold on!" he said, putting up both hands. "That ain't needed. Sit tight." He got up, with the quilt folded around himself, and groped for his trousers.

Amparo made a little click of scorn with her tongue. Then she grinned at his discomfort. "*¡Qué niño!*" she said.

James knew 'niño' meant 'child'. With his face flushing red, he started to stand erect, an angry retort on his lips. Then it occurred to him that if Amparo thought he was such a baby, nothing was likely to happen between them.

"All right. I'm coming," he said, turning away to button his trousers.

Amparo giggled. James sighed again, then grinned and went around the fire.

"Women!" he said, and slid cautiously under the covers beside her. She snuggled her back against his chest and curled into a ball, radiating heat. James lay stiff and straight, his muscles tensed. But soon, his limbs relaxed in the warmth from her body, and before long he fell asleep.

∽

It was late afternoon when James and Amparo neared Trinidad, one of the towns along the trail to Santa Fe. They crossed the Purgatory River beneath the looming height of stair stepped, flat topped Fisher's Peak, then pulled their horses to a stop on Main Street in front of a store.

Amparo craned her neck to one side to look down the street, then to the other side, and glanced back the way they had come. "*Aquí estamos,*" she said.

James shrugged his shoulders at her words. "This is Trinidad. I hope the storekeeper has a good warm blanket he'll sell me cheap."

After he got down and tied the horses and mules to a rail set into posts, he put up his arms to help Amparo to dismount.

Behind him he heard a loud cackle, followed by a rude laugh. Then a slurred voice called out, "Looky here. A new boy in town. And he's brought his own fancy girl."

James's back stiffened as his body tensed, but he tried to keep his face clear so Amparo wouldn't see there was a problem.

"A dirty Mexican, at that," rasped a second voice. "Hey girlie, guess what I got for you." The voices joined in ugly laughter.

James lowered Amparo to the ground. One part of his mind appreciated the lightness of her body, the swirl of her cape as her feet touched the street. Another part thought, *I'm not minded to pick a fight today, but when a man takes on a duty, he has to protect his stewardship.* He turned to face the challenge, keeping the girl behind him and to his left side as his right hand dangled handy to the gun he wore in his holster.

Two men sat on barrels in front of the store, sharing a bottle of whiskey. They kept up their nasty talk, laughing and pointing at James and Amparo.

"Excuse me, gents," James began. His voice sounded mild in his ears, but he didn't feel mild. He felt mean—mean and ruffled—for these men had said some harsh things about the girl at his side. "I like a good joke, but I reckon I missed yours. Tell it again so I can join the merriment."

"He can talk." One man nudged the other. The two held their sides, laughing fit to bust a gut and rocking from side to side.

"That's a mighty fine greaser gal you got there," the second man hooted. "She belong just to you, or do we get a sample?"

As the man talked, Amparo caught a quick breath. *She must have heard the word 'greaser' before*, James thought. Her sandal slid in the gravel as she backed up a step.

James took one step forward. "She's a lady," he said with a brittle edge on his voice.

"Yeah. Sure she is," the first man said, leering and winking at Amparo. "Ain't you gonna share her?" He took a pull from the whiskey bottle.

"We'll be glad to pay you," the second man said, then he fished a coin from his pocket and tossed it at James's feet.

The bright circle plumped into the dust, and James stared at it, feeling the nerves pinging in his tight jaw. He had to concentrate to keep his hand from pulling the gun.

"She's my wife," James declared. He heard his words echoing off the front of the building back to him. They had a ring like a fine and shining quarter thrown on a marble countertop.

"The devil you say," the first man sneered, then giggled.

"No white man needs to marry a Mexican," tittered the second. "Not when he can get it free." He collapsed from the barrel to the ground. The first man bent over to raise up his friend, and fell in a heap atop him.

The trouble was over. *These men are harmless enough*, James reflected, although their words bit deep into his soul. He kicked the coin aside, took Amparo's hand, and stepped past the men into the store.

"*Malditos.* Bad mans," she whispered, and her hand shook in his.

When he looked at her to see if she was frightened, the angry set of her chin and the fire in her eyes cleared up his worry. His chest expanded as he drew in a breath of relief mixed with pride.

"That-a girl. They're only drunks." James smiled and watched the corners of Amparo's mouth inch upward, then he squeezed her hand and led her deeper into the store.

At the back counter stood a man with a large nose and a green visor over his eyes. He looked up and cleared his throat. "We don't serve Mexicans," he said, sniffing through his nose.

"She goes where I go," James answered.

"Then take your business out of here. I don't like greasers."

That fine, proud feeling left James, and he clenched his teeth to stifle a hot retort. He could feel muscles bunching along his jaw, down his neck, and through his chest to his belly. Despite the tightness of his body, an oath got through his teeth, and he grabbed Amparo's hand and hurried her along as he stalked down the aisle.

"This town must be full of Yankees," James muttered. "You don't deserve this kind of treatment."

As he stepped from the door, several gunshots brought him up short, and he moved sideways to shield Amparo behind him. He couldn't see who had fired, due to the stinking gray cloud of smoke that drifted over to them, but there were no more shots, and soon he saw the results of the gunplay lying crumpled in the street.

The drunks from the front of the store lurched to the edge of the boardwalk to stare down at the body, and James turned to block Amparo's view. "This town is roaring," he told her between his teeth. "There's no safety for us here."

He helped Amparo to mount, then untied the animals, swung into his saddle, and gigged the sorrel to a trot.

Chapter 14

The cold clamped down on James and Amparo as they climbed the grade toward Ratón Pass. Evening would soon catch them, and James kept his eyes open for a place to build a fire for the night.

There was a chill in his bones, and he didn't know if it was from the patches of snow along the road and up under the junipers, or from the trial they'd been through in Trinidad. Then too, gray clouds scudded across the sky, and the possibility of a snowstorm worried him.

Not too long after they passed through Uncle Dick Wootton's tollgate, James felt like talking. It didn't seem to matter that Amparo didn't know what he said. He started telling her about the first time he'd been through Ratón Pass.

"My pa took us boys down to Texas to buy cattle. We were all mighty green in the ways of the West when we started out, but by the time we got home, I reckon we'd been down the river and over the mountain." James glanced at the girl. She was listening real hard; maybe she could pick up a word or two. "We bought trouble that trip. An outlaw and his pals trailed us back to the Greenhorn—that's the mountain where we live—and stole my sister and . . . my girl."

Thinking about Ellen brought a lump to his throat, so he stopped a moment to swallow it down. "We buried those rowdies in a cave," he continued, breathing kind of ragged. "We lost a good cowhand ourselves, and near lost my brother."

James rearranged a few strands of his horse's mane, anxious to see how he felt when he thought of Carl. Holding his breath, he found himself wondering if Carl had mended good. Carl had been shot up a fair bit. The pain he felt was for his brother, not for himself, and he whistled at the discovery.

Looking back over the wide, misty plains below them, James continued, "Anyway, it was a warm spring day last time I came through here. I'm glad I made you that cloak. I reckon this high country isn't so pleasant in winter."

At the end of their day's travel, James chose a spot near a close-grouped stand of oak trees for their campsite, making a shelter against a rocky ledge. A wind blew through the clearing, chasing the temperature down. Even though James built a reflecting fire with firewood stacked up to send the heat toward the bedding, he knew he would suffer from the cold that night, alone in his one-quilt bed.

As he got to his feet, James glanced at Amparo. She had taken off her cape so she could use her arms freely, and she shivered as she clapped her hands around a mite of cornmeal, fashioning it into a tortilla. James found the cape, brought it to her, and placed it over her shoulders.

"The weather's right nippy up here, girl," he said. "You need to keep covered. Tomorrow, God willing, we'll get through the Pass and down the road off this mountain." He looked through the trees toward the gray clouds covering the sky. "God willing and the snow don't fall."

After supper, Amparo sat among her blankets, close to the fire, while James checked the animals. When he returned, he threw more wood on the flames, then sat down near her.

"I don't know why I feel like talking so much. I reckon I need to hear somebody's voice, since you an' me don't chat back and forth the regular way." A strange thought came to his mind. "Tarnation. I reckon I miss my family."

"Fa-mi-ly? *¿Familia?*" Amparo turned her head away, and her words came back muffled. "*No tengo familia.*"

"There's so many of 'em, it never was quiet at home."

James scraped the ground bare in front of them with his hands, took a slender stick from the pile of wood, and drew a small circle on the rocky ground. He put a hat on the circle and traced a stick figure beneath it.

"Look here, Miss Amparo. This is my pa," he said, and she turned to watch his moving stick. He made another body figure beside the first. "Here's Ma." He added hair and a skirt. Then he made another man's figure below the couple.

"Rulon's my oldest brother. He has a mujer and two young'uns." More figures joined Rulon.

"Niños," Amparo said.

James nodded. "Niños. Then Benjamin." He drew a figure and crossed it out. "*Es-ta muer-to.* And Carl." After he drew another figure he tapped Amparo's ring with his stick. "He got wed a while back."

Slowly he drew a woman figure beside Carl. "That's his mujer, Ellen. She was pledged to me."

Amparo's chin jerked upward, and she stared at James. "*¿El-len?*" she said, choking. "*¿Elena es la mujer de tu hermano? ¡Santa María!*"

James looked beyond the fire for a long time before he drew another figure and covered it with an x. "Peter. Then me, James," he said, adding another man, then slapping his chest.

"*Che-mes*," she said.

"That's close. Try it again."

Amparo put her head to one side. "Che-mes," she repeated.

"James. And this is my twin, John." He crossed out John's figure. "*Es-ta muer-to*, too. Then there's my sister, Marie. Then Clayton, Albert, and Julianna."

"*¡Qué cantidad de niños!*" the girl said, and stopped his moving stick. "*Dáme el palo.*" She took the stick from his hand. "Amparo," she said firmly, and added a woman figure alongside the drawing of James. "Amparo," she repeated.

Her way of saying the name is so different from mine, he thought, *with two a's just alike and a little roll of the r. I wish I could say it like that.* Then he realized what she'd done with the stick.

"Yes," he agreed slowly. "Amparo. Till Santa Fe."

She looked at James with those great huge eyes, then slowly turned to look at the fire, and her shoulders slumped. He bit his lip, tasting ashes in his mouth.

James put a hand on her arm. "Don't take it so hard. I'm sure your ma will be glad to see you."

Amparo shook her head. "*Madrastra. No es mi mamá. Y es una mujer sumamente malvada. Le odio.*"

"Hold on there," he said, lost among so many new words, but knowing bitterness when he heard it.

She tapped the stick on a log sticking out of the fire, and James knew she was impatient that he didn't understand. She was angry, too, but somehow he didn't think her anger was directed toward him.

Then "*¡Ah!*" she said, and sat upright. Amparo smoothed out James's family and sketched a man figure. "*Ésto es mi papá.*"

"That's your pa."

"*Cierto. Y ésta es mi mamá. Ella murió.*" She put an x on the woman she had completed.

James chewed the inside of his cheek. "*Es-ta muer-to?*"

"*Sí, está muerta. Y mi papa se casó de nuevo.*" She drew another woman beside the first.

"This is you, Miss Amparo?"

"No." She showed the ring. "*Otra mujer se casó con mi papá. Otra mujer. Ella es mi madrastra.*"

"*O-tra* mujer? That's your pa's wife, but your ma is dead. Six little beans! She's your stepmother."

Then tension went out of Amparo's body with a rush of air. "*Sí. 'Madrastra' es* 'stepmother'." She spit out the word.

"But she's a widow woman, according to Tom O'Connor. Your pa *es-ta muer-to?*"

"*Sí.*" She put a fist to her mouth and turned away again.

"Amparo?" The straight name came out so easily, in such a natural manner. James laid his arm around her shoulders. "I'm sorry about your pa," he said.

Amparo turned to nuzzle her face against his neck, and he heard a choked little sigh, and something wet slipped down inside his collar.

He held her against him for a long time, whispering her name, rocking her like a baby in his arms, watching the fire die and smelling smoke in her hair as her tears watered his neck inside his coat. He hoped his comfort eased her grief and loneliness, because suddenly he knew her state of mind mattered to him, more than just her being a sad little stranger in a place far from home. Whether he liked it or not, he was growing feelings for her, stirrings beyond his manly needs, and confusion took root next to resolve.

After a long spell she got quiet, and James figured she'd gone to sleep, so he pulled her blankets over them both, and lay down with her in his arms. Being so close to her soft curves, a hunger rose in him, but he beat it back with his newfound sense of protecting her, and lay still with her head nestled under his chin. Then he listened to the wind moaning through the branches above them on the lonesome shoulder of the mountain.

&

Amparo lay quiet for what seemed like hours, bound to the Anglo's side by his encircling arms. When he finally moved in his sleep, releasing her, she eased herself to her knees and pulled her mother's rosary from her skirt pocket.

After she had said her prayers, she whispered, "Holy Mother of God, I miss my papá so much. The Anglo is kind, though. He was sad when he learned of my sorrow. Blessed Virgin, I know his name. It is Che-mes." She sighed. "And the name he cried out in the night, it belongs to a woman he must not love. It is the name of his sister-in-law. Holy Virgin, you must not look down with horror. I think she is but recently wed to his brother. Perhaps he travels to flee her memory, and the pain and anger it brings to him. Most Favored Mother, smile upon me. Let me have power to soothe his pain. Let me be the haven where he can forget Elena."

The girl waited a moment with bowed head, then replaced the beads in her pocket and slipped beneath the covers. James sighed and rolled from his back to his side, facing her, and she scooted against his coat-clad chest. *My gentle Anglo, Chemes*, she thought. *Will you not touch me again? Will you not find solace in my arms?*

&

James yawned awake the next morning when the night sky lightened to gray. An insect was tiptoeing through his beard, and he stuck a hand out from under the blankets to bat it away. The bug didn't scare off, for it was Amparo's hand. She was awake and playing with his whiskers.

She laughed as James caught her hand, and he turned and tickled her on the ribs, chuckling to see the surprise in her eyes. She squirmed and giggled, then snuck her hand under his coat to get him back, and they teased like a couple of seven-year-olds for a while, messing up the bed and enjoying the frosty morning while the dog romped around them, barking and wagging its tail. When they had made an untidy heap of the bed, they lay there panting, getting back their breath and their age, while the dog licked their faces.

"Chemes," Amparo said.

James lay on his back, sprawled out as he breathed deeply, and when the girl said his name, he raised up on one elbow and looked down at her. She swallowed, and he watched the action of her smooth brown throat.

"Chemes," she repeated. "*Creo que te amo.*"

He didn't know what she said, but he sure liked the way she said it, along with the tender look she gave him. Before he knew what he was doing he was stroking her cheek, rubbing his thumb over her lip, and bending down to kiss her mouth.

While they shared the kiss, it came to James of a sudden what he was up to, and he raised his head and shuddered.

"Amparo, don't do this to me," he pleaded as he got to his feet and backed away, his chest heaving with the pain of leaving her. One look at her stricken face and he gave himself a lecture: *James, don't do it to her, either.* He turned and grabbed his hat, and fled from the camp.

As he gathered in and saddled the horses, he repeated to himself, "I made a vow, Ma, I said I'd get her home. God help me, I'm a man of my word."

After that, as they journeyed through the Pass, off the mountain, and down into New Mexico Territory, James didn't dare share Amparo's bed. He did the best he could to keep warm alone, moving the fire to one side come bedtime so he could make his bed on the hot ground, then heaping wood on the fire all night.

Shortly after twilight one night, near the end of the trail, James lay in the cold darkness, biting his lip, biting back the yearning that stirred his belly—the yearning to lie in the bed on the other side of the fire, with Amparo held close to his heart. Cicadas whirred in a mesquite tree nearby, and the old dog snuffled in its sleep. James turned his head and his eyes caressed the girl's outline under her blanket. He tried to swallow the lump that almost closed his throat.

Ma, you always taught me to keep to a task I gave my word to do. I never figured it would be this hard. Ma, I wish the mountains could swallow up Santa Fe!

Chapter 15

"Hush. Look at that sky!"

Light passing through the clear air above Santa Fe made the colors of the ridges and peaks surrounding the village brighter than natural. James had never seen such a blue expanse of the heavens. He looked to the left as he and Amparo rode from the south toward town. Sunset encroached upon daylight like a powder burst from the mouth of a crimson cannon—orange and gold ribbons shot forth to wage a battle against the clouds. The western horizon was obscured by a glow like a living thing. Such a sight on another occasion would have brought James joy, but his soul had an ache to it like black rot in a back tooth.

"I reckon we'd best get a hurry on if I'm to put you in the hands of your stepmother tonight." James held his body straight in the saddle, for the keen blade of loss lay in his belly, and if he was cautious, he could keep it from stabbing him.

He looked back over his shoulder at Amparo. Even though she had dark half circles under her eyes from the strain of traveling long and hard, her chin was up, and pride in her strength and will fingered his heart. Then he said, "We're nearly to the end of the trail." He had to swallow before he went on. "Here's where I stop being your 'marido'." His eyes lingered on the curve of her shoulders under the homemade cape.

She looked from the sky to him, and something too tender to bear was in her eyes as she urged the horse forward to come up even with him. James looked away—not daring to face her—and remembered some of the blacksmith's words.

"Tom said 'Amparo' means shelter," he muttered. "You've been a shelter and a refuge, like a house made of stone where I could hole up and heal." He inhaled sharply, dragging the crisp, cold air of twilight into his lungs. "I reckon you made a wounded boy into a whole man." He breathed out sharply, then swallowed. "You helped me forget I wanted a certain red headed gal, but I won't ever forget you."

Amparo tilted her head to one side, and he knew she didn't understand him, but it eased his hurting to talk to her.

"Chemes." The name was never so gently spoken as by her lips. He looked at her. "*Sé feliz, mi* marido," she said.

James wrenched his eyes away. "Where do you live? House. Where's your *casa?*"

Amparo pointed down the narrow streets toward the square. "*Vivía al otro lado de la plaza. Mi padre nació en la misma casa.*"

"You take the lead." James reined in his horse and motioned the girl to go before him.

"*Está bien.*"

As Amparo urged her horse to the front, the head covering James had made fell back, and he watched as the light of a passing torch gleamed on the twists of her braids.

Hair to be touched, he thought. *Tarnation*! He looked at his hand—fingers threaded through the reins—resting on his thigh. *I've done my touching, and now I'm left with the recollection of that silk wrapped around my fingers.*

Amparo led the way around the plaza and beyond, and James followed to a house similar to others they had passed: square and earthen and blank faced to the street.

"*Ésta es la casa de mi papá,*" she said, and stopped her horse.

He dismounted and approached the door, an unexpected tightness binding his chest. His throat burned, and he cleared it as he stood there, staring at the carved wooden figures that stared back at him. He shifted his foot, then turned back toward the girl, his girl, his wife, chest heaving like he was on a bucking colt.

A little crease showed between Amparo's eyebrows. "*¿Qué pasa, Chemes?*"

"I can't leave you here." The battle deep in his gut was worse than hand to hand fighting. "You're not her girl any more. You're mine." His mouth was open, gulping air. "I'll knock, and tell her we're wed, then say 'goodbye'."

James turned to the door. It shuddered under his fist as he thumped it. No one responded to his first knock and he tried again, shook his head, and looked at the toes of his boots.

After a moment he turned to speak to Amparo, and a sliver of light fell on her face. He heard "What is it?" and turned to the door.

"You speak English," James blurted to the small, white haired man who stood in the doorway.

"Of course. I was born in Ohio. What do you want?"

"I reckon I've got the wrong place. I'm looking for Catarina viuda de Garcés. Can you point out her house?"

"This was her house, young man, but I bought it a while back. As to finding her, you've got a long trail ahead of you. She took off for San Francisco."

James stared at the stranger for a long time before he turned and lifted his chin to look at Amparo. "She's gone, cleared out," he said, and felt a little grin tugging up the ends of his mouth. "She's down the river and over the mountain, and I'm not chasing her to San Francisco just to say 'howdy', girl!"

"Is that your woman?" asked the man.

He whirled around. "My wife!" he said. "She's my wife! Thought we'd look in on some relations, but San Francisco's a mite far to go." James couldn't keep that grin off his face, nor inventions from spilling out of his mouth.

The man squinted into the darkness. "I hope the widow wasn't a near relation. The lady vamoosed with a male friend of dubious repute. She's been playing hob with her husband's memory."

"I reckon she was not close to the young lady." From the heated way Amparo had talked, James knew they hadn't got along well.

"I'd say I was sorry you missed her, but I'm not. No offense, you understand."

James shook his head. "None taken." There was growing in his soul a need to whoop out loud, and he shifted weight from one leg to the other. "Would you know of a place we can put up for the night, seeing we missed the widow?"

"Go back to the *plaza*," directed the man. "On the southeast corner there's an adobe inn. It's called *La Fonda*. They'll put you up."

"Much obliged." James nearly yelled the words. As the American closed the door, James turned towards Amparo and let loose the whoop, shaking his fists in the air as he did so. The door opened again and the American stuck his head out, saw James grinning at him, shrugged his shoulders as he said, "Young people!" and shut the door.

James nearly ran to the horse. "Amparo, your *madrastra's* gone. Vamoosed, like the man said."

"¿Vamoosed? ¿Vamos? ¿Me dices que ella se fue? ¿Para dónde se fue?"

"*Pa ra don de se fue?*" he repeated. "Tarnation, I don't know what you're asking, but she went to San Francisco with a man friend."

"*¿Se fue a San Francisco?*" Amparo's face twisted up with anger. "*Con Juan Pablo Fuentes, me imagino. ¡Ay de mi!*" she cried out, looking wildly around. "*¿Qué será conmigo?*"

James looked at the distress on her face. "I wish I could talk to you, girl. This ain't a time for grief. I got such a great joy bubbling inside of me." He laughed into the empty street, and whooped again. "Yahoo! I'm gonna keep you, girl!"

"*No entiendo nada de esto,*" she replied, lifting her chin and setting her face into a blank expression.

"Don't you get stony faced on me, mujer. Mule tails! I got to get somebody to help us talk. This matter needs clearing up." James swung into his saddle. "But first we'll go find that hotel."

଼ଠ

James turned the animals over to the hostler at the livery stable behind the inn, then, carrying his war bag and Amparo's bundle, joined his wife where he had left her in the lobby. After he arranged for lodging, he escorted Amparo down a hallway, opened the door to a small room, and entered, dumping the gear on the bed. Amparo sat down in the one chair in the room, hunching her shoulders as though she were in pain. The look on her face made James ache to erase the confusion he saw there. He went over to her and stood before her.

"I sold your mule. That'll pay for our stay and get us supplies for the trip home." She didn't look up, so he bent down and picked up one of her hands. "Come on. They're setting up the comida. Let's go eat." James took her other hand and pulled her to her feet, then held her by the shoulders. Her head drooped, and she wouldn't look at him. "Amparo, girl, I ain't going to leave you off here." He bent his head to let her see his smile. "You're going home with me, to mi casa. Tarnation! I wish you took my meaning."

She started a slow wagging of her head, back and forth, back and forth, with her eyes squeezed tight shut. "*Estoy confundida,*" she said.

James bit his lip. "Mules tails! We got to get this straight. I'll find somebody here that speaks both lingos, like Tom. But first, let's eat. My belly thinks my throat's been cut."

He took her hand and moved her through the door and off to the dining room, then after he helped her with her chair and sat down himself, he looked around at the other diners in the room.

At the next table a man of middle years sat alone. His black broadcloth suit was an American style, but his face—thin skin tightly stretched over fine bones—was from the Mexican mold. His eyes met those of James, who nodded politely. The man seemed surprised, but gave James a nod of his own.

I wonder if he talks English, James thought, and opened his mouth to speak, but the waiter came to take the man's food order, and the chance passed.

Then the waiter came toward James. When he finished ordering, James looked around the room again. Five Mexican men sat at another table, discussing their business in Spanish. An old man and his wife, whom James took to be Easterners from their dress, huddled over their plates, never glancing up from their food. *That's the whole bundle,* he thought, and decided that the man at the next table was the most likely prospect.

The food arrived: steak, potatoes cut in wedges, with crisp fried eggs on the side. James took a bite. He chewed, swallowed, then winked at Amparo. "I like your comida better, girl." Her cheeks glowed pink, and he wondered if she blushed for the words or the wink.

Oh, my pretty wife. James gulped, thinking of all the things he had in his heart to tell her, yearning to share the deep buried feelings that came bubbling up under his skin. "Tarnation," he said softly. "I can't take this anymore."

He took a full breath and turned to the man at the next table. It took a while to get the man's attention, so James cleared his throat, and when the man looked up through black, heavily hooded eyes, James said, "Excuse me, sir. Do you speak English?"

The gentleman jerked his head, slowly wiped his mouth with his napkin, then said, "I have good English."

James sighed. "That's fine. That's mighty fine. I've got to beg a favor of you, sir. Can you come sit with us for a spell?" The man nodded once, got to his feet, and took the chair James rose to pull out for him. When he was settled he said, "I am Peter Chaves. How may I be of service?"

James cleared his throat again as he sat. "My name is James Owen. I'm from up in Huérfano County, Colorado Territory. This here's Amparo. I've got a little problem talking to the young lady, me not knowing much of her lingo and all. I know it's a lot of trouble, but can you tell her what I say, you know, in Spanish?"

"You want me to interpret?"

"I reckon that's what it's called. I'm sorry to keep you from your meal, but I got to tell her something real important and know she understands."

Mr. Chaves blinked, then waved his hand in agreement. "Certainly," he said. "I will do my best."

"Fine, fine. I'll talk on, then, if you're ready?"

"Go ahead, young man."

James took his wife's hand. "Amparo. I was wrong, back there at the church. I lied to the priest, and I'm mighty sorry." He stopped to get a breath, and felt a drop of sweat plop from his jaw onto the skin of his throat and run down to his collar where it soaked into his shirt. The stranger took his turn, a sour look on his face, and when he had finished speaking, James continued.

"I want things right between you and me, so here and now I make my vows for the regular term. Till death takes me away from you, I'll be your husband." He shifted in his chair. "All I got is the clothes on my back, the grub in my pack, and the skills in my hands, but you won't go hungry as long as I live."

James glanced at the man, who moved his mouth without words for a moment, then got out, "You are married?"

"Yup."

Peter Chaves sat up straight for a minute, his thin skinned fingers twitching on the table, then he drew his brows together as he spoke to Amparo. When he stopped, James began again.

"Your madrastra left town, but you know that. What you don't know is . . . I got to dreading the day I would meet her. I thought I could do my duty by you and turn you back to her without a second thought, but I got to where I was hating the idea. I didn't want to let you go." James sucked in a deep breath. "I'll never do it now, and we can go home to the Greenhorn and have us a passel of kids, and you can meet my family and—"

"*Déje, joven*. Let me catch up."

James watched Amparo as the man spoke to her. Wonder flickered in her wide eyes. Then she threw back her head and laughed, and a flush—wondrous and warm—moved over James's body as he heard the joy in her start low and chuckling like a stream of water growing and boiling out of an underground spring. Amparo tucked her chin down again, shook her head and answered the man.

Peter Chaves looked at James and spread his hands on the table. "She seems very happy, as you can see. She says she feels like she already knows your family." The man lowered his gaze. "And she is eager to have many niños, babies with your laughing eyes." He shrugged his shoulders. "I translate the best I can."

Amparo's laughing spring seemed to be inside of James. He did his best to keep it from gushing out, holding it private and precious, but he grinned broadly in spite of himself.

"Ah, you did a good job. Thank you. Thank you. Wait." James swallowed hard. "Tell her—no, tell me how to say 'I love you'."

The man rubbed his pink earlobes. "Say '*te amo*'. It's very easy. Just '*te amo*'."

James bit his lip and practiced a couple of times in a whisper. Amparo looked at him and squeezed his hand. Then he gazed at her, his pretty little wife, and there was a feeling in him like water seeping in to fill a dry well—gradual, but steady—rising with life giving moisture. He felt no more need to practice, so he said straight out, "Amparo, *te amo*, today, and yesterday, and tomorrow. Te amo all my days."

The man rattled off a few more Spanish words to fill in the gaps, and Amparo listened, her lips parted and eyes melting into James's soul, then she tugged on Chaves's coat and motioned for him to bend down. She whispered her wants, and got his reply, then a smile blazed from her face.

"Chemes, I lahv you for-e-ver," she said. She put her hands to her mouth and giggled. "I lahv you, *para siempre*," she repeated, and her hands pounced on his and squeezed tight.

Mr. Chaves got to his feet. James stood and shook his hand.

"Thank you for all you've done for us. I'm obliged for your help."

"Good luck to you, young man. And may you quickly learn much Spanish. Such things as you said are for private times and private places."

James swallowed. "I know. It couldn't be helped. I'm deeply obliged, Mr. Chaves."

The man returned to his table and his meal, and James sat down and tried another bite of food, but the sight of Amparo's glowing face in front of him made it hard to chew. He pushed his plate to the center of the table. "Are you hungry?" he asked.

Amparo pushed away her plate. "Vamos," she whispered, holding his glance with those dark eyes of hers.

"Yeah, vamos," he answered, getting to his feet so hastily that he knocked over his chair.

&

James opened the door of the room for Amparo and followed her in, then caught up the chair and tilted the back of it under the doorknob. He shook it to check the fit, then turned and laughed.

"Six little beans! I'm kinda shaky, like I was sprawled out behind a bush, waiting for the Yankees to come down on me." He took off his coat and crossed the room to hang it on a hook. "But there ain't no Yankees, only a gentle little gal, sweet as sugar, waiting for me to right my wrongs." James took Amparo's shawl and hung it over his coat, talking toward the wall. "I got a sorrowful feeling for the way I lied to that priest. But hush, I'm so full of happy, it likes to drive the sorrow away."

When James turned back to the room he noticed that Amparo had not moved, but stood there in the center of the room, a smile playing with her lips.

&

Madre Santísima, he has said he loves me! I thought he found me ugly after the first time, but he does want to hold me, to touch me.

&

"I'm scared, Amparo. I reckon it's like we got wed right there at that table." James stopped for a breath. "Tarnation, I'm nervy as a tied up coon dog with the fresh smell of varmint tweaking his nose. It's like . . . we ain't ever . . . been together," he stammered.

&

Holy Mary, is this the happiness that comes of doing duty? See how his eyes soften. My papá looked at me in that manner. Yet, there is more in my Anglo's eyes. I am not ugly to this man, my Chemes, my beloved.

&

James held his arms wide, and Amparo stepped into them. "*Bésame, mi amor,*" she whispered, and James replied, "Bésame," and bent his head and kissed her.

After a moment he straightened up and said, "My sweet girl, you're such a wonder, with your eyes all soft an' shining, and your hair—" He untied the cords binding her braids. "Out there on the street, before we got to your house, I craved to touch your hair one more time before your madrastra took you away from me." Amparo's hair started to come unbound from the plaits. "Oh, my pretty girl, your hair is just like I remembered it, smooth as silk in my hands." His fingers separated the strands at her temples, and the ear bobs caught his eye. He touched them, then motioned. "Take them off. I want to get you some different aretes, gifts from me."

Amparo had a puzzled look, so James touched the backs of the ear bobs. Then he remembered a word. "*Quita,*" he said.

&

He has learned many words from me, Blessed Virgin, just as I have learned much from him.

Amparo smiled and removed the jewelry from her ears. As she did so, James saw the ring on her finger, and caught her hand. Amparo dropped the ear bobs into his palm.

"You can't wear that *muerto* fellow's pledge," he grunted, pulling the circle from her finger and putting it and the other jewelry on the chest of drawers. "I don't want his ghost in my bed. Not on my rightful wedding night."

Amparo giggled. "*Noche de bodas*," she whispered.

"Noche de bodas," James repeated. "Our noche de bodas," he said, and picked her up in his arms.

"This here ring is my pledge."

James stood in the open doorway of the room, looking at his yawning bride lying snuggled in the bedclothes. He had left the room early that morning to sell the wedding ring and earrings to a goldsmith, and buy new gifts. In one hand he carried a large parcel. Between thumb and finger he held out another result of his shopping trip.

A laugh came out of James's mouth at the sight of Amparo's eager face as she sat up. He realized she wasn't presentable, so he pushed the door shut with his boot. Then he tossed the package onto the chair and crossed the room to the bed, picking up her dress from the floor and handing it to her.

James stood and waited while Amparo got out of bed and hurried into her clothes. He caught her hand and kissed each finger, stopping at the ring finger and holding it a prisoner. Then he slid the gold circle down the length of her finger, and it shone in the light with a warmth that reminded him of the hearth at home. Amparo caught her breath.

"That joins us official," James said, and grinned at the little-girl pleasure on her face.

"*¡Este anillo es magnífico!*" There was a wonderment in her voice that matched the feeling in his belly as he looked at her, hardly believing that she was his.

He kissed the top of her head, breathing in the perfume of her hair. Amparo was warm, she was here with him, and she loved him. His chest ached with the joy of finding a treasure where he'd only seen a duty.

James pulled back a bit to look at Amparo, and caught her admiring the ring again, moving her finger and hand to catch light on the polished surface. "*¡Qué belleza!*" she said, and kissed the ring. Then she turned her attention to the large package on the chair. "*¿Que es esto, mi amor?*" she asked. James laughed and cut the string tying up the package. He spread apart the brown paper and lifted up a gray wool cloak.

"You won't be cold going home, girl. Try this on quick. I've got to go out again to buy supplies so we can get an early start on the trail."

"¡Oh!" she cried, and slipped the cloak around her shoulders. "*Es muy bella.*" She hooked the fasteners and twirled to spread the fullness around her. Then she clasped her hands together in front of her chin and lifted teasing eyes to his.

"*Gracias, mi amor, ¿pero no me traes* aretes?"

"Aretes! Six little beans! I almost forgot." James stood and shoved his hand into a pocket, then brought out a twisted square of paper. "I bought the prettiest ones I could find, gold, with little red and green stones," he said as he unwrapped the ear bobs. "Puts me in mind of Christmas coming." He tucked the paper into Amparo's outstretched hands, then touched his jaw below his moustache. His skin was still tender from shaving his beard in a hurry that morning before Amparo awoke. Now that he had admitted he was a married man, he wanted to look presentable for his wife.

She pushed the tiny earrings around the paper, watching the colors that reflected from the gems. "*¡Qué maravilla!*" she breathed. "*¡Qué lujo!*" Then Amparo walked to the washstand, shoved the china bowl and pitcher to the rear, and put the paper on the edge she had cleared.

James came up behind her, adding his grin to her smile in the cracked mirror over the stand. He lifted her hair away from her ears, stroking her neck a bit as he did so. "Put them on, mujer. I want to see my ear bobs shining through these black tresses."

"*Hombre,*" she said, and held the decorations to her ears. "*¿Te gustan, mi amor?*" she asked, laughing at him as he nuzzled her neck.

"Just put them on, pretty wife. We got to hit the trail this morning. I'm hankering to get you home to Colorado."

Amparo finished putting on the earrings and turned to him, giggling. "*Te amo, mi amor,*" she whispered, and pulled his face down to hers.

He kissed her, muttering, "Te amo, Amparo."

They didn't start for home until way past noon.

Chapter 16

Amparo and James took joy in being together, whether it was riding side by side on the trail so they could hold hands, or lying close together in their bed watching the dog capering in the dawn as the sun rose over the prairie, or looking for a camp sheltered enough to put them out of sight of other travelers. An ice bound wind blew off the mountains and swept the valleys, but the hot blood coursing through James's veins kept him warm from dawn to dark, and his wife warmed his bed from dark to dawn.

One morning they stood together in their camp in the dark before dawn, next to the ascending trail to the mountain pass men call Ratón, and looked back on New Mexico as the sun came up and filled the valleys with rosy light. The dog caught a scent and dashed away from its place beside the horses, going off the side of the road and down the mountain.

"Pretty place," James muttered into his wife's hair as he stood behind her with his arms wrapped around her middle. "But I know a prettier one. Let's go home."

As he packed the mule, he noticed that the bag of cornmeal was nearly empty. "Tarnation. I didn't buy a new sack in Santa Fe. I missed that," he said as he boosted Amparo onto her horse. "My head must be turned inside out 'cause te amo so much. Hush, we'll have to stop in Trinidad, girl." Then James swung into the leather, whistled for the dog, and looked again at his wife.

Ma'll be proud to know Amparo. I reckon she will be a mite surprised. Pa likely told her how I wasn't fit for human company when I left.

"And now I have a wife!" he said aloud.

Amparo looked at him. "*¿Eres feliz, hombre?*"

"I got a great joy in you," he said. "And you look so fine, just so fine."

She smiled and James grinned. He nudged his horse, and they rode into the pass and toward Trinidad.

☙

"There are a mighty lot of folks going armed." James craned his neck to look behind as he and Amparo rode into town. "There's no womenfolk on the street. I wonder *¿qué pasa?*" He turned to the front again. "Whatever it is, we ain't going to meddle in. We'll get the grub and be on our way."

"*Necesito comprar algunas cositas,* Chemes," Amparo said. "*Quiero comprarte un regalito para el Año Nuevo.*"

"Every white man I see is walking with another man, and they're stepping wary. This town is full of weapons."

James leaned forward a bit in the saddle, easing the stiffness in his back. Rolling his shoulders, he loosened joints that creaked from the cold, windy journey they had made through the Pass. Then he spotted a 'general store' sign nailed to the front of the Colorado Hotel, and guided his horse over to the side of the street.

"We'll buy our goods here." He dismounted and tied his horse and the mule to a post, then looked around as Amparo's horse came up beside him. "There's a crowd across the street. Rifle barrels around that adobe house like quills on a porcupine's back. You stick close to me, Amparo." He took a turn around the post with the tether from her horse.

"*Eres tan serio. ¿*Qué pasa?" she asked, stretching out her arms for him to help her down. James put her on her feet between the horses.

"Don't move," he told her, gesturing with his hand. He looked over his saddle toward the street. "I don't like the feel of things, girl."

Across the way, two men stood at the corners of an adobe building, shotguns held ready to level and fire. A third man guarded the door, and James caught the man staring back at him. Other men wandered back and forth in front of the building, carrying their weapons in front of them across their bodies. Some of the guards were whites, and some were Mexicans, and there didn't seem to be rhyme or reason for the mixture.

"Somebody's a prisoner in that house," James said. "Those hombres don't want him busting loose, neither." He slid his rifle out of the saddle boot. The men across the street tensed up, and James turned away to show he was no threat.

"Why's there a mixed crowd over there?" James frowned as he put his left arm around Amparo's shoulder and guided her up onto the stoop of the hotel. He opened the door, looked around the interior and motioned to Amparo with a sideways jerk of his head. "It's empty. Go ahead in."

I can't figure it, he worried. *Last time we passed through town, seemed like the whites had a pure hatred for the Mexicans. Why are they joined up together across the street?*

James looked into the hotel store. The owner had not yelled at his wife to leave. *Good*, he thought. *Maybe I can get her in and out of Trinidad without trouble this time.*

Noise on the street caught his ear, and he glanced at a group of men coming down the road, shouting at the townsfolk who huddled against the walls of the buildings. "Going to leave him to rot?" one man yelled before James turned and entered the doorway, shaking his head.

Spices! he thought, inhaling deeply. The overwhelming scent of cinnamon mixed with ginger and nutmeg entered his nose as he walked between rows of store goods toward where Amparo waited in the middle of the room. He grinned and strode to her side. *Ma's going to take to you like a setting hen to a glass doorknob.*

Amparo brushed dust from the sleeve of her dress with her little brown hand, then smoothed her black braids. *My little bay filly. I always was partial to bays.*

"Chemes, *necesito comprar harina de maíz.*" Amparo patted her hands together like she was fashioning tortillas from cornmeal.

"Yes—*sí*," he said as he reached over and smoothed the wrinkles out of the back of her skirt, giving her a little pat. "Putting on weight with all them tortillas, ain't you?"

Amparo jumped forward at his touch, and a pink stain darkened her cheekbones. "¡Chemes! *¡Qué vergüenza!*" she gasped, then brushed past him toward the clerk at the back of the room.

I reckon I shouldn't have done that in public, James thought. He tried to catch her elbow with his free hand so he could make things right, but she moved faster than he did, and he was left with a handful of air.

"Six little beans, mujer. I meant no harm." He wondered if his face showed color like hers, then he joined her where she was halted in her flight by the back counter and stood shrugging her shoulders like a hen ruffling her feathers.

"Can I get you something?" the clerk asked, easing off his stool to greet James.

"I reckon." He leaned his rifle against the counter, barrel upward. "The little woman needs fifty pounds of flour and fifty pounds of cornmeal. And a big tin of lard." James turned as he scratched his thumb along the side of his jaw. "Amparo. Do we need more frijoles?"

She shook her head, then the counterman spoke again.

"You don't speak much Mexican lingo?"

"No, but I'm picking up words as I need 'em."

"And she don't speak English."

"A little."

"Then why are you carting her around with you?"

James felt his back tighten, and he reached out to grip the cold metal of the rifle barrel. "I reckon I got a good reason. She's my wife."

The clerk shook his head and moved around behind the counters to fill his order. "I can't believe a nice boy like you would hitch up with a Mexican. You'd best ride right through Trinidad. Things have been a touch uneasy here before, but after that little fracas last week, well, you just ride on out of here."

James loosed the rifle. "I was meaning to ask why folks are going armed out on the street."

The man paused to hoist a flour sack down off a shelf before answering.

"You see, last week it was, a driver for the stage line was drinking with some friends at the saloon down the street." The man thumped the flour sack onto the counter. Flecks of white dusted the wooden surface. "It was a real nice day for December, Christmas Day, as I recall. Well, Frank Blue, that's the driver's name, he likes to gamble a bit. He got tipsy, and offered a wager that he could beat any Mexican in town in a wrassling match." He put a tin of lard alongside the flour.

"Did he get any takers?"

"Well, there was a group of Mexicans standing nearby, and one of them took his challenge. The two of them went out to the crossroads, Main and C Streets, and started their match."

"That sounds harmless enough." James leaned his elbow on top of a box on the counter.

"Not the way they was fighting." The clerk drummed his stocky fingers against the top of the lard tin. "This was grappling and punching and no holds barred. Being a holiday, everybody gathered around to watch, the whites on one side of the street, and the Mexicans on the other."

"There does seem to be a contrary feeling in this town," James said.

"Been that way for years." The clerk grunted as he lifted a sack of cornmeal off a pile in the corner of the store. "I try to stay away from the bickering, what with the hotel customers to keep out of harm's way." The cornmeal joined the sack of flour on the counter. "Now, the Mexican fellow got right into the spirit of the match, you see. I guess he had a deal of experience with that sort of fighting, and he was getting the best of Frank Blue."

"Then what happened?"

The man rested his forearms on the counter. "Old Frank didn't much like that. He fancies himself a sort of champion. So then he and this Mex tore into each other." He paused, dipped a steel pen in his inkwell and scratched some figures on a scrap of paper. "Is that all you want to buy?"

"I think my wife wanted something. Amparo, *quieres* more?"

She pursed her lips, then looked at the store clerk. "Señor, *necesito espuelas de plata para mi esposo. Espuelas. Para sus botas.*" She frowned, then pointed to James's boots.

"I don't need boots. These'll do me for another season."

"*No son* boots," she said, shaking her head. "*Quiero comprarte espuelas de caballero.*" Amparo looked around the shelves. "*Allí las tiene,*" she said, pointing to a display of horse tack.

"She wants to buy something for the horse?"

"I don't think so. What else you got up there?"

"Bits and bridles and spurs."

"Spurs." Amparo's face beamed. "*Quiero comprar* spurs."

"Show her the spurs," James said, grinning. "She picks up words real fast."

"I guess she'd better, if you're going to keep her around."

James felt his face muscles setting into tight bunches. "She's my wife legal and proper. Church wed in the bargain. I don't plan to set her loose."

The man threw up his hands. "No offense, no offense." A loud noise came from the street. "Jumping Jericho! What's that commotion out there?"

James turned at the sound of angry shouting that came from the street outside, grabbing the barrel of his rifle as he moved. Amparo was right behind him. "You got another wrestling match going?"

The clerk came from behind the counter and walked to the door to peer out. He brought his head back into the room, a scowl on his face. "It's just that noisy John Dunn trying to stir up trouble. I thought we got rid of him for good when he took the stage south a couple of days ago. But no, here he comes back on this morning's stage, and five or six buddies with him. All we need is another ruckus. I got enough troubles, running the hotel, the store, and the stage station, and one driver short, to boot."

"What happened to your driver?" James put his rifle back against the counter.

"It's Frank Blue. He's over yonder in the jail."

"They got a heavy guard on a man arrested for street fighting."

"That ain't the half of it."

Amparo tugged on James's sleeve. "Chemes, *las espuelas*."

"Can you get them spurs for her to look at?"

"Oh. Sure." The man took a step into the room, then glanced out the door again. "You know, Frank got going so dirty that he twisted that Mex fellow's leg from here to yonder, sat on it, and snapped it clean in two." He came toward the counter. "You never saw such a to do. The Mexican's friends took offense at the leg breaking and commenced to chasing old Frank, throwing rocks and yanking out their guns. Mister Blue pulled his pistol and fired back. Then Frank's friends got in it, and one of the Mexicans went down, shot through the brisket. Died on the spot." The clerk went behind the counter and got down an assortment of spurs.

"Here you are, little lady."

"So Mister Blue got blamed for the killing?"

"Not so fast, young man. There's a lot more to the tale."

"I reckon we're not ready to go, yet," James said, looking at Amparo, who stood by the counter, turning the spurs over and over in her hands.

"Old Frank took to his heels, with a whole posse of angry folks right behind him, and he tried to hole up in an adobe down the way a piece. Well, the Mexicans started to tear off the doggone roof, they was so riled. Old Frank kicked out the fireplace and got into another part of the building. He locked himself in a room, but the Mexes were still electing to string him up when the sheriff stopped them from ripping the house down."

"They must have been related to the dead man."

"May be, may be. The sheriff put Frank in that adobe over yonder, since we don't have a proper jail." The man nodded his head toward Amparo. "Say, she always take this long to make up her mind?"

"Can't say that I know. We haven't been wed overlong. Tell me, why's the sheriff got Mexicans guarding Frank Blue if they're the ones so mad at him?"

"Well, the sheriff's a Mexican, you see. He's a good man, and I guess he figured it might cool things down if both sides was to take a hand in the guarding." He scratched his ear.

"Does it work?"

"I don't know. The dead man's brother and some others have been seen at night, just about when shots are fired into the jail, but nobody's done anything about it. It's let up, here lately. Been quiet at night twice in a row."

"That's good." James walked to the door and looked out. "Your Mister Dunn has gone off down the street. What's he fussing about?"

"He's a friend of Frank's. He was worried the Mexicans would lynch old Frank, so he took the stage down to Cimarron. Wanted to bring troops back from Fort Union. I guess they told him no, 'cause the soldier boys didn't escort him back. Now he's trying to get folks to make a run on the jail and let Frank loose."

"Six little beans! Can't he let well enough alone?"

"That's the size of it."

Amparo came toward James and put spurs into his hands.

"Chemes, *éstas son tus espuelas de regalo. ¡Feliz Año Nuevo!*"

The silver rowels felt cool to his palms, and he turned the spurs over to admire them.

"Mighty pretty, girl. But I can't figure why you want me to have them."

"I think she wished you a happy New Year, son. Today's January First. "

"New Year's Day. Say, do you have any fancy side combs, maybe silver, or that shell stuff?"

"Right over here." The man went to a glass case and brought back several pairs for James to examine. He chose a silver set with little red jewel flowers worked into the backs.

"Now it's my turn, girl," he said, holding the combs out toward his wife. "Happy New Year."

She took the combs, and looked at him with those great dark eyes, and his insides moved like butter down a hot cob of corn. *Maybe this fellow has a room free*, he thought. *No, we'd best get out of town, like he said.* "Put them in your hair."

Amparo pulled a comb through the thick black strands at one side of her head, then stopping short of the place where the braids began, turned the comb and pushed it snug against her head. Then she did the same at the other side, and posed her head for James.

"Ah, they look fine, just fine." He turned to the hotel man. "You got the bill made out? We'll settle up and pack our gear out of here."

The man scribbled some more and said, "It comes to twenty dollars even. Best wishes to you and the lady, and don't forget, when next you come through, stop here to trade."

James fished coins out of his pocket to pay the bill. "I don't figure to pass this way again. We're heading home to the Greenhorn."

The man put the money in his strongbox, then loaded the sack of cornmeal onto his shoulder. "I'll help you out."

James hoisted the flour over his shoulder, nodded for Amparo to take the spurs and the lard tin, and picked up his rifle. "I'm obliged," he grunted, and followed the man toward the door.

A bullet shattered a pane of the storefront, and glass tinkled onto a display of milk cans. James's heart started drumming, near popping out of his chest as the firing continued, and he dived at Amparo, pulling her down to the floor. They rolled behind a stack of cracker barrels, away from the open area where he'd dropped the flour. He looked back, and the sack lay there, sifting a white halo onto the floorboards around it.

"Keep your head down," he hissed at Amparo, motioning with his hand. Then he turned her loose and skinned his way across the floor to the hotel man, who was taking shelter behind the cornmeal. "Are you hit?" James asked him, but the man shook his head.

"That glass cost me a fortune," he moaned. "I thought a man had a right to property hereabouts."

"Make your claim later." James listened for a moment to the shouting and gunfire. "Sounds like both sides are excited. Who's making all those threats?"

"The sheriff," he groaned. "I'll never get money out of the county to pay for that window."

"Who else is out there?"

The man swore. "It's that John Dunn. He must have stormed the jail and got Frank loose."

"Sure sounds like a big bunch out there."

"And they're coming this way!" The man's face grew pale.

James looked back at Amparo. She had her head down, but she was watching him. "Amparo, te amo," he called across the floor.

She raised one finger to her lips and blew him a kiss. *I should have taken that room*, he thought. *We'd be out of reach of this lead throwing contest with four walls close about us.* Then his head jerked around to face the door as five men tumbled through the opening.

The hotel man rose up on his elbows and protested. "Take your fight back out on the street, Dunn."

"Shut up, Philo," a big man grunted. "Gutiérrez has three hundred greasers out there, all riled up and after my blood."

"They're welcome to it, Frank Blue. Get out of my hotel. You're fired off the stage," Philo yelled.

More men from the street backed into the doorway, firing at the crowd outside, drowning out the argument between Philo and Frank Blue. During a lull in the shooting, James crawled to Amparo, grabbed his rifle where it lay on the floor, and got himself and his wife behind the back counter.

"Are you in one piece?" he asked her, looking hard into her eyes.

"Chemes, *tengo tanto temor*," she whispered, trembling, sinking her fingers into the meat of his forearm.

James took her chin in his free hand. "We're not in this fight. Soon as we hit a breathing place, I'll yell for that sheriff to let us go free." He rose up a bit and peered into the room over the counter. *There must be fifty men in this lobby*, he thought.

Philo, the hotel man, sat in a corner, glaring at a man who had a rifle trained on him. Several men hauled flour sacks to make a barricade at the front of the store. Three others were chipping holes through the wall with their belt knives.

They're forting up for a regular siege, James thought. A drop of sweat ran down his neck and into his collar. He pulled his head down and slumped against the counter. *I can't let her know we're in a pinch.*

Amparo grabbed his arm again. He looked her way and felt his mouth pulling up at the corner as he shut his eye in a slow wink. "We'll wait out the storm," he said, and wondered if there was a back way out of the hotel.

Then several shots from outside the rear of the building sealed off that route. James felt the pounding of boots on the floorboards underneath him as men ran down a hallway to his left. The thump of his heart matched the echo of the boots.

"Philo, you keep your hands in view and we'll let you go set on your stool," growled the voice that belonged to Frank Blue. "We wouldn't use your stupid flour 'lessen it was an emergency." The voice stopped, then after a shot was fired, it continued. "See there, we have to have something in front of us so's we can shoot at those filthy greasers. Now git, Philo. I don't want you accident'ly coming into my sights."

Philo came stumbling around the counter, hands held high, muttering to himself. "Thinks I'm foolish enough to set up on that stool, does he? Catch a stray bullet myself, that away." He ducked down beside James and Amparo and lowered his hands. "I may be old, but I ain't lost my faculties yet."

The crowd outside continued to shoot at the hotel, and then there were answering shots from the men in the store. James heard a yell from the street, and a loud conversation between three men huddled against the front wall. A horse whinnied from the hitch rack out front, and he thought of his animals, wondering if any of them had been hit.

I've got my rifle. I could bully my way out there and turn them loose. Then he thought better of the idea. *I'd be a target for either side in this ruckus. I've got a wife to think about now. She doesn't need to be left a widow in this unfriendly town.*

"Rice, get me some more of those cartridges back of the counter." John Dunn was talking. "And while you're at it, see if Philo's got a bottle under there."

The man came thumping across the floor toward the end of the counter, then into the narrow space between the counter and the wall of shelves. James looked up as the man gave a grunt of surprise, then yelled.

"How'd this greaser woman get in here?"

Chapter 17

Rice's boot moved faster than James could scramble upward, and Amparo's yelp filled the shelves and echoed back to his ears. As James got to his feet he rammed his fist into the man's fat belly, and Rice cried out, "Frank!" James stepped backward and the man fell forward as he doubled up. James's heel came down onto the stock of the rifle that lay on the floor, and he slipped and fell against the edge of the counter.

Rice scrabbled to his feet. He clutched at the front of James's coat, grabbing his lapels and lifting him, bending him backward over the counter. Then another man's arm curled around James's neck, and as Rice let go, the arm pulled James off the counter. Tobacco stink filled his nose and he tried to get fresh air, but the arm tightened, squeezing against his throat, cutting his wind, then somehow dimming the sunlight filtering through the . . .

હ

Rice grabbed Amparo's arm and yanked her to her feet.

"*¡Madre Santa!*" she cried, pulling her arm back from his grasp.

"Shut up, you filthy greaser," the man growled, slapping her across the face. "There'll be none of that heathen talk." Amparo's head snapped to one side. Light flashed before her eyes. She felt something warm trickle from her nose as the man hit her again. She grasped his hand, bit it, felt sinews moving between her teeth as the man howled in rage and pain. Then he yanked his hand loose and hit her in the stomach. Amparo bent double, arms wrapped around herself as the man dragged her from behind the counter.

"Colley, give me a hand with this Mex."

Another man took her left arm, and a sick feeling of panic washed over Amparo. She screamed out in Spanish, "Help me, Blessed Virgin," as she struggled in the men's grasp. "Give me aid, Holy Mother. They are going to violate me!"

હ

. . .sound he'd ever heard, like the Rebel yell pitched higher than any man he'd served with could keen it. The noise came again, passing outside the hotel, then faded into the distance.

James opened his eyes and tried to swallow, but something was caught in his throat. He fought it, struggling to clear the clog, and finally squeezed through a drop of saliva. Then he relaxed, the clog eased up, and he knew what it was that had choked him: his neck and throat were swollen from Frank Blue's chokehold.

When James went to lift his hand to his neck, both of them rose up, and he discovered that his two hands were tied together at the wrists. He stared at the binding, then shifted his focus to his ankles and found them tied, also. His tongue was crowded by a wad of cloth, which was held in his mouth by something that passed between his opened teeth, then went around to the back of his head.

I don't know this place, James thought. *Barrels and crates. Some kind of storeroom, I reckon.* He closed his eyes, trying to recall— Something horribly important was gone from his mind, and he strained to pull it back.

For a while James sat and thought, but the more he thought, the less he remembered, so he started to work on getting loose. He found that if he raised his arms high above his head and lowered them a bit behind, he could get his fingers into the knot holding twisted-up cloth around his head. He tried to move the whole binding upward, but it wasn't loose enough to slip from between his teeth.

James craned his neck to one side, got one thumb and finger around the knot, and worked the fabric back and forth. After several minutes, a knife-sharp pain in his shoulders made him lower his arms and rest a bit.

Malditos, he thought.

He rested, breathing in a raspy, ragged way. His nose told him the pieces of cloth gagging him had gone a long spell since the last laundering.

Malditos. Bad men. Amparo! James's body went stiff, and he looked around. *She's not here with me.* He recalled her cry as the man Rice kicked her, and raised his arms to try the knot again. The pain came back, but stronger still was the recollection of her cry echoing through the store, and he remembered a laugh he'd heard. James started to sweat, and worked harder at the knot.

The cord-like cloth fell to his lap, and he pulled his arms back over his head and down and dug the gag from his mouth with his thumb. Now that his teeth were free, he picked loose the knot around his wrists, and then untied his ankles.

The door was unlocked. James opened it a crack and saw two men reloading weapons in the corridor between him and the front of the hotel. An angry voice shouted threats from the street.

" . . .meddling Indians or not, you send out my prisoner or we'll storm you from all sides. This is the last chance I give you."

Then, "You call that justice? You'd hang a man for spitting on the sidewalk," yelled Dunn from the store. "We'll take our chances the way we make them."

The men were finished reloading. The two hefted the guns onto their shoulders and moved out of James's view.

He took a breath, held it, let it out slowly, and pulled the door wide open. Before he stepped into the hall, James glanced toward the rear door. The defenders there had their eyes pressed against cracks in the door, so he eased through the opening and toward the front of the hotel.

The sheriff turned loose his mob.

James ducked into a door space halfway up the hall, then crouched over and ran to the front room, dived behind the counter, and crashed into Philo, who had his hands tied behind his back.

"Where's my wife?" James grunted as he undid the old man's knots.

"They argued some after they carted you off, then old Frank slapped her around a bit before the Indians came into town," Philo whispered.

"Where is she? Indians?" he yelped.

"Shh. I think Frank put her in one of the rooms."

"Did he . . . touch her?" James watched the color drain from his clenched fist and felt a muscle throbbing along his swollen neck.

"He beat her some, but he ain't had time to take liberties. Them Utes rode in and riled Gutiérrez right proper. Kept Dunn and old Frank guessing for a spell."

"How long they going to exchange lead?" James found his rifle under the kick space at the base of the counter.

"Till one side runs out," Philo hissed. "And my hotel won't ever be the same again." He swore. "Them scalawag politicians won't pay for this mess."

∞

"I think somebody ran out of bullets."

Philo's voice woke James. He blinked, listening to the screaming quiet in the darkened room. *Hush, Pa won't believe I slept through this battle. Ma won't believe I'm bringing her another daughter, neither.* He reached out to touch Amparo's hair and felt a leathery bald spot fringed with spiky tufts.

The hotel man pulled James's hand down from his head. "She's still in the other room, son," he whispered. "I think it's the first one on the far side."

"No offense meant," James muttered, knowing his cheeks were blooming.

"None taken. You been dreaming a handsome dream of your little lady, I can tell. I remember how it was when I was young and had a new wife. That's a long time ago, but I recollect it's a good feeling. Yes, and it's never the same with a second wife."

"I reckon I'll never know."

"Listen to the old man," Philo said. "He prattles on while you chafe to have your woman safe at your side again. Look here. Dunn and Blue have been over in the corner discussing something for quite a spell. If you was to dash over into the hall, they'd never know you'd been and left."

"I reckon," James said, and crouched into a ball, preparing to rush into the hallway.

"Good luck, son," Philo said, very low.

James patted his shoulder and left as quietly as he could, carrying his rifle. The door squeaked a little as he eased it open, but the dog howled in the street, and James hoped the animal noise covered the sound he made opening the door.

The room was black as the inside of a cook stove, and James stood by the closed door for a moment, letting his eyes get used to the dark. Soon he saw the outline of a bed with Amparo lying on it, bound as he had been bound. He crossed the room to her side and loosed her, and she came into his arms and huddled against his chest.

"¡*Válgame Dios! Eres tú*," she sobbed.

"Shh, shh," he whispered. "We're not safe yet."

James's fingers searched her face, finding a lump next to her eye and dried blood under her nose. His rage shook them both, and he swore, "The man who did this to you—he will pay!" He put his face into Amparo's disordered hair, breathed in her warmth and rubbed her back. "My pretty wife, my sweet girl, he will pay!"

"Chemes, *salgamos de aquí, por favor*," she said. James recognized the pleading tone to her voice.

"I've got to vamos you out of this room. If he comes back, you won't be here to put up with his filthy paws."

James took Amparo's hand and stepped to the door, listening to the men moving around in the lobby of the hotel. "It's quiet right now," he whispered, putting his finger to his lips. "Best we move silent down the hall."

He recalled that the door hinges creaked, so he opened the door slowly, holding his breath so he wouldn't draw in a noisy lungful of air. Then the door was open and the hall stretched black before him. He waited until he had the storeroom door located, then inched forward, holding Amparo's hand as she followed behind.

We're going to make it, he thought, and put his hand out to unlatch the storeroom door. Then the hall filled with dim, pushing, shoving figures. The crack of a pistol echoed in James's head. Amparo slammed against his back.

"Who's that?" Dunn rasped. Then James was jostled and bumped as several men swore their way down the hall, and he slipped his arm around Amparo and drew her close to keep her from falling.

"You're safe now," he grunted as the men passed through the back door and out into the alley.

Hush, my shirt's all wet, he thought, loosening his hold around Amparo's back. She slumped against him, her body slack and falling. *Warm and sticky*, his mind urged. *Blood. They shot her!*

"A light, bring a light!" James bellowed into the gloom as he fell to one knee and eased her to the floor. "Amparo?" He turned toward the store. "Philo! A lamp, man."

A glimmer of light bobbed down the hall toward James, then came to floor level as Philo knelt. He asked, "What's the trouble, son?" then inhaled sharply.

James watched the bright red stain spread on Amparo's white blouse beside a small, powder black hole, heard her cough, sigh "Chemes," slowly take in a breath, then hold it.

He yanked his handkerchief from his pocket and balled it in his hand, pressed it to her chest, and grunted, "Breathe, breathe, take a breath."

Somebody was trying to lift him away from Amparo, and he wrestled loose. "Amparo, breathe!" he commanded, and pressed the cloth to the wound.

"It's no use, son," someone, Philo, he guessed, muttered in his ear. Gentle. It surprised him. Then, "She's gone. Give it up, son." Hands hauled him to his feet.

Chills and horror and black, rending pain swept his body. James looked down on her, lying still in the flicker of the lamp on the floor; silent, peaceful, her eyes closed by someone's hand, coins placed to weight the lids shut. Black and brown and white. And red: awful, blinding, jolting red. He felt her blood drying on his hands, binding his shirt to his chest, smelled the rank sweet odor of her blood mingling with the reek of sweat and the heavy gunpowder fumes in the hall.

James crumpled his fingers into fists, and rage took over his soul. *They will pay*, he swore. *Upon my word as an Owen, they will pay!*

ജ

"They favor lots of candles around the departed."

Philo climbed down the ladder with a fistful of candlesticks from the top shelf. Thick blood pounded in James's temples, hot from his heart, and he thought, *I don't know the rites of her church, but she'll have the candles until a priest comes.*

As he watched Philo put candles into the holders and set the wicks ablaze, James remembered the few minutes he had gained alone with Amparo's body. He had called for water and a cloth, picked her up and carried her into the storeroom, and kicked the door shut behind him. A moment later someone brought the water and the gray cloak he'd bought for Amparo in Santa Fe. Then James closed the door on the world.

He bathed her face, soaking the blood from around her nose and mouth, and ran his thumb over her lips, still soft and giving. Then he took off her ruined blouse and washed all the stiff blood from her body, looking on her beauty one last, hurtful time.

His soul cried out to her, *Amparo, my girl, my wife. We were just beginning.* Now there would be no homestead to prove up, no cabin in the pines, no fireplace tended by a caring wife, no little niños giggling in the twilight. The sense of loss, the dark sorrow, cut deeper when James thought of his never born children, and he wondered if his bride's body had sheltered a growing babe.

He had wrapped her in the gray cloak, then laid her on the cleared off side counter in the store while Philo lighted candles to put at her head and her feet.

James took a step backward, and something clinked under his heel. He stooped, picked up one of Amparo's silver spurs, then looked for its mate and found it in the litter on the floor. The rowels glistened in the candle light, cool in his burning hands. Then he knelt and put the spurs onto his boots.

The men who had sprung Frank Blue from jail gathered in little groups around the lobby, hats off, twiddled in their hands. They come up during the night, in knots of twos and threes, curious at the dead stranger in their midst. James watched their hard faces turn soft, and there was more than one man with a need to blow his nose after looking on her. James kept an account. Dunn and Blue and Rice and one other man were missing, and he drew their features on a black slate in a corner of his mind marked vengeance.

Through the hours of the night he kept a death watch, standing close enough to the counter to hear the plop of wax on the wood, the crackle of the wick. The taste of sulfur in his mouth from the thick air in the corridor brought thirst, but he set it aside.

The air cooled in the room, and James knew dawn was near. The chill worked into his flesh, and he stretched his shoulders to rid them of tightness.

"Hello in the hotel."

Men came awake around the room, and James turned his eyes toward the street, where the shadows of night were turning gray. Two men in suits stood in the road. One held up a ramrod with a white bit of cloth tied to the top.

"We want to come in and talk," one man yelled. The other man waved the ramrod back and forth.

"Is that you, Alton?" One of the hotel defenders rose up and looked out the broken window. "Come in. We got something to show you."

"We're unarmed, Archie."

"You showed your white flag," Archie said.

Several men hauled the flour sacks away from the door and let the outsiders come in. The man called Alton took off his hat and stepped into the room. He saw the candles burning on the counter.

"That's a lot of wax going up in—" Alton stopped and stared at Amparo as James stepped backward to protect her body from mischief.

"Why, it's a girl, a Mexican woman. What's going on here?"

"My wife." James measured out his words, working to keep his voice flat and steady. "The men who escaped last night shot her."

"Escaped? Who escaped? Nobody could get through those lines out there."

James raised his chin. "Frank Blue and John Dunn and two others left last night. If they couldn't get through, they're out in the alley, but they're not in the hotel." He clamped his jaw to keep from saying more.

"And who are you? Are you new to these parts?" Alton didn't like James. James didn't like Alton.

"Just passing through."

"Well, I don't know what to tell you. Looks like you passed through on the wrong day of the year, stranger. Sorry you lost your . . . wife. We'll see to it that she's buried in the town plot, at town expense."

James caught hold of the counter behind to steady himself, to keep his hands from tearing open the man's throat. Then he spoke, but the voice was a stranger's.

"I reckon my Amparo girl couldn't rest good in the ground of this trash heap you call a town. Your hellish little fracas took her away from me, but you aren't going to keep her."

He had to stop and get a breath, to ease the choking that made his voice shred his ears. "You get me a priest to see her soul to the other side, and I'll take care of laying her body to rest."

"I can't get a priest in here, man. You're under siege by the sheriff!"

"Allowing as how I had no hand in this uprising, I expect you to take a message to your sheriff for me. I'm taking my wife out of this town today, shriven or not, so tell him to hurry that priest on in here." The strain of keeping a hold on his temper shook his body.

Alton blinked his eyes several times. "All right, all right. I'll talk to him." He backed away from James and went over to Archie, who seemed to be the leader now that Blue and Dunn were gone.

The two of them talked, discussing what to do now that the prisoner had fled. Alton pulled out his pocket watch, muttering about a time limit. Archie's face set in hard lines. James turned his back, gripped the edge of the counter, and rocked backward, his arms extended. He looked at Amparo, took several deep breaths, closed his eyes. Then Archie said, "You do that. We'll wait here."

James cleared his throat and called out, "Don't forget the priest." He didn't look around at Alton as the man and his companion left, banging the door behind them.

ಐ

James felt as though his head were stuffed with cotton. He knelt on the floor by a splintered keg of nails as a brown robed priest worked through a service that confused him. Philo stood beside James, patting his shoulder. Men whispered from their groups against the walls.

James shut his eyes. *Amparo!* his soul cried. *Amparo, don't leave me. Don't leave me alone!*

Chills racked his body as he bowed his head. *Dear God, send her back. Ma. Ma, she can't be gone. I need her. God in heaven, I need her!* Sweat poured from his brow.

Philo tapped him on the shoulder, and James looked up. The priest had finished, was turned toward him, looking at him with pity, no, compassion in his eyes.

"*Paz, mi hijo,*" he said, his arm looping in the air. Then his hand was on James's shoulder, patting, then coaxing him to his feet.

"Thank you." James rose, stiffly, then put his hand into his pocket and drew out a coin. "For your trouble," he said, giving it to the padre.

"Fo' the poor," the priest answered in halting English. "Go in peace, my son."

James closed his eyes and shivered. What peace was there for him now? When would he ever have peace again?

Philo led him toward Amparo's body. "You'd best get gone while the sheriff's still of a mind to let you go, son. I'll see to it your supplies get packed and loaded."

James nodded. *Amparo.* He put out his hand and covered her face with a flap of her cloak. *My wife. I'll bury you on the mountain.* He straightened his shoulders and shook off the lethargy that tempted him to sit amid the ruins of the store goods on the floor. Then he took Amparo's body in his arms and turned toward the door.

ℛ

James held the sorrel down to a walk as it ascended the steep mountain trail that led to Ratón Pass. In his hand he held the lead line tethered to Amparo's horse, which carried the gray shrouded burden of his wife's body. Next in line, the mule plodded along, and the Mexican's dog trotted mournfully behind them all. Before mid-afternoon he reached Uncle Dick Wooton's tollgate.

"I'm looking for four men," he grunted as he paid the toll to the keeper. "They would have passed through here last night."

"Uncle Dick would know. You'll have to wait a couple of hours to talk to him. He's gone on an errand."

"I can't wait," James said, taking a fresh grasp on the sorrel's lead rope. "I'll find them myself."

The man shrugged. "Suit yourself." He eyed Amparo's body as he lifted the pole, but didn't say anything further as James and his animals passed through the gate and proceeded along the toll road.

Although the icy afternoon wind blowing off the mountain slashed at James's nose and froze his cheeks, the furnace blazing in his belly kept him from feeling the cold. He could think of nothing but the cloak-wrapped girl behind him.

"Amparo!"

It surged out of him from down deep, across his lips, then was gone into the valley behind him on the cutting wind. Nothing was left but the hole in his heart, and the burning rage, and the task at hand.

"Soon," he cried. He couldn't say more than one word at a time. He had no yen to try. "Soon," he repeated, looked at the pistol he wore belted to his hip, then touched the second gun thrust into his waistband. It was the one he had given to Amparo for protection when he had to leave her alone and go back along the trail for his runaway horse. He stroked the hard wood of the handle, wanting to feel something she had touched, yearning to feel her hand under his. Then he thrust the yearning aside. He had much to do.

As James neared the summit of the pass, he veered off the trail toward the stand of trees where he and Amparo had camped on their first trip over the mountain. Sight of the place loosened his tongue, and he half turned in the saddle to speak.

"Hush, girl, it's cold, rocky ground up here, but there's wind enough to keep the stink of hate out of your nose." Then James reseated himself and squinted against the wind that whistled through the trees just as it had on the night they camped there.

He recalled how Amparo had laid aside her home made cloak to prepare their meal, how she shivered as she cooked, and how he then had retrieved her cape to keep her warm.

"You won't have to abide the cold now that you've got that warm cloak. You'll lie snug here, girl."

James dismounted, tied his horse, and tightened his nerves for the job ahead. Loosening the ropes binding Amparo's body to the horse took more time than he'd thought with his fingers stiff from the cold, but he finally lowered the gray wrapped load from the horse's back and into his arms.

She was all he had, and he held her close to his chest for a long moment, breathing in long, shuddering gulps. Now he was obliged to put her to rest, so he walked a few feet beyond the site of their old camp and went to one knee to lay her body on the ground. Then he returned to the animals and twisted the pick and shovel free from the pack. Two paced steps gave him the length he needed, and he marked the measurement with two large rocks.

James lifted the pick, swung it overhead, and plunged it into the earth. A sudden flaring of his rage fed his strength, and as he worked, he began to grunt in time with the blows, "They . . . will . . . pay. They . . . will . . . pay!"

He hacked the grave into the shoulder of the mountain, stopping once to remove his coat. The ground was frozen, and the pick seemed reluctant to bite, but he forced it between the earth and rocks with regular swings. The shock of the blows chased up his hands, his arms, and into his back, but the pain of his muscles never matched the hurt of his grief. It was a live thing, growing within him, and from time to time it frightened him.

Once, he rested the pick to catch his breath, with his chest heaving to regain the air stolen from him by the robber wind. His lungs ached, burned by the frozen vapor he sucked into them. He looked over to the horses, which stood nose to tail, huddled together to wait out the wind. The old dog poked his nose between the pair of animals to get warmth from them.

Then James tossed the pick aside and took up the shovel, digging and flinging the rocky earth over his shoulder to deepen the hole. The sweet odor of blood pricked his nostrils, and as he hauled himself out of the hole to find the pick again, he noticed that his palms, worn beyond blisters, were bleeding.

A movement in the forest drew his eye, and he thought, *Wolves. I've got to go deeper to keep her safe from varmints.*

As he worked with the pick, James tasted sweat flowing into his open mouth. He was breathing with great gasps, and the salty liquid dripped off his chin and froze in icy streaks on the blood-soaked front of his shirt.

He looked down at the brownish stain. *That's Amparo's blood*, he thought, and wiped his bleeding palm across his chest, adding new stains. *Now my blood and her blood are mixed.* Then he wondered if the wetness running down his cheeks was sweat or tears, but it didn't matter . . . it didn't matter at all.

Sometime later, he stood in the hole, panting from the effort of squaring the grave, and his mind wandered to the whisper that had come to his ears before he left the town.

"They went south, bound for the fort. Someone will notice four men on three horses."

"They will pay," he muttered, and climbed out to finish his work.

James knelt beside his wife's body and bared Amparo's face to run his fingertips along the angle of her jaw, storing up forever the feel of her smooth brown skin. He forced his voice to be calm and whispered, "Goodbye, little wife. Our time—" He had to swallow. "Our time was so short."

Smoothing back a stray bit of hair from her face, he noticed that one of her ear bobs, the aretes he'd given her in Santa Fe, was missing. He felt the loss like a physical blow to the pit of his stomach, and hunched over for a moment. When he recovered, he removed the remaining adornment, closing his fingers over the gold and emerald and ruby arete, warming the cold out of it against his palm. Then he knotted the earbob into a corner of his handkerchief and thrust it into his pocket. He left the silver combs in her hair where she had placed them.

He covered her face, lifted her body and carried it to the grave. The dog stood at the edge of the hole, whimpering and sniffing. Then it howled. James suppressed a shudder.

When he had eased Amparo down into the hole, James laid her body flat along the bottom and climbed out to stand at her head. The mourning dog nudged his leg, and he reached down to comfort it with a stroke on the head.

"First your master, then your mistress, old dog," he whispered. Then James shrugged on his coat, removed his hat, and recited words he'd learned to read in childhood.

"Who can find a virtuous woman? For her price is far above rubies. The heart of her husband doth safely trust in her, so that he shall have no need of spoil. She will do him good and not evil all the days of her life."

His voice cracked on the final words, and he squeezed his eyelids tight for a moment. Then he muttered, "She'd have done all the rest, if she'd had a chance."

James stooped to gather a fistful of cold earth, and held it a while to warm it before he scattered it onto Amparo's body. Then the pain built up and exploded out of him like a field piece, and he cried out, "Amparo! Oh, Amparo, te amo all my days!" He listened, but there was no whisper of her sweet voice returning the vow.

The shovel worked awkwardly in his hands as he filled in the grave, for he was shuddering with a weariness that came up from his toes. The sun was near to going down when he mounded the earth and piled stones on top as an extra protection against animals. He picked up his tools and retied them to the mule's pack in the last light.

Bunching the lead ropes of the spare horse and the mule in his raw fist, he mounted the sorrel, whistled up the dog, and rode along the shoulder of the mountain to the road leading into New Mexico. The trail of Frank Blue.

Chapter 18

James rode most of the night. When the moon rose, he stopped to chuck Amparo's saddle into the brush and cinch his own in its place on her horse's back. He also took an hour's rest when he feared he was so tired he would slip from the saddle.

As the light increased with coming dawn, he slowed down to check the tracks on the road. When he'd gotten about fifteen miles from the tollgate, he pulled up to dismount and sort the hoof marks into patterns.

The tracks that caught his eye were at least a day old, but that was the right time, and three horses made them, including one with deep tracks, possibly from the weight of two men. He studied the length of the horses' strides and the shape of the shoes, then he mounted and settled Amparo's black horse into a ground eating trot. Before long, he was out of the pass and onto the flat land below it.

James stopped at mid morning to grain the animals and water them in a stream. He stood back a ways and waited for the horses to fill up. Then he hobbled them and turned them loose to graze on the weeds growing beside the water while he rested for a spell, hat over eyes, back against a stunted tree trunk.

His grumbling stomach woke him about noon. He saddled the sorrel, ignored his hunger, and stepped into the stirrups. Then he cut sign, pleased—as far as he could be pleased—that the prints he was following still showed on the road. A short way along, the tracks moved off the road and swung north a bit until they arrived back at the stream. James followed, riding warily.

"Well, old dog, do you reckon they've seen our dust and wonder if I'm Gutiérrez?" asked James. He thought about his question for a while, then answered it out loud. "No. I reckon they'd not expect anyone to be coming after their hides in New Mexico." He loosened his rifle in the scabbard anyway.

He followed the tracks for an hour. They still lay along the bank beside the stream. Soon, however, James noticed that the horses had taken shorter strides. He got down to look over the hoof prints.

"Maybe those men are looking for a camping place," he muttered over his shoulder to the dog. James glanced to the west where the snow-capped Sangre de Cristo Mountains angled up to meet the sky. Another, smaller range lay closer to hand. "I reckon they're heading for the mountains, not the fort, but they couldn't make it in one day's ride." He stood up, easing the cramps in his belly by drinking from his canteen and walking around for a moment.

After remounting, James rode forward at a walk, looking for sign that the men had holed up along the river. When he found a place where their horses had gone down the shallow bank, he dismounted and took the rifle from the boot. Then he walked the animals a few yards back the way they had come to a side canyon where he could hide them. There he tethered them—including the dog—then he walked nearly all the way toward the place the horses had disturbed, stopping five yards short of the spot. He carefully went down the bank to the creek side, keeping trees between him and the likely location of the camp.

In the brush at the edge of a cleared spot, James stopped to make sure the men had gone. Then he circled and looked for sign. Boot tracks and trampled grass around a blackened circle of stones told him where the fire had been. He counted four sets of man tracks and three places where horses had left their mark. The bit of black broadcloth snagged in a bush could have come from John Dunn's suit.

Before James could give himself up to satisfaction, he had to know these tracks belonged to the men he was after. He went over the camp again. The tinned tomato cans scattered near the fire could have come from any store besides Philo's.

A worry gnawed his belly like a hungry gopher, and he nudged one of the cans with his foot. It skittered off into the ashes. Then he looked down, and grunted in surprise.

Something picked up the afternoon light in the place where the can had been, something small and shiny. James bent and lifted it in his fingers, then almost dropped it again.

It was Amparo's missing arete, the gold and emerald and ruby ear bob he had thought was lost from the pair he bought her on the morning before they left Santa Fe! A feeling cold as a cavern seeped into James's bones as he straightened up.

"Frank Blue, sure as I stand here," he muttered. The earring cut into his clenched fist. "Amparo didn't let this go without a fight." After a moment, he opened his hand and looked at the earring again, then fished his handkerchief out of his pocket, and tied the precious find beside its mate.

He stepped into the trees and followed the tracks that appeared to have been made when the men left the camp. The signs went back up the bank and continued west. Satisfied, James returned to his animals.

"We're on the right trail, old dog," he said as he settled in the leather. A hot craving mounted in his chest, a raging lust to see blood spilled. He didn't shove it aside. Instead he breathed with it, his heart thundered with it, and he whispered, "I reckon we can catch them before nightfall."

80

The sun slid behind the mountains, leaving a glow like lamplight on the land before dark came down. James swung off the sorrel and led the horses into a covering of trees beside the stream. Off to his left, a small trickle of a creek came from a canyon and joined the main stream.

They're ahead. I can taste the dusty air. Frank Blue, I'm coming for you.

James wanted to shout the challenge into the dusk, but he banked the yearning like a nighttime fire and took care of the horses instead. After he picketed them on the dry grass under the trees, he stroked the dog's head and told it to be silent, cradled the rifle, and started back to the trail to read the tracks in the last light. He was hunkered down in the middle of the path when the sound of metal on metal hit his ears. He arose and moved into the rocks rising to his left at the mouth of the canyon.

As he settled into a crack between two rocks, he picked out the man sounds— boots scraping on rock, rifle stocks thunking against the earth, pots clinking, heavy yawns, the low murmur of voices. He had to get closer before the moon rose.

The dog at his side gave a low growl, and James put his hand on its head, shushing it, smoothing its raised ruff. He peered out of his shelter into the darkness, figuring how far he could get into the canyon before he was spotted. He tried to find a place of concealment, but the darkness was too deep.

He grunted, and squatted to remove his spurs and lay them on the rocky ground. "You stay quiet too, dog," he said, then stood up and stepped out of the crack that hid him.

James took a few slow steps into the canyon, easing his weight onto his toes as he walked. Stopping once to listen, he continued until he found an outcropping of rock that he could slip behind. The dog followed him, ears pricked.

James slid into the shelter of the rocks, biting his bottom lip, listening for the man sounds once more. The only thing that came to his ears was the growling of his belly and the slight panting of the dog. He searched in his pocket for the leather pouch, but there was no more jerky, and the foodstuffs were back on the pack saddle. James slumped against the rock and shut his eyes to keep the edge of the outcrop from dancing.

At length, James forced his eyes to open, fighting against the exhaustion that threatened to overwhelm him. He had caught up to his prey. Frank Blue. John Dunn. A man called Rice, and one other. Well-armed men who didn't know who he was or even that he trailed them. Hard men, who wouldn't care that his wife lay with a bullet in her breast, wrapped in a gray cloak shroud and covered with a ton of earth and rocks.

It matters to me, he thought, watching his fist shake against his thigh. *I married her, yearning for another gal, and she worked magic on me.* James opened his hand. *Then just when our life was laid out smooth as Ma's wedding quilt, she was gone.* "It matters to me," he whispered, spitting on the rock between his wide braced feet. His mouth held a taste like rotten meat.

James looked around the edge of the outcrop. Another crack in the rock lay ahead, and it was the work of only a few moments to move into it. There was barely room for him and the dog, but they crowded together. He peered toward where the murmuring voices came from. Four men sat around a low fire, their conversation verging on a quarrel.

"I still say we missed the road. You can't bring a wagon up this trail."

"We should have made Cimarron by now."

"It don't matter. We can circle around and come into Taos from the back."

"I don't know. This track gets smaller and smaller. Are you sure it even goes over the pass?"

"It don't matter, I say. We'll find our way in the morning. Turn in and get some sleep."

James heard the men settling down into their bedrolls. He gave them some time, his heart thrumming wildly in his chest, then was about to move closer when the crunch of footsteps came toward him. He flattened back against the rock.

The unknown man—maybe his name was Colley—passed him, looking up at the moon rising into the sky. He stopped, and was unbuttoning his trousers when James hit him on the temple with his pistol butt. Colley went down.

Working fast, and as silently as he could, James gagged the man with his own handkerchief, and half dragged, half carried him to the mouth of the canyon. He stopped where he had left his animals to get rope, and tied the man up. He left him in a heap out of reach of the hooves before he returned to the canyon.

The light from the moon diminished, and James looked up. Clouds scudded across the moon, and the temperature dropped. Taking advantage of the lowered light, James crept back to his hiding place, and slumped into it, the dog beside him. He had captured one of the men; maybe it was all right to close his eyes for just a few minutes.

"Vengeance is mine, saith the Lord."

What? James opened his eyes. Nobody was there but the dog. He shut his eyes. Hard. The dog whined.

"The Good Book preaches forgiveness, son. I know you been hurt grievous sore, but you got to forgive."

His ma's face shimmered in his mind. He blinked, then swallowed.

I can't do that, Ma.

There were lines coming out from around his mother's eyes, gouging furrows along her cheeks.

"You got an obligation, son. Might don't make right."

They beat my wife, Ma. They shot her dead.

"The Lord said to love your enemies, son. You been through Hell's own fire, but if you plant seeds of vengeance, you'll reap a harvest of hate all your life, and end in Hell's fire on your own account."

But Ma. My . . . wife's . . . dead! She was the sweetest little girl. I was bringing her home, and you never got to as much as set eyes on her.

"Living with hate is like eating bitter herbs every day of your life, boy. You don't want that. She don't want you to live like that. Wasn't she gentle, good?"

She was that.

"Trust the Lord, son. You keep her memory bright."

When James's chin hit his chest, he woke up, cold and hungry. The moon was heavily veiled by clouds, and the campers' fire was nearly out. Two of the three men snored into the night air. The dog could find the third man. It was time to make them all pay.

"Dog," he said to the animal. "Those are bad men, malditos." The dog's ears pricked, and it growled deep in its throat. "Let's go get them."

James stepped out from the rock cleft, his left hand holding the animal by the scruff of the neck so it could guide him to the camp. He left his rifle behind in the rocks, and had his revolver in his right hand. His heart drummed in his ears.

When he was within five feet of the sleeping men, he turned the dog loose. It bounded into the camp, snarling and snapping at whatever it could find. The men came awake, shouting and groping for their guns. One man stood up, and another brought him down with a snap shot. James kept low, his senses dulled by exhaustion, waiting for a good target. The downed man yowled and cursed, thrashing against the pain. The other two tried to roll up in their bedrolls to avoid the teeth of the dog.

James stood over the wounded man, sighting down the barrel of his revolver. Its weight dragged at his arms, and he had trouble keeping it steady. Then he heard his mother's voice echoing in his mind: "Vengeance is mine, saith the Lord."

Ma, I can't let them go!

"You'll do it, son, in memory of your sweet wife."

Amparo! She'll never forgive me. I swore an oath of vengeance on her grave.

"You quit a hasty oath once before, my boy."

No, Ma! Go away. Leave me be!

The wounded man had quit struggling, and lay still, moaning slightly. James found his gun and threw it into the rocks. Growling and snapping, the dog had one of the other two men pinned down next to the fire. James looked around, but the last man had fled the camp, leaving behind his pistol.

He saw that the dog had captured John Dunn, and kicked the revolver that had fallen out of the man's hand into the darkness. The other gun was small, and he put it into his pocket. Unless the escapee had picked up a rifle, he was unarmed.

James stirred up the fire and put some wood on it, called off the dog, and then tied up John Dunn.

"Who are you?" the man sniffed before James gagged him.

"Nobody you know," James answered, tied a handkerchief over the man's mouth, and went to inspect the other man's wounds. It was Frank Blue.

The gunshot wound was not life-threatening. James tended to it. First light broke as he finished the last knot on Frank Blue's ankles. Then he followed the last man's boot prints into the trees along the creek. At one point, James's legs wobbled so badly that he had to sit down, and he must have slept or passed out from exhaustion. Sometime later he opened his eyes, hearing a rustle to his left. He came fully awake; something was in the trees with him, but the dog was nowhere to be seen. His eyes moved slowly around, looking for the source of the noise, then a man's figure came up big before him, and James's eyes went to slits.

It was Rice, the man who'd kicked Amparo, and he came at James until he stood above, so close that his sweat smell and fire smoke odor mixed into a stink that made James want to retch. The man held his rifle barrel straight ahead as he bent over and looked at James, then poked his shoulder with the barrel.

James grabbed the rifle barrel with his right hand, startling Rice so badly that when he wrenched the gun from the man's grasp, it came away with little effort. James kicked up with his legs to tumble Rice onto his back, then quickly knelt astride his enemy, pinning his arms, pulling his revolver and holding it pressed up to the man's throat.

"Don't move. One blink, one sound, and you're gone to hell, Rice."

The man's eyes showed white around the faded blue color in the center. He nodded his head, very slowly.

"You hellions have caused me a world of grief," James panted, glaring down at his captive. "You'd best know my temper's ready as a pistol with the trigger filed down to a short pull. Tarnation!" He shifted his kneeling stance slightly.

Rice stared. He moved his mouth, trying to swallow, but the gun pressed against his throat worked against him. Finally, he got enough saliva together to whisper, "Who are you?"

"It doesn't matter who I am. Just a stranger. But you folks did me evil when we met back in town. One of you beat my wife. Another killed her when you busted loose." Thick bile rose in James's throat. He swallowed hard.

Rice swore softly. "You're the kid from the hotel—the one with the greaser woman." His eyes narrowed. "We didn't kill nobody!"

James jabbed the pistol, and his voice came in a rush. "You didn't kill nobody? You cowards was in such a hurry to light a shuck and get shed of the town and the sheriff, you don't know what you did? You just killed the sweetest, most loving creature it was ever my good fortune to know. You didn't kill nobody!" His voice rasped harshly, and he rocked back on his heels to spit out the vile tasting residue in his mouth.

Rice took courage as the gun left his neck. "Kid, I swear, I didn't know anything about your wo—about your wife. Do I look like a man who'd kill somebody's wo—wife?"

"Quiet!" James snapped. "You talk too much. And yes, you do look like that sort." He adjusted his weight and his weapon, leaning close over the man's sweating face. "Listen to me, Rice. I got you now, you and your friends, and you need to be mighty quiet while I figure what to do with you."

The man whispered, "You mean to kill me?"

James expelled a harsh sigh and slumped his shoulders as he turned his head. The pistol stayed next to Rice's bobbing Adam's apple, never wavering as James heaved air in and out of his chest with quick pumps of his lungs. Rice closed his eyes.

Then James straightened his shoulders and returned his gaze to Rice.

"Look at me!"

Rice opened his watery eyes. His head bobbled slightly as he shook. "You gonna kill me?" he gasped.

James squeezed his thighs like he was riding a horse and squinted at the man. "I'm doing the talking now. You listen."

Rice's head came up as the dog came through the trees with a rush, growling and snapping at the man lying beneath James. The man sucked in his breath to scream, but James waved away the dog with his free hand, and Rice subsided. The animal whined, turned in a circle, then took up a menacing stance a few feet away, teeth bared at the man.

James shifted his weight again. "I can kill you, Rice, but I won't. If I was to shoot you, I'd be the same breed of man as you—a killer." James shook his gun in Rice's face. "That's not my kind of life. I got a pride in being a law abiding man," he grunted.

Rice rolled his eyes in the direction of the growling dog. "You don't have to kill me. You'll just leave your dog alone here and it'll do your dirty work."

"There's a sheriff looking for you who wouldn't like that. I reckon I'll take all y'all back to him."

"I don't want to go back to that greaser sheriff. His jail stinks of dirty Mexicans," Rice whined. The dog advanced and snapped at the man's arm. James lifted his free hand and swatted the air above the animal's nose.

"Down, boy! Get back!" The dog whimpered and backed away. James turned back to Rice. "You talk too much!"

Rice shut his mouth. James twisted off the man, covering him with his revolver as he stood. "Get up. Head back to your camp. And keep your arms raised in the air." James marched the man back into the camp, where he found rope, tied him up, and gagged him with his own dirty handkerchief. Dunn watched silently.

Weariness made James slump to the ground. He shoved the pistol into his holster. A picture of Amparo, still and silent, flooded James's mind. Pain seethed over him, Amparo's pain. "Y'all gave her no mercy." He spat out the words and sat up straight. "I've changed my mind. Forget the Lord's vengeance. I'll take it myself."

Rice squirmed against his bindings.

"She was my church-wed wife!" Anger cracked through James's voice.

Rice moaned, ashen faced.

James jumped to his feet. White heat rose in him, a passion to destroy, a melting, eating torment that racked his belly. He shook as Rice shook.

"You kicked her, Rice!" As James raged, he drew his pistol, raised it, and stepped forward.

Rice gave a muffled scream, then the gag flew loose before a gush of white and yellow and brown vomit.

"You don't want to live with coward stink smeared on you, son."

James blinked as Ma's words cut across his mind.

"Blessed are they that mourn."

James backed up.

"For they shall be comforted. Blessed are the merciful, for they shall obtain mercy."

James looked at Rice. He looked into his own soul.

"Whosoever shall smite thee on thy right cheek, turn to him the other also."

For a long time, James sighted down the barrel of the gun, feeling his anger seeping away. Then he sighed, and lowered the pistol.

"Killing you ain't worth losing my soul."

James picked up the rifle, turned his other cheek and stumbled toward the edge of the trees where the men's horses were tied. The dog followed him, whining. Dropping the rifle in the dry grass, James began saddling the horses. Despite his weariness, he felt scrubbed and clean and whole. He went about his tasks with a lighter heart and increased energy.

When the four men were secured on horses, James hoisted his saddle onto his own sorrel.

"We ride to Ratón," he said to his animals, wondering at the mildness of his voice, "ride to Ratón to tell Amparo I've been merciful. To see if she minds."

∾

A day later, James stumbled off his horse a hundred yards from the clearing on the brow of the mountain where Amparo lay.

"Ain't we getting down, too?" asked Dunn.

"No," said James.

Dunn started to say something more, then looked at James's set face and shut up.

James dropped his reins, but kept hold of the line that connected his captives' horses together. He wrapped and tied the line around a stout tree trunk, set the dog to guard the prisoners, then walked the path toward his wife's grave. He took off his hat and held it in his hand. Amparo's silver spurs clinked as he walked into the clearing, noticing that the mound of earth he'd left piled up was settling a bit.

James came to a halt before the burial place. He whacked his hat lightly against his thigh, then moved it back and forth next to his leg. "Amparo," he said, looking up through the boughs of the over-hanging tree, "I quit my oath. I found those killers up the trail a ways, but I didn't spill their blood." He kicked aside a small stone, looked down at the tips of his boots, and jutted his chin into the air, sucking in a long breath. "I'm taking them back to Trinidad, to justice. I reckon the sheriff will be glad to see them."

He opened his fist and examined the torn, but healing flesh of his palm. "I turned mercy for ill use. Amparo, I hope I've done right."

James turned to look down the shoulder of the mountain toward the Santa Fe Trail, checking the view. After a while he put his hat on, turned back to the grave and moved a rock into place. A fallen branch or two called him to carry them away, then he swept around the mound with a handful of leaves. Last, he sat on a rock, elbows on knees, twirling his doffed hat between his twitching fingers.

"Amparo, you taught me so much in our short time. I reckon you guessed about Ellen. She hurt my pride so sorely, and you bound up my wounds and gave me a shelter place." He bent his head, inhaled, then gave a great, shuddering sigh. "You didn't know my heart was banged up, besides my pride. Pa made me leave a girl behind in the Shenandoah. Her pa lost his legs in the war, and Pa wouldn't bring him west. I thought my heart would break when I parted from Jessica."

James had to get up and walk around, his hand over his mouth. After a bit, he returned to the rock and sat.

"I thought I knew love then." He shook his head. "You brought that to me, my sweet girl. Now my heart is truly broke, and my soul, too." His shoulders sagged, and he sat with his head bowed for a long time. He finally spoke again.

"I'll be going now. Not to the Greenhorn—that's my pa's dream, since I don't have you to build for." James leaned down and brushed a speck of grit from his boot. "I don't have a notion to work Uncle Jonathan's claim. I can't bear any more digging right yet." He looked at one of his hands, then rubbed his chest with it. "I heard tell I got kin over amongst the Mormons. Maybe I'll pass through their country and see what they're all about."

James passed his hand over his face, then straightened his shoulders. "I can break horses wherever there's such work, so I reckon I'll drift till I heal some wounds and rub off my raw edges."

The wind from the summit swept through the trees, brushing against the leaves. James listened to the sighing sound for a long time, then whispered, "I hope you forgive me for letting your killers live, my sweet girl." He listened again to the sighing wind, then stood, biting his lips to keep his control.

"Amparo!" he called out. His breath came hard, ragged. "Amparo, *te amo*. Always and always."

He clapped his hat on his head and listened, knowing as he did it, he would never hear her voice again. But as he listened, the wind blew soft and gentle around his body, and brought a faint whisper to his heart.

"Chemes, *mi amor, gracias. Te amo para siempre.*"

෨

As he descended into Trinidad, James sighed and half turned to glance behind him to be sure the four men were still secure on their saddles. They had long since quit complaining, and rode sullenly in his wake, hands bound and tied to their saddle horns, and feet tied together with ropes slung under the bellies of their horses. The dog brought up the rear. James turned to the front again, fighting the overwhelming urge to tumble from his horse and sleep where he lay.

He forced his eyes open to look for the sheriff's office along the strip of road that formed Trinidad's main street. Black spots danced before his eyes. He looked down, blinking to drive away the spots, and noticed that his hands trembled from fatigue and the crushing strain of the last few days. When he looked up, he squinted down the street. Three large wagons, bows covered with soiled canvas, were pulling into the other end of town, and he wondered who was traveling cross-country at this time of year. He shook his head, then located the sign he was looking for.

The sheriff's small adobe office was opposite Philo's hotel and mercantile. James gave an inward shudder and reined his horse to a halt. The wagons were across the street now, pulled to a stop. A young woman shook dust from her shawl and climbed down from the seat of the third wagon. She pushed back her sunbonnet with one wrist, exposing hair the color of wheat. He looked away, sitting still a moment to summon the strength to swing his right leg over the cantle of his saddle to dismount. *I hope I don't fall on my face*, he thought, his jaw tightening.

As he concentrated, he heard a gasp from someone across the street, followed by an explosive "James!"

He turned in his seat, shaken to his toes. He knew that voice.

"James," came his name again. It was the young woman speaking. "I thought I'd never see you again!" She bit her lip and started across the street.

He heard a strange, guttural cry, and realized it came from himself. Moisture slid down his cheeks; his throat constricted. The ache of Amparo's loss swelling in his chest blocked his breath. A measure of calm grounded him at last, and he finally could inhale. He looked down at the young woman who had come to stand next to his horse. After a moment he extended his left hand to her. The calmness increased, loosening his tight throat. He exhaled, took another breath, and held it a moment before he expelled it softly.

"Jessica."

: : : : :

Spanish Glossary and Phrase Guide

I've added a Spanish Glossary to this box set, which I hope will give you a bit of the flavor of the language used by Amparo. ~Marsha Ward

adios - Good-bye, literally, go with God.

Allí las tiene. - There they are. Literally "there you have them."

amigo - friend

Amparo - This is a female given name meaning shelter. Yes, it ends with an "o." That's because it's a noun. Another female given name ending in "o" is Consuelo, meaning consolation. These are in the category of names like Faith, Hope, Charity, etc. in English.

anglo - non-hispanic person

Aquí estamos - Here we are

arêtes - earrings, or as James calls them, "ear bobs"

Ave María - Hail Mary (Latin)

¡Ay! - An interjection meaning alas or ouch.

¡Ay de mi! - My goodness, oh my, etc.

Bésame, mi amor. - Kiss me, my love.

caballero - horseman

¡Callate! - Be quiet!

Chemes, mi amor, gracias. Te amo para siempre. - James, my love, thank you. I love you forever.

chica - girl

Cierto. Y ésta es mi mamá. Ella murió. - Certainly. And this is my mama. She died.

comida - food

Con Juan Pablo Fuentes, me imagino. ¡Ay de mi! ¿Qué será conmigo? - With Juan Pablo Fuentes, I imagine. Woe is me! What will become of me?

Creo que te amo. - I think I love you.

Dáme el palo. - Give me the stick

Déjame acabarla. - Let me finish it.

Déje, joven. - Hold up, young man.

digo - I say

Don - A Spanish title of respect, roughly equivalent to Sir.

¿Él está muerto? - He is dead?

¿Elena es la mujer de tu hermano? - Elena is your brother's wife?

¿Eres feliz? - Are you happy?

Eres tan serio. - You're so serious.

¡Eres tú! Gracias a los cielos, eres tú. - It's you! Thanks to the heavens, it's you.

Es mi placer. - It's my pleasure.

Es muy bella. - It's very beautiful.

Es un anillo nupcial - It's a nuptual (wedding) ring

está bien - that's fine

Esta capa es tan fea. - This cloak is so ugly.

Ésta es la casa de mi papá. - This is my papa's house.

está muerto - (he/she) is dead

¿Estás herido? - Are you injured?

éstas son tus espuelas de regalo. ¡Feliz Año Nuevo! - These spurs are my gift to you. Happy New Year!

¡Este anillo es magnífico! - This ring is magnificent!

Ésto es mi papa - This (stick figure) is my papa.

Estoy confundida. - I'm confused.

familia - family

frijoles - beans

gracias - thank you

Gracias, mi amor, ¿pero no me traes aretes? - Thank you, my love, but you don't bring me earrings? Note that in Spanish, the upside down punctuation may occur in the middle of a sentence, and that's okay.

Hize un convenion sagrado. - I made a sacred vow. By the way, "h" is silent in Spanish, so "hize" is voiced "eezay."

Hombre - Man. When Amparo used it, it was a little comment on her man being amorous.

jornada - journey

Leones - lions--the historic name of Walsenburg, Colorado, was La Plaza de los Leones (Lion's Square), which was named after the Leon family who lived on the north side of the Cuchara (spoon) River.

lingo - (English) slang term for words or language, probably a derivative of lengua, meaning language

listo - means both "bright" and "ready"

¿ 'Ma'? ¿Quieres decir 'mamá'? Ella no es mi mamá. Es mi madrastra. - Ma? Do you mean 'mama'? She is not my mama. She's my stepmother.

Madrastra. No es mi mamá. Y es una mujer sumamente malvada. Le odio. - Stepmother. She is not my mama. And she is a really evil woman. I hate her.

Madre de Dios - Mother of God

¡Madre Santa! - Holy Mother!

maldito caballo - damned horse

Malditos - bad men

mama - mama

María Santísima - Holiest Mary

mi - possessive adjective my--in Spanish, a noun is always preceded by an article or, in this case, a possessive adjective: mi mamá, la chica, el niño (my mama, the girl, the [boy] child).

mi esposo - my husband (Amparo uses this form between herself and Molly, but when talking to James, she usually calls him "mi marido.")

mi papa se casó de nuevo. - My papa married again.

mi pobre marido - my poor husband (marido is a less formal, more intimate form of "husband," almost "lover," so if you're going to refer to one's husband to her face, use "esposo.")

mi pobrecito - my poor little one (male)

muchacha - Another way to say "girl," "lass" or "young woman." Chica is for a younger girl, or is more slangy.

muerto - dead

mujer - woman, also a slang term for wife

Necesito comprar algunas cositas. - I have to buy a few things.

Necesito comprar harina de maíz. - I need to buy corn meal.

Necesito espuelas de plata para mi esposo. Espuelas. Para sus botas. - I need silver spurs for my husband. Spurs. For his boots.

niños - children

¿no? - Spanish sentences in dialogue may end in "no," if the speaker is wondering if you understand or is asking you a question.

No entiendo - I don't understand

No entiendo nada de esto. - I don't understand any of this.

no seas estúpido - don't be stupid

no tengo familia - I don't have a family

Noche de bodas - Wedding night

Otra mujer se casó con mi papá. Otra mujer. Ella es mi madrastra. - Another woman married my papa. Another woman. She is my stepmother.

Padre - Father, often used in reference to a priest.

pan dulce - sweet bread

papa - papa

para siempre - forever

pobrecita - poor little thing (female)

por supuesto - of course

¡Qué belleza! - What beauty!

¡Qué cantidad de niños! - What a lot of kids!

¿Qué es esta cosa? - What is this thing?

¿Qué es esto, mi amor? - What is this, my love?

¡Qué maravilla! ¡Qué lujo! - What a wonder! What luxury!

¡Qué niño! - What a child!

¿Qué pasa? - What's happening, what's up?

¡Qué vergüenza! - How shameless!

querida - dear (female)

Quiero comprar - I want to buy

Quiero comprarte espuelas de caballero. - I want to buy horsemen's spurs for you.

Quiero comprarte un regalito para el Año Nuevo - I want to buy you a little gift for New Year's.

¡Quita la ropa! - Take the (your) clothes off!

rancho - ranch

salgamos de aquí, por favor - Let's leave, please

sangre - blood

Santa María - St. Mary, Holy Mary, Blessed Mary

¿Se fue a San Francisco? - She went to San Francisco?

Señor - Mr.

Señora - Mrs.

Señorita - Miss

¡Siéntate! - Sit down!

te amo - I love you

¿Te gustan, mi amor? - Do you like them, my love?

Tenemos visitante - We have a visitor

tengo tanto temor - I'm so frightened

Tienes frío. Ven aquí o yo tendré que ir allá. - You're cold. Come here, or I'll have to go over there.

tortilla - flat corn cake

¡Válgame Dios! Eres tú. - God help me! It's you.

¿Vamos? ¿Me dices que ella se fue? ¿Para dónde se fue? - Let's go? You're saying she's gone? Where did she go?

¡Vaya! - (literally) Get out! (figuratively) Yikes! Ack! Shoot! or similar exclamations

¡Vaya de mi esposo! - Get away from my husband!

ven aquí - come here

Virgen Santa - Holy Virgin, Blessed Virgin

viuda - widow

Vivía al otro lado de la plaza. Mi padre nació en la misma casa. - We lived on the other side of the square. My father was born in that same house.

Voy a lavar tu cara - I'm going to wash your face
¿Y cuál de nosotros es listo? - And which of us is bright?
¿Y qué de mí? - And what of me? What will become of me?

: : : : :

Trail of Storms
Author's Note

Several years ago, I was solicited to donate something of value for an auction to benefit the local Scout troop. I offered to name a character after the winning bidder. My friend Jeff Julander bid high, and threw in five dollars more if I would name a goat after his friend. Thanks Jeff! A pivotal character bears the name of Jeff Julander, and the Julander family's goat is named Mike. I rounded out the fictional family by using some actual family names, as well as some fake ones. Be it known to all, however, that beyond names and general physical descriptions, my Julander characters are not the same as the actual people whose names they bear. The characters are purely a product of my imagination.

Albuquerque, New Mexico Territory, is mentioned frequently in this work. At the time in which our characters lived, it was called "Alburquerque," with an extra "r." In 1706, Don Francisco Cuervo y Valdés, the provincial Governor of New Mexico, named the settlement in honor of the Viceroy of New Spain, Don Francisco Fernández de la Cueva, Duke of Alburquerque. It is generally believed that sometime after the coming of the railroad in the 1880s, an Anglo station master dropped the first "r" because he couldn't correctly pronounce the Spanish name of the town. "Albuquerque" became the common spelling thereafter.

Despite the historical time frame, I have used the modern spelling as a convenience to my readers (and also to prevent Microsoft Word from going crazy with spelling error underlines as I typed).

One of my characters speaks Spanish only a little, and that badly. The word *henti* is his approximation of the correct word *gente*, meaning "people."

Chapter 1

"You girls stick tight together. Those blasted Yankee riders are still bothering folks."

Jessica Bingham paused outside the bakery's front door, letting Ma's words roll off her shoulders as she rearranged the loaves of freshly baked bread in her basket. She looked down the quiet street. The rising sun's pink and gold rays chased night's shadows from the cracks and crannies of Mount Jackson's storefronts. She inhaled the fresh scents of the morning to clear the heavy odor of yeast from her nose. Spring was here. "Hmm," she sighed, and felt a smile of satisfaction lift her mouth. Ma was wrong to worry. This perfect day could hold no danger to her or her sisters.

And yet . . . the previous week, two young married ladies had been knocked to the ground by a band of cavalrymen of the occupation force. One merely had the wind knocked out of her, but the other had lost her unborn babe. Her husband had protested. He'd been badly beaten. A feeling of unease crept over Jessica. Perhaps there were no perfect days in Virginia anymore?

Her older, recently married sister, Hannah, pushed past, saying, "Jessie, get yourself out of my way. This bread won't deliver itself."

Jessie stepped aside and let Hannah pass, since she always seemed to be in a hurry. She had to take the lead in every endeavor, and couldn't abide being late. Maybe that's why she was born first of the twins.

The other twin, Hepzibah, came out of the door and stopped at Jessie's side. She nudged Jessie and said, rolling her eyes, "Hannah's just so rude. Don't give in to her. Ever since she got married, she thinks she's the queen of the world."

Jessie shrugged and stepped out into the street, Hepzibah following after. "Maybe she is, in Robert Fletcher's eyes. He treats her like a fine lady."

Hepzibah made a small, anguished sound. Jessie looked around at her sister, whose expression had changed to chagrin.

Jessie said in a rush, "Oh Heppie, don't mind my prattle. I reckon George loves you just as much as Robert does Hannah. He's bound to say so real soon."

This time, Heppie's sound was definitely a sigh, and her eyes began to redden.

Jessie, trying to divert Heppie from having a crying spell in the middle of the street, called out to Hannah, who strode along five yards ahead of them. "Wait for us. Ma will have a conniption if we don't stay together." She looked around the deserted street, her nerves beginning to twang. "Do you see any riders down the road?"

"No," Hannah replied. "It's too early for those lazy bums to be out. Besides, I ain't seen 'em for days. Ma's just got a bug in her ear." Hannah carried her basket of baked goods on her hip. She stopped walking and gave it a little hitch to make it ride higher.

"Do you reckon they've left town?" Heppie asked Jessie as they followed Hannah.

Jessie shrugged. "I don't know. Maybe a customer told Ma they're still here." She turned her head to look behind her. "I don't see them."

"That don't mean they're not around the corner," Heppie said, sniffing, then wiping her nose with a tiny scrap of a handkerchief. "Look sharp."

Jessie shivered. Her stomach began to ache, and she felt vulnerable and unsafe. The Yankees had already won the war, ravaging the country in the process. It was terribly hard to make ends meet these days. She'd heard Ma crying at night on that score. Why didn't the Yankees go home and leave the people of Mount Jackson alone?

She thought of Hannah, who lived with Robert in a house on the other side of town. During the time he worked at the bank, Hannah was all alone. *She may lord it over Heppie and me for not being married, but maybe she's afraid too. She does spend an awful lot of each day at our house.*

Jessie stepped over a stick in her path. *I reckon I don't blame her*, she thought. She hesitated a moment, sniffing the air. Was that dust she smelled? *Don't panic. Likely a wagon passed on the Valley Pike.* At that moment, the sound of hoof beats coming up behind them raised chills along her spine. She whirled and faced four mounted Yankees, who had seemed to rise out of the very ground.

The men caught up and circled the three women before they could take another step. Two of them spat tobacco juice near the girls' shoes. One failed to launch his mouthful properly, dribbling juice down the front of his shirt.

"Cal, you can't hit a tin can with a turnip," said one man whose dirty red hair poked out in points where it escaped his cap. His laughter rang through the empty street.

Jessie grabbed hold of Hannah's arm with her free hand. She felt Heppie clutching at her skirt band. Jessie looked around, frantic. Where were the Miller brothers? They were always up early, coming down the street as the girls left the bakery.

"Sez you, Red," the Yankee named Cal said, spitting a fresh stream that landed on Heppie's shoulder.

Heppie screamed, dropped her basket, and tried to wipe the juice off.

Cal chewed on his wad of tobacco, turned, and shot a spurt of juice in Hannah's direction. She shrieked as it hit her cheek. Red laughed again, and waved his cap in the air.

"Hannah!" Jessie shouted, and pulled her sister closer to her. The stink of the tobacco filled her nose as she dashed it away from Hannah's eye with her hand.

The third man, whose black moustache contained bits of food, said to Heppie, "Here, let me wipe that for you." He leaned down and grabbed a lock of Heppie's blonde hair. She cried out as he yanked on it, pulling her closer to his horse.

"You need a knife, Bull?" asked the fourth Yankee, reaching into his pocket.

Bull swore. "I can get my own trophies, Foster. Put away your knife."

"Get away from her!" Jessie shouted. Her heart thrummed in her chest. She tried to think of what to do even as she shoved at the man's arm, getting the juice from her hand on his uniform sleeve. He let go of Heppie's hair and turned on Jessie, trying to swat at her hand, but she evaded his reach. Hannah was cowering away from Foster, who called her unpleasant names. The other men rode in circles around the three young women, laughing, whistling, and making rude talk.

"Go back to the store," Jessie urged her sisters. She stripped the white towel from her basket and flapped it in the face of the nearest horse. It reared, dumping Red, and galloped off down the road. The girls pushed their way through the interrupted circle and ran for the front door of the bakery. Behind them, Jessie heard the laughter and catcalls the other men showered on the unseated rider, who swore at them, his horse, and Jessie herself.

Heppie made it to the door first, wrenching it open. Hannah followed hard on her heels, and Jessie brought up the rear.

"Lock it, Jessie," shrieked Heppie. Her big blue eyes seemed ready to leap out of her face.

Jessie twisted the lock, wondering if it would keep the men out if they wanted to enter. "Ma," she cried out as her mother rushed into the shop from the kitchen. "Those Yankees! They spit tobacco juice at us. Just look at Heppie's dress!"

"They're so crude," Heppie moaned, swiping at her shoulder. "I'll never get this stain off me!"

"There, there, girls." Ma gathered the young women into her arms. "Did they hurt you?" Jessie felt her mother's body shaking.

Hannah loosed herself from Ma's grasp and dabbed at her cheek with a handkerchief. "I hate tobacco!"

Ma let go of the girls. "Jessie? You ain't been harmed?"

"No, Ma." Jessie started to hug herself to control her quaking, but remembered in time that her hand was still smeared with slime. She walked behind the bakery display case, found a cloth, and wiped her hand with it. The day had just begun, and already it was a disaster.

Ma went to the window and looked out. "Are the Yankees still out there?" She craned her neck to the right. "Looks like they're going off down the street," she said. "One of 'em is chasing a horse. What happened?"

"Jessie spooked his mount and got us out of there," Hannah said. Her voice sounded calmer. "Heppie, let's go clean ourselves up." She took Heppie's arm, and the twins went into the kitchen.

"Ma." Jessie joined her mother at the window. "Do we have to go out there again?"

Ma took a deep, shuddering breath, then let it out slowly. It seemed to steady her. "Folks'll be lookin' for their bread and pastries. If you leave by the back door, it's most likely the Yankees won't even spot you." She gave Jessie a pat on the shoulder. "I know those Yankee louts are mighty rude to folks, but I don't think you'll come to real harm if you stay together. When Hannah and Heppie have cleaned up, you three scoot."

Jessie sighed. *Ma's right. Folks need their baked goods, and heaven knows we need the money.* She shivered. They would have to go back out. Without a protector. Her brother Luke was too young to do much good. Her heart pounded in her chest. *Oh Pa! Why did you have to die and leave us so helpless?*

❧

Jessie looked over her shoulder at Hannah and Heppie, who walked away from her toward the street corner, leaving Jessie to collect payment for a pie. Mrs. Wiggins, however, seemed inclined to chat.

Please just pay me, Jessie thought, looking the other way down the street. *I don't want us running into those Yankees again*. She turned back to Mrs. Wiggins, anxious about the distance between her and her sisters. She didn't want to be alone, even for the few seconds it would take her to catch up.

Mrs. Wiggins looked at Jessie expectantly. She must have asked a question.

Shrugging her shoulders to shake off her reverie, Jessie said, "I'm so sorry, ma'am, I fear I was woolgathering. What's that you said?"

The stout little woman sighed. "Jessie dear, I was askin' if your ma could bake me a loaf of sourdough bread for tomorrow morning."

"I'll need payment for the pie first, ma'am," Jessie said, hoping it didn't sound too rude.

"Can't y'all wait to the end of the week?" Mrs. Wiggins looked flustered.

"Times are hard, ma'am. Ma needs to buy supplies." Jessie glanced over her shoulder again. Hannah and Heppie were a half block away. A cold chill ran through her.

"That's right, Jessie dear. Times are hard indeed, but Mr. Wiggins wanted an apple pie for his birthday." Mrs. Wiggins sighed. "I'll get your money." She turned her back, left the door open, and took the pie into the house.

Jessie tapped her toe as she waited, watching her sisters grow smaller and smaller. Her stomach tightened on her breakfast and made her queasy. *Hurry up!* she thought, and mentally berated the twins for leaving her here. She was the "little sister." More often than not, they stuck together and left her to do the more distasteful things like collect money from customers.

After what seemed like forever, Mrs. Wiggins returned with a few coins and counted out the price of the pie.

"Thank you, ma'am. I'll tell Ma about your bread," Jessie said as she put the money into her pocket.

Mrs. Wiggins closed the door forcefully, as if to protest Jessie's insistence on being paid.

Jessie snorted. *Silly old bat! Of course she has to pay Ma now. How does she expect—* Jessie left the thought alone and went on to her more immediate worry. With one hand she scooped up the basket she'd put on the porch while she waited, and with the other she grabbed her skirt, racing off after her sisters. "Hannah," she called out. "Heppie! Wait for me."

Jessie had covered half the distance that separated her from the twins when she tripped on a root and fell, landing on the hard dirt with her forearms straddling the basket.

Pain lanced through her arms but was instantly supplanted by the smart of her embarrassment. *Oh, what mortification! You'd think I was twelve years old instead of eighteen, tripping over a danged root.*

Heppie had looked back in time to see the fall. "Jessie," she cried out, and started toward her, motioning for her to get up—as if Jessie were perfectly content to lie sprawled across the path as she was. Hannah continued on to the corner, then turned and waited while Jessie scrambled to her feet and Heppie helped her brush off her skirts.

"Jessie! Are you hurt?"

She rubbed her sore arms, getting the dirt off. "I reckon I'll be—"

Jessie saw the man at that moment, the rider the Yankees called Red. In what seemed only a few seconds, he jumped off his horse, grabbed Hannah around the waist, and was back in his saddle, having thrown Hannah over the front of his horse like a sack of grain. Her basket tumbled through the air, spewing loaves of bread onto the ground. Jessie cried out and pointed, unable to form words to describe what she was seeing. Heppie turned and began to scream. Jessie lifted her skirts and ran toward the corner as fast as she could. *He can't be taking her*, she thought, her heart pounding in her ears.

ഔ

Jessie shoved open the door of the bank with such force that it banged against the wall. Several customers turned to gaze at her in surprise. The clerks and tellers looked up from their work.

Jessie located Hannah's husband, Robert Fletcher, in the teller's cage at the end of the row. She ran across the tile floor and pushed aside the woman standing opposite him.

"You must come, now!" Jessie said to the man, gasping as she struggled to draw air into her burning lungs.

"Miss Jessica—" He turned to his customer. "I'm sorry, Miz Addison. I'm sure she didn't mean—" He broke off and faced Jessie again, frown lines deeply creasing his face and sweat breaking out on his forehead. "What happened to you? You're quite . . . untidy." Robert took out a handkerchief and dabbed at the brow on both sides of his pronounced widow's peak.

"Mr. Fletcher—Robert—Hannah's been taken!" Jessie put out a shaking hand and grasped the counter to support herself. "We've got to get help."

Robert took in a sharp breath. He stuffed the handkerchief in his pocket as he turned and leaped over the gate separating the teller's cages from the customer area.

Before Jessie could blink, he grasped her by the elbow and shook her arm. "What do you mean, 'Hannah's been taken'?"

Jessie's trembling almost overcame her. She forced herself to find her voice, still breathing with difficulty as Robert's grip tightened. "You know those Yankee riders? One of them grabbed her and took her off. Oh, Mr. Fletcher, Heppie's in such a state I had—"

An oath escaped Robert Fletcher's lips as he dropped her arm. "Take me there," he grunted, barging through the door to the street. She caught up to him and led off at a run, lifting her skirts out of the way of her feet.

They cut across the street, darting between vehicles and horses, bumping without apology into passersby, their silent haste fed by adrenaline and fear.

When they arrived at the street where Hannah had been abducted, Heppie bolted out of Mrs. Wiggins's door, crying into her handkerchief. "Oh, Mr. Fletcher, I'm so glad to see you."

Robert nodded briefly to Heppie, then turned and asked Jessie, "Which way did he go?"

Jessie pointed south on the Valley Pike. "It's the redheaded one."

Robert thrust Jessie into Heppie's arms, saying, "Go to your ma's. I'll bring her there," and ran down the street.

"Jessie, did you see his face?" Heppie wailed.

Jessie shook in her sister's embrace as new fear enveloped her. "Yes. I'm afraid he'll kill that Yankee."

Chapter 2

Hannah screamed as the Yankee carried her away from her sisters. She took a breath to scream again. The odor of tobacco and sweaty clothes worn too long without washing almost gagged her.

"Don't bother yelling. Nobody's going to help you," said the man in a rasping voice. He jammed his free arm underneath her stomach and yanked her roughly against him. "None of your yellow-bellied rebel men have the guts."

Hannah twisted and turned in the man's grasp. She tried to get her fingers to his face to gouge his eyes, but he swatted her arm down with his rein hand and pinned it to her side.

"No more of that, missy," he growled, and prodded his horse to a faster pace with a few kicks.

"My husband will come. He'll find you, and he'll kill you," Hannah gasped, struggling anew to find a way to hurt the man.

"You won't be worth the bother when I'm done with you."

The Yankee's words ripped through Hannah's mind. *Oh dear God, no! Help me! Don't let him do this.* "Robert!" she shrieked between sobs that seemed to tear all the flesh from her throat.

"Your Bobbie-boy can't help you, missy," the man growled, and punched Hannah on the side of her head. "Behave now. We've got a ways to go."

Pain sent Hannah slumping forward against the horse's neck as she tried not to lose consciousness. Her ears rang. Her nose filled with dust thrown from the horse's hooves. She closed her eyes and coughed. *I won't let him kill me, she thought. I'll be strong. No matter what he does, I'll be strong until Robert comes.*

After a long time, the horseman pulled up and pushed Hannah to the ground. She rolled to her knees. Three startled chickens ran into the brush at the edge of a stable yard. Before she could arise and follow them, the man was beside her, grasping her around the waist. He dragged her to her feet and into the stable, tugging on a rein to make sure his horse followed. He kicked the door, but not hard enough to close it, and it stood open a ways, letting in a stream of sunlight.

Hannah screamed, lashing out at the man, pulling his hair with both hands. *I'll mark him, she thought. If he's gone when Robert comes, I'll tell him what to look for.*

The Yankee hit Hannah across the mouth, and she lost her grip on his hair with one hand. She tasted salt against her tongue and knew she was bleeding, but she tugged on the man's rusty-colored hair with her other fist. They whirled around, struggling back and forth in the alleyway of the stable. Hair came loose in her hand. She spit her blood on his shirt. He hit her again and she spun and went down onto the straw-covered floor of a stall.

Hannah choked and coughed at the dust her fall had raised. She heard the man coming toward her and tried to curl into a ball, but he knelt on top of her, ripping her blouse until her flesh was exposed and pulling at her skirt. She smelled his rank breath as he tried to kiss her. "No!" she screamed. He slapped her, but she only cried out again. "Help me!"

The man swore at her, calling her vile names as he unbuckled his belt and slid down his trousers. Hannah thrashed back and forth, clawing him with her nails and calling for help as he tore at her skirt, ripping it open nearly to her waist. She screamed again when he shredded her underclothes, then wrestled with her until he restrained her hands above her head.

The pain of his assault wrenched through her body, tore at the sanctity of her womanhood, and bludgeoned her soul until she believed that neither her body nor her spirit would survive. She clenched her eyes shut, as if that could hide what was happening, and felt tears leaking from the corners of her eyes. *He is a fiend of hell,* her thoughts shrieked as he slumped on top of her.

Hannah shivered under him, too spent to cry out any longer. She could not avoid inhaling the stench of his hair lying on her face. It seemed that hours passed while his loathsome body pinned hers into the straw. At last he raised himself above her. She kept her eyes closed, but couldn't hold back the sob that rose in her throat.

"What's the matter? You don't like my looks?" he growled. "That's too bad, missy. You've got to bear them until I'm finished with you." He reached down and touched her breast, laughing at her. "I told you no one was coming for you. I've got as long as I want."

℘

Robert ran down the Pike, his heart thudding in his chest. Where would the man take Hannah? If he was intent on doing her harm, he'd want a private place, like a barn or a grove of trees, even though the occupation soldiers and cavalry were doing pretty much as they liked these days. He'd have to ask if Hannah and the rider had been seen passing by. That might be useless—folks were staying out of each other's business. His breath rattled in his throat. His side burned with pain. His legs seemed made of lead. *No matter,* he thought, and continued his headlong dash. *Hannah needs me.*

When he stumbled and fell, Robert lay with his face in the dust for a moment, then raised his head and eyed the road. The marks of horses' hooves mocked him. *I don't know how to track. I don't know what's fresh and what might be five days old.* He scrambled to his knees, got to his feet, and looked around. He was outside of town and had passed two farms already. *Have I gone too far?* He took a steadying breath. No. Those farms had been burned out by the Yankees. Their barns hadn't been rebuilt yet and the woodlots were gone. No privacy there. Robert began to run again. George Heizer's dairy farm was next. He had a barn.

Robert approached the Heizer place. From the lane he could see two men standing by a wagon in the barnyard, talking. They seemed calm, not looking over their shoulders or fidgeting. *No Yankee's been there*, he decided, and continued down the pike. *I'll try at McNeely's.*

Robert ran another two hundred yards, turned into McNeely's farmyard, skidded to a stop at the door of the house and rapped. His windpipe wheezed and his lungs burned as he sucked breath into them. After a moment, Mistress Maude moved the curtain to one side and peered out. She opened the door a crack, her white face telling of her fear.

Before he could say a word, the woman began.

"Mr. Fletcher! Oh, please, can you look? My Patrick won't be home until after dark."

"Look where, Mrs. McNeely?"

"Oh my! Out in the stable. There's been the most horrid sounds coming from out there for such a long time. Screams, very terrible sounds, they were."

He ground his teeth. "Do you have a gun?"

"A gun? Oh, no, Mr. Fletcher. We had to give it up."

"A knife, then. Lend me your butcher knife."

Her gasp told Robert how she felt about that idea as she closed the door in his face. He heard the lock snapping into place.

He found a stout stick of firewood he could wrap his fingers around, not thinking what he would do with it, but somehow needing to feel the wood's heft, needing to have a weapon. He strode toward the stable.

The door stood open enough to let him through, and he stopped a moment to let his eyes adjust to the semidarkness. The Yankee's horse munched straw to one side, still saddled, reins hanging loose. A rack of farm implements hung on the wall, next to a couple of saddle blankets arranged over a rail. The burly redheaded Yankee knelt over Hannah in a stall, pants at his ankles.

Hannah! What has he done? I'm too late to spare you that—

Robert swallowed hard, his thoughts a torment. The sight of Hannah's bare knees being forced apart for the brute's pleasure enraged him, pushing him past reason, past honor, and he ran toward the man, raising his bludgeon to strike him from behind.

Hannah opened her eyes. With his last vestige of wits, Robert saw hope spring into them, then she turned her head away, but not before he recognized the look of shame on her face.

Robert swung his club down toward the Yankee's head, but Hannah shrieked at his attack. The sound startled him, causing him to miss his target. The blow glanced off the side of the man's skull, and he fell on top of Hannah. Robert threw away his club, grasped the back of the man's jacket, and hauled him to his feet.

Robert turned the Yankee around. Hannah had done damage with her nails. One of the man's cheeks was striped with raw lesions.

The Yankee groaned, wagged his head, and then spat in Robert's face. "I'll kill you, rebel scum," the man rasped through his patchy beard. He threw a punch at Robert, striking him on the chin and knocking him backward. Robert crumpled to the floor. The Yankee loomed over him, and gave a gargling laugh as he pulled up and buttoned his trousers. "She wasn't even that good," he said, and stomped on Robert's cheek. "I've had better times with a whore."

A red blur swam before Robert's eyes. *My sweet Hannah, compared to a whore?* He cried out, "She was good at defending herself." Rage flashed through his body, giving him strength he didn't know he possessed. He leaped up and connected with a blow that sent the man staggering into the aisle of the stable. Robert followed, punching him time and again until his knuckles bled. He jabbed the man's ribbon-slashed cheek with a thumb. The man yowled.

Robert's fingers closed around the man's throat. "I'm here to finish the job."

The Yankee clawed at Robert's fingers, finally breaking their hold. Then he retreated, stumbling backward until he found a pitchfork and jabbed it toward Robert, murderous intent glittering in his bloodshot eyes. "You'll finish nothing, you slimy reb. I ain't through with you, nor with her."

Robert lunged back in time to avoid the lethal tines. *If he kills me, he'll continue with Hannah until she's dead. I can't let that happen.*

The man came at him again, and Robert's hand closed over the handle of an ax that he swung blindly at the oncoming fork. The clash of metal on metal split the air. The pitchfork flew from the man's hands and landed against a partition near where Hannah crouched with her hands covering her ears, shrieking.

Robert swung the ax once more to keep the Yankee at a distance, but underestimated his strength and turned himself half around.

The man rushed Robert, grabbing him by an arm and a leg, then spun and threw him against a wall. Momentum carried the man in another circle, until he screamed in agony and fell silent.

Robert lay in a heap, wondering at the cessation of the man's cry. He pushed himself to his knees, his own panting sounding loud in his ears, louder than Hannah's hysterical sobs. The Yankee hadn't returned to the fray. Robert staggered to his feet, wary, looking for his enemy.

The man stood close to a partition, bent over a bit, his face a mask of astonishment. His mouth gaped open, and his arms hung at his sides, but he didn't move.

Robert could hear Hannah, weeping uncontrollably, but he couldn't see her anywhere. *I've got to deal with him first*, he told himself, struggling with his instinct to find her, to gather her into his arms and console her.

Robert searched for a weapon, located and picked up the ax from where it had fallen, and approached the man, on guard. "You ain't through with me, you say?" he challenged. Hannah's cries filled his ears, louder than ever, but the Yankee made no reply. A fly buzzed down from the ceiling and settled on the man's eye. He didn't blink.

Robert did blink, finally seeing the streams of blood trailing down the front of the Yankee's chest from where small black iron points emerged from his shirt. Hannah squatted behind him against the partition, the handle of the pitchfork clutched in her hands.

Almost stuttering between crying and speech, Hannah gasped out, "Is . . . he . . . dead?"

Robert nodded. He dropped the ax, reached behind the man and forcibly uncurled Hannah's fingers from the pitchfork so he could push the Yankee aside. He pulled her to her feet, dragging her away from the sight. As they reached the other side of the stable, he snatched up a saddle blanket, and drew her into his arms.

"Hannah," he crooned in her ear. "Hannah love." He pulled her blouse closed and covered her with the blanket.

His wife shook in his embrace, sobbing out, "I wanted him to stop hurting you."

He stroked her hair. "I . . . Hannah, he can't hurt anybody anymore."

"I killed him." Hannah's cry came out strangled.

Robert swallowed, wishing he could take her burden upon himself. He glanced over at the dead Yankee, face down in the straw. Bile rose in his throat, and he wanted to vomit. Instead, he steeled himself and said, "We have to leave."

He stood up and helped Hannah to her feet. She stopped crying, but swayed against him, at the point of collapse. He picked her up, but his own strength was spent and he staggered, almost dropping her. How would he get her home?

The Yankee's horse.

Robert set Hannah down and went to the wild-eyed animal. "Hey, boy, quiet now. Come here." He mounted with some effort, then kneed the animal forward to where his wife stood. "Put your arms up, love," he murmured, and as she did, he reached down and, grunting, pulled her onto the horse.

As Hannah settled against him, he stiffened involuntarily. Hannah whimpered, "You're hurt, ain't you?"

Robert bit his lip against the pain throbbing through his head and body. "Some little bit," he agreed. "But I reckon we can make it as far as the Heizer place."

Chapter 3

George Heizer leaned his head against the warm flank of the cow, his fingers squeezing in the age-old rhythm of milking. When the knock came on the barn door, he paused, not sure he'd heard it. When it came again, he stood up and grabbed his pitchfork. Who knocked on the door of a barn?

Before he had sorted out in his mind whether the visitor could be a customer or someone bent on doing harm, the knock came again. He waited a moment, but no one spoke to offer him a greeting.

George crept out of the stall, stepping as quietly as he could. "Who's there?" he called.

"Robert Fletcher. George, I need your help."

Robert Fletcher was his good friend. They'd seen action in the same company during the war. Robert had come home unwounded, but George's right ear was half gone from a close shave with a Yankee bullet. Robert had tied his own handkerchief around the bleeding ear. Later, in the same battle, he had saved George's bacon when he was wounded in the leg.

George went to the small door and wrenched it open. A horse stood in the shade before the opening, two people hunched over its withers. One slid to the ground, fell to one knee, and struggled to get to his feet. It was indeed Robert, his brown hair darkened by sweat, and—was that blood?

Robert held out his hands to the other figure, still sitting on the horse. That person half fell into his arms, and the two of them went to the ground.

The horse moved aside. Again, Robert climbed to his feet, stooped, and tried to raise the other person. At length he stood, his arms around what was clearly a woman in a high state of disarray. Robert had married not long ago, and George finally recognized the second person as Robert's wife, Hannah.

George cried out in dismay. Robert had taken a beating, and Hannah had obviously suffered a great deal of misuse. Her pale yellow hair was matted to her head. Her face was bloodied. Her clothing was torn. Although she tried to clasp the pieces about her, she was having difficulty remaining covered. George stared at her, knowing he should look away, but unable to do so.

He finally shook himself free of the fascination and asked, "What happened to you? Yankees?" The mere thought of the occupation forces made him shudder and look down the lane. "Come inside," he said, backing through the door.

Robert bent to retrieve a saddle blanket on the ground. When he straightened up and draped it around Hannah, he grimaced in pain. "Yes. I had a set-to with one of those riders." He shepherded Hannah through the door, paused and coughed, then examined a spot on his head with careful fingers.

George slammed the door shut. "I hope you killed him."

"He's dead," Robert said, and spat out a gob of blood. "Can you help us get to Mrs. Bingham's bakery?" He paused, wiped the blood from his lips, and blurted out, "I hate getting you involved in this, George, but I don't know where else to go." After a moment, Robert continued, "Unless you can't see your way clear."

George swore to himself. Yes, helping Robert was risky. The Yankees would find their crony dead. If they discovered Robert had killed him, then learned that George helped Robert, who knew what they would do in reprisal.

Hannah moaned in Robert's arms.

Robert had pulled George off the battlefield when he'd been shot in the leg and lay bleeding and stunned by the force of the blow and the pain. No matter what happened, he owed Robert a debt.

"I'll hitch the team to the milk wagon. It's covered, so no one will see you."

"Thank you," Robert said.

George said nothing, but shook his head as he hurried to get the harness.

80

A hard knock on the back door made Jessie jump. She looked through the curtain of the back window. "Oh, thank God," she said, unlocking the door and throwing it wide. "Hurry in," she whispered, unable to take her eyes off her bedraggled sister, who sagged between Robert Fletcher and George Heizer. "Hannah?" she asked as she locked the door behind them. But she couldn't continue. She didn't know what words to use in asking what had happened.

Jessie followed the group into the kitchen. Her younger brother Luke sat at the table, fiddling with a half-eaten plate of food. George said to him, "Give Hannah your chair," and Luke hopped up as Heppie screamed. George and Robert get Hannah into the seat, then George stepped away and went to Heppie. "Shh," he said, putting his hand on her shoulder.

Jessie heard her mother gasp repeatedly behind her. *Ma isn't dealing well*, she thought. *George is distracting Heppie. Who's going to tend to Hannah?* She threw back her shoulders. *Me*, she told herself, and went to her sister's side. Hannah's head hung low, but her hand flew up and gripped Jessie's forearm.

"Steady," Jessie said. "You're home safe."

"There's nowhere safe," Hannah got out through lips crusted with blood. "Nowhere in Virginia."

"Oh, my dear daughter," Ma said, breathing in great rasping breaths. She elbowed Jessie to one side, and hugged Hannah around her head.

Jessie peeled Hannah's fingers from her arm and went to find a cloth to wet. She heard her mother's wild questions to Robert, and his soft answers.

"She was in McNeely's barn. I pulled the Yankee off her, and he's still there."

"Still there?" Luke asked. "Didn't you fight him?"

Jessie came back with the wet cloth and caught Robert nodding in answer to Luke's question. *Luke's stupid question*, she thought. *Anyone with eyes can see Robert's been in a fight!* She said a quiet word to her mother and got her to release Hannah. She started cleaning the blood from her sister's face. Her eyes smarted as she struggled to hold back tears. What kind of monster had done this? Her stomach lurched as she cleaned a clot of blood off Hannah's ear. She'd always had an aversion to blood. *This isn't so bad*, she told herself, trying to contain her tendency to gag. *It's dried, not flowing.*

"How come he's still there? Isn't he looking for you?" Ma's voice soared, and Jessie wanted to hush her as she would a wailing child.

"He's dead."

"Thank the Lord. Thank the Lord." Ma stood by the stove, rocking back and forth, her voice uplifted in prayer.

"Ma, softly now," Jessie said. She glanced at Heppie. "Can you get some water for Mr. Fletcher to clean up?" What an impossible event, having to prompt her older sister into action. The whole world was coming apart.

Ma finally stopped praying, came back to Jessie, and took the cloth from her. Jessie began to pace, rubbing her arm where Hannah had clasped it so hard, wondering what would happen to them, how they would go on.

"Now everything will be fine," Ma said.

Robert shook his head as he took a basin of water that Heppie gave him. "I have to leave, Mrs. Bingham. As soon as someone finds that dead Yankee, the commander will investigate. Mrs. McNeely knew I was there, and with so many Yankees still around—"

"No. We'll be safe now that the Yankee is dead." Ma said. "You did the right thing, Mr. Fletcher, exactly the right thing." Her voice broke, and she blinked back tears, wiping Hannah's face vigorously.

"That hurts, Ma." Hannah's voice was feeble.

"Ma'am, folks will remember Mrs. Fletcher was kidnapped. When Miss Jessie fetched me, the bank was full of people. They all saw us leave in a hurry." Robert put one of his hands into the water to soak and with the other scrubbed his face with a cloth. "Folks are frightened. Someone's going to say something."

"But what of Hannah?" Mrs. Bingham asked.

Robert looked up, his face hard with offense. "I'll not leave her behind!"

As the buzz of the discussion continued behind her, Jessie paced between the stove and the back door, trying to wrap her mind around how different her world was from what it had been when she woke up this morning. Hannah had been carried off in broad daylight. From the looks of her, she had been terribly abused by the Yankee. Could Heppie, could Jessie herself expect any better treatment in the months to come? Jessie kneaded her hands together. What could they do to keep safe? Nothing. Hannah was right. There was no safety for women in Virginia. They were all subject to Yankee whims and carpetbagger tricks. If the Yankees didn't leave Mount Jackson, why couldn't the whole family leave instead? She stopped pacing and stood still. She held her breath. What if they left with Mr. Fletcher and Hannah? Yes. Yes! That was the answer.

"Ma!" she interrupted. "Do you have that letter Max sent you?"

Mrs. Bingham turned her head sharply. "What?"

"The letter. Didn't Max ask us to join him in"—Jessie made circles beside her head with her fingers, frustrated with the mental fog the day had brought to her mind—"that town with the strange name?"

"Oh Jessie, you don't mean—"

"Ma, let's all go. George, I mean Mr. Heizer too, if he wants—if he must."

"Albuquerque is far away, Jessie," her mother argued. "It's almost to California."

"Isn't that a good thing? We'll get lost to these troublesome, hateful—" She couldn't think of a word bad enough to describe their tormentors. Her eyes settled on Hannah, her broken countenance. "Conquerors!" she spat.

"Miss Jessie," George began. He stopped and pursed his lips for a moment. "I'd like that better than anything, but I can't leave. I've had a letter from my brother Ned. He was in the hospital for a long time, but they finally released him. He's not very strong, but he's on his way home." He glanced over at Heppie with a somber expression on his face.

Jessie looked from George to Robert, who was bent over Hannah, patting her on the arm and murmuring soothing words to her. He straightened up when George finished speaking. One of his eyes was swollen and blackened. His lips were cracked.

"As many of you as wants to go with us can do so, but if you're coming, you need to pack up right away. We're leaving tonight. Miss Jessie's right. After all—" He looked at Hannah again, and Jessie thought she might have seen tears in his eyes before he regained control. "After all that's happened, leaving this place, leaving all of this behind is the only way to go on."

Heppie gave a little shrug. "I'm going with you. Hannah needs nursing, and I can do that."

"Heppie," George said, disappointment strong in his voice.

She looked at Hannah, then back to George. "Hannah needs me more," she said, her voice cracking.

Jessie knew that was not an easy thing for her sister to say. Heppie whispered to her each night before they fell asleep about her growing affection for George Heizer. Leaving him behind was no trifling act on Heppie's part. But what else could they do?

"Ma," Jessie said. "I'm going too. There's been nothing here for me since . . ." She stopped herself, unwilling to say it out loud. The wound of James Owen's leaving her to go west with his family was still raw, even if it had been almost a year ago. "What about you and Luke?"

Ma clasped her hands together. Jessie saw her knuckles turn white with the pressure. Her shoulders hunched together. At last she sighed and let them relax. "Lucas, cut your pa's picture from the frame. We're going to New Mexico."

෨

Heppie sat with George on the floor of the darkened bakery, her knees drawn up to her chin. The others were still packing, but he had insisted they take a little break and talk one more time.

George lifted her hand and stroked it. "Stay here with me, Heppie," he whispered. "We'll get married and you can help me run the farm. I'll keep you safe from the Yankees."

Tears ran down Heppie's cheeks as she blinked her eyes. What should she do? Hannah needed her so desperately. Besides, she was Hannah's twin. Hannah's marriage had caused the greatest parting they'd ever experienced, but they still managed to see each other almost every day. George was complicating her life with his plea. If she married him and stayed here, she'd never see Hannah or her family again.

"My family needs me. I want to be with them. They love me." She swiped at the tears.

"I love you, Heppie. I've loved you for years."

She shook her head and took her hand away from George's fingers. "You never said that before. You talked of us marrying but never declared yourself to love me. Maybe that's why I didn't give you an answer." Her words trailed off into the void between them.

George hung his head. "That was wrong of me. I meant not to pressure you." He looked up at her, his blue eyes pleading. "Heppie, don't go off and leave me alone."

"You won't be alone for long. You said your brother's coming home. You said that's why you can't leave." Her voice sounded flat, expressionless, devoid of hope.

"Heppie, please. He's still not recovered. How can I up and take off when he expects me to welcome him home? And the cows. I wouldn't do them a service to leave 'em without someone to take care of them."

Heppie waited for a long time before she spoke in a terse voice. "I need to be with my family. You need to take care of your brother and your cows. I reckon that puts us on different paths, Mr. Heizer."

"Heppie, don't say that."

She struggled to her feet, and he also arose. "Good-bye, George," she managed to say, and walked back into the kitchen.

Chapter 4

George headed back to the farm in the milk wagon. He'd had a busy morning making deliveries, just barely busy enough to keep him from thinking too much about Heppie. She and her family had been gone for several days, and every single one of those days had been an agony of despair to him. He should have told her a long time ago that he loved her. He should have insisted that he needed her more than her sister did. He should have, he should have, he should have.

Hoof beats drummed on the road behind him. His baleful thoughts faded into the protective recesses of his mind as he wondered who was coming down the Valley Pike in such a hurry. Whoever they were, they were riding hard and quick, not sparing their horses. He craned his neck to see around the box of the milk wagon, and spotted three men, lashing their mounts unmercifully.

I'd best get out of their way, he thought, and guided the team to the side of the road and halted them. He waited for the riders to pass by, but instead, he heard rough voices yelling as they drew near.

"It's him," one said. "Catch up that team."

A man rode up and grabbed hold of the harness. Another, whose dirty blond hair flew around his face, circled his mount in front of the team, blocking their way. The third, wearing a full black beard that covered the collar front of his Union uniform blouse, reined to a stop beside the seat and hit George in the face with his fist. "Where are they, rebel scum?"

George recoiled from the blow, almost toppling off the other side of the seat. "Who?" he grunted, trying to catch his breath.

The black-bearded man swore. "You know who. That bastard banker, that's who, and his whore of a wife." The man struck George again, then hauled him off the seat and dropped him in the road. He dismounted and kicked George, who curled into a ball to absorb the blow.

By this time, all three men were off their horses. The one with the blond hair unhooked the team from the wagon, and gave the horses a swat on their rumps so they ran off, dragging the lines behind them.

"Don't kill him, Bull," said the man who had grabbed the team. "He knows where they are."

"Where did they go, you miserable rebel dog? Tell me now." Bull kicked George again, reached down, and pulled him to his feet.

"Where's that bakery lady at?" asked the man with the blond hair. "Did they all go off together?" He punched George over the kidney, and he reeled across the roadbed, moaning with the pain that radiated throughout his body.

"Cal, let me beat him some," whined the third man to the blond.

"No, you grab him and hold him, Foster," said Bull. Foster shrugged, then caught George by the arms. He wrestled him back to Bull, who hit George in the jaw, muttering "Where is Fletcher? We know he killed Red." His black beard twitched as he clouted George again.

"I don't know what you're talking about," George mumbled through the pain, just before Cal hit him in the eye.

"We know different," said Bull. "People saw you making a late delivery to the bakery. We figure it wasn't milk."

"Bull's right, Heizer," said Foster, twisting George's arms. "You helped him get away."

"We want to know where they went," Cal said, and followed his words with a punch to George's belly.

George yelled, "I don't know where they are," and tried to keep himself upright, tried to raise a foot to kick one of his tormenters. He failed, as another fist plowed into his face. The blows came without much talk from the riders. His mind focused on trying to blank out the pain. At last it overwhelmed him, and he wished for death before he betrayed his friend . . . and Heppie. These men would treat her as their crony had treated Robert's wife.

Bull planted another blow on George's other kidney, and he sagged in Foster's grip. "Where did they go?" the lout asked again.

"I don't know," he shouted with the last of his strength. "I don't know." He heard sobs and, after a few more punches landed, realized they were his own. His lips were swollen from the blows that had split them. He could barely breathe, but he sucked in air and forced out a word. "Richmond."

"Ha," Cal said, with another jab. "If you're lying, we'll come kill you." He turned away, then back again, "We're done, Foster. Let him loose."

Foster released his grasp, and George staggered forward and collapsed in the dust. He dimly heard the creak of leather when the men climbed into their saddles. The sound of hoof beats on the hard pike receded as they rode back the way they'd come.

He didn't know how long he lay there before he mastered the pain enough to get to his hands and knees. His face throbbed. His ribs ached where he'd been kicked. His kidneys burned. A question flitted through his mind. Would he pee blood? Anger roiled into his body, and it gave him the strength to get one foot flat on the road. He couldn't get the other under him, and he fell back onto his knees, feeble from the pain.

At least I bought Heppie a few more days, he thought. *They'll look in the wrong direction.*

He crawled to the side of the road, wondering if he had the strength to get home. Probably not, but he'd be damned if he didn't try. The cows would need milking by the time he could get there. The infernal cows he'd chosen over Heppie. No, it wasn't only the cows. Ned was coming home. Ned, who would need tending to finish healing up. Ned, who had gone North at the beginning of the war. Ned, the Yankee officer.

"Hannah love, you have to eat," Robert said, holding a spoonful of gruel to his wife's lips.

Hannah moaned, closed her eyes, then opened them. "I'll just lose it again," she whispered.

"Heppie tells me you haven't eaten much of anything for three days." Robert found Hannah's mouth by the light of the campfire and tried to put the spoon inside her lips.

She shook her head. "Don't make me."

"You're so weak, darling. You won't mend if you don't eat something."

Hannah gave a tiny negative shake of her head. "Who cares if I mend? I don't. God don't. If He cared I wouldn't have . . . That man . . . I killed him, Robert."

Robert swallowed down the bitter gall that rose in his throat as his mind flashed over that horrible day. He put down the bowl and started to cup his hands around Hannah's face, but she turned away. He looked at his scabbed-over knuckles and dropped them to his sides. When he tried to speak, his voice seemed to choke on a lump in his throat, but he pushed the words through, noting how hoarse they sounded in his ears. "He deserved to die," he said. "If God was there, He had you pick up the fork. You were defending me."

"I should be sorry I killed him." Hannah was sobbing, gulping for breath. "I'm not. It's all mixed up. He hurt me so much!"

Robert reached out to gather Hannah into his arms, but she froze with her arms crossed over her chest. Again, he dropped his hands, wondering how long she would lock him out, rejecting his consolation. She didn't want his comfort.

No, she doesn't want your touch, he thought. *You're a man. Her mind was hurt as badly as her body, and a man did that to her.* His stomach churned. *How long will it take for Hannah's mind to heal?* He took a deep breath, remembering his wedding vows. *In sickness or in health.* He let out a long, shuddering sigh. *However long it is, however long it takes, I've got to stand alongside her, ready to help her fight the trouble in her mind.*

Hannah choked back her sobs as Robert walked away, banging one fist into the other. She longed with all her heart to feel his arms around her, but she couldn't bear that. Not now. The violation of her body had damaged her spirit and her mind, as well. Perhaps that was the worst part. She couldn't abide the comfort that she needed the most.

She flinched, gagging, and turned on her side to locate the basin Heppie had placed there. Hannah brought it to her mouth, but her heaving stomach was empty. She had nothing to throw up, not even bile.

Finished, Hannah dropped the basin. Retching had left her too weak to hold it. *Am I dying? Has that wicked man mortally wounded me?* Her eyes leaked tears that she had no strength to wipe away. *I don't want to leave Robert alone. What will he do without me? Who will take care of him? No one can cherish him as I do.*

As she lay there, exhausted and feeble, a seed of determination grew in her heart. *I won't let that evil Yankee kill me*, she thought. *I must hold on for Robert's sake.* With a jolt, she realized she had made similar oaths on the day she had been attacked. *I had the strength at that time. I'll find it again.*

She rolled onto her back and slid her hand toward the bowl with the gruel Robert had tried to feed her. She knew if she tried to raise it, she would spill the contents, so she located the spoon, filled it, and lifted it toward her mouth. The nearer the spoon came, the more she feared she would drop it, but when she did, most of the gruel ended up in her open mouth.

She closed it, holding the cold, mushy liquid on her tongue until she dared to swallow. Her hand fell to her side as her body shook from the effort she had made. The spoon slid down her cheek to her bosom. She ignored it and the gobs of gruel on her face and in her hair. They didn't matter. Someone would come back soon, and they would clean her up. All that mattered was that she had eaten a bite of food. She was not going to die.

෩

George made it to the narrow road leading to the farmhouse after dark had fallen. He'd rolled into the ditch beside the Pike every time someone came along. Crawling up the lane on bleeding hands and elbows, and knees that poked through his trousers, he saw lamplight streaming through a crack in the shutters covering the kitchen window.

He stopped. *What on earth?* He blinked, not trusting the sight of his injured eyes. Yes, that was light, not an illusion. Someone was in the house. *Who is it? The Yankees didn't come back down here by the pike.*

There was no ditch to roll into for protection. Only trees lined the path. He hunkered down to the ground, not knowing what else to do to. He waited for an eternity.

At length, a hunched figure carrying a lantern stepped out the side door and limped toward the barn. He stopped once, turned toward the lane, and held the light high. Then he continued on his original path, whistling a few bars of a tune.

Ned!

If the fleeting look at the man's face hadn't been enough for George, the tune was confirmation. His brother had made up that melody years ago when they were boys playing games in the dusk. *Ned is home.*

George pursed his swollen lips, but couldn't manage a whistle. He tried again, but it was useless. He'd have to cry out, if he had enough strength. He tried breathing deeply, and pain penalized his efforts. *Busted ribs.*

"Ned," he exhaled, and thought he saw his brother pause. "Ned," he tried again, with a little more force.

This time Ned turned around and held up the light again. "Who's there?" he asked, his other arm sliding down to a holstered weapon.

"George. Come get me," he whispered, rising to his hands and knees.

"Who's out there?" Ned asked again, setting down the lantern and drawing his pistol. George heard the click of the hammer being pulled back.

Weakness overwhelmed George, and a sob came out of his throat. "Help . . .

me," he tried again. Unable to look up, he heard Ned's hesitant footfalls as he approached. They stopped a fair distance away.

"Friend or foe?" Ned challenged.

"Friend," he moaned, trying to raise his face out of the dust.

Footsteps. Ned had gained courage. George sensed, rather than saw, a circle of light through his closed eyelids. Ned must be carrying the lantern. Something settled into the dust nearby. Maybe the lantern. A hand turned him over. He heard the creak of the lantern's handle and the light rose above him.

"George!" Ned exclaimed, and swore. "What happened?" George heard him ease down the hammer on his pistol and holster it.

"Riders," he said, trying to open his eyes. "The occupiers." He coughed, and his ribs flamed with pain.

"Why?"

George shook his head a fraction. This was his brother, but the war might have changed him into someone he couldn't trust. "Can you . . . get me . . . to the house?" he gasped.

"I can try." Ned blew out the lantern and set it down. "No point in borrowing trouble," he said, and knelt on one knee, grunting as he got his hands under George's shoulders. "Hold on, brother. This is going to hurt."

"Me, or you?" George could see the shape above him dimly outlined against the dark.

"Ha!" Ned barked a laugh. "Both of us, I reckon." He began to haul George slowly toward the house, stopping every few paces to catch his breath.

When he reached the stoop at the house, Ned stopped and stood up. He swiveled his neck and shook his arms, then opened the door and bent to help George to his feet. "Come on up. Lean on me."

George shook his head and said, "I'll have to crawl. I don't reckon I can stay on my feet, even with help. Go fetch the lantern, but hold off lighting it until you're inside."

Ned went back down the lane to get the lamp, and George got into the house and was working at getting onto a chair in the kitchen when his brother returned. Ned put the lantern on the table, tugged George onto the chair, and lit the lamp. He said, "You weren't around when I got here and I was some worried. Then the team came trotting into the yard by itself, and I worried a lot more." He positioned the lantern on a hook hanging from the ceiling of the kitchen and began to examine George's wounds. "I put up the horses, but was trying to decide which way I should go to look for you when the cows started making a fuss to be milked."

George sighed. "You chose right." He gasped in pain as Ned's fingers probed his side.

"These ribs is busted, brother."

"Tell me something I don't know," George said, his breath rasping.

Ned frowned. "Here's the news from town. I reported to the commander of the occupiers, as you call them, before I came here. There's a big fuss about a cavalryman who got killed a few days back. Looked like he was in a fight. He died quick from a pitchfork in his back." He eyed George. "They're searching for his murderer."

George said nothing. He fingered his swollen eye.

"I reckon the war is past business. I'm home now. You're my brother. Those are the two things that matter to me." He found a rag and water, and began to clean George's face. "Why'd they beat you up?"

George swallowed and breathed through his mouth while Ned worked on his nose. Could he trust Ned? Tell him why he'd been beaten? No. It was too early to settle on where his loyalties lay. He had to let Heppie and the Bingham family get clear out of the South.

"They must have had a reason."

George groaned as Ned found a tender spot—split skin over his cheekbone. "Do they need one?"

Ned grimaced. "It's a wonder you're alive. Whatever their reckoning, they didn't care if they killed you or not."

"No. I don't guess they did."

Ned suddenly sat down.

George squinted at him. Ned's face had gone gray. "Where does it hurt you?" he asked.

"Mostly my legs. I lost a lot of muscle when the shell exploded." He shook himself.

"Where else?"

"I get kinks in my back. Spasms."

"Anything I can do to help?"

Ned laughed, a bitter sound. "Not in your shape, brother. Let me take a minute to rest, then I'll get back to nursing you."

"I had it all worked out that I was going to nurse you," George said. "I let Heppie leave here—" Aghast at his slip, George shut his mouth and let his head hang down to hide his face.

After a moment, Ned asked, "Who's Heppie?" When George didn't answer, he paused for a long moment, and finally said, "Hepzibah Bingham? Are you sweet on her?"

George said nothing, his heart sick. If his brother put the pieces together and reported them to the occupation commander, his own stupid big mouth might mean a prison sentence for the girl he loved. She didn't do anything wrong, either. *No, please*, he thought, and realized that he was shaking, but not from the pain of his injuries.

Ned was speaking again, wringing out the bloody cloth over a bowl of water. "When I came through town, I didn't get a brass band and a 'welcome home' speech." His voice sounded strained. "Folks didn't seem happy to see me. Old Man Calkins spit on me before I made it out of town." He paused for a moment and began again, his intonation carrying a note of despair. "I stopped at the Bingham's bakery to see how Miss Jessie would receive me, but it was locked up, so I didn't get to see her."

George looked up. "James Owen edged you out of the running with Miss

Jessie last year," he said. "I heard tell they were fixin' to marry. Ended up he went west with his folks."

Ned's face twisted in anxiety. "James Owen? Jessie's gone with him?"

George shook his head. "No. He left her here."

Ned called James a few choice names even as he heaved a sigh of relief. He straightened up in his chair, his face furrowed. "Where is she? Nobody was at the bakery. It looked"—he compressed his lips for a moment, then blurted out—"abandoned."

George shook his head again. "I don't know where she is."

Ned swore. "George, you're hiding something. You'd know where she was if she was anywhere nearby. That means she's gone. What happened?"

George licked his split lips. "I can't say."

"Does it have anything to do with those riders beating you near to death?" Ned was hovering over George, looking intently into his eyes. "Don't tell me you don't trust me."

George put his hands over his face. "War changes folks," he muttered, ashamed of his misgivings. "I don't know where you stand." He heard Ned's sharp exhalation and the creak of the chair as he sat once more. After a while, George dropped his hands into his lap and looked at his brother. To his surprise, tears trickled down Ned's cheeks.

Ned swiped at his cheeks before he opened his mouth and said, "I fought for the Union because I believe in it. That didn't make me love my family less than I did before I left. George, you're all the family I got now, and I don't want to be at odds with you." Ned swallowed, his Adam's apple moving up his throat, then down again. "I won't press you more than to ask this favor. If you know Jessie's in trouble, and you know where she is, you've got to tell me."

Chapter 5

During the next few days, Hannah fought her fears and strengthened her resolve to live. She ate everything Heppie gave her, and soon she became strong enough to walk for short periods.

The morning was bright and sunny when Hannah decided she wanted to get off the wagon seat and see how long she could keep pace with the others.

"Luke," she said to her brother, who was driving. "Can you pull up for a minute? I'd like to walk."

"Are you sure, Sis?"

"I reckon so."

He halted the team and helped her down. "Holler when you're tired out," he said. He slapped the lines on the rumps of the horses and yelled, "Hi-yup! Get up there!"

Hannah took a deep breath of spring-scented air as the wagon lumbered into motion. Soon, however, she coughed, as the dust left in the wagon's wake filled her lungs. She moved to the side of the road, coughing and gagging, and clutched a sapling for support.

The air cleared as the wagon and its brown cloud moved on down the pike. Hannah stood straight, breathing in the newly freshened air. Suddenly she bent double and threw up her breakfast.

No! she thought, as her head and stomach roiled in a crazy dance. *Not again. I can't be ill again.* But the nasty sickness came down on her, forcing her to gag and heave until she had no strength to stand. With her last bit of energy, she wrenched herself away from the foul results of her ailment and fell to her knees, forehead against a tree.

She took shallow breaths, trying to avoid vomiting again. After a while, her stomach calmed, but she couldn't get to her feet. She let go of the tree and fell sideways, then rolled a bit away from the pool of vomit.

As Hannah lay by the side of the pike, she began to worry that the wagon and her family were getting farther away each moment. *Will they miss me? Luke will daydream. He won't take notice that I'm gone for hours.* Her anxiety increased until she had to wrap her arms around her stomach to keep herself from vomiting again. Then she thought, *Robert will come for me.* She sighed, relief sweeping through her body.

Why do I feel ill? she asked herself. *I'm not feverish. Not even a little bit. These spells come out of nowhere.*

Half-hidden thoughts ran like skittering mice through the hallways of her mind. She swallowed, dipping her head and making a grand effort to force saliva through her dry throat. Half-recalled whispers, timidly giggled from the mouth of a girlfriend into her conspiratorial ear wafted by her consciousness. One thought took root, and she shuddered violently. *No!* She rolled into a ball. *This is impossible!*

She lay curled on the earth and leaves, unable to believe the caprice of her brain. "No!" she cried out, feeling like her body would explode. The awful truth bombarded her realization, but she thrust it from her, out of her thoughts, out of her actuality. Her fists flew to guard her ears, as though someone were speaking to her in gross, disgusting words. "No!" she shrieked. "No, I won't let it be so. You can't make me. God, you can't make me bear a child from that loathsome, hairy monster! It's not true! It's not true! It's not true."

She began to sob wildly. What would Robert think of her, bearing a bastard child? The child of a bastard Yankee? *He'll never love me again!*

Chapter 6

Several days after he'd met the Yankee riders on the turnpike, George hauled himself into the milk wagon, wincing at the pain in his ribs. Although Ned had wrapped them well with strips of soft cotton material, any movement of his torso gave him sharp reminders of the beating he'd taken. Just as George gathered the lines, Ned came into the barnyard and stood in front of the horses, glowering as though he'd drunk sour milk.

"Where do you reckon you're off to?" He took hold of the headstall of the nearest horse.

George took a shallow breath. "I'm sick of you pouring most of the milk down the garden rows 'cause I can't deliver it."

Ned shook his head. "Come down off that seat. You're not healed up enough to drive into town. I'm sorry I don't know the customers, but that can't be helped."

"I'm going, Ned. If you want to come spell me on the driving, climb up. If not, step out of the way."

"Do you deliver to the Yankee camp?"

"Ha," George barked, a single laugh at Ned's reference. His brother, the Yankee. "Yes, I do. They pay on time, too."

Ned moved aside, hesitated a moment, then got up onto the wagon seat. "I'll go along. I have business there."

George got the horses underway before he handed the lines to Ned. "Do you reckon you remember how to drive?"

"Does the sun come up in the east?" Ned countered, his face serious.

George arranged himself more comfortably on the seat, and after Ned had turned the team onto the Pike, he asked, "What's your business at the camp?"

Ned's face was blank and he didn't answer.

"Are you fixin' to tattle on those riders?"

This time, Ned grimaced. After a bit, he nodded. "You're the only brother I got, George. Those louts ain't my brothers-in-arms. I got no loyalty to them." He paused to guide the horses around a pothole in the road. "If my service as a Union officer counts for anything with the commander, I'll use it."

"You reckon he'll shake his finger at Bull and them and give 'em what for?"

"I'm hoping for more like a court martial."

"A court martial? For beating a Johnny Reb?" George laughed. "You been cooped up in that hospital for too long, Ned. Mount Jackson, hell, the whole Shenandoah Valley is occupied territory." He touched his swollen, yellowing cheek. "They'll probably get medals."

Ned growled, "The war's over. The troops are supposed to treat the population with respect."

"You're asking too much." George sat back on the seat. "Those riders are rough men. I know they don't care about giving respect. Not after what I seen."

Ned looked sideways at George. "Are you ready to tell me what you seen?"

"I'm thinking about it."

"It was pretty bad?"

George's face twisted at his memories. "My friend's wife was . . . raped!" He looked over at Ned. "You can't say that to the commander. I'll let you tell him I was beaten, but that's as far as it goes."

"Tell me their names."

"Bull, Cal, Foster. I don't have first and last names for you. That's all I heard."

"I reckon that will do." Ned shook the lines over the backs of the horses and lapsed into silence for the rest of the trip to town.

Their first stop was at the Union camp. Gritting his teeth against the pain in his ribs, George hauled down the milk cans and delivered them while Ned talked to the commander.

George returned to the wagon and waited on the seat, his hands tightly gripped together. What was Ned telling the commander? Would he mention Mrs. Fletcher's violation? Ned was no dummy. George figured his brother had made out most of the story from the bits of information George had let slip. How much would he reveal to the Union commander?

When Ned finally limped toward the milk wagon, his set face didn't give away much of what was in his mind. He climbed aboard, and George slapped the horses' backs with the lines, urging them to get started into town.

After a period of silence that stretched into forever, George asked, "Well?"

Ned leaned over and rested his elbows on his knees. "He listened. He's likely going to drum them out of the army. There's been reports about their cruel deeds before, and I reckon this was the final straw." He picked at a thread of weed clinging to his boot. "I still should have taken you in with me to show what they did."

"What does it matter if you convinced him they're treating folks poorly?"

Ned threw the weed onto the passing roadway. "No matter, I reckon. You'd have made an almighty good witness, though, just to look at you." He grinned at last. "I might not have had to jaw at him so long."

George clucked to the team, and they went about their deliveries. They were finished by midafternoon, and headed back to the farm.

Ned saw the smoke first, black and billowing, far down the Valley Pike.

"No!" he exclaimed, and swore.

George shouted at the team, but the horses were weary and couldn't keep up more than a shambling trot. Ned threw himself out of the wagon seat and ran along the pike. Soon, the injuries to his legs proved too much, and he pulled up at the side of the road, bent over and panting.

When George reached him, Ned climbed aboard and gasped out, "I reckon it's our place."

George bellowed "Damn Yankees!" and then looked at his brother's white face. "No offence," he muttered.

"They're louts," Ned replied, shaking his head.

George turned into the lane, and pulled up the horses when they were halfway down, aghast at the devastation. The barn had burned to the ground, the wellhead had been tipped over, and the house had been set afire. Being made of stone, it had not burned entirely. Smoke drifted on a breeze. George sat in stunned silence for two minutes. At last he got out of the wagon to follow Ned, who was attempting to enter the barn.

"It's still too hot to get inside," Ned said, wiping sweat from his forehead. He kicked a timber that had fallen into the barnyard with the collapse of the roof and swore bitterly. "How many cows did you have?" he asked.

"Six. They should be in the pasture."

"I don't see any out there."

"Where are they?" George stumbled toward the pasture fence.

By then Ned was inside the barn, moving debris out of his way. He stopped working and let loose a string of impassioned swear words, beckoning to George. "You have to see this."

George followed Ned, his stomach roiling at the stench. His six cows lay on their sides, throats cut, the hair on their hides burned. George emptied his lunch onto the embers of what had been a stall.

Once he could stand upright, he wiped his mouth with the back of his hand and looked at his brother. The bleak, yet outraged expression on Ned's face helped him make up his mind. He cleared his throat and said, "I reckon I can tell you where Miss Jessie went. The Fletchers and all the Binghams are on their way to St. Louis. They're heading out for New Mexico Territory."

Ned let out a whoosh of air. He looked around and spread his hands. "There's nothing of value to keep us here, George. Let's follow them at first light."

ဆ

As the glow of coming dawn lightened the eastern sky, George and Ned left the burned-out farm and walked their horses toward the Valley Pike. George rode the better of the two wagon horses, and used the other as a pack animal. Ned was astride the Union mount that had brought him home. They carried a bare minimum of supplies: a change of clothes, water, whatever food they could find in the ashes of the kitchen. George dug a hole in the garden to retrieve a buried rifle and ammunition he'd managed to bring home, and Ned had his weapons.

When they reached the end of the lane, George turned south and Ned turned north.

Wheeling his mount, Ned whistled a note to halt George, who waited for him to catch up.

"Where you going?" Ned asked.

"To Staunton."

"Wouldn't Fletcher take the Northwestern Pike out of Winchester? It would get them into West Virginia quicker."

"I reckon they took the Staunton and Parkersburg Pike." George slid his thumb along one of his reins.

"What makes you think that?"

"Miss Heppie sometimes talked about her cousin in Monterey. They used to visit every couple of years before the war. Mrs. Bingham knows that road."

Ned rubbed the back of his neck. "The Northwestern is better traveling."

"Don't matter," George said. "I followed them a mite, and they turned south out of town."

Ned exhaled. "Let's get moving."

They gigged their horses to a trot and followed the pike south, and soon approached the McNeely farm. Mrs. McNeely stood in the yard, throwing feed to her three scrawny hens. She stared after the brothers as they passed.

"That's a bad piece of fortune," George muttered.

"Old Miz McNeely?" Ned shook his head. "She's harmless."

"No, she'll make mention of our leaving. The dead rider was found in her barn, and I expect the other Yankees scared her pretty fair. I reckon she's afraid not to tell them anything they might be curious about."

Ned looked back over his shoulder. "She's just standing there, watching us."

"We'd best be watchful, ourselves."

Neither brother said much the rest of the day. They reserved their strength for the journey, pressing forward as hard and as fast as George's ribs could bear.

On the third day, they passed through Staunton and turned northwest toward Monterey. Late in the day, they forded a stream that hadn't been re-bridged since the war ended, and found a camping place back in the forest away from the road. They kept their campfire low, just hot enough to warm the beans they'd cooked the night before. After they ate, they doused the fire and made ready for bed, aided by the light of a quarter moon.

George stood up from rolling out his bedroll. "Ned, my ribs ache something fierce. I'm going to scout around a bit before I turn in. Maybe I can work some kinks out with a walk."

Ned gave a nod and said, "I'd join you if I wasn't so tuckered out. Mind you, don't make a lot of noise and wake me up when you come back."

George chuckled. "You wouldn't hear a bear stumbling into camp over your snoring. Rest well, brother."

He left the camp and walked a short distance through the woods. Silver moonlight streaming through the trees dappled the ground before him. He wondered how Heppie would look with the light of the moon falling on her hair, over her shoulders, on the soft white skin of her throat. He swallowed hard. Heppie was somewhere on this road ahead of him. He would find her, maybe inside of a week. How would she receive him after the dim-witted things he'd said? Would she turn her back? Refuse to look at him? Meet him with harsh words?

How could a woman with such a fair face say anything unkind? Yet she had left him behind, coldly turning his loyalty to his brother and the dumb creatures in his care into ashes with a few stark sentences.

George leaned against a tree. He could see Heppie's face in his mind's eye as clearly as though she stood before him. Pale yellow hair rippling beside her cheek, nose turned up a tad bit on the tip, lips pink and soft—He backed away from that thought. She had chosen Hannah over him. They were like two halves of a split apple, those twins. Ever since he'd known them, he'd puzzled to figure out a way to distinguish which sister was who. Finally he had discovered the small pink spot on the side of Heppie's neck; a spot that pulsed with the beating of her heart.

He imagined he could hear her heart beating, throbbing, drumming like horses' hooves on a road. Her voice seemed raised in a strident complaint, then it lowered, then came forth again with a different timbre. He closed his eyes. Was this an omen of what lay before him?

He shook his head to clear away the unwelcome discordant noises and stood upright as he realized that he actually heard a party of riders coming along the road. He could hear them not only because of the usual sounds of horses traveling, but because the men were arguing as they rode along.

"All right!" one voice yelled, frustration evident in the shrillness of his voice. "We'll stop."

The road was not far from where George stood, and the riders turned off on his side of the track. He stepped behind the tree he leaned against, wishing he'd brought his rifle.

The quarrel continued as the men dismounted and prepared to camp.

"They're still at least a week ahead," one man grumbled, and George recognized the voice as that of the frustrated man who'd called the halt in spite of wanting to continue on.

"Nah, we've made up time," another said.

"If you'd let us sleep once in a while, my stomach would be in better shape." This objection came from a different voice, so there were at least three men in the party.

"If you'd stop nipping at your flask, your stomach would have no complaints," the first man bellowed.

"If you'd brought proper rations, my stomach wouldn't have a quarrel with you."

"Shut your trap, Foster. Bull's right. We can't make good time if you're too drunk to sit your horse."

George froze as the men continued wrangling over their differences. These men were the Yankee riders. How had they known— Of course. Mrs. McNeely had reported seeing Ned and him passing by. His mind whirled, sorting out what he heard the men say. He and Ned hadn't been on the road for a week. Somehow, they'd tracked down Robert and his wife . . . and Heppie. Cold chills ran between his shoulder blades. The men were close by. Would they hear him as he moved away toward his own camp?

" . . .Heizer!" one man said, and spat. "It's all his doing."

George inhaled sharply and held his breath. They were after him, too.

"Thinks he's so high and mighty. Captain bloody rebel-born Heizer! When I get my hands on him, I'll snap his scrawny neck!"

"Not if I get to him first, you won't. That damned turncoat cost me my back pay."

George let out his breath slowly and crept away. He and Ned had to ride out immediately. They had to escape the wrath of these ruffians. They had to warn Robert and the Binghams.

⁊ↄ

George knelt beside Ned's bedroll, gently shook his shoulder with one hand, and rested his fingers on his brother's mouth with the other.

Ned came awake with wide eyes.

"Shhh," George warned. "Them riders caught up with us."

"Riders?" Ned blinked. "Those occupiers?"

George nodded. "They know Robert and the family are on this road." He paused, then continued in a lower tone. "They're after you, too. And me, I reckon."

Ned was on his knees, rolling his bedding. He threw a whisper over his shoulder. "Well, we'd best not let them catch us or the girls. I'll saddle the horses while you break camp."

℥

After leading their animals along the pike for a mile, George and Ned rode the rest of the night, the turnpike ever climbing into the foothills. As dawn broke they entered the outskirts of Monterey. George pulled his horse to a stop and looked to the west. Pink light coming from the east flooded the hills as far as his eyes could see. *What a fetching sight*, he thought. *A pity I won't be back to see it again.*

"Do you know the cousin's name?" Ned asked as he dismounted. He lifted one of his horse's hooves and took a look at it. He pried a stone loose with his thumb. "That should feel better," he said to the horse, then lowered its leg.

George had finished consulting his memory. "Emmy Lou. Emmy Lou Pitkin. This town ain't so large that we can't find her."

"Where do we start?"

George looked around. It was too early for the stores to be open, but a farm woman might be a good source of information. "How about over there?" he asked, pointing to a nearby house where light came through a window.

Ned mounted, and they rode to the dwelling. George knocked on the door, found a cautious reception, but got the information he sought. When he joined Ned, he said, "The lady told me the Pitkins live on a farm the other side of town. She gave me good directions. We don't need to bother anyone else in finding 'em." He yawned. "After we learn if they have news of the Binghams, I want about two hours sleep."

"Dang it, don't yawn, or I'll start in doing it," Ned protested.

George grinned, but sobered as he climbed into his saddle. "Let's get going."

They found the Pitkin farm, as directed, and came upon several members of the family finishing morning chores before breakfast.

"How do," George called out, as he and Ned halted their horses in the yard. "Is this the Pitkin place?"

"Howdy, strangers," said an older man, looking the brothers over. "I'm Pitkin. You look like travelers." He gestured for George and Ned to alight from their horses, and they did so. Three teenage boys gathered nearby.

George offered his hand. Mr. Pitkin squeezed it in a farmer's grip.

"We are traveling, sir," George said, "hoping to catch up with the Bingham family. How long ago did they come through here?"

"Well now," said the farmer, eyeing George's face. "That cut there on your cheek looks recent." He paused, took a pipe of his pocket, and stuck it in his mouth. "What puts you in mind that the Binghams passed by?"

"I was at their home when they left Mount Jackson. I'm Miss Heppie's beau, sir."

"Well now," Mr. Pitkin repeated. "If you're Miss Heppie's beau, why aren't you at her side in her adversity?"

George felt himself flush. He took as deep a breath as he could manage and said, "I would have gone with the family, sir, except they left so sudden. I had obligations to take care of."

"Obligations." The man chewed on the word, squinted at the sky, took the unlit pipe from his mouth, and put it in his pocket again. "Did you get shed of your obligations?"

George nodded.

"Someone chasing you?"

"Yes sir. Three cashiered Yankee riders. They're also after the Binghams." George paused, and then added, "Robert Fletcher, mostly."

"Miss Hannah's man." It was a statement rather than a question.

George nodded again.

"By the age of his scars, you didn't beat on each other."

"No sir."

Mr. Pitkin nodded in his turn, appeared to be satisfied, and said, "My sister and her kin came in six days ago. Spent a night and left. I gave them my extra pistol and a shotgun. I figured they had more need of them than I do." He abruptly turned on his heel, then stopped and threw over his shoulder, "Want breakfast?"

"Thank you kindly, sir," said Ned. "If it's no trouble to the missus, we'd be pleased to join you for a bite."

They left before noon, fortified by a solid country breakfast and a couple of hours of sleep.

଼

About a week into their travels, the brothers arrived at a small stream just before the sun went down. Exhausted, they made camp, keeping a good distance from a fire that told of other people nearby.

"Do you reckon they're friendly?" George asked.

Ned snorted. "I don't propose to find out. Mind you, give them plenty of space to move around."

"A man can't be too careful about his neighbors," George agreed. He arose from where he'd been scraping a bare spot for a fire. "I'll bring in some wood." Before Ned could offer a caution, he added, "Yes, I'll be wary."

George ranged about in the half light until he located a dry limb as thick as his arm. He put his foot in the center and lifted one end. It broke into two lengths with a snap. Somewhere behind him, a voice drew in a sharp breath, followed by, "Luke, is that you?" The voice was young, and female.

He whirled around. A bush screened most of a female's figure from his sight, but he could see a part of her skirt spread against the ground. "Sorry, ma'am, no, I'm not Luke. I'll be going on now." He turned away, his face burning at interrupting the girl at her private task.

The skirt rustled, then the voice came again, clearly Southern, not frightened, not embarrassed. A little amused. "You sound like someone my sister would like to see. Hmm, maybe not. She's riled that you prefer your cows over her."

George couldn't move. His arms had gone stiff as stone. His legs refused to shift to let him face the girl. He tried his jaw. It moved. "Miss Jessie?" he guessed. In case he was wrong, he tried again. "Miz Fletcher? Did we find you?"

"I'm Jessie. What took you so long, Mr. Heizer?"

Chapter 7

Heppie could scarcely believe the news Jessie brought her. George had come. Heppie smiled. He had followed her after all. He did love her! She'd started off to greet him, but Ma interrupted, fussing about getting the evening meal together in a hurry.

Heppie's fingers seemed to belong to someone else as she tried to do her part in carving venison steaks from the deer her brother had come across and shot just as they made camp. What would she say to George? Should she maintain her grievance against him, or should she welcome him with all her heart? Following several mishaps, and after she'd fumbled a chunk of the meat off the cutting board and into the grass, her mother thrust her to one side and gave her a different task: to clean up the wooden mixing bowl.

"You can't possibly hurt that, Heppie," Mrs. Bingham had said, irritation sharpening her voice. "Jessie, put this meat in the frying pan. No, you'll have to wash it a mite first. At least brush the dirt and grass off."

"Ma, I didn't mean to—" Heppie began, but her mother cut her off.

"Luke brought down that deer by the grace of Providence, and we need every last shred of the meat. Especially now that the Heizer boys have joined us."

Heppie sighed. Ma was going to talk all night about her clumsiness. As if that wouldn't make her all the more bungle fingered. All she could hope for was that George would pay Ma no mind. If Heppie forgave him, surely he would cast his thoughts on the future, and not on Ma's speech. Heppie smiled and played with a curl of hair that hung down her cheek. George was going to want to get married now that he had caught up with her.

She took a deep breath. Married! She thought of his broad shoulders and long arms. He would put those arms around her, cuddle her to his chest, maybe kiss her. She exhaled, her lips burning at the thought of kissing George. What else did married folks do? She knew very little of their amorous ways. Surely they didn't behave like mating animals! She shrugged. Hannah hadn't shared that part of her life. Heppie only knew about the occasions back in Mount Jackson when she'd caught her sister glowing with happiness after spending time alone with Robert. Being married must be . . . pleasurable.

Heppie dropped the bowl, startling herself back to reality. George might have come after her . . . no, them . . . well, maybe her, but he took his sweet time, and that proved she was second on his list of importance. No, make that third, she thought as she stooped to pick the bowl out of the weeds. *First the cows, next, his brother. I come third!*

Determined to punish George for his disloyalty, Heppie scowled all during supper, not once looking at him. She gave him the cold shoulder whenever he tried to make conversation with her. She frowned as she washed dishes. She wondered how on earth she was going to avoid him after cleanup was finished.

Maybe she shouldn't avoid him. Maybe she should give him a piece of her mind, straight out. She attacked a pot with her brush, glaring into the dishpan.

"Heppie?"

Heppie jumped and dropped the brush. She knew that voice behind her, deep and resonant. She hunched her shoulders for a moment, then relaxed them, took her hands out of the water, wiped them on her apron, and faced George.

"George Heizer," she began, "you are a scoundrel!" She called him several other names.

He seemed concerned, but not repentant.

"That's not all. I don't know why you have the nerve to come after me when it's obvious to a pumpkin that you don't give me any thought." She half turned away, then faced him again. He stared back at her, almost somber, but strangely steadfast. He wasn't hanging his head under her onslaught of bitter words, scuffing the dirt, or fingering the poor little remnant of his ear. He should look more beaten down.

The resin in a log at the campfire flared up. Bright light played on George's face for a moment. He *did* look beaten down, physically. He had a cut on his cheek and discoloration around one eye, and his lips seemed to be misshapen. Heppie took in a quick breath and almost reached out to him before her anger overcame her again.

"How dare you come all this way to bother me with your protestations of love!" She resisted stomping her foot, feeling guilty that he hadn't, in fact, had a chance to make any such protestations since arriving. "And you brought your brother! I'd have thought you would leave him behind to tend your cows."

"You're throwing it in my face that I chose my brother over you." George's voice was so soft that Heppie strained to hear it. "Ain't it a fact you chose Hannah over me?" George bent his head and looked at the toes of his boots. He raised his eyes to look at Heppie again. "It appears we've both made mistakes."

Heppie sucked in her breath as her thoughts whirled. What was George saying? Her legs went mushy and she needed to sit down, but she steeled herself and stayed on her feet, although she swayed a bit.

"So I'm a pot calling the kettle black?" Heppie's hand went to her mouth. She'd said that too forcefully, too much like a challenge, when she'd meant it as a confession. She bit her lip, wanting to call the words back. A deep sense of sorrow engulfed her, making her shiver.

George stepped forward. He looked haggard, drawn down to a fine strand. He took her by the upper arms and held her still.

"That's enough! The cows are dead, the barn got burned, and the house is a shell. Those Yankee riders got thrown out of the army for"—he made a deprecating movement of his head—"beating me some, and they're coming after Robert and y'all." He took a breath, and Heppie thought he grew taller. "Maybe I did wrong to stay behind, to put my brother and my animals over you. I've regretted that choice every day since you left. Every moment was misery, knowing I'd lost you. That hurt more than the broken ribs." He let his hands fall from Heppie's arms and turned away as though he'd said too much.

Heppie touched his sleeve, and he turned back, his eyes burning with reflected firelight.

George stared at her, long moments passing before he spoke in a low tone. "I'm here now, come to save your life if I can. And marry you at the next town, if you'll have me."

Joy thrummed through her like a plucked fiddle string. She moved toward him, and his arms encircled her, those long, strong arms she'd been thinking about. *He loves me*, she thought. *As much as a practical man can. I reckon that's enough love for now.*

He held her still, not moving, and she realized he waited for her reply.

"Yes, George," she said, and wondered that her voice trembled. "If you can abide my mistakes and forgive me for them, I'll gladly have you."

ℂ

Once they knew they were being followed, the Bingham party traveled on as quickly as they could. Hannah had recovered her strength enough to walk behind the wagon. The day after George and Ned found them, Robert strode along beside her, carrying a rifle. From time to time she glanced over at her husband's grave face.

"Do you reckon they'll catch up to us soon?" she asked.

Robert looked at Hannah, then directed his gaze forward again.

"It's likely. George said he and his brother were just a bit ahead of them." He turned to look back at the road they'd already traveled. "That's why they're riding behind us. They're what you call a rear guard."

Hannah tried to swallow the tightness in her throat. "What will they do to me for killing that . . . man?" Nausea built in her as she remembered the shock to her arms, to her whole body as her attacker's body hit the tines of the pitchfork. She wanted to clutch Robert or fling herself into his embrace for safety, and wondered if she would be able to stand having his arms around her. She fought with her fear and revulsion and kept walking.

"Hannah," Robert said. His voice was so tender that Hannah's breath caught in her throat. Robert paused for a long time before speaking again. "First of all, they're not going to do anything to you. We have four armed men, counting Luke. There are only three of them."

Hannah looked sideways at Robert. *He must be clenching his teeth,* she thought. *His jaw muscles are bunched up like grapes.*

"But you're worried?" she asked. The rhythm of her breathing increased with her anxiety, until Robert laid his hand on her hair.

"Concerned," he admitted. A shadow of a smile flitted over his mouth. "A man would be crazy not to have some reservations about a coming fight." His fingers dropped to Hannah's cheek and stroked it. "They don't know anything about your part. They think I killed that monster."

Hannah shivered, both at the venom in Robert's quiet voice and at his touch. He hated that man called Red. He surely must hate what had happened to her. Did he still love her? She stared at the tailgate of the wagon as Robert removed his hand. His actions said he did, but his voice was so . . . bitter, and he hadn't tried to share any physical intimacies since—

She shivered again. *How will Robert feel when he finds out that vicious cur planted his seed in me? He won't be able to love me when he learns of it. How can I keep this horrible baby a secret?*

A noise from behind brought Hannah out of her thoughts. She looked back, but it was only Ned Heizer on the road. The riotous curls of his yellow hair made a halo around his somber face. Her spine prickled with dread of the battle that would engulf them. The Yankees were coming.

஧

The first hint that the riders had caught up to them came in the afternoon with the sound of rifle fire from back down the turnpike. Robert and Luke got the wagon stopped and pulled off into a screening stand of trees and brush. Luke unhooked the team from the wagon tongue, swatted the near horse on the rump, and the animals ran off.

The firing moved closer, but came sporadically. Robert got the shotgun from the rear of the wagon and handed it to Mrs. Bingham with a few words of instruction. He swept his arm toward the forest. "Ladies, get into the woods. Keep out of sight. George and Ned are bringing the fight to us."

"Robert—" Hannah started to say something, but he cut her off.

"Run, Hannah!"

Robert and Luke hunkered down behind what little shelter the wagon box gave them. "Don't fire until George and Ned are clear," Robert said. "If you can't get a good bead on a man, shoot his horse and bring it down. A moving man is a hard target."

Luke's voice shook when he answered, "I ain't shot a man before."

Robert felt as though his words would strangle him. "These are monsters. When you aim, think on what their buddy did to your sister."

Luke swallowed hard and nodded. He whispered, "Is she going to be all right?"

Robert didn't answer for a minute. Outwardly, Hannah looked the same. She had begun to eat better. Her bruises were healing. However, the light hadn't come back into her eyes. Instead, she looked haunted by bad memories. *It's going to take time*, he thought. He cleared his throat and said, "I don't know yet. Keep a good watch down that pike."

Hooves pounded. A bullet whizzed through the air. George came down the road, whipping the reins against his horse's flank. Ned was close behind, but turned and fired his sidearm before he approached Robert and Luke's position.

George pulled up his horse and vaulted to the ground where the wagon had turned off. He shoved his animal in the direction of the trees, then flopped to the ground behind a bush. "There's still three of them," he shouted to Robert. "I winged one, but he didn't fall."

Robert nodded. Luke screamed beside him, "Look out! Look out!" Ned wheeled his horse toward the forest. Luke's rifle boomed as three horsemen came into view.

One of the three horses faltered and bucked sideways, trying to unseat its rider. The man fell, but one foot didn't clear the stirrup, and the horse dragged him by, screaming.

"He's your lookout, Luke," Robert said. The boy turned and stood, bringing his rifle to his shoulder. The weapon spoke again. Luke raised his voice in an imitation of the rebel yell, then shouted, "I got him!"

The other two riders turned their horses in the road and sought shelter. Robert fired, but the bullet didn't find the target. He berated himself for wasting his shot, then ducked at evidence that one of the riders had taken up a position and thought well of shooting him. A yelp behind him made him turn. Luke lay sprawled on the side of the road. His hand flew up to clasp his left arm above the elbow. Blood seeped between his fingers.

George ran to the boy and dragged him into the brush. "I'll tend him," he called to Robert. "Ned, where are you?"

"Shh," came a soft response.

Robert squinted into the dust raised by the horses. Where had the two remaining men gone? He thought he saw movement in the woods to the left of where the men had turned off the road. Was that one of the men, or both? His stomach cramped with tension as time passed and the lull in the shooting grew longer. Where were the Yankees? Were they hunkered down as he was, or had they chosen to creep closer under cover of the trees? His back was exposed if the men passed his position. Did it matter where he was? Should he move? No, he wouldn't be able to spot movement down the turnpike if he abandoned his post. But who would choose to charge down the middle of the road into the rifle fire of your enemy? He wouldn't, and the men had already gone into the protection of the forest. Maybe it would be best to retrench back in the trees.

Robert lowered his weapon, and was in the act of shifting his feet to move when the shot came from across the road and down a piece, cutting a splinter of wood loose from the tailboard of the wagon.

He jerked his rifle to his shoulder and shot in the direction of the muzzle blast. One of the men in his party—Ned, maybe?—shot back as well.

An enraged cry came from a Yankee. Was he hit? He didn't fire again, and Robert took that moment to remove himself from the side of the wagon and back into the woods.

He came upon George, crouched beside Luke. The boy's arm bore a crude bandage and splints made from segments of tree branches.

"How is he?" Robert asked.

"His arm's broke, but he'll live."

Robert nodded and looked around for Ned. Soon he spotted him to his right. Ned raised his hand and motioned toward the Yankee across the road. Taking the movement as a question, Robert shook his head and shrugged his shoulders. There was no telling if the Yankee was injured or not.

☙

Jessie knelt in a circle of oak trees, her eyes darting from the direction of the road to her mother and sisters. Ma stood upright, her back to a tree, holding the shotgun so tightly in front of her face that her knuckles were white. Hannah and Heppie huddled together, their arms around each other. *The men will protect us*, Jessie thought. *There are four of them now.*

An errant thought flashed into her mind. *I'm glad I'm wearing this light-colored dress. It doesn't stick out like Ma's widow's weeds.* She looked down at her skirt, sprigs of flowers aligned in rows on a tan background. She shook her head slightly. *What on earth does it matter what I'm wearing?* she chided herself. *Three hell-raising Yankees are after us and I'm thinking about my clothing?* She looked at Ma again. The black clothes would be visible for a long distance.

A crashing noise in the woods behind them brought Jessie to her feet. She turned around to face the sound, aware that one of her sisters had caught her by the ankle.

"Leave go!" she said, shaking her foot at the same time as she tried to stay upright on her other.

"What is it, Jessie?" Hannah said in a wailing voice.

"Let me go so I can give attention to finding out," she said, hopping to keep her balance. As soon as her sister turned her loose, she said, "Ma, give me the shotgun and sit down!"

Her face white, her mother obediently handed her the weapon and sank into a heap.

Jessie lifted the shotgun until the barrels faced in the direction of the noise. Someone was walking toward them through the trees, and whoever it was didn't care how much racket he made. In a few moments, she would be able to see who it was.

She felt the strain in her arms and her back of keeping the weapon in position. Sweat dripped off the tip of her nose. Out of the corner of her eye she sensed movement within the circle of the oak trees, but didn't dare glance down to see what her sisters were doing. Someone was coming, and he probably wasn't one of their traveling party.

What if it's someone who lives around here? She thought. *Maybe he heard the shooting and is coming to investigate.* Dread of shooting a stranger filled her chest, squeezing her windpipe nearly closed.

A large man stepped out of the cover of the nearest copse of trees. His black-bearded face was familiar, seared into her memory by the tobacco-spitting incident in the street. "Bull!" slipped from between her lips like a swear word. She bit her lower lip to prevent saying more. This man wasn't a stranger come to see what was happening on his lands. This man had spit on Southern women, beaten Heppie's George, and now he was surely coming to hurt as many of them as he could.

In the next instant, a malevolent grin splitting the man's scruffy beard told Jessie he had seen her and the other women.

"Yep," he said, almost chortling in his glee, "we found you, all right. This is going to be fun." His voice became more threatening as he lifted his rifle in his hands. "Sort of a memorial for my brother, Red. I hope he got his licks in before that banker killed him." His voice turned into a snarl as he took notice of the shotgun in Jessie's hands. "Put down that scattergun, little lady. It won't stop me."

Jessie tightened her grip. Mr. Fletcher had told Ma to aim low and squeeze the triggers. She could do that.

The man advanced toward the circle of oaks, speaking in a wheedling tone of voice. "Give me the gun, sweetheart. It'll break your shoulder. You don't want a broken shoulder, now, do you?"

Better a broken shoulder than the horror your kin dealt to my sister, she thought.

The man put out his left hand, reaching for the shotgun, saying, "Give me the gun, sugar! I got a better plan for you."

Jessie's eyes locked on the man's leering face. He wanted to impose the same indignities on her as his brother had on Hannah. She squeezed both triggers and felt herself being thrown backward as the man disappeared from her view. The metallic smell of blood filled her nostrils, and she knew for certain the man named Bull was not a threat to her or her sisters any longer.

ಇ

Ned heard the blast of the shotgun and looked over his shoulder in the direction of the noise. He half rose to his feet and looked back at Robert. "You get that one across the road," he shouted, then spun around and sprinted into the trees.

"Jessie," he cried out, wondering at the vehemence in his voice. He dodged a hanging tree branch and leaped over a downed log. A woman's high-pitched shriek came from ahead, and he adjusted his course, weaving between the trees as he ran. Someone ran behind him, but he figured it had to be George or maybe Robert, and he didn't look around. At last he could see the women, sheltered by oak trees. None were standing, and he increased his speed, drawn by the sharp wails made by one of them.

"Jessie, Miss Jessie," he called. In five more steps he skidded to a halt. Jessie lay on her back, blood spotting her dress. She clutched the shotgun with one hand and rubbed her shoulder with the other, while her sisters and mother crowded together, arms about each other. One of the twins continued to wail.

At that moment, Ned saw the mangled remains of a body on the opposite side of the tree circle. He shuddered at the nearness of the carnage and turned to stare at Jessie.

"He came so close," he said, the tightness of his throat almost strangling him. Jessie was trying to sit upright, and Ned took her hand to help her. Once she got situated, Ned reached for the shotgun. Jessie let it go without a word.

"That blood?" he asked, motioning to her dress. "Is any of it yours?"

Jessie shook her head. She didn't seem able to talk yet.

George came through the trees and went immediately to Heppie, quieting her outcry. Mrs. Bingham turned her loose, gathering Hannah to her bosom.

"Stay low," Ned said. "There's still one other man alive out there, but Mr. Fletcher's seeing to him."

"Luke?" Jessie whispered. She rubbed her neck.

George answered. "He took a slug through the arm. It's broken because he fell wrong when he went down, but he'll mend."

Ned removed Jessie's hand from her neck. "Do you mind if I test out your shoulder for injury?" he asked.

Jessie turned wide eyes to look at him. "He said"—she took a gulp of air—"he said it would break my shoulder. Maybe he was right. It hurts pretty fair."

"Let me check," Ned said. At Jessie's nod, he felt along the bones of her arm and shoulder with gentle fingers. Finally he smiled and patted her arm with great care. "No broken bones. You'll bruise up and probably hurt like you do now for several days, but there are no broken bones."

Jessie must have been holding her breath, for she let out a long, shaky sigh. "Thank you, Mr. Heizer."

"You called me Ned back in school days."

Jessie slid a glance toward Mrs. Bingham and then looked back at Ned. "That was when we were children. Ma would take a switch to me if I did that now."

Ned chuckled. "Don't let her hear you." The smile she gave him warmed his soul.

ℴ

Robert looked at Ned running toward the sound of the shotgun blast. *He's got the situation in hand,* he thought. *I've got someone to worry about across the road.*

He squinted through the brush but could detect no movement. He crouched and sidestepped to his left until he reached Luke's position.

"How are you doing?" he whispered to the young man.

Luke looked up, his face white. "It hurts a mite, but Mr. Heizer says I'll live."

"Good lad." Robert motioned down the road. "How far is your man?"

"About two hundred feet. The horse quit dragging him when it fell over dead."

"I'm going there to check."

"The Yankee's dead."

"Good. Making sure will give me a chance to get on the other side of the road."

"Oh." Luke nodded.

As Robert left Luke with a pat he heard, "Be careful."

Both man and horse were indeed dead. Robert crossed the road and started toward the spot from which the last Yankee had fired. He heard thrashing sounds. Huffing. Snorts. Not the man. He slowed his pace, peering into the underbrush before he changed position.

After a time, he came upon the horse, down on its side, barely moving. He gave it a pat and looked around warily. A breeze came through the trees, blowing against his face, bringing with it an acrid odor.

The man must be down. He's fouled himself. He continued in the direction of the smell, using the trees and bushes for cover. A few steps farther along, he spotted the Yankee propped against a tree trunk. He held his belly with blood-stained hands. The ground beside him was discolored with red pools.

Robert stayed where he was until he located the man's rifle. It lay out of reach in a blackberry bush, so he approached the man, watching for sudden movement toward a hidden weapon.

"What's your name?" Robert asked, standing over the mortally wounded Yankee.

"Jace Foster." He squinted at Robert. "What's yours?"

"Robert Fletcher." He looked around for the man's canteen. Instead, he found a flask half full of liquor. He squatted and held it to the man's lips.

Foster slowly took a sip, then spoke in a whisper. "You're the damned murderer we came after?" His drawn-out words spoke of coming death.

Robert shook his head. "He died in a fair fight. If it soothes your sensibilities any, I would have killed him for what he did to my wife."

"You killed me." Foster's voice faltered.

Robert considered for a long time. "Maybe I did." He shrugged one shoulder. "Maybe it was Heizer's bullet."

"Which brother?"

"The Yankee."

Foster choked, and blood spilled from the corners of his mouth. When he could speak again, he asked, "Where are my buddies?"

"You're the only one left."

"Finish me off!"

"No."

"I'll bleed to death."

Robert swirled the flask. "You'd better drink this down. It'll take the edge off the pain."

"Slit my throat. You'd do it for a dog."

"No. But when you're gone, I'll do it for your horse."

With a burst of energy, Foster reached for the liquor. He tipped the flask, rinsed his mouth, and spat. Then he drank, his Adam's apple bobbing in a steady rhythm. When he had drained the container, he threw it away and slumped forward.

Robert watched for a long time, but when Foster didn't right himself, he touched the man's neck. Then he walked away, drawing his knife.

಄

When the riders were buried, Robert called the group together around Luke, who sat propped against a tree trunk.

"I don't want us to camp here for the night. My question to you is which way do we go, now that those . . . men are dead?"

Hannah asked, "What do you mean, 'which way'?"

"Do we go back to Virginia, or continue west?" He motioned with his head toward the common grave they'd dug back in the woods and filled with the remains of the Yankees. "They're not a threat to us now. We could go back." Robert looked at the somber faces around him. "Each of you has a vote. It's 'Virginia' if you want to go back, and 'west' if you want to go on." He stopped speaking for a moment, then gestured down the road. "Let me say it's a long journey to New Mexico Territory, and right now we're ill prepared for such an undertaking."

No one said anything, so Robert continued. "We'll start with Mrs. Bingham. What's your vote, ma'am?"

Mrs. Bingham looked down at her hands, clasping the edges of her apron. "West," she whispered. "Let's join Max."

"Mrs. Fletcher?"

"West!"

"Miss Hepzibah?"

Heppie looked at George, then down at her toes. Finally, she said, "West."

"Miss Jessica?"

"I want to go west."

"Master Lucas?"

The boy shifted his broken arm with his other hand. "I reckon Ma needs me. West."

"I vote to go west," Robert said, and turned to the Heizer brothers. "Mr. Ned?"

Ned glanced at Jessie, and said "West," with an emphatic nod of his head.

"Mr. George?"

George reached for Heppie's hand and drew her toward him. "I've asked Miss Heppie to marry me, and she has agreed. I'll go west with her."

"It's decided. Let's hitch up the team."

Chapter 8

Ned offered to drive the wagon in Luke's stead. "The youngster can't handle the lines with that busted wing," he reminded Mrs. Bingham. "If he's careful, he can ride my horse. If he'd rather, he can sit in the wagon." He looked around for Jessie. "Miss Jessie should ride until her shoulder stops hurting so much."

"Thank you kindly, Mr. Heizer," said Mrs. Bingham. "Luke, a few days in the wagon bed should speed your healing. See if you can crawl up there."

"Let me help," Ned said, and got Luke positioned to his liking in a few moments. Ned jumped out of the back of the wagon box and walked to the front. "Now Miss Jessie, let's get you up on the seat."

Jessie cradled her right arm with her left and shook her head. "I reckon I'd rather walk."

"But Miss Jessie—"

"I'm fine as can be, Mr. Heizer. Really I am. I'll tie something around my arm to keep it still, and I'll be fit as a fiddle. Besides, I don't want to displace Ma."

"I think Mr. Heizer is right, Jessie," Mrs. Bingham said. "Just you rest that shoulder. A few days of walking won't put me out none."

"Ma," Jessie protested, but Ned had his way, and soon Jessie was ensconced on the seat with Ned settled down beside her.

"Hi! Get up there!" Ned called to the horses. Once they were on the road, he turned to Jessie. "Your ma's walking back there with Robert and Miz Hannah. You can call me Ned now." He watched a pink glow light her cheeks.

"I haven't seen you for so long," Jessie said, ducking her head to one side.

"Yup." Ned moved his foot onto the brake lever. "I'm sorry I let some years get between us."

Jessie didn't reply.

"Do you remember that time I brought you a peck of mulberries, and we climbed the tree behind Miller's barn and ate the whole thing?"

Jessie smiled but said nothing.

"Our hands got all purple, and my belly ached something fierce, but the company was fine."

Jessie laughed. "As I recall, you threw up all over my skirt, and I had to hide it from Ma and wash it myself."

Ned grinned. "I don't remember that."

"It happened."

"Nah, it couldn't have. I was always a model citizen around you."

"It did."

"It didn't!"

"Did too!"

"Did not!"

Jessie gave Ned's arm a gentle shove as her laughter filled the road. "The purple stain never did come all the way out of my skirt. I had to cover it with an apron until I outgrew it."

"It does my heart good to hear you laugh, Jessie. I don't reckon you've had much to laugh about the last few years."

She shook her head. "Ma always tells us life ain't meant to be fair."

"But a fine-looking girl like you should have little things that give you pleasure, like fancy trinkets and good memories." He looked over at Jessie. She was blushing again. "Memories are precious gifts. I have a store of them I could share."

Jessie said nothing. After a while, Ned began to whistle a tune, and she turned to him, her face a picture of delight.

"That's the firefly song. You made it up."

"I made it up for you." Ned avoided looking at Jessie. He hadn't told her that, before now, and couldn't predict how she would react.

"You did?" A low chuckle escaped Jessie's throat. "I never knew." She tried out the tune, then laid her hand on his arm. "You never told me. What other secrets are you keeping from me?"

"Oh, lots and lots." Ned grinned, relieved. "Like the time I shut the Owen boys in the Bates's cellar for teasing you. Remember, I took you and Ellen Bates and Marie Owen into town on the buckboard to get candy at the store? That's so you wouldn't hear them rascals fussing to be let out."

Jessie snatched her hand from Ned's arm. He looked at her. She had turned her face away again.

"Did I say something wrong?"

"N-no," she said, stumbling on the word.

"Are you in pain?" he asked. "This road ain't too smooth."

"Um, I'm a little tired," she said.

"I don't wonder," he said. "That shotgun sent you flying. Fear is mighty fatiguing, as well."

Jessie said nothing in return, and Ned lapsed into silence.

Jessie hadn't thought about James Owen for more than a week, but Ned's remembrance of secrets he'd kept had reopened the wound that never quite seemed to heal. *Precious mercy! Will I never stop thinking about him!* A cold chill ran through her body, and she shivered, fighting tears that she wouldn't be able to explain away.

Ned Heizer. Big-brother substitute Ned. Protector and friend while her own big brother, Max, played beau to the girls. Ned was acting like he wanted to court her.

That can't be. Ned is my friend. How can he possibly want more than that?

Trying to get her mind to think about a different sort of relationship with Ned, Jessie compared him to her vanished James. He and Ned were about the same height, but while Ned's hair was light colored and prone to corkscrew curls, James Owen had dark, crisp hair that curled around his ears only if it grew too long. How she'd loved to run her fingers through that ink-colored hair! James was handsome in a thoroughly different way from Ned, who limped when he walked. She'd heard Ned had received serious injuries to his legs. James had two perfectly good legs, although he had received a bayonet wound in one shoulder. His impairment had not kept him abed for long. Within two weeks of his return home, he had come courting, smiling and joking and singing songs of love that won her heart.

She sighed, remembering the nausea that had swept through her when James told her he was being forced to go west with his family and he could not take her with him. They clung together, hidden behind a clump of lilacs, tempted to fulfill their love, but when James's kisses grew hot and insistent, she pushed him away, weeping.

"I can't, James. You know why. You could leave me with a child. That'd be a dreadful situation for me." Tears ran down her cheeks, and she allowed him to kiss them away, but kept her body from touching his.

"Ah Jessie, Jessie." James's groan seemed to come from his toes. "How can I leave you?"

"It's your pa's doing. I'll never forgive him." Jessie inhaled sharply as James kissed her neck. "Don't, oh, don't!" She struggled to think clearly. "The Bible says you've got to obey him, even if you don't like it. Go and take care of your ma," she whispered, and gave James a soft kiss and a shove. "Go away, James. Don't come again. Just go." She fled for the house.

James was gone, lost to her. She'd never see him again, and a sob rose in her throat, choking her. Even knowing Ned sat beside her, puzzled at her strong emotion, couldn't keep her from letting it free, for just a moment.

Ned watched Jessie that night. She surely had acted strange earlier, falling silent when he brought up memories they shared, then starting to cry. Oh, she tried to keep it secret, but he knew she was upset about something he said. He simply didn't know what had set her off.

She sat on the ground beside Luke, feeding him soup, a spoonful at a time. Her face, lit by the firelight, danced with animation, first smiling, and then frowning when Luke refused the remnants of the soup. She set aside the bowl and pulled up his blanket, patting it into place around his chin. She smiled again, and started to hum.

Ned recognized the tune. It was a lullaby, an old one his mother used to sing.

Jessie finished one hummed verse, then began to sing in a low voice. "Golden slumbers kiss your eyes, smiles awake you when you rise . . ."

He grinned in the dark. How was Luke taking this, a lullaby from his sister? He looked at the boy. His eyes were closed, his face slack. *No shame there*, Ned thought. *He's already asleep.*

Chapter 9

Several days later, Heppie stood at the altar in a strange church and gave a nervous giggle. *At last!* Her face felt warm, and she wondered if she was blushing. She took a deep breath to suppress another giggle. George stood, ramrod straight, clothes brushed free of dust, sandy hair combed carefully into place over his half ear, looking like he'd keel over if he didn't wiggle something soon. Heppie looked at the minister, who was thumbing through his prayer book. She couldn't read his expression and wondered if he objected to marrying two strangers. *Two shabby strangers.*

She wore the same dress as every day. It was all she had to wear. Ma had brushed at it with her hand, trying to get the worst of the dust off, before they stepped through the church door. Heppie wished she'd been able to wash her dress or at least take a bath, but time had run out when the bustling little minister arrived, shepherded by Robert Fletcher. Several curious townsfolk came in their wake—drawn by gossip that a traveling couple had asked the minister to marry them—and accompanied the wedding party into the church.

Fortunately my hair looks nice. Hannah had brushed it, braided it, and coiled it intricately at the back of Heppie's head. *I'll make a good appearance from the back.*

The minister looked from his prayer book to them and opened his mouth to begin the wedding ceremony. At first Heppie didn't hear a word he said. She knew he was talking, because his mouth moved, and she could hear a droning sound like a thousand bees circling her head, but nothing made sense because George was looking down at her, and she was drowning in the depths of his blue eyes.

When George finally broke eye contact to look at the minister, Heppie got her ears working again. George stuttered, "I . . . ah . . . do," and the minister looked at Heppie.

"Do you, Hepzibah Bingham, take George Heizer for your husband, to love, obey, and cherish him so long as life lasts?"

Heppie stared at the little man in the frock coat. Did she want to marry George? She swallowed, panicked. *Will I love him until I die? Do I have to obey everything he says?* She looked at George, her eyes drawn to his right ear. *Can I cherish that little half-shot-off ear as long as I live?* George squeezed Heppie's hand and smiled down at her. His touch steadied her, and she knew he loved her. *Settle down, Heppie,* she thought. *You can do this. Just be quick about it before you change your mind again!*

She turned to the minister and said in a rush, "Yes, I do. What's next?" As soon as the question left her lips, she gasped and clapped her hand over her mouth, mortified at her audacity.

The minister looked surprised and slapped his prayer book closed with his hand still inside. After a moment, he opened it again, moved his finger down the page, and found his place.

"By the power given to me by God Almighty, this county, and the state of West Virginia, I proclaim you husband and wife, duly and legally married according to the rite of the church. Two dollars, please."

As Robert took up a collection for the money, George wrapped his arms around Heppie. "The preacher forgot to mention this," he whispered, and lightly kissed her on the lips. "I'll never put cows ahead of you again," he vowed, then kissed Heppie with a thoroughness that dizzied her brain.

She clung to him, warmth spreading from her lips to the core of her being, a tingling wave that awakened an overwhelming need to somehow knit her body together with his. Frightened by the intensity of her feelings, Heppie broke away, her breathing short and quick. George winked at her, and she looked at her hands, still gripping his shirt. She dropped them to her sides, wondering, *Did Hannah feel like this on her wedding day?*

&

After the ceremony, the townsfolk gave the newlyweds energetic congratulations and several bits of advice. Heppie smiled, nodded, and wished they were on the road again, away from well-meaning strangers. She wanted to wash, to get at least her hands and face clean before nighttime came and George— What *was* George going to do? After they'd set up camp, Ma had taken Heppie aside for a moment and said that after the wedding Heppie would give herself to her husband. Tales she'd heard and things she'd seen crowded into her mind, but surely that wasn't what people did?

They finally arrived at their camping place with the other members of their party. George patted her hand and said, "I'm going to wash up a bit, but I'll be back soon." Heppie smiled in relief and took herself into the woods with a pan of water to do the same.

Later, the last supper dish had been dried and put away and everyone had gone off into the darkness, leaving the newlyweds alone at the campfire. Heppie sat beside the fire, stirring it back to life whenever the flames weakened.

After a time, she got up and leaned over the fire with her stick, and George asked, "Heppie, what are you doing?"

She jumped backward, righted herself, and looked at her husband. "Keeping the fire going."

"Why, my girl?"

"I like the light." She sat back down, fidgeting with the stick and wishing Hannah or Jessie would step into the firelight.

"Let it go out. It's time for bed."

"Allow me a few more minutes."

George got to his feet, moved behind her, and squatted down. He put his lips to her ear. "I'd rather you came to bed, my love," he whispered.

"It's dark away from the fire," she whispered back.

"That's fine with me. The darker the better." He slipped his arms around her waist.

"George!" she whispered. "What a thing to say!"

"Come on, honey. We have to get up early."

"I don't like the dark." She thought of animals in the darkness of the forest beyond their camp. Animals that lumbered through the trees, making noise.

"You'll be safe with me." He nuzzled her neck. "So safe and warm." He drew out the words, tantalizingly slow.

"Will I?" she asked, moving her neck slightly. "I'm fearful."

"Of me?"

She remembered seeing a tom cat mount a female at a friend's farm. The tom had been rough. "No, of things I don't know much about."

George kissed her throat. She thought her skin would melt.

Heppie swallowed hard. "The things I feel."

"Don't be afraid. I'll take care of you."

"Will you?"

"Yes." His drawl made the single syllable go on forever. His breath stirred the hairs below the coils of her tresses.

Heppie closed her eyes and took a deep breath. Yes, her skin was melting, and if he kept kissing her, she would want to flee into the darkness with him. *I'll be safe from these feelings beside the fire.*

George stood up and stepped to one side. Heppie also stood, bending toward the embers to stir them again. *I'm a married lady. I can have these feelings.* She put down her stick. She paused, thinking, *What if this is lust? Lust is sinful!* She picked up the stick again and stirred the fire. Sparks flew up, and she stepped back to avoid them. George moved in, took the stick from her hand, and led her away from the fire.

Those cats made a fearful racket. Heppie felt a bit of panic rise in her stomach. *Do married folk make noise? Will all the camp hear us?*

George drew her closer into the circle of his arm as they walked toward the bed she knew he had prepared for them. *He is strong*, she thought. *He is brave and warm and safe. I love him. I want to be with him.* An idea dawned on her. *This is what Ma meant.* Her panic diminished.

He chuckled. "You're so deep in thought, my dear. Where are you wandering?"

"Hold me close," she begged, suddenly clutching him around the neck.

"That's what I had in mind," he said, enclosing her in his embrace.

"No. Hold me for a minute or two right now." She let out a gust of air as he complied.

He bent his head and kissed her under the ear. "There's nothing to fear."

"Wolves?"

He shook his head against her.

"Bears?"

Again she felt the negative movement.

"Making noise?"

He was still for a moment, then whispered, "I can't guarantee that."

"George!"

"I *can* guarantee I'll take good care of you." His hug tightened.

The last of the panic left Heppie, and she let him lead her through the darkness toward their marriage bed.

Chapter 10

Several weeks of travel brought the Bingham party within sight of the Mississippi River. When they reached St. Louis, they rented quarters in a rooming house. Everyone got jobs to improve their condition. Robert hired on at a bank, while Ned took a job as a guard at a warehouse, and George joined the police force. Luke ran errands for a grocery, Mrs. Bingham sold dry goods, and Jessie worked in a millinery shop. Hannah took in mending and sewed men's shirts.

One day, Hannah sat in a chair, her still hands lying on trousers that needed mending, when Jessie returned early from work.

"Hello, Hannah," Jessie said, taking off her bonnet and hanging it on a hook by the door. "Miss Huckaby gave me a few hours off, as we've caught up on the latest piece work." She walked over to Hannah and looked down at her. "You look so pale. Why don't you take a stroll around the park, if you're finished there? The fresh air will do you good."

"No." Hannah glanced at Jessie, and then down to her lap. "I haven't finished the mending." One of her hands twitched, and she clasped both together. "Nothing will do me good, Jessie. Not a walk in the park, not a journey across the country, not anything!"

Hannah's voice had risen, and her sister stared. "What do you mean?" Jessie asked.

"I mean I'm not all right. I'll never be all right again." She turned her head away from Jessie. "You can't know what I endured that awful, horrible day. Why did you and Heppie leave me on that corner alone?"

"Hannah, I'm sorry. You can't know how bad I feel that you were . . . taken. And hurt so." Jessie knelt by the side of Hannah's chair and tried to grasp her hand.

Hannah pushed herself sideways in the chair, her back to Jessie. "You'll never feel as bad as I do. Never!" She bit off her words.

"I know that," Jessie said, getting to her feet. "It's been weeks since that happened to you, Hannah. Past time for you to get over your troubles." She squared her shoulders. "I'm going out. You may not want to walk around the park, but I do. Tell Ma I'll be home before dark." She rushed to the door, grabbed her bonnet, and left the room, slamming the door behind her.

Hannah stood up. The trousers and her mending supplies tumbled onto the floor as she ran into the bedchamber, snatched the pitcher out of the washbasin, and threw up.

After spewing her luncheon into the white ceramic bowl, she slowly raised her head, picked up the towel, and wiped her mouth. *That's twice today*, she thought, wringing the cloth in fisted hands. *It's getting so hard to keep this a secret.* She blew out slow breaths through pursed lips, hating the smell of the vomited material. She wrinkled her nose, but picked up the basin, went to the open window, closed her eyes, and threw out the waste. Someone below yelped in protest, and Hannah felt shame that she hadn't looked before she tossed out the vomit, but she moved out of sight and put the basin on the stand.

The odor remained in the room, filling it like the noxious fumes from a pile of manure. Taking small, slow actions so as not to alarm her stomach, Hannah poured a little water from the pitcher into the bowl, rinsed it with a slow swirling motion, looked out the window to be sure no one was below, and emptied the foul brew into the street. She lit a candle, blew it out, and moved it slowly through the air to kill the odor.

When she put the candle on the washstand, she sighed in relief. The air seemed to be cleaner. Now no one would know she had thrown up.

Hannah backed to the bed, and slowly lay across it. *I'll just rest for a minute. Mrs. Coley won't be here for the mending until five o'clock.*

She woke to footsteps in the sitting room. The pall of sleep still rested heavy on her body and her mind, but she pushed herself to her feet and staggered from the room to see her mother taking off her bonnet.

"Ma! Why are you home?"

"It's time for me to be here, daughter. I imagine it's almost five."

"Oh no!" Hannah stumbled across the room to her chair and bent to retrieve the mending and her sewing materials from the floor. "This batch is due to be finished by five. How on earth did I nod off?"

Mrs. Bingham took the trousers from Hannah. "What is needed besides mending this hole?"

"That's all. I've finished everything else, but I went into the bedroom to—" Her eyes went wide, and she stood still.

"I'll complete this work, my dear," her mother said, sitting down. "You seem somehow frazzled. You say you were sleeping?"

"Yes. I just lay down for a moment, and I don't know what happened to me."

"You have suffered quite a deal of tumult, my dear. If you wish to finish your nap, I don't mind whipping a few stitches into these britches." She smiled, evidently pleased with her joke, and sat herself in the chair Hannah had occupied an hour previously.

"Thank you, Ma." Hannah stepped backward, turned, hurried into the bedroom, and approached the washstand.

"Oh," she gasped. Her stomach clenched, but there was nothing within it to come forth, so she heaved helplessly as the convulsive waves racked her body. A small part of her mind wished she had closed the door behind her. *What if Ma hears?* she thought. *I can't bear it if she comes in and sees me.*

At last the nausea passed. Hannah went and shut the door, and sat on the bed. *If this baby were gone, I wouldn't throw up.*

The thought buzzed in her head, twisting and turning, mixed with denial that her mind had conjured such an idea. "That's a sin," she said, clapping her hands over her mouth, afraid her mother had heard. Afraid that if she came in, she would read the wicked thought hanging in the air.

If the baby were gone, I'd be rid of the shame.

Oh God, oh God, she prayed. *Take this evil thought out of my mind. I'll give the baby away. Some barren woman won't mind having the child of a monster. I won't tell her that's what it is.*

But if I carry the baby, Robert will hate me. He'll hate the child. He'll be so disgusted. Maybe he'll leave me. I can't bear that.

Hannah covered her eyes and sobbed, beaten down by her ghastly situation. *I can't tell Robert!* she thought, and mourned the loss of her close relationship with her husband.

∞

At the table in the family's combination cooking-eating-sitting room one Sunday afternoon, Robert paused from doing sums with a stubby pencil and scrap paper and watched George count coins into stacks. Mrs. Bingham wrote a letter; Luke whittled softwood by the front door; and the young women on the sofa took turns modeling an unfinished shop hat Jessie had brought home. Meanwhile, Ned dozed in a window chair, and his soft snores punctuated the others' conversation.

"Do we have enough?" George asked.

Robert took up his pencil and finished the calculations. After a minute, he stood up and stretched. His shoulders ached, and the motion felt good. He twisted his head from side to side, and his neck cracked. "Ahhh," he said, letting his shoulders fall into place. Then he sat down.

"You're doing that to keep me in suspense," George said, grinning. "Do we have enough?" His words were deliberate.

"Nearly so." Robert gave a short, barking laugh. "In all honesty, I want to purchase that prairie schooner from Mr. Grant." He moved a coin back and forth on the tabletop with his fingertip. He looked at the figures on the paper. Then he nodded at the pot of bean soup that stood on the stove. "I reckon if we work another week and continue to eat plain food, we can make our deals for wagons and supplies, and depart within a fortnight."

George smiled hugely. "That is good news, Robert. Thanks for doing the sums." He clapped Robert on the shoulder. "I can figure how much seed is needed to sow a field, but real money figures are beyond my understanding."

George rose from the table and looked at the women. "I'm going for a walk. Will you come with me, Mrs. Heizer?"

Heppie looked up, a smile quirking her mouth. "Yes," she said. "I think it's a lovely day." She got off the sofa and removed the apron she still wore from preparing dinner. "Will any of you come with us?"

Amid a widespread shaking of heads, George and Heppie prepared to depart for their stroll.

"Wait just one moment." Mrs. Bingham stopped them. "Can you post this letter for me? I've written at last to let Maxwell know we're on our way."

Heppie took the letter, and she and George left.

Robert scooped the cash and coins into a canvas bag, drew the cords shut, and knotted them together. He hid the bag behind a cracker tin on a shelf, and turned to survey the room.

Hannah and Jessie still sat on the sofa, measuring a feather affixed to the side of the hat.

"Is it just a mite too long?" Jessie asked. "Shall I snip it down?"

"I suppose it's fine," Hannah said, shrugging. "It's not to my taste. I've never liked feathers on a hat."

"You've never *had* feathers on a hat," Jessie joked, wiggling the plume against Hannah's upper lip.

"Don't do that!" Hannah shouted, and bounced to her feet. "You know I can't abide tickling."

Robert crossed the room and took Hannah by the hands. "I also need a walk, my dear. Come with me so I won't be alone."

"I don't want to—" she tried to protest, but Robert shushed her with a wave of his hand.

"I think you need the air," he said, gently tugging her toward the door. "You're looking a bit pale."

As Robert wouldn't listen to her protests, Hannah gave in.

Once outside, Robert bent his head to speak to Hannah in a low tone. "No feathers? No tickling? No taking the air? Where is the agreeable wife of my heart?"

She gave a huff and lifted her chin. Robert stopped. She looked away, avoiding his gaze.

"Hannah, have you lost flesh? Aren't you eating enough? You don't need to leave off eating to make our savings grow." He touched her hand, lifted it, and inspected her fingers. "You're too thin. Look how your wedding ring spins around. Hannah, you must eat. You would not want to lose that off your finger."

"Most days I have no appetite," she said, pulling her hand free. "If we must walk, let's get to it. I still have a bit of mending to accomplish."

"Not today," he said. "The customer can wait for a weekday."

"It's your mending," she murmured. "How did you manage to tear your sleeve so badly?"

"It was merely a slit a month ago. I don't know how it grew."

"Was it neglect? Wearing it each day? Not showing it to your wife in good time?" She seemed to make an effort to put on a jovial countenance.

"There's my smile," he said, coaxing the bud into full blossom with his fingertip. "You have such beautiful lips, my dear. Curving them into a smile makes them even more lovely."

"Robert, someone will see you. And you mustn't say such things. They'll hear you."

"Who?"

She looked around, but the street was nearly empty. She shrugged.

"Let's go to the park," Robert said. "There are several benches we can sit on if we grow tired. In fact, I know of a bench that's hidden in a grove of trees. I can say anything to you there." He grinned at her, and she ducked her head away from him. "Maybe I can get you to say something indiscreet back to me." He winked.

She shrugged again but let him lead her to the park.

Chapter 11

Ned awoke a few minutes later. He scrubbed at his face with one hand, feeling the stubble prickling his fingers, and looked over at Jessie, who sat on the sofa showing her mother a hat. *She sparkles like the evening star at twilight*, he thought. *She always has.* He dropped his hand on his thigh. *She's taking a lot of joy in that hat. I wish I could buy it for her.* His pockets were empty, all his wages tossed in the common pot to purchase supplies for the journey ahead. He looked around the room. Only the two women and young Luke were there with him.

"Where is everybody?" he asked, getting to his feet.

"Mr. Heizer," Mrs. Bingham said, smiling up at him. "Did you enjoy your nap?"

Ned fidgeted with his thumbnail, embarrassed that he hadn't gone into the next room to sleep. "Ah, yes, ma'am," he said. "I hope I didn't disturb y'all."

"Certainly not. A little snore now and then can be curiously comforting."

He smiled and gritted his teeth. *I was snoring? Just the impression I want to leave on Jessie.* "What's my brother up to?"

"He went for a stroll with Heppie," Jessie answered. "It's a lovely day." She looked down at the hat in her lap, put it on her pale yellow hair, and fiddled with the feather.

Ned's heart turned over, and he caught himself breathing hard and fast. "Whew," he said in a whisper, then added aloud, "Would you enjoy a walk in the park, Miss Jessie?"

Jessie looked up, a slow smile spreading across her face. "I would, Mr. Heizer. Are you asking me to accompany you?" She took off the hat and gave it to her mother.

Ned gulped. "I am. That is, if your mother is willing." He turned to Mrs. Bingham. "Is that agreeable with you, ma'am?"

Mrs. Bingham pushed herself to her feet and nodded. "I think Luke would enjoy stretching his legs. Wouldn't you, Luke." Her tone made her last words a statement.

Jessie rose to her feet. "It appears we will have company, Mr. Heizer." She turned to Mrs. Bingham. "Are you coming, Ma?"

"No, dear." Mrs. Bingham smiled as she shook her head. "Luke will be companion enough to make things proper. You young people have a good time."

With Jessie beside him and Luke following after, Ned limped down the stairs leading to the street. Once they were walking toward the park, Ned turned to look at Luke. He glanced at Jessie and waggled his eyebrows. Jessie grinned back at him, then looked over her shoulder at Luke.

"Lukie, I believe I left my little purse behind. Will you go fetch it? Please?"

"Ah sis, you're kidding me. You don't need a purse for a walk in the park."

"Yes I do."

"Do not!"

"Do too!"

"Do not."

Jessie stopped, turned around, and pointed her finger toward the rooming house. "Yes I do. Go get it for me, and I'll do one of your chores tomorrow."

"Take out the rubbish?"

"Well . . ."

Luke pulled his knife from his pocket and picked at the whittling stick he still held in his hand. "You don't need your purse. You're trying to get rid of me. I'll get rid of myself if you'll take out the rubbish tomorrow."

Jessie laughed. "I'll do it. Maybe Mr. Heizer will help me."

Ned nodded, and Luke grinned. "You promise?"

"I promise, Lukie." Jessie put out her hand and shook Luke's. "Good-bye."

Luke turned around and left. Ned took Jessie's hand and pulled it through the crook of his arm. "Ready for our walk?"

Jessie smiled. "It will be delightful, now that our chaperon is gone."

Ned grinned. "You got rid of him right handily, missie." He inhaled deeply as they entered the park, breathing in the heady scent of the lilacs lining the path.

"I've had lots of practice," Jessie said, almost skipping a little as she tried to keep up with Ned's longer stride. "Whenever Ma sent him out with us girls, we would take turns inventing errands to send him on." Her smile grew wistful. "It was more fun before he figured out we didn't want his company."

Ned threw back his head and laughed. When his mirth was spent and he had wiped tears from his eyes, he said, "Jessie Bingham, you're a caution. Poor Luke. It must be hard living with a bunch of girls. I'm glad I grew up having George."

Jessie looked thoughtful. "I reckon you're right. Max was so much older. By the time Luke wanted someone to play games with, Max was interested in girls, being a hero, and such. He didn't pay Luke any mind." She looked at Ned. "Do you suppose I'm being cruel to Lukie?"

Ned looked at Jessie and wanted to touch her on the nose, but he resisted, instead saying, "Maybe."

"Oh, do you think so?" She frowned. "I don't want to be mean. We've had good times together. We're the two youngest, you know."

"I know." They arrived at a bench situated in an intimate circle of trees beside the winding path, and Ned stopped and turned to face Jessie. "Shall we sit a spell?"

Jessie plopped on the bench and smoothed her skirt.

Ned watched her face as her emotions played over it. *She's got a tender heart*, he thought. "Luke will be all right," he said, sitting beside her. *Will she let me take her hand?* He decided to wait. "What do you think of St. Louis?'

"It's so much bigger than Mount Jackson," she said, crinkling her nose. "The river smells. If I lived here, I'd have to be away from the river."

Ned laughed. "I thought you were going to New Mexico Territory with your ma."

"I am," she said tilting her head to one side. "I wonder if Max found a wife out there. When he left, his head was filled with notions of making his fortune. I hope he did so."

"From what I remember of Max, I'm sure he's doing fine." *Making a big impression with the ladies, no doubt*, he thought. *Max always liked the girls.*

"He wrote to Pa, inviting us to join him, so I reckon he's set up in some kind of business." Jessie looked down at her feet. "He didn't know Pa had died."

Ned looked at Jessie's somber face. He reached over and took her hand, sliding his fingers between hers. "What happy memory can I bring to your mind? You're thinking too hard on your pa."

"Not just Pa. All that's happened to us. That . . . man I killed back there. Is God angry with me?"

Ned gave Jessie's hand a little squeeze. "You been stewing about that since it happened?"

"It comes and goes. Some days I think I did the right thing. Some days . . . I don't know."

"Like today?"

"Yes."

Ned wondered if he could put his arm over Jessie's shoulder. It might comfort her. Then again, it might well offend her. He decided to wait. He was, after all, holding her hand without any protest from her.

"Here's what I think," he finally said, when Jessie had turned anxious eyes to him. "God ain't in favor of tyrants. He don't like bullies. I don't reckon he looks on rapists and such with high regard. From what you said at the time, he was threatening you and your sisters—maybe even your ma—with vile acts. Am I right?"

Ned felt Jessie's shiver through her hand. He squeezed it again and said, "I'm right. I reckon God knows your heart, that you were defending yourself and your kin. You did purely the right thing, Jessie Bingham. You did the right thing." Ned took in a lungful of air, and capped his speech by bending over and kissing the top of Jessie's head. She responded by laying her head on his shoulder.

"Thank you, Ned. You're such a good friend."

Ned tightened his gut as though he had received a blow. *A good friend? Ned, my boy, you have a long row to hoe*, he thought, resisting a sigh. Another thought came and brightened his attitude as he looked at their entwined hands. *Yes, and you're on a long, long journey. You have time to make her think different of you.*

Chapter 12

Several days later, Hannah cut flannel pieces to sew a man's shirt, then gathered the scraps to use during for her monthly. As she tucked them in a dresser drawer, she stopped short, her hands suspended. *I haven't had my monthly since we left Virginia. I won't have it again for a long time. I've got this horrid lump of clay in me, this bastard baby.*

She backed away from the dresser, wringing her hands, and paced beside the bed. *I'm trapped here with the mending and sewing. How can I find someone to get rid of this curse?*

She sank on the bed, feeling wicked for letting the appalling thought come again. *I'm already dirty, and unworthy of my husband for letting that Yankee dog rape me,* she thought. *Now I'm sinful, as well.* She wanted to scream, to vent her outrage and her anguish, but the walls of the boardinghouse were too thin. It was bad enough that she dared cry when she was alone. She wouldn't even have that release soon. Robert said they would leave St. Louis the following week. They'd be out on the trail again. She'd have no privacy for weeping.

Hannah got up and shut the drawer. She went into the main room, picked up her needle and thread, and began to sew together the shirt. When she pricked her finger, she began to cry, pretending it was because the puncture hurt.

഻

When Robert purchased a team of mules and the canvas-topped wagon he'd been eyeing for weeks, Mr. Grant's broad face beamed with delight. Although the conveyance was not new, it had proved its worth on the trail to Kansas several times.

"You'll make better time with this vehicle and the mules than with that tumble-down farm wagon you folks brought with you," Mr. Grant said.

"Oh, we're still taking the old wagon, and another, as well," Robert said. "We've laid in a store of food sufficient for the journey, and we'll need every inch of space."

"Your brother-in-law bought a wagon?" the man asked.

"He found one to his liking down yonder," Robert answered, nodding toward another business. "He thinks there's enough grass on the plains, so he's using horses. Big ones."

Mr. Grant shrugged. "They pull strong, but they eat a lot. You'd best be taking grain along."

"Grain?"

"Yep. You're bound to come to places along the trail where the grass is eaten down. When you do, you'll have something to nourish your animals. That's the thing to keep in mind. Always look out for your animals."

"Hmm," Robert said. "I thought we'd simply be letting them graze."

"A couple hundred pounds of grain is a good thing to have along, just in case. You might even run into a big spot where a prairie fire's gone through. You'll need grain."

"Thanks for the advice. We'll buy grain." Robert shook the man's hand and climbed to the plank seat. He gathered the lines, took up a whip, and yelled, "Get up there," to his team. When the mules lurched against the collars and put the wagon into lumbering motion, Robert grinned broadly. At last he possessed his own means of transportation. Just as he predicted, they'd be on their way in two weeks.

☙

One night, soon after their departure from St. Louis, Robert accompanied his wife into a wooded area to gather kindling and fuel for their campfires. When they were well hidden from the others, he took her shoulders in his hands and drew her to his chest. She went stiff in his embrace, and he lightened his touch on her arms.

"Hannah love," he whispered in her ear. "Calm yourself." His voice was very low, almost inaudible, but he deliberately made it gentle. "You went through a horrible time. I only want to hold you in my arms for a little while. Won't you let me smell your hair?"

"My hair is filthy," she muttered.

"Your hair is beautiful, like you are. Beautiful and soft and sweet."

"No!" Hannah tried to pull free, but Robert held her tight. She struggled against him for a moment and then gave up, her shoulders tensed. "My hair is filthy. My skin is filthy. My female parts are filthy. My womb is filthy, because it carries a filthy child. A dirty, rotten, misbegotten Yankee child. I'm filthy through and through!" She was almost screaming at him, and he shushed her with his hand over her mouth. "Don't. Do. That," she gasped, wrenching herself from his grasp.

He grabbed her before she ran away, and pulled her to him, his mind whirling. *A child!* "We're having a child?"

"No! I'm having a child. It has nothing to do with you."

"Hannah. It's my child."

She averted her eyes and sobbed out, "You don't know that."

Robert looked over Hannah's head into the deep woods, struggling with his conflicting feelings of joy and dismay. He kissed the top of her head. "Hannah, I'm your husband. It's my child."

"Robert. Don't." She took a deep gulp of breath. "It's a Yankee bastard."

He stopped her with two fingers lightly pressed against her lips, and bent down to look at her. "Don't say that. The only Yankee bastard is the one we left in that barn. The vile . . ." He had to stop to get air and calm himself. After a moment, he said, "That child is most likely mine. I've been a husband to you all along."

"We'd been wed six months with no sign of an infant coming!"

"But this spring"— He ran the back of his knuckles along her arm.— "Don't you remember how sweet it was to be in our own home at last? Not have to share a house with your mother?"

Hannah stood still, rubbing her arm where Robert had touched her. "How do you know we created the child? How do you know this babe isn't from that

Yankee's depraved, foul, revolting seed? He debased me." Sobs raked her body. "Why do I feel so soiled?"

Robert dropped his hands and released her. He chose his words carefully. "I can't pretend to know your reason for thinking that way. Perhaps a doctor could explain it. Or your mother."

"Don't you talk to my mother," she cried out. "Don't you dare." She pounded on his chest with her fists. "She can't know about this evil, wicked baby, this sin I've done against you."

"Hannah." He captured her fists in his hands. "Your mother will know about the baby. Everyone will know about the child coming as time goes by. Scarves and such only conceal for a while."

"Rip it from me! Tear me asunder!" She wept into his chest.

Robert felt the blood drain from his face. He swallowed and straightened his shoulders. "Hannah," he barked. "Hannah, come back to your senses." He softened his voice. "Hannah, you are very dear to me, every part of you is dear to me." He struggled to say something to touch her soul. "Can I cherish you more than I do now? My heart is knit to yours. Any child you bring forth will be sweet and clean. I will love it with all my being. We two are one, and the acts of a despicable man have no bearing on our union."

Hannah burrowed against Robert, sobbing. "I want to believe that. I want to." She began to shiver. "I cannot fathom such a thing."

He squeezed her hands. "I must consider that in time, you will believe me." He turned one palm upward and kissed the center of it. "There, I have cleaned a little part of you with my love. Trust in it. Feel it. Let it grow."

"Oh, Robert," she moaned. "You have no sense to be so good to me." Her body went slack against his, and he caught her before she fell.

He held her close for a long time, until her breathing slowed and she was restored to a state of calm. Then he released her with a sigh, bent down, and picked up a fallen branch.

"We'd better get on with our job. They'll be wondering where the wood is."

Chapter 13

After a matter of weeks, the party made camp near a spot where the westward trails divided. The northern branch led to Utah and California and Oregon. The southern track was still renowned as the Santa Fe Trail, which connected to old Spanish trails that continued through New Mexico Territory all the way to California, following a wagon road pioneered by a party of Mormon volunteers during the War with Mexico in the '40s.

Jessie stood over an iron skillet, frying bacon. She looked up from her task when Ned stepped into the firelight.

"Good evening, Jessie," he began.

"Hello, Ned." She tucked a lock of hair behind her ear. "Ma's not nearby, so I can call you that."

Ned smiled and nodded. "You look very nice tonight," he said. "Do you mind if I sit a spell?"

Jessie rolled her eyes in mild annoyance and said, "Suit yourself." She turned the bacon with a fork.

"Thanks." He found a box and lowered himself onto it. "Lovely night. Stars out and a full moon."

"Uh-huh," she said, laying down the fork and lifting the lid on a pot of beans. It needed stirring, so she picked up a wooden spoon and thrust it into the savory mixture.

Ned shuffled his feet

At the sound, Jessie looked up to see him gazing at George and Heppie, who were teasing each other near their wagon.

Ned cleared his throat, then spoke. "Married life seems to suit my brother and your sister."

"They do seem over the moon."

"Have you thought about getting married?"

Jessie cast her eyes down to her work. She hadn't given the topic much thought since . . . since she'd been left behind when James went west. She bit her lip. It didn't help. Her heart still hurt more. Slowly she looked up. Ned was sitting there, waiting for her to answer. She shrugged her shoulders. "Not for a long time."

Ned bent over and fiddled with the top of his boot. "Do you know what double cousins are?"

Jessie frowned. *What a strange question!* "No."

"That's when two brothers marry two sisters, or a brother and sister marry a sister and brother. Their youngsters are double cousins."

Jessie stirred the beans so vigorously that they sloshed over the rim of the pot.

"Jessie." Ned paused, fiddling with the lacing on his boot. "I, that is, you, I mean . . ." His voice trailed off. "Oh, confound it," he said, rising to his feet. "Will you marry me? We'll run into a town sooner or later, and we can scare up a preacher or a mayor or a judge to say the words over us—"

"Mr. Heizer," Jessie interrupted.

"Please, Jessie, hear me out. We're good friends, that's a fact, but I've got strong feelings for you. I thought of you a good deal during the months that I was lying there in the hospital up north. When I got back to Mount Jackson and found out you were gone, it tore me up inside. I want to be with you now."

Jessie turned and faced him. "Mr. Heizer, Ned, I—"

"If you don't want to answer yet, I'll understand." He stepped forward and took her hand. "Take all the time you need."

Jessie looked at Ned's hand holding hers. She looked into his eyes. She looked away. "Ned, we're only friends. I've never thought of marrying you."

Ned dropped her hand and shuffled his feet. "I think friendship is a good start for marriage."

Jessie stared at him. "But what about love?"

"I've never loved anyone but you, Jessie."

Jessie smiled wryly. "That's on your side of the matter, Ned. Don't I need to love you too?" Her smile slipped away as Ned jerked upright, his throat working as he swallowed several times. "Being in love matters to a girl."

She turned to the bacon and poured the grease into the bean pot. She whacked at the crisp bacon. It shattered into pieces that she scooped into the pot. She looked up. Ned was staring at her, his face somber.

After a moment, he spoke. "Don't misunderstand me, Jessie. Naturally I want you to love me, but I'm sure that will come in time. For now, consider taking a good, hard look at your feelings for me. See if they ain't sufficient for marriage."

Jessie laid down her spoon and moved to face Ned. She put her hand on his arm. "I been in love before," she whispered. "I don't feel the same about you."

Ned looked down at the ground, then up again. Finally he spoke, his voice dark. "James Owen?" he asked.

"Yes."

"Is he anywhere around?"

"No."

"Then marry me."

"I don't love you like that. You're my friend."

"It doesn't matter to me what kind of love you bear me now." Ned took her hand from his arm and brought it to his chest. His heart beat strong, hard. "I hope that will change in time. I care for you enough for both of us." He nodded sharply, only once, then added, "You think about what I've said."

Jessie lowered her eyes. Her heart thumped in her throat, matching the rhythm of Ned's. *Maybe I do love him*, she thought. *Maybe I should think about marrying him.* Slowly she nodded. "I'll give thought to your suggestion." She looked up. Ned was watching her face. "It may take me some time to . . ." She swallowed, took her hand from Ned's chest, then said in a gush of air, "To think it through."

Ned's eyes looked like the depths of a deep pool. He gazed at her for a long time, not moving, frozen in place. Then he nodded, again only one time. "I'll wait."

He strode off, his long legs barely limping, and Jessie wondered how hard it was for him to damp down his pride and give her the time she needed.

଼ଓ

Riding in the wagon several days later, Robert watched Hannah out of the corner of his eye. She seemed wilted, like a bunch of wildflowers plucked in the morning and set aside without water by a careless child. The wagon lurched, and she gave a little gasp.

"Have you told your ma about the baby?" he asked.

"No." Hannah's shoulders rose and fell with her sigh. "Has Mama been asking nosy questions?"

"A few. I try to remember she's concerned for you, darling." Robert slapped the lines over the backs of the big mules.

"Are you?"

"Am I what?"

"Are you concerned for me?"

"Oh, darling, how can you ask that?" He looked over at Hannah. Her hands lay gripped tightly together against the growing mound of her belly. "Mercy! Hannah love, you know what I did to that man when I came after you."

"I have nightmares nearly every night. Will they ever go away?" Her voice dropped. "Will you ever forgive me?"

Robert swore softly. Nothing he said or did seemed to make a difference to Hannah. He pulled the mules to a stop and wrapped the lines around the brake handle. He grabbed Hannah's shoulders and kissed her, firmly, possessively.

He let her go, took up the lines again, and slapped them against the animals' rumps a little more forcefully than was necessary. When they were once again on the move, he looked over at her. Hannah stared back at him with wide eyes. "You're my wife," he said, softly. "I love you with all my heart and soul, and no matter what happened in that barn, no matter what happens in the future, nothing will change that."

"I want to believe you," Hannah said, beginning to sniffle. "I just—it's so hard."

A feeling of helplessness washing over him, Robert sat dumbly on the wagon seat. If only there were something more he could do to assure her of his love. Theirs was the last wagon of the bunch, and he didn't dare stop again for fear they would fall behind. How dearly he would have liked to halt the wagon, lift Hannah down from the seat, find a scrap of shade, and tenderly show her how much he loved and needed her.

He grabbed the whip, uncoiled it, and cracked it with vigor above the ears of the mules. *That'll have to wait*, he told himself. *She's not ready for me yet.*

Chapter 14

Heppie watched the sky all afternoon as she walked beside the wagon. White clouds built into towering giants, filling the horizon. They loomed there, first turning gray, dark and ominous, then becoming almost black as a wind pushed them toward her. Soon they would be overhead. Prickles of gooseflesh raised the hair on her arms under her sleeves. Would rain come to dowse them as they struggled west? Lightning slashed to earth several miles ahead of the travelers. Heppie cried out, even before the deafening thunderclap filled her head. *Dear God in Heaven*, she prayed. *Not a lightning storm!*

Rubbing her arms with her hands, she looked over at George. He was standing in the wagon, gripping the lines hard to keep the four big horses from bolting. His lips were drawn back from his teeth, and she couldn't tell if he was grinning or focusing on the task. *He's probably grinning because he faces life like an adventure.* She shook her head. *Will I ever be brave like him?*

Another bolt of lightning struck ahead of them. Heppie shivered, bracing herself for the thunder, biting her lower lip to keep herself quiet. She could see rain falling in the distance, sheets of it, accompanied by wind lashing the grass. The sun had gone into shelter behind the menacing clouds. It was probably time for her to seek shelter as well.

Pulling up her skirt so her feet wouldn't get caught in the hem, Heppie dashed toward the wagon. "George," she screamed above another rumble of thunder. "Stop and let me get up."

George turned his face toward her. She saw that he was battling with the horses. He yelled back, "Stay clear! They want to run."

Heppie stepped out of the way, thinking, *No! He'll be killed if they run off.* Her heart banged against her ribs. *George, hold on to them*, she pleaded silently, watching the wagon lurch along the trail, gathering speed, until the animals broke free of George's control.

Heppie cried out, a long gusty "No!" that the rising wind swallowed.

From behind, noise pounded on the prairie like another roll of thunder. Heppie looked over her shoulder. What new danger was upon them? A horse approached with Ned bent low over its neck, driving forward to catch up to the runaway wagon. He passed Heppie. Clods of earth fell around her, stirred up by the horse's hooves. A small chunk of sod hit her cheek, sticking in place, and she batted at it as if it were a bug. She had to see what was happening to George.

She realized she was running, half falling over the furrows of churned-up earth left behind by hooves and wheels. Her throat felt raw, filled with her high, keening cry. Her lungs burned as she filled them with air that seemed to have been singed by the lightning. The wagon was so far away!

Another horse blew by, whipping up a dust cloud, pressing the thick yellow air against her. Mr. Fletcher. Luke sprinted by, his arms pumping with effort. She squinted her eyes, trying to find the wagon. Trying to see George.

At last she broke out of the dust. Ahead of her, the wagon lay on its side at the end of a plowed-up rut in the earth, one wheel smashed, the other spinning crazily. Ned Heizer and Robert Fletcher were off their mounts, struggling with horses thrashing on the ground. Luke ran toward them. Where was George?

Raindrops began to pelt her—needles on her flesh—but she kept running. Was George under the wagon? Her head seemed to reel as the storm grew in ferocity. Someone was screaming, "George!" over and over. She finally recognized her own voice.

The sky closed in, black and threatening. Sunlight had gone, fleeing from the violent flashes of lightning. A dark figure rose from the prairie floor and caught at her as she passed it.

"Heppie!"

She whirled around, screaming her husband's name, clutching at his arm.

Blood slid down George's cheek from a gash above his eye. It mixed with the rain to become a pink flow. He moved cautiously, as though he were checking his body for injury. His arms wrapped around Heppie, and she nuzzled against him, drawing in great panting breaths of air.

"Are you hurt?" she asked.

Heppie sensed George shaking his head. His body trembled, and she burrowed into his chest, trying to buoy him up.

"I have to see to the horses," he said in a tight voice. "And the wagon."

The tremors of his body frightened her. "Hold me a minute, then you can go," she said, still panting, willing him to stop shaking. After a moment, she turned him loose and watched him limp toward the overturned wagon. He bent to retrieve his hat, but the bending was slow and awkward. *Oh George,* she thought, *are you hurt in your innards?*

Lightning struck, much closer this time. A great roll of thunder followed.

Heppie jumped, stifling a shriek, wiping rain out of her eyes so she could see. She pressed her lips together, trying to settle her nerves. *Hepzibah Heizer, you stop that*, she told herself, making her inner voice as firm as she could manage. *George needs you.* She began to walk toward the group of men gathered around the horses. *This storm will pass. Sooner or later, they'll fix that wheel and set the wagon upright. After that, George will expect you to put our things to rights inside.*

℘

Favoring his right leg, George trudged along the water-filled ruts toward the wagon. The leg didn't seem broken. Probably got bruised when he landed so hard. His side burned something fierce, though, so he sent his fingers to explore. Maybe he'd busted a rib or two. *Holy Nellie!* he swore, at the thought of going through that botheration and discomfort again.

Ahead, the wagon wheel on the rear axle still spun. Just like his head. The cut on his forehead smarted, but he figured the rain would wash it clean. He shut his eyes briefly, still walking, and tripped on an upturned ridge of earth. He didn't go down, catching his balance, knowing that Heppie was following behind, probably wide-eyed and breathless with fear for him.

A smile twitched at the corner of his mouth. Heppie. She was certainly grabbing hold of the spirit of being married. The previous evening she'd teased the tiredness out of him. His smile widened. It had been a good night.

Ahead of him, Robert and Ned had succeeded in quieting the team, despite continuous flashes of lightning that made the air sizzle and cracks of thunder that seemed to rip the sky from stem to stern. Luke knelt on one knee, bending forward. He got to his feet and stepped aside.

Three of George's horses were on their feet, but one lay on the ground, struggling weakly, flailing a leg that was clearly broken.

His mouth went slack and he began to run, his feet splashing into pools of water standing on the prairie.

Robert heard him coming and looked up. He rubbed his jaw and shook his head.

George uttered a curse. They'd barely started their journey across the Great Plains, and here he had a horse down. If that leg was busted, there was no hope. He'd have to shoot the animal.

When he reached the back of the wagon, he stopped running and walked the last few feet with lead in his chest. Heppie was depending on him to get her safely to Albuquerque. How was he going to do that with three horses in a four-horse harness? Maybe they'd have to limp to the next settlement and plant themselves there.

No, that would never do. Heppie set a lot of store by her family. She was determined to get to New Mexico Territory. *It's my job to see that she does*, he thought. *Come hell or high water.* He set his jaw. *We've been through hell just getting out of Virginia. I reckon we can survive high water too. Just so long as them three other horses stay sound.*

Ned looked at George and said, "The leg's broke. Do you want to shoot the horse, or shall I?"

"Hold on. I want to see what's what first."

"The rifle's yonder, when you're ready." Ned nodded at his horse.

George looked over his team. Someone, probably Luke, had cut the harness from the wounded horse. He wondered if he could repair it. *I'll probably have to realign it, put the odd horse between the other two. Or maybe in front, in the center of the rigging. That'll be a job of work. We're going to be here for a while.*

"Well, let's unhitch them other horses from the wagon. I reckon we should move them off a piece so they don't take fright again when I shoot this one." Bitter regret washed over George. He hated to see a good animal lose its life, especially because of an accident like this one, right out of the blue. Rain drummed on his hat, matching his bleak mood.

Ned went for the rifle while the others took the sound horses away. Ned gave the gun to George.

George looked over Ned's shoulder. Heppie stood at the rear of the wagon, one hand resting on the wheel that had been whirling. He wondered if she had stopped it. She looked down at her shoes.

Behind him, the injured horse breathed with a whistle.

George shut his eyes. When he opened them again, Heppie was looking at him. He couldn't tell if the water coursing down her cheeks was from the rain or from her tears.

"Cover your ears," he said, his words sounding thick.

She nodded and whirled, bringing her hands up to do so.

George turned to the horse. Ned moved away and George took a breath, bringing the rifle to his shoulder. "Damnation," he said into a lightning flash, and squeezed the trigger. The sound of the shot was swallowed in the next thunderclap.

શ

Heppie sat under Hannah's wagon, out of the storm, watching George and the other men as they struggled with the smashed wheel, trying to get it loose from the axle. George didn't want anyone to climb on the sides of the wagon lest they snap the bows with their weight. This left the wheel up in the air, the pin almost unreachable, making their task more difficult than it had to be. Robert and Ned had both argued with him about it, but he couldn't be persuaded.

Although it was only about five o'clock, the clouds were so dark and the rain so fierce that they'd had to light a lamp to continue working.

Why don't they wait until tomorrow? she wondered, shivering in the cold wind. *They're going to be struck by lightning if they don't stop.*

Luke held a broken spoke of the wheel to steady it. George sat on Ned's and Robert's shoulders, a mallet in his hand, banging on the end of the pin.

Heppie let out an exasperated sigh. *Is he daring the lightning to hit him? Luke weighs less. He should be up there, if anybody has to do this foolish job tonight.*

Lightning ripped through the clouds, hitting the ground a hundred yards away. George was swinging the mallet when it struck. The men below him must have shifted, or jumped at the sudden explosion of energy released so close at hand, for he tumbled to the ground, landing with a splash in a rivulet of storm water. Robert leaned over to help him up.

"We're done for tonight," Ned said, grabbing the lantern and moving toward the Bingham's wagon. Luke followed him, and Robert came toward his own vehicle.

George threw the mallet to the ground beside the wagon and stalked away, stamping his feet on the wet ground.

"George!" Heppie called to him. "Come here!" More lightning banged into the ground. The roar of thunder followed almost instantly, the concussion in the air hurting her ears. George winced, then turned and hurried toward her. When he arrived, he bent down and slid under the wagon, grumbling to himself.

"You can't do more until the storm lets up," she said, laying her hand on his mud-caked arm.

"I wanted to get that wheel changed."

"Not tonight."

"I know," he said, and added a curse word.

"George!"

"I'm sorry, Heppie. I'm tired and sore and wet and muddy, and my wagon is tipped over with who knows how much damage besides the wheel." He slapped mud off his hat. "And I had to kill a perfectly good horse." His voice had dropped to a rough whisper.

"A horse with a broken leg," she said, wondering at how clearly her mind was working amidst the chaos.

"Yeah," George said, releasing a gusty sigh. "Yeah, broken."

"We'll be all right," she said, patting his arm. "I know you'll get us to Albuquerque, somehow."

George turned his head. Heppie met his gaze.

"Somehow," he repeated.

Chapter 15

Several days later, the Bingham party got underway again. In the meantime, George had butchered the dead horse, saying it was a shame to leave the meat to rot when they could use the flesh in their diet. Heppie balked at first, but finally helped salt the meat and pack it into a barrel. At last the men had changed the wheel and put the wagon upright, Heppie had straightened up the goods and gear inside it, and George had mended the harness. The rain clouds, along with the lightning and thunder, had moved east across the prairie, leaving sunshine and a mild breeze.

On the morning they left their forced camp, Mrs. Bingham chose to walk. She and her daughters set off in a group, but soon Heppie and Jessie lagged behind, gathering wild flowers. Hannah stared straight ahead, answering Mrs. Bingham's attempts at conversation in single syllables.

Mrs. Bingham pointed to the sky. "Look at that hawk, Hannah. Did you ever see such a wide wingspan?"

Hannah glanced up, then down again. "No."

"These plains birds are so much bigger than the ones at home."

Hannah shook her head slightly. "Home?"

"Well, I mean the Valley. You know that."

"Yes." Hannah's word came out sharp and breathy.

Mrs. Bingham said, "I reckon home is the wagon while we're traveling."

Hannah didn't reply.

Mrs. Bingham was looking at Hannah when a strong gust of air cooled her face and tightened Hannah's skirt against her abdomen. Mrs. Bingham took in a quick breath. *Oh lordy, lordy!* she thought. *There's a baby in that belly!* She'd worried ever since they'd left Mount Jackson that the Yankee had planted a seed. She closed her eyes against the proof while waves of nausea roiled in her stomach. *Oh my dear Hannah.* She wanted to weep. They hadn't left all their troubles behind, as she had hoped. Hannah was carrying trouble with them in her body.

What will Mr. Fletcher do? she asked herself. *Surely he knows. Oh, what can I do? I can't let Hannah carry this burden alone.*

When Mrs. Bingham opened her eyes, Hannah was staring at her, hostility clear in her face. Mrs. Bingham looked away, clamping her lips against crying out. Hannah had read her expression.

"Ma!" Hannah barked. She had her hands splayed out on the top of the small lump, as though she would push it out of her.

Mrs. Bingham turned her head, feeling like she was twisting a stubborn stopper on a crock of sauerkraut. "Yes, daughter?" Her voice sounded strained, shaky, as though she'd been down in bed for a week with a fever.

"Don't say a word!"

The intensity in Hannah's voice made Mrs. Bingham take a step away from her.

Hannah spoke again. "I won't discuss it."

"No?"

"No! Now leave me be."

Mrs. Bingham stopped walking, and Hannah strode on, her head down and arms wrapped around herself.

Mrs. Bingham let out a ragged sigh. *I've got to speak with Robert Fletcher.*

ଚ

Ned tethered his horse to the back of the Bingham wagon and strode in Jessie's direction. She was alone for the moment, walking along with a free stride, carrying a bunch of wild flowers in one hand. Her yellow hair hung loose, blowing a bit in the breeze. He wished he could twirl a tendril of it around his fingers. He snorted to himself. *Forget it, Ned. She ain't given you an answer yet.* He took two more steps. *Maybe today she will.*

He caught up. "Hi," he said, grinning down at her.

"Hi, yourself." Jessie smiled, bringing the flowers in front of her. She raised them to her nose and sniffed.

"Smell good?" he asked.

"Very good. Want a try?" Jessie thrust the bouquet at Ned.

He inhaled. "Pretty nice. Prairie smells. Like rain and fresh breezes."

Jessie made a face. "I've had enough rain for now." She ran her free hand along her neck under her hair, then tossed it. "I'm glad I can dry out."

"Me too." Ned grinned. "Your hair is pretty today. Kind of shiny. Bright too."

Jessie laughed and ducked her head. "Well, it's yellow. That's a bright color."

Ned chuckled. *Good. She's in a happy mood.* He matched his stride to hers. How could he bring the conversation from bright colors to marriage? He walked along, thinking.

"What's on your mind, Ned?"

Her question caught him off guard. "What do you mean?" he countered, stalling until his thoughts made sense.

Jessie laughed. "I can almost see your thoughts floating out behind your head, silly."

Silly? Uh-oh. "I was admiring the picture you made with your hair blowing," he said, choosing the honest approach.

"You were?" Jessie had dropped her smile, but seemed willing to let him talk.

"Actually, I was wondering if you have an answer for me."

Jessie's face went guarded, and Ned mentally kicked himself.

"No, Ned." Joy in the day had gone from her countenance. "I don't. I haven't decided yet."

"But you're giving it thought?" He hoped a little pressure wouldn't send her skittering off toward her sister.

She nodded. And swallowed. "I'm sorry it's taking me such a long time." Her voice came out muffled.

Ned's chest squeezed, tight bands choking off his air. He didn't want that unhappy look on her face. Not when she was contemplating marriage to him. That wasn't how he wanted her to feel. Thinking on marriage should bring her pleasure.

"Well, you take all the time you need." He stopped walking and Jessie passed by him. Then she stopped and looked at him, hesitating like she was going to speak. She faced forward, glanced back momentarily, then walked away.

Ned took in a breath. He let it out slowly. His thoughts ran rampant. *By now Jessie should welcome the chance to wed. She knows she'll never see James Owen again. I'm twice the man he is, even stove up like I am.* A bitter fluid rose through his throat and into his mouth. He spit it out and trudged toward his horse. *I'd never run off and leave her.*

∾

Robert hobbled his mules to graze and bent to pick up the harness he'd stripped off them. He looked toward the wagons, wondering why Mrs. Bingham was walking out to him. She usually left Hannah and him to their own devices, but she approached, calling his name.

"Mr. Fletcher, I must talk to you."

"Ma'am?"

"Tonight, after supper."

"In private?"

"Yes, please." She twisted her apron in her hands. "I don't want Hannah to know."

"To know what, ma'am?"

"That we're talking together."

Robert tilted his head. "That might be difficult to arrange."

"Perhaps after she's gone to bed?"

Robert winced. How many others had noticed that he and Hannah shared the same place at night, but not the same schedule? These days he almost always gave her time to go to sleep before he went to lie beside her, yearning to reach over and touch her. Knowing she would reject his touch.

He nodded and agreed. "After she's gone to bed."

The camp was quiet when Mrs. Bingham sat down by Robert beside the fire, puffing a bit as she bent over.

Robert was grateful that the firelight had died down as the wood went from embers to ashes. He twirled a stick in his hands, waiting for Hannah's mother to speak, wondering if she blamed him for the harm that had come to her daughter.

When Mrs. Bingham began, it was in a voice so low that Robert had to lean toward her to hear. He shifted in his seat so that he was closer.

"Hannah," she said.

"Yes?" He could hear her breathing, sucking in gulps of air as though to fortify her body against a lack of it.

"Do you know . . . are you aware?" She stopped, raised her shoulders, and let them drop. "Hannah."

He waited.

"She's going to have a baby."

He waited again, time stretching thin between them. When she didn't go on, he said, "I know." The air seemed thin too, and he caught himself breathing as Mrs. Bingham had. He said, "I know," again, and lapsed into silence. Mrs. Bingham would talk when she was ready.

"Do you reckon it's the Yankee's?"

"I do not!" His denial felt forced, a little too strong, but he had to make it. For Hannah's sake.

Mrs. Bingham examined her hands, spreading her fingers and staring at them. She rubbed her palms together as though they were covered in glue. "How do you know?" she whispered.

"The baby's mine. No matter what Hannah bears, the child is mine."

"You will claim . . ." She paused. "Anything?"

"Hannah is my wife. Whatever happens, the child is mine," he repeated. "I will give it the love of a father."

"You're a decent man, Robert Fletcher."

"I love Hannah. She suffered much at that man's hands." He felt tears filling his eyes, but resisted swiping at them. Perhaps Mrs. Bingham couldn't see the tears in the fading light. "She fought him hard," he said, envisioning the terrible scratches on the man's face. He raked his nails down his own cheek. "She tore at his hair." He put a hand to his head, imagining the pain. "It must have hurt, but he deserved all she did to him," he added, and knew his mother-in-law would perceive the husky note in his voice.

Mrs. Bingham sniffed and put her apron to her nose.

"Then she . . ." He stopped talking, reconsidering what to tell about the battle in the stable. He loosened his shoulders. "When the fight was over, the man was dead."

"My poor Hannah." Mrs. Bingham wiped her face. "You're a saint."

"I'm her husband." He leaned over, resting his forehead on his hand, bracing his arm against his chest. He remained that way for a time, then straightened up and blurted out, "She's so angry!"

Mrs. Bingham inhaled sharply. "Not at you?"

"At the babe. She won't love it." He turned away, suddenly needing to hide his expression. "That breaks my heart. She must love her child. Sometime."

"Oh, Mr. Fletcher! Someday she will. I will speak to her."

He said, "Hmm," and could feel the sound buzzing in his head. Would Hannah's heart be changed by a conversation with her mother? He doubted that would do the trick.

"Where there's life, there's hope, Mr. Fletcher," said Mrs. Bingham, getting to her feet.

"Ma'am," he said, rising as well. "I'm sure you can do some good." He could say that to comfort Mrs. Bingham, but he knew the burden in his heart belied his words.

Chapter 16

Two hard months of travel brought the Bingham party to Pueblo City, Colorado. They camped on the outskirts of town in a meadow surrounded by trees that were just starting to show a hint of color. Before night fell, a buggy drew up near the wagons.

"Hello, the camp," called a round little man with a top hat perched on his sandy hair. "May we visit?"

Robert walked forward from the fire. "Visitors are always welcome. Step down and sit a spell."

Three men exited the buggy and moved forward. "Thank you," said the man who had hailed them. He was accompanied by a tall man in a black coat and by a man of medium build wearing a patterned vest over his shirt.

"Come to the fire," Robert said, gesturing toward the half circle of three wagons. "Will you take supper with us?"

"No, no, we've already et," said the short spokesman. He doffed his hat and nodded to George and Ned. "We've come to give you welcome to our fair city and to inquire if you will be staying hereabouts. I'm the mayor, Abraham Louis, by name, and these two men are members of the city council." He motioned to his companions.

Robert escorted them to what seats were available, and answered Mayor Louis's question. "We're mighty pleased to be here, but we're only passing through, heading on south. If no one takes it ill, we'd like to rest our animals for a few days, and the ladies would like to do laundry."

"That's acceptable to us. There's a fine creek about a mile in that direction, if you want to remove there tomorrow."

"Thank you. That's mighty kind of you to suggest it."

During the conversation, the tall man had been staring at Robert. He spoke up, his voice mimicking Robert's drawl.

"Say, haven't I seen you before? I'd swear I know you."

Robert drew himself up. "Sir? I'm newly come to this place. I don't know where we could have met."

The man turned to Mrs. Bingham and held his pursed lips between his thumb and knuckles as he stared at her. At length he snapped his fingers. "You're Joseph Bingham's wife! Where is the man? I'd like to greet him."

Mrs. Bingham turned white. Robert moved to her side, and she grasped his sleeve. "Sir, why would you know my husband?"

"Hell's bells, begging your pardon, ma'am, don't you know me? You've been in my store many times."

"No sir, we've barely come here."

"I don't mean the store in Pueblo City." The mayor and the second man tugged on the speaker's coat, but he persisted and pointed at Robert. "You're the Fletcher boy, and aren't you the, hmm, the Heizer lads?" He gestured at the brothers and snapped his fingers again. "I've sold both of you many a piece of penny candy."

ℰℴ

Jessie gasped, and the men turned toward her. "It's Mr. Hilbrands. You must remember him. The storekeeper in Mount Jackson. They left with . . ." She let out her breath in a loud sigh. "He and his family . . . when the Owens left."

"Mr. Hilbrands," Mrs. Bingham said, looking him up and down. "You've done well for yourself, getting onto the city council in so short a time. To answer your question, my Joseph died shortly after you left."

Randolph Hilbrands shook his head mournfully. "I'm most sorry to hear that, ma'am. You better let Rod Owen know when you pass by. He set a lot of store by your husband."

"We'll pass by?" she asked.

"Yes, ma'am. He took up land south of here. He's raising cattle and grandchildren." Rand grinned and continued. "The Owen place is about two days' journey south of here, toward the mountains. Rod and his boys are building that big dream he always had."

Jessie took a breath and stepped forward. "His boys?" she asked.

"Yes. There's Rulon, of course, who wed my daughter Mary. They have two fine children, young Roddy and a little baby girl. And Carl and his wife Ellen, you know, the Bates girl? They're helping out. Clay and Albert are too young to marry yet, but they pull their weight." He winked at Robert.

Jessie looked at Heppie, then back at Mr. Hilbrands. "And James? You didn't mention him."

"Well now, James is away from home. Ellen Bates was supposed to marry him, but she chose Carl. James took it hard. After the wedding, he had a dustup with his pa and he left. He stayed with us for a couple of weeks, sorely wounded in the side from a shootout with some Irish fellow." Rand put his hand over his right side in illustration of the location of James's wound. "After he mended, he refused to stay on as my freight driver. He went back south, and that's the last I heard of him."

As Mr. Hilbrands told his story, Jessie hunched her shoulders in shock. Heppie placed a hand on her arm, but Jessie shrugged it off, making fists.

"Chester Bates and them are raising wheat down along the Apishapa." He snapped his fingers. "I recollect that I told James of a job, breaking colts for Angus Campbell. Maybe he's still there." He looked over at Jessie and cocked his head. "You might hear more about him from the folks south of here, if you're curious," Mr. Hilbrands said.

Jessie looked up. "No," she said. "I'm not curious in the least."

The mayor took control of the conversation, said good-bye, and gathered his companions into the buggy. The man in the vest had not said a word during the entire encounter.

☙

After supper, Jessie left the firelight. Heppie followed and found her sitting some distance away on a hill of sand, two hands over her mouth.

"Jessie, Jessie," Heppie said, sitting down and patting Jessie's arm. "What a liar you are! Not curious in the least! I'm sorry you didn't get any more news of James than what Mr. Hilbrands gave you, but that's probably for the best. Don't cry."

Jessie dropped her hands from her mouth. "I'm not crying," she said in a firm voice. "I'm screaming. How dare he?"

"How dare who do what?" Heppie asked. "What do you mean?"

"James! How dare he ask Ellen Bates to marry him. He loved me!"

Heppie shifted, adjusting her dress under herself. What on earth could she answer to sooth Jessie's anger? It seemed justified. James had been so attentive back in Mount Jackson. Once he'd recovered from his war wound, he'd come into town every chance he got so he could pay court to Jessie. Jessie had whispered that James was mentioning marriage. Heppie felt the heat of anger rising in her chest on Jessie's behalf. How dare he, indeed!

Heppie patted Jessie's back. "It appears James got his comeuppance when Ellen married Carl instead of him. Don't think about him. You got over caring about him once, and it's best to stay that way."

Jessie raised her face. "That's my difficulty," she said. "I never did. I reckon that's why I've kept refusing Mr. Heizer."

"Ned? He asked you to marry him? I didn't know he cared for you."

"He's always been a good friend, and now he declares he loves me. A while ago he asked me to consider marrying him. I reckon I'm still considering."

"You should snatch him up, Jessie. If he's as good a man as George is, why, he'll treat you very well. I'm sure he'll make a good living for you, once we get settled."

"I suppose so."

Something in Jessie's voice made Heppie turn to look at her. Jessie's lips were quivering. Heppie straightened her back. "I reckon he can make you forget James Owen." Heppie pressed her own lips together and frowned. "James didn't treat you right, going off to the west, then fixing to wed Ellen."

Jessie sniffed as if her nose were dripping. "That was probably his pa's doing. Making him ask Ellen."

"That's neither here nor there! He's gone, and Ned wants you."

Jessie sighed. "I suppose so." She looked up. "I don't feel affection for Ned, at least not the kind to want him for a husband."

Heppie shrugged. "Many girls marry a man without caring for him. You can do that."

"I'm not certain I can." Jessie tucked her chin into her chest, and her voice came out muffled. "I don't want to marry a man unless thinking about him makes my knees go weak. Thinking on James still does that to me."

Heppie shook Jessie's shoulder with one hand. "Mercy sakes, Jessie! You ought to consider Ned's offer real hard and forget that James." She dropped her hand and sighed. "Come on. It's nearly bedtime, and we have a wagonload of wash to do tomorrow."

"Oh, yes, that's a better subject to think on. Doing the wash." Jessie laughed as she got to her feet, but there was no mirth in her voice.

∞

A week later they camped below the Wet Mountains. Crickets chirped in the distance. A soft breeze blew down the side of the hills, bringing with it a chilly touch of autumn.

Mrs. Bingham sat in the flickering light of the waning fire, forking up a last bite of beans. When she'd swallowed it, she put down her fork and looked to Hannah, who sat nearby. Her daughter played with her half-eaten food as though her thoughts were a million miles away.

Mrs. Bingham cleared her throat and asked, "Dearie, did you take enough to feed yourself right? That little babe needs good nourishment."

Hannah stirred in her seat. "Ma, I don't want to talk about this . . ." She paused. "This mound of flesh. I can't stop it from supping at my vitals, but I don't have to talk about it."

"Daughter," Mrs. Bingham remonstrated, getting to her feet and collecting plates and forks. "Don't be unnatural. You must count your blessings."

As others drifted off to do their chores, she carried the dinnerware to a dishpan near her wagon. She got boiling water from the fire, poured it over the dishes, and called out to Heppie, "It's your turn to wash."

"Yes, Ma." Heppie came up and dipped her hand into the water, pulled it out, and shook it. She blew on her fingers. "This water is still too hot, Ma."

Mrs. Bingham rounded the fire and sat beside Hannah. "It'll cool down soon enough," she called.

Hannah clutched her hands together, her head bent over the abandoned plate. Her body seemed to vibrate with tension.

Mrs. Bingham straightened her shoulders. "You have many blessings, Hannah. Chief among them, you didn't die at that wicked man's hand. Mr. Fletcher says you punished him gravely."

Hannah interrupted. "I scratched his face and pulled his hair. That's not so much."

"Your husband told me a tale of great bravery on your part, dear. I got him to talk about it one night, and he wept as he told how you struggled."

"Robert doesn't weep."

"Mr. Fletcher has very deep emotions about that day, Hannah. He grieves that you were hurt. He grieves that your heart is so hard toward your babe. He loves you. He swears he will love your child, no matter what."

"How good he is," Hannah said, scorn tingeing her words. "How noble. How fine."

"Hannah! You must not talk that way about your husband. He deserves your respect."

"He is not the one carrying this bastard child!" Hannah blurted out. "No one blames him. Everyone will praise him to the heavens for his forbearance toward me."

"Hannah." Mrs. Bingham's voice rose firmly. "Robert Fletcher is one of the greatest blessings in your life. Once upon a time you knew that, and cherished his love. You returned it. It grew into a fine, shining thing. Don't debase it because you had a misfortunate experience with a vile man."

Hannah's face went white. "I can't forget that day."

"You must try. You must turn your thoughts to your babe, to being a good mother and a good wife. Give thanks each day for your blessings and for your family."

The anger in Hannah's face crumbled away, and her hands flew up to hide her face. "Mama," she said in a little-girl voice. "Don't scold me so. I can't bear for you to hate me. I hate myself enough for all the world."

Mrs. Bingham got up and gathered her daughter into her arms. "There now, dearie," she crooned, as Hannah cried deep gulping sobs. "Leave go of hate. Where there is life, there is hope. Your dear Robert knows that. He has been strong enough to carry you through this terrible time. Bear him a grateful heart for his fortitude. Don't turn your back on that gift."

Hannah turned her stricken face to look up at Mrs. Bingham. "Oh, Mama, I've been a dreadful wife."

"Yes, you have." Mrs. Bingham stroked Hannah's back.

"How can I cure that?"

"If you open your heart, you will know what to do, and when the time is right, you will be knit together as one soul again."

Hannah sniffled. "Can that happen, Mama?"

Mrs. Bingham stood still for a moment, looking at the moon as it rose over the meadow. She turned back to Hannah and hugged her tight. "Your Robert is fixing a snug bed under yonder stand of trees. I am confident he will receive you with all his heart." She looked again at the moon. "There's good luck in that light, daughter. Don't let it go to waste."

Hannah sat up and got free of her mother's encircling arms. She took a deep breath and stood up. She seemed to stand taller. "Thank you, Mama. I won't."

Mrs. Bingham stepped back and made a shooing motion. "Go on with you," she said. As Hannah walked away, she whispered, "Good night. May God be with you."

Chapter 17

By the middle of November, the Bingham party had reached the valley of the Apishapa River below the Mexican town of Leones. They pressed onward, anxious to cross Raton Pass before snow came upon them.

Late one afternoon, they approached a neat farm with fallow fields, pastures, grazing horses, corrals, and outbuildings surrounding a sod house. A teenage boy sat on the top rail of a fence and watched as their caravan drew near. Tied inside the fence was a saddled mouse-colored mustang, its sides flecked with sweat from recent exercise.

"Hello," Robert called out to the boy as soon as they were in voice range. "Is your pa at home?"

"Yep," the boy replied. "He's over yonder in the stable. I'll go fetch him."

"Wait a moment," Robert said, pulled up his team, and wrapped the lines around the brake handle. He smiled at the boy, jumped from the seat to the ground, and walked up to the fence. "We're looking for a place to spend the night and heard that the Campbells live somewhere around here. I figure you can give us directions."

The boy said, "Well, I reckon you've found it without my help. I'm Andy Campbell. My pa's name is Angus." He grinned down at Robert. "You sound a mite familiar."

Robert took off his hat and brushed at the dust on the crown. "We come from Shenandoah County, Virginia, same as you. Is your pa nearby?"

Andy got off the fence and waved toward the barnyard. "I'll take you over there."

"No need, Andy. I'll find my way. Looks like you're working with that horse. Is he new broke?"

"James Owen worked him some, but he had to go south, so I'm finishing up the job." He took a deep breath and stood straight, his shoulders back.

"James Owen, huh?" Robert tilted his head, looked at the boy, and nodded. "It's a good thing to take pride in a job well done." George and Ned had joined Robert by this time, and they watched Andy climb the fence into the corral, mount the mustang, and gently kick it into a series of turns before they strode off toward the stable.

♋

"Angus Campbell?" Robert asked as they entered the stable.

Angus turned his head at the sound of his name, rose from his seat, and extended his hand.

"Welcome, gentlemen. By your voices, I'd say you're from my old neck of the woods."

"We are. I'm Robert Fletcher, and these men are George and Ned Heizer."

"From Mount Jackson?"

Robert nodded. "I worked there in the bank. George and Ned had the dairy outside of town. We're traveling down to New Mexico Territory with Mrs. Bingham and her boy Luke. George and I married the twin daughters."

"Mrs. Bingham? Alone? I take it Joseph didn't survive his wounds?"

"No sir," Robert replied. "Mr. Bingham took sick and died soon after y'all left. Max Bingham went west before his pa died. He sent word to invite the family to join him."

"Your timing is off. Most folks come through here in the summertime."

George jumped into the conversation. "Well sir, we planned to leave next spring, but things got hurried up a mite. The old town wasn't pleasant for us anymore."

Robert nodded, shifting his feet a bit.

Angus said, "It's getting on toward suppertime. Will you and your party take nourishment with us and stay the night?"

George grinned. "We was hoping to ask you for a place to camp tonight on your land."

"You'll have it." Angus hung up the harness he'd been mending and put away his tools. "Come with me. Molly will be glad for the company. We don't get enough to suit her, seems like." He started for the house.

Robert matched his pace. "Womenfolk like to be sociable. I know Mrs. Bingham has enjoyed seeing her old neighbors again as we've passed by."

Angus pulled the door open and paused before entering his house. "Come say hello to Molly, then drive your wagons into the dooryard and water your animals at the well. You can make a proper camp after we eat."

"We'll bring food to contribute," Robert said. "Mrs. Bingham likes us to add to the meals we're invited to."

Angus laughed. "Fair's fair, I reckon. Molly!" He ducked his head and strode through the doorway. "Molly, we have company."

ജ

Jessie's spirits lifted as she helped prepare the meal. Molly Campbell was a jolly woman who laughed and told jokes and shared news of all the people who had come west from the Shenandoah Valley with the Owen family. The laughter untied the knot that had cinched Jessie's innards since Randolph Hilbrands had spoken of James and Ellen. *Maybe I'll hear some news of James*, she thought. *Mr. Hilbrands said he came south.*

Since there were so many people, the men took seats at the table first, while the women stood aside, serving the food and chattering to each other. Jessie was content to let the conversation roll over her.

Young Andy mentioned the horse he'd been training. "Pa, I think that mustang is about finished up. Do you want me to start on the horse that bucked James off?"

Jessie's ears pricked up at the mention of James's name. Finally some news.

Angus laughed. "You're sure eager to follow in his dust," he said.

"You have horses to break, Mr. Campbell?" George asked.

"I do. James Owen came through and he started them off, but he was in a hurry to get through the Pass, so I let him go on. He's supposed to come back and finish the task, but I need a horse gentled down right away for Molly to ride."

"That James Owen!" Molly said with a click of her tongue.

Jessie's ribs ached as she held her breath, waiting for more information, but Molly only put a pie on the table and stood back.

"I can gentle a horse for you," George said. "That is, if you don't mind."

"Pa," Andy protested, "I can finish the horses."

Angus held up his hands. "It don't matter to me who does the job, so long as it gets done." He cut into the pie and served himself a large piece before sliding it down the table. He turned to the boy. "I have plenty of other chores for you, Andy." Then he turned back to address George. "If you want to tackle working the kinks out of the colts, I can pay you in cash or supplies."

"We have use for both, if you're willing to split up the payment when I'm finished."

"The deal is done." Angus stuck his hand over the table and George shook it, then attacked his piece of pie.

Jessie felt like screaming. The men finished their dessert and vacated their seats so the women could eat. As they filed out the door, she tried to think of a way to bring the conversation back around to the topic of James. Molly had information, and she wanted to hear it.

The women sat. Molly launched into a story. Jessie passed her plate down the table for stew, then added a biscuit at the side when it came back to her.

When Molly finally finished her tale of the wedding of her brother, the blacksmith, Jessie asked, "Do you get many visitors here?"

"Not so many as I'd like, Jessie girl. There'll be even less as winter comes on." Molly spread a bit of jam on her biscuit and raised it to her mouth. She lowered it to say, "I reckon the last visitors we had were James Owen and that Mexican girl he had with him." She put the biscuit to her mouth again and took a bite.

The bottom dropped out of Jessie's stomach. She swallowed hard and asked, "Mexican girl?"

"Yes. He said he was taking her down to her folks in Santa Fe. She got stranded somehow at the church up in Leones." She paused to take food and chew it. Finally she continued. "I suspected there was more to it than that. Amparo—that was her name, Amparo—looked at him in a special way, like they had a secret he wasn't sharing with us. Later on, I got a letter from Muriel Bates. She said my brother Tom told her husband that James and the girl were married."

Molly must have kept on talking, for Jessie's ears buzzed. Her head felt hollow, but throbbed, as if it were expanding and contracting. White dots filled her vision, then black dots, and she knew she was going to throw up, if she didn't faint first.

She left her seat so suddenly that the chair overturned, but she couldn't stop to put it upright. She had to leave the kitchen. She had to escape the heat and the talk. James Owen had got married!

Jessie wiped her mouth on her apron. Getting rid of her supper had relieved the pain in her stomach, but the hurt in her heart remained. She couldn't stop sobbing. Even though the news of James's betrothal to Ellen Bates had cut into her soul like a hot knife, knowing that he was free and somewhere in this country had given her hope. Jessie shuddered. She couldn't think of James anymore. No use crying over him.

She wiped her eyes and looked around. She'd been lucky when she left the kitchen. No one had been around. Just then, two men came out of the stable, laughing and talking. George and . . . Ned.

Ned! Ned wants me. James doesn't. Ned does. He'll take care of me, and I'll never have to think about James Owen again.

She ran toward Ned, forcing a smile. *He'll be happy. I've got to be happy.* "Ned," she called.

"Jessie?" He smiled at her, and left George, taking long strides to meet her. "What is it?"

Jessie halted and let Ned approach. *He says he loves me. He'll never leave me.* She grabbed her upper arm with the other hand and waited. *He'll make me happy.*

Ned smiled down at her, and she lifted her head. "I'll marry you," she said.

Ned's smile widened to a grin. "You mean it?"

"Yes." She waited, her fingers gripping her arm. She'd be safe with Ned.

Ned picked her up by the waist and swung her around. She clutched his shoulders to keep her balance.

"Jessie, I'm the happiest man in the world. We can get married at the next town." He put her on her feet.

Married? So soon? She hadn't thought beyond her acceptance of Ned's offer. *What if I get pregnant?* She thought of Hannah, and the physical discomfort she was going through in carrying her child. "I think we should wait until we get to Albuquerque to wed. We have so far to go. I don't want to be . . . like Hannah is." She watched disappointment mask Ned's eyes. Then he accepted her condition, though his shoulders sank a bit.

"I reckon you're right, honeybunch. I wouldn't want you to be burdened by—" He pressed his lips together, sighed, and nodded. "We'll wait."

Chapter 18

It took George a while longer than he'd bargained for to gentle all the horses to Angus's liking, so it was already far into December when the Bingham party got on its way again.

A few days into their renewed journey, Hannah asked Robert to stop the wagon so she could walk for a while.

"I can't stand the jostling for a minute more!" she exclaimed when Robert protested, so he put her off the wagon on the side of the trail and climbed up to the seat again.

"You're sure?" he asked her again.

"Yes!" She began to walk, or rather to lumber, beside the wagon. After a while, George rode up with a long stick that he offered her.

"Miss Hannah, this might make it easier to walk."

Hannah accepted the stick and laughed. "I reckon I make a comical sight."

George grinned. "Your sister worried you might fall and lay beside the track for hours before you could get up."

"You tell Heppie that I'm going to laugh at her when she's as round as a tub and can barely walk."

"What?" George's face went slack.

"She is bound to be in my state someday, and I'll tease her back. You tell her I said so."

George smiled, tipped his hat, and rode away toward the front of the wagons.

Although Hannah struggled to walk, being on her feet for a while was preferable to enduring the jarring motion of the wagon. She stopped to rest from time to time, leaning on the stick, and eventually the three wagons pulled ahead of her.

During one rest, Hannah rubbed the top of her belly after the baby inside kicked her. *Robert will love you*, she said to the child. *No matter who you are, he will provide for you and treat you as his own. You are my flesh, and that is good enough for him.*

She looked ahead, and saw one wagon pulling off the road. A figure descended from the wagon seat and came toward her. She stood and watched him for a while, a smile playing with her mouth, and then she started toward him, swinging the stick in time with her steps. He began to lope. She continued her clumsy gait. She could see his face, and he was grinning broadly. She stopped, and he broke into a run. She waited.

Robert skidded to a halt and stood in front of her, his breath coming in great heaves. "If you can't ride, I won't either," he gasped.

She put her hand on his bearded cheek and sighed. "You are impossible."

He took her hand and kissed it. "I'm impossibly in love with you, and I miss you."

She laughed. "I haven't been off that seat more than an hour."

"The longest hour of my life," he said, and enveloped her in his arms. "Come, walk with me."

She laughed again, shrugged out of his embrace, and dug her stick into the ground. "You came to walk with me!" She started toward the wagons.

He hustled to catch up and laid his hand on top of her belly. "Baby, you have the most obstinate mother in the world."

"Robert," she said, pushing his hand away, "don't do that. Somebody might see you."

He looked around, then up in the sky. "Who? That hawk circling up there?" He pointed. "I doubt it cares."

She giggled. "I care." She tripped a bit on a stone she couldn't see, and he steadied her.

"See how you need me around?" He put his face close to her stomach. "Mama needs me, little one."

She stopped and turned her glowing face toward him. "Yes, I need you. I think I've walked enough. Carry me to the wagon."

"It's just over there!"

She bent over, breathing heavily. "I know it, but I can't go any farther on my own."

"You're a caution, Hannah Fletcher," he said, and scooped her up. He carried her the five yards to the wagon, and helped her onto the seat, laughing all the time. He hauled himself up, took the lines in his hands, and looked at Hannah. "You are so very dear to me." He yelled at the mules and got them into motion.

Chapter 19

Jessie rode on the wagon seat beside Luke as they approached the next town on the trail. The weather had steadily grown colder, and she clasped a shawl around her shoulders. The sunbonnet she wore was for warmth as much as for shade, and she shivered as they crossed the stream that lay in their path.

Ahead of them, a long street meandered under the shadow of a stair-step mountain. They were the last wagon in the little train and the dust had been bothersome, so Jessie was glad they would soon stop for the evening. George had mentioned something about spending some of his cash on rooms in a hotel. Perhaps that was too wasteful of him, using his hard-earned money on hotel rooms. However, the closer they got to their destination, the more excited she grew at the thought of sleeping in a real bed. Of course, she would have to share it. Probably not only with Ma, but with her sisters, if the room only had one bed. The women would have one room, and the men another. She laughed at her mental picture of all of them jumbled together. The bed better be soft!

When Luke pulled up their horses at last, Jessie waited for the wagon to stop lurching, shook dust from her shawl, and climbed down from the seat. She pushed back her sunbonnet with one wrist and let the sunlight warm her hair. As she looked around, she saw a worn-looking, bearded man on a black mare across the street. He sat with his head bowed, his hat shadowing his face, and clutched a rope that extended back to the mounts of four other men.

"Luke," she said as her brother got down from the wagon. "Look at that. Those men are tied on their horses. Do you suppose they are outlaws?" She whispered the last word, cupping her mouth between her hands.

"Maybe," Luke said. "Do you figure that man is the sheriff?"

She shrugged her shoulders. "Why is he just sitting there?"

"He looks played out to me. Could be he's afraid he'll fall off his horse if he moves."

The man shifted in his saddle, and Jessie saw his face. She hugged herself, taking in a great gasp of air. Before she could help herself, she let it out in an explosive, "James!" Her hands flew to her mouth as he turned toward her. "James," she said his name again, calling out this time. "I thought I'd never see you again!" As a great rolling joy enveloped her, she bit her lip and started across the street.

She heard a strange, guttural cry, and realized it came from his mouth. Moisture slid down his cheeks. She watched him struggle, trying to catch his breath, and finally, he inhaled.

She reached his side, and he looked down at her from his seat atop the mare. After a moment, he extended his left hand, exhaled, took another breath, and held it a moment before he expelled it softly.

"Jessica."

Jessie looked at James's face for a moment. He looked as used up as though someone had hit him on the head with a shovel, then beaten him into the ground. Her gaze shifted, and she stared at the hand he held out to her, red and work roughened. The joy sank from her heart and drained from her body, leaving her cold and desolate. That hand had probably held Ellen Bates's hand. It had most certainly led his wife to their marriage bed. It was the hand of a married man, not the carefree James from her past.

"Jessica," James repeated, whispering. "Jessie Bingham."

Jessie watched James struggle. What was wrong with him? He should be happy, with a new wife and all his life in front of him. She looked around, fearing his wife would come out of one of the doors that lined the street. How could she bear to meet the girl named Amparo?

"Jessie," he said again, dropping his hand to his thigh. "Miss Jessie," he amended formally. "I left you in Virginia." He closed his eyes and shivered. "How did you get to Trinidad?"

Jessie started to speak, but broke off as a large man with a closely trimmed black moustache appeared in the doorway of the sheriff's office. She stared at the badge on the man's vest. She looked up at his face. His skin was brown, darker than the leather of his vest. *This man is the sheriff?* She wasn't sure she was interpreting what she saw correctly. What sort of place had brown-skinned people in authority?

The sheriff looked over James's train of captives. "What is this, young man?" he asked, his accent thick, nearly unintelligible. "Who are these *hombres*?"

"They're the men who escaped the hotel shootout, Sheriff. I tracked them down. Yonder is your escaped prisoner, Frank Blue." James motioned to one of the men. "I brung him back for justice," he said. Jessie hunched her shoulders at the flatness of his voice.

"I must thank you, *joven*." The sheriff removed his hat and held it over his heart. "Please receive my condolences on the loss of your wife."

Jessie furrowed her brow, unsure of what the sheriff had said in his heavily accented English. *Did I hear right? Did he say "loss of your wife?"* She put a hand to her abdomen, rubbing a bit at the lump of dread growing there. She looked from the sheriff to James.

He was nodding, his eyes glazed. He dismounted from the black mare with great caution, took careful steps toward the sheriff, and handed him the lead rope. A brown dog trotted up and thrust its nose into James's dangling hand. Next it sniffed at Jessie's skirt before it caught a new scent and followed it around the building.

"Can someone tend to my animals?" James asked the sheriff. "This mare and that there sorrel are mine, and the pack mule too." He rubbed his forehead, eyes closed. "They took the other three horses from the town."

"Sí, joven." The sheriff nodded, looking closely at James. "You have not slept, *no*?"

"No." James shook his head and tethered his horse. "If you need me, I'm going to see Philo about a room."

"*Está bien*," the sheriff said, and went to see to his prisoners.

"James," Jessie began. She stopped speaking to glance over him again. *He looks so tuckered out*, she thought. *He's worn down to a frazzle. Something mighty bad has happened to him.* Her stomach clenched.

As Jessie paused, James ducked under the reins to the other side of the horse, untied a worn satchel resting behind the cantle of his saddle, slid his rifle from the boot, and turned to face her.

She almost cried out at the pain in his eyes, but stopped herself, her insides churning around her own pain. She blurted out, "James, that brown-skinned man, that sheriff. Did he say something about your . . . wife? A loss?"

A look that terrified her flickered across his face, but was gone in an instant. "Yes, he did," James said. "She's dead, about a week past."

"Dead," Jessie echoed. Her heart quaked, and she felt herself shaking. She needed to say something, some word of condolence, of comfort, but the only thing she could think to say was, "How horrid!"

James looked away, out into the street. Jessie wondered what he was looking at so intently. Then he spoke in a hollow voice, stretching out the words as though to the rhythm of a slow heartbeat: "It . . . ain't . . . been . . . pleasurable."

Jessie heard footsteps behind her, a man clearing his throat.

Ned.

She had told Ned she would marry him.

Ned's hand came down on her shoulder. His grip felt like a trap snapping on her flesh.

"James," she said, her voice shaking, pitched low. Ned's hand on her shoulder must have weighed a hundred pounds. "James," she started again. "Do you remember Ned Heizer?"

James nodded his head one time. "Heizer." Once more, his voice had no inflection.

"My family is traveling to join my brother Max in New Mexico Territory." She hesitated, then took a steadying breath and said, "I have agreed to marry Mr. Heizer when we get to Albuquerque."

∽

James flung his "war bag" satchel onto his shoulder. "I reckon manners say I should stop and chat, but I need to catch up on my sleep. Y'all will excuse me?" He started across the street, feeling Heizer's eyes boring holes in his back.

Jessie Bingham. She was the last person he'd expected to see in Trinidad. She'd said her family was here too. That meant he had to talk to folks from his past, folks he'd left behind like ghosts. He wondered if Mr. Bingham was strong enough to horsewhip him for the shameful way he'd gone off and left Jessie behind in Virginia. Maybe a whipping would get rid of the agony that was consuming his soul.

"Amparo!" he whispered. Grief overcame him, and he stumbled a bit as he walked between the first and second wagons of the three parked in front of the hotel, and gained the wooden sidewalk. Planks of wood crisscrossed the gap where a glass window had been broken out of the frame.

A woman stood in the hotel doorway, peering out into the street. Her face lit up and she called out, "Jessie, Mr. Heizer, there you are. Come inside." She stepped back as James approached. Then her face changed and she gasped, "Oh my! You're James Owen! What has happened to you? You look wrung out."

"Hello, Miz Bingham," he mumbled. "I been on the trail without much sleep for most of a week."

"You poor thing! Come inside and find a seat. I'll send for a nice cup of tea to revive you."

He shook his head. "No, ma'am, I only require sleep. Excuse me." James pushed past Mrs. Bingham and strode into the room filled with mercantile goods, his legs quivering like jelly.

"Philo," James greeted the proprietor standing behind the counter. "I'll take a room today." He put his rifle on the planks and set his war bag on the floor.

"My boy!" The balding man looked startled. "I didn't think I'd ever see you again. Welcome, welcome."

James grimaced. Philo meant well, but this place would never hold a welcome for James Owen. He wanted to finish his business and get out of town, back to the clean air of the trail . . . to somewhere else. Anywhere else. Just so it wasn't Trinidad.

James touched his rifle barrel. The cold steel seemed to burn his fingers, and he pulled them back and made a fist instead. Maybe that would help him keep a rein on his feelings for a few moments more.

"I brought them four escapees back to the sheriff," he said at last. He shook his head. "I don't know which one of those jackals shot Amparo. Maybe a jury can figure it out." He put both hands flat on the counter and leaned on them, his arms shaking. "I know I swore an oath of vengeance against them all, but in the end, I couldn't kill 'em."

Philo nodded. "You did right, my boy."

"I know." James's voice was no more than a whisper. "She approved."

Philo raised an eyebrow. "She did?"

James tapped his chest over his heart. "Yes. I can feel it here."

Philo stood in silence for a moment, then said, "Take the last room on the right, end of the corridor." He clapped James on the shoulder. "I already filled up the front two rooms with those folks." He gestured toward Mrs. Bingham.

"Thank you, Philo. I'm falling-down weary."

"You look it, my boy." Philo leaned across the counter separating them and whispered in James's ear. "The room is yours as long as you need it. My compliments."

"Thank you." James tapped his rifle. "Will you mind this for me?"

"Of course, my boy."

James started toward the corridor, then looked back at Jessie. She was talking to her mother. Heizer was nowhere in sight.

Ned Heizer, he thought bitterly. *The turncoat.* He shook his head, wondering why it mattered to him who Jessie Bingham married.

℘

Jessie watched James cross the street. His gait reminded her of an old man, struggling for each step. Her thoughts whirled. She could feel Ned's breath on the back of her head, stirring her hair. *I'm going to marry Ned*, she reminded herself. *James means no more to me than a rock on the trail.* She swallowed, wondering why her mouth was so dry. *We'll be gone tomorrow, and James will go . . . wherever he's bound.*

Ned's grip on her shoulder hurt, and she turned to look at him. His face was set, jaws clamped so tightly that corded veins stood out in his neck. His breath rasped in his throat. She touched his clawed hand. "Ned?"

He expelled his breath in a short "Hah!" then loosened his fingers and dropped his hand. After a moment, he said in a hard voice, "I reckon I didn't figure to see him again."

I didn't either, Jessie thought. *I didn't want to. Now here he is, disturbing my peace.* She frowned. *He shouldn't be able to do that. I've settled on Ned. I'm going to marry him. James can go take his ragged grief and . . .* And what? Did she wish him ill? *No. No. That's mean spirited of me.*

Despite her disgust at letting her encounter with James turn her emotions inside out, Jessie knew her peace was disturbed. *Am I angry? Yes! Feeling betrayed? Yes.* Agreeing to marry Ned should have put an end to this way of thinking. But it hadn't. Hearing about James had been a misery. Seeing him had tilted her world off beam.

Jessie heard her mother calling them, and looked toward the hotel. "Ma wants us," she said. She turned back to Ned. "If you don't want to see . . . Maybe you should stay here."

Ned's face went grim. "I won't let the likes of James Owen keep me from going about my business."

Jessie's body recoiled at the vehemence in Ned's voice. She jerked up her chin and started across the road. She heard Ned coming along behind her, his limping walk accentuated by the quickness of his step. When she stopped at her mother's side, Ned passed her and entered the hotel. She gave her attention to her mother.

"Jessie," Mrs. Bingham said, clutching Jessie's arm. "Did you see him? It's James Owen!" She looked over her shoulder. "My, he looks done in. What do you reckon happened to him?"

Jessie's face burned. She licked her lips. What could she say to her mother? *"James Owen survived losing me, but looks like he's at death's door because he lost his wife?"* Anger stirred in her. She wasn't sure she could speak, but she finally found her voice and a few words. "His wife died."

Mrs. Bingham's eyes widened. "What?"

Jessie shrugged her shoulders. "You heard me, Ma. She died. The Mexican girl he married."

"Oh my! Oh my!" Mrs. Bingham seemed incapable of saying anything else. She squeezed her eyes shut and said, "So many people dying!"

"Ma!"

"How did it happen?"

"He didn't tell me. I heard him say to the sheriff that he'd brought back an escaped prisoner and men from a shootout here at the hotel." She gestured at the wood covering the window. "That must be why the glass is gone."

"That sounds real bad." Mrs. Bingham crossed her arms as though she were hugging herself. "Real bad." She rocked backward and forward for a while, and then said, "They weren't married long."

"Long enough that he mourns her."

"Jessica!"

The reprimand in her mother's voice snapped Jessie to attention, her back stiff.

Mrs. Bingham took a few quick breaths, her nostrils flaring. "I know you was hurt when James left. I reckon he was hurt too. That old reprobate Rod Owen had a lot to do with that, and James was just a boy. He's been a lone man out here, never thinking to see you again. Don't begrudge him a bit of happiness because it didn't include you."

Jessie didn't reply. Ma had had the last word, and Jessie felt sick at her own ill will. *What's wrong with me?* she asked. *Can't I leave it be?* She wished she could, and suddenly knew that the thing she wanted most to do in the world was to go and take James Owen into her arms and comfort him.

ଈୠ

Robert came out of the hallway, passing a young bearded man on his way down the corridor. He seemed familiar, but his face bore such a look of anguish that Robert didn't stop him to strike up a conversation. Instead, he approached the proprietor. "Nice rooms," he said. "They'll do us fine."

"I'm glad you like them," the owner said.

"Say, that man." Robert hitched his head toward the hall. "I think I might be acquainted with him. Do you know his name?"

"That's my young friend, James Owen."

Robert nodded and smiled.

"Ah, I see the name rings a bell with you. From your manner of speaking, I believe you come from the same part of the country."

"Yes, we do. The Shenandoah Valley of Virginia. I'm a bit older than James, but we associated a fair amount."

"I knew it! I just knew it." Philo slapped his hand on the counter with a thud. An answering thud echoed from the hall, and he swung his head toward the sound. "I thought I heard something drop. Hold on. I'm coming back for some talk. I like to get to know my customers."

Robert nodded once more and looked around the room as Philo moved toward the corridor. Mrs. Bingham and Miss Jessie stood near the door, their conversation animated. Luke came out of the hall and went through the outside door. George followed a moment later. Philo came back, shaking his head.

"Your friend," he said. "He's had some real troublesome times of late. He and his new little bride was coming back from Santa Fe, intent on going home to his pa's place. We had a ruckus hereabouts, and the consequence of it all was the girl died of a gunshot. He's sure tore up about it. Wouldn't even use the cemetery to bury her." Philo expelled a gust of air and shook his head again. "I don't know if you saw them killers he tracked down and brought back to the sheriff. Bad *hombres*. That word, *hombres*, means 'men,' you know."

"I didn't." Robert felt his mouth quirk. Now he knew why James looked so bad. Losing his wife? He'd almost lost Hannah. Maybe tomorrow he could say a comforting word to James, give his condolences.

"He and I had conversation during the ruckus. He has mighty strong feelings for that girl. It's so sad to see him in this state."

"Why did you use that word, hombres?" Robert asked.

"Half our town is Mexican, including the sheriff, and I reckon I picked up a bit of their lingo in the natural course of life. You'll encounter a lot of Mexicans in this country. They owned it before we won the war with Mexico in '48. That was my war." Philo shrugged and wiped his nose with a knuckle. "But I forget myself. Is there anything I can do for you? Some comfort I've forgotten?"

Robert waved his hand negatively as he pushed himself off from where he'd been leaning against the counter. "No. I wanted to see if it truly was James Owen. Thank you for enlightening me."

Philo spread his hands. "No charge." He craned his neck toward the hallway. "I hope he'll get some sleep."

ဆ

Jessie stood not far from the counter, her cheeks burning. She shivered as though she had a fever. If the dark-skinned sheriff was Mexican, that meant James's Mexican wife had been dark skinned too.

ဆ

The memories that welled up as James walked down the corridor toward his room clogged his throat with nausea. Only a week past he had come to consciousness in the storeroom of this very hotel, finding himself bound and gagged.

Was that faint brown spot on the floor of the hallway the remnant of Amparo's blood? She had lain there with a grievous wound, the crimson life force staining her white blouse. *No!* his heart cried, riven with pain. *Not my Amparo!*

James stepped across the spot, stumbled, and fell to one knee, dropping his war bag. He gripped the nearest doorjamb and scrabbled his way to his feet.

Oh dear God in Heaven! This doorway led to the room where he had found his wife tied up, huddling on the bed in the dark. She was terror stricken and in pain from a beating she'd received at the hands of Frank Blue, whose cronies had invaded the hotel after they broke Frank out of the town's makeshift jail.

James untied Amparo, comforted her, and led her from the room into the dark hallway. They came so close to escaping from the dreadful experience of the sheriff's siege in which they'd been caught.

We only stopped in Trinidad to buy supplies, he thought. *If only them four men hadn't picked that same time to make their break for freedom!*

Memory crowded upon memory. Men hustling down the corridor toward the back door. The sound of the errant pistol shot that still rang in his ears. Amparo going limp in his arms. The lamp Philo had brought at his call. The wrenching sight of his wife's blood. Her final, whispered version of his name as she died: "Chemes."

James covered his face with his hands and fled down the hall, bouncing against the wall in his blind flight. He bumped against the back door before he uncovered his face, found and turned the doorknob of the last room, and entered it: a room of which he had no memories to harrow up his soul.

James flung off his hat, unslung his revolver, sank onto a cot, and wrenched off his dusty boots. Philo knocked on the door, calling, "Here's your bag, my boy."

James said, "I'm obliged. Please leave it outside the door." He couldn't bear to see the man's face.

"Do you want a candle?" the proprietor asked through the door.

"No. I want rest." His voice sounded gritty in his ears, but he repented of his brusqueness and went to the door to acknowledge Philo's kindness.

With the bag in the room, James shucked his clothes and left them in a heap. He turned down the blankets and lay on a bed for the first time in many weeks.

He could not sleep. His arms were empty. His body yearned for the gentle young woman who had been his wife in the last bed he had occupied, at the Inn of La Fonda in Santa Fe. That was the site of their *noche de bodas*, the real wedding night he had proclaimed once he acknowledged his love for Amparo.

"Oh my sweet girl," he groaned, his mind in torment. "I can't love you less because you died."

Thinking the cot was too soft since he'd become accustomed to sleeping on the hard ground, he tried pulling the blankets from the bed and wrapping them around himself on the wooden floor. Then the makeshift bedroll reminded him of the blankets and quilts he had shared with Amparo as they journeyed on the trail back toward his father's home. James shook with fatigue, but his mind would not let his body rest.

At length, he sat up, came to his knees against the side frame of the bed, bowed his head, and cried to heaven, "Oh God! Oh God, my ma says you love all your children. If you love me, let me have peace. Let me have rest!" He sobbed against his arms folded on the bed. "Dear God, I love her. She is my own soul. God in Heaven, when I die, let me be with my Amparo again."

His sobs gradually quieted, and he crawled onto the bed again, his body shaking with exhaustion.

Chapter 20

After the Bingham party ate dinner, Heppie kissed George good night and retired to the women's room with her mother and sisters. Giddy happiness surrounded her. Tonight she would sleep in a bed! She had to share it, but wonder of wonders, the room contained *two* beds, so she and Hannah would share the one shoved under the window, and Ma and Jessie would take the one by the door.

I wish it could be George instead of Hannah, she thought. Even in St. Louis, they hadn't shared a bed. They had lain together only on the trail, in blankets spread on top of rocks, small plants, and other discomfiting items on the cold, hard ground. The wide open sky had been their roof and the far horizons their walls.

Even though their privacy had been scant, George had not stinted in his matrimonial duties. Heppie wondered if a bedstead and four walls would make any difference in their lovemaking. *If I had my own house, I could yell all I wanted.* She smiled, unbuttoning her blouse. Being with George was almost always pleasurable, and that included wanting to yell out when he— *Well, not tonight*, she told herself. She asked aloud, "Hannah, which side of the bed do you want?"

"I think I need the outside," Hannah said. "This babe is taking up a lot of room, and I'm likely to use the chamber pot. You don't want me climbing over you to get to it."

Heppie laughed. "No, I surely do not."

Hannah patted her stomach, then winced.

"What ails you?"

"The child kicked me."

Heppie finished undressing and put on her nightgown. "Does it do that often?"

"Kick? Often enough. Hard too." She pressed her lips together and clasped her stomach. "I might have a bruise later. The little one is active tonight."

Heppie got under the covers and slid over to the wall side of the bed.

Hannah dropped her skirt and petticoats, revealing the extent of her stomach. It jutted out from her body, stretching against the fabric of her pantaloons.

"Oh my," Heppie said as Hannah's abdomen seemed to change shape. A knob stuck out, then receded. "What on earth?"

"That was probably a foot. Or maybe an elbow," Hannah said, grunting as she lay down. "I may not sleep well tonight."

"Will you let me feel your belly?" Heppie whispered.

Hannah sighed. After a moment, she said, "I reckon you won't quit asking until I let you. Give me your hand."

Heppie stuck it out and Hannah guided it to an area of activity. The baby rolled and flung out its appendages under Heppie's palm. "It's alive inside you."

Hannah sounded irritated as she answered, "Of course it is. Get some sense, Heppie."

"I never dreamed a baby would feel like that."

"You're only getting the half of it. It kicks inside too."

Heppie took back her hand and lay in silence for a long time. Was Hannah annoyed because she had asked to feel the baby? Did her anger come from not knowing if this was Robert's baby or that horrible man's? Perhaps all pregnant women got bothered, just from their condition. *I hope not! Life can be disagreeable enough, without feeling out of sorts all the time.*

"Hannah?"

"Um?"

"I hope you won't get riled at me for asking you something. I really want to know about it, and I don't want to ask Ma." She paused, and finally asked in a rush, "How did you know you were with child?"

Heppie listened to Hannah taking in air in short, sharp puffs. Maybe she wouldn't answer, given the circumstances. Maybe she didn't want to remember that time. *Maybe I shouldn't have asked*, she thought.

Just when Heppie was about to turn over and go to sleep without an answer, Hannah spoke. "I threw up a lot. My breasts swelled and hurt. When I was . . . violated, I worried that I might get pregnant. When I missed the monthly, I knew for sure I was." Hannah paused. After a while, her voice came again, barely audible. "I didn't have a chance to find someone to help me in St. Louis."

"Help you?" Heppie stopped breathing.

Hannah's voice sounded hoarse. "It crossed my mind to destroy the baby. I knew it was a terrible sin to think about that, Heppie. I couldn't help it."

"Oh Hannah!" Heppie's heart lurched. She wanted to vomit. How could her sister even think about getting rid of her baby? Maybe her mind wandered that way because she thought the child was the spawn of that monster?

"Working on that awful mending and sewing, I didn't have time or energy to find someone. I didn't know how to find someone. Before I could do anything, we left St. Louis." Hannah fell silent.

Heppie didn't want to say anything. She'd told George she would go west to take care of Hannah, and she hadn't even known the terrible times her sister had been going through. Shame ran through her body like a torrent of hot blood.

Hannah surprised her by continuing.

"I wondered what roots or weeds I could eat to be rid of the baby. But when Robert found out I was pregnant, he insisted that it's his baby. What if it is, Heppie? I couldn't kill my husband's child!" Her quiet breaths went on for a time. At last, she said, "He's almost convinced me to love it."

"Even if—"

"Even if it's not truly flesh of his flesh. Whatever it is, half of it comes from me. I must love at least that half, he says."

Heppie lay beside Hannah, partly ashamed that she had no such quandary in her life. She touched her swollen breasts. She cupped her belly. Despite her sister's tumultuous situation, she let joy leap into her heart.

Chapter 21

Robert looked around the Ratón Café. It was a light and airy place, with the morning sun shining in through clean windows. Red checked oilcloth covered several tables arranged in rows. He patted Hannah's hand, which was tucked into the crook of his arm. "Judging by the appearance of this place, the food should be nourishing, at the least."

Hannah smiled, and Robert's heart lurched at the brilliance of it. "Do you suppose they can put tables together for all of us?"

"I'll find out," he said, and letting loose of her hand, he went in search of someone to ask. Nearby, he found a middle-aged waitress, who wore a gingham checked apron that matched the tablecloths. She smiled, and he said, "Good morning. We have eight people coming for breakfast. Can we move a couple of tables together to seat all of us?"

"That's easy enough done," she replied, and went toward two large tables in the back of the room. "These will set up against each other, sir." She looked up at Robert. "Would you mind lending a hand?"

"I don't mind at all," he said, and helped arrange the tables and chairs until the waitress was satisfied.

"There now," she said, standing back to view the place settings. "There's room for ten, but I can take away the extra chairs on the ends."

"We might have nine people, so leave them be," he said. "Thank you for your help."

"My pleasure." The waitress turned at the creak of the front door opening. "Are these your people?"

Robert looked. "That's them." He beckoned to Mrs. Bingham and the others, and they all sat down.

When they had given their food orders, Robert stood up and spoke to the group.

"Most of you know James Owen is here in Trinidad."

Almost everyone nodded. Ned scowled.

"He's had some hard luck lately, but he used to be a neighbor." Robert paused to look at the faces around the table. He went on. "We should look out for him. I propose asking him to accompany us to Albuquerque."

Ned swore, and Heppie clicked her tongue at his indiscretion in mixed company. Robert held up a hand against the tumult of replies.

"He knows the trail from here to Santa Fe, so he'll be of use to us. He's also a good hunter, if I recollect rightly."

Mrs. Bingham said, "It's the Christian thing to do, to give him the comfort of our company."

"Does he want our company?" George asked, eying Ned.

"We'll have to ask him that." Robert looked down at Hannah, and up at the group again. "His wife died not long ago. We can at least offer him the chance of a new start in a new place."

"He'll be in the way," Ned muttered.

"He'll be an extra gun when we go through Indian country past Santa Fe," Robert replied. "Think on it, but don't take too long. When he comes to breakfast, I want to invite him to go with us."

After the food came, Robert polled the group. Almost everyone agreed readily. George looked at Ned again, but eventually nodded. Jessie whispered a reply that Robert chose to interpret as yes. Ned's objection was voted down. Robert grinned. He'd always liked James Owen, and the prospect of having him along for the rest of the journey warmed his soul.

∞

The next thing James knew, he awoke—ravenously hungry—to light filtering through the window, and he knew God had answered his petition for rest.

The knowing lifted his spirits, and when he had washed up, he sought out the proprietor. Philo moved a broom about the floor of his store.

"Philo, where can I get breakfast?"

"Good morning, my boy. The only decent place is the Ratón Café down the street. It's clean, and the grub's good. Go out the door and bear left. You can't miss it."

"Is that where the Binghams . . . where the folks who came in last night went to eat?"

Philo nodded. "They're heading to Albuquerque, they told me. Joining a relative, I hear. Now then, have you made plans?"

James scratched his cheek. His week-old beard itched. "I only want to find a place that has work for me to do. Hard work will help ease me, I reckon."

"What can you do?"

"Break horses. Work cattle. I'm a crack shot, rifle or pistol."

Philo resumed sweeping. "You ever think of becoming a lawman?"

"It hadn't crossed my mind."

"There are plenty of rough towns hereabouts. You could find work along those lines easy enough, my boy."

James's stomach growled. Loudly. He gave a rueful chuckle. "Thanks for the talk, Philo. I'd best find that café."

The man waved him out the door. James walked along the wooden planks that butted up to the storefronts, slowing slightly as he approached the café's sign. He tried to swallow, but his throat felt like sandpaper rasping together.

James, he told himself, *Mr. Bingham's in there, fixing to set you straight for hurting Jessie.* He came to a stop and put a hand against the clapboard wall next to him. He leaned on it, his head drooping, shoulders bent. *Maybe now she's got herself pledged to Heizer, her pa will go easy on me.* He raised his head and stared into the distance toward the stair-step mountain, but his eyes refused to focus. It would be hard to eat a meal comfortably with the Bingham family in the same room. *I reckon I owe them the courtesy of trying,* he thought.

James got himself under control and entered the café. Half the tables were occupied. Two others had been put together to accommodate the Bingham party. Two chairs at the long table remained empty. Mr. Bingham was nowhere in sight.

Upon seeing James, Mrs. Bingham stood up and beckoned to him. "Come over, you dear young man. Sit with us."

He moved in that direction and put his hand on the back of one of the empty chairs. "I don't want to intrude on your kin, Miz Bingham."

"It's no intrusion, James Owen. What would your mama say if I let you sit apart, all alone, when I was here to make you welcome?" She looked around the room and took her seat. "No, indeed! You just set yourself down."

James hesitated, confused that neither empty place had silverware or food at it. He said, "I don't want to take Mr. Bingham's seat."

Mrs. Bingham's face went from smiles to a pinched look and back to a forced cordiality in a matter of seconds. James waited, uneasy at not knowing the cause.

Mrs. Bingham looked down at her lap, then up at James. "Mr. Bingham is no longer with us," she said in a low tone. "We miss him a great deal, but must go forward, doing him honor with our courage in continuing on."

The bottom seemed to drop out of James's stomach. Joseph Bingham, dead?

"You must sit down, young man. You look quite overcome."

James pulled out the chair with shaking fingers and sat, surrounded by the oppression of death. Would he never be free of it? He looked up. "I'm very sorry to hear it. Last thing I knew, Mr. Bingham was getting better."

Jessie cleared her throat, and James realized too late that he had sat down beside her.

She said, "He sickened shortly after you left. It was a blow to us all." A rattlesnake dripped less venom than Jessie's voice.

Mrs. Bingham glared at Jessie, but jumped back into the conversation. "James, I want to reacquaint you with my family. We have added several members." She gestured to Robert and Hannah. "You may remember my eldest daughter, Hannah. This is her husband, Mr. Robert Fletcher."

Robert grinned. "James and I are acquainted."

"Rob," James said, nodding.

Hannah, who was clearly expecting a child in the near future, wore a scarf draped along the front of her dress, but it did not successfully hide a prominent bulge. She murmured, "Hello, Mr. Owen."

James nodded again, saying, "Miz Fletcher."

Mrs. Bingham continued her introductions by motioning to the young woman next to Hannah. "You may recall my second daughter, Hepzibah, twin to Hannah. She is the wife of Mr. George Heizer."

George's mouth tightened as he pressed his lips together, but he gave a slight wave of his hand in James's direction.

James nodded to George. Blood was thicker than water. The man would back his brother Ned to the grave.

Mrs. Bingham gestured to the gangly youngster seated to her right. "Possibly you remember Lucas, although he kept to himself when you were . . . calling at the house."

James craned his neck to see the boy and said, "Luke."

"I don't know if you remember Mr. Ned Heizer. Jessie has recently accepted his proposal of marriage."

James growled his acknowledgement, "Heizer," but didn't look at Ned. He didn't want to spoil his appetite, now that his stomach had returned to normal.

The waitress appeared at James's elbow and laid silverware, a cup, and a napkin before him. He gave her his order for eggs and a stack of pancakes. She poured him a cup of coffee, and he took an exploratory sip, surprised at the genuine aroma that arose from the blue enameled cup.

"I ain't had real coffee since, well, since the war." He brushed a drop of the hot liquid from his moustache. "It's been a long time," he said, and took another sip.

When the waitress had returned to the kitchen, Mrs. Bingham spoke again. "My son Maxwell left the Valley not long after you folks did. He established himself in a town in New Mexico Territory." She paused, fussing a bit with her food. "Some months ago we received a letter asking that my husband and family come to join him. He did not know his father had died."

James looked up from his coffee, but didn't reply.

"Life became hard to bear in the Valley. We worked to leave for some time, then matters were—" She stopped and looked fleetingly across the table at her daughter, Hannah, and took up her story again. "We left quite suddenly in our farm wagon, and have been taking on odd jobs as we traveled." She sighed and put her fingers to her forehead.

Since Mrs. Bingham seemed exhausted by the strain of her narration, Robert added, "I had a bit of trouble with the Yankees, and we thought it best for all of us to leave."

"You said you had one wagon?" James said. "I counted three when you drove into town. One of them has an odd setup with the team."

"Our luck changed in St. Louis," George said. "We worked jobs and earned enough cash to outfit ourselves." He shrugged. "That's my team with the odd rigging. I lost a horse on the prairie."

"That's lamentable," James replied. "Clever rigging, though. Does it work?"

"It does the job so far."

Robert leaned forward. "James, I spoke with the family before you arrived for breakfast. I understand you know the trail to Santa Fe and where to find game. We've all agreed . . ." He stopped, looked at Ned, then backtracked. "We voted to invite you to go to Albuquerque with us."

The waitress appeared, and James waited while she put his food on the table. He took a bite of eggs, put down his fork, and chewed.

After he swallowed, he said, "I can't see my way clear to go with you. I have a job waiting for me back yonder, some colts I promised to finish breaking."

George gave half a smile, his left eyebrow pointing toward the tin ceiling. "Would that horse-breaking job be for Angus Campbell?"

James rubbed his mouth in surprise, then smoothed down his moustache. "It would."

"I'm sorry to take bread out of your mouth, Owen. When we passed through, Mr. Campbell mentioned the colts, and I said I could do that task for him. The job pushed our schedule back some, but we hope with fair weather we'll reach Albuquerque without mishap."

"Did you finish up the job to his satisfaction? All the colts are gentled?"

"Yes," George said. "He was a pretty hard taskmaster, checking on me all the while I was working."

"Does he think ill of me?"

"Doesn't seem to. Mr. Campbell figured you were delayed by storms. He was glad the job is done and his wife has a saddle horse to ride."

James speared the stack of pancakes with his fork and cut into it with his knife. While he worked at the food, he considered. *I have nothing to show Pa to make up for laying into him. Ma has plenty to keep her busy, and I'm not bringing her new kin after all.* His stomach clamped down on the grief that arose momentarily, and he took a steadying breath to clear his head.

When he let out the air, he laid down his knife and said, "It appears I'm at liberty. I reckon I can go with you to Albuquerque."

&

"George," Hepzibah whispered when they had finished the meal, "I need to do a little shopping."

"Didn't you get your dress goods yesterday?" he asked, sliding her chair back from the table.

"Yes, but I discovered I need some other things."

"Like what?"

"Not here," she whispered, squirming a little under his gaze. "I'll show you in the store."

George accompanied her back down the boardwalk to the mercantile area of Philo's hotel. "What do you have such a pressing need for, Mrs. Heizer?"

"Flannel."

"Flannel?"

"And muslin."

"Flannel and muslin?"

"And maybe some linsey-woolsey."

"I cannot guess what you have in mind, Heppie."

"Clothes. Special, tiny clothes."

"No!" George looked shocked.

"You're going to be a father!"

"No!" repeated George, and fainted.

Chapter 22

When James left the café, a small brown man rose from the boardwalk across the street and came toward him. He was attired in loose white trousers and a tunic-like shirt, covered with a brown, everyday serape for warmth. When he came up to James, he took off his wide-brimmed straw hat and gave a slight bow. James stopped and nodded to the man.

"Señor, please, *venga conmigo*." He pointed down the street.

James hesitated, not sure what the man wanted. He tried a word or two of Spanish, knowing it was poorly spoken. "*Quiere habla* with me?" He tapped his mouth and hoped for the best.

The man cracked a huge smile and nodded.

"*Venga conmigo, por favor*." The man beckoned James to follow him.

"*No . . . hablo . . . bien*," James said, but the man only tugged on his sleeve, smiling and gesturing. "I go with you?" he asked.

"*Sí,* señor. *Queremos hablar con usted*." The man dropped James's sleeve to move both hands in quacking duck fashion.

"I'll come," James said. Somebody wanted to talk with him.

The man moved in front of James and led off toward the center part of town. Soon the bell tower of an adobe church came into view. A group of brown-skinned men were gathered in front of the church, watching his approach. A vague feeling of apprehension stirred in his belly, but it disappeared as beaming smiles appeared on the men's faces.

The sheriff was among the men, but he hung back, as though this wasn't his show. James nodded to him anyway.

"Sheriff."

He nodded back, most solemnly. "Señor Owen."

James recognized the priest who had come to give last rites to Amparo. The man gently pushed through the crowd and came to stand before James.

"Señor Owen," said the priest, "we praise you because you honored *una de la gente,* one of our people." His voice was hesitant around the vowels and consonants, but James understood his meaning. "We are talking much about your kindness to our little sister *en Cristo,* but we talk a very much lot of your bravery, your courage. You are Anglo, but you leave the town to capture the outlaw Anglo and his *amigos . . .* friends, I mean to say. You are a hero for us."

James shook his head. "She was my wife, my mujer. Church wed." He pointed toward the church.

"That is also a very brave thing, Señor Owen. In this town, Anglos do not marry our women. We praise you for your honor treatment to her."

James let out the breath he didn't remember holding. "You are fine people," he said, slowly, looking at all the faces turned toward him. "Good *henti*. Amparo teach me *mucho*." He felt a blush creeping up his face at the way he knew he was butchering the words, especially the one for "people." He put his hand on his heart and took in air. He continued, slowly, softly. "*Amo Amparo siempre*. I love Amparo forever."

"*Sabemos . . .*" The man stopped and began again. "We know you must soon travel, leave *nuestro pueblo*—our town—and we give you this *regalo*." The priest looked a question back at the sheriff.

The sheriff said, "Gift."

"Gift," the priest echoed.

The priest turned behind him, to a man who handed him a sack. He faced James and held it out to him.

"We have collect *moneda*, I mean, money, to help you, eh, travel to your home, to your people. In this way, we honor you. Please accept our offering to you."

James took the surprisingly hefty sack and stood silent for a time. He nodded and said, "Thank you. *Mucho gracias*." The kindness of the men built a large lump in his throat that kept him from swallowing for a time. He remained as though he were rooted in the road until he could clear it out. Then he said, "You are good *henti*."

At length, he turned and walked slowly back to the hotel, to the accompaniment of good wishes from the men. At least, that was what they sounded like to James, as he swiped at his eyes and cheeks to remove his tears.

SO

Philo stood in the hotel passageway when James arrived. He held up a finger, called out, "My boy!" and ducked into the storeroom door. James waited until the man reappeared with a large parcel in his hands.

"This is for you," Philo said. "The town council is giving you a token of peace. And their thanks, of course, for bringing back those runaways. I'm left to make the presentation. They were too cowardly to do it themselves, seeing as how you don't like them much." He shoved the package into James's hands.

Unsuccessfully juggling both items, James dropped the money sack, which thunked solidly onto the wooden floor. Several coins spilled out of the mouth of the sack, spinning erratically on the worn surface.

"I'm sorry, my boy. What's that you have there, a treasure trove?"

James knelt, put the package on the floor and started to pick up the coins. The irony of the situation struck him. He'd received a gift of money, given with sincere gratitude, and very likely offered at great cost, from the brown-skinned people of the town. Here was a backhanded peace offering from the white town fathers, probably given more through guilt than appreciation. He began to laugh, feeling a bubbling relief of his tension. Dropping the coins, he sprawled out against the corridor wall and threw back his head, banging it hard enough to bring tears to his eyes. He whooped, rubbing his hands up and down the stubble on his cheeks. "Six little beans!" he said, letting his hands fall into his lap.

Philo reached for his broom and swept up the errant coins. He knelt on the floor and put them into the sack. When he had finished, he sat back on his heels and waited. "Will you explain the joke for an old man with a slow brain?"

After several false starts and renewed guffaws, James regained his composure.

"Philo, it seems I am the hero of the day. This cash money is from the Mexicans, in honor of my kindness to my wife and my bravery at bringing back those ruffians. You give me a mystery package from the council to cool my rage against their town. Do you know what's in it?"

"Yes I do. Alton come by a while ago to pick through my goods." Philo tapped the package. "He found this in the storeroom, and asked me to wrap it up for you. It's a small tent the Army put on the market a few years ago, after the doings, and all." He slapped his knee. "He actually paid me money for it."

James straightened his face. The time for laughing had passed with Philo's mention of the war. "Alton's hustling me out of town, isn't he? I had breakfast with the Bingham family. They asked me to accompany them on their travels." He touched the parcel. "A tent will come in handy enough on the road. I don't know if we'll come upon snow or sunshine, but shelter can't hurt." He gave a little grimace, remembering that Amparo's name meant "shelter."

"So you're going with them." Philo found a leverage point on the wall and got to his feet. "Give thought to what I said about taking up a career as a lawman, my boy. I think you'd do well as a sheriff or town marshal or the like."

"The dog did half the work of capturing those men," James said. "Mayhap he can get elected." A grin creased his face. "Give me a hand up, Philo. I've got to make a list of provisions."

₧

When James had gathered the items on his list and paid Philo, he took the supplies to his room. The kindness of the Mexican people had brought him a thought that he should be kind and set his mother's mind at ease concerning his welfare. For that purpose, he had purchased a few sheets of writing paper and a pencil. These he brought out, and sitting at the small table, he began a letter to his mother.

"Dear Ma," he wrote, then put down the pencil. His head bent forward as his hands came up to hide his face. *Oh Ma! How do I say good-bye to you?*

He hadn't done it when he'd left home all those months ago. It pained him now that he'd likely caused Ma a deal of worry. He'd let his anger at Pa drive a wedge between him and his family, but when he acknowledged his love to Amparo, he pulled that wedge free, looking forward to taking her home with him. She was gone, and he now understood the heartache of not being able to say good-bye.

James bit his lip and took up the pencil. "I am well," he wrote, "although troublesome times have plagued me. I set off to dig out Uncle Jonathan's mine, but only made it as far north as Pueblo town. Ask Mr. Hilbrands for the particulars next time you go there for supplies.

"I traveled as far south as Santa Fe town, but arrived back here in the city of Trinidad, intending to return to the bosom of the family with my new wife. To our great misfortune, she met Death's grim fingers in this place.

"I own to having had good times, but they are presently overshadowed by the bad. I wager you won't see me again until time knocks the corners off my sorrow. Receive a kiss for yourself and my sisters, and an embrace for my brothers. Tell Pa I have learned much from his example.

"Your affectionate son, James Owen"

When he had folded the letter and addressed it, he left the hotel and put the note into the care of the sheriff, along with money to pay the next traveler north to deliver it.

Chapter 23

Although he had been invited to stow his gear and necessities among the wagons, James preferred to leave them on his mule. Not only were the wagons showing hard use, but the livestock—two teams of horses and one of mules—was wearing down. Surely George Heizer's team of three was under a handicap in the cut down harness. If he could spare the animals having to pull extra weight during the ascent ahead, he would do so. His grief also kept him apart from the other travelers, so he tied his mule and spare horse behind a wagon and rode alone, his coat collar turned up and hat pulled low over his ears in the cold wind.

This time when James climbed into Raton Pass, the dog trotting alongside his black horse, he felt empty, knowing Amparo's grave was ahead, knowing that unless some happenstance brought him this way again, he would soon see her final resting place for the last time. It wasn't likely he'd be back. His connection to his family had been cut by his leaving as surely as Amparo's life had been cut short by that bullet.

Robert rode up beside James in the late afternoon, on a mount with Union markings. James wondered how Robert had acquired it. *I'll ask him about it sometime*, he thought.

"Hey, James."

"Rob." He felt comfortable with Robert Fletcher. They'd crossed paths many times in Shenandoah County. There had been some memorable escapades. Boys had been boys.

Robert explained why he wasn't on his wagon box. "Luke's taking a turn driving the mules. That boy does like a challenge."

"Who's driving Mrs. Bingham's wagon?"

Robert turned, grinning. "Your old nemesis, Ned. He's trying to get in the good graces of my mother-in-law."

James frowned, rolling the new word around in his mouth. Finally he asked, "What's a nemesis?"

"That's a fancy word for an enemy."

"Huh," James retorted. "He was your enemy too. Not to mention George's. It's a wonder you never met in battle."

"God works in mysterious ways." Robert rode in silence for a moment, and then changed the subject. "Say, how many times have you been through this Pass?"

James counted off the occasions on his fingers. *Texas, down and back. Santa Fe . . . and chasing down Frank Blue and his lot.* "I reckon about six times, now. This will be my seventh trip over, if you count coming and going both."

Robert nodded. "That's quite a few for the amount of time you've been in the country. What's the most likely camping spot? We should set up in daylight, if that's possible." He looked around at the gathering clouds. "Looks like we're in for a storm."

"Yep. I reckon it's rain coming in. Not cold enough for snow." James remembered a meadow beyond Amparo's clearing that would hold the party, and his heartbeat quickened. "I'll ride ahead and see about a place I know."

"Good. Thanks." Robert nodded again and wheeled his horse.

James touched his spurs lightly to the flanks of the black mare. "Let's go take a look at that big meadow," he said to the dog, leaning forward to pat the horse on its neck. "It's close enough to . . . go visiting tonight."

A mile along the road, James slowed the horse to a walk. *Oh my sweet girl*, he thought, *you're lying all alone just around the bend. Thank God you got that warm cloak I bought you in Santa Fe.* Shudders swept through his body that had nothing to do with the cold wind that blew down the mountainside. He felt a strong impulse to guide the mare off the road and into the clearing ahead, but he resisted. *I can't stop now, but I'll come back tonight.*

The dog had no such control. It whined and crept off the trail, but James rode past it, and it crouched in the underbrush at the edge of the path, whimpering, until he whistled it back to his side.

Once he was past the turnoff to Amparo's gravesite, James put the horse into a lope, and they went on until a flat meadow opened out to his left. He turned into it and slowed again to a walk, circling the area to look for windfalls of dead branches. There was enough firewood for the party, but it would be a dry camp.

"It'll do for the night," he grunted. "Come on, dog. This should please Robert."

James turned his mare and went back to the wagons and reported.

"Good!" Robert said. "It doesn't matter about the water. We have enough in the barrels for tonight."

℠

James untied his animals from the tailgate of the wagon where he had tethered them, then rode back to the meadow and dismounted. He unsaddled the mare, removed the pack from his mule, and watered the animals from a canvas bucket before hobbling them in an area of good grass. James found his lantern, made sure it was full of kerosene, and set it to one side, ready for nightfall.

By then, the wagons had pulled into the meadow, and the travelers made camp, the men seeing to the livestock while the women brought in wood for cooking fires. Night overtook them just before they settled down to supper, and the men lit the lanterns. When supper was finished, the women gathered up the plates and utensils and started to clean them, using as little water as possible.

James told the dog to stay put, took his lantern, and walked out to the road. He knew the light would draw attention, but hoped any curious soul would think he was following nature's call. He headed down the road, anxiously watching for the break in the trees that indicated the path he sought. The night fooled him once: he thought a wide space between two trees was the turnoff, but soon retreated to the road and walked on. The second spot was the true path, and at last, he stood over the grave of his wife, holding the lamp in front of him.

"*Amparo*," he said, using the Spanish way she had said her name. "*Amparo, te amo para siempre.* I love you forever."

The lamp sputtered in the wind, and James shifted it a bit to shelter the flame. He sighed as grief poured into his veins, icy, but not numbing. A muscle throbbed in his jaw, and he unclenched his teeth.

"Amparo, I'm moving along, going to a new place called Albuquerque." James sighed and knelt on one knee at the head of the grave. "I'm going there with some folks I know. I reckon I won't come back this way to visit, but I will love you forever. Oh my girl, my sweet girl, I miss you sorely." His voice fell to a whisper. "I want to be with you when I die."

The mound of Amparo's grave had settled a bit more since James had last visited it. He rose and tidied the grave one last time, wishing he had a marker to place at the site. He said, "I don't even know how you spell '*Garcés*,' but you were 'Amparo Owen' when you died, and that's what matters."

A small explosive cough attracted his attention, and he turned toward the path from the road. A figure stood a few yards from the foot of Amparo's grave, and James held up the lamp to see who was there.

He groaned involuntarily. "Jess . . . Jessie!" he stammered, and took several steps in her direction. "You followed me. How long . . .?" Anger welled in his chest, and he stopped talking to keep from lashing harsh words at her.

Jessie let her hand fall from before her mouth. She looked stricken, but stood her ground. "A few minutes. Is this . . .?" She cleared her throat and began again. "This is your wife's resting place?"

James nodded. A clash of emotions made him weak—annoyance at being overheard in his deepest agony, relief that Ned Heizer was nowhere to be seen, and a very odd visceral reaction to the pain on Jessie Bingham's face—and he half staggered as he covered the rest of the distance to where the girl stood.

Jessie asked, "Her name was Amparo?" James watched the motion of her throat as she swallowed after speaking the unfamiliar name.

"It was." Why was Jessie biting her lip?

"You loved her? A Mexican girl?" Jessie's hands curled into fists that she brought up in front of her mouth.

James set down the lamp, then bending over it, fussed with it, giving himself time to find the right words, trying to quell his resentment. He never thought he'd have this conversation with Jessie. He never thought he'd see her again. Why was he so angry with her? He straightened up and said, "I loved her. I still do."

"A Mexican with black skin?" Jessie's face blanched, then began to redden.

James shook his head and his words spilled out in a rush. "Her skin wasn't black. It was brown. She put me in mind of a bay horse, with her black hair and—"

James broke off as Jessie flew at him and began to drum against his face and chest with her fists.

She cried out, "You left me. You said you loved me, but you left me behind. You chose Ellen Bates over me. When she threw you over you married a nigra!"

His anger flared. "Don't say that," he grunted as she struck him on the shoulder. He struggled to capture her fists, but she fought him hard, her voice choking on her vehement words. Finally he trapped her flailing arms at her sides. His body shook at holding onto a woman he had once loved. Her sobs cut into his heart, and the anger drained away as he realized he *still* cared for her. The insight rocked him. After so long a time, and in spite of her flinging such an ugly word at Amparo, he still loved Jessie Bingham.

"You said you loved me," she managed to get through her tight-clamped teeth.

"I did," he murmured, letting the vagueness of his answer hang in the air. Reason cried out that he should explain: he did say it, and he did love her then. He concentrated instead on trying not to betray how her closeness affected him now. How could this be happening? Amparo lay in her grave not two steps behind him. Jessie stood here, crying her eyes out. He barely could keep from pulling her into a tight embrace. How could a man care for two women at the same time?

He ached to tell Jessie the truth. As much as he loved Amparo, he loved her too. He opened his mouth, but he couldn't force out the words.

Nothing he said would matter.

Jessie had promised to marry Ned Heizer.

A clap of thunder made them both jump, and rain began to pelt them. Lightning blazed in the sky. "Get back to camp," James shouted over another roll of thunder. "Take the light." He held the lantern out to her.

Jessie looked at him with desolate eyes, accepted the lamp, and with a final sob, bolted toward the road. James turned to Amparo's grave, the sky lit by intermittent flashes of lightning.

Confusion swept over him. "Amparo," he whispered, hanging his head at his easy betrayal of his newly buried wife. He stood there, silent for a long time, gazing at the recently dug earth with its adornment of rocks. He could hold his silence no longer and yelled her name into the storm. "Amparo! Forgive me! Te amo! Te amo!" He spread his arms out wide, then sank to his knees and prostrated himself on the rocks of the grave, sobbing with grief and frustration that she was dead and he had been disloyal to her memory.

※

Jessie stumbled into camp, her skirt muddy and her eyes wild. As she passed the tarpaulin that sheltered the members of the group, her mother put out a hand to stop her.

"Jessie! You're sopping wet, girl. Where have you been?"

"Oh, Mama," she gasped, pulling her mother with her into the storm. "Oh, Mama, I've done something terrible."

"Terrible?" Mrs. Bingham exclaimed, slipping free of Jessie's grasp so she could yank her shawl up to cover her head. "Get in the wagon," she yelled over the din of the rain hitting the tarpaulin.

Jessie climbed up the spokes of the front wheel and put her hand down to help her mother ascend. The women ducked through the opening in the wagon cover. Jessie slumped against the goods piled on the floor of the vehicle.

"Tell me," Mrs. Bingham demanded. "What terrible thing did you do out there in the wind and the rain?"

Jessie was crying, tears choking her, but she managed to gulp out a few words at a time. "I followed James. He went to a grave. His wife's. He talked to her. Said her name. Oh, Mama!" She bent her head and hid her face in her hands.

"There, there. It was a bit indiscreet of you to follow him, but not terrible." Her mother patted Jessie's head.

"I beat on him. Hit him. Called her a name." Jessie snuffled. "I told Ned I would marry him."

"What?" Mrs. Bingham's hand stopped moving. "Not just now?"

Jessie shook her head. "In spite, in spite of all . . ." She couldn't seem to get her breath, so she raised her head and forced the sodden air deep into her lungs. "Mama, I still love James."

Mrs. Bingham said, "Well now. Mr. Ned Heizer will take that as ill news."

"Ned?" Jessie said in a low voice. "What of Ned?"

"You're to marry him, dearie."

"Oh. Yes." She paused to think. "No, I hate him!"

"What? You hate Ned? I'm confused, daughter."

"No, no, I hate James."

"Well now . . ." Mrs. Bingham began.

"Ned is reliable," Jessie said in a rush. "He's safe. He'll take care of me and won't leave me."

"Jessie girl," Mrs. Bingham said. "Hush." She sighed, stroking Jessie's hair. "Albuquerque's a long way off. You have time yet to sort it all out."

Chapter 24

James arose well before the sun to get himself together. Of all times of the day, he liked morning best. The hush and the soft air always drove away the demons of the night. As he tended to his animals, the twitter of the awakening birds soothed his soul, smoothing away the anguish of his encounter with Jessie. Last night's storm had left the air clean and crisp. The temperature had fallen, and the cold worked its way into his ungloved hands. James enjoyed seeing the mule's breath streaming out as it put its head down into the feedbag he held under its nose.

Soon, the rest of the travelers got up and began the day's work. Luke Bingham had a cook fire started by the time the four women had breakfast preparations underway. Ned fed the stock while Robert and George inspected the worn-down wagons. James walked over and joined the two men where they were looking at the loose iron rim of one wheel.

"Good morning," Robert said. George scowled, but nodded an acknowledgement of James's presence. "You figure that rim will stay on till we reach the next town?" Robert asked.

James ran his hand over the rim, wiggling it back and forth. "I don't reckon it will. You need to shim it until it's tight." He looked around the ground for a stick, and pulled his clasp knife from his pocket. As he worked with the wood, the other two men followed his example and whittled out several wedges that they shoved into the crevices.

"Nah," said James. "You need to space them out." He eased two or three of the wooden slivers out and gestured with his head, "Just lift up the wagon bed there a bit, and I'll put these in where they'll do the best job."

"The wagon jack's broke," George said, bending down to put his shoulder against the side of the wagon. "You take the front, Robert." The two men heaved together, and James turned the wheel, hammering the wooden shims into place.

"There. That ought to hold until you can get a blacksmith to tighten that tire. They should have one in the next town over the pass." James picked up another stick or two as the men let the wagon bed down. "Just the same, I'll whittle up a few more shims in case any of these work their way loose as we go along."

Robert wiped his hands on his trousers. "I'm pleased to have you along, James. You know a great deal more than I do." He tilted his head, gesturing toward the wagon. "The livery and the blacksmith took care of my vehicle problems back home, and clerking in the bank didn't fit me for all this outdoor work. I've learned plenty, but it's a comfort to have you along." He put out his hand, and when James extended his, he clasped it. "Thanks for coming with us."

James shrugged. "I don't have a home. Albuquerque is as good as any other place to light for a while."

George strode off to hitch up his team. Robert looked fidgety.

James asked, "What's bothering you, Rob?"

Robert took in some air. "You may have noticed my wife is carrying a child. The babe will be born soon. I'm not sure when. I reckon I'm wondering if the road through this pass is safe." He let out a short laugh. "That may seem foolish, but the thought of a runaway wagon makes my stomach hurt."

"You have dear ones to protect," James said, wishing his own stomach didn't ache as he thought of his loss. He no longer had anyone to protect.

Robert's voice shook a bit as he said, "Hannah means the world to me. And the babe." He paused, looking off into the distance. "I'm a mite anxious to see what we have. Whatever happens, I want to give Hannah and the baby a good life in a new land. A clean start."

"The road is good," James said, laying his hand on Robert's shoulder and squeezing it. "Steep in some places, but if we need to do it, we can chain logs on the back as extra brakes. Don't fret. We'll be fine."

James headed back to his animals, making sure he didn't cross paths with Jessie. After last night's experience, he thought avoiding her would be the best way to keep clear of any awkwardness.

Breakfast came and went, and the party got on the road, moving through the pass at a steady pace. James always took the forward position. He liked it there. Not only was there no dust, but he didn't have to talk to anyone, since the dog and the horse didn't make conversation. He could be alone with his thoughts.

The farther he got from Amparo's grave, the more he thought of her sweetness, her self-sacrifice, and her unconditional love for him. It was as though she had decided to love him from the moment he said he would marry her. Shame suffused his body as he recalled his intention to take her back to her home and abandon his vow of marriage. How could he have been so ignorant, so selfish? How could he know his marriage would last such a short time?

Grief hit him anew, grief so tangible that he rocked in the saddle from the blow. *Oh God*, he cried in his heart, *let me be with her again!* Fire seared through his limbs at the despairing thought of never being able to see Amparo again.

God, please, he prayed silently. *I love my dear little wife. How can I ever be happy on earth, if I can't have a mite of hope of having her by my side again? How can love end with death? Oh God, it don't! And it hurts so powerful much!*

Suddenly, he realized this love was like that his parents shared. Yes, Rod Owen was arrogant, overbearing, and brusque, and James would have fought him to a standstill if he had the chance, but Rod loved his Julia, and she loved him back. James recalled the exchanged glances, the occasional touches, the muffled laughter in the night. *How would Ma or Pa get along without the other?* The question had no answer.

At noon, James returned to the wagons and called a halt to rest the teams and get a bit of dinner. Soon the trail would dip downward, and they would be in New Mexico Territory. An ache started as he remembered all the joy and pleasure he had known with Amparo in that part of the land.

He dismounted and took care of the black mare. Then he went to the mule and dug around in the pack until he found the bean pot. He didn't bother with a fire, but stood by the mule as he spooned up and ate a few cold mouthfuls of beans. The dog had hunted down and killed his own lunch, and lay nearby, chewing on bones.

Back in the saddle, James made circles with his shoulders, loosening his clenched muscles, and put his spurs gently to the black's flanks. The wagons creaked behind him as they got underway.

"James," floated out to him, but he disregarded Jessie's call and continued to ride in front of the wagons. As she called his name again, he recognized the desperate tone of her voice. It was the same one he used when he called on God.

"Jessie," he muttered through clenched teeth, "I don't have room for you now." Shame flowed over him once more. "Maybe God don't have room for *me*," he said under his breath, and a guttural groan escaped his lips. He squeezed his eyes closed, and then opened them and turned the black mare back toward the wagons. The dog bounded up to James.

Jessie walked alongside the Bingham's old farm wagon, so James maneuvered the horse in a circle that brought him up beside her.

"You called me?" James strove mightily to keep a blank expression as Jessie halted beside his mount.

The dog put out his paw, and Jessie took it in her hand. She shook it, then peered up at James. Her face looked pinched and hollow. She took a deep breath and held it for a moment. Finally she spoke. "I'm sorry for what I called your wife."

James must have clenched the muscles of his legs, because the black danced sideways, almost tangling legs with the dog. James was obliged to bring the horse back beside Jessie before he spoke. "Six little beans! I got feelings I can't get shed of, Jessie. It pained me to hear you pin that name on somebody I hold so dear." He laid his free hand on his thigh and rubbed up and down its length, working out a cramp.

Jessie was silent for a moment. When she spoke again, her voice was so low and anguished that James had to lean forward to hear her. "I'm sorry. It was almighty rude of me. Can you forgive me? Forget what I said?" The dog perked its ears, came up to Jessie, and licked her hand for a long moment before it loped away down the trail.

James nodded acceptance of her apology, holding his emotions in tight rein. "Hush," he breathed to himself, put his spurs against the black's sides, and rode out to join the dog at the front of the company.

As the afternoon wore on, the trail began its descent out of the pass down onto the flats. James passed the point where he had stood with Amparo, gazing down over the plains of New Mexico, making plans to see his family again, to start a family of his own. He gritted his teeth and rode on, through juniper and stunted oak trees bordering the trail.

A small bird whirred out of a juniper bush and flew toward the east. It startled the black and caused the dog to bark after it, but James soothed his mount, patting and rubbing it on the neck. "Whoa, there. Easy, easy. *Cállate*, old dog. Quiet down!"

Soon James rode on a flat trail. A creek on the right burbled through rocks as it wound its way south.

I turned off about here.

James touched his forehead as though his head had begun aching. His thoughts continued about the hours he'd spent tracking the men who had killed his wife. He squeezed his eyes shut to blank them out. *Mule tails! Am I going to remember everything that happened to me all along this trail?* Some of the memories would be sweet, he considered. *Amparo made my life sweet. We were happy. She was a shelter place to me, just like her name means.* He sighed, remembering her playfulness in their camp on the prairie that lay spread out far before him. *Oh, Amparo*, he thought, feeling the hole in his soul that her absence left.

He realized that yes, he would remember every occurrence that had burned into his memory during their journeys together, every happening along the trail's twists and turns. As he covered the same miles again, he would remember it all, the apprehension, the joy, the guilt, the laughter, the struggle to communicate without a common language.

He clenched his fists in an attempt to get rid of the longing to touch her hair, the hunger to run his fingers through the black strands framing her little brown face. He closed his eyes and swallowed hard as remembrance of the feeling of her smooth skin beneath his hands swept over him. His body ached as he recalled the desire, the relief, the joy of being with her as a committed husband, rather than as a reluctant bridegroom.

"Oh God," he cried out to Heaven. "She's gone!" Unashamed, he wept in the middle of the trail, bereft at her loss. Without his Amparo, life had no purpose. He had nothing to do except take some folks to the end of their trek because they were people he knew.

Chapter 25

Early in the afternoon of the next day the travelers came into Raton and found the blacksmith shop. The burly smith took off the wheel with the loose rim and left the wagon jacked up while he began his work, saying it would take him all afternoon to tighten the tire, and they might as well park their vehicles on the flats by the creek overnight.

George and Robert drove the other two wagons out of town and, with Ned, began to make camp. James prepared his own campsite a little apart from the main one. It being too early to start dinner, the women pulled up seats and rested, after finding mending that could be done as they sat.

Jessie, who had decided to explore the town, got her mother's permission to go, if someone went with her, and set about persuading Luke to accompany her. "Come on, Lukie, you really want to see the sights, don't you?" she said, tilting her head to one side.

"Ain't no sights here, Sis," he muttered. "Just another little town on the road."

"Please," she said, looking up at her younger brother, who had grown a couple of inches since they'd left St. Louis.

"Ain't nothing else to do," he said, agreeing to join her in her ramble.

They set off down a road so dry that puffs of dust rose from each step they took.

"I hope Ma's planning to cook something filling for dinner," Luke said as they walked along. "My belly's fixin' to whine, it's been so long since I last ate."

Jessie gave him a little shove as they entered the main street. "You're always hungry, Luke."

"Am not."

"Are so."

"Only at meal times."

Jessie laughed. "All day long!" She looked sidelong at him. "Who was asking Ma this morning if she had any extra biscuits tucked away in the wagon?"

Luke made a face. "You heard me?"

"I have good ears."

"What you have are long ears, great big hanging donkey ears."

"Do not!"

"Do too."

"Do not."

"No, you don't," said James, passing them by with long strides. The dog followed behind, its tongue lolling out of its mouth.

Jessie took in a quick breath, feeling her body flush, and turned to Luke. "See? An impartial party disagrees with you."

"What's 'impartial' mean?"

Jessie stopped walking, waiting until James was out of earshot. Luke turned to her, folding his arms across his chest.

"Well?"

"'Impartial' describes someone who has no interest in a dispute or the parties involved. Judges are impartial." She continued softly, "James Owen is impartial." She watched him as he strode away.

Luke shrugged. "That may be. But your ears are still long."

He cuffed her gently on the arm, but Jessie's joy in the banter was gone. "Not now, Lukie," she said, and turned down a side street.

Luke followed, his stomach rumblings reaching Jessie's ears. Soon they found themselves in a narrow byway made up of connected whitewashed houses facing each other, with doors set flush to the street. When they had walked nearly to the next intersection, they saw an old, brown-skinned woman sitting in an open doorway. She wore a colorful shawl against the cold breeze that swept down the lane. Luke's stomach took that moment to complain. The woman looked up, grinned, and hailed them.

"*Jóvenes, vengan,*" she said, gesturing them to approach, and went back to what she had been doing, patting something white between her weathered brown hands.

Jessie put her hand on Luke's arm and clutched it tightly. At the same time, she drew him along toward the wrinkled woman, who wore her white hair in a braid wound around the top of her head. *That style's real pretty,* Jessie thought.

"*¿Tienen hambre?*" asked the woman, gesturing toward her mouth with her fingers close together.

Luke caught on right away. He mimicked her motion, saying, "Yes. I'm hungry." His stomach chose that moment to agree, loudly, and he hung his head. "Sorry!"

The woman laughed, and reached back into her home to lay down what she'd been working on. "*Tengo tortillas,*" she said, and brought her arm back, holding a plate covered with a cloth. She removed the cover, and revealed several round, flat, white patties, about six inches across. "Uuu eeet," she said in broken English, extending the plate toward the two, while making her eating movement with the other hand.

Luke grinned. "Thank you, ma'am," he said, and reached out to take one of the patties. "*Tengo tortillas?*" he asked, repeating the woman's words.

"Jes. Tortillas," she answered. "Ver, very good eeet."

Luke ripped off a piece of the tortilla and put it in his mouth. He chewed, and his face brightened. "It's good, Sis," he said. "Try one." He turned back to the woman, and speaking around his next mouthful, thanked her again.

Jessie bit her lip, took a tortilla, and popped a piece into her mouth. It was warm and tasted of corn and lard. She smiled. "It's like corn pone, only different," she said to Luke. "Thank you, ma'am." She put another piece into her mouth and bobbed her head at the woman.

"*No hay de que,*" the woman said, flipping her free hand above her shoulder in a self-deprecating gesture. "*Coman todos,*" she said, indicating the rest of the tortillas.

"Oh, we couldn't eat them all," Jessie exclaimed. "I haven't got any money to pay you." She turned to her brother. "Luke, do you have any coins?"

He shook his head as he ate another tortilla.

"Luke! We have to pay her."

"I don't reckon she wants money, Sis," he answered. "She's being nice."

"Ma'am, you're very kind," Jessie said, as the woman pressed another tortilla into her hands. She took it and tore pieces off, wondering why a brown woman would share her food with two strangers. White strangers.

When Luke had eaten his way through the plateful of tortillas, he thanked the woman another time and she laughed, her eyes narrowing into massed crinkles.

"Uuu good boy," she said, and patted Luke's hand. "Uuu good girl." She looked at Jessie. "*Vayan con Dios.*"

Jessie was quiet as she and Luke continued their exploration around the town. When they were nearly back to the wagons, she tugged on Luke's arm to stop him.

"Why did she feed us?" she asked him.

He shrugged. "There's no doubt she heard my gut rumbling. Likely she took pity on me. You were there, Sis, so she gave you food too." He grinned. "Just being polite, I reckon."

"But why did *she* feed *us?*" she asked again, emphasizing her words. "She as much as invited us into her home and gave us a meal. But she's a Mexican, and we're white."

"You worry on such things too much," Luke said, and turned away.

"Yes, I do," she muttered to herself, and immediately followed it with a thought: *Aren't Mexicans different from us?* She followed her brother back to camp, not sure she knew the answer anymore.

Chapter 26

During the next few days, Mrs. Bingham kept a close watch on Hannah. Robert had told her that his wife had been secluding herself in their wagon, hauling herself over the load to find bits and pieces of cloth and sack toweling and arranging a bed in an empty crate she'd insisted they not burn.

"She's nesting, just like a broody hen," Mrs. Bingham told him. "Her time is near, I reckon."

Robert drew his brows together. "What can I do to help?"

"Stay out of her way, Mr. Fletcher. Perhaps I need to sit on the seat tomorrow and see what she's about."

"I'll welcome your presence, ma'am," he said, sighing. "She's snappish with me."

Mrs. Bingham laughed. "I thought you'd be used to that by now. Hasn't she been off in her behavior during the whole journey?"

Robert blushed. He compressed his lips, and nodded his head positively. "Yes, up until lately. Then she . . ." His head motions went from side to side. "One night she . . ." His voice trailed off, and after a pause, he tried again. "Well, ma'am, matters between us got better. I'd have to say, they got much better." He nodded up and down once more.

Mrs. Bingham patted Robert on the arm and smiled. "I'll put my eye on her, my dear, and let you know what I think."

The next day, Mrs. Bingham sat on Robert's wagon seat, while Hannah fussed around in the bed, after her initial remonstrance against her mother's company went unheeded.

At the noon stop, Mrs. Bingham touched Robert on the arm and said, "She has only a few days left, Mr. Fletcher. If she complains of continuous pains, we'll need to pull up and make camp."

Robert let out a short gust of air. "Then the baby will come?"

"I figure so. See, she's carrying low now. Her time is near."

"Need I let her know?" Robert fidgeted with a thumbnail.

"I'll do you the service, if you don't mind."

"Please, go right ahead. I'd rather a woman tells her." He worried at the thumbnail with his teeth, and when he had got the rough edge torn off, he added, "I hear childbirth is mighty painful."

"It is that, Mr. Fletcher. Dangerous and painful. Ever since Mother Eve."

⁊

The company traveled on, striking southwest toward the town of Cimarron, where, a few days later, they crossed the river without incident. Having done so safely, James had no end of irritation when a day later the sorrel pitched him into the icy water as he crossed Rayado Creek.

"Damn horse," he muttered, along with all the other animal-related curses he could think of as he regained his feet and slogged through the water to the creek bank. The dog stood hunched down with stiff front legs, barking excitedly at him. Ned stood nearby, doubled over with laughter.

As Robert and George built a fire on the south side of the creek, Luke retrieved the sorrel, and asked if he could clean and reload James's rifle.

"I reckon," James sputtered, water coursing down his face from his wet hair. He reached to his side, loosened the thong holding his handgun in his holster, and gave it to Luke. "Thanks, Luke. Do my pistol too, will you?" he said, swiping water from his eyes.

Heppie brought James a blanket from his bedroll, which had made it safely across on the back of the mule. "Come to the fire," she said, holding out the blanket.

"Hang on to that a moment," James said. "Let me get my boots off. They're full of water."

He sat near the newborn fire to remove and dump his boots, then, shivering, took the blanket from Heppie.

Robert came up to him, but waited to speak until Heppie had moved away. "You need to strip off, dry your clothes," he said.

James shook his head. "I don't want to hold up the party while there's daylight."

"We'll take the time to let you dry out. Don't you have a tent packed away? You can use that to preserve your modesty."

"I'd forgot. It's in the bundle on the offside of the mule."

Robert unpacked and set up the tent while James huddled near the fire. When they had finished, he hustled in to take off his clothes. The men outside strung a rope line across the fire and hung his coat, shirt, and pants over it as he handed them out.

"Let's have your underclothes, too!" Robert demanded, thrusting his hand into the door of the tent. "If everything ain't bone dry in this weather, you'll take sick."

James, teeth chattering, complied, and Robert draped the underwear over the line. "Tell the ladies to stay away from the fire," Robert said to George.

George laughed. "What's the use of that? They've all seen a man's small clothes, one time or another. If not on a body, at the least, hanging on a line."

"These could use a good scrubbing with lye soap."

James stuck his head out of the tent flap, clasping the edges together, in time to see Jessie taking his underwear off the line.

"Rob, don't let her—Jessie! Don't you touch my things!"

"They want washing," she replied. "They reek something fierce. I have a crock of soap, and I'll use a little creek water to—"

At that point, Robert kept her from getting any more clothes off the line, but she remained in possession of James's undergarments.

"Jessie! Hang those back on the line," James yelled at her as she turned around to depart. "Six little beans! You remind me of Rida O'Connor."

Jessie spun around. "Who's that?"

"The blacksmith's little girl in Leones. She stole my clothes when I was—" James stopped short, remembering the occasion had been his marriage day. Probably not the best thing to bring up with Jessie Bingham. "Never you mind. Leave me be." He pulled his head into the tent and sat on the ground, wrapped in the blanket.

The next thing he heard was Ned's angry voice. "What are you doing?"

Jessie replied, "A little laundry."

"His laundry. You don't do mine."

"You never asked."

"It's not fitting!"

"What, washing a few things?"

"He didn't ask you to."

"Humph."

James could imagine Jessie shrugging her shoulders and turning her head away from Ned. That should have ended the quarrel, but Ned pressed on.

"He didn't ask, and you shouldn't have offered. You're spoken for." Clothes rustled. Jessie's skirts. Was Heizer fool enough to lay hands on her?

James almost got up, but reflected that he was not in a suitable state to go rescuing young women from their folly.

"Ned Heizer, get away from me." Jessie's voice was low, carrying a threat that a thinking man should take heed of.

After a long pause, Ned said, "Stay away from him, Jessie. He treated you poorly."

Looks like everyone shares that opinion of me. James waited for Jessie to counter Ned's statement.

When she did speak, her voice was low, but had a somber tone to it as she agreed, "Yes, he did."

Ned made a sound like wind rushing through aspen leaves, but he didn't say anything.

Jessie spoke again. "I begun this. Let me finish, Ned."

"Keep clear of him in future," he said. Ned's boots crunched on the gravel of the creek bank as he moved off.

James heard Jessie sigh. He pulled the newly learn word out of his mind. *Nemesis.*

Later, when the clothes were dry, Robert brought them to James, including the stolen—and washed—undergarments. "It's a pity you have to put this dirty shirt on over such sweet-smelling small clothes," he said. "Maybe I shouldn't have stopped the young lady." He turned away.

James glared at Robert's departing back. "They'll be dirty enough when the week's out," he said, and began to dress.

₧

Robert kept his eye on Hannah during the forced halt. She couldn't seem to light and sit down, but roamed around the wagons, twisting a loose rope end here, patting a horse there. Sure she would tire herself out, he approached her.

"Hannah love. You must sit down and rest. We'll be on our way soon, and you'll miss your chance." He caught her hands, gently holding them still. "Come over here. Sit yourself down."

"I'm restless," she said, glancing around the temporary camp. "Ma said I'm about due to, well, she said, my time's nearly up for, you know . . ." Her voice trailed off as she finally looked at Robert.

"She told me the baby would come soon," he said.

Hannah's mouth twisted. "I'm frightened," she whispered.

Robert drew her toward him. "Don't you be," he said to sooth her. "I'm here. Whatever happens, I love you. I love our babe."

"Even if . . ."

His firm statement cut her off. "No matter what happens." He tugged her toward a barrel.

"I've been having pain," she admitted when she had sat down.

Robert knelt beside her. "What kind of pain?"

"Cramping. Here." She laid her hand on her abdomen. "Oh!" She tensed up and moaned. "Like that one."

"Do they keep coming, love?"

"They have since morning."

"That long?"

"I didn't want to trouble you. They weren't much at first."

"But now?" Robert got to his feet.

"Now I reckon I'm troublesome."

"Mrs. Bingham," Robert called out. He caught George's eye. "Make camp. The baby is on its way!"

The mad scramble that Robert's words brought on would have been amusing to him, except that Hannah had doubled over, and her initial moan had turned to a keen that ripped through his heart.

James came striding up, a look of concern on his face. "Use the tent," he said, and was gone so fast that Robert doubted whether he had been there at all.

"Luke! Find our bedding and take it to Mr. Owen's tent," Robert barked. He didn't want to move Hannah while the pain was upon her, but he figured she should get settled into a private place for her laboring. James's tent seemed the ideal location.

"Heppie," Mrs. Bingham called. "I need your assistance. Jessie, set a kettle on the fire. We'll need wash water by and by."

Robert felt his innards quake at the sounds that came from Hannah's throat. She was counting on him to be strong for her. Could he do that? *Will I let her down at the last moment?* he wondered. *I've been saying I'll love the baby, even if that brute was its father. Can I actually manage it? Or did I say that only for Hannah's sake?* He let out a long sigh, just as Hannah straightened up, her face shiny with sweat. "Can you walk?" he asked.

"I don't know," she said, wiping her eyes. "I'll try."

Robert got her to her feet, his arms supporting her, and they took a few steps.

"Don't leave me," Hannah said in a throaty growl. "Ma will try to make you go. Stay with me! Uh!" She bent over, and Robert stopped walking her along, waiting for her pain to pass.

"I won't go," he said, rubbing her back in small circles.

"Lower," she grunted.

"Not out here," he replied. "Let's get you into the tent. I'll do whatever you say, once we're sheltered."

"I don't care," she moaned. "Rub lower!"

Robert looked around, shrugged his shoulders, and furtively moved his hand lower on his wife's back.

"Yeees," Hannah said on a long outward breath. Then she stood upright and asked, "Where's the tent? Get me to it."

Robert half stumbled, half walked with Hannah to the tent and through the open flap. Luke had brought the bedding—*blessed boy*—and arranged it on the ground.

Mrs. Bingham came through the tent door, Heppie in her wake. "Thank you, Mr. Fletcher," she said as Robert helped Hannah get situated on the quilt. "You can leave now."

"I'm staying," he said.

"But you can't," said Mrs. Bingham. "This is women's work."

"She told me to stay," Robert said.

"At least be useful. Help me take off her clothing." Mrs. Bingham looked over her shoulder. "Take off her shoes," she told Heppie, whose face had paled since she had come into the tent.

Robert began unbuttoning Hannah's blouse. Mrs. Bingham untied her skirt, and Heppie attacked her shoes. Between them, they removed her outer garments.

Hannah cried out. Mrs. Bingham felt her belly under her petticoat. "That's a hard cramp. Breathe, dear. You need air. There, that's right." She looked at Robert. "I need to take a look at her, Mr. Fletcher. Please turn your head." He gave half a smile, but acquiesced and looked away.

Mrs. Bingham lifted Hannah's petticoat and examined her. "You have a ways to go, dear, but you're doing fine." She covered Hannah with a blanket. "Keep breathing between the pains. I have to fetch some things from the wagon, but I'll return shortly. Heppie, come with me." The two women left the tent.

Robert stroked Hannah's hair. "What can I do to help?" he asked.

"Get behind and hold me up. Rub my shoulders," she gasped out in a small voice.

Robert raised her torso and sat behind her on the quilt, his legs extending on either side of her body. "Like this?" he whispered as he massaged her neck and shoulders.

"Oh yes," she said, then screamed and curled forward.

Robert ran his hands down Hannah's arms and touched her belly. "It's hard as rock, love. No wonder you're screaming." He rubbed her stomach.

"Oh, don't touch me, not now. Later," Hannah said, catching her breath and pushing his hands away. "It hurts so much." After a moment she leaned back against his chest, panting.

"It can't go on much longer," he murmured.

"Hours and hours," she said, bending forward and clutching at his hands.

In a few moments, Mrs. Bingham returned with Heppie and an armful of supplies. Hannah was in the throes of another pain, doubled forward. She caught her breath and screamed.

Heppie gagged. "Ma, I can't help you," she choked out as she fled the tent.

"Send Jessie," Mrs. Bingham flung over her shoulder. "There's no help for it. I need someone here," she grumbled to herself as she sat down and arranged the supplies.

"What can I do to assist, ma'am?" Robert asked.

"Now, you keep right where you are," Mrs. Bingham said, motioning him to stay put with her hands. "You're doing fine right there."

Robert chuckled. "You want me out of the way."

"Yes sir, I do," Mrs. Bingham said. "This here will always be woman's work." She turned her head and hollered out the door of the tent. "Jessie! Where are you, girl?"

଼ଠ

Jessie came reluctantly into the tent. Not only was Robert Fletcher in there, but Ma was likely to raise up Hannah's skirt, and that was a sight she wasn't prepared to gaze upon. *There's going to be blood. I know it!* Hannah was panting, and Jessie turned her head, ashamed of the revulsion that swept over her.

She had little concrete idea of how babies came into the world, except that it involved a woman's secret parts. She'd been too young to learn much when Luke came along. As far as the process for making a baby went, she'd seen the occasional dog and chicken matings, but gave little credence to the notion that

---

humans did the same thing as the lower animals. Ma's warnings about kissing boys had not prepared her with actual useful information about what came afterward between a man and a woman. Even James's persistent kisses, which had stirred her to the core, had done nothing to reveal the mystery. All she knew was that babies came after couples did something together that had to do with lust.

She'd visited the Owen farm, years ago, where she and Marie had spent a lazy afternoon lying on the side of a stack of hay as they chatted. When she heard loud whinnies and snorts coming from a small corral, she'd climbed up to the top of the hay to see what the commotion was about. She barely caught sight of a stallion mounting a mare when Marie pulled her back down the slippery stack, saying, "I forgot Pa was breeding the mares today. You don't want to see that."

"Don't I?" she asked.

"No. It'll spoil your wedding day, worrying about that big long thing coming at you." Teasing was one of Marie's great pleasures in life.

The size of the stallion's "thing" had been truly impressive, but Jessie hadn't thought much about it through the years. The only time she'd seen the result of such an encounter was when a pregnant cat had sped into the house through a carelessly opened door and given birth to its kittens behind the stove. She'd watched the cat's convulsive expulsions of slimy sacs, one by one, each followed by a barbaric eating of that kitten's protective coating. She shuddered at the remembrance. Surely a human birth was more, well, humane?

Jessie sat down to one side of Hannah. What did Ma want her to do? Was this baby going to have red hair and a grizzled, bearded chin, dripping tobacco juice? A feeling of dread settled on her. Would Hannah turn away from such a baby and let it languish from neglect? Surely Robert wouldn't allow that.

Jessie looked at Robert, tucked away behind Hannah, supporting her body with his own. *What's going through his mind? He's said over and over how this baby is his own, no matter what. Will he be able to follow through on his talk? I hope so. He's a good man. Hannah's been lucky to have him. Steadfast, that's what he is. Would James be steadfast, stand by me if I was in such a fix? No, I mean Ned. Would Ned do that?*

"Jessie, hold this towel." Mrs. Bingham's demand cut through Jessie's thoughts.

She took the piece of flour sack and let it dangle between her hands. Her sister was doubled over again, cupping her belly with white hands, gritting her teeth and grunting. *Is this why they call it labor? She's doing a lot of work.* Ma had her hands down by Hannah's private place, mopping at something. *Ah! That's blood!* Waves of nausea hammered at Jessie's body, threatening her consciousness, but she kept above the black pool by wrapping the cloth tightly around one hand and biting her lip.

What is Ma doing now? Jessie quit biting herself and craned her neck. It looked like Ma was holding a head, a tiny head covered with blood and a white gooey substance.

"Now push!" Ma said to Hannah.

Hannah took three quick breaths and bore down, her face turning from white to crimson with her effort. Jessie watched in amazement as Ma's hands suddenly contained not only the wee head, but a baby's body, followed by a long twisted cord that seemed still attached to Hannah's nether regions.

"I need more hands," Mrs. Bingham said in a grumbling voice. "Jessie, that towel!"

Jessie leaned forward and gave the cloth to Ma, who wiped up the blood on the baby's face, scooped something out of its mouth, and tapped it on the chest.

The infant let out a squall that filled the tent. It continued crying as Mrs. Bingham fired instructions at Robert and Jessie.

"The string, Mr. Fletcher. Here and here." Robert tied twine around the cord in two places, pulling it tight at Mrs. Bingham's direction. Then he picked up a pair of scissors.

"Now?"

"Yes, cut."

Jessie turned away, bile rising in her throat.

"Give me that blanket beside you, girl."

Jessie fought down the acrid gall and found the blanket.

Ma wrapped the child, swiping at its little face once again. She held out the bundle to Robert. "He is your true son, Mr. Fletcher. See how his hair grows?" She touched the infant's forehead tenderly. "Now Hannah, you have a bit more work to do."

A few moments later, the afterbirth came, and Ma started tidying up.

"Can I go, Ma?" Jessie asked, and without waiting for an answer, got up and flung herself through the tent flaps and into the sweet, cold air of the late afternoon.

Chapter 27

James looked up as Jessie stumbled out of the tent door, her face white and drawn. *What's amiss?* he wondered, and caught up to her in three strides. Hannah had stopped screaming, and he was sure he'd heard a baby cry. "Jessie?" he asked, touching her arm.

She shook him off, rushing toward a circle of trees, when she bent double and wretched. James dug out his handkerchief and pressed it into her hand. "Does your sister live?" he asked. "Is the babe well?"

"The blood," Jessie choked out. "It unnerves me." She paused to wretch again, and James held her arm to keep her from falling.

"All is well?"

She heaved, and vomit splattered the ground. After a moment, she spit out, "Do I look well?"

"With the birth, I mean." James stifled a chuckle at Jessie's heated tone. She looked pathetic, but he wasn't going to mention that fact. That was Ned's concern.

Jessie took a breath and mopped her mouth. "The boy is born. Hannah lives."

"Thank God," James said, just as the hand he'd been expecting clamped down on his shoulder.

"Turn her loose," Ned growled.

James did so, and Jessie staggered a step away. He turned to Ned, making his face into a bland mask.

"Why were you touching her?" Ned barked.

"She would have fallen," James answered. "A man doesn't like to see that happen."

"That's my lookout."

"You weren't looking out for her." James felt a churning in his gut. *Nemesis!*

"You got in the way."

"You weren't around."

At that jibe, Ned swung, hitting James on the cheekbone and knocking him backward. "Leave her be!" he shouted. "She's my girl."

James shook his head to clear away the ringing. He'd known Ned was spoiling for a fight. He shouldn't have pushed him toward it, even accidentally. But Ned had thrown the first punch, and *hush!* James was ready to oblige him. He put his head down and charged, butting Ned in the stomach. They both went down, rolling on the ground, fists flying. Jessie shrieked.

৪০

Mrs. Bingham laughed, a great trilling sound that filled Hannah's senses with relief. "All our worry was for naught, Hannah. He's a splendid boy, the spitting image of his papa." She gathered up the soiled cloths. "You had a short delivery, for a first-time birth," she added. "That's another blessing to give thanks for. God's compensation, I'll warrant." She got to her feet and went to the doorway. "What's that row?" she asked, and turned back with a shake of her finger and a word of command, "Rest!"

"Robert!" Hannah exclaimed as her mother left the tent. "Show me the baby."

He touched the child on the tip of its nose, then handed the bundle to Hannah, who took the infant into her arms. "Oh!" she said, wonder filling her breast. "Oh, he's so tiny." She looked at his hands, made sure five fingers sprouted on each one; inspected his feet, his legs, his obviously male parts. "He's a boy." She glanced at Robert, blinking away tears.

"Yes."

"And look at his hair. There's so much of it. Just like yours. Oh, Robert! He does look like you."

Robert stroked the baby's forehead where the hair grew in a point like his own widow's peak. He nuzzled Hannah's neck and whispered in her ear. "I am the father of our babe. There is no doubt."

Hannah looked sideways at him and nodded, joy leaping in her soul. She turned her attention to the wiggling infant. "What shall I do with this howling boy?" she asked. The feelings of her heart expanded to enclose the three of them in a soft cocoon of love. Then her body shook as great peals of relieved laughter came from her throat.

"Feed him," Robert said, and chuckled. "You know he's hungry."

"Poacher!" Ned shouted, his fists flailing at James.

"Turncoat!" James replied, catching Ned on the ear.

"Get up!" Jessie screamed. "Stop it this minute!"

James got to his feet, dragging Ned up from the ground. He punched him again, and Ned reeled backward. James followed, ready to pound him with another well-placed fist, when Mrs. Bingham shoved between them. Her stiff arm stopped James in his tracks.

He pawed the dust out of his eyes and watched Ned come to a halt, his face wary.

"You men!" Mrs. Bingham's voice sounded like a clap of thunder. "Acting like little boys, rolling in the dust, fighting each other like heathens! You will stop it this instant. There's a baby to think about, and y'all are causing nothing but turmoil."

James winced at the vitriolic burn of her words. Of course she was right. He hadn't meant to lose his temper. There was just something about Ned that rubbed his fur the wrong way.

"Shake hands, now. There'll be no more antics like these," Mrs. Bingham scolded.

James held out his hand. Ned briefly touched it, his eyes challenging James against gripping it in amity. James shrugged and turned away. *Ned's bad humor is Jessie's concern now, not mine*, he reflected as he walked toward his horses. Even so, his stomach churned at the thought of Jessie's having to placate an angry man.

"Do you feel anything growing?" George whispered, his hand caressing Heppie's stomach. He lay on his side in their bed under the wagon, propping himself up on one elbow.

"I just feel sick," she said, snuggling beside him. "Not now, but sometimes."

"Did your sister feel sick?"

"Oh, all the time," she answered. "She tried to hide it, but she did, and she had this . . . smell. I hope I don't get like that."

"We're all smelly," he said, kissing her ear. "We can't help it much."

"George! Do I smell?"

He chuckled. "Don't I?"

"Well, yes, now that you speak of it."

"Think of this. Every day we travel, we get closer to a bathtub. And regular weekly baths." He kissed her nose.

"That tickles."

"Does this tickle?"

She took a quick breath.

"How about this?"

She moaned. "I don't think . . . you're supposed . . . to do that!"

"Why not?"

"I don't want to faint."

George drew back. "You're cruel to bring that to mind, Heppie. I didn't faint on purpose!"

Heppie let out her breath in a short puff. "I wasn't thinking of that, George, but you were such a sight, toppling over like a great felled tree. Good thing you landed on the dry goods." She giggled.

George lay back. Heppie cuddled up to him.

"You stopped," she whispered.

"Yep."

"Don't."

He said nothing.

She poked his chest. "George."

He turned his head. "What?"

"Don't stop."

George sighed. "I can't do nothing now, Heppie."

"You can't?"

"Nothing takes the air out of a man's sails like knowing his wife is making fun of him."

"I wasn't, George."

"Sounded like it."

"I wasn't even thinking about that time. When you tickled me like that, it took my breath away." She curled closer to him, and her voice sank to a murmur. "I felt like I was up in the trees, floating, kinda hanging there, breathless and all quivering and losing control of myself. George, don't stop. Even if I faint, don't stop taking me up to that place in the trees, where—"

He turned and kissed her, impeding the movement of her lips. After a moment, he whispered, "You like that?"

"More. Do more."

George chuckled. "You won't talk about fainting?"

"Don't stop."

"I don't reckon I will."

Chapter 28

Several days later, James was leading the Bingham party down the road when, ahead, he saw a train of wagons winding its way along the trail toward him.

"That's odd," he said aloud to the dog. "We ain't met other travelers for a long while."

James looked to the south. Off in the distance a hawk soared in an afternoon updraft, looking for a meal. To the north, snow-covered peaks loomed on the horizon.

When he looked west again, James could see that the party coming toward them wasn't making any progress. A few minutes later, he realized that one of the wagons in the band lay toppled on its side. He turned his horse and bellowed toward the wagons. "Robert, George, Ned! Come quick!" He put the black mare into a canter down the road.

As he drew near, James saw several men working to pull the wagon upright. They had unhitched the team, tied ropes to the side of the wagon, and were using the animals to haul on the ropes to get it back on its wheels. Although the animals strained at the lines, the vehicle didn't budge.

James rode on to offer his assistance. He could see several women standing to the side, small children hanging on their skirts or aprons. Older children stood around in knots or helped with the upset wagon. Arriving in earshot, he heard screams coming from the vicinity of the wagon. Someone was caught underneath. James reined in the mare, got down, and led the horse to where the animals were sweating and straining to right the wagon.

"Add my horse," he said to one of the men. "She's strong."

"Thank you. We're obliged," a man said, and took over the task. James strode around to the other side of the wreck to see if he could help in the lifting effort. A woman knelt there, tears streaming down her cheeks as she crooned to the young woman caught under the wagon.

"Laurie Sue," she said over and over. "Laurie Sue, we'll get you out. Please, don't scream, Laurie Sue. Think of Zion. Praise God for your blessings. Laurie Sue, don't cry."

James found a place among three other men and put his shoulder under the wagon box. "Push," cried a man, and James heaved with all his strength. He was aware that Robert and George had joined them. They all gave a second mighty heave, and the wagon tilted skyward. With a great rattle and a cloud of dust, it settled back on its wheels.

Laurie Sue had stopped screaming, and the woman on her knees wailed, "She's gone. Lord have mercy, she's gone to Jesus."

James bent to raise the woman up, but she struggled until another man came and took her in his arms. "Eliza, hush. Hush your crying, honey. We'll join her to us in Zion." Tears muddied the man's cheeks.

What does he mean, "join her to us?" James wondered. He retrieved his horse, whistled for the dog, and would have mounted and left, but another man hailed him.

"Stranger, wait up, there." A tall thin man with high cheekbones and a wan smile approached James. His black hair was worn slicked back from his forehead, and he smoothed it down before he put on his hat. He offered James his hand. "I'm Jeffrey Julander, leader of this company. We're obliged for your help, and that of your friends." He nodded toward Robert and the Heizer brothers, who had come over to stand near James. "Will you stay and partake of supper with us tonight? It appears we're obliged to camp until we can have a service for our sister and bury her."

"My condolences about your sister." James blew out his breath, and turned to the other men of his party. "What do you say, Robert? Are we ready to camp? We've come a goodly lot of miles today."

Robert nodded. "We have. Is there water nearby? We need to fill our barrels."

Mr. Julander answered. "We've been following a river up from the south. It runs alongside the trail over there." He gestured toward a thin ribbon of water.

Robert nodded, satisfied. "I reckon we can join you for supper, Mr. Julander. I'm also sorry for the loss of your sister."

Mr. Julander pumped the hands of all the men, and said, "Laurie Sue isn't my blood sister. She's my sister in the gospel. We all belong to the same church, and we call each other Brother and Sister. You can call me Brother Jeff, if you've a mind to."

James shrugged. "If that's what you'd rather we name you, I can get my mouth around it." He looked back toward the river. "There's a flat piece just along there, if you want to pull your wagons off the road. We'll camp the other side of you." James made as though to leave, then turned back to the man. "You'd better check that wagon for damage before you try to move it. It might fall into a wreck and block the whole road."

"We'll do that. See you at supper."

℘

James rode behind the Heizer brothers and Robert to the Bingham's halted wagons. When Mrs. Bingham saw them coming, she inquired about what was going on.

George said, "The party coming this way had a misfortune." He pulled on the lobe of his half ear. "One of their wagons overturned, and a young lady was . . . well, wounded mighty bad. They'll have services for her tomorrow."

"Services? You mean she's dead?"

George nodded. "That's right. She didn't make it through."

"Merciful heavens! Let's get down there and help them poor people. They'll need a warm meal and a pot of tea to steady their nerves." She arranged herself on the wagon seat, and said to Luke, "Let's go, boy. Time's a-wasting."

"Yes, ma'am." Luke got the team underway, and the rest of the party followed.

When the Binghams arrived, they found the Julander camp already set up, with fires going and bubbling pots hanging from tripods.

James sought out Brother Jeff and introduced Mrs. Bingham and the rest of the party to him.

"We're obliged for the help your men gave us this afternoon," Brother Jeff said to her. "We're beholden and would like you to partake of our meal with us." He beckoned to a tall, calico-clad woman with fine dark eyes. "This is my wife, Becky Julander. Mrs. Bingham, ladies, she can show you where we're going to serve the food."

Mrs. Bingham nodded to Mrs. Julander, looked around the tidy camp, and turned back to Brother Jeff. "Mr. Julander, you seem to have matters under control."

"Yes, ma'am. We've been practicing a good long time now. We've come from Mississippi."

"Why, we're from Virginia, ourselves."

"Is that a fact? Come with me, ladies," Mrs. Julander said, and Mrs. Bingham and the women moved off after her.

James said, "Your people aren't weeping and wailing like I expected they would."

Brother Jeff pursed his lips. "It's hard to lose a friend, that's for sure, but we have a bright outlook with our faith and our teachings. I'd like to tell you a bit about them after supper." He motioned to the other men. "You gentlemen are included in the invitation."

James stroked his moustache. "I reckon I'll listen," he said.

Robert nodded. "I don't mind talking a bit of religion."

George and Ned looked at each other. George made a sour face, but Ned quirked an eyebrow. "I reckon our souls are saved, but we'll hear what you have to say."

"It appears you'll have a crowd," James said, and went to look after his animals.

Chapter 29

Ned grabbed a tin plate from a stack and got in the line of men that approached a kettle at the first fire. Jessie wasn't in sight, or he would have cut the line to be with her. *She's likely serving food down the way*, he thought. When he got to the kettle, he sniffed the aroma of stew, and his mouth watered. He looked up to hold out his plate, and nearly dropped it.

A tall girl with long brown hair stared back at him, a smile playing on her lips. "How do," she said, and ladled the stew onto his plate.

Ned tried to return her greeting, but his heart seemed to have left his chest to clog up his throat. He swallowed, nodding to the girl. The firelight swirled in her dark eyes. "If you need more, come back, you hear?" she said, and gave him a slow wink.

Ned nodded again. Although he couldn't speak, his body seemed more alive than it had ever been, warmth spreading through his vitals and limbs. He moved past the girl, looking back to memorize her face and form. Who was she? What was such a beguiling creature doing in the wilderness? He kept his gaze on her as long as he could, and when the line came to the next fire, he accepted a biscuit from Jessie's hand and hardly knew it. Then he realized who she was: his betrothed, his beloved, his Jessie. He pushed down the warmth and tried to smile at her.

"Jessie," he said. The smile finally came, feeling forced and false. Before he could say more, the press of the man behind pushed him along the line.

Jessie. I'm going to marry Jessie. I love her. I've always loved her.

His head turned, as though he had no volition, to stare back at the dark-haired beauty at the first fire. *Who is that girl?*

&

Maggie felt a touch on her sleeve. For a moment longer she let her gaze follow the handsome, curly-haired man who had just stood before her, but was passing down the food line. She locked her knees to keep from falling, from melting away into a puddle. Her heart raced.

"Maggie!"

The voice in her ear made her snap upright, the ladle waving in the air. She let out her breath in a rush and looked up at her mother. Mama looked sad.

"Maggie, what are you thinking?" Her mother's voice was so low a whisper that Maggie leaned sideways toward her to hear it.

"Come again, ma'am?" Maggie replied in an equally low tone.

"You winked at that young man."

Maggie's eyes widened. She blinked. "I did?"

"You did, missy. He's going to think you're a bold flirt."

"A flirt? Oh no, Mama. I didn't mean anything of the sort." She dished a ladleful of stew onto the plate of the next person who came through the line. She could feel the heated flush of embarrassment on her face and neck. "I reckon I . . ." She stopped, then started over, still whispering. "He seemed so nice, but kinda shy-like. Tongue-tied. And so nice. And shy." Her words came out in fits and starts.

"Nice. And shy." Something caught in her mother's voice, and she coughed.

Maggie glanced at her again. Mama looked like she was trying to stifle a smile.

"So you winked at him."

"If I winked, I couldn't help it, Mama. He appeared to be so . . . nice."

"And shy?"

"Yes, shy. I reckon I was surprised into winking. I had no thought to be bold or brazen, Mama. He's just . . . so nice."

Her mother's light touch on her arm became a pat. She said in a strangled voice, "He does seem nice," and walked away as if she had an urgent errand to attend to. Maggie heard her coughing again. Mama surely was acting odd. Maggie sighed and looked down the line, but the fair-haired stranger was gone.

Chapter 30

Due to the combined efforts of both parties, the meal was tasty and filling. Soon the women began to clear away the food and the dishes.

Jessie found herself in the company of Mrs. Julander, who stood over the dishpan. The older woman handed Jessie a tin plate to wipe dry, and said, "I feel too young for you to be calling me 'Mrs. Julander,'" she said. "I hope you'll call me 'Sister Becky,' or 'Miss Becky.'" When Jessie nodded her assent, she continued. "It's odd that both of our parties are traveling in wintertime. What puts you folks so late on the trail?"

Jessie took the plate and swiped at it with a worn tea towel. "We've had hard luck with our wagons, Miss Becky, and sometimes we had to stop and work for supplies." She sighed. "It's been a long journey."

Miss Becky laughed. "It that a fact? It sounds like your luck was similar to ours."

"Yes. Now we're crossing paths. You're going up the trail and we're headed down." Jessie handed the plate to Hannah, who made a stack of the tin plates with one hand while she cradled her baby in the other.

"Maybe we're meeting because God has a purpose in mind."

"What do you mean, Miss Becky?"

"Maybe he wants us to talk together," Miss Becky said, and smiled. "You know, He loves us and wants the best for us."

"He does? I always thought God was a sort of gruff spirit who likes to torment us." Jessie wiped another plate and gave it to her sister.

"Oh my, no! God's not like that at all, my dear. He's your Heavenly Father. He loves you like your earthly father does."

"My father's dead. That's one reason we left Virginia. His legs was shot off, and he couldn't defend us from the Yankee louts invading our town. Then he died, and my sis—" She broke off speaking, glanced at Hannah, and straightened her shoulders. "Here we are, a long time later, and we're nearly to Albuquerque. I'll be so glad when I can sleep in a real bed again."

Miss Becky shook water from her hands. "I'm sorry about your father, and the trouble you've had on your journey. God does love you, and he won't ever give you more trials in this life than you can handle with His help." She took up the water-filled dishpan, swirled it a bit, and tossed the water behind her toward the rear of her wagon. A goat's offended bleats cut through the air.

Miss Becky laughed, and called out, "Sorry, old Mike." She turned to Jessie and Hannah. "I forgot our billy goat was tied to the back of the wagon just there. He's a bit of a rascal, and we have to tie him up or he'll eat everything in sight." After a bit, the animal fell silent. She put away the pan, grabbed up a flour-sack towel and dried her hands, then said, "Let's go sit and talk a spell. Do you mind that?"

"Oh, no. You say things that make sense."

Hannah asked, "May I come too?"

Miss Becky smiled. "Certainly. I want to get a better look at that precious babe."

ᔕᗞ

James sat down off to the side of a campfire, absently patting the dog on the head until it lay down with its nose between its paws. Robert came over and sat near James. George and Ned joined them.

Brother Jeff took a seat, placed a Bible in his lap, and said, "We had a pair of preachers come to our county several years before the unpleasantness started. My wife and I were new married, but we let them stay with us for a while." He smiled. "They gave us a book to read, and they held meetings around the countryside for a few weeks. Becky and me felt convicted that we should become Saints."

"Saints?" Robert raised his eyebrows.

"We believe that the same gospel Jesus Christ preached has been restored to the earth again. The members of Christ's church called themselves Saints, and we do, as well." Brother Jeff rubbed the Bible. "A lot of folks 'round about took exception to that. We lost a few friends."

"That's a hard thing," James said.

"We found other friends in the members who joined the church. Most of them are in this party."

"Where is it y'all are going?" George asked. "Oregon? Wyoming?"

"We're bound for the Great Salt Lake Valley."

George sat back. "I thought only Mormons lived in that country." His voice had a hard edge.

Brother Jeff moved a bit in his seat, but didn't seem to take offense at George's manner. "That's a name we're given from time to time. We're members of the Church of Jesus Christ of Latter-day Saints. Like I said, we call ourselves Saints."

James stroked his beard. "So you're Mormons. I have a relative who followed that path, or so my ma told me. That was twenty-odd years ago, before I was born."

Brother Jeff laughed. "Our path, as you put it, has many doctrines to recommend it. We believe our first prophet, Joseph Smith, received a vision while he was just a lad. He saw God and his Holy Son. Brother Joseph was chosen to restore Christ's Church and the power of God to earth. That power is called the priesthood."

Robert said, "You say he's a prophet, like the ones in the Old Testament? I thought all the prophets were dead."

"The old ones are for sure, but many of them prophesied that after a falling away, the truth would come again to men. We believe that began to happen in 1820, when Brother Joseph had his vision."

"So he's a prophet, living and breathing and talking to God?" Robert moved his foot around in the dirt for a moment before he spoke again. "That's an amazing thing."

"It is amazing and wonderful, for a fact, but he was reviled and hated, and finally killed by a mob."

"I have some experience of mobs," James said, and looked away, a bitterness descending over him at the thought of the men rushing down the hall of the hotel in Trinidad.

Brother Jeff gazed beyond the fire. "We heard about Brother Joseph's death, his and his brother's, while we were trying to get up funds to move to Illinois to join the Saints. That news set us back some." He looked down at his clasped hands. "We didn't know what would happen to the Church with the prophet dead. We had contact for a while, and kept saving our traveling money. We found out Brother Joseph had given the power of God to lead the Church to others, so it kept on going. Later, we heard the Saints had been driven out of Illinois and went west."

"Why didn't you join them?" Ned spoke for the first time.

"We tried, but with crop failures, and one thing and another, we couldn't ever seem to scrape together enough money. We had our young ones and it took a lot of doing to raise them. Finally, we got the cash together, and were fixin' to leave, but the fighting started, and we were stuck in Mississippi."

The dog stood up and woofed, and James patted it on the head and said "Quiet, now," but it slipped from under his hand and left the fire. James looked at Brother Jeff. "It must be sweet to you folks to be so near your goal at last."

"We've had our hard times, but you're right. In a few more months, we'll be safe with the Saints."

The men spoke together for several minutes. James recalled something that had caught his attention when he heard it said at the accident scene.

"When your young sister died, a man comforted Miz Eliza by saying, 'We'll join her to us in Zion.' What did he mean by that?"

Brother Jeff tipped down his head and stared at his feet for a moment. After a while, he looked directly at James and said, "I'll tell you that, but first, let me give you a little background." He hesitated a moment as he looked around the circle. "You might find some of our teachings a mite odd. For example, we believe that husbands and wives can be bound together in marriage for eternity, by the priesthood power given to men. Love doesn't stop when someone dies, so why should a marriage end?"

Startled, James half rose to his feet. His heart pounded in his chest. This was exactly what he'd been telling God. He sank to his seat again, heaved a great sigh, and said, with a voice that sounded to him as though he were being strangled, "I don't find that odd at all."

Brother Jeff peered at him. "You've lost your wife," he said. It was a statement.

"Yes. About New Year's. She was a good girl, and didn't deserve to die so young."

Brother Jeff leaned forward and squeezed James on the shoulder. "I'm sorry to hear of your loss, very sorry."

"Much obliged," James said, looking up at last. "Please, won't you tell me more about marrying forever?"

Chapter 31

The three women found seats beside one of the fires. Miss Becky asked, "May I hold your dear little one?"

Hannah nodded and gave her the baby.

As Miss Becky cradled the baby in her arms, James's dog came up to sniff at her, then lay down beside Jessie.

"Ooooo, you are so precious," Miss Becky cooed to the infant, counting its fingers. She kissed him on the forehead, then cuddled him against her bodice. "I'd forgotten how good it feels to hold a baby to my breast," she whispered. "Mrs. Fletcher, you are so blessed to have this sweet little bundle fresh from the arms of God." She admired the child for a few more moments, then passed him back to his mother.

"Do you really believe what you said before, Miss Becky?" Jessie stroked the dog's head. "That God loves me?"

"I do. You two are sisters, isn't that right?"

Jessie and Hannah nodded.

"Think about your feelings for each other, for your family members, for that baby. How do you suppose you got those feelings of love and kinship? God put them there. You are his children."

"Doesn't God punish us when we've done something wrong?" Hannah asked, looking down at her baby. "Something really bad?"

The expression on Miss Becky's face softened as she looked at Hannah. After a moment, she said, "I think sometimes we punish ourselves enough that God doesn't have to. I reckon you've had rough experiences in your life. Maybe some you're regretting. Our loving Father provides a way to wipe out all our sins and blunders."

Jessie fidgeted with the fringe of her shawl, thinking about the man she had killed way back in West Virginia. Hannah's mention of doing wrong things had suddenly brought an apparition to her mind of the man's grotesque form splayed out before her on the forest floor. Ned had said the man needed killing, but a foul taste filled her mouth. Would she go to hell for shooting him?

Miss Becky had continued talking, and Jessie shook her head to free her mind of the evil remembrance so she could catch up.

"And his true church is on the earth again. Baptism into his church brings forgiveness from God, a newness of soul, a cleansing as though you had just been born. You need faith in the Lord Jesus Christ and his restored church, and a repentant spirit, to receive baptism in it."

Hannah stirred in her seat, and Jessie glanced over at her. Hannah's face held hope for the first time in months, Jessie thought. *What did she do that was so awful she needs a baptism? The bad things happened to her.* A thought struck her, and she sat upright. *Did Hannah kill the man who attacked her? Robert always says the brute was dead when it all ended, but he never gives details.* She looked away. Were she and Hannah both murderers?

Hannah voice broke into Jessie's thoughts. "You're right about me having a rough life. I've done regretful things, and I want to know more about receiving forgiveness."

Miss Becky stared off into the distance for a moment. She looked at Hannah and said, "I have a little book I treasure a great deal. I would like to give it to you. It will show you how other families have gone through many hard trials, and how God has helped them to bear their burdens." She got up and left the fire for a few minutes. When she returned, she had a small book in her hand.

"This is called The Book of Mormon. It's scripture, just like the Bible. It will help you know that God and his son Jesus Christ are real, and that they love you. When I read it, I received much comfort in my heart. I hope it will do the same for you." She leaned over and held out the book.

Hannah took it and stroked its cover. She looked up at Miss Becky and smiled wistfully. "I don't know if I can take your precious scriptures, Miss Becky." She tried to give the little volume back.

"I'll get another book in Zion," Miss Becky said, her hands up to refuse the return of the book. She stood up. "Now then, my husband is talking to your men about our faith. I reckon we should go over and let him tell you more."

∞

"We have another teaching that might give you comfort," Brother Jeff told James. "We believe that we can perform ceremonies like baptisms and marriages, and such, by proxy, for our dead loved ones. A living person stands in for the dead. That's what Brother Martin was talking about when he spoke to his wife."

James thought for a long time, digesting the man's words. "I recall Paul mentioned baptizing for the dead in the Bible. I don't understand about Brother Martin, though. What kind of proxy ceremony will they do for him in Zion?"

"That's the third teaching I want to tell you about. Do you recall in the Old Testament that Isaac had more than one wife?"

James nodded. "I recollect several of the ancient prophets who did that."

George hooted derisively. "Solomon had so many he needed to build himself a palace to keep them in."

Brother Jeff chuckled, but sobered as he spoke. "We believe God gave a commandment to the Saints to do likewise, for a few of the men to provide homes and look after more than one woman. Laurie Sue is Sister Eliza's blood sister. Brother Martin meant he's willing to have Laurie Sue sealed to him as a wife, if the new prophet, Brother Brigham, gives permission, of course. That is a comfort to Sister Eliza, to know that Laurie Sue will belong to someone forever as a wife, even though she's dead."

"That's an astonishing thing, Brother Jeff," James said.

George got to his feet. "Astonishing? Unbelievable. I think I've heard about all I care to. Heppie is wife enough for me."

Brother Jeff rose as well and thanked George for listening. George made a face, tugged on his brother's coat sleeve, and said, "Come along, Ned. I don't reckon we're cut out to be Mormon converts."

James saw confusion on Ned's face as he got up. He agreed with his brother, though, and the two strode off toward their camp.

When the three remaining men had taken their seats again, James said, "Let's back up a tad bit. What you're saying is that God wants our marriages to last forever?"

Brother Jeff nodded. "I do say that."

"And He gave your prophet the power to do that? 'Seal,' you said?" James noticed that Robert was leaning forward, intently taking in the conversation.

"Yes," Brother Jeff agreed.

"And if that wasn't done before a body dies, it can be done afterward?"

"Yes."

"I could be a married man forever?" James paused, tugging on his beard, then smoothing it. "Could I take another wife besides, a live one?"

"Since your first wife is dead, you wouldn't need the prophet's permission to marry again."

James rubbed his chest slowly, feeling the explosive pounding of his heart. "The things you tell me burn like a fire."

"That's the Holy Ghost witnessing to you," Brother Jeff said.

"Do you reckon I can join your church?" James asked.

Brother Jeff opened his mouth, but a voice in the darkness interrupted. "I'd like to join, have the baptizing," Hannah took a step into the firelight. "Robert? Please?"

Robert jumped up and went to her side. "Yes." He looked at Brother Jeff. "I would like that, as well."

James and Brother Jeff were on their feet as Miss Becky and Jessie entered the circle of light.

"I can arrange that," Brother Jeff said. "I'll find a place in the river, and we can baptize you tomorrow, after the funeral service."

"How much water do you need for that?" Jessie asked.

Miss Becky put her hand on Jessie's arm and said, "John the Baptist used the Jordan River for Our Lord's baptism. He was immersed, totally covered. You might remember, the Holy Ghost came down like a dove, and then God Himself spoke."

"I've read that," James said. "I'll take the baptizing." He looked over at Jessie, uneasy that she was present when he had another question burning in his soul.

The baby let out a cry, and Hannah began to rock him back and forth. "He's hungry." She gave a great sigh. "I look forward to tomorrow," she said, smiling at Robert. "Good night, Miss Becky. Good night, Brother Jeff. Jessie, we'll walk you back to camp."

Jessie looked from James to Hannah, uncertainty showing in her face.

James thought, *Does she want the baptizing too? I reckon Ned will tell her no if she asks his permission. That's not my concern.*

She hesitated, finally walking away with Robert and Hannah. He turned back to Brother Jeff and his wife.

"How do I get Amparo—that's my wife, Amparo—sealed to me forever?"

Brother Jeff said, "That takes a bit more work. You'll have to go to Zion with us to see about that. I can scarcely wait to get there and have Becky and the kids sealed to me."

James's head fell forward and his words trickled slowly from his lips. "I gave my word to take these folks to Albuquerque. Maybe after that . . ." He felt a constriction of his heart as hope diminished.

"At least we can get you started with baptism, Brother James." Brother Jeff took Miss Becky's hand and nodded to James. "It's not full dark yet. I'll go find a fittin' place in the river and maybe dam it up a bit."

છ

Jessie looked back as she walked away. James stood beside the waning fire, talking to the leader of the Mormon group. His head was down in a dejected pose, and she stopped for a moment to watch him. Brother Jeff took his wife's hand, gestured with his head, and left the fire. James ran his fingers through his hair, and Jessie ached to go to him, to comfort him, to hold him close to her heart. Remembering her promise to Ned, she balled her fists, turned away, and followed Hannah and Robert back to the wagons.

Chapter 32

After he left the fire with George, Ned checked the picket pin on his horse and spread his blankets near the Bingham's wagon. He chatted a bit with Luke, and looked around for Jessie, but she wasn't back from the Mormons' camp yet. He shrugged his shoulders and sat on his blankets, preparing to bed down.

Before he pulled off his boots, a thought struck him. James Owen hadn't returned either. Had he enticed Jessie to listen to Julander's outrageous claims? He had better go over and bring her to safety.

Ned pushed himself to his feet and shrugged into his coat. He wouldn't be surprised if it froze tonight. The Mormons would be hard-pressed tomorrow to dig a proper burial hole for that young girl who had died.

Once Ned was past the Bingham's fire, he walked in darkness. The stars glittered above, but the light they shed wasn't much to navigate by. A couple of people, Robert and Hannah, from the sound of the voices, passed him at a distance, going the other way.

Ned moved up to the fire where he'd sat with the men, talking to Julander. It smoldered by itself. Julander was gone. Owen was gone. Jessie wasn't there.

He stopped, unsure what to do next. Maybe Jessie had slipped past him in the darkness and was safely out of harm's way. He felt a bit foolish, chasing her all over the landscape like this, but he'd always been her protector, and he wasn't about to stop that now. Especially with Owen in the picture.

Maybe I'm making a mountain out of a molehill, he thought. *Owen's got that dead wife he's moping after. If he wants to join the Mormons and go with them, it's all the better for me.*

A figure came toward the fire, carrying a bucket that sloshed water over the sides. It was the girl he had met in the food line. Ned felt his body tightening, but tried to ignore it as he hurried to help her with the bucket.

"Here now, let me carry that for you," he said, stretching out his hand to take the handle.

The girl smiled in the waning light. "I ain't going no further," she said in a melodious voice that cut deep into Ned's soul. "I come to put the fire down."

"I can take care of that," he said, reaching out and taking the bucket from her slender hands. She stood still and surrendered it, and when their fingers touched, Ned felt as though he'd been lightning-struck. The girl was so close that when he inhaled, her scent filled his nostrils. He noted that she smelled of wood smoke and violets. *Violets? Here in the winter wilderness of New Mexico Territory?*

"I'm Ned Heizer," he said, listening to his voice rise up the scale into a boyish octave. What on earth was happening to him? Why didn't he step back out of her way and let her get about her business?

Ned figured the moon slipped up the horizon behind him, because the girl's face gradually glowed with a soft light.

"My name is Maggie," she said, taking air in a fetching manner that raised and lowered her shoulders and chest. "Maggie Julander."

Ned swallowed. This beautiful girl was Jeffrey Julander's daughter, and all that separated them was a bucket of water. He stepped sideways to get a bit of distance, put the pail down, took her hand, and said, "I'm very pleased to make your acquaintance, Miss Maggie." He was also very pleased that his voice stayed in a normal register this time.

"Mister Heizer," she acknowledged, giving his hand a tiny squeeze before she let it go.

Everything about Miss Maggie's comportment was pure innocence, but there was a heady undertone of bewitching backwoods humor, a quirk to her mouth that told him she liked to laugh, to take joy in life.

Joy in life. That's something I've been missing of late. The admission scared him, made him feel disloyal and a bit out of sorts. Digging into the mass of his fears, he discovered that the thing jolting him the most was that he truly *had* been missing joy in his life. He should be over the moon with happiness. Not so long ago, Jessie had finally said she would marry him. He'd agreed to her condition of waiting, but even the prospect of having to damp down his desire to be her husband hadn't dismayed him.

Or maybe it had.

Whatever was going on in his courtship, it didn't seem to matter right now. Miss Maggie's very presence expanded his senses and made him feel glad to be alive.

Ned shook himself mentally. Staring at Miss Maggie wouldn't finish her chore.

He bent and picked up the water bucket, smiling at the girl. He couldn't stop smiling at her. He circled the fire, pouring water onto the margins, then into the heart of the blackened coals. Wisps of steam arose, and his nose sampled the odor of ashes.

"Did I do that right?" he asked, handing the bucket back to Maggie.

"I reckon that took care of the job," she answered. "I'm obliged, Mr. Heizer."

Ned realized that he hadn't let go of the bucket when Maggie put out her hand to take it back. Their fingers both curled around the wire bail, side by side, their thumbs touching. Her skin was cool, but his hand felt like fire. He stopped breathing.

When he straightened his fingers at last to release the thick, curved wire, the empty bucket swung down to hang in Maggie's hand at her side, rocking back and forth so slowly that it seemed as though time had been altered by his suspended breath.

The moon bathed Maggie's face in white light. She was smiling. Ned knew he was smiling. Pixie lights danced before his eyes until he become conscious that he was in danger of passing out. He took a long, gasping breath, nearly strangling with the desire to touch her again. He must not do that. The moment had passed. All that was left was to wrench himself away, back to his camp, and let her go about her nightly routine.

"Miss Maggie," he said in a shaky voice. "Good night to you."

"And to you, Mr. Heizer," she replied, her voice barely above a whisper.

Maggie turned away, slipping off like a phantom and breaking the spell that had kept Ned rooted to one spot. His jaw felt slack, his legs rubbery. He'd never before experienced the lightness, the elation that permeated his very skin. He wondered how he was going to survive until he saw Miss Maggie again.

&

Hannah put the baby to bed, touching the tiny widow's peak with a kiss. She turned to Robert. "I'm going to have my sins washed away," she said, breathless at the wonder of it.

"Sins, my love? I find no sins in you." Robert stretched his length in the quilts, holding out his hand to help Hannah down beside him.

"I have a great many. That man, killing him. Not wanting the baby. Turning you away from my affections." She ticked them off on her fingers.

Robert took her hand and kissed each finger she had touched. She quaked with joy, but lest he misunderstand her quivers for fright, she turned her head and kissed him on the mouth.

"I shall be clean," she murmured against his lips. "Jesus will wash me in his blood."

"And I—"

"You have no faults, Robert."

"I warrant I can conjure a good many."

"No you can't," she said, kissing his neck, listening to his sudden intake of breath. "Isn't lust a sin?" She giggled.

"Not in the marriage bed," Robert whispered, and tickled her until she laughed out loud.

"You'll wake the baby," she gasped.

"That *would* be a sin. Good thing it will be washed away tomorrow."

Chapter 33

James awoke to a faint rhythmic thump that he later found out was several of the Mormon men swinging pickaxes to dig Miss Laurie Sue's grave. He sat, rubbed the sleep from his eyes, and got to his feet. Grabbing his boots, he tipped them upside down, shook them to remove any nighttime visitors, and put them on. He rolled his bed into a tight bundle and tied it onto the mule's pack that sat beside his saddle.

He gathered the rest of his gear and packed it up. Then he remembered. The Bingham company wasn't traveling anywhere today. After the Mormons held a funeral service for Miss Laurie Sue, he, James Owen, was fixing to walk down into a pool of cold river water and wash off his sins. It was a first step toward making Amparo his wife forever—no matter how long it might take to have it done.

He realized that for the first time in several weeks, he wasn't experiencing the never-ending grief he'd been carrying like a sack full of rocks tied around his heart, the grief about Amparo's not being with him. He figured it still would hurt later, but right now, thinking on his baptism, his heart jumped in his chest, free of restricting pain.

James took a deep breath and let it out slowly in a white plume. His lungs tightened around another breath of the crisp, cold air. Last night, he'd made this decision a matter of prayer. He had a comforting feeling in his chest about his choice to join the Mormon faith. If only Amparo were here—he knew she would receive the preaching about marrying forever with joy and acceptance. *Para siempre*. She was big on the notion of forever.

The Bingham women pooled their supplies with the Mormon ladies that morning, and breakfast consisted of boiled salt pork, beaten biscuits, and milk gravy. James got in line for the food behind Brother Jeff. He heard the man ask that four biscuits be tied up in a cloth, and when Jessie handed him the bundle, he put it in his coat pocket.

Jessie glanced up at James and put three biscuits on his plate, but she didn't say anything to him. He wondered again if she had the urge to become a Mormon. It'd seemed like she wanted to say something last night before Hannah whisked her away.

James looked at her a moment, wishing Ned Heizer had stayed in the north after the war. That might have uncomplicated things a tad bit. He asked, "Will you be at the baptizing service?"

Jessie's eyes darted from side to side. She straightened her shoulders and put on a smile. "I wouldn't miss seeing you lose your sins for all the world," she said. Her light tone seemed forced. As he moved down the line to get his gravy, he wondered why it mattered to him if she would be there or not. How could he yearn for Amparo one moment and the very next be concerned about Jessie's whereabouts? *Life is complex*, he thought, and stuffed a biscuit into his mouth.

&

After breakfast, James joined the parade of people carrying seats to the spot where the Mormons had dug a grave off the side of the road. As he settled himself on his saddle, four men brought Laurie Sue's body, which had been sewn into a shroud made of canvas, to the front of the gathering. He got to his feet in respect for the dead as the men laid their burden beside the grave, and he sat down as they took places in the congregation beside their wives.

Jeffrey Julander went to the front, turned to face the crowd, and directed the Mormons to sing an old familiar hymn, "Rock of Ages." A woman in the audience gave a pitch, the Mormons began to sing, and the members of the Bingham party joined in. A hush fell on the group as Brother Jeff called on one of the men to offer a prayer.

The man arose and took off his hat. The other men followed suit, and as the Mormon got deep into his prayer, he spoke of being grateful for their trials along the trail and of their faith in a loving Savior. He asked for comfort for the family who had lost their kin, and peace for the hearts of all assembled there. He ended the prayer and sat down. The congregation followed suit.

Brother Jeff took charge again. He breathed slowly for a moment, and James wondered what he was waiting for. At last he said, "We're gathered to mourn the sudden passing of our sister in Christ, Laurie Sue Purdy. She may not have made it to Zion, but now she's in Paradise, greeted by Our Lord, Jesus Christ.

"We are left to wonder why she was taken and to do our duty as Saints to comfort each other, particularly Sister Eliza, who is mighty heartsick."

Brother Jeff took a slim book from his pocket and opened it to a part that he'd marked with a scrap of paper.

"Thus saith the Lord about the last days," he said, and began to read from the book. "'Mine indignation is soon to be poured out without measure upon all nations; and this will I do when the cup of their iniquity is full. And in that day all who are found upon the watch-tower, or in other words, all mine Israel, shall be saved. And they that have been scattered shall be gathered.'" Brother Jeff looked over at Laurie Sue's shroud for a minute, then resumed reading. "'And all they who have mourned shall be comforted. And all they who have given their lives for my name shall be crowned. Therefore, let your hearts be comforted concerning Zion; for all flesh is in mine hands; be still and know that I am God.'

"Brethren and Sisters, in this passage the Lord God of Israel declared that the day will come when all who mourn will be comforted, in that day when he gathers us in. We look forward to that blessed event." He closed the book over the scrap of paper, put it into his pocket, and spoke again. "The prophet Alma proclaimed that we as members of God's kingdom have a deep feeling and a sacred duty to comfort each other in our times of grief. He was speaking to the people at the waters of Mormon, urging them to take heed of their Christ like feelings of love and concern and to be baptized and become His Church."

Brother Jeff put his hand into another pocket and drew it out empty. He frowned, patting all his other pockets. Whatever he sought wasn't to be found, and Brother Jeff walked over to Miss Becky and asked, "Do you have your Book of Mormon?"

"Oh," she exclaimed. "I don't have it. I gave it to Mrs. Fletcher." She turned in her seat and asked Hannah, "Did you happen to bring that little book to the meeting?"

Hannah blushed, but nodded, took the Book of Mormon from her pocket, and handed it to Miss Becky.

"I'll give it back to you," Miss Becky whispered, and delivered the volume to her husband.

Brother Jeff opened the book, found the place he wanted, and read, "'Behold, here are the waters of Mormon and now, as ye are desirous to come into the fold of God, and to be called his people, and are willing to bear one another's burdens, that they may be light; Yea, and are willing to mourn with those that mourn; yea, and to comfort those that stand in need of comfort, and to stand as witnesses of God at all times and in all things, and in all places that ye may be in, even until death, that ye may be redeemed of God, and be numbered with those of the first resurrection, that ye may have eternal life— Now I say unto you, if this be the desire of your hearts, what have you against being baptized in the name of the Lord, as a witness before him that ye have entered into a covenant with him, that ye will serve him and keep his commandments, that he may pour out his Spirit more abundantly upon you?'"

James restrained himself from rising to his feet and calling out, "Yes, this is the desire of my heart!" He shifted in his seat and looked around, saw Jessie staring at him, and wondered if he had said it out loud. He broke into a sweat despite the coolness of the morning.

Brother Jeff shut the book with a thump and gave it back to Miss Becky.

"Are we not commanded to be faithful in carrying out our duty? Yes, and we do it out of love, one for another, even as Christ loved the Church for our sakes.

"Now we will lay the body of our sister in the grave, here beside our trail, but the memories we will take with us are of a sweet sister who was faithful in all her dealings, kindhearted, hardworking, and cheerful in adversity. We will commend her spirit to the keeping of Our Lord, and pledge to remember our time with her on earth with glad hearts."

Brother Jeff gestured to the four men who had earlier carried the body to the graveside. They came forward, took up the shrouded body, and gently laid it in the bottom of the grave. Then they picked up shovels and scooped the earth into place.

James looked away while they filled the grave, remembering all too clearly the similar labor he had performed just days before, in a place not so far away. His heart thumped hard in his chest, and he gripped his hands together until they ached.

When the men returned to their seats, Brother Jeff spoke again. "We have among us today several who wish to be baptized like those people of Alma's day and time. When we have concluded this service, those who wish to do so may gather on the side of the river to witness the baptisms," he said.

Brother Jeff ended his sermon with a few more thoughts and scriptures that James had never heard before. He led them in singing another song, one that the Bingham party didn't know. It included a verse about dying "before our journey's through," but all being well, as it was a happy day, free from toil and sorrow. James felt buoyed up, even though he had nothing to do with the family who mourned.

Another Mormon gave a prayer, and at the "Amen," the people rose to their feet and gathered around Sister Eliza, who dabbed ineffectually at her streaming eyes.

As the Mormons comforted the woman, James felt the grip of conflicting emotions. Grief, joy, and apprehension swirled together in his head, and he hoped he could maintain a steady countenance among these strangers.

Brother Jeff approached with the Fletchers close behind him and touched James on the elbow. "Are you ready?" he asked. "If so, follow me." He turned and strode toward the river's edge, taking off his coat as he walked. He stopped at the bank to remove his boots.

James hesitated a moment, his stomach churning. Then he went after Brother Jeff, stripping off his coat, as well.

The rocks put in the stream yesterday had done their work, and a fair-sized pool of water stood behind the temporary dam. Brother Jeff greeted those who had approached and called for another prayer.

This time, the Mormon who prayed asked for blessings upon the converts, that they would be able to have clear minds to learn more of the doctrines of the kingdom, and for a safe journey through life until they could join the Saints in Zion.

James stood stiffly alongside Robert and Hannah. He looked over at them. Their heads were bowed as they followed the prayer. Hannah, in particular, seemed relaxed and serene, patting her child on the back and swaying. James shut his eyes and bent his head.

The prayer ended, and Brother Jeff waded into the pool. He put out his hand and gestured for James to join him. James took off his boots and followed. The shock of the cold water when he entered the stream ran up his legs and spread into his chest, but James persevered until he stood beside the Mormon leader.

Brother Jeff smiled at him, and gave him quick instructions concerning stopping up his nostrils when the time came. He raised his arm and called James by name, said he was commissioned by Jesus Christ to do this baptism, told him to hold his nose, and laid him down in the water. James's weight pulled Brother Jeff off balance on the slick rocky bottom, and he went under too. They both came up sputtering and laughing.

"Whew! I do feel clean!" James said, shaking his head. Water drops spattered into the creek's flow. "So now I'm a Mormon?" he asked, and began to shiver in the chilly breeze. Oddly, his heart felt warm, though his skin bristled with gooseflesh.

Brother Jeff smiled. "Almost. We'll give you a confirmation by the laying on of hands. After that, you'll be a Saint." He turned James toward the water's edge, and James picked his way across the rocks. Brother Jeff beckoned to Robert to enter the water.

When James reached the creek bank, Jessie surprised him by holding out a blanket. He took it, thanked her, and wrapped it around himself. Ned came and took Jessie's arm, as though he wanted to remove her from the area.

James heard her whisper, "I want to watch, Ned." The man dropped his hand, but stayed at her side.

By then, Robert had made his way to Brother Jeff, who repeated the process of praying and baptizing. Robert came out of the water, shouting for joy. Brother Jeff patted his arm, beamed, and sent him back to the bank. As he approached, Hannah handed the baby to Mrs. Bingham and stooped to pick up a blanket. She gave it to Robert and stepped into the creek for her own turn.

"Watch your step, ma'am," Brother Jeff said, as he helped Hannah enter the pool of water. He repeated the same ceremony and, when he had finished, helped Hannah out of the water. Robert embraced her and wrapped her in the blanket, wiping a few tears from her smiling face.

James looked around. Where would the laying on of hands that Brother Jeff mentioned take place? Several Mormon men had moved away from the river and surrounded a chair someone had brought to the site. Brother Jeff joined them after toweling the water off his legs and torso and shrugging into his black coat. He waved a hand at James.

James gave the blanket back to Jessie and went to sit down on the chair. The men put their hands on his head. The hands warmed him. Brother Jeff spoke, his voice soft, but firm, as he pronounced the words that confirmed James a member of The Church of Jesus Christ of Latter-day Saints and gave him gifts and blessings from heaven.

At the end of the prayer, Brother Jeff patted James on the shoulder. He leaned over and whispered, "You are a member of God's Kingdom. Now we're going to give you the priesthood and ordain you an elder. Remember, we spoke of this power of God," he added.

James nodded, a lump in his throat.

Again, Brother Jeff's voice was soft and steady as he prayed and gave James the priesthood.

James was no longer cold. He sat beneath the warm hands of his brothers, soaking in the words and the feeling of overwhelming strength that caused him to shake a bit. The simple words seemed to come from God Himself, and sank forcefully into his soul.

Brother Jeff said, "Amen," which the other men echoed.

James said, "Amen," rose to his feet, and embraced Brother Jeff. "Thank you," he whispered in his ear. "I'm mighty obliged."

"You're welcome," said Brother Jeff. "I am most pleased to do it. Be faithful and true, and the desires of your heart will be met, if it is God's will."

James's heart soared, remembering his most precious desire: being one with Amparo forever. But that was a future promise, for a future time.

The other men embraced James in their turn, and he would have stepped away, but Brother Jeff said, "Join us in the circle to confirm the Fletchers. You have that right and duty now."

James expelled a lungful of air as the surprise hit him, but did as he was bidden, and placed himself between two brothers who had made room for him.

Robert sat in the chair. Brother Jeff confirmed him as a new member of the Church and gave him the Holy Ghost. Then he gave Robert the priesthood, as he had done with James, and invited him to join the circle for Hannah's confirmation. James and Robert looked at each other.

Robert grinned. "This is good," he murmured. "Very good."

James nodded. The strength he felt in the circle of men—brethren, he reminded himself—filled his chest with awe. He'd been a lone man for so long, all the way back to when he'd left his family. He'd missed his brothers, even after he married Amparo and gained her company. Falling in love with her had not driven out the yearning for family, for brotherhood. He sensed it here, the bonds of men united in purpose. His heart swelled throughout Hannah's confirmation until, when the brethren all said "Amen" together, he thought it would burst the walls of his chest. A few deep breaths helped calm him. This was very good.

A few moments later, Brother Jeff sat on a barrel in the Mormon camp and put a few blank pieces of paper on a makeshift desk in front of him. "Brother Harris," he asked, "you got that calendar you're keeping handy? What's the date today?"

Brother Harris went to fetch his calendar and proclaimed the day was Saturday, January 17, 1867.

Brother Jeff wrote out a certificate, stating that he, Jeffrey Julander, Elder, had baptized and confirmed James Owen on that date, and wrote another certificate as proof that he had ordained him an elder. He gave the two pieces of paper to James. "Keep them safe, now. When you make it to Zion, you'll need the proof of your membership and priesthood office in Christ's Kingdom."

"Thank you. I will do that." After reading the certificates over twice, James folded them carefully and thanked Brother Jeff again.

The man wrote other certificates for Robert and Hannah. "Please join us tomorrow at eight o'clock for Sabbath services," he said to the new Mormons as he passed one of the papers to Hannah. "We'll have the sacrament of the Lord's Supper."

Robert said, "I was hoping we could be on our way tomorrow."

"You'll be on the road before noon," Brother Jeff promised.

"Good. I reckon we'll be there," Robert promised.

Chapter 34

To James's surprise, Brother Jeff involved Robert and him in the Sabbath service the next morning. He asked Robert to offer the opening prayer. He knelt beside James and read a prayer over crumbled biscuit pieces that represented the body of Christ. After other men had given the bits of biscuit to the congregation, Brother Jeff pointed out the verse in a book of scripture called the Doctrine and Covenants that was the prayer James was to read. He did so, holding a large cup of water that stood in for the blood that Christ shed for mankind. This was passed to the Mormons as well.

James watched as Hannah sipped from the cup and passed it on. Her face glowed with joy. A feeling of comfort enveloped him, and he knew his decision to become a Saint was right.

After the Lord's Supper had been celebrated, Brother Jeff announced that their meeting would include testimonies from the assembled Saints. Then he sat down.

James looked around. What an odd statement. Wasn't Brother Jeff supposed to give a sermon?

A man got up and said how glad he was to take the sacrament of the Lord's Supper and renew his baptismal covenants with God. He had kind words for James and the Fletchers, accepting a new way of life and new beliefs. After a bit, he sat down.

Brother Martin arose and gave his testimony of love for the gospel of Jesus Christ and of all it meant to him. When he'd had his say, he wiped the moisture from his eyes, sat down, and took Miz Eliza's hand in his.

She stood up beside him and, weeping, spoke of her hope in everlasting life and of the comfort she had in knowing her husband held the priesthood of God and that at the end of their journey, they could be sealed together for eternity. She wiped her nose on her apron, slipped a book from her pocket, and come toward James, who stood at her approach.

"This is Laurie Sue's Doctrine and Covenants," she said, holding the book out to James. "I reckon she don't need it now, and I think she would like to see it put to good use by a new brother in the gospel. Please take it in remembrance of her."

James received the book in both his hands and stood still, rubbing one thumb over the worn cover. "I thank you, Miz Eliza. I will keep it safe and study it carefully."

As she returned to her seat, James knew he couldn't sit down. He had to say something to these people. He made his way to the front and turned to the congregation.

"I want to give all of you thanks for the kind fashion you've received me as one of you. Brother Jeff thought I'd find odd the beliefs he told me about, but I have a burning conviction that they are God's truth. I'm mighty sure I don't know all your ways, or God's ways, but I mean to read and follow all the commandments in this book.

"I reckon I'm supposed to give a testimony here. I know my love for my wife didn't die when she passed on, and I'm mighty grateful to God to hear that He gave you a way to bind a man and wife together beyond the grave. I reckon that'll keep me sane for a good long time, until I can join you in Zion and make that happen for me and Amparo. In the name of Jesus, Amen."

His legs quivering like jelly, James headed back to his seat before they could collapse. As he walked, he glanced over the congregation. Jessie sat at the back, and he didn't know how long she'd been there. She didn't meet his eye. Her head was bowed a little forward, and her wheat-colored hair rippled beside her cheeks.

He bit his lip and took his seat. Hearing him profess his love for Amparo in a public meeting probably cut her to the quick, he thought, but reminded himself that Jessie was pledged to marry Ned Heizer. His feelings about another woman shouldn't be any bother to her. Still, he struggled to reconcile the facts with his emotions.

Unsettled, James turned his gaze to the front and gave attention to the other Saints who spoke. Hannah abruptly handed the baby to Mrs. Bingham and stood.

"I'm so grateful to have my sins washed clean," she said, and sat down as fast as she had popped up. She grabbed the child and kissed his tiny brow.

After a while, Brother Jeff called for a hymn, and the meeting ended with another prayer.

Before James could leave to tie the pack on his mule, Brother Jeff clapped him on the shoulder and shook his hand.

"Well done, Brother James. I thank you for your help during the meeting."

"I wondered why you asked me. You have so many brothers who know what they're doing."

"Y'all needed to learn how to administer the ordinances in the Church. I've called Brother Fletcher to be the presiding elder to the Saints in your party. You're going to be a mighty small congregation, but I hope you will be able to learn more about the gospel and convert a few others before you come to Zion."

James bit his lip. "That may be," he said, and straightened his shoulders. "Thank you for your instruction, Brother Jeff. It's been a great enlightenment to me to have come across you folks. I'll surely miss you." He half turned, but Brother Jeff stopped him with a hand on his arm.

"I've told you all I can think of that you need to know. Let the scriptures be your guide when you have a question, Brother James. Have a safe journey."

James clapped Brother Jeff on the shoulder and moved away. Across the road, the dog was running around the wagons, and George had the teams hitched up and waiting. James walked swiftly to his horses and mule. Although he cherished the knowledge he had gained during their several days' stop, it would be good to be on the trail again. The sooner he got the Bingham party to Albuquerque, the sooner he could be on his way to Zion.

Chapter 35

After the birth of Robert's son, James gave his tent to the Fletcher family. His new custom was to bunk down beside one of the fires. Several nights after they parted ways with the Mormon travelers, Robert had pitched the tent near their wagon.

The baby cried at midnight.

James awoke and lay listening to the intimate sounds: the wail of the hungry infant, Hannah waking and rustling around in the tent as she picked up the baby, the sudden cessation of noise, then hungry gulping sounds as the child nuzzled at her breast. His belly tightened.

Rolling over in his bedroll, he decided it wasn't lust that inspired his unease. He had no eye for a married woman, especially not one nourishing her young babe. It wasn't the thought of her breast that bothered him. He had seen women nurse their children before. He closed his eyes and tried to get back to sleep, but the feeling persisted. Suddenly he knew what rankled him.

I want children.

His longing deepened and turned into an ache. He had always wanted to be a father, to teach his children what he had been taught through his growing years. Ma had made him a God-fearing man. Pa had taught him practical skills. Dealing with his brothers, both the older and the younger, had helped him learn to get along with others, and that family was the best, the most important group of people he could associate with.

Family. Robert looked forward to the birth of his child. I want that same pleasure.

He had talked a bit with Robert, and admired the man's enthusiasm for providing a good life for Hannah and their baby. "A good life in a new land," he had said.

Robert will do that, he told himself. *He has the gumption for it.*

James turned the other way in bed.

I want a family forever, he thought. *Amparo's taught me that.* A cold wave raised bumps on his skin as it passed through him from head to toe. *I want a family, a wife to give me children, a woman I can love as I've loved before. Not someone to replace Amparo—no one can take her place. I need someone to stand by my side and share the rest of my life.*

Jessie's face loomed before his mind's eye. He sighed deeply, recalling the passion he'd once felt for her. *I surely was a lustful young stallion. Six little beans! I hurt Jessie so bad by leaving her behind in the Shenandoah.* Another sigh quivered through his frame. *If I'd stayed, I'd likely be a father now.* A knot of regret wrapped around his heart. He moistened his lips. *I want a living, breathing passel of kids I can hold in my arms, teaching 'em how to rope and gentle a horse, and comforting 'em when they fall down. I want Jessie there, birthing 'em, mothering 'em, kissing their skinned knees and . . .* He held his breath until he felt dizzy, then exhausted the air from his lungs and took in a great, shivering chestful of air. *Kissing me in the night. I want Jessie back, and Ned Heizer can go—*

Mules tales! He didn't want to swear, now that he'd got God's forgiveness for his sins, but the thought of Ned Heizer holding Jessie in his arms made his head feel near to exploding. *I may not be good enough to kiss Jessie's little finger, but I'm a danged sight better for her than Ned Yankee Heizer.*

A resolve started to grow in him, a commitment to make things right with Jessie, to somehow show her the depth of his affection. He had to turn her heart away from Ned. He had to make her love him again.

Chapter 36

James scouted the trail ahead of the wagons, keeping a sharp eye on the sky as it grew dark with heavy clouds. The wind began to rise, cold and fierce, gusting against him and the horse, and threatening to push them off the trail. He tied his neck scarf over his hat to keep it in place and pulled gloves from his pocket. Then he turned the sorrel's head out of the wind and started back toward the small train.

George rode out from the wagons, his eyes dark slits in his face. By the time the two met, the wind was howling, and flakes of snow were swirling around their heads, dusting the shoulders of their coats.

"What's up ahead? We need a campground."

"There ain't a good, sheltered spot, except . . ." James stopped shouting for a moment, adjusting his collar.

"Except what?" George held on to his hat with one hand and kept a firm grip with the other on the reins of his dancing horse.

"Down a piece there's a big Mexican outfit, a *hacienda*, my wife called it. They're good folks." James's muscles tensed as he awaited George's response.

George frowned. "Mexicans? Are they honest?"

"Don Pedro is a big landowner and a kind, decent man." James covered his lower face with his hand and breathed into it to warm his nose and mask his dismay at George's prejudicial attitude. "He helped me out once."

"I reckon we can't be choosy in a storm like this."

"No." His voice was flat as he continued. "We don't dare be choosy."

"Lead the way." Luke was driving the first wagon, and George turned around to inform the boy about the change of plans.

James headed his horse straight into the wind, fighting it as it wheeled around to escape the icy blast. "Hi! Get up there, horse!" he muttered. "You'll be in a nice warm stable soon." He slapped the sorrel on the flank. The animal bucked a bit, but it was weary, and James was determined, so it soon followed his direction and continued along the road. A popping sound drew his attention, the impact of the horse's hooves striking the frozen snow.

A few minutes later, James turned the tiring horse into the lee of a small stand of trees where a trail left the road. The shelter wasn't enough for all the wagons, and James didn't dare stop. Luke drove his team in James's wake, and the other two wagons followed.

The temperature fell rapidly as the snow swirled around in the icy wind, leaving the ground white in some places and bare in others. George rode forward and told James he was going to spell his wife at driving the team.

"Mrs. Heizer can't feel her hands. How much further do we have to go?"

"I ain't been to the house, George, but I reckon it can't be too distant."

"Well, keep us on the trail. If this wind dies down, the snow will cover the path."

James barked a laugh. "It would be warmer, though." He could feel the hairs in his nostrils freezing stiff in the cold, and he covered his nose with his hand for a moment. His old wounds ached, and he rubbed his side. "Go take care of your wife," he said, and George rode back to the wagons.

James moved closer to the first wagon and used a rope end to chivvy the lead horses onward. "Luke!" he called out. "Use your whip, boy. We got to get out of this storm."

The boy nodded, handed the lines to his sister, and turned to get his whip from the wagon box. Jessie slapped the lines on the rumps of the horses, and James called out, "Hi! Giddap! Hey!" to the horses before he went ahead to pick out the trail.

Fifteen minutes later, the half-frozen travelers arrived at the arched gateway to the Chaves headquarters. James dismounted to open the wrought iron gate. It screeched as he pushed it aside. When all three wagons had passed through, he closed the gate, got back into the saddle, and rode up the white lane behind the wagons.

When the wagons stopped before the long, low adobe buildings, he approached the house. Don Pedro Chaves stood on his porch out of the storm, bundled in a bearskin coat.

James got off his horse.

"I know you, yes?" Don Pedro asked when James approached.

"Yes, sir. I'm James Owen. I was in Santa Fe some weeks back." He took off his right glove and held out his hand.

The older man's face lit up as he recognized the name as well as the face, and he extended his hand to James. "Oh yes, yes." He shook hands with warm regard. "At La Fonda." Don Pedro craned his neck to look at the people getting out of the wagons. "Tell me, where is your dear wife?"

James made a harsh sound. "She met with a . . . bad . . . accident," he said, pain pinching his voice. "She died in Trinidad."

"No!" Don Pedro crossed himself. "That cannot be!"

James plunged ahead, ignoring his rising grief. "This is the Bingham family and their kin. I'm taking them to Albuquerque." James gestured at the Binghams. "Can we shelter here?"

"¡Cómo no! Yes, of course! Please, bring your friends inside."

"Thank you." James turned to the family. "He says we're welcome. Go ahead in. I'll look after the stock."

"No, *joven*, my men will see to them. You are frozen. Please enter. Tell me of your misfortune. *¡Ay!* Such a young girl to die!" He crooked a finger and gave an order to the man who appeared, and the servant hurried off to do Don Pedro's bidding.

଼

Jessie stumbled down the wagon wheel. Her fingers were numb. She couldn't feel her toes. Would she ever be warm again? She shuddered as she approached the covered porch, rubbing her fists along her arms, trying to regain feeling in them.

Her first sight of the man who stood greeting James made her open her eyes wide. Although he must be very old because his hair was silver, his brown face bore few deep wrinkles. He carried himself straight and tall, almost like a general, she imagined. She couldn't sense any malice in the man, for he smiled and made gestures of welcome to her mother, clearly inviting her inside the house. *Mighty gracious of him*, she thought.

When everyone was out of the storm, the man stood beside the roaring fire in a massive fireplace and spoke to the party in accented but formal English.

"I am Pedro Chaves, Peter Chaves in English. Everyone calls me Don Pedro. Welcome to my humble home. It is at your service for anything you will need. Come to the fire, ladies. Get warm." He turned to James and beckoned toward the women. "Now, who are these lovely ladies, Mr. Owen?"

James made introductions, including the men of the party, as well as Luke. Don Pedro turned to Mrs. Bingham. "Señora, my wife and the cooks will have a meal ready very soon. May they bring you hot chocolate?"

Jessie watched as Ma's look of apprehension fled, replaced by astonishment. "Chocolate! My lands, Mr. Chaves, it has been years since I tasted chocolate! You are very kind, sir."

"It is nothing, señora, a small token to offer my guests." He motioned to a leather armchair in front of the hearth. "Please, sit and warm yourself."

"Thank you, sir. Girls, come around and thank Mr. Chaves for his generosity."

Heppie went and made a curtsey, and Hannah nodded to the man as she held her baby close. Jessie hesitated and glanced around. James had stepped back to allow the women to approach Mr. Chaves. Ned and the other men ranged themselves at the back of the group. How did James know this man?

Jessie put away the question to ponder later and stepped forward. She thrust out her hand to shake his like a man would do and said, "Thank you, sir. We appreciate your hospitality."

Don Pedro took her hand and shook it, grinning broadly. "You are most welcome."

Jessie smiled, ducked her head, and turned away. The man's openhandedness puzzled her. *Why's he being so kind to us? We showed up unannounced and unexpected. How did he come to know James?* As she wiggled the questions around in her brain, Jessie moved over to stand beside her mother, who had sat down in an armchair.

Jessie rubbed her hands together and looked around the room. Hannah and Heppie were seated on stools close to the fireplace. George knelt on one knee beside Heppie, spreading his hands to the fire's warmth. Across the room, Don Pedro gestured toward a leather couch, and Robert and James took seats on it.

Jessie felt a touch on her elbow. She turned her head to meet Ned's gaze.

"Are you getting warm?" he asked. "I worried that your fingers would get frostbit, not having gloves."

Jessie looked at her hands and waggled her fingers. "I reckon they're doing fine," she said. "Still a mite cold, but I've got feeling in them now. I was worried when they were numb."

Ned took Jessie by the elbows and turned her around to face him. He cupped his hands around one of hers and chafed it. "This will take the chill off, honeybunch," he said.

Jessie allowed him to rub her hands, first one, then the other, and back to the first. He moved his hands up her arm, and she felt a twinge of uneasiness. Ned was being overly friendly, especially with her mother sitting right there beside them.

"Ned," she murmured. "Leave off. I'm all warm now."

One of the corners of his mouth moved slightly downward. He opened it as though he were going to reply, but closed it again and dropped his hands from her arm. He nodded, and said, "As you wish."

Jessie rolled her eyes toward her mother, hoping he would take a hint. She wasn't sure Ma could see what Ned had been doing, with Jessie between them, but the touch of his fingers on her upper arms had unsettled her. Yes, she had promised to marry Ned, but that didn't mean he was permitted to become so familiar. He probably wanted to kiss her, but she hadn't allowed that intimacy. Only one man had kissed her, and— She put her hand to her lips. *Only James Owen.* She looked behind her. James sat on the couch across the room, his fingers twisting against his thighs. She could tell he wasn't listening to Don Pedro or Robert. He looked up, meeting her eyes.

She turned her head, feeling guilty as she pushed away her tumbling thoughts. She shuddered, aware of Ned's concerned eyes on her. Glancing sideways, she caught sight of a stool like the ones her sisters sat upon. She took a breath and smiled brightly up at the man who would be her husband.

"Ned, will you draw up that stool for me? I'm a bit weary."

"Of course," he said, and went to do her bidding. She bit her lip. *How can I forget about James Owen? He's always nearby.* She rubbed a cold spot on her arm. *How am I ever going to make a life with Ned if James stays on in Albuquerque?*

Ned put the stool at her feet and Jessie sank onto it. The leather seat had absorbed warmth from the room, and the heat felt comforting through her skirt and undergarments. "Thank you."

He settled down cross-legged on the floor beside her and jerked his head in acknowledgement of her thanks.

Words jumped out of Jessie's mouth when she noticed that Don Pedro and the other men had stood up. "Why is that man being so good to us?" She took a sharp breath, annoyed at herself for letting her thought free.

Ned looked surprised, then scowled. "He seems friendly with Mr. Owen. Maybe he owes him a favor."

Jessie shrugged. "I reckon there's no way of knowing."

"Honeybunch." Ned reached up and put his hand on her arm. "You appear puzzled at Mr. Pedro's kindness, but I reckon he won't do us any harm."

"I wasn't worried about harm coming to us. He's mighty generous to a pack of strangers."

James left the room, following a servant man. She yanked her eyes away from him, focusing on her betrothed.

Ned patted Jessie's arm. "Don't go twisting your brains into a knot, honeybunch. Sit there all comfy cozy, soak up the warm air, and quit thinking so hard."

Honeybunch? Is Ned going to call me honeybunch all our lives? Jessie shuddered. *I don't like that pet name.*

"You're shivering. Shall I rub your arms again?" Ned asked.

"No, no, I'm fine." She folded her arms across her chest. *Honeybunch? James never called me that. He had more sense. Drat! Why am I thinking about James again?* She put her hand to her forehead and rubbed a spot above her right eyebrow. *Jessie, you hate and despise James Owen. Because of that, you gave your word to Ned to marry him, and that's all you need to think about.* She stopped rubbing her face, looked down at Ned, and gave him half a smile. *I reckon we'll do as well as most folks, pulling in the same harness, as long as he doesn't call me honeybunch!*

&

James sat at Don Pedro's invitation and looked at the other side of the room. Ned stood close to Jessie, chafing first one hand, then the other between his own. His hands wandered up her forearms, rubbing circulation back into them. Each intimate gesture felt like it drove a thorn into James's flesh. He wanted to leap up, cross the room, knock Ned Heizer on his backside, and take Jessie away from him.

This is how Carl felt, watching Ellen and me. A jolt of fire flashed through James's veins at the thought of the woman who had been betrothed to him, and had married his brother. *I tried so hard to forget Jessie, to learn to love Ellen.* He looked at his hands, twisted together against his legs. *I should have seen the way of it and given her up to Carl with a bit of grace. Now I've lost Jessie to a Yankee. No, worse than a Yankee. A Virginia turncoat.*

Don Pedro said something to him, but James couldn't tear himself away from his thoughts to answer. He looked across at the folks arranged around the fireplace once more. He realized Jessie's eyes were fixed on him, and he felt a rush of blood into his head. *She don't love him. She gave him a promise, but she don't love him. Just like Ellen promised to wed me, not giving me her love with her word.* The bitter irony hit him like a physical blow, and he rocked backward in his seat. Grim truth took possession of his soul. *Jessie don't love him, but she's wary of me. I hurt her when I left her behind. Pa set me up to marry Ellen and I lost her to Carl, but later I did marry someone. A gal I didn't yet love.* He swallowed down the gall that had risen in his throat as he listed his sins against Jessie.

Now Don Pedro and Robert had risen to their feet, and James scrambled to stand.

"Gentlemen, you are weary. I am selfish to keep you from your beds." He addressed himself to a servant who had come into the hall. "Ramón, are the fires lit?"

"*Sí,* señor. *Todo está listo,*" said the man, and James mentally translated his words as assent. But he remembered *listo* as signifying bright or quick. That couldn't be right.

He screwed up his courage and asked, "Don Pedro, what does *listo* mean?"

"Ah *joven,* it can mean clever, but Ramón intends to say that all things are in readiness. If you will go with him, my young friend, he will take you to a sleeping room." He turned to Robert. "Please, if you will wait a moment longer, Ramón will bring you, your señora, and your little one to another." He turned back to include James. "We have many rooms here in the *hacienda.* We don't often have the opportunity to fill them with guests. This occasion is a great joy to me." He put out his hand and shook with James. "Thank you for coming."

As James followed Ramón down the long corridor, his thoughts turned to the girl he'd married. *Amparo, I came to love you dearly. What Brother Jeff told us gave me a lot of comfort. There's a way I can be with you again when I'm dead. But girl, there's something you got to understand. I'm still alive, and I want Jessie!*

Ramón opened a door and ushered James into a small bedroom with a fire burning at one end. He bowed slightly to James and left the room.

James went right to the bedstead and put his war bag down beside it. He stood above the bed, remembering how he'd thought his life was at an end when Amparo died. His body stiffened at the remembrance of laying her to rest. That ordeal was over, he reminded himself. Now, because of the new ideas he'd accepted, he could go on living. He could have hope.

I'll need to win Jessie back, he decided, and thought of how he'd gotten her to love him before. His cramped shoulders gradually loosened as he recalled the sweet days of courting Jessie, singing to her on the swing in her folks' backyard, kissing each one of her fingers between verses of his love songs. How long had it been since he'd raised his voice in song?

"I sang to Pa's Texas cows," he said aloud. "I never sang to Ellen, nor to Amparo, but I sang to those dim-witted cows."

He sank to his knees to offer up his nightly prayer, asking for calm in his soul and for a way to gain back Jessie's trust so he could win her from Ned.

ॐ

They stayed the night, and the next day too, as the blizzard roared on for nearly twenty-four hours. Don Pedro had made sure everyone was comfortable in snug rooms of both the house and a guesthouse. The animals were housed in tight adobe barns and suffered no ill effects of the cold. The dog, after making the acquaintance of Don Pedro's dog pack, spent most of its time lying in front of the warm hearth.

When the storm blew itself out, James ventured from the house to look around. Where was the road? All signs of the trail they had traveled yesterday lay under deep snow. He went back into the house, stamping his boots on the tile floor.

Don Pedro met him in the great room and took him into his office, where a desk with a pile of ledgers stacked on a leather blotter sat comfortably close to a potbelly stove. He ushered James to an armchair in front of the desk and went to a sideboard where stood a decanter of brandy and several glasses, one with an inch of liquid already in the bottom. "Such a storm we had, no? You will stay again this night." He offered James a drink.

Declining the liquor, James said, "We don't want to put you out, sir."

Don Pedro picked up his glass and took it to the desk, where he sat in a swivel chair. "*¡Ay, señor!* We enjoy our guests. You are no trouble. None whatsoever." He smiled and twitched his moustache. "You can help me improve my English."

James laughed at that. "I'm no great shakes as a scholar, sir."

Don Pedro chuckled. "You learned English at the knee of your *mamá, joven.* It makes a difference."

James nodded at that thought. "I reckon it does, at that. My ma tried her best to raise us up as good, Christian citizens, with a lot of country wisdom mixed into the ABC's."

"I think, *mi jovencito*, that your mamá is a very great lady." He lifted his glass. "Cheers, my friend James. That is what they say, *no?*"

"No. I mean yes. In polite company, that is."

Don Pedro sipped his drink and smiled again. "My language is somewhat confusing, *no?* When I say no at the end of a sentence, I ask you to agree with me."

James smiled. "Confusing, yes, but awful purty. Sometimes, when Amparo got going speaking your tongue, the sound was musical, like bells tinkling." He rubbed his chin. "I miss her. I miss her a lot, sir."

"I can see that, joven. If it helps to know it, when you lose a loved one, as the years go by, the pain is less. You begin to remember only the good times, to cherish the sweet memories." He stopped and gazed into his tumbler. "My youngest son died many years ago."

"I didn't know that, sir. I'm sorry for your loss."

"He was a good son, very obedient, very kind. Since that time, I have tried to live a worthy life to enable him to enter heaven." Don Pedro moved his hand through the air. "That is what the priest counseled me to do, along with giving liberally to the church, of course. Surely my sacrifices have made that difference to my son."

James held silence, wondering if Don Pedro's religious penance bore any relationship to the circumstances leading to his own marriage.

Don Pedro smiled. "My memories of my son are now sweet, as I said, joven, but it has been many years. I wish that you may find peace sooner than that."

"Thank you, sir. I have a question for you. Is it a common practice in your religion to pledge to do something to get your loved ones to heaven?"

"It is. Why do you ask?"

"I reckon that's what my wife took on her. Her pa was recently dead, and when we met in Colorado, she was mighty insistent that she had to marry someone, anyone. The blacksmith said she'd made a vow. Do you reckon she was worried about getting her pa to heaven?"

Don Pedro pursed his lips. After a long moment he spoke. "You have made clear some of those words you had me translate at La Fonda, joven. You married the young lady to fulfill her vow?"

"That seems to be the case, sir."

"So, you made a convenient marriage."

James tucked his chin into his chest, then looked up at Don Pedro and squared his shoulders. "I reckon. At first."

"You grew to cherish your wife?"

"That's so."

"Were her last days happy ones?"

"I—I reckon so, sir. They were for me."

"*Bien. Muy bien.* That is good. I renew my wish that you may find peace and comfort as time passes." Don Pedro stirred in his seat. "Will you remain alone? It is not good for a man to be alone."

"I'm thinking on that problem, sir. Turning so soon to someone new seems like being unfaithful to all Amparo meant to me."

"You must take your time to grieve, joven, but not too long. Find a good woman to marry."

"I'm working along those lines."

"There is someone in your company? The bold *señorita*, perhaps?"

"She's spoken for."

"Ah! But is she married? May not a woman dance with anyone she chooses until she is at last wed?"

James felt his body tighten at the thought of Jessie's marrying Ned. "Perhaps, sir. I'd purely hate to see her end up with the man who claims her hand."

"You know her well?"

A memory of Jessie's sweet lips under his swept over James. "She's a friend from long ago," he said, knowing he was blushing. He hoped his beard hid his reddened face.

"Ah." Don Pedro let his breath out in a long sigh. "More than a friend, I believe. Or so your face tells me."

James leaned over to hide it, clasping his hands between his knees.

"You have good words, my young friend. Use them. Convince her you are the better man."

James looked up. "I reckon I need to try." He rolled a shoulder. "My feelings are tied in knots, sir."

Don Pedro nodded, and suddenly he chuckled. "They will be forever, joven. Remember, women are incomprehensible. We cannot know their minds. We can only strive to bring them happiness."

James quirked his eyebrow. "Is that meant to cheer me, sir?"

Don Pedro laughed, picked up his glass, and drained it. "At the root of all, your heart is happy, my friend. You should not stay in misery." He got to his feet and James joined him. "I have enjoyed our conversation, but I must get back to work. Please, tell the others of my invitation to stay another night. If you cannot tell which way to travel, you must remain here a little while longer, yes?" Don Pedro's eyes twinkled. "We also say yes at the end."

James chuckled. "I'll tell them of your offer. Thank you, sir. *Your* heart is very large."

Chapter 37

The weather warmed during the night, and the travelers left the following morning, after expressing their gratitude to Don Pedro for his kind hospitality. The wagons jolted along the snow-covered path that led to the main trail. With the snow melting, fence posts marked the way to the main gate. Don Pedro had sent a rider ahead to greet them when they reached the portal, and he guided them along the track toward the road and saw them on their way.

The party spent two days pushing through windswept plains and snow-clogged passes. On the third day, James rode ahead of the wagons, checking the trail for any remaining drifts. He turned in his saddle to look at the wagons trundling along a half-mile behind him. The snow had held off, and they were making good time along the road. Glorieta Pass was ahead of them. Soon enough, they would be in Santa Fe.

As he settled straight in the saddle once more, James clucked to the sorrel horse, and it sprang forward at his urging. He wanted to see what was along the road. If he found water, their night camp would be much more pleasant. His thoughts drifted over his many camps, both in the South and here in the West. The night camp before the fight at the courthouse, waiting for the Yankees to come up to battle. The camp on the prairie where he watched his fiancée Ellen leave the fire with his brother Carl. The camp at Fort Union with Amparo in his arms and joy in his heart. His cheeks reddened at the memory of their lovemaking, sweet and tender. *Oh God!* he groaned to the heavens. *How can she be gone? How can I bear being in Santa Fe without her?*

He closed his eyes, letting the feeling of desolation sweep over him. When it had reached his toes, he lifted his head and squared his shoulders. God had a promise of joy for him. Someday . . . someday Amparo would be his again, for all time! As his heart lifted, he stood in his stirrups and gave a shout of exultation, punching the sky with his fist.

The sorrel shied, and James sat in the saddle again, chuckling at his exuberance. *Ain't I the silly one! Robert is going to come see what I'm yelling about, for sure.* He patted the animal's neck. "Sorry, boy. I didn't aim to startle you."

Several miles on, James found an inviting location for their night camp. Water flowed from a crack in the side of a wall of rock, creating a pool that invited travelers to stop and refresh themselves. A stand of oak trees offered shelter and wood. If he remembered correctly, Santa Fe was but ten miles or so along the trail, and they would be able to reach it tomorrow.

When he rode back among the wagons to let Robert know he'd found a campsite, James noticed Jessie walking along the trail, heedless of the mud, braid-crowned head bent down, a serious expression on her face. She carried a book and glanced at it from time to time. Her arm dropped to her side, and she bit her lip in concentration. Ned Heizer was nowhere in sight.

He remembered Don Pedro's advice, and his stomach flipped over. A short time ago he'd been thinking of Amparo. In a few minutes he'd have to turn his whole attention to Jessie while Ned was elsewhere. He gulped and went to find Robert.

When James had finished giving his report, he rode up beside Jessie. Dismounting, he walked beside her for a few paces, holding the sorrel's headstall in his right hand so the fractious horse was a good distance from the girl.

"Something worrying you?" he asked.

She jumped and said, "Ah!" and he realized that she had been so engrossed in her thoughts that she hadn't known he was present.

"I didn't mean to alarm you," he said, putting out his hand to steady her. His fingers shook as he touched her back.

"James," she said. They no longer walked. He no longer touched her.

"Were you woolgathering?"

She looked at her feet. "Hannah loaned me the book Miss Becky gave her. I been reading in it about a young man named Nephi." She stopped talking, lifted her head, and looked sideways toward James.

He said, "Robert told me about him. He was a prophet."

"Robert told Hannah about your prophet, Brother Joseph, and the new one, Brother Brigham." She looked at her feet again. "She told me about them. I reckon it's a good thing to have a prophet."

"Are you studying on the Mormon religion, Jessie?" James's chest felt tight with anticipation.

She looked him square in the face. "Maybe."

"Is Ned going to permit that?"

Jessie's eyes went wide. "Ned's not my keeper! I can decide for myself what religion I'll follow."

James felt like dancing a little jig at her gumption, but restrained himself. Instead, he dropped his chin and looked at his boots. He thought maybe a smile was in order, to go with the "good words" he'd selected to say, and when he lifted his head, his lips curved upward.

"I'd show respect for your choices, if I was your man."

Jessie inhaled sharply.

He knew he'd surprised her. He could only hope she wasn't put off by his daring words. She began to walk again, and he strolled along beside her, matching his stride to her shorter one.

She stopped abruptly, and he turned to face her.

"You know I told Ned—"

"I know," he said, cutting her off. "You haven't married him. Not yet." He let the bald fact hang in the air, and watched as she digested it.

Jessie lifted her chin.

James suppressed a groan. She intended to be contrary.

"You have other concerns on your mind," she said. "You love your wife."

"I do," he agreed, and instantly knew he'd stepped in a deep hole. *Hush! That was the wrong thing to say.*

Jessie's face went pale. She turned away and raised the book in front of her eyes. After a moment, she said in a voice as cold as the wind, "Good day, James," and walked away.

James almost felt icicles forming on his eyebrows. He mounted his horse and took his post at the front of the wagons again.

∾

Ned rode up from the rear as soon as he noticed James Owen talking to Jessie. Before he reached the two, Jessie walked away, her face in a book, and Owen got on the sorrel and left. Much as he'd like to pound Owen's face into the mud, Ned felt relief at not having to confront him. The day's weather was ideal for traveling, cold and crisp, the only detriment being the muddy condition of the road. The sooner they got to Albuquerque, the sooner he and Jessie would be wed, and Owen would be out of the picture.

The thought of marrying Jessie made Ned grin, and with that expression on his face, he caught up to her.

"Afternoon, Jessie," he said. "Was Mr. Owen bothering you?"

She lowered her book and shrugged. "No. Not so much a body should take notice."

Her words, though spoken in a mild tone of voice, seemed like a reproof, and Ned felt his grin stiffen.

"Just you call out for me if he vexes you again," Ned said. "I don't want him hassling you."

Jessie looked at him. "He wasn't hassling me, Ned. Only conversing a bit."

"Well, don't let him become a problem." He rode along beside her as she put the book in front of her face again. "What's that you're reading?"

"A book Hannah lent me."

A guarded note in her voice made him crane his neck in an attempt to see the title.

"When did Hannah come by a new book? It's not from those Mormons, is it?"

Jessie closed the book and put it in her pocket. "What if it is?" She walked forward, not looking at him.

"You want to be cautious of those Mormons, honeybunch. They've got some strange ways."

"What are you saying, Ned? They seemed like normal folk."

"Well, for one thing, I count baptizing a body entirely down in the water on a mighty cold day powerful strange."

"Hannah wanted that, washing away her sins."

"I'm glad you have more sense."

"Don't make light of Hannah."

She spoke sharply, and Ned drew back, regretting his choice of words.

"I'm sorry. I didn't mean to slight your sister. I misspoke."

They moved on in silence for a time. Finally Ned said, "Jessie, honeybunch, we're drawing nigh to Santa Fe. Don't you think we could get married there?"

The furious face she turned on him took him by surprise. Her words shook him no less.

"I told you we'd wait until we got to the end of the trail, Ned. You agreed. Let's not be hasty in changing things around."

"Albuquerque's not that far distant, Jessie. You wouldn't run much risk of, well, getting in a family way and being all discommoded."

Jessie's face flushed. "Don't linger here, Ned. I don't want a disagreement between us."

He nodded, and turned his horse aside, flustered at her show of temper. Whatever was making her irritable? *I'll wager Maggie Julander is more tractable*, he thought. *She would heed my cautions about odd folk.* Ned let his thoughts dwell on Maggie for a moment, then clapped his hand against his cheek. Maggie was already one of those "odd" folks. Maggie was a Mormon.

He rubbed his jaw. The stubble of his beard felt like sandpaper on his flesh. Jessie had spoken the truth: the Mormons had seemed to be normal, not according to the tales he'd heard of them having horns and tails and the like. He'd seen no horns coming from Maggie's head, no tail proceeding from her shapely— He stopped himself from following that notion, but his wayward body was already warm from thinking about the dark-haired girl.

What ails you? he castigated himself. *Jessie's going to be your wife, not Maggie Julander. After all the work it took you to win her over, you'd best fix your fancies on the prize.*

୪

He called me honeybunch again! Jessie thought as she walked away from Ned. She repressed her desire to scream into a slight "Ahhh!" *Won't he ever learn?*

At once she felt ashamed. She wasn't being fair. She hadn't mentioned to Ned how much she disliked the pet name. She would tell him tonight. She reflected a moment, whether she'd also treated James a bit too sharply, and decided she had, although with good reason. *I did trick him into saying so, but he still cares for that dead Mexican girl.* She took a deep breath. *His wife. What business does he have making up to me, anyway, telling me how he'd respect my selections in life? I'll stick with Ned, thank you very much, James Owen. Ned loves me!*

Jessie spent the rest of the afternoon walking along with her nose in Hannah's book, fascinated by the account of ancient people taking a journey of their own. Once, she stumbled and fell, scraping a knee, but the burn of the abrasion seemed small compared to the trials she read about.

That evening, Ned came around and joined her where she sat beside the fire, mending a tear in her skirt. She didn't look up as she said, "I'm sorry I snapped at you today."

Ned patted her hand. "That's fine, honeybunch. I reckon we can wait to get married."

Jessie sighed and bit her lip. "I simply cannot abide you calling me honeybunch, Ned." She gave a shiver. "Can you please refrain from saying it?"

Ned must have seen her slight convulsion, for he put his arm around her, saying, "Are you taking a chill? Can I bring you a blanket or the like?"

"Ned," she persisted. "Stick to the point. Will you stop using that pet name?"

"Of course, honey—" He stopped himself abruptly. "I reckon I can if I'll put my mind to it." He grimaced. "Anything else about me you've taken a dislike to?"

Finished with the mending task, Jessie bit through the thread, wove the needle into the cloth and flexed her fingers. "Well now, you do seem a mite prickly when James Owen is around. I'd favor seeing you two on a more affable footing. He is your old friend."

Ned compressed his lips, then licked them. After a moment, he spoke in a rough voice. "That's not something I can promise. We don't see eye to eye."

"You can be civil to him."

Ned cocked his head sideways. "I reckon I can do that, so long as he understands that when this journey's done, you're marrying me."

"I said so, didn't I?" Jessie replied, shrugging. "What James understands or doesn't understand is not in my power to guarantee."

Ned seemed satisfied, and after spending another quarter hour in Jessie's company, he went off to check the stock.

When Ned had gone, Jessie took the needle from the cloth and flicked it with her thumbnail as a thought came to her. *What does James understand? It's certain that he made a point to seek me out this afternoon. And the thing he said! If he was my man.* She brought her hand toward her face, remembering the long-ago touch of James's lips on hers, but she pricked herself with the needle and dropped it.

"Oh drat!" she said, cross with herself. She pulled a piece of wood out of the fire to light her search for the needle, then got on her knees and carefully felt over the ground beside her seat.

"What's amiss?" James Owen stood beside her. He leaned over and took the wood from her hand. "Have you lost something?"

His voice brought her upright, and her face flushed as she recalled where her thoughts had recently strayed. When she tried to speak, nothing issued from her throat. She cleared it and tried again, dismayed at the squeaky sound. "I dropped my needle. It's the only one I have."

"I'll help you look." He knelt down alongside her, holding the firebrand first high, then low. Though they spent several minutes going over the ground thoroughly, the needle remained lost.

"That is so vexing," Jessie said as she climbed to her feet, ignoring James's proffered hand. "But I thank you for making the attempt." She turned her head away from James and wiped her eyes, not wanting to share with him that her frustration had brought out tears. She glanced back at him just as he spoke.

"It's the least bit a man can do," he said with a lingering look at her, and walked away into the darkness. He left Jessie feeling faint and breathless, wondering what he'd meant to imply. The warmth in her vitals confirmed her notion that he'd continued his tactic from the afternoon. James had set out to court her.

Chapter 38

The next day, James arose early and checked the same ground he and Jessie had covered the night before. He found the needle and was about to seek out Jessie and give it to her when he noticed that Ned had her attention.

James gritted his teeth and carefully wove the needle into the inside lapel of his coat. He had plenty of time later to give it back.

He went to saddle the black mare, but he found that another horse had bitten her on the hock during the night, and she was not fit to ride without treatment and rest. He shook his head over the matter, patched up her wounds, and saddled the sorrel.

Just as James put his foot in the stirrup, the dog chased a raccoon into camp, and they both ran under the sorrel's belly. The horse began to buck, and James, losing his grip on the saddle horn, flew into the air.

He woke up some little time later to the sound of Heppie Heizer's screams, seeing Jessie's anxious face leaning over him. Actually, Jessie had two faces, and they swirled in front of him, along with those of the rest of the party who crowded about him.

"She-ah," he said, trying to rise up.

Jessie pushed him back to the ground with gentle hands. "Lie still," she said. "You busted your head."

"I've got to hunt." His voice came out in a croak, startling him. His fingers explored his head, and came upon a knot wet with blood. He looked at his fingers. There were several too many of them.

"Not today," she insisted, although her voice shook. She turned away for a moment, saying to the crowd, "I'll get his bed made up, if some of you will carry him over."

James closed his eyes, heard the voices of assent. His head did ache. So did his back. He flexed his extremities and they all worked. None of his bones seemed broken. He opened his eyes again and raised himself up on one elbow. "Jessie?"

Again, she pushed him down. "James, don't you rise up and hurt yourself more. Stay still. Soon's I lay out your bedroll, Robert and George will bring you to it."

"Stop dancing around, Jess."

Her forehead—foreheads—furrowed in concern. "I'm still as a statue, James. It's your eyes that are rolling around. Stay still, now. You'll be right as rain after you take a rest." Her voice still shook a bit.

He shut his eyes, dizzy from the effort of trying to sort out which image of Jessie was the true one. He knew he would regain his strength by and by, but right now he felt that emptying his stomach might settle it down. He fought the impulse. He'd mess up Jessie's dress. That wouldn't do. That wouldn't do at all. Six little beans, but his head hurt!

James sensed movement as Jessie stood up, but he kept his eyes closed. He remembered how much she disliked blood and wondered if she, too, was battling with her stomach. Still and all, she seemed determined to take care of him.

After a while, somebody grasped him under the arms and someone else grabbed onto his legs, and they lifted him off the earth. Except for a moment when his trousers bumped against the dirt, the trip seemed uneventful. Be that as it may, James was grateful to be on solid ground again. The swaying motion had increased his nausea to the point that he didn't know if he could keep down his breakfast or not.

He couldn't.

Hush, he hadn't felt this weak since, well since he'd been laid up in the jail in Pueblo Town.

A cool, wet cloth touched the corner of his lips, wiping away the muck he'd vomited up. He opened one eye. Jessie was beside him again. One-and-a-half Jessies, now, not two. Seeing any number of Jessies was a long sight better than looking up from a jail cot and seeing Rand Hilbrands's face.

"There now," Jessie said. "Feel better?"

James closed his eye and nodded, then wished he'd kept his head still. He breathed out to keep the nausea at bay. After a few moments, he whispered, "Anytime you're around, I feel better."

He felt a fleeting pat on his shoulder, a little shove. "Go on with you, James Owen! Here you lay with a broken head, and you're trying to sweet-talk me." Even as she spoke, Jessie lifted his head slightly and dabbed at the wound.

"Nah," he said, teetering on the edge of a black void. "No sweet talk. I want you around for all my life and always."

Jessie inhaled sharply.

James felt light as air, his head suspended in Jessie's still hands.

He felt the wash of her breath on his face as she let it out. Her fingers began to work quickly to bind up his head as she said, "I'm betrothed to Ned."

He opened both eyes, lifted his hand, and touched her cheek. He let his hand fall to his side. "He don't give you enough respect."

"James!" The whispered word exploded in the still air. "Is the pot calling the kettle black?"

He understood her meaning, and struggled against the looming darkness to find words to lay her worries to rest. "I've always found you irresistible, Jessie."

"How can you? You love that . . . Amparo girl." She bit off the words.

"Don't you care for Hannah and Heppie both?" James closed his hands into fists, fighting to stay conscious. "Luke and Max? Your ma and pa, as well?"

"Oh," she said, her voice a quiet squeak. "I reckon I do."

"I have mighty tender feelings for the two of you," he whispered. "But you're here, warm and alive. You can't say . . . flat out . . . you're not fond of me." His voice trailed off, but he made a final effort and added, "I need you."

James felt his hands relax. He let the blackness enfold him.

ⅆ

Jessie tried to say, "I'm not fond of you at all," but her voice wouldn't come out of where it lodged in her dry throat. When James's muscles went slack, she gasped and put her hand over his heart to see if it was beating. The rhythm was strong and regular under her palm. He still lived.

She hastened to finish the bandage around James's head, his last words echoing in her heart. *I need you.* What was a body supposed to say to that? Ned had never said he needed her. She didn't think he needed anyone to get along in life. He always carried an air of self-assurance. Maybe he could manage without her. *I said I'd marry him, though.* She rocked herself up onto her feet and looked down at James. *Even if James needs me, I gave my word to Ned.* A frantic feeling came over her, and she felt her face creasing into furrows. *Who do I need?*

ⅆ

Ned hurried over to take Jessie's arm when she moved away from James Owen's bedside. "Can't you let your ma tend to Owen?" he asked.

Jessie looked up at him and shrugged off his hand. "I'm handy at taking care of wounds," she said.

"What was all that talking about?" Ned felt his face settling into a frown.

"Ain't you full of questions."

"Yep. I see what's going on. He's always hounding you."

"The man took a fall, Ned. He's half out of his head. Concussed, I reckon. A little talk might keep him lucid."

"Just take care he doesn't hog all your time."

Jessie made a motion of denial with her hand. "I reckon I'll spend most of it catching up on the laundry. There's a good washing pool here. A day or two off the trail won't harm us."

"Well, I don't agree. We could pack Owen into a wagon and keep traveling on." He smiled down at Jessie. "I'm anxious to get to the end of the trek."

Jessie put her hand over her mouth. He could see a frown behind her hand. "Don't be unseemly, Ned."

"What's unseemly about wanting to get married? I do look forward to that, missie." He had more to say, but Jessie had started off, walking away from him. "Hey!" he said. "I mean no disrespect."

"Disrespect. Humph!" Jessie said, putting her head down and striding quickly toward her wagon.

Ned threw his hands into the air. "Jessie?" She didn't answer.

Another traveler came down the road late that afternoon, a slovenly man riding an ungainly roan horse and leading a string of three sorry-looking pack horses and a haltered gelding. Ned, who was pouring water from a bucket into the water barrel on the Bingham's wagon, watched the fellow ride up to the Bingham party's encampment. Robert strode out to meet him, and the man asked for permission to stay nearby. Robert gave it.

The stranger settled his animals for the night before he wandered over to Mrs. Bingham's fire when suppertime drew near. Ned, still hauling water, saw him approach.

"Howdy, ma'am," the stranger said, stopping and tipping his beat-up felt hat to Mrs. Bingham. "My name's Lester. Alphonse Lester. I have a clutch o' hen fruit here I'd be willing to trade for a meal." He held up a once-blue bandana, lumpy with eggs, and looked around the camp, counting the people with little nods of his round head. "They won't stretch for omelets to feed your kin, ma'am, but you could make a nice cake with 'em."

"Mister Lester, set down and take a load off your feet," replied Mrs. Bingham. "I ain't seen eggs in a long while. Fresh, are they?"

"Two days old, ma'am. I traded for them back a ways."

She tapped her nose with one finger. "You've had them two days. How long did they sit before you acquired them?"

"Oh no, ma'am. They're next thing to fresh. I saw them laid, bunked down in the stable as I was." He scratched his nose with his free hand and added, "I'm a trader, traveling these parts, making one trade here, another trade there. Folks know I'll be around from time to time."

Mrs. Bingham nodded. "As the eggs are reasonably fresh, I reckon we can deal. That is, if you don't mind beans and venison for supper."

"I'd be mighty pleased with beans and venison, Mrs . . .?" The word hung in the air.

"Bingham. Mrs. Joseph Bingham."

Mr. Lester nodded. "Pleased to acquaint myself with you," he said, handing over the bandana.

"Ned," she called over her shoulder. "Would you be so kind as to stow these in the grub box?"

Ned took two steps and relieved Mrs. Bingham of the parcel. "Surely, ma'am," he said, not taking his eyes off the trader as he did her bidding.

"Your son, ma'am?"

She hesitated, then said, "Near kin."

Ned approved of her not spelling out the relationship. It was none of the man's business.

Mr. Lester took a seat on the ground, again looking at the camp, his eyebrows raised in a speculative manner.

Ned thought the man was a bit too interested in his surroundings. A sense of unease raised prickles on the back of his neck. Instead of moving off toward the spring to get more water, he grabbed a stick, sank down on his haunches, and stirred the fire. When he got up, he noticed that Mr. Lester's eyes were fixed on one location. He looked in that direction. Jessie sat beside James Owen's bed, blowing on a spoonful of gruel. She'd unbraided her hair after wearing it up all day, and it rippled down her back like a waterfall made of sun-kissed wheat.

"Now that's a mighty comely sight!" Mr. Lester said, and Ned whipped his head back around toward the man.

The hungry look on the trader's face surprised Ned, and his distrust strengthened. He hovered around the fire, looking for tasks to keep him in camp so he could watch the trader.

After supper, instead of getting to his feet and going to his own campsite, Mr. Lester drew a pipe out of his pocket and lit it. Ned gritted his teeth. *Will the man never leave?*

"Are you folks traveling far?" Mr. Lester asked. "Winter ain't the best time for making good progress."

Robert answered him. "We're nearly to our destination."

"Oh, would that be Santa Fe?"

"No."

Ned felt his respect for Robert Fletcher growing. Being closemouthed was the proper way to treat this interloper.

"The hot springs down yonder?" Mr. Lester tilted his head and gestured with it in a westerly direction.

"We've got kin waiting for us where we're going." Robert had a slight frown on his face.

He's getting irritated with the man, Ned thought. *Good.*

"Hmm," said the man. "I can see you folks been having a hard time of it. You know, I'm a trader. Maybe I can help you on your way."

"How's that?" Robert asked.

The man leaned back. "You're short a horse. I have a nice gelding I picked up along my way. A first-rate draft animal. Strong. Pulls good, and all day long, sweet as you please. You wouldn't go wrong trading for it."

George bent forward. "We don't have much in the way of goods. What kind of trade are you talking about?"

"You have something here in camp that brightens my eyes." The trader motioned with his head. "Sitting right over there. That young gal." He stared at Jessie.

Ned bounded to his feet and stood above the man. "You disgust me," he shouted. "Get out of our camp!"

Chapter 39

A few days later, James led the party into Santa Fe. They parked the wagons in the plaza, the historic end of the trail from Missouri.

Robert came up to James and said, "You've been here before. Where's the best place to buy foodstuffs? We're low on flour."

James moved his head carefully to look around and get his bearings, relieved that his head had stopped swimming during the day's travel. "I wasn't here long. Just a couple of days." He pointed. "If I remember right, there's a mercantile shop two or three blocks over."

"Do you need anything? I'd like the company," said Robert.

"I'll go with you. I have a few things to buy."

"Good. Ned and George want to stay with the wagons, in case that trader they ran off shows his face in town."

"What was that all about, anyway?" James asked. "I was fairly well out of touch when the yelling started."

As they walked along, Robert told James about the disgraceful proposal the trader had made. "Ned was all for dumping him in the pond, but George talked him out of it. He said it would ruin the water for all time."

"Six little beans!" James exclaimed. "Did Miss Jessie find out what was going on?"

"I believe young Luke teased her about it."

"I wish I'd been up to pounding the fellow. Sounds like my nemesis did a good job on his own."

Robert's face took on a quizzical look. "The man's manners were lacking, that's sure, but what's your interest in the subject?"

James didn't say anything for a couple of minutes. His teeth tugged at his bottom lip. He released it and said, "I want Jessie back."

"What?" Robert stopped in the street.

James turned around to face him. He nodded. "I want to marry her."

"But you've recently lost a wife. Isn't it early to want another?"

James took a step closer to Robert. He kept his voice low when he replied. "I reckon some would say that. It's a fact I'm not finished grieving for Amparo, but I'm running out of time, Rob. Heizer's anxious to marry once he gets to Albuquerque." He smacked his leg. "I care too much for Jessie to let her go into a marriage she's dreading."

"Dreading? Are you sure?"

"Watch her with Heizer. They quibble all the time. There's not the air of a loving couple hanging about them."

Robert began to walk again. "So you're rescuing her?"

"No." James strode along beside Robert for a few steps before he spoke again. "It's not that at all. I have a great . . . tenderness for Jessie. I regret leaving her behind when I came west. I took the coward's way, letting Pa run roughshod over our wishes."

"Your pa's a mighty commanding figure of a man."

"He is that."

"Hard to stand up to a man so strong."

James snorted. "I'm shamed that I didn't. Now I have a chance I never thought would come my way. I need to win Jessie back."

"To ease your pride?"

"No. I love her so much I ache inside. I can't twiddle my thumbs and let Heizer have her."

Robert slapped James on the back. "Luck to you, my friend."

James responded in kind. "Thanks." He gestured toward a side street. "Down that way is the grocery shop."

ℴ

James drifted around the store, his heart turning into a leaden lump in his chest. He'd been in this place only weeks before, stocking up on food to make the trip back to his pa's homestead—with Amparo. The small span of time since that occasion held such a range of shattered hopes, broken dreams. Now he was here again, harboring altered expectations, different desires. *Hush! Life ain't easy.*

He mentally shook himself, noting how he'd been blessed during the past weeks. *I never thought to see Jessie again. Nor to take upon me a new religion with power and promises.* The sweetness of the two events drove the hard lump from his chest. *I'm a lucky man. Besides Ma, there are no finer women on earth than Amparo and Jessie.*

James trailed his fingers over a bolt of cloth and smiled at his fanciful notion. *I don't have no guarantee yet that Jessie will have me*, he thought.

An idea hit him, and he felt inside his coat for the needle he'd pinned there a few days before. It was in place. The fall from the horse hadn't dislodged it. What was it Jessie had said? This was her only needle. He grinned and started toward the back of the store.

ℴ

Ned watched Robert Fletcher and James Owen walk back into the camp with parcels. He limped toward where Jessie stood near the fire, helping her mother with supper. He wanted to be nearby in case Owen had any thoughts of approaching her. "Whew," he said to himself. All this watch-care over his intended bride took up a lot of time and energy. If only he could be certain Jessie wouldn't have her head turned by Owen's fancy words.

"Evening, Jessie," he said when he reached her side.

"Evening yourself, Ned." Jessie stirred the soup in a large cauldron hanging on a tripod

"Is there anything you need? Water?"

"No, Luke filled the barrels this afternoon."

"That's good. He's a hard worker."

"Aren't we all," Jessie answered.

Ned bit his lip as silence fell upon them. How come it was so hard to strike up a conversation with Jessie? After all these years, surely they had a lot to talk about. Mrs. Bingham was in earshot, though, as well as Heppie and Hannah, and strolling down memory lane didn't seem the thing to do with a passel of listeners. Neither he nor Jessie had been out of camp to explore the town, so that didn't offer a new topic of discussion.

He tried again. "Nice sky."

"It does appear to have a clear light," Jessie said.

Ned could only agree. He looked around. Owen stood over his pack, giving him a look of exasperation. *Good!* He would remain here whether he could find a task to do or not. Anything to thwart Owen's desires.

He took a step away from Jessie and squatted near the edge of the fire, spreading his hands to it as though they were cold. They weren't, but no one needed to know that. He rubbed them together, acting out his role for the women.

"You should wrap up in a quilt if you're cold, Ned," Jessie said.

"No need," he said. "I'll be comfy in a minute or two."

Just then, James Owen approached the fire and began to whistle an old tune. Ned looked up in time to see shock registering on Jessie's face, driving out the color. *What's going on?* Ned wondered. *What does "Annie Laurie" mean to her?*

"Ned," she said, her voice urgent. "I believe I need more firewood. Please, would you fetch me a big ol' log?"

He looked at the woodpile a few yards away. "You have wood."

"I need more. Please?"

He nodded and stood up, knowing he was being sent away. *Damn James Owen!* he thought. *What's he got up his sleeve?* He glowered at his rival as he passed him. Owen smiled back and took a step closer to Jessie.

∞

As soon as Ned walked off, Jessie turned to James and hissed, "Don't be foolish, James Owen."

In reply, he softly sang, "'Maxwelton's braes are bonnie where early falls the dew. And 'twas there that my fair Jessie gave me her promise true.'"

Jessie felt a touch faint. "That's all past and gone."

He shook his head and continued in a voice so hushed he almost whispered the words: "'Gave me her promise true that ne'er forgot shall be. And for love of my fair Jessie I'd lay me doon and dee.'"

"Stop it. Ma will hear you."

"Does that matter?"

"You left me behind." Jessie tried to turn away, to give him her back, but she made the mistake of looking at his eyes, and a quiver ran through her body, rooting her in place.

"I own to being foolish several times in my life, but never so much as then. When I heard you tell me to go, I lost heart."

James stood so near that Jessie could have reached out and touched his cheek. She struggled with that impulse as he continued. "I was a fool to listen to you and to Pa. I should have stayed with you or fought Pa to bring you along."

"James." She shook her head in confusion as her insides churned. *Ned loves me, Ned loves me,* she repeated several times in her mind. *James is simply jealous.*

"I have something for you," he said.

She shivered at the intensity of his voice.

He pointed to the center of the plaza. "Meet me at the town well after supper, and I'll give it to you."

Before she could refuse, James was gone, striding away with a confident air as he whistled the refrain to "Annie Laurie" again.

"Six little beans!" she muttered, using one of James's favorite exclamations. Curiosity zipped around the corridors of her mind as she tried to imagine what James would bring her. It suggested first one thing, then another. *If James is really jealous* . . . She gave the soup a vigorous stir and knew that, despite her misgivings, she would be at the well.

୫

After supper, Jessie's reservations nearly got the better of her curiosity.

James only wants to turn your head, she told herself as she dried her hands on her apron. *If he cared a fig, he would—* Her thoughts in disarray, she wondered what he *would* do if he truly loved her. Well, one thing was clear. If she didn't go meet him, she never would know what he had in mind. For sure, she wouldn't receive whatever he had bought for her in town.

At last, curiosity won out. Jessie took off her apron, unbraided and brushed out her hair, and slipped away from the camp.

Although the plaza was large, it took her only a few moments to find the town well, with its washing troughs for accommodating laundry day. She spotted James sitting on the edge of one of the troughs, a lighted lamp at his side. She stopped for a minute, a flood of memories making her heart leap into her throat and constrict her breathing. She almost smelled lilacs. *No!* she thought. *I don't want to remember that!* She nearly turned to run, but she must have made a sound. James looked up and saw her, and he smiled, lamplight caressing the creases on the lit side of his face. *If he says my name, I'll be lost*, she thought.

"Jessie," he called. His voice matched his smile.

"Hello," she managed to say, wanting to run and hide at the same time that she desired above all things to be swept away by her memories to a past that should have been her present.

James got up and approached, took her hand, and brought her to the circle of light. "I wasn't sure you'd come," he said. "I'm mighty pleased you did."

His smile had not faded. In fact, it seemed to Jessie to be wider than before, brightening his eyes. Even so, he seemed oddly vulnerable.

She hesitated before answering. She didn't want to seem petty, but finally the only thing she thought of to say was, "You said you had something for me."

James laughed. "I did say that." He let go of her hand, indicated that she should sit down and, when she had done so, sat beside her.

He reached inside his coat and wiggled something loose from the facing of the lapel. "I found your needle," he said, and held it out so she could see it. A short tail of thread trailed from the eye.

"You did?" Jessie smiled. "You found it! Thank you, James."

Instead of giving it to her, he leaned back and thrust his free hand into his pocket, bringing out two small objects. One was a packet of pins that he transferred to his other hand. "I didn't want you to lose the needle again, so I bought you this." He unfolded a scrap of cloth to reveal that it was pierced with three bright new needles. "It's sort of a sewing kit, without the scissors and thread." He paused. "Maybe I should have gotten you those too?" His voice trailed off, uncertain. He asked, "Did I do wrong?"

Jessie held herself very still, afraid to answer, but her immobility was in vain. His thoughtfulness made tears spring to her eyes. She wiped at them, but they trailed down her cheeks. She looked up. The anxious, little-boy expression on his face was too much to bear. She began to sniffle, caught in a whirlpool of gratitude, tenderness and affection.

"Hush! Now I made you cry," James blurted out, his face crumpling.

"No! You done . . . That was so sweet. You didn't have to. But you did."

"Don't cry, Jessie. This is all backward. I wanted you to be happy."

"I am," she bawled, unable to stop the tears and the emotions that fed them.

"But you're crying."

"Yes," she agreed. She wished James would put his arms around her, but sensed that his confusion had him spellbound. She had no claim on asking him to comfort her, so she kept on crying, and he kept making soothing sounds. He didn't touch her, which she realized was because he had his hands full of prickly objects. That thought struck Jessie as funny, and she began to laugh.

A moment later, James joined her in merriment. He stuck the found needle into the cloth with the others, and put the cloth and the pins into her hand. "Ah, Jessie," he said, after one long spell of hoots and chortles, "It's mighty nice to laugh with you. I wish you'd marry me."

Jessie shot to her feet. That would not happen, much as she wished it could. She'd promised— *Oh Lordy, why did I promise Ned I'd marry him? Did he hear us laughing? He'll come over and find us making merry together!*

"I must go," she said, and gathering up her skirt in one hand, ran back toward the camp.

Chapter 40

The party left Santa Fe the next morning amid flurries of snow that continued intermittently throughout the day. They made ten miles before coming to a water hole edged with white. Ned went to fill his canteen, but James warned him off and led the wagons past the water. When James had left, Ned turned his horse and approached the hole. He was kneeling to get water when James rode up.

"Don't drink that!" he called.

Ned got to his feet, feeling the rise of irritation in his stomach. What gave James Owen the right to tell him where to whet his thirst? "What's your problem, Owen?" He balled his hands into fists.

"That's bad water. You don't want to drink it."

"Who says I don't?" Ned blustered.

"See that white rime?" James was off his horse, kicking the coating that rimmed the water tank.

"A little ice. Maybe snow."

"No. It's alkali. I saw the like in Texas."

"I've never heard of it." Ned bent over, scooped up a handful of water, and drank it. The taste was noxious, but he couldn't spit it out in front of his rival. He did allow some to dribble out the side of his mouth.

"No!" James exclaimed, and pulled Ned away from the water tank. "It poisons the water."

Ned swallowed, then shook himself away from James's hold. "It's not so bad."

"Don't be a fool, Heizer." James got the canteen from his saddle and held it out to Ned. "You'd best get some good water into you and dilute that mouthful you took. You're going to be sick, but you probably won't die if you'll do that."

"I'm never sick," Ned shouted, angered at being called a fool. Then he fell to his knees and retched, his mouth burning. He heard James's sharp inhalation of air. Ned cursed himself for letting his ill humor lead him to reckless behavior. When he'd finished throwing up, he wiped his mouth with a shaking hand and whispered, "You have the right of it. Will you help me get on my horse?"

"Gladly," James replied, offering the canteen again. "First, drink deep."

Ned took the canteen, washed out his mouth, and spit. He took another mouthful and swallowed it, regretting his hard-headedness as he realized the alkali water had burned his throat as well as his mouth. He chugged down the liquid in the canteen, mentally blessing James Owen. The man could have shrugged his shoulders and left him to do what he wanted, but he stepped in and tried to prevent the injury.

Ned handed back the canteen and said, "I am a fool. I'm beholden to you."

James nodded once, but didn't say anything as he helped Ned get on his horse.

෨

By the time Ned dismounted in camp that evening, he knew he was in trouble. He'd been dealing with retching and the trots ever since the incident at the water hole. James Owen had always seemed to be nearby to help him get on and off his horse, never saying much, but assisting when he was needed.

Ned slid to the ground, unsteady on his feet, wanting to collapse into a heap, but knowing he couldn't do that before he found privacy for another bout of affliction. He limped toward a stand of trees at the edge of the clearing, one hand clutching his cramping belly. Beads of sweat trickled down his cheeks. *Where's George when I need him?* he thought.

"Heizer?" came James Owen's voice from behind. "Do you need aid?"

"No," Ned groaned. "Send my brother."

"I'll do that," James said. Ned heard the crunch of his boots on dry twigs as he retreated toward the camp.

Ned went about his business as best he could while clinging to a tree to keep from falling. When he'd finished an attack of dry heaves, he fell on his hands and knees and gave himself up to the weakness that caused his entire body to quiver. A moment later, George came running through the grove.

"Ned? Where are you?"

"Here," he said, his voice rasping in his ears. "I'm here."

George hauled him up and got himself under Ned's arm. "Holy Nellie, what ails you?"

"Bad water," Ned managed to whisper.

"Water? You didn't drink that alkali poison Owen pointed out, did you?" George half walked and half carried Ned toward the camp.

"Uh-huh."

"No wonder you look like a calf with the scours. Let's get you bedded down. I'll ask Mother Bingham if she has a remedy."

"It burned my throat," Ned muttered.

"Don't talk. Heppie! Miss Jessie!" George called. "Make up a bed for Ned. He's bad off."

Ned winched as George pulled him over rough ground at the edge of the clearing. "Hold up. Belly hurts," he said, panting.

George held him while he fought against the gripping pain in his gut. Thankfully, his body had run out of perfidious fluids, and after great effort, he found enough strength to assist in getting himself into camp.

After a time, he found himself lying in his blankets with Jessie pressing a cool, wet cloth to his cracked lips. "Oh, Ned," she exclaimed. "Didn't you know that water was bad?"

He shook his head a fraction of an inch, without strength to speak.

Jessie said, "Thank you, Ma," and twisted to accept something from Mrs. Bingham. She put a spoonful of liquid against his mouth. "Sip this. Ma said slippery elm and chamomile will ease your burns. She knows her remedies."

Ned accepted the liquid and felt it slide down his throat as he swallowed. Jessie spooned it into his mouth until the cup was empty, murmuring all the while, "Is that better? Does it soothe?" without waiting for an answer. She set the cup aside and began to wipe the sweat from his forehead with her cloth.

After a while, she patted him on the shoulder and said, "You need to sleep. Rest will restore you." Then she began to croon a lullaby in a soft voice.

A lullaby? Something about having Jessie sing him to sleep disturbed Ned, but he drifted off before he could work it through.

છ

Robert decided they would remain camped until Ned had recovered. They spent the next two days tightening harnesses and mending clothes.

Ned drifted in and out of sleep, hearing scraps of conversation, feeling the soothing slippery elm tea roll down his throat, knowing Jessie came to tend him when she noticed he was awake. Where was she when he was asleep? Letting James Owen court her?

Jessie hadn't accompanied him to the trees. George, or occasionally, James, had done that duty. She'd know what he had to do and when he had to do it, though, and that unsettled Ned. A body should have some privacy, even from the girl who loved him.

When he awoke from a nap on the afternoon of the second day, Ned's mood matched the dark gray clouds overhead. The only light in the sky diffused through the clouds on the western horizon. *Late afternoon*, he thought. He assessed his health. His mouth and throat no longer burned. His bodily functions had regularized. *Tomorrow we can push on.* He looked around. No one had noticed he was awake. *Good. Time I proved I'm up to traveling.*

Ned threw the quilt aside, got to his feet and, wavering just a tad, limped away from the camp. Nature was calling, and he sure wasn't going to let Jessie know how unsteady he felt. He couldn't put himself through any further discomfiture.

How much frustration can a man stand? he asked himself. *Does Jessie care for me or not? You'd think James Owen hung the moon, the way she talked to him when he was laid up. "James, don't you rise up and hurt yourself," and "I blew the heat out of this gruel for you." Sounded like a cat purring, her voice all soft and sweet as cream, like that Maggie talked to me.*

He stopped short. Maggie. What made him think of Maggie Julander? Memories popped into his mind. Maggie. Tall—almost as tall as Ned himself. Slim, with dark hair falling over her shoulders like a waterfall in deep shadows. Sun-browned arms. That Mississippi lilt to her voice. The yearning way she had looked back toward him when the Mormons left. *No, Ned*, he told himself. *You're going to marry Jessie.*

"Jessie," he moaned as his mind reviewed the past days when he'd lain abed, mouth and throat burning until she'd brought him the tea. *She sang me lullabies. Lullabies! Same as she did Luke! I'm not her man. I'm her big brother!*

He chewed on that thought for a moment as he took care of his business. *Does she love me? Maybe. Maybe like I'm her protector, yes, her big brother. I've looked out for her for years, made sure she didn't come to any harm ever since we were youngsters. Don't we suit each other?*

A biting question entered his thoughts. *Do I love Jessie?* "Of course I do!" he exclaimed to the wooded landscape. "There's no doubt of that."

"Ned?"

He stiffened at Jessie's voice behind him.

"What's there no doubt of?"

"Jessie," he said, his brain whirling with the enormity of the idea that came upon him, the vastness of the consequences of what he knew he was going to do. He turned slowly to face her, the girl he thought he'd adored forever. The bottom seemed to drop out of his stomach. "Jessie," he said again. "We've been friends for a long time."

He watched the expressions changing on her face. Wariness. Doubt. Fear. Knowing he brought her to fear was like a punch to the head. He swallowed hard.

"Jessie. You don't have to marry me."

"What?" Her face reflected horror. "Ned, what are you saying?"

What would be better? Blaming himself or her? He watched Jessie shaking her head back and forth. Himself. That was the right notion. He squared his shoulders. "I'm releasing you from your promise."

"No. No no no! You can't do that! We're getting wed soon. When we get to Albuquerque." Her hands balled into fists, almost as if she would strike out at him in another minute.

He gulped. "I don't love you, Jessie. Not that way."

"You're daft! You do love me. You always have."

"Like a friend, Jessie. Like a good habit."

"A habit! I'm not a habit. I'm your—I'm almost your wife. You can't simply shuck me off like a dirty shirt."

"I'm not shucking you off, Jessie. I'm letting you go. You fancy James Owen over me."

"James Owen? What's he got to do with anything? He—I don't—he don't care a fig for me!"

Ned shook his head. "You're hiding behind me, Jessie. Using me to keep Owen at a distance so you won't get hurt again." He felt a slow burn of anger rising in his gut. "All a body has to do is look at his eyes to know he worships you."

"No." Her voice took on a mournful tone. "He loves that dead wife."

"He loved you first, dammit!" He stood as tall as he could, considering that his soul was bent over, crouching and curling into a ball at having to admit the truth. "Get it into your head, Jessie. We're done. James Owen has a better claim on you. He knows it and now I know it."

"I don't know any such thing! I won't let you throw me over."

He didn't see the slap coming, and it snapped his head to one side, stinging his face and his dignity.

Anger flared in him. "I should have traded you for the gelding," he said. At the look on her face, he compressed his lips and regretted his words, but they were in the air. He couldn't take them back.

"I hate you," she said, flinging the phrase like another slap.

"Good. You won't want to marry me." Ned turned and started toward the camp, his harsh thoughts blinding him to his surroundings. The last thing he knew was a tremendous pain at the back of his head, accompanied by a flash of red behind his eyes.

&

James heard the scream, recognized the fear in it, knew it was Jessie's voice. She'd slipped into the woods, following Ned Heizer. As James jumped up and headed toward the trees he wondered what was happening between them to make her shriek like that. Even Heizer wouldn't—

He almost stumbled over Ned's body. That raised the short hairs. *Hush, where's Jessie?* Her cries had been cut short as though someone's hand had clamped over her mouth. He peered into the trees ahead, and started as the old dog rushed past him, growling deep in its throat. He ran forward, keeping it in sight. George and Robert raised a cry behind him as they discovered Ned.

James heard a muffled wail ahead and to his left, and he turned in the direction of the sound. "Jessie," he hollered. "I'm coming!"

Whoever had taken Jessie moved through the woods at a quick pace, and James wondered if he was in a race with a horseman. Fear gripped his heart with a tight fist, but he dug deep into his strength and ran faster, dodging around trees, hurdling fallen logs, slapping brittle hanging branches away from his face.

Jessie screamed again. A man's harsh voice told her to shut up, but she disobeyed him, giving James a beacon to run toward.

Time had no meaning as he fought his way through the vegetation, his chest heaving, the puckered scar on his side burning in agony. *Jessie!*

The Complete Owen Family Saga   Page 785

He caught sight of her white apron through the screen of tree trunks. She was just ahead, beyond that copse of oaks. She struggled with a stout man on horseback. *Is that the trader?* James gulped air, found his second wind, and sped toward them.

The dog was barking, growling. A horse screamed, reared as the dog nipped at its legs. Jessie was falling, crying out as the man landed on top of her.

ဆ

Oh God, oh God, oh God, Jessie thought. *Not like Hannah!* She flailed with her elbows, scrambling from under the man's heavy body. *I won't let him!*

The man grabbed her ankle, dragging her toward him. She bent her other knee and kicked at him. He let go for just a moment, then clutched at her again before she could get free. He stood up and pulled her to his feet, swearing at the fleeing horse. She shrieked, and he put his hand over her mouth once more.

"None of that!"

Jessie shuddered as her captor yanked her along, kicking at the dog that nipped him. She'd been angry before this brute hauled her onto his saddle, angry at Ned for his imprudent, thoughtless words, for jilting her after all this time. Now she felt the anger rise in her again, beating back the fear that had partially paralyzed her brain.

She bit the man's hand, grinding her teeth into the flesh, tasting the brine of his blood. She gagged, and her teeth lost their grip as the man thrashed his arm in pain.

Despite having to take a second to spit out the trader's blood, Jessie grabbed at the man, wrapped her arms around his waist, and hung off him, a dead weight, trying to hinder his progress until James could catch up. The man tripped, flailed around, and halted, trying to beat at the dog with a club.

She'd stopped him, she realized, triumph surging through her body. She had the upper hand. She and the dog, she recognized, as it tore at the man's leg. Because of her efforts at hampering the trader, his stupid club wasn't having much effect on the dog.

James burst between two saplings and skidded to a halt. Jessie laughed at the astonished look on his face.

He launched himself into the fray, hitting the man over and over with his fists, and getting a glancing blow on his head from the club for his troubles.

The sight of blood streaming down from James's scalp almost choked her, but it didn't seem to deter him from playing the hero. He soon overpowered the man, bringing them all down to the ground in a heap.

"Jessie, turn him loose," James said.

She unwrapped her arms from the man and spit again, shuddering, but she wanted to laugh at James's commanding tone. She and the dog had got the best of the trader.

"*¡Quita!*" he told the dog. "Get off there."

Jessie scrambled away, and the dog sat on its haunches, still growling.

As James lugged the man to his feet, he said, "See if you can find his horse. Bring a rope."

"You ain't gonna hang me?" yelped the man.

"What outlandish notion took hold of your senses?" James shouted at the trader. "You can't kidnap a woman!"

"Your head!" Jessie said, reaching up with a corner of her apron to dab at the blood pouring down James's cheek. "You're bleeding all over."

"Never mind my head. Get me a rope."

"I wasn't going to hurt her. I only wanted a bit of female companionship," the man whined.

"You picked the wrong female," James said, twisting the trader's hands behind his back. "She's mine."

Jessie sucked in her breath, not sure if she was annoyed at James's statement, or overjoyed.

80

After they got the trader to camp, Jessie stood on one side of the fire, patching up James's scalp wound. Hannah and Heppie huddled together on the other, working over Ned. Jessie noticed that as Heppie twisted to pick up Ma's remedy basket, a small round lump stuck out from her belly. *Heppie? With child?* She sighed. How long would it be before her turn came? Ned didn't want to be her husband. Was James in earnest, or had he merely been flirting with her?

Robert and George stood sentinel over the trader, who slumped on the ground nearby, his hands tied behind his back.

"What do we do with him?" George asked.

"We can't let him go." Robert scowled at the ground. "He's apt to go looking for another young lady to prey on."

James said, "Let's take him in to Albuquerque and let the law deal with him. We're only three days out."

Ned roused himself, shaking his head a bit. "Santa Fe's closer."

"We've passed Santa Fe," James said.

"I'm going that way," Ned replied in a quiet voice. "I'll take him with me."

George walked over. "What do you mean? We're bound for Albuquerque."

Ned got to his feet. "Y'all are bound for Albuquerque. I'm headed the other way."

Jessie felt James go still under her hands. As she listened to the hubbub of voices raised in denial, a sick feeling formed a knot in her stomach. *He knows Ned's leaving me.*

She turned her head, willing Ned not to continue, not to shame her, but he looked her way and pressed on. She held her breath.

"Miss Jessie and me ain't right for each other. I was wrong to hound her into giving me her pledge." He spoke to her. "I beg you to forgive me." He paused for a moment, waiting.

Ned's gracious words brought her no dishonor, no embarrassment or disgrace. She recognized his gift of freedom, and managed a nod and a thankful smile as the knot in her stomach untied.

Ned returned the smile, one side of his mouth tilting higher than the other. He faced the others again. "There *is* a little gal in the Mormon bunch I reckon is right for me. I aim to catch up to them and see if she feels the same."

George spoke up. "Are you sure, Ned?"

"Sure as I'll ever be."

"Well, brother," George said softly, "let's get you some provisions together so you can leave in the morning."

Jessie looked down at James and noticed that her fingers were covered in his blood.

He caught the direction of her gaze and picked up one of her hands. "I thought blood made you sick," he said.

Jessie ducked her head. "Not yours, it appears."

James got to his feet and pulled her away from the camp into the trees.

As Jessie went with him, she realized that his manner was much different from that of the young man who had paid her court in that faraway town in the Shenandoah Valley. His soul had grown. When the horse bucked James off, he had struggled to stay conscious long enough to convince her of how vast love could be. "I have mighty tender feelings for the two of you," he had said of her and Amparo, and she knew it was true.

There would always be Amparo, but she had left Jessie a gift. Because of her, James's heart was larger, deeper, big enough to hold Amparo and Jessie too.

James stopped and turned to face Jessie, his eyes glowing with intense feeling.

"Marry me," he whispered. "Soon as we get to town."

Joy flooded over her, wrapping her in warm swirls of emotion. She was free to say yes. She nodded, slowly at first, then quickly, bobbing her head until she felt giddy. "I reckon you're the only one who wants me."

James reached over, stilled her face, and wiped a smudge off her cheek. "More than life, Jessie Bingham." He began to sing, so softly that no ears but hers could hear, "'And for love of Jessie Bingham, I'd lay me doon and dee.'"

"That would be a great trial to me," she whispered, wiping James's blood off her hands with her apron. "But you came after me. You proved you're willing."

Jessie looked around. Lightning crackled in the clouds to the west. Everyone in camp was gathered around Ned, arguing, discussing . . . ignoring the two of them.

She looked at James. He smiled at her, taking her breath away, filling her soul with wonder and elation.

He took her face in his hands and said, "I'm willing to live for you, and with you, forever and always."

"Oh, James," she said, clinging to him. She closed her eyes. Sometime soon she would tell him that she knew how much Amparo had blessed her life. *She sent you back to me a much better man. My James*, she thought, feeling the warmth of his affection surrounding her heart.

He gathered her into the circle of his arms. Then he kissed her: long, and hard, and joyfully, and drove away the troubles of their trail of storms.

The End

Thank You!

Please post a review of this book on your favorite review or purchase site. Reviews from readers, even as few as twenty words, make all the difference to those browsing and buying.

Remember to recommend this book to your friends, telling them what you liked about it. Word-of-mouth recommendations are valuable rewards for authors.

Finally, subscribe to Marsha's VMA Readers email list to receive advance notice of coming book releases. https://is.gd/rBXkA4

About the Author

Marsha Ward writes authentic historical fiction set in 19th Century America, and contemporary romance. She was born in the sleepy little town of Phoenix, Arizona, in a simpler time. With plenty of room to roam among the chickens and citrus trees, Marsha enjoyed playing with neighborhood chums, but always had her imaginary friend, cowboy Johnny Rigger Prescott, at her side. Now she makes her home in a forest in the mountains of Arizona. She loves to hear from her readers.

Connect with her at:
Website: http://marshaward.com
Blog: http://marshaward.blogspot.com
Email: marshaw@marshaward.com
Facebook: https://www.facebook.com/authormarshaward
Twitter: https://twitter.com/MarshaWard

Join Marsha's VMA Readers' email list to receive advance notice of coming book releases. https://is.gd/rBXkA4

www.ingramcontent.com/pod-product-compliance
Lightning Source LLC
Chambersburg PA
CBHW070340030726
47504CB00001B/16